The Collected Stories of Sean O'Faolain

An Atlantic Monthly Press Book

LITTLE, BROWN AND COMPANY · BOSTON · TORONTO

FIRST AMERICAN EDITION

ATLANTIC – LITTLE, BROWN BOOKS

ARE PUBLISHED BY

LITTLE, BROWN AND COMPANY

IN ASSOCIATION WITH

THE ATLANTIC MONTHLY PRESS

MV
*Published simultaneously in Canada
by Little, Brown & Company (Canada) Limited*

PRINTED IN THE UNITED STATES OF AMERICA

The stories on pages 320–345 and 484–499 are from
THE MAN WHO INVENTED SIN,
reprinted by kind permission of
Devin-Adair, Publishers,
of Old Greenwich, Connecticut —
publishers of Irish Literature since 1911.

Contents

Unpublished Stories (1982)

The
Collected Stories
of
Sean O'Faolain

Midsummer Night Madness

I

For a second I looked back into the city, down through the smoke at the clustered chimney-pots and roofs on whose purples and greens and blues the summer night was falling as gently as dust, falling too on the thousand tiny beacons winking and blinking beneath me to their starry counterparts above. It was just the curfew hour and the last few laggard couples went hurrying past me, their love-making ended abruptly for the night, lest the Tans in their roaring Lancia patrol-cars should find them conspicuous on the empty white streets of the city. Then I turned to the open fields and drew in a long draught of their sweetness, their May-month sweetness, as only a man could who had been cooped up for months past under one of those tiny roofs, seeing the life of men and women only through a peep-hole in a window-blind, seeing these green fields only in the far distance from an attic skylight. Mounting my bicycle I left the last gas-lamp behind, and the pavement end, and rode on happily into the open country.

Yet, though the countryside was very sweet to me after all those months among the backyards, worried and watchful lest I should run into a chance patrol or raiding-party, I kept listening, not to the chorus of the birds, not to the little wind in the bushes by the way, but nervously to every distant, tiny sound — the chuckle of a wakeful goose or hen in a near-by farmyard, or the fall of water coming suddenly within earshot, or some animal starting away from the hedge where I surprised its drowsing heavy head, and once I halted dead, my grip tight on the brakes when a donkey brayed suddenly and loudly as if he were laughing at the intense quietness of the night. Fallen hawthorn blossoms splashed with their lime the dust of the road, and so narrow were the boreens in places that the lilac and the dog-rose, hung with wisps of hay, reached down as if to be plucked, and under the overhanging trees I could smell the pungent smell of the laurel sweating in the damp night-air. And all about me the dead silence of the coming night, unless a little stream trickled over the road and my wheels made a great double splash as they crossed it; then once again the heavy silence, drowsy with the odours of the night-flowers and the cut meadows.

I was on my way to the townlands of Farrane and Kilcrea, to see why to all appearances the local battalion had been completely inactive for the last three or four months. That portion of my task I did not relish for I had known and been friendly with Stevey Long, the commandant, ever since the chances of revolution threw us together. Still I should be free of the open fields for a few days, and there was enough romance left in the revolution for me to be excited at the thought that I was to stay at a house I had known and wondered at since childhood; I might even see and meet, if he were still alive, its strange mad owner whom as children we thought more terrifying than any of the ogres in the fairy-books – Old Henn of Henn Hall.

But I could hardly credit that he was still alive, for even when we were very young my mother always spoke of him as 'that old devil' or 'that old cripple' of a Henn. And an old devil he was, living up there all alone, in what she used to call his 'rooky-rawky' of a house, never married but always in a state of marriage with some woman or other. He began, I could well believe, with women of his own class, officers' wives from the barracks at B——, or Cork, or perhaps with what we used to call 'horsy women' from some neighbouring English hunt. But, judging by his later life, he cannot have been over-particular at any time in his choice of women, and many a tinted London beauty must have walked his fields, looking in utter boredom at the gulls flying after the plough or the rain hanging in the bare trees, until finally, like all her predecessors and successors of many years, she in her turn cursed Henn and his Hall, and Ireland and all belonging to it, and went back gladly to the flickering city-lights and the back streets, and the familiar loved smells of gas-lit theatres and stuffy hansom-cabs. Clearly, a man who lived by the things of the body – women, wine, hunting, fishing, shooting. My mother often told us how as she and a crowd of schoolgirl friends were returning from their first Communion one cold autumn afternoon they entered his fields to take a short way by the river to their homes, removing their new shoes and stockings as they always did when they left the high road, and they came on Henn – and he was a grown man then – standing in his pelt by the river, ready for a swim. She used shudder as she told how he chased them, and they ran from him, screaming with fear, throwing away the new shoes and stockings as they ran, their legs all torn on the withered rushes of the bog and the furzed hedge-tops, not daring to look back to see if the naked 'madman' were catching up with them, until, as she said, they had left his fields 'forty miles behind' and panting and exhausted they ran into their homes. Henn must have been delighted with his frolic, and I can see him, running back for his swim, his long legs and his long neck, that gave him the nickname of 'Henn's Neck,' cutting through the air as he ran. And he must have been especially delighted when in the late evening the fathers and brothers of the children came looking here and there timidly for the little blue or red socks and the black shoes. It was only one of many such escapades that my mother knew, all spreading the name and legend of madness that clung to him through his life. We needed few such warnings to avoid him and his estate, but we used to say to each other, some-body's warning half-understood, that if Henn caught a little girl 'he'd salt her', and we went in mortal terror of him and his salting for years. No wonder we used say that he had wires hidden under his fields and if you crossed even one of his ditches bells would ring up in the Hall and he would come galloping on a white horse with his hungry hounds to salt you.

It was a wonderful old house to look at, and often we looked at it from far off, sitting up on its own high hill, its two gable chimneys like two cocked ears and all its empty windows gazing wide-eyed down the river-valley – very tall, with a wide door whose steps curled down and around like moustaches. The place was a pale rain-faded pink at the end, but it was often called the Red House, and if it was ever really the *Red* House it must have been visible for miles to anyone driving westward to Crookstown along the valley, following the little river and its dark line of woods. Yet, as I tried to recall it now, only one impression remained, for we came into the city when I was quite young and there I soon forgot the Hall; but at least two or three times afterwards my father took me on an unusually long walk in that direction, and each time when he returned he said to my mother – 'We could just see the Red House up the valley beyond Kilnaglory'. And each time she said

'Glory be to God, I wonder is that old devil Henn alive yet?' and told us all over again how he chased them in his pelt when they were little children. One of these walks was on a soft wintry day with packed clouds threatening to drop rain every minute, and the Lee and the Bride in flood, and the tall bare beeches with the rooks' nests in their tip-tops swayed and swung in the hard wind. The roads were muddy in places and there were many pot-holes full of rain or liquid dung and they were all wrinkled in the breeze and the flooded river ran frothing and brown and storm-blown by the very edge of the road. Off up the sodden valley, high on its rounded hill sat Henn's house, and it was really more red than pink that day because of the rain, and as we looked at it one solitary window showed a light. At the same time the cold, yellow sky behind it was turning to a most marvellous red as of blood, and the scarlet light blackened every leafless twig and already rain-black and rain-green tree-trunk that stood against it and every ditch and scooped riverbank, and lastly the road and the very sky itself became swarthy, and there was light only in the waves curling the river and the potholes of the road. When the solitary window shone my father said, 'That's old Henn,' and I pictured him as an old man with a beard and long claw-hands half into the glowing ashes, so that I said, 'I think, father, it's going to be thunder and lightning,' and he looked back and said 'it might,' and to my joy we turned our backs on Henn and his house and faced for the lights and the crowds and the shop-windows of the city.

Really, I am sure, that was not Henn; he would certainly have been down at the bridge-head with his rods and his basket and his gillie. But when those same winter rains streamed down the cur-tainless windows now, would he not have to stand watching it, backbent – if indeed he still lived – shivering in the bay, and return to crouch sadly – not so far removed from my childish picture of him – over his perpetual summer-to-summer fire?

You may pity him as I tell you of him, but I, riding along the darkling lanes that night, had nothing in my heart for him but hate. He was one of the class that had battened for too long on our poor people, and I was quite pleased to think that if he lived he lived only in name; that if he had any charm at all left he would need it all now to attract even the coarsest woman. For no London light-o'-love would be attracted to his ruin of a house now for other reasons.

Perhaps he was beyond all that, and if he was not, he would be like Juan in old age, for the farmers' daughters for miles around would shun him as they would the plague, and for such a man as Henn to descend to the women of the passing tinkers for whom alone his house would appear even yet a big house, was out of the question. And yet not even his maids who came from a distance would be in the house a day without hearing all about him from the neighbours. Perhaps, after all, the tinkers would have to suffice? But, thinking of the big Red House, with its terraced lawns, and its cypresses and its yews, and its great five-mile estate wall, all built by the first Henn, the founder not only of his line but of an industry – glass-making, and long since disappeared from Ireland – I could not believe that even such a house would fall so low.

2

As I came to a crossways where my road dropped swiftly downhill the tenting chestnuts filled the lanes with darkness as of pitchy night, and under my wheels the lain dust was soft as velvet. Before I took this last turn on my way I looked back the road I had come and saw upthrown behind the hill that distant glow of the city's lights, a furnace-glow that made me realize how near and how far I was to the roofs and chimneys I had left. But as I looked I saw, too, how the clouds were gathering like pale flowers over the inky sky and even as I dropped silently downhill the first drops beat the fronded layers above. On my left, high as two men, rose the estate walls that had once kept the whole countryside at bay but could not now (gapped and crumbling as they were) keep a fox out or a chicken in. I passed two great entrance-gates sunken in the weeds. Then the pale ghostlike pillars of the third gate came in view across a gap in the tunnel where the rain was beating down the dust, gradually changing its pattering blows for the hissing sound of a real downpour. Head bowed I raced across the unsheltered patch and edged my bicycle through the creaking gate and was just abreast of the little Gothic door of the lodge when it swung open and a woman stepped suddenly through the laurels and caught my arm, saying roughly and passionately as she did so :

'Stevey, why did you go away? Henn was down again tonight. Stevey, I . . .'

Astonished, I made no sound. The rain beat down on us, blotting out stars and moon alike.

'Stevey,' she went on, 'I can't help it. . . .'

Then she saw her mistake, and dropped my hand.

'I'm sorry,' she said. 'I thought . . .'

I laughed to put her at her ease.

'You thought I was Stevey Long.'

She turned and went back to the door and seeing me from there look after her she cried out roughly :

'Go on !'

And because I was slow in moving for all the falling rain, she cried again :

'Go on about your business. Go on !'

'What a rough, passionate creature!' I was saying to myself; only by degrees recovering from my surprise as I began to wheel my bicycle up the avenue, when I heard her steps behind me and felt her grip on my arm once more. She beckoned and drew me back into the shadow of one of the sheltering trees beside the little house and with the only grace she was capable of leant insinuatingly close to me, fingering my lapel, and said in her hollow mannish voice :

'You know Stevey Long?'

'Yes, of course, I do.'

'Are you the boy he was bringing to the Hall to stay ?'

'Yes.'

'He told me about you. You know him well, don't you?'

'I know Stevey for a long time.'

'He told me you were in jail with him once.'

'Did he tell you that? I was. Oh yes! Stevey and I had many a bout together.'

She paused. Then in a low trembling voice she said, 'Do you know his girl?'

'His girl?'

'Yes. He told me all about her. He said you know her too. Tell me . . . where is she?'

Her voice was strained against the leash, become passionately intent in spite of her. I did not want to be caught by her country trickery, and I looked into her face by the light of the little window, as one always looks into the face of a person one doubts, from eye to eye searching for the truth. Seeing me hesitate she caught my arm the more fiercely.

'Tell me!'

'Why, I suppose you are Stevey's girl,' I bantered.

'Tell me, boy! She sent him letters to jail, didn't she? Oh, for Christ's sake, go on and tell me!'

She had me by the two arms now, her full bosom almost touching mine, so close to me that I could see the pouches under her eyes, her mouth dragged down wet and sensual, the little angry furrow between her eyebrows. The wind shook the heavy leaves of the chestnuts and as they scattered benediction on us the light from the little Gothic window shone on their wet leaves, and on her bosom and chest and knees. For a second I thought her blue apron drooped over her too rich, too wide hips. But when I would not speak she shook me like a dog and growled at me so fiercely that I could not refuse to reply.

'I don't know,' I said. 'She just sent letters to us, to Stevey of course, and cigarettes and fruit and things – that's all. I don't know!'

She threw me away so that I all but stumbled over my bike.

'I knew it was true,' she moaned. 'I knew it was true when they said it.'

'But anyone might write him a letter. . . .'

'He denied it. He denied he ever got a letter from her.'

In open country it is surprising how the voice sometimes echoes. Under those trees her voice resounded so that I feared she would be heard up at the Hall or down in the village.

'The liar. He's going to marry that wan. That's the wan he wants. The shcut! And look what he's going to do now.'

Her great bosom rose and fell in rage.

'Do?' I asked. 'What is he going to do?'

'Who'd mind Henn? I ought to know. But Stevey. But Stevey, with his grand talk. He said *he'd* never harm me. But I won't marry him. I won't marry him. I won't. I won't!'

And she turned and ran in to the lodge, leaving me with the feeling that this Hall and estate and countryside had an unpleasant, real life of its own, a life that would spoil for me the few days of quietness that I had been dreaming of this last hour as I cycled between the hedgerows. I scarcely noticed that the sudden summer shower had ceased as I made slowly up the mossed drive, dark with unpruned trees and black laurel. Everything here too seeming to send up its sweetness into the soft wet air, even the weeds bursting through the gravel, and when I came to the front of the house the great dark cypresses might in the wet failing light have been plumes of billowy smoke that rose against the sky. I was now on the terrace before the Hall, and as I looked down into the valley to where the sound of the waters of the Bride rose murmuring through the air purified by the shower, I almost expected to see the old libertine come floating up like a spectre or a long-legged ogre through the hills.

I found my way, as I had been instructed to do, to the rear of the house and in by the servants' quarters to the great kitchen. The pale still light of a candle on the table filled the room, and at the foot of the table beneath it was a basin of dusty milk, and before the embers an old sheep-dog yawned and stretched his legs. I sat down by the fire and, glad of the rest, began to try to understand what it was that so troubled the girl at the lodge, with her passionate raging outburst against Stevey, her cry 'I won't marry him, I won't marry him.' But almost on my heels I heard the sound of feet mashing the gravel outside and she came in to the kitchen.

'Put on some turf, boy,' she said at once. 'And blow up the fire.'

As I laid on the brown peat and sat by the side of the machine turning its handle she began to lay the table for my supper. Then we heard somebody else approach outside, and with a sudden shake of her fist to me by way of warning, she opened the door to Stevey. To her he gave a mere 'Hullo, Gypsy.'

To me he gave a cordial, 'Here we are again,' and he shook my hand several times and told me how glad he was to see me safe and sound. Sullenly the girl broke in on us with :

'Put the kettle on, Stevey, for the boy's supper,' and sent me out to the rain-barrel for some water. I rose and went, and as I passed the window, there she was struggling out of his arms like a wild animal. But when I returned she was again by the table, and he was bending down over the fire, swinging the great iron kettle forward on its crane to be filled. I lay back in the old basket chair and watched him move silently about the kitchen, finding everything where he expected to find it, his fair flock of curls all about his neck and brow like a mountainy sheep, his knees flinging apart at every step as they always did, and his hangdog head and his rounded shoulders more slouched than ever.

Since they would not speak to one another I began to ask random questions; the name of this or that townland; whether this or that family were still alive, and they answered civilly enough but would never talk a word to one another.

A nice companionable house I have come to! I was grumbling to myself; and a nice pair of quarrelsome suspicious lovers! And I was wondering if I should really have come to this house at all, or if I was to have any pleasure in my few days of freedom, when suddenly Gypsy broke silence to say that a lorry-load of Tans had gone past two hours ago on the valley road, 'roaring,' she said, 'with the great venom and the drink,' shooting over the thatch of the houses in the village; they had, she even heard, killed a child and gone on without a thought, laughing at the terror of the villagers. At that Stevey burst into a terrible profane rage, but he caught my eye and fell silent. He knew my thought – if he had not been so inactive for the past four months the Tans would not be roaring their way so daringly through his territory now. 'Did any-one come to warn me?' he asked.

'Aye. The girl of the Mullinses.' And she added, 'The boys are wild tonight.'

I wished Stevey would turn to see me sneering at him. I had something to go on already I thought, and I was looking forward to my talk with him, when the girl would leave us to ourselves. But his mind began to wander from the Tans and he began to hum moodily to himself like a man with something gnawing at his brain, until, at last, unable to keep silent any longer he came out with a very casual,

'Was, eh, was Henn down tonight, Gyp?'

I could see her turn towards me as she answered with a brazen 'No.'

Then she said under her breath to him :

'He knows what he'd get if he came.'

At once everything changed. Stevey burst suddenly into a wild roar of song, his old favourite 'Night of Stars and Night of Love,' the barcarolle from *Hoffman* – and he echoed it through the empty house so that even Gypsy gave me a wry smile as she bade me sit up to supper.

'By God, John,' he cried at me, 'we'll give those bastards of Tans something to think about. Won't we, girl?'

And he caught her up whirling her into a corner of the room so that she screamed with sudden delight and in mock fear of his rough hands. Stevey drew a long comical face at his stupidity and she smoothed herself down and said she was all right, and so they sat in a corner of the huge fireplace while I, with my back to them, ate my salted rashers and my country bread and butter.

'Ate up, there, John,' he said; and then I heard them kissing secretly.

'I am tired,' I said.

'That's the man,' said Stevey, and they kissed again and she giggled to herself, and turning I found her tousling his already wild mop because he was making too free of her where she sat on his knee.

'She has great titties, John,' said Stevey coarsely, and she slapped his face for that, and as I went on with my supper I heard him kiss her in return. So they made their love in the dark corner, shamelessly, until I was almost finished and ready for Stevey, and then they rose suddenly and left me, to walk, as they said, down to the village now that it was so fine in the heel of the day. Stevey waved me aside when I wanted to detain him, saying the night was long and tomorrow was good too. So I was alone in the Hall, listening to the corncrake at his last dim rattle in the meadows and the doves fluting long and slow in the deep woods through the fallen dark.

As I lit my pipe and smoked under the shadow of the fireplace I began to feel that I should not have come to this house at all. True it was safe because it was the home of one of the 'garrison' people, one of those thousand unofficial blockhouses of the English on Irish soil, the last place to be suspected of harbouring a rebel. But with Stevey's girl – or rather, knowing him as I did – one of his girls in the same house, this was not a suitable place for the investigator of Stevey's shortcomings. But, as when I came along the road, the quietness and the peace gradually drove all other thoughts out of my head. The city, I thought, would by now be as empty as if it had been deserted, the Lancias booming along the naked streets, their searchlights shooting down the dark lanes and the side alleys, and the funereal tramp-tramp, tramp-tramp of the patrols taking with them from every door they passed its heavy sigh of suspended fear. All this Stevey had escaped. Not for him as for us, for months on end, the sight of a rusted roof in a city back-yard, the stale odour of airless bedrooms. Strange to think that one could work better in that sort of a room than where the walls were deep in lush grass and the springtime rain green-dripping from the trees into the water-butts and the cupped flowers.

The great front door banged, its echoes thundering, and steps clanked in the front hall. Another door opened and was closed again. The night had settled down about the Hall, seeped into the woods, calming the doves, and only the old tireless croaker kept up his ceaseless cry. A door opened again and steps shuffled along the passage and halted; then an old man's voice coughed and called wheedlingly.

'Gypsy?'

I was silent and again the old voice wheedled, now almost at the kitchen door :

'Is he gone, Gypsy? Are you there, my pretty?'

And as I said nothing the shuffling came nearer and the stick-tapping and coughing, and Mad Henn stood peering at me around the candle-flame. I knew him at once by his long collarless neck and his stork's legs and his madman's face beaked and narrow like a hen.

Even here indoors he wore a little faded bowler-hat cocked airily on one side of his head, and over his shoulders and draping his body a rug. He had the face of a bird, mottled and bead-eyed, and his hair, tawny in streaks with the glister of oil, had one lock at the back that stood out like a cock's comb. As he looked at me for a moment he pulled the loose flesh of his throat or scraped with one finger the tawny scum about his lips as if he were trying to remember whether he might not have asked me to come there or had some business with me that he had forgotten. I stood up awkwardly.

'Gypsy is gone for a walk with Stevey, Mister Henn,' I said.

'And who might you be, young man, if I might ask a polite question?' his eyebrows working up and down with irritation and the strain of having to speak.

'I . . . I'm a friend of Mr Long's.'

He sniffed so that a drop fell from his beaked nose.

'Mister Long,' he muttered in scorn. 'So you're another one of 'em are you? Eh? Are you?'

'I don't quite understand,' I said, and mentally cursed Stevey for not having arranged things better than this for me. For the old fellow began to pound with his heel on the floor and his legs and hands twitched for rage so that I expected him every second to turn me out of his house at the point of his stick.

'I suppose, I say,' he piped sardonically again, 'I suppose you're another one of our new patriots? Eh? Eh? I suppose you think you can walk into any man's house and sit on his armchair and drink his liquor, eh? And threaten him if he protests against you for a cad and a bully, eh? You're another of those, are you?'

He held a decanter in his right hand, and it was filled with dancing liquor. I thought it best to humour him.

'I beg your pardon, indeed, Mister Henn,' I said as humbly as I knew how, for I did not want a quarrel with the old devil. 'I'm sorry if I have intruded. But I didn't mean to. I think I have made a mistake – and I'll try if I can find the servant, or . . . find Stevey, that is . . . wherever they are . . . just now'

It was a very undignified speech, but it seemed to strike the old man with astonishment.

'Ho!' he said. 'This is a new one. Quite polite in fact. You're not very long on the road, young man,' he added with an air of bitter experience.

'That's all right,' I said, as I turned sullenly to go.

He halted me as I laid my hand on the door-latch – where I was going to I didn't know.

'Here! It is all right. Your apology is perfectly all right. Don't go, boy. Don't you go.'

At the word 'here' I noticed how tenderly he said his r's – *here*, and *your*, and *perfectly*. It was the last bit of blazonry he preserved, making him off for all his degradation as one of the conquering race.

'Did you call me?' I asked.

'Yes,' he said.

We looked at one another silently; then, in quite another tone, as coolly and politely as if he were speaking across his decanter in a club:

'Will you have a drink?'

I looked at him in surprise.

'Come along. I should like to talk to you. You are the first of your kind that I have met who seems to have any bit of education. I'd like to talk to you for that reason. We'll have a whisky and soda. Will you join me?'

I returned, no doubt a little flattered, but largely because I did not know what else to do; and our feet went clanking on the hall-flags as if the whole house were a vault, and indeed there was everywhere a musty smell of rooms long abandoned or never tended. His drawing-room was just as I expected, a good room but battered and unkempt like a tramp. At the farther end was a great super-fluous fire and standing by it he poured me out a jorum of whisky in a glass whose crevices were brown with the encrustations of years, all the time peering at me around the side of a pink-bowled oil-lamp whose crude unshaded light made everything look even more drab and dirty – the bare uncarpeted floor, the fine marble fireplaces mottled and cracked, the china cabinets with broken glass and no china in them; and I remembered the look of the yards with their rusted churns and staveless barrels, and everywhere and on everything the fur of mildew and green damp.

'Here! Drink that,' he said, pouring himself another glass and throwing it off at a gulp, raw.

'That's the way to take your liquor. I suppose you'll empty the siphon in yours, eh? Hum! If you didn't have a revolver stuck in your back pockets what would you young fellows have over us? Oh, you're stronger – but have you more grit? Let me look at you.'

I stood up for the drink, and he peered at me.

'Ah!' he wailed. 'There's only one thing I regret, one thing I've lost and that's clear eyes. The whole year is all like foggy autumn to me. I see the trees and the woods as if they were clouded in mist. It's a great blessing. I go out on a fine evening like this evening and it's like an evening in winter to me when the light fails at four o'clock in the afternoon and every hill is a valley and every tree is twice as far away as it really is.'

His streaming eyes strayed to the caverns of the fire, but the flames shone dully in the milky cataracts of the old fading pink-shot pupils.

'Why are you in this business, tell me?' he asked of a sudden.

'I . . . I believe in it,' I said awkwardly.

He threw up his hand in disgust.

'I believed in things once,' he said. 'I had ideas about the people, the people on my land. I thought I'd get them to do things with their land – I was ready to help them with loans and advice. I'd tell them how to drain it, how to grow more variety of vegetables, and how to make money out of their gardens selling the produce in the city, and how to make better butter and keep their eggs clean . . .'

He sniffed a long sneer at himself and pulled his throat and looked absently into the fire.

'Look at them, today. As dirty as ever, as poor as ever, as backward as ever, and I suppose they blame people like us for it all. If they had my land they'd know how to farm it, they think. But why haven't they done anything with their own? Why? Why?'

He was a hot-tempered old fellow, flying into a temper at a second's warning.

'But you're a city boy, you know nothing of the people. It's people like us who know Ireland. We belong to it – we who've grown up on the land and know it and the people on it.'

'Your people were merchants,' I said rather timidly.

'They made their money on bottles,' he said reaching for the whisky. 'And I've spent their money on bottles,' he added with the air of a man who has often made the same joke and grown serious over it. For as he began to pour the liquor out tremblingly he turned savagely on me.

'And who makes glass in Ireland, now?' he wheezed.

'When we stopped, why didn't somebody else take it up? They could make lovely glass in Ireland at one time. It might have become a great, distinctive national industry, and everywhere you'd see the men blowing the glass into lovely shapes. People would be coming from abroad to see them. I've seen them as a lad. Pouf! And there you had a globe of glass, shining, coloured, glowing. Oh, no, Oh, no! What do we see in the shop-windows, now?' he cried, leaning forward and baring his rotting, easily-moved teeth. 'Cobblers! Yah! A race of cobblers. That's what we are – a race of cobblers! They hadn't it in them. They hadn't it in them!'

I saw for the first time how deep the hate on his side could be, as deep as the hate on ours, as deep and as terrible, and although he angered me there was so much contempt in his face and voice that I could scarcely muster up the courage to meet his eyes. His whisky was rising in my head.

'Oh, that was all begun two centuries ago,' I cried back at him. 'It was the Union with England that ruined us and our industries. Can't you see that? It ruined you. It ruined your glass-business. Aren't you part of Ireland as much as us?'

'Ach! It's always the same. This ruined us, and that ruined us, and the other ruined us. I tell you I'm ashamed to be called an Irishman, and in fact I'm not an Irishman. I'm a colonist – a planter – whatever you like, one of those that tried to come and do something with you people. Why didn't the people fight for their rights when they had a parliament?'

I tried to answer but he wouldn't let me, spilling his liquor all over the hearth in his rage.

'I know what you'll say. But look at the Welsh, and look at the Scotch. They haven't a parliament and they have prospered. What's to stop us from making our linens and our woven silks, from weaving patterns into them like the Indians and the Slavs? Where are our crafts? What can we show? What have we ever done? Except dig patches and plough fields? Why haven't we stuffs, yes, stuffs, stuffs, stuffs, of our own – stuffs (how he spat it out!) that any woman would love to fold around her body, stuffs she'd love to feel against her flesh? Coloured, brilliant, delicate stuffs?'

And he began to rub his little hands down his thighs.

'Oh, fantastic!' I said, and leaned back from him smiling.

'Ah, there's your revolver man talking. But it could be done. Or why don't we export bulbs or cut-flowers like the Dutch and the French and the Channel Islanders?'

'It's impossible – the climate.'

'Pah! It's on our side. The Gulf Stream would do.'

'The Gulf Stream?'

Mad Henn!

'Yes! It warms our southern shores. You can grow acacias in Kerry in the open air in mid-winter. (A rush of delicate r's here.) I've picked London pride on the mountains in early March. Jasmine, lilacs, fuchsias....'

'Fuchsia isn't a cut flower,' I taunted. 'Nor a bulb!'

He twitched in every limb, dashed his glass in the fire and banged the hearth with his stick, and stuttered all the rest he had to say to me.

'It grows, it grows, I tell you it grows wild in mid-winter. In the open air. You're a damned obstinate young fellow. And wallflower, lily of the valley, freesia, gardenia, arbutus, mignonette. And all sorts of delicate ferns. A marvellous but a lost opportunity. These things will bring them in more money than potatoes. But they tread on them. It's so silly, really, because it's just like treading on gold.'

'But the people are farmers.'

'What are the Germans, the Dutch, the Belgians? Ah! (It was a long-drawn-out Ah! of sweet memories.) I know the people. You city fellows don't know them.'

Then his voice fell.

'I know their women,' he said.

He rubbed his little hands again and tapped me on the knee.

'I know every sort of woman: English women, French women, Italians, I've even known a Russian woman. The Russians are like the Irish, you know. But too stubborn and too obstinate and too proud. Prouder even than the Irish. And not one of them all can equal the Irish woman – of the right sort. But they're airy. You have to bind them down with a brutal religion or they'd fly over the fields from you. Don't you feel that too, eh?'

And he cocked his hat even still further over on one ear and laughed a little elfish laugh of delight and his loose lock behind almost curled like a drake's tail. He poked the embers with his stick. He filled my glass in spite of me – delighted like all old bachelors whose club-days and dancing-days are done to have anyone at all who will talk with them.

'Ah! Yes,' he sighed as he poured my whisky, 'the women are all right. So lovely and plump. Muscular from the fields. Arms . . . right! (He moulded them with the bottle in his hand.) Breasts like tulips. Lovely! Lovely! But you don't know. You only know the city. The city! Puh! I wouldn't give that much for a city woman.'

I threw off his whisky neat.

'Why shouldn't I know the country?' I cried. 'By damn but I do. As well as you, better than you. I know their women. Many a mouse I moused with their women. What's more than that, I was born in the country and born right here in this townland. My mother was born and is buried and my grandmother and all her people before her down there in Kilcrea churchyard. I lived in the townland of Farrane myself, as a child and my father lived there before me.'

I thought he shrank into himself at that, pulling down his long neck like a snail or a tortoise at the approach of danger.

'What's your name?' he asked quietly.

I told him.

'I remember your mother well,' he said. 'She held land from me. And I remember your father. He was stationed at Kilcrea. I met him first at an eviction on my land. They shoved a red-hot poker through the door at him and he caught it; and by God he pulled it from them, so he did. A fine man.'

'I remember that,' I said, quiet myself, too, now.

'No, boy, no,' he said sadly. 'That was a long time ago.'

'Oh, but, I do well,' I cried. 'I remember the bandage on his hand.'

'Not at all,' and he smacked the stick on the side of the marble fireplace. 'This was a long time ago. Forty years or more. Forty years or more' – and as he said it his eyes strayed, rheum wet, from me to the fire and back again as if he were trying to see my father in me and those dead years that were gone from him for ever.

'Where is he now?' he asked.

'He's dead,' I said.

'Ah, and is he dead?'

'Yes.'

'And your mother?'

'She is dead,' I answered quietly.

'Ah!'

He looked into the embers and they seemed to glow but faintly on his all but sightless balls – a quietness more than the night fallen on him secretly and unexpectedly. Just then a step resounded on the hall-flags and the door opened and in came the dark, muscular Gypsy, behind her Stevey, slouching as ever. He did not see me at first, and he approached the old man with a low 'Good-night' and I thought the long neck drew into itself again. Henn did not reply, but he raised a feeble hand and took the girl's fingers in his palm. His was as tiny as hers – and the fire shone pink between his bony fingers, ridged with the veins and threaded with the thousand wrinkles of age. As their eyes met the swan's neck curved up to her lovingly.

'Have you had a nice walk, pretty?'

'Yes, down to the bridge at the pub.'

Before him how delicately her lips said, *down*, with a voluptuous upward curve at the corners of her mouth so that they swept into her cheek as the curved initials on his ring swept into the gold. Her sullen eyes were soft and in this light she almost looked beautiful. His hand wandered over her arm as he asked the next question – a question as familiar as Sunday. She smiled as she replied.

'Was there anything rising?' he asked.

'Down be the bridge they're leppin,' she said.

'It's the breeze. There's always a breeze fluting down that side of the valley.'

Stevey laughed loudly at them both, and his voice was rough and coarse beside the rich voice of the girl and the cultured voice of the old man.

'Leppin'? Rise? Rise, how are you! That was me spittin' when she wasn't looking.'

'Oh, then, there was a rise,' she cried. 'I saw their silver bellies shining as they leaped.'

'Ooh!' mocked Stevey. 'Bellies! Naughty word! Ooh!'

Henn gripped his stick until it trembled and his knuckles strained the skin white. He stamped at Stevey.

'If the girl says there was a rise, there was. Aren't you enough of a gentleman not to contradict her?'

But his voice trembled as if he were half afraid of his own daring. Well he might. In a second Stevey was in one of his violent passions, almost raising his fist over the old bowler-hatted head.

'I don't want any English pimp to tell me what to do or not do with the girl – or any girl. Mind that!'

Henn's hand shook, and all his legs as he pulled himself up on his stick, taller when he stood than any of us, his bent back straightened, made gigantic by the great shadow that climbed the wall behind him. I could see what a man he was in his heyday, what a figure on a horse, wielding the rod from the top of a rock, a wiry, bony giant. There was almost majesty in him as he pointed his trembling stick to the door and faced down to Stevey with;

'Leave my house, sir. I'll not be bullied any longer by you – not an hour.'

'And I'll leave it,' cried Stevey, 'when and only when I choose. I'll not be ordered by *you*. Who the hell do you think you are ordering? Do you think you can order *me*? Ho, and but let me tell you, Mister Alexander Henn, I'm *staying* here.'

I could see he had taken drink while down at the pub, and the devil was in his eyes: he skipped across the hearth by the side of Henn and flopped mockingly into the chair the old man had just left. Then he stretched out his hand for Henn's glass on the mantel-piece, and wiping the side of it on his coat-sleeve raised it in mockery of the old man. There was silence for a second and then Gypsy laughed, and the laugh cut through Henn. He raised his stick and lashed at the hand that held the empty glass in the air, and as the splinters fell I leapt, Henn thrusting his face across my arm into Stevey's face, Gypsy barely holding back Stevey's fist before it crashed into the old rheumy, half-blind eyes. Henn was all but weeping for vanity, for that laughter of the girl at his age and infirmity. All he could say between his sobs was 'You young ruffian. You ruffian. You ruffian. . . .'

I thrust Stevey back. Henn turned to me.

'This young woman. If anything should happen to her, which God forbid . . .'

'Oh, you hypocrite,' cried Stevey, turning to the empty air for somebody to appeal to. 'Oh, listen to that, God! God forbid! Oh, the hypocrisy of it!'

'Yes, yes, yes,' I appealed and implored Gypsy to take him away and pushed him from us, and the girl dragged him, and pushed him, and persuaded him out of the room. She was strangely cool as if abuse and quarrelling and coarse talk were nothing to her. I put the old man in his chair and filled a glass for him and left him and found Stevey sullenly akimbo on the top of the steps. He was ashamed, I felt, to have played his heroics opposite me and I thought he might not have quarrelled with old Henn if he knew I was there. So I stood beside him without speaking until he said he was sorry he had broken out like that since it would ruin my chances of staying at the Hall. I could not tell of what else he was thinking, but I was thinking to myself: Where shall I go now? For I could neither remain in the Hall nor go with Stevey. My hopes of a quiet, serene night were already vanished, and I felt to Stevey as one feels towards some hooligan who breaks in on lovely music with his loud shouting and laughter. We stood in silence and looked down into the night. A frightened bird fluttered in the woods; a star fell in a graceful, fatal swoop, vanishing in mid-air as if a mighty hand had scratched the sky with light.

Biting his nails, Stevey said, 'Tell Gypsy I want her.'

I went back to the drawing-room where the girl and the old man stood by the window.

'Stevey wishes to speak to you,' I said; and when she went tramping wearily, heavily, from the room I looked at Henn and he looked back at me and neither of us spoke. As I looked away again through the shining window I could see the old man's eyes fixed on me. At last I buttoned my coat about me and turned to him.

'I suppose I'd better be going,' I said.

'Going? Where are you going?'

'I don't know really, but . . .'

'Hum! You were to stay here, I take it, eh?'

After a long hesitation I answered, 'Yes – I was. I was. I may even stay in your hay-barn yet, for all you know. Good-night,' I concluded, 'I'm glad to have met you.'

'No, boy. I won't say good-night. And you won't stay in my hay-barn, because I have none. Stay where you intended to stay. Even though you didn't choose to ask me, stay. If not for your own sake, for your father's and mother's sake.'

He rose and went slowly and feebly to the door, his half-emptied bottle in his hand.

'Could I stop you,' he said, 'if you wanted to stay here a month? Stay! And be damned to ye!'

'I won't,' I said.

He turned to me at the door.

'Please do stay,' he pleaded, nodding his head many times to encourage me. 'Stay, stay, stay.'

He was maudlin with the excitement and the liquor.

'Will you stay?' he asked again.

I looked out into the dark.

Stay! I thought to myself it must be near to eleven or midnight.

'Thanks very much,' I said; and being satisfied he waved his bony hand, slipping his bottle into the great pocket of his swallow-tailed coat; then he turned and went, his little hat perched on one side of his head and his rug trailing after him on the uncarpeted floor.

I sat by the table and looked about me again: at the table-cloth like a gypsy's shawl, at the threadbare carpet on the floor, at the dusty lace curtains dragged to the ends of their poles, and everything my eyes fell on mocked him and his desires. Lovely woven silks, he had said, and woven linens, and stuffs such as women might love to feel? And such strange flowers and bulbs as the Dutch and the Channel Islanders grew, as freesia, gardenia, mignonette? What a liar, I thought; and bitterly I was pleased to end the triad, calling him (as the farming folk had called him for fifty years) a lunatic; and he would not deny he was a libertine as well.

Gypsy returned, and I told her I was staying in the house, and once more she went and returned. We heard Stevey's steps vanish down the drive, and then silently she took a candle and lit me upstairs to bed. As we went I asked her what her name was, and she said:

'My name is Gammle.'

'Indeed,' I said, thoughtlessly.

'Why *indeed*?' she asked, halting in her step and looking at me.

'Nothing,' I said. 'It's just a strange name.'

But I did not tell her I was thinking that the name was well known in North Cork for a tinker tribe, in Charleville and Doneraile and the borders of Limerick and up into Clare, a name few decent men or women ever bore.

'Good night,' she said, and left me in a great empty musty room, the bed all tousled and the bed-clothes soiled, and yellow. I lay down as I stood, and to the sound of the branches of the trees tapping on the bare window I dozed and slept.

3

I awoke, wide-eyed of a sudden insomnia, to the rusted, wailing drone of an old phonograph in the room below me. By the light of the moon I looked at my watch, it was past twelve o'clock, an hour when cities begin to live and the fields are fast asleep. How many times had I not lain awake for hours listening to the quietness of the city, or to late parties singing their way homeward, before the war and curfew sent us all to our beds, I would be awake now almost until the dawn broke. Rising peevishly I went to the door, opening it in time to hear a new record begin its nasal introductory speech – This is an Edison Bell recawrd; number one seven nine nine; songs from the Awpera of Dawn Giovanni by Mozart. And then through the hollow-sounding house the stifled music of one of the loveliest of operas; and humming with the singer, or rather behind the singer, came old blear-eyed maudlin Henn's cracked and drunken voice :

'*Batti; batti . . .*'

I bade sleep good-night, and dragging on my pants sat on the edge of the bed, my coat about my shoulders, smoking a cigarette. Or watched the branches beating on the panes, or the laurels shivering and shining in the tangled garden beneath my window, or the Bride rain-laden far below glinted between its ancient gall-black alders under the starry sky.

> '*Questo é il fin di chi fa mal,*
> *E de' perfidi la morte, alla vita è sempre ugual!*'

The pair and their song died slowly, and when silence fell Henn kicked his enamel chamber-pot until it rang. Croaking and humming the love-song he shuffled out on his landing. From my door I watched him almost stumble headlong down the stairs, out of the house, on to the gravelled drive and out of sight into the dark.

One by one I began to hear them – those innumerable, inexplicable sounds that are to be heard at night in a house when all the casual day-sounds are still; timbers that stretch and contract, little insects that make a great creaking noise. And feeling that I had rather be in the open air than alone in this empty house I pulled on my boots and went down to the open door and out on the avenue and down towards the cottage in the track of Henn. Here a chill wind was blowing last year's leaves high in the air, but near the lodge where the drive fell sharply down to the gates between the trees on their high ditches the dust lay in soft whispering drifts – soft and white as snow under the moon, so soft that as I stood by the little deserted lodge peering curiously in through one of the windows I might have been a rabbit or a fox for all the warning

I gave anyone who might have been inside. Only a shaft of wavering light lay thrown across the tiny hallway from another room.
Moving cautiously to the other window I peered in again. There they
were, Gypsy and Henn: she with her skirt drawn above her knees,
an old coat over the warm skin of her bare shoulders, toasting her
shins to a little flickering fire – Henn, as he did the first time I saw
them together, holding her fingers in his palm and leaning forward
over her round knee to see into her eyes.

Strange to watch the unequal pair looking at one another so long,
so silently, seeming not to say one word to each other, her dark
head bowed sidelong to his lips, her fallen lashes on her cheeks, her
parted lips that never moved, he, with a smile, foolish yet tender,
sagging his quivering mouth apart, his old hat cocked forward on
eyes that streamed their water to his cheeks; and yet, though Henn
was old and decaying, and she warm-fleshed, white to her teeth,
full of the pride of youth, and – Henn, was right – her breasts like
tulips fully blown, if anything too magnificently full, too Jewess
soft, yet he could for all that, raise his hand now with so much
languid grace to feel their roundness, hold the precious globe for
one moment, so lightly, so fondly on his fingers before his withered
hand fell as if in despair into her lap, that finer woman than Gypsy
might well have smiled, even as she smiled now, with head turning
slow from that flattering gesture of the epicure, with long slow-
drawn sighs at the uselessness of such praise from him. To which
of these men, I wondered, had this girl given herself? For now with
her hair dragged on the ridge of her chair and her head falling
lower and lower on her bosom until her eyes caught in the embers
of the fire, she permitted him to move aside her skirt, ever so little,
from her bare knee, and caress it with his withered hand as softly
as if it were swans-down, caress it even after the glow of the fire
shone on her eyes drowned in tears, caress it while she sat rigid
with misery, her moans breaking out in trembling waves to the
whispering night outside. And yet not a stir or word from Henn,
but as if hoping that his old hand could quiet her childlike sobs, he
caressed and caressed and looked and looked dog-like into her face.
Alas! each exhausted sigh was but the prelude to a new shuddering
burst of tears like waves that are silent for a while and then burst
suddenly and inevitably on the shore.

I could not bear those dog-like eyes of the old libertine, nor those sighs and sobs of the young girl; and stumbling away from the light of the little window and out of the creaking gate I found myself walking on and on under the tenting chestnuts in the windy dust-blown lane, up and along the highway I had come that evening, too moved to return and sit alone in my unkempt bedroom in the Hall. For somehow country and freedom seemed a small thing under this austere darkness with that pair, heavy with one another's sorrow, down in the weather-streaked decaying cottage; and with the memory of those drooping mother's breasts and that large mother's belly on the young girl, and the look of pity on the old libertine's face I find myself walking aimlessly on and on.

But suddenly across the black valley there rises a leaping yellow flame, and through the night air on the night wind comes the crackle of the burning timber, joists moist with the damp of years, burning the vermin in their cracks and the resinous veins.

The flames through the trees flickered like a huge bonfire and running down the lanes toward Henn Hall I could see from time to time as I ran the outline of windows, of a gable-end, of a chimney silhouetted against the glowing air about it. At the lodge the little light was still shining in the window but without looking through I knocked and knocked until bare padding feet came along the floor and the girl's voice said:

'Who is it? Who's there?'

'A fire,' I cried. 'What can we do? Across the valley, a big house.' And in my excitement I cried out, 'Where's Mad Henn?'

She answered through the door.

'He's not here. Isn't he at the Hall?'

I was, I admit, a fool that night.

'I don't know,' I shouted back to her.

'You don't know?'

She opened an inch or two of the door and looked out at me with frightened eyes.

'Whose house is it?' she asked.

'I don't know. It's straight over the river – straight across there.'

Holding her clothes about her body she stepped to the corner of the lodge and looked across at the blazing house.

'It's Blake's,' she said. 'We can't do anything. They may come over here. Where's Henn?' she asked then, suddenly terrified.

'I thought he was here.'

She stared at me, astonished, yet full of cunning that was mingled with fright for Henn.

'Isn't he at the Hall?' she insisted nervously.

'Maybe,' I stuttered, 'yes – perhaps he is – I suppose he *is* at the Hall.'

'Did you try?'

'I was out walking,' I said.

'Walking!'

There was a pause.

'What time is it?' she asked.

As I peered at my watch, saying, 'It's well after one o'clock,' I could see her eyes looking at me with fear and suspicion, and having spied on her I was ashamed to look up. But slowly I understood why she was watching me in that way, she thought that my coming there that night, a man 'on the run,' had something to do with this burning house, that I had caused it, as a reprisal, an act of revenge, and that in some way Henn too would suffer by it, and that Stevey, probably, had been the man who carried it out. How stupid I had been – but such reprisals were as yet rare in the country and it had never occurred to me that this was one until in her eyes I saw fear and distrust and hate.

'A nice time for walking,' she said shortly, and raced down the slope of the ditch and up to the Hall and there she knocked on the heavy hen's-head knocker until the countryside resounded and even a dog, somewhere across the fields, began to bark-bark at our knock-knock-knock on the echoing door. I tried to explain myself.

' 'Tis why I came to the country – to sleep. I get insomnia. So I got up and came out.'

'How did you get out? Henn keeps the key in his room.'

'The door was open.'

But I was now concealing something from her and she would not believe me.

'My God,' she moaned, 'what's happened him?'

Then in her fear and rage and suspicion she turned on me, a tigress robbed of her mate – and even in that instant I remember saying to myself, Oho! So it's Henn, is it?

'Where is he?' she cried. 'What did ye do with him? Christ blast ye all, ye set of ——s. What did ye do to him?'

Her voice was echoed by the stony face of the house, thrown

back into the fields and echoed there again and again by the barking
dog.

'I know nothing about him,' I said angrily. 'He's probably dead
drunk. Knock him up.'

And I clouted the hen's head until my hand ached. Not a sound
replied but the dog over the fields, now thoroughly aroused, and
the crackling of the flames across the valley, and, within, the old
sheep-dog, who stirred and howled mournfully.

The girl caught my arm in fear.

'Oh, it's the dog crying before somebody dies.'

'Sssh! Is that a window?'

'Is it the I.R.A that burnt it?' she asked, looking up and then
over her shoulder.

'I know nothing about it. How can we get in?'

'It's for the child the Tans killed. Oh! Ye've done something to
Henn. Ye've surely done something to Henn.'

We found a little scullery window open and through it I clambered and let her in at the front door. Up we climbed the dark
stairs, the dog flopping along behind, and up to his room, and into
it. We found him there in his bed, snoring on his stomach with the
weight of drink, his night-shirt crumpled above his bare knees, and
on his head a fluff-laden night-cap of scarlet wool. Ashamed of the
sight of him with his dirty toes and the engrimed creases across the
base of his neck and half-way up his skull, Gypsy shook him madly
into a gasping wakefulness; and seeing me, in the faint glow that
filled the room, smile at his comically stupid look she straightened
his cap on his head as if he were a child, and covered his shoulders
as he sat up in bed looking about him at the angry waving light –
like a picture of Juan in hell.

'Are you all right?' she asked.

'I – yes – oh, I'm all right. But . . .'

'Look.' She pointed, and he looked.

'My God!' he cried. 'Totty Blake's.'

His eyes bulged as he looked, and trying to master himself he
shambled across the floor to stoop in the open window in his
shirt.

'Oh! My God! My God!' was all he could say, and then, 'Do you
hear them? Do you hear the noise?'

'The flames?' I said.

'No! The rooks. They'll never nest there again. They're ruined with the heat.'

And he began to tousle his cap and sank on his knees crying like a child. Gypsy stood over him where he knelt.

'The Blakes will be likely coming here for the night.'

He stood up at once like a hardened toper, and turned to us.

'Go down,' he said, 'and lay the table for them, and set the fire going. And you, boy, go, like a good fellow, and give her a hand.'

Gypsy went but I thought he was unable to look after himself and tried to coax him from the window.

'I'll stay here,' I whispered. 'It's cold, you know. You must dress, now. I'll help you. Come on.'

But when I tried to lead him back to the bed he flung my arm aside, peevishly.

'Am I a child?' he cried.

So I left him in a palsy of trembling, dragging his nightshirt over his head, rump-naked, fumbling for his clothes by the pale light of the candle and the fluttering light of the burning house.

In silence we set about blowing the seed of fire on the hearth into flame, and I dipped the kettle in the dark water of the butt and the crane swung it slowly over the fire. The false dawn of the fire and the distant rooks cawing with fright had awakened the doves and all the birds on this side of the valley and the night was sweet with their music. From time to time as we passed from kitchen to parlour with ware or food we halted to look at the fire that sometimes seemed to have died away and sometimes flared up more madly than ever before. There Henn joined me and we waited there, wondering if the Blakes would come or if we should go back to bed and try to sleep out the end of the night. At last he drew me into the room and filled out a drink for himself, while I yawned, dry-eyed for lack of sleep.

'I don't know where else the Blakes can go,' he said. 'Though if there was another house within three miles of them they'd rather die than come under my roof. I'm sorry for his two tits of sisters, though.'

'Only two women?' I asked wearily.

'Philamena and Agatha. Two sour tits. And the Captain, their father. That's all that's there. Oh, but Philamena *is* a sour creature. I chalked that very word on the door of the church about her when

I was six – got whipped for it too. And she never spoke a word to me after. And I gave Agatha a penny at the age of eight if she'd let me swing her so high that I could see her drawers. They would never let her see me after that. I once went,' he said, throwing back his liquor, 'I once went to church to a Handel service, and I had to run out of it when I saw the two virgins singing away *"To us a child is born; to us a son is given."* But, ah!' he snarled, 'they're sour titties. Vinegar for milk they have. Sour and old and virginal.'

He was getting angry with them, I could see.

'They'd just raise their hands in horror at a girl like . . . at a girl that would, that would . . .'

I stood in the corner of the window watching the sparks rising and falling endlessly like fireflies, silenced as one is always silenced by a raging fire, to think of calamity on one's doorstep.

'Gypsy,' says Henn, suddenly rising and going to another window, 'Gypsy was sick tonight.'

'Bad?' I asked sleepily.

'Bad? Oh, no! Not yet.'

'Not yet?'

'That's what I said. Didn't you hear me?'

'Yes.'

He came shuffling over to me on his stick.

'The girl is ruined,' he said, peering into my eyes that filled with shame as he looked at them.

'What do you mean by that?'

'Gypsy is going to be a mother next month or after.'

I answered his stare.

'Who do you think is to blame?' he asked.

For answer I looked angrily over the valley at the house. What did it matter to him what I thought? What would all the country think when they heard it? Another servant of Henn's – it was an old story – about to bear a child.

'I'll not be blamed,' he cried and his tubes were hoarse with passion. 'I am not to be blamed.'

'What does the girl say?'

'How does she know?'

And he went back to his glass and his fire.

And then up the avenue in a shadowy mass, singing and shouting, came the incendiaries, Stevey at their head, ready for anything, drunk with whisky and triumph. Had it been six months later, he could safely have burnt half the houses in the district and we should not have dared, nor cared, nor had the time, nor even wished in the heat of passion – for things grew very hot by then – to question any such act of his. But tonight I ran to the door determined to thwart him. He faced up the steps and shouted for Henn, Henn the whore, Henn the cock, the Henn's neck, and all about him shouted with him out of the dark in their rough, country accents:

'Henn! Henn! Come out, you whore. Henn! Come out, Henn!'

There was a glint of a revolver in one man's hand as I ran down the steps and faced up to Stevey.

'What rotten sort of soldier are you?' I shouted at him.

'What do you mean?' he cried.

'Is that what you call soldiering?' I shouted into his face, pointing across the valley at the burning ruin. For an instant he looked at it, and then to his men and at me.

'Ah,' he shouted. 'We burnt the bastards out; didn't we, boys? And damn right well they deserved it.'

They shouted it back to him, their memories full of the days when their people died of starvation by the roadsides and the big houses looked on in portly indifference. Again and again they echoed it back to him.

'And we'll burn Henn out,' cried Stevey, and made a dive for the steps. I caught him and swung him about while Henn hung over the iron railings and croaked down at us:

'If I had a gun. Oh, if I only had a gun.'

'Shut up,' I shouted at him. The crowd was nasty enough without this.

'Oh, for a gun,' he persisted. 'Just for one minute . . .'

'Go in, blast you,' I shouted at him while Gypsy tried to drag him from the steps.

'You're fine fellows. Oh, you're great fellows,' I taunted them. 'You haven't, between the lot of you, fired a single shot in all this district for four months. Unless you shot a sitting hare or a tame fox. It's what you'd do by the look of you. And now you go and burn a couple of women out in the middle of the night. Oh, you're grand soldiers entirely. You cowardly mob!'

'You keep your tongue quiet'; from Stevey. He was a head higher than me.

'I'm here to talk to you,' I said, 'and I'll give you and your men my talk now, if you want it. Let me tell you you have the reputation of being the tamest commandant. . . .'

He flew into a passion at once and drew his revolver at me. At once the country fellows skipped aside – they didn't at all like this business of drawing a gun on one of their own, and they began to mutter and pluck at Stevey, and to signal me to hold my peace; but I knew my man.

'Now, now, Long,' they muttered. 'Be aisy now, Long.'

'You won't bully me,' I said. 'Why don't you use your gun on the Tans?'

He turned to them.

'Are you going to be stopped by a city caffler?'

And to me:

'We know what Henn is.'

'What am I?' croaked Henn who was still grasping the railings, with Gypsy trying to persuade him to come in.

'What did Henn ever do to *you*?' I asked.

'Aye, what did I ever do to you?' gasped Henn, hoarse with excitement, sweeping his little hat off his head and leaning down over the railings like a man giving a speech. 'What did I do to you? What did I ever to do you or yours?'

'Ah,' shouted Stevey up to him. 'Ah, you whore-master' – and I thought he'd blow the old man's brains out. 'What do you know what's mine or yours? You blasted father of thousands.'

Utterly beyond himself he pointed with his gun at Gypsy, and shook his fist in the old man's eyes.

'Look at that girl. What did you do to her? Answer that or you'll not have a house by morning.'

Then quite without warning the rest of them turned and raced over the lawn into the surrounding night. Only one waited to pluck Stevey by the arm and whisper:

'It's the Blakes. They're coming. Come away out of this. They'll know us.'

'I don't care about the Blakes,' said Stevey, too intent on having his way with Henn that night to care about anything else. 'Ask him,' he said to me, 'Ask him what did he do to that girl? Ask him that?'

'Stevey, Stevey,' implored the girl as she tried still to induce Henn to move.

I drew Stevey to one side as Henn, who had also seen the Blakes come up the drive swaying with the weight of the bundles they bore, stood down on the steps to meet them, his hat in his hand like an ambassador or a prince receiving his guests, his head like a gander's head, jigging up and down as he bowed them in; and as the two old maids came timidly up to him, peering here and there in their fear, and the portly captain, their father, brought up the rear, peeping over their shoulders because he was almost as blind as Henn, they all looked more like frightened ganders and geese than human beings able to look to themselves. They clustered together on their way up the steps, Henn wheezing about not being 'quite up to the tip-top of readiness,' and saying, 'You have me at a disadvantage, Miss Blake. But come in. A cup of hot tea, now. A shot of Martell's, captain? Most regrettable! Terrible! This way, now. Allow me. This way. That's right – there we are. . . .' And so into the hall with his visitors.

When they were gone the dark figures gathered about us again, like wolves, or tormenting flies that had been driven aside for the moment.

'I'll make that man marry the girl,' said Stevey under his breath to me, 'or I'll burn this house to the very ground.'

'We'll burn him out,' they growled, the lust for destruction in their blood.

'He'll marry the girl, or he'll have no house over his head by morning.'

'But the man is eighty if he's a day,' I implored, 'and the girl is a mere slip of a girl. Is she twenty itself?'

'Well, he ruined her,' said Stevey up to my mouth as if he would force the words into it.

'I do not believe it,' I said.

Another shower had begun to fall by now, growing heavier drop by drop, dimming the starlight and shimmering dark about the distant fire. Stevey waved his hand to his fellows.

'The city fellows are a lot of help to us,' he said. 'But I'll show you. I'm not going to stand here all night in the rain talking with you.'

He rushed past me up the steps and into the house with his

mob after him. I managed to stop him at the door of the drawing-room and we parleyed there for a while, whispering as we peeped through the cracked door. There, where fifty years ago he had leant across the shining walnut to his perfumed lights-o'-love, smiling quizzically down on them from his swan's neck, approving the painted lips, the tilted eyebrows, always gracious to them, however cynical, perpetually on the smile, only leaning back from his scandalous whispering when the butler laid a new course or refilled his glass – there, now, he offered his smoke-tainted tea, with the airs of fifty years ago, though they creaked and stuttered a little from lack of use, to the two silent, miserable old maids.

'Oh, yes, do drink a cup of tea, Miss Blake,' and he puffs out his cheeks to encourage her. 'Just one?'

'Thank you. I don't believe I really want one, Mr Henn.'

'Oh just one cup. Just one.'

But they sat very straight-backed and unbending, trying hard not to keep looking over the valley at their ruined home. They looked instead at the soiled table-cloth, the unequal ware, the tarnished silver, or at one another, or at the old captain, their father, who sat sucking his brandy, heavy jowled and heavy bodied, by Henn's fire. Or they looked at Gypsy, who, careless of her ungainly, ungirlish shape, danced superfluous attendance on them, full of pity for their misfortune, glad to be in the presence of real ladies even for an hour.

So they were sitting when Stevey burst in on them, calling on Henn so loudly that they almost screamed.

'Henn,' he said. 'We want you.'

'Don't go, Henn,' said the captain at once, as if he felt as much for his own sake as for Henn's that it was better they should all cling together now.

'What do you want, now?' stuttered Henn.

'I want you to come too, Gipsy,' said Stevey.

'Oh, Stevey, Stevey,' said the girl, utterly ashamed before the company.

'Come on, Henn,' bullied Stevey. 'Or will I tell my business here?'

'Out with it,' says the captain.

'One minute now,' pleaded Henn.

I thought it best to get the matter over, and went up to the old man and whispered that it would be best to come – I could not keep those fellows in hand for him any longer.

'Don't go Henn,' said the captain again.

'No, no,' said the old maids, with the same thought as their father in their minds that even Henn was better than nothing in their extremity, homeless as they were at this hour of the morning.

But he rose and went into the kitchen and Stevey and Gypsy and I after him. There he turned and faced us, looking down over us all, even over Stevey himself. And Stevey alone returned his glare, for the girl sat with her head in her hands by the fire and I looked at the rain spitting on the dark window. When Stevey had finished, all Henn could say was, 'You liar, you liar!' And all the girl could do was weep and say, 'My misfortune. My misfortune. My misfortune.' Even when I went to her and put my hand on her shoulder she only burst away from me and cried to let her alone, let her alone in her misfortune; for God's sake to let her alone in her misfortune, and sate at the table hiding her face in her hands, shaken with tears.

'You liar!' muttered Henn.

'I'm no liar,' cried Stevey.

As the girl wept with renewed shame that no man would own now that he ever loved her, Henn looked at her and said very gently to me:

'Supposing I won't marry her?'

'No harm will come to your person,' I said, and faced Stevey on that.

'Your house will go the way of Blake's,' said Stevey and faced me on that, 'If not tonight, tomorrow night, and if not then the night after. But if I have to wait a year to do it, up it will go.'

I shook the wretched girl by the shoulder.

'Do you want to marry this old man?' I cried into her ear.

She gave no reply.

'Speak up, Gypsy,' said Stevey. 'You will marry him, won't you? You said you would.'

She said not a word now.

'I'll not marry her,' said Henn.

Stevey had cunning enough to play his last card.

'Then tell your Blake friends to get out of this house, if they have sense. Or, you needn't – I'll do it.'

Henn stopped him at the door.

'Stop. Don't! Don't!'

And thereupon he sank into a chair with a sudden dizziness, and I had to hold him up from falling sidelong to the floor.

'Gypsy,' I said. 'Get a sup of whisky.'

'Alec!' she said, going to him, and he took her hand, her little hand in his when she stood by his side and said his name. 'Alec! Will I get a sup of brandy?'

There was silence for a few minutes, with only the noise of the rain cat-pattering against the window and the three of us over Henn. At last he began to whisper through his fingers, and I leaned down to hear him.

'Will she marry me?' he was whispering while the spittle dropped like a cow's spittle between his fingers to the flagged floor.

'Now!' cried Stevey triumphantly. 'Gypsy! Will you have him?'

In her deep man's voice she replied:

'And who else would have me now? Since others won't – others that have their own life and their own plans and plots?'

And seeing that the old man was not in need of help she went out of the kitchen, holding her stomach in her little palms, murmuring as she went,

'I will, if he will.'

I pushed Stevey before me from the kitchen and leaving Henn to himself we drove the rest of the herd before us from the hall, into the darkness, so rain-arrowy and cold. From the great front door I watched them go tramping down the avenue and as I, too, turned to go upstairs to my bed I heard Henn, back in the drawing-room, trying once more to play the host, after his fifty years' interval, with his smoky tea and his patched ware. I wondered as I tramped upstairs if he was thinking that, with this young wife, he might begin life again.

From my bed I heard the summer downpour drip about the house and occasionally spit down the chimney on the damp papers stuffed in the grate, tainting all the room with their sooty reek. Not until late noon did I hear another sound, and then it was the birds singing and the croaking corncrake and the doves in the high woods, and when I rose the whole house was radiant with sunshine reflected from the fields and the trees. There was nobody about the house but Gypsy. The Blakes had gone since early morning and Henn did not leave his bed for several days. Stevey I could find nowhere and the local men said he was gone into Kerry, swearing he would only return to make Henn keep to his promise. Two days I waited for him and searched about for news of him, and then I called a meeting of his battalion and replaced him by a new commandant.

One evening I left Henn Hall as I had come, but before I went I visited Henn in his room to say good-bye and I found him sitting over his fire, drinking punch and reading an *Anglers' Annual* of thirty years ago.

'Be careful of yourself, boy,' he warned as I turned to leave him.

'Oh, yes,' I said. 'I'll be careful.'

'Do you believe Long's story?' he said, then, leaning forward to me.

'I have no cause,' I parried, 'to believe or disbelieve anybody.' He leaned back and stared at the fire.

'Anyway,' he said after a while, 'I'm going to marry her. She's as good as the next, and better than some, even though she *is* only a tinker's daughter. Besides,' he added proudly, 'if it's a boy 'twill keep the name alive.'

As if he were a Hapsburg or a Bourbon!

One night two months or so later we heard in our back-yard bedroom that a strange pair left Cork for Dublin that afternoon on the Mail Express, all their dozen or so of trunks and bags labelled forward to an address in Paris. The woman, in a massive hat with a scarlet feather, had flaunted her way to her carriage – the old man, her husband, hobbling and shuffling along yards behind her. His travelling coat almost completely hid him, its tail touching the ground, its coat-collar up about his ears, and so weak did his eyes appear to be that even in the dim filtered light of the station he had cocked his hat forward over his eyebrows and shaded his eyes with his withered hand as he walked. But I find it too painful to think of him, there in Paris, with his scraps of governess-French, guiding his tinker wife through the boulevards, the cafés, the theatres – seeing once more the lovely women and the men gay in their hour. Life is too pitiful in these recapturings of the *temps perdu*, these brief intervals of reality.

Lilliput

On those nights when curfew came at ten o'clock and people were hastening within doors, locking doors, bolting doors, chaining doors at a full quarter to the hour, the poor alone were leisurely. Shandon had therefore struck ten before the last of the apple-sellers began to drag her basket after her into the lanes, but once she was gone the bridge was as empty as a plain.

There had been a fragrance in the air as long as the apples lay there exposed but the smell of the river was about to conquer again. A light fog had crept up the valley of the Lee from the harbour mouth and the lamps on the bridges had gathered from it a rich and reddish hue, while their dagger-like reflections trembled but slightly in the cold and glassy river-water. Farther down the quays the lovers were parting in the darker nooks, the men with one eye raised for the coming of the patrols, the women drawing their shawls closer around their lovers for the last embrace. Where the nets were drying there hung an odour of tar, and where they wash the sheep-skins the slips and pavement smelt in the night air. Already in the side-streets where there lie stables and storehouses and an occasional dwelling-house it might have been the first hours of the morning. But in one of these streets which lead from the quaysides to the centre of the city through a middle-class quarter, there stood, and had stood all the day long, a cart surmounted by a black box-like erection – a sort of miserable caravan without windows, without chimney and without an animal to support the slanting shafts. It might remind you of the little cart of the Poor Shepherd Nuns, or of a small-scale fever-cart intended to carry away the infected clothes from a condemned house. Inside were three children fast asleep. Clothes and cloths and mere rags filled this box of a house. Straw, a bucket, a board, chains – these with some huge stones at the wheels were scattered around it on the street. The cart carried no lamp. The open doorway facing the shafts was curtained by an old yellow coat, but at this hour the whole was a black mass inviting collision from the last-minute jarvey-cars careering past with their drunken passengers clinging to the seat.

It was now several minutes past the forbidden hour, and any moment the first lorries would be heard tearing along the quays and through the principal streets. None the less you could hear in the square near-by a war of words and distinguish them if you chose to listen. A woman was answering two or three male voices, young and soft in spite of their jeering tones, and as they parted farther and farther from one another, and the steps of the woman came nearer, and the voices of the others more shrill in the distance you might have heard every swear.

'Aha! The Kerry porther is the best porther, I can tell ye.'

They answered with a crying call such as a savage might use in battle.

'Go home to yeer mothers,' she responded, and followed with a cry as wild as theirs.

Just then the lorries began to whir in the distance and the boyish feet scampered for safety. Indifferent to them she sang herself back to her cart, sometimes muttering between the lines about her husband, and the police, and her donkey-ass. She sang out,

> 'O-o-oh!
> Will anybody tell me where the Blarney roses grow?
> Is it over in Kilmurry South, or yonder in Cloghroe?'

and tumbled into her cart, and sank at once into a profound sleep. The people of the quarter, however, sate up in their beds for an hour waiting for the patrols to come and take her, and when she was still there in the morning, they said such ungenerous things as 'The devil always looks after his own'; or, 'Look how a good person wouldn't have been so fortunate'; and went by to church with disapproving eyes.

At the first Angelus the haze still hung over the city, but the morning broke in sunshine shortly before the second bell rang in the noon. From that onwards there were ding-dongs all over the city at intervals of hours or half-hours. Finally when all the children were returning from their usual Sunday Mass she was arisen and had made some slops of tea. The city children gathered around her in wonderment as she washed the little girls' faces in the water she had borrowed near-by. Unperturbed, she combed their hair, peering at the scalp.

She was a sturdy woman with fresh colour in her cheeks, but her dun-coloured hair hung around her in contrast to the neat little figures that watched her and her cart in wonder. She saw this herself and eventually sate down on the sloping shaft to examine their spotless muslin frocks, their white shoes, their frilly lace, and sky-blue ribbons. She began to tell them disconsolately of her husband who was in Moore's Hotel – they knew Moore's Hotel was a jail – and she spoke pityingly of her three children and of the donkey-ass whom 'Cruelty' had led away when her husband was taken. So, all the day long she sate there, only rising at intervals. Once she picked and plucked at the three children, and went off with them to the jail. But she soon returned like a huge liner with three small tenders on her flanks, and began speaking of their father to some women that had gathered around her. The 'polis' had taken him for beating the donkey-ass 'till he brayed and died.' It was a tree fell on the donkey-ass, she said. They asked her had she come far, and she said from Headford. They said she was a pity, and one of the poorest came to her with a pot of soup and vegetables and potatoes. But her eldest child knocked it over by accident, and her mother called her a jade, and sate down for a spell.

All day long there was a changing little crowd around her. Patiently she told again and again of the donkey-ass and *their* father, and Moore's Hotel. She had once lived in Blarney Street and was four years on the road. Or she had lived in Barrackah and was ten years on the road. Or she had been born on the road and didn't know what a roof-tree meant. She told all her stories with her cheek on her fist, occasionally cocking her eye at her listeners but with a bored air. Each one of her listeners said she and her three children were a pity. She told them of the blackguards who called her low names last night, and they promised to keep guard for her, even to go to the sessions with her, and she answered she must rely on the help of God and her neighbours in all things. Some of the women did not like her and asked her questions that she refused to answer, but the other women said that these things were her own business.

At tea-hour the crowd did not slacken. The children from the streets all around became more noisy and familiar and had to be hunted away by the women. She borrowed water again, and a passing man bought her the last two loaves from the nearest huckster's shop. She gave tea to her three little girls within the cart, she herself eating from the roadway like a photographer behind the curtaining yellow coat, just as if her cart were a huge black camera.

At dusk and dark the people of the district became very nervous, and wondered why the police did not come to move her away, and complained that the whole country was in a shocking state, and feared above all, saying so to one another from door to door and window to window, that she would attract the attention of the Tans and the patrols to their quiet street and they would have no wink of sleep at all that night. At last the police came, but they had no mind to argue with her, and they merely told her to take her cart to hell out of that street even as she brought it in, and then because they knew she would begin to ask how was she to do that, they went away at once so that they should have the last word.

Then the children around began to enjoy themselves in earnest. They laid themselves under the shafts, and, shouting, began to strain and pull, or they heaved the huge stones from beneath the wheels and cried out for orders from the woman. The hoydens from the lane-ways told her to wheel her cart to this place or that, and the children chimed in that Harper's Lane was not at all like this street, but was a small narrow lane, down below there. The women gathered around her again and again, or sank on their haunches before her children and returning, told the mother that they were chatting away to themselves. Amid cries the cart began to move, and the loose chains to swing and ring in the dark as the children dragged it from the kerb. But the woman hailed them, and they ordered one another to wheel it back again, and there it stayed yet another night. She lit a candle and put the little girls to bed and its light shone brightly from the interior of the cart until she drew the yellow coat across it.

It was now almost ten o'clock and the women began to scatter, talking among themselves and asking her if she would be all right there. She walked away with a few of them and the wind blew the

candle out and the night moulded the cart into the blackness of
the street, and the street became as quiet as early dawn. A man who
asked the children who owned the cart, and where she was now,
had to chase them because they pelted him with stones and called
out ribald answers. Then the street settled down to the night again.
But a priest walked down the street from the riverside, showing like
a statue in jet under the lamps above him. Three girls clasping one
another's waists cried out that he was coming and retired to a
corner of the square. He looked around when he reached the cart,
and down the street ahead of him, and tapped politely at the side of
the cart, and looked to the right and then went home tapping his
silver-headed stick on the flags. The girls ran another way to watch
him and all was still again until the lorries began to whir in the
distance as Shandon struck the hour and the girls raced for their
homes.

The woman returned shortly after and crept into the cart on her
knees. An old woman shuffled along and asked her if she were there
last night also, and asked why was the poor man taken, and prayed
God to help us all. The woman within spoke out to her to go away
for Virgin Mary's sake and let her sleep – which the old woman
did, looking back several times as she padded away on her bare
feet, the woman within snoring out loud snores that might be heard
by a passer-by long before he distinguished the cart from the darkness around it.

Towards midnight a patrol of military tramped slowly down
the street while the wakeful householders held their breath. The
patrol halted at the cart, and the officer flashed his torch into the
interior. Then he murmured something to his sergeant and the
sergeant ordered his men to move on.

'Blimey!' whispered the sergeant to the corporal, and he passed
on the word to the men. 'Blimey, if it isn't a woman.'

'Oo is it?' asked a stupid private.

'Mary Mac and the Holy Trinity,' said the corporal, who was an
atheist; and sniggering they all tramped away – quietly and slowly
as if they would not disturb her sleep.

Fugue

The clouds lifted slowly from the ridge of the mountains and the dawn-rim appeared. As I stooped low to peer over the frame of the little attic-window I whispered to Rory that it was pitch-dark; and indeed it was far darker than the night before when we had the full moon in the sky. Rory leaned up on one elbow in bed, and asked me if I could hear anything from behind the river.

The damp of the dawn was everywhere that I might look. It softened the lime gable of the out-house beneath me, it hung over the sodden hay in the barn and, like the fog and mist last night under the blazing moon, it floated over the rumbling river to my right. I could imagine the flow taking strange courses in its flood, swishing in this neither dawn nor day nor dark, through all the alders and the reeds and the rushes and, doubtless, covering the stepping-stones that we hoped would give us an escape to the mountains beyond.

So I whispered to Rory that I could only hear the water falling in the weirs, and tumbling out of his bed he called a curse from Christ on the whore of a river that was holding us here to be plugged by the Tans for a pair of Irish bitches.

As I peered, standing in bare feet on the timber floor, I recalled last night with a shudder. We were retreating from Inchigeela by the back-roads and we two had lost ourselves in the barren and rocky place they call the Rough, a difficult place by day and almost impassable by night. We had tramped up and down and up and down until I felt my eyes closing as I stumbled along, and scarcely had the energy to push back my bandolier when it came sliding around my elbows. Rory, a country fellow, seemed tireless, but my shirt clung to my back with cold sweat. The fog lay like a white quilt under the moon, covering the countryside, and black shadows miles long and miles wide stretched across the land. Up and down we went, the fog growing thicker as we stumbled into boggy valleys, our feet squelching in the sodden turf, and fear hovering round our hearts. Earlier in the evening before the night fell, I had heard a noise before us in the lag, and had clicked a bullet in my rifle-breech and fallen flat, but Rory swore at me and asked me in amazement if I meant to fight them? After that I had no guts for anything but to get away from the danger of an encounter, to get across the river and the main road before the dawn, and up to the higher mountain on Ballyvourney beyond. So we trudged on and every natural night sound terrified us, a bird's cry, a barking dog with his double note, bark-bark, and then silence, bark-bark, and like that now and again the whole night long from one mountain side or another. People say the most lonely thing of all is the bark of a dog at night, but to us the most lonely sight was the odd twinkle of a light, miles away, one dot of light and all the rest of the land in darkness, except for the moon in the sky. The little light meant friends, a fireside, words of advice, comfort – but for us only the squelching and the trudging that seemed never to end, and maybe a bullet in the head before the dawn.

Once only we rested when Rory lost all patience and flung caution to the wind to light a cigarette in the hollow of his palms. I stretched out on the sodden mass – God, how restful to sleep there for an hour or two – but Rory muttered to himself, and I tried to keep awake by watching the coming of the red glow in his palm every time he drew in a fresh puff. The moon was a few nights from full roundness, and I thought it looked like a jolly wench laughing at us both and the missing segment like a bonnety tam cocked on the side of her fat head. The devil would look after his own, Rory was saying, blast them, two again' twenty, we couldn't fight them. Rory pulled me up and we went on, and I cursed Rory for not knowing the lay of his own countryside and he cursed me for a city snot that had no business out here in the mountains. Then we heard the cattle plunging in the boggy hollow beneath us, and we plunged ahead ourselves down a sharp descent where the river must have cut its way centuries ago: down we went sliding and running until the heavenly sight of trees broke against the sky and the dark mass of a house against them. Rory knew it for Dan Jamesy's house and we hammered with our rifle butts on the door, anxious only for sleep, and food, and the sight of friends. From an upper window she called to us and Rory spoke his name. Used to this sort of thing, and pitying us, she came down; barefooted, her black hair around her, a black cloak on her shoulders not altogether drawn over her pale breast, a candle blown madly by the wind slanting in her hand.

Rory had dressed himself while I peered out at the wall of mountain before me, and slinging his equipment over one shoulder he went down to eat something before we faced the river and the road – both half a mile away now. I followed him in a moment and found the old woman of the house and a little boy seated on the settle, his eyes wide with interest, hers full of uneasiness at our being in her house, a danger to her sons and husband. The young woman who had opened the door the night before stood like a statue before the wide fireplace, her bright arm bare to the elbow, and – curious gesture – her hand on the crown of her head as if to keep in position the hair brushed and close-combed around her skull like a black velvet cap shining in the firelight. She smiled at me as I entered, but I was too anxious to reply with more than a wan smile. Rory asked her many questions about the encircling troops, and she replied, looking down at his ruddy earnest face, that some lorries had passed by an hour ago, and when he asked about the river she said that it had risen over the stones and could not be crossed. She stooped down to reach the teapot, keeping one hand on her hip as she poured the tea: before the hour was out I recollected how she looked at me while she poured me out a cupful, and at the recollection I felt just as when I saw the night before an odd, twinkling window-light heading a deserted valley full of moonlight and mist. Stooping again she replaced the pot and went to sit on the other side of the little boy, and laying one hand on his knee spoke to him.

'That fir Tom brought last night has no fire in it.'

'Tis a bad fire, God bless it.'

'Get a good log, now, Jamesy, will you? Will you?' The little fellow looked at us only, and said: 'I will,' but he did not stir. The old woman broke in irritably:

'Wisha, Jamesy couldn't.'

'Indeed, Jamesy is a great man, isn't he, Jamesy? Imagine Jamesy not to be able to carry a baulk of fir! Will you, Jamesy?'

But Jamesy sat with dangling legs watching us eat and she rose and with easy steps went out: the old woman stirred the wood fire; one of the sons handled my revolver with dull curiosity, and another fumbled in a rope-loft over Rory's head and replied that another lorry was gone by. We prepared for the river and the road, on our guard, not so afraid as when the night was all around. I went to the door to see if it rained, and stood looking into the dark archway of the stables and at the dark hollows under the thatch – nowhere else could I see the soft, silent fall. As I looked at the dark archway she appeared in it with an armful of logs and raised her head towards me and smiled once again and then approached pulling her blue apron over her head to protect her from the rain. I saw her smile and it tortured me. But Rory and the old man of the house came out and went towards the stables, arguing about a horse to carry us over the flood, and I followed them, and we came at last to where the river was tearing madly over the drowned stones.

As I sat behind the old fellow on his white mare clasping him firmly about the waist, and trying to keep my eyes from the swirling water that tore the gravel from the unsteady hoofs, I saw from the corners of my eyes the drops that splashed up and flashed in the sun as they fell again on the prancing knees and the brown water. I saw at the identical moment the young woman in the blowing wind of the night, and her looks at me twice, thrice that morning. I longed for an end to this vagabond life, longed for I dared not think what; but there was in it the scent and light of flowers and the scent of woman and her soft caresses. She had looked at me as if we had between us some secret love: not one woman in ten thousand will look so at one man in as many thousand, perhaps not one in all his life, never more than one I would have said a day ago, and now one such had looked at my eyes and I thought at once of the evening glow of the city streets when the sun has gone behind the tallest houses, when the end of the day is near, and the canyon-alleys are suffused with dusk and slow-moving lights: when men waken from the sleep of day and returning in upon themselves think of love, and the darkness where love is, and wander out from the city to the dark fields seeking a secret loneliness for their pain.

Rory had forgotten that he must not look down and he fell sidewise on the horse's back, and when he reached the opposite bank he began talking of his foolishness and never ceased reverting to it the whole day. He looked down, you see, he looked down into the flood, he forgot, man, he looked down, and, by God, if he hadn't looked, but he looked into the water, he knew he shouldn't, – wasn't it I myself was telling you not to look at the flood, but whatever happened I looked down. And Cripes! when I did. . . . To stay him and have peace for my own thought I told him that he had but little talk the night before : but he did not heed my jibes, and chattered on, glad of the morning and reckless about the last mile between us and the foothills. He was a little bellied fellow, his mouth like a crack across a potato, his cap distended by a cane hoop just like a plate on the top of his head. He had pinned a coloured minature of the Virgin to the front of his queer cap, and when in the mood, his talk bubbled from him in anything but a virginal flow. How he had sworn at me yesterday when he sighted the enemy troops, and I could not see at all the tiny khaki figures below us on the lower slopes!

'Do you see them?' he had cried with equal stress on each word after the manner of his dialect. 'Christ, can't you see them?' he had shouted in rage, saying it as if it were spelled in two syllables, Chi-rist. 'Will you look at them, Christ, will you look at them when I tell you?'

I used to wonder at his affection for me in spite of such failures as this. In better mood now he jabbered on while we made our way up against the sprung wind and a hilly place. At last we heard the incessant knocking of a threshing engine on the bald summit in front of us, and we made our way to it. Up here the wind was a storm, and it blew the chaff about the sky like yellow snow blown before the wind. First the blue slate-roof, then the white walls of the house, the yellow stack of corn, the stone-wall fences of the fields, and at last the little black engine jumping like a kettle on the hob, while all the time the men swung their arms to and fro in labour : soon we were amongst them telling one group after another of the night's and day's adventures. Rory gabbled between every pant after his climb, telling about the horse and how I could not see the little grey figures when they came around us the evening before. From where we stood, the Rough looked like a flat plain and the distant mountains like hunchbacks in a row. I watched the whole country change with the shadows of the flying clouds, listening to the engine, with its disyllabic knocking, ceaseless since the dawn, and the wind's cry, and Rory shouting above all.

'There was the bloody mare in the middle of the river, I'm not in the habit of horses, you know, a man that was used to horses wouldn't mind, but I wasn't in the habit of them and I never was, and what did I do and the bloody mare there in the middle of the river, what did I do, what did I do? The thing I did! What should I *do*, I ask you, but look down at the flood, so look down at the flood I did. I looked down and only for the lad got a grip of me I was down. Cripes, I was. I was! If I would only not look down at the flood, you see, but I looked down, and by Christ!'

Here Rory began to shake in his excitement, too moved to be articulate.

The chaff was always driving away before the wind, and now and again someone would look up and around at the sky and say to the man whose stack was being threshed in this communal fashion of the mountains :

'Maybe, it will hold dry.'

The other would look up and around and say :

'Maybe it will. It might then. It's a strong wind.'

Then they would set to work again, piking and tossing the broken sheaves and we moved down at last to the road.

The road twisted eastward behind the rocks, and nothing but the tops of the telegraph poles showed where it ran after that. It was bare and empty, so we ran for it, crossed it, and in another moment Rory was crying that a lorry was coming around the bend. Heart-leaping, we doubled our pace and fell upon our bellies in the moss, squirming around like legless things to face the road. In a moment more the shots began to whine away over our heads, and I saw two awkward figures firing at us as they ran : I fired wildly in reply until my bolt jammed, and then rolled away into a hollow that by the fortunes of war lay behind me : thereupon I ran through the rocky place, through the bracken and the bog, more madly than ever in my life before, and raced for such a lengthy spell that when at last I fell helpless upon the ground my breath pumped in and out painfully and my heart beat against my side like a thing trying to leave my body. I heard the shots still ringing and the bullets whining high up in the air, flying no doubt in a great parabola so that I fancied that I heard them thud when spent into the soft earth, a rainbow curve completed.

When at last they ceased and our hearts returned to a normal beat we were come to a little lowflung wood of birch and rowan, the silver bark peeling black stripes horizontally from the birch, the red berries of the rowan wind-blown on its delicate branches. Grey rocks covered the interstices of the trees and the sun fell sometimes on the rock to warm the cold colour : a stream twisted through the rough ground and its sound was soft and bass, and up on a sudden promontory silhouetted against the sky was a single figure who was working in a series of vigorous thrusts on a spade. We remained in the little wood for many hours, listening to the bass-viol of the falling water, to the wind pulling at the larchtops and shaking the tender rowan, and sometimes listening with attention to the drumming of a lorry as it passed in and out of earshot in the near distance.

Excited by danger, and by the beauty of this calm place, the falling stream beside me, the trees moving all around, I began to think again of the young woman in the black cloak who had become aware that I too lived just as much as anyone she had hitherto known at church or fair. I saw her always as she had come to us in the night, her black cloak hanging heavily against her skin as she led us to the quiet kitchen and the dead embers on the hearth. Surely life had a less miser purpose in this encounter than in the thousands of thousands of meetings when men cross and recross in towns and country places? Time and again they had appeared barren and futile, but rather than believe them fruitless, rather than feel as a spool revolving in a shuttle, I had lived instead in the unrest of a chessman fingered by a hesitant player. Now sloth of mind, as sometimes before, drew down my heart to the beauty of this life, and in this little birdless wood, I began to dream. When the stream had carved itself a majesty, passing barges and lights on the barges would ride the brown smoke of the evening air, each crossing the scurrying wake of waves from swifter hulls to disappear slowly through the dusk while men sat on each deck and smoked in content with life, and recalled all the dead among my acquaintances who have suffered too willingly the futility of life. There is an owl in the Celtic fable who had seen each rowan as a seed upon a tree, and its length seven times fallen to the earth and seven times over raised in leaf; it had seen the men whose bones were washed from these boulders when the rain was rounding them to pebbles from seven hundred times their height this dropping evening; it had seen the men for whom the promontory above me was a bottomless valley and the hollow place where Rory and I sat was a high mountain before the Flood. Such an owl called out of the dusk at me and its cry filled me with age and the peace that comes when we feel the wheels of the passing years turn so slowly it is almost complete rest. I dozed as I lay – life stopped for me while my eyes swayed and fell.

But Rory, his mind whirling, sang of passionate life. He sang of the old Newgate murderer, the song found scrawled upon his New-gate cell after they hanged him and buried him : how eerie to see him ghosting like this in Ireland, his disjointed spine rattling Rory, not aware that before the night had fallen death would have got him, too – his body plugged full of English lead – sang cheerily : –

> My name is Samuel Hall, Samuel Hall,
> My name is Samuel Hall, Samuel Hall,
> My name is Samuel Hall,
> And I've only got one ball,
> Here's my curse upon you all,
> > God damn your eyes !
>
> I killed a man 'tis said, so 'tis said,
> I killed a man 'tis said, so 'tis said,
> I hit him on the head,
> With a bloody lump of lead,
> And I laid the buggur dead,
> > God damn his eyes !

I did not heed the words, but the sense, entering my mind, broke my drowsy dream in part. Looking up I saw the West grow cold and saffron as if the threshers of the morn, reduplicated in valley after valley had blown a storm of corn-sheaves against the falling cape of night. A score of birds fulfilling their ancient ritual flew home-ward in formation : as they passed into the blazing sun I dropped my eyes again to the stream, but while I had turned away it had changed to silver against the dark stones. Night was dropping upon us secretly and we must move onward to some house where we could sit before the flames and doze before a chimney-wall browned with soot and old invading rain and sleep quietly while the night passed by.

We tramped ahead, keeping to the backroads still, but quite without fear now that we were so many miles from the enemy, and at last, high up among the hills, walking in the reaches of the wind we came to the little roadside house that was shop and post office in one, and we sat there wearily by the fire.

The land was cold and windswept here, and the few elms that stood outside, landmark for many miles around, were torn by the wind and being blown to pieces like the clouds in the sky. Rory was to stay here for the night, but I must move farther on, and I sat by the fire waiting impatiently for the cart that was to carry me part of the last few miles to a supper and a safe bed. At the end of the kitchen the old carter was whispering across the little counter with the woman of the house; the young daughter of the house stood beside them lighting an oil-lamp that hung from a beam overhead, and presently the two grey pates were lit from above. The light fell in a warm glow on the unpainted counter, plain as when its planks first arrived from the town of Macroom twenty miles away and were flung on the kitchen floor for the admiration of the little fat woman with her little fat baby. The glow fell on the soiled and mutilated bank-notes, on the silver and copper coins and on the blue sugar-bags and the dun surfaces of the remainder of Saturday night's groceries. I waited while they talked in a secretive whisper, perhaps over the account, perhaps about their oldwives' gossip of the countryside. Perhaps they were wishing us wandering guerillas farther on and wishing the fighting at an end lest their barns be burnt over their hay or their thatch over their heads. Outside in the windy night the old horse was tethered to an elm, its head bent low and its eyes heavy with sleep like a Buddha's. Thinking of it I sat by the fire and raked in the ashes with the muzzle of my rifle. I felt it would rain heavily tonight though the wind was getting stronger, and once again I thought of the girl in the black cloak; but already she had slipped many miles into the things of the past, and in another day she would have slipped wholly from my mind not to be recalled unless in some odd place at some odd time when I would wonder about our strange encounter, and in sentimental mood wonder if she ever asked a comrade where I had gone, saying that I was a nice boy, perhaps more than that. She had been at such a door as this in her mother's arms and would as her mother had done stand there again in one, two, three years' time bidding farewell to the very last mocking couple of her bridal party, and looking at the sky with her young husband, see the coming of the rain and lock and latch the door upon it, and returning to the dying fire would hear the first drops fall on the warm core, and the rising howl strip the elms; he would draw her toward him and she, feeling her youth passed for ever, would weep softly and secretly in the dark and then smile for her first ungirdling. What sad weavings the old Weaver of life can think of, as if all will not fray away and moths rise from the eyes of his dears, and all his storms crumble at the end in dust.

I heard Rory chant some passage from a hedge-school memory, and turning I saw the young girl of the house watching him, ready for a burst of laughter at the end.

'This,' chanted Rory, 'is a man, the beauty of whose eloquence and the wisdom of whose conversation is balanced only by the impeccability of his character and the noble qualities of the mind wherewith God has endowed him, for it is abundantly clear to me,' continued the emperor in a graver tone, 'that wherever the original refulgence of the human mind is neither adumbrated in its infancy nor adulterated in its maturity, the unique powers of the will of man must inevitably produce in every individual, no matter in what clime he has been born, nor under what star he has first seen the light of day, if only he be true to what is right and turn from what is wrong, the genius of an Alexander, the oratory of a Cicero, the wisdom of a Solomon, or the sublime skill of a Leonardo da Vinci, as the case may befall.'

The little bellied fellow finished with a breathless rush, and turning to the girl clapped his hands and clapped her hands in applause at his own performance.

I found that this child was to accompany me a little way on the road and we snuggled into the back of the cart and sat shouting our farewells as it jolted away from the two yellow squares of light and from the figures crowding the open door. Then as we entered the spacious dark, silence fell on us three. I stretched back on the floor of the cart listening to the braggart storm. I felt young and wilful under its breath; I loved to hear its impotent whine: off behind the ridge of mountain through which a pass had been cut maybe five centuries ago by roadmakers rotted in the grave there came the great spreading light of the moon. We were following the direction of the racing clouds, they flying beyond us in the sky. My eyes were beginning to close with the rough swaying of the cart when suddenly the child clasping my hand said :

'Are you afraid of the pookas? I am!'

And fell upon my breast and laid her head by mine and I put an arm around her and we lay so, jolting along under the stars and the driving fleeces overhead. But as suddenly, when about a mile had passed she pressed nearer and swiftly kissed me. Then she rolled away from me to the other side of the cart, though still grasping my coat-sleeve in terror of the black night all around.

Presently I left them, and the old cart was soon out of earshot. Jogging on through the dark, my thoughts wandered at will. I pictured the bed where I would sleep – I had slept in so many hundreds that it might be any size or shape, but I chose from my set of images one bed most suitable to the stormy night. It was the marriage bed of the peasants, made of plain wood, closed on back, side and top, and but only the front left open, and that sometimes covered by a curtain on a string : it was like a beehive with a flat crown and sloping roofs, shallow at head and foot, so that a man could stand in comfort only in the middle of the bed. The storm might howl for all I cared, the rain might drench the stooks and fill the yards with pools of dung; the windows might rattle – I would sleep the night through and wake to find the skies clearing in the morning. I was hungry for food and sleep, and in this bed I would lie for a while thinking over the day's happenings, trying to find a scheme for things in the true dreamer's way, a scheme into which everyone would fit as by nature, the woman of the cloak, the little girl, myself, the dead husband, the carter, the crowds that meet and remeet, as it seemed aimlessly, blindly – and all these would jumble in my mind and quaint combinations occur and confuse me, and my reasoning fall under the sway of interweaving images and sleep come secretly with her hood.

At last the bright square of window-light slid into view, quartered by the crucifix framework, and I found the causeway to the door and groped my way to it after the window vanished in its own recess : I played blindman's buff with the door and at last with outstretched hands I stumbled against it and grasped the latch.

Fire-flames, a settle, and maybe a white cloth and something to eat other than dry bread and tea with goat's milk. I lifted the latch and looked in : a young woman stood with her back to me stiffened in a posture of surprise as when I first fumbled at the door, but relaxing and turning when I spoke, touched her soft hair and bade me enter : it was the young woman of the morning.

'Is there e'er a wake here?' I asked seeing the lone kitchen, my voice trembling as I spoke.

'Devil a wake then!' She was smiling at me again.

'Yeer very quiet then,' I said, looking around at the cleanswept kitchen, and then at her skin like a boy's under its first white down.

' 'Tis quiet, wisha,' she answered making way for me as I moved to the settle. I asked if there would be room for the night, and she said there would be and welcome.

'And a bit to eat for a hungry man?'

'Surely, if you don't mind waiting for just a moment or two.' I wanted to ask how she came before me to the hither side of the country twelve long miles away from her last night's hostel. I flung aside my bandolier and raincoat; I laid my rifle and pack and belt in a corner. She went to the end of the kitchen and I heard the splash of water and the paddling of hands, and when she returned to me by the fire, wiping her fingers, they were rosy when the apron fell. She half knelt before the fire to blow it with a hand-bellows, and as she worked her body formed a single curve, one breast on one knee, and her arms circling the knee while she worked lustily at the bellows. I could see the little wrinkles at each corner of her lips – laughter wrinkles, maybe?

'Are the old people in bed?' I asked.

'Yes.' Her voice trembled, I thought.

'And the rest? Where's the rest from you?'

'There's nobody else. Tom, my brother, is on the run in Kerry.' I leaned back on the settle and the flames crackled into life.

'Well, you must be very lonely here all alone.'

'I have got used to it,' she answered, patting her hair with the fingers of her hands : how soft it looked! Then she stood up and began to spread a white cloth on the white table, and then to lay a milk jug, a cup and saucer, a sugar basin, a pot of jam.

'Do you live here?'

'Yes.'

'But you're not always as desolate as this – surely?'

'Desolate, just as you say; this is a lonely district, you know.'

'Well it's not so bad at all now,' I said. 'I shouldn't mind if I lived here – the mountains and the valleys. . . .'

She halted in her step and faced me: the little mouth was gathered into a hard white button of flesh.

'You would soon tire of these mountains! The city, though, that's where I'd like to live. There's company there, and sport and educated people, and a chance to live whatever life you choose!'

She had put two eggs into a little black pot of boiling water, and the water bubbled and leaped around them with a hissing. A blast of wind came down the chimney and drove a cloud of firesmoke into the kitchen. We sat silent and presently went to the table and she poured me red tea to drink and I cut the brown loaf and plastered it with butter and jam, and ate greedily. She sat before the fire, and I asked her why she did not like the district, but she only looked at me and said nothing. I asked again, pleading that I wished to know, really and truly. She answered:

'Because this farm is bare and high. The land is poor. And this townland has a Northern aspect.'

A heavy drop of rain fell on the fire – the storm was howling. I saw the sea of discontent and unrest that these words were born of, saw the drizzling rain and no sun shining on it, saw her looks steal round her to this farm and to that and back from them to her own home. Another gust of wind blew the smoke around her and she turned away from it and clasped my knee to prevent herself from falling from the low stool.

'You'll be choked,' said I, and her eyebrows stirred and she smiled at me. I laid my palm on her hand and thought of the whole livelong day I had spent, the rick that must be threshed before the wind fell, the carter jogging through the wet night, the sea of darkness outside the door. How many days could I live without a complete revolt! I spoke earnestly.

'It's a cruel country to have to live in.'

She spoke kindly to me then.

'I think you are honest,' she said.

'Do you think that?'

'I think you *are* honest. *Really* honest,' she said again.

Looking at her soft eyes, and at her soft hair my eyes wandered down to the first shadows of her breasts: she caught my glance and looked down at her warm bosom and then at me and she smiled. As I moved to her I saw the little broken corner of her tooth; I had no word to say; so I sat beside her before the leaping flames and put my arms around her and felt in the cup of my hollow palm the firm casque of her breast. Smiling at me as a sick woman might smile upon a doctor who brought her her ease from pain she slipped my hand beneath her blouse to where I felt the warmth of her skin and her warm protruding nipple, and I leaned to her for a kiss.

A rush of feet came to the door and the little girl from the roadside house flung it wide with a cry to me to run, to run; Rory was shot dead; they were coming West for me! I bundled up my equipment, ran in a flash through the open door into the dark night, and raced on and on – stumbling and falling and going I cared not where but away from the flashing lights to the North. When I fell into a panting walk I was like a man who has been listening to music the livelong day and after it his mind is full of strange chords, and ill-recollected they torture him with a sense of something lost. On my bare head the rain fell heavily and aslant, now and again it was blown into my face by the wind, and the clouds totally blotted out the moon. Full of terror for such a death as I knew Rory's was I filled every house with armed men, fierce men to whom killing was a little thing and torture but little more, and my imagination and the stories I had heard drove me blindly on through the sodden night. I trudged a way through the pathless bogs and tore through briery dikes: all that night I found no shelter from the lashing rain and I met not a single tree in leaf: long after midnight I saw a little glinting window leap suddenly out of the dark about a mile away, and as I thrust away from it, away to safety, into the rain, the memory of its light tortured me as the memory of cool winds must torture the damned of hell.

At last I came upon a lonely ruin upon the mountain, three walls, and I lay on the lee side of it while the rain dripped on me from the remnants of its eaves. When I awoke a dim radiance lit the falling haze, but whether it was the dawn or the sinking moon or any hour past three or before three I could not say. No sound was to be heard: no living thing moved: no bird stirred the wet air: the falling haze made no sound. I rose chattering and trembling, and my feet splashed through the wet earth and the drowned grass, and when I halted there was quiet. I crossed a little stone wall and one of the stones fell with a mighty sound. I might have been the last human creature to crawl to the last summit of the world waiting until the Deluge and the fortieth night of rain would strain him upwards on his toes while the water licked his stretched neck. Yet everywhere they slept sound abed, my dark woman curling her warm body beneath the bed-clothes, the warmer for the wet fall without, thinking if she turned and heard the dripping eaves – that the winter was at last come.

Cold till doom!
The storm has spread.
A river is each furrow on the slope,
Each ford is a full pool.

Each lake is a great tidal sea,
Each pool is a great lake,
Horses cannot cross the ford,
Nor two feet.

The fish of Ireland are wandering,
There is no strand upon which the waves
    do not pound.
Not a town is in the land,
Not a bell, not a crane's whining cry.

The wolves in the wood of Cuan cannot rest,
They cannot sleep in their lair:
Even the little wren cannot shelter
In her tiny nest on the side of Lon.

Keen wind and cold ice
Have burst upon the little world of birds.
The blackbird cannot shelter its side
In the wood of Cuan.

Cosy was our pot upon the nook,
In the crazy hut on the slope of Lon:
The snow has crushed the wood,
And toilsome is the climb to Ben-bo.

The ancient bird of Glenn Rye
Is grieved by the cold wind :
Her misery and her pain are great,
The ice will get into her throat.

From flock and from down to rise
Were folly for thee! Take it to heart.
Ice heaped on every ford,
Wherefore I say 'cold till doom.'

Down below me in the valley I heard an early cart; the morning wind, light and bitter, sang occasionally in the key of the flooded streams. The dawn moved along the rim of the mountains and as I went down the hill felt the new day come up around me and felt life begin once more its ancient, ceaseless gyre.

The Small Lady

I

Three days after the disappearance of Mrs Sydney Browne this scandalous ballad – I dare not give it in full – was being sung in every market town in Munster. The groups that listened to it in the side-lanes listened with averted faces as if they feared to be interrupted before the end, and when it was finished there would be a scramble for copies of the song and everyone would then move quickly away, the women hiding the green sheet of the ballad between their breasts, the men stuffing it into their clasped purses among the silver and the dirty notes:

ON THE SIX SINN FEIN BOYS SHOT IN CORK
BARRACKS BY DRUM HEAD COURT MARTIAL

(*Air*: Canada-io!)

Come all ye brave Sinn Feiners
And listen to my song,
How six brave Irish rebel boys
Were murdered in the wrong.
An English woman that sold them,
A servant of the crown,
And the name of the cursed she-spy
'Twas Mrs Sydney Browne.

She drove to Aughameelinn
And told the English Tans
To come and take these brave young boys
With all their armed bands.
They came and took them by surprise

And caught them where they lay
And shot them by drum head court martial
In Cork at the dawn of day.

The name she had was the Small Lady,
Five foot in her scarlet gown;
God's curse may light upon her
And fall from heaven down,
For she sold our boys to England's Tans
So they fell without a blow
Face to face with a firing squad
All standing in a row.

But now the Tans are searching wide
For our Mrs Sydney Browne
In Cork and Kerry and Tipperary
And up to Dublin town.
The Small Lady is hard to find;
And why do you think 'tis so?
They've searched the whole of Irish soil
But they haven't searched below.

Dig five by two by two foot five
For yeer scarlet hat and gown,
But ye will never find her alive –
The servant of the crown.
She's in bed with her fancy serving man
Where the pissabeds do grow . . .
So, dig down and down and down, me boys,
Dig down and down and down,
And the Tans will never find her
Till they meet her in Hell below.

She heard a version of it, her death-song, the night they took her
from her home and drove her into the mountains in the car they
stole from a nearby garage, singing as they tore through the village
into the night. How the car ever carried its load nobody ever knew,
for it had stood under the rains by the side of the road ever since
old Lord Bandon had made a jesting gift of it to the garage pro-

prietor winters ago. Its roof and upholstery were torn and tattered, and fouled by roosting hens; it had four flat tyres and all its parts were loose; but they filled it with petrol and pushed it until it started and so it screamed out of the village with its load of singing guerillas, and the little red-coated woman sitting at the back, beside her butler, almost buried under the trench-coated riflemen clinging to every aery perch they could find on roof and wing. Of course after a mile the first tyre whirled off but when the driver halted to replace it the captain would have no delays and ordered him to drive on. When the second tyre bounded into the ditch the driver looked enquiringly at the captain, but the captain only grinned and jerked his thumb forward. So that at the loss of the third and the last tyre, and mile by mile of the other loose parts, the tool-box here, the bonnet there, a window, then another window, the crowd only roared with delight, interrupting their ribaldry for the moment, and even the butler grinned feebly. But to the woman, who loved cars as she loved her dogs and her horses, it was almost terrifying to hear this skinned thing screaming up through the silent hills in its cloud of boiling steam and burning oil, and when it halted finally, a bearing burnt clean through, throbbing and choking like a winded hack, she was gone white – even the little red spots under her eyes were pale and you could see through the rouge the blue of her lips. But her rage did not last long; it vanished as she stepped from the car. The well-known valley stretched beneath her eyes.

The sun was setting not beyond one but several horizons that reached to the ultimate haze where sky and land swam together. In the valley the sun was set and the river shone there like silver, and a tree-crowned islet floated in it like a black ship. Down there was her house and her dogs yapping for their supper and her servants, forgetful of them, talking of her before the red glow of the kitchen fire. If the yards were cold and silent and wet underfoot, there was, too, the pleasant drip-drop into the hollow waterbutts, and by the river's edge the willows dragging their tender buds of March in the milk-smooth tide. A mist was coming up the hills like an advancing army, and she pulled off her hat and bared her throat to the breasts for the fall of the gentle pricking rain, slipping insensibly into what her friends used call 'her O Goddam mood,' indifferent to, even contemning anything that could happen her. She had loved this day of clouds moving low in the sky, of soft showers streaming down the air, a day of aqueous light that seemed to have nothing to do with sun but came and went like cold waves, a radiance rather than a light, as if the white clouds were luminous by nature and carried their pale glow within them as they moved. She had made love to it since morning when she plunged naked into the icy river, racing back barefooted in her scarlet dressing-gown over the soaked lawn. She would not care now if they made her spend the night wandering over the mountains – she even laughed quietly to herself to think of the game rising against the moon, the little fishes darting out of their sleep – she would not care if they sate the night out watching the embers dying in some farmer's kitchen, not even care if they then shot her in the dawn for 'a cursed English spy.' Only she must have a few more hours of beautiful and passionate life, and then, 'O Goddam all, good-bye green fields, blue sky; off I pop into the great Has-been!' Yet when the gentle fall began to trickle across her lips and down the channel of her breasts she shivered: it was cold up here even where the sun still shone, cold with the coldness of the sweating earth, and when she turned to look at her captors she thought they looked like homeless animals clustered in a storm. They broke up even as she looked at them, and the young fellow set off as her special guard motioned her with them into the woods. In here the pine-needles clung to their boots and every leaf bore a bright drop, and though there was light in the sky above, the evening star shone like a lantern through the swaying tops of the pines. When the car had stopped they had hurled it with shouts of glee over the edge of the road, but she had noticed that they fell at once into a gloomy silence when the quiet murmur of the stream rose again, uninterrupted out of the dusk. Now again she noticed how they moved in complete silence, their rifles at the ready, looking nervously left and right into the dark alleys of the wood. She knew that there was no likelihood of meeting anybody here, miles away from anywhere, in the heart of the hills, but as they went up and on in this furtive manner, the branches caressing their faces, swishing back after they had passed, she began to feel less confident. When some bird or a bat squeaked past her face she even caught her guard's hand for a second in terror, and soon the damp smell of rotting leafmould and dead-wood that made this place heavy like a tomb sucked her last drop of courage from her and left her, like them, glancing to and fro into the dim shadows. A branch crackled and they stopped dead as if every man were turned to a statue; whereupon as they listened the silence became ponderous and rang in their ears. A bird fluttered but gave no cry. Then through the darkness a bell tolled with long pauses after each deep stroke, and as they quickened their paces the trees rolled away and there was the darkening blue of the sky and the first bright stars.

In the monastery it was not so much a fine soft day in spring as Friday, a day of hard Lenten fare. In the refectory there was only one guest, a drunkard, one of those wretches whom the city sends periodically to the monastery to be cured of sights and mad visions. The monks receive the poor creatures with a kind of sardonic pity, feeding them with ever-dwindling drams of the whisky that has maddened them until they can be finally weaned of their lust for it and turned loose on the healthy food and drink of the monastery farms. Then there is no escape from penance, the realization of sin, the promise of reformation. In the refectory, watching this shivering wretch pick sadly at his dry bread and sip sadly from his mug of black tea, was also Brother John the guestmaster, his temples deep-hollowed, his cheeks scooped, his beard white and scanty, his lips thin and bloodless from a life of penance and hard living. Absolved as guestmaster from the rule of silence he gabbled so incessantly to the drunkard at the table-head that he might have been making up for time lost when as a young fellow in brown cloth he tamed his lusty blood with silence and fasting and praying and the flagellations of his cincture on his rump as he sang in the choir-loft at his Hours,

> . . . *de coelo praestiti eis,*

and a blow,

> . . . *delectamentum habentem.*

Often he washed the blood from his thighs before he lay to rest, and could not sleep. *He* could tell topers how to tame the heat of the flesh : if they only would, he often told them, lower their breeches nightly for twenty or thirty years to the knots of a stout rope they would, presently, become different men.

The drunkard was still on his diet of whisky though the allowance was down to a glass every morning and night now, but Brother John thought it great fun to watch him nibble his Lenten fare. It was good March fare for any Christian man, and Brother John had himself eaten little more during the whole day and he had not tasted meat for many weeks, even on Sundays when he might.

'Aha, me boyo,' said Brother John, stroking his white whiskers upwards and outwards with back of his bony hand, 'if we had you here a twelvemonth we'd soon make a monk of yeh.'

'It's poor fare for any man,' whispered the toper. 'It's the poorest bloody fare I ever ate.'

'No "bloodys" now. No bad words in the monastery. Do you want to destroy all the virtue of your fast? God can withhold his grace even as he can give it.'

'Excuse the language, father. . . .'

'Brother. Just plain Brother John,' said the monk, fearful of the sin of vanity at his elbow.

To the drunkard every frocked man was a priest – his was not a mind to distinguish half-ways and go-betweens, it must be with him a feast or a famine, the highest throne in heaven or the lowest pit in hell. So he was by turns either a total abstainer or a hopeless bib.

'Yes, father; I mean – yes, brother. I do forget.'

He sighed deeply and sucked his black tea.

'I dunno how we'll ever get to heaven, brother. When I sees all the monks do in here I gives up all hope of ever attaining salvation.'

'That's despair,' warned the guestmaster with a bony finger. 'It's a sin to say the like. Even to think the like is a sin, one of the greatest sins that may be committed. It's one of the seven deadly sins. It's almost a sin against the Holy Ghost, and the sin against the Holy Ghost will never find forgiveness. Beware of the sin of despair. God is infinitely merciful to us all. One sinner returned to the fold who enters heaven rejoices Him more than the ninety-nine blessed. Let me never hear you say the like again,' he concluded, easily slipping his palms between his belt and his empty stomach.

'It is a sin, father, I mean brother. Sure God is good and He will forgive us all.'

'He will forgive us all,' said Brother John, with a gentle mockery in his voice at the drunkard's lapse now into the contrary sin of

presumption. 'He will if we do penance and seek the means of salvation. If we do penance, I say. Do you hear me? How do you find
the bread now?'

'Ah, it's bloody dry, father. I mean it's a dry mouthful.'

'Did I hear you say "bloody?" Do you want to be without your
little glass of John Jameson, tonight?'

'It's dry, father, it's dry. Sure God knows it's dry. I mean no
harm in the world, father; sure you can see for yourself I'm as
gentle as a lamb. Only for the wan failing I mean no harm in the
world. I beg your pardon, father. I mean the bread is dry.'

'Ahadee, but you were the unlucky man, I think,' said Brother
John, pausing to look out of the black glass of the window at shining
Hesperus, 'the unlucky man, that is to say, to come to Mount
Melleray for a cure in the month of March.'

The drunkard forgot himself so utterly at the bitter truth of this
that he banged his fist on the table and cried out in earnest blasphemy:

'Jasus, wasn't I though!'

At the profanity Brother John flew into a sudden rage and his
white eyebrows gathered into a knot above his weak, dimmed eyes
and his beard rose as his lips tightened. The drunkard had realized
the transgression of his oath even as he made it, and he raised his
hand cringingly like a dog expecting a whiplash. He glanced in
fright right and left of the old pink-cheeked brown-cassock, down
at his skirts, at his hairy ankles, into the dark corners of the room,
anywhere but at the hard fur-rimmed eyes that glared down at
him in silent contempt. But just then feet began to crunch on the
gravel walk outside and the window frames shook under a blast
of mountain wind and splashes of sudden rain broke against the
windowpanes like the crackling of empty sea-shells. The guestmaster's bell rang in the kitchen and Brother John swished around
from the drunkard so that his beads rattled and his personal odour
scented the air, and he walked off into the gloomy shadows of the
hall where on each side of the door two blue side windows cut in
the darkness graded lengths of a somewhat lesser gloom. As he
undid the bars and put the door on its chain the drunkard peeping
out after him saw through one of the side windows a very bright
star and lowered his head slowly, so slowly that it might have been
the hour-hand of a clock, for at his heels he had suddenly seen a

gleam of light on the pitch-pine leg of the hall-stool and behind it he could hear a real rat gnawing in the dark. When the bell rang loudly again he jumped with terror, and his heavy lower lip began to dribble. Then the door opened gratingly, and he was staring beyond the flame of the monk's guttering candle into the rain and dark at the wet glitter of arms and the crowding faces of hunted men. He did not see the guestmaster's stern face soften in welcome, but the next minute the hall seemed full of dripping figures whispering and clustering about the old monk and his blowing candle. The drunkard smiled too, for he always declared he was a fierce-minded man and he hoped that one or other of these 'shinners would have a half a pint of whisky in a bottle in his pocket to wet a fellow-patriot's whistle.' But as he was lost in rumination of the golden liquor and its labelled bottle they pushed past him into the fire where he followed, to hover disconsolately about them, giving his pipe to one, his matches to another, his tobacco to a third, but getting no smell of the whisky he craved so much. Now that they were safe and sheltered they showed by their sudden relaxing into careless comfortable positions, on the floor, on the chairs, by the walls, that they had been through a great deal in the past few days; they dried their knees wearily before the little fire, smoked with the heavy pulls of men long denied a smoke, and ate and drank ravenously of the poor leavings of the supper-table. The toper left them in a bad humour and went off, peeping into the hall again, where besides Brother John and the captain he found only another young fellow and a ladylike sort of little woman in a red coat bending over an old hatless man collapsed on a hall-bench. But he slid away when the old monk looked at him and, though he returned now and again to peep at the woman in the red coat and even once whispered to her timidly to ask what was 'up with the old four-eyes,' he never remained, and at length, unnerved by his own caution and the dread of the monk's eyes, he disappeared by a back door and was seen in the refectory no more that night.

The rain dripped outside and the wind blew in under the door and chilled Brother John's bare ankles, and the wet feet and the thighs of the woman. She had left the old butler, for she could not bear his apologies, and she stood in the centre of the hall looking at the monk picking at the candle until his fingers became engrimed, and at the captain picking at the monk's vest in his eagerness to convince him that there was no harm in housing her there for a night. But the old monk argued the rule *contra mulieribus* and scratched his poll with his grease-covered nails and the captain blew his nose between his fingers in exasperation. In disgust she turned to the boy at the door and seeing his face clearly for the first time she was delighted to find herself looking at the eager uplifted face of a boy of the cities. She let her eyes wander over his long tapering hands that clasped his rifle, his waist like a colt or a greyhound, back to his eyes that looked at her with a frank and open look, and at once she felt she could speak to this boy: she felt the same thrill she had often felt as a young woman in Africa or India when she saw the pale cheeks of a European traveller or tourist in a boma or bazaar, a thrill that used set her thinking sadly of England and home, her parents and her sisters, loved bits of town and country and all that home meant to a young girl exiled on her marriage-day. So she looked at him now, with what her male friends had dubbed her 'please-please eyes,' and before he could gather his wits against hers he had smiled back at her, and in a minute he was promising to get her something for her butler and later on, if he could manage it, a cup of tea for herself if they remained there the night. She was much older than he, but her hair was still flaxen and wavy and the pink spots under her cheeks had returned, and he could not refuse those appealing looks and her slightly whimpering voice. But she could get no farther just then for Brother John tapped her on the shoulder and beckoned her to follow him, and she had to go after the bony heels down a long whitewashed corridor into the monastery. As she passed the refectory door she saw the merciless eyes watching her, and (as a painter might realize the drabness of life by seeing in passing a face in a photographer's showcase) she realized her position for the first time when one face among those that looked at her grinned cruelly to see her go: he was a black-faced fellow with a row of jet curls low across his forehead, a black-eyed brute that looked up at her like a bull ready to charge, and, as she passed down under the Gothic arches of the corridor, that face remained in her mind with her other pictures of the dirty hands and head of the monk, his dirty underclothing showing at the neck, the stain of spilt tea on the cloth in the refectory, the cold emptiness of the hall, so that as she entered the guests' corridor, now deserted, she felt that everything here was stale and dirty, that her footsteps left circles of dust on the long brown carpet, that every cranny was filled with spiders' webs and dead flies, and she hated the feeling that ugliness had descended on her and that she might die surrounded by it. Then the monk ushered her into a high musty room and, leaving her the dirty wick, locked the door after him and padded away out of earshot. The silence of the night enveloped her and her ears began to ring with it again until by degrees she began to distinguish the dripping of the rain on the sill outside the window, and the occasional whisper of the light wind in the trees beneath it. Wearily she moved to the window and lifted the heavy frame to let in the night air. The rain had ceased, and she leaned her elbows on the wet sill and looked over the dark countryside and up at the blowing clouds. There she remained a long time, perhaps an hour, listening to the distant fall of waters, and watching the come and go of the moon edge the saw-toothed pine-forests. Then for sheer weariness and hunger she lay on the great damp bed to rest and because she was afraid of the dark she did not blow out the smelly wick. She found herself reading over and over again the typed script tacked to the timbered wall beside her head. Clearly it was intended to be the last thing one saw before falling asleep, the first on waking. It said :

  You
are alive tonight. *You* may not see another night. Before the next night has passed you may be dead.

ETERNITY, ETERNITY, ETERNITY!

Every idle thought, word, deed and omission will be judged against you. By the result of that judgment *you* will either be in heaven with God or in Hell with the devils for all

ETERNITY, ETERNITY, ETERNITY!

Will *you* barter a few short years in this Vale of Tears against all ETERNITY? Life is short, but the joys and the terrible pains of Eternity go on

For ever and for ever and for ever.

ETERNITY, ETERNITY, ETERNITY!

Will *you* barter the brief lusts and passing pleasures of the few moments of this life to be in the flames of Hell for all

ETERNITY, ETERNITY, ETERNITY?

Burning without cease, without a second's rest, without one single moment's pause, in torment, taunted and tortured by demons, aching and suffering, writhing with the pain of loss and the pain of the flesh, through

ETERNITY, ETERNITY, ETERNITY!

As she read the dead quiet began to smother her and she would cough or swallow loud spittle to break the silence. She waited for the regular fall of the drops outside, but when she moved her feet they made a terrifying rustle at the dark end of the bed. She tried to sleep, but sleep would not come, and so she read and reread the hateful script until she felt that they were already stealing her life from her before it was time. She sat up in bed to see the great monastery stretching away in black straggling masses; with its daily round it had killed the years one by one which she in the valley had sucked as one sucks an orange dry, flirting, smoking, drinking, hunting, playing bridge for high stakes, one long empty round of pleasure. In spite of herself she thought of the old guest-master, walking down the corridor, his candle throwing wavering shadows on the white arches of the ceiling as he swished along; he and all of them would be there tomorrow and after, year after year at their changeless routine, and she lying dead. She feared them because their sureness was snatching from her the only world she had ever known, and as she thought of them, staring out at the monastery buildings, she could almost feel it falling away from her as a field falls away from a soaring bird. The drops fell incessantly from the roof; the cold wind stole along her body. Words from the script seemed to jump out to her as the dying flame leaped and fell. 'You are alive tonight . . .' Sinking in the ooze of a bog, the rain would fall on her as she lay, but not for her; the sun would set over the waves of the horizons, but she would not know it. Others would see the willows swishing their pale hanging leaves in the rain-high tide and love them the more for knowing that *they* lived in their time, whoever else might be dead; and she remembered how on days when the sun glittered in the middle of the blue air she used think of the most passionate people she knew, of Baudelaire and Toulouse-Lautrec and the harlots he used to paint, of La Goulue and Mimi *patte en l'air* and of Yvette Guilbert, and how she used rejoice to think that they were dead and she lived. But now no more? An

end to her too? To live no more? In a passion she jumped to the
floor and began to undo her frock and smock, and tearing aside all
her silks and soft clothes, some falling pale on the dusty carpet as
the candle died and blackness folded her she stood and faced the
night and the open fields and the straggling buildings, as white then,
naked to her breasts, as the moon that came swimming out of a
cloud to look at her.

Somebody was tapping at the door for admittance. She ran to it,
heard the key being turned, felt the door opening, saw by the light
from the sky the boy she had spoken to in the hall. He was carrying
a tray of food, and he came in holding it out before him awkwardly.

'You are in the dark,' he said.

'Is that you?' she whispered.

'Have you a match?' he said.

'No.'

'Do you mind taking this tray while I get a candle?'

'We don't want a candle.'

When sitting in the window she had thought of him too, of his
long pale hands, of his boyish gestures when he spoke, of the down
just curling on his lip, and above all, of his inexperience that seemed
to her so infinitely charming. Coming now behind him she found
his shoulders and laid her arms about his neck while he stood non-
plussed holding out his tin tray.

'What have you for me, dear?'

She wondered if she were being too daring.

'Some cocoa and dry toast. It's all I could get. A fast day.'

Whereupon she tousled her hair with one hand and laughed
at him, and because it amused her to think of him standing there
with his tray she refused to let him go until he promised he would
stay and talk a little: she said she was frightened of the dark, and
he believed her, and unaware of what she had done, laid down the
tray and came to the window to answer a question about one of
the buildings across from her room. It was the chapel, and she
spoke of the dim light shining in its ugly red and blue windows
and asked if that meant a special service for the Sunday, but he
reminded her that it was Friday and explained that it was the
sanctuary lamp that never dies before the high altar and the host.
Looking sideways where she pointed a white arm in the starlight

he touched her soft bosom with his elbow, and to his nostrils rose the scent of her breasts and looking at her he saw her white body. He was only a boy yet, and she who had known many men and travelled far, seeing in his eyes the old troubled look thought he was fallen into her net. But instead, with an extraordinary gentleness and tenderness, he said to her that she must put on her clothes. And this, all unwrought by the experiences of the past few hours, she did with trembling hands and lips, finally beginning to weep silently in pity of herself like a very tired child. Then in a voice more gentle than she had ever heard since her husband courted her so long ago with whispered words, he said to her :

'Won't you eat your cocoa and toast?'

Again she did what she was bidden, and felt again like a child overcome with some small misery, but in her tears she hated the lukewarm cocoa, and could see ahead of her the return of her gloomy mood and tried to keep him by her with little talk. She could not swallow the coarse grains of the cocoa, made without any milk because of the double fast; she asked him to try for a cup of tea or a little glass of wine and some meat after midnight when the fast would cease, and he promised to try. She found him very boyish, and they spoke a little longer of this and that, trifles like the size of the monastery and the guestmaster's name and the drunkard's. His own name was Denis. Hers was Bella. Since he left college he had been fully a year tramping around the mountains with the rebels, and he said he often spent the livelong night walking up and down, up and down under the moon, or watching the rain-pitted mountain lakes, rather than go down to comfort in the dangerous valleys where the roads were. Their talk was like the talk of children telling one another of different worlds. She would have wished him to talk on and on but there was not time and he was extremely shy and became more awkward still when she would speak of her own life. The countryside was very dear to him too, and for so long wandering about in it his body and mind had become as it were soaked and bathed in its beauty, and all physical desires dropped away leaving behind only a calm, placid, thoughtless mind. She believed him completely, even when he spoke to her of the most extraordinary things, just as she used believe her children coming to her without any thought of deceit with their childish tales, and she flooded up with a love for this inexperienced youth such as she had not felt for any male thing since she had her first son; and when he spoke to her of his virginity she believed him and would have loved to take his head on her breasts and weep over her own lost youth. Tears were very near her as she sat in the dim silence with him, but she knew he would go away if he saw her weep, and her throat heavy with their surge, and the corners of her mouth trembling from the effort, she forced them back and tried to talk a little longer of indifferent things. She would have loved to talk of young love and late love, but she only said that she hoped he would come back again before the night ended, and that she would try to be a good woman and not tempt him. But to hear herself say these foolish words was too much for her, and she began to cry to herself, hoping he would not notice. The thought of the irrevocable years overcame her: the thought that all was now gone, marriage and motherhood. Even her friends, her last link with life, were drifting away from her like the dropping leaves. He rose and began to move away, carrying his tray, and she did not know how to keep him before he would have gone, maybe (like so much she had known) never to return.

'Denis, I am not really a sensual woman. But my life – one makes these, so many compromises, one bargains with life to be let live. I suppose I was like you when I was your age. O God, you just don't know it all.'

But he, not even yet begun to live, knowing as yet no great unhappiness or misfortune, thought that these tears of hers were unwomanly, sentimental; he even thought of them with secret contempt as Sassenach tears; and ignorant of the heart-weariness of the woman holding his hand in hers he edged out in silence and, awkward, shut to the door.

She left her door unlatched hoping he might return, and lay on the bed listening. Shortly before Lauds she was awakened from a drowsy sleep by a knocking on the outer door but her heart fell to see the drunkard grinning at her across a tray of tea and cold ham. She asked him to wait for the tray, and to hear him gabble she nibbled at the food. Sitting on the bedkerb he told her in confidence, his breath coming in odorous waves, how with the help of her 'old four-eyes' next door he had stolen a bottle of whisky from Brother John's tallboy. As he spoke, his pig's eyes bulged out till they were like great red-speckled gooseberries, and when he told of the white china handle on the monk's door, creaking as they turned it stealthily, he gripped her arm tightly, and his eyes threatened to burst as he told her of the little red lamp always burning before the altar in the monk's room, and his mouth dribbled on the edge of her tray as he drank again in imagination the hot golden liquor. As he described how they stole away down the corridor in their stockinged feet he lifted his feet in turn, and then he laughed loudly at it all, rubbing his hair up the back of his poll so that it stood on his head like upturned whiskers. She drew him on to talk of Denis.

'Yoy! It was all thanks to the chiseller that kep old Johnny talking Irish to him. Ould Johnny 'ull be looney. Ould Johnny is a bloody ould sham – God forgive me for saying it. He don't know is it on his head or his feet he is, with the column in on him and he keeping it quiet from the abbot. You know Johnny is a great Irishian. And he's a learned man too. He was a lawyer, don't you know, up in Dublin and they say he was a divil entirely for his drop. And it was all over his mother dying he came into the monks. God betune us and all harm, didn't she come to him in her graveclothes and he on a batt. He got a terrible turn. And no wonder! He was in the D.T.s for a month after it. Sure me heart goes out to him. But anyway he came here to the monastery for a cure, and if he didn't make up his mind to go for a priest. So bedad he was for years going for a priest. But sure God didn't call him, and he left the priests and he went back to Dublin and of course, I needn't tell you, he met his ould cronies and he was sousing for a month after, and back he kem to the monastery and weights on his hands and legs for fear he'd tear his gullet out with the desire for it. . . .'

Patiently she drew him back to Denis. He told her how Brother John was even then talking to the boy, delighted to have a listener for his endless Irish verses and riddles and proverbs.

'Oh, but Johnny has great Irish, don't you know. And as vain as you like about it. With his "ahoo, eminent min have complimented me on my facility in the tongue of my fathers." '

And the drunkard put on a very refined accent to imitate the old man.

'And his, "ahoo, I have a remarkable gift of extemporizing on a given theme." Not but that he haven't clever sayings, in Irish and

English. He'd say to you, and you trying to get away from him – ahoo, let me gather me wits now for a specimen. " 'Twas fate they say – ahoo, 'twas fate they say, 'twas wayward fate our web of discord wove, and whilst our inimies jined in hate we never jined in love. Is not that apposite," he says. And now he says, "I wish to give the same thought in an entirely diferent manner. 'Twas fate they say, a wayward fate, that wove our web of discord, and whilst our inimies jined in hate – we never jined in concord. . . ." The bloody ould sham. God forgive me for saying it, but that's all he is. . . .'

She got tired of the wandering gabble of the drunkard and sent him away without the tray, and when he had gone sniggering and jerking his shoulders with a hiccuping delight in his own humour, she sat thinking of the old monk – vain, cocksure, glad to have heard about him since he helped her to think that all there were like him, cocksure and vain. But her thoughts wandered off to Denis, bored by the old monk, and she sniggered to think of his annoyance, and then she wished he would return and talk about it all with her.

When at last Denis broke away from the old monk, under the plea that he must see if his prisoner were safe, it gave him great pleasure to think that he and the guestmaster were the only people awake in all that great monastery among the mountains, and it elated him to think that he alone was enjoying the loneliness of the late hour. He wandered down the guests' corridor as if he were in a deserted building, opening doors at random, and finding every room empty would halt and look through its dark and through the window opposite at the windy, starry sky, and rejoice again that he had the night to himself and that none but he and the wind were awake. When he came to a foxy photograph on the wall, a group of pilgrims taken somewhere in the nineties, he might have been a *revenant* coming looking at the relics of his past world. Pensively, then, listening to the falling rhythms of the wind, like waves falling on a shore, he opened another door and found himself looking at Bella, sleeping on the bed, but as he stood watching her, the night breeze rushed through the room and she opened her eyes wide and with a curved arm drew him down to kiss her. Then the door banged to in the breeze and they were alone in the dark, listening where, through the open window, a dull singing of voices rose up from outside. By the radiance on the ceiling she knew the chapel was lighted up and these the monks chanting their Lauds. She drew him down beside her and though she could not speak for the choking of delight not a shadow of desire entered her; yet, when they heard a short, heavy breathing pause outside their door like a dog about to scratch for entry and Denis moved as if to leap to his feet – her arm held him firmly, until the breathing passed away.

'Who is it?' she whispered.

'It must be Brother John going to Lauds,' he said, and his voice trembled.

'How long will he be away?'

'An hour at least.'

'My darling boy!' and she kissed him and began to murmur love-talk to him.

But it was not Brother John who had crept past the door : it was the drunkard, his thirst grown frenzied now as the pleasure of the stolen liquor evaporated, stealing along the corridor like a tiger, his eyes on the china handle of the guest-master's door.

She lay smiling beside her boy, murmuring such words as no young girl had ever murmured to him, calling him gently by his name as if he were her son, and kissed him again and again with brimming happiness, wishful only that the night should never end. But in him desire moved like a slow serpent, and when she stirred and the musk of her body came to him it circled in his brain like a drunken vapour. His hands grew passionate and she did not resist – rather, gently, almost humbly she permitted his love, never so moved as when she felt his body tremble at the meeting (terrible to him as she knew) of their limbs.

They remained in one another's arms for so long that she lost all feeling of time, and it was at last a wild cry that broke the charm, rising time after time in the corridor outside where the drunkard ran howling past, beating with his fists on their door and every door, crying out in the horrors of drink, 'O Lord God have mercy on me a sinner, Lord God! Lord God! For all Eternity, for all Eternity, for all Eternity!' and so he cried until somebody dragged him away by main force, perhaps some of the guerrillas in their shirt-tails, and there was silence again but for the dull murmurs of the choir below and their own breathing in the dark, except when stopping his mouth with hers, she kissed him long and slow, and even then the choir was silent, until they breathed again. He told her that when she kissed he could only hear a singing within him, and she said it was the eternal singing of the sirens that sit upon the seven turning spheres and whose song we hear only when we make silent love. But she regretted having said this : she had said it too often before to other men, and she genuinely loved her boy.

They parted before the praying had finished below, and that he might not by any chance be suspected she sent him down to the chapel. He hated to enter it, and shy and ashamed he crossed to his pew under the eyes of all the monks, kneeling to the host as he passed over the wide, empty spaces of the nave, a sinner before God and man. When he was kneeling in his place he found he was the only layman in the chapel, and as he looked about him he felt a reproach in everything he saw. The monks of the choir were pale and worn and they sang in brittle passionless voices. The bare planks of the church, every nail hammered by the dead, were as the boards of a coffin, and the altar, bare because of the Lenten time of any flower or ornament except the brown candles shrouded in the purple of sorrow, was as a bier of death. Everywhere he looked was the sign of adoration of the Ender of life. This chapel was the temple of the bodiless, and as the monks sang on and on, he felt more and more the grossness of his own body, and that he, foul flesh, was cursed in the presence of his God. A very tall monk came before the great altar – one of the tallest men he had ever seen, drawing the high scarlet curtains. His long brown sleeves, long and wide as they were, did not cover his red wrists, and as he bowed his head abjectly before the Host his long neck above and his calves below showed as thin as reeds. When he turned and showed his temples, broad and bony and skin-drawn, and his eyes sunken in them, a death's-head. Denis could not bear to look at him or to think of what his life in that monastery was and had been, and bowing his head in his hands allowed himself to sink into the dark ocean of despair as a doomed swimmer will at last abandon hope, and sink into the depths. If he could have wept he would have, or run into the darkness of the woods to bury his unhappiness, but the tears would not come, and even the thought of the moaning trees outside filled him with fear. When all had filed out he, too, rose and passed from transept to transept with averted head. Brother John was waiting for him outside eager to recite another quatrain, but he saw that the boy was tired, or worried, and mercifully he did not approach him and allowed him to pass to his room where he lay awake almost until the dawn came, alone with his despairing heart.

2

So in the morning, when he was sent to bring his prisoner to breakfast, he was silent and shamefaced, and she, seeing him so, went down gloomily after him. She was given breakfast in a little locked room where there was dried spittle and unswept cigarette-ash in the grate, and the cloth wrinkled by many elbows and ring-marked by many a dribbling cup of tea. The early morning had risen in mist and hoar but she could see over the edge of her thick-lipped mug through the window of the breakfast-room little patches of blue, and she heard Brother John say to the captain that it would be a fine day after all; and sure enough as they descended the farther side of the mountain the blue and white patches were chasing one another and the bog-cotton at her feet blew slantwise. But beside her Denis walked in complete silence and as her eyes roved from one to other of his companions the immanence of her fate began to oppress her. Once she saw through a bare, black thorn-tree the wrinkled surface of a mountain-tarn blown yellow with froth by the night, and she so ached that she could not point it out to him that a feeling of loneliness settled heavily on her, a smother about her heart. When she nudged his arm and smiled, he looked sullenly where she nodded her head and then without pleasure to the valley beyond, and moved aside from her so that she should not accost him again. They were now walking on the edge of a shut-in valley or coom and to try him again she spoke, saying it did not seem to her that men and women could live in so desolate a place, but he made no reply and she fell into a sad silence herself. It was a stretch where there was not a tree, not even hardy shrubs like holly or haw, to be seen for miles around, and the only living thing they saw was an occasional stare or snipe rising suddenly from the coarse grass beneath their feet, and once a flock of sheep in the distance that made echoing moan through the valley as they tumbled like grey maggots down the opposite mountain-side. About an hour later, almost perpendicularly beneath them they saw a dirty white

cabin all but buried in a bit of sandy level – a household clutching
its patch of earth that the streamlets had in the course of the
centuries brought down grain by grain from the high slopes. She
looked down at it and thought it was more suitable as a tomb than
a dwelling-house, and glancing all about the deserted country that
circled this hidden coom shuddered at it. Several hours later they
had clambered down the monster heap of sodden moss and sweating
rocks that lay behind this farm-house and they confined her under
its high thatch in a loft with one cobweb-covered pane that faced
the valley-end, where, all day long, wherever else there was blue,
low clouds trailed slowly past and were followed by more that had
endless more in train. So that as the early dusk began to fall, and
she was permitted to walk abroad for an hour, she was utterly surprised to find the western air fall sharp and clear about every rock
and fence and pool and every stream that ran tinkling over the
drowned stones. Down the valley some holly clustered under the
grey rocks, and even a rowan drooped, and even a beech or two,
though small and weakling here, stood motionless as if there were
no air, and farther on, edging a broad loch, were flags that stood
by the blue water as if they were part of the mountain that hung
ponderous above them in the clear air. It was not at all like an
evening in spring : it was one of those evenings that defy the order
of the seasons, for though the road and all things – trees, rocks,
walls, and bushes – were heavy and wet the sky seemed as if it held,
suspended aloft blowing through the upper regions of the air, a
light-as-feather fall of early October snow. Denis accompanied her
but was so evidently unwilling to speak that she tried to lose herself
in the beauty of the fading light and the purity of the air, until
seeing across the lake a fire or two and twin pillars of dove-grey
smoke, she asked who these were, and he replied in a low, tired
voice that these must be travelling tinkers going to Nantenan beyond
the hills where there was a pattern on the following day. She stood
watching the flickering fires with a passionate envy welling in her.
The voices resounded across the lake, a cart-wheel jolted, a laugh
echoed among the hills, and as if delighting in the replication of
their voices, they laughed and laughed or cried long haloos. Then
because the darkness was gathering about them they had to return.
Denis told her that her case would be decided that night – the
adjutant and quartermaster were come – but he said it all without

pity or interest in his voice as if it were a message he had been told to give her, and as he spoke he looked away beyond the edges of the coom so that her eyes should not look into his. She did not try; and when they were returned to the cabin and she climbed to her loft and he called after her as if wishing to speak to her, 'Can I do anything for you, Mrs Browne?' only her heavy footsteps replied. And when the wee girl of the house came to her with her evening meal she was lying on her bed, her shoulders gathered up about her as if she would cloak her head with them, gazing through the little dirty window to watch the darkness come down from the heights, covering in the valley and the great rocks until all had become blacker than the night itself. Before the light failed completely she felt rustling in her pocket a crumpled ball of paper and pulling it out read on it a portion of a letter she had been writing to her husband the morning before when they took her suddenly from her house. She read those thoughts of yesterday as one might read an old diary, her mind again shaping those memories first called up there, of how, unlike this winter, other winters had been empty and lonely and pitiless, with wild winds that rushed wave-like through the sponge-heavy trees, nights when the moon was almost always obscured by mist and haze; mornings when, as she lay thinking enviously of Indian or African sunshine, she used hear from her bedroom an occasional creeper leaf stealing like a thief along the gravel in the little winds that blew before the light came. And yet, this night drew her back into the mood of those old winters, and what her letter said seemed false and a pretence. 'My God! The Malabar coast for you in April? You poor dear Jack! And the heat coming! I can see the heat-haze shimmering along the red mountain-tracks, the roses and acacias and petunias drooping in the midday sun, the greasy gum-trees dripping in the grizzling sun. But here! Oh, Jack! The lashing rains of March and the rivers in flood, our willows hanging their hair in the curling tide. You know me? I went out last night on the balcony and stood absolutely naked in the downpour until I was soaked. It was godly. I shall do it again.'

Below a door opened and shut, and a shaft of light streamed out and was gone. It was dark night and she could read no more, but other sentences came back to her as she gazed into the black valley-head. 'All the winter there has scarcely been a day when there has not been on the road before our gate, two or three, once there were even six powerful Lancia motor-cars.' Or, another bit. 'They are my boys, these fine, black-bonneted, tight-breeched, khaki-coated, pipe-smoking, six-shooter men. It has been a different Ireland with them. The old lonely winters are dead. I am in love with three of them at once. You don't mind, dear?'

She could see the chinks of light through the timbers of the floor and hear an occasional dull sound from the kitchen beneath. She lay on her bed where all was dark and quiet, and only the wind outside roaring in the streams.

Denis wandered back along the dark lake-side where the wind was gathering the brown spume about the rushes and heavy with the night-scent of the bog-myrtle.

Farther on was a little lime-washed, green-streaked church among the rocks and farther still the pink house of the curate, its bright window staring at him through the dark. For a long time he walked by the edge of the water listening to its rippling waves and whisper-ing flags. At first the far-off mountain was dark and the sky was dark and only the near waters gleamed when they fell in ripples with a light that came from nowhere, but after a while he sat on a rock by the edge of the loch and the mountain slowly outlined its dark head. He looked often at the brightly lighted window but he dared not go into the bright room face to face with the priest. He longed to go into the little chapel and lay his head on the lap of his Christ and weep out his sin and be comforted, but only the rustling and the lapping answered him, and across the loch the impenetrable yawning darkness of the mountain and the wind roaring down the coom filled him with a terror at his own littleness. Moving a foot he felt the shell of a snail crackling under his boot and he removed his foot hurriedly with the fear of a greater One than himself to Whom he was no more than the dead creeper. The pinprick glow of a cigarette and a man's steps approached along the shore; he was smoking fitfully himself and knowing he was discovered he did not stir. It was the priest taking the night air before he turned in. The voice came through the dark – a young man's voice.

'Any luck tonight, Paddy?'

'Goodnight, father.'

'Oh. who's that?'

'One of the boys.'

'I didn't know any of ye were around.'

'We're moving in the morning.'

'Have ye cigarettes? Can I give ye anything?'

Denis did not hear the question – he was glad of the dark. The priest stood beside him and they both looked silently across the water.

'What about confession, father?' he murmured.

'Any time ye like,' said the priest willingly. 'Come up to the house.'

'I . . . I'd like to make a confession, father,' said the boy flinging his cigarette end into the water where it hissed in the foam between the reeds.

'Come up to the house, my child,' said the priest, falling into his professional voice.

'No. It doesn't matter.' He felt his chance of happiness slipping from him. There was silence for a minute, and he noticed that the priest had stopped smoking, and he rose as if to go. The priest stepped forward and caught him by the arm.

'Will you promise to wait here while I go and get my stole? Will you?'

'Yes, father.'

The priest's footsteps crunched rapidly away. Now he must tell his secret. How could he say it? The mountain wind came down the valley in one of its sudden gusts – the faery wind they called it among the mountains when it came like that without warning churning the lakes into storm before it passed on. 'Father, I was with a woman.' The very thought of anything so coarse and ugly made him step rapidly away into the dark. Then he halted. 'Father, I have sinned with one of the opposite sex.' At that he shuddered and turned and ran into the dark away from the priest's house and the chapel followed by a voice shouting: 'Where are you?' He halted and came slowly back, ashamed, and knelt silently on the pebbly shore. He could see the purple ribbon of the stole falling in an arc about the priest's shoulders. Then it was: 'Well, my child, tell me your sins,' and with the cold faery wind circling his head he murmured out his dark secret, in what words he could never remember, but they were an old formula worn into an easy smoothness like a coin long in use. As he walked back in the teeth of the mountain wind he felt like a colt turned loose from a stable: he almost choked with happiness; he actually laughed out at the crying wind, and the night and the mountains were clothed in beauty without end.

At the point where the carcase of the abandoned car lay damming the murmuring mountain stream the headlights of a Lancia motorcar shone along the rising road and into the pinewoods where the road turned. The engines were silent and the black-bonneted occupants sat with rifles at the ready listening tensely to every sound borne on the wind. On the dark road behind the car an officer conversed with his guide, an old grey-pated constable who whispered out all he knew of the roads and by-paths leading to the monastery. When they had finished half of the party went with the old man up through the woods where the night before Bella and Denis had clambered along on their way to the guest-house door; the other half, with lights dimmed and engines racing, cut through the wind to the gates of the monastery avenue, and up between the swaying elms towards the outer gates of the guest-house. The old constable scarcely needed to look right or left, he knew the way as the palm of his hand. He tramped on staring before him into the dark between the trees, finding his way by sheer memory, his present thoughts turning unhappily on the ungrateful task they had set him, making of him a spy on his own people – on the monks who had been so good to him, whom he loved so much. It was only last July he had come down that path, enjoying the cool shade of the trees, the nutmeg scent of the crushed leaves, the soft carpet to rest on when weary. It was harvest time, and he loved to walk down after breakfast among the fields where the monks were at work, and lying under a cock of hay draw out his brown beads or his prayer-book and in the presence of the beauty of the coloured country stretched before him praise the good and great God who made all. He had never been so happy as during those two weeks of retreat, and he grew to love and be loved by the monks working silently day after day in the fields, and to whom he would talk without expecting a reply and tell the latest news from the world outside without ever a question. Smiling he would take up his position in the silent row that bound the grain after the clanking reaper and work with them, halting and straightening his back when he remembered a piece of news he had not told them before. He might say :

'There was a terrible earthquake in Japan and there's thousands homeless. A terrible business entirely. I believe houses fell on all sides of one Catholic church and the church wasn't touched at all.'

Or,

'There's terrible work in Morocco and the Spaniards have great trouble there with a fellow called – oh, some queer name – that they can't catch like the English with Kruger in South Africa – Ah, yes! Abdul Krim!'

Or,

'There's to be an election in Cavan and the Irish Party have stood down for the Sinn Feiners. I believe the Government intend to interfere with it in some shape or form.'

Or he might tell some innocent joke about the latest cure at the monastery and the monks would all raise a silent laugh and go on with their binding and stacking, but keeping an eye open for any attempt of his to begin again, when they would straighten and listen with eager faces. But he would soon have no more to recount, and then he would sidle up to one of the older monks and say to him shyly:

'Father, I have a son, Denis; he's a bit of a wild boy. He's up and down with them Sinn Feiners, and his poor mother is worried to death over him and it is his last year at the University. Won't you say a prayer for his success for God's sake, for I've done all I can for him now? God bless you, father.'

Whereupon he would smile over them all a silent good-bye and taking his coat in his arm – a fine well-built man he always was – stride off down the valley to where a little tarn stood edged by a few whispering reeds, and a bent thorn-tree, and walk on around it, his chin lifted as if the whole countryside were a flag and he marching past, his mouth sometimes opening to drink in great draughts of air. Often a well would lie in his way and he would drink deeply of its precious wine and if his way lay by an outlying ploughland of the monastery he would always stop to examine the work. And so back at evening time to the simple fare in the filled refectory – life for a couple of weeks in her quietest mood, every moment of those regular days a new delight, the praying, the eating, the long walks, the snoring sleep under trees or in bed when the last bell tolled over the pines for all the community to come to rest. Thinking of it all he tramped up the well-known path, sucking

in his white moustaches and chewing their ends in his bitter unhappiness at his present task. It was a fresh bitterness to see – even
in that darkness – such little changes as a tree cut here and there
to widen the way, or at one sharp point a few rough steps made
with flat stones and driven stakes. But the familiar was even worse
– the sudden slow tolling of the distant bell going through him like
a spear, the rolling away of the trees at the summit of the wood and
the sight of the distant buildings dark on the hill-top against the
sky.

In the monastery the drunkard sat in the guest-house refectory,
shuddering at the roaring wind that shook the avenue elms and all
the trees about the house. His hands were in a continual tremble
and his pig's eyes winked and blinked without stop as if he were
semaphoring with them across the room to something in the gloom
beyond. For a long time there had been silence in the room and
when Brother John began to speak suddenly the toper put his cup
of black tea into the slops of the saucer so roughly that they flowed
over on the cloth in a circular wave and dyed the edge of his dry
bread a pale beer-brown.

'Even Saint Pether,' continued the guestmaster sternly, as he
stroked his empty stomach by way of assuring himself that his
remarks had no personal application, 'Saint Pether did penance for
his sin in betraying our Lord. He wept for it until the tears made
furrows in his two cheeks. Yes, and Saint Mary Magdalene, the
holy fathers say, never stopped weeping from the day Christ died
until she died herself.'

'Well, well, well,' muttered the drunkard, as if these remarks had
no personal application to him either.

'And yet,' continued Brother John, his pitiless eyes on the wretch
blinking away beneath him at the imaginary semaphorist in the
opposite corner, 'and yet do you know what some of the fathers
hold? They say she is even to this very moment burning in Purgatory,
and will continue to burn there until the last trumpet releases her,
for all the terrible sins committed before she was converted.'

' 'Tis hard on the poor woman,' murmured the toper miserably.

'What hard?' grumbled the old monk. 'The woman was nearly
damned for all Eternity but for the great goodness of God.'

'Yes,' whispered the toper, completely cowed.

'Ah, penance! Penance is the only cure for sin. Forgiveness washes away the guilt of sin, but not the temporal punishment due to it. Do you hear that? Not the temporal punishment due to it.'

He paused as the wind blew past in a violent gust.

'Do you hear that,' he asked so suddenly that the toper all but leaped with terror and shouted out that he did, indeed.

'They say,' murmured the old monk quietly, 'that the wind is the crying of lost souls.'

'God help us all,' said the toper fervently.

'May God help each and every one of us then,' said the monk.

Another pause followed. The coals fell suddenly in the grate and the blind flapped and Brother John sucked at his teeth and gazed down at the dark ebb of tea in the drunkard's cup. Then he came up out of his deep meditation with –

'I wonder, may a man (and he paused) eat between his collations (pause) the food that sticks between his teeth . . . since the last meal? We had an orange for supper,' he explained in conclusion.

'Damn little sticks in my teeth, then,' said the drunkard angrily.

'Huh!' said the monk and began to laugh quietly at the joke.

Silence fell on them again, even more profound since the wind had fallen into a momentary calm, then beginning again to tap at the blinds and ripple the window blinds into a cat-like patter. Then it seemed to scream up the avenue towards the guest-house and a second later, there was indeed a thundering on the door that made the old monk whirl off the candle to the hall with a benediction of grease on the table-cloth as he went, fearful that this noise would awaken the whole community from their beds. In a second torches were flashing into the hall and armed men behind these bayonets of light rushed into the refectory. Black-bonneted devils out of the deepest pit of hell they seemed to the drunkard so that he choked when he would speak.

'I – ah – uh – you – gentlemen – ah – ah pathriots! Always was a pathriot! Genl'men, one of yeerselves. Don't shoot don' wan' to die. Not ready. Haven't made confession. Stole a bottle of Johnny Jameson. Holy Father, Mary mother of God! Genl'men, we're all wan!'

'Who's all one?' said a great elongated officer, jabbing the wretch's swollen stomach with the long nose of his black Webley revolver. 'Who do ye think we are, eh?'

The toper, utterly confounded, semaphored madly and shook like a scarecrow in the wind. The old constable, whispering like a man in a church, intervened mildly.

'That's Jerry Kane of Cork. He's in the D.T.'s. He's a simple man and there's no harm in him.'

'What's that,' growled the officer. 'Speak up man. Do you know him? What's he doing here? Is this a hospital?'

'He's on a cure. He's in charge of him,' said the old constable, pointing almost shyly at the guestmaster, an El Greco figure in brown watching them intently over the heads and fists and murderous faces and whirling torches of the black-bonnets moving around him. The officer glanced at the monk, and looked back at the toper who, almost sobered with fear stared up at him from under his knotted eyebrows with the intent stare of a frightened cat or bird. With his revolver the officer motioned the constable to one side.

'Take that fellow away,' he said, 'upstairs or somewhere and lock him in until I come.'

With bitter, disdainful eyes Brother John watched the pair go, the old constable and the drunkard. He knew that whatever the drunkard knew he would tell, and when the abbot came and, on hearing the officer's angry explanation of the raid, ordered the old monk to his cell for the night, he did not close an eye or rest for one second, pacing up and down thinking of the danger to the rebels sleeping unsuspectingly in the coom. He imagined them surprised, surrounded, shot to pieces in that valley-trap and he kept moving to the window to listen for the sound of starting motors, hoping the storm would continue, wishing for a night fog, downcast when the clouds parted and every field showed almost as bright as day, pleased when a dark cloud swam across the sky and the great fields filled with shadows and heavy drops fell. He was kneeling red-eyed and weary at the open window when the first pale ring of dawn circled the horizon, and he only slept on his arms in the window recess, when the moon sank and the stars waned and the little birds began to chirp in tune. By then the cars had not yet left the monastery courtyard.

What did happen in the end he never knew, for in the morning the abbot sent him back to silence among the cloistered brothers, and there he remained for so many years that with time he forgot it all, and nothing remained in the end but one meaningless picture of a heavy-coated policeman leading one of the drunks down the guest's corridor. It might be ten years after that he and the drunkard met again, the aged monk again guestmaster, the old toper still a toper, and they talked of that night that both had all but completely forgotten. The toper could only remember scraps of their conversation.

'He was a dacent man, God rest his soul. But that boy of his – I could tell you a thing or two about him. Somehow I haven't it clear at all now. But there was that woman they killed – what was her name? Wasn't I watching the two of them. God forgive me I was mad for the drop you had in your room. There he was tryin' room after room for her and he got it at last; and did he come out? Good-bye to you, says I, you're all right for the night and I seein' him shut the door after him. . . .'

But the monk had forgotten the boy and only gathered roughly that the toper was telling him of some indecency and would not listen, bidding him sternly to speak no evil in that room if he didn't wish to be without his little glass of John Jameson for the night. So they ended their talk of that night so many years ago, the toper murmuring apologetically that 'he was only sayin' how he was tellin' the constable, God rest him, about the goings-on of his boy.' He might have remembered more if he had seen the constable stealing out after Lauds, bent under his heavy coat and helmet, into the empty chapel to pray. The high red curtains were closed before the high altar and for light only the little tongue of flame in the red sanctuary lamp that cast its leaping shadows into the dark and moted well and womb of the empty nave, and threw no beam at all – unlike the occasional moon – into the choir stalls where the old man knelt, his bald pate bent and all his body with it fallen in utter despair into the shelter of his crooked arms. He remained there muttering so fervently that he might have been talking to some real person through the gloom.

'O immense passion! O profound wounds! O sweetness above all sweetness,' came his heartbroken litany, 'O most bitter Death, grant him mercy. May the most sacred and loving heart of the good, kind Jesus, the good, kind, loving Jesus, grant us all and especially poor Denis Thy mercy. I beseech Thee, O good Jesus, O good, sweet, kind, and loving Jesus. . . .'

Until he fell asleep there, and he too awoke chill and stiff in the dawn to hear the little fluttering birds chirping outside in the branches of the trees.

3

In the coom at dawn a chill wind came over the edge of the mountains and Bella was wakened by it in time to see the cold light spreading southward in the sky. She stood in her bare feet under the thatch and rubbed the damp pane with her hand. Like magic a waterfall appeared high up in a crook of the mountains and the golden morning star above it in the sky and below it in a pool on the floor of the glen. As she stood listening to the silence and watching the dark sky grow grey she heard faintly the distant sound of the falling waters, and from a distant cock there came echoing through the valley a long forlorn crow. As she leant her forehead on the cold pane the inevitable repetition came trailing and wavering as if the morning mist choked it. Everything looked bedraggled and shaggy after the storm but indifferent and timeless as the stones of the hills, indifferent, deathless, going on and on without end. The cock shrilled again, but its cry wavered and was lost in the silence. Even the cock, she thought – red-eyed, red-combed, bedraggled – was indifferent to everything but the rhythmical return of the dawn and the ritual of welcome. When she heard the little girl of the house tramping up the stairs she smiled to hear the feet halt on every step, but when the child entered the room and she looked at its wide frightened eyes, wide like a deer or pet cat, fear surged up around her beating heart. At the same moment the melancholy bird outside called again, as if to say to her, 'Here's-to the-end-of you, oh, here's-to-the-end-of you-u-u!'

The child laid her breakfast on the window ledge and almost crying from fear turned to go, but with a sudden motherly impulse she caught at the little trembling shoulders and kissed the white face and plucked the pink frock into shape. Then she found her gold compact and dabbing a bit of powder on her cheeks and glancing for the last time at her hair she snapped the case to and pressed it into the tiny fist.

'To go with your frock,' she said, trying to smile gaily.

'It's me new dress,' said the mite shyly.

'Oh?'

'I have it on for to go to Mass in it.'

'To Mass?'

Footsteps passed by behind the house, resounded for a moment and were out of earshot. Far up the opposite mountain-side a group of people were moving down to the valley. The child, fingering the gold toy, had forgotten its fears, but it remembered a message and said of a sudden, pointing to the food on the tray.

'If you want more of that stuff you can have it and welcome.'

It was a big tumbler of whisky.

'What is it for?' she asked in a low voice.

'It's the min have it below in the kitchen. They're dhrinkin' it since the morning. . . .

All but sickened she faced the window. There she spoke to the child without turning.

'I want paper and a pen. I must write a letter.'

The little steps went from the room, halting on each knee of the stairs as they clambered down. She tried to grip herself, summoning up her thoughts in order: Dearest Jack, or Darling Jack, or just plain Jack: To say good-bye. I thought it would be easy but it's hateful. I thought I'd just go. I can't. But I shouldn't complain. Life has been good while it lasted. Dot and Billie are happy. We have done our duty. Say good-bye to them for me. They are good girls. I'd love to see you again. But it isn't to be, is it? I have had my time. Yes, she could go through with all that – it was easy to say good-bye to him – he would understand, and if there was an after he would follow in his time. Don't worry about these people, they will meet their end too. It isn't worth while. It has been good fun while it lasted. My time, I mean. You, too, make it spin. It soon goes. So cheerio. Oh, it would be very easy to write a cheerful letter just like that, to him. But there were other things, things that would not hear, and would not follow after, the ancient eternal things she loved, that morning star, the sinking moon, the hours of change between night and day, the lovely, lovely light, the beautiful, beautiful dark, the various hours, so lovely, all so cruel, come and go, come and go, for ever, as if she had not so much as been. Heavier steps tramped up the little stairs and there was a knock at the door and turning she saw Denis. He came in and with shame-heavy eyes laid a penny bottle of ink and a sheet of notepaper and a child's pink-handled steel pen on the table.

'Have you been drinking?' she said bitterly.

'No. I am going to Mass.'

'Mass?'

'To Communion.'

'Come and go, come and go.'

'I will pray for you.'

'You can go to hell!'

'I'm sorry.'

'Oh, all right.'

'I am sorry about all this. I could do nothing. Headquarters were against it, are against it. But there's the six boys. They are all drunk.'

'Go to Communion.'

'Can I take a letter?'

'Will you?'

'I promise.'

'Though I shall know nothing about that.'

'I promise. Write another and give me the one you want to go.'

'You mean, write two?'

'Yes.'

'You mean two letters.'

'Yes.'

'I hope you will be very happy, boy.'

'I am happy.'

'You will be very happy, I think. I liked you. Lead your life, child, while it lasts.'

'You'd better write.'

He felt a prig as she turned and knelt by the window and wrote. But he had laid out his course and he must follow it. The church-bell began to ring up the valley and he hoped he would not be late for the Communion. They would ask him below-stairs what she said but they were too drunk to notice if he told an awkward lie. He was glad he was going to Mass and they had let him out of the whole hateful business. Afterwards he would leave the column for a few weeks and go home to the city to see his father and mother. God had been very good to him so far. He must keep good always now. Always and always, for ever and ever, without a single lapse. It would take a long time to forget that night in the monastery but he must not think of it again, and he was glad the priest had forbade him to go back over it. He must just take it for a lesson. He must remember that life was a hard struggle but with the help of God he would spend the remainder of it as pure as he was at that moment. She handed him her letter and he put it in his pocket. Then he said good-bye and went down to Mass.

As he entered the little weather-beaten church the bell ceased its insistent ringing. He gave his rifle to a boy among the crowd kneeling outside the door and took his place farther in; yet from where he knelt he could see over his shoulder, through the great open door that filled the entire rear wall of the church, the sharp rise of the mountain, dark green save where the shaggy clouds swept their lower edges along its slopes. These bare mountains were infinitely beautiful to him, and as he waited for the Mass to begin he pictured how the church would appear from their summits, set by a bowl of lead in the mountains. It was a place where old hermits were said to have lived in complete silence while the storm howled down about their huts and stirred up the lake to an angry sea. They, too, weathered by the rains would have looked like rocks or withered bushes or old worn statues – the church itself would seem from the hills as if carved out of the tumbled stones, even down to the worshippers clustered shoulder to shoulder outside the door, the peasants in their green-black frieze, all on one knee, facing forward to the altar as their forefathers must have before the altar-rock of Christ or Crom.

The Mass went through all its phases to the Communion time and Denis, following each movement of the ceremony of adoration, and preparation and final miracle, with eyes closed and his head and all his body bowed forward into his hands felt as he had never before the great calm of harbourage, the peace of the anchor-hold in from the surge of the sea. But far up the coom there reverberated through the echoing hills a volley of rifle-fire. As the echoes vanished so did the peace within him, and his heart was once again in storm. Not so easily, not so quietly was life to be left behind. O Immense Passion, O profound wounds, O sweetness above all sweetness, grant her eternal rest. Then the boy to whom he had given his rifle was

pulling at his shoulder and all the little congregation were looking
with frightened eyes up along the dark-green slopes where a scattered
line of troops was moving slowly down out of the shaggy fog. In
a second he had his rifle in his hand and was out of the chapel and
was racing under the shelter of the graveyard below the mountain
out towards his comrades in the coom. It was a long way and there
were innumerable turf-cuttings and dikes hewn out of the bog and
he splashed in and out of brown bog-water and sank to his knees
many times in the spongy mould as he ran his way. The shoulder of
the mountain now hid the advancing figures and he could not see
how widely they were deployed or how near they came as he ran.
When he passed the cabin not a soul was to be seen but as he
entered the shadows of the coom he could see far up the glen the
cluster of men coming and going with little steps as about some
special task. His voice as he shouted made but little noise in the
wide, ravine-high place, for his throat and palate were dry and his
heart beating madly against his side and his gasping breath robbed it
of all energy. But soon they saw him stumbling toward them and
he waved his hand behind him and made for the nearest stream to
clamber up its course out of the trap of the coom. They understood
at once and scattered up the slopes and for a long while he saw
nobody, climbing up hand over hand, resting as long as he dared
like a hunted stag in the trickling water, drinking it up as he lay.
After a while, less than an hour, he caught sight of a group of his
fellows struggling upwards to the head of the coom and he changed
his course to meet them but before they could come together he
saw from his higher position a scattered group of khaki figures top
the coom-head not more than five˙hundred yards away, and open
fierce bursts of fire down the slopes. Up here he was better sheltered
than the others, and as he climbed he fired; it was not his first fight
and he was not frightened, and he was full of the knowledge that
he was never in his life so prepared to die.

More conspicuous than the other figures at the coom-head was
one tall officer, long-legged against the sky as he directed his men.
Denis chose him for his target and repeatedly he fired at him. He
emptied his clip and shoved in another and emptied that. Finding
a good position behind a rock he loaded his breech once again, and
first looking behind him and above him to make sure that he was
not in danger from these quarters took long, careful aim and

fired in rapid succession. Long-legs was not aware of him and now stood up to change his position and at the same moment there was a sudden lull in the volleying so that even the echoes had time to die away. Once more the boy aimed, and his shot rang out alone. This time the tall figure stumbled and with one hand flung high fell prone.

Just then the clouds, as they often do in these high mountains, sank down slowly like white fleecy curtains on the whole valley, and (enveloped in the driving fog) the boy clambered away to the north, elated at his success, and drove on until he found the ground levelling under his feet. He was on the edge of the plateau above the coom, and to the south the cabin and farther west the little leaden lake and the tiny chapel at its white edge were still occasionally visible. What looked from below like white clouds was here wet flying mist, and here it was the rocks not the bog-water pools that were the contrast with the wraiths flying heedlessly past him. The pools were as mirrors breathed on, the rocks were storm-polished to ebony. He could see in his mind's eye this region as it appeared on the maps – marked only by the trailing ends of tributary streams and petered mountain paths or by the ultimate peak-circles of the contour lines, or such homeless words as Stone Circle or the long Irish names of the mountains, a pathless waste; and knowing the danger to be gone – yet taking no chances – he struck away northwards to the heart of it, sure that before the night ended he would reach the next valley-stop and find rest and shelter by some peasant's turf-fire or in the odorous warmth of a farmer's winter hay.

And as he tramped on, straight as an arrow for fear of losing his sense of direction, through every little obstacle, pool or clustered tuft, his thoughts slowly gathered and he let them gather at their will for they were, he had often found, the best protection against rough weather and long marches – thoughts of the city, thoughts of home, other thoughts not so welcome that made him drive faster on as if he would leave something that hurried with him behind, until unexpectedly there loomed out of the mist another figure which, before he had time to be startled he recognized as one of his comrades – the black-browed, black-eyed fellow they called Rory, and Rory was singing a song that he barely interrupted for a greeting, a song that he would for no pleadings of Denis cease to sing, adding verses to it as he sang, each new verse more hateful than the one before.

> Will anybody tell me where is Inchigeela's shore
> For there's a bed new-made down there for somebody
>   we know,
> The blanket is of Irish green, the quilt it is of red,
> But she that's lying underneath is dead, me boys, is
>   dead . . .
> Her coat was red and her blanket's red . . .

And so they tramped on through the driving fog, quiet only until a new verse broke the profound silence, tramped until the sun gleamed silver through the lightening mist, very low because it was sinking, and then as the new night came to turn the world from light to dark they both were walking on in utter silence. Their feet squelched over the pebbly places and the withered gorse rustled dry in the wind, slanted perpetually away from the prevalent blasts. A little light in a window miles away glinted out of a sudden and Rory spoke.

'That was a narrow shave, Dinny. We left it go too long.'

'What?'

'That bloody she-spy. Do you know where we are?'

'No.'

'That's Knockane down there, I know a domn fine girrl down there will give us a warm bed for the night. By God the shtars is out.'

'Hesperus.'

'What?'

'The evening star,' said Denis.

'I know a pome about the wreck of that wan.'

'That was a ship. But it was called after the star.'

'It's very bright, by God.'

'Aye,' said Denis, 'it will be a lovely night.'

'Do you know, Old Johnny sent a message while you were at Mass?'

'Why didn't ye tell me?'

'We left it go too long. We were nearly caught ourselves.'

'I plugged the Tan that led them,' said Denis.

'Are you sure?'

'I saw him drop.'
'The son of a bitch.'
'He nearly finished us. He'll talk no more.'

In this valley it was another world. The sky was cleared and the stars winked and shone firmly one by one – a lovely, lovely night.

'Chi-rist,' said Rory, 'I'm domn tired.'

'It's my back,' said Denis, moving his shoulder-blades.

'We'll have a good sleep *tonight*,' said Rory.

'Aye. We need it,' said Denis. 'I need it sorely.'

Talking like that they dropped into the valley with all its lights, and by the time they were at the door of the 'domn fine girrl' they were in a gay mood, rejoicing in the loveliness of the night, and their own youth, and the promise of infinite days yet to come.

The Bombshop

At first it was easy to work steadily in the Bombshop, all day long
and into the night too. They found all the pleasure they needed in
making the bombs and there was a special malicious pleasure in
knowing that while they made them there were the markets, so
fussy, so noisy, beneath their windows, too busily engaged selling
their fish to suspect anything. The three would chuckle when they
thought of it and say to one another with a wink: 'If they only
knew!' and return with vigour to their deadly tasks. There was
never any question, then, of going out into the streets, not even
after dark or in the early dawn, or if they thought of it they were
ashamed to mention it. Even when the work began to pall on
them, when they began to halt in the middle of it to lounge and
smoke in the front room, or to peep through the drawn blinds at
the streets, they returned shamefaced with a joke about the Freedom of the City that would one day be conferred on them. And
when they did at last confess to one another that they would
like to go out into the streets it was a long time before they talked
of it as something that might possibly be done. When they did they
found that only two things prevented them – the danger to themselves and the danger to the Bombshop; they might easily be
recognized by a spy and arrested, or, worse still and more likely,
they might not be arrested at once but watched as they went back
to their lair. So they abandoned the idea, only to return to it again,
and abandon it again, and return to it and abandon it, until the very
thought of the streets tormented them. In this way they discovered
something that nobody else could have taught them – that it is
easy to do anything at first, no matter how difficult or dangerous,
but the inevitable desires of the heart swell and burst in the end
like a well gathering beneath the surface of the earth.

They came to fear special hours of the day, and the nights
tormented them. They feared especially the early cock-crow when

the market-life began and their sleep ended, the dark hours of the morning when the carts went rumbling in beneath their windows from the fields and the seashore. Leo, the youngest of the three and who should have slept better than any of them, was the first to admit that he often rose on his elbow to watch the loads go by, the cabbage glistening, the fish crates brown, the domes of hay darkened by the rain falling on them so heavily from the great leaking sieve of a sky that the fish almost swam in their boxes and the cabbage-heads cupped the water and splashed it on the fishwives who unloaded them from their places in the carts. Once he saw a drenched carter look enviously up at his window and angrily flick his horse's glistening rump with his whiplash. 'If he only knew!' said the boy, with a bitter self-pity, and leaned back wearily in his bed wishing he could sleep again. Their work would not begin until the angelus bells began to chime, here, there, everywhere, over the city, and from that on the roar of the spirit-lamps and the rattle of the pestle in the mortar, and the hiss of sifters kept the city sounds at bay, except alone the cries of the fishwomen outside that they could not stifle – the 'Here's the herrings, here's the herrings, here's the herrings' in a torrent of words, or the wail of 'Fine cod a' hake, oh, fine cod a' hake'; but at lunch-hour the lamps would fall silent and all the city enter through the windows, and from that on they toiled as best they might through the long afternoon. Then the markets would gradually be dissipated and the dark fall, and they too cease work, and old memories and old habits recur.

On wet nights – almost every night that is for the two months since they came – they sat before their fire in the sitting-room while the rain dripped musically on the tin roof in the yard, and Shandon tower struck out the hours from the wet dark above their heads. They could see it through the window in the landing if they chose to look, a tapering mass, dark against the wet luminous sky, its golden weather-fish swimming endlessly through the aqueous air. They sat there, almost always in silence, playing chess, or reading, or writing long letters until Norah – their courier and housekeeper – returned with dispatches, and the dispatches almost always taunted them to hurry, to get finished, saying that everything and everybody was ready for the attack but the Bombshop. Or if there were no dispatches, one of them wishing to be alone would go to his room till the following morning (as Leo did more often than any of them) or another down into the yard to sit on the ash-bin, to smoke and look up at their square of sky, returning with his hair wet with points of mist like dew.

On the few fine nights there were, they could see, by peeping carefully through the front windows, the lane-children racing and shouting under the lit lamps, or hear a group of girls circling arm in arm about the markets, singing as they went the mournful harmony of old sentimental numbers – those songs from the Edwardian music-halls that are remembered in the provinces long after they are forgotten elsewhere.

> Come over the garden wall,
>   Little girl to me.
> I've been lonely a long, long time,
> And the wall isn't hard to climb.
> Just jump up and then jump down,
>   I won't let you fall.
> We'll play at sweethearts
> And then we'll be married, so,
> Come over the garden wall.

Or they would sing something from the *Prince of Pilsen* or *Florodora*; and Sean, with his great awkward body, would leap up and imitate the girls of the chorus with their fleshy, pink-tighted thighs that popped in and popped out like the mechanical men on circus roundabouts, and the others would laugh at him and at them. But hearing the voices come from the distance and vanish into it as the girls went round and round the squares the three bomb-makers would hum in turn after them.

> 'I've been lonely a long, long time,
>   Little girl of mine. . . .'

Or they would read the evening paper over and over again, sharing it between them until it became a wrinkled ball. Then Norah would come and draw the tiny envelopes from her bosom and they receive them still warm from her flesh – and, reading them, forget her.

Sometimes, indeed, they were merry, if there were many dispatches from Norah. Or if she brought much news they would gossip for hours on end. Or they would be coaxed from their silence on the rare nights when they were visited by Mother Dale. She was the owner of the house, the only other woman who knew of the Bombshop; she kept the old-clothes shop beneath them, and lived between them and it.

She rarely troubled them – as if she knew that they did not want her old woman's talk, but now and again of nights the door would open and there she would stand under the lintel, tall in the gloom like a slender statue from a Middle Ages porch, a spear carved into woman-shape. She was a wonderful old woman; even Sean and Caesar, rough fellows as they were, could find no other word for her but that, and as she peered down at them, with child-soft eyes and inclined brow, unbuttoning her little mouth, that was wrinkled like cloth, into a smooth gentle smile they would wink at her or smile foolishly, not knowing whether to believe those open mother's eyes or her torture-tightened lips.

One wet night she came, early in the night, not going out that one night of all her nights to pray in the chapels for them, and as they looked up at her wet spangled bonnet, Norah ran and gently removed it from the lowered pate before her, pretending to be exasperated that she should have been out in such weather. But she only removed her wet cloak, and smiling at them said:

'Sure the best night of all to be out is the wet night when there's nobody to follow me. If it was a fine night I'd be rounding the markets for an hour before I'd come to my own door-bell, and all for fear of a fellow that warn't watching me at all, but only out for a drink after hours. But a night like this there's none abroad but the lost cats and the night police. And how is Leo?' turning to the boy amongst them.

He grinned back at her.

'I went out to pray for ye,' she continued, 'and to pray for the good work, but I got a pain in my side and I came home. And what need is there to pray for ye or the work when God is always on the watch for the boys of Ireland. Look what I brought ye, Sean.'

It was a bottle of invalid's wine. Out went his great hand, and back she snatched it in her bony one.

'Oh,' he wailed in mock despair, 'and I that haven't been in a pub for two months.'

'Ye'll get none of this then.'

'Oh, oh,' from Sean as if he were the most crestfallen man in the world.

'Not a drop! If I was to let you put your big mouth to it the bottle would be empty in a flash.'

Then she laughed at him.

'Ah, no. Sure no? I don't mean that at all. Take it, Norah. It's for all of ye. I pray for yeer souls and I bring wine for yeer bodies. Norah understands me, doesn't she? Norah?'

'Yes I do, Mother Dale,' from Norah, her prominent teeth bared, her soft lips spread.

'Mind yeerselves though, boys,' she said, as she rose and turned to go. 'They say the city is full of spies.'

She laid an envelope of new records on the table for Sean's gramophone.

'I nearly forgot them. Good night, Sean.'

He raised his big paw.

'Good night, mother.'

'Caesar?'

'Good night, mother.'

'Leo?'

'Good night, mother.'

'Good night, Norah.'

'Cheerio, mother,' said Norah, who always had a special 'good night' to herself, the last of all. The old woman had to stoop her lofty head to leave the room. Down she went to her own room below, and they opened the wine and sipped the weak juice in a returning silence while Norah went out quietly for her nightly batch of messages. Even as she closed the hall-door behind her she could hear the opening bars of the 'Turkish Patrol' ('As played by the band of the Highland Light Infantry') come blaring from the great brass-horned gramophone. She was glad that Sean had something to occupy him for the night, but as she thought again of the great maw of the gramophone, pasted all over inside and out with postage stamps, and of the rusted needles, and the cracked sound-box, she strode gladly away, into the drizzling rain, crunching savagely over cabbage stumps and the heads of decapitated fish. But the wind over the bridges blew her umbrella inside out and the rain seeped into her shoes and her body became chilled in the cold womb of the chapel, where she exchanged dispatches with the

Headquarters courier, and on her way back she felt so miserable that she almost thought of the Bombshop as 'home.' Once inside the door, however, there was the 'Turkish Patrol' still blaring away as if they had all gone out and forgotten to shut off the record and it had ever since been repeating and repeating itself while the needle wore to a stump. She raced up the stairs in a rage and found Caesar hanging over a chess problem and Leo staring mournfully and without interest at the gramophone. By this a new record had been set in the machine and as she entered the room Sean caught her up in his great hands and set her down right before it – he had the hands and body of a navvy and the concave profile of a prize-fighter, and as she glared at him he laughed at her, and winked behind Caesar's back. Before she could speak a nasal whine of song scraped and whined in the horn.

'It's just one line,' roared Sean, 'one line we can't make out. It's called – "Where the old horse died."

> 'In the lag behind the hollow.
> Where the grath ith golden red,'

cried a deep basso from the depth of the gramophone.

'Now,' cried Sean.

'And the coopoo gooloo moonoo nuroon,' said the basso.

'What do you make of it?' roared Sean, the gramophone whining on and on.

'There we sometimes hear the churchbells,' roared the basso.

> 'There no more we hear them now.
> In the place where the old horse died.'

'Well?' repeated Sean.

'Not a word of it,' said Norah, wearily removing her hat and damp coat, while the chess-player groaned and Leo shook his head and sighed.

'Slowly now this time,' said Sean, and as for a moment he held the needle from the record to adjust the regulator they could hear the rain drip before the wind on the tin roof outside and Shandon booming out the quarter. Then the rite began once more.

'In the lag behind the hollow,
Where the grath ith golden red.'

sang the basso for the hundredth time in the house that night, now
with the slowness of a dead-march.

'Now,' roared Sean towering over her.

'And the coopoo gooloo moonoo nuroon,' said the basso once
again.

'No,' said Norah, and she shook her head.

'We think,' he said, 'that it's either "and the grey grass blooms
upon the lawn," or "and the church-bells bloom through the dawn."
But wait. Twice as slow this time.'

The silent chess-player looked up and in a low voice of bitterness
he said :

'Stop it!'

Caesar was quite different from the prize-fighter – a long slim
figure with the eyes of an ascetic or a fanatic, one of them slightly
askew so that he always had an impenetrable look; but it was his
pendulous nose and his hollowed cheeks and his elongated neck
that had christened him.

'Ah! Caesar!' mocked Sean at him. 'One more little bouteen
now. One more now. All listen with the utmost attention and
devotion, and in all moments of temptation danger and affliction' –
he quoted blasphemously from the Catechism as the rite began again
and the chess-player leaped to his feet and thrust out his hand to
the machine.

At once broken-nose grew dark-faced and stood up to him.

'For God's sake give it a rest,' said Caesar.

'Why should I?' cried Sean. 'What else have we here to occupy
our minds?'

'Sean!' implored the girl, while Leo sat still and looked gloomily
at the three of them. This was what life had been like in the Bombshop for a month now.

'Let it alone!' cried Sean.

'In-the-lag-behind-the-hollow,' wailed the dying basso.

'Stop it or I'll smash it,' said Caesar, and with his fist he smashed
the whirling black circle, and the rain dripped audibly on the
corrugated roof. The prize-fighter was furious. He thrust his fist
into his hip-pocket and the nickel of a revolver flashed. Norah was

between them in a second but as they struggled two deafening shots rang and the air was hot-flavoured with the smell of powder. At once they all grew quiet, looking at one another to see if anyone was hurt, and then they returned to their places. Caesar fingered his chessmen; by the fire Sean ejected the empty shells, and dropped the broken record bit by bit into the fire, frowning as each morsel melted in acrid flame. Secretly we were all listening for some sign that the shots had been heard in the street. Norah removed her shoes and felt her damp feet, and to fill the uneasy silence she turned to the boy.

'Not a single dispatch tonight,' she said. 'But I met Frank Boland.'

'Where has he been?'

'He's been in the mountains, and in Dublin and Kildare, too.'

'My home counties,' said Leo. 'Where was he? Clane or Sallins or Celbridge? Has he any news?'

'He said it was very wet weather there.'

'Yet the beech would be out by now,' said Leo.

'He said something was out. He watches things like that.'

'He does.'

'Maybe it was the beech, he mentioned,' she said. 'But he preferred the mountains for all that they were cold and harsh. He said every road there is a bog and the torrents pouring down the mountain-cliffs like snow.'

They could see that Caesar was listening, and Sean held a piece of broken record poised on his fingers.

'Out there,' said Leo wistfully, 'every pool is a big lake.'

'And every pub,' said Sean, 'is a filled room.'

He was thinking of the frieze-coated peasants, with their pints before them and the smell of the bogs and the byres from their clothes and their twisted bits of ash-plants scraping the spittle into shapes on the sawdust floor. Leo turned to him.

'Wouldn't you scoff a frothy pint now, Sean?' he mocked timidly.

'It's not the pint I want,' he said, and he rose and went to bed.

When he was gone they looked at one another as people might who have heard a strange sound and wonder if their companions can explain it. And as none of them had anything to say Norah leaped up and went down to Mother Dale. They knew she would be wondering what had happened, frightened by those sudden shots.

The two heard Norah's steps go down the stairs, the old woman's door open, and then a brief silence.

'I was once in Sallins,' Caesar was saying, when they heard scream after scream ring through the silent house. They heard Norah pounding up the stairs and when she stood panting before them her face was as pale as her bosom. She pointed through the floor and as they looked stupidly down at it they saw two neat little holes drilled there by the passage of Sean's bullets.

They found the old woman seated as if asleep in her armchair, not a rib of hair askew, her arms lying on the arm-rests, her body as erect as a Caryatid supporting a great weight on its head, but as Leo laid his hand on the back of her neck his fingers grew wet and sticky with blood, and her blood was warm still though the flesh was already rough with the chill of death. There they left her, for all that Norah could say, with tears of pity and rage, half-mad with both, protesting against Caesar's orders that he gave through his tight fanatic's lips. Not a priest nor a doctor would he have; she was dead, cold as a stone already; priests and doctors could do her no good. He stood and looked coldly while Norah applied a mirror to her lips to see if there was any life at all, and then as the glass came away untarnished he looked at the girl and shrugged his shoulders as if to say, 'I told you so.'

'Let us kneel and pray for her,' he said, perhaps with some thought of easing the girl's pain, perhaps to think quietly while we prayed. But at any rate he could not lead our prayers but stumbled and stuttered at them, and Norah rose and pleaded again.

'The work must go on at all costs,' said Caesar. 'Unless she can be removed secretly she stays where she is. Lead the Rosary for her, Norah.'

But Norah cursed him and all of us for a pack of cowards, while Caesar placed a crucifix between the dead woman's fingers and laid a cloth over her face, and as they went up to bed Norah followed them step by step taunting them as she went.

All night long Leo heard her turning uneasily on her pallet and in the morning she was heavy-lidded and her hands trembled. That day they were so long in beginning work that before the lamps began to boom the country carts were long trundled away and the parallelograms of sunlight disappeared from the tiles of the kitchen floor. Then Sean discovered that a jar of his acid was cracked behind its straw and had leaked empty and there was nothing for him to do but fall idle for the day.

Those idle hours finished him. He wandered aimlessly about the house, and they even heard him enter the dead woman's room. He came to Norah where she sat in the kitchen cutting the cotton-wool in long strips for the incendiaries and tried to gossip with her about his children, and when she would not he went poking in the old disused front room. When she followed, after listening for a long time for any sound from him, she found him at the window watching the children playing in the sun; there, she at one side of the window, he at the other, they stood watching them, delighted, until the musty air began to choke her and she fled to her work. It was an old lumber-room, crowded to the door with boxes, trunks, and packing-cases, in which and on which every kind of useless but cherished household god was living – or rather dying, malodorously. To her, too young to care about anybody's past, these sea-shells stuck on velvet, those rows of cracked decanters, the fox under the glass dome (with a special hole cut for his long tail), all those long-cherished useless things commemorated the breaking one by one of the heart-strings of the dead woman. Mother Dale, she knew, had kept them – and all women keep them – because they hope that as long as they look at them their past is not yet dead, their lives not yet spent. During the long ennui of those empty days passed in hiding in whatever house opened its 'front drawing-room' to her, she had become artful, and hated herself for being so artful, in smelling out the faintest musk of those private and particular gods of her woman friends – the chinaware shoe (from Youghal), the filigree plate (from the Royal Oriental Exhibition), the tarnished silver teapot presented at marriage or retirement, the specially-bound prize book (from Sister Joanna to dear May), the *Cabinet of Literature* never cut, the *History of all Time* never read, memories all, mortuaries of the dead past. When she would be older, she well knew, she too would have her monuments and love them as old men love antiquity that is musty like their hearts and she would look fondly at them and carefully preserve the photograph of her marriage-day and the marble clock with the tarnished brass-plate commemorating the first step in the ending of her youth.

'Sean,' she called into him, 'come out of that bloody charnel-house.'

But he had found a red velvet-covered, brass-bound, gilt-latched photograph album, with a musical-box buried in it so that as one looked at the pictures of one's antecedents it ping-ponged out its sad meowing tune:

'Oh, there's, no, place, like, home; oh, no, place, like, home.' Guffawing at it, he opened it again and again, and would not come to her.

As if to mock her and tempt him the sun burst on the city at noon, and the damp of three months rose in curling exhalations from the pavements. Feeling the sun she returned to peep into the streets and found them filled with points of light that leaped from the scales of the mackerel, the white bosoms of the women, their arms diving among the flat fish and the sprats and the slender plaice. She looked up and the seagulls turned their white breasts to her and the vegetables below shone like polished ware; she looked up into the sky where the clouds were lifted slowly up through the blue air like flock for gods to lie on, and below the onion-girls and the lane-children were crying louder than ever, screaming as they ran, the one for customers, the others as for pure joy in the sudden parturition of the year. Even the wail of 'Fine cod a' hake' became faster and more joyous, and even this dim blind-drawn room filled with warmth and light, the great sun glowing through it like fiery bronze. But in the gloom of one corner behind her the musical-box iterated its dozen notes, and Sean, in his fine baritone voice, sang the same few notes over and over again:

> 'Mid pleasures and palaces,
> No matter where we roam,
> Be it ever so humble,
> There's no place like home.'

She turned and swore at him. 'For Christ's sake, stop it, Sean.'

He only laughed at her, and the others, hearing them, left their work to join in the fun. Before them Sean donned a bonnet and a wrap.

'But I haven't the wasp waist,' he roared at them, 'nor the puffed shoulders. If I had the waist it would only be after a month of pulling and hauling on the laces with the maid cocking her leg on the side of the bed for leverage.'

'No, you haven't the waist,' said Leo, imitating his capers.

'The corset wasn't made that would circle your belly,' said Caesar more coarsely than he had even before spoken in that house.

'To be sure women have narrower waists than men,' said Leo, and then he blushed; he saw Norah bite her soft big lips with her prominent teeth, and look at up him through her hair that had fallen forward over her bowed head. In his confusion he spoke foolishly.

'Who do you think, now,' he said, 'wore them things last?'

They broke up at that, silently, like men parting in a church or at a funeral – one going one way, another that, overcome by the thought of the passing away of something they had loved.

The sun moved downward so slowly and so brightly that they noticed without difficulty the lengthening of the day. They talked of the spring while they worked, Leo speaking often of the beech-woods of Kildare, Norah of the smell of the furze and the bracken hot and damp in the mountains. When the dusk fell Sean was still in the old lumber-room watching the scattering of the markets, and when the dark came he packed his bag and despite Caesar's furious taunts he left the house. Norah accompanied him, hoping it might be safer for him, and Caesar and Leo spent the night examining their secret dump under the stairs to see how little they had yet done. There was yet not a third of the amount required, and Caesar, rather than receive another taunting note from the quarter-master when Norah should return, went in despair to his room and Leo sat alone before the empty grate, watching vacantly where a yellow slug, tempted by the sudden heat, drew his silver trail inch by inch to the open window.

It was not the market-people who awoke them the following morning but the milkman thundering on the door. After he had made the whole street resound they saw him stand back from the door and survey the house and then whip up his pony in wonderment, looking back many times as he went. For the first time they realized the risks they were taking. The old woman had few friends, but one of the few might come at any time to visit her, and be astonished at the shutters on the shop-windows and the closed door. At once Caesar went rummaging in the dead-room for a specimen of the old woman's script – finally breaking open a tin safe where she kept her money and her private papers. He winked at Leo with

his impenetrable eye and smiled at his own cunning as he copied
her hand in a notice for the shop-door: *Gone to the country for a
fortnight, May Dale*. If they could now get a man to replace Sean,
get a new jar of acid, and arrange to remove the body of the old
woman they might bring their work to a successful end. But there
was no longer any excuse now for bringing a packing-case or a trunk
to the shop as they formerly did whenever they needed raw material,
and headquarters complained that it would be even more difficult to
get a new man for them than to get a case in or a coffin out. But
Caesar threw their taunts back at them in a long dispatch that
Norah carried out that night, and he made extreme plans and
preparations like a successful general who has received an unexpected defeat. Norah was not to leave now until quite late at
night; he would have the Scouts extinguish the lamps near him
in the markets so as to give additional darkness; they would rise
earlier and finish later. He over-flowed with a rash self-confidence
and he always said afterwards that he would have won through if
the unexpected had not happened. For his plans did not get very far.
Norah actually went out the following night quite late, and the
Boy Scouts extinguished every light in the markets – that was
Thursday, the third night after her death – by shooting every bulb
to pieces with their revolvers; they thereby attracted the attention
of the patrols for the first time to the markets and attracted to
themselves Caesar's rage, for he sent their Master a long profane
dispatch pleading for a 'less spectacular method of hastening the
gentle night.' He need not have been so sarcastic with the boys.
Even while they were making cock-shots of the market-lights there
occurred, at the very gateway of the police headquarters over the
river, an ambush in which three Tans and two soldiers were killed,
and as a punishment an instant curfew was imposed to the very
boundaries of the city, and every man and woman was ordered to
be within doors from five o'clock in the afternoon until five o'clock
on the following morning, and so nightly 'until further notice.'
Until further notice read to Caesar like – *For Ever*.

The first afternoon of curfew the foot-patrols were doubled and
armoured-cars roared through the deserted streets, leaving as they
went from earshot a silence as of death in their wake. In the Bombshop they feared to continue working after the silence of Curfew
fell and they peeped through the blinds at the bare markets where

the only live thing was a cat quietly washing its face in the warm
sun, and a dog crunching a fish-head. Beyond the end of the square
a section of main street stood empty as if it were early dawn instead
of an hour before sundown, and the naked tram rails in the distance
and the closed warehouses made it appear as if every clock in the
city had stopped and all Cork had forgotten to rise.

Then night came and there was no moon, and in the markets not
a lamp was lit; everything was impenetrable shadow out to the
farthest end of the distant street and the cold light of a street-lamp.
Once towards ten o'clock a lorry roared into the square and a
searchlight flooded the place with a sudden blaze as of protracted
lightning. The cats stood still and glared into the light, the cabbage-
stumps and the fish-crates leaped out of their black shadows as if
they were alive. Then the light swooped and the lorry moved slowly
to another street. As they returned to sit by the empty grate they
thought to themselves that it would be like that now for weeks to
come. They looked at Caesar questioningly, and Caesar shrugged his
shoulders and returned to peep again out of the lumber-room; in
their hearts they felt defeat gradually approaching. As they listened
to the strange quietness they felt themselves islanded in an empty
sea.

It was plain to Caesar that he was in the position of an outpost
whose communications had been cut, and so, at eleven, promising
to return if the luck were with him, he gave his revolver to Leo,
put a battered hat on his head – it was his only disguise – slipped
a half-filled whisky bottle in his pocket, first taking a dram to fume
his breath. Then he stole quietly out of the house and the door was
closed to behind him. When he and Leo met again, months afterwards, in the mountains he merely said that immediately he sat
down that night in his own house, unnerved by the danger of the
journey, he saw at once 'how impossible it all was.' Leo asked him
if he attempted to return, but he shook his head and looked at Leo
out of his impenetrable eye, and Leo nodded, and they spoke of
other things.

But that night in the Bombshop they waited patiently, certain
that Caesar would return. Shandon tower alone struck, and struck
the hope from their hearts. It was their first night sitting awake in
that house and as the hours came and went into eternity they remembered that another besides themselves was sitting, waiting also,

below them. To distract the girl, Leo talked and talked of the beauty of the driving clouds and said that it was many a month and more, it seemed like many a year, since he had the peace of mind to look up at the sky at night and marvel at its beauty, while she said passionately that he seemed not to care whether Caesar returned, and called them cowards again, and wished Ireland were better served than by such soldiers.

'Caesar will return in a few hours,' said Leo, almost glad to see her angry because it kept her mind free of thinking on other things. Oh, yes, Caesar would come back, he was a fine fellow, he was sure to return if it could possibly be done. Last night when there was a moon he wished they had been alone. There were four squares of moonlight under the lobby window and they were good to look at, better to stand on, he in one square, she in another.

'There must be beauty in a thing to make it worth fighting for,' he said trying to make her argue. 'A man won't die for a mere abstraction. Keats said Truth was Beauty. I say Freedom is Beauty. Christ was not really the Son of the God of Love, he was the Son of the God of Freedom. He freed men because He knew that in Freedom all beauty has its source. Shelley was wiser than Keats, more human, more true. If Keats had not been a poet, a sensuous youth, he would have been an abstract rationalist. With his "truth is beauty"! A Manichean, a bloody Manichean he'd have been, like all abstract thinkers – like Augustine. *Gaudium de veritate*, your eye-brow! I say *Gaudium de libertate*. The whole Irish church is on the Augustine tack. They herd us in, they circumscribe us, they herd us up the gangway to Heaven, they take us by the scruff of the neck and shove us into Heaven whether we like it or not. They always did it, so overcome by the fear of Hell-fire that they have no time for the love of the Christlight. Scholastics without the scholastic brains, medievalists without the medievalists' sense of beauty. If man could only be free, truly free, if he could only be as God made him. . . .'

But Norah could have hit him in the face. And she left him because she could not hold her temper in, going upstairs, with that strange attractive waddle she had, to lean recklessly with arms akimbo on the moonlit window-sill, thinking that the dead woman sitting below was happiest of all, wishing to the dead Christ – she swore in her rage and despair – that she was lying on her hands

and face on the green fields she could see across the city in the light
of the rising moon. As she leaned there the quarters and the halves
struck, and she listened to them with a sinking heart, thinking of
the men on the hills, seeing the quartermaster trudging through
the boglands to his dumps, marking up his smudgy note-book by
the light of a farm-house fire – so few incendiary bombs, so few
cartridges for the grenades and cursing them and everyone else that
they could do no better with the lives of men depending on their
efforts, and the success of a great cause in the balance. She went
wearily to bed, feeling so lonely as she lay, that before she slept she
sobbed at the darkness and the emptiness of the house like a little
child.

It was only by pure will-power that she rose from bed that
Sunday morning. On looking at her watch she found it was only
half-past five, and suddenly hearing the first chapel-bell toll faintly
across the streets she decided she must go out to mass. The dawn
was so dark that she had to light a candle and it reminded her of
Christmas time when one lights the lights over the Christmas dinner,
even in the daytime. She stole down past Leo's door, and as she
glanced at it she noticed that it was open. Peeping through the
slit of the hinges she saw the bed was empty and she could hear
no breathing. She opened the door cautiously and found the room
deserted. She tried every other room – she even opened the dead
woman's door and peeped through. There in the dim light of the
curtained room sat the corpse, still and statuesque as they left it.
Fright overcame her and she fled thundering down the stairs and
out into the markets, and not daring to think of her or of Leo
or of anything, she hurried across the intervening streets to the
monks' chapel. It lay at the end of a great sweep of grazing land:
on the grass a soft mist like frost, and through the morning dusk
the little Gothic windows of the chapel glowed yellow like the
windows of a toy house. When she reached it a stream of people
was passing in from the Incurables hospital across the road, the
blind, the crippled, the stumbling, the maimed – people whose
disease was hidden from the eye. Nobody spoke as they hurried
into mass – all cold and silent but for their feet on the damp gravel-
path, around them the city lying quietly asleep. They were like a
meeting of the dumb and sleepless ones of Cork hurrying to a gift
of peace that sleep had denied them, hurrying as if to snatch that

gift before the morning should come, for overhead the sky was still dark and the larger stars were shining and the night wind swept through the higher regions of the air.

The chapel was full when she entered, and as if Death were never to be avoided a coffin on trestles stood under a black and silver shroud in the centre of the flags. She sat on a bench that faced the pall, peeping nervously around, half afraid for having ventured out, beginning to wonder where she should go when mass had finished. Two young people attracted her for a long time, a young man and a young woman who prayed so seriously, for their youthful looks, that she wondered at them in her heart. They seemed as if they had only recently been married, or not married for very long, but they were here at the earliest mass in Cork, on a cold April morning, kneeling shoulder to shoulder and praying to what Leo once called a problematical God with an earnestness that frightened her. It was not beautiful to see in the body such young people so fanatically pious – it made her fear God. Meanwhile the ceremony went on, the priest genuflecting as he passed the tabernacle, the acolyte tapping the low-booming bell at the consecration of the Host. Then there was a general scurry as people rose to approach the altar rails. There, as she looked at them, she saw among the crowd the youthful face of Leo; he knelt, he waited for the priest to come with the Host, he raised his head, and the age-old ceremony was fulfilled. Christ the God, the God of Love or the God of Freedom – which she thought was Leo thinking of? – descended on earth to lie on the boy's tongue. She hid her face as he passed back and the next thing she heard was the organ playing tremulously and the priest saying: 'Your prayers are requested for the repose of the soul of Brother Senan who has died at the age of twenty-one.' The congregation murmured pityingly in reply: 'May God have mercy on his soul and the souls of all the faithful departed, Amen.' She rose and slipped out, and when she stepped on the gravel path the sky was bright and the east was red and all the stars were gone. She hurried back to the Bombshop, looking over her shoulder many times, to see if Leo were in sight, and then to her room where she lay on her bed fully dressed, listening for his return, listening to the city wakening by degrees from its night's slumber, to the bells of the city churches, to the occasional footsteps returning from or going to the early Mass.

At last he came, and when she descended he was already at work, and as she fried the rashers for their breakfast the tang of the potassium rose in the air. She entered the workshop smilingly to call him to breakfast, but immediately she looked at him she noticed a change. The Mass that had filled her heart with peace, a serene and happy peace, had filled his with far other feelings. He would not talk to her; and when she ventured a question or two – as whether the incendiaries would be finished in time – he replied with a short No.

'Why not?' she asked.

How could they? Anyway, why should he care? What a small business they were engaged in! A dirty business. Bombs? Incendiaries? He would do the grenade cartridges. He would do that. Others would have to do the bombs. And when, because she did not understand what he was driving at (and woman-like seized the practical objection first), she protested that he had never done the grenade cartridges which were always Caesar's job, he flared up and his tongue loosened, and he became argumentative.

'Can't do them? I'll tell you how to do them. Empty the old Mausers first of all. Now listen!'

As he spoke he jabbed his greasy fork in the air, so that she had to draw back from his whirling hands. Afterwards when she realized that the well had merely burst through his clay also, she was sorry for him, but now as he argued that she had neither sympathy nor patience left.

'Weigh out the grains,' he cried, 'with the utmost care. I know what I'm talking about. Clean the old cartridges with dilute nitric, and when they're ready cut them down and file them down. Then the cardboard wads. And the cotton wads. Then after that you just coax the little grains carefully, one by one, a single one might make twenty yards of difference in the cast, and ram the wads tight, and the paper wads, and close the lot with your tweezers.'

'But, Leo, what is it all for? What do you want to change for?'

'Now, let me finish. I'll show you if I know.'

'But even if you do know, Leo?'

'Now, the cap. Shellac for that. And a trick to dry them is to put them on a hot plate over a Bunsen. Yes, well, now, the caps. The caps. Oh yes! They must be impressed. Tight. And that's not all. . . .'

She looked at him, and he saw she was looking at him as one looks at somebody one has known for a long time and trusted for a long time and suddenly begun to doubt or suspect. He fell silent, and returned her look in kind. There they sat, all about them the monuments of their hopes, the bags of chemicals, the roughly-fashioned ovens and heating trays, the books of instructions, the jars of acid. Beneath them the silent statue in her chair. Outside the awakening city and the climbing sun; there at least was peace, or the appearance of peace, with the shadows slanting from the houses, the bells falling into silence.

Knock, knock, knock-knock! Like cringing curs their tongues sank down in their throats and they swallowed hard with fear, staring at one another and listening for the next bold knocking on the door below. Knock! And after it a series of running knocks in the rhythm of the cry of 'Here's the herrings, here's the herrings, here's the herrings.' So they had come for her? Or was it a raid? If so this was the end. For some reason Norah wondered why the old woman did not rise up and go down to that insistent knocking and say 'Here I am, and long enough I waited for you.' A long silence was followed by a single knock. They stole on tiptoe to the lumber-room window and peeped out, half-expecting to see scattered figures in uniform thrown in a half circle before the house, rifles at the ready. All they saw was a man passing by on the opposite side of the square look across in the direction of the door. Nobody came forward to look up at the house, but after a while steps moved away from the door beneath them and they returned and sat as before. Then Leo jumped to his feet.

'This puts a finish to it,' he said.

'I don't see that,' persisted Norah, flinging her hair back from her brow.

'Are we to wait to be taken? Who was that at the door?'

'They're gone.'

'Do you think they won't return? Do you think she has no relations or friends who don't know she never went "to the country" like that before. Let's clear out. Come on quick.'

Panic had seized him. He caught up the sweeping brush with some wild notion of leaving the house tidy as they found it, the death below left unexplained.

'You are afraid,' she taunted.

'Sean and Caesar were right to leave you,' he retorted, 'with your bickering tongue.'

'How soft the men leave their posts! Wait till the story spreads on you. Leo, Leo! Aren't you thinking of the men on the hills waiting for the stuff? They must have something to fight with.'

'For God's sake. . . .'

She laid her hand gently on his shoulder. He could not bear that – after all he was only a boy.

'Leo,' she pleaded, 'I know you dearly love Ireland. . . .'

'Oh, vomit on Ireland,' he cried. 'Vomit on her.'

He began to sweep the workroom, the silver powder and the grey powder and the red, the curls of cotton-wool, the brass-filings, and she began to work on the incendiary cartridges at the bench by the window. But he followed her, packing away the things she needed, brushing the dust around her feet, he even knocked the brush-end deliberately against her ankles. He put the matches in his pocket, saying they were his, and when she went to the kitchen for more he snapped them up, saying he believed they were his also. When she changed her place over to the other window, he followed her and flung open the shutters and chanted some song out to the back-yards that had never heard a man's voice in that house as long as the oldest resident could remember. At that she turned on him in a rage, and he in a rage turned to face her. She gripped the shutter to close it; he held it to keep it wide. They could see a woman looking across at them in amazement from the window of a slum-house opposite. Tears came to the girl's eyes, and her flaxen hair fell around her shoulders so that the sun made an aureole of it about her trembling features, and looking at her the boy released his grasp and blushing with shame he left the room.

As she began to work on the little caps, dropping warm shellac one by one into each, she could hear in the distance a group of merry-makers leaving the city for the day in cars, the sound of the horses' hoofs and the sound of their concertina playing gaily, and those happy, indifferent sounds dispirited her. The room now grew warm, and she felt the sweat gather on her brow, and the sky darkened until presently her spirit lamp was throwing leaping shadows on the benches, and her hands as they moved were shadowed on the ceiling. Between the room and the murmurs of the city there seemed to hang a heavy curtain dulling all sound, and what light came through the chinks of the shutter was livid. One by one she filled the caps, arranging them when filled in a neat little row before her. Once the lamp threw a strange shadow high in front of her and she leaped around in terror to see who was in the room, and from that on she kept glancing right and left, listening to know where Sean was, looking over her shoulder at the door, looking down at the floor as if she thought she heard some noise below her. At last she seemed to hear something clearly, and she rose and faced the door; she had heard the heavy steps come slowly up the stairs, step by step, to each landing, to the last landing, to the very handle of the door.

'Leo! Leo!' she screamed. 'She's coming. She's coming!'

'What is it? What is it?' he cried and ran in to her.

'Look at her! Look! Look!'

A frightful rattle of thunder crashed over the room as if mighty billiard-balls were cannoning in the sky. He clasped her to him and she clung to him – she could see the fish-head eyes of the corpse staring at her through the linen cloth. Then the soft rain outside changed into a downpour so that they heard it on the iron roof in the yard. Leo flung open the shutters again so that they could see the sun shining through the falling water, and as she continued to tremble he kissed her right on the lips. She did not try to prevent him. She heard him whispering that this was the best end of all, and she did not try to deny it, for as he whispered she grew calmer and knew that an end there must be.

So they spent that morning cleaning the house, packing everything away in the secret dump, ready to be removed if the chance should offer. Last of all they unlocked her door and dusted and tidied her room, and they set a great fire going on front of her, and they poured fresh milk into her glass and put their own food in her cupboard. The last thing they did before they left was to remove the linen cloth from her face. Then they walked boldly out into the markets and the city streets just a little before curfew when everybody was hastening home. They spent the night in a country house on the hills that lay just outside the city to the south-west, sitting silently together as soon as they could be alone, hand in hand. Norah flung her shoes from off her feet, and to please Leo she let her hair down about her shoulders.

'I am afraid, darling,' she said to him, 'there are streaks of grey in it.'

'I cannot see them,' he said gallantly.

'I shan't search for them,' she said gaily, holding his hand tighter than ever.

If they wished to raise their eyes from under the glow of the old reading-lamp they could see through the open window the fire-flies of the city far below them, a thin row of footlights to the night, but where they could smell the country smells of budding-time they had no wish to look down into that dark hollow with its thousand blinking eyes. No city should they see if they looked, but a house in the centre of the markets, vegetable and fish refuse around it, dogs barking in the yards behind it, and the one occupant they left there seated before the warm fire, staring into its flames.

The Death of Stevey Long

Macroom Castle was built somewhere in the sixteenth century by the MacCarthys, a building of great height raised on a solitary outcrop of rock and with a moat and a demesne reaching down to the river-edge. As Macroom is the last town on the western road through the mountainy divide of Cork and Kerry the castle has always become a barracks in troubled times, the last outpost for the wild, disaffected country beyond. It has a long history: it suffered at least one siege, and passed through several hands. The O'Sullivans lost it in 1606 to the Earl of Cork and in 1675 the crown confiscated it and put troops in it to overawe the rebels to the West, that broken land impenetrable to everyone but tories and raparees. It had its dungeons and its secret passages, and in fact when the Tans took it over as a barracks, in their time, they thought it best to close up several doors that, it seemed to them, led nowhere. But it was not a suitable place to imprison anyone; the river bred too many rats and moles and beavers, and when the mountains sent their rain-water churning down the rocky valleys the floods rose so high that they overflowed into the basement, and from the later-built cells a little higher up a prisoner could see the trees and the hedges growing out of the water almost on a level with his eye.

In one of these cells, his elbows resting easily on the window-sill, stood Stevey Long gazing westward to where the faint blue of the mountains was barely discernible against a white sky. Beside him was a little man whose finger-tips barely clutched the stone edge on which Stevey leaned, and as he strained up to peep at the mountains Stevey looked down at him with amusement.

'They'll shoot you tonight, Fahy,' said Stevey suddenly.

'Ah, shtop that talk now, Long,' said the little man with an imploring upward glance.

'Oh, but I hear them saying it,' said Stevey. ' "Bring out that fat murderer of a teacher," they'll say. Or they'll say, "Bring up that assassin of a teacher, and we'll teach him".'

'Oh, suffering Heart!' wailed the teacher. 'Me nerves is all upsot. Shtop it now, Long. It's not fair.'

As Stevey gazed off contemptuously at the mountains the teacher defended himself.

'Anyway,' he said, 'I never let on to be a fightin' man. And it's all very well for you. You haven't a wife and seven children.'

'Seven children?' asked Stevey. 'Is that all you have, teacher? You ought to be ashamed of yourself.'

'Isn't it enough? You're mocking again, Long. Saying your prayers would befit you betther. That dirty tongue of yours will bring the wrath of God on us.'

'My tongue,' said Stevey vehemently, 'is our only hope.'

'Then why,' said the teacher peevishly, 'don't you get round that bastard of a jailer for us?'

'Oh! Oh! Bastard? Naughty word, teacher. Naughty word!'

'Go to hell,' said the little man in an agony of anger and fear, and he retired to a corner of the cell, by now almost in tears.

Stevey went to the iron door of the cell and listened for any sound in the passage-way. Then in one of his sudden rages he stooped over his companion.

'Haven't I told him enough lies to drown a cathedral? Said I was at Festubert? Said I had an English wife? Said I knew Camden Town and Highgate like the palm of me hand? Told him every dirty story I ever read or heard? And what have you done but sit there and cry?' – and he raised his hand as one might to a child – 'you long-faced lubber!'

Stevey returned to the window.

'And after all that,' he continued, 'all he says is, "Aow! How interesting!" God, how I despise the English!'

'It's no use, Stevey,' said the teacher. 'We can't get round him.'

The teacher would have been secretly pleased if Stevey would believe it. For two weeks he had had to sit in that unsanitary cell listening at all hours of the day and night to Stevey and the Tan who had been on cell-fatigue since they came, exchanging indecent stories. Stevey poured them out without an effort of memory: stories he had heard in the pubs and garages and lavatories of Cork, stories he had read in the *Decameron*, the *Heptameron*, French joke-books, Maupassant, the Bible – at first to the amazement, and gradually to the horror of the little teacher. He had read nothing since he left his Training College ten years before, and he still talked of Dickens on the strength of the one novel he was obliged to read there. What horrified him most of all was to find himself gradually inveigled into listening to these stories, and (with a start) he would find himself grinning with delight before he realized that the sewer-stream had been let loose once again. Stevey was a plumber by trade – he was always saying how proud his father was of 'the profession' – and he would begin to talk of red-lead or three-inch pipes, and proceed slowly via lavatory-traps, the sewers of Paris, chronic constipation, tablets for anaemia, or cures for impotency, to the brothels of the world or the famous courtesans of history – all with great seriousness and a show of modest indignation – and he would illustrate with a vast amount of inaccurate, and even for his subject, defamatory detail at which the teacher's eyes would swell and his fat head would shake with wonder and sudden enlightenment. Or he would spend a whole night hinting at his affairs with the loose girls of the city, returning quickly to the cess-pools or chloride-of-lime if the teacher showed disapproval, or to Margaret of Navarre or Boccaccio as if his life, too, were one long legend and romance. But he could pollute even the sweetest women of literature, and the teacher would find himself trapped again when Stevey would fling Madame Bovary or Boule de Suif or Tess into the same bawdy-box as Mata Hari or some creature out of the *Rat Bleu et Jaune* or some local beshawled laneway light-o'-love just previously removed to the city madhouse. To the Tan he was as the Shahra-zade to her Persian king. The Englishman heard such stories from him as he had never heard in tap-room or barrack-square – even an old story would become fresh and vivid in Stevey's mouth, and weak with laughter he would scarcely have enough strength to turn the key in the door as he staggered off roaring with delight to retail what he had heard to his comrades upstairs. Then Stevey would, as now, return to the window muttering contemptuous curses under his breath and appeal to Fahy for something to add to his stock of bawdry. When Fahy would reply with an apologetic wail that, 'I was always on the althar, Stevey,' or , 'I was a great Confraternity man, Stevey,' the gunman would lose himself in gazing at the pale, far-off horizons, wave after wave of land, paling into the all-but-invisible peaks of the real hinterland fifty miles away. Since the days of the Earls of Cork a hundred rebelly Irishmen must have gazed just as longingly at those changeless mountain-tops, thinking first of the misfortune of their capture, then of wives or friends, then of the fate in store for them, but soon reduced, as they looked out on the unattainable freedom of the hills, to thinking of nothing at all, waiting only for the dusk and the dark and the forgetfulness of sleep. None can have spent his hours, as Stevey did, thinking to coax his English jailer with bawdry, but few, if any, can have been as cruel, and as cunning, and (it must be admitted) as fearless, as Stevey Long.

Suddenly steps clanked down the passage-way and the cell began to taint of gas – the jailer had turned on the tap outside the door, and the little blue flame leaped up on the shelf above the lintel, and the circle cut in the centre of the door was filled by an eye.

'Hey!' whispered the Tan.

'Yes,' said Stevey, at the door in a flash.

'You two blokes are to be moved.'

'Where?' asked Stevey while the little teacher crowded up against him to listen.

'Cork Male Prison,' said the Tan.

Stevey groaned. There was an end to his hopes of escape from the castle, and he knew Cork Jail well enough not to like it. The eye disappeared and was replaced by a pair of lips.

'But you ain't goin'!' they whispered cautiously.

'Why not?' asked Stevey, excited with hope.

'Cos' I 'ave other plans for you,' said the Tan, blinking a wink at them. 'I won't 'ave it. 'Ere's the order,' he said curtaining the circle for a moment with a buff paper. 'There's two deserters here from the Wiltshires, higher up than you, right upstairs, and I'm jolly well going to run them out on this order. They came in an hour ago and they're blind and blotto with Irish moonshine.'

'Oh,' said Stevey, 'but you can't. . . .'

'See if I don't,' said the Tan, and he opened the door and entered the cell. He cornered Stevey by the window and prodded his chest with his finger as it were a revolver or a knife.

'Hark at me!' he said.

'Yes?' said Stevey and the little teacher put in his fat face to listen.

'Go away, you,' growled the Tan, and Fahy retired like a kicked dog. 'Go and stand by the door and hear if anybody's coming.'

He turned to Stevey.

'You know about my wife?'

Stevey did indeed know about the wife. She had been, he always knew it, his main hope. She was London-Irish and a Catholic, and it was she who made Stevey declare his wife was London-Irish and a Catholic too, by Heaven.

'Yes,' said Stevey.

'She keeps on nagging at me in her letters,' complained the Tan. 'She's delicate, and she has nerves, and she's a Catholic.' (This last seemed to be a great grievance with him.) 'I was proud of all that when I married her. It's so romantic, I thinks to myself, to have a delicate wife that's a Catholic into the bargain. But now! She says I'm earning blood-money. I told her about you, and she writes and says she weeps to think of you. But that's all right. She weeps to think of anything, she does. I don't mind that. But now she says such things about leaving the kids and going to live with her married sister that I don't trust her.'

'I wouldn't trust her,' says Stevey.

'How I 'ate married sisters,' said the Tan; and then, 'Why wouldn't you trust her?'

'She's all alone in London,' said Stevey in a gloomy voice.

'She's got her kids. She's got her married sister.'

'Ah,' said Stevey in a hollow voice, 'but where's her husband? From what we know of women,' he continued seriously, 'and especially married women,' he added with an air of sad wisdom, 'you can't trust a woman that's separated from a man that she thinks isn't fond of her.'

'Nor I don't trust her,' said the Tan. 'And I'm goin' home. That's where you come in.'

'Yes,' said Stevey like a shot. 'I could get you out of this country within ten hours, without anybody knowing it – if I were free.'

'You've said so. Dozens of men – deserting, if you like to put it that way.'

'It's my job,' said Stevey. 'City of Cork Steam Packet to Liverpool. Think you were travelling first-class. Easy as that.'

'I'll chance it,' said the Tan. 'Back to London I must get. To tell you the truth I'm sick of this bloody place.'

From inside his uniform he pulled a hacksaw and a length of stout rope. Stevey took them in a grab.

'After dark,' said the Tan. 'I'll bring supper as usual. Now get to work and quietly. If that blade cracks I can't get you another one.'

As he opened the door to go Stevey's mind flamed; as fast as a bullet it flew to the old coach road south-west of the castle where they would probably begin their trek west or east.

'Sst,' he called.

The Tan turned.

'Take a message for me to the village,' said Stevey.

'No,' said the Tan.

'You must,' said Stevey. With a stub of pencil he wrote on a sheet of paper from the Tan's pocket-book, and gave it to him. The Tan read it and winked back at Stevey.

'It's the little bicycle-shop just across the bridge,' said Stevey.

'You're a clever fellow,' said the Tan. 'Of course we must have bikes.'

When he was gone Stevey wound the rope round the belly of the teacher and put him with his back to the door so as to cover the spyhole and listen for approaching feet. Then he began, stealthily at first, to saw at the first of the three bars in the window.

'This scratching,' he said, 'will be heard all over the town of Macroom.'

'If we only had a bit of grease for it,' said the teacher like a fool.

'I once read about Casanova,' said Stevey, and then he stopped talking and hacked away.

'By God,' cried the teacher, 'I once heard a story about that fellow. . . .'

'Eat it,' said Stevey, working like a madman.

The evening was now falling, and as Stevey worked the interior of the cell grew dark. Away to the south-west the sun was sinking over the distant mountains and as she sank they grew first a rich, deep brown, and then purple, 'their very peaks became transparent,' and lastly they paled into an unreal mist. The last level rays threw Stevey's shadows on the iron door and the limed wall, and the little teacher's face was warmed to a ruddy glow. As the air grew cold and rarefied they heard all the sounds of the village life, the children that cried out in their play and the cart that lumbered over the cobbles of the bridge.

About half-past six o'clock the teacher, weary and stiff for so long standing in a fixed position, was almost glad to announce the approach of footsteps. By that time Stevey had cut to within a feather's breadth the top and bottom of two of the bars, filling with clay from the floor the shining track of the saw through the steel. The clanking steps came to the door – it was their friend the Tan. He laid their supper on the bench and bent his head to whisper.

'I'm going with you,' he said to Stevey. 'Mind you promise to get me out of it safe and sound.'

'I swear to Christ,' said Stevey like a shot.

The little teacher was like a kettle on the hob with excitement.

'Naow!' said the Tan. 'No swearing. Parole. Give me your parole, word of honour.'

'Word of honour,' said Stevey, without a thought.

'Oh, God, yes, word of honour,' said the teacher heatedly.

'Shut up, you,' said the Tan angrily, and the little fellow piped down miserably, fearing to be left behind if he angered either of them.

'The Tommies are gone to Cork,' said the Tan with a grin. 'There'll be hell to pay when they get in with the Shinners in Cork Jail. When will we go?'

'When is sundown?' asked Stevey. 'Is there a moon?'

The Tan consulted his diary.

'Six forty-six, sun sets. Full moon, eight-ten.'

'It'll be dark at eight,' said Stevey. 'We'll go then.'

'Is he coming?' said the Tan, pointing to the teacher.

'We'll bring him,' said Stevey.

The Tan looked at the teacher and then he went away without a word. They ate but little that night and Stevey kept going and coming in a corner of the cell.

'God,' he said nervously, 'I'm like a cistern tonight.'

'Will we go wesht?' asked the teacher, stuttering with terror.

'You'll go wesht if you're not careful,' said Stevey. 'Remember that bastard has a gun in his hind-pocket. And we have none.'

They kept watching for the faint moon but the reflected glow of the village and the fluttering light of the gas-jet confused them. All the country to the west was now wrapped in night and the mountains could no longer be seen. With the fall of darkness their ears became sharper and they could hear now the last cries of the children quite plainly and the murmur of the river far below. A mist spread itself over the land before their window, and a faint mooing of cattle occasionally came out of the darkness. As he peered into it Stevey made up his mind that he would not go west – he was sick of that wild, broken country where, as he used to say, 'they ploughed the land with their teeth,' sick of the poor food, the dry bread and jam, the boiled tea and salted bacon, sick of the rough country girls. He was pining for the lights and gaiety of the city and he decided he would do a little 'deserting' of his own. When the Englishman came down, sharp at eight, he had donned a civilian's coat over his green-black policeman's trousers and a wide-brimmed bowler hat that pressed his two ears out like railway signals.

'Ready?' he whispered.

Stevey nodded. From outside he extinguished the jet and plunged the cell in darkness. Stevey unwound the rope from the belly of the teacher, and the Tan pressed with all his might on the cut bars. They would not give. Stevey dropped the rope and threw his weight on them and still they held. The Tan swore, the teacher entangled himself in the rope, and Stevey searched in the dark for the saw. At last he found it and with a few sharp rasps the blade broke through the steel. It was easy then to bend the bars up on a level with the higher coping, and when the rope had been tied to the uncut bar and flung out into the dark they were ready.

'I'll go first,' said Stevey, 'and signal with one pull on the rope if everything is clear below. Send him after' – pointing to the teacher. 'And come last yourself.'

'Oh,' moaned the teacher, as he looked at the aperture, 'I'm too fat to get through that.' But they paid no heed to him.

Stevey wriggled out first, his feet scraping the wall as he was pushed behind by the other two.

'I'll never get through them bars,' wailed the teacher in a deep whisper to nobody in particular.

Stevey vanished downward, swaying as he went, hand over hand. He landed in a great bed of stinging nettles and resisting an impulse to turn and run for it he listened for a second. The little river gurgled noisily below him; he could distinctly hear the quiet munching of cattle just beyond the mound where he stood. He pulled the rope once and stood looking up. A faint white radiance was beginning to appear where the moon was rising on his left. Stevey saw the teacher's fat legs waving in the air and his fat bottom squirming skyward. But there he remained, not advancing an inch, and after a long pause he was pulled in again, and Stevey saw the bare shins of the Tan, then his black trousers dragged up to the knees, then his body following after. In a second he too was among the nettles.

'Where's Fahy?' asked Stevey in a whisper.

'Come on,' said the Tan fiercely.

The fat pale face of the teacher appeared at the window.

'I can't get out,' he wailed in a loud whisper.

'Use the saw,' said Stevey. 'We can't wait.' And he clambered down the mound, grinding his teeth as a pile of loose stones rumbled after him down the slope.

'Ssh!' said the Tan. 'The sentries will hear us.'

'Lie still,' said Stevey, and they dropped on the dew-wet grass. They heard a sentry's voice call to his mate, and the mate's reply. They heard the grounding of arms, and then the noisy river, and the wind in the willows above them shivering and whispering incessantly by the river's edge. After a while they rose and in a stooping posture they half-walked, half-ran along by the edge of the river through the grass, feeling the ground (when they left the river) rise steeper and steeper, and when they fell panting again on the ground, there below them was the black pile of the castle and the hundred eyes of the town.

'That bloody teacher nearly ruined us,' said the Tan.

'He'll never get out,' said Stevey.

But he soon forgot him, and he did not in fact live to know what happened him in the end. They were now standing on the soft dust of the old coach road, below them the next valley, and, as if it were standing on the tip of the distant ridge beyond, the great ruby moon. To Stevey it was all familiar and congenial, but to the Englishman it was cold and desolate.

'We're out of it,' said Stevey gaily, and he slapped the Englishman on the back.

'I'm in it,' said the Tan gloomily. 'Well, where are the bikes?'

At that Stevey squared his shoulders and clenched his fists. He looked up and down the narrow, shaded road, and then at the Tan.

He looked down at the far-off lights of the town and at the Tan again. Then he jerked his head onward.

'This way,' he said. 'They should be here.'

He went on ahead, peering right and left, whispering in a low voice as he went 'Jimmy? Jimmy?' When he passed a blasted oak a bicycle fell clattering on the road at his feet. He peered up and there was a gaitered leg and the tail of the inevitable trench-coat. Everything was happening just as he expected it.

'Here's one,' he shouted. 'Try is the other there,' and he pointed backwards to the opposite side of the lane. As the Tan groped in the far ditch Stevey whispered madly to the hidden figure.

'Have ye the skits?'

'Yes.'

'Get 'em ready.'

'How many are there?' said the voice.

'One.'

Then Stevey shouted back to the Tan.

'Have you got it?'

'No.'

'Here,' called Stevey. 'Hold this one.'

The unsuspecting man came forward to hold the bicycle, and as he took it Stevey passed behind his back. The bicycle crashed as Stevey leaped like a tiger at his neck, roaring at the same time to 'Jimmy' to give a hand. Two trench-coated figures leaped from the hedges at the cry and fell on the struggling shouting soldier, and in two minutes he was bound with Stevey's trousers belt and his kicking legs held and tied with a bit of cord. Finally his yelling mouth was stoppered by Stevey's handkerchief and then, except for their panting and an occasional squirm from the helpless man at their feet everything was deadly quiet again.

'Gimme his skit,' said Stevey.

The captive looked up with the light of terror glaring in his eyes. Stevey stood over him for a second with his finger wavering on the trigger.

'Here,' he said then to one of the two. 'You do it. I gave him my word I wouldn't.'

He made for the bike, dusting himself as he went, and threw his leg over the saddle. A horrible double sound of a revolver being discharged tore through the night.

'Gimme that,' said Stevey.

The revolver was handed to him, and he thrust it in his pocket.

'Are you sure he's finished?' he asked.

'Sure,' said the other.

'Good-bye boys,' said Stevey, and he pedalled swiftly along the dark lane.

Presently he freewheeled on to the lower road and came to a dimly-lighted pub. An old cart and a sleepy horse were tethered outside the door. This was the pub known as The Half-way House, and Stevey decided that he needed a free whisky. First peering through the glass door he entered. There was nobody inside but the bar-girl and an old farmer leaning in the corner of the counter and the wall; the girl said nothing, and the old farmer merely nodded. Those were tough times, and they had heard the double shot.

'Any Tans about?' said Stevey when he had ordered his drink.

The girl only shook her head silently and poured the drink, watching him as he swallowed it. The farmer lowered his eyes to sip his porter whenever Stevey looked at him, raising them slowly whenever he felt he was not being watched, nodding and smiling foolishly whenever Stevey's eyes caught him. A tiny clock among the whisky bottles ticked so loudly in the silence that Stevey looked up at it startled. It was nearly nine o'clock.

'By God, it's late,' he said.

The girl nodded and said nothing, and when Stevey looked at the farmer he was turning his glass round and round in its own wet circle, his eyes shooting side-glances towards Stevey all the while.

'Christ,' swore Stevey, 'you are a talkative pair!' And putting down his empty glass he strode out between the swinging doors and walked to his bicycle. Then it occurred to him to return on tip-toe and listen at the glass-doors. The old farmer was speaking:

'Aye,' he was saying, 'a bit o' money is a great thing.'

'Yes,' said the girl listlessly.

'Sons how are ye!' said the farmer.

'Aye,' responded the girl. There was a pause, and then:

'Money is betther than sons any day,' said the farmer.

'Yes sure,' said the girl with a sigh.

With a superior grin Stevey mounted and rode away.

Had Stevey kept his word with the Englishman he might be alive today. He would certainly have avoided Cork that night. But now, knowing nothing of what awaited him and with nobody to warn him, he covered, in less than four hours, the forty odd miles that separate Macroom from Cork. He had cycled along the winding roads among the bogs where the mountains come down to the plains, and when the mountains vanished from sight he pedalled over a bare, high plateau where he measured the distance not by prominent hills or valleys but by a tree here and a tree there, or a cross-road, a familiar house, or a school. At last he came to the valley of the city river and for miles he cycled above it, straight as a crow's flight to the edge of the city. It was about one o'clock when he stood looking down over all its sleeping roofs as over a vale of quietness, a slight drizzle of rain beginning to fall, a gentle wind blowing it in his eyes as he peered across to the uttermost farthest light that marked the remote side of the city to the north where his father lived. He might have made a long detour to reach Fair Hill, but why should he? Had he known the city was under curfew he would never have dared to do anything else, but his two weeks in Macroom Castle were two weeks cut off from the world, and now, flinging his bike into the ditch, he dropped downhill into the danger of the streets.

After his three long months in the mountains it was sweet to feel the ring of the pavements instead of the pad-pad of the mud roads, to see the walls and the gas-lamps all about him, so sheltering after the open darkness of the country nights. But as he went on the streets were so strangely empty, even for one o'clock in the morning – there was not even a wandering dog abroad – that Stevey became worried and ill at ease. As he approached the open business section of the city especially he began to realize what a grave risk he was taking in coming back into the city at all where he was well known for a gunman; but to come late at night, with no crowds to mingle with, and the police on the alert for late wanderers was doubly dangerous. Still, as the mist thickened, became heavier, finally changed into a wind-blown downpour, it did not occur to him that any reason other than bad weather was required to explain the strange emptiness of the streets, until suddenly, not more than a few blocks away, a dozen rifle-shots broke through the hiss of the falling rain, loud above the river purling in its narrow bed. Stevey halted in his stride. Then as there was no repetition of the sound he went on, down to the quays that shone under the arclights webbed with moisture.

The rain hissed into the river, cold and spearlike, and his calves were now wet, and his face and shoulders and he could feel his coat was sodden through. Then, in and out of the glow of the lamps on the pathway in front of him he saw a girl racing in his direction, calling as she ran to another girl to hurry, the other calling to her to wait. It was a relief to Stevey to meet somebody, but when the first girl, who ran against the rain with lowered head, rushed into his arms and then screamed and cowered away from him into the wall – he stood angry and astonished.

'Oh! Sir, sir!' she wailed. 'I'm goin' home.'

'Hello, hello!' said Stevey. 'What's up with you?'

'I'm goin' home, sir,' she said again, trying to cower past him. 'I am, honest.'

'Well, go home!' cried Stevey exasperated, and passed on. The other girl, he found, had turned and fled from him as from the devil.

Stevey now observed that the houses towering about him were almost pitchy black. All the erect oblongs of light had long since moved up nearer the roofs, wavered there for a while, and then vanished suddenly; the sitting-rooms had become bedrooms and then been blotted out, and now only red eyes of light showed bedroom walls where one could no longer see bedroom windows. Once a moving candle-flare showed the turn of a stairs, a landing, a high window. Bare boards, thought Stevey, under bare feet unheeding the silver of hammered nails in the white wood, long white neck-frilled night-dresses bending over the balustrade to call to a tiled hallway for surety of locked doors. A blind sank down, squares walking up its yellow ground. A pair of gold parallelograms disappeared, and then began to reappear and vanish, faint or defined, but never steady for a moment, and to Stevey's thought a woman curved over the flames, her fingers slipping her shoes from her feet, silken stockings falling after. All the while the rain lashed the shining pavement – a real mixture of March wind and April shower – and the spouts poured their overflow across the cement flags. Everyone was asleep in bed but he. He possessed the whole city, as if it had been made for him alone.

Again the rifle-shots rang out and this time they were followed
by a rattle of machine-gun fire and a few isolated explosions. Again
Stevey halted, drawing into a door and peering along the quays.
He felt that after his fortnight in prison and his three months in the
hills he was become a stranger to this city-world in which he had
once moved so easily and safely, and he wished he had made a
call in some friendly house before entering the city – it almost
seemed to him as if something strange and unusual were occurring
around him. He left the quays at this thought, and began to dodge
among the side-lanes and the back-streets, but to cross the river
he finally had to come into the open. As he crossed the railway bridge
he saw on the opposite quay, spread across the street, a squad of
soldiers whose accoutrements and arms glinted in the rain and the
arclights, and seeing their weapons at the ready he drew back behind
a girder and waited. They were approaching gradually and he knew
that he would certainly be discovered if he remained there. He
moved in quick bird-like leaps across the bridge, from the shelter
of one girder to the shelter of another, peeping all the time at his
enemy. Then he had to leave the bridge and cross the street. His
heart beat faster; he breathed quickly. He heard a cry of 'Halt' and
he took to his heels. Over his head, by his very ears it seemed to
him, whistled the bullets. At once he took to the side-lanes, up and
down and in and out until he had lost his pursuers and himself
thoroughly, and exhausted he fell back into a doorway to think.
It did not take him long to realize this time that it was Curfew,
long threatened even while he was in the mountains, suddenly
clapped on the city while he was in jail, and he had walked like a
fool into the net. His hand stole to the revolver in his pocket. If
he had been caught with that it would have meant anything. Now
completely unnerved he left the door, halting at the slightest noise,
looking around every lane-corner and down every passage-way
before he dared pass them by. Gradually he began to recognize
where he was – in the network of lanes between the river and the
fish-markets, an isolated quarter to leave which would bring him
into the open streets once more. A lecherous pair of cats made him
leap for an arched alley-way. He laughed at himself the next minute
but he realized that he could never hope to reach Fair Hill in this
way, across the other bridge and along another set of naked quays.
Over his head Shandon boomed out two o'clock – there would be

at least three hours more of Curfew. He wiped the sweat of fear from his forehead and peeped cautiously out of his alley-way, thanking his good-fortune that he did so, for the next instant the heavens seemed to open with light and every cranny and crevice of the lane was flooded by a powerful searchlight. At the same moment he heard the soft whirring of a car and low voices. He was taut and trembling like a string that has been made vibrate by a blow. He thought he heard steps approaching and he slunk backwards down the alley, halting in doors and watching the flooded light of the lane, beyond the tunnel of the arch. He came to the alley-end and his feet crunched on the head of a dead fish, the guts oozing under his heels. He glanced about the great pitch-dark square – he was in the markets. In the limelight of the arch far down the alley he saw two khaki figures who turned towards him and entered the arch and faced the wall. It was enough for Stevey – he turned and crouched his way along the markets, slipping on the rotting vege-tables and the slime of fishgut, resting in door after door with some-thing of the feeling that he had walked into the wrong region, that here were troops of men, that in any other part of the city it would have been far different if not entirely safe. But he felt his last turn taken when a whirring lorry roared suddenly around the corner and its floodlight poured into the street, lighting the very pavement at his feet, where he stood with his back to a door; and as if to give him no possible chance he saw, and cursed as he saw, that the jambs and lintel and panels were pure white. With the instinct of the trapped man he crushed back against it and the nearer the car came the more he crushed. Slowly, as he pressed against it, the door swung open behind him. He passed in and closed it behind him and listened, not even breathing, while the car passed slowly by. Then he began to breathe tremblingly, and panting, and with his hand to his heart, he laughed quietly to himself. Trust Stevey, said he to himself, to get out of any corner.

The hallway was blackness unbroken, and with his two hands out, one grasping his revolver, a crucified gunman, he groped his way in. His feet struck the first knee of the stairs, and he began to climb. A window-sill and an empty pot – he passed it by. A lead-lined sink and a dripping tap – he moved on upwards. A door. Was this a man or a family, or a lone woman? Damn dangerous business this, thought Stevey to himself; but not half so dangerous as the streets. What should he do? Sleep in the hall? Clear out? Neither. Was it Stevey Long not to get himself a good doss for the night? As his father would say, he must think of 'the profession.' He moved up higher and came to a landing window. Through it he could see Shandon dark against the glowing sky of the city. Across in another house he could see a back-window all lit up, and framed in it two men, both in pants and shirts. He could hear their quarrel, see the bigger of the two crash his fist into the face of the other, see a ragged-haired lane-woman drag them apart. Then the light vanished as she moved away upstairs with the candle, and the small man wiping the blood from his cheeks stumbled downstairs out of sight. Looking up diagonally Stevey saw a landing; looking down, the dark well of the stairs; through the window a tin roof on which the chutes above dripped and dripped. He went up to the landing and here he noticed a streak of yellow light at the base of the door. He tapped softly, hardly knowing what he was doing. He knocked again and still there was no reply. He peeped through the keyhole and there before a warm fire he saw an old woman sitting bolt upright in her chair.

Even to Stevey the old woman was a touching sight, her corrugated hands clasping her crucifix, her mouth all wrinkled and folded, her eyes lost in the firelight. He was moved by the peace of this room high above the markets and the river, warm after the rain. How cosy she looked! – no, not cosy, but how calm, and yes, how holy! How holy! Stevey smiled and shook his head at her. He looked at her more closely. Then he entered, closing the door softly behind him. He laid his hand on her shoulder – on her face – on her left breast. She was dead.

He looked around him slowly, and slowly he removed his wet coat, hanging it on a chair before the glowing fire. Then he sat quietly warming his hands to the flames, stretching his long legs, and drying his face. He chuckled quietly to himself. Here was joy!

He awoke before dawn and thinking he felt a little cold he threw fresh coals on the fire. Feeling thirsty he drank half the milk in the glass beside him. Then he fell asleep again until a church bell tolling faintly in the distance gradually percolated through to his senses. For a full two minutes he stared sleepily and in wonder at the corpse seated beside him, and then, as the cries of the market-girls came to his ears his mind reverted to the city. He realized at once that he was back among his own people, as safe as a house.

He rose stretching his stiff shoulders and began to move through the house. As for the old lady, he did not trouble himself about her – heart disease no doubt or a sudden stroke, and he remembered the warm fire and the fresh glass of milk. One room was full of strange lumber, and as he peeped at the markets through the drawn blinds his hand fell idly on an old album. When he opened it and it began to ping-pong out its little tune he shut it with a fright and hoped nobody heard. The back-room was an ordinary sitting-room. He saw a chess-board and wondered cunningly who played chess in that seemingly empty house. Surely there must be a man somewhere he thought, and he felt certain of it when his eye fell on a great brass-horned gramophone, every inch of its dark maw pasted over with foreign postage stamps. He felt it best to get out of the house as soon as possible and hearing Shandon bells strike eight he decided that now was the best time – it was Monday morning and he could mingle with the crowds going to work; they would be too preoccupied to notice his wet, wrinkled clothes, his dirty boots, his unshaven face. First, however, he returned to the dead room to look for food. He found bread, and a pot of jam, and milk that was only just a little sour. He was raising the milk to his lips when his eye caught a black-japanned tin box by the window and the glint of silver in it. He strode across and looked down at the wad of notes and the loose pile of florins and shillings and half-crowns and little worn sixpenny pieces. The lock, he noticed, had been broken at some time previously. Without a thought he put his hand on the thick roll of notes and filled a fistful of silver into his pocket. Then, abandoning the food he had prepared for himself he turned and tramped down the stairs, opened the hall door and walked right into the arms of a raiding patrol as it alighted from a lorry. He looked right and left and made one step as if to attempt an escape, but in a second a dozen rifles were pointed at his heart. In another second he was seated high on the car with a crowd of market-people gathered wonderingly about him.

In a dream he found himself smoking one of a bundle of cigarettes handed him on all sides from the sympathetic fish-women. All they knew was that he was a 'Shinner' and they cheered him repeatedly for it. As he sat there in a daze one woman actually put a little tricolour rebel flag into his hand, and he waved it feebly from time to time, and the fish-wives and the onion-girls cheered him wildly as he was driven away. As they turned the corner of the markets one of the guards smiled grimly and said 'Good-bye-ee,' and Stevey smiled weakly in return and stuffed the flag into his pocket.

It was the last smile Stevey Long smiled on this earth. The search of the house discovered, hidden under the stairs, a conglomeration of explosives, bombs and grenades and incendiaries, finished and unfinished. It took the military an hour to remove them all, and to crown the amazement of the market-folk, they then brought up a coffin, carrying it in lightly, carrying it on four bending shoulders. At his court martial, which they held an hour later at drumhead – martial law was in force – question after question was fired at Stevey and he dodged and twisted like a hare, but he was a hare in a net. By degrees they wearied him, and finally cowed him.

'Where did he get that revolver?'

'I found it,' said Stevey.

'Where?'

'In the fields.'

'There were two bullets discharged?'

'Were there?' said Stevey innocently.

'When did you find it?'

'Last night.'

'Where did you come from last night?'

At that Stevey paused, feeling that these questions were leading back to Macroom Castle, realizing that he could not substantiate any statement he might make as to his whereabouts the evening before. The President repeated the question testily.

'Where did you come from?'

'East Cork.'

'Where in East Cork?'

'Midleton.'

'What were you doing in that house?'

To this Stevey replied truthfully, and though it was the only true thing he said that day, they did not believe him.

'Do you mean to say,' asked the president, 'that the people of Midleton didn't know a curfew order was in force in Cork?'

A few such questions drove Stevey to the wall, but it was when they told him that the woman was shot by a point four-five bullet, of the same calibre as the gun found on him, and charged him with the murder of the old lady that he paled and grew thoroughly confused and realized the danger in which he stood. His advocate did his best for him but it was no use, and when in the end Stevey was asked if he had anything to say he grew excited and began to talk foolishly, leaning forward and waving his hands, swearing that he would tell the whole truth this time, and contradicting almost everything he had previously said. His advocate tried again to save him but the president intervened; he had caught his man and now he would have a little sport with him.

'Let the prisoner speak,' he said, and leaned back in his chair and glanced at his colleagues. They, in turn, glanced back at him and drew their fingers over their mouths and looked down at the table – the old man, they thought, was in a good mood today.

The truth was, said Stevey, that he was coming from East Cork and he was ambushed by Sinn Feiners. He fired two shots at them. . . .

'At your own people?' asked the colonel.

'Well they fired at me,' cried Stevey with an oath.

'Go on,' said the colonel politely.

'The bastards fired at me,' said Stevey in a towering rage at his imagined enemies.

'One moment,' said the president. 'Where did you really get this revolver? Do you admit possessing it?'

'Ain't I telling you?' said Stevey. 'It was a Tan that gave it to me.'

'Indeed?' said the colonel politely. 'Go on.'

'I fired at them, once, twice. And then, I'm sorry to say, I ran.'

'To Cork?' asked the colonel sarcastically.

'I got a bike,' said Stevey sullenly.

'Where?' asked the president, leaning forward. 'Can we substantiate that?'

'Well, to tell the truth,' said Stevey, 'I – I stole it.'

'Like this money we found on you? You admit you stole that, too?'

'Yes, I stole it, I took it,' admitted Stevey.

'Can we even confirm that you stole the bike?' asked the president. 'Where did you steal it? Where is it now?'

Stevey told six more lies in his efforts to avoid admitting the bicycle was in a ditch on the wrong side of the city. The old colonel lost his patience here.

'Where did you steal the bike?' he roared.

'It was in the dark I stole it,' muttered Stevey and the court rocked with laughter.

'It's true,' wailed Stevey.

'Remove the prisoner,' said the old colonel in disgust.

In order to disgrace him as well as punish him he was sentenced for murder and robbery under arms.

The Patriot

It was doubtless because of the inevitable desire of man to recapture
the past that they went to Youghal for their honeymoon. Their
friends expected them to go at least to Dublin, if not to London or
Paris, but they both knew in their hearts that they had spent the
gayest days of their lives in this little town, and so as if to crown
all those early happinesses to Youghal they went, like true volup-
tuaries deliberately creating fresh memories that would torment
them when they were old.

Across there on the little stone promenade, when they were as
yet little more than girl and boy, they had met for the first time.
She was on holiday with her sister; he had come with his aunt for
the day. In the train they had met Edward Bradley, his former
teacher, and Mister Bradley had walked about with him (in spite
of his aunt) for a few hours, and given them tea. He had been
flattered, he remembered, because old Bradley stayed with them
so long, and afterwards he pretended to Norah that Mister Bradley
was really a great friend of his. Off there at the end of the promenade they had sate, the three of them, because his aunt was too
old to walk far without a rest and as they sate there Norah and her
sister came and halted opposite them to lean on the wall. A liner
was passing slowly, almost imperceptibly, along the horizon and
everybody was looking at it, and his aunt was asking him to tell
them – he was young, God bless him, and had the better sight –
was it two funnels or three it had. He had stood up, pretending to
look at the liner, but he was really trying to look at Norah's black
hair and her jet-black eyes without being seen, growing irritated
because he and she could not be there alone, and growing more
irritated still because he saw that she too was trying to look at him
without being observed, turning her back frequently on the sea
to look, as it were, up over their heads at the crowds on the cliffs,
curving herself backwards over the wall and standing on her toes

as if to show herself off to him. In the end her sister drew her
away as the ship became too faint to be seen and Bernard became
so disconsolate and silent that his aunt plucked at him and said,

'What on earth's wrong with you, Bernie? Are you tired, or what
is it?'

But Mister Bradley cocked his eye at him and winked without his
aunt seeing. Old Bradley was a cute boyo, he had thought, and
flushed because he felt he had been observed. After tea he and his
aunt were alone again, and she who had been so sweet to their
companion, was now abusing him roundly for a firebrand who
was leading all the young men into wild politics. 'Some day,'
Bernie defended, 'that man will be Lord Mayor of Cork and then
you'll sing a different song,' but she would have none of it and as
he just then caught sight again of his dark girl in the distance and
wished to walk on and catch up with her he did not argue further.
Alas! his aunt got tired once more, saying that tea was like a load
on her stomach, and they had to sit on another bench. His dark
vision passed out of his sight and he felt she had merely floated
before him and he would never meet her again.

When he did meet her again it was several years after and she
was again on holiday in Youghal, and it was only by degrees they
realized they had seen each other before. On this occasion he was
an Irregular guerilla – doubly a rebel – seated high up on a lorry,
with his rifle across his back and his coat-collar turned up, and his
cap thrown back and upwards from his forehead to let his curls
free to the wind. Seven other lorries were roaring along behind
him through the streets and as they tore their way under the old
clock archway, there on the pavement, smiling up at them, and
waving her green handkerchief to them, was the loveliest dark-haired
girl he had ever seen. Their lorry halted just beyond the arch to
wait for the troops marching in from the railway, and he alighted
and by virtue of being a soldier was able to approach her on the
pretence of wanting matches or cigarettes. By the time the troops
came into the town they were in a little tea-shop, and he was flirting away with all the bravado in the world. As the men passed outside, four by four, they sang their rebelly songs, waking as he said
to her, the ghosts of old Raleigh who had once lived there, and of
the stiff Earl of Cork from his tomb in the Christ's Church, and the
ghost of every Elizabethan sailorman who had cast a rope ashore

by the crumbled quays they could see through the rear door of
the shop, edging with their fallen stones the glittering blue of the
bay.

There were descendants of those seadogs in that town still, she
told him, for having come there year after year on her holidays
since she was a little child she knew Youghal as if she had been
born there. She chanted the names to him, the Merricks, the
Gurneys, the Boyles, the Brisketts, and at each name he swaggered
his cup on high to curse them, so that it was a profane litany that
finished their tea.

'The Yardleys too,' she said, laughing at him.

'God damn them for ever!' he swashbuckled.

'Of course the Townshends are Cromwellians,' she smiled.

'God damn them for ever!' he cried again.

Her eyes wandered to the bay. A brown sailed yawl was floating
past on the blue water as gracefully as a yacht.

'Isn't she lovely?' she cried, flushing with the delight of it.

'Not as lovely as you,' he bantered.

'Oh! Come and watch her,' she invited, and away they went.

When he found his way to the abandoned military barracks they
had taken over, it was late night – discipline was a joke in those
days – but he did not sleep for many hours, standing at the window
of the great deserted mess-room watching where the moon poured
down across the face of the shimmering ocean, into the little harbour.
It lit up as if it were day the shouldering furze-bright hills, and the
white edge of motionless surf at the base of the distant cliffs, and
every sleeping roof in the town clustered beneath him.

It was curious that it was there in Youghal, too, that same summer,
that Norah had first met Edward Bradley. There had been a public
meeting in the market-place while the guerillas held the town and
one of the chief speakers was Bradley. That day he had spoken
with a terrible passion against England, and against the Irish traitors
who had been cowed by her, and his passionate words caught and
flared the temper of the people so that they cheered and cheered
until their voices echoed across the smooth surface of the water
into the woods beyond. Bernie had cheered like the rest where he
stood beside Norah, proud to be that man's friend. After the meeting
the three met, and the teacher, flushed with his success, walked
between them along the tumbledown quays. He found that he knew

Norah's people quite well, though he had not seen them for many years.

'But I'll call on them often now,' he said, looking at Norah and he began to take her arm, and then he remembered Bernie and he took his arm – like a grandfather Bernie had said, jokingly, to him, and was angry with himself for saying it for a deeper blush crept over the face of the older man and halting he had said,

'Maybe I am too old to be walking with the like of ye,' and cocking his eye at the girl again he had laughed, half-bitterly as Bernie thought, and with a 'God bless ye, my children,' turned and walked away. Wasn't he a very nice man, Norah had said, and stood looking after the teacher so long that Bernie almost thought he was going to be jealous; but he had not thought long of it. It was a warm autumn day, and so clear that they could see across the channel where the hay garnered in for the winter had left white patches on the clovered meadows. Tempted by the fields beyond they had rowed slowly across the bay to spend the afternoon on the other side. The geese had cropped the grass of the foreshore until it was as close and clean as a golf-course, except where a few odd straws lost to the granary lay strewn about and with them, cast up by the tide, bits of reedy sea-wrack, and here and there the dark-grey droppings of the fowl. The air was so rarefied that as they crossed the low stone walls on their way into the oak woods the stones fell with a gurgling sound like water, and far away the ocean boomed deeply into the crannied rocks. They had gone deep into the woods to lie there while the misty darkness fell, bringing in the night wind a little rain, to lie there in their deep love as still as corpses, as still as fallen leaves. They returned late at night to the town whose yellow windows, bright across the channel, spoke to them of sanded floors in quayside pubs and the first fires before the winter warming the cold chimneys of summer.

But before that week was out the town was abandoned and Norah had to stand under the shelter of the old town-walls watching the great barracks smoking against the fading sky and the distant mountains, themselves so faint that in their greyness they blended and were lost in the darkness and the smoke.

It was the way of that guerilla life that for months on end a man never even thought of home or friends, and for months Bernard wandered among those grey mountains to the north of Youghal,

as aimlessly, and he used to feel more uselessly, than a lost sheep.
Once only did he use his rifle in those seven months of guerilla life
and that was when sniping from fifteen hundred yards a village
supposed to contain enemy troops. He slept in a different bed each
night and never ate twice in succession from the same table so that
most of his time was spent in going from place to place in search
of food and rest. He did so less from a sense of danger than a sense
of pity towards the farmers who had to feed and shelter him and
his fellows, never thinking that as all his fellows did as he was doing,
it saved nothing to the flour bin lying lightly on the loft, or the
tea-caddy on the high mantel-shelf, emptied almost daily. The days
scarcely existed for him and the weeks flew over his head as unnoticed as birds homing at night, until as a human being he almost
ceased to be, enveloped by the countryside as if he were a twig, a
stone, an ear of corn. And then, without the slightest warning, as
suddenly as the breaking of a thunder-shower, he remembered
how lovely Youghal had been, and how lovely Norah, and he hated
to look up at the cold and naked mountains. It was late February
with the rain falling as by the clock, and for a month they had been
hunted through it, day and night. Thinking of that and thinking of
the summer his memory began to work on him like a goad. All
about him on the night he thought of her, sitting alone by the
embers of a turf-fire after the family had gone to bed, the mountains
lay black and silent, wet as if they had been dipped in the sea,
and overhead a white path of stars more clear in the washed air
than if there were a frost abroad. Out there, too, he felt was danger;
he was listening so intently that he almost leaped when a little
cricket chirruped in the dark warmth of the hearth, and yet he
feared even to stir so great a noise did every movement make –
almost as great, it seemed, as the resounding drop-drop of the
leaking thatch beyond the door.

In his pocket-book he had her one letter, reminding him of that
little wood where they had loved :

'I went specially to Youghal to see our wood again. The autumn
is over it and over all the land. The days are shortening, farmers
are threshing, thatching turf-ricks, digging potatoes, culling sheep
from their flocks to barter in fair and market, fields are decaying
with grief for the loss of their fruits, and grief is a brown and
withered hag, nuts are ripening, black-berries are rotting, holly

berries are reddening, leaves are dropping yellow. Mists cover the
mountains like a hooded cloak, grey rocks ooze tears of desolation,
green ferns on the hill-side are withering, and purple heather is
turning grey. Birds are silent, winds rustling in denuded boughs. In
Youghal tourists are departed – no more the hum of the motor, nor
the flash of fashionable attire. In my little hotel Mrs M—— is
resting and knitting, K—— turning over stacks of McCall's Journals
and Home Gossips, the serving-girl is considering her return to her
mother's home, P—— L—— wearing her shoes "going aisht and
wesht," B—— twinkling with gestating jokes, and R—— counting
the takings of the season. Norah is at the moment writing to Bernard;
at other moments? – thinking, reading, peering into a dimly-lit
future. . . .'

He smiled at that letter, so full of life as it was. Then he thought
of the night outside and went to the door. He could hear the streams
swirling down the dark *leaca* and as he listened their roar mingled
terror with the desolation of the black silence, and he wished
passionately to be away from so lonely and cruel a place. Three
miles across the hills, in a little fishing hotel by a mountain lake,
was the head-quarters of the Division. There, he hoped, he might
get money – a few shillings would do – to help him on the road
home, and maybe they would give him a clean shirt and collar,
and a better hat and trousers than these guerilla's rags that, up to
now, he had been flaunting as with a deliberate joy in their torn
dirt. Above all he might meet Edward Bradley there, for he too
had been hiding for several months in the mountains not daring
to stay in the city for fear of arrest. He felt he wanted to talk to
somebody like Bradley, someone who would persuade him that this
struggle of theirs was not hopeless, that all their humiliation of
poverty and hunger was not, as he had long since begun to feel, a
useless and wasted offering. Quietly he unbolted the door and stole
through the yard into the sodden starlit fields.

It was midnight when he saw the lake below him and to his
surprise every window in the little hotel was lit. He approached
warily, alert for a sentry's challenge, fearful of an ambushed enemy
patrol – for he might, he knew, be shot as easily by either. But he
continued to walk unaccosted past the sleeping farmhouses and
the great strewn rocks until he came to the lake-side edge and the
lighted windows, and all the way he did not meet a living soul.

Inside the steamed window the room was filled with armed men, smoking, drinking, arguing in groups. He recognized the faces of three or four officers. There was the adjutant with his eyes swollen with too much drink and too little sleep – it was common knowledge that he lived like that. By the fire was Boyle, a great black-faced commandant from Kerry; under the lamp in the largest group he recognized Tom Carroll from East Cork – clearly a meeting of the officers of the Division.

He entered unchallenged where a group of men were lounging in the dim candle-lit hall. Three officers strode out of the room – it was the dining-room – with empty glasses in each hand, returning gingerly when the glasses had been filled to the brim with black stout or porter. He saw the quartermaster coming out of the kitchen with a pair of black pint-glasses dripping their froth about his wrists, and he went over to tell him how dangerous it was to leave the back road unguarded. But the quartermaster only growled,

'Well, what are you doing here then? Go up yourself and sentrify it,' and passed on.

The column captain came out from the bar with a tray of divers-coloured glasses and to him also Bernie told how the North road was unprotected. But the captain flew into a rage and glared at him over the tray.

'I've told off six men, there, to go,' he said, jerking his head at the loungers in the hall.

One of them spoke back at him, a fellow with only two walrus teeth above and below in his gums.

'We won't go. Why should we go? Ye're all dhrinking. Why don't we get a dhrink?'

'Go into the kitchen and get it,' said the Captain.

'Where'll we get the money.'

'Ask the quartermaster.'

'Damn the quartermaster.'

'I want the quartermaster,' said Bernie. 'I want a couple of bob to get home.'

The loungers scoffed at him in a loud chorus, and Buckteeth called him Sweet Innocence. Two more joined them, swaggering in their belted and ragged raincoats, out from the glow of the dining-room into the dark hall. As they came they deliberately crushed against the captain's tray all but upsetting his yellow and purple argosy. With a curse at them he raced like a waiter balancing his tray into the dining-room, returning to grab Bernard and put him standing in the between-passage outside the dining-room door.

'Stand there, you,' he growled. 'And let nobody into this room unless he has business there.'

The loungers cheered.

'Will ye go up, for Christ's sake,' the captain implored them, 'to the North road and watch it or the whole Division will be caught?'

'Oh! It's always deh Division, aw!' piped up a little fair-haired sprat of a boy from the foot of the stairs. 'What about deh men, aw? Dere's never any talk about deh men?'

'For God's sake get us a drink, Jim,' appealed the man with the walrus teeth.

'Go on, Jim,' joined in three or four more. They seemed to have no sense of pride left.

With a sudden air of intimacy the captain stepped into the middle of them, bending his neck right and left among them like a pecking hen.

'Go in,' he said, 'and take it. Say the quartermaster will fix it up. They'll never know in the hotel.'

Buckteeth turned away in disgust.

'No! They feed us, and they sleep us,' he said, 'and we're not going to soak drink from them as well.'

'Well I have no money for you,' complained the captain.

'Deh quartermaster have buckets of it,' declared fair-hair.

'*Buckets* is deh word,' sneered a tall man in spectacles from his dark corner at the door.

They laughed at the word in spite of their anger : it measured the quartermaster's thirst.

'Well, I can do no more for ye,' said the captain in a temper, and left them.

Bernie stood where he had been placed by the dining-room door and everybody passed in and out without paying the slightest attention to him. The quartermaster, already flushed with drink, returned to fill his glasses once more, and timidly Bernie touched him on the shoulder.

'Well? Are you here still?' said the quartermaster.

Bernie had not the courage to face the refusal of a loan so he asked instead for cigarettes. The quartermaster thrust a package into his hand.

'Here,' he said. 'You fellows do nothing from morning to night but bum and soak for cigarettes. Why don't ye do something?'

As he passed by a piece of black and white paper fluttered gently to the ground in his wake. Bernie picked it up. It was a hundred pound note. For a moment he thought of rushing out to his fellows in the hall and waving it in the air before their eyes; for another moment he thought of using it himself to get home. Then he realized he could not steal money like that, and even if he did nobody would change so large a note for them or him. As the quartermaster returned he tapped his arm once again. A wave of whisky belched into his face as the fellow turned on him and stuck his potato nose into his face. Bernie held up the note, saw him look stupidly at it, without a word thrust it into his vest pocket and stride into the dining-room with his dripping glasses. What a hopeless sort of army they were, Bernie thought, and he made up his mind that he must at all costs go back into the city out of these bleak mountains where they did nothing for month after month but eat the substance of the people and lounge over their fires like sleepy dogs. Things were still happening occasionally in the city. If he could rest for a while and see Norah, he would become invigorated by her and be of some use again. Suddenly there was a great stirring in the room and the captain returned to tell him close and guard the outer door. Bernie did not have the energy to tell him that all this was so much utter foolery. Instead he begged a match from him and lit a cigarette and leaned into the corner of the passage to think. He had waited so long he could wait now another couple of hours until the dawn.

By the glow of the lamps in the room beyond the passage-way he read Norah's letter again, scarcely hearing the talking and arguing rising hotter and hotter at the meeting, though he faintly gathered as he read the letter by the dim light that they were considering the whole military situation in the south and that some were for laying down their arms at once, and others for fighting on. He was hardly interested. He was thinking only of the summer that was gone and of every little incident of his last meeting with Norah in the woods beyond the bay at Youghal. Gradually the discussion in the room changed to an argument about men and ammunition and money and as the voices fell his thoughts wandered freely to the brownsailed yawl they saw floating past the frame of the restaurant door, the sun shining on the blue and white sea in its wake and the curling foam at its bows. He remembered how he had whispered an old song to her as they lay among the leaves and to himself he hummed it over again :

> 'O beloved of my inmost heart
> come some night and soon,
> when my people are at rest,
> that we may talk together;
> my arms shall encircle you
> while I relate my sad tale
> that it was your pleasant soft voice
> that has stolen from me heaven.
>
> The fire is unraked,
> the light extinguished,
> the key is under the door.
> And do you softly draw it.
> My mother is asleep,
> but I am awake.
> My fortune is in my hand
> and I am ready.
> I will go with you. . . .'

He heard Edward Bradley's voice addressing the meeting. Why he should be there he did not know, for he was not an army man. But afterwards he told Bernie that because he was older than anybody there and they wanted to hear what the politicians had to say they allowed him to speak. He was imploring them not to lay down their arms – far better to be defeated, at a blow or by degrees, though that would be slow and terrible for them all. As on that day at Youghal his passion carried the meeting with him and they cheered him loudly when he finished. When he came into the passage he was flushed and trembling, and when he saw Bernie he drew him with him out into the hall, and because the loungers were still there, out into the cool air by the side of the lake. A sedge of broken reeds had been washed ashore by the storms, reminding Bernie of the sedge of sea-wrack on the foreshore across Youghal bay, but across the lake the mountain-streams made a ceaseless desolate moaning as they fell, and a night mist was blowing in their faces so that they had to shelter in the pitchy darkness of a gable-wall. He told Bernie how terrible things were all over the country – so everybody at the meeting had said – and Bernie told him what he knew of the state of the men among those hills, all of them weak and scabby and sore, not a penny in their pockets, not a pipeful to smoke, nothing to do from one week to another but run when danger approached, never together, badly led, beaten all but in name.

'And in this hotel,' said Bradley, 'the officers taking their break-fast at six o'clock in the evening and drinking in the dawn.'

Suddenly Bradley said :

'Do you hear at all from that girl now ?'

'What girl?'

'The girl in Youghal.'

'A long time ago. I got a letter.'

He hated to talk of Norah. It was as if she were a secret part of him and he would not bare it.

'She is a very intelligent girl,' said Bradley.

'Yes,' said Bernie as if he were not really interested, but he felt his breath come in heavy waves.

'Oh, yes!' said Bradley. 'I saw a good deal of her before I came out here. I stayed at her house for safety several times before I took to the hills. And she's a very nice girl.'

Bernie shivered, his blood turning over in his body, but it was not from the cold.

'Well I'm leaving in an hour or two,' said Bradley. 'This place won't be safe for twenty miles around after the news of this meeting gets to the military.'

In the hall the candle was guttering out but the loungers still remained. To say something to them as he passed in Bernie told them what Bradley had said of the conditions about the country and of the officers in the hotel.

'Puh!' taunted the tall bespectacled fellow. 'And what does he do himself but hang over a book in the comfort of the hotel fire from dawn to dark?'

Bernie returned to his position in the passage. He was sick of these tauntings and tale-bearings, and he wondered how a man like Bradley could remain out there where he must hear them and notice them day after day. And if Bradley chose he could go back to hide in the city any day – there would be many people glad to receive and shelter him, and Bernie wished he had asked for the loan of half a crown and a clean collar and tie. He must see Norah again, and the city, and his people, and friends. The quartermaster was talking now, in a thick but fierce voice.

' "No surrender" must be our cry,' he was saying. 'I'd rather be shot any day than surrender. Let those that are tired of the fight go into the city and surrender!'

He peeped in to the long room. One lamp was guttered low to a smoking circle of red wick. The other glowed like a yellow ball through the skeins of smoke woven in heavy layers from table to ceiling. Beer bottles and empty glasses were everywhere. The men were yawning and stretching themselves, some talking among themselves, paying no heed at all to the speaker, and the chairman was drawing idle circles with a pencil on the table before him.

Somebody silenced the quartermaster with a question and by degrees the talk fell again to a drone as they discussed men and money and ammunition. He leaned back into a corner of the passage and while he thought of the road home, of every wind and turn in it, of every side-road and back-road he could take, he fell into a doze where he stood. He awoke to hear Boyle from Kerry cry out in a fury at somebody :

'Let them that want to rat, do it. Myself and John Jo Sheehan will hold Kerry anyway. Won't we John Jo?'

The meeting seemed to be ending. Sheehan was standing huge against the window with his back to them all, in spite of the lamp, black-shouldered against the pale glimmer of the dawn hanging over the mists on the lake outside. In taunting and utter disbelief he cursed over his shoulder at Boyle.

'Hold Kerry, how are you? You and Kerry may go to hell!'

The meeting broke up in laughter, men standing and talking in little groups, edging around their Chief to discuss private questions of their own. It seemed as if they would never come out and Bernie sate on the ground to sleep. The first few officers leaving the room poked his stomach with their boots in mockery of their sleeping sentry. He made his way out to the kitchen where the loungers were strewn asleep on the settle, the table, on chairs or about the floor near the grey embers of the fire. He rolled a porter barrel in from the bar and sate on it and through the sounds of the departing officers, horses stamping, carts trundling out, searchings in the dark for last drinks, calls and farewells, he slept in the corner of the cooling hearth. When he awoke the morning had come and the loungers were like him shivering together over the grate where Buckteeth was blowing the seed of fire into a fresh sod of turf. Seeing him open his eyes they asked him :

'Well? What was deh end of deh meeting, aw? Are we to go home or stay here? Aw?'

'Fight on!' said Bernie.

They looked at him too tired to mock the phrase.

'Stay here, he means,' said Buckteeth. 'Stay bloody well here.'

Bernie shared his cigarettes about and they smoked in silence while the fowl awakened by the echoing crow of the cock began to clatter and suckle in the rain-water of the yard, for the rain was now darkening the window, pouring straight down into the dung-filled haggard. Looking out at it Bernie saw again the mist hanging in the woods of Youghal, and Norah running down the slip to the ferry, her black curls swinging as she ran. Their hunger began to stir in them, but they could not find a scrap of food in the house – it had all been eaten by the crowd just departed. In their search they found the quartermaster snoring on the sofa of the dining-room, a roll of bank-notes hanging from his pocket. At once they grabbed them, sharing out the smaller notes, leaving the twenty-fives and the fifties and the hundreds, but as they argued over the division the quartermaster awoke and in a fury he demanded the money. Buckteeth who held the fistful of notes showered them over the furious man's head, and while he clambered under the tables and the chairs to collect them they mocked at him. Beside himself with rage he cursed them for lazy, useless louts and rushing off to tackle his horse and side-car in the yard he left through the blowing rain while in a crowd they cheered him from the door. But money would not buy them food and they went about draining the ebb of porter in every glass, then wandering over the hotel from floor to attic to see what they could find. There was not a soul there but the people of the house sleeping heavily after the long hours of work the day before, and they returned to the kitchen to wait.

At last the girls of the house came down the ladder-like stairs, their legs thrust bare into their dung-covered boots. They sate on the settle by the fire, bowed over their knees until their mother followed.

'A bad morning, Mrs O——,' said Bernie to the mother.

She stood by the low window and looked sadly at the rain.

'Isn't it a bad morning, thanks be to God?' she sighed.

Not a word of reproach was said, or of enquiry about the meeting, or of complaint at their long labour. The girls sate looking at the fire or out at the rain. There was nothing for them to eat, and nothing to do on such a wet day. The mother set to scrape the bins and the bags for flour and when the boy of the house came in he milked the cows. The dough was dampened with spring-water and fresh milk. It was kneaded and shaped and put in to the bastable while they all looked on. Through the open door they could see the rain splashing the causeway outside and a duck poked his eye in by the jamb. Buckteeth spat at the cocked eye and the duck clattered out, but nobody laughed. The bastable was over the fire and they had all turned to it to watch it whilst it baked. While they waited six other men came to the house, sodden with rain, arm and thigh and chest, searching for a breakfast and news of the meeting, but when they found the others before them they moved on patiently to the next farmhouse a mile off. They said they must be in Mill-street, twenty miles away, before night. Then they would walk on into Limerick along the Feale. For Limerick, they declared, bare and open though it was, was safer now than Cork. One of them, a Kerry lad, had no socks and his feet were torn by the bare leather of his boots. He had no overcoat, his very shirt clung to his back with wet, and he coughed ceaselessly. The woman of the house took pity on him and asked him to stay, and when he heard the others argue that Limerick was a far more dangerous place than Cork he sate down wearily by the fire and began to cry, telling his companions between his tears that he was afraid to go on with them and would hide here among the mountains. All the while Buck-teeth and the others looked awkwardly at him. They offered him cigarettes and tried to cheer him by assuring him that that place was as safe as a house, and while he and they drank the scalding tea and the soft hot cake the girls searched him out a pair of socks and a dry, if torn, shirt. But while they ate they were less sure about the safety of the glens and they argued and argued as to what they should do next. The Kerry lad could say nothing but 'We must hide. We must hide in the holes of the mountains,' and the little fair-haired city gamin kept whining plaintively 'But where are our officers? Where are our officers from us now? Aw?' At intervals the boy of the house assured them again and again that it was madness to stay there another day with the valleys filled, as he said, with 'people taking the heels from one another with the news of the meeting to the military in the next village.' So when the rain lightened they scattered, some going to the north, one declaring that the safest thing was to skirt the village to the east, and Bernie found he had lost courage to attempt the journey home. Tomorrow he would go, he thought, and with Buckteeth and Kerry, as they christened him, he went up among the cliffs in search of a cave to hide in. The boy of the house, though he kept assuring them it was madness to stay there, showed them a dump that had been made in a cleft between the rocks, a grave-like place dug out of the earth and covered with a sheet of corrugated tin and hidden by stones and withered brushwood. There was barely room for the three to lie in this dark, damp tomb, but as Kerry implored them to go into it at once, they lay down there, shoulder to shoulder, peering up and out all day long at the grey spears of the falling rain.

At dark, in spite of their hunger and the cold they slept, and so tired were they, they slept past the following dawn, past the rising of the sun and past the late morning, and all the while it rained and the whistling of the rain seemed to lull and keep them asleep in spite of encircling danger. They were awakened by the shattering echoes of machine-gun fire and the impact of hundreds of bullets tearing at the rock above their heads. When the first volley ceased the echoes carried its rat-a-tat-tat across the cliff-top to where another echoing air seized upon it and its thunder was reduplicated fainter and fainter into the heart of the mountains before it finally died into silence. There was such a long interval that it seemed as if everybody were listening to that last faint replication so high up and so far away. Then they heard the shouts below them:

'Come out! Come out, ye snipes! Come out or we'll bomb ye out. Come out!'

Those cries were echoed, and then a brief silence followed. The next minute the gun seemed to tear the tin roof from over their heads where they crouched helpless, their faces to the clay. They had placed their boots to dry, the night before, on the ledge before their dump and these now shot in on their foreheads torn to pieces by bullets. Again the echoes were reduplicated to the farthest uttermost glen and again the shouts came, mingling with those echoes and their own that followed after.

'Yeer last chance! Ye whores! Come out!'

The Kerry boy began to weep again.

'O God!' he shouted. 'Leave us out. Leave us out.'

'Throw down yeer guns,' cried the echoing voices below.

They did so, and Buckteeth tearing a sleeve from his shirt raised it before him as he crawled out into the rain. Below them was a score of sturdy green-clad riflemen and in a minute the three were among them, shivering with fear and excitement – broken, timid as children.

They passed through Youghal as prisoners, standing high on a lorry, conspicuous in their rags, and as it roared its way under the old clock archway, there across the windblown bay Bernie glimpsed his woods shrouded in mist, growing, as it seemed, out of the grey-green bay. Never did anything seem so definitely past to him as his summer flirting under those trees. It might have happened to him in another life, it might have been something he read of in a novel, so distant did it seem.

They drove him to Cork that night and there he remained in prison until the winter was passed and another winter had come again. Norah wrote to him many times while he was in jail – at first briefly but kindly, sending him gifts as she might to any other prisoner, later on long letters at greater length, as to a special friend. After a while she brought herself to reproach him for his long silence of that lonely winter, a winter in which she had tried hard, and vainly, to be as he had been forgetful of the sweetness of their early summer and autumn love. It was Christmas when he received a letter from her confessing how miserable and unhappy those months had been, and he was glad of the confession though it was a torment to him to be reminded, in the place where he was, of his foolishness when he had been free. And when she wrote that Edward Bradley often stayed with them, and spoke kindly of him, it was a double torment – that worst torment of all prisoners – to think what lovely things life could have given him, too, had he been out in the world and part of it. When he was freed he was very ill and weak and the doctor ordered him to the sea and he went, as a matter of course, to Youghal. It was February again, just a year since he had passed through it as a prisoner, and the woods and the bay were again shrouded in haze, but because Norah came to see him, and walked with him there, and showed him the rain in the cob-webs among the branches, and – it was so mild there by the sea – an early celandine hiding under a root, he thought those woods even more beautiful than they had been almost two years before when they watched the red globe of the autumn sun sinking behind its black branches.

Small wonder then that they should come back years after to this little seaside town for their honeymoon, the consummation of their love. It was Easter and so late in the spring – the fifteenth of April had been Easter Sunday – that the catkins' furry paws were already raised to the sun, and the long tails and the tiny wet noses of the lambs protruded from the red and blue creels rumbling in to the lamb-fair. The yellow furze was ranged high against the blue sky along the slopes of the hills, and over the surface of the sea beneath there was a cold layer of air that made the waves break with a brittle noise such as one never hears in the soft, dead heat of summer. They went about that first day, their wedding day, noticing everything with new delight – the spears of green grass shooting through the dead fields, the primroses and the violets clustered near the grey stones in the ditches, the beech-buds swollen red, the patches of hawthorn green lighting the withered hedges. The long country lanes were empty; they had the ocean to themselves. The summer visitors had not yet even thought of coming and all the length of the old stone promenade was bare. They even felt a delight in the shuttered windows and the bathing-boxes nailed up since last autumn. On the sands stretching for miles in front of them, lost in the end in the spume of the incoming waves far off in the distance, they saw only a sandpiper or two strutting by the skirts of the spreading sea, or peewits in their swoop turning as if to command on their white bellies, turning again their dark wings low over the thunderous sea. When they lay under an early blossoming blackthorn high above that singing sea and in the long silences of deep love gazed over the empty horizon, or back at the clustered smoking chimneys on the farther shore, Bernard felt, and knew that his young wife felt, that if another gull should wheel through the blue air, another distant lamb call out to its dam, their cups of ecstasy must overflow and roll upon the ground. They crossed back then, as of old, to the points of light that marked the town through an early sea-haze and sought out that little restaurant where so long ago they had cursed the Elizabethans and the Cromwellians, and there they had their tea, watching back through the open door at the rear of the shop the channel darkening with the fall of night. As they ate they suddenly saw beside them a little green poster bearing that day's name and date. They read it with interest:

SINN FEIN ABU

A

Public Meeting

will be

addressed in

the Town Hall

at 7 p.m. by

EDWARD BRADLEY. . . .

'Shall we go?' asked Bernard.

It was almost the hour as they made their way down the wandering sidelanes that lead to wharves and the Town Hall. There, hidden deep in the crowd they stood by an open window through which they could see the ever-present channel and the waters of the bay. The gas-lights in the hall hummed like flies, huge green luminous flies that had floated in from the half-night outside, so blue and lovely where it sank down, darker and darker over the masts and the brown sails of the fishing smacks in the harbour, and far in the distance the peaked mountains that Bernard knew so well. It was so lovely to watch the hollow night fall outside, and through it now and again a green light climbing up a mast, and to turn from it to the pale pink-washed green-lit room within, that they paid but little heed to the speakers until their friend the teacher rose. The years between that night and the day in the market-square had not dulled his eloquence, and though his temples were gone quite white now – premature for his years – the terrible passion of the man blazed like the fire of burning youth. Yet as he talked the lovers did not join in the cheers of the audience. The night had

C.S.S.O.—F

fallen now and nothing showed beyond but the eyes of green or
red on mast and poop. The mountains had vanished. The far woods
were gone. They barely heard the lapping of the bay. As by one
thought they moved quietly out through the cheering crowd into
the darkness. But, shyly, they did not go back directly to their hotel.
Wrapped in their own silence and the silence of the night they
wandered about the quays or in and out among the lanes as if prolonging the night to the very last moment. The meeting was over
before they returned to their hotel, and the lights of the houses in
that street, and doubtless of every street in the town, were gone up
to the second storey. When they entered their room they saw that
the pale light of the gas lamp outside the window fell on the high
old-fashioned ceiling and from there glimmered down on the wide,
carved bridal-bed, and needing no other light they used none. Across
the street was another row of sleeping houses, and beyond that the
bay, widening to the ocean, and when they stood without stirring
they could hear the low boom of the waves on the cliffs and across
the bar. As they undressed the faint hum of a motor rose in the
distance and approached along the street.

'Bernard,' she whispered.

Over his shoulder he could see her pale form in the dim light,
but where he stood by the window with one hand raised to the blind
his eyes fell on the passing car. He saw the white hair of their orator-
friend, the old bachelor, the patriot, driving out of the town into
the country and the dark night. The hedges would race past him;
the rabbits skip before his headlights on the road; the moths in the
cool wind would fly round his flushed face and his trembling hands.
But that wind would not for many miles cool the passion in him to
which he had given his life.

'Bernard,' she whispered again, and her voice trembled a little.

He drew the blind down slowly, the lamp shadowing the framework of the window on it, and slowly he turned to her where she
smiled to him in the dark.

A Broken World

'That's a lonely place!' said the priest suddenly. He was rubbing the carriage-window with his little finger. He pointed with the stem of his pipe through the window, and the flutter of snow and the blown steam of the engine, at the mountainy farm to his right. He might have been talking to himself, for he did not stir his head or remove his elbow from its rest. He was a skeleton of a man, and the veins of his temples bulged out like nerves. Peering I could barely see, below the pine-forest of 'The Department,' through the fog of the storm, a lone chapel and a farm-house, now a tangle of black and white. Although it was the middle of the day a light shone yellow in a byre. Then the buildings swivelled and were left behind. The land was blinding.

'Aye!' I said. 'It is lonely. But,' I said easily, 'sure every parish is a world in itself.'

He grunted and pulled at his cherrywood pipe and kept looking out the window at the whirling dots of white.

Then, without looking at me – looking down at the flap of my trousers, instead – he leaned forward, one bony hand gripping his left knee, and his elbow resting on the other knee so that he might still hold and smoke his pipe in comfort. I could see that he spoke less for the sake of conversation than from a desire to instruct me, for he seemed to get no other pleasure out of his talk.

'That used to be a credo with me, too,' he said, 'that every parish is a world in itself. But where there is no moral unity there is no life.'

'Moral unity?'

There were ten notes in the wind, boom and whistle and groan and sigh. Listening to them I hardly heard him. The snow had stopped.

'Yes.' He was cock-assuredly positive. 'Life is a moral unity with a common thought. The *compositum* of one's being, emerging from the Divine Essence, which is harmony itself, cannot, unless it abdicates its own intelligence and lives in chaos, that is to say, in sin, be in disunity with itself. Since society, however, is an entity composed of many members, life becomes a moral unity with a common thought. You can see that?'

'Yes.'

He went on, while I wondered if he was a professor in some seminary trying out something he had been studying. He enunciated his ideas with indrawn lips. That gave him a hellish, pedagogic look. The glare outside turned him into marble.

'In places like that – you have a broken world, and there is no unity.'

In spite of this abstract way of talk the next thing he said showed me that he was not a professor.

'Let me give you an example of what life is like in those isolated places,' jerking his head. 'When I was ordained my first parish was a lonely parish in the County Wicklow. From my presbytery window I could see the entire coast, a long straight beach, miles to the north, miles to the south, with a headland at each end stuck out into the sea. By the sea it is marsh. Then comes the first wave of high land around villages like Newtownmountkennedy. The land isn't bad on those hills, though it isn't what you would call really good land. They grow good turnips and potatoes and mangolds; the greens are not bad; but they cannot grow wheat. You need a good marl bottom for wheat. I was a young man then, and keen, so I studied these questions.'

(Whatever else you were, I said to myself, you must have been a bloody bore.)

'Look!' he said, pointing through the opposite window.

A vast, white plain, level as a sea, mapped with black hedgerows, all diminishing in size, spread away and away, maybe twenty miles, to a much lower range of mountains.

'My parish was in the same relation to that good land as these mountains here (nodding over his shoulder) in relation to that plain. That is to say, it was mountain bog, reclaimed by much labour, but always badly drained. Last of all, beyond me, was the utterly, miserably,' – his voice was almost oratorical here – 'wretched moor. Miles and miles of it on the plateau of the mountain-tops. The native tribes lived as freebooters up there as late as the end

of the eighteenth century. It was wooded then, and untouched by
any road. Then, in Ninety-eight, two so-called Military Roads cut
it across and across like a scissors. They were fifty miles long, and
straight as rulers. By the way,' he asked suddenly, catching me
looking idly out through the window, 'were you ever in County
Wicklow?'

'Oh, no, father,' I replied, as suddenly. I forced myself to attend.
Just then my eyes caught the eye of an old farmer seated opposite
me in the carriage; he was midway on the same seat as the priest,
and, so, near enough to hear everything. A pool of water had
gathered around each boot. Spits starred the dry patch between.
Seeing me look at him he took from his mouth, with his entire fist,
a bit of a cigarette he was smoking, and winked at me. Then he
put back the cigarette and contemplated the priest's face with an
air of childlike wonderment. At that wink I began to listen more
carefully. Evidently my priest was a local 'character.'

'They are remarkable roads,' went on the priest. 'Well, the people
of my parish were all poor. The interesting thing about them is
that there were two sets of names – either the old tribal names,
like O'Toole or O'Byrne or Doyle, or foreign names like Ryder,
Nash, Greene, Pugh, Spink, Empie, Gascon, Latour.'

A little smile took the corners of his mouth as he said those names;
but he never raised his eyes.

'The Greenes and Ryders and Pughs, and the rest of them, were
soldiers who long ago trickled down into the houses of the poor,
intermarried there, and became poor themselves as a result. However, they brought the people respect for law and order. Or; if you
like, they knocked the last bit of rebel spirit out of them.'

'Interesting!' I said, politely. I was beginning to enjoy the joke,
for I could see the old farmer getting cross, and at the end of that
last bit he had spat out his butt-end of cigarette.

'But the middle land, the good land, remained in the possession
of the big people who never intermarried. When I went there to
take over my duties I looked up the history of those wealthy people
in *Debrett* and *Who's Who*, and *Burke's Landed Gentry*.'

His palm became an imaginary book, and with his pipe-stem he
followed the lines and pretended to read:

' "Lord Blank, family name of Baron Blank. Fifth baron. Created
in eighteen hundred and one. Lieutenant of the Seventeenth Hussars.

Married Dorothy, oldest daughter of, let's say something like James Whipple Teaman of Grange House, Dilworth, Dorsetshire, you know the kind of thing. Succeeded his father in nineteen-eighteen. Educated at Eton and Sandhurst. Address, Grosvenor Square, London. Club – Travellers' or Brooks's. Recreations? Oh, as usual, hunting, shooting, fishing, racquets, riding." '

Again the thin smile. The farmer was gob-open.

'My parishioners were their stable–boys, gate-lodge keepers, woodmen, beaters, farmhands, lady's-maids, etcetera. *They* were always intermarrying. *Their* bits of farms, reclaimed from the furze, were always being divided. I've seen people live on a bit of land about twice the size of this carriage.'

The farmer leaned forward, listening now with great interest. Our three heads nodded with the jolt of the train.

'Then there was emigration. In the five years I spent there I had one solitary marriage. I had sixty schoolchildren on roll when I went there. I had thirty-five when I left. Last year I heard they were reduced to eleven, and five of those were all one family. No wonder the county is full of ruins. You come on them in scores on scores, with, maybe, a tree growing out of the hearth, and the marks of the ridges they ploughed, still there, now smooth with grass.'

'Begobs, then, they're here too, father,' said the old farmer. The priest nodded sideways to him and proceeded :

'I liked the people. They were clean; hard-working; respectful. Too respectful – tipping their hats to everybody. They were always making what we call "the poor mouth" – a mendicant habit of centuries, I suppose. They gave me no trouble, except for two things. They had a habit of writing anonymous letters, and I couldn't stop it. They were at it all the time. They wrote them to one another.'

He paused. I prompted him. The farmer leaned closer and closer.

'The other thing?' I asked.

'The other thing?' he said irritably to his pipe-bowl. 'In every one of these cabins they earned money by taking in boarded-out children – children unwanted by poor parents, or simply illegitimates. There was hardly a cottage without one, two, or three of these stranger children. They were well looked after, and the people often grew so fond of them they wouldn't part with them; and, I suppose, that was a nice trait too. But the point is that the only fresh blood coming into the county was . . . Well . . . a curious county, as you can see, and the morals were a bit curious too. However, that's enough about them.'

And he had at least enough sense to go no further with that.

'Well, there you are. That was my parish, and you can't say it was a world in itself. It was too incomplete. Too many things left out. The human dignity of men is always impaired when, like that, they're depending on other people who can make or break them. They weren't men. They were servants. That's the whole of it.'

'But did that make their lives lonely? You said they were lonely?'

For the first time he looked up at me. The veins on his temples, swollen from holding his head down, throbbed with relief.

'I didn't say *they* were lonely.'

His eyes wavered sideways to the farmer. I easily followed him over the hiatus when he jumped to –

'One day, after three years without stepping out of the parish, I decided to see if the neighbouring parish was any better.' (When I heard the personal note come into his voice I wished the farmer was not there; as it was he kept to his cold, factual description.)

'Do you know, the contrast was amazing! When I climbed down to the valley and the good land! And it was the trees that made me realize it. Beeches instead of pines. Great, old beeches with roots like claws on the double ditches. The farm-houses, too. They were large and prosperous with everything you might expect to find in a sturdy English farm – barns, ducks in the pond, thick-packed granaries, airy lofts, a pigeon-croft, a seat under an arbour, fruit-gardens.

'All that was good. But it was those beeches that really impressed me. They were so clean and old, not like the quick-growing pines of the mountains – dirty trees that scatter their needles into the shoots of the houses and block them up three times every winter.'

'Oh, they're buggurs, father!' agreed the farmer earnestly.

'I climbed lower still and came to the gates of the houses where the gentry used to live.'

'Used to?'

'Used to. I should have expected it, but somehow it hadn't occurred to me. It's funny how we all forget how time passes. But there they were – the gate-posts falling. The lodges boarded up.

Notices, *For Sale*. Fifteen years of grass on the avenues. You see?
"Owns ten thousand acres in Ireland. Address, Grosvenor Square,
London." '

The pipe-stem travelled across the palm.

'I met an old man who took me down one of those avenues to
see the ruins of a big house burned out during the troubled times.
It was a lovely spring evening. The sky was like milk. The rooks
were cawing about the roofless chimneys just like the flakes of soot
come to life again. I spotted a queer little building at the end of
a cypress avenue. The old man called it "the oftaphone." He meant
octagon. It was a kind of peristyle. He said, "The Lord" – just like
that, "The Lord used to have tea-parties and dances there long
ago." I went into it and it had a magnificent view, a powerful view,
across the valley over at my mountainy parish, yes, and beyond
it to the ridges of the mountains, and even beyond that again to
the very moors behind with their last little flecks and drifts of snow.
They could have sat there and drunk their tea and seen my people –
the poor Ryders, and Greenes, and O'Tooles, making little brown
lines in the far-off fields in the ploughing time.'

'They could! Oh, begobs, father, so they could!' – and a mighty
spit.

'Or at night, of summer evenings, they could have sipped their
brandy and coffee and seen the little yellow lights of our cabin
windows, and said, "How pretty it is!" '

'Begobs, yes! That's true!'

If anyone entered the carriage then he would have taken us for
three friends, we were huddled together so eagerly. The priest
went on :

' "They must have had good times here, once?" I said to the
man who was with me. "The best, father!" says he. "Oh, the best
out. The best while they lasted. And there were never any times like
the old times. But they're scattered now, father," says he, "to the
four winds. And they'll never come back." "Who owns the land,
now?" I asked him. "They own it always, but who wants it?" says
he. "The people here don't want it. They'd rather live in the towns
and cities and work for wages." '

'That's right,' said the farmer, as if we were really discussing his
own county. 'Begobs, you're talking sense now, father!'

' "The land was kept from them too long," says he. "And now

they have lost the knack of it. I have two grown sons of my own," says he, "and they're after joining the British Army." '

'Begobs, yes!' said the farmer, leaning to catch every word; but the priest stopped and leaned back.

The white, cold fields were singing by us. The cabins so still they might be rocks clung to the earth. The priest was looking at them and we were all looking at them, and at the flooded and frozen pools of water divided by the hedgerows. By his talk he had evoked a most powerful sense of comradeship in that carriage, whether he meant to or not: we felt one. Then, as quickly, he proceeded to break it.

'Well!' I asked eagerly. 'Well?'

'Why, that's all!' said the priest. 'I came back from my voyage of exploration, much refreshed. Much improved in spirits. You see, I had extended the pattern of life of my own poor parish. I saw how, how – I mean, how the whole thing had worked, hung together, made up a real unity. It was like putting two halves of a broken plate together. As I walked up another one of those hill-roads on my way home I passed more prosperous houses – smaller houses this time, what you would call private houses. They had neat, green curtains with fine, polished brassware inside on the polished mahogany. And through another window three aluminium hot-water bottles shining on a dark hall-table, signs of comfort as you might say . . . Yes! I had completed the pattern. That parish and my parish made up a world, as neither did by itself, rich and poor, culture and . . .'

'But,' I cried angrily, 'where's your moral unity? Your common thought? It's absurd.'

'Oh, yes! I realized that even before I got home. I just tell you the thing as it happened. But they in their octagon and we in our lighted cabins, I mean to say, it was two halves of a world . . .'

The farmer was looking at us both with dull, stupid eyes. He had lost the thread of the talk.

'Yes, I suppose so,' I agreed, just as lightly. 'But now that the gentry are gone, won't the people, the mountainy people, and so on, begin to make a complete world of their own?'

He shook his head. The farmer listened again.

'I refuse to believe they won't,' I said.

He shrugged his shoulders.

'And is there no possible solution, then?' I asked him.

He was looking out of the window, his poll to the farmer. He rolled up his eyes under his brows – a warning look, and faintly indicated the man behind him. Then he actually began to laugh, a cold, cackling laugh, an extraordinary, inhuman, kind of laugh that ended in a noise like a little groan.

The train slowed up, and we were in a station, and he was gathering his bags. He got out without even saying 'Good day' to us, and his face was coldly composed. A manservant, touching his cap, took the bags. The station-master touched his cap to him. The porter receiving the tickets touched his cap to him. The jarvey, who was waiting for him, bowed as he received the bags from the manservant. Black, tall, thin, and straight as a lamp-post, he left the lit, snow-bright station with every down-looking lounger there bowing and hat-touching as he passed. When I turned away the train was moving out, and the old farmer, in his own place, had lit another cigarette.

2

'Do you know his reverence?' I asked – as irritated as somebody from whom a book has been snatched before the end of the tale.

'Oh, aye!' said the old man, and he added, without interest : 'He's silenced.'

There was a touch of dread in that word, 'silenced.'

'What did they silence him for?'

'Politics.'

'Oh? He was too extreme?'

'Aye!' Still without interest.

'A clever man?'

No answer. His mind had gone to sleep. I looked at him in annoyance.

'What kind of ideas had he? I mean, what did he want?'

'Begobs, I dunno.'

Then he added, as if it was a matter of no importance –

'He wanted the people to have the land.'

'What land?'

'The land. The gentry's land.'

I leaned to him eagerly –

'But isn't that what ye want? Isn't that what the whole trouble is? Isn't that what the Government wants?'

'Aye. I suppose it is, you know? But he wanted it to be a sudden business.'

'They didn't silence him for that?'

'Maybe they didn't. Ach, he's odd. Sure, he took ten or twenty foolish young lads and, one night, he thrun down the walls of Lord Milltown's estate. He started some sort of a League, too. He's odd. God help him.'

'What did he want to do with this League of his?'

'I dunno. It was some kind of faddy business. He wanted halls . . . and . . . some kind of halls he wanted. Halls. I dunno what he wanted 'em for. Ah, he's a decent poor man.'

I tried another line.

'I suppose it's true for his reverence – ye have a hard time of it up here on the poor land?'

Puffing at his ease he was looking idly at the passing fields. A woman and two small boys, crushed into the doorway of a cabin, waved to us. He looked, and when they were gone his eyes were still fixed, seeing whatever passed beneath them with equal interest – or disinterest?

He tilted his head, but he said nothing. I made one last effort to shake him from his lethargic mood – possibly, most likely indeed, the mood in which he spent the greater part of his life.

'You know,' I said, warmly, 'I think I'd die in this lonely place. That priest is right!'

He looked at it, and scratched his ear, and said :

'Aye!' And then, suddenly, he added a second 'Aye!' – and then, when I thought he was finished, he actually added – 'I suppose 'tis quiet,' and relapsed into indifference.

Angrily I burst out at him –

'But damn it all, don't you mind, or is it that ye don't want to stir, ye're too damn lazy to stir?'

He took the butt-end from his mouth, and he looked at me, and by the way he looked up and down at me, I was hoping he would say something bitter and strong. But his stare was childish, and the eyes wavered, as if he was very tired. He just dropped one last, vast spit on the wet floor, snuggled into his corner, and went to sleep under his hat.

In his sleep he was as motionless as a rock; but you could not say he was 'like a rock' because he was like nothing on earth but himself, everything about him was so personal to him. Unless, because he was so much a random accumulation of work and season and all that belongs to the first human that was ever made, I chose to say, as I glared at him snoring in his corner, that time and nature had engendered something no more human than a rock. So I thought, as the dusk drew down, and the wind moaned in many keys, and the snow blew horizontally and stuck to the edges of the window. It was as if we two might have been jolting into a blank beyond either sleep or night, and I wanted to get up and kick him. I felt that if I did he would only moo.

We halted at several stations, with their one or two silent white-shouldered figures. He slept on. I was just wondering if I should wake him when suddenly, at a station, identical with every other station, as if some animal magnetism in the place stirred him, he rose and stumbled out. He did not speak. He did not raise his head to see if it was his station. He saluted no one. Anyway, there was no one there but a muffled porter who silently waved a lantern over his head. As we moved off he was trudging in the middle of a road that glimmered with its own strange afterglow, passing between a row of pines whose sheltered sides were red and raw as with the cold. He was exactly like an old black mongrel loping home.

3

So I was left with the pool of water on the floor, dark under the carriage-light, and the snow crumbling into the corners of the windows outside, and beyond that only the light leaping and falling along the hedges. And in another two hours or so, when I got out, the carriage would be racing along, empty, through the night – three bits of separateness, the priest and the farmer and myself, flung off it like bits of the *disjecta membra* of the wheel of life.

For those two hours I tried to refute the talk of that priest, thinking that he had merely spoken out of the snowy landscape, which above all other conditions of nature is so powerful to make life seem lonely, and all work futile, and time itself a form of decay; or thinking that, had it been the green-dripping spring or the hot summer, we might all have shown different and more happy sides of our worlds; or thinking that the thin cheeks and the throbbing nerve of the man were nothing but the sign of twenty years of self-corrosion, and that even when he was a young man in his first parish, his heart must have been so bitter and vain that, like a leech, it began to destroy everything to preserve itself; or thinking that because of it he had joined us for a few moments until we seemed to crouch over a fire, and then deliberately scattered us and left us with his pox. But, though that might be all true, I could not deny to the wintry moment its own truth, and that under that white shroud, covering the whole of Ireland, life was lying broken and hardly breathing. His impress remained even when the train swished slowly into the city, where the arc-lamps sizzled in the snow, and the sounds were muffled, and through every street a sharp, pure wind blew down from the Wicklow hills. Once their distant convex gleamed, far away, beyond the vista of a street. There were few people abroad, and as they walked against the wind with huddled backs they, too, seemed to be shrouding something within them that slept, and barely palpitated, and was hurt by the cold. What image, I wondered, as I passed through them, could warm them as the Wicklow priest had warmed us for a few minutes in that carriage now chugging around the edge of the city to the sea? What image of life that would fire and fuse us all, what music bursting like the spring, what triumph, what engendering love, so that those breasting mountains that now looked cold should appear brilliant and gay, the white land that seemed to sleep should appear to smile, and these people who huddled over the embers of their lives should become like the peasants who held the hand of Faust with their singing one Easter morning? Perhaps it was foolish to wish for such an image – so magnificent that it would have the power of a resurrection call? Yet, there are times, as when we hear the percussion of some great music, or when we feel the shrivelling effect of the cold wind and snow, that leave us no other choice but to live splendidly, or gather up at least enough grace for a quick remove.

The train could be heard easily, in the rarefied air, chugging across the bridges that span the city, bearing with it an empty coach. In the morning, Ireland, under its snow, would be silent as a perpetual dawn.

The Old Master

When I was younger, and so, I suppose, in the nature of things, a little more cruel, I once tried to express John Aloysius Gonzaga O'Sullivan geometrically: a parabola of pomposity in a rectangle of gaslight. The quip pleased everybody who knew the reference – it was to his favourite stand, under the portico of the court-house, his huge bulk wedged into the very tall and slender doorway.

I said *'gaslight'* because John Aloysius rarely came to work before the afternoon when they lit the gas in the dim entrance-hall, and its greenish, wateryish light began to hiss high up in the dome. There he would stand, ten times in the afternoon, smoking, or watching the traffic, or gossiping with some idling clerk. He had a sinecure in the fusty-musty little law-library, a room no bigger than a box. He used to say, in his facetious way, that he left it often because he exhausted the air every half-hour.

As the Assizes came to us only four times each year, and the library was rarely used between the sessions, he was not hard worked. He was always at liberty to practise at the Bar, but he never did – he was a bachelor without attachments and he had a small private income.

The last time he took up his stand in the doorway was the Tuesday of the week the Russian Ballet came to town. That day he became a next-to-permanent feature of the portico. He wanted to talk to everybody about it, until we were sick of the sight of him.

Higgins the door-keeper got the brunt of it; he also got a relay of John A.'s best Egyptian cigarettes. Peter Cooney, Secretary of the Poor Law Guardians, got the remnants – invited specially to drink coffee with John Aloysius in the library, and look, for the thousandth time, at his naughty prints of Ingres' *La Source* (the naked girl with the pitcher), or Fragonard's *The Swing* (the shepherd-ess-lady being swung much too high above the gentlemen in silk knee-breeches and ribboned shirt). They were good listeners, the one because he had nothing else to do, the other because he liked the coffee – it was good coffee, ground in a special little French hand-mill, and flavoured with a fine liqueur brandy – and because, too, he loved the romantic flavour of the tiny library with its books stacked to the ceiling, and he really admired John Aloysius, and thought him a most cultivated man, and a most refined man – even if he did tell smutty stories and had a bad name with the women.

To Higgins the door-keeper, John Aloysius would say – with the cigarette poised before his mouth, and the fat, little finger cocked in the air – 'Higgins, I am outshone. Up to last night, Higgins, I was the sole particle of colour in this diminutive jakes of a town. I alone brought colour and culture into this kraal that goes by the name of Cork. But I am honourably outshone. Russia has eclipsed me.'

That was his regular way of talk. And if nobody took it seriously, nobody took it comically, either. For he always talked with a slightly cynical air, an ambiguous kind of self-mockery, and he never smiled. God alone knows if ever he said to himself, in the silence of the night, 'John Aloysius Gonzaga O'Sullivan, you're a sham!' Such men have no life but their own drama, and if you had dared say that to him he would probably have replied: 'Is it not as good a life as another?'

'Look at this court-house, Higgins!' John Aloysius would go on. 'Look at it! I have seen the Lord Chief Justice enter this building between files of cuirassiers with shining breast-plates, uplifted sabres, snowy plumes. A vision of scarlet and ermine, Higgins. But that was in the good old days, before these yahoos from the heath, these bog-trotters of Gaelic Leaguers, these bag-men, these Attacotti, these tin-pot patriots with the smell of dung on their boots, set the grass growing on the streets. But now, Higgins, what do we see? We see Justice arrive in a bowler hat and flannel-bags. My God, Higgins! It's a symbol. And I am left! I am left! I am left, Higgins, like an old master, lying forgotten in a deserted mansion.'

'Aye, aye, sir!' Higgins would respond, like the old navy-man he was.

And John Aloysius would pat his third and hairless chin, and tip his deep-bayed collar, with the tips of his pink fingers, and, in disgust at the changed world, fling his cigarette on the mossy steps of the court-house, lingering for a second to watch some ragged-pants pick it up – his jewel flung in largess. Then he would stalk away, his great torso swaying like a young elephant from side to side, and he would bid Peter Cooney come to the library, and lolling in his arm-chair, take up the tale again.

'Cooney, that fellow Higgins is a boor, a gun-room lout, a deck-swabber. Why must John Aloysius Gonzaga O'Sullivan associate with such offal? Can you tell me that, Cooney? You at least, however ignorant, have been to the ballet once – you have made your obeisance to that loveliness of which these, and these' (indicating the naughty prints, at which Cooney would be trying hard to look objectively), 'are but the whispering echoes. Think of it, Cooney! Russia is at our doors – the greatest civilization in the world, crushed under the elephant feet of these yahoos of Bolsheviks, these hairy moujiks from Siberia, these Circassian Huns who never knew what beauty was – that Russia is come to our city. And what happens, Cooney? Pwah! The swine do not even smell the pearls. Last night – a first night – the theatre – you saw it yourself – was *empty*!'

'O, bejaney, John A.,' Peter would mumble, ' 'tis a bloody shame.'

'My dear boy, we are ashamed before the civilized world. How can I lift my head again in London? Or in Paris? The name of this city will stink in the nostrils of every artist in Europe. Saint Petersburg comes to Cork – for so, in my dreams, I sometimes call that lovely city, and think to see again her lovely streets. . . . And Cork ignores her. The Nevsky Prospect, Cooney; the sleighs on the Voznesensky; the Gorokhovaya Ulitsa, lit from end to end by the rising sun! (It runs due south-east, Cooney.) The Neva frozen and glittering! All that! And Cork ignores it!'

(That was typical John Aloysius – he devoured travel-books to the point of believing himself that he had travelled the world.)

'Cooney! Will you tell me why do I live here? Why does John Aloysius Gonzaga O'Sullivan live in a sewer? You say nothing? I know why. You are saying to yourself – "But what an error!" you are saying. "Surely," you are saying, "the sewers of Paris, as compared with this chamber-pot of a town, are as a translucent Pierian spring?'' And you are quite right. My boy, you show great intelligence.'

And so, having smoked Peter, and eased his own heart, off with him again to Higgins, and back again to his office, as restless as a hen with an egg, all that Tuesday afternoon, waiting until he should be seated again in the stalls, in his starched shirt and his tails – the only man, he was certain, who would dress for the event.

He knew he would be rubbing his paunch around and around, in an ecstasy, watching the limbs twine and untwine, the waves of *Les Sylphides* advance and retire, the heads nod, the knees rise, the arms upflinging. . . . In his library he blew little secret kisses at his vision. As he dressed he promised himself, 'fore God, that he would go around after the show to the stage-door and congratulate them in person. He might even take one of the ladies to supper. . . . He trembled at the thought. . . . And he knew that he was the only man left in all Ireland with a sense of beauty . . . the old master deserted in the abandoned house.

What a phrase! 'The old master on the walls – silent and dignified – while the bailiffs below-stairs drank their gin. . . .' As he walked to the theatre he polished the phrase, and he swayed on his hips like a young elephant.

2

Nobody knows if he said all that, but we can well infer it from what happened. For at the door of the theatre John Aloysius got a shock. He heard his name pronounced in full at his elbow – 'John Aloysius Gonzaga O'Sullivan,' spoken in a cold, malicious voice. Turning, he saw two men looking at him, one with a scornful frown, the other sheepishly. The frowner held a note-book in his hand and he was writing down the name. The other, of all people, was his satellite, Peter Cooney.

'What may this be?' stormed John Aloysius.

Cooney blushed and fidgeted, but the other spoke up.

'We're taking down the name of every man who enters the theatre tonight.'

He was a fine, healthy young man, with red, high cheek-bones, blue eyes, a soft mouth. John Aloysius recognized him; he was a doctor named Quill.

'And for what purpose, in the name of heaven?' asked John A., with a sick feeling beginning to crawl around his stomach.

'We think it's an indecent performance,' said Quill.

John Aloysius looked where he pointed and saw a little procession of young men marching around the square; among them were, also, some young women and boys. One man carried a placard which said:

MEN OF SAINT MARK

We have Them Marked!

DOWN WITH IMMORAL PLAYS!

He thought quickly of his job. It was a nice job. But it had to be renewed by the County Council every year, and that was sometimes a delicate business.

'Dear me,' he said, and for Cooney's benefit he tried to say it as facetiously as possible. 'And is it as bad as all that? Have you, I mean to say, have you seen the performance?'

'I wouldn't be seen supporting it,' said Quill.

Cooney was restive. He drew John A. aside.

'To tell you the gospel truth, John A.' he said, wrinkling up his nose apologetically, 'Doctor Quill can say anything he likes, but it's the way I *couldn't* be seen supporting it. I'm in this all on account of Canon Paul. As you know, what he says goes. But take my advice now, John A., and let it alone. 'Twill be better for you.'

'And do you mean to stand there,' stormed John Aloysius, 'and admit to me that you are such a craven wretch . . .'

'None of that,' threatened Quill, turning on them like a flash. 'Mr Cooney has made up his own mind and you can make up yours, too, and as a matter of fact, I'm sure Mr Cooney doesn't really approve of this performance at all.'

It was on the tip of John A.'s tongue to abuse them both. As he caught the flaring lights of the foyer, the gold paint, the smell of the theatre's musk, like burned toast, he wanted to ask them if they realized that all the loveliness of Russia was behind those doors, to talk of the Gorokhovaya Ulitsa lit from end to end by the rising sun. He even thought of arguing that the ballet is, by nature, anti-Communistic. Rage swelled his neck. He thought of ten bad words to call Cooney – a moujik, a pimp, a blister, a PILE. . . .

'I see,' he said. 'Dear me. I must think it over.'

As he walked away from the door he heard the wretched Cooney say, 'Cross out that name. Mr O'Sullivan is with us.'

He felt he would choke, or cry. He went around the corner, and to a small newsboy who tried to sell him a paper he said all the ten bad words in a rush. Then he bethought himself and walked quickly to the stage-door, casting many glances behind him as he entered. He presented his card and a florin to the door-keeper, and was finally shown into the dressing-room of the dancer who did the part of the Rose in *Le Spectre de la Rose*. The room was full of excited men and women, all talking in loud voices at the same time.

'I have come, sir,' said John Aloysius to the dancer, 'to congratulate you, and to protest on behalf of my city against these disgraceful scenes outside. I do not wish you, sir, to form the idea that this city is an ignorant city, or a boorish city. It is a most cultivated centre of the arts. It always was. I am but one of thousands who feel that your ballet is a glorious thing, and if I may say so, an uplifting thing.'

The dancer was a small, lithe Lithuanian named Rachmanoff. He was no Nijinsky. Where Nijinsky would have hurled himself through the window, ten feet through the air, on to a mattress held by four scene-shifters, poor Rachmanoff jumped like any man. He was thirty-eight – near the end of his race as a dancer, and he was touring the small cities of the world, trying to lay up a little store of money against the time when he would dance no more. Eagerly he interpreted to the others, as they crowded around them to know what it all meant. John Aloysius saw the glowing lips, and coloured cheeks of the girls, their bare arms, their white backs, and smelled the scent of the powder. He felt the air in the musty dressing-room grow quick, as when lightning is about to explode the sky.

'It means so much to us,' pleaded Rachmanoff. 'It will ruin us. Last week in Sheffield we did not do well. And *Cardiff* – you remem-

ber *Cardiff?*' He turned to them all, and they all groaned the word
'*Cardiff!*' 'Who are these young men?' implored Rachmanoff.

'They are young fools,' said John Aloysius. 'In fact, they are
mere scum! In fact, they are the lowest of the low! As a matter
of fact, they're really . . . what you might call, revolutionaries,
That's what they are!'

'Not Communists?' begged Rachmanoff.

'Worse than Communists! Perhaps you might call them Fascists.
Or Nationalists. It's very complicated.'

'What can you do for us?' pleaded the little dancer, and the girls
put their white arms around John A.'s shoulders and peered at him
beseechingly, as if he were their saviour.

'Pay no heed to them,' said John Aloysius, feeling the scent fume
through his brain. 'I am a lawyer. There are ways and means. Tomorrow night, I, John O'Sullivan, guarantee it, they will be swept
off the streets. I can only apologize for them, now. As an old master,
as one of the very few old masters, left on the walls of modern
times, from the great eras, my friends, as you are of those great eras,
I speak, so to speak, and I apologize for them. They will be swept
from the streets like the dust before the wind.'

Then, hearing the singing of hymns outside the windows, and
fearing the young men might come in and find him, he dragged
himself away, followed by their beseeching eyes, their pleading
smiles, their looks of fear and doubt. His heart was thumping as
he left them. But he felt justified. He had given these yahoos their
answer. The old master, so to speak, had leaned down from the
walls, reproved their ignorance. . . .

3

So thinking he found himself at the front of the theatre again. The
procession had swollen to twice its size. Crowds of people were
watching it circle round and round. Seeing them all, John Aloysius
felt his resolution ebbing away. Suddenly he heard his name spoken
again; this time it was Canon Paul, a lean, hollow-browed man with
spectacles. With distaste John Aloysius noticed that the glass of
the spectacles was dusted with little grains, and browned in the
crevices of the frame.

'Mr O'Sullivan,' said the canon, 'Doctor Quill has told me how you refused to support this wretched business when you heard of our protest. That's the spirit. I'm so glad you are with us. Only three men have gone into the theatre – and, believe me, Mr O'Sullivan, we'll teach them a lesson.'

'Why,' muttered John Aloysius, 'I mean to say, it's . . . I was thinking . . . after all, it's all right for . . . adults, don't you think, Canon?'

'Ah, but it's the bad example, Mr O'Sullivan. That's what counts. The young people must be given good example.'

'Quite so,' said John Aloysius.

'And now, Mr O'Sullivan, we're going to start. We'll march through the city. Come with me.'

Gently but firmly he took John Aloysius by the arm, saying something about the value of educated men, and about ending this sort of thing, and before he could get out of it John Aloysius found himself beside Cooney in the procession with a hymn-book in his hand.

'Now, men!' shouted the canon.

At once John A. imagined himself standing out and denouncing them all. What a great story it would be! And while he thought of it the procession shuffled off and he had to march with it. He saw the crowds fall in behind, marshalled by stewards. They were singing. Cooney was bawling in his ear like a trumpeter. In his white paunch, he himself was the most conspicuous of them all, he was so big and fat, and his tall hat stuck up in the air.

The canon fell in by his side and smilingly urged him to sing. Then as the procession circled around towards the drawn doors of the theatre he saw the dancers clustered inside, overcoats over their shoulders, peering out, and they were gesticulating madly and pointing direct at him. He tried to hunch down his shoulders, and bend his knees. He took off his hat. But that looked as if he were trying to put more gusto into his singing, so he put it on again.

'Sing up, Mr O'Sullivan,' urged the canon, singing away himself right into his ear (as Cooney did on the other side), and banging his breviary to mark the time. Viciously John Aloysius sang.

'*Hark*,' he piped.

'Out with it,' from the canon.

'Hark, hear the sound
Those blessed strains are telling . . .'

'Fine,' said the canon. 'Louder!'

'Of that new life,' sang John Aloysius,
'When sin shall be no more. . . .'

They debouched out of the square into the principal street. Crowds gathered on the kerbs. Old shawled women bobbed to the canon, and said what a grand man he had with him.

'Somebody is waving to you,' cried the canon.

It was Higgins the door-keeper, waving cheerfully from the kerb. John Aloysius looked sideways out of his pince-nez and bawled away at the hymn, pretending not to see him at all. Presently the canon said :

'We're going to hold a protest meeting in the Grand Parade. You'll say a few words, of course?'

John Aloysius groaned. Sweat clamped his dress-shirt to his back. He felt he was going to assassinate the canon, pull out his lean neck the way you pull the neck of a hen. He saw, down a side-street, a little green, iron building. Pointing shyly to it, he excused himself to the canon, dived from the ranks, and with his tails in the air, raced down the street and took refuge inside the privy.

As he turned into it he saw Cooney racing after him.

'You vomit!' cried John Aloysius, mopping his brow inside the building.

'The canon wants you to speak!' protested Cooney.

'I have a colic,' said John Aloysius. 'A bad colic. I get them often,' and he began to unfasten his vest. 'Go away, you scoundrel, you . . .'

'But the canon!' cried Cooney.

'I'll follow after you,' said John Aloysius. 'Go now, please go. It's so embarrassing. I'll join you in five minutes. I swear it!'

Unwillingly Cooney went. There was an old man there, too. He had a belt across his knees. John Aloysius peered out.

'Wha's all the singin' about?' grunted the old man.

'Some damn yahoos!' said John Aloysius. 'Clod-hoppers! Protesting about something or other! Saying something is immoral.'

The old man grunted. John Aloysius decided it would be safer to join him. They were now sitting side by side.

'All nonsense, of course,' said John Aloysius. 'As one of the old world – an old master – left by the tide – as you might say. . . .' He peered out carefully and saw the procession pass the end of the street. 'They know nothing. The beauty of the world. The grace of the human body. All lost on them.'

The old man grunted. John Aloysius looked at him in disgust. He lit an Egyptian cigarette and thought of the white arms of the dancers.

'The rhythm of the human form,' he murmured. 'Lost to them. Its life. Its colour. Know nothing. Never will.'

The sun streamed down diagonally into them. It was September and it had the softness of spring in it. Far away they heard the singing, the clear voices of boys and young women rising through the air, and they were – though John Aloysius hardly thought so – also springlike and clear, sweet as a shower through sunlight.

'The Gorokhovaya Ulitsa,' murmured John Aloysius.

The voices sang:

> 'Though our hearts be wrapt in sorrow
> From the hope of dawn we borrow,
> Promise of a glad to-morrow,
> All through the night.'

John Aloysius was left alone. The sun faded, but he was afraid to stir. He heard the sound of cheering. He formed the phrases he would use tomorrow to denounce Cooney. 'A man of no courage. I, at least, made my protest. Spoke my mind. To the dancers. Defended beauty.' It grew darker, and the soft voices rose again in another hymn. He stole away, wandering down devious side-streets, polishing his invective, swaying as he went.

In the end he never said a word to Peter Cooney. He got his death of cold out of it, and within two weeks pneumonia had him whipped. But the strange thing is that, somehow or other . . . John Aloysius had a good time . . . amused everyone . . . enjoyed life . . . but nobody ever thought of him as anything but a free, public show while he was alive, and we only began to think of him as a human being when he was gone.

Sinners

The canon, barely glancing at his two waiting penitents, entered the confessional. From inside he looked wearily across at the rows of penitents on each side of Father Deeley's box, all still as statues where they sat against the wall, or leaned forward to let the light of the single electric bulb, high up in the windy roof, fall on their prayer-books. Deeley would give each about ten minutes, and that meant he would not absolve the last until near midnight. 'More trouble with the sacristan,' sighed the canon, and closed the curtains and lifted his hand towards the slide of the grille.

He paused. To banish a sudden restiveness he said a prayer. He often said that prayer – an Aspiration against Anger. He had remembered that on the other side of the grille was a little serving-girl he had sent out of the box last Saturday night because she had been five years away from confession and did not seem to be a bit sorry for it. He lifted his hand, but paused again. To add to his difficulty – for it was no help to know what, under the *sigillum*, he must pretend not to know – he had just been told in the sacristy by her employer that a pair of her best boots was missing. Why on earth, he sighed, did people reveal such things to him? Did he *want* to know the sins of his penitents? Was the confession being made to him, or to God? Was it . . . He lowered his hand, ashamed of his irritation, and repeated the prayer. Then he drew the slide, cupped his ear in his palm to listen, and saw her hands clasping and unclasping as if her courage was a little bird between her palms trying to escape.

'My poor child,' he said, ever so gently, dutifully pretending to know nothing about her, 'tell me how long it is since your last confession.'

'It's a long time, father,' she whispered.

'How long?' To encourage her he added, 'Over a year?'

'Yes, father.'

'How much? Tell me, poor child, tell me. Two years?'

'More, father.'

'Three years?'

'More, father.'

'Well, well, you must tell me, you know.'

In spite of himself his voice was a little pettish. The title 'father' instead of 'canon' was annoying him, too. She noted the change of voice, for she said, hurriedly :

' 'Tis that, father.'

' 'Tis what?' asked the canon a shade too loudly.

'Over three years, father,' she prevaricated.

He wondered if he could dare let the prevarication go; but his conscience would not let him.

'My dear child, how much over three years is it?'

' 'Tis, 'tis, father, 'tis . . .'

The canon forestalled the lie.

'My dear child, how much over three years is it? Is it four years? And would you mind calling me *canon*?'

The breathing came faster.

' 'Tis, father. I mean, 'tis more, *canon*, father.'

'Well, how much? I can't make your confession for you, you know.'

' 'Tis a bit more, father.'

'Two months,' lied the maid, and her hands made a flutter of whiteness in the dark.

The canon almost wished he could break the seal of the confessional and reveal to her that he knew exactly who she was, and how long she had been away; all he dared say was :

'I suspect you're telling me a lie.'

'Oh, God, father, it's gospel truth.'

'But,' the canon tapped the cushion, 'there's no use in telling me if it's not the truth. For God's sake, my poor child,' he controlled himself, 'maybe it's five years?'

' 'Tis five years,' admitted the maid in so low a voice that he barely heard it.

He sighed with satisfaction. He straightened his hair on his forehead. Then he leaned nearer to hear her sins, nearer and nearer until his ear was pressed against the lattice.

'Now,' he warned, 'that is a long time, my child. But, thank God,

you have come back at last. You must try hard to remember all –
all – your sins. Let me help you. My poor little child! Take the first
commandment.'

But when he heard the shudder of her breath he knew he had
made a bad mistake; she would be seeing a long list of broken commandments before her and she would slur over many of her sins
in order to shorten the ordeal.

'I mean to say,' went on the canon, annoyed with his own
stupidity, 'that is one way of doing it. Do you wish to make your
confession that way?'

'Yes, father.'

'Very well.'

'The first commandment . . .' She stopped in confusion and he
realized that she did not even know what the commandment was.

'Did you ever miss Mass on Sundays?' he helped her out, although
his knees were beginning to dance with impatience.

'Oh, never, never in my whole life.'

'Good. Did you ever swear? Take the Lord's name in vain?'

'Tututut!' said the girl in horror at the very idea.

'Did you ever disobey your parents, cause them pain in any way,
give back-answers?'

'I have no parents, father. Mrs Higg – my mistress got me from
the Orphanage.'

'Ah! Well . . . er . . . Lies? Anger? Have you told lies, or given
way to anger?'

'Wisha, I suppose I did, father. I suppose I told a little lie now
and again.'

'How often in those five years? On an average? I mean, is it a
weakness you have? A habit?'

'God help us, father, I don't tell many. I only tell 'em when I
do be afraid.'

'Well, we will say you told lies occasionally. Now the sixth
commandment. Have you ever sinned in thought, word, or deed
against Holy Purity? The opposite sex, for example. Have you ever
misbehaved in any way with men?'

'Oh!' gasped the maid, and her voice thickened.

'Stealing?' prompted the canon, and he waited for her to say
that she had stolen Mrs Higgins's boots.

'I never in my life, father, stole as much as the head off a pin.

Except when I was small I once stole an apple in the nuns' orchard. And then they caught me and gave me a flaking. And they took the last bite out of my mouth.'

'You never stole articles of dress?' threatened the canon, and he suddenly realized that there were only three very unlikely commandments left. 'Clothes? Hats? Gloves? Shoes?'

'Never, father.'

There was a long pause.

'Boots?' he whispered.

Suddenly the girl was sobbing violently.

'Father,' she wept, 'Mrs Higgins is telling you lies about me. I hate that wan. I . . . I . . . I hate her. I do. She's always prying and poking and prodding at me. She took me from the nuns five years ago and she never gave me a minute's rest. She calls me low names. She tells me I can't be good or wholesome to come out of an Orphanage. She is picking at me from dawn to dusk. She's an old bitch . . .'

'My child! My child!'

'I did take the boots. I took them. But I didn't steal them. Sure I haven't a boot on my foot and she has lashings and leavings of 'em. I was going to put them back.'

'My child, to take them is the same as to steal them.'

'What does she want them for? But she's that mean. Her own daughter ran away from her two years ago and married an Englishman who's half a Freemason. The poor girl told me with her own mouth, only last week, how she's half-starved by that husband of hers and they have no money to have a family. But do you think her mother would give her a penny?'

The girl sobbed on. The canon groaned and drew himself up to ease his chest. He could hear the wind whistling up in the roof and he could see the long queue on each side of Father Deeley's box, all still as statues in the dusk of the aisle. Seeing them he groaned again as much as to say, 'What's the use? They all deceive themselves. They all think everyone is sinful but themselves only. Or if they say they are sinners, and feel it – it only lasts while they are in the church. Then they go out and are filled with envy and pride and they have no charity.' He leaned back.

'My child, my child, my child! For five years you have stayed away from God. If you had died you would have died with that mortal sin on your soul and gone to hell for all eternity. It's the law of the Church, and the law of God, that you *must*, you *must* go to confession at least once a year. Why did you stay away? Look at the way your mind is deformed so that you can't even recognize a sin when you commit it. Is there some sin you haven't told me that you were ashamed to tell?'

'No, father.'

'Didn't your good mistress send you to confession at least every month during those five years?'

'She sent me every week. But it was always of a Saturday night. And one Saturday night I didn't go because I wanted to buy a blouse before the shops shut. Then it was six months before I knew it and I was afraid to go. And, anyway, sure what had I to tell?'

The canon waved his hands weakly and with great sarcasm he said:

'Did you *never* commit a sin?'

'I suppose I told a lie, father. And there was the apple in the nuns' orchard.'

Furiously the priest turned to her, determined to wring the truth from her. In her compartment he heard Lady Nolan-White, his second penitent, coughing impatiently.

'My dear child, you simply must have committed sins during those five years. Be honest with yourself. Come now! Look! Take the most common sin of all. Have you, ever, had what we, vulgarly, call a . . . er . . . call a boy?'

'I had – once – father.'

'Well, now!' He rubbed his forehead like a man in a great heat and he strained towards her as if he were struggling with her demon. 'You were, what do we say . . . er . . . walking out with him?'

'Yes,' panted the girl. 'In the back-lane.'

'Well, what shall we say? Did, what do you say, did, er, did any intimacy take place with him?'

'I don't know, father.'

'You know what it is to be immodest, don't you?' cried the canon.

Her breath was panting in and out. She said nothing. She stared at him.

'My poor, poor child, you seem to have small experience of the world. But we must get at the truth. Did he – did you – did either of you ever go beyond the bounds of propriety?'

'I dunno, father.'

Loudly the canon expelled his breath. He was becoming exhausted, but he would not give in. He rubbed his hair all the wrong way, which gave him a wild look. He took off his pince-nez and wiped them.

'You understand plain English, don't you? Now, tell me, tell Almighty God the truth of the thing. Did you ever allow him to take liberties with you?'

'Yes, father. I mean no, father. We were in the lane. No, father. We didn't do nothing. Nothing much, I mean.'

'Five years,' moaned the canon, and he hammered his thigh with his fist. 'And nothing to tell. What kind of Christians . . .' He determined to make one last effort – just one more effort. 'Did he ever touch your body?' he asked bluntly.

'No, father. Well, I mean – no, father.'

Seeing that she was beginning to whimper again he threw up his hands.

'All right, child,' he said gently. 'Say your Act of Contrition and I'll give you Absolution.'

'Father,' she whispered, her eyes black through the grille, 'I was in bed with him once.'

The canon looked at her. She drew back. He leaned away and looked from a distance at the criss-crossed face behind the grille. Then he began to smile, slowly expanding his mouth into a wide beam of relief.

'My child,' he whispered, 'did anyone ever tell you that you were a little deficient in the head? I mean, you weren't very smart at school, were you?'

'I was always at the top of the school, father. Mother Mary Gonzaga wanted to make a teacher of me.'

'And,' growled the canon, now utterly exasperated, and dancing his knees up and down on the balls of his feet like a man in the agony of toothache, 'do you kneel there and tell me that you think it no sin to go to bed with a man? Who,' he added, casually, 'isn't your husband?'

'I meant no harm, father,' she palpitated, 'and it's not what is in your mind at all, for we didn't do nothing, and if it wasn't for the thunder and lightning that terrified me, I wouldn't do it at all. Mrs Higgins was down in Crosshaven with Mrs Kinwall, that's her daughter, and I was all alone in the house, and I was afraid of the dark and the thunder, so Mickey said he'd stay with me, so he stayed, and then it was late and I was 'fraid to be by myself in the bed, so he said, "I'll mind you," so I said, "All right, Mikey, but none of that," and he said, "All right, Madgie, none of that," and there wasn't any of that, father.'

She stared at the canon, who was blowing and puffing and shaking his head as if the whole world were suddenly gone mad.

'It was no harm, father,' she wailed, seeing he did not believe her.

'Once?' asked the canon shortly. 'You did this once?'

'Yes, father.'

'Are you sorry for it?' he demanded briefly.

'If it was a sin. Was it, father?'

'It was,' he roared. 'People can't be allowed to do this kind of thing. It was a serious occasion of sin. Anything might have happened. Are you sorry?' – and he wondered if he should throw her out of the box again.

'I'm sorry, father.'

'Tell me a sin of your past life.'

'The apple in the orchard, father.'

'Say an Act of Contrition.'

She ran through it swiftly, staring at him all the while. There were beads of perspiration on her upper lip.

'Say three Rosarys for your penance.'

He shot the slide to and sank back, worn out. From force of habit he drew the opposite slide and at once he got the sweet scent of jasmine, but when Lady Nolan-White was in the middle of her *Confiteor* he waved his two hands madly in the air and said, hastily:

'Excuse me, one moment . . . I can't . . . It's all absurd . . . It's impossible . . .'

And he drew the slide on her astonished, beautiful, rouged face. He put on his biretta, low down on his nose, and stalked out into the aisle. He parted the curtains on Lady Nolan-White and said:

'It's quite impossible . . . You don't understand it . . . Good night!'

He stalked up the dim aisle, and when he met two urchins gossiping in a corner he banged their little skulls together, and at once he became disgusted with himself to see them cowering from him in fright. He passed on, his hand under the tail of his surplice, dancing it up and down. When he saw two old women by the great Calvary, rubbing spittle into the Magdalen's foot and then rubbing spittle to their eyes or throat, he groaned out, 'Oh, dear, oh dear,' and strode on towards Father Deeley's box. There he counted heads – fourteen penitents on one side and twelve on the other, looked at his gold watch and saw it was a quarter-past eight.

He strode back to the centre compartment and flung aside the curtains. Out of the dimness the warm, cherubic face of the young curate looked at him – a pink Italian saint. Slowly the glow of spiritual elevation died from his face as the canon's insistent whisper hissed down at him :

'Father Deeley, it won't do. I assure you it's absolutely impossible. Half-past eight and twenty-six people yet to hear confession. They're just deceiving you. They want to gabble. I am an old man and I understand them. Think of the sacristan. Electric light, too! And gas going until midnight. The organization of the Church . . .'

And so on. All the time he kept stretching and relaxing the mechanical bow of his genteel smile, and he spoke in the most polite voice. But Deeley's face grew troubled, and pained, and seeing it the canon groaned inwardly. He remembered a curate he had once who played the organ every day for hours on end, until the parishioners complained that they couldn't pray with the noise he made; the canon recalled how he had gone up into the loft to ask him to stop, and the curate had lifted to him a face like an angel, and how within one half-minute it had became the face of a cruel, bitter old man.

'All right, Father Deeley,' he said hastily, forestalling protests. 'You are young. I know. Still, you are young . . .'

'I am not young,' hissed Deeley furiously. 'I know my duty. It's a matter of conscience. I can sit in the dark if you are so mean that you . . .'

'All right, all right, all right,' waved the canon, smiling furiously. 'We are all old nowadays. Experience counts for nothing . . .'

'Canon,' said Deeley, intensely, putting his two fists on his chest, 'when I was in the seminary, I used to say to myself, "Deeley," I used to say, "when you are a priest..." '

'Oh,' begged the canon, cracking his face in a smile, 'don't, I beg you, please don't tell me your life-story!'

Whereupon he whirled away, his head in the air, switching on and off the electric light of his smile to penitents he did not know and had never seen in his life before. He found himself before the high altar. He saw the sacristan standing on a step-ladder before it arranging the flowers for the morning, and he thought it would be well to apologize to him for Deeley's late hours. But the sacristan kept turning a vase round and round and round, and at last he realized that the little man was cross with him already, was deliberately delaying up there, and would not come down until he was gone.

Sighing he went away, and after writing some letters he realized that his stomach had ceased to belong to him and would be out on its own devices until morning, like a hound that escapes from its kennel. Wearily he took his hat and cane and decided to take a long walk to calm his nerves.

It was tender night of floating moonlight, cosily damp, and it soothed him to look down on the city and see the roofs as white as if there was frost on them. More calm, he returned home. The river was like milk. The streets were asleep. He hummed quietly to himself and felt at peace with all men. The clocks of the city chimed at one another in a good-humoured mood, slow and with silvery, singing echoes. Then he heard a woman's voice talking from the high window of a cement-faced house, and he saw that it was Mrs Higgins's house. She was in a white nightdress.

'That's a fine story!' she cried down to the pavement. 'Ha! A cockalorum of a story! Wait until I see the canon. At confession, indeed! Wait until I see the nuns! Oh, you jade! You unfortunate, poor sinner!'

He saw the little girlish figure cowering down in the doorway.

'Mrs Higgins,' she wailed, 'it's gospel truth. The canon threw me out again. I told him all sorts of lies. I had to go to Father Deeley. He kept me half an hour. Oh, Mrs Higgins,' wailed the child. 'It's gospel truth.'

'Aha!' prated the nightdress. 'But you're a nice thing. Wait until I tell...'

The canon felt the hound of his stomach jump from the kennel again. His entrails came bodily up to his neck. He marched by, blowing and puffing.

'Oh, my God!' he whined. 'Have pity on me. Oh, my God! Have pity on me!'

He turned towards the dark presbytery deep among the darkest lanes.

Admiring the Scenery

From between the little wayside platforms the railway shot two shining arrows off into the vast bogland where they vanished over a rise that might have been imperceptible without them. It was just before sunset in early spring, a soft evening of evaporating moisture and tentative bird-song; for the birds seemed to be practising rather than singing, twirling and stopping, and twirling and stopping, and when the bold thrush rolled out a whirl of sound he might have been mocking all the other eager, stupid little fellows like the bullfinch or the tits who had not yet learned their songs.

The three men, leaning on the wooden railing along the platform, looked at the blush of the sun on the last drifted snow of the mountains, and though every rail was cut into an A shape on top, uncomfortable for arm or elbow, they found it restful to lean and look over the bog, speaking hardly at all. They had been walking all day and now were dog-tired. They were waiting for the last train to take them into the country town where they all three taught in the Diocesan College.

The priest stood in the middle, a young man, too fat for his years, with drooping lids, puffed lips, and a red face as if he suffered from blood pressure. The same features on another man might have suggested a sensual nature, but there was in his heavily-lidded eyes a look that was sometimes whimsical and sometimes sad, and that look, with the gentle turn to his mouth when he smiled, gave him the appearance of a man who had gone through many struggles and finally solved his problems in a spirit of good-humoured regret. So, now, as he pulled at his pipe and looked down into a cold bog-stream that flowed beneath them, his chin and his piggy jowls rested on his Roman collar, expanded around his little mouth as if he might at any moment break into a little, silent chuckle. Only, you might have felt, those tired eyes would not even then have changed : they would have mocked his own smile.

On his left, carrying the haversack, was a small dark man, with a slim small body and a button of a head and clipped dark moustaches. The main thing about him was that he did break occasionally into sudden talk, and when he did he banged the hard railings repeatedly or lifted his two fists in the air and slapped his forehead. He did all these things, suddenly, when he cried out:

'Why on earth is this ten-thousand times accursed station three miles from the village? What's it here for at all? My God, what a country! What – is – it – for?'

'To take us home,' said the third man, and the priest's belly shook a little, too tired to expel laughter.

There was nothing remarkable about this third man except that he had handlebar moustaches and a long black coat and a black hat that came down low on his forehead and shaded his melancholy face; when he spoke, however, his face was gentle as the fluting of a dove. There was nothing resigned about him; his oblong face was blackberry-coloured where he shaved and delicate as a woman's where he did not. His eyes were lined with a myriad of fine wrinkles. They were cranky, tormented eyes, and his mouth was thin and cold and hard.

'I know,' cried the small man. 'It's some bloody Czar that did it. Some fool of an Under-Secretary long ago or some ass of a flaming Lord-Lieutenant who took a ruler and drew a line across Ireland and said, "That shall be the route of the new railway!" God, what a flaming country!'

'I wonder,' said the sad man, Hanafan, in his slow voice, 'do the common people ever admire scenery?'

'Now that's very interesting, Hanafan,' cried the small man across the priest's chest. 'That's a most extraordinary thing. I often thought of that. Isn't that a coincidence.'

'Well,' said the sad Hanafan, blushing modestly, 'it's a common enough idea, you know.'

'Of course they do,' said the deep basso of the priest.

'But do they, do they, do they?' shouted the little man, hammering the railing.

The priest nodded, never taking his eyes from the stream or his pipe from his little mouth.

'How do you know?' demanded the small man, leaping backward

and whirling his head left, right, and up in the air, as if the answer were a bird.

'Why wouldn't they?' grunted the priest.

'I know what you mean,' interrupted the small man, and he wagged his finger into the priest's face. 'I know. I met men like that. Our gardener at home, for example. I'd say to him – he was an awful old drunkard – he'd be lying of a hot summer's afternoon under an apple-tree – a lazy old ruffian, "Grand day, Murphy," I'd say. "Oh, a grand day, God bless it," he'd say, "and isn't it good to be alive?" But that's not admiring the scenery,' went on the small man. 'It's not being *conscious* of it. It isn't, if you understand me, projecting the idea of the beauty of the scene, the idea, into one's own consciousness. Is it, now, Hanafan? And that's what you mean by admiring the scenery.'

'Well,' said Hanafan, and his words were like prize pigeons that he released one by one from his hands, 'I don't know. I'm not sure I mean that.'

'Then what the hell *do* you mean?'

'If a man said to me,' went on Hanafan, in his downy voice, ' "I do be sometimes sitting here, Mr Hanafan, enjoying the cool of the evening," I'd say that that man was enjoying the scenery even though he might not know he was doing so at all.'

The priest nodded. The small man looked contemptuously at Hanafan who now began to quote from Gray's 'Elegy' in his round, womanly voice, all the time looking sadly at the warmth of the sun fading from the distant grains of snow, and the mountains becoming black and cold:

'The lowing herd winds slowly o'er the lea....'

'I know, I know,' interrupted the other, but Hanafan went on quietly:

'The ploughman homeward plods his weary way;
And leaves the world to darkness, and to me.'

'You see I feel,' he said, 'that the ploughman responded to the sense of the end of the day, and the way the fields were all gentle, and dark, and quiet. Just like that bog there ... is ... all ...'

His voice died out.

'Ah, damn it,' said the small man in disgust, 'that has nothing to do with it.'

'It has, Mr Governey,' murmured the priest. 'In a sense it has.'

'Every man,' cried Hanafan, aroused with such vigour that the other two glanced at him, 'lives out his own imagination of himself. And every imagination must have a background. I'll tell you a queer thing. It's about the station-master in this station a few years ago.'

The priest nodded and chuckled aloud.

'He was nearly sixty-five,' said Hanafan, 'And he was married, and had a grown-up son in New York, and a daughter, a nun in South America.'

'I sent her there,' said the priest. 'A nice poor girl she was, God rest her.'

'Did she die?' asked Hanafan, and when the priest said, 'Yes,' he fell silent and forgot his story until the other teacher reminded him crossly.

'Yes,' said Hanafan. But, again, he stopped because the station porter came out with two oil lamps, one of which he put into the frame of the standard near them.

'It's a grand evening, father,' he said as he turned up the wick.

'Is she late again?' asked the priest, and the porter looked up the line at the signal, and said :

'Aye, she's a trifle behindhand, I'm thinking.'

He got down and drew a great silver watch from his corduroy vest and held it up to the setting sun, peering through the yellow celluloid guard.

'She's due, bedad. Ah, she'll be here in a quarter of an hour all right.'

The small man groaned and said, 'What a country !' The other two looked up at the lamp and then away, and Hanafan said :

'Isn't it dark !'

The porter had walked away.

'Well,' resumed Hanafan suddenly, 'this old station-master ! His name was Boyhan. He thought he had a great voice for singing. He was stationed at N——' (he mentioned the town where they all lived and taught in the college), 'and he used to come and sing in the choir with us. That was before your time, Mr Governey. And he sang in the parish choir. And he'd have sung in the Protestant choir and the Wesleyan choir and the tin-hut choir if they let him. There was not a concert in N—— that he wasn't the head and tail of it, and he always sang twice and three times, and it was all they could do to keep him from giving encores all night long. For,' sighed the teacher, 'he had no sense and the people used to make a hare of him. He couldn't sing any more than I could. He had a small little voice, a small range too, but it had no strength or sweetness; there was no richness in it.'

The teacher said these words, *strength, sweetness, richness*, with a luscious curl of his thin lips around the fruit of sound. His eyes widened. Clearly he was seeing nothing but the old station-master. Earnestly he went on, a small glow on each cheek:

'That was all right until they shifted poor Boyhan to this God-forsaken place. And if N—— is a lonely hole, this is the back of beyond. At the same time they started the new Broadcasting Station in Dublin and Boyhan conceived a great ambition to sing there. He formed the idea that some day or other a passenger would be on his way to Dublin, or from Dublin, and he would hear him singing and say, "My Heavens, who is that with the grand voice?" And he would make inquiries – some director or Government official – and stop the train to seek out Boyhan and say to him, "What's the meaning of this neglect? Why haven't you been asked to sing over the Radio?" Then there would be paragraphs in the newspapers about Discovery of Great Irish Baritone, and Romance of a Chance-heard Voice, and so on.

'The result of this was that whenever a train rolled in, Boyhan used to come out of his office singing. He'd be singing little trills up and down the scale, or a bar of *The Moon hath raised her Lamp Above*. He was known to all the passengers and, sure, they used to be looking out for him. And there he would always be, rubbing his hands and pretending he was doing his *Dohsohmedoh*, just for delight and jollity.

'Well, one hard, moonlight night in December, I was here, like this, waiting for the last train back to N——. The snow was white on the hills. It was blazing. There wasn't a sound but the wind in the telegraph wires. The clouds were in flitters, in bits. I well remember it. A rich night. A deep, rich night, and no harm in the winds but they puffing and blowing.'

Again Hanafan's cold thin lips sucked the sound of those words, *rich*, *deep*, and his eyes dilated under his black hat with the image of his memory. His eyes were not cranky now, but soft and big.

'I was here with a – a – I was here with a – a friend.'

He stopped for a second. The small man's eyes pounced on him, observing at once his strange embarrassment. He glanced at the priest, but he had lowered his face and his mouth was clamped. In that hesitant second he saw at once a piece of Hanafan's secret life revealed, a memory of something known also to the priest; the thought of a dead friend – or perhaps a woman – something or somebody that made the memory of that night so precious to Hanafan that he could not speak of it openly.

'Was this long ago?' probed the small man inquisitively.

'We walked up and down,' said Hanafan, 'looking at the snow under the moon and the clouds tumbling. Then Boyhan came out and he took us across the line. He had a fire and we sat around it. The smell of the peat, thick and slab, was stuck into everything in the room.'

'Was it only two of you?' prodded the small man, eager to know if it was a woman.

'He showed us photographs of his daughter, the nun, and of his son, Timsy, with, as he said, a lawn-tennis in his hand. He had no wife. She was dead. And there he was living alone, in the station, three miles from the village and his only two children in the world away in exile. I quoted Sir Thomas Browne for him, the passage in *The Quincunx*. We all looked out the little window at the stars of the Plough. "Think!" said I, "*The quincunx of heaven runs low and 'tis time to close the five ports of knowledge. . . . The huntsmen are up in America and they are already past their first sleep in Persia. But who can be drowsy at that hour which freed us from everlasting sleep, or have slumbering thoughts at that time, when sleep itself must end. . . .*"

'Then, by way of no harm, he began to talk about music and singing and he gave us one song after another. He sang us, *Oft in the stilly night* – and, you know, he sang it well. He sang, *The Moon hath raised her Lamp Above*. I heard the signal bell ring as he was in the middle of it and far away the train began to purr. He was singing it so heartily we didn't like to interrupt him, and as the train became a roar across the bog and the lights went flashing across the window, he rose and went out to the platform. By Heavens, that man saw the trainload as a vast audience whirled before him. He stood out on the platform singing to them.

'We rushed for the bridge, we had no tickets, he gave us no tickets, and as I ran I shouted back at him, "Hold the train!" He paid no heed, and when we were up on the middle of the bridge he got to the grand burst, the last crescendo, of –

"I come! . . . My heart's delight"

and waved the train on. We were left looking at it vanishing up the line. I roared at him for a fool, and a vain fool, but he only bowed to us, and he bowed to the porter, and he bowed his way backward to the office like a Caruso. The train purred into the distance and there we two were with the wind in the wires and the white moon on mountains.

'I went back to abuse him – it was the last train – but he only looked at me like a child you'd strike and said he couldn't hold back a train for anyone. The porter paid no heed to us. He outed the lamps and locked the place up. We left the old fellow alone in the station. We had to walk home. It was a grand, bright night. A lovely, thick night. . . .'

Hanafan's voice broke. Just then a signal bell rang. It was dark over the bog where far away the train murmured and it could easily be heard because the birds had stopped singing. There was nothing but the deep scent of the night air, and below them in a marsh, still deep from the March rains, a prattling as of a thousand tiny frogs.

'This is a lonely place he lived in,' whispered Hanafan. 'A lonely life. No children. No wife.'

The priest rose up and knocked out the ashes of his pipe as the train roared nearer.

'Yes,' he agreed.

'But,' cried Governey, 'what has all that got to do with admiring the scenery?'

'He sang to the night,' cried Hanafan passionately. 'He sang to the whole night. The moon was up.'

His voice fell and they barely heard him over the rumbling train at the end of the platform.

'We saw the moon in the flags of the Liffey as we left the station. In the flags of the river, through the trees.'

'Still and all,' cried the small man, 'he didn't form any intellectual concept. . . .'

The train drowned his voice and its lights flitted across their faces. When they climbed into a carriage the windows were speckled with rain and the three men inside, who leaned back to let them pass, had a cold, damp look. They had been talking when the train stopped, but when they saw the priest they fell silent; looked at him under their brows; and shyly tipped their hats.

'Raining up the line?' asked the priest in a friendly voice.

'Oh, pouring in Dublin, father,' said one of the three men – an elderly, soldierly-looking man, probably a warder in the jail at M——.

The three teachers fell silent, sensing that they had interrupted a conversation. Then they were rolling through the night, looking at the lights racing along the little hedges beside the line. Suddenly the rain that had hit Dublin half an hour before swept down on them across the mountains, slapping the windows like a bucket of water. It kept trickling and shining on the windows.

'He died there last year,' said Hanafan suddenly, looking at the trickle outside the pane.

'I once asked him,' the priest leaned forward to say to the small man, 'what his favourite song was. Do you know what he said? *Scenes that are brightest.*'

The priest leaned back and gave a merry little laugh.

'Still,' cried the small man, thumping his knee, 'I can't see what this has to do with the question we were discussing!'

The priest looked at him, and kept looking at him, as he swayed with the carriage, but he said nothing. Angrily the small man looked back, and then he looked angrily at Hanafan, whose eyes had become cranky and tormented once more. He began to wonder why Hanafan was always so sour, and why he remained on in N—— if he didn't like the place, and why he had never married. His eye lit up a bit at that and he determined to get it all out of the priest when they were next alone. He tapped Hanafan on the knee and he began to ask him some question, but when he saw that Hanafan's eyes were

closed he leaned back again. The priest was still looking at him, so
he nodded towards Hanafan and winked. The priest's lidded eyes
were as immovable as an owl's.

As they rolled on through the bog the small man kept looking
around him restlessly, and at last he shifted over to the three countrymen, determined to find out if the common people really do admire
the scenery. He started a conversation about turf-cutting, but before
he could lead up to the question the train halted at a small station
and the strangers got out. Then the three friends were left alone in
the cold, damp carriage, listening to the battering rain. Tired and
sleepy, nobody noticed that, in his corner, Hanafan was weeping
to himself, the drops creeping through his tightly closed eyes.

Egotists

The young sailor was making his way hiking from Galveston to 'Frisco, and the professor was motoring east, from 'Frisco, with his niece. They met at the little hamlet of Santa Rosa, in Texas, not far from the border of New Mexico.

The professor halted his car there, because although Santa Rosa is little more than a handful of shacks, and he would have to sleep in the wayside camp, there is nothing much better in the four hundred miles between Santa Fé and Fort Worth. The sailor halted there because he was tired. It was hot and sticky. The sky was bronze with clouds sparring slowly around one another, promising storm during the night. Besides, he was afraid of snakes, and he had passed three of them on the road earlier in the afternoon, and they, like the slugs at home in Ireland, were a sure sign of rain.

Down beyond the six wooden huts of the camp was a makeshift bathing-pool under a group of magnificent maple-trees, and there he heard a girl's voice shouting and laughing. It was an English voice. He went down in the dusky light and saw the girl splashing about in the muddy water, and, on the grass bank, a tall elderly man watching her. His face, beard and bald head made a perfect egg-shape. His mouth was so soft that when it was closed it did not look closed.

'Very stuffy tonight, sir,' said the sailor.

The professor looked with interest at the man who had called him 'sir,' and said :

'It is very warm.'

The sailor looked down at the girl, and in his loneliness her English voice began to dissolve his bowels.

'I'm thinking it will be a storm, sir,' he said.

'I guess it will,' agreed the professor, looking southward at the brazen sky. Just then the girl scrambled up the ladder and ran dripping across the livid grass towards the huts.

'The young lady is English?' said the sailor.

'My niece is English,' said the professor, 'but,' he added pleasantly, 'she's been all around the world. I should have thought she'd have lost some of her accent by now. Are you English?'

On the vast edge of the Texan plain, quivers of lightning waved their hands madly, to and fro, and the thunder-pig came grunting across the horizon. The flashes lit up the *mesa* and its flat top stood for a second black against the sky.

'Yes,' said the sailor, 'I've hiked up from Galveston, down on the Gulf. I landed there from Southampton.'

A drop or two began to fall, so the professor edged towards the huts, and the sailor with him.

'Galveston? Where are you aiming for?'

' 'Frisco. I have a brother there that I didn't see for twenty years. But I won't make it. I'm turning back from here. Ah, I was dumb. I didn't realize how big this country is. I must have done up to seven hundred miles. Two weeks' walking, and still in Texas!'

He looked back south over the plain where it rolled down behind a fence, farther than a man could run without resting – and yet, that was not more than a mile away.

'Ah!' he went on. 'This country is too big.'

'It's big,' said the man who owned the camp.

They saw him sitting inside the netting of his porch, smoking at his ease. He was a powerful blond, probably a Swede. He looked at them, stolid, expressionless. The sailor gave him a dollar. The professor took out his wallet.

'Are you a Texan?' asked the professor as the man began to write out a receipt for the sailor.

'No,' said the man, without looking up. 'Chicago. I was a postman there for twenty-five years.'

'Oh, my!' murmured the professor. In his gentle way he was interested, but, as his training had long since put him beyond surprise, he was only mildly curious. However, as he considered the matter, he nodded and said again, 'Oh, my!' (It was as if he had said, 'That is surprising,' and then said, 'That is an interesting fact,' the tone of voice for each 'Oh, my!' had been so entirely different.)

'But,' cried the sailor, 'Chicago is thousands of miles away. It's a big city. Full of streets and people and . . . streets, you know, and . . . people.'

The ex-postman handed him his chit and took the professor's two dollars.

'Yeah,' he said, with interest. 'I remember the streets.'

'Still!' protested the sailor. 'You must want to get back!' Then thinking of what twenty-five years meant, he said : 'Yes – I suppose it was a long time.'

It was raining now, and the rain, as always at night, seemed to be murmuring and muttering to itself as if a vast crowd had suddenly filled the world.

'Still!' protested the sailor again, and then he stopped, thinking that a postman's life was a dull one, or, perhaps, impressed by the complete certitude of the man. 'Well, I suppose so,' he said, and scratched his curly hair.

The English girl raced in, laughing at the rain. She was firm-jawed and fair-haired. Flinging back her damp hair she smiled at them all. She looked down at the camp proprietor and said to her uncle :

'What about supper, uncle?'

'Yes,' he agreed, dreamily. 'Do you know, Helen, that this man has been a postman in Chicago for twenty-five years and he's not a bit lonely here.'

'Really?' cried the girl. 'Aren't you a bit lonely after all the gaiety and the noise and the fun and the excitement?'

'Why should I?' asked the man, leaning back in his rocker and looking from one to the other of the three people standing before him.

'How long are you here?' she asked, her eyes bright and wide, her white teeth showing, her r's very faint, her question put with a typical English mixture of assurance, politeness, kindness, and insolence.

'Twelve years,' he said easily. 'How old are you and where do you come from?'

'Berkshire, in England. I'm twenty-five.'

'Is that a big town?'

'It's not a town. It's a county. I live in Abingdon.'

'Big place?'

'Not very big.'

'Well, would you like to spend the next twenty-five years of your life there, without moving out of it?'

'Perhaps not without moving out of it.'

'I said,' he insisted, 'without moving out of it. If you got the chance, at the end of twenty-five years, of changing to some little place like this – in England – wouldn't you take it?'

'I don't think so, at all,' she said with assurance. 'For one thing I should miss my relatives. Didn't you when you left Chicago?'

'Young woman,' he said, 'in twenty-five years' time you won't have any relatives.'

She was going to say something, but instead she gave a little scream as the porch was illuminated by the lightning. They all looked out in time to see the *mesa* rise up and out of the darkness, and at the same instant the rumble broke, swelled, cracked. Iron doors were opening and shutting inside the mountain.

'Besides, I have friends here,' said the postman.

The girl stared at him unbelievingly, thinking of the vast distance between her and the sea, of the dull, wide boiling stretches of Arizona, and how the road since they entered Texas had become more and more uninteresting. In the clammy heat she lifted her breasts to breathe.

Then, as if to show that he was indifferent to company, the Swede said, in the same stolid voice:

'There's a café down the village. You'll pass the padre's bungalow on the way, at the turn of the road. You ought to call on him. He'd love to see you. He's a funny little cuss.'

The professor thanked him and they went out. At the porch he invited the lone sailor-man to eat with them and the old man said, 'Sure, that's nice of you,' and they scrambled into the car. Over their cold tea, ham sandwiches, and apple-pie, the professor said:

'Do you know, Helen, this man is walking from Galveston to 'Frisco. He came from Southampton. He's English.'

'Really?' said the girl. 'How nice!'

'Well,' explained the young man, 'I'm not really English. I'm Irish. But here it doesn't mean anything to say you're Irish. So I say I'm English.'

'My goodness,' cried the girl, 'but I always heard the Irish ran America! Isn't that so, uncle?'

'East,' he agreed, 'it would mean something to be Irish. In Texas, not so much. Though there are many fine Irishmen here, too. The man who owns the hotel in Albuquerque is named Murphy. I guess that's Irish enough.' He smiled with his mouth that was not so much a mouth as a loose opening above his neat beard.

'Are you going back to Ireland?' asked the girl.

'I am, that,' said the sailor. 'And,' he said, 'I'm going there now. You see, I wanted to see my brother here – I haven't seen him for twelve years. Then, I had a kind of idea, too, that I wanted to see the Mississippi. That's why I took a boat bound for Galveston. I thought it would be near the Mississippi. Somebody said it was near New Orleans, but you can't get any idea how big this country is until you begin to feel it. So now, I'm turning back from here. And I won't see the Mississippi, and I won't see the brother. Of course, I can always say I saw Texas. But I never wanted to see Texas.'

'And are you walking back to Galveston?' she asked.

'I must get to the coast,' he explained. 'Galveston is the nearest port. Well, I have plenty of time. I'll make it in a month. This country is too damn big. I don't like it. I come from County Cork. I thought that was a big county, but look at this place. Of course, I can always say I saw Texas,' he repeated, 'but I didn't want to see Texas, I wanted to see the Mississippi. And my brother.'

'It is big,' agreed the professor.

'It *is* big,' agreed the sailor warmly. 'It's big, and there's nothing in it. There's the Mississippi, of course. But I won't see the Mississippi, now.'

He laughed and she laughed.

'Yes!' cried the sailor, drawing out the word in a warm tone of approval. 'I'm going *back*. If it takes me a year! It's all in a day's work. Only I'd have liked to see the Mississippi. You see, I have a ferry in Cork, and I take an interest in rivers.'

They finished their meal and looked out at the empty plain. It was dark night, now, and the whole place was saturated and the thunder grunted continually. Their foreheads were damp with sweat.

They went down to the padre's bungalow, then, as the camp-man had suggested. He was sitting in the dark with an old Mexican who left when they came in. He was a very small, fat, jolly little priest, very dirty, without a collar, and his shirt was brown with snuff. He looked as if he washed in oil and then rolled in dust. The room was incredibly untidy but comfortable. With his easy smile and his *pantoufled* air of complete indifference to such things as cleanliness, or order, the little man had clearly rooted himself in that place as a thistle might root itself in a ditch. He was entirely at his ease with his visitors. He greeted them as if he had known them all his life. While he lit a candle the girl asked him about Texas. As he talked of it, he laughed and sighed by turns.

'You understand,' he explained, 'I'm not a Texan. I am French. I can never go back to France, now, because I did not do my period of military training, and I did not go to the war. Even if I could, it is too far.' Then he laughed, almost with pleasure, 'I have plenty to do here. My parish is three hundred square miles. Every Sunday I say three masses in different churches. Some of my people I say mass for only once a month. Some, once in three months. I ride horseback. The roads,' he chuckled, 'aren't there at all.'

He sighed deeply then, and went on :

'I would like to be here fifty years ago. It is all too quiet now.'

'Aren't there snakes and things?' asked the girl.

'Yes, there are snakes.' The padre shook all over with delight. He flung his fat podge of a hand out to the *mesa*. 'Up there. Thousands of them. When I came home in the old days I always shook my rug before I went to bed. Then I looked under the bed. Once there was a snake coiled on the handle of the door. But there are not so many now.'

'What makes it, as you say, quiet?' asked the professor.

'I don't know,' sighed the little priest. 'No bad men nowadays. But in the good days there were many of them. In the time of Billy the Kid. He was a dreadful scoundrel,' he chuckled. 'Of course,' he added quickly, trying hard to be solemn, 'he was a ruffian. He did terrible things. His father was shot by a red-headed man, so he went about shooting every red-headed man he met. Once' – the fat hand waved to the south – 'in a saloon in Estacado, on the Llano, he met a red-headed man. When he came in, everyone got out of the way and the bartender moved the glasses. "You drink with me," said Billy. He was a boy about eighteen. "No," said the red-headed man, "I don't know you." "You drink with me," said Billy. To avoid trouble the red-headed man drinks. When his head is lifted to drink, Billy shoots him, right through the mouth. The glass stuck in the unfortunate man's palate.'

The priest smiled broadly. But then he grew sad to think those wild days were gone.

'What about Indians?' asked the girl.

'Yes,' agreed the padre, and his voice grew cold. 'I have one small *pueblo*. But they are just like children and I let them go their own ways. They have a *kiva*, for instance (you have seen the *kivas* in New Mexico?), and they have their little practices in the *kiva*. I don't know what they do. No one knows what they do. I don't mind,' he smiled benignly. 'They do all sorts of little things. They put food in the coffins when they bury their dead. They are good people. They give no trouble.'

It was clear that he had small interest in these poor, mild Indians.

'Are you a Catholic priest?' asked the sailor with sudden suspicion.

The priest laughed so long at that that they all smiled.

'What else do you think? he cried. 'And what are you? You are not an American?'

Again the sailor talked about his brother, and about the Mississippi, and Galveston, and how big the country was, and how he was turning back in the morning. He spoke sadly. All this talk about strange people and strange doings made him feel more lonely than ever and the night was oppressive and the darkness mysterious.

'An Irishman?' said the fat padre. 'It was an Irishman that shot Billy the Kid. He met him and he just shot him. A dreadful scoundrel!' he chuckled.

'My uncle,' explained the English girl, 'knows all about the other Indian people. We are both back from there. We came by San Francisco.'

The professor nodded.

'Yes,' he said in his mild voice that they could hardly hear. 'Naturally they are wiser and more cultivated than our Indians here – even in the days of Cortez.'

'Them bloody Red Injuns,' said the sailor crossly, 'are savages.

'No, no,' reproved the professor in a whisper. 'They had a very high level of civilization until we white men reduced them to savagery. The race that came from below the Gulf, wandering like that storm that is blowing now over Mexico ...'

They all looked at the curtains blown in on the wind.

'They came up to the Great Lakes. They were, often, a noble people who believed in one God, the Father, and saw in all earthly things a manifestation of His goodness.'

The padre rose and put out the guttering candle.

'God's candles will do,' he smiled, but the room was more musty than ever, and all they could see was the little beard of the professor. The white fire kept fluttering far away. 'You have studied their religion?' asked the padre, wiping his hand on his tail, and the sweat from his forehead, and again wiping his tail.

'Yes,' said the professor. 'For many years. I was for five years in Benares and for five years in Allahabad. I wish I could live there always. Noble poetry . . . noble imagery . . . In Allahabad; where the Jumna and the Ganges join – the holiest spot in the world. You wished' – he turned to where the sailor sat, heavily and silently, in the dark – 'to see the Mississippi. Since I was a boy I wished to see the Ganges. I have gone back there again and again. But now I am old, and I do not think I shall go back again. I shall not see the great festival when the pilgrims gather from as far away as the Himalayas, into the streets of Allahabad. And in the sun, after weeks of fasting and praying, they go down to the sacred river, all white-robed, to bathe . . .'

His voice was a mere breathing and they could hear the tremble in it. They were silent. The rain was silent.

'Never mind,' comforted the little priest innocently, 'if men are good-living, I always say, it doesn't matter what they do.'

Below the maple-trees was a great noise of cicadas, rubbing their thighs in a perpetual whistling, and far away the whiplash of a whip-poor-will. The thunder-pig had gone grunting off to the west.

The girl touched her uncle's arm as if to waken him from a trance.

'We should go to the camp,' she said softly.

The padre did not rise; he just waved his hand to them like a Pope and began to take snuff.

'Back?' said the man from Chicago. 'Did you meet the padre?' The girl said 'Yes,' and he added: 'He's a funny little cuss, isn't he? But he's a grand fist at dominoes.'

The girl and her uncle were gazing at the wind in the maples.

After a while she found herself sitting on the steps of her hut, and when she looked down the line, there was the eye of the sailor's cigarette at his door, and she could hear the ex-postman rocking quietly on his porch. She sat there for a long time, occasionally lifting her whole chest to breathe more easily.

Then she got up and walked down to the young sailor's hut to ask him for a light, and she sat on the step below him and smoked. He smiled down at her and she smiled back. She made him talk about Ireland because she wanted to hear an even slightly familiar voice and speech, and she liked the rough gutturals and the way he said 'I ran' as if it was 'I wron,' and his 'sure' that was so buttery after her uncle's twangy 'sheure.' Actually what he said she hardly knew. She kept lifting her chest. Her throat was heavy and her inside moved. She rose and gave him her hand and said 'Good night.' She wanted him to put his arms around her and crush her. Then shrugging a little – as if at him, and herself – she walked back to her hut.

For a long while they all sat there in silence, three of them smoking, and the postman rocking patiently on his porch. When he stopped, there was nothing. Or nothing that human ears could hear.

Kitty the Wren

I

The first thing the French sailor noticed about Connemara was that
it smelled like a hospital. That was the reek of the turf-smoke, strong
as iodoform.

But other smells were mingled with that smell of the turf-smoke;
and when he leaped ashore and put his hand on a sod from the stack
on the pier – his fingers went into the sod and he dropped it as if it
were dung – those other smells made him straighten his back as if
he had been kicked. He sniffed them, the uncovered seaweed, the
hot summery air from the mountain at evening, the hundred scents
of the little meadows, limed by the sun. He put out his chest, shook
his ear-rings until they danced. He took a deep breath. He felt suddenly that they had put a hole in his stomach. They made him want
something. And what he wanted was a girl.

'Before I meet Kitty the Wren,' the sailor used to say on that
afterwards, 'turf remind me of a hospital. After – a hospital remind
me of turf.'

Down the pier he went, and along the boreen to the pub. Inside,
there were four fishermen, but the French sailor, without hesitation,
selected an old but powerfully built man who was leaning over the
counter, talking to the girl of the house. He greeted the pair of them,
noted with distaste that the girl had a chest as flat as the back of your
hand, and stood the man a pint of porter.

'My name is Peter,' he said, grinning.

'It's a damn good name,' laughed the old man, showing his rotted
teeth. 'For Peter means a rock.'

The sailor smacked his chest, threw his roundy hat into the air,
and laughed so merrily that the old man took a great liking to him.

'And what is your name?' asked Peter.

'My name and surname is Jamesy McCann. But the people all

know me around these parts as Jamesy Dinny John. That,' he explained solemnly, 'is after my father, and my grandfather.'

'Aha! Jamesy Dénijon!' flattered the sailor. 'That is a magnificent name. Have a cigar!'

Then the old man and the girl began to probe the stranger, and he told them so many entertaining lies that by the time the girl had brought a third drink – all paid for by the sailor – the three of them had their arms around one another, enveloped in a fog of cigar-smoke, and the talk was where the sailor wanted it.

'Is she a good girl?' he asked Jamesy Dénijon, winking at the barmaid.

'Is it Mary Con Jo Dubh?' asked the old toper, with his lower lip out in a blister of mockery, his eyes almost lost up under his ancient hat. He leaned down over the sailor's singlet, with one eye cocked up at the girl, who listened in delight, and he said, 'Listen to me, young man. You're inquiring now about a heifer would nuzzle no kish of brogues. It isn't today nor yesterday that one's tail waggled under her mother's belly!'

And while she screamed with laughter, and hammered his old hat with a glass-cloth, he prodded his head upward in imitation of a sucking lamb. Nevertheless, when it was all over, and the old lad was still laughing and sucking his cigar, the sailor persisted.

'But are you a good girl?' he asked her.

'I'd be very bad, now, then' (she tossed her head and flicked his cheek lightly with the cloth), 'if I'm not half as good as whoever you left behind where you last drew anchor.'

He could not catch that, so he tried to chuck her under the chin, and as she stalked away haughtily he cried out after her:

'And, my little one, if you are so good as all that, then I waste the beginning of a good night with you!'

That sealed the friendship between himself and Jamesy, who roared fit to burst, and slapped the counter, and took another pint.

'Jamesy,' sighed the sailor, coming to the point, 'when a man is on the sea he has no wife.'

'The divil a wife, by Jawsus!' croaked Jamesy at the top of his palate, 'but you're betther off not to be breaking your melt keeping time with them.'

'Jamesy,' coaxed the sailor, after as much polite laughter as he could manage for a joke of which he understood not a word, 'I have a feeling' – putting his lean hand on his stomach – 'that I want my arms to be around a girl.'

'A bad disorder,' commiserated Jamesy, 'but,' looking forward to a grand night of porter, 'we have the right way here to drown it.'

'Jamesy,' appealed the sailor, in exasperation, putting his two hands on his stomach, 'I am certain that many a time you have squeezed a girl under a bush.'

'The divils of hell hoist ye,' roared Jamesy in a rage that eddied at once into high good-humour. 'But maybe I did. I wouldn't say I didn't. I'd say again' it for no man. But, Pether, my lad, my son, my poor boy! There's no Kitty the Wrens in this part of the world.'

The sailor cocked his ear.

'Kitty the Wren? That is a nice girl? Where is she? Why is that her name? Tell me, quickly.'

'Aye!' nodded Jamesy wisely. 'You could hould her in your fist, she's that small. But,' daintily holding the cigar, whose end was by now a bog, horizontally under the sailor's eyes, he began to recite,

> ' "On Saint Stephenses day
> She was caught in the furze,
> Although she be little,
> Her family's great . . ."

That is, if all we hear is true!' With a mighty wink. 'And as tidy, and as nate as a bullfinch, so she is. And living all alone where you wouldn't hear a sound but the stones falling on the mountain.'

'Jamesy,' whispered the sailor, 'where does she live?'

'Away behind Croghan.' Jamesy nodded his hat across the estuary that was already dark as a field. 'Twelve miles away. Behind in the hills.'

It took a great deal of whispering before the sailor found out all he wished to know. When he left the pub he left Jamesy staring down into his glass, whose froth and lees might have been an image of his youth – so deeply did the old man sigh as he stared into them.

2

The French sailor had a bicycle – he had borrowed it from one Jamesy Dinny John in Croghanbeag – and for two hours now he had been cycling over the mountain road. At first he sang. But as the glen grew dark, and the clouds gleaned the light of day, he grew silent. All he could hear was a sheep far up the valley. Still he went on, bumping and swaying. He crossed a railway, so covered with weeds and rust that it looked as if it had not been used for fifty years, and entered another valley. There he got tired of being bumped and walked for miles. Still the last cabin seemed hours ago, and still no sign of the grey rock by the mountain lake, that, so Jamesy said, was 'as near the house as if it fell out of the window.' Instead, he saw nothing around him, or before him, but grey rocks, and grey grass, and bog-pools the colour of porter. He rode on again, trying to avoid the slabs of outcrop, until the light grew so dim that he kept jagging into them. All he could see was black Croghan to his left. All he could hear was a lake clapping the stones, muttering to its froth.

There he met her, driving two spancelled goats whose beards almost touched the ground, and whose hair hung down like sails. He fell off his bicycle, flung it heartily into the ditch, cried out a *Hello!* and tried to see her face.

She was a slight creature, with handsome dark eyes – the only noticeable thing in her face – about forty, very shy but friendly. Her yellow hair thrust out about her in a bush. She walked with a slouch that reminded him of a little dinghy plunging in a fluking sea. He was greatly attracted by that gait of hers, and in anticipation of the fun before him he forgot the glen, the night, the distance from his ship.

'Kitty?' he said.

'Good night, sir,' she said, and she seemed to blush.

'I came to see you,' he smiled.

'To see me, sir? And what is your name, if you please?'

'My name is Peter. Your name is Kitty? I bring you a little present.'

He drew a parcel from his hip-pocket and held it out. She looked at it and at him. She hesitated, with many glancings all over him. At last she said: 'What is the message?'

'It is Jamesy Dénijon. He say to me – "Kitty is a nice girl. If you are lonely, talk to Kitty." '

Even in the dark her face went sullen, as if a cloud had slipped over a moon. Her head drooped away. Suddenly she cried out to the goats and slouched away after them.

'Kitty!' cried the French sailor, hastening after her. 'I am a poor sailor. I am a long time on the ocean. I have traversed the whole mountain, all the long way, to see you!'

She had seemed to him to be childish, undeveloped, in spite of her years, immature; he had thoughts she would be easy game because of that sluttish gait of hers. Quickly, now, he felt the fo'c'sle stove might be all he would have in the heel of the night. She paused on one leg.

'They're making a hare of you in Croghanbeag,' she muttered. 'So go back with yourself. The night is falling.'

A wind came rushing across the lake, bringing a mist out of the dark against his face. He saw her move away. In his mind's eye he saw rain over the mountains, and Jamesy Dénijon laughing loud at him. . . . He threw out his hands before her.

'Twelve miles! You say "Go back." I come over the hills and the valleys. All on an accursed road. On an accursed bicycle. Blessed Virgin! I cannot do it. I am tired out. Oh, my little one, please, I beg you, let me rest a while.'

She looked at him, weakening.

'Let me sit by your fire for a while,' he begged. 'For a little time. All I ask is to rest and talk with you for a little time.' He smiled his best smile, and finished – 'Then I go.'

'All right,' she yielded. 'But then,' she warned sternly, raising one finger, 'you take your road on yourself, sure and certain.'

'Of course!' he assured her. 'What else?'

3

They were sitting by the fire, each holding a cup of goat's milk. She had no tea, she said with a blush. She sat with her knees spread like a man, and held her cup like a man in her fist, and she leaned her elbow on her knee like a man. She pleased him just because she was so like a man, though afterwards he thought she did everything like that merely because her brothers and her father did it in that way.

He coaxed her, casting his line gently lest he should as much as ruffle the quiet moment.

'I'm sure you're never lonely here,' he said.

'Why do you say that?'

'I'm sure you're never lonely. You must have lots of fine lads calling in to give you the time of day.'

She sipped her milk and looked at the glowing turf.

'And living all alone,' he said, drawing out the words seductively.

'Tell me,' she said, 'what things do they be saying about me in Croghanbeag?'

'They say,' the sailor leaned eagerly towards her, 'that you are a fine girl, a lovely girl, warm as a thrush, and that you live alone. That is all. And it is all true.'

'Aren't they the bitter people in Croghanbeag!' she mused. 'And it isn't all true, nor half of it.' Her mournful glance held him. 'I don't live alone.'

He looked over his shoulder to where the firelight edged a few bits of delph on some kind of shapeless dresser. His straw-rope chair creaked as if the angry hand rattling the door from across the lake had shaken the whole cabin. The wind died down.

'But what matter?' she sighed.

In the silence there came from the room, beyond the darkness, a little wail. Hugging her elbow to support her cup-hand she was looking at the stranger with curiosity, forgetting her shyness. She was examining with her eyes his curious dress – the blouse, the round cap, the blue trousers, the canvas shoes.

'That's my brother,' she said. 'He does be here always. He goes out when the wind changes. Then I stay awake the whole night although I go to bed.'

'Where does he go to?' whispered the sailor.

'He goes down to the school. It do be shut, of course; but he has a wish to be there. I always find him there, in the morning, sitting by the wall.'

'Is he . . . is he not well?' whispered the sailor.

'God help us, he's not himself these ten years.' Suddenly she leaned forward to his blouse and began to finger it with pleasure. 'That's a queer yoke of a jacket you have. Where did you get it?'

He wanted to go away. He spoke shortly, not caring if she understood. 'Marseilles.'

'I'd like a blouse of that stuff. Why do you wear them things? – pointing to his ear-rings. 'Show me.'

He took one off and put it in her palm. She turned it over and over, and looking at it forgot him. As she did so, he looked into the heel of the kitchen. She laughed, and it frightened him. She was wagging her head to feel the ear-ring against her cheek.

'Give me the other,' she smiled.

She put that on, too, and because she had no mirror in the house he took out his little pocket-mirror and she looked at herself in it, and kept looking at it, and putting it down, and taking it up.

'You like pretty things?' he said. 'To wear in the village.'

'I never leave the glen.'

'You go to the village?'

'No.'

'But you go there sometimes?'

'No.'

'But for food – you must, sometimes.'

'The brother do go, when he's any way well. Sure, what would we want? There's always the goat's milk and the bit of flour. Times, there doesn't be any flour. But what matter? God is good.'

'Still,' insisted the sailor, 'sometimes you go?' And when she could no longer turn aside his whys and why-nots, she said she had no boots. The sailor's eye fell on a crucifix on the wall, and he said:

'You go to the Holy Mass?'

'I don't.' She hung her head over the mirror. 'And sure a person might as well be an animal if they don't go to Mass. But you're a Protestant, I suppose?'

'I am not. I am a Catholic.'

'You're a liar.'

'But I am a Catholic,' he protested, and, for the first time, saw something like fear creep into her eyes.

'But you couldn't be!' she cried.

'But I am,' he said.

'You came here,' she muttered, 'tonight, with bad things in your head.' He waved his hands at that.

'It's no harm,' he tried, with a last flicker of playfulness, 'to come to see a nice girl.'

As if it climbed up from the bottom of her mind the answer took a long time to come.

'It's no good thing people learn in foreign countries.' Again she delved and said, solemnly, 'It's a mortal sin.'

Thereupon she gave him back the mirror and the rings, one by one. To return the mirror to his pocket he had to take out a folded paper story-book he had been reading. She put out her hand for it.

'I do read too,' she said. 'But I have only one book.'

Leaning forward under the tarred, soot-caked log that was the chimney-tree, she drew, from a clevvy in the wall, a book with black shamrocks printed all over the green cover. It was a school-reader with her name inside, in childish handwriting.

Kitty Canavan,
Carrigadoura National School,
Lochawnaphooka,
Connemara.

'I read that often to myself.' She took the book from him and turning the pages began to chant in a high monotone, with rests after each group of words, just as if she were reciting it in the class-room. ' "The rhineoycayros – is a wild bashte – he would ate – a human being – he is the largest – and the strongest – of all the bashtes – that inhabit the earth." '

'If I ever come back to Ireland, Kitty,' murmured the French sailor, 'I will bring you books to read.'

'Oh, God, do !' she cried. 'Books with pictures.'

'Yes,' promised the sailor, wishing he had all the books in the world to give her at that moment.

'I forgot,' he said, then, bringing out again the little parcel she had refused earlier, 'It is for you.'

She unfolded the paper. It was a pair of slippers, so soft as to be quite useless to her – living as she did. They had furry edges and a design on the instep. Her face grew transparent with delight as she held them in her hands.

'Try them on,' whispered the sailor.

Biting her lip as if she was afraid to speak, she put her foot into the slipper. She arched her foot, and moved it this way and that, and admired it, so utterly a child, that the French sailor leaped up, dug his two fists into his hair, then shook them up to the roof, and sitting down, groaned into his palms.

'Kitty,' he cried, taking her knee, 'I come tomorrow, and I bring you shoes. I bring you clothes. That is Saturday. I bring you all the bloody shoes in Croghanbeag. Then, on Sunday, you go to Mass! It is settled? Yes, it is settled!'

And, after a little while of arguing, it was settled. He said good-bye, kissed her hand and ran out of the door. As he ran, the wail from the room came to him, the wail as of a sick man, and the wind sighed a little when he opened the door, as if it had intended to roar but remained to watch. Indeed, when he had closed the door and was becoming accustomed to the dark, the mountain seemed to be leaning forward over him, and the white mouth of the lake whispering up to him from the shore.

He opened the door again to give her the mirror. She was standing with her dress over her bare knees, gazing at the slippers on her feet. She laughed out.

'I'm looking at them.'

He gave her the mirror, and looked at her and looked at her, and even then he wondered could he coax her, but he knew that all he wanted, now, was to kiss her and hear her laugh. He banged the door and raced down the boreen, where he groped for his bicycle, and rode the twenty miles back to his ship, torn by emotions as dark and twisting as the wind.

It was the first dawn before the bog-myrtle gave way to the old stink of the sea. The clouds were blue-black over the hills.

4

In the afternoon of the Saturday he went to the pub; but as soon as he mentioned the name of Kitty Canavan the barmaid's lanky face grew as cold as the rain spattering the windows.

'Who was blathering to you about Kitty the Wren?' she asked sharply.

'It was Jamesy Dénijon. But I think he told me a lot of lies.'

' 'Twouldn't be much harder for him than to tell the truth.'

'Where does this girl live?' he asked.

'Away back in the hills.'

'With her father and mother?'

'Her father is dead. He wasn't right when he died.'

'Does she never come to the village now?'

'I never saw her. Is there anything you want?' She let her eyes rove over the shelves.

From her he went down to the shop, where he bought three red handkerchiefs that he didn't want. There, beginning to learn the ways of the country, he tacked against the wind towards his question. Yet, even at that, the man's face grew into a knot when her name was spoken.

'Aye!' he said, as if he grudged having to admit that she as much as existed. 'There is such a family.'

'Are they well off?' asked the sailor.

'They were one time,' admitted the man, and stopped dead.

Then, as if in a sudden gush of confidence, he leaned forward with a great show of secrecy.

'There was a class of a dispute about land. And then . . .'

He touched his forehead, and winked, and said no more.

'But this girl? Is she not . . . what do they say here?' – and the sailor fluttered his fingers towards his forehead.

The man beckoned and whispered around the corner of the sailor's ear.

'She's sound enough in the head. But she got into trouble, thereabout ten years ago. There was a child. One of the lads from around this place it was, as a matter of fact. He ran to America. 'Twas then her father, poor man, went wild. He drank himself into a fury and he was missing for three days. They found the body, God help him, in a bog-hole. Ah,' cried the man, reverting to his work at the counter, 'not a nice business at all, no, not nice at all, at all. Women like that,' he muttered, 'should be hunted out of the country.'

A dark wind from Kitty's night-valley might have crept over the sailor, he shivered so violently. He saw he would get no more from this man, so he left him in search of Jamesy Dénijon. But when the old toper saw him he turned away up the road, was lost behind a thorn hedge, and the sailor never saw him thereafter. From that the sailor went, idly, towards the little whitewashed chapel on the hill, and sat there smoking under the lee of the wall, looking out moodily. The hairy clouds brushed the sea with rain until it seemed covered with dust. He cursed aloud.

There the old priest came on him, and they talked for a while, and the old man was so kind and genial that the sailor burst out with:

'Father, do you know a girl called Kitty Canavan?'

The sailor thought he would say, 'Yes, what about her?' Instead the priest stroked his nose with his finger and thumb, and said, slowly:

'Tell me. What do you know about Kitty Canavan?'

The sailor talked so fast that the old priest lifted a fin of a hand.

'One moment. What I want to know is, did you ever meet Kitty Canavan?'

'Yes, I did,' said the sailor. 'I went out to her last night.'

'Why?' asked the priest, and the look that came whenever her name was mentioned darkened his face.

'Because,' cried the sailor with bravado, 'I wanted a woman. But I got nothing for my journey except a sore behind. She said it was a mortal sin.'

The old priest grunted between derision and satisfaction, and looked long at the sailor.

'Tell me, young man,' he said, 'how long is your boat going to be in Croghanbeag?'

'Until the high tide tomorrow morning.'

'And tell me this. What do you propose to do with yourself tonight?'

'I had thought that I would take her a pair of shoes so that she could come to Holy Mass. But – '

'Yes?'

'I think I will get drunk instead.'

There was a long pause.

'I see. Tell me, my child. How drunk do you get when you get drunk?'

The sailor flew into a rage and waved his fist under the priest's nose.

'I get so drunk that I cannot stand,' he shouted. 'I become a dead pig.'

'I see.' Then, patting the young man's shoulder, the priest said, 'You could do worse.'

'But,' shouted the sailor, as the old man began to move away, 'what about Kitty the Wren?'

Half turning, the old priest took the sailor by the arm. He spoke so gently and earnestly that the sailor was impressed.

'Are you a Catholic, my child?'

The sailor shrugged his shoulders and said, 'Yes.'

'Have you talked at all to the people hereabouts – I mean talked about this girl?'

The sailor shrugged again, eloquently.

'My child, I am her priest. Regularly, once a year, I visit this girl. I go to her for my dues – I don't want them – they are a shilling or at most two – but I take them from her. I go every May Day, and she is expecting me, and she is fasting, and I hear her confession, and I give her Holy Communion. I cannot tell you what she confesses to me, but, young man, if you had as little to confess as Kitty the Wren it would be well for you. Yet never once have I asked that girl to come here to Mass, and never once has she asked me about it. The poor girl will never enter this village again.' The old priest looked at the mottled stones of the graveyard as he added: 'And 'tis better that way.'

'She told me,' grumbled the sailor, 'that there is nothing on earth she would like better than to come to Mass.'

'No doubt,' sighed the old priest, as he looked away over the sea. 'But it's the least part of her punishment. Leave her, my child,' he patted, 'to her solitude. It's a lonely glen, but it can be lovely. God, my child, deals with His little creatures in His own way – a more kindly way than our way. Take her from where she is, and . . .'

His eyes roved to the handful of houses that made up Croghanbeag. Then they grew bright and a wickedly merry glint appeared in them.

'My child, if you get tired of Flaherty's liquor, come up to me. We'll make a night of it.'

Tottering, he went away, while the sailor leaned over the stone wall and waited until the mist that was making Croghan invisible damped him. Then he cursed, dreadfully, Jamesy, and the priest, and the barmaid, and Connemara, and he tried to understand why the priest should be so lenient with him and so stern with Kitty, and he ended by cursing the whole of Ireland, lock, stock and barrel, and he went down to the pub, where he drank himself into the darkness of the night – the worst bout of drinking ever seen in Croghanbeag; so that, afterwards, they would say of a man 'he was as drunk as the French sailor.'

He woke when the people were crowding down the hill from Mass on Sunday morning, their faces shining and their clothes as black as the gale that was howling up from the north. The tide was soon at the full. A rain-squall, in the afternoon, veered the wind to the west, and they sailed on it. He sat at the tiller until the sunset was holding up its five fingers to the clouds, and then he went below.

When he looked out again they were veering towards land, but he could see nothing, for dusk, but the water clapping against the prow and a few faint pricks of light along the coast. They came nearer and nearer until they could smell the peat-smoke, and they finally moored in a little harbour that might have been a smaller Croghanbeag. After the supper the sailor sat before the stove crumbling a lump of turf between his hands. The captain joked him, but his replies were growled.

'*Tu vas t'amuser ce soir? Une bonne petite femme?*'

'*Ca n'existe pas dans ce pays.*'

'*Tiens, tiens. Tu le crois?*'

The sailor tore the turf to pieces, and said :

'*Non. 'Ny a pas des filles en Irelande. Mais les hommes. . . . Ce sont des crevasses, des moules, des . . .*'

'*'Ta gueule!*' roared the captain at the filthy words.

With any angry look he beckoned the third man of the crew. They went ashore and left him by the stove, still grinding the little bit of turf into tiny fragments. When they came back, he was lying asleep in his bunk, his face as gentle, his lips as soft as a child's.

My Son Austin

I suppose very few people here now remember poor Father Tom Owens. He left the priesthood in or around 1921, when the Troubles in Ireland were at their height. He told the Bishop he was suffering from nerves and must go away for a rest, and the Bishop, like a decent old skin, gave him twenty quid and told him to go off to London for a month. The truth of the matter was that Father Tom's mother died just about that time. Right enough, he suffered from nerves too, though not so much on account of the shootings and the ambushes and the rest of it as because, simply, he had known for years that he was a square peg in a round hole. He told me himself when I met him in London that his mother had made him become a priest; so that, when she died, he felt it was now or never. He said goodbye to the Bishop – he did not tell His Lordship what he was going to do – and he set out for London, intending never to return. He had about six months of freedom, and then, one morning, he was found dead in bed from heart disease.

All that is another story – the devices he employed to get a lounge-suit; the fibs he told his tailor; how he never did destroy his black trousseau; the time it took him to knot his tie every morning; the way he worried about his investments; above all, the extraordinary ideas he had about women – terrified out of his wits of them. I mention him only because it was from him, and in London, that I gathered the truth about Dinny Fagan and his son Austin.

I had called one morning on Father Tom . . . I must mention that I never could get used to calling him plain Tom. I had known him as Father Tom ever since I was a child, when I used to imitate his earnest, lugubrious, up-and-down way of saying the prayers, running clean up the scale until he spoke with the intake of his breath, and then down the scale again to take in more breath at the very bottom. It had a great effect of piety and impressed every parish he went to.

I had called on Father Tom, then, in his flat on Primrose Hill one morning in June, just as the postman on his second rounds left the house. He greeted me, finished reading the letter, stuck it into his pocket, filled me out two jorums of Irish, and at once began to fiddle nervously with his glass. It was about eleven o'clock in the morning, and the wireless was braying out its music from some wretched cinema organ in Shepherd's Bush. Down the hill a delivery van was jolting quietly from door to door, and the clank of milk-bottles told us that the dairyman was still on his rounds: from time to time we heard his cuckoo cry of Mi-ULK . . . Mi-ULK. Whenever the cinema organ paused, the hum of London rose from the distance like a dust.

'You mentioned ould Dinny Fagan the other night,' said Father Tom suddenly.

'That's right. You said you didn't know much about him.'

'A priest,' said Tom – *Father* Tom (I can't help it!) – 'knows every-thing. And he knows nothing. I have a letter in my pocket, now, that refers to him. You know,' he went on, nervously, 'I was never quite easy in my conscience about that family. I know I did my best for them. But . . .'

While he shook his head and looked out at the sun on the limes I saw old Dinny Fagan. He was just another like Crainquebille, in that lovely story of Anatole France, only, being Irish and Catholic and reared in Kerry in the Black Forties, he was ten times more stupid, and gentle, and shy. When I knew him he was already old, barely able to run his rounds for a city butcher. Under each arm he would have a lump of meat wrapped up in newspaper (which he would sometimes pause to read, lifting the leg of mutton close to his nose). I used to see him, too, every Monday night toddling down the nave at the Holy Family Confraternity, his phiz screwed into a rictus from peering, his face as scrubbed as a butcher's block on a Saturday night, and his fingers trying to unfold his red ribbon and leaden medal from the bit of brown paper in which he kept it clean from week to week. It was, I used to think, the widest, brightest, cleanest ribbon in the church. Sometimes Father Tom, who conducted the Confraternity in his easy, lazy way (reading us, maybe, a bit of Dickens instead of a sermon, and keeping us together more by the way he roared out the hymns and banged his breviary on the pulpit cushion, than by good advice), would stop the old man in his toddling haste and in his hearty way greet him loudly as the oldest member of the Confraternity. But Dinny would look up at him, in fright, and go red, and hurry on, as if he were afraid even of his priest.

'You remember,' Father Tom interrupted me suddenly, 'how he used to come to the Holy Family Confraternity? Well, now, there's a case in point. Would you believe it, I used to hate to see him there? I knew, too well, the kind of family life he had in Harper's Lane. Eight of them living in two rooms – Dinny and his son Austin, and his son Bill, and his daughter-in-law, Bill's wife, and their four children. What with Bill drinking, and the wife drinking, and the pair of them nagging at him, and even beating him, it's no exaggeration to say that the old chap lived the life of the damned in that house from the time his own wife died. And – Godfathers! – the dirt of the place. . . . The only years of peace he had were the last few years of his life, when his son Austin took him away from it all over to the North side of the city. Did you ever talk to Dinny?'

I nodded, and said, 'A few times.'

'Then you know all about him. Because, apart from that home of his, which he was always – poor fellow – trying to keep secret, there was little enough to know. I used to often stop him in the street for a chat, and I'd mention the weather, or politics, or something that happened in Dublin or London, a murder or a procession or something big like the coronation. And he'd know about them, all right, too . . . he'd know they happened, anyway. But he'd mention every single thing, Dublin or Timbuctoo, king or criminal, in exactly the same tone of voice. I don't really believe that he was quite convinced that they existed. You know the feeling you get when you read about witchcraft in the Balkans? That, I imagine, is the way Dinny felt about everything outside his native Cork.

'But . . . if you mentioned his son Austin! The eyes would stop peering, and the voice was as soft as a hand laid on the head. He'd say "My son Austin" the way a man would mention his birthplace. You'd have to listen, then, to all the books on history that Austin had at home in the lane, the maps of old Cork that had been copied from books in the Free Library, the plaster model of the old city, painted "*by hand*," the modellings of flowers and designs, and all the rest of it – for Austin, you know, was a very fine modeller. Dinny would tell you things that never appeared in any books; and never would – some of them; and always it was "So my son Austin tells me," until you could never be sure whether what you heard came from the mind of the son or the mind of the father.

'He'd say, shifting the leg of mutton (God forgive me, I often thought of the dinners we delayed with our old gossiping):

' "Did you ever know, father, that this street, here, Paul Street, has a river flowing underneath it? D'chever know that before? It was a quay, long ago, d'chesee? Ships from all parts of the world used to come up to it. Oh, it was the most famous river in history. And, since by, look!"

'He'd shift the lump of meat to the other arm, then, and begin to list on his fingers.

' "Look, father. Look at all the tradesmen that are in it! There's a cork-maker. There's a frame-maker. There's a boot-maker. A basket-weaver. A tinsmith. A statue-maker, a cabinet-maker, and a wood-carver! And around the corner, there's a farrier . . . and a man makin' vinegar. And," suddenly remembering in huge delight, "bejimininy, there's ould Carey the cooper!"

'And mind you, those tradesmen were there, just as he said, and I had never noticed them for all my years in the parish. Another time he stopped me, and he said without preamble –

' "Father, do you know who was a great man? Aristotle."

' "He was, indeed, Dinny," says I.

' "Do you know who was another great man, father? Plato."

' "So he was, Dinny."

' "Ah, a great man," sighed Dinny. "And my son Austin tells me he's up in the Cork Madhouse, now."

'Another time:

' "Father, I suppose you do be reading a lot at night? I wonder now, could you tell me where I'd get a good lamp cheap. That son of mine is a terror for the books."

'I knew,' added Father Tom, here, 'what books Austin was reading. A priest, as I say, knows everything. Lessing's *Laocoön*, Renan's *Life of Jesus*, the atheistical one. Books from the Rationalist Press, Bob Ingersoll, and such-like.

' "He's a terror for the books," says Dinny, "and the poor boy do be complaining how he can't come out to the Confraternity with me on account of all the study he wants to do. For my son Austin isn't going to be a common plasterer all his life, father."

'And then,' sighed Father Tom, again nervously turning his glass round and round, 'the last touch to the story – the old chap would appear about twice a year with his face all cut and his eye a deep purple. Always he made up some lie about it (and I suppose he'd confess the lie after to me in confession) concealing that foul home-life, the termagant daughter-in-law, the boozing eldest son – concealing what we all knew. Ah, dear! Ah, dear!' said Father Tom. 'And worse later on, when he got too old for the butcher and he was bringing no money at all into the house. Yes,' he sighed, 'yes . . .'

I could see that, to him, that old man babbling out his innocent lies was not merely the contents of one life, but the contents of all human life – a tiny purse of it, with all the coins there, well rubbed, much treasured. And I knew that even if I rebelled for Father Tom, supposed this old babbler a youth, a courtship, a love-making, some-thing more than he seemed ever to have had, it wouldn't make a scrap of difference; because I never could have supposed the old man enough ambition to make either youth, or courtship, an act of his own will, something grabbed by him from life to add to – *to what*?

'Well,' I said, 'that's one subject, anyway, that you seem to know everything about.'

Again he let the sun on the limes outside mesmerize him, staring at them with those fine, sad eyes of his that, once upon a time, made him such a popular priest with the women and children.

'Yes!' he said. 'But take that son Austin! There was a fellow no one ever fathomed! I always said Dinny was a saint. I say, now – though you might think it a strange thing to say – that Austin Fagan was a bit of a saint, too, in his own queer way.'

The mild eyes grew very troubled as he said this, and he had the bothered air of a man who, in acknowledging that there are more worlds than one, acknowledges also that he can never decide which one of them he will choose for himself. Suddenly his eyes cleared as he went on, smiling:

'One good thing that young man did, anyway, for which I'll always be thankful to him – he married Lily Long. In fact, the night we heard it, there were five of us in the presbytery, and we opened a bottle of sherry and the five of us drank his health. For Miss Long, not to put a tooth in it, was the loose lady of the parish, and for years she had us crucified running after her. And we weren't the

only ones who celebrated. The night he proposed to her in public
– yes, in public! – became a legend in the lane, and I suppose it's
still a stock story in the parish.

'I knew it was coming, because Dinny had me worried about it
for weeks beforehand. When I'd see him coming along the street, at
his snail-pace, and his face...'

Father Tom threw up his hand.

'I used to try my best to comfort him; and had he only foreseen
it, it was the best thing ever happened to him; but they had the life
pestered out of him down in Kelleher's pub. They'd say ... A priest
knows everything,' winked Father Tom. 'They'd say, "Well, Dinny,
that's a fine hoult of a daughter-in-law you're going to have,
aw?" Or, "Have she him hooked yet, Dinny-boy; have she him
clammed?" '

(Tom was excellent at the sing-song, slender, Cork accent, and
he trolled it with delight. He must have been a grand priest for the
lanes.)

'Or they'd say: "Have she him out tonight, Dinny-boy? A good
night for the larks in the fields, aw, Dinny?" And poor Dinny, what
between not knowing the half of what they were hinting, and not
daring to ask, and not knowing where to turn for comfort, and
being afraid to go home to the other termagant, would come wandering round to me, his heart as heavy as lead. So he was, one evening,
when the three met in the lane. It was a grand summer's evening
and I was stuck inside on duty listening to the kids howling around
the streets...'

The eyes were lost, once more. In their pupils, Cork ... the slender
finger of Shandon, plumb against the clouds, rising across the river,
exactly in the centre of the canyon lane ... Dusty streets ... The
old crones and the young girls sitting in their doorways on each
side of the passage-way; the girls with their flaxen hair caught into
a wave at the nook of the neck by their shawls...

'The old man saw the two of them coming along the lane, arm-
in-arm. And he began to cry.

' "What's wrong with you, now, da?" says Austin.

'The old man said nothing, only looking down at the ground.

' "Is there somebody tormenting you?" asks the son.

'Still, Dinny couldn't get a word out of himself.

' "Speak up, da!" says Austin.

('My spies told it well,' said Father Tom. ' "At that moment, father dear, didn't Shandon strike the hour and the dead-bell in the chapel begin to toll?")

' "Austin," says Dinny at last. "Who's the girl?"

' "Is it Lily?" says Austin. He was a queer, mocking, cheek-sucking kind of fellow. "Lily is my girl," says he. "She's going to marry me. Aren't you, Lily?"

(' "Father dear, it was the queerest proposal you ever heard. And, father dear, sure if we all begin to laugh, who'd blame us?")

' "Ooh, Austin!" says Dinny. "Not marry!"

' "Come on up home, da," orders the young fellow, at that, "and we'll talk it over."

(' "And when we made for to follow them, father dear, what does he do but turn on us with a look that'd skin you, and says he, as if he was God Almighty – This is our affair, says he, and we intend, says he, to discuss it in private.")

'You know,' chuckled Father Tom, now thoroughly enjoying the story, 'it was like a scene in the French Revolution. There was I, up in the presbytery, and the gossips running in with despatches every five minutes. "Oh, fader, dere'll be holy war in deh lane tonight." And, "Fader, Bill Fagan and deh wife is paralatic." And then, "Fader, he's clammed, he's done, she have him, fader, there's not a winda in the lane but have three heads in it. Fader, fader, poor Dinny is out of his mind – dey're inside in deh house this last two hours and dere's ructions going on with Bill and the missus."

'It was four o'clock in the morning before I was finally called out. There was Dinny, stretched out inside in the house, and he was, indeed, *paralatic*. Everyone was gone home, by then, except Austin and his future wife – a shy, soft, foolish sort of a girl. I gathered that not only was Dinny persuaded into agreeing to the marriage – and agreeing was a good word with a fellow like Austin Fagan who'd have had his will of Satan – but *delighted* with it! For Austin had money saved, and was going to start as a builder himself, and he was willing to take his father with him to a new house. At that point his brother and sister-in-law had raised the ructions; the Guards had been called in; they all, apparently, went down to Kelleher's until Kelleher threw them out at closing-time, and then they took a half-tierce into a stable, and made a night of it.

'What between the excitement and the drinking it was all too much for Dinny, and I was very much afraid it might well be his last night on earth.

'It was the most extraordinary scene I ever saw. There in that room, while I anointed him. The dawn all blue and white, and the blessed candles were lighting, and the girl stood like a beautiful madonna looking out the dirty window at the sky. Austin sat in a corner, reading a book, and by the way he glared at the page, and his two cheeks meeting inside his mouth, I could see he wasn't reading a word of it. I spoke in a whisper, when I spoke at all, for the rest of the Fagans were snoring next door and there wasn't a cackle in the lane. When I went away it was about five in the morning, and there wasn't a window lit but theirs.

'A month later Austin married the girl, and there was very nearly a scandal about that too, because the fellow actually wanted to marry her in a Registry Office . . .'

Father Tom was so cross at the bare memory of it that I had to smile. He saw me and grew red. He waved his hands. I stopped him by patting his knee and saying :

'I'm only teasing you. Go on.'

'You can see, of course,' he expostulated, 'what a scandal it would be for these poor people. In the end I married them myself, and when they were in the sacristy signing the book, Austin says, very sarcastically, "Well, I suppose you expect the usual twenty pounds for this?" "I want nothing whatever," said I, "only to see the pair of you happy. But I think you should pay ten shillings, anyway, to the parish." He looked at me very hard – and he gave me three quid. It was the decent streak in him breaking out in spite of himself. He took his father with him, then, up to the North side of the city, and the old man was in the seventh heaven.

'They had a nice little house, with a yard where Austin put his building materials. Lily turned out quite well – at first, at any rate, when I visited them – and there was Dinny, inside in the spotless little kitchen, sitting beside the fire, gazing into the bars, one palm on his knee rubbing it round and round, and the old cat, inside the fender, washing its puss. One little thing only troubled him. He was too far from the centre parish ever to come to the Confraternity. And also he used to sometimes miss the little things that had meant much to him in the lane – a hole-in-the-wall where he bought his baccy and had a little chat, or the fishermen tarring their nets who'd give him the time of day, and so on and so forth.

'But he wouldn't go back! Many times the other son and his wife invited him – for they felt the disgrace of his being away from them, and once he actually did go there for a week; he left it after two nights, old and infirm as he was, with the drum of his ear broken. After that, so I was told later, he would wake the house, crying out like a little pup, thinking he was shouting: "Don't hit me! Don't hit me!" Austin would have to come in to him and shake him out of the nightmare and he would sink back then breathing relief.

'The years went by. Two, three, four . . . I forgot all about them, and then, suddenly, a message came to me from one of the priests on the North side to come up and do something with the Fagan household, for the sake of the children and the sake of the parish. I went up, and I called into the house on my way, and though there wasn't any great difference there – except that now there were four children, and it's not so easy to keep a house tidy with four small things crawling around it – I very quickly sensed that there was something wrong.

'There was Dinny, sitting by the fire, the hand rubbing the knee as always, but though I could see he was dying to say something to me he never let out a word. I talked, then, to the wife, and at once she began to defend herself . . . It is hard to blame girls of that type. She was a warm-blooded piece, and she liked her bit of gaiety, and on the other side her only anchor was the Church and the priest – and Austin, he derided the Church. Then, too, the building was not going too well. Austin considered himself too good for it, and if a city contractor asked him to come down and do a bit of modelling for him, an acanthus leaf or a trellis of vine-shoots for some wine-merchant's shop, he would drop whatever bit of plastering he had on hand and race away at once. The result is that here and there all over Cork you can still see examples of his work on other men's houses, and not a building, not even a slum cottage, built by himself. As for the children, he simply said two of them weren't his, and he paid no attention to them, and he was never at home any night before twelve or one o'clock. He used to go to the School of Art every night to draw from the model. Nobody there, except one other student, seemed to know him well. That other student was a clever young draughtsman with a queer, twitching, sensitive face.

I remember he had a magnificent profile. They called him The Knight of the Rueful Countenance. Those two used to go home together, and at the bridge they would halt, wet or fine, and stand for hours plastered into the parapet. Once, coming back from a sick-call at two o'clock on a February morning, I passed over the bridge, and there were the two of them, hunched against the wind and rain, talking, their fists in one another's faces. I asked The Knight, after, what on earth the dispute was about.

' "Ha!" he laughed, and he smote his forehead, and his face twitched all over, "the old dispute. Adams or Franchini. We were studying the Georgian stucco-work in the big houses of Cork and Dublin, and it was the 1740's against the 1790's all over again. Fagan is very good on Adams, and his own designs and his own modelling are topping – first-class. It's a crime to have that man plastering houses. But, in Cork, well . . . You know Cork . . ." And The Knight twitched his face and shrugged his shoulders and ate his moustache and then, in sorrow for Fagan, he made a terrible face and nearly tore his ear and walked away, tails flying, hands flung up into the air.'

Father Tom's sorrow expressed itself in a three-step descent of the scale.

'Yes,' he sighed, and he turned off the music. 'Yes,' and the faint clacking of a lawn-mower. 'Yes,' and we heard a fly on the pane. 'And I should have helped Austin. But . . . ah, well . . . I didn't. The thing went its way and 'twas on a Christmas Eve it finished. I went up there, in response to another appeal of the canon's – a hard, frosty morning it was, with the holly piled along the kerb for sale. I came to the old wooden gate just as Shandon blared out the nine o'clock – the old blistered, grey gate, with the half-circle on it – *Austin Fagan*, and the line underneath – *Builder and Contractor*. There was a little crowd of people at the gate watching the milkman hammering at it with his measure.

' "What's wrong here?" said I, and the milkman told me he could get no answer, and some of the neighbours began to tell me how the dog had been wailing all night long, and the hens cackling since dawn.

' "Father," says one old woman – and she whispered it – "I think we'd better burst in that gate, I don't like the look of things at all."

'I borrowed a step-ladder and the milkman climbed in and unbarred the gate. In we went, about ten of us, up the cinder-path; and when we came to the house the blinds were down. We went around the back, and there was the old dog in his kennel, growling at us, and in the hen-run the fowl lined up clucking for food.

' "Father," says the milkman, "look at this."

'I looked in the window and there was Dinny, in the kitchen, sitting by the cold range, his hand motionless on his knee and a suitcase on the floor by his side. Leaning against the case was a little plaster cast of Shandon tower. When we got in, there wasn't a soul in the house, nor a stick of furniture but the chair he was sitting on.'

Father Tom was a man who suffered from blood pressure, and his face was normally like a ripe strawberry. Now he was dirty and grey. I filled him a glass and he took it, shaking.

'But where were they gone to?'

'Somewhere in America. The day before, a van had gone in and come out. That was, no doubt, the furniture. All they left Dinny to take back to the home in the lane was the suitcase – it had a few books of Austin's in it – and the little plaster model. He had taken them. And when they were gone he packed his few little traps, and took the model of Shandon in memory of the great cleverness of his son. Then he sat down for a last warm by the old fire.'

'And went back,' I said, 'to live in the lane . . .'

Father Tom looked at me out of his big, soft dog's eye: a beaten dog. He said:

'The fire was gone cold . . . I buried him on Boxing Day. The only mourner. It was a damn windy day.'

'I know the Cork wind.'

' 'Tis cold.'

'Up from the harbour.'

A Born Genius

Prout Lane (better known as Little Hell) was wrapped in a softly-waving veil of mist and Pat Lenihan, leaning against his doorpost, was staring into it; even as earlier in the afternoon when he had been caught by old Phillips, at the office-window of the vinegar factory, staring down into the darkening marshes.

'Lenihan,' he had raged, 'if I came into this office twenty times a day I'd find you eating your pen with your gob to that window. What the blazes do you be looking at, anyway?'

And shoving up his glasses, he had peered out at the brown evening fog rising through the pollarded willows, mingling as it rose with the barely descending rain. Then he had looked back at Lenihan, and as if slightly in doubt of his clerk's sanity, he had left the room with a low, minatory 'Get on with it.'

Lenihan smiled to himself as he recalled the question. What had he been looking at, indeed, but at his boat – when it would be finished – chugging out between the forts at the harbour mouth, cutting through the waves and the mists over the open sea.

He was clerk to the old vinegar factory – an easy, even a pleasant job. There was not a great deal of work to be done; the factory was on the outskirts of the city, one might almost say in the country, and Phillips, the manager and owner, was easy to get on with. Besides, Lenihan knew he was not a very satisfactory clerk and not every employer would have put up with him. That afternoon incident at the window was typical. There were other times when Phillips had been known to roar up from the yard to the office-window:

'Lenihan, will you stop that blasted singing?'

And the sweet, tenor voice, that like a thrush in full music had been trilling up and down the scales with swollen throat for the last half-hour, would fall silent in the middle of a run. Then old Phillips would sniff through his great red beak of a nose and with a sigh the workmen would take up their shovels or their hods again, and up in his office Lenihan would raise his shoulders as if to bear a sudden weight before he returned with a sigh to his ledgers.

Even the workmen knew he was not a satisfactory clerk. When they came to the office-window on Saturday for the week's pay they might find him sweating with excitement and nervousness over a pile of notes and silver, counting the amounts over and over again, forgetting to which envelope each little pile belonged, making wrong calculations, and finally getting so utterly confused that the men themselves would have to come to his aid before he got it all correct.

In return he occasionally sang for them. If he passed by as they lay resting after the midday meal they would grasp his hands and sleeves and legs and beseech him for a song. They did not care what song he sang – anything so long as they heard him. Not that he always agreed : he would explain that a singer must be very careful of his voice, *so* careful. If he did sing, he would draw himself up, take the key from a tuning-fork, puff out his voice in a little cough, face the marsh, the sluggish stream and the leaning poplars, as if they were an audience, and with as much care as if he were in the greatest theatre in the world, sing for the four or five old workers lying about him, all stained white with magnesia. He would give them *Flow on thou Silent River*, or *The Gypsy's Warning*, which is, he explained, really a song for a contralto, or their favourite, the tenor's part from *The Moon hath raised her Lamp Above* out of Benedict's *Lily of Killarney*. Gently he would sing :

> 'Do not trust him, gentle maiden,
> Gentle maiden, trust him not . . .'

while the men swung their heads in time and winked at one another in delight and admiration.

> 'Over in the green grave yonder,
> Lies the gypsy's only child . . .
> Soon she perished, now she's sleeping,
> In that cold and silent grave. . . .'

When he finished he would go away at once with a little bow and a
military salute, blushing faintly if he overheard their praise as he
went.

'Ah! God!' one would say. 'He have a massive voice.'

'A marvel!' they would reply in unison.

'But, of course,' the first would lean forward to whisper confidentially, 'he's a born genius!'

Only Flyer, his brother, would lean back very stiffly, silent as a
waxwork image. Presently, he knew, they would turn to him for
the latest news of Pat's doings, and then he would tell them – what
matter if they had heard it all fifty times before. Meanwhile he sat
silent, his two hands holding his paunch, his two swivel eyes gazing
sadly into one another.

'Well, Flyer!' they ask at last. 'What is he up to now?'

Before he began Flyer would shake his head mightily by way of
emphasis, as if he were trying to shake his eyes straight or fix his
head down properly into his shoulders.

'Pat,' he whispers very solemnly and oracularly, 'is a marvel!'
Then with a sudden roar he leans forward to them – 'He's after
painting two swans,' he bellows dramatically, 'on deh kitchen win-
das. Wan is facing wan way and d'oder is facing d'oder way. And
I swear to God,' Flyer continues with the gestures of an orator
speaking to thousands, 'I swear to God dis day' – here he looks both
ways to the sky – 'ye'd tink dey'd fly away while ye'd be looking at
'em. And what's more, he's after making a sunny-house outside o'
deh winda, and he have geraniums, and lilies, and posies, and nasturtiums and I dunno what else put growin' dere. So dat so help me
God dis day' – again Flyer implores the sky – 'you'd tink deh swans
was floatin' in a garden! And deh garden was floating in through
deh winda! And dere was no winda! But you all flowers' – here
he swims through the air with his outflung hands – 'and all swans
and all garden . . .'

He never finished his account of anything, his head taken by a
kind of gigantic Vitus's dance and his eyes starting from his head.
He was subnormal, the factory liar. Pat scarcely ever spoke to him,
he was ashamed of him.

The men firmly believed Flyer's tales; wasn't there, at the back
of the drying-shed where the white chunks of magnesia were stacked

on shelves to cake, and had been, for years now, the monument he carved for his sister's grave? It was a huge block of grey vermicular stone which the rains of winter had begun to peel and crumble as if it were plaster. For almost a year he had toiled at it, day and night, in every spare moment, lying on his stomach on the cold stone, kneeling beside it in the clay, getting into all sorts of postures as he hacked away. For that year he never went to a concert or exercised his voice. He worked so hard that old Phillips, seeing him tapping away at the stone during the spare moments of the lunch-hour, used to sniff and say, 'If you worked as hard as that for me, Lenihan, by George, you'd nearly be worth your hire!'

But when it was all ready except the inscription he had spoiled it. He went at his sister's name in a fury of impatience to be finished, working into the night by candlelight, with the bull-frogs croaking below him in the moon-blanched marsh. Then he stared in horror at the result: all the S's and N's were upside down – it read like Russian script. A month later he began at the name again, carving out a horizontal piece to obliterate what he had done. This time, he got all the S's and N's right, but by some accursed fate he forgot everything else, and the name now read,

SUSANNANAN LENINAN.

He never completed his task and the monument now lay – as he said bitterly, like a huge letter-box to Heaven for *Susannanan Leninan* – covered with a sack, forgotten, unfinished behind the drying-sheds. And now, wasn't he making a motor-boat!

*

The veils of mist continued to float in from the sea, as solid as a fog. With a sigh he closed the door and returned to the fire. Summer was ending. He took up a piece of wood-carving that he had begun last winter and with a small gouge he scraped at the vein in a leaf. He had the house to himself – Flyer was boozing in the pub at the end of the lane and his mother was gone to the chapel to her Confraternity. He laid the piece of wood aside and lit a cigarette and hummed a bar or two from a song – Schubert's Serenade. Then he turned to his baby grand piano, and when he had searched for and found the key and shook out the music, he dusted the worn keys with his silk handkerchief.

⁕

2

Directly opposite the narrow mouth of Little Hell, or so it appears to the eye, are the slopes of Montenotte – tonight no more than a crowd of winking lights hanging, like the stars, but in a lower darkness. From where she had stepped on a mound of ruins somewhere behind Prout Lane, Mrs John Delaney looked across at those hundred faint lights of which at least a couple might be the windows of her home and the lamps at her lodge-gates. She could even distinguish the lay of her own road where the lamps curved in a steady series. Far down to the right, too, she could see through the mists another faint line of lights where the river swung out to meet the harbour, and she halted for an extra second to stare into the impenetrable darkness beyond all, from where the wind blew chill about her legs and blew the mist into her eyes and penetrated her furs. It would be hard for her to say which view of the harbour was more familiar to her – from this side of the city, a narrow ribbon of river threading between factory chimneys and the roofs of houses; from her garden, there across the valley, widening and narrowing to river-lochs, the great country-houses scattered deep in trees into which she could almost fling a pebble. For it was not really so long ago since, from a lane-way door not a mile from this lane, she had stood as a young girl looking at this self-same night-view, taking a breath of air after hours of practice at the piano, and at the Jewel Song from *Faust*, and *Absent*, and *Flow on thou Silent River*, and *The Gypsy's Warning*, and all the rest of them, to be allowed to sing one of which was her reward for an hour Oh'ing and Ah'ing at the scales. Leaning against a crumbling wall she hummed to herself :

> 'Do not trust him, gentle maiden,
> Gentle maiden, trust him not . . .
> Soon she perished – '

She pulled herself up suddenly – at this rate she would not get her calls finished by midnight. She saw a solitary lamp ahead of her at the end of a passage and made for it: perhaps Ninety-Two B was at that end of the lane, and for the sixth time she smacked her lips in annoyance at not having had the sense to ask for precise directions, or, at least, to bring some kind of torch.

And yet they were always telling her at the Society that she was their best woman for dispensing charity. Occasionally she wondered why. There were occasions on which she forgot she had been a lane-child herself, or tried to persuade herself that the Society and the lane-people did not know that it was her voice, and the help of the nuns in her school, that had lifted her out of the rut, that it was her voice alone that had opened the way for her into amateur theatricals where she met her husband. It was her one vanity, her one hopeless self-deception. For even if they had not remembered her, the lanes would have seen the mark of their kind in her deep chest, and her strong arms, and her frosty complexion, and her hard lips – her only inheritance from her mother, a woman who had carried a basket of fish on her back around Cork, day after day, for thirty years. That was the real reason why the Society always sent her to the worst lanes; they knew well that the lane-people knew, and would not try to impose on her with a sorrowful tale and a whining voice; that the only weapon left to the poor people was flattery, and that would not succeed with such as her. It was because of that lane-cunning, as strong in her as in them, that she would not knock now at a door to ask the way. It was old wisdom to her – 'What they didn't know didn't trouble them.'

But when she reached the lamp and its light fell on the number to her left, she knew she was utterly lost in this forest of slummery. She was about to walk back the way she had come when suddenly from behind the lighted cabin-window by her shoulder a piano flung out in great strong drops of sound the prelude to an old familiar arrangement of Schubert's Serenade and immediately a fine tenor voice opened the duet, though where the contralto or baritone should reply there was silence except for the gently throbbing beat of the accompaniment. Her heart beat faster than the time of the music as in one of these half-silences she knocked at that door. The music halted and the door opened. Because the light was strong behind him she could not see Lenihan's face.

'Can you tell me,' she said, 'where I can find number Ninety-Two B?'

At the first word she recognized the voice.

'Yes, of course. But I'm afraid you won't find it yourself. Wait one minute,' he said, diving back into the kitchen, 'and I'll get my hat and show you.'

She lowered her head to step down into the earthen-floored cabin. She saw the baby grand, almost as long as the whole room; it was grey with a layer of dust and coal-ash. A smoke-darkened plaster-cast of an angel hung over the wide, low grate. Pieces of wood shaped like monstrous bones leaned in a corner – the ribs of his boat. When he turned she gave him one quick look, and he, caught by the full shock of surprise, cried out:

'Trixie Flynn!'

'Pat Lenihan!' she reproached. 'Why did you never come to see me and welcome me home?'

Her voice was deep, rich, pouting.

'I couldn't, Trixie. I couldn't somehow. What brings you here at this hour of the night?'

'The Saint Vincent de Pauls sent me. Mrs Cahill in Ninety-Two B is sick.'

She had recovered completely from her surprise and she arranged her hair as she looked at him from under her eyebrows.

'Sit down!' he said.

His voice was shaking and he shut the door and leaned against it.

'The old favourite,' she said, looking at the score on the piano.

'I haven't sung for nearly a year and a half,' he said.

'Why?'

'I'm making a boat,' he murmured, almost as if he were a child caught wrong-doing.

'A boat!'

She was shocked.

'Pat Lenihan! A boat! And you with your voice!'

'Ah!' he cried miserably. 'It's all very well for you, Trixie. You caught the tide. You've been to Paris and Milan. I read about your concert last March, below in the Opera House.'

She grimaced with lips and eyebrows and shrugged her shoulders in disdain.

'*Un rien.* A bagatelle.'

'And you got married, too,' he whispered.

'Aha!' she trilled. 'I often thought we'd get together, Pat. But, *chi lo sa?*'

His lips twitched and his eyes strayed to a photograph on the piano. She went over to it, and he followed. There she, as a buxom Marguerite, knelt and looked up at Lenihan in the tights and doublet of Faust.

'And you've been singing in Manchester and Liverpool,' he said, looking at her as she looked at the photograph.

'It's my wonderful year,' she laughed. 'Back from Milan! Married! Several recitals! But' – she pouted again in a deep, said voice – 'you never came to see *ta petite* Marguerite!'

'See what?' asked Lenihan.

'Me!' she pouted, swaying before him.

'Oh! You don't want me now,' cried Lenihan.

He slammed down the lid of the piano. The wires vibrated.

'I'll never sing another song!' he declared.

She was about to argue with him, but he interrupted her savagely.

'What's the use?' he cried. 'Who hears me? And if they did, what difference would it make? Who could tell in this hole of a city whether I was good or bad? I suppose if the truth were known I wouldn't be taken in the chorus of a travelling Moody-Manners.'

'I heard you outside the window,' she said. 'You were in good voice.'

'I'm not. I couldn't be. I haven't practised for eighteen months. It's all a lot of damned tomfoolery. Look at all the hours I've wasted – the nights. And what good did it do me? I know I have a voice. But it isn't a great voice. I never even got as much as a penny out of it. Not that I want it. Of course the Opera House is a bagatelle to you, as you call it. What are we here but a lot of country boys playing at amateur operatics?'

'Why don't you sing in a choir, Pat?' she asked. 'You'd make some money that way.'

'A choir!'

His voice was like the sour beer that stank in the vinegar factory.

'And what would I sing in a choir?'

Through his nose he began to intone horribly :

'Tantum ergo
Sacramentum

                              Novo cedat
                              Ritui . . .'

'Stop, Pat!'

They were silent for a minute or two.

'I want to sing my old part in that serenade, Pat,' she said gently.

'No.'

'Please, Pat!'

'No! No! No!'

She went to the piano and, leaving a wave of scent in the air as she swished by him, began to turn the music with the ample gestures of a *prima donna*. As she sat, and with her white fingers plucked out the modulated sounds, the music seemed to mingle sweetly with the scent. She saw, looking over her shoulder at him, that he was wavering.

'Have you never been to any of my concerts, Pat?'

He shook his head. She flung out a few notes like a blackbird full of pride in its song.

'Come on, Pat!' She smiled at him again.

He flung his mood aside and stood by her, his hands clasped tremblingly across his chest, his eyes lost in the dark corner of the room. They began:

              'Leise flehen meine Lieder
                Durch die Nacht zu dir,
            In die stillen Hain hernieder,
                Liebchen komm zu mir' . . .

Her rich, finely trained voice poured into the room and out of it through the lanes. Responding to it his body swayed to and fro as he drew up from his chest the most powerful volume of song he could command. Once where she had a bar or two to sing alone he glanced down at her. Her great bosom, too, rose to the notes, and it was white and suède-smooth in the lamplight. Looking at her, he almost missed a note. He sang with an almost uncontrolled passion the remainder of the song.

When it was finished he fell into a chair by the piano and covered his eyes with his hands.

'My God!' he said. 'What a voice! What a marvellous voice!'

He thought he caught the vibration of triumph and pity in her throat as she said:

'Pat! You really have a very nice voice.'

Outside the window, in spite of the rain, they suddenly heard a chattering group of men, women, and children, trying to peep through the window-slits and the key-hole. He was glad of the interruption and, jerking his head, he led her to the back-door and across the yard to another lane.

'Come and see me, Pat!' she said. He did not reply. From time to time she said, 'Isn't it wet?' Or, 'Mind this hole!' But still he did not reply. At the door of Ninety-Two B, she said again :

'Won't you come to see me? Ah! *S'il vous plaît? Mon cher* Pat? *Mon petit Pat?*'

'Yes, yes, yes,' he said shortly. 'I'll come. Maybe. Good night, Trixie.'

'Au revoir, *mon petit* Pat.'

The light of the cabin windows fell on him at intervals, as he went. Then the mist and the dark covered him from her sight.

3

To her surprise, when she heard from him, three months later just before the Christmas holidays, he was in New York. It was a picture postcard of the New York Philharmonic Orchestra with his address and two sentences :

> *Having a grand time. Richard Trübner has taken me in hand and has great hopes of me. Pat.*

With the cunning of the born guttersnipe she went at once to Little Hell on two or three entirely superfluous calls and at each house she said when leaving – 'I hear you've lost Mr Lenihan from the lane.'

Before she left the slum she had heard more about him than he would ever have written to her in a hundred letters, and as she was driven back to Montenotte she smiled to think how neatly everything she had heard fitted in with all her previous knowledge of Pat Lenihan – his silence about himself, his poverty, the strain of bitterness and irreligion in him. He had never told her, for example, that he lived in Prout Lane or that he had for years supported his mother and sister. And she recalled, suddenly, how when five years before they were meeting frequently for some amateur operetta he had told her of the monument he was going to carve for his sister's grave. She had said, probing inquisitively :

'And you'll put your father's name on it, too, of course?'

'No! I will not,' he had snapped back, and, flushing, walked away. Well! Here was the secret out at last.

'Ah, sure, Mrs Delaney,' they had said to her in Prout Lane. 'That boy could do any mortal thing he liked. D'ye see his house? 'Twould take the sight of your eyes, Mrs Delaney. It's massive. Oh, sure, his father will make a Cruso out of him. The two of ye will charm Cork.'

She had to halt their flattery several times. She wanted to hear about Pat Lenihan.

'His father? 'Nt ye know? Fifteen years ago – No! I'm tellin' a lie – twelve years ago his fader ran away from his mother to America. He left her with five children, the blackguard. Three of 'em died since. Susie was the last to go. An' all this time the father is sending for the boy. His mother says, an' Flyer says – but you wouldn't mind Flyer – his mother says the father is rotten with money. But the blackguard never sent a penny since the day he left. Oh, Pat's future is cut out for him. Sure he's a genius. He'd charm the married women. And' – with a burst of hypocritical and delighted laughter – 'sure you'd charm the married men, Mrs Delaney!'

She envied him. She was to have her first child in the spring and her singing days, she felt, were nearly done. For all her promise of triumphant nights and audiences applauding in the gloom across the footlights, she was falling into the routine of a little tawdry provincial city. From this on the most she could hope for would be an occasional recital in Cork, with more frequent gratis appearances at charity concerts to help her husband to get contracts for churches or convent buildings or for hospitals or schools managed by religious. She did not reply to the postcard.

4

New York was wine to Pat Lenihan, and because it was under snow the silence of it filled into his heart. All he could hear above the perpetual whistling of the chains on the automobiles, and the muffled honk of their horns, was the long sad squawk of a train-siren cleaving the frozen air, and the low tolling of a bell where an engine drew its load through Manhattan, somewhere to the north. The air was cold, exhilarating and pure. A few last gentle flakes were added to those clotting the trees in the Park, and the low sun, a burning moon, blazed on every twig. The tall, tapering buildings, dim and pale, glittered with their own thousand lights as they rose through the sky.

He was driving in a taxi, back from his singing-lesson, to his room in a little down-town Theological Seminary on Ninth Avenue and Twenty-First Street. He had laughed to think what they would say in Cork if they heard he was living in such a place. But two weeks after his arrival in New York his father had got him a letter to the Dean, and because it was cheaper and less frigid than a hotel he had stayed there ever since. Not that he saw his father; the introduction was sent to him, and though that was nearly four months ago he was about to meet his father tonight for the first time.

Ever since the tender disappeared into the early-morning mist at Queenstown four months or so ago, leaving him on the liner, he had been filled by that miracle of elation that comes only once in life to every man, that fills him when chance at last opens for him some long-desired road. He had never in all his life been so excited as when he stepped off the boat and looked expectantly around the wharf; for half his dreams had been of the day when his father would return with him, successful and wealthy, to live, reconciled to his mother, in Ireland. But he saw nobody and nobody came to meet him. He was planning to go to his father's business address, the only one he knew, when at the customs desk they handed him a letter in which his father explained that he had been called away suddenly to Cleveland on business and they would see one another in a few weeks' time.

'There is, to be sure,' his father wrote, 'a good deal of money in singing and my Pat must have the best teachers money can buy. Meanwhile you must have a good time.'

The letter mentioned several theatres; one called *Earl Carroll's Vanities* was a 'real bully show.' Lenihan smiled at the Americanese, and because he could not meet his father, went that evening to see something that his father had liked. He came out, unhappy and troubled, his eyes and mind soiled by gaudy images of red and purple curtains and sham marble pillars and naked women. Had he not come by chance on a symphony concert and snatched an hour filled with the thunder and whisper of a Beethoven concerto (it was *The Emperor*) he would have had nothing but an unpleasant memory for his first night in New York, a memory that might have shattered his miracle for ever.

After that he lived his own life and the miraculous elation of hope blossomed once more. After another three weeks his father wrote again. He was now in Chicago and in a few weeks they would meet. Meanwhile Pat must begin to study; 'for my Pat must make a name for himself and I'll help my boy to it while I have a dollar left.' Things went on like that for another three months, some of the letters containing large cheques, and still Lenihan had not met his father. By now, too, his mother was writing long letters from Cork, charging him in an agony of fear with hiding something from her, and Lenihan spent a good part of his leisure time writing long letters to both of them. But his master was by now much more hopeful, and even enthusiastic, and Lenihan could already see, a year away, perhaps, the night of his début – the little concert-hall, for it would be a very modest beginning, the accompanist looking to him for the signal, the scattered audience of connoisseurs and critics, and then the notices the following morning in the Press giving him the taste of fame or failure.

It was characteristic of his elation that he found even Ninth Avenue beautiful. And yet, at any rate around Twenty-First Street, it is merely a dirty, paper-strewn cobbled street, darkened and made raucous by an overhead railway. There is the usual Greek fruit-store, the usual wide-windowed restaurant and lunch-counter, white-tiled like a public lavatory at home in Ireland, and with such names as *Charlie's Lunch* or *The Coffee Pot*; an old-clothes shop, a cheap Sicilian haberdasher strayed up from MacDougall Street; there was a *Palmist and Phrenologist*, with big-breasted Polish gypsies always offering themselves in the doorway. The tram-cars raced along the avenue under the thunder of the overhead railway. Only when the snow covers the dirt and the smells and dulls the noise is the place really tolerable. Yet, to Lenihan, it had the charm of a foreign city, the one place that remained indelible in all its details on his memory when he returned to Ireland, that filthy avenue banked in snow, made doubly white by the black girders of the overhead; and side by side for all its length all those vital struggling immigrant homes. That long noisy street remained with him as a poignantly lovely memory, a thing more vital and brutal than he could ever explain.

And it was all the more poignant and bitter when he discovered that for all the four months he was in New York his father had watched him coming out of the archway of the Seminary in the morning and going in, often very late at night, getting no more in return for his patient vigil than the briefest glance at his son's face raised questioningly to the sky, or, after dark, the outline of his son's back under the lamplight.

In the hall, now, by the telephone booth he stood waiting, and though it was twelve years since they had met, and the old man had grown scant-haired and yellow-skinned and hard-mouthed, they recognized each other at once. But they could say nothing but, 'How are you, my son?' and, 'How are you, father?' – looking shyly at each other, smiling and saying nothing, because they had nothing in common they dared talk about.

'Let's go and have a cup of cawfee,' said the father at last, and he took his son by the arm and led him across to the white counter of *Charlie's Lunch*.

In the bright light of the restaurant Lenihan noticed that his father's hands were trembling, and that they were rough with work, and that his suit was odorous of the steam-press.

'You've come from Detroit, father?'

'What?' said the father, taken by surprise.

'You wrote me from Detroit last time, father,' said Lenihan.

'Yeah!'

As the white-hatted curate brought them the coffee the father spoke about Detroit to his son, inventing the names of the streets and the squares and the parks.

' 'Nt you like New Yawrk?' he asked then, and in spite of the succession of nasals his intonation was pure Cork.

'I do, indeed,' said Lenihan. 'It's marvellous!'

The old man began at once in a very fast voice to make his confession to his son, but he went round and round it and he could not approach the actual point. He talked instead in a confused way about America and its customs, about democracy and the liberties of America, about freedom of thought and tolerance and cosmo-politanism, and though Lenihan tried very hard to follow him he could not, and finally he gave it up and, barely listening, merely said, 'Yes,' or 'No,' or 'Indeed?' or 'Do you say so?' He was trying to think how he could get to the point of suggesting to his father that he ought to return to his home and wife in Cork. Suddenly he observed how excited and nervous the old man was, and how his eyes were shifting here and there as his talk grew slower and more deliberate. He felt his father was coming to the point, and he waited for his opportunity, almost trembling himself with hope and expectation.

'Of course,' his father was saying, 'you are a young maan still, Pat. A very young maan. And in Ireland a maan has little chance of meeting with experience. But you are a clever young maan and I hope you have understanding.'

'I hope so, sir,' said Lenihan.

The old man looked at him from eye to eye, and said solemnly and deliberately :

'A maan's married life is sacred to him.'

'Father!' said Lenihan, grasping his father's hand. How rough it was and how it shook as he held it !

'Yes, Pat?'

'Father, come home to my mother.'

With a shock he realized that he had often and often said those words before to his father when he used to meet him as a child, wandering drunk in the streets. His father looked at him. There was silence for a moment and then an overhead train thundered by.

'Pat!' said his father.

'Yes.'

'Pat, I want you to stay here.'

'But you can go home without me,' he was beginning to argue when the old man interrupted him.

'Pat, boy, I'll make a success of you. I'm very fond of you, and I always was. Aren't you my first son, and why shouldn't I? I have a father's love for you, Pat. My boy ! I've done a lot of rotten things, Pat, but you don't hold them against me? You wouldn't hold things out against your old dad?'

A group of men came in and sat at the counter near them.

'Come upstairs, Pat,' said the father, taking his hand.

'Upstairs?' said Lenihan.

'Yes,' said the father, leading him through the shop. 'I know the man here,' he explained.

He was like a hare doubling before the dog. He lied at every hand's turn. Upstairs in the room over the shop the first thing Lenihan saw was a panorama of Queenstown and in surprise he turned to his father.

'Yes, Pat?' faltered the old man.

'Queenstown!' said Lenihan in delight.

'Aye,' smiled his father, still unable to confess.

'How did it get here?'

'Yes, Pat.'

And he laughed with foolish delight, in spite of his nervousness, because at last someone else besides himself was enjoying the old familiar scene.

'Look at the old Deepwater Quay!' said Lenihan. 'And look at Spike! and Haulbowline! Isn't it grand!'

Then he stopped, his eyes wandering to the fireplace over which hung an Irish flag, the old green with the yellow harp, and crossing it an Italian flag, the quartered shield in the white centre. Beneath it on the mantelpiece was a photograph. He went towards it. It was himself and Trixie Flynn as Faust and Marguerite. When he wheeled on his father the old man was looking up at him like a dog about to be kicked or a schoolboy waiting for punishment. But before the confession could come the door was flung open and in raced two lovely little black-haired boys, and after them strode a dark-eyed, big-chested Italian woman.

'Whoo! Pop!' cried the children, leaping up joyously at old Lenihan. 'We been shoppin'!'

And they began to show him their New Year toys until, seeing the stranger, they fell suddenly quiet.

'Anita!' said old Lenihan. 'This is Pat.'

It was plain that he had told her at least some of the truth – how much Lenihan never knew; probably that he was a widower and this was his son. Afterwards it tore Lenihan's heart to think the old man had not been able to keep it secret that he had a son whom he loved. Now, however, as the woman looked at him, searching his face for the face of his mother, Lenihan began to think of Prout Lane, wrapped in its veils of mist, and of his mother, hurrying to the chapel to her Confraternity at night, and he let his eyes fall, and taking his hat he went slowly out of the room. His father raced down the stairs to stop him, persuading and entreating him, step by step, as he insisted on descending to the street.

That night when he had at last got rid of his father Lenihan packed his bag and took the Shore Line midnight to Boston, his taxi racing with whistling chains through the snow-covered avenues, past the great flood-lit towers of the city's buildings, closed for the night, past the theatres he had begun to know so well, dark now and silent, and empty, the shops at rest, the side-walks deserted, into the great station where the foyer was full of light and life, and the waiting line of Pullmans beyond stood silent and dark, ready for its journey, under the sad whistle of the siren and the low tolling of its bell.

He stayed in Boston for the better part of a year, abandoning all his ambitions and hopes. There was no looking out of the office window here, no singing at the lunch-hour for the workmen, no intervals in which he might at his ease exercise his voice. Having saved his fare, and a little more, he returned to Ireland for Christmas.

Not until he was seated in the train from Queenstown to Cork did it occur to him that in those four months in New York his father must have spent on him the best part of his life's savings, that his father was a poor man – that his father probably was truly fond of him. A light snow, rare event in Southern Ireland, was blowing past the carriage windows, and in it he saw Ninth Avenue and the black girders of the overhead and, for the first time, his father's face at the window of *Charlie's Lunch* peering out anxiously to see him leave the Seminary in the morning, peering out at night in the hope of seeing him return, and doing that day after day, week after week, afraid to meet his son, and yet aching to talk with him and maybe persuade him to stay with him for the rest of his life. The old fellow, thought Lenihan, must have gone to a great deal of trouble and humiliation persuading the Dean to allow me to stay at the Seminary; and then he thought of all the devices, all the lies, all the subterfuges his father had employed, and all to no greater result than five minutes' painful argument as they stepped down the stairs of the restaurant-cum-haberdasher's shop in Ninth Avenue; and, afterwards, still more painful because bitter and insulting, the pleading and the quarrelling in the little room of the Theological Seminary over the way. Through the whirling snowflakes, curling about the bare beech-boughs, and melting on the dark drooping laurels and the tattered hedges, he saw only, and now with a sudden but tardy pity, that his father's sin had borne bitter fruit.

The train rolled into the city, over the red bridge into the railway station, and as he stepped from it and saw his mother coming forward in search of him through the crowd, full of joy at the thought that she was about to see her son again – the sorrow of her husband's early desertion long since forgotten – Lenihan realized that he was divided in pity between these two, and that, for being divided, he could never as long as he lived be at ease again with either.

In the old covered car, as they drove into the city, and up the hills again to Prout Lane, Lenihan told his mother the truth about her husband. But when she began to weep for herself and curse her husband with sudden blasphemy, Lenihan found that he had no longer any hate or resentment left in him. After that, when the news spread through the lane, he refused to talk of it with anybody, and if they insisted on upbraiding his father he would merely say 'I pity him sometimes.'

5

All that day a stream of lane-people kept trickling in to welcome the genius home. They had expected a night of jollification, but they were just as pleased with the drama of the weeping mother, Flyer drunken and fractious on the porter intended for the feast, and Pat sitting glum and silent by the fire. His piano he had sold before he went to America, never thinking to need it again; his window-flowers were withered stumps; the fire had taken his wood-carvings one by one, as well as the unfinished portions of his boat that used to lean in the corners of the kitchen.

'Didn't I have a clean kitchen for you, Pat?' his mother wailed. 'And what news you brought me! Look at that lovely red marbled wallpaper we got for you, fourpence a dozen, and Flyer to put it up for you with his own two hands. Oh! What a home-coming!' she wailed at each new comforting gossip, until at last he drove out of the house and down to the river's edge to look at the skeleton of his boat, and to look, in the dusk, at the marshes of the vinegar factory. Then the only shelter from the night and his loneliness was the dark lights of Montenotte and Trixie Flynn.

It was no pleasure to him to visit her. Earlier in the afternoon he had observed from an old poster that they were now calling her 'Madame Flynn-Delaney, Cork's Own Nightingale,' and as he read it he had groaned aloud, like a man in pain. This rat-eaten place still had, he thought bitterly, as he walked through its tawdry front streets whose finery was only the thickness of a brick, and into its warehouse back streets that looked as if they had been rusting and crumbling for centuries, all the mannerisms and unconscious humour ascribed to it by the sniggering Levers and Prouts and Thackerays of a hundred years ago. With a kind of sour joy he began to roam about the city, trying to keep from visiting Montenotte – O romantic mount of Night! – associating his own misery with the shades of the Spensers and the Warbecks and the Walters – for he refused to ally even his thoughts with the people themselves – the Dukes and Earls and Lords-Lieutenant and Secretaries whose petty glories were the only ones the place had ever seen. Everywhere he went he sought with deliberate malice for the signs of decayed grandeur – streets of Georgian houses full of cheap shops, a puny bridge called after Wellington, a wide street dubbed a Square and given to Nelson, a horse-trough presented to a Berwick, a wretched slum street to the whole House of Hanover, and every sooty, mud-deep quay partitioned off here to a Grenville, or a Wandesford, or a Camden, or a Lancaster, a George, a Charlotte, an Albert. Every exiled down-at-heel sighing for St James's and Pall Mall, with their flea-bitten servants and tarnished finery, had been offered the immortality of their names on the walls of a jakes in this city of exile. But all the time, as if in spite of himself, he approached nearer and nearer to Montenotte. The bored souls of provincial towns are all like that – feeding on one another without pleasure like leeches.

He had been afraid that she would ask him too many questions about his father and his òwn plans. She seemed far more interested in showing him her baby and in telling him about the contract for the new cathedral that all the architects in Cork were trying to wheedle out of the Bishop. Then her husband came in for dinner and with him her sister-in-law and her brother, and they prevailed on Lenihan to stay. It was a good dinner but noisy with cross-talk, and

Delaney bored them with talk about the cathedral – the people who
were manoeuvring for the contract, distant relations of the Bishop
that were being approached by this person and that, the best sites
for the cathedral, the soil, the stone, the style, explaining the advantages of Romanesque with his knife and his napkin and a loaf of
bread, deriding Pugin because he had filled Ireland with plaster
Gothic.

'My God! I'd rather concrete,' he would declare. 'Though concrete
wasn't as popular once as it is now. That's what your Americans' –
to Lenihan – 'did for us. I remember a competition twelve years ago
and I was the first student to suggest a concrete church. "How in
the name of God," said the adjudicator – it was Sir Edward Lutyens
– "how in the name of almighty God," says he, "could that roof
stand?" "Oh, it's concrete, Sir Edward," says I. "Indeed," says Sir
Edward, "an' I suppose the spire is made of cast-iron?" But, you
know,' Delaney went on in spite of the laughter, 'you could have a
concrete roof in a Romanesque church. And it wouldn't be a smaller
church. You'd make in the height what you'd lose in the width; you
could have galleries . . .'

And so on and on Lenihan kept thinking, 'I'm back; back in garrulous, windbag Cork.' And his mind filled with images of New
York and Boston and he ceased to hear Delaney's talk except as the
babble of a stream.

After dinner, whisky and port and coffee were handed around
and there was much sniggering in a corner over a *risqué* French
pictorial. But Lenihan put such a good face on things that he managed to lift out of his mood into a good humour, and while the rain
blown up from the harbour lashed the streaming panes and the fire
crackled with drops falling in the chimney he and Trixie sang a
comical duet from the *Yeomen of the Guard* while Delaney pranced
around the room holding his glass to the ceiling, coming in on the
refrain very flat and out of tune. Then he went off to drive his
guests home and Lenihan and Trixie were left alone, boasting by
the fire in a darkened room, of the great singers they had heard, she
of Melba, and Patti, and Tonnalerre, and Clara Butt, he of Kennerley
Rumford and Caruso and his master Trübner. She began to complain
sadly of her life in Cork and he said he could well believe her.

'I have my child, of course,' she said, 'and I'd die for her. I'd lay
down the last drop of my blood for that child,' she declared with

flashing eyes, and her bosom panted and her voice rose.

The wine was going to both their heads, and Lenihan found himself telling her that her sentiments did her great honour. But then, there was her husband, she said, and her voice fell. There was John gone off to the club now and he wouldn't be back until morning; and she allowed Lenihan to kiss her on the hand. He felt he had never liked her so much as tonight, and as she leaned forward and encouraged him to speak he told her readily all about his father. As he left they halted in the door to hum a bar from the Serenade, and he kissed her hand in goodbye.

Then, as he tramped in a midnight downpour back up to the little sleeping cabins of Prout Lane he felt that he had no right to betray the old man's shame, and late as it was he wrote and posted a letter to his Trixie warning that she had his confidence and imploring her to tell nobody what she had heard. She wrote a long and warm letter in reply saying that she was honoured by his confidence and would respect it. She wrote:

'Don't I understand, Pat, only too well that such things are best kept quiet in a town like this. There are always people trying to dig out your past in Cork. As for your father, have nothing to do with the old devil. You never know what he'd try to make out of this. Leave him severely alone, neither writing to him nor communicating with him in any way...'

Again Lenihan saw his father peering out of *Charlie's Lunch* for that morning and evening glimpse of himself leaving the Seminary, and thinking of it he decided he would never again visit this coarse woman, wandering instead at night, in and out of the back streets, searching always for old names and old memories, sometimes for snatches of accidental beauty where the shadows of a lamp in an archway made a design of glooms, or lights that were more like shadows, or where an empty blank gable-end towered dark over a lane, or a whitewashed cottage shone like snow under its purple roof. What was he, after all, but another like those Sydneys and Coburgs and Adelaides and the rest of them, whoever they were, another exile tortured by empty days and the companionless nights?

In the end he went back to her. After all, they were the only two people in Cork who really knew what singing meant. And when he did go, late one evening, she was so childishly glad to see him, and so unhappy about her husband, that he felt he had been harsh and unkind and readily agreed to sing with her at a forthcoming concert. But it happened that just that night a priest called to bless the house. ('Father Shanahan,' she whispered to Lenihan as he came in, 'the Bishop's secretary;' and, as he went upstairs to pray over the house, 'God forgive me I have my house blessed by half the priests in Cork.) He was a pale-haired saturnine man, with a voice as high-pitched as a girl's, and his eyes were soft with innocence or humility, and immediately he entered the room Trixie began to be charming to him and flirt with him in a loud voice and with much winking. His answers, however, were so awkward that to Lenihan Trixie's talk seemed improper and gross. He pretended to be playing with the baby, leaning over the pram and glaring down at it as if he were about to choke it. Presently he found himself being intrigued into giving a half-promise to sing the *Adeste* with Trixie at the parish choir next Sunday, though it enraged him to see his half-promise passed on at once as if it were a personal gift of Trixie's to the parish. But she was so charming about it that the little priest grew more and more awkward and finally took his leave, and Lenihan, who had disliked priests at all times, preferred to go with him. Yet the following night he was back at her house again. Again she was delighted to see him. After that he took to visiting her regularly. There was no other house open to him.

6

In April he was taken back in the vinegar factory, and little by little the marshes under the office window began to sprout in green patches, and at the lunch-hour he could walk abroad in the fields more and more often under dry skies and broken clouds and work longer and longer in the evenings at his boat. He began to feel less resentful of Cork. The loveliness of the country encroaching on and compensating for the empty town, the promise of long Sundays in summer among the inlets within and without the harbour, where the bright green hills dipped down to the blue sea, and the white line of waves seemed never to move – all this weaned him gradually back to his old self, and the memory of the heavy winter passed from him.

He was in that happy mood one Sunday as he went to sing at a charity matinée with Trixie. She was waiting for him in the corridor and at once she called him aside to her dressing-room. In the artificial light her hair shone – so much bronze wire piled on her head – and her rich bosom displayed generously in her low-cut evening-gown of pink and silver looked as if a touch would reveal that it had a nap on it like a peach or snow-white suède. He took her by her bare, braceleted arm.

'Is it the contract?' he asked eagerly.

'No.'

She was awkward. He felt there was something wrong.

'Pat! They are beginning to talk about us. You mustn't come so often.'

The music of the orchestra rolled up to them as the stage-door was opened and shut.

'Who is talking about us?' he asked, flushing with shame.

'Well! Father Shanahan is dropping hints.'

'Oh!'

'My husband says it's unwise.'

'It's the contract you're thinking of, Trixie.'

'I'm not, Pat. But you know Cork?'

With a sudden impulse of defiance of the mean, tattling city he put his arms around her and kissed her, and she did not resist him, returning his kiss even more warmly than he gave it. It seemed natural to her to kiss him, to hold him in her great maternal arms. A knock on the door called them to their duet and they went down the corridor to the stage whispering to each other to be calm, to be calm. But as on that first night when she came to his house in Prout Lane, they sang the duet in a rivalry of almost wild passion, accelerating the tempo of the melancholy serenade until the accompanist found himself never nearer than a quarter of a bar behind. The audience sensed their emotion in Lenihan's flushed cheeks and in the woman by her high-flung chin and flashing eyes, and sharing in that emotion, several seconds before the song ended, they sent their clamorous, thundering applause up from the gloom beyond the bright encircling footlights. In the wings, Delaney, trembling

for his contract, waited for his wife: he implored her to be careful
– the Bishop was in the house and Shanahan was somewhere on the
stage. But beyond the billowing curtain the applause rose and fell
in wave on wave until they came forward to sing again, choosing
with an almost incredible lack of discretion the love-duet from
The Lily of Killarney. By the prompter's box Father Shanahan
looked on with tightened lips and disapproving eyes as Lenihan rose
breathlessly to:

> 'I come, I come, my heart's delight!
> My heart's delight!
> My heart's delight . . .'

sung so feelingly that when it was over and he reached the side of
the stage he collapsed in a chair. They brought him a glass of water,
and as he sipped it mechanically he saw Delaney come in from the
auditorium, in a fury, and lead his wife to her room, and little
Father Shanahan looking at them with a cold look in his innocent
eyes.

After that painful scene he dared not visit her again, and indeed
she wrote to warn him not to come to her. Fortunately it was
summer and he could now work for long hours in the evenings at
his boat. As he saw it, as it were, come to life under his hands he
became as happy as a woman with child. July came and the trestles
under his boat were deep in buttercups, and as he worked the salmon
leaped up the falls, splashing, bow-bent silver. During those days he
seemed to be tireless, and when the darkness drove him home to his
cabin-kitchen he worked late into the night making cabinets to
exchange with a local firm of furnishers for the timber and the brass
and iron and glass fittings he needed. It was August and a woodbine
trailed its tendrils from the hedges over the flank of his boat. As with
his sister's tombstone he worked in a fever of impatience to be
finished. It was so hot that he had to put a tarpaulin over the keel
and it burned his hand to lean on it. September came and under his
boat the yellow musk, and the wild-arum in its tight wrapping.
October followed and the denuded trees showed the red berry of the
dog-rose, burning like the holly-berry on its branch. It seemed as if
he would not have his boat launched that autumn, but before the
month died he had painted the name on her prow – *The Trickster*;

and dared write to Delaney asking if he and his wife would come to launch his boat.

That Sunday, after singing in the choir, she came, and the boat was lowered down the slip and it breasted the water and floated there in broken ripples of colour. Lenihan rushed forward to thank her, but her husband was impatient to be gone and she would not delay.

All he could say was:

'Thanks. Is he still angry?'

'Yes. He says you lost him that contract.'

'Didn't you get it after all?' he cried.

'No,' she said. 'We heard last night that Cassidy got it.'

But Delaney sounded his horn impatiently and she turned to go.

For a week Lenihan was delighted with his boat. He almost slept in it. He visited it before his work every morning. He raced down at the lunch-hour to see and fondle it. Then the engineers from whom he had ordered the engine told him it would never be of any use to him. He argued with them for hours, but they only shrugged their shoulders at him. The timbers were too far apart and flimsy to bed the engine on them; the stern-post would not bear piercing for the propeller-shaft; the sheer of the quarter made it impossible to lead the shaft through at the proper angle.

As in the case of his sister's tombstone he never went near it again. It lay moored under the alders until marauding boys knocked a hole in it, and sinking half-way in the shallow mud, it grew slimy and green and hulk-like. You can see it there today – for it has out-lived poor Lenihan – but only if you peer closely enough into the fibrous shadows of the bank, where it is almost indistinguishable from the air-searching roots of the trees.

The evening Lenihan discovered that it would never take him out to the misty sea, never nuzzle the swaying flowers that glisten in the carmined inlets of the harbour, it was grey with the first cold rains of November. He stood by his door in Prout Lane, biting his nails, and staring across the dark valley of the Lee at the hanging lights of Montenotte, while the slowly waving mist veiled the moon – a warm haze floated up from the sea, persistent as a fog. Winter had begun again, and again the boredom of the empty days and nights. He could hear the people talking beyond the dividing wall. His mother was gone to the chapel to her Confraternity. Flyer was boozing in the pub at the end of the lane.

Searching for the key of his piano – a second-hand, cheap affair – he wiped the dust from the yellow keys and sat to play the Schubert Serenade. As the worn keys plucked out the drops of sound his voice rose gently to the words. Suddenly he stopped and listened. He rushed to the door and flung it wide. He saw the mist curling about the gas-lamp overhead and the lighted cabin-windows as they vanished down the winding lane. Slowly he closed the door and returned to his song. The voices in the next house had fallen silent: his fingers drew the notes in slow procession.

> 'Lass auch dir die Brust bewegen,
> Liebchen höre mich,
> Bebend harr' ich dir entgegen,
> Komm, beglücke mich . . .'

He could not finish. Was that a tapping at the door?

Sullivan's Trousers

I

When I first came to know poor Roger Sullivan he had the reputation and the face of a jolly man. He travelled for cured pigs' heads and he had a face like a pig's head, only his face was red, and a pig's face, when cured, is pale, and nothing would cure Sullivan's face but a régime that he could not have borne : he loved his drop.

It is the misfortune of fat people, with red faces, and a quick tongue, that nobody takes them seriously. But during the troubled times in Ireland it was a useful misfortune to Roger. Nobody on earth could have suspected that men 'on the run' used Roger's house even in the toughest times; that he had secreted guns for them, carried messages for them, collected money for them, guarded, at one time, under the floor of his bedroom, as much as ten thousand pounds in gold coins.

But time came when it was a misfortune to be a traveller for pigs' heads. There was only one thing worse than pigs' heads that he could have peddled, and that was English boots, clothes, furniture or anything else forbidden entry into the country. It meant that he saw revolutionary politics in terms of hard-cash. And this, in a country which was gone mad on them, was aggravating to himself, and more aggravating to the patriots he tried to persuade to his point of view.

'But,' Roger would argue, 'the trade of the country-shops is being ruined. There's no credit. There's no buying. . . .'

'Credit,' they would reply, 'is a fetish. People will buy what they need. They can do without what they don't buy.'

'But there's no money in circulation,' Roger would cry.

'Money,' they would say, 'is a fetish. Values are correcting themselves at last.'

'But I can't get my debts in,' Roger would shout. 'I can't pay my own creditors.'

'Debts,' they would point out, 'are a fetish. You cannot collect your debts. Well, what of it? This man, from whom you cannot collect your debts, cannot collect his debts from some other man who cannot collect his debts from another man who cannot collect HIS debts from you. You see, it all adjusts itself quite easily in time. Let us all wipe out our debts and begin again on a cash basis. Nobody will really suffer.'

At that stage – and such arguments were as common as sunrise – Sullivan would become sarcastic and the bitter side of him come out.

'I see,' he would say. 'Well, *you* will begin, no doubt. You are owed a month's wages by your employer. If we decide to consider all debts wiped out, will you forgo the wages of that month?'

Blandly they would agree.

'Why not? My grocer will also agree to forgive my debts. It could easily be done.'

'And then you will not allow your employers to go into debt with you again? Eh? And if a trader orders a hundred pigs' heads from me he will pay cash? Eh? And if a miller orders four hundred tons of wheat from the Argentine, will you tell me when will he pay, and where will he pay, and at what rate will he pay? Eh?'

'My dear chap,' they would smile, 'we shan't import any wheat. And as to the price of it – the Government will control all that. I don't think,' they might add gently, 'that you have quite thought it out.'

'And what about the stuff you export?' Roger would say between cold terror that the world was going mad and rage that was threatening to drive himself mad.

'Pooh! We shan't have any exports. We shall be absolutely self-contained.'

'I see,' Roger would whisper. 'And by that time I suppose we'll all be drinking spring-water for tea, and reading the newspapers of twenty years back for news. Yes. Perhaps I haven't thought it all out. It will be a very interesting country. Very. Hahahahahaha!'

And off he would go in a perfect whirl of laughter that was so acid and so rancid and so scornful that they would turn red with irritation and declare the fellow was a danger to the State and should (like all debts) be 'wiped out',

2

Finally, after twenty years of selling pigs' heads, Roger found he could sell no more. Why that was so nobody could tell. There were no more Danish pigs or Russian pigs or Chinese pigs, and the price of bacon went up, and yet the farmers couldn't sell their pigs and began to eat them. Everybody said that was sensible except Roger. However, he gave up selling pigs to the towns and began to sell seeds to the farmers, and for a while that worked just as well. But then the farmers stopped buying seeds, also. They were now so poor that they garnered their own seeds. And everybody pointed out how sensible that was, too.

'Imagine the folly of the old system,' they said. 'A farmer goes into the town to buy what's growing on his own land! Towns are clearly a fetish. The land is the only reality.'

'It may be,' Roger would cry. 'But where am I? I'll tell you where I am. I'm up the bloody spout.'

And he would think of his wife and child at home living on what their relations could give them and go mad with rage. He came to cursing the Government and the shopkeepers joined him in his cursing and enjoyed themselves immensely. But it meant that Roger would find himself outside their doors just as poor as when he went in.

He now looked what he was becoming, a dangerous man. He would start an argument in the best possible humour, trying to get to the bottom of the new economics – for he was a serious man, and he had a real interest in his country – and he would end by tearing open his coat and crying :

'Me shirt is made in Ireland. Me vest is made in Ireland. The hair on me chest is like catgut from Irish whisky. Me very skin is made out of Irish food. But do ye know what it is? I'm turning to hate the bloody country and all in it. As for this so-and-so Government, and its so-and-so president, and its so-and-so ministry, well, be heavens, my, you, oh!, then, I, ah! . . . Oh!' he would groan, 'if Roger Sullivan was only God Almighty for five minutes!'

And then – after one of his worst quarrels . . .

3

I remember the quarrel well – on the journey to Limerick. I got in at the Junction and the carriage was already steaming with argument. Every place was full and they all with faces as long as a wet week. It was a dismal journey and a dismal day and a dismal argument. Roger was in one corner and he was talking to a black-faced man diagonally across from him – old Phil McCarthy, who travelled for Irish beer.

'Dev's New Economic Policy,' says the black-faced commercial – in the most melancholy voice imaginable, 'is a Christian policy.'

'Primitive Christian,' snaps Roger. 'The sort they had in the Libyan desert.'

'And what's wrong with the Libyan desert?' challenged the melancholy man, almost with fire. 'I suppose a man could be happy in the Libyan desert too?'

'You'd be happy there, I suppose,' said Roger to McCarthy, 'selling your Irish beer? Bloody stuff that'd take the paint off a door. But would I be happy there trying to sell me canary-seed?'

'Ah, no!' said the melancholy man with the suavity of one of the saved. 'Under Dev's policy you wouldn't be selling canary-seed. After all, canaries are a fetish. For instance, now, during the War I had a cousin in Liverpool who had three parrots. And for patriotic reasons do you know what she did with them?'

What Roger said she did with them is not printable.

'She did not,' said the melancholy McCarthy. 'She killed them and ate them. And they were dear to her. And in that way she was able to save quite a few shillings on seed every year. Now, why haven't we that spirit? Our forefathers,' he wagged his lean finger solemnly, 'were happy, and they had no canaries. They had no parrots. They lived simply and they were happy.'

'Happy-me-arm,' roars Roger. 'Living on rotten potatoes in 'forty-seven?'

'That,' said the sad man with a mild reproof of his finger, 'was due to English policy. We exported our corn while we were starving. But under Dev's New Economic Policy we'd export nothing.'

With fury and contempt Roger jumped up and down on his seat.

'In the first place,' he cried, 'if we export nothing we can import nothing. We can have no machinery. In the second place, if we begin to manufacture machinery the price of every machine-made product would go up like a rocket. In the third place we couldn't manufacture machinery. In the fourth place we'd be living in a state of barbarism. We'd have no motor-cars, no motor-buses, no lorries, no trains, no aeroplanes, no big guns, no fountain-pens, no watches, no safety-pins, no nothing. Isn't that right?' he implored the whole carriage-load of commercials.

All those who were travelling for safety-pins or watches or the like hummed a cautious agreement.

'What need have we,' asked the beer-man pityingly, 'for these things? Our forefathers had no buses, and they were happy. If I were the President I'd pass a law forbidding the use of all motor-vehicles. Why can't we use horses? Look at the help that would immediately give to the horse-breeding industry. Take yourself, for example. You'd be far better off riding a horse than travelling in this stuffy train. And what do we want with safety-pins? Our fore-fathers had no safety-pins, and oh!' he groaned with his eyes to heaven and in a rising wail, 'they were good and they were happy . . .'

'You can't get on without watches!' shouted Roger in despair.

'Our forefathers,' said the commercial traveller.

'Your forefathers-me-arm!' howled Roger.

'I remember,' said the beer-man . . .

'Ah, yes, and I remember,' said Roger. . . .

'I remember,' said McCarthy, unperturbed, 'my own poor mother to say, I think it's dinner-time, children, because the sun is on the dresser. And she was a good and holy woman who . . .'

'Begobs,' gritted Roger, 'then it's kind son for her. What we'll be saying now is the sun is on the dresser, children, but there's nothing on the table. Oh, yes! Oh, yes! I know the sort of Ireland ye want. We'll all be going around living in beehive huts and wearing kilts and having our newspapers like the Book of Kells on goatskin. Yah! Do you know what I'd do with that sort of country? I'd run out of it to the Isle of Man.'

'I am informed,' said McCarthy with a joyous misery, 'that last summer twelve people committed suicide in the Isle of Man. You see – they're not happy. They don't lead the simple life. They live like pagans and they die like pagans.'

The whole carriage murmured approval at that and looked sadly at Roger as at a pagan already doomed to die.

'Pagans my so-and-so!' said Roger, and he went out to the corridor lest he should say worse, while they all looked pityingly after him.

'That man,' said the beer-traveller, 'is a danger to the country.'

'As a matter of fact,' whispered McCarthy to the carriage, 'I heard the man is being watched by the police, and not for that.'

'As a matter of fact,' said a traveller for school requirements, 'he's in the pay of the British.'

'As a matter of fact,' said the jeweller confidentially – but he said nothing else, only tapped his head.

Three days after he did go mad. We were travelling back from Limerick for the weekend on the morning train, and when the train halted at Mallow who should we see on the platform but Roger, and he dressed in kilts, with a feather out of his bonnet and a big card in his hand – BUY ONLY IRISH GOODS. We hailed him and he got in.

'I was down in Tralee,' he began. 'It's a noble town, but decadent. Oh, quite decadent. The heart of Ireland gone rotten. I thought I'd hear nothing but Irish spoken. Not at all. Anglicized. I ran out of the place in disgust. I went to Dingle. The most westerly town in Europe. Was that Irish? Did they talk Irish? Not a bit of it. Most disheartening. I ran out of that. I went on out to Dunquin. It was a dark night and the breakers were roaring under Slea Head. And the lights of Blasket against the black Atlantic. There I was at home. The O'Suileabháin blood in me boiled with delight. Do ye know what I did? I walked down to the rocks and I took off every stitch I had. I thrun my duds into the sea. They were made in Ireland, but the cut was the cut of Cromwell. Naked I ran to the priest's house and naked I knelt to him and naked made him rechristen me in the tongue of my forefathers. He rose me up and he said – "Ruadhri O'Suileabháin, put on your pants." "Never," says I. "Well," says he, "you'll catch yer death of cold." "Nothing but kilts will I wear from this day on," says I, "if I was to die for it ten times over." '

Well, apparently they searched Dunquin high and low with Roger sitting in his pelt by the fire and the housekeeper peeping through the keyhole, and by the grace of God there was a boy there was a piper in Killarney once and for the sake of decency they gave Roger the suit. He tore the buttons off one by one. 'Our forefathers,' Roger cried, 'had no buttons and neither will I.' He showed them then how to use pieces of twigs for clasps and with that he was prickly with twigs all over him.

'And are you still in seeds?' they asked him in the carriage.

He produced a clay pipe made in Tralee, and filled it with tobacco grown in Millstreet, and lit it with a flint and steel he got in an old curiosity shop in Killarney.

'All commerce,' he explained patiently, 'is a fetish. Our fore-fathers didn't have commercial travellers and they were happy. There is no record of Irish coinage before Elizabeth. It will all adjust itself according to the natural life. This is my last journey in a train,' he apologized, 'and I wouldn't be taking it only I'm in a hurry to bring my wife and child to Sceilg.'

'The Sceilg,' cried McCarthy the beer-man. 'Is it the Sceilg Rock?'

'It is,' said Roger. 'I'm gathering a community of Irishmen who'll be prepared to live the life our forefathers lived. Away with all forms of paganism. Away with trousers. Back to the desert!'

In no time there were all sorts of accounts of Roger's community in every paper in the British Isles, for, naturally, it was better than either a murder or a monster. But of course his wife wouldn't go with him and she had him pestered with priests and policemen trying to persuade him to come home and have sense. However, so far he was breaking no law, and though the Government didn't like it at all because it was bringing their Economic Policy into disrepute, they saw no way to interfere. Then, unfortunately, Roger began to reeve. He and the other lunatics began to go out at night and drive the cattle from the mainland farms down into the sea. That was the end of him. He was arrested and they gave him six months' hard in Mountjoy. After his release he became a familiar figure around Dublin, with his bonnet and his kilts and he living down in the Iveagh House with what pennies people put into his hand for the love of God. And then . . .

4

I remember well the day we heard it. We were travelling up to a Congress of the Commercial Travellers' Benefit Society when McCarthy bought an *Evening Herald* at Ballybrophy and the next thing he was crying out that Poor Roger – as everyone called him now – was dead.

'Is it Roger Sullivan who used to sell pigs' heads?' says we.

'Oh, it is, indeed, the poor lad,' says McCarthy in his miserable voice. 'And he died nobly, too, in the end of all. It appears there was an ambush down in Ballymuggena – a foul attack on the President's car. There by Cooney's pub (sure ye all know it). "And the deceased," he read out, "rushing forward recklessly with outspread hands, faced the attackers. The firing, however, did not cease until the car had passed. The man was then picked up dead. On inquiring at the police-barrack our correspondent was told the matter was well in hand." '

'But is the President safe?' says everybody in one breath; for everybody loved the President.

'Quite safe, thank God.'

'Well, well,' they sighed. 'So there was good stuff in Poor Roger all through.'

'And to think,' says a traveller for ready-mades, 'that it was only under a year ago since we were arguing with him that day on the Limerick train about the New Economic Policy. He was an upright fighter whatever he believed. I had to admire the poor fellow that day the way he stood up for his point against us all.'

' "Imports," says he' – put in the traveller for jewellery, ' "must pay for exports." We can't progress without machinery. I felt the truth of it at the time. But I said nothing.'

'I think,' said the traveller for school requirements, 'that we have a lot to answer for. It was you, now, for example,' he challenged McCarthy, 'that put it into his head to go back to the ways of our forefathers. And have you gone back to the ways of your forefathers yourself? I think he was at his best when he stood for the development of a modern Ireland.'

'Ah, no,' said McCarthy, 'he was at his peak when he put on the kilts at Dunquin. I say here and now, without fear of contradiction, that when Roger Sullivan took off his trousers the course of Irish civilization was changed. It was an historic date. And an historic spot. He was a pioneer.'

'Yes!' protested the jeweller (who was beginning to find it hard to sell even Ingersoll alarm-clocks). 'But why the hell don't you take off your trousers?'

'In time,' defended McCarthy, flushing. 'All in good time. Bit by bit is the keynote of progress. We can agree to differ on his merits. But we can all agree to commemorate him and I propose we do something about it here and now. I am going to move a motion at the Congress that we institute a collection at once to erect a monument on the Rocks of Dunquin showing Roger Sullivan taking off his trousers and casting them into the sea, under it to be written :

HIBERNIA JUGUM ANGLICUM DEPONET.'

'Never,' said the jeweller hotly. 'I'll oppose it. The man's trousers are a symbol. He was right about exports. I believe when he threw his trousers into the sea he was symbolizing the folly of Ireland in abandoning its export trade.'

'Let's have the monument, anyway,' said McCarthy. 'Every comer can interpret it as he wishes.'

'Agreed,' said the jeweller. 'It's a long time, anyway, since anyone had a statue in Ireland.'

Well, the thing was proposed and it was passed, and more than passed, for nothing would do McCarthy but to march four-deep to College Green and have a public demonstration in memory of Roger. At first they did not approve of this. But when McCarthy put in the bit about 'four-deep' he swept the crowd with him. For there isn't an Irishman living who would not march from here to Hong Kong if only he is allowed to do it in military formation.

Of the meeting little is remembered now but its queer ending. McCarthy was in grand oratorical form, and at the critical moment he had just come to the question of the monument.

'And there, a cháirde, near where Grattan points to the future,' he was saying, 'and in the presence of the figures of Goldsmith and Tom Moore, we propose to raise a mighty monolith, to commemorate eternally the moment in which Roger Sullivan on the peak point of the peninsula of Dingle, in the name of Ireland and the future, took down his trousers. Though it's a deed, mind you, I wouldn't, and few of us would, be prepared to do here in College Green. He is to be commemorated not merely for his courage but for his honesty, because he expressed his opinion without rancour or rant – (hear, hear) – because he was a man of independent judgment – (hear, hear) – and because in agreeing to commemorate a man who differed from many of us we erect a monument for ever, also, to the spirit of Irish tolerance. (Cheers.)'

And then McCarthy stopped dead. For there through the excited and cheering crowd he saw coming towards him the furious face of the Man that Died. About his head a neat bandage, and over it a bowler hat, and, worst of all, he was wearing his trousers!

'Ye bloody set of yahoos,' yelled Roger. 'I'll have ye up for libel.'

'What's wrong?' cried the crowd. 'Who's this man? What's this about?'

'It's Roger Sullivan,' shouted McCarthy. 'He's safe. He's with us again. Three cheers for the saviour of his country!'

And the crowd cheered like mad, and McCarthy threw his arms around Roger, and dragged him up on the wagonette, though all he wanted to do, really, was to hide the fact that Roger was wearing trousers like everybody else.

'A speech, a speech, a speech!' howled the mob. 'Tell us about the ambush.'

'Ye Hottentots of Hell!' screamed Roger, and he beside himself with rage. 'There was no ambush. I'll have ye all in jail for this.'

'But you saved the President,' cried McCarthy, and he trying to drape his overcoat around Roger's waist, for he knew that if the crowd saw the trousers the whole lot of them would be killed dead.

'There was no President,' screamed Roger. 'We were just having cockshots at a porter-bottle on the ditch with an airgun. And as for saving the President, do ye think that I'd lift one solitary finger to save a scoundrel that's ruining the country? Do ye know that for wan six months I didn't sell a single package of canary-seed? And for the six months before that I only sold two and a half pigs' heads.'

Then he turned in a fury to McCarthy, who was behind him all this time trying to take down his trousers, unknown to him.

'That policy,' howled Roger to the crowd (and it was clear that whether with the wound, or with all his previous sufferings, he was back to sanity once more), 'that policy is the policy of retrogression. It is a return to barbarism.'

By this time McCarthy had all the buttons open and he was now down on his knees and he pulling like blazes at the legs of Sullivan's pants.

'No, no,' he cried, poking out his head between Roger's legs.

'If you don't balance your exports and imports,' howled Roger –

too excited to take notice – 'you are heading for economic ruin.'

'No, no!' cried McCarthy, who had by now got Sullivan's pants down to his ankles.

'Stop, stop,' cried the crowd. 'This is all wrong. That's not Roger Sullivan. Where's his kilts? His bonnet and feather?'

'Wages,' shouted Roger, hammering the side of the wagonette, 'will fall and prices will rise.'

'Traitor,' shouted the crowd. 'Pull him down. Tear him. That's not Sullivan. That man is a fraud. He's an impostor.'

'He's no impostor,' poked McCarthy, giving Roger a sudden heave, and whipping the trousers off him he waved them in the air.

'Sullivan's trousers!' he cried triumphantly. 'Sullivan's trousers!'

Whereupon the crowd, carried completely away, cheered fit to split the sky. But, unfortunately, at this point some apple-women near the wagonette caught sight of Roger and they screamed out murder when they saw he had no trousers on. And when Roger began again at exports and imports everything went to pieces. The crowd rushed the wagonette. McCarthy shouted to Roger to run. And Roger ran. He broke through the people and bebbled down a side street and off down through the slums near Trinity College, with his shirt-tails flying and the slum-women after him, their hair waving like mænads, the men hurling paving-stones after him, the children screaming with delight at the man's white legs twinkling in the sun, and down from the windows of the brothels the pious prostitutes flung flower-pots at the man without any pants.

A Meeting

Many towns in Ireland, after fifty or sixty years of prosperity, suddenly begin to decay; and 'decay' is the word for it, because they become not so much old as, in literal truth, decayed. Houses fall idle. Then they fall down. The street becomes gapped like an old man's mouth.

Burnt Hall is like that. From being a mere coach-stop on the road to Limerick it suddenly became quite a large town after the Crimea when the English cavalry began to train there. Now, the English cavalry is gone. The barrack (Crimean tent-canvas become stone) is crumbling to pieces. Facing this metamorphosed canvas is a broken line of shops – the sutlers' booths – staring emptily at the mirror of their own future.

I walked down this melancholy street one afternoon this summer. The river was as calm as a dream; it slept among the pebbles of the shore. Fishing was out of the question, so I decided to go for a walk on the bogs, where I heard the hum of a hay machine. Outside one shop (one of the few with any real purpose now) were the usual bundles of hayforks and rakes and spade-handles, tied in lots, all sunburnt. My mind was so idle as I smelled the dinner-bones burning in the cabins, and looked at the loungers extended on the grass under the barrack-wall, that I struck against these farming implements. At the clatter every door became a cuckoo-clock. A man strolled out of the mossy gateway of the barracks and looked at me with suspicion. The loungers actually turned their heads and peeped under their caps that had been shading their faces from the sun. Then I saw a woman staring at me, and I realized that, after twelve years, I was re-meeting Sally Dunn.

When I first knew Sally she was up to her eyes in the Revolution. If there was a dangerous despatch, or a bomb or two, or a gun to be carried through the British patrols, she was the safest girl in Limerick for the job. If there was an important mission to Paris or

America, she was certain to be chosen – the tomboy, the dare-devil, the travelled woman, and the best story-teller I ever met. We used to look up to her, then, as a woman of the world – she was about thirty, older than most of us – so that we always fell silent when she began.

I shall always associate her with her marvellous yarn about her school-days in Paris when, at the age of eighteen, she lost her companions in some big hotel. She took the wrong stairs and found herself suddenly in what must have been a basement *brasserie*, surrounded by red-coated cavalrymen. Her hands would flag as she talked:

'I was flattened, I needn't tell you. Imagine! Only eighteen! I had long golden hair . . .'

'You still have,' somebody would admire.

'Oh, but then it was yards and yards! Down to my knees, girl! They gathered about me. Big men with black moustaches and clanking sabres. They made a circle around me, and they drew their swords and they held them in the air. One of them wound my golden hair around my throat. Then they caught hands, and danced around me. I was limp. Limp!'

Or her story about the Persian princess, told with the most casual reference to Wagons-Lit, the Interlaken and Kandersteg, F. D. trains, the Engadine Express, and 'I said to the gendarme at the frontier' – or, 'Then, at Linz, her maid came in with the coffee' – ending with:

' "*Gar nichts,*" said I, and "*Gar nichts,*" said she. So he went through our things. And the two of us trying to keep looking out the window! He found nothing and he went away and we nearly lost the connection trying to pack at the last moment and dodge out. "Well, anyway," says I to her, "if it hadn't been for your damned old diamonds in the wash basin I could have washed myself." And says she, "If it hadn't been for your stupid papers down my knickers I could have dressed myself." "Pooh to you," says I. "Pooh to you, whatever it is," says she, and I never saw her after. Of course, I don't believe she was a princess at all. And anyway, I'm *sure* she was up to something underhand.'

Even now, as we strolled along the street of Burnt Hall, she talked and talked, and she said she would love to walk with me over the bogs. But first we went to her home; she had married into the little town – her husband was a dentist – and she had three children. It was only when we sat in the front parlour of her little villa (originally built by some English colonel) that I began to feel a lack in her talk. She would drop a subject almost as quickly as she took it up, and race off on a bit of domestic gossip. There were embarrassing pauses.

Once, she went out of the room to appease a crying child, and as I looked about me I felt the same lack. Only on the little book-shelf did I find any memories of the old days – pamphlets from Russia, poems by this rebel leader who was shot in action, and that one who died on a hunger-strike – and even they were down on the lowest shelf behind the armchair. When she ran in to say she was ready she caught me fiddling with them, and she just laughed and lifted her eyes comically to the ceiling, and shook her head a little as if to say . . . I did not know what. I promised myself to find out while we walked in the fields.

The bog was dry as dust and in the heat it trembled like a mirage. For miles and miles it stretched across Ireland, dark purple with heather, and bright with furze. Only a few tattered poplars broke the horizon. There was one little hill – the cone of Cobdur, lonely as a stranded bottle on a beach. The only sign of life was the occasional plume of smoke from a turf-cutter's fire. It was all as quiet as the waters of the shallows back in the village, asleep among the stones. But although it was lovely, not merely old but immemorable, not merely unchanged but unchangeable, it began to weigh heavily on me; and to that feeling, partly of the day, partly of doubt about my friend, was added a sense of other hidden lives when I saw the bog-cabins with the dark water lapping to their doors, just like arks, all sinking back into the mould. We saw a woman inside one door, her eyes as dark as bog-pools, and as patient and as still.

Not, again, that Sally was not full of talk – except for those sudden pauses – and delighted to have somebody to fill with old tales; and I made her tell me again the yarn of the Persian princess, and I tried to rouse her with talk of current politics.

'Aha,' she cried, 'we're still good at heart!'

But then she asked me some question or other that showed me that she had not read a paper for days. She was passionate and angry, too, about the village life, saying that it would drive a saint to sin; but she did not play golf ('an English game'), or play cards ('the women are as silly as geese'); or even go to the annual Point-to-Point that everybody associates with Burnt Hall.

Repeatedly I drew her back and back to the old rebelly days and nights. Once or twice she told a grand story – like that one about the morning she woke up to see a man on the platform at Munich being greeted by an absolutely infuriated woman; simply because on his fur collar was *her* Spanish comb. It had got stuck there when she slept with her head on his shoulder during the journey.

'And you know, I said to myself, I must not lean over that way if I begin to fall asleep. I simply mustn't. And all the time that I was nodding I was keeping myself from that lovely fur collar! But wasn't he a dear to have let me sleep there all the time? For of course he had a private sleeping-compartment of his own – only – The dear! he wouldn't disturb me.'

'How do you know he had?' I asked, sceptically.

'Good Heavens, didn't I tell you who he was? It was only a year after I found it out. I saw his photograph in the papers.'

'Who *was* he, Sally?'

'My child, it was Basil Zaharoff!'

I always did enjoy that story; although the first time she told it to me the man was Fritz Kreisler.

Once or twice, too, she took out her old battle-weapons and, as it were, spat on them saying:

'We're having an auction on Monday at Lady Banks's place in Mount Prospect. That's one of the last of the old gang to leave the country. Thank God for that, anyway.'

'Sally, girl,' I protested, 'don't say you're gone Bolshie?'

There was a pause. She turned and waved her hands wildly, and let them fall.

'I don't know. We are going to have a factory now in the disused barracks. The slum-people have taken over all the living-quarters. And they're turning it into another slum. I don't know. Honest to God, I don't know! I wonder ought we have factories spreading like that all over Ireland? We might end with cities like Manchester or Glasgow? And look at all these vulgar people making money out of it all. It's hard to tell . . . You know, it's . . .' – another pause.

So we talked for an hour, sitting low under one of the high causeway roads, chewing dry rush-stalks. Somehow it was she who seemed to do most of the listening, until I felt like a person giving a transfusion of blood. She was draining me. Life – these few hours of it, anyway – was become like music in the distance, as quiet as the bees wandering near us into the thistle-flowers and the furze. As we walked back our talk was like the dusty smell of the boreens – a musk – hardly a scent, something so faint and slight that it really hardly touched the senses. It was just pleasant, companionable talk – getting its meaning from old memories – nothing more. We might otherwise be strangers.

Then she was suddenly imploring me to meet her again, some day, in Limerick, when we must talk and talk.

'Oh!' she cried. 'We'll talk like the old days. There's so much I want to talk about I can't remember it now. We'll talk until the cows come home! And then talk again until the cocks begin to crow! Won't we?'

'We will!' I laughed. 'Of course we will!'

I knew that if I had met her six or seven years before I could have said:

'Sally, are you really happy here?'

And she would have said:

'Jesus, I'm fed to the bloody eye-teeth with this bloody hole and all in it!'

As we walked to the station a faint, sweet, evening wind came down over Ireland. When I had waved goodbye and was looking back through the window there was already, behind her, a light or two in the little country town, and the bog into which it all sank behind the train was already whispering and dim.

We never met again. I doubt if either of us wanted it or expected it. You cannot have your memories and eat them.

Discord

At the square and low-pitched window of the priest's room high under the eaves and overlooking the city, the two lovers – they had been married only yesterday and were in Dublin for the honeymoon – clutched the window-frame level with their chins and saw the field of roofs. The moving panorama of the sky had blown with it all but the final dusk of smoke. Down in the street a tin-can rolled on the flags with a bright clanking. Behind them Father Peter, his black arm pointing between their heads, led their eyes over the aerial plain.

'That's Saint Michan's with the spire. There's the Protestant Saint Michan's with the square tower.'

Always awkward with the newly-wedded, he had led them straight to the window immediately they entered his room. He now said Pro*test*ant for a joke, hiding his own shyness.

'That?'

To a query of the girl's.

'The Dominican Church. But there now is a very interesting old place, Saint Mary's Abbey. Its real name is Saint Mary's Ostmanby – the East Men, do you see, the Danes. It was a Benedictine church to begin and then the Cistercians took it over. It's all the old Dublin as you know, there in front of us across the river.'

'Girt around by prayer,' said the young man, whose eye picked out the spires and towers all around the horizon.

'And girt around by pubs,' said Father Peter cynically. 'It's wonderful there at night, though, with all the lights. It's like Paris from Montmartre. Those old roofs of that slum-house there between us and the river . . .'

One could have spat down across the narrow street at the humped and twisted dents and downs of the roof-top.

'. . . they're ugly enough with their lumps of plaster between the slates, but you have no idea how lovely they are if there's a fall of snow. Oh, it's very lovely. Last winter there was a heavy fall and those little crevices of roofs were ... Ah!'

They could almost see the whirling gentle fall darkening over Dublin as they heard him gurgle behind them with delight. He was forgetting his shyness. Through the windows of the slum-house they could see three floors and on each floor iron bed-legs. Seeing the poor drabness of it Angela turned away.

'Well, well,' teased the girl as she looked over the cosy room with its big mannish furniture and its low roof, 'who wouldn't be a priest?'

They sat down in the deep armchairs, their minds brought back by her to the present.

'This is the best of it ye're seeing now,' laughed Peter. 'Not that I have such a bad time, mind you.'

'Are you kept very busy, father?' she asked kindly.

'No,' he said, a bit doubtfully; and then, more positively, 'No!' He poked the fire, and leaned back in the capacious settee, and supported his paunch, for it was a cold autumn and he liked his comfort. He lit a cigar and gave them cigarettes, to celebrate the occasion as he said. 'I have two Confraternities, the women's every Monday night, and then the first Sunday of each month I have the Bona Mors. That,' he explained, 'is for the old people. For a happy death. It's mainly the old weak people who come to that, as you might understand.'

The young lovers nodded as if they did understand.

'Then we have a week on and a week off on duty, sick-calls and the like. We share that between us. Day and night. I'm unlucky at that. I seem to get more sick-calls than any other priest.'

'That's because you're so popular, father,' laughed the girl.

'Faith, 'tis not. 'Tis just the way things come. I have one old lad there now in Watling Street and he gets uræmic fits. Even if he had me in twice that day and it was three in the morning he'd have me in again.'

'And you have to go?' asked the youth.

'Oh,' said the priest solemnly, 'you couldn't refuse.'

'Some of them are divils,' commiserated the youth.

'Aha,' teased his girl, 'wait till you're on your bed of death and you'll be howling for a priest like the worst of them.'

'Bedad,' laughed Father Peter, 'a uræmic fit is a pretty bad thing.'

'I suppose,' she said, 'you'd wish sometimes for a little parish down the country?'

'I do,' he agreed eagerly. 'I do. It's good here. And I meet all sorts of people. And it's interesting work. But – ah, you know . . .'

'Still,' said Frank with equal eagerness, 'I envy you. You meet people, you're in contact with life. There's that fear always over me – being isolated – getting away from life – getting wrapped into myself. Everyone living in the country has that feeling sometimes. It's a bit terrifying.'

His eyes wandered to the sea of roofs. His girl looked at him, as if surprised by some cavern in him that she had not seen before and must, maybe, yet explore. She did not guess that in his mind that image of a vast Dublin, growing and decaying, was still dilating like a smoke in wind.

'There's that indeed,' said the priest. 'You must keep on meeting people. But, then, you know, too, here it's always a certain kind of people. Sad stories. Rotten stories. Down-and-out stories. Always the same. Drunks, paupers, prostitutes – ach!'

'You have a lot of books?' said the girl, again drawing their minds back with hers.

'I'm bankrupt from them. But they're a great refuge for me. As you see, I have no room for any more.'

He rolled out of his settee and picked out a volume.

'This *Life of Mangan* reminds me. This room is full of associations. Mangan wrote most of his poetry here: he and Davis and the rest of the writers of *The Nation* used to come here and talk and argue into the dawn. John Mitchel was in this room. That was when the famous Father Meehan – C. P., you remember – lived here. He kept open house for the lot of them. It was called The Attics. They had Attic Nights!'

'Is that a fact?' cried the youth. 'James Clarence Mangan in this room?'

He rose and walked about it excitedly. It would have been just the same then – the low ceiling, the windows crushed under it, the green baize door, the cosy fire, the books from floor to roof, and all that poor, decayed city full of life and fashion and movement and colour. His mind flooded with vague associations of eighteenth- and nineteenth-century Dublin.

'Surely Wolfe Tone was born somewhere hereabouts?' he pointed.

'And Lord Edward Fitzgerald, where did he live?'

His hands seemed to grope with his memory.

'Why, man,' cried Father Peter, 'Thomas Street is just behind us. Emmet had his depot for making bombs a stone's-throw away. They hanged him in the street – you can see Saint Catherine's spire just over the spot from my bedroom window. The street between us and the Castle is Lord Edward Street.'

'Mangan!' said the young man, and he recited, moodily but finely, while his wife looked at him, troubled, and at the priest almost with distrust:

> 'I saw her once, one little while, and then no more:
> 'Twas paradise on earth awhile, and then no more.
> Ah, what avails my vigil pale, my magic lore?
> She shone before mine eyes awhile and then no more.
> The shallop of my peace is wrecked on Beauty's shore.
> Near Hope's fair isle it rode awhile, and then no more . . .'

'He was a fine poet,' said Father Peter, and then, thinking this too melancholy for honeymoon days, he said, 'They had one great night here, I believe, when they had an argument on Shakespeare. Davis was reciting Antony's speech to the mob, "Lend me your ears . . ." "What nonsense," cries Mangan. "That's a misreading. He said, 'Lend me your cars.' Sure, they were going to a funeral." '

They laughed lightly at that, but the fume of memory was still in the young man's brain.

> 'I saw her once, one little while, and then no more;
> The earth was Peri-land awhile, and then no more.
> Oh, might I see but once again as once before,
> Through chance or wile, that shape awhile, and then no more!
> Death soon would heal my griefs! This heart now sad and sore
> Would beat anew a little while, and then no more . . .'

'Aye,' said Father Peter, 'and the O'Hussey's *Ode to the Maguire* is magnificent.'

> 'An awful, a tremendous night is this meseems,
> The floodgates of the rivers of heaven, I think, have been burst
> wide . . .'

The girl had fallen silent. The priest noticed it.

'Come and see the chapel,' he said. 'Or the crypt.'

'What's there to be seen?' asked the girl distrustfully.

'Why,' cried the priest, 'it's most historic. There's maybe a hundred people buried there. Great huge vaults there like wine-cellars. Do you know who's buried there? Leonard MacNally.'

MacNally the spy. The scrubby lawyer who was the friend of the Earl of Clare, the traitor who used to eat his nails and was so dirty the bar-mess would not admit him. The friend of Tone. The friend of Emmet. He had defended him and betrayed him. Not until he was dead did the people discover it. The priest laughed.

'Yes, he's down there. And his coffin falling to pieces. Every time I go down I give it another kick. When he was being brought there I believe the poor of the city crowded the vaults to be sure he wasn't laid near or nigh to one of their own. Come on and let's have a look at the church.'

After descending the long dark stairs and entering the chapel by a side-door they were surprised to find the high altar so marble-white and glittering. As they looked reverently at it a young man with his hands joined and his eyes cast down approached the priest. The lovers moved away, but they heard the man's request; his wife was outside and she wanted her baby to be baptized. Father Peter gruffly told him the name of the priest on duty. In one place an old woman was muttering prayers under her shawl. An old man told his beads under the light of the candles by the Virgin's altar. They were all poor and ragged. Suddenly they saw a wild-bearded, hollow-faced man standing away back in the nave, praying devoutly. His beard was soft but tangled; his hair was to his shoulders; he held his two arms aloft as he prayed; his eyes shone. Curiously they watched him, a little frightened.

'Who is he?' asked the girl of the priest.

'He's daft,' whispered the priest. 'An ex-soldier. He sometimes preaches to the empty church. Come this way.'

'He'd terrify me,' said the girl.

Peter laughed again as he led them down another flight of stairs through an old trap-door.

'You'd go off your nut here if you took too much notice of things. Wait till I light this candle.'

Down they went and the air was close and it was pitch-dark beyond the candle gleam. In that little light they saw the vaults open right and left of the great supporting arches. She took her man's hand as the shapes of the coffins emerged out of the dark. A hanging bit of rusted wire caught in her hair and she gave a little scream.

'That's a bit of wire,' said the priest cheerfully.

Two eyes of light from the street-level stared at them.

'Do you see those holes?' he said, and they were all stooping. 'The cats come in there from the street.'

Before them the wall under the high altar was pierced by two tiny arches. Behind was a tiny enclosure in which they barely fitted. 'Here we are.' He held the candle sideways to show the lettering on a coffin-plate. With his spittle he tried to rub the name clear.

'*Philip Betagh*,' he read out. 'That was the first man to be buried here. He was a hedge-schoolmaster who brought the property and set up a school here. This (he was speaking like a guide), I forgot to say, is the site of the old Smock Alley Theatre where Peg Woffington used to foot it one time. Betagh bought the site and afterwards the church was built on it. The land belongs to the Protestants, so we still pay them a hundred and sixty pounds a year for ground rent. Think of it – nearly two hundred thousand pounds they have from us by now. Isn't it a shame!'

They felt hot and clammy. The candle smelt of its own grease. They clambered out of the place, and he showed them another and another coffin.

'I smell putrefaction,' said Frank.

The priest showed them a pile of tiny coffins.

'There's something the Gas people never put in their front window. An explosion that wiped out a whole slum tenement.'

The girl clung, horrified, to her lover. She thought of the young wife whose baby had to be baptized, as she looked at the tiny little boxes, now falling apart and immovable.

'Oh!' she cried. 'Come out, come out.'

'I want to see MacNally,' said Frank obstinately.

'There you are.'

It lay all alone in a great vault. It was unusually large because of the lead casing. The wood was a fine red dust. A finger on it left a hole. To show them that it was of lead the priest kicked it, and for bravado the young man kicked it.

'Come, come,' said the girl. 'I'm baking.'

They went back as they had come. The wild eyes of the mad soldier had not deflected from the high altar. The youth who had intercepted them still stood by the side-door, his fingers peaked, his eyes downcast.

'Why didn't you come at the right time?' said the priest to him as he passed out to the windy, sunny September air: outside the young girl waited with her baby in an old battered pram.

The priest spoke to her more gently. 'You should have come at twelve o'clock,' he said.

'We were late, father,' said the girl humbly. 'I was workin'.'

They re-entered the presbytery and Father Peter challenged them to race him up the stairs. He took it three steps at a time. He left them in the room while he went for his hat and overcoat. He was going to take them out for a 'bit of fun to celebrate.'

They did not speak while he was away. She sat looking into the fire and he stood by the window, looking over the city. A light or two had begun to twinkle. The roofs were melting into one another. Somehow since they had met the priest several years had been added to both of them. They had come upon one of those moments of life when, like the winter butterflies in the high corners, they felt the hurt of cold. Breezily the priest returned, coated, buttoned, slapping his hands.

'Well, now, boys and girls, we'll see what Dublin has to offer in the way of life.'

Meekly and slowly they followed him and on the stairs they groped for one another's fingers. and when they met they held and clutched. Outside the dusk was fallen and the night air was blue and the water of the river held an autumn mist.

While they were with him they tried hard to be gay, and they delayed him when he wanted to go, and Frank even made him promise to meet them in the morning; but, once he was gone, they hurried to their hotel along the quays, faster and faster, their hands clasped like children lost in a wood. Not until they were quite alone, and he had drawn down the window-blinds, and closed the windows, shutting out the faint cry of a barking dog, did they begin to laugh; and they laughed and laughed over Peter, with his penny candle, until they had him turned into a fat Punch like the Devil in the play.

Then he closed the old-fashioned plush curtains so as to shut out the last glow from the arc-lamp. They lay beside one another in the dark. Their passion was wild in its unrestraint.

In the morning the river glittered in the sun, and she made him bring Peter to the Zoo. There she was so gay and comical with the animals that they were delighted by her innocence, and Peter, leaving them at the gate of the Park, took Frank by the arm and said, 'A grand girl, Frankie, boy!' However, nobody but she saw the joke, and even she, in her wisdom, as women do with their wisdom, never thought about it when she recalled it, as she never forgot it when it had long passed out of her silly little head.

The Confessional

In the wide nave the wintry evening light was faint as gloom and
in the shadows of the aisle it was like early night. There was no
sound in the chapel but the wind blowing up from the river-valley,
or an occasional tiny noise when a brass socket creaked under the
great heat of a dying flame. To the three small boys crouched
together in a bench in the farther aisle, holding each other's hands,
listening timidly to the crying wind, staring wide-eyed at the candles,
it seemed odd that in such a storm the bright flames never moved.

Suddenly the eldest of the three, a red-headed little ruffian, whispered loudly; but the other two, staring at the distant face of the
statue, silenced him with a great hiss like a breaking wave. In
another moment the lad in the centre, crouching down in fear and
gripping the hand on each side of him, whispered so quietly that
they barely heard: 'She's moving.'

For a second or two they did not even breathe. Then all three
expelled a deep sigh of disappointment.

It was Monday afternoon, and every Monday as they had each
heard tell over and over again in their homes, Father Hanafin spoke
with the Blessed Virgin in the grotto. Some said she came late at
night; some said in the early morning before the chapel was opened;
some said it was at the time when the sun goes down, but until now
nobody had dared to watch. To be sure Father Hanafin was not in
the chapel now, but for all that the three little spies had come filled
with high hope. The eldest spoke their bitter disappointment aloud.

'It's all my eye,' he said angrily. The other two felt that what he
said was true, but they pretended to be deeply shocked.

'That's an awful thing you said, Foxer,' whispered the boy in the
middle.

'Go away, you, Philpot!' said Foxer.

'God! I think it's a cause for confession, Foxer!' whispered Philpot again.

'It's a mortal sin, Foxer!' said the third, leaning over to say it.

'Don't try to cod me, Cooney, or I'd bust yer jaw!' cried Foxer angrily.

Philpot hushed them sternly and swiftly, but the spell was broken. They all leaned back in the bench.

Beside them was Father Hanafin's confession-box, its worn purple curtain partly drawn back, his worn purple stole hanging on a crook on the wall inside, and as Foxer gazed into the box with curiosity the Adversary tempted him in his heart.

'Come on, Cooney!' he invited at last, 'come on, and I'll hear yer confession.'

'Gor! Come on,' said Cooney, rising.

'That's a sin,' said Philpot, though secretly eager to sit in the priest's chair.

'You're an awful ould Aunt Mary!' jeered Foxer, whereupon all Philpot's scruples vanished and the three scrambled for the con-ressor's seat. But Foxer was there before either of them, and at once he swished the curtains together as he had seen Father Hanafin do, and put the long stole about his neck. It was so nice in there in the dark that he forgot his two penitents waiting beyond the closed grilles on either side, and he was putting imaginary snuff into his nostrils and flicking imaginary specks of snuff from his chest when Cooney's angry face appeared between the curtains.

'Are you going to hear me confession, Foxer, or are yeh not?' he cried in a rage, eager for his turn to be priest.

'Go back, my child,' said Foxer crossly, and he swished the curtains together again. Then, as if in spite, he leaned over to the opposite grille and slowly and solemnly he drew the slide and peered into the frightened eyes of Philpot.

'Tell me how long since your last confession, my child,' he said gravely.

'Twenty years,' whispered Philpot in awe.

'What have you done since then?' intoned Foxer sadly.

'I stole sweets, father. And I forgot my prayers. And I cursed, father.'

'You cursed!' thundered Foxer. 'What curse did you say?'

'I said that our master was an ould sod, father,' murmured Philpot timidly.

'So he is, my child. Is there anything else?'

'No, father.'

'For your penance say two hundred and forty-nine rosaries, and four hundred and seventy Our Fathers, and three hundred and thirty-two Hail Marys. And now be a good obedient boy. And pray for me, won't you? Gawd bless you, my child.'

And with that Foxer drew the slide slowly before the small astonished face.

As he turned to the other side his hand fell on a little box – it was Father Hanafin's consolation during the long hours spent in that stuffy confessional listening to the sins and sorrows of his parishioners. Foxer's awkward fingers lifted the cover and the sweet scent rose powerfully through the darkness as he coaxed the loose snuff down from the cover. Then drawing the slide on Cooney, he gravely inhaled a pinch and leaned his ear to the cool iron of the grille.

Outside a footstep sounded on the marble floor, and peering out Foxer saw the priest walk slowly up the farther aisle, turn and walk slowly down again, his breviary held high to the slanting radiance of the Virgin's altar.

'It's Father Hanafin,' whispered Foxer to Cooney; and to Philpot – 'Keep quiet or we're all ruined.'

Up and down the solemn footsteps went, and high above their heads in the windows of the clerestory and along the lath and plaster of the roof the wind moaned and fingered the loose slates, and now and again they heard the priest murmur aloud the deep, open vowels of his prayer, Gaudiamus Domine, or Domine, Domine meo, in a long breathing sigh.

'He's talking to the Virgin,' breathed Cooney to Foxer.

'He's talking to the Virgin,' breathed Foxer in turn to Philpot.

'Amen,' sighed the priest, and went on his knees before the candles that shone steadily and were reflected brilliantly in the burnished brass.

The three spies had begun to peep from their hiding-place when the snuff fell on Foxer's lap and the grains began to titillate his nose. In agony he held his mouth for a full minute and then burst into a furious sneeze. In astonishment the priest gazed about him and once again Foxer held his breath and once again he sneezed. At the third sneeze the priest gazed straight at the box.

'Come out!' he said in a loud voice. 'Come out of that box!'

And as the three guilty forms crept from the three portals he commanded again, 'Come here!'

Awkwardly they stumbled forward through the seats, trying to hide behind one another, pushing and upbraiding one another until they stood before him.

'What were you doing in there?' he asked Foxer.

'I was hearing their confession, father,' trembled Foxer, and half raised his arm as if to ward off a blow.

For a moment the priest glared at him and then he asked, 'And what penance did you give?'

'I – I gave three hundred and thirty Hail Marys, father, and I think it was four hundred Our Fathers, father, and two hundred and forty-nine rosaries, father.'

'Well!' pronounced the priest in a solemn voice, 'go home and let each one of ye say that penance three times over before nine o'clock tomorrow morning.'

Stumbling over one another's heels the three crept down the dark aisle and crushed out through the green baize door and into the falling night that was torn by the storm. The street-lamps were lit and under one of these they halted and looked at each other, angry and crestfallen.

'Nine hundred and ninety Hail Marys!' wailed Philpot, and Cooney squared up to Foxer with clenched fists.

'Yerrah!' said Foxer. 'It's all a cod!'

And he raced suddenly away to his supper, followed by the shouts and feet of the other two.

Mother Matilda's Book

I

In their starched and pointed coifs, beak-like, their winged blue sleeves, their skirts pouched about them like balloons, the sisters of Saint John of the Cross look for all the world like geese. As they talk their cowls slew about in the air. They move as if on castors.

But, in her hey-day, Mother Matilda simply was a goose. She was shapeless as a ball of fur; she clucked and stuttered – her teeth never fitted her – and as the smiling novices hopped about her, she was for ever waving her hands up and down in the air as if she were winging water through the air from the tips of her little fat hands. And as in her youth she had been a goose, in her years she was a wretched little gosling. Her clothes hung from her, she had developed a dropped eyelid, her cowl fell over her blind eye; her voice was a pip-cough. When she slept in the sun, with her breath coming in gusts through her mouth, her face red with sun and sleep, her bibulous coif, and her teeth sinking slowly down to her lower lip, she was a picture nobody in the convent, least of all the novices over whom she once held power, cared to look at. She was become one of those pensioners of religion that you find in every convent, and whose doings are a constant worry to their House. She was come to that stage when the new Reverend Mother – the third since her day – began to conspire with the sisters against her; as she had in her time conspired against the pensioners above in the graveyard.

Daily they gossiped about her, looking over their shoulders lest she should come on them unawares; they said, nodding many times over it, that she was a dear old soul, everyone in the convent knew that. But after all (we get old, and she can't help it, poor dear), this latest habit of losing her teeth was too much. Why, you might walk on them! And Sister Eunice said that if she straightened Mother Matilda's coif once a day, she straightened it twenty times. And

Sister Agnes whispered behind their backs that it was a pity she dropped tea on her gimp. And Sister Ignatius thrust in her red, country face with the two buck-teeth, and cried that yesterday as she was walking by the oratory with Father Kennedy they almost fell over her legs, where she had them stretched out right in front of her like a man, and she sitting on the grass-bank snoring like a trooper. They all laughed at that, but Mother John sighed impatiently and hushed them away to their tasks. They were no help to her.

Then as she stood in the green distempered hall and looked up at the portrait of their foundress, her eye fell on the list of Mothers of this House framed beneath it. There was Matilda's name and two other names after it, and then, last of all, her own name, Mother John O'Connell. Poor old Matilda had inscribed that list herself, in a firm uncial hand with grotesque Celtic capitals – she had been drawing mistress in her day; and as the name *Mother John O'Connell* showed – clear and soft and flowing – inscribed only a few months ago, she had not yet lost her skill. Mother John noted all that; but she noted, too, with a little start of fright, the date beside the first name of all. In five years' time that house of the North Abbey would be seventy-five years in existence. At once she turned and went smiling in search of Matilda.

She found her telling her beads in a shady corner, sheltering from the summer sun and wind. She straightened her coif and, holding her hand, led the talk to the history of the Order. From their nook the city roofs fell into the valley, hung there in a swaying hammock of smoke. From the near backyards, with the shirts and shifts drying in the wind, and the cries of the lane children and the mothers calling them at the tops of their voices, that aerial plain narrowed out and up to the farthest smoke-rim beyond. There they could barely see another piece of churchyard calm, the second house of Saint John of the Cross – the South Abbey.

'Do you realize, mother,' said Mother John, 'that in five years' time it will be the Jubilee of this House?'

'I do,' said Mother Matilda.

'We must begin to prepare for it,' said Mother John.

At the word 'we' Matilda looked up with a faint hope; then she said humbly :

'Indeed, you must, mother.'

Quickly John began to talk about their foundress, the wealthy and charitable spinster Georgina Tinsely, whose people had made their money out of sweet Kerry butter and lived, through the last century, in the North Abbey. That was her portrait in the hall, a sharp, long-jawed face, shadowed by its frilled coif. Mother John began to complain that in spite of the interdictions of generations of Reverend Mothers, the frame beneath was worn shapeless by 'the lanes' about.

'Year after year,' she wailed, 'they rub their dirty fingers on the wood. I even saw a woman scraping off a piece of gilt the other day and blessing herself with it. As if it were Holy Water or a bit of the True Cross!'

'Ah, wisha, sure,' soothed Matilda, 'it's no wonder. She did great work for them.'

'They don't do it in the South Abbey,' said John, looking across at it.

'She didn't live in the South Abbey,' said Matilda.

'She founded it,' said John.

'Well, in a way she did,' said Matilda, 'but it was her sister gave her wealth to it.'

Gabbling away, while John listened cutely, she began to trace the spread of the Order all over Ireland, recalling how a third house had been founded by a convert, how a parish priest in Kinsale had asked for a fourth, because he wanted free schools for the soldiers' children, how a bishop gave land for a fifth near Cashel, and how the Order had prayed night and day when a lawsuit was being fought to get money for a sixth.

'I often heard Mother Mary, God rest her,' said Matilda, 'tell about the Novenas they said that time. If we lost that case we'd be beggared for the next fifty years, aye, and longer!'

John looked at her – she was a bright old woman, yet, she thought. Yes, she could do it all right. And if she didn't, what harm was done.

'Mother Matilda,' she ordered, and she straightened the dropped coif once more, 'you shall write the history of the North Abbey and the Order. The book will be like the Book of Kells. It must be ready for the Jubilee, and every house in the country will see it and pride in it.'

She rose and looked down smilingly at the old pensioner. Matilda, like an old cat rejoicing in a sudden wave of sunshine, had stuck out her tongue between her teeth and was gazing over the city and the hills beyond. She clapped her little hands and waved the tiny sausages of fingers up and down in the air. Then her hands fell and she sighed.

'I'll begin it, mother. But I'll never live to see the Jubilee, mind you.'

'You'll live to see the Centenary,' laughed Mother John, as she raced away, delighted with her plan.

2

For the first couple of years Matilda did quite well at the History. She got a huge vellum book, bound in tooled leather, a book so huge and heavy that she always had a novice beside her to lift and move it. (This was part of Mother John's cunning – it gave her an excellent excuse for putting a warder over the old nun.) With the most per-durable inks, of scarlet and violet and gallblack, with Chinese white and tiny drops of gold, Matilda framed each small block of hand-writing. She would spend a month tracing out the convolutions of the patterns in which she bedded her capitals, peering at them for hours through a magnifying-glass held out by the trembling hand of the novice. She copied these designs from Irish manuscripts of the tenth and eleventh centuries, the great period of manuscript illumination, and she expended so much patience in making her plant-like animals brilliant and glittering, after their long voyage through their own deformities, that by the time she had spent three years on the book and covered twenty years of history, there was not a convent of the Order that had not borrowed the unfinished manuscript, to show it to their sisters and patrons. Nobody cared now if she snored over her work, or if her coif fell on her neck, or if she mislaid her teeth. For she did all these things in the privacy of her cell, and if she escaped to do them elsewhere they could chide the novice to their hearts' content.

Alas! she then grew ill and her eyes began to fail her, and she grew weary of her work. She had copied all the more interesting pieces of illumination and she grew perverse and headstrong and began to invent designs for herself. But they were always the same kind of thing – vines twined about a trellis with bunches of purple grapes and great vine-leaves wandering into the body of the text. A little later on she ceased to make capitals, and her round uncial declined into a ragged minuscule, from that into an angular running hand, and lastly into a childish typescript of her own. Because she was too lazy to rule her page it sloped out of the horizontal. There were several errors in spelling and the leaves were often smudged.

It grew so bad that by the time Mother Philomena succeeded Mother John the book could no longer be sent out of the North Abbey. They tried to suggest to her that she was tired and should allow somebody else to finish the book, for by now it had become, in their minds, a prized possession of the House. They would cluster over her as she worked, sighing at one another behind her back, while the novice stared at them all with a stony face, or looked at the old nun as one might look at a strange animal. Or they would hint that she needed more light; or one of them would lend her a ruler that was 'nicer than her own'; or the more daring ones brought new pieces of illuminated work that they 'thought she might like to get ideas from.' She would just raise her fat face with the greying moustaches and smile her thanks and go on ruining the book.

With the approach of the Jubilee the last step was reached. She hurried and scurried over the page like a rabbit, scarcely seeing what she wrote. Her vines became leafless; their staffs sagged; the grape-bunches were either pills or big as onions. She did not even notice if her sleeve suddenly swept a whole page into a mist. But that was not the worst of it. She talked of nothing but the Jubilee day. Clacking her teeth like an enraged monkey, she would peer up suddenly at the novice through the thick lenses of her spectacles and cry :

'I think we ought to exhibit it in the chapel!'

Then she would turn the half-filled page, with a stuttering, tremulous :

'Where did I leave off? What last? What last?'

Or she would jump up and, wrapping her glasses in her sleeve, hobble off to search out the new Reverend Mother – Philomena.

'The hall, mother,' she would grin. 'That's the best place. I just thought of it. In the hall! Can I show it in the hall?'

Whereupon Philomena, who was a shrewish city woman with a cocked nose and a lisp, would see His Lordship stooping in amazement over the childish efforts of the old nun, or the visiting Mothers smiling sweetly at her and telling her what a great work the mother-house had done for the Order, and how well they could understand now why the book was kept from them during the last three years.

'No, dear,' snapped Philomena – red to the summit of her nose – 'it is a very bad place. Do straighten your cowl, mother dear. What? In the hall? In everybody's way! Sister Agnes!' (she calls out to a nun flitting by). 'You know, dear, you have no right to be . . .'

So she leaves the old pensioner drooping like a broken plant, and that afternoon three separate sisters come privately to her to tell her that 'poor Mother Matilda is weeping all alone in the oratory and will not leave it for anybody.'

'Why,' she implores Mother John (already sinking to the stage of pensioner herself), 'why did you ever suggest to that poor soul to write a history of the Order?'

'Oh!' cries John. 'How can you be so hard on the old dear? Why, the whole convent knows she is a born saint. Please, mother, let me tell her you will exhibit the book somewhere.'

'Tell her anything you like,' cried Philomena. 'This Jubilee will be the death of me.'

And before she could retract her promise, off goes John to fetch the scribe, and off goes Philomena to conspire against the pair of them. From her office-window she could see them, a few minutes later, coming hand-in-hand down the rosary, Matilda shining like a moon, as she unwrapped her glasses to add a few more smudges and a few more monstrous grapes to her manuscript.

3

It was the Reverend Mother, as usual, who settled the problem. She took Matilda aside and told her she had made special arrangements for the book. They would have a lectern sent up from the North Cathedral. They would drape it in purple velvet. She could have candles about it and flowers. They would give her the best room in the school, where everybody could see it in comfort.

The result was that the novice watched in terror while Matilda madly filled page after page, composing now as she went, making the most loving personal remarks about everybody in the convent, down to the new washer-woman, whose steam was even then rising from the basement.

'A most praiseworthy and Christian woman,' read the novice

over her shoulder. 'She is married, we are informed on the best authority, to the most disgraceful . . .'

'Disgraceful?' popped Matilda back at the novice, while her hand made impatient circles over the page. 'What else is he?'

'Mother, I don't know him!' wailed the novice.

'Oh! What else? What else? Disgraceful? What else could he be?' Her hand raced on.

'. . . and disreputable drunkard of a man. She has ten children, she tells us, all by different husbands. But the hand of God has watched over her and lighted her a way out of the . . .

'The what?' she cries. 'The what?'

'I don't know, mother?'

'What do you get lit out of? What? What?'

'. . . pit!' writes the hand.

'Pit of what?' she cries again. 'Of what?'

'. . . iniquity,' writes the hand, while the novice groans and tells her beads.

They finished the book so late on the eve of the Jubilee day that Matilda was too exhausted to question if anybody would ever come to the Geography Room to see her masterpiece. It was three storeys up, and all that evening they tramped up and down stairs, carrying flowers and candles, and bickering with other nuns who wanted the same flowers and candles for something else.

They barely had the room and the book prepared as the first guests arrived the following morning. The lawns were green after a providential night of showers and a morning of burning sun. The Chinese lanterns barely swayed on their strings and the tablecloths barely flapped a lazy wing under the jellies and the wines and the teacups and the cones of sweetcake. The gentle wind had cleared the city roofs of smoke and the clouds were building castles in the air. The two nuns, the old nun and the young novice, remained for hours watching the greens grow black with priests as if a flock of crows had alighted there and were pecking on the lawn. They all had shiny tall-hats; a neat circle of white cuff on every wrist; here and there a warm ribbon of scarlet marked out a canon or a dean.

Then His Lordship came with Mother Philomena on his right and her second-in-charge on his left, and the Mistress of Novices accompanied his secretary behind. As he passed through the crowd of clergy and lay people, he was like some giant walking through a field of rushes; at every step they sank before him on a half-knee. Then he went indoors and the two nuns fluttered about their book and lit the candles and tipped the flowers.

But he did not come to their room – and no priest came to their room, and through the livelong day nobody came. Until, several hours after lunch, Mother John managed to round up two giggling schoolgirls who looked and blushed at one another, and were heard giggling louder than ever as soon as they got outside the door. John had tried hard (so she whispered to the novice), but Philomena had her cohorts so well deployed that it was impossible to get anybody even as far as the door of the school.

4

Then, from their window-perch, the novice suddenly saw a friend of still earlier novitiate days entering with the Reverend Mother of the Kilcrea House. After being cooped up in that room all day, far from the fun and excitement below, her flesh weakened and she ran to seek her. ('Just for one minute, mother dear, you won't go away, will you, his lordship might come?') It was ten minutes, however, before she did find her, and then, hand-in-hand, the two young nuns went wandering under the lilacs by the gardener's shed, pressing one another's fingers under cover of their long sleeves, and smiling foolishly, as if they were both a little tipsy, and sometimes pausing to kiss when they recalled some particularly happy morning in Kilcrea. They were so full of joy that they lost all sense of time.

Left to herself, Matilda blew out the candles and wandered down, painfully, step by step, to the main parlour, and from that to the guests' parlour, and so from room to room. One or two nuns, sitting there with friends, smiled at her coldly and she retired at once. Then she heard voices in the Common Room, and peeping in, she saw that it was filled with priests, standing or sitting about comfortably, sipping tea or wine or smoking cigarettes. There were two or three nuns there, but though they stared at her, she did not retire. With a little croak of joy she had spied old Father Mulligan in a far corner, a parish priest she had known years ago, and she was beckoning to him and making noises like a bird to attract his attention.

At last somebody pointed her out to him and with delight he came forward and drew her in. He was a hearty, rude-faced man who had been given a small parish twenty years before in a village by the sea and he had never left it. Whiskers stood out of his ears and a kind of invading wilderness of white hair was stopped on each cheek by the razor. He was the only priest there smoking a pipe. He bowed over her and flattered her, and they talked for a while over everybody they knew – though it was one long litany of God-rest-them! – until his curate came by and he was led forward to meet the old nun.

'The oldest sister in the House,' boomed Father Mulligan.

'Interesting!' murmured the curate humbly. 'It should be commemorated. The doyen of the House.'

The next thing Matilda knew was a sudden fall in the clamour of talk about her and they were all listening to old Father Mulligan calling on them to drink 'in wine, whisky, or good strong tay' the health of the doyen of the North Abbey.

'And she's still at work, I may say. She had completed the History of the Order of Saint John of the Cross.'

'History?' one or two murmured with interest.

'Illuminated like the Book of Kells,' palpitated Matilda. 'It's on exhibition in the Geography Room and I wish you'd all come and see it.'

'Let's all go and see it,' said Father Mulligan, while the three nuns looked at one another in horror.

'This way,' piped Matilda, turning round and round like a peg-top, unable, in her excitement, to find the door.

But then she clapped her hands to her mouth and stared around at them in fright.

'What's wrong, mother?' asked the curate in his miserable, whining, too-humble voice.

'My teeth,' wailed Matilda. 'I've lost my teeth. I think I had them in my hand when I came into the Common Room.'

'Let's find them,' cried a merry little man with a bush of curly hair.

He had drunk just a shade too much Beaune in the wine-tent.

'A search! A search!' he cried.

Whereupon they all began to wave their hands in the air and lift cushions and flower-pots, and stooping, they raised their behinds

before armchairs and peeped under settees, and they opened cupboards that they should not have opened, while the three nuns fled
for Philomena and her cohorts, and above all for the wretched novice
who had allowed Matilda to escape.

'Lost! A row of delf!' cried curly-mop.

'Aurora's pearls,' said the classical scholar.

'Upper and lower?' teased Father Mulligan, while Matilda in a
corner searched herself all over.

The fun and scurry was at its height when His Lordship entered,
ushered in by Philomena's second-in-charge.

'Oh, my!' he said in his gentle country brogue that broke every
word into an iambic sigh. 'O-oh! m-my!'

'It's Mother Matilda,' explained Father Mulligan's curate in a sad
voice, dropping his cigarette behind him where a friend deftly
crushed it under his toe. 'She has mislaid her denture,' he went on,
and he said it like a naughty schoolboy, looking up at the bishop
under his fair eyebrows.

'Oh, my!' groaned his lordship sympathetically.

'And who,' he croaked in his graveyard voice, that with time had
become gentle and slow, because nobody had ever dared to interrupt him, 'who may Mother Matilda be?'

'She is Father Mulligan's friend,' said the curate wickedly, as if
he were saying, 'It's poor old Mulligan at it again, milord.'

But Father Mulligan did not mind. He led her forward.

'The oldest sister of the Order,' he said. 'The doyen of the
abbey.'

Matilda dropped on her two knees and kissed the extended ruby,
once, twice, three times.

'Once for a man,' murmured the curate under his breath, 'twice
for a woman, three times for a fool.'

'Well, well!' smiled his lordship, and the first 'well' was up in a
tree, and the second 'well' was as deep as a well. 'Well, well!'

'Give me your blessing, your lordship,' pleaded Matilda.

His hand wavered it over her crooked coif. The priests gathered
near, away from the wine-glasses, and watched with interest.

'I hope, my child,' smiled the bishop, 'that you will have many
more long and happy years.'

The face of Philomena appeared in the door, behind it a bunch of
dismayed faces peeping over her shoulder.

'Dear Mother Matilda,' greeted Philomena, coming forward. 'I hear Sister Kieran left you. It was naughty of her.'

She smiled at the bishop and led Kieran forward.

'Sister Kieran wants to show you a pigeon's egg,' she went on to Matilda.

The round face of the little novice was pale as a mushroom.

'A lovely little pigeon's blue and white spotted egg,' she babbled, 'such a lovely little egg, come and see it.'

Matilda looked blankly at her.

'Go,' croaked his lordship, and he smilingly patted Matilda's arm, 'go and see the pigeon's EGG!'

'It's green with blue spots on it,' said the novice eagerly. 'It's marvellous! It's lovely!'

She led her charge out and away down the corridor. She almost dragged her in her haste.

'But my teeth,' wailed Matilda, stumbling after her. 'And the book.'

'In the Geography Room,' said Kieran. 'You left them there, maybe.'

'And the book?' wailed Matilda. 'They are coming to see the book.'

'You left that in the Geography Room, too. We must light the candles. Hurry. Hurry.'

Matilda was panting before she reached the room. While Kieran lit the candles she drew her breath at the window. From there she saw the bishop go out into the garden and then down the alley to the main gate. The priests, like cockchafers, flowed in his wake. Matilda said nothing, but her coif slewed after them as they passed out of sight.

The rumble of the evening of the city came to her, and near at hand a mother calling loudly to her child. A gentle mist was beginning to fall and Matilda lost herself in gazing out through that shimmer of haze. The novice was looking at the flame of a candle, and her eyes were soft and her mouth trembling. She snivelled.

'He's a lovely priest,' said Matilda suddenly. 'And he gave me his blessing. But,' she gulped, 'he never saw the book.'

Suddenly she noticed the tears in the novice's eyes.

'Never mind, dear. We'll show the book another day,' encouraged the old nun.

'It isn't that,' wept the novice, who was thinking of her little friend in Kilcrea. 'But Sister Mary Michael is – is – is as thin as a latch.'

And she wept openly at the thought that her friend might die.

For a moment Matilda tried to understand, but then she began to pick at her back tooth and look over the misted roof and her eyes, once more enlarged with her own little grief, went grey with the light of the falling rain.

'Ja-a-a-anie!' screamed the mother below in the lane. 'Come ho-o-a-ame! I'll give you lamb-and-sally when I ca-a-a-atch yeh! Ja-a-a-anie!'

Faintly in the distance a child's voice replied. Then they heard, far away, the rumble of the town. One by one the novice extinguished the candles and led the old nun down to the babble of the refectory for her supper. As she had not found her teeth, however, she could eat nothing, so she spent the whole hour listening vacantly to everyone talking of the excitement of the day.

There's a Birdie in the Cage

1

While the case was being tried at the court-house, Lolly Black thought it would be a good time to see Pomfret's house. Her father would be at the court; the town would be at the court; poor old Mrs Pom would be at the court. So with her Phil she went there.

Immediately they got inside the house they realized it was too big for them. It rose like a Norman castle from the garden, a square of red brick like one of the grain elevators down in the harbour, or the queer concrete thing at the chemical works, all red from iron ore. It was lavish in its waste of space – wide passages, many cupboards, two dozen or more rooms. They could never hope either to furnish it or make it look cosy. What Pomfret wanted it all for they could not guess.

'Well,' said Lolly, 'it's easy to see what ruined this fellow.'

Their feet resounded across the bare corridor.

'Look,' she said.

It was a small, square room on the second landing. It was papered in deep blue, walls and ceiling, with golden stars stuck all over the paper, and in between them some silver butterflies. The glass in the arched window was a livid yellow and red. The floor had been painted black at some time; the mark of a square of linoleum or carpet was in the centre of the floor. Candle-grease spotted the floor in one corner.

'Was he a Freemason?' he asked.

'Was he a Catholic?' she whispered. 'It looks like an oratory.'

'*Was* he? Why *was*?'

'Well, is he?'

'They both are. Or rather, she is – or was – I don't know . . .'

They laughed. In a big room facing the sea they came on a mantel-piece laden with books. They fingered one or two. Byron's works.

A cream-covered notebook like a bank pass-book. It had to do with the distillery.

'No wonder he messed your father's affairs,' said Phil. 'Look at the scrap of a book. Poor devil – he let it all go to blazes at the end. Didn't even clear out of the house properly.'

He was pointing to the back of the door where trousers hung on a peg. A little wind from the sea made it wave feebly as if in a Pomfretian protest.

He lifted the window and they sat on the sill and looked out where the two brigs in the little harbour swayed and a cart rolled over the hump-backed bridge. In a backyard a cock crowed. A beech shed two leaves.

'Was it drink?' asked Phil.

He came from the city and he knew little about the town or its people.

'He drank,' said Lolly. 'But she drank like a blooming fish. But it wasn't that, I think. Just expensive living.'

'In Barronloe! But what is there to spend money on, here?'

'This house, parties, an expensive car, and two pianos, and holidays abroad: cruises, tours, expensive education for the daughters, clothes. The town says he gave a party last summer down there in the garden. At supper one of the fireworks went down instead of up – they were probably tipsy – and burnt a hole in the tablecloth: it had to be sent away to Brussels to be mended and cost twenty pounds to repair.'

He thought he caught a note of envy in her voice.

'He enjoyed himself?' he tested.

'Chinese lanterns in the apple-trees,' she went on, 'and he had three kind-of-tramp musicians in the summer-house, playing the melodeon and the concertina. The town was up till all hours, watching the fireworks, and listening. They talked of it for weeks. I heard the parish priest hinted at them in a sermon. Helen and myself were walking the Harbour Road that evening and we saw a good deal of their goings-on.'

He knew what 'walking the Harbour Road' meant. Every time he came to Barronloe and found the sisters out he was told he would be sure to meet them 'walking the Harbour Road.'

'How much did he get from your father per annum?' he wanted to ask. Instead he said:

'Had his wife money?'

'Ph!'

'Had he private means?'

'I knew his father when I was a child. He was a cobbler.'

'Isn't that amazing?'

'He speculated. On grain. With father's money. That will all be coming out by now in the court. He left pappy with fifteen thousand tons of maize, with the market falling. Too clever!'

'Where did he get the high notions?'

'I say it is from her. She was really a nobody. She can be very grand, but sometimes a terrific cockney accent jumps out. I believe it is true she used to dance. He said she was famous at one time, and that her name was Violet von Evremont. But I never met anybody who heard of her. Helena says her name was Lizzy Boggs. If she ever danced, it was a long time ago.'

'What a wicked little puss we are!' he teased.

'She made an awful show of herself on the beach at that party, I'm certain. She's forty-five if she's a day, and fourteen stone, and they say she was half-undressed, doing Greek dances.'

'Did you like her?'

She looked at him.

'What does Helena see in her?' he asked.

'Helena is soft.'

They closed the window and went down into the garden. It was gone wild already. Pomfret had been arrested in April, and everything collapsed at once. One good wet spring had turned the place into a jungle, docks three feet high, giant nettles, bishopsweed in the beds, speedwell, dandelions seeding on the wind. Apples lay rotting on the paths. Here and there they shone white in the high grass. Lolly Black could not stop talking of Mrs Pomfret.

'Really, she's an awful heap, and the town is well rid of her. He isn't a bad fellow. He keeps himself well. I have often seen him with a different suit every day. And he told me he ordered his shirts direct from London. (He has good taste and good manners.) But she *was* a heap. The first time we called on her she was all right. But the next time Helena and I dropped in unexpectedly. We were sick of the Harbour Road. She was all frowsy, with a dirty old dressing-gown on her, smoking cigarettes and drinking whisky. That at

twelve o'clock in the day. She began to tell us – phew! the smell of
the whisky – all about Buenos Aires, and how you pay five shillings
for a bottle of Bass there. "And you must 'ave it, dearie. You come
out from a hard night with the ballet and you're just simply dying
for it. Of course, we didn't always have to *buy* it, dearie!" '

'Ho-ho!' whistled Phil.

'You may well ho-ho. It angered me to hear her talk that way,
especially to Helena. "Hellow, Helen, dearie. Aren't you looking
clean and fresh! That dress shows off your figure, Helen. You know,
Helen, you have a lovely figure." And Helen would blush, and try
to look at some picture or other. "What are you staring at, Helen?
How warm you look. Let me hold your hand. Oh, that? That's *The
Tweed*. A clipper that licked the steamer from Hong Kong to Singapore by a day and a half. That other one was decorated by the
Viceroy of Madras from this-or-the-other. You know, Helen, I can't
keep my eyes off you. You have a lovely body, darling. Let me look
at you . . ." Ach! Then the way she'd pull her dressing-gown tight
around her and shiver. And lean on the mantel, looking you up and
down with heavy lids, talking of marriage and men, and the way life
goes slipping away from you, and the loneliness of Barronloe, and
what a lovely body Helen had if she only knew it, and she blowing
smoke through her nose at every sigh.'

'Forty-five? Fifty? Fifty-five?'

'At least. She married twice, you know. Her first husband was a
planter in Sumatra. That house' – they both looked up at its bald
red back – 'was full of things from the Indies. Lumps of teak and
ivory. The shipyards of Johore, dearie. Heads of wild beasts. The
Burmese jungles, dearie. All mixed up with spears and skin shields
and pictures and bottles of sacred water. Straight from Lourdes,
dearie. That day she offered us whisky before she thought of herself,
and then tea. Then she ended up by producing an enormous box of
chocolates. The outside smelt of eau-de-Cologne. She pulled it out
of a drawer in her bedroom. It was awful. Please don't ask me to
remember it. The chocolates cost at least a pound. Have 'em, dearie.
I don't eat 'em. A boy-friend gave 'em to me. She said he was a silly
ass. I couldn't touch them. Straight from her bedroom, dearie. But
Helen didn't mind. She said I was a silly ass.

'The barracks in the town knew her like a bad penny. The jarveys
were always driving officers to the house. And the extraordinary

thing is that Pomfret never seems to have known about her goings-on. He was too often away.'

'Shall I be too often away?'

She slapped his hand playfully.

'Our gardener, who knows everything about everybody, told pappy, when he had Pomfret arrested for embezzlement, that the clerks in the distillery always knew they could be late if they saw light in Pomfret's windows after twelve. That meant *he* was out of town. And he told me that: "Yerrah, sure, miss, the poachers on the river used her house for a lighthouse!" He said, too, that the priests were always taking maids away from the house.'

'It sounds a nasty kind of house to me,' said Phil. 'Where did Pomfret meet this woman? He's a town boy, isn't he?'

'Yes. He met her here. One summer when she came on holidays with her first husband. He had some job connected with oil. He was a Major Gilfillan. They took the house for two months for their children. Pomfret was only a clerk with us, then. The first time anyone ever heard of her was one pouring wet night – she must have taken the house for August and September – when the Rowleys, they're the only neighbours we speak to, heard a most frightful row coming up from the beach. Then they heard a window being smashed and Violet von Evremont, or Mrs Gilfillan, or Mrs Pomfret, or Lizzy Boggs or whatever the creature's name is, screaming out at the top of her voice that her husband was killing her. The next thing there was her ladyship, breasting in the door with the two older children, Bel and Pickaninny, by the hands. She sobbed out that Gilfillan had stabbed her with his sword and that nothing but her corset saved her. And the maid running off with Donna in a blanket to the police barrack. We didn't hear about this until long after, for it was hushed up, or, I needn't tell you, we shouldn't have called on her. I think it was very wrong of the Rowleys. But once she told Helen that *she* had first stabbed *him* with the carving-knife, in the hand! And one of her maids that came to us told me it all began when the dog ate her false fringe and she beat the dog. I think the truth of the matter is that she was drinking his brandy. Though the gardener says it was the way he found her with an officer in the house. One doesn't know what to believe. That was when Pomfret met her. He used to play cards there. I suppose he had nowhere better to go – it's a small town. Then when the Major died suddenly he met her again and married her. That was twelve years ago. They had two children. That's five altogether. But now she does nothing but mope and drink, and race off to Dublin. She just let herself go to pieces. Honestly, she lives half her life in a pig-sty. And, of course – officers always. Helena and I, when we go for a walk down the Harbour Road, see her hanging out of the window, smoking and mooning, her hair done up beautifully, rouged, and all the rest of it. But we always said she was probably in rags from the neck down.'

'She probably hadn't enough to occupy her time,' suggested Phil, who was tired of the subject. 'We must give you enough to keep you busy.'

Lolly looked at him and then began to blush slowly, deeply, and not knowing where to look, until suddenly understanding her blush he caught her to himself and kissed her hair and brow. With soft, dreamy, sensuous eyes she looked over the sparkling sea, all her little pert and youthful hardness dissolving in her love.

2

Her hands and her hair lit by the sun through the slats of the venetian blind, Helen strummed with too much *rallentando* and too much *molle* and *piano*, at her favourite largo from her favourite Beethoven – the *Concerto in C Minor* – a thing more soft and more tender than air or dew, humming where the flute and the bassoon should moan out the *andante*. But then, instead of going on to the *rondo*, she lifted her hands from the keys as a mother might lift her hands from a cradle. She looked at the dust-motes in the barred sun.

'It's too sweet,' wept Mrs Pomfret from the sofa. 'Thank you, darling.'

Helen rose, on her mouth a twisted smile. She clicked the blinds level so that the sun poured in, and she could see the heat-haze on the ocean, and far away through it as through milky water the clouds falling like rose-petals in late autumn. A cart lumped over the bridge. On the hillock, in the chapel grounds, to her left, the chapel-woman was tolling a dead bell.

Behind her Mrs Pomfret blessed herself hastily, and when Helen turned suddenly and saw her, she explained :

'The Angelus is such a lovely thought. It always reminds me of Fra Angelica. Like the Rosary. The hours I've spent with thee, dear heart.'

Helen twisted her fingers passionately.

'It comforts me in my misfortune, Helen. I didn't know the hardness of human beings. You know I always thought you Irish were so kind and soft. But it isn't so ! I dropped into the bank just now to cash a cheque I got from a good friend. You don't know, Helen, what it is to be looked at the way they looked at me, and at that cheque, and the questions and the delay. I had to sell our Bechstein this morning for ten pounds, Helen, to pay a lawyer for my husband. Think of it! My Bechstein in Murphy's front parlour. You know what that skinny daughter of his will do with it. She'll play 'ymns on it. And put a red antimacassar on it, and the family photographs. Anytime . . . Oh, well! It does rile me! And I sold my last bit of jewellery to Cooney for another ten. My engagement ring that Jim bought in London for fifty guineas. And if I didn't sell 'em Jim wouldn't have any counsel at all to open 'is bleedin' mouth for 'im.'

'I'm sorry, Violet.'

'It's nice to hear you call me Violet,' groaned Mrs Pomfret.

'I wish I could lend you some money,' sighed Helen.

'That's good of you, dearie; but we owe nearly five hundred in town.'

At that Helen, in spite of herself, gave a little gasp of annoyance and disapproval, and at that sign from so young and ignorant a critic Mrs Pomfret's dams began to crack.

'Oh, I know it ain't nice. But everybody does it. It isn't that that worries me. I don't mind for my own sake. I've been through it before. I don't give a damn even for Jim's sake. He'll come through it in his good time. It's the kiddies. Mary and Patrick are just ready to get something out of their schooling now. And Donna, in the middle of her course at the university. But wot can I do? Where can I take 'em? I can go and live with my sister in Blackpool. But you cawn't fit children reared in an Irish village, I might say, into an English town.'

She banged her fist into the sofa and let herself go utterly.

'Oh, Christ, wot a fool that man was ! Wot a bloody fool I was

to marry 'im. Oh, don't look at me like that, dearie. I know I didn't
ort to use bad language opposite you. You're so good. But it's the
bad stuff comin' out. I don't care. I don't care. I must 'ave a good
cry. And damn, damn, damn, damn, damn! So there! Think of me
what you like.'

And the big, fat, powdered and painted wreck of a danseuse broke
into a storm of tears. Suddenly she stopped and dried them.

'Here I am, after all my years, and I haven't as much sense as
one of the chorus in her first pantomime. Here I am. And wot
brought me 'ere? I ask you. I *awsk* you! Even if I was back in
Sumatra with my old man I'd be better off – and I know it's hell,
the sweating heat, the stink, the water that's always hot and tasting
of iron. Though you should 'ave seen me, Helen. I was slim. You 'ad
to be slim in them places. The heat made you slim. I'll tell the world.
All in white. Pure w'ite. He called me 'is lily. Ha, don't make me
larf. And look at me now; yes, do look at me. I see you looking at
me, and I know what you're thinkin'; you're thinkin' I'm a fat,
coarse lump of a woman, with false hair and sweaty armpits, and a
complexion at two-and-six a jar. And you're right. It is right. It is
so. But time was when the Johnnies in the stalls threw golden
sovereigns at my feet. You should have seen me do the can-can. I
could kick me legs as high as that bloody chandelier, I could. Swish,
frouf, kick, boys, kick! And the Johnnies in Rio shouting at me to
kick it higher. I'll say I kicked. I did it though I bust me braces!
Last year I tried to do it on the beach, for our tin wedding. I know
I made a fool of myself. I didn't need Jim to tell me that. I saw
them smirking at one another while I did it. And yet I just couldn't
stop. And why couldn't I stop? I couldn't stop because I thought I
was back in Java, doing it for my old man for our tin wedding on
the beach, and the niggers beating with their feet and clapping hands
like a lot of bloody lunatics. Oh, Helen! The moon, and the water
making a little – you know – hush – hush . . .'

And again the tears. With Helen staring at her, between shame,
and horror, and pity.

'Come, now, Mrs Pomfret,' she stammered. 'It's all – I mean –
Java is . . . Well, your husband is dead now . . .'

'Ho, indeed? Is he? I bet he ain't. Yes, yes, yes, yes! I know he's
supposed to be. That's the yarn I spread about here. I suppose it's
bigamy. But I don't care. What a show I'm after making of myself

before you, girlie. But somehow – I don't know – I've always found
you so – so innocent, Helen. Coo! The things I've done. What's the
differ now? I came here to try and give you a bit of advice, and
here I am splitting on myself, and you'll hate me all your life. Well,
I deserve it.'

'But why . . .'

'Oh, I was down and out – that's why. I had three kids on my
hands. My old man left them to me, and he left me, that's all. Then
Jim Pomfret came along. And I say it's all his fault. He had no right
to marry me. I didn't know wot kind of life was before me, with
him. He ought to have known. It's all right for him. He had his
business at your daddy's place. He had his friends at the club. But
wot about me? I used to sit up in the window of our bedroom, day
after day after day after day and look out. And wot would I see?
I tell you. I see an empty ocean. Or I see a little ship come now and
again with pyrites for the chemical factory. Ships from Rio Tinto.
And I've been in Rio Tinto. And when I'd look at them through the
bloody rain I'd see Rio Tinto. Or else wot would I see? The harbour
lighthouse in the fog of the water. That's all. That's my life for ten
years. Do you know wot I've done? I've done the Stations of the
Cross. I used to look up at the Virgin's face and say – yes, I'm a
mother of sorrows, too. I've looked up at the face of Father
McCarthy giving sermons to the Women's Confraternity – me in the
Confraternity! Think of it! – Shades of Rio! – and I'd say to myself,
"Gawd bless you, father, you're a bleedin' innocent," I'd say, "and
if that's sin then I'm a bleedin' saint." '

And she tried to calm herself, but her hair was crooked and her
hat was crooked, and her eyes were gone red and her lips wet.

'Oh, well. Never mind. I shouldn't talk like this to you, Helen.
You're such a kid.' There was a pause. 'Helen, you ought to get
married. It's so easy for you. You've got such a lovely figure, and
with your hair. All men are alike when it comes to that! You could
get any man you liked – if you – you know – don't be so shy. That's
what I came to say. And I say it 'cos I like you. You've never turned
your back on me. Of course,' she said bitterly, 'you might if you'd
known.'

Helen said in a low voice:

'I did know.'

The woman peered at her.

'Wot did you know?'

'I knew everything. Bel told me.'

'Wot's everything?' cried Mrs Pomfret in terror. 'Whatche mean? About my husband?'

'Yes.'

Mrs Pomfret rose in a fury.

'Bel didn't tell you. Bel's my son. Bel didn't know. What you bloody well mean? Come off it. He didn't know. I tell you he didn't know! How could he know? Bel's my son – my son, my son!'

The girl grew pale.

'I shouldn't – I shouldn't ...'

The big woman stood over her. Her fist was clenched.

'What did Bel tell you?'

But she, too, was going pale, and there was fright and shame in her eyes.

'Bel knew. I knew about the house. I mean. Bel knew. That's why he left.'

The woman looked at her, peering furiously, searching her young face.

'I don't believe Bel knew. You're telling me a lie, Helen.'

'I am not telling you a lie,' said Helen angrily. 'I beg your pardon, Mrs Pomfret; but I am not telling you a lie.'

Pomfret collapsed.

'Don't be angry, dearie,' she wheedled. 'But Bel didn't really tell you, did he? I mean, you picked it up from him. Guessed like. Isn't that all?'

Helen shook her head. The older woman sank into a chair.

'So you *were* great with him? I was right about that anyway. You're all together. You're all one. You're all just the same! The only person in the whole damn' town to stick by me was that little rat of a Shinnick woman. A rat of a woman. The cook's wife in the asylum!'

Again she collapsed.

'Oh, I wish I 'adn't come to say goodbye to you. But I'm not sure, mind you. No, I don't care what you say; I don't believe it. I don't believe Bel knows. It's all lies. All lies. I'll tell you why Bel went away. I sent him away. Now!'

The girl looked at her, doubtfully.

'Yes, I did. I'll tell you the way of it. If you get my meaning. Just about the time the trouble came with the distillery, Bel told Jim right off the bloody reel that he wanted to marry you. That he was in love with you. You're . . .'

'Yes?'

'Well . . .'

'I know what you were going to say.'

'I wasn't going to say it.'

'What?'

'Oh, don't be an idiot, girl. He said he was going to ask you some day to marry him. His father – I mean – well – if you must know it – told Bel to remember you are a Protestant. I don't mind so much really about religion myself. I have my own way of getting on. I don't always hold with the Church . . .'

Helen was looking at her wildly. The old woman went on hurriedly with her lies.

'Anyway, his father and I and he had a hell of a row. Jim was on bail at this time, remember. I said: "Send the boy away for a year or two and then see if he still wants the girl." It so happened I had an offer of a job from a friend in Sumatra for any young lad that wanted a start in life. And I put it up to Bel.'

'I see,' said Helen in a dull voice.

'I pity the boy. It's no place for a white man. Bad enough for a white woman. Out at dawn to get something done before the heat of the day.'

She shook her head at the thought of it.

'No wonder I'm what I am. Only time I ever slept in that place was between noon and half-past four in the afternoon. And sweat? Only for the nights I couldn't have stuck it. I tell you, we made them hum!'

Helen turned on the piano-stool and sank her head in her hands. The keys jangled under elbows, horribly.

'I'm getting batty,' said Pomfret. 'I wanted to tell you about Bel.'

'I don't want to hear about Bel.' Helen whirled proudly. 'I'm not interested.'

Pomfret leaned over her and took her chin in her palm and looked at her face as at a mirror.

'Helen! Are you still in love with him?'

One second's hesitation would have meant yes. Helen hesitated far longer. Pomfret dropped her hand.

'I'm sorry, Helen. It's all Jim's doing. Though it's not that either. You're . . .'

'You said it before,' wailed Helen.

'What?'

'You said I'm too old for him.'

'Well, it is the truth. There – you have it at last.'

Helen shook her large and lovely head, knowing that she would never know the truth from this woman.

'You were always telling me I should get married!' she cried. 'Why did he go?'

'Yes, but . . .'

'Yes, but not to Bel. Is that it?'

'Well . . .'

The old woman was silent. The girl had hit on the only piece of truth left in that heavy carcass. The woman was proud of it, and she was ashamed of it. But because it was a piece of truth she decided to surrender on good terms.

'He's my only boy, Helen, dearie. If you married him he'd be sure to find out everything. You see – your daddy knows all about me.'

Revelation broke on the girl. It was her father who had sent Bel away. She tried hard to hold her pride, but her pride broke her. Pomfret bent over the child and kissed her quivering neck.

'Darling!' she said, 'I came to give you advice and I've made a mess of it. Everything comes out in the wash. Your daddy sent him away.'

Then she stole from the room. In the hall she pulled herself together and walked like a lady down the Main Street of Barronloe, thanking her stars that she had not, at least, confessed that she had sold the girl for twenty-five pounds and the education of her own daughter.

3

Through the slats Helen looked across the bay, where the sun was pouring shadows into the little valley of the distant river. The cottages on the far shore were like mushrooms. There, only last April in the late afternoon of a day so soft that between the tides the surface of the mud cracked in the sudden heat, she and Bel had

gone exploring the first open tributary of the Barron Beag. They
had sighed with pleasure to see the cool breeze come crawling over
the water and race suddenly down their spines. As they passed under
the cold slimy bridge, the waters rushed at them around the quoins.

'Floods after the rains,' grunted Bel.

On either side the woods swept down to the edge of the gravel.
Far ahead the smoke of a village clung to the pine-tops. It had been
hard pulling against the current, so that they were glad to moor by
the steps at the back of a pub and drink lemonade that Bel brought
out in two enormous glasses. It was a picture she would never
forget – the boy standing there, balancing the glasses, in a doorway
set in a pink, sunlit wall. For, as she had looked up at him over the
necks of the hens pecking corn on the landing-stage, she had realized,
with a flooding of sudden excitement in her throat, how young and
manly he was, with his fair glib of hair falling into his eyes, his
soiled shirt climbing out of his baggy trousers, and in his ways plain
almost to rudeness. He did not take the slightest notice of her as he
handed her the glass and with a grin slugged down his own, spitting
afterwards with gusto at the clucking hens.

Leaving the boat there they had walked through the village and
sat on a tree-trunk outside a sweet-shop and sucked bull's-eyes. Bel
fired pebbles at the sweet-shop hens until the shop woman strode out
to them and called them 'little Proteshtant shnots' and other rougher
names that made them fly, red with laughter, back to their boat.

'Though why,' chuckled Bel, 'I should look like a Protestant!'

'Do I?' she had challenged.

'You have their cold look about you,' he taunted.

Then they had pulled slowly into the stream, smooth and colourless in the after-glow. They were stopped by the weirs of an abandoned mill, where the tide, dim with corn-dust, curled as slowly as
the hands of a clock.

Far away across the distant lock they heard the clanking of the
last train out of Barronloe, and coming on the clear air from the
hills above the rattle of a cart.

'Nice place,' commented Bel, where he lay chewing sweets on his
back in the prow.

' 'M,' said Helen, and she remembered how she had tried to write
her name in the dust of the water.

'Must have a picnic here,' he nad suggested then. 'Will you come?'
'I'd love to.'

She bent lower over the water, afraid she had said it too eagerly.

'Are you cold?' he asked. 'You have a thin dress on. You look like a lump of ice to me.'

'Lump?' she bandied. 'Thank you.'

He laughed and scratched his stomach and giggled again over the joke.

'Pole us home,' he suggested.

She stood and poled them around easily, and they began to float back through the grassbanks to the village.

'You're not really a lump,' he said critically.

She blushed, remembering how often Mrs Pomfret had said the same thing, though more nicely. She tossed her head.

'Getting dark,' she said.

The Harbour Road would be deserted, the lovers gathering under the trees. Bel was now poling beside her. It would be lovely on the estuary as they rowed back. Suddenly he saw the reflected lights of the village were dulled by a mudbank.

'Cripes!' he said. 'The tide is falling.'

Down they floated lower and lower between mudbanks, where tributaries now opened right and left, wide almost as the main stream. When he stood on a thwart to see ahead a star twinkled in a ring of mud.

'Safer to let me pole,' he advised, and as he stepped back the boat rocked under his feet.

'Shall I try to steer?'

'No, no, it can't be done.'

It was quite dusk now. The stars were coming out. The pinewoods might have housed wolves, so black they were. They ran aground.

'Blast!' she heard him curse under his breath.

He stood up and heaved the nose free. The stern ran aground now. The stars shuddered in the water.

'Can't see much!' he muttered.

His voice sounded hollow and distant, and when he paused to wipe the sweat from his brow she heard only the mud whispering in its ooze. He pushed off and for the last time she stuck.

'Bel! Swing her stern into that side-stream.'

'What good is that?' he snapped.

'We can sail out again,' she mocked, as shy people always mock.

He shoved her about and her stern fouled again. He sat down, and in despair flung his oar into the boat.

'We're done,' he said. 'We can't get off until the tide rises. I am a fool. That wasn't the floodwater pulling against us at the bridge. It was the falling tide.'

'We can't stay here all night,' she said firmly.

He was drying his face with his handkerchief.

'There's nothing for it but to get into the water. It's deep enough at the prow. But it's damnably cold. Just turn around, Helen, I'm going to undress.'

A few moments later she heard the splash of his body descending into the water, and the blubbering sound he made with his mouth at the cold. She saw his ten fingers clutching the side of the boat and his naked shoulders heaving against it.

'No good,' he shouted at last. 'I'm coming in. Turn away.'

She felt him clambering in and the smack of his wet feet on the thwart and his teeth chattering. She turned her head slowly – against her will – to look. She saw him forked against the stars, the water glistening on his thighs, one arm whirling to bring back the blood. Her cheeks burned, but she continued to look.

'All right, I'm dressed,' he said at last.

Almost in a whisper, she asked :

'When does the tide rise?'

'About dawn I should say.'

He took out a diary and lit several matches to see. They sizzled when they fell.

'Four twenty-two,' he said. 'Can you swim?'

'No. Why?'

'Ach!' He snapped. 'What does it matter if you can't? We might try to swim ashore up a side-stream. Wade, rather. Nice sight we'd be then, though, and a mile to the village after.'

He seemed to be turning over all possible plans in his mind.

'It's no good. Have a bull's-eye.'

'No, thanks!'

He crunched.

'Sorry, Helen!' he mumbled at last.

'It's all right. Father will be worried to death.'

They sat silent for about half an hour. Then her teeth began to dance.

'Take my coat,' he commanded, peeling it off.

'No.'

He thrust it at her. She flung it back.

'No!'

They sat silent for another spell, and he guessed she was holding her jaws tightly because when she took a breath her teeth chattered again. He went forward to where she sat and put his arm on her shoulder.

'Helen, you'll get your death of cold.'

He took off his coat and put it about them both and sat near her. She was too miserable to remove his arms. Across the far mouth of the valley a faint moonlight came from behind the clouds. About half an hour more and he suggested they must lie on the floorboards, and began to bale. She said she would not, but when he was beside her again an owl screamed suddenly in the woods, and she shivered violently in his arms. He became serious then and made her lie down. She said he must share the coat, so they lay side by side. She thought of the Harbour Road again, and the lovers clinging together under the trees. ('Helen, dearie, you have a lovely body.') When she felt his arms pressing her more closely she did not resist, nor when she felt his mouth pressing on her hair and forehead. They lay like that all night, and from time to time his hand strayed gently over her. That was when he told her all he knew of his mother's life.

When she awoke they were in the middle of the loch, the sky clouded over, the estuary filled as with milk, and the houses on the far shore watching her. The mist clung low on the shore.

As she was ill for three weeks after that she did not know that he had gone until she received his letter from Cairo. That lovely May night she went down the road to the strand, slipping on the stones and the slime, out to the very point and the first ripple. A yawl was entering the harbour, its boom creaking, a light from its hold cast upward on the brown sail. There, with a dead dog to her left and a stranded basket to her right, she looked where the tide held the winking town of Barronloe on a plate, and again and again she returned to that letter and its opening words – 'Darlingest Helen.' Of course she would wait for him. Sumatra? She would go to Siberia with him. He was the first person she had loved. She felt he would be the only one she would ever love. She spent all the following day writing a reply, but to that she received only a long letter telling about life in Sumatra, the loneliness of plantation life there, and he wondered many times if she would ever be able to exist there. That was the only letter she received from him since he landed. As she watched another sunset filling the valley across the bay with its shadows, she knew she would not hear from him again.

*

Her father came in. With a start she turned from the window.
'That's over!' he said.
'Did – what . . .?' (She had lost all sense of time and place.)
'Three years he got. I'm glad it's finished.'
'Oh!'
He sank into the sofa and wiped his cheek wearily with his palm.
'Play me something, Helen.'
For a minute she sat without playing. He thought she was deciding what to play. She was thinking, really, if she ought to speak to him about Bel. Then she remembered that Bel had not written for four months.
She began again at that pathetic largo, music that is like the sound of human tears. She played it gently and slowly, but with more understanding than she had ever played it in her life before. When she had finished, she went to the window and sat there for so long a time without stirring that she did not notice her father go. Quite clearly, and with absolute honesty and accuracy, she saw her life stretched out before her; and she faced it with courage, for there were many dreams that allured her by the way, and many hopeless possibilities that delayed her. If she had not known Mrs Pomfret – if she had met Bel far sooner – if Mrs Pomfret were a good woman, that above all – if her father had not found out about Mrs Pomfret – she even thought wildly of going off to Sumatra, and thereby came to the end of her vain turning and twisting. It wasn't that she didn't even know where his place was, thousands and thousands of miles away, lost even on the largest map. It was just that he was gone.
He was gone. And she was here, and would be here always. He was free – yet. But she was caught as, sooner or later, all human beings are caught in that coil of things from which there is no escape.

Now and again she saw the dumb gulls fly inland over the house, and in the harbour the fog breathing on the full water. High over the tide the clouds, warmed by the sunset, were bursting like roses, and as she, a statue by the window, looked at them over the ocean, she saw, without moving either eye or head, the antique lamplighter on the road beneath confess the autumn evening.

*

The door opened gently and the maid appeared.

'Tea is ready, miss. Your father is waiting.'

The statue scarcely nodded. Then, dissolving into a woman, it went downstairs to tea. Lolly and her young man were there. Her father sat quickly to table. She could see that they were all irritable for being kept waiting.

'You know I like you to pour,' chided her father.

Absently she poured. As she sipped, she saw the moisture on the window-panes.

Teresa

I

On the platform at Dieppe, at a corner so near the sea and the boat as to be part of the quay, there stood a small nun, flanked by three shapeless bags of that old-fashioned kind known as portmanteaux. Lovely as a black wallflower, large-eyed by nature, her eyes were now enormous: for she was looking across the quays with delight at the sun-blazing confections of houses on the other side. Now and again an old nun came hobbling up to her from the busier end of the platform, muttering something that drew a shadow across the lovely face, and then hobbling away again, head down, to this official and that official, wavering around like a top as each one hurriedly threw a few words at her and rushed past. At last the old nun came back to the novice, with her two hands out in appeal. The novice, followed by the old nun, at once walked straight down to the first official she saw and said in clear English:

'Where is the train for Rouen?'

The official glanced at her, then smiled, then bowed, and said politely, indeed with deference:

'There it is, mademoiselle,' and pointed to it.

'Mais non, non,' babbled the old nun. 'Pas aller à Rouen! Aller à Leesoo!'

'That's all right, Sister Patrick,' said the other. 'We change at Rouen.' And taking charge of the situation, she led the still-protesting nun up to the waiting train, put in the bags, helped – almost pushed – the old woman before her, and settled herself for the journey. The old woman clambered out again, red with fluster. Once more she ambushed official after official, all of whom said a word so like 'Wrong' that she insisted on hauling out her companion.

'Listen, Sister Patrick,' begged the novice, with saintly patience. 'I know the route backwards. It's Dieppe, Rouen, Elbeuf St Aubin, Serquigny, and then Lisieux. This is the train.'

The guard confirmed this, as far as concerned Rouen, and they clambered in at the last moment; but the old woman was still saying that they would never get to 'Leesoo', that they would find themselves landed in Paris in the middle of the night, that she had told Mother Mary Mell not to send her, that thirty-one years is too long out of a country for anyone to remember the language, and so on and so on, while the younger nun gazed wide-eyed out of the window at the passing fields.

'Our pilgrimage has begun,' she said in a dreamy voice, almost to herself.

'And what's going to be the end of it at this rate?' snapped the old woman. But then she gave a frightened look at the little face before her. The big eyes had lowered. A tremble was flitting across the red lips. The old woman immediately calmed down, laid a rough hand on the novice's knee, and said, gently, 'Sure, don't mind me, Sister Teresa. I'm all of a flusther. We're on the road now. Just as you say. When we get to Leesoo, 'twill be all right, a gilly. Saint Teresa will look after you and . . . Look't, I have no sense. We should be eating our lunch.'

'I'd love a cup of tea!' said the girl. 'I have a raging headache.'

'Tut tut,' clucked the old woman, and then she grabbed the girl's flank. 'Are ye wearing your double petticoat, Sister Teresa?'

'Yes, Sister,' said Teresa, with a blush and a warning look into the corner of the carriage, where an old Frenchman was devouring a roll and slugging red wine.

'Have ye the red-flannel drawers on ye?' demanded the old nun.

'Yes, Sister. Sssh!'

'There's nothing like red flannel next the skin,' said the nun, fiddling with the lunch-parcel. ' 'Tis a touch of cold you've got.'

' 'Twas the heat down under that deck,' said Teresa, and big floods of water entered her eyes. Her chaperone did not notice. 'I never saw Dieppe from the sea,' she whimpered. 'And Mother Mary Mell says that it's lovely from the sea.'

'Will ye have egg and cress, or tomato?' asked the old woman, too intent on her own appetite to take notice of anything else. 'We earned it,' she laughed, with a happy look about her and a country-woman's smile and nod to the old Clemenceau in the corner. He just dug a chunk of his roll off with his penknife, wiped the back of his hand right and left across his moustaches, and with an idle

C.S.S.O.—L

glance at her, opened both mouth and eyes simultaneously to devour the chunk.

The nuns began to nibble their food. Two hens could not have pecked more nimbly or neatly. Their travelling-companion finished his lunch almost before they had well begun. He carefully stowed away his bottle, produced a long cheroot, and began to fill the carriage with smoke. Then, to the dismay of the novice, he leaned across and closed the window tightly. By the time she had finished eating, she had already begun to lean her aching head on her palm. In minute imitation of the Frenchman, the old woman rubbed her moustaches and her beard clean of crubs, leaned back, closed her eyes, began to eat chocolates and to breathe through her nose. She woke with a start to hear Teresa say to the Frenchman :

'C'est assez chaud, monsieur. Veuillex bien ouvrir la fenêtre.'

The old tiger-face glared, growled, tapped his chest fiercely, poured out a flood of uncompromising French, and leaned back. His sideward glare thereafter was like a cat ready to pounce.

'What's that?' asked the old nun apprehensively.

'My head,' groaned Teresa.

'Offer it up, girl,' advised the old woman. 'Offer it up to Saint Teresa for the success of your intention.'

'I've offered it up on the boat the whole way over,' retorted the novice.

' 'Tis a cross,' said the old woman easily. ' 'Tis put on you by Saint Teresa to try you. Suffer it for her sake.'

The girl looked at her coldly. Then she observed that they had a second travelling-companion. He was a cavalry officer, who, with more consideration than their 'Clemenceau', was walking up and down in the corridor to smoke his pipe. Each time he passed the door he glanced up at his luggage on the rack. She raised her eyes appealingly the next time he passed. He paused, glanced at her, was about to pass on, paused again to look. A tiny gesture of her hand, a widening of her eyes held him. He came in, sat down, looked around him, and stared at her.

'Monsieur,' she begged. 'J'ai mal à la tête. La fenêtre. Est ce que nous pouvons l'ouvrir?'

'With pleasure,' he said, in English, stalked over to it and slapped it down.

A raucous argument started up at once between the officer and his fellow-countryman. Sister Patrick sat up, glared at her charge, and drew herself in from the combatants. The argument ended with the abrupt flight of the old man, cursing as he went, a laugh from the officer, and a frightened smile from the novice, accompanied by a glance at her chaperone, who, in the greatest suspicion of the officer, had lowered her head to look crookedly at him, like a duck, out under her coif. He was stroking his little line of moustache and smiling at Teresa. When Patrick slewed full around to survey her charge, Teresa had cast her eyes down demurely on her clasped hands.

Presently the officer got up, and went out to smoke another pipe. Every time he passed, he bowed in to the two nuns. Teresa never looked higher than his knees. When he had passed for about the sixth time, Patrick said:

'Sister, do you realize that officer is bowing to us every two minutes?'

'He is very kind,' said the little nun. 'Everybody is very kind,' she sighed, and began to pray on her beads.

But when he passed again, and bowed, the old nun said crossly:

'I believe you're looking at him, Sister Teresa!'

Teresa shook her head sadly and looked out of her big eyes at her chaperone.

'It is sad,' she said. 'He will be killed in the wars,' and her eyes swam with tears.

'And what's that to you?' whispered the old nun angrily.

'He reminds me of my brother, Jim, in the army,' said Teresa. 'He will be killed on the battlefield too. Oh, let us pray for the pair of them.'

The old nun could not refuse to do this, so they prayed together, and when the officer passed, and bowed, and smiled, the two nuns bowed and smiled back, and went on with their prayers for the repose of his soul when he would be killed in the wars. But he was useful at Rouen. He bought them two lovely cartons of café-au-lait, with buttered rolls, and showed them where the auto-rail would start. Then for the last time he bowed, and smiled, and went away, and they never saw him again.

2

It was the fading hour of day before their little auto-rail came and took the two travellers (and about eight others) trotting out of Rouen. A light haze of rain began to float down through the air. They passed a village deep in trees. There the first lights were beginning to contest the supremacy of the day. Soon the rain shone in rivulets on the lighted windows of the auto. The other travellers leaned closer together in a kind of animal companionship and chattered in loud voices, as if to keep the night at bay.

'I wonder,' murmured Teresa, 'what are they doing now back in Saint Anthony's?'

'Ah, yes!' sighed the old nun wearily. 'It makes England seem very far away to think of Saint Anthony's now.'

'And Dublin?' smiled the novice sadly.

'Ha!' said the old nun, with a yawn that dropped the subject into vacancy. Her youth and her friends were too remote for serious reflection.

'I know what my sisters are doing now in Dublin,' whispered Teresa. 'Having tea and making plans for the night.' And she looked out at the evening shower and the thickening night. 'I wish I never came,' she said suddenly. 'I feel terribly lonely.'

'Sssh! Tut tut!' chided the old nun; she had begun to eat more chocolates, and did not want to talk.

'It's all right for you,' complained the novice. 'You're going to meet your aunt. I'll know nobody in Lisieux. And if I find out there that I have no vocation, what'll I do?'

'Now, now, now,' grumbled the old woman, 'you know you'll get peace and calm in Leesoo. The saint will reveal your heart to you. You'll quieten down. You'll know that all these scruples of yours mean nothing at all. Sure, we all had them!' In spite of herself she became impatient. Her soothing voice gradually took on an edge. 'And anyway, goodness knows, you were eager enough to come! And let me tell you it isn't every Reverend Mother would let you. And it's not a holiday you're on, Miss. It's thinking of the holy saint you should be, and not of gillygooseys in Dublin.'

The novice withdrew into herself. She was too tired to pray; from sheer repetition the words were becoming meaningless.

Presently the old nun said, as if she were thinking aloud:

'And even if I have an aunt . . . Ha! . . . I suppose she won't know me.'

She stopped again and folded her hands deep into her sleeves.

'Thirty-one years,' she mused to the window.

The auto-rail rattled along for several miles. Then, Patrick leaned over and said comfortably:

'A terror for the hot milk at night. She'd drink two pints of it. Sure, 'twas enough to kill a plough-horse.'

From that on she kept on letting occasional little gasps of laughter escape her. It was as if somebody tickled her every three minutes. Then, after a protracted giggle out of each side of her mouth, she went off into a beatific sleep and the broad smile never left her face until they stopped abruptly in Lisieux.

As they left the station and emerged on the great square, Teresa cried in delight:

'But it's really a big place!'

Through the rain the little town shone into the station like a prismatic waterfall. She saw a green neon light flitting through the wetness over the hotel door. She saw a vis-à-vis crawling shiningly across the Place, and it made the town seem both cosy and intimate, and at the same time enormous and important. But Patrick had flown into a hurry and scurry, fumbling with her umbrella, and clutching her bags, and gazing all around her in a new rush of timidity; the two, in this conflict of absorption, nearly lost one another in the crush. The novice said:

'Oh, Sister Patrick! Couldn't we have one cup of tea in a restaurant before we go to the Hostel?'

'Wha-a-t?' cried Patrick, hunching up her shoulders, and laying her hand on her guimp like a stage Frenchwoman. 'Mon Pethite, que dites vous? Du thé? Vous savez bien . . . Vous savez bien que nous . . . Il faut . . . Il faut . . .' She groaned furiously. 'I can't talk French. I told Mother Mary Mell . . . Are you talking about tea? Do you realize, Miss, that you're on a pilgrimage? Gosthering in the middle of the street! Hurry! Hurry!'

They did hurry, under their black umbrellas, like two ants with top-heavy loads. Suddenly Teresa stopped and sneezed resolutely; once . . . twice . . . four times. Patrick towered over her. She started to gibber at her like a baboon.

'You're after getting a cold on me! That's yourself, and your window, and your fine officer!' Teresa sneezed a fifth time. 'Are you sure,' demanded Patrick, 'that you have the double petticoat?'

The novice's big eyes were directed miserably into a confectioner's window. It was bright with the brightest cakes.

'Dear Sister Patrick!' she wheedled. 'Don't you think we could have one small, tiny little cup of tea?'

The nun opened her mouth to say 'No,' looked at the window, looked at Teresa, and after a struggle said:

'Well! Since you have a cold coming on you, I'll let you have just one hot cup of coffee. Just one, mind you!'

It was warm in the café. Patrick had an éclair. Over their heads a radio kept weaving waltzes that made the novice sway gently on her chair. Patrick had two éclairs. The novice made her coffee last as long as possible. Patrick had a third éclair. Then, in spite of a fleck of cream on her jaw, Patrick's face was unusually forbidding as she looked up and said:

'Well, Miss, I hope you're feeling better now?'

'Thank you very much, Sister,' said Teresa, and rose with an air of firm resignation. 'We must go to the Hostel.'

A bell rang eight o'clock as they emerged. They wasted ten minutes searching for the Hostel, a bald faced house rising plumb from the pavement. Its brass tipped, reed-woven half-screens were damply inhospitable. Its closed door and iron grille were shining with the rain. The lay-sister who drew the slide of the grille spoke in unintelligible, provincial French, of which they understood only one word, 'Impossible!'

'Quoi?' squawked Patrick, clawing the grille, as the slide shot to in her face. 'What did that wan say?'

The bell jangled down the hall again. This time the lay-sister was even more emphatic, and therefore even less intelligible, and she became still less intelligible as Patrick hung to the grille and blustered in Franco-English. Teresa firmly pushed her aside, with a calm sanity:

'Vous ne comprenez pas. Tout est bien arrangé. Notre mère a écrit une lettre à votre mère....'

The lay-sister interrupted. She said, 'Trop tard.' She said, 'Huit heures.' She said these words several times. She closed the grille with the slowness of a curiosity that commented on the folly of the two foolish virgins who had come too late. Teresa turned to Patrick, and burst into peals of laughter at the look of horror on her face.

'We're too late!' she cried, joyously. 'Now we must go to a hotel!'

Patrick rent her.

'You and your tea! You did it deliberately! Wait until we get back to Mother Mary Mell! I'll tell her you're not fit to be a nun! You're a little flitthermouse! You're a gillygoosey! What a pilgrim we have in you! There's your answer for you! You're not fit to be a nun! You're a slip! You're a miss! What're we going to do? What'll my aunt say to me? What'll Mother Mary Mell say to me? What's going to happen to us?'

Teresa began to cry. Patrick at once hushed her tirade, unfurled her umbrella (it was as big as a bookmaker's), dragged up two of the bags and set off, in a mouth-buttoned fury, to find a hotel. The rain was now a downpour. Their bags weighted them down. She halted. She gave the girl a look that was worse than a blow, shoved her into a doorway, and said, 'Don't stir from there till I came back.' She left the bags in her care, and butted out into the rain.

Men kept approaching the door, and seeing the nun, they would stop dead, and push away. At first this merely frightened her for she did not realize her predicament: but suddenly a cistern flushed noisily behind her and she recognized that she was standing in the doorway of a *cabinet*. Clutching her bags, she fled down the street, down a side street, another side street, and halted panting under a café awning.

The old proprietor came out and looked at her, cocked his head to one side, bowed, considered her, smiled, said that it was a bad night, and wiped his indifference on to the tabletop. Then he gazed around him, looked at her again, shrugged, and went indoors. More men passed her, on their way in or out, always pausing, after the first glance, to smile and bow. Twice she got up to fly, wondered whether Patrick would ever find her, sat again on the damp iron chair. A drunken old man with a beard finally put her to flight by taking off his hat, leaning on the tabletop, and starting a flowery speech. She ran into a gendarme who was accompanying Sister Patrick down the street. Patrick threw her two hands up to the sky preparatory to a tornado of abuse. She was soaked; her guimp was a rag; her coif hung around her face like lace. Before she could speak, Teresa hurled herself on the old woman's breast and sobbed out all her awful adventures, so that the gendarme and the nun calmed her with diffi-

culty. They took her bag, then, and led her, whimpering, to the little
pension-pub that Patrick had chosen for their night's lodging. There
Patrick put her into bed, in a cosy little room all to herself, with
red stuff curtains and a dusty-looking carpet – it was nearly threadbare – and with her own two hands Patrick lit a fire, brought an
omelette, rolls, and coffee, and tucked her in for the night; and all
the time Patrick kept begging her pardon for that outburst at the
hostel. What with the comfort, the kindness, and the vestigial excitement, the little novice was melted to tears of happiness.

'Our pilgrimage is beginning,' she whispered happily to Patrick.
'Isn't it, dear Sister Patrick?'

' 'Twill begin in the morning,' temporized Patrick. 'And then the
saint will smoothen everything out.'

Right cheek touched right cheek, and left cheek touched left
cheek, in the way of all nuns kissing. Old fingers laid out her glossy
black hair on the pillow. The light went out. A rough palm smoothed
her forehead. The door clicked. The flames flickered on the ceiling.

In Kent, at Saint Anthony's, the only sound around the convent at
night had been the crackle of twigs in the damp wood, the hoo-hoo
of an owl. Here she heard footsteps in the street below, an occasional
motor-car swishing over the cobbles, the soft, whispering downfall
of April rain. Looking up at the wavering ceiling, she attended to
those sounds, whose tumult, and whose unfamiliarity, and whose
suggestiveness made England and her convent, Dublin and her home,
utterly remote – less part of another country than part of another
life. More than anything else they said, 'The pilgrimage has begun!'
They said, 'O dear Saint Thérèse, I will leave all things in thy hands.'
They said, 'O most omnipotent God, I yield all the world to Thee.'

'I want to be a saint!' she cried out, and beat the coverlet with
her palm. And at that fell asleep, curled up in bed as softly as a cat.

3

Only the hens were awake as they walked to first Mass at Saint
Pierre. The sun was glittering in the water between the cobblestones.
Teresa felt that she alone possessed the town. She felt that all things
converged on the forthcoming visit to the shrine. Even the warm
prophecy of the steam rising from the streets and the cloudless

whiteness of the sky seemed not something general to everybody in the world, but particular to her life alone. She whispered to Patrick, 'Thérèse is calling! I hear her!' Patrick nodded, too excited to speak.

After breakfast they began the ritual of Lisieux. Les Buisonnets, the Martin home (Saint Thérèse Martin), was exactly as they had foreseen it, just like all the photos and descriptions in biographies of the saint. They saw the 'trim lawn in front of the house', and 'the useful kitchen-garden at the back'. From the attic windows there was the expected 'distant view over the plain'. Teresa said to Patrick, with a sign of happiness:

'It was all made for her. If I had lived here, I, too, would have been a saint!'

Patrick nodded in agreement with the general proposition. For the novice to say that she could have been a saint was merely a way of saying that God had chosen one and could easily have chosen another.

' 'Tis Heaven!' she murmured, and clasped Teresa's hand.

It was the same in the sacristy of the Carmelite convent, where the saint's hair lies strewn under glass in its reliquary, and the walls are covered by mementoes of those who have paid honour to her memory – decorations, orders, swords, letters from all over the world. Here, where Patrick became almost incoherent at the prospect of meeting her aunt, thirty-one years after, now a Reverend Mother in the Carmelites, Teresa filled with sadness.

'The folly of the world!' she murmured, sighing again and again. 'They honour her now. They did not know the sorrow of her heart while she was alive.'

The two touched cheek to cheek again.

A Carmelite lay-sister next led them to the grave of the saint. From that they would go on to the convent proper to meet Patrick's aunt. They began to palpitate in mutual sympathy. The grave calmed them by its simplicity.

When they rose, the aunt stood beside them. Patrick toddled to her with cries of joy. The aged woman, her head a mere skull, her hands bony and ridged, gave no sign of recognition other than to say, 'God bless you, my child.' Old Patrick drew back like a frightened child. Timidly she introduced the novice. She explained falteringly why they had come.

'She's not sure if she wants to be a nun, Mother.'

The Carmelite looked at the novice. She, too, at once drew back. But the Carmelite smiled to hear the English name, Teresa, and took her hand gently and led her (Patrick following) across the garden to the convent ante-room. On the way she talked of simple things like the budding shrubs and the blessing of the rain. They sat in the ante-room and the Carmelite rang a bell.

They talked of the price of vegetables, until a faint passage of light in one wall drew their eyes to the grille – the last portal of the inner Carmelite hermitage. Behind the grille was a gauze, and presently Teresa's eyes made out, behind the gauze, a still face from which the gauze had eroded all recognizable character. All she could see was the vaguest outline of a countenance. As if she realized in that second how the discipline of the Order must have likewise eroded from the little girl of Les Buissonets all human emotion, and in a flash of understanding knew what sacrifice really means, she flung herself at the Carmelite's knees and cried out hysterically :

'Ma mère ! I have no vocation !'

Patrick intervened hurriedly :

'Pay no heed to her. She's upset and sick in herself. The child doesn't know what she wants.'

The aged Carmelite waved her aside and lifted the novice to her feet. Looking into her face with a clear eye, she said, after a frightening silence :

'Could you be a Carmelite?'

'No !' panted the novice, and she drew back, as if she were at that moment about to be imprisoned behind the grille.

'If you cannot be a Carmelite, my child, you can be nothing.'

'She'd be happy enough,' intervened Patrick comfortably, 'in an easier Order.'

'She will be happy – we will all be happy – only in Heaven,' said the Carmelite coldly. 'Could you not even try to be a Carmelite?' asked the aged woman.

'No !' begged the novice. 'I couldn't do it !'

'Why not?'

'To be always shut in?' trembled the girl.

'It is an enclosed Order,' agreed the Superioress calmly.

'I couldn't stand it !'

'How do you know?' catechized the Superioress.

For answer the girl burst into such a sobbing wail that Patrick drew her to her broad bosom and turned on her aunt.

'Ye have no heart!' she upbraided. 'Badgering the poor child! 'Tisn't that we expected from you! Don't heed her,' she comforted Teresa. 'My poor little girsha! Don't mind her. Sure we can't all be saints. You'll do your best. You can't do more.'

'But,' sobbed Teresa, 'I want to be a saint. 'Tis to . . . to . . . to be a saint I joined the nuns.' Her voice came out through her nose, miserably. 'If I can't be a saint, I don't *want* to be a nun!'

The old woman comforted her, and finally restored her to a whimpering silence. Looking up, they saw they were alone. The grille was closed. The veil was hidden. The Superioress had gone.

The two pilgrims went back to their pension. That afternoon, without discussion, they went on to Saint Malo. There the novice was expected to find bodily rest, as at Lisieux she had been expected to find calm of soul.

4

Saint Malo faces across a wide estuary the modern watering-place of Dinard. At night they saw the lights in the hotels, and cafés, and more coloured lights beaded all around the roof of the casino; and sometimes they heard music across the still surface of water. Steamers from Southampton and the Channel Islands floated in the bay at anchor. Patrick was charmed with her room in the convent where they stayed. It looked directly across at Dinard. She wrote to Mother Mary Mell that she had a 'grand-stand', and that she was thinking of going across in a row-boat some night to gamble in the Casino and make the fortune of the Order. Becoming serious in a postscript, she said that Teresa had not yet made up her mind, but that she was 'behaving with the most edifying devotion'.

Not only did the novice attend every service in the convent, but she had become pious beyond description, daily spending long hours alone in adoration in the chapel. But when Patrick noticed that she left her lunch untouched on her table on the third day of her arrival, and went up to the novice's cell to ask if this were wise, she made a frightening discovery. She found that the mattress and bedclothes had been rolled up and put away under the bed, and all the girl's flannel underclothing was hanging in her cupboard. At once she went down to the chapel, and hissed at the solitary worshipper to come out, beckoning madly with her bony finger.

'Sister Teresa,' she said severely, 'you are refusing your food. Is there any reason for this?'

The novice hung her head and said nothing.

'Answer me, Sister.'

Still the novice kept her eyes on the parquet.

'I command you, Sister, to answer me.'

'There is no reason,' whispered the novice.

'Then eat up your food in future,' ordered the nun. 'Do you want to make a skeleton out of yourself?' And she added more easily, 'Don't you know right well I'm supposed to bring you home as plump as a duck?'

The novice raised two large, sad eyes.

'Sister Patrick,' she begged, 'I will obey if you command me. But I want to do penance for my sins, and for the sins of the world. I feel I have received a higher command.'

'What higher command?' blustered the old woman, taken aback. 'What on earth are you talking about, Sister?'

Teresa sighed.

'The sins of the world are all about us,' she smiled sadly. 'I see them every night from my window, across the water, in the dens and gambling-houses. All lit up like the fires of Hell to lure poor souls astray. I dreamed the first night I came here that the Devil lives over there. I saw his red eyes in the air. I saw that this convent was put here specially to atone for the wickedness that surrounds it.'

'Holy Mother!' cried the nun. 'What are you talking about, girl? Sister Teresa, let me tell you that if you ate a proper supper . . . And by the same token, Miss, no wonder you have dreams if you sleep on the laths of the bed. Do you,' she threatened, 'sleep on the laths of the bed?'

The novice once more hung her head, and once more she had to be bullied into replying.

'I do, Sister,' she confessed unhappily.

'Well, then, let there be an end of it! What right have you to be going on with these andrewmartins off of your own bat? You know right well you must ask permission of your superior before you do the like. And that reminds me,' she cried, grabbing the girl's flank, and then standing back from her in horror, with her gummy mouth open. 'You haven't a stitch on you! Go upstairs at once, miss, and dress yourself properly. I'll be after you in two minutes. I'm worn out and tormented with your vagaries! Ten times I told Mother Mary Mell . . .'

She pointed upstairs – a figure of Justice.

The novice went, tearful, head-hanging. In two minutes the old nun followed. She opened the door of the cell. The girl lay on the ground, her arms stretched out like a crucifix, her dilated eyes fixed as on a vision over her head. The old nun entered the room, closed the door, and thundered:

'Get up out o' that!'

The novice did not move.

'Miss!' said the old woman, pale as a sheet, 'how dare you disobey me!'

The novice trembled as if a wind had ruffled her spirit. With her heart battering inside in her, Patrick walked over and looked down. The big brown eyes, so strikingly dark in that pale pink-and-white face, stared up past her. Patrick looked up at the electric light bulb. She looked all about her. The thick-moted afternoon sun slanted in across the bed. A hissing suspiration below the window was followed by the little groan of the gravel dragging back under the wave. Then she saw a slimy brown insect, with wavering head, creep to the white ear of the novice, and she screamed:

'An earwig! Climbing into your ear!'

Teresa sat up as if she was stung. The fright passed. The two looked at each other with hate in their eyes. At the door, Patrick said:

'I'll wait in the garden.'

In complete silence they walked four miles that afternoon. They did the same the following morning. That was their last full day. On the final afternoon Patrick spoke:

'We will be in Saint Anthony's tomorrow night. Do you know, yet, my dear, if you have a vocation?'

'I have decided to join the Carmelites,' said the novice.

They halted. They looked across the sea-wall into the blue of Dinard. A few lights were already springing up over there – the first dots in the long, golden necklet that already they had come to know so well. A lone seagull squawked over the glassy water. The sunset behind the blue pinnacles of the resort was russet.

'And what's wrong with our own Order, Sister dear?' asked Patrick of the vacancy before her.

'I feel, dear Sister Patrick,' judged the novice, staring ahead of her, 'that it is too worldly.'

'How is it too worldly?' asked Patrick in a whisper.

'Well, dear Sister Patrick,' pronounced the novice, 'I see, for example, that you all eat too much.'

The little wavelets fell almost inaudibly, drunken with the fullness of the tide, exhausted and soothed by their own completion.

'I shall tell Mother Mary Mell that you think so,' whispered the old nun.

'There is no need, dear Sister. It will be my duty to tell her myself. I will pray for you all when I am in the Carmelites. I love you all. You are all kind and generous. But, dear Sister, I feel that very few nuns really have the right vocation to be nuns.' Patrick closed her eyes tightly. The novice continued: 'I will surrender myself to the divine Love. The death I desire is the death of Love. The death of the Cross.'

They heard only the baby tongues of the waves. The evening star blazed in the russet sky. The old nun saw it, and she said, in part a statement, in part a prayer, in part a retort:

'Sweet Star of the Sea!'

Teresa raised her dark eyes to the star and she intoned in her girlish voice the poem of Saint Thérèse:

> 'Come, Mother, once again,
> Who camest first to chide.
> Come once again, but then
> To smile – at eventide.'

The old nun fiddled with her beads. She drew long breaths through her nose. She tried several times to speak. She gestured that they must go back. They turned and walked slowly back to the convent, side by side; the old nun as restless as if she were in bodily agony, the novice as sedate and calm as a statue. After a while Patrick fumbled in her pocket, and found a chocolate, and popped it into her mouth. Then she stopped chewing, and threw an eye at her companion. At the look of intense sorrow in the face beside her, she hunched up her shoulders and as silently as she could, she gulped the fragments whole.

On the journey homeward they did not speak one word to each other : all the way to Rouen in the trotting auto-rail; in the clanking train to Dieppe; on the boat; in the English train. In silence they arrived at Saint Anthony's, among the dank beechwoods, now softly dripping, in time to hear the first hoo-hoo of the owl, and to troop in with the rest of the community for evening chapel. Mother Mary Mell barely had time to ask the old nun how she had enjoyed her holiday – that first holiday in thirty-one years. Patrick's eyes fluttered. She recalled the lights of Dinard.

'It was lovely, Mother !'

Mary Mell caught the flicker of hesitation. Just as they crossed the tessellated threshold of the chapel, she whispered quickly, 'And Teresa ?'

Patrick who had been waiting for that question ever since the final afternoon in Saint Malo, and yet had no answer ready, took refuge behind the chapel's interdiction of silence. She smiled reassuringly, nodded, smiled, nodded again, and then, very solemn and pious, she walked in with her head down. She said her prayers badly. She slept hardly at all that night. She heard every crackling branch and fluttering night-bird. For what, in the name of the Most High, was she to say to Mary Mell? And what was she to say to the community in the morning? As she tossed and tumbled, she thought of Teresa sleeping peacefully in her cell, and the old woman burst into tears of rage.

In the morning there was no Teresa. She had left the convent, through a ground-floor window, before anybody was awake, and gone on the milk-train to London. She had walked across the city at that hour when the sun emphasizes the position of the East End, and the sleepers in the parks that she traversed are unwrapping their newspaper-blankets. A sister-in-law coming out to collect the morning milk found a nun sitting on the doorstep. She had breakfast, in a tennis-frock, along with the family.

She saw the convent only once again – about two years later when she brought her husband to see it. As they got out of the train she looked up into the familiar beeches at the steam of the engine caught in the branches, and she remembered how every train used to make the woods seem infinitely lonely and the convent darker and more melancholy, because that white steam suggested people travelling, and the luxury of the world she had renounced. Her George, who was a Protestant, and who was much excited by this expedition, nodded solemnly, and began to get an uncomfortable feeling that he was married to a nun. They were entertained politely. Old Sister Patrick did not appear. As they left, the starting train again sent its gushes of steam into the branches, and now those branches again seemed to Teresa to clutch not only at the white smoke but at her own heart. She felt that the woods enclosed a refuge from the world of which she had, irrevocably, become a part. As she snuggled down into her fur collar she gazed out of her big eyes at her husband, and said, with a shake of her little head :

'Ah, George! George! You will never know what I gave up to marry you!'

He smiled adoringly at her as, in obedience to a gesture, he leaned over to put a cigarette between her rouged lips.

'My precious Teresa,' he murmured softly, and patted her knee.

She shook her head at him again, with a pitying smile.

'Has it upset you, my sweet?' he asked dismally.

Saying never a word, she kept gazing at him fixedly, as if he were a stranger. He huffed, and hawed, and hedged himself behind his newspaper, looking as despondent as he considered proper. For as he explained to his colleagues in the morning, his wife was 'a very spiritual woman' and on occasions like this she always made him feel that he had the soul of a hog.

The Man Who Invented Sin

In our youth when we used to pour into the mountains to learn Irish, places that were lonely and silent for the rest of the year became full of gaiety during the summer months. Every day there were picnics and expeditions; every night there were dances, moonlight boating parties, sing-songs in the cottages. The village street became a crowded promenade; its windows never went black before one in the morning; the pub was never empty. Where once you could have been utterly alone half a mile off the road, in the bog or up the mountain, you could not now be sure of privacy anywhere. If you went up the mountain to bathe naked in some tiny loch you might suddenly see a file of young students like Alpineers coming laughing down on you over the next scarp; you might turn the corner of a lonely mountain-pass courting your girl and burst upon a bevy of nuns sedately singing choruses among the rocks – for every kind of teacher, laymen and women, nuns, priests and monks were encouraged in those years to come out into the hills.

How we all got accommodation I do not know. The priests took lodgings in the villages. The monks and nuns purchased derelict houses which had been abandoned by the landlords after the Revolution. The people gave up their best rooms to the rest of us, turned lofts into dormitories, one or two even set up second-hand bell tents. One July, so stifling was the house where I stayed – six at least to every room – that I used to take a rug every night and climb into the high hay in the barn; and there were always four or five like me who preferred to be bitten by the ticks and wakened early by the birds and the mountain air than to be half-suffocated in feather-beds under the baking slates. By the end of the month, however, I got so tired of digging the little crab-like ticks from under my skin that I moved two miles out the road to a place called Ryder's, a small house on the lower lake, which usually took nobody at all. Indeed, only by great cajoling did I persuade Mrs Ryder to take me in. My only fear, then, was that I might be lonely. But before she knew what had happened Mrs Ryder had not merely one lodger but five, for with the beginning of August the monks' hostel overflowed, and the nuns' hostel overflowed, and she had to take in two of the monks and two of the nuns.

There was nothing remarkable about my fellow-students, except, perhaps, that little Sister Magdalen was so dainty and gay and spirited that it seemed a shame to lock her away from the world in a convent. Sister Crysostom was tall, delicate, with big hands and a blotchy skin, and she walked with her toes turned in. She was a bit of a Miss Prim, and I think she had been chosen as companion for Sister Magdalen because she was so prim. Brother Virgilius was a countryman with a powerful frame and a powerful voice, round red cheeks, and no nerves, and why he had chosen to be a monk was hard to understand. It seemed to me that he would have made a better farmer than a teacher. However, I found that he was a fine hurler and I am sure the boys loved him for his natural ways. Brother Majellan was very different, a gentle, apple-cheeked man with big glasses, a complexion like a girl, teeth as white as a hound's, and soft, beaming eyes. He was an intelligent, sensitive man. I took to him immediately.

At first we saw very little of one another. They had their principal meal at their own hostels, were studying most of the day, and the only time we all met was in the evenings, when we sat in the little garden and passed discreet remarks across the path about politics or the weather; or, if there was rain, we would meet in the drawing-room where there was a turf fire, and talk of the day's lessons. They kept convent hours, were off to their rooms by nine at the latest, and long before I rose were gone down to the village to morning Mass. That year, however, the weather broke suddenly in the middle of August so that we found ourselves in the drawing-room almost every evening, over our notebooks and dictionaries and grammars. We had, by then, become like travellers on a long railway-journey who have broken the silence and are beginning to chat companionably. We might still sit silent for, say, a quarter of an hour, but then somebody would say something and we would all get going. One night for instance, Majellan lifted his eager, earnest, doggy eyes, and said :

'Sister Magdalen, how do you pronounce the word which I call *cearrbhach?*'

'Oh, Brother Majellan,' she laughed, shocked at herself, entertained by her own folly, 'I am afraid I do not even know what the word means!'

Virgilius clapped his two big countryman's paws together and roared out laughing.

'Sister Magdalen, I'm surprised at you! I'm surprised at you! Not know the word *cearrbhach*? It means a card-player or a gambler.'

'And is that what it means? *Cearrbhach*.' And she pronounced the guttural word as daintily as if it rhymed with *peruke*.

She was a city-girl and had never before heard Irish spoken by anybody but city-people.

'No! You're not saying it right at all. You're too ladylike about it. Say it the way the people say it. *This* way.'

'I see.' And again the dainty pronunciation like *peruke*. 'Like that?'

'Listen, Sister. I'll show you the way to talk Irish. If you'll pardon the expression, make a great big shpit inside in your mouth and gurgle it. Like this. Carrrwoochhhk.'

Crysostom immediately protested.

'Please, Brother Virgilius! If we cannot speak our own language like ladies let us not speak it at all.'

'But,' from Majellan, 'that really is the way the people speak. It is a guttural language. Like German.'

'Not Bavarian German. It is true that the Prussians . . .'

And off they went into a heated argument – the sort of argument we were always having in those days, about whether Ireland must always be a peasant country, and what other countries had achieved, and Virgilius, who hated arguments, blew out his lips and looked gloomily at his two big feet stretched out before him, and Majellan and Magdalen got so excited that Crysostom had to stop it with her usual : 'Sister, I really think it is our hour to retire.'

One day at the College, as we called the sunbaked tin building where we studied from ten to one, we were asked to write an essay on a proverb to which the nearest Saxon equivalent is 'The Child is Father to the Man'. I remember, that evening, how the mists lifted from the hills, and the sun began to raise gentle wisps of steam from the rocks, and the trout were leaping from a lake as blue as the patches of sky between the dissolving clouds. We spread newspapers on the two damp garden seats, and as we discussed the proper Irish terms to be used, the four of them began, without noticing it, to speak of their own childhood; where they had been born, where they went to school, and so on. Sister Magdalen sucked the end of her silver pencil and said :

'I know the Gaelic for "I was born", that is *Do rugadh mé*. And the place – Templemore. Of course, that is *An Teampall Môr*. The Great Temple. Or the big church. Though the Lord knows there's no big temple in Templemore.' She sighed. Then she cocked her head suddenly. 'I suppose you were never in Templemore, Brother Majellan? But, sure, why would you! It's an out-of-the-way little place.'

Crysostom tapped my fingers irritably with her pencil. I was idly pulling a fuchsia flower to pieces :

'How would you say that, Sister?'

'Which? What? What was it you said, Sister Crysostom?'

' "It's an out-of-the-way little place." You see I want to say that, too. I was born in a small little place like Templemore.'

'Where was that?' asked Virgilius idly. He had been staring solemnly at the fuchsia that I threw into his lap.

'Kilfinnane,' said Crysostom, 'in County Limerick.'

At once Virgilius whirled and slapped her thigh.

'Yerrah, Crysostom, do you mean to tell me that you come from Kilfinnane!'

'Brother!' And she held his arm excitedly. 'Do you know Kilfinnane?'

'Do I know my own father? Wasn't I born just below in Kilmallock? Oh, wisha, then, 'tis many the fine Sunday I took the old bicycle out to Kilfinnane hunting hares behind the rath. If you come from Kilfinnane you must surely know the rath?'

'The rath is on our land!'

'Ah, no?' – in a huge childish delight.

'Often and often I stood on the rath and looked down at the smoke of the train coming into Kilmallock – in and out of the woods – the little white smoke. And I could watch it again for another half an hour after it left Kilmallock, puffing away down towards Cork.'

'I well believe you! It's a wonderful view. They say you can see six counties?'

'For a whole hour,' she remembered. 'The little white smoke. I used to wonder who might be in it, and would I ever travel away in it myself.'

'Didn't I go every night to meet it at the station and gather the Dublin papers, for my uncle kept a paper shop in the Main Street? The Cork train we called it. Majellan, you're a Corkman, aren't you?'

Majellan was not listening to us. He was gazing across the darkening lake whose headlands were faint as smoke.

'My father,' said Sister Magdalen thoughtfully, 'was a doctor. I know how to say that, too. My mother died when I was fourteen ... I was a lone child ... My father married a second time.'

Majellan kept staring over the lake. She said something about a notebook and flitted indoors. I got tired of listening to Virgilius and Crysostom and got up to go to the dance. It was only then I noticed that Majellan and Magdalen were in the hall. She was dabbing her eyes with his big red handkerchief.

When I came back from the dance the half moon had vaporized the moist land with a melancholy, filmy light. The house was black and silent.

I think it was Virgilius who first began to play pitch-and-toss along the garden path, and it was that evening that Magdalen called Majellan 'Jelly'. I came on them laughing over the game, which Brother Virgilius was trying to teach to the other three. Brother Majellan was, by then, calling Sister Magdalen 'Maggie', Crysostom naturally became 'Chrissy', and Virgilius, of course, joined Jelly as 'Jilly'. How they laughed over that! I crowned the night for them by taking them up to the drawing-room piano and teaching them all a song with a chorus:

'*Bab Eró 'gus O mo mhíle grá.*'

And Chrissy so surprised us by the strength and sweetness of her voice that at the end Virgilius clapped his hands and shouted, 'I wouldn't doubt you, Chrissy. I knew you had it in you,' and made her sing the song again alone. As she sang we heard a clear echo: it was a boating party out on the lake. They took up the chorus and gave it back to her until they faded around a headland still singing.

'But you know,' gurgled Magdalen, 'I really don't know what it all means. Can you translate it for me, Jelly?'

'No trouble at all,' said Majellan. 'It is a young fellow singing a song to his lady and this is what he says.'

As he translated he gradually blushed redder and redder, and Virgilius winked at the big, rolling eyes of Magdalen, and her rounded little mouth, just ready to burst into laughter. When Majellan stuck his head right out through the window to look at the lake Magdalen burst. Crysostom said : 'I really think, Sister, it is our hour to retire.'

'Jelly,' said Virgilius, when they were gone, 'you big gom! You have as much sense as a child of two.'

When monks and nuns quarrel, I found, they seem to be astonished and shocked rather than angry : like children who have bumped against a door or a calf who has tried his first nettle. Grown men would have ended it with a curse or a clout. I escaped down to the kitchen to practise my Irish on Mrs Ryder. She was baking a cake, and humming 'Bab Eró . . .' Her cousin, who was the clerk in the Post Office, was sitting on the settle. She asked me which had the lovely voice. Mrs Ryder said her house was blessed.

'The creatures! Isn't it grand to hear them enjoying themselves? Four saints I have in the house.'

'Only four?' I protested.

'What time did *you* come in last night?' she asked, and the conversation became exuberantly coarse.

The next evening too, was exquisitely silent. The tiny trout-splashes could be heard clearly, and the cattle lying on the dry strand across the water chewing the cud. We were all upstairs, I playing the piano, Virgilius seated in the open window singing and beating time with a silver tankard that young Ryder won in a tug-of-war, Jelly and Maggie trying to waltz, and when Crissy was not laughing at poor Jelly's efforts to learn the steps she, too, was singing, at *Bab Eró*, like a blackbird. The music must have carried a long way over the water.

The door was slashed open with a bang that made the piano hum, and there was our local curate's black barrel of a body blocking the opening : for though he was not more than twenty-five – I believe it was his first parish – he was very fat. He was also pompous and cocksure. In the College we called him Lispeen, which is the Irish for a frog. For that second it was as if a camera-reel stopped dead – the tankard held in the air, the two dancers like a waxworks, and Crissy with her mouth open.

'Glory be to God,' he moaned. 'So I have been informed correctly.'

(It was only after that I thought of the postmistress on the settle the night before; you might as well talk to a microphone as to a postmistress.) 'To think that this kind of thing has been going on under my nose for weeks.' He let his voice fall solemnly, even secretively. 'Unknown to anybody!' He roared then: 'To think I cannot go for a summer walk to read my office without hearing this kind of caterwauling!' His voice fell again. 'If Martin Luther could only see this! What's your name?' he stabbed at Crissy. She had turned as pale as her coif.

'Sisssster Cryssossostom, father.'

'And your name, Sister?'

'My name is Sister Mary Magdalen,' said Maggie, very dignified and entirely self-possessed, and looking very angry.

'Well-named,' he growled. I saw Jelly grow red with fury. 'Go to your rooms, please. I'll talk to these gentlemen.' With a scornful emphasis on the last word.

They fluttered out obediently, Magdalen with her head in the air, Crysostom with terror in her eyes. Majellan turned on him. I held his arm. He was only a monk, and no match for a curate in his own parish.

'You had no right, father, to talk to the sisters like that.'

The curate swelled.

'Are you daring to answer me back, young man?'

Majellan's voice shook but he held his ground.

'We are doing no harm.'

Even Virgilius spoke up, though more respectfully – he knew the power before him.

'Sure we were only having a bit of sing-song, father?'

The curate gasped, melodramatically – I swear he had taken a prize for elocution at his seminary – then dropped into a wonderful tone of sarcasm.

'Only having a bit of a sing-song? *Only* having a bit of a singsong? Well, well!' He put his stick behind him like a shooting-stick and teetered back and fro on it. He was very sure of himself. 'Perhaps, gentlemen, we think that we are back in the days of the Reformation?' Then he did his roar again. 'Singing? Dancing? Drinking?' He whirled his stick and cracked the tankard.

Virgilius stared into the tankard, and sighed: 'Shweepstake Tickets.'

That sent the blood to Lispeen's forehead.

'I'll talk to you young bucks in the morning when I've had a word with your Superior. Good evening to you.'

The door slammed. We heard him go downstairs. His voice boomed in the kitchen at the Ryders. Then we saw his shadow passing across the paling sheen of the lake.

'The bosthoon,' hissed Majellan.

'Jelly,' moaned Virgilius, who had seized the situation at once, 'we're for the long drop!'

With that we stole down the corridor and tapped at the sisters' doors and conferred in a huddle, and Virgilius and Crysostom blamed Majellan for speaking back but Magdalen said, 'You were quite right, Brother. He is no gentleman.' But Crysostom kept pulling her fingers and looking at each of us in turn. She knew, too, how all this would appear back in the city where the Bishop and their Superiors would say, 'What is this! Nuns and monks living in the same house? Dancing together? Singing choruses? Playing pitch-and-toss out in the garden? And what's all this about *a tankard*?'

Magdalen said next morning that she heard Crysostom crying late into the night.

Actually nothing at all happened. Old Ryder and the Parish Priest between them must have put a stop to the curate's gallop. After all curates come and curates go but parish priests, like the brook, go on for ever. But the story spread, and the students gathered round the four to comfort and encourage them, and of evenings people started to walk out to Ryder's and, in spite of Sister Crysostom's warnings and tremors, we began to have regular concerts in the garden. The four even began to go out on surreptitious boating-parties, and the bed-at-nine rule gradually became bed-at-ten, and even bed-at-eleven, until they were soon having as happy a time as anybody. Or should have, if their consciences were at ease. But were they? For, looking back at it now, I think I understand what had occurred. The Serpent had come into the garden with the most wily of temptations. He had said, 'How dare you eat this apple?' And straightaway they began to eat it. They swallowed the last morsel of their apple the night before they were due to return to the city, perhaps for a lifetime, among the smelly slums about their schools.

We were moody that evening in the garden.

'I suppose this will be the last time we'll see the moon on the lake,' said Sister Magdalen.

But the moon would not be up until after eleven, and a fairy-wind in the reeds, ruffling the stars in the water into a fuzz, meant that even then there might be a clouded night.

'Our bus goes at seven,' said Sister Crysostom. 'When does yours go, Brother Virgilius?'

By anticipation they were already becoming formal with one another.

'Half-past seven,' Brother Virgilius.

'Who'll walk as far as the lake?' suggested Brother Majellan.

They went down the white road. Autumn was coming already. A white mist hung low over the river. The lake was dim as a ghost. They stood at the edge of it and looked at the low hills beyond.

'Sure, we can be looking forward to next year,' said Brother Virgilius cheerfully.

'If there are any summer courses next year,' murmured Sister Magdalen.

The soft sound of oars was heard and a boat appeared out on the water. The people in it were singing quietly; a last boating-party. It was one of those big, barge-like boats built for excursion parties, and there must have been twenty people in it, crushed shoulder to shoulder. Majellan hailed them and they approached and when they invited the four out for a row even Crissy hardly demurred. The presence of the two monks and the two nuns seemed to cheer them up, for as they rowed away towards the narrows, making for the upper lake, the songs became louder and more merry. The lights of the village overflowed into the lake. Promenaders there heard them and sang back. Doubtless the curate heard them, too, and thanked God they would all be gone in the morning.

Time ceases to exist on a lake: every fisherman knows that. Somebody said that the moon would be up at eleven and would light them home. Crissy whispered to Maggie that that would be very late, and what would happen if some message came from the Hostel? But Maggie hushed her passionately, and Virgilius cried, 'Let the last night be the longest.'

It was much later than eleven before they got through the narrows – the old barge stuck there as it always did. Then the grey mountain slowly swelled up like a ghost against the spreading moon, and the whole land became black and white. On the bright side of the land the white cottages shone under their tarry roofs, and on the dark hills their scattered yellow lights invited us home. It became cold on the water. Rowing back against the current was a slow business. Heavy drops of phosphorescence fell from the blades. Presently a voice said, 'It is near twelve, lads, put your backs into it.' Now they were not singing at all; nor did they sing again until they saw the remaining village lights – only one or two left now. And they did not sing Irish songs, which are nearly all melancholy, but old music-hall songs like *Daisy, Daisy*, and *The Girls you Can't Forget*, and *I'm One of the Knuts of Barcelona*. The barge was not much more than twelve feet from the shore when they saw, clear in the moon-light, the black figure standing on the causeway. Majellan yelled, 'Backwater!' The barge slewed around.

'I suppose, my dear ladies and gentlemen, that it does not matter to you that you are keeping the whole village awake?'

Nobody replied. The rowers set off for the opposite shore. The two brothers turned up their coat collars to hide their Roman collars. The two nuns hid their guimps and coifs with borrowed coats. Every-body was feeling cross and tired. As they neared the far shore the same black figure awaited them. He had raced round by the bridge, and gone leaping over heather and bog-pool.

'You won't land here tonight until I have the name of every person on that boat!'

The midnight mountains cried back, 'On – that – boat.'

The boat pushed off again and in mid-lake they held a conference: for even lay-teachers do not like falling out with a priest. And the four religious? There was only one thing to do. It was easy to dis-guise Majellan and Virgilius: caps for black hats, and the Roman collars ripped off. The nuns had to remove guimps, and cowls, put on kerchiefs and pin up their skirts. Then the boat again rowed to the landing-place, the men crushed around the priest arguing loudly, and the rest ran. In five minutes he was alone on the causeway. At his feet he saw a white object on the stones: a nun's starched guimp. As he looked at it he trembled like a dog.

He was no longer alone by the moon-flooded lake. He was roaring in the pulpit, holding up the guimp: he was in the Bishop's Palace quietly unfolding a pale linen object out of brown paper: he was in the Parish Priest's sitting-room and the white thing lay between them on the table : he was knocking at Ryder's door – yes, even if it was nearly one o'clock in the morning. He might have done all these things if, when he got back to his cottage, there was not a sick-call before him, and he had to get out his car and drive at once three and a half miles into the heart of the hills. Half an hour later he was tearing back. He had been hoaxed. The window of his cottage was open. The guimp was gone. It was the one good deed I did for my four friends.

I was awakened by the supernaturally bright light : it was not the sunrise : it was the sinking moon. My watch showed me that it was barely turned five o'clock. Dew and mist were all around the silent house : the lake was frosty; the sky pallid. The trees were weighted with sleep. Only the ceaseless mountain-stream and the deceived birds made a sweet noise. Below in the garden, by the wooden gate, stood Majellan and Magdalen, talking . . .

I never saw Magdalen again; I never saw Virgilius again; I never saw Crysostom again.

That was nineteen hundred and twenty, and not for twenty-three years did I meet Majellan. He was, of course, still a monk, and will always be : he was greying, and a little stooped, and much thinner. His eager, doggy eyes lit up for me : until I began to joke about those days, and then the light faded. I asked him about the others, and he told me that Virgilius was now a Principal somewhere. He had not heard of the two nuns since that night on the lake.

'Ah !' I sighed. 'Great days ! But nobody wants to learn the language now. The mountains are empty.'

'Yes. The mountains are empty.'

'What a shame !'

'Mind you,' he said, after a moment, 'I'm not sure that I altogether approve of young people going out to these places. I hope I'm not being puritanical or anything like that, but . . . well, you know the sort of thing that goes on there.'

I was so shocked that I could not reply for a moment.

'But, surely, it's all very harmless ?'

He shook his head seriously.

'Maybe. You *never* know.'

I said something idle. Then I asked him did he go out there at all nowadays.

'That was our last year.'

'I hope it wasn't any trouble with your superiors?' I asked anxiously.

'Oh, nothing like that. No. It was just . . .' He looked away. Then he said over his shoulder, 'I didn't much want to, really.' Then he looked at me, and in a little gush of confidence he said, 'You mightn't understand it, now! But it's not good to take people out of their rut. I didn't enjoy that summer.'

I said I understand that. After a few more words, we parted. He smiled, said he was delighted to see I was looking so well, and went off, stooping his way back to his monastery in the slum.

By coincidence, two hours later, I found myself side by side with Lispeen, looking into a bookshop window. He was scarcely changed, except for a faint brush of grey at each ear; he wore a tall silk hat and carried a silver-headed umbrella. When I spoke to him and he turned, the sunset struck his rosy face and lit the sides of his hat so that they glowed and shone. With difficulty I brought his mind back to those years, but when I did he greeted me as heartily as if I was his best friend, and laughed so merrily at the memory of those old days that I almost expected him to clap me on the back.

'Of course, you know,' he confided, with wide eyes, 'they were only children. Such innocents!' He laughed at the thought of the innocents. 'Of course, I *had* to frighten them!' And he laughed again, and then threw up his head and said heigh-ho in a big sigh. Then he shook my hand, and beamed at me, told me I was looking grand, and went his cheerful way. He bowed benevolently to every respectful salute along the glowing street, and when he did his elongated shadow waved behind him like a tail.

Unholy Living and Half Dying

Jacky Cardew is one of those club bachelors who are so well-groomed, well-preserved, pomaded, medicated, and self-cosseted that they seem ageless – the sort of fixture about whom his pals will say when he comes unstuck around the age of eighty, 'Well, well! Didn't poor old Jacky Cardew go off *very* fast in the end?'

For thirty years or so he has lived in what are called Private Hotels; last winter he said to his friends, 'These bloody kips are neither private nor hotels, I'm going to take a flat.' What he got in the end was the sort of makeshift thing that goes by the name of a flat in Irish cities – two rooms (that is, one room cut in two), with the W.C. on the ground floor and the bathroom on the top floor; and in the bathroom an unpleasant, greasy-looking gas-stove such as Prince Albert might have unveiled at the Great Crystal Palace Exhibition of 1851.

But Jacky was delighted. At least he now had privacy. Nobody lived in the house but himself and his own landlady, for a tinsmith had the ground floor (rather noisy and smelling of solder), there were solicitors' offices on the second floor, the old lady lived under the slates, above Jacky's flat, and he hardly ever saw her except when he paid his rent.

About two o'clock one bad February morning just as Jacky and a few friends were settling down for the fourth time to their last game of solo they gradually became aware that a dog was beating his tail on the floor above. There was no other sound then – for a while – but the flick of the cards and the rain spitting on the window and the slight exclamations of the players. Then they heard the rapping again.

'Better go easy, boys,' somebody said, playing a card, 'we're keeping the old lady upstairs awake.'

They played on intently. Again they heard the rapping, this time insistent and loud. Jacky glanced around at the lifted eyebrows, at his wrist-watch, at the dying fire, at the drops sparkling on the pane in the arclight of the Square below, and went out with the sort of frown he would have turned on a junior in the bank who had not been soapy enough. Striking matches he climbed the stairs. The nail-heads shone. Hearing him stumble and curse she called his name, and he made his way towards the voice, stooping under the great rafters of the attics, elbowing aside the damp washing that she had hung there to dry, feeling the cold within a few inches of his poll. He found her room, a bare attic. He was affronted by its poverty, its cold stuffiness, its sloping attic-window that wept in ripples with the lights of the city.

In the matchlight he saw her pale eyes staring up at him in terror from the pillow; he saw her hollowed cheeks; the white beard on her chin; her two pigtails tied with bits of red wool. The match burned his fingers. Through the dark he heard her whisper:

'Mr Cardew, I'm dying.'

He was so frightened that he immediately lit another match. He was even more frightened by what she replied when he asked her if he could call in one of her friends:

'God help us,' she panted. 'Friends how are ye? I haven't a friend to wet me lips. Not a friend. In the world.'

He raced down the stairs. One of his pals was a doctor; he went up and examined her, soothed her, came down, said there was nothing much wrong with her except old age and perhaps a touch of indigestion, and ordered two aspirins and a hot-water bottle on her stomach. They made her comfortable for the night and the party went home, heads down to the rain, shouting commiserations all round.

Jacky came back to his dishevelled room and sat by the cold fireplace. He heard every quarter-hour strike from the City Hall, sometimes bold and clear, sometimes faint and sad, according to the mood of the wintry wind. He suddenly remembered that his own mother had gone on a night like this. He wondered who would attend to the old woman if she died, and for the first time he took notice of the family photographs hung around the walls, mainly young men and women and vacant-looking babies with their mouths open. There was a big black enlargement of a man with a grey moustache and a bald head. He reminded him of old Cassidy, his last Manager, who now dined regularly every Tuesday of the year with another retired banker called Enright. As Jacky poked the dead

cinders it came to him that Cassidy probably had no other friend in
the world, and, begod, anyway, once you turn fifty what is it but a
gallop down the bloody straight?

At half-past three he went up to have another look at her. She was
asleep, breathing heavily. He tried to feel her pulse but could not
remember what a normal beat is and felt hers was as low as a hearse.
He returned to his cold room. The rain still spat. The Square outside
shone. He felt a dull pain in his groin and wondered, could it be
appendicitis? He thought that he should have called in the priest to
her and he counted the years since he last went to Confession. At
half-past four he had another look at her and found her breathing
easily and decided she was all right. As he pulled up his pyjamas he
gave his paunch a dirty look.

He was awakened at his usual hour by the old lady herself, bringing him his usual hot cup of tea and buttered toast. She had a prayer-
book under one arm and was dressed for the street.

'Good Heavens,' he gulped, 'I thought you were . . .'

Her tall lean body swayed over like a reed with the gusts of
laughter.

'Mr Cardew, 'tis well known you can't kill a bad thing. My little
hot seat in Purgatory isn't ready for me yet. Ah, I knew I'd pay for
that load of bacon and cabbage I ate yesterday.' An inelegant gesture
from her stomach to her throat made him hastily lay down the
buttered toast. 'I was all swelled up with it the day long.'

Jacky dressed, blaspheming. On his way out he decided to have a
serious word with the woman. She had returned from chapel and
was sitting in her kitchen sucking up a big basin of soup.

'Look here, Mrs Canty,' he said severely, 'is it an actual fact that
you have no friends whatsoever?'

'I have plenty friends, Mr Cardew,' she smiled happily. 'The best
friends any woman ever had.' She laid her bony hands on a pile of
prayer-books – there must have been about twelve of them, a pile
a foot high, all in shiny black cloth coverings. 'Haven't I the souls
suffering in Purgatory? I have Saint Anthony.' Her glance directed
his to a big brown-and-cream statue on the dresser. 'And haven't I
the Sacred Heart?' He eyed the red-and-gold statue over the sink
with the withered palms of last Easter crossed before it. 'Look at
the Little Flower smiling at me. And what about Saint Joseph and
Saint Monica?'

Jacky's head was going around like a weather-cock.

'And amn't I only after coming in from praying to the Left Shoulder? Friends, Mr Cardew?'

She smiled pityingly at him. He strode out, to prevent himself from saying, 'Then why the hell didn't you call on them last night instead of rapping me up to you?' Instead he took it out of his secretary at the bank.

'Pure damn superstition, that's what I call it. Craw-thumpin' by day and bellyachin' by night. The usual Irish miserere. All based on fear of hellfire and damnation. It would turn anybody into an atheist!'

The girl talked up to him; they almost quarrelled; she told him he should be ashamed of himself; she even told him his 'day would come'; she drove him beside himself by telling him she 'would pray for him'. At lunch he got into a violent argument about religion during which he kept on using the word, 'Benighted! Benighted!' He was still at it that night in the club, but he had to go easy there as most of the members were Knights of Columbanus and business is business. He took the middle line of:

'Mind you, I have a great regard for what I call *real* religion. And, mind you, I'm no saint. I'm honest about that. Though I suppose I'm no worse than the general run, and maybe a bit better if the truth were told. And I'll say this for it, religion is a great consolation for old age. But if religion doesn't go with *character* – character first and before all – then it crumbles away into formalism and superstition!'

They all considered it safe to agree with that. He surveyed his cards contentedly.

'I think it's your lead, Maguire.'

He found himself strolling homewards with Maguire: a gentle night after all the rain, and a delicate spring touch in the air.

'We won't know where we are now,' said Maguire, 'until Easter is on us.' And he gave an uncomfortable little laugh.

'What's the joke?'

'Wisha, I was just thinking there tonight when you were gassing about religion that . . . begod, do you know, 'tis a year since I was at confession. With Easter coming on now I suppose we'll have to get the ould skillet cleaned again. Easter Duty, you know. Where do you go? I always pop up to Rathfarnham to the S.J.'s. Men of the world. Nobody like 'em.'

'I usually go there, too,' lied Jacky. 'You can talk to those fellows.'

And he began to wonder, would he or would he not make a dash for it this year?

On the Thursday of Holy Week, just after midnight, Jacky and the boys were in the middle of a hot game of nap when a faint knocking percolated through the ceiling.

'No bloody fear,' he grunted. 'Once bitten twice shy. More cod-acting.'

They gathered up their hands and began to play. Through the slap of the cards the rapping came again, this time more faintly.

'That one now,' said Jacky. 'You play, Jim. That one . . . God, have you nothing but the Ace? That one is a typical example of the modern Irish crawthumper. Behind all this piety, believe you me . . . Who said I reneged? What are you talking about, didn't I put the seven on Redmond's deuce? Behind all this so-called piety there's nothing but a child's fear of the dark.'

Maguire laughed at him.

'Now, Jacky, there's no earthly use your beefing about religion. The stamp of the Church is on you. 'Tis on all of us. 'Tis on you since the day you were born and sooner or later they'll get you and you may as well give in and be done with it. Mark my words, I'll live to see the day you'll have holy pictures all around your bloody bedroom! The stamp is on you! The stamp is on you.'

Jacky flared. Here was a fellow who barely confessed once a year and he was talking as if he were a blooming saint.

'Stop wagging your finger at me, please. And, anyway, with all your guff, when were you at confession last, I'd like to know?'

Maguire laughed smugly.

'I don't in the least mind telling you. I was there three days ago. A grand old priest.' He clicked his fingers and looked around him at the group. 'He let me off like that. I think if I'd told him I'd committed murder all he'd say would be, "Any other little thing troubling you, my child?"'

They laughed approvingly.

'Ah, there's nothing like an S.J.,' Maguire went on. 'Listen, did ye ever hear the one about the fellow that went to confession the time of the Troubles here and said, "Father, I shot a Black and Tan." Do you know what the priest said? "My child," says he, "you may omit your venial sins." Honest to God, I believe 'tis a fact.'

They all laughed again although they had heard the yarn many times before : it is the sort of story every hardy sinner likes to hear. Through their laughter the knocking came again.

'I'm afraid, Jacky,' said another of them, a commercial named Sullivan, 'you'll have to have a look at the ould geezer.'

With a curse Jacky flung down his cards. He climbed to the attic. He struck a match and gave one look at her and at once he knew that she was bad. Her forehead was beaded. Her chest rose and fell rapidly.

'Mr Cardew. I'm finished. Get me the priest. For God's sake.'

'Certainly. Certainly. Right away. And I'll get the doctor.'

He belted down the stairs and burst in on them.

'God, lads, 'tis no joke this time. She's for it. I can tell it. I can see it. Maguire, run out for the priest like a good man. Sullivan, there's a telephone down by the kiosk, call the doctor, get Cantillon, Hanley, Casey, any of 'em. Hurry, hurry!'

He brought her up a stiff whisky but she was too weak to sip it. When the priest came, a young man with the sad eyes and bent head of a Saint Francis, the gamblers huddled outside under the rafters, looking through the skylight at the wide Easter moon. They were all middle-aged men, younger than Jacky, but replicas in every other way.

'Oh,' whispered Maguire. ' 'Tis true. Just as the old priest told me. Like a thief in the night. We never know the day or the hour.'

' 'Twas a terrible winter,' whispered Sullivan. 'I never saw so many people popping off. I see where old Sir John Philpott went off yesterday.'

'Ah, God, no?' begged Jacky, shocked at the news. 'You don't mean Philpott of Potter and Philpotts? I was talking to him in the club only three days ago.' (He said it as if he were affronted at Sir John's giving him no previous warning of the event.) 'But he was a comparatively young man ! Was he sixty-two itself?'

'Heart,' whispered Wilson. 'He went off very fast in the end.'

'Here today,' sighed Maguire. 'Gone tomorrow.'

'The best way to go,' murmured Sullivan. 'No trouble to anybody.'

'That is,' whispered Maguire, 'provided our ticket's been punched for – ' And he pointed respectfully upwards. 'I heard a preacher say one time that he knew a man who came into his confession-box after being twenty years away. He said he had just lifted his finger and said the *Absolvo te*' – here Maguire lifted his two first fingers – 'when the man dropped dead at his feet in the box! There was a close shave for you!'

Jacky moved uneasily; he knew the story was just a preacher's yarn, but he had not the spirit to say it.

'The best death of all,' murmured Sullivan, 'is the soldier's. I believe, just before a battle, a priest can give a whole regiment a General Absolution, and if a man is killed he goes straight up to heaven. That's what makes Irishmen such good soldiers. Straight up to heaven!'

'Grand in attack,' said Jacky judiciously, 'not so good in defence.'

'And that's why!' said Sullivan. 'And, what's more, I wouldn't be surprised if that isn't why the English are better on the defensive than in the charge. Sure any man would fight like a divil if he knew what was coming after? Death has no terrors for a man in a situation like that.'

They fell silent. A cloudlet crossed the moon. Then all their faces were illumined again. The city's roofs shone. The priest's voice murmured softly.

'He's taking a long time,' said Jacky. 'And it isn't,' he whispered, trying to make a little joke, 'as if she had so much to tell. *She's* all right anyway.'

'And,' said Maguire piously, 'on Good Friday. A lovely death!'

'So it is,' said Wilson. 'Good Friday!'

They all sighed deeply. The priest came out, stooping under the beams, removing his stole and kissing it. Maguire asked him, 'Will she last, father?' The priest sighed, 'A saint, a saint,' as if he were sighing for all the sinners of the world. Jacky showed him out, and as he walked away the doctor came down. Jacky shut him into his car and shoved in his head anxiously.

'Is she bad, doctor?'

'Anno Domini. We can't live for ever. The works give out – just like an old motor-car. All we can do at that age is wait for the call,' and he beckoned with one finger. Jacky drew back hastily. The headlamps whirled and the car purred away across the empty Square as if its red tail-lights were running away with somebody.

Jacky was left alone in his room. He sank into an armchair by the open window. The spring night was gentle. The blood of life was pulsing through everything. Even the three old London planes in the middle of the Square had their little throb and the high Easter moon was delicately transparent as if with youth. He leaped up and began to circle the room. He had never seen anything so lovely, it seemed to him, as those little babies gazing at him out of their big eyes, with their soft little lips parted. He was looking again over the shining roofs and the blank chimney-pots, and as if a shutter flicked he felt for one moment the intense vacancy and loneliness of his life and saw it, as the years went by, becoming more lonely and more empty. And when he was gone, the moon out there, the old trees below, would still be there, still throbbing. A little wind scurried furtively in the dust of the Square. He looked at the decanter. Low tide. Like his own life. He'd be able to rest tomorrow anyway. He paused before the black enlargement. Good Friday morning. One more day to Easter. A veined, red face with a blue nose, thin ruffled hair, bags under the eyes was looking at him out of the mirror. He licked his lips and got a horrible taste in his mouth and felt an uneven thumping in his heart.

He sat down heavily by the open window, before the moon's indifferent beauty, and began to go back over the years. There were a couple of things it wasn't going to be too easy to . . .

'Not, mind you,' he assured the empty Square, with bravado, 'that I'm going to hand myself over to some bogtrot from the County Meath. Pick the right man and . . . "Well, Father," he rehearsed, flicking a grain of ash from his pants and pulling his ear, "I'm afraid, er, I've got more than a few little peccadilloes to tell you. We're only human, Father. Children of Adam, and all to that and so on." That was the ticket. Frank and open. Two men of the world. "Of course, there's been a spot of liquor, Father. And, er . . . Well, er . . . I mean, er . . ."' Jacky coughed and ran his finger around inside his collar. This thing was going to take a bit of doing. He closed his eyes and began to think of all those nights that had seemed such grand nights – at the time.

When he opened his eyes again the sun was warm on his face, the Square was gay with sunlight, somebody was shaking his shoulder. It was his landlady smilingly handing him his tea and buttered toast.

'Well, Mr Cardew,' she cackled, 'since I didn't go last night I'll live to be a hundred!'

As Jacky looked blearily down at the three plane trees the misery of the night flooded on him. He gave her one maddened look, banged down the cup, and started up to tell her just what he thought of her. An unholy gripe pierced a red-hot needle through the small of his back.

'Oh, Mr Cardew, what on earth made you sit by the open window!'

But now the pain ran across the back of his neck, and with hand to his back and a hand to his neck all he could do was to crawl away moaning and cursing to his bed.

As he lay there through the holidays he found himself being petted and cosseted as he had never been in his life before. She rubbed his back and she rubbed his chest and she brought him hot punch and fed him with Easter delicacies until, gradually, if sourly, he decided that he would be a fool to change his landlady. At the same time, and especially on Easter Sunday morning as he lay with the sun slanting warmly across his chest, his hands behind his head, smoking his after-breakfast cigarette, his Sunday paper on his lap, listening to the silvery bells of all the churches of the city, he was aware of a certain slight feeling of discomfort – nothing much, just a coiled shadow at the back of his mind, the merest hint of apprehension. Cautiously he turned his stiff shoulders to look at the mantelpiece where she had placed a little spray of Palm in a glass vase, and beside it a little glass bowl of Holy Water. He grunted as he considered them. He'd get rid of those things all right when he got on his feet again! Just then he remembered Maguire, and all that about the stamp being on you. He smiled uncomfortably. Oh, well! He flicked his ash on the carpet. Some day, no doubt. Some day.

How lovely the sun was. It was nice to hear all the footsteps across the Square below, going to Mass. Their shadowy reflections passed softly on the ceiling, and the silvery bells went on calling everybody to be happy because Christ was risen.

He took up the paper and began to study Form.

The Silence of the Valley

Only in the one or two farmhouses about the lake, or in the fishing hotel at its edge – preoccupations of work and pleasure – does one ever forget the silence of the valley. Even in the winter, when the great cataracts slide down the mountain-face, the echoes of falling water are fitful : the winds fetch and carry them. In the summer a fisherman will hear the tinkle of the ghost of one of those falls only if he steals among the mirrored reeds under the pent of the cliffs, and withholds the plash of his oars. These tiny muted sounds will awe and delight him by the vacancy out of which they creep, intermittently.

One May evening a relaxed group of early visitors were helping themselves to drink in the hotel-bar, throwing the coins into a pint glass. There were five of them all looking out the door at the lake, the rhododendrons on the hermit's island, the mountain towering beyond it, and the wall of blue air above the mountain line. Behind the counter was an American soldier, blond, blankly handsome, his wide-vision glasses convexing the sky against his face. Leaning against the counter was a priest; jovial, fat, ruddy, his Roman-collar off and his trousers stuck into his socks – he had been up the mountain all day rough-shooting. Leaning against the pink-washed wall was a dark young man with pince-nez; he had the smouldering ill-disposed eyes of the incorrigible Celt – 'always eager to take offence' as the fourth of the party had privately cracked. She was a sturdy, red-mopped young woman in blue slacks now sitting on the counter drinking whisky. She sometimes seemed not at all beautiful, and sometimes her heavy features seemed to have a strong beauty of their own, for she was on a hair-trigger between a glowering Beethoven and The Laughing Cavalier. Sometimes her mouth was broody; suddenly it would expand into a half-batty gaiety. Her deep-set eyes ran from gloom to irony, to challenge, to wild humour. She had severe eyebrows that floated as gently as a veil in the wind. She was a Scot. The fifth of the group was a sack of a man, a big fat school-inspector, also with his collar off. He had cute ingratiating eyes. He leaned against the opposite pink-washed wall.

In the middle of the tiled floor was a very small man, a tramp with a fluent black beard, long black curls, a billycock hat, a mackintosh to his toes, and a gnarled stick with a hairy paw. The tramp (a whisper from the priest had informed them all that he had once been a waiter on the Holyhead–Euston Express) held a pint of porter in his free hand and was singing to them in a fine tenor voice a ballad called *Lonely I wandered from the Scenes of my Childhood*. They heard him in quizzical boredom. He had been singing ballads to them on and off for nearly two hours now.

Outside, the sun was seeping away behind the far end of the valley. From the bar they could see it touching the tips of the tallest rowans on the island. Across the lake the tip of a green cornfield on a hillock blazed and went out. Then vast beams, cutting through lesser defiles, flowed like a yellow searchlight for miles to the open land to the east, picking out great escarpments and odd projections of the mountains. The wavelets were by now blowing in sullenly on the shore, edging it with froth.

The tramp ended. They applauded perfunctorily. He knew they were sated and when the red-headed young woman cried, 'Tommy, give us *The Inchigeela Puck Goat*,' he demurred politely.

'I think, miss, ye have enough of me now, and sure I'm as dry as a lime-kiln.'

'More porter for the singer,' cried the priest with lazy authority, and the lieutenant willingly poured out another bottle of stout and rattled a coin into the pint-glass.

'I suppose,' asked the Celtic-looking young man, in a slightly critical voice, 'you have no songs in Irish?'

'Now,' soothed the school-inspector, 'haven't you the Irish the whole bloody year round? Leave us to take a holiday from it while we can.'

'I had been under the impression,' yielded the Celt, with a – for him – amicable smile, 'that we came out here to learn the language of our forefathers? Far be it from me to insist pedantically on the point.' And he smiled again like a stage curate.

'Tell me, brother,' asked the American, as he filled up the tramp's glass, 'do you remain on the road the whole year round?'

'Summer and winter, for fifteen years come next September, and no roof over my head but the field of stars. And would you believe it, sur, never wance did I get as much as a shiver of a cold in my head.'

'That is certainly a remarkable record.'

The proprietor of the hotel entered the bar from the kitchen behind it and planked a saucepan full of fowls' guts on the counter. He was accompanied by a small boy, long-lashed, almost pretty, obviously a city-child, who kept dodging excitedly about him.

'Have any of ye a match?' he asked. He was a powerful man, with the shoulders of a horse. He wore neither coat nor vest. His cap was on his poll. His face was round and weather-beaten as a mangold. He had a mouthful of false teeth.

'What do you want a match for, Dinny?' asked the priest with a wink at the others.

The American produced a match. Dinny deftly pinched a fold of his trousers between the eye of his suspenders and inserted the match through the fold: there it effectively did the work of a button. The priest twisted him around familiarly. A nail had performed the same service behind. They all laughed, but Dinny was too pre-occupied to heed.

'What's this mess for?' The American pointed to the stinking saucepan.

Dinny paid no attention. He stretched up over the top of the shelves and after much fumbling brought down a fishing-rod.

'Give it to me, Dinny, give it to me,' shouted the child.

Dinny ignored him also as he fiddled with the line. He glanced out the door, turned to the kitchen and roared:

'Kitty cows coming home tell Patsy James have ye the buckets scalded blosht it boys the day is gone.'

Or he said something like that, for he mouthed all his words in his gullet and his teeth clacked and he spoke too fast. They all turned back to watch the frieze of small black cows passing slowly before the scalloped water, the fawny froth, the wall of mountain.

'The cobbler won't lasht the night,' said Dinny, pulling with his teeth at the tangled pike-line. The priest whirled.

'Is he bad? Did you see him? Should I go down?'

'Still unconscious, Father. No use for you. Timeen was up. He was buying the drink.'

'Drink?' asked the Scots girl grinning hopefully.

'For the wake,' explained the Celt.

'Well, do you know what it is, by Harry?' cried the inspector earnestly to them all. 'He's making a great fight for it.'

'He may as well go now and be done with it,' said Dinny. 'Gimme the guts. We're fishing for eels.'

'Gimme the rod, Dinny, gimme the rod,' screamed the child and taking it he dashed off like a lancer, shouting with joy. Dinny lumbered after him with the saucepan.

'I reckon these people are pretty heartless?' suggested the soldier.

'We Irish,' explained the Celt, 'are indifferent to the affairs of the body. We are a spiritual people.'

'What enchanting nonsense,' laughed the young woman and threw back her whisky delightedly.

'It is none the less true,' reprimanded the Celt.

'You make me feel so old,' sighed the young woman, 'so old and so wise.'

'Are you a Catholic?' asked the Celt suspiciously.

'Yes, but what on earth has that to do with anything?'

'Well, I reckon I don't know much about the spirit, but you may be right about the body. Did you see those hens' guts?'

The priest intervened diplomatically.

'Did you ever see them fishing for eels? It's great fun. Come and watch them.'

All but the tramp walked idly to the edge of the lake. The waves were beating in among the stones, pushing a little wrack of straw and broken reeds before them. Dinny had stuck a long string of windpipe to the hook and the boy had slung it out about twelve feet from the shore. To lure the eels a few random bits of guts had been thrown into the brown shallows at their feet and there swayed like seaweed. The group peered. Nothing happened. Suddenly Dinny shouted as fast as a machine-gun's burst.

'Look at 'em look at 'em look at the divils blosht it look at 'em look at 'em.'

A string of intestines was streaking away out into the lake. Dark serpentine shapes whirled snakily in and out of the brown water. The eels had smelled the rank bait and were converging on it.

'By golly,' cried the American, 'they must smell that bait a mile away.'

The reel whirred, the line flew, the rod bent, they all began to shout, the child trembled with excitement.

'You have him pull him you divil,' roared Dinny and seized the rod and whirled a long white belly in over their dodging heads. The girl gave a cry of disgust as the five men leaped on the eel, now lashing in the dust, and hammered savagely at it with heels, stones, a stick, screaming, laughing, shoving. The eel seemed immortal. Though filthy and bleeding it squirmed galvanically. The child circled dancing around the struggling group, half-delighted, half-terrified.

'Well, Jo,' said the young woman as she looked disdainfully at the last wriggles of the corpse, 'it seems that boys will be boys. Dinny, do you really eat eels?'

'Christ gurl I wouldn't touch one of 'em for a hundred pounds.'

'Then why catch them?'

'For fun.'

Her face gathered, ceased to be The Laughing Cavalier and became Beethoven in Labour. She saw that the men had now become absorbed entirely in the sport. The American had thrown out the line again and they were all peering excitedly into the water. The sun left the last tips of the mountains. The lake grew sullen. Its waves still hissed. They did not weary of the game until eight eels lay writhing in the dust.

Just as they were becoming bored they observed a silent countryman at the edge of the ring looking down at the eels. The priest spoke to him saying, 'Well, Timeen, how is he?' He was a lithe, lean, hollow-cheeked young man with his cap pulled low over his eyes. He lifted his face and they saw that he was weeping.

'He's gone, Father,' he said in a low voice.

'The Lord have mercy on him,' said the priest and his own eyes filled and the others murmured the prayer after him. 'The poor old cobbler. I must go and see herself.'

He hastened away and presently, tidy and brushed and in his Roman collar, they saw him cycle down the road. The child called after him, 'Will you roast the eels for me tonight?' and over his shoulder the priest called, 'I will, Jo, after supper,' and disappeared wobblingly over the first hill.

'By Harry,' cried the inspector, 'there'll be a powerful gathering of the clans tonight.'

'How's that?' from the American.

'For the wake,' explained the Celt.

'I'd certainly like to see a wake.'

'You'll be very welcome, sur,' said Timeen.

'Did he go easy?' asked the inspector.

Dinny threw the guts into the lake and took Timeen by the arm.

'He went out like a candle,' said Timeen, and let Dinny lead him away gently to some private part of the house.

The group dissolved.

'I do wish,' said the American, 'they wouldn't throw guts into the lake. After all we swim in it.'

'It's very unsanitary all right,' the inspector agreed.

'What are we all,' said the Celt philosophically, 'but a perambulating parcel of guts.'

The girl sighed heavily and said, 'The lamp is lighting.'

In the hotel window the round globe of the lamp was like a full moon. A blue haze had gathered over everything. They strolled back to the bar for a last drink, the child staggering after them with the heavy saucepan of dead eels.

The cobbler's cottage was on the brow of a hill about a mile down the road. It was naked, slated, whitewashed, two-storeyed. It had a sunken haggard in front and a few fuchsias and hollies behind it, blown almost horizontally by the storms. On three sides lay an expanse of moor, now softened by the haze of evening. From his front door the dead cobbler used to look across this barren moor at the jagged mountain-range, but he could also see where the valley opened out and faded into the tentative and varying horizons of forty miles away.

When the priest entered the kitchen the wife was alone – the news had not yet travelled. She was a tiny, aged woman who looked as if her whole body from scalp to soles was wrinkled and yellow; her face, her bare arms, her bare chest were as golden as a dried apple; even her eyeballs seemed wrinkled. But her white hair flowed upward all about her like a Fury in magnificent wild snakes from under an old fisherman's tweed hat, and her mobile mouth and her loud – too loud – voice gave out a tremendous vitality. When she was a young girl she must have been as lively as a minnow in a mountain-stream. The priest had known her for most of his adult life as a woman whose ribald tongue had made the neighbours delight in her and fear her: he was stirred to tears to find her looking up at him now like a child who has been beaten. She was seated on the long settle underneath the red lamp before the picture of the Sacred Heart.

He sat beside her and took her hand.

'Can I go up and pray for him?'

'Katey Dan is readying him,' she whispered, and the priest became aware of footsteps moving in the room over their heads.

She lumbered up the ladder-like stairs to see if everything was ready. While he waited he looked at the cobbler's tools by the window – the last, and the worn hammer, and the old butter-box by the fire where the cobbler used to sit. Everything in the kitchen had the same worn look of time and use, and everything was dusted with the grey dust of turf – the kettle over the peat fire, the varied pot-hooks on the crane, the bright metal of the tongs, the dresser with its pieces of delph, a scalded churn-lid leaning in the window to dry. There was nothing there that was not necessary; unless, perhaps, the red lamp and the oleograph of the Sacred Heart, and even that had the stiff and frozen prescription of an ikon. The only unusual thing was two plates on the table under the window, one of snuff and one of shredded tobacco for the visitors who would soon be coming down from every corner of the glens. The only light in the cottage came from the turf-fire.

As he sat and looked at the blue smoke curling up against the brown soot of the chimney's maw he became aware, for the first time in his life, of the silence of this moor. He heard the hollow feet above the rafters. A cricket chirruped somewhere behind the fire. Always up to now he had thought of this cottage as a place full of the cobbler's satirical talk, his wife's echoes and contradictions. Somebody had once told the old man that he was not only the valley's storyteller but its 'gossip-columnist'; the old chap had cocked a suspicious eye, too vain to admit that he did not know the phrase, and skated off into one of his yarns about the days when he had cobbled for the Irish workers laying rails out of Glasgow along the Clyde. The priest smiled at the incident. Then he frowned as he looked at the fire, a quiet disintegration: a turf-fire never emits even the slightest whisper. He realized that this cottage would be completely silent from now on. Although it was May he had a sudden poignant sensation of autumn, why he could not tell.

The old woman called him up. After the dusk of the kitchen this upper room was brilliant. She had lighted five wax-candles about her husband's head. Snowy sheets made a canopy about his face. The neighbour-woman had just finished the last delicately fluted fold on the lacey counterpane that lay ridged over the stomach and toes. Silently the three knelt and prayed.

When they rose the old woman said, looking down at the calm countenance on the pillow:

'He's a fine corse and a heavy corse.'

'He was a great man. I loved him.'

'He had a fierce veneration for you, Father.'

They lumbered down the steep stairs. She was as quiet as if the business in hand was something that had happened outside the course of nature. She thanked God for the fine weather. She asked him were there many staying at the hotel. When he told her, she muttered, 'We must be satisfied,' as if she were talking about the hotel and not about her man. When two more neighbour-women came and stood looking at them from the doorway, he took leave of her saying that he would return later in the night.

The hollies at the door were rubbing squeakingly against each other. The moon was rising serenely over the Pass to the East. He felt the cold wind as he rode back to the lake.

They were at supper when he entered the hotel. He joined them about the round table in the bay window through which he could barely discern the stars above the mountains. The rest of the long room, beyond the globe of the lamp, was in shadow. He mentioned that he had seen the cobbler, that they must go down later to the wake, and then set about his food. He paid small heed to the conversation although he gathered that they were loud in discussion over the delay in serving supper.

'Just the same,' the American was saying, 'I cannot see why it would not be perfectly simple to hang up a card on the wall announcing meal-times. Breakfast, eight to ten. Luncheon, one to three. And so on. It's quite simple.'

'Just as they do,' suggested the young Scotswoman, 'in the Regent Palace Hotel?'

'Exactly,' he agreed, and then looked in puzzlement at her because she was giggling happily to herself.

'You must admit,' the inspector assured her, following his usual role of trying to agree with everybody, 'that they have a wonderful opportunity here if they only availed of it. Why don't they cater more for the wealthy clientèle? I mean, now, suppose they advertised Special Duck Dinners, think of the crowds that would come motoring out of Cork for them on summer afternoons. It's only about forty miles, a nice run.'

'Gee, how often have I driven forty miles and more for a barbecue supper down the coast? I can see those lobster suppers at Cohasset, now, two dollars fifty, and the rows and rows of automobiles lined outside on the concrete.'

'What does our Celt say to this perfectly hideous picture?' asked the redmop.

'I can see no objection – provided the language spoken is Gaelic.'
She broke into peals of laughter.

'We,' the Celt went on, dark with anger, 'envisage an Ireland both modern and progressive. Christianity,' he went on, proud both of the rightness and intellectual tolerance of his argument, 'is not opposed to modernity, or to comfort, or to culture. I should not mind,' his voice was savage, for she was chuckling like a zany, 'if seaplanes landed on that lake outside. Why should I? All this admiration for backwardness and inefficiency is merely so much romantic nonsense. Ireland has had enough of it.'

She groaned comically.

'Fascist type. Definitely schizoid. Slight sadistic tendency. Would probably be Socialist in Britain, if not – ' she wagged her flaming head warningly and made eyes of mock horror – 'dare I say it, C.P.?'

'You,' cried the Celt scornfully, 'merely like the primitive so long as it is not in your own country. Let's go to Nigeria and love the simple ways of the niggers. Let's holiday in Ireland among the beautiful peasants. Imperialist!'

'I beg your pardon,' she cried, quite offended. 'I am just as happy in the Shetlands or the Hebrides as I am here. Britain's pockets of primitiveness are her salvation. If she ever loses them she's doomed. I very much fear she's doomed already with all these moth-eaten church-wardens in Parliament trying to tidy us up!'

And she drew out her cigar-case and pulling her coffee towards her lit a long Panatella. As she puffed she was sullen and unbeautiful again as if his hate had quenched her loveliness as well as her humour.

'Well, now, now, after all,' soothed the inspector, 'it's all very well for you. Your country is a great country with all the most modern conveniences . . .'

'Heaven help it!'

'. . . whereas we have a long leeway to make up. Now, to take even a small thing. Those guts in the lake.'

'O God!' she groaned. 'What a fuss you make over one poor little chicken's guts! Damn it, it's all phosphates. The Chinese use human phosphates for manure.'

The priest shook in his fat with laughter – it was a joke exactly to his liking – but the other three took the discussion from her and she smoked in dudgeon until the priest too was pulling his pipe and telling her about the dead cobbler, and how every night in winter his cottage used to be full of men coming to hear his views on Hitler and Mussolini and the Prophecies of Saint Columcille which foretold that the last battle of the last world-war would be fought at Bally-lickey Bridge. The others began to listen as he retold some of the cobbler's more earthy stories that were as innocent and sweaty as any Norse or Celtic yarn of the Golden Age : such as the dilemma of the sow eating the eel which slipped out of her as fast as it went into her until, at last, the sow shouted in a fury: 'I'll settle you, you slippery divil!' and at one and the same moment snapped up the eel and clapped her backside to the wall.

Laughing they rose and wandered, as usual, into the kitchen for the night. They expected to find it empty, thinking that everybody would be going down to the wakehouse; instead it was more crowded than ever, it had become a sort of clearing-house where the people called on their way to and from the cobbler's cottage, either too shy to go there directly or unwilling to go home after visiting their old friend.

The small boy was eagerly awaiting them with the saucepan of eels. The priest set to. He took off his clerical jacket and put on a green wind-jammer, whose brevity put an equator around his enormous paunch, so that when he stooped over the fire he looked like one of those global toys that one cannot knock over. When the

resinous fir-stumps on the great flat hearth flamed up – the only light
in the kitchen – he swelled up, shadows and all, like a necromancer.
He put an eel down on the stone floor and with his penknife slit it
to its tail and gutted it. The offal glistened oilily. While he was
cutting the eel its tail had slowly wound about his wrist, and when
he tied its nose to a pothook and dangled it over a leaning flame and
its oil began to drip and sizzle in the blaze the eel again slowly
curved as if in agony. The visitors amused themselves by making
sarcastic comments on the priest as cook, but four countrymen who
lined the settle in the darkness with their caps on and their hands in
their pockets watched him, perfectly immobile, not speaking,
apparently not interested.

'Aha, you divil, you,' taunted the priest, 'now will you squirm?
If the cobbler's sow was here now she would make short work of
you!'

That was the only time any of the countrymen spoke: from the
darkness of a far corner an old man said:

'I wonder is the cobbler telling that story to Hitler now?'

'I sincerely hope,' said the Scots girl, 'that they're not in the same
place.'

The old man said:

'God is good. I heard a priesht say wan time that even Judas might
be saved.'

'Jo,' said the inspector, steering as usual into pleasant channels,
'do you think that eel is alive?'

The small boy was too absorbed to heed, lost in his own delight.

Now and again a handsome, dark serving-girl came to the fire to
tend the pots or renew the sods, for meals were eaten in this house
at all hours: she seemed fascinated by the eel and every time she
came she made disgusted noises. The men loved these expressions of
disgust and tried various ways to provoke more of them, offering
her a bite or holding up the entangled saucepan to her nose. Once the
American chased her laughingly with an eel in his fist and from the
dark back-kitchen they could hear them scuffling playfully. By this
time many more neighbours had come into the kitchen and into the
bar and into the second back-kitchen, and two more serving-girls
became busy as drinks and teas and dishes of ham passed to and fro,
so that the shadows of the men about the fire, the scurrying girls,
the wandering neighbours fluttered continually on the white walls

and the babble of voices clucked through the house like ducks clacking at a nightpond.

Above this murmuring and clattering they heard the tramp singing in the bar a merry dancing tune, partly in Gaelic and partly in English :

> So, little soldier of my heart
> Will you marry, marry me now,
> With a heigh and a ho
> And a sound of drum now ?

'So the little bastard does know Irish,' cried the Celt much affronted as the song broke into Gaelic :

> A chailin óg mo chroidhe
> Conus a phósfainn-se thú
> Agus gan pioc de'n bhróg do chur orm . . .

'Perhaps he suits his language to his company?' the red-haired girl suggested.

> I went to the cobbler
> The besht in the town
> For a fine pair of shoes
> For my soldiereen brown,
> So-o-o . . .
> Little soldier of my heart,
> Will you marry, marry me now . . .

The girl peered around the jamb of the door into the bar and then scurried back dismayed. The tramp had spotted her and at once came dancing fantastically into the kitchen on her heels. His long mackintosh tails leaped, and their shadows with them. His black beard flowed left and right as his head swayed to the tune and his black locks swung with it. His hands expressively flicked left and right as he capered about the girl. His billy-cock hat hopped.

> But O girl of my heart
> How could I marry you
> And I without a shirt
> Either white or blue ?

'Would you ate an eel?' asked the green-jacketed porpoise by the fire holding up the shrivelled carcase to the dancer, who at once gaily doffed his hat (into which the priest dropped the eel) and went on his way back to the bar dancing and singing, followed in delight by the boy:

> So chuadhas dti an tailliúr
> The besht to be found
> And I bought a silken shirt
> For my saighdiúrin donn

'Come, lads,' cried the priest, suddenly serious, 'it's time for us to visit the poor cobbler.'

It was full moonlight. The lake crawled livingly under it. The mountains were like the mouth of hell. It seemed to the priest as if the dark would come down and claw at them. He said so to the Celt who had become wildly excited at the sight of the dark and the light and the creeping lake and strode down to the beach and threw up his arms crying,

'O Love! O Terror! O Death!' – and he broke into Balfe's song to the moon from *The Lily of Killarney*:

The Moon hath raised her lamp above.

'If you don't stop that emotional ass,' growled the girl as she wheeled out her bicycle, 'he'll start singing The Barcarolle,' and showed her own emotion by cycling madly away by herself.

'Grim! Grim!' said the American and the inspector agreed with, 'In the winter! Ah! In the winter!'

They were cycling now in single file switchbacking up and down over the little hills until the glow of the cobbler's window eyed them from the dark. Near the cottage dark shapes of men and boys huddled under the hedges and near the walls and as they alighted drew aside to let them pass, fingers to caps for the priest. The causeway to the kitchen door was crowded, unexpectedly noisy with talk, smelling of turf-smoke and pipe-smoke and bogwater and sweat and hens.

In her corner by the enormous peat-fire, the little old woman seemed almost to be holding pleasant court, her spirits roused by the friendliness and excitement of the crowds of neighbours.

The babble fell as the strangers entered. It rose again as they disappeared up the ladder-stairs to pay their respects to the cobbler. It sank again when they clambered down. Then gradually it rose and steadied as they settled into the company. They were handed whisky or stout or tea by Timeen, and the priest began to chat pleasantly and unconcernedly with the nearest men to him. To the three Irishmen all this was so familiar that they made no wonder of it, and they left the American and the girl to the cobbler's wife who at once talked to them about America and Scotland with such a fantastic mixture of ignorance and personal knowledge – gleaned from years upon years of visitors – that all their embarrassment vanished in their pleasure at her wise and foolish talk.

Only twice did her thoughts stray upstairs. A neighbour lifted a red coal in the tongs to kindle his pipe: she glanced sharply and drew a sharp breath.

'Light away, Dan Frank,' she encouraged then. 'Lasht week my ould divil used to be ever reddening his pipe, God rest him, although I used to be scolding him for burning his poor ould belly with all the shmoking.'

Once when the babble suddenly fell into a trough of silence they heard a dog across the moor baying at the moon. She said:

'Times now I do be thinking that with the cobbler gone from me I'll be afraid to be by meself in the house with all the idle shtallions going the road.'

It was her commonest word for men, shtalls or shtallions, and all the neighbours who heard her must have pictured a lone tramp or a tinker walking the mountain road, and she inside listening through the barred door to the passing feet.

Elsewise she talked of things like hens and of prices and several times seemed to forget the nature of the occasion entirely. Then, in her most ribald vein she became scabrous in her comments on her visitors, to the delight of everybody except the victims, who could only scuttle red-faced out the door without, in respect for her, as much as the satisfaction of a curse. It was after one of these sallies that the priest decided to close his visit with a laughing command to them all to kneel for the Rosary. With a lot of scuffling they huddled over chairs or sank on one knee, hiding their faces reverently in their caps.

Only the soldier did not join them. He went out and found more men, all along the causeway and under the hedges, kneeling likewise, so that the mumbling litany of prayer mingled with the tireless baying of the dog. All about them the encircling jags of mountains were bright and jet, brilliant craters, quarries of blackness, gleaming rocks, grey undergrowth.

The journey back was even more eerie than the journey out, the moon now behind them, their shadows before, and as they climbed the hills the mountains climbed before them as if to bar their way and when they rushed downward to the leaden bowl that was the lake, and into the closed gully of the coom, it was as if they were cycling not through space but through a maw of Time that would never move.

The kitchen was empty. The eels lay in the pot. Two old boots lay on their sides drying before the fading fire. The crickets whistled loudly in the crannies. They took their candles and went in their stockinged feet up the stairs to bed, whispering.

The morning was a blaze of heat. The island was a floating red flower. The rhododendrons around the edges of the island were replicated in the smooth lee-water which they barely touched. As the American, the girl, and the Celt set off for their pre-breakfast swim from the island they heard the sounds of spades striking against gravel. They saw the tall thin figure of an aged man, with grey side-chops, in a roundy black hat and a swallow-tailed coat, standing against the sky. He held a piece of twig in his hand like a water-diviner. He was measuring, taking bearings, solicitously encouraging the grave-diggers below him to be accurate in their lines. He greeted the strangers politely, but they could see that they were distracting him and that he was weighed down by the importance of his task.

'For do you see, gentlemen, the cobbler was most particular about where he would be buried. I had a long talk with him about it lasht week and the one thing he laid down was for him to be buried in the one line with all the Cronins from Baurlinn.'

'But,' demurred the American, 'would a foot or two make all that difference?'

'It is an old graveyard,' the old man admonished him solemnly, 'and there are many laid here before him, and there will be many another after him.'

They left him to his task. The water was icy and they could only bear to dive in and clamber out. To get warm again they had to race up and down the brief sward before they dressed, hooting with pleasure in the comfort of the sun, the blue sky, the smells of the island and the prospect of trout and bacon-and-eggs for breakfast. As they stepped back on the mainland they met a mountainy lad coming from the depths of the coom, carrying a weighted sack. His grey tweed trousers were as dark with wetness to his hips as if he had jumped into a boghole. He walked with them to the hotel and explained that he was wet from the dew on the mountain-heather and the young plantations. He had just crossed from the next valley, about two hours away. He halted and opened the mouth of the sack to show them, with a grin of satisfaction, the curved silver and blue of a salmon. He said he would be content to sell it to the hotel for five shillings and they agreed heartily with him when he said, 'Sure what is it only a night's sport and a walk over the mountains?' Over breakfast they upbraided one another for their lie-abed laziness on such a glorious day.

The day continued summer-hot burning itself away past high noon. The inspector got his car and drove away to visit some distant school. The American took his rod and rowed out of sight to the head of the lake. The girl walked away alone. The Celt went fishing from the far shore. The priest sat on the garden-seat before the hotel and read his Office and put a handkerchief over his head and dozed, and when the postman came took the morning paper from him. Once a farm-cart made a crockety-crock down the eastern road and he wondered if it was bringing the coffin. In the farmyard behind the hotel the milk-separator whirred. For most of the time everything was still – the sparkling lake, the idle shore, the tiny fields, the sleeping hermit's island, the towering mountains, the flawless sky. 'It is as still,' thought the priest, 'as the world before life began.' All the hours that the priest sat there, or walked slowly up and down reading his breviary, or opened a lazy eye under his handkerchief, he saw only one sign of life – a woman came on top of a hillock across the lake, looked about her for man or animal and went back to her chores.

Towards two o'clock the red-headed girl returned from her walk and sat near him. She was too tired or lazy to talk: but she did ask after a time:

'Do you think they really believe that the cobbler is talking to Hitler?'

'They know no more about Hitler than they do about Cromwell. But I'm sure they believe that the cobbler is having nice little chats with his old pals Jerry Coakley and Shamus Cronin – that's Dinny's father that he will be lying next to – up there in the graveyard – in a half an hour's time.'

She smiled happily.

'I wish I had their faith.'

'If you were born here you would.'

'I'd also have ten children,' she laughed. 'Will you join me in a drink?'

He could not because he must await the funeral and the local curate at the chapel on the island, and, rising, he went off there. She went alone into the bar and helped herself to a whisky, and leaned over the morning paper. She was joined presently by the Celt, radiant at having caught nothing. To pass the time she started a discussion about large families and the ethics of birth-control. He said that he believed that everybody 'practised it in secret', a remark which put her into such good humour that, in gratitude, she made him happy by assuring him that in ten years' time the birth-rate in England would be the lowest in the world and for the innocent joy he showed at this she glowed with so much good-feeling towards him that she told him also how hateful birth-control is to the poor in the East End of London.

'I always knew it,' he cried joyfully. 'Religion has nothing to do with these things. All that counts is the Natural Law. For, as I hope you do realize, there is a Law of Nature!'

And he filled out two more whiskies and settled down to the unburthening of his soul.

'You see, I'm not really an orthodox Catholic at all. To me Religion is valid only because and in so far as it is based on Nature. That is why Ireland has a great message for the world. Everywhere else but here civilization has taken the wrong turning. Here Nature still rules Man, and Man still obeys Nature. . . .'

'As in the East End?' she said.

He hurried on, frowning crossly.

'I worship these mountains and these lakes and these simple Gaelic people because they alone still possess . . .'

'But you were angry last night when I defended primitive life. You wanted sea-planes on the lake and tourists from Manchester in Austin Sevens parked in front of . . .'

'I have already explained to you,' he reproved her, 'that to be natural doesn't mean that we must be primitive! That's the romantic illusion. What I mean to say is – that is in very simple words of course . . .'

And his dark face buttoned up and he became ill-disposed again as he laboured to resolve his own contradictions.

She was about to fly from him when, through the wide-open door, she saw a dark group top the hillock to the east. As the sky stirred between their limbs she saw that they were a silhouette of six men lumbering under a coffin. Its brass plate caught the sun. They were followed by a darker huddle of women. After these came more men, and then a double file of horsemen descended out of the blue sky. On the hermit's island some watcher began to toll a bell.

'I'm going to the island,' she said. He followed her, nattering about Darwin and Lamarck.

The priest stood under the barrel-arch of the little Romanesque chapel, distent in his white surplice, impressive, a magician. The two went shyly among the trees and watched the procession dissolving by the lakeside. The priest went out to meet the local curate.

Presently the coffin lumbered forward towards the chapel on the six shoulders and was laid rockingly on four chairs. The crowd seeped in among the trees. The widow sat in the centre of the chapel steps, flanked on each side by three women. She was the only one who spoke and it was plain from the way her attendants covered their faces with their hands that she was being ribald about each new arrival; the men knew it too, for as each one came forward on the sward, to meet the judgment of her dancing, wicked eyes, he skipped hastily into the undergrowth, with a wink or a grin at his neighbours. There was now a prolonged delay. The men looked around at the weather, or across the lake at the crops. Some turned their heads where, far up the lake, the American in his boat was rhythmically casting his invisible line. Then the two priests returned and entered the chapel. Their voices mumbling the *De Profundis* was like the buzzing of bees. The men bowed their heads, as usual holding their caps before their faces. Silence fell again as the procession reformed.

In the graveyard the familiar voices of the men lowering the dead into the earth outraged the silence. Nobody else made a sound until the first shovel of earth struck the brass-plate on the lid and then the widow, defeated at last, cried out without restraint. As the earth began to fall more softly her wailing became more quiet. The last act of the burial was when the tall man, the cobbler's friend, smoothened the last dust of earth with his palms as if he were smoothening a blanket over a child. The priest said three Aves. They all responded hollowly.

They dispersed slowly, as if loath to admit that something final had happened to them all. As each one went down the path he could see the fisherman far away, steadily flogging the water. But they did not go home. They hung around the hotel all the afternoon, the men in the crowded bar, drinking; the women clucking in the back-kitchens. Outside the hotel the heads of the patient horses, growing fewer as the hours went by, drooped lower and lower with the going down of the sun, until only one cart was left and that, at last, ambled slowly away.

It was twilight before the visitors, tired and not in a good temper – they had only been given tea and boiled eggs for lunch – could take possession of the littered bar. They helped themselves to drinks and threw the coins into the pint-glass. Drinking they looked out at the amber light touching the mountain line.

'It's queer,' murmured the priest. 'Why is it, all today and yesterday, I keep on thinking it's the autumn?'

' 'Tis a bit like it all right,' the inspector agreed pleasantly.

'Nonsense,' said the red-haired girl. 'It's a beautiful May day.'

'Thanks be to God,' agreed the inspector.

A frieze of small black cows passed, one by one, along the beach. They watched them go. Then Dinny put his head in from the kitchen.

'Supper, gentlemen.'

'I hope we'll have that salmon that came over the mountains,' smiled the Celt.

Nobody stirred.

'In America, you know, we call it the Fall.'

'The Fall?' said the priest.

'The fall of the leaves,' explained the soldier, thinking he did not understand.

The priest looked out over the dark lake – a stranger would hardly have known there was a lake if it had not been for the dun edge of froth – and, jutting out his lower lip, nodded to himself, very slowly, three times.

'Yes, indeed,' the inspector sighed, watching his face sympathetic-ally.

'Aye,' murmured the priest, and looked at him, and nodded again, knowing that this was a man who understood.

Then he whirled, gave the Celt a mighty slap on the back, and cried, 'Come on and we'll polish off that salmon. Quick march!'

They finished their drinks and strolled into the lamplit dining-room. As they sat around the table and shook out their napkins the soldier said, 'I reckon tomorrow will be another fine day.'

The red-haired girl leaned to the window and shaded her eyes against the pane. She could see how the moon touched the trees on the island with a ghostly tenderness. One clear star above the moun-tain wall gleamed. Seeing it her eyebrows floated upward softly for sheer joy.

'Yes,' she said quietly. 'It will be another grand day – tomorrow.'
And her eyebrows sank, very slowly, like a falling curtain.

Innocence

All this month the nuns have been preparing my little boy for his first Confession. In a few days he will go in a crocodile from the school to the parish church; enter the strange-looking cabinet in the corner of the aisle and see in the dusk of this secretive box an old priest's face behind a grille. He will acknowledge his wickedness to this pale, criss-crossed face. He will be a little frightened but he will enjoy it too, because he does not really believe any of it – for him it is a kind of game that the nuns and the priest are playing between them.

How could he believe it? The nuns tell him that the Infant Jesus is sad when he is wicked. But he is never wicked, so what can it matter? If they told him instead of the sorrow he causes the Weasel, or Two Toes, or the Robin in the Cow's Ear, all of which live in the fields below our house, he would believe it in just the same way. To be sure he tells lies, he is a terrible liar, and when he plays Rummy with me he cheats as often as he can, and when he is slow and I flurry him he flies into furious rages and his eyes swim with tears and he dashes the cards down and calls me A Pig. For this I love him so much that I hug him, because it is so transparent and innocent; and at night if I remember his tears I want to go into his room and hold his fat, sweaty hand that lies on the coverlet clutching some such treasure as an empty reel. How, then, can he believe that God could be angry with him because he tells lies or calls his daddy A Pig?

Yet, I hate to see him being prepared for his first Confession because one day he will really do something wicked, and I know the fear that will come over him on that day – and I cannot prevent it.

I have never forgotten the first time I knew that I had committed sin. I had been going to Confession for years, ever since I was seven, as he is now, telling the same things time after time just as he will do. 'Father, I told a lie . . . Father, I forgot to say my morning prayers

. . . Father, I was disobedient to my parents . . . And that is all, Father.' It was always quite true: I had done these things; but, as with him, it was only true as a fable or a mock-battle is true since none of these things were any more sinful than his childish lies and rages. Until, one dim, wintry afternoon, not long after Christmas, when I went as usual to Confession in an old, dark, windy church called Saint Augustine's, down a side-lane, away from the city's traffic, a place as cold and damp and smelly as a tomb. It has since been pulled down and if they had not pulled it down it must soon have fallen down. It was the sort of church where there was always a beggar or two sheltering from the weather in the porch or in the dusky part under the back gallery; and always some poor shawled woman sighing her prayers in a corner like the wind fluttering in the slates. The paint was always clean and fresh, but the floor and the benches and the woodwork were battered and worn by the generations. The priests dressed in the usual black Augustinian garment with a cowl and a leather cincture. Altogether, a stranger would have found it a gloomy place. But I was familiar with it ever since my mother brought me there to dedicate me to Saint Monica, the mother of Augustine, and I loved the bright candles before her picture, and the dark nooks under the galleries, and the painted tondos on the ceiling, and the stuffy confessional boxes with their heavy purple curtains underneath which the heels of the penitents stuck out when they knelt to the grille.

There I was, glad to be out of the January cold, kneeling before Saint Monica, brilliant with the candles of her mendicants. I was reading down through the lists of sins in my penny prayer-book, heeding the ones I knew, passing over the ones I didn't know, when I suddenly stopped at the name of a sin that I had hitherto passed by as having nothing to do with me.

As I write down these words I again feel the terror that crept into me like a snake as I realized that I knew that sin. I knew it well. No criminal who feels the sudden grip of a policeman on his arm can have felt more fear than I did as I stared at the horrible words. . . .

I joined the long silent queue of penitents seated against the wall. I went, at last, into the dark confessional. I told my usual innocent litany. I whispered the sin.

Now, the old priest inside the confessional was a very aged man.

He was so old and feeble that the community rarely allowed him to do anything but say Mass and hear Confessions. Whenever they let him preach he would ramble on and on for an hour; people would get up and go away; the sacristan would peep out in despair through the sacristy door; and in the end an altar-boy would be sent out to ring the great gong on the altar-steps to make him stop. I have seen the boy come out three times to the gong before the old man could be lured down from the pulpit.

When this old priest heard what I said to him he gave a groan that must have been heard in the farthest corner of the church. He leaned his face against the wire and called me his 'child', as all priests in the confessional call every penitent. Then he began to question me about the details. I had not counted on this. I had thought that I would say my sin and be forgiven: for up to this every priest had merely told me that I was a very good little boy and asked me to pray for him as if I were a little angel whose prayers had a special efficacy, and then I would be dismissed jumping with joy.

To his questions I replied tremulously that it had happened 'more than once' – How soon we begin to evade the truth! – and, I said, 'Yes, Father, it was with another.' At this he let out another groan so that I wanted to beg him to be quiet or the people outside would hear him. Then he asked me a question that made my clasped hands sweat and shake on the ledge of the grille. He asked me if any harm had been done to me. At first I didn't know what he meant. Then horrible shapes of understanding came creeping towards me along the dark road of my ignorance, as, in some indistinct manner, I recognized that he was mistaking me for a girl! I cried out that nothing at all had happened, Father. Nothing! Nothing! Nothing! But he only sighed like the south wind and said:

'Ah, my poor child, you won't know for several months.'

I now had no desire but to escape. I was ready to tell him any story, any lie, if he would only stop his questions. What I did say I don't know but in some fashion I must have made the old man understand that I was a male sinner. For his next question, which utterly broke me, was:

'I see, I see. Well, tell me, my poor child. Was she married or unmarried?'

I need hardly say that as I remember this now I laugh at it for an absurd misadventure, and I have sometimes made my friends laugh at his questions and his groans, and at me with my two skinny heels sticking out under the curtains and knocking like castanets, and the next penitents wondering what on earth was going on inside the box. But, then, I was like a pup caught in a bramble bush, recanting and retracting and trying to get to the point where he would say the blessed words '*Absolve te . . .*' and tell me what my penance would be.

What I said I cannot recall. All I remember distinctly is how I emerged under the eyes of the queue, walked up the aisle, as far away as I could get from the brightness of Saint Monica into the darkest corner under the gallery where the poorest of the poor crowd on Sundays. I saw everything through smoke. The scarlet eye of the sanctuary lamp – the only illumination apart from the candles before the shrine – stared at me. The shawled woman sighed at me. The wind under my bare knees crept away from me. A beggar in a corner, picking his nose and scratching himself, was Purity itself compared to me.

In the streets the building stood dark and wet against the after-Christmas pallor of the sky. High up over the city there was one tiny star. It was as bright and remote as lost innocence. The blank windows that held the winter sky were sullen. The wet cement walls were black. I walked around for hours. When I crept in home my mother demanded angrily where I had been all these hours and I told her lies that *were* lies, because I wanted to deceive her, and I knew that from this on I would always be deceiving everybody because I had something inside me that nobody must ever know. I was afraid of the dark night before me. And I still had to face another Confession when I would have to confess all these fresh lies that I had just told the old priest and my mother.

It's forty years ago, now : something long since put in its unimportant place. Yet, somehow, when I look across at this small kid clutching his penny prayer-book in his sweaty hands and wrinkling up his nose at the hard words – I cannot laugh. It does not even comfort me when I think of that second Confession, after I had carefully examined those lists of sins for the proper name of my sin. For, what I said to the next priest was : 'Father, I committed adultery.' With infinite tenderness he assured me that I was mistaken, and that I would not know anything about that sin for many years to come, indeed, that I would have to be married before I could commit it – and then asked me to pray for him, and said I was a very good little boy and sent me away jumping with joy. When I think of that and look at this small Adam he becomes like that indescribably remote and tender star, and I sigh like that old, dead priest, and it does not help to know that he is playing a fable of – 'Father, I told lies . . . Father, I forgot to say my morning prayers. . . . Father, I called my daddy A Pig.'

The Trout

One of the first places Julia always ran to when they arrived in G—— was The Dark Walk. It is a laurel walk, very old, almost gone wild, a lofty midnight tunnel of smooth, sinewy branches. Underfoot the tough brown leaves are never dry enough to crackle : there is always a suggestion of damp and cool trickle.

She raced right into it. For the first few yards she always had the memory of the sun behind her, then she felt the dusk closing swiftly down on her so that she screamed with pleasure and raced on to reach the light at the far end; and it was always just a little too long in coming so that she emerged gasping, clasping her hands, laughing, drinking in the sun. When she was filled with the heat and glare she would turn and consider the ordeal again.

This year she had the extra joy of showing it to her small brother, and of terrifying him as well as herself. And for him the fear lasted longer because his legs were so short and she had gone out at the far end while he was still screaming and racing.

When they had done this many times they came back to the house to tell everybody that they had done it. He boasted. She mocked. They squabbled.

'Cry babby !'

'You were afraid yourself, so there !'

'I won't take you any more.'

'You're a big pig.'

'I hate you.'

Tears were threatening so somebody said, 'Did you see the well?' She opened her eyes at that and held up her long lovely neck suspiciously and decided to be incredulous. She was twelve and at that age little girls are beginning to suspect most stories : they have already found out too many, from Santa Claus to the Stork. How could there be a well ! In The Dark Walk? That she had visited year after year? Haughtily she said, 'Nonsense.'

But she went back, pretending to be going somewhere else, and she found a hole scooped in the rock at the side of the walk, choked with damp leaves, so shrouded by ferns that she only uncovered it after much searching. At the back of this little cavern there was about a quart of water. In the water she suddenly perceived a panting trout. She rushed for Stephen and dragged him to see, and they were both so excited that they were no longer afraid of the darkness as they hunched down and peered in at the fish panting in his tiny prison, his silver stomach going up and down like an engine.

Nobody knew how the trout got there. Even old Martin in the kitchen-garden laughed and refused to believe that it was there, or pretended not to believe, until she forced him to come down and see. Kneeling and pushing back his tattered old cap he peered in.

'Be cripes, you're right. How the divil in hell did that fella get there?'

She stared at him suspiciously.

'You knew?' she accused; but he said, 'The divil a know;' and reached down to lift it out. Convinced she hauled him back. If she had found it then it was her trout.

Her mother suggested that a bird had carried the spawn. Her father thought that in the winter a small streamlet might have carried it down there as a baby, and it had been safe until the summer came and the water began to dry up. She said, 'I see,' and went back to look again and consider the matter in private. Her brother remained behind, wanting to hear the whole story of the trout, not really interested in the actual trout but much interested in the story which his mummy began to make up for him on the lines of, 'So one day Daddy Trout and Mammy Trout . . .' When he retailed it to her she said, 'Pooh.'

It troubled her that the trout was always in the same position; he had no room to turn; all the time the silver belly went up and down; otherwise he was motionless. She wondered what he ate and in between visits to Joey Pony, and the boat and a bathe to get cool, she thought of his hunger. She brought him down bits of dough; once she brought a worm. He ignored the food. He just went on panting. Hunched over him she thought how, all the winter, while she was at school he had been in there. All winter, in The Dark Walk, all day, all night, floating around alone. She drew the leaf of her hat down around her ears and chin and stared. She was still thinking of it as she lay in bed.

It was late June, the longest days of the year. The sun had sat still for a week, burning up the world. Although it was after ten o'clock it was still bright and still hot. She lay on her back under a single sheet, with her long legs spread, trying to keep cool. She could see the D of the moon through the fir-tree – they slept on the ground floor. Before they went to bed her mummy had told Stephen the story of the trout again, and she, in her bed, had resolutely presented her back to them and read her book. But she had kept one ear cocked.

'And so, in the end, this naughty fish who would not stay at home got bigger and bigger and bigger, and the water got smaller and smaller. . . .'

Passionately she had whirled and cried, 'Mummy, don't make it a horrible old moral story!' Her mummy had brought in a Fairy Godmother, then, who sent lots of rain, and filled the well, and a stream poured out and the trout floated away down to the river below. Staring at the moon she knew that there are no such things as Fairy Godmothers and that the trout, down in The Dark Walk, was panting like an engine. She heard somebody unwind a fishing-reel. Would the *beasts* fish him out!

She sat up. Stephen was a hot lump of sleep, lazy thing. The Dark Walk would be full of little scraps of moon. She leaped up and looked out the window, and somehow it was not so lightsome now that she saw the dim mountains far away and the black firs against the breathing land and heard a dog say, bark-bark. Quietly she lifted the ewer of water, and climbed out the window and scuttled along the cool but cruel gravel down to the maw of the tunnel. Her pyjamas were very short so that when she splashed water it wet her ankles. She peered into the tunnel. Something alive rustled inside there. She raced in, and up and down she raced, and flurried, and cried aloud, 'Oh, Gosh, I can't find it,' and then at last she did. Kneeling down in the damp she put her hand into the slimy hole. When the body lashed they were both mad with fright. But she gripped him and shoved him into the ewer and raced, with her teeth ground, out to the other end of the tunnel and down the steep paths to the river's edge.

All the time she could feel him lashing his tail against the side

of the ewer. She was afraid he would jump right out. The gravel cut
into her soles until she came to the cool ooze of the river's bank
where the moon-mice on the water crept into her feet. She poured
out watching until he plopped. For a second he was visible in the
water. She hoped he was not dizzy. Then all she saw was the glimmer
of the moon in the silent-flowing river, the dark firs, the dim mountains, and the radiant pointed face laughing down at her out of the
empty sky.

She scuttled up the hill, in the window, plonked down the ewer
and flew through the air like a bird into bed. The dog said bark-bark.
She heard the fishing-reel whirring. She hugged herself and giggled.
Like a river·of joy her holiday spread before her.

In the morning Stephen rushed to her, shouting that 'he' was gone,
and asking 'where' and 'how'. Lifting her nose in the air she said
superciliously, 'Fairy Godmother, I suppose?' and strolled away
patting the palms of her hands.

Shades of the Prison House

The village kids said that they fell out with Inch Moran because she had 'levelled' Padna Calla with a stone. That, as far as they knew, was the truth. They had really outlawed Inch because of the things their fathers and mothers were saying about her father. They had turned against him because he was a warder in the jail; because Bantry the tramp was going to be hanged in a week's time for the murder of Boody Bess; and because they were all terrified of everybody and everything connected with the hanging.

Up to the very last day of the trial they had talked only of Bantry and Boody. Did he do it? Would he get off? Would he be certified? Or they would go back and look again into the pond under the alders where she had been found with her red hair spread on the water and her eyes open and her forehead staved in. Or they would stare into the cave where the police found Bantry staring out at them with the starting-handle still clutched in his fist. But on the night of the verdict when they looked out at the jail-tower, and saw the solitary light, somebody said, 'I suppose Moran is in charge of him'; and from that on they began to see Moran locking Bantry into his cell, feeding him his breakfast every morning (for some reason vaguely connected with the idea that condemned men get anything they ask for on the last morning they thought only of his breakfast), and they saw Moran leading Bantry by the arm to the drop, and they even saw Moran holding the greased rope for Pierpoint the hangman. At once, even the man's uniform, that did not have as much as a silver button on it, was connected with death in their minds. They spliced everything he did into their own horror of the hanging. He was a great hand at fretwork, and when they saw his light shining late at night they saw it as a kind of counterpart to the solitary light in the tower. Mrs Calla said it gave her the shivers to see him digging in his garden.

So, for two long weeks, up to the very eve of the hanging, the kids outlawed Inch. It meant imprisonment; for since the murder no child was allowed to go alone outside the village. It meant that she sat, all the livelong day, in the house, or else in the tiny garden high on top of an outdoor stone stairs that climbed for ten steps and stopped in mid-air: the remains of some vanished structure. She was like one of those coloured gnomes that people buy for gardens – fat-legged, rosy, a red row of sausage curls across her forehead, in an old-fashioned coat with many capes like a dwarf highwayman, and her two grey eyes wide and a divilment that had no outlet.

On a level with her lofty throne, staring out through the dormer window, were her two sisters, side by side, two statues with blank eyeballs, facing across the river at the baths where the bodies of the city lads gleamed in the sun. The two mild-faced creatures never spoke to her, or to anyone. When they did speak they spoke to the air, never above a whisper, and never finishing a sentence. One would say, 'We want to.' And the other might reply, 'This is the.' Inch, high among the madder of the valerian, the stonecrop, the budding lobelia, was hardly aware that they were there. The only people who ever spoke to her were the mothers filling their ewers and buckets from the pump below on the pavement. They would say, 'Why don't you go out and play with the childer, Inch? They're all gone out to the quarry.'

She would say, 'I am quite happy where I am, thank you. I have my thoughts to think. They are very interesting thoughts, and very typical.'

At which the women would bend down and pump convulsively.

It was very quiet in the village on the eve of the hanging; Inch, broody on her aerial perch, could hardly hear a sound. The river was at ebb. The turbines in the waterworks, whereby the village lived, were stopped. The only sound was when somebody threw a bucket of slops across the road, or when she heard the voices of the gang ringing in the distance. Always up to now when she fell out with the gang – as, being a little boss, she often did – she won them back after a few days; enticed first one, then another, until she finally had them all with some grand plan they could not resist, such as promise of a marvellous picnic (she was a born organizer), or news of a gorgeous new 'plank', their word for a secret haunt of blackberries, or mushrooms, or wild-crabs. This time not a soul approached her. And there were the wide fields breaking with whitethorn, and celandines, and wild arum. There were the clouds stealing away over the hills, saying, 'Come on, come on.' While she was left there, as she told her father in a fury the night before, like an abandoned female.

Suddenly she saw Rory Baked Beans below her on the road. He was hardly one of the gang, too young to be initiated. At any other time she would have told him to run along and wipe his nose. This time she seized her chance like lightning.

'Hullo, Rory boy!' she greeted, the title the basest flattery.

'Hullo, Inch girl!' said Rory.

'How's yeer cat these days?' asked Inch politely.

He lighted up instantly. 'She have hundreds of kittens. But,' – sadly – 'they're all blind.'

'All kittens is blind,' explained Inch. 'Pups is blind, too. That's because they're born in the dark and aren't used to the light.'

'Gor!' said Rory, in wonder at her vast knowledge. Then, recollecting himself: 'What dark were they born in?'

'In the coal-hole, of course, you fooleen,' said Inch. 'All kittens and pups is born in coal-holes.'

Rory agreed, pondering on the interesting fact. Inch began to tempt him.

'I know,' she whispered, 'where there's a nest of young larks. Larks is never born blind. Will you come out along with me in the morning and we'll see them?'

Rory hesitated but looked fondly up the river at the softening tops of the beechweeds. Inch went on: 'I have a cocoa-tin that we could boil tea in. I have tuppence my Da gave me. We could have a massive picnic. Them too,' pointing to her sisters, 'would come with us, though the Lord knows they're not much use to God or man.'

'Where is it?' asked Rory.

Inch swept out her arm with a gesture worthy of a generalissimo.

'Were you ever out to the tip-top of Pike Hill?' she asked.

'What's there?' he bargained.

'Mrs Calla,' said Inch, and it was a sign of her ruthless genius that she did not even think of the Calla child she had levelled with the stone, but that her eyes dilated instead with the vastness of her indefinable image, 'Mrs Calla says that when you'd get to the top of Pike Hill and look down you'd see *Nothing*! Imagine it, Rory boy – out and out as far we can go, and look down, and see Nothing!'

'Is it out beyond the wood where they caught Bantry?'

'Miles farther,' said Inch, without a tremor.

'Is it out beyond the quarry where they found Boody Bess?' whispered Rory, fearful of giving offence even as he said it.

'Miles beyond that,' laughed Inch. 'Out and out and out!'

That silenced them both, it broke the power of their own imagination. The far cries of the gang sank away. The setting sun caught only the ripples by the gravelled islands of the river. Somebody called Rory's name but he did not stir.

'We'll start in the early morning,' she lured. 'Come up and sit here and we'll plan it.'

He came in and up. The two vacant sisters still gazed away at the slow dusk with the patient eyes of cows. Inch put her arms about him.

'We'll go out and out,' she crooned.

'Out and out?'

'And we'll climb. And look down.'

'Yoy! We'll look down, Inch.'

'And see Nothing.'

'Nothing!'

Again the mother's voice called, despairingly, to Rory. Dark was fallen. The two statues did not budge. The river had become more audible with the fall of night. Beyond the tree-tops, the rounded domes of the sycamores, the sea-weedy elms, the serrated pines, the unrecognizable furry fuzziness of the farthest woods, there rose the hexagonal tower of the jail. The solitary light shone in its tower. Inch smiled down at Rory.

One of the sisters, said, 'Who will put the?' And the other answered, 'Sometimes.'

The next morning the four of them were already approaching the round hill-top before the dew was yet dry on the grassy margins of the roads. She had seen the village kids look with envy after her as she led her opposition down the street. She knew that when she came back she would have such stories that she would have no trouble in leading a larger expedition the following morning. Within three days she would be King of the Castle again. Her thoughts levitated her so that she kept the three of them fast on the march, and before they realized it they had left the village far behind and were looking on unfamiliar country.

The river was now far below them; cattle stood in it, tiny and black. To the west, forty miles away, they saw a neat row of mountains, eight or ten little blue hunchbacks, with white caps on their heads. Hand in hand the four of them left the road and marched up the slope to the globe of green hill, as to a sacrificial altar.

'We'll picnic on the top,' panted Inch, and the grouped trees right and left of the dome of grass invited them.

At last they were on top, sweaty and worn but triumphant. They saw more mountains beyond the hunchbacks. The river crept like a cat through the land. A breath of mist revealed it when the woods hid it. Inch recovered first of all, threw out her hand and said grandly to Rory Baked Beans, 'Well? *There* you are!' If it was not Nothing it was as endless and as bottomless.

It did not occur to the children to turn and look the way they had come until a man and a woman came walking slowly up the hill, and, reaching them, nodded and smiled, and began to look towards the village through a pair of field glasses. Then Inch turned to the familiar spire, the familiar web of smoke, and the hexagonal tower. The four kids listened to the grown-ups.

'*There* you are!' said the man suddenly, with the field glasses stuck to his eyes. 'I see it!'

'Show *me*, darling,' said the young woman, and she took the glasses, focused them, and said, 'Yes. It's quite clear now. I can see it fluttering.'

'It *is* black, isn't it?' said the man.

'It's black all right,' she mumbled, still staring, fascinated.

'If Pierpoint really didn't come,' he said, 'I wonder who they got to do it.'

'Some warder,' she said idly. 'I believe they have to give him ten pounds to do it.'

'May I have another look, dear?' said the man testily.

He looked again. Then she looked. Then they got tired of looking at the flag and began to focus idly this way and that. At last, with another smile for the kids, they wandered away downhill.

Inch, like her two vacant stepsisters, was staring away at the mountains, and at the river that gently turned its white belly like a fish whenever the sun through cloud passed slowly across it. Rory was stitching daisies into a chain. Silently they prepared the picnic. Then they played a game. Then Inch wandered off by herself. The long day leaked away. Rory got tired and wanted to go home, but she would not and would not. He kept saying, 'Why?' She kept saying, 'Just because!'

They quarrelled and she abused him and he cried. At last he said, 'There's nothing to see here,' and sank down and fell asleep under a tree. The hunchbacks became transparent as the sun sank behind them and the sky widened with mackerel backs and pink mare's tails. Rory went off and then came back from some lonely expedition. Inch waked up the two mad sisters who were asleep in one another's arms.

'We must go home, now,' she said, and gave one last long look at the vast West where only the river was bright. They packed up, and dragged their legs home along the dusty road and finally came to the first cottage. Like lambs to the stall the two sisters went into their house. Rory went to Mrs Calla's for his tea. Inch would not go with any of them. She stood in the dark and kicked stones with her boot toe. Mrs Calla came out and made her come into her house for her supper.

The gossips dropped in one by one, but seeing Inch they did not talk. From time to time Mrs Calla kept rubbing Inch's poll and saying, 'Poor child! God help you!' Dadda Calla, whose job it was to scrape the wrack from the waterworks gratings, asked her where she spent the day. She said, lightly, 'Over the hills and far away.'

'Whatdeyeat?' said Dadda, all in one word, which was the way he always talked, as if he had marbles in his mouth and was afraid they'd all fall out.

'Sweets and cakes,' said Inch, very grand in her manner.

'A hake-o'-fish'd-be-betthher,' growled Dadda. 'Hake-o'-fish-and-aloado'spuds!'

'And what'd ye see, childeen bawn?' asked Mrs Calla, stroking the small fat hand.

'Oh, nothing,' said Inch. 'Nothing. But it was quite interesting, thank you,' she added primly. 'It was very typical and interesting to all of us.'

'And will you be going out there now soon again, a grah, with the rest of the children?' asked Mrs Calla, pressing the little hand.

'No thank you,' said Inch, getting up. 'Now I must be going. My father will be expecting me.'

They let her go. At the door she looked up at the sky, and said, 'It's a starry night. A starry night for a ramble.' And fled, choking.

She stayed out as long as she dared. She kicked more stones. Then she got afraid. Tossing her curls she went into her home.

He was by the fire, in a heavy sleep. A piece of fretwork hung dangling from his hand. It had got as far as *God Save Our Gracious Ki.* She smelled him, and said, 'I suppose it's the whiskey.' She went up to bed. The two sisters were awake, staring at the ceiling, side by side. She got into bed beside them. The ripples of the river under the lights of the Waterworks shimmered on the ceiling. The night turbines throbbed softly. At long last she heard him come heavily up the stairs, go to his room, and after a while bed springs creaked. She heard a faint sound of water over the weir, and wondered at it because of the drouth. Then she realized that it was him whimpering in his sleep – like a little dog.

The End of a Good Man

*

Men who go into competition with the world are broken into fragments by the world, and it is such men we love to analyse. But men
who do not go into competition with the world remain intact, and
these men we cannot analyse. They are always contented men, with
modest ambitions. Larry Dunne was that kind of man. All that there
is to say about him, therefore, is that he bred pigeons and was
happy.

And yet, this unconditional lump of reality, this unrefracted
thought in the mind of God, suddenly did fall into fragments. He
fell for the same reason as Adam. For when God was saying,
'Orchards for Adam', and 'Finance for J. P. Morgan', and 'Politics
for Teddy Roosevelt', and 'Pigeons for Larry Dunne', He must have
added (sotto voce), 'But one pigeon he must never control.' And it
was to that one pigeon, that one ambition that Larry Dunne gave his
heart. The pigeon's name was Brian Boru. Larry got him on his
thirty-fifth birthday from his father.

Any evening that summer you could have met Larry at the pigeon
club – it sat every night under the canal bridge on the towpath – and
you might have guessed in what direction his heart was already
moving by the way he talked endlessly without ever mentioning the
fatal bird. You might have heard him, towering over the rest of the
club, talking of his runts, tumblers, pouters, homers, racers, without
ever mentioning Brian Boru; you might have heard how he had a
jacobin, and nearly had a scandaroon; how 'Pigeons, mind you, must
never be washed, only sprayed with rain-water. And what's more,
pigeons should be sprayed from the shoulders down – never the
head, unless you want them to die of meningitis.' What a scoundrel
the man in Saint Rita's Terrace was, a low fellow who kept budgerigars and had once actually said that pigeons were mere riff-raff.
How his father had stolen a sacred pigeon out of an Indian temple,
when he was in Rangoon with the Royal Irish, and how the rajah

chased him into the jungle for two miles trying to catch him. 'And what's more, you should never dry a pigeon, unless, to be sure, you wrapped him up in warm flannel – which isn't the same thing.' And anyway, what were budgerigars, only pups off parrots? 'They are not even called budgerigars! They call them budgies – as if anyone would ever dare to call a pigeon a pidgy! Doesn't it show yeh?'

But whatever he spoke of, or whomever he spoke to, you might notice that he never spoke to one little runt of a man who always listened to him with a sly, sneering smile on his face. That was the club-member whose Michael Collins the Second had beaten Larry's Brian Boru in every race since the season began – beaten the bird that had laid its beak on Larry's heart.

Nobody knew the history of this Brian Boru. Larry's father swore he was the great-grandson of the Indian rajah's sacred pigeon, but that, of course, was a tall yarn. Whatever his pedigree, the bird was a marvel. Such speed! Such direction! Such a homer! A bird that had only one flaw! Time and again, when there was a race, Larry had seen that faint speck of joy come into the sky over the flat counties and the chequered market gardens where he lived, each time half an hour, at the very least, ahead of every other bird in the team; and on one occasion as much as fifty-eight minutes ahead of them, and that in the teeth of thirty-mile gale.

For while other birds had to follow the guiding shore line, or the railway line that dodged the hills, Brian came sailing over mountain top and moor like an arrow from the bow. Time and again, after greeting him with an adoring shout, Larry had gone tearing back down the lane to his tumbledown cottage, roaring to his Da to get out the decoys, and to light the primus-stove for some new concoction whose smell was to tempt Brian Boru down to his loft. Back then to the bridge, waving to the sky, calling the bird by name as it came nearer and nearer to the parapet on which stood the club's time-piece – a clock with a glass front on which there was a blue and green painting of a waterfall. (A bird was not officially home until its owner had tipped the waterfall with its beak.)

But . . . time and again the one flaw told. Brian Boru would circle, and Brian Boru would sink, and inevitably Brian Boru would rise again. After about thirty minutes of this he would come down to the telegraph pole over Larry's backyard; and stay there until some slow coach like Michael Collins the Second had walked off with the race. The bird so loved the air that it could not settle down.

'Oh!' Larry had been heard to moan, as he looked up at the telegraph pole. 'Isn't it a sign? Isn't it a symbol? Isn't that poor Ireland all over again? First in the race. Fast as the lightning. But she won't settle down! That bird has too much spirit – he's a high-flyer – and aren't we the same? Always up in the bloody air. Can't come down to earth.' And then he would beseech the bird, as it looked down at him over its prima-donna chest with a bleary eye, rather like an old damp-nosed judge falling asleep on his bench: 'O Brian Boru! Yeh sweet limb o' the divil, will you come down? Look! I've custards for yeh. I have sowanies for yeh. I have yer loft lined with the sweetest straw.' And he would start clucking and chortling at it. 'Coordle-coordle-coordle, Brian Boru-u-u-yu.' Or: 'Tchook, tchuc, thc, thc, thc, thc. Tchook, thc, thc . . . oh, but I'll tchook you if I lay me hands on you, you criminal type from British India! Brian, my *darling*, aren't you *going* to come *down* to me?'

Brian would snuggle his beak on his chest, or make a contemptuous noise like a snore.

Then, that night at the bridge – for on race nights Larry simply had to talk about Brian Boru:

'It's not fair,' Larry would protest. 'The rules should be altered. That bird is not being given his due. That bird is suffering from injustice. Sure, it's only plain, honest reason. The bird is first home in every race – will any member of the club deny it?'

'No, Larry!' they would reply, appeasingly. 'No! He's a grand bird, we all admit it, but a bird who won't settle is no good. And, for another thing, as we're sick and tired of telling you, supposing two birds come into sight at one and the same time, who the blazes is going to tell which one of them is first past the winning post – if there's going to be no winning post?'

'Ah!' Larry would roar, 'But sure this bird is home hours before any of your so-called pigeons – cripples I call them.' And then, true to his happy, light-hearted nature, he could not help laughing and making a joke of it. Six feet two, and as innocent as a child. 'Did I call them cripples? Cripples is too good for them. The one-half of ye must be breeding yeer birds from a cross between penguins and pelicans!'

At which he would recover something of his natural good humour again, and go off chortling – a chortle that would die as he remembered what began it.

As the season approached its end the bird got fat, and Larry got thin; but the bird retained his speed, and Larry became slow-moving and sullen. Those who had always known him for a gay fellow shook their heads sadly over it. He still entered Brian for the races; but each Saturday, now, he would barely stroll to the bridge when the regular two hours were passed since the birds had been released down the country. And when he saw the familiar speck in the sky he would actually turn his back on it.

It was the Easter Monday race that brought things to a head. That day a passing stranger said to him, as Brian Boru came into sight, 'Whose bird is that?'

Larry, leaning with his back and two elbows on the parapet, gave an idle glance over his shoulder at the sky.

'Him? He's my bird. But – eh – he's not in the race, you know. He's what you might call a gentleman pigeon. He's doing it for fun. That bird, sir, could win any race he wanted to. But the way it is with him, he couldn't be bothered. Pride is what's wrong with that bird, sir. Pride! Pride, they say, made the angels fall. Maybe it did. I wish something would make that fellow fall.'

Whereupon, Larry, as if a new understanding of the nature of pigeons had suddenly been vouchsafed to him, turned and gave the circling speck a terrible look. It was the look of a man struck by rejected love. Just at that moment it was that the man who owned Michael Collins the Second said the fatal word, as they all remembered and often recounted long after. He was a shrimp of a creature, a Tom Thumb of a man, who worked as a Boots in a hotel and bred his pigeons out of his tips. Seeing that look of misery in Larry's face he laughed and said, 'Why don't you breed budgerigars, Larry? At least you could take them out of their cage and kiss 'em?' The row of pigeon-fanciers, staring up at the sky, chuckled. They did not see the look of hate in Larry's face, or notice the way he slouched away home to his cabin.

There, as he was at his tea, he suddenly heard the clatter of wings like tearing silk and, looking up through his cabin window, he saw his bird in its loft among the custards and dainties, and now and again it glanced indifferently towards the cabin door. Pushing aside his cup, Larry said to his father – the old man recorded it when there was no use in recording it – 'I wish to God, Da, you never gave me that pigeon. That bird isn't human. He despises me.' And he put his head between his hands.

Later in the night, while the drizzle of rain fell on him, and the red reflections of the city illuminated the sky, he stood outside until his hair was pricked with the dew of the drizzle, talking now to himself, now to Brian; and though his father kept coming to the door, telling him not to be behaving like a child of two, Larry would not stir. He was like a boy hanging about under the window of his beloved.

'Is it the way you're faulting me?' he whispered. 'Is there something you think I ought to do? But what is there I can do? I can't alter the rules, and you won't come down! I know it's a dishonour. It's a dishonour for both of us. I know that, Brian my darling, just as well as you know it. But honest to God, I don't think it's my fault. I brought you up well. I did my best for you. I swear to God above this night I'd lay down my life for you. But, bar flying up in the air myself and bringing you down, what *can* I do?'

From the loft no reply, except the deep breathing of sleep.

Once more he entered the bird. Once more the pigeon scorned the earth. Once more the Boots mentioned budgerigars, and this time he added that canaries can at least sing. Once more, Michael Collins won the race. That finished it. Larry went home, and on the following Monday he sold every bird, box, loft, packet of food, and medicine bottle that he possessed. With the money he bought an old Smith and Wesson, thirty-two bore, and five rounds of ammunition from a former pal of the I.R.A. Then, for the last time, he entered the bird, saw it come, as always, first of the team up against the clouds that floated like bridesmaids over the hedgerows; saw through the veils of the sun how Brian swerved, and circled, and sank . . . and rose again; and did so its usual number of times before making for the inaccessible perch on the telegraph pole. While the dozen heads along the bridge shook their commiseration, Larry gripped his revolver in his pocket, and waited for the Boots to laugh. The Boots laughed. At that Larry's body took on the old fighting slouch; he pulled his hat savagely down over one eye; he buttoned his coat across his chest; he became the old down-looking gunman he had been fifteen years ago when he was in the I.R.A. Then with a roll of his shoulders like a militia man, a trick learned from his soldier Da, he looked at the Boots between the shoulder blades, put on the final bit of the gunman's manner – the ominously casual strolling gait – and walked quietly down the lane. There he found Brian on the pole.

'Brian,' he whispered, but without hope. 'Will you come down to me now?'

The bird rose and flew away, circled and came back again.

'So yeh won't come down?' whispered Larry out of the corner of his mouth. The bird looked haughtily over the lane roofs, as if contemplating another circle of flight. Before it could stir the shot cracked. With one head-sinking tumble it fell with a plop to the ground. Larry stooped, lifted the hot, twitching body in his palms, gave it one agonized look, and pelted back to the bridge, roaring like a maniac.

'By the Lord Almighty!' they said, when they saw him coming, screeching, with the bird in his palms. 'Brian Boru is after winning at last!'

Shouldering their cluster right and left, Larry snapped the beak to the glass of the clock, displayed the celluloid ring on the stiff ankle, and shouted, pale as the clouds, 'Has he won?'

It was only then that they saw the blood oozing down between his trembling fingers; but before they could tell him what they thought of him they saw the mad look in his eyes, and the way his hand stole to his pocket.

'Well?' yelled Larry at the Boots. 'Has he won? Or has he not won? Or maybe you'll say there's a rule that a dead bird can't win a race?'

'He's w-w-won, all right,' trembled the Boots.

'Gimme his prize!' said Larry.

In fear they gave it to him. It was a new dovecot, painted a lovely green. ('Eau-de-canal' the Boots called it afterwards, being the sarcastic brute he was.) Larry took the dovecot, and with the reddening beak hanging from his fist he slouched away. On Monday he sold the dovecot, had the bird stuffed, and put in the window of his lane cabin for the world to see.

You never see Larry Dunne at the canal bridge now. He walks moodily by himself along the towpaths, idly flicking a little twig against the hedges: or he sits with his father at the other side of the fire, learning off bits from his favourite book, *Who's Who,* or he sits gazing into the dancing devils of flame. The sky outside is lurid with the lights of Dublin. And in the little curtained window, the pigeon looks with two glassy eyes out over the damp market gardens, and the heavy, odorous night-fields, at the bloody sky.

Passion

Dearest Love. When will we meet again? It is only a few hours since I left you, and I am already full of melancholy thoughts.

Why on earth did I think tonight, after I had left you, of Conny Hourigan, and of that soft, wet night when the lights of Cork down in the valley were weeping through the haze, and everything as still as before dawn; and not a sound but the jolt of an old tram over the worn points, or the drip of the rain on the old tin shed in the backyard?

I think it was because I went to my window and saw the far away lights of Dublin, and at once I was again listening to that silence of twenty years ago drumming in my ears. I was waiting for my aunt to play the next card, and looking across the cosy eye of the fire in the kitchen-range at Conny breathing contentedly over his evening paper and stroking his Moses beard.

He suddenly lifts his eyes to look over his spectacles at the tiny window, and he says – 'Them bastards of slugs will be out in their marching orders tonight.' And he is just about to heave himself up and go out to his beloved patch of a garden to kill some of them when we hear a ratatatat at the hall-door. With a look over his glasses at my auntie, and a look at the clock, and a 'Who on earth can that be?' he goes shuffling out along the little hall. My aunt suspends her card. We turn our heads when we hear the voices rising sharply and Conny shouting, 'No!' And again, 'I tell you, no!' – and then more loud voices and the slam of the door.

He came back, flushed; gave a hitch to his belly, sat down, growled, 'Bloody cheek!' and tried to resume his reading.

'Who's that, Conny?' said the auntie, still holding up her card.

'Three buckos from Blarney Lane. Asking me to give 'um me six Easter lilies.'

'Oh, law! And why so?'

'Some kid that's dead up in Barrett's Buildings. Name of Delurey.

Molly Delurey. Died up in the Fever Hospital. The best I ever heard.
God Almighty! Asking me to cut me six Easter lilies for some wan
I never heard of in me life before. Did you ever hear the beat of
that?'

His sister, of course, wanted to know all about it. Cork may call
itself a city, but it is really a big town made up of a lot of little
villages, and in each 'village' everybody wants to know everything
about everybody else.

'Delurey?' she says. 'I don't know any wan now of that name. To
be sure, we had a little apple-woman used to come here . . . Ah, but
she was a Minny Delaney. And how did they come to know that
you have the lilies?'

'You may ask. Your brave milkman. Spotted 'um every morning
coming in with the milk. I knew that fellow had his eye on me
garden. I always said that fellow's too sweet to be wholesome. "Oh,
Mister Hourigan, haven't you the grand geraniums! Oh, isn't the
verbena massive, Mister Hourigan!" Making a big man out of himself. "Flowers? I'll get ye the flowers. Go up to Mister Hourigan and
tell him I sent you. Ask him for his lilies." The cheek of him! The
cool, bloody pig's cheek of him!'

My auntie played her card without looking at it. She forgot to
take her trick. I suppose she was seeing the little deal coffin, or the
child laid out on the bed in the back bedroom. The rain played its
harp strings in the yard. The fire purred.

'What they usually do,' she ventured, 'is to make up a collection
for to buy the flowers.'

'That's what I said to 'um.' – Over his spectacles. 'They wanted to
blind me that there's none in the shops. I don't believe wan word of
it. And if there isn't,' his voice kept rising and rising, 'why did they
come up to *me* for *my* poor little flowers? How fair they wouldn't
go down to Bolster has a glasshouse full of 'um? Oh, no! Up to the
foola! Me poor little six Easter lilies that I reared, that I looked after
as if they were me own children, that I . . . But these buckos have no
consideration. "Go up to Mister Hourigan and tell him I sent you."
The . . . But what . . . Me poor little lilies. Who ever . . . God
Almighty, I . . .'

He choked off into incoherence.

I said, 'Your trick, auntie?'

She gently swept the cards aside with her hand and breathed

rather than whispered, 'The poor child.'

Down with his paper, off with his specs.

'That's all very fine, woman, but am I going to give me six Easter lilies because . . . And aren't they me own property? Or aren't they? Amn't I entitled to do what I like with 'um? Or amn't I? And if I don't want to give 'um to 'um what right have them cafflers to be coming up to me own hall-door giving me lip?'

'Conny, I hope you didn't have *words*.'

'And am I going to let a pack of Blarney Lane cafflers tell me up to me puss that there won't be luck nor grace about the house if I don't give me flowers to 'um?'

'Conny! Conny! Conny! You refused the dead.'

He dashed down the paper and tore out of the kitchen. We heard the front door opening. I could imagine the dark and the haze and the smudgy lights down in the valley. He shuffled into the bedroom and struck a match. That was for the candle. I saw how the lilies outside the window would be pale against the smudgy lights of the city.

The wind wailed down from the convent grounds behind the backyard. My auntie was slowly putting the cards back into the old cigar-box. The candle clattered against the basin and ewer and then he came shuffling in along the linoleum of the hall. He blew out the candle, took up his paper firmly, and began to read it. The aunt closed the cigar-box and folded her arms about her and turning to the fire was lost in the little fluttering puffs coming out of the coal.

'The loveliest funeral I ever seen was the time of Lord Mayor MacSwiney. All the bands of the city. And the pipers. And the boys marching. And the Dead marching Saul. And the flag on the coffin. And all the flowers. And people in every window crying down salt tears.' Conversationally she inquired of him: 'Isn't Packey Cassidy buried up there with the Lord Mayor?'

'How do I know where he's buried?'

'Sure aren't they all together up in the one plot?'

'I dunno who you're talking about, let me read me paper, woman.'

'Yerrah is it pretending you don't know Packey Cassidy from the Glen worked with you down in the gas-house? Oh then many the night he brought you home when you had a sup taken. Didn't the two of us stand outside there in the garden and the pipers playing him up the Western Road to the Republican Plot?'

Conny pretended to read. The wind brought us the soft broken tolling of the nuns' bell. Conny looked over his specs again at the window and gave a poke to the cosy fire.

'That's a nor'-wester. There'll be a flood in the river tomorrow.'

'Ah, God look down on us. 'Tis no harm to say it – once we're dead we're soon forgotten.'

'You'd betther be beatin' your way home, boy, the last tram is gone.'

I hated to leave the warm kitchen. Somehow this talk of processions and bands and floods in the river and the nuns' bell and the squeaks of the last tram had wrapped me into a cosy nest of Time and Memory, and I remembered with pleasure how somebody had said that 'All Cork is out of the wan eggshell', and I understood for the first time what that meant. I wanted desperately that Conny should give the lilies to the dead child, and I felt bitter of him that he wouldn't do it. Timidly I said, 'Wouldn't you give her three of them, Uncle Conny?' He roared at me, 'No, nor wan nor half a wan.' The aunt's face got pale and venomous and miserable and she stabbed at him :

'No nor I don't think you'd give them to meself if it was a thing that I was stretched in the next room !'

After a moment he said, quietly,

'Go home, boy.'

As I left his patch of a garden – it was about as big as a table – I saw the six lilies, calm as sleep, by the pale light of the hall. The dead child's face would be just as pale. Down in its hollow the little city seemed to have locked every door and window against the storm and the rain. There were few lights.

That was twenty years ago. Why did that wet night flash on me when I walked into my bedroom tonight and saw the land under the full moon?

The sky is bleached, the fields are white, the lights of Dublin are bright as youth. They drained me so that I had to lean on the window-sill and let it all pour over me as if I were a stone under a river. It was like hearing an old, old tune on a brass-band; or the sound of church-bells on a wet Sunday morning; or the hoot of a ship's siren on Christmas Day. Frightening shadows under everything – under the gooseberry bushes, under the cabbages, under an old ash-can. And nothing between those shadows and that high moon but those lights of the city, low down, and poised over them, one long narrow cloud stretched from east to west like a scythe about to sweep the sky. It is the sort of night that might make a man ache for love, and I was suffused with you, dear heart, and should have been full of joy and content.

That night, so long ago, was very different to this serene moon. All through that stormy night the drums of the rain beat on the roofs of Cork. In the morning the river was in flood. Rafts of branches and wrack and reeds torn up by the storm sailed on the muddy water through the city. And Conny's lovely white lilies were battered into the mud. When he saw them he just went back to bed and he stayed there for three days. The aunt didn't say one word to him. But outside his window he could hear everybody who came into the little garden – including the milkman – loud in commiseration. After that I no longer envied him his hobby, as I once used to. I began vaguely to understand that his garden was a sort of torment to him.

Or is it, dearest one, that all passion is an unhappiness? Are we always looking forward to our joy, or thinking back on it, or so drunk with it that we cannot realize it?

The night is nearly finished. The moon is going down. The lights of Dublin are still bright. The shadows are long and pale. You are asleep, with your dear red hair spread on your pillow. I hear a little wind creeping up from the north-west.

Dear Love, when will we meet again? Let it be soon, Dear Love, let it be soon!

A Letter

As she cycled out of the village along the bog-road she was aware of
the heads popping out over the half-doors. She was not ruffled. She
knew that if she had been a native they would have considered
where she might be going, and why, the state of her health, the price
she paid for her hat, her general character, her prospects of marriage,
the condition and fortunes of her father and mother and brothers
and sisters and all her known relations. As it was they would look
after her down the road, and look up the road, and return to their
affairs.

Just beyond the creamery she passed the three bank-clerks. She
threw them a gobbet of pity. What on earth had they to talk about,
day after day? They were always together in the bank, always taking the same walk, out by the bog-road, back by the New Line, home
to tea to their digs. She saw nobody else until she came to Cappagh
Cross where she passed the tall young Franciscan with the umbrella,
striding along, kicking his brown habit before him. When she turned
under the beeches up the dark road to the Commons she saw the
sun at the far end of the tunnel gaze at her with a brilliantly vacant
eye.

At the top of the long slope she came out into the sun and saw the
rocky landscape of the Commons spread out beneath her. It wavered
under its own miasma. The little lake in the centre of it glinted all
over. She turned off the road down her favourite boreen, wobbling
intently between the cart-ruts, avoiding the overhanging briars that
trailed lost threads of hay from the rank hedges on each side.

The boreen wound and dropped until it came to an abrupt end at
a gap stuffed with furze bushes. There she threw her bicycle into the
hedge and drank from the icy well, noticing how the dribbled water
dried on the flagstone. She delayed to admire the line of poplars
beyond. She looked for the distant spire of the village. It was so pale
that it was almost invisible. She clambered over the gap and thrust

through the scrub that borders the lake until she came on open water between tall reeds. She crunched forward on the strand, dazzled by the whiteness of its minute crustacea. When she lay down the water glittered level with her eye.

For a while she lay still, her satchel for pillow, enjoying the heat of the strand, sleepy with rest, hearing nothing but the clucking of invisible coots. Then she squirmed about and pulled out a book and paper from her bag. The paper was a New York periodical several months old: the book was Balzac's *Père Goriot* in English. She read reviews of plays that she was never likely to see, and notices of books she was never likely to read. Then she opened her novel and began to read the description of Eugène de Rastignac's first ball.

From time to time, as she read, her eyes wandered, distracted by a coot zig-zagging across the water, or hypnotized by the mirage shimmering above the violet rocks beyond the lake. A trail of steam from a distant train – too far away to be heard – sieved out of Cappagh woods. Her eyes did not return from the vacant sky into which it evaporated until, with a sudden gesture, she pulled out her writing-pad and her pen and began to write:

Dear Ann,

Here I am back again in B—— after the long summer holidays. I am only a month back today and already I am overcome by the feeling that I am all alone and no one writes to me and I am fed up with my eternal state of being a B.A. teaching kids in a convent school. I am in a rebellious state against God and man at finding myself an economic slave while all the rest of the world is going places and doing wonderful things. Oh! For gondolas, lights and music! I have made up my mind definitely and finally to clear out of this place as fast as I can. I have felt like this ever since I returned. The only reason I haven't written sooner is that I cannot without putting myself into my letters and I loathe whining. (If you dare commiserate with me I'll cut your throat.) You are in London and probably having a much better time. But don't dare to pity me! Now I . . .

The ink in her pen gave out. She lay back again, full length on the hot strand, frowning at the bright sky. She tried again to read but gave it up. She walked back to her bicycle and pushed it back along the boreen to the main road and cycled away around the lake, and on and on as if she were chasing the setting sun. By the time she had turned for home this fickle Saint Martin's heat had been followed by an evening chill, and with a pang she noticed the briefness of the day and the watery crackle of the trees.

The first lights had already sprung up in the village pubs. In the window under the tin roof of the cinema the blue glare of the carbons matched the bruised blueness of the flying clouds. She was too exhausted to do more than sit to her tea in the kitchen of her lodgings listening indifferently to the chatter of the landlady and her mother who was now sitting in her cocoon of shawls by the unnecessary fire. The young husband wandered aimlessly in and out of the kitchen and the talk.

The old woman in the corner was over eighty. From her armchair in the corner she was now surveying life as amusedly and ironically as if she were sitting on a cloud in Olympus. She had kept a lodging house for years in the city and had known some of her student friends.

'Miss O,' she suddenly said, 'do you remember a wild divil of a girl in the University by the name of Kitty Cooney? You do – you know her well. She came easht from near Cloyne. Her father was a vet.'

'I seem to remember the name . . .'

'Yerrah, you can't but know her. Gold hair on her. A fine looking girl. I tell you that wan was a hot piece. She had a boy called Looney. Cooney the Looney we used to call her.'

'Of course! I remember her now. She was a lovely girl.'

'Listen to me, child, she had boys after her like autumn crows in a wheat-field. Every night coortin' in the front room with the lights out. Wan night didn't I go in there forgettin' all about her and I turned on the light. Wasn't Looney inside there and his two hands inside her blouse!'

To hide her blushes she stooped for her writing-pad and prepared to write. Her daughter saw her blush and laughed aloud. The old woman gurgled. The young husband tactfully turned away to switch on the wireless. It cut in on a bit of Mozart.

'Wan time didn't she buy a shtatue of the Blessed Virgin to put in her bedroom. It was as big as herself, aroo. Looney had to carry it up from the shop in his two arums. All the way up the stairs he took it for her. Half an hour it took them to settle it, moryah!

"Ambaisthe, you divil you," says I to him, when they came down, "weren't your arums tired enough from carrying it?" He gave me wan look and he ran out of the house near choked with the laughing. He knew what I was up to. But do you think her ladyship minded? Tell me what happened her at all? Did he marry her?'

'She went to America. She married a French count.'

'Glory be to the lamb of God do you mean to say that wan is a countess? Cooney a countess? Minnie, do you hear what Miss O is after saying?'

Hearing the music rather than their talk she wrote:

. . . These digs are a gift. A bit of our old lives. They are West of Ireland people who kept a lodging-house in the College Road. I am enjoying their yarns about the inner lives of ones we knew at college. They are talking this minute about Kitty Cooney. Do you remember her? She married a farmer in County Cavan and had twins the first go off. I have made up my mind. I am going to live here in Ireland and enjoy it. These people are marvellous. They have a wonderful idiom. Just now the old woman, talking of the cuteness of the local kids, has said, 'They'd herd geese for you at a cross-road.' Isn't that wonderful? Oh, the people who leave Ireland have no sense, yourself included. Life is delightfully intimate in Ireland. I must . . .

The old woman in the corner, finding that her lodger was not in the mood for talking rose painfully and assisted by her daughter and son-in-law made for bed. When her groaning had died away up the little stairs the silence of the night enveloped the kitchen. Sometimes when the music sank away she heard kids in the street rolling their iron hoops on the concrete. So as not to disturb the old woman she turned down the music until it became a delicate whisper in the air.

She wrote on:

I must tell you something. I have an overwhelming desire to lose myself in some grand passion. I believe that it will be music. Not just to hear it and listen to it. No, that wouldn't do. It wouldn't be enough. It wouldn't satisfy me. I want to play it myself. I want to lose myself in it. If I want to live outside a convent or an asylum

I must do this. I have nothing else to do that's DEVOURING enough but read and read and read. I am reading Balzac now. He fills me with a great desire to . . .'

The husband came in again and began to poke for something in one of the drawers of the kitchen-dresser.
'I thought I had a bit of rope there somewhere.'
She leaned back.
'You're writing?' he said over his shoulder.
'A note to a friend.'
The one drawback to these lodgings was that the little house had no parlour: the only place where she could be alone was her bed-room and that was tiny – there was not even room for a chair in it and she had to sit on the bed.
' 'Tis a great night outside, thank God,' and he rummaged away. 'The sky is a riddle of stars.'
'That's a good sign.'
'Mind you, there's a touch of autumn in the air. Where the divil did I put that yoke? There's a right frosty look in the stars.' He found the bit of rope and jammed back the drawer. As he went out he said, with a smirk, 'Don't forget to put in the kisses.'
' 'Tis to a girl,' she said bitterly, but he laughed unbelievingly as he latched the door.
She looked at her letter. 'Fills me with a great desire to . . .' She crossed it out roughly. She leaned to the back window, shading her eyes from the light of the room to look out. The sky was white with starlight.
The music danced on gently. She scribbled :

In another week I will be seeing the leaves wafting down silently and the mists lurking in the trees and floating like grey water in the hollows, a time I dread. How lovely it would be then to have a book-lined room of one's own, with a friend, and deep glasses of old red port, a spider-guarded ruby, and talk, and old songs and . . .

Her hand fished for cigarettes and failed to find them. She rose and dragged on her overcoat and went out and down the street towards the stream of light falling from the window of the paper-and-sweets shop. The stars were like snow. A horse and cart stood outside the shop, his breath enveloping his drooping head. As she left the shop and walked around the block the horse and cart were already rattling out of the village, carrying her mind to the white bog-roads radiating from it under the vast indifference of the night. In her circuit she met nobody.

Back in the kitchen the wife and husband were talking in low voices beside the dying fire, their usual nightly chat, the only time when they had the kitchen to themselves. She bade them goodnight, and sat on her bed, smoking and writing:

I'm afraid this letter is all blether, but if I don't blether I'll relax the reins. For the love of God send me something exciting to read. I have made a tremendous plan which is going to ruin my good looks and destroy my adipose. I'm going to get up every morning at seven and go to bed at twelve and have plenty of time for study and reading and thinking and living inside myself. I don't care if I get scraggy and withered with a thin wrinkled neck. It will give me the pleasure of being FREE, of being DIFFERENT to those other females who carefully do their best to preserve their youth and keep up their market value. I object to this and ALL OTHER TYRANNY.

Your friend,

Joan.

She directed the envelope and folded the letter into it. She threw the red cinder of her cigarette out the window, undressed, and climbed into the deep feather-bed. The pair downstairs stole upstairs. She heard them whispering next door. Far down the village street somebody's footsteps faintly grew out of the hum of the silence, became louder, passed metallically underneath the window and faded slowly away. With them she faded into the night and sleep.

About two months later as she lay in bed with a cold she opened the Balzac and found the letter inside it. November rain fell heavily and crookedly past her tiny window. She could hear it gurgling across the pavement from a rainspout, and she imagined it beating the ruffled lake, and the poplars swaying before it, and the woods of Cappagh dripping, and the little steely pools in every field and how all the roads out across the plain must be blank and bitter.

She tried to recall that lovely, burning September afternoon, but it came to her only in disconnected patches and she thought how, in a year's time, it would probably have vanished as completely as if it had never been lived.

'Why,' she wondered, looking at the crooked rain, 'do I remember these scraps? The drops were drying on the hot flagstone of the well. The spire was so dim against the sky that I barely saw it. The steam of the train evaporating.'

And she began to wonder whether there is any special meaning in what we remember, or is it all a mere chance whether we remember or forget. She looked about her and considered what she was likely to remember of that day, or would she remember anything at all except, perhaps, the crooked rain. Contemplating it where she lay curled up to the pillow she began to wonder what might be the significance of the crooked rain.

Vive la France!

It took Alec Forbes nearly twenty years to notice that his pals began to wink at one another whenever he began to talk about his travels. That was why he folded into his beard all the lovely words that started to burst inside him when he heard the French rugby team was coming to Cork – such as Le Havre, Ostende, Marseille, café-au-lait, cognac, monsieur, mam'selle, and à la bonne chance. Instead he let the clodhoppers around him blether away to their heart's content, while he winked into his glass.

But he made it his business to be at the railway station the night the team arrived. He knew there would be an address of welcome from the Mayor and the Aldermen and the Chamber of Commerce, and he knew that if there wasn't somebody present who knew the ropes they would make an unholy mess of the whole thing. He wore his best bowler hat, his best cravat, cuffs and butterfly collar, and his gold links that gleamed in the arclights. He had brushed and combed his mosaic beard a dozen times. He held his walking stick up on his shoulder like a gun. The reception committee scowled at him.

Sure enough, when the train roared in and the team hung out of the windows waving tricolours through the steam Alec began to run up and down the platform and wave his stick and shout, 'Vive la France!' and when the team fell out of the carriages like bags of apples he was right in the middle of them handshaking all round and shouting, 'Vive la France!, que'st que vous dee dong, millo quattro chinko quaranto. Cognac! Cognac!' – at which they all cheered and laughed and shook his hands and kissed one another and shouted, 'Vive l'Irlande!' and 'Cognac! Cognac! Cognac!'

'Gintlemin,' said the Mayor shouldering Alec to one side, to read his address of welcome.

'Messieurs, mesdames,' corrected Alec out of the side of his mouth. His face was glowing with happiness, his hat back on his poll, his stick on his shoulder like a gun.

'Gintlemin,' said the Mayor sternly. 'I have . . .'

'Blasht yeh,' says Alec, giving him a poke in the back, 'can't yeh say messieurs?' And to cover up he shouted, 'Vive la France!' and they all shouted, 'Vive l'Irlande!'

'Gintlemin,' cried the Mayor, 'I have the greatest honour . . .'

'Yerrah, for God's sake,' cried Alec, 'can't we cut out all this ould guff and go and have a drink somewhere? Listen to me, boys!' he shouted at the team, and waved his stick like a serpent and enveloped them with his arms, his voice, his beard. 'Come on and have a drink at the Railway Arms. Follow me every man Jack of ye. Comme ci, comme ça? Drinko? Oui, oui?'

'Gintlemin,' bellowed the Mayor glancing around wildly, 'I have the greatest honour to say to ye tonight . . .'

But Alec had managed to detach four of the team's followers and although three of them came back to hear out the Address of Welcome he succeeded in hauling one young fellow away with him, down the ramp and out of the station, gesticulating so passionately as he pointed onwards that the young man stopped resisting and decided with a shrug that his benevolent-looking guide was probably the town-pimp.

In the Railway Arms, across the tramlines, Alec said, 'Cognac?' and the young man said, 'Cognac.' They had to be satisfied with Irish whiskey. Alec said, 'Vive la France!' and the young man said, 'Vive la France!' Alec said, 'Toujours la politesse.' The young man, already a little bored, agreed philosophically, 'Toujours la politesse.' A deep silence followed. Alec drummed the Marseillaise with his fingers on the counter but he didn't feel equal to singing it. After a while the young man said, 'Cognac?' so they had some more Irish whiskey.

'You from Marseille?' asked Alec, shaping a whole continent with his hands and stabbing southward at the spittoon to indicate Marseille.

'Marseille?' asked the young man.

'Oui? Vous? Non? Oui? Yes? No?'

'Comprends pas.'

'Look,' said Alec.

He laid his bowler-hat on the marble counter. He stooped over it and like a magician he moulded fantastic air about it with his fingers.

'La France. Comprenez-vous?'

'La France,' agreed the young man, picking a dead fly from the rim of the hat.

'Bong,' said Alec. 'Now watch.'

He laid his walking-stick in front of the hat. Swiftly he spread his hands along the stick, east-west, as if he were drawing it out like a telescope.

'La Mediterranean Sea,' he cried, and gazed hopefully into the eyes of his guest, who at once picked up the stick and returned it with a smile and a bow.

'Votre baton.'

Alec put back the stick a little irritably. Once more he embraced the hat. The barmaid was now watching them both suspiciously. Once more he leaned towards the youth. Once again he indicated the hat.

'La France!' he cried. 'Your country. Comprends?'

The young man sighed as who should say, 'Do we have to do this all over again?' However, he nodded to indicate that he was prepared to agree, for the sake of argument, that this peculiar hat was France.

'Bong!' cried Alec.

Once more he laid out the stick. He placed his two palms in the middle of it. He stared fiercely at the youth. He extended his palms slowly and magnificently along the stick and gazing wrapt into the young man's eyes he intoned –

'La Mediterranean Sea!'

At this the youth began to examine Alec's countenance all over, very seriously and minutely. Finding no explanation there he looked at the barmaid who gazed at him with a half-witted expression. At this the young man looked pensively out the door as if contemplating immediate flight.

'No comprends?' implored Alec. 'Look!' he roared. 'La Mediterraneano! The Meditabloodywellranean Sea!'

'Vive l'Irlande!' said the young man and raised his glass.

Alec looked coldly at his guest. He tipped his beard. He put on his hat.

'Cognac?' he said listlessly.

'Cognac,' the young man agreed so they had some more Irish whiskey.

Now and again Alec stirred as if to speak but sank back each time frustrated. Then he gave the youth a slap on the back that nearly knocked him over the counter.

'Well, honest to God,' he assured the barmaid, 'I'm a proper ould gom and there's no harm to say it. The poor noddle,' he explained to his friend, 'is gone to hell. Off the rocker altogether. Listen! Sure I have two daughters at home that's learning French for the last three years until you think 'twould come out through their eyes. Look, boy, you come along with me. And anyway, what you want inside your belly band is a good bit of hot grub. That stuff you're drinking there is no damn good to you. Bilge-water! I have deux daughter. Two! Two filles!'

He held up two fingers. The young man demurred. He held up one finger.

'Two!' insisted Alec. 'Blast it, don't I know meself how many daughters I have!'

One finger. Two fingers. One. Two.

Alec led him aside. He ate aerial food. He carved it. He devoured his moustaches. He rubbed his stomach. He waved his hands. The young man gave it up and Alec marched him off arm in arm.

They boarded a little rattlebox of a tram in which they swayed and rocked away from the city's lights, between crumbling Georgian terraces, into the dusk. The yellow glow of the tram fell on the blue evening haze. Now and again it touched another yellow stream falling from the door of some little shop, and whenever that happened the young Frenchman would look back at the bright window and glance at Alec, talking fifteen to the dozen, and give a little sigh. They passed tiny terraces where only the fanlights were bright – the sort of houses where a sea-captain might live. High on the hills above were the lighted windows of big houses, and above these were the first stars which were not quite so bright.

'That's Montenotte,' said Alec, seeing his upward glance.

'Le Mont de Nuit? C'est charmant.'

'All the nobs of Cork live up there. That's if you want to call 'em nobs. I wouldn't. Johnny-jump-ups I call 'em. Thick in the head and strong in the back. In from the heath. If you take my advice you'll steer clear of them blokes while you're here. A lot of bloody yahoos – never went nowhere – never saw nothing. That's their ticket.'

The river opened before them, wide and sullen. Across this sullen water a noble avenue led its long linden line down and down to a darkening loch where a river-light winked fitfully. A steamer was chugging outward on the high tide, trailing its red and green mast-lights through the stars. Alec waved his stick across the river at the dusky avenue.

'That's the Marina. The next village down there is Tivoli.'

'La Marina? Tivoli? Mont de Nuit?' cried the youth. 'Mais ce n'est pas l'Irlande. C'est l'Italie!'

The tram disgorged them. They leaned on the quay-wall and looked after the diminishing steamer. From here the rumble of the city was faint and its maze of lights were as yellow as wine or candlelight. They suggested friendship, warmth, company. The young foreigner looked at these suggestive lights, looked at the feathery avenue over the river, looked at the little ship which was by now silent in the distance.

Alec suddenly threw one arm around his shoulder.

'Look, monsieur! I want to tell yeh something. Me. Sailor. I've been all over the world. Do you know what my address for forty years was? I'll tell yeh. "Alec Forbes, First Mate, Malta, Gibraltar, Port Said or elsewhere." That's me. Moi. Toujours. Everywhere. Marseille, Ostende, Le Havre, Genoa, up the Black Sea, down the Black Sea, Constanzia, Constantinople, Leghorn, every bloody place. But them blokes,' arm up to the dark hills, 'never saw nothing. Know nothing. Comprends? Ici? Toujours, ici!'

'Vous?' said the young man miserably.

'No, God blast it! Them! All of 'em. Every man Jack of 'em. Little Jackeens that never went farther than th' Isle o' Man for two weeks in the summer. Fellows that wouldn't know the difference between vin blank and vin rooge. They wouldn't even know how to *ask* for cognac! And they don't believe wan word that I tell 'em. Oh,' he groaned, 'will I ever forget the first time I drank cognac. Forty . . . what am I talking about? . . . 'tis forty-three years ago. In a place called Angers. Up the Rhône. Comprends? Were you ever there?'

'Angers? Mais oui. La Loire. Une petite ville ravissante.'

'The café was called "Le Roi René". I remember it as well as . . . And no wan believes me! Not even me own daughters believe me!'

The young man gazed at the yellow lights of the city and sighed deeply.

'Café,' he whispered. 'Le Roi René. Je m'en souviens. Je veux dire

c.s.s.o.—o

Le Roi René,' he explained. 'Pas le café. Le duc d'Anjou. Sa fille, je crois, est devenue reine d'Angleterre?'

He looked gloomily into the water at the upturned belly of a drowned dog. He looked dejectedly at the stars. He looked at the pin-point of the lighthouse winking at him indifferently. Abruptly he laid his hand on Alec's hand and spoke to him at great length, with considerable feeling, even with passion. He shook him twice by the lapels. Then he gave him a long distasteful look and folding his arms on the quay-wall contemplated the upturned dog again. Behind them the old tram departed for town, crickety-crockety, taking its light with it, leaving them to the dark, the sucking water, the chill wind. They fell silent.

Alec also looked morosely at the drowned dog. Then he glanced across the road at the city's last pub – it is called 'The Cosmopolitan Bar' – and said, 'Cognac?' The young man agreed, so they went across the road and had some more Irish whiskey.

'Constanzia, now,' declared Alec, 'is a grand port!'

But he saw that his guest was rolling his whiskey around in his glass and paying no attention.

'Allons,' Alec sighed. 'C'm on home! Grub.'

In silence they marched across a little wooden railway-bridge up a steep hill, between the damp walls of an alley whose rare gaslamps flickered on the ivy that glistened beneath them. Far behind and beneath, to the turned head, the walls framed the little city's distended glow. They halted at a tiny lodge, an Elizabethan cottage, the rear entrance to the grounds of somebody's suburban mansion. There was a fluttering of trees overhead. There was a smell of damp laurels and woodsmoke.

The door of the cottage opened on a burst of light and an overheated kitchen. Two red-headed girls of about sixteen and seventeen looked up at them. Both were warm, puffy, negligent, and handsome. The elder and slimmer was standing over an ironing board in the strained pose of any girl ironing – the elbow bent, the knee crooked, one shoulder lifted. Her eyes made the young man think at once of green rock-pools. The younger one was curled in a battered basket-chair before the little stove, her red hair tumbled over her book. She had those gently voluptuous lips that rest perpetually apart like a little trumpet, as if she were always whispering, 'Goose, goose, goose.'

Alec waved introductions: 'That's Molly. This is Jenny. This is ...'
He looked at the youth.

He was staring around the little kitchen, at the girls, at Alec. A
long, slow blush was mounting to his forehead. It retired swiftly as
if a glass were emptying and he became quite pale.

'Je m'appelle Paul Demus.'

'We'll call yeh Paul.'

The young man bowed respectfully to the girls. They grinned so
eagerly that he could guess no boy had so far done anything but
chase them in the dark until they screamed, probably down that
steep hill, under the gaslamps, their red hair flying.

'Sit down, Paul. Grub, girls! Prestissimo!'

The youth watched while they sat their father on the basket chair,
unlaced his boots, brought him his slippers, handed him his evening paper
and his glasses. He gazed restlessly about him, and once he half-rose
as if to go. But now they were talking to him in a macaroni of which
he recognized one or two English words, bits of French, and a tongue
which nobody ever told him was Irish. However, as they glanced
at him, tossed back their curls, made him lay the table, passed
him the jam or the pickles or refilled his cup, they also spoke a
language which occurs in no dictionary but which he found
entirely intelligible and which he soon began to speak just as
volubly.

He showed them photographs from his wallet, of his mother, his
two sisters, his friends in l'équipe. To explain the word he had to
borrow their dictionary and that started a game which moved
faster and faster as they became adept at flicking the pages and
passing the book to and fro across the table.

'Regardez, mesdemoiselles.' He nicked a word. '*Oriflamme.*'

'Quoi?'

'Vos cheveux!' Tipping Jenny's hair.

'Oriflamme? Oh! Oh!'

'What are ye laughing about? What's that? What's he saying?'

'He says the weather is very close tonight, daddy.'

'Then why don't ye open the window?'

'Regardez, monsieur. Vous êtes un *rogue.*'

'Quoi? Coquin? Moi? Non, non! Regardez. *De tout mon cœur.*'

'What does that mean?' seizing the book. 'Oh! Oh! Regardez!
Heartless.'

'Moi? *Sans cœur?* Non, non! Regardez. *Qui a le cœur navré, brisé, mort.*'

'What's all this about regardez? Is that window to his liking? What the divil are ye all up to?'

But the three paid no attention. They were leaning over the table in a jumble, laughing, pushing, hair tumbling. The girls pointed to the words:

'*Qui a le cœur libre!*'

He replied: '*Si le cœur vous en dit!*'

'Oh! Oh! Look! *Loin des yeux, loin de cœur.*'

'Oh! Mesdemoiselles!'

Alec laughed happily at their laughter, and returned to his paper. The noise became louder. He shouted:

'Regardez yerself, Paul, is that window all right?'

At once, gleefully, Paul seized the book and nicked, '*Vue, elevation, perspective, scène,*' and for answer to his question Alec beheld Molly and Monsieur Paul go out into the porch with so much laughing that he demanded, 'What on earth is it all about, Jenny?'

'I think he just wants to see the view of the city,' Jenny explained demurely.

'Sure that's what the boy is at all the night with his regardez. Is that all the French ye have? I could have told ye that meself,' and he resumed his reading.

When Molly returned her hair was like heather on fire. Then Jenny showed him the view, and then Molly showed him the view again, and each time they took a little longer at it, and the next time Paul wanted to see the view Alec got up and declared that they did not know how to show him the view at all and went out with the three of them.

There the four of them stood in the dark, in a line, their arms about one another's shoulders, looking at the thousands of little lights, and the occasional lightning flash when, somewhere, a tram-trolley hopped the wire.

'Do you know what it is, Paul? It's a damn nice little city. It reminds me sometimes of the view over Marseille. Comprenez-vous, monsieur?'

The youth did not reply. It seemed at first that he was considering what Alec had said. Then he shook himself and cried abruptly, 'Faut que je file!'

'Go?' Jenny cried. 'Oh, no, no! Paul, not yet!'

And Molly wailed,

'Oh, but not yet?'

Alec cried,

'By no means! Not yet! You and I are going to have a long talk together. Parlez beaucoup. Vous, moi. Lots of things!'

He insisted. He was almost rude about it. They held him. He tore himself away. They gave in. The two girls went with him, down the dark alley, over the city, swinging out of his arms, gabbling about the nuns, and Mother O'Brien who had once been to France, and about the rugby-match, and when they got to the tramstop he refused to part with them unless they first came with him into the Cosmopolitan Bar.

There they sat in a corner and over hot whisky punch – it was their idea; they said they had it every Christmas – he explained to them at great length something which was evidently of great emotional importance to himself. To everything they nodded seriously and said, 'Oui', and 'Non', and kept making beseeching frowns at one another across the table, and lifting their eyebrows behind his back and shaking their heads, but when he finished and shook their hands over and over again and said, 'Vous comprenez maintenant?' they said, 'Parfaitement', and merely shrugged at one another like Frenchwomen.

He rose. They had to help him up, and all three were laughing as they shoved him into the tram. From the step he kissed them both, to the delight of the conductor and under the frowning eyes of a severe looking priest sitting inside. When the tram was jolting away their friend was deep in explanations to the priest who kept staring at him like an image.

All the way up the dark laneway they argued heatedly. Jenny said he was a Count. Molly said he was engaged to be married to a girl whom he did not love. But they did not quarrel over it and when their Da looked up at the two of them, standing side by side in the porch, the eyes that gazed down at him were starry and golden.

His were not, and seeing his melancholy look they drooped a little.

'Didn't he go off a bit early?' he complained. 'I thought we were getting on fine. I hope ye didn't say anything to offend him?'

Jenny hurled her green beret on to the sofa, and leaned her elbows on the windowsill and looked tragically over the diamonded city. Molly slowly lifted her tam-o'-shanter from her red mop, until it was like a chef's hat, and then sank slowly at his knees in a ball and softly said, wrapping her arms about his legs :

'Fa'rer. Why donsh yeh tell ush shomethin' about Marsheille?'

Alec started up, glared at the two of them over his specs and opened his mouth to say something. Just then, far below on the river, a ship, sailing outward on the tide, hooted softly. He leaned back.

'Marseille?' he murmured.

He looked into the fire. Smiling, he began to stroke his moustaches and his beard. What was he remembering?

The Woman Who Married Clark Gable

She should have lived in Moscow. If she had been a Russian she would have said: 'O God, life is passing and I have yet to live. All last Easter when the baby clouds were passing over the birch-woods, and the streams were whispering of the coming of summer, and the bells were dancing and singing in the monastery towers, I sat at home and drank vodka and longed for love. I do not know whether life is angry with me because I do not live it, or whether I am angry with life because it will not let me live. Ivan Ivanovitch, for God's sake, meet me tonight by the frog-pond and tell me what is this pain in my heart.' And Ivan would have met her and told her in very simple terms. Instead of that she lived in Dublin (South Circular Road, small red house, red terrace, small garden, near the Old Woman's Hostel – full – and Kilmainham Jail – disused). She nagged her husband virtuously when she should have got drunk with him and poured her virtue down the drains. She went twice a week to the movies, hoovered the house until she had all the pile sucked off the carpets, bought a new knick-knack for the mantelpiece every week, washed the dog, polished the windows, slept after lunch, read *Chit Chat* and *Winifred's Weekly*, went for a walk, and then sat around waiting for her husband to come back from the job.

Every night the conversation was the same.

'Had a hard day, darling?' – from her.

'Not so bad, dearie' – from him.

'What did you have for lunch?'

'A very nice lunch. Pork chop, spinach, chips, rhubarb pie, coffee. Very tasty.'

'I washed Herbie. Look at him. It was an awful job. But he is a pet. Aren't you, Herbie?'

'Nice old 'Erbie. Like your bathie. Soapy-soapy? Not tired, dearie?'

And she would always say she was, very tired, or that she had a stitch in her side, or a pain in her head, and she would put on a miserable face, and he would tell her she ought not to do it, not really, and she would tilt her eyebrows and ask sadly for the evening paper. He would suggest a stroll, or a movie, or have a pipe, or tell her a dirty story, and so to bed, and *da capo* the next day and the next. Before she got into bed she would always say the Rosary, and then she would curl up next to him and wait for him to snore. She liked him; he was an honourable, hardworking, straightforward, generous man; but she did not love him. It must be added that they had no children and she worried about that. It must also be understood that he was a Methodist and went regularly to the tin chapel along the road, and she worried about that too. She was always praying that he might be converted: that was why she said the Rosary every night, though she never told him that. He was English and was rather stubborn about religious matters.

One morning as she kissed him goodbye at the gate of her little garden she drew back hastily and peered at him.

'Darling, you haven't shaved?'

He grinned fatuously, lifted his bowler-hat, said: 'I'm growing a moustache,' and ran. For weeks after that their nightly conversation had an extra five lines:

'I don't like that moustache, darling.'

'It's coming on. Chaps at the works rag me a lot abaht it. But I don't mind. Jealous, I say.'

'But it tickles, darling.'

'Aain't that nice, dearie?'

One night they went to the movies to see *San Francisco*, with Jeanette MacDonald and Clark Gable. This picture dealt with a rake and a good man and a singing heroine, friends in spite of everything, even the singing and the fact that the good man (Spencer Tracy) was a priest. The rake had a squabble with the priest, and although the priest – he was a Boxing Padre – could have knocked him on the canvas for twenty he merely wiped the blood off the corner of his mouth and looked sadly at the rake. In the end there is an earthquake and the earth opens and all sorts of things fall down into holes and the rake kneels down and is converted. They show Mr Gable's boot soles because nobody looking at his face would believe it. Then they all join hands and march down the hill into the camera and the closing, gauzy iridescent curtains of the cinema, singing the theme-

song, 'Sa-a-n Francisco, Open your pearly gates . . .' (etc.), and everybody goes home happy.

She walked home that night in a dreamy silence. She heard none
of his remarks about the picture, and when they were back home
she kept looking at him in a strange, distant way. She went restlessly
in and out of the parlour, threw guilty sidelong glances at him, did
not seem to want to go to bed, hardly said a word in answer to his
chatter, forgot to pray for his conversion, and lay awake for hours
looking out at the tops of the London plane waving faintly against
the dull upthrown glow of the city.

She went to the same cinema, alone, the next day; and that night
she made him take her to it again; which he was pleased to do
because he wanted to know how they got all those things to fall
into holes in the ground. All through the picture she held his hand
and stole sideward glances at the black line of his Gablesque
moustache. That night she put on her pink chiffon nightgown – the
one she bought the time she thought she was going to have a baby
and only had a miss; and she had worn it again the time she had her
gallstones out; and the time she had the appendix; and the time she
went to the nursing home when she tumbled down stairs. She put
scent behind her ears and looking at herself in the mirror said,

'Darling, did I ever tell you I had rather a good voice when I was
. . . I mean before I married you?' And she swayed and began to
hum, 'San Francisco, Open your pearly gates!'

'It sounds like hydraulic pressure,' he ruminated. 'You know, like
a lift going down.'

When she lay beside him she looked at his profile and whispered.

'Darling, supposing this was San Francisco. You and me? And the
earth begins to shake?'

'Lummy,' he cried. 'Like this?' And he began to bounce up and
down on the springs.

She gave a frightened scream.

'Why, dearie, what's wrong?'

'You're so rough,' she said adoringly.

'My poor little upsydaisy, isum frightened?'

She put out the light.

For about two weeks they were happier than at any time since
their honeymoon, in that little redbrick house on the South Circular
Road. She bought a record of *Open your pearly gates*. She asked him

questions about earthquakes and he began to read them up. One Saturday she heard the film was at Bray and, under pretence of a day's outing by the sea, made him take her to it again. This he found a bit boring, but being a kind-hearted chap he humoured her. When it moved on up to Malahide and she wanted to follow it he demurred. To his surprise she crumbled at once and said that if he hit her she wouldn't blame him, and that she probably deserved it. He did no more than tease her when he found a picture of Mr Gable garbed for the boxing-ring pinned up in their parlour the next day. But he did begin to get a bit worried when she bought him a cravat, an old-time three-cornered collar, asked him to take up boxing-lessons, and wanted him to meet her priest and become great friends with him. He drew the line at the priest and the boxing but he did wear the cravat and the collar in which he looked like a horse in demi-harness.

She noticed the worried look on his face the first morning he wore this contraption and decided that he was unhappy because he guessed that she was deceiving him with Mr Gable. She went off to consult her priest.

He heard her problem in complete silence and then said, 'It's a very fine point, I think you'd better give me a week to think it over.' So at the end of the week she went again, this time in a black veil, and he explained to her that the chief end of marriage is, of course, the bearing of children and that what we call Love is, naturally, secondary to this great end. And after all, he said, what *is* Love? Indeed, what are all those curious human manifestations which lead to the great end (which he had already defined)? To a mere celibate these things were all very strange. But then, he added quickly, who are we, anyway, to question the devices of Providence which, indeed, as we may see, are frequently not merely puzzling but baffling? At all events, he hurried on, be that as it might, it appeared to him that, theologically speaking, and always provided that she kept that great end in view, and had no other end in view at any time – he stressed the words *at any time* – there could be no objection to her deciding that she was living with this Mr Mark Cable. Indeed, he added testily, for the matter had caused him a great deal of worry, and caused him to read a great many dull Latin volumes, she could (always provided she kept that great end in view) go on believing that she was living with her grandfather; and he dismissed her

abruptly. She left him, a little hurt by the reference to her grandfather, but more content with the propriety of her behaviour than
she had ever been since her wedding night.

Her joy was brief. It was on her way home that she purchased
the film-magazine which reported, with a large portrait of Mr Clark
Gable, that there were rumours flying about New York to the effect
that 'our Clark' had lately been seen in gay places in the company
of a well-known oil millionairess.

That night she saw at once that her George was giving her worried
looks; as well he might since she kept looking at him in a very
peculiar fashion.

'Tired, dearie?' he asked.

'A fat lot you care,' she cried tragically.

'But I do care, dearie!'

'You,' she charged with passion, 'care nothing whatsoever for me.
What did you have for lunch today?'

'Why,' he mumbled, a bit taken aback by this divergence, 'I 'ad
a spot of steak-and-kidney, rhubarb and cuss, black coffee, all very
tasty too.'

At this she laughed scornfully.

'Alone?' she challenged.

'Wotcher mean, alone?'

'Were – you – alone?'

'Well, not quite alone. A couple of the chaps as usual.'

'Chaps!'

She uttered what she considered to be a strangled cry, gave a
broken sob, ended up with a groan of despair and made a fair shot
at hurling herself from the room. He, staring at the dog wagging its
tail hopefully, began to examine his conscience; and as any man
can always find some little thing somewhere in his conscience, even
if it is only a pinched bottom, he played a good deal at finger-under-
the-collar before he went up to bed. She did not speak one word to
him. Once he asked her if she had a cold, because she was sobbing
into her pillow; at which she moaned as if her poor little heart
would break, causing him to beg her to tell him if she had a toothache. His patience gave out when she refused to get up and cook his
breakfast, for an Englishman will stand much but he will not stand
for a breakfast of cold milk and dog-biscuits. He drank neat whisky
at lunch and he drank neat whisky (several times) on his way home

in the evening, and he tore off his horse-collar and dropped it into the canal, and he had a haircut and shave, and he even had the barber shave off his moustache, and when he squeaked open the garden gate he was full of fight.

She was not. She had bought another film-magazine that afternoon which scornfully denied the story about Mr Clark Gable and the millionairess; said that Mr Gable was very cross about it, in fact. In a high state of nerves she awaited his return and she was trembling when she opened the hall-door. She gave one look at the bald face and collarless neck before her, realized simultaneously that she was being confronted by her husband and had been abandoned by Mr Gable, and the next thing she did was to sink in a faint on the mat and give her poll a terrific wallop off the lino.

It took poor George an hour to bring her around and calm her down, and by that time all the fight had gone out of him. Besides he was too relieved to find that she was her old self again – moaning and groaning at him to his heart's content. When she wanted the evening paper she asked for it (to his great joy) quite snappishly. When, as the night was near ending, he ventured to tell her a dirty story and she laughed loudly and then put on a shocked face and said he ought to be ashamed of himself, he almost winked.

They lived unhappily ever after in complete marital satisfaction.

Lady Lucifer

The three friends had rowed very slowly down-river – half-floated, indeed – seeing only the withered thistles in the fields, cows standing to their ankles in still water. There was not a speck in the sky. Not even a bird; as if they had taken shelter from the humming heat in the pine-forest that rose on one side, dark and cool as a cave. The only sound they heard for a mile was the fall of water in the canal-lock; and when they passed through the lock and were lazily poling along the slim perspective of the canal, everything was again sloth and softness and sun. The narrow road of canal was a dreaming slip of water. They were secluded, lost, tucked-away. The world had died.

The doctor was poling. He wore brief cream bathing-trunks: a finely-built, sandy-haired man, serious but not severe. He had studied in Vienna, New York, and London; he was a specialist in mental diseases; he was just back from six years with the British Army in the East; he bore himself with the authority of experience and power. In the stern the priest lay like Velasquez's picture of 'old Silenus lolling in the sunshine', his bare paunch, immensely pink, spilling over his black trousers. On his brow a garland of purple loose-strife lay crookedly. Malachy, the bank-clerk, was stretched jammed in the prow, both hands in the water, head back, eyes closed, gob-open to the sun. It was he who had said that the priest was like old Silenus. To demonstrate, he had torn the garland from the luxuriance of wild-flowers along the edges of the canal. As they rocked gently along, these two jungles of river-plants undulated faintly – balsam, golden flags, willow-herbs, coltsfoot, purple loose-strife: their delicate pungency scented the warm air. Nobody spoke.

Presently the canal rejoined the river. Here it was wide and smooth. Its width was broken by so many eyots into a network of bayous that there was no main channel and the river could barely stir. In front they saw a toy lock-house perched beside a tiny hump-backed bridge; that, and the much-tarred warehouse nearby, meant that another shallows lay ahead and another canal to by-pass it. They moored by one of the smallest eyots, winding the chain around a clump of flags. When they had clambered ashore they found themselves in a plum-orchard and idly they plucked the fruit. A trout leaped with a splash that startled them. The three lay beside a hay-cock, facing the barely-moving river, and ate the plums. Malachy looked sideways at the lock-house.

'If somebody gave me that house and a job as lock-keeper I'd be happy for ever after.'

The clerk was only a bank-clerk by avocation: his inward life was in his writing; he wrote novels and stories, over the name of Malachy Lucas. The priest agreed with him, rolling over heavily on his belly, pulling a strand of hay to smell it, murmuring, 'Yes – away from everything.'

It is a lost corner, barely coming to life, some dim noise half-heard through sleep, a moth on a window-pane at morning, an occasional barge slowly dud-dudding along the river, disturbing the coots and the wild-flowers with its arrowy wake. The very air of this deep valley seems too heavy to move. Even then a little cloud lay on the tip of the far line of mountains, too exhausted to persist. The doctor threw a plum-stone into the water. A heron rose from the island and flapped away in bored sloth into the woods.

'You'd have to live on your innards. There's nobody to talk to for miles around. I know I couldn't do it. It's a pipe-dream. And think of the winter nights.'

'I can see it at night with my fire and my lamp lighting and not a sound but the rain pocking the canal. A barge nosing the water like an otter. Like an otter. Greasily. Almost silently.'

'It's a pipe-dream. The river rises six feet in winter and turns this place into a lake. You'd go crackers.'

The priest was fingering the hay under his nose.

'There's nothing like the smell of new-mown hay.'

The doctor glanced downwards sharply and said, 'Hm,' in a voice that made them look at him. He laid down the plums and leaned back into the haycock.

'Lucas, you're not much over thirty. Isn't it a bit early to want to renounce the world?'

The priest grinned.

'I renounced the world at twenty-four.'

'I want to write – to work.'

'You could work in the city.' His voice had sharpened a little.

'I do work in the city. I work to exist. I don't want to exist. I want to write.'

The doctor grinned at him and began to bait him, at first amiably.

'Robinson Crusoe! The commonest Irish complex. Hermitage. People wanting all the time to leave the world and live in a convent or a monastery or in a little village at a little job. Sanctuary.'

The priest looked up.

'What about all our emigrants?'

'They're mostly country-people. Peasants don't have complexes. They have the natural, healthy, human urge to seek their fortune. You must have noticed that most folk-tales, things made-up by peasants, are all about men who travel the world to seek their fortune. But I agree you get both types. We Irish are always either the one or t'other. Our saints were all either hermits or adventurers. The sane ones travelled and kicked up holy murder. The daft ones stayed at home and went into the woods and wrote poetry. Take care, Lucas.'

Malachy laughed.

'You are one of the sane ones who travelled and kicked up holy murder?'

'No wonder you fellows write such sleepy books. Why don't you give us books like Balzac, full of guts and vigour?'

Malachy demurred, and mentioned Liam O'Flaherty.

'Now there's a very interesting case. All his characters are slightly mental. He describes the fellows who stay at home and go around the bend. All your stories,' and his voice was not amiable now, 'are about little spurts of passion. Faint gestures. You should call your next book *Faint Gestures*.'

The priest tried to come to the assistance of the clerk who was now blushing with chagrin.

'After all, nothing much happens in Ireland?' He held up the fistful of hay to be smelled. 'Isn't it gorgeous'

The doctor slapped it down irritably. It was plain that something had broken the calm peace of his day.

'I'm sorry, Father,' he apologized instantly. 'You reminded me of somebody.' He jumped up. 'What about a swim?'

Racing down the bank he hurled himself with a great splash into the pool and struck powerfully for mid-river.

'What's biting him?' asked the clerk.

The priest lumbered up and grunted. He dragged off his trousers and tumbled with a crash into the water. The clerk followed diving cleanly. The whole place was suddenly noisy. The sky from water-level was a desert. The tiny cloud had laboured up the sky, dragging a veil after it, too diaphanous to screen the sun. The treetops of the forest seemed to be watching them. A woman at the door of the lock-house. A blue vein of smoke from the chimney.

When the three were drying themselves and feeling the after-water heat the doctor stopped rubbing and looked affectionately at the water. 'I've been dreaming of that swim for five years. In the heart of the jungle I'd think about it. I'll swim in the Barrow, I used to say. Down at the Clashganny Lock, I used to say.' He threw down his towel in sudden annoyance. 'Damn it, why didn't we bring tea? And after it, I used to say, I'll have some damn good Irish tea. I wonder would that lock-house woman give us tea? I'm going to ask her.'

In his flannels and white shirt he strode off across the lock-gate and over the humpty-dumpty bridge, a fine soldierly figure. In five minutes he was back.

'That's all right. She'll do it. By the way, Lucas, you wouldn't really like it there. It's dark and poky.'

The three, glowing and cool, strolled into the lock-house.

The plain, low-ceilinged kitchen was so dim that the usual red lamp before the usual oleograph of the Sacred Heart was a brilliant eye of scarlet. It was cool after the great heat outside. A gun and fishing-rod hung over the mantelpiece; thighboots broken-necked in a corner; a scythe behind the door; over a pannier of plums wasps rose and sank and folded their wide wings to glut. The young woman was friendly, but shy.

'She should get her teeth attended to,' murmured the doctor. 'And what do you do,' he said to her, 'when the floods come?'

He spoke to her in a loud commanding voice as if to wake her up and dominate her.

'Ah, sir, we have to live upstairs.'

'And how do you get out for food and so on?' he shouted.

'We have a boat, sir. We moor it in the garden.'

The doctor smiled in the direction of the clerk.

'Still,' the clerk protested, 'I'm sure they could do something about it. A flood-wall or something.'

'I expect they could, really. Anyway it would be a lovely place for three months of the summer.' He was plainly trying to make up to the clerk for his earlier rudeness. 'But,' he shouted, 'wouldn't you rather live in the town?'

'I dunno, sir.'

He started to carve the bread in disgust, muttering, 'My God, look at that lump of butter. I haven't seen so much butter together for five years. Well, well, perhaps there's something to be said for being a Crusoe after all.'

The priest poured the tea: it was as black as his sleeve. As they ate they heard the muted dud-dudding of a barge and the young woman went out to attend to the gates.

'Travellers visit the desert island,' laughed the priest.

'Pirates,' said the doctor. 'Bold seafaring men.'

'She should come back leading Man Friday?' laughed the clerk.

They were all happy again.

Through the tiny window they saw the barge nose into the lock. One of the crew leaned his back against the beam of the gate and slowly slewed it against the flood. Another, at the other end, worked the winch. It took a long time. Slowly the stovepipe began to sink below the level of the lock-wall.

'How nice to think,' mused the clerk, elbows on the table as he sipped his tea, 'that they've been doing that for a hundred and fifty years. No wonder life gets into a little rut.'

'Aye, to be sure!' the priest agreed contentedly, lighting his pipe. 'Everything here is old. Old and traditional. That turf-fire. The fishing-rod. The scythe. They don't need much to live. A bit of turf, a couple of fish, a wild duck, a bite of hay for the cow. It's an attractive sort of existence, Doc. And isn't it better anyway than a slum in Dublin?'

'I'm not saying that everybody should leave the country and go into the city. That would be absurd. What I'm talking about is people deliberately trying to bury themselves away somewhere.

Lucas here imagines he'd like it. You really wouldn't, you know. Anybody like you with ambition has to live a full life. Anybody with a bit of pride in him. You'd run out of it in a month.'

'Pride,' smiled the priest, 'can be a dangerous thing. It is one of the Seven Deadly Sins.'

'I have to disagree,' said the doctor stiffly.

'I mean, of course,' the priest leaned forward earnestly, 'pride of intellect.'

It was the first time during the whole day that he had stirred himself.

'I still disagree. There isn't enough pride of any sort in this country. There's too much damned humility.'

'Listen to me, now.' The discussion had suddenly become serious. 'I worked for seven years on the English mission. In Liverpool. You're a doctor, I'm a priest, and between us I suppose we could list every known sort of human horror. I saw them all. I came to the conclusion that there are only two mortal sins in this world, the inordinate love of money and pride of intellect. Pride, Covetousness, Lust, Gluttony, Envy, Sloth . . . You notice that they're the first two in the list.'

'And I still disagree. I'll tell you why. Pride and humility aren't opposites. They're two sides of the same thing. I've seen it over and over again. If a man is born proud he must feed his pride. It was something given to him. Once he starts the humility tack he's lost. Lost and damned. Drowned in the opposite of his own pride. Show me your humble man and I'll show you the pride coiled up in his humility devouring it like a worm. Show me your proud man and I'll show you the humility flowering beneath his pride like a crocus under the snow.'

'You are almost suggesting,' cried the clerk, 'that there is no such thing as humility!'

'Nor is there!' said the doctor with arrogant certainty. 'All our emotions are a tension of opposites. It depends from hour to hour which way the balance swings.'

'I do not follow you,' sighed the priest, as if he were suddenly depressed by the feeling that he was talking to an unbeliever. 'Or do you say that even in the saints there was nothing but a random balance of opposites?'

'The most that any man can achieve.'

'Are you saying,' asked the priest, glowering a little under his eyebrows, 'that Christ was not humble?'

'If Christ was a god who came on earth to show men how to live then that was a mortal man who must have suffered everything that we suffer, all the temptations and allurements of the world, a man who had the same pride and passion that we have, who may have sinned as we sin. . . .'

The priest waved his hand in angry dissent.

'Then,' cried the doctor, 'where was the example? If Christ could not sin. . . .'

'Christ as man could sin but, being also God, he did not. God cannot contradict Himself. It is the only thing which He cannot do.'

The doctor shrugged.

'I cannot follow you into these realms. It seems to me that you destroy the simplicity of the Gospel story with metaphysical explanations – and the value of it!'

He fell silent. He took one of the clerk's cigarettes. They could hear the laughter of the woman as she flirted with the bargemen. The wasps hummed over the plums.

'Father! I was rude to you a moment ago. There on the island.'

'Yerrah, what nonsense. Forget it.'

'You reminded me of somebody. A woman I used to know about twenty years ago. I'll tell you about her. It was the new-mown hay reminded me. She was a nurse in the Asylum at M——, the first post I took the summer I returned from Vienna. She was a beautiful girl. Tall as a spear. Dark as night. Her two eyes were two brown jewels set under her forehead. She was one of the most beautiful girls I have ever known.'

He looked at the ash of his cigarette which glowed in the dim kitchen.

'That place was a little village. The Asylum itself was as big as the village, out on the edge of the filthy little place, beyond the doctor's house, beyond the cross-roads, out where the country began at the end of our wall, where the footpath stopped. I won't tell you her name but I'll tell you what they called her in the Asylum. Lady Lucifer. They had names for everybody, always satirical. They never dared call it to her face, but they were cute enough to have their mean little joke just the same. They shortened the nickname to Lucy, then they lengthened it again to Lucy Lockit, then they lopped it again to Lockit, and they called her that to her face. As nurses in these places are practically warders it wasn't a bad name. But the real humour of it, for them, was that she never knew that the other nickname lay behind it. You know, Lucas, I imagine all hermits have bitter jokes like that?

'The first time I saw her she was up in the female recreation-field, behind the buildings, overlooking the whole level country, its woods and demesnes and its white winding roads. The staff called that place Khartoum, another of their jokes.'

'Khartoum?' from the priest.

'You remember? After the British Government refused to relieve it, the Mahdi took it and sacked it? The desert city where Gordon died. She was standing up there, in her nurse's uniform, the billowing apron, the coif flowing about her head in the breeze, the white expanse of bosom, the skirt blowing between her thighs. She was like a goddess dressed in a wave. She was talking to her best friend – I think before I came he was her only friend – a male nurse named Davidson, Larry Davidson, a gentle drooping fellow with a girlish complexion. They met up there because they were protected from all interference by the patients.

'I know what they talked about because after a while I used to join them. I used to enjoy their talk because it was a kind of talk that nobody else in the institution ever talked. It was an extraordinary mixture of mysticism and ambition. They had stockphrases, mostly hers, like – "Man must conquer the tyranny of material things; The humility of the spirit is the All Powerful; We must turn emotion into spirit before we can get peace"; and tags like "The wide-open spaces; Do or die; Venture and win".

'They were always adding new phrases to the list. One day I heard her fit the theory of evolution into her own gospel by maintaining that "the most highly evolved creatures are the world's outcasts, because they alone have defeated the material world." As she said it she got up – she was a very effective nurse – to quieten, very tenderly, very kindly – she was most kind – an old woman who was striding up and down the gravel with her white hair streaming behind her crying, "The cake is baking, the cake is baking." She came back to us with, "That poor woman sacrificed herself to her family as Christ sacrificed his life for us."

'I thought I would challenge her that day. I said, "What about

Long Bow?" Long Bow was the worst maniac in the place, a poor wretch who had G.P.I.'

'What is that?' from the clerk.

'Not nice. General paralysis of the insane. Its symptoms are usually delusions of grandeur. Of course lots of people have a *folie de grandeur* without being in the least insane. In fact,' he laughed, 'I think I have a touch of it myself! but it is a symptom of disease if it is part of a general condition: they think they are millionaires, or that they have titles, and so on. This poor devil was homicidal. He had been brought into the place in coils of rope. She didn't burk at my question. "Nobody knows," she said, "what evil that man inherited or what good he may have done in the world. It will never be known until the Last Day, when all our secrets are exposed, what his drop of goodness may have done in the whole stream of life. Just as the smile of a child might alter the life of a king and change the history of an empire."

'I remember I laughed, but Davidson took fire from her, as he always did, and supported her excitedly: they could always agree on any idea that derided the meaning of worldly success and exalted what Dostoievsky calls "the insulted and injured". One of the reasons she liked Davidson, for example, was the way he squandered his salary like grain the first day he got it, and was a pauper for the rest of the month, which was very different to the way the rest of them hoarded up their shillings, cautiously, like all peasants.'

'Is this a parable of humility?' smiled the priest.

The doctor ignored the question.

'Mind you, that wasn't the end of their talk. They always ended by switching over to some plan or other for getting away from that sleepy plain, whose roads were always empty, where you never heard anything but the hum of a mowing-machine or the gabble of hens. They said they wanted to conquer their lower nature by facing the hardships of the world. She certainly did. I always felt it was only a matter of months before she would hand in her resignation.

'Well! We were chatting like that one July day – I remember they were just beginning to cut the hay in the grounds – when we saw a well-dressed stranger come in the iron gate at the far end of Khartoum. Davidson went off to meet him.

' "I seem to know that man," she said, and we watched him shake hands with Davidson and slap him on the back and laugh so loud that all the patients stopped their gabble for a moment. Davidson pointed up in our direction and the man came striding up. By his clothes I thought that he was a returned American. "Why," she cried, "it's Jim Motherway. He was a nurse here six years ago." She ran to meet him. "Jim, where the divil have you come from?" He took both her hands and he stood back to approve her. He paid no attention to me. "Straight from 'Frisco. All around and back again. Shanghai, Bombay, Capetown. By Gosh! You're lookin' marvellous, Lockit!" "And you look as if you've been seeing life?" she said enviously. "I've seen it raw," he laughed, "and I've seen it cooked. And you're still stuck in the same old job? Gee, nothing's changed here. Not a blooming thing. No more than if I'd walked out of this place yesterday morning."

'I left them.

'From that day our talks in Khartoum stopped. Every free day she had after that a grand glittering Packard would come hooting up the avenue, triumphant as a cock-crow. She'd run down the steps, her long legs taking them three at a time, and jump into the car and be whirled off, and she wouldn't come back until the last second before the front gates clanged for the night. Several times I saw the headlights pick out Davidson in the lodge-porch – he'd be keeping old Michael the porter in talk in order to give her a last few minutes.'

The barge began to chug heavily out of the lock into the smooth river: they could see it moor by the wooden warehouse on the tiny quay. The crew began to unload barrels of porter for some inland pub. They did it as leisurely as if they had the whole day before them.

'What sort of a chap was this Motherway?' asked the priest.

'He was a powerful looking fellow. He was a Gaelic-speaker, a Kerryman: the adventurous type. But he had waited just a little *too* long before starting on his travels – he was already grey, about fifty. I went with Davidson several times to chat with him – in the village local – it was for Davidson's sake, really, because I hated to see the poor devil hiding away in corners, pretending not to see the winks and smirks all around him. We used to sit in the little front parlour and all the time Davidson would keep drawing him out and drawing him out, as if he was trying to find the secret of this fellow's success. It was pathetic.

'One morning I remember Davidson asking him about Africa, in his soft, drooly voice.

' "And what part of Africa were you in, now, Jim?"

' "Everywhere. All over the place. Jo'burg, Capetown, Durban. I've been up in the interior. But it's no place for a white man, I tell you. There's places in Africa that'd remind you of the end of the world. God, I'll never forget one time I went up to a place called Beira. That's Portuguese East Africa. A fellow I met was trying to interest me in a proposition he had up there. The dregs of India, the dregs of Egypt, the dregs of East Africa meet there. I went on the worst skite I ever went on in all my born days in that hell-hole. Do you know, Doc, what finished that skite? Funk. Sheer funk. I went into a joint one morning for a drink and I started to hang my hat on the wall. The wall was grey. That whole wall came out to meet me. It bulged! It bulged! It bulged with beetles, that's what made it grey. I went out on the seashore with a bottle of brandy. The shore was scarlet. What made it scarlet? Crabs, millions and millions of them. They call them soldier-crabs out there. I took off my hat to wipe the sweat off my forehead and honest to the Lord on high that shore stirred. It stirred, Larry. No, you needn't laugh, it wasn't the drink. Every bleeding crab on that shore took a pace to the right and a pace to the left. I ran for my life. I didn't wait to finish my business. God, will I ever forget it? I can see it now. . . ."

'And by the terror in his eyes I knew he was speaking the truth. Davidson asked him then, very gently, "And how did you get out of that wild place, now, Jim?"

' "How did I get out of it? Ho, that's a story. No train for three days. No boat for a week. I found a couple of half-breeds from Madagascar with a sort of a sailing-boat down at the harbour. Take me up to Aden. Take me down to Durban. Take me to India! Take me anywhere! I offered them ten quid. No! Twenty quid? No! Thirty quid? No! I bought the bloody boat off them and I sailed it myself. It's hanging off a rotting rope somewhere in the docks of Durban this minute. What a voyage! What a voyage!"

'That morning I had to drag Davidson away. I was becoming frightened at the look in his face, all knotted up, and a stare in his eyes like a fellow that's going to die. Damn it, I've cursed myself a hundred times since for being so stupid about it, but it was that queer look on his face that deceived me. I was concentrating on it. Even the other nurses noticed it and mentioned it to me, and anyway a child could have noticed his changing mood.

'He used to have that queer stare when the Packard would come squeaking on the gravel in the morning and she stood laughing on top of the steps and raised her wrist in greeting to Motherway. And when the car whirled, and she waved to us over the back of it, all Davidson would do was take the pipe out of his mouth and tilt it slowly at her. His eyes never lost their fixed stare as they followed the car. As he waited for that car to come back every night he still held that stare. He gave her the same slight greeting with the pipe, as if he had never stirred since morning. "There'll be trouble, yet," the staff began to say, and they stopped mocking Davidson. Afterwards, of course, they said, "Why didn't he speak up? Why didn't he say something and not keep it bottled up inside him?" '

The doctor fell silent for a moment.

Through the window a pale warm evening light had begun to stream into the kitchen from the west. The woods outside had become darker and the river seemed more calm and glassy. The noises of the barrels made little hollow echoes.

'Then, one weekend, she went with Motherway to Killarney. When she came back I was the first person she told what happened. She came into my office and she sat down before my desk, and she pretended she was asking my advice.'

Again the doctor fell silent.

'The two of them had climbed up a headland over the lakes just as the sun was going down. A bad hour. The time of the evening when – Ah, I've often seen it in the East! – there's a sort of toneless residue of the daylight that breaks your heart with the loneliness. "We were sitting there, Doc, with all the lakes spread out for miles and miles below us. It got cold and he spread his coat over my shoulders. There was a stream behind us and all of a sudden it got so loud that we looked back at it, and when we looked at the lakes again I thought somebody had switched out a light. Jim kept looking and looking but he didn't seem to be paying any heed to anything, and then he began to hum a song to himself. It was in Irish. Then he stopped. Doctor," says she, "and I wouldn't tell a soul but you. He began to cry. He said he'd wandered all over the world and he hadn't a friend and he had no home. You see, Doctor, he's only a kid under it all. He was afraid of the night coming on. Just as if he was a kid. And when he put his two arms around me I had to comfort him, Doctor. I couldn't help it. I couldn't refuse him, now could I? Did I do right, Doctor? Tell me I did right. We're to be married next week."

'She was trembling like a racehorse. But she was the racehorse breed. You don't get many like her. I don't remember what I said to her. All I know is I got her back to her quarters, but I can still see a bloody big red star rising in front of us, and the mist over the plain, and I can smell the smell of the new-mown hay, and I can still feel the feel of the ring on her finger when I shook hands with her.

'That was the worst night I ever spent in that Asylum. Whether it was the heat of July that upset the patients, or whether it was that she had set up some sort of restlessness among the staff, I could feel the whole Madhouse raising its bristles. At supper-time the main dining-room was like a nest of wasps. Two of the good patients, as we called them, had to be dragged out, and when their heels squeaked along the parquet that great hall jibbered like the bloody jungle when a moon rises late to waken the animals. Down in the west wing Long Bow was screaming with laughter. I could hear him out in the grounds when I went out for a smoke to keep my own nerves quiet. The moon was full. It made the sky look tiny. And that blanket of mist on the valley. And that sweet smell of the new-mown hay.

'That night we saw nothing of Motherway, but about ten o'clock Davidson came in to me to report for night-duty and he told me he was down in the village standing champagne all round. I stayed up late visiting the wards waiting for the place to quieten down. About midnight somebody came in to tell me that Motherway was sitting outside on the front steps, and they thought he had taken too much liquor. I went out to send him home, he had no business being there, and there he was, singing quietly to himself, in Irish. And sitting beside him was Davidson. They were like two old friends enjoying the night, and the smells, and the whole plain bright before them. I could see he was drunk so I sat down on the other side of him.

The three of us began to smoke. Nobody was saying a thing. After a while he said,

' "You know I'm taking her away. Doctor?"

' "Is that so?" I said. "And where are you taking her to?"

' "I'm going to make a queen of her. I can do it. Who says I can't do it?"

' "Nobody, Jim," says Davidson, "nobody at all."

' "I know I can do it. Did you," turning to me, "did you say I can't do it?"

' "No," I said. "I'm sure you can do it, Motherway, provided you have the cash!"

'He looked at me, and his eyes were two red moons, inspecting me as if he doubted my sanity. Then he threw away his cigarette and he laughed, and,' cried the doctor, 'it was at that laugh that I knew what an idiot I'd been, and when I looked across at Davidson I saw that he knew too, and what is more that he had known all the time. A nurse, a male nurse, knew it, and I, the doctor, a specialist, back from Vienna, back from the Rockefeller Institute, had noticed nothing at all. Motherway got up, we all got up, and he dived his hand into his pocket and hauled out a wallet. He tore out a wad of dollar bills and flicked them under my nose: he might have had a couple of hundred dollars in all.

' "There's a thousand pounds there," he shouted. "I've ten times as much in my trunk. And ten times as much again in the Bank. I'm worth millions," he shouted. "Millions!"

'He fished in his wallet, and he clawed out a printed visiting-card.

' "Read that!" he screamed.

'By the moonlight I read it plainly. It said, *James Hugo Motherway, M.D., Ph.D., D. Litt., D.Sc., Barrister at Law, Long Island, New York.*

'I looked at the man His hat was on his poll, his grey hair was wild, his eyes were dilated and squinting. I threw the card away. He saw it swim through the air and he let out a roar. Davidson jumped on his back. The dollars fluttered about them. They crashed down the long flight of steps, rolling over and over. A knife glinted. They were both yelling. Before I could get at them Motherway had wriggled from under and he was flashing into the shrubberies and Davidson was clutching his bleeding throat. We searched and we searched for him. I had a whole posse of attendants out all night after him. But we couldn't track him – he knew the grounds too well. While they searched I sat in my room and wondered who was going to tell Lucy.

'I decided to tell her just before the dawn broke – we were certain to get him pretty soon after that. I knocked at her door just as the first bird began to sing, and the first light was touching the windows like a fog. She didn't answer. I opened the door. She was standing by the window in her dressing-gown, with her long hair in two black plaits down her back, leaning out on the sill, her face in her hands, staring over the plain. She barely looked at me over her shoulder as I came in and stood by her. Then she went on looking into the distance.

' "Doc," she said, and she was talking as if our conversation the night before had never been interrupted, "do you know that I've been thinking? I've been thinking of one Christmas morning, when I was a kid and I got up specially early to open my presents. I forget now what it was that I had been expecting, but when I opened the package I found something that wasn't at all what I'd been promised. If I was ever asked what was the most unhappy moment of my life I'd say it was that Christmas morning. But," she turned and blazed at me, "I'm not going to cry now. I thought I had a hard, strong, unbreakable man. I thought he was like iron. It never even occurred to me that there was a soft streak in him. But I don't care! I don't care! I'm going to bring out all the strength that's inside in him. The two of us, side by side, Jim and me, we'll conquer or die!"

'A bird sang just then, in the meadow below us. She saw me listening. I was certain I heard his voice, croaking feebly at some cock-eyed tune that might once have been a love-song. Another bird sang. He came out from behind the great rhododendron, dressed in his shirt and trousers, his hair wild, his eyes searching a treetop. In that instant all the birds burst into a hymn of praise and the first rays of the sun lit the sky. He looked around him, caught a glimpse of white in her window and he ran forward, with his hands outstretched.

'She turned. In the corridor she saw the two attendants waiting for me, one of them with a coil of rope. She whirled back and looked down at him. I have never in my life seen any man or woman acknowledge a fact as instantaneously as she did. I have never seen, under my eyes, as if I could touch them, a woman's supports rush bodily to defend her citadel as her courage rushed to her. Oh, she was a woman! She was a real woman! She shoved me on one side. She ran down the corridor, her pigtails flying, her gown floating, and down the big winding stairs, and through the hall. The sun on the great glass doors flashed right and left as she raced out into the grounds. By the time I got there she was leading him in by the hand, up the steps, and he was gurgling at her like a child. . . .'

A curious light had begun to add a cold gleam to the woods; a delicate, glistering light that made the trees look pale and unreal. Later, when they went out, they were astonished to find that it was the rising moon. On the river, the barge had finished its unloading. The men had tied down the tarpaulin on the hatches and were beginning to cast off. The doctor rose and stood looking out the door at the barge.

'Well, that's all. I moved on. Davidson went to an uncle in California. She remained behind. I saw her two weeks ago. She is the Matron now. She will soon be there nearly thirty years. When I shook hands with her I saw that she was still wearing her engagement ring. He stayed there. He is still there.'

'Well, Father?' the doctor turned from the door. 'Which would you say she was? Which is *her* folly? Humility or pride?'

The young woman came in from the lock carrying a newspaper.

'Would ye like to see the paper?' she asked shyly.

The doctor took it, thanking her, and glanced at the headlines; he looked again, puzzled; then he smiled and handed it back to her.

'It's yesterday's.'

'Ah,' said the girl easily, 'sure it's all wan to us.'

He paid her, and they said goodbye to her. The sinking sun dazzled them. In the distance of the canal they saw the barge drawing its arrowy wake after it, and all along the way as it receded the river-plants on either side bowed their heads deep into the water and slowly swung upwards again when the arrows had passed on. The three men unmoored their boat silently and the doctor rowed them into the calm river, where, now, the trout were leaping on all sides. The clerk lay jammed in the prow, looking back at the toy lock-house, the still pools, the humped bridge, and over them all the moon, enormously red, reflected in the water. The priest lay in the stern, his heavy chin on his chest, his eyes fixed heavily on the clerk.

'Life is a divil,' breathed the clerk.

They entered the dim lane of the canal. It was now a long soft smudge – the flowers, the water, the woods. Only the ridge of the woods caught the sun. Their deeps were warmed by the moon. The evening birds were singing like mad. As the doctor poled he let out a deep sigh of joy.

'Dear God,' he gasped. 'This is heaven! Heaven!'

Childybawn

When Benjy Spillane's mother got a letter signed 'A True Friend' informing her that Benjy had been 'carrying on' for years with a young lady in the bank she at once sank beneath all the appropriate maternal emotions. She saw her treasure looted, her future imperilled, her love deceived. She saw her poor, foolish child beguiled, his innocence undermined, his sanity destroyed. At this time Benjy was just turned forty-one, a cheerful man-about-town with a winy face like a Halloween turnip with a candle inside it, a pair of merry bull's eyes, a hint of grey at his temples, and his overcoat hung down straight from his paunch as if he was going to have a baby. He was an accountant at the bank, his rank and his cubicle next to the manager's.

For two weeks Benjy could not go out for a walk or open a letter at the breakfast table without evoking long, anxious, secretive looks from his mother. At last she could stand it no longer, and put the question point-blank to him.

'Benjy, lovey, is it true what I heard? That you're thinking of getting married? Not, of course, childybawn, that anything would give me more joy than to see you settled down. But, of course, you have time enough, too, and I'd like to see you happy. It isn't a thing you'd rush into, you know.'

Benjy's eyes were normally *à fleur de tête*. At this they protruded as if he had goitre. His little mouth was open like a toy fish. Then he hooted loudly.

'Me? Married? In the name of God where did you get that yarn?'

'I dunno now what put it into my head,' she said, her heart beginning to glow with relief and joy. 'I wonder could it be something that ould jade Ma Looney said to me the other night at the chapel? About how I'd soon be losing you, or something like that. She was always a bad-minded ould rip.'

'Well, you can tell her from me she's talking through her left leg. I know, Mammy, when I'm well off,' and he slapped her knee. 'Aren't you better to me than any wife? And amn't I as good as a second husband to you?'

Which, natural functions apart, was quite true; for, like all Irish mothers, she had him fastened to her with hoops of comfort, and he was so devoted to her that his young lady at the bank once told him that it made her sick to see the pair of them together. So she thought no more about it, beyond petting and spoiling him worse than ever, until she got another letter, this time signed 'A Well Wisher', a few days after he came home from his Easter holidays, informing her that the young lady at the bank had gone with him to Paris and Cannes. At this she began to steam open his correspondence. Since Benjy and his ladylove were at the same bank it was over a month before she was rewarded. She was scarlet before she finished the first sentence: 'Darling Benjy Wenjy, Your poor little Angela is in bed with the flu, and isn't it a shame, a show and a scandal that 'tis only the flu I'm in bed with. . . .' As she watched Benjy reading the letter that evening over dinner, with a foolish smile on his fat face, she wished that his Angela would get double pneumonia and never rise from her bed again.

The first thing she did was to toddle off to her father confessor. He annoyed her exceedingly by advising her to pray for her son's early marriage. She thanked him. She said she would. But she had no intention of doing anything of the kind; firstly because it was the last thing she wanted herself, and secondly because she had to face the fact that it was the last thing Benjy wanted either. She thought up a much more satisfying plan. She had always had an intense devotion to Saint Monica, the mother of Saint Augustine, and she now started to make a novena to the pair of them. She hung up their pictures in Benjy's bedroom. One day she went so far as to borrow a copy of *The Confessions of Saint Augustine* from the free library, and laid it casually under the *Sporting Chronicle* on Benjy's armchair. It was the night he usually took her to the pictures, so when she said she was a bit tired and would rather stay at home he naturally sat down on the book.

'Hello!' he said, lugging it out. 'Where did you get this?'

'That?' she said, peering at it over her specs. 'Wisha, I dunno now where did I get that? Ah, yes, I remember now I got it in the free library. I suppose 'tis edifying, but . . . Anyway, the old print is too small for my poor eyes.'

'Would you like me to read a bit of it for you?' said Benjy, who used sometimes to read aloud to her on their nights at home.

'If you like,' she said without enthusiasm.

He humoured her, but after a few minutes he began to ruffle the pages.

'Why doesn't he come to the point?' he asked impatiently. 'This is all crawthumping stuff. There's not as much as a bottle of stout in it yet. I mean, what did he do anyway after all his old guff?'

'Not much, then,' she said, and gazed sadly into the fire. 'God help the poor creature!' she sighed. 'That's all I have to say – God help her!'

'God help who?' said Benjy. 'Oh, but you're right, didn't he go off with a woman or something?' – and he began to turn the pages more hopefully.

'I'm referring to Monica,' said his mother severely. 'He broke his poor mother's heart. But,' she said cheerfully, 'he mended it again, God bless him and protect him. When he turned from his bad ways! Ah, that was a lovely scene, the two of them sitting in the window, and the sun going down over the sea. Hand in hand. Mother and son. Lovely! Ah! Lovely! Lovely!'

'You seem to have the book off by heart. We didn't come to that at all yet.'

'Yerrah, what book, childybawn? I don't need any book. Amn't I going to the special anniversary sermon on him every year for the last forty years down in Saint Augustine's? And that was another lovely scene, the day in the orchard. When the poor boy was feeling down in the dumps. His conscience at him, I suppose. And the voice said, *Tolle lege, tolle lege*. And there and then he took up the book, and what did he read in the first line?' She fixed her eye on Benjy, who was looking at her in astonishment out of his cheerful, ruddy, turnip face, and she let him have it full blast: '*Not in rioting nor in wantonness, not in chambering nor in drunkenness, but put ye on the garment of the Lord Jesus Christ.*' She said it so dramatically that Benjy thought she was going to begin the next sentence with 'Dearly beloved brethren.' 'Aha!' she went on. 'That was when the arrow struck him. As it strikes each and every one of us sooner or later. Even the hardest hearted amongst us. *I come*, says the Lord, *like a thief in the night, seeking whom I may devour!*'

Benjy looked at her sourly.

'There was a great preacher lost in you,' he said, and went on looking for the spicy bit.

She was silent for a while. He had succeeded in finding a not-too-bad description of what he took to be a bullfight, so he did not see the sharp looks she was giving him. Then he heard her say, lightly, to nobody in particular:

'I was at confession today.'

Benjy grunted. That was nothing new.

'Father Benignus I went to. Over at the Capuchins.'

Benjy was now deeply interested in the bullfight, so he said nothing to this either.

'He says he knows you.'

At this Benjy looked up.

'Me? I never laid eyes on him.' And he looked down again.

'He laid eyes on you, then. He says he knows you as well as a bad ha'penny.'

Benjy laid down the book. The crawthumping stuff had begun again.

'Oho? So ye were talking about me?' with an ominous note in his voice which she nervously observed and dared to ignore.

'No, no! Sure, amn't I telling you it was inside in confession? 'Twas only just how we were talking about poor Saint Augustine.'

'Is that so?' says Benjy, giving her a long look. 'Tell me! Is there, by any chance, any other priest who knows me like that?'

'Father Semple at the South Chapel told me he often saw you at the bank. And Father Milvey up in the Lough Chapel says you have a great future if you'll only mind your *p*'s and *q*'s.'

At that Benjy flared:

'I see you have me well bell-a-ragged around the town! I suppose you're telling them all that I'm a trial and a torment to you?'

'Oh! Benjy! What a dreadful thing you're after saying! All I ever said to anyone, and I'd say it to the Pope himself, is that you're the best son ever trod shoe leather. As you are! So far as I know!' A hurt came into her voice as she added, 'What do I know about your affairs? Only what you tell me.' A long pause. 'Your life is your own.' A still longer pause. 'To make or to mar.'

There was a long silence between them after that.

'I think,' said Benjy, 'I'll take the ould dog out for a walk.'

He got no farther than the local, where he had a couple of brooding drinks. He needed them. So did she, and had them. For it was one of her little habits – which she never mentioned to Benjy; it would be only troubling the poor boy – to have a nip of brandy every night, or if the poor heart was weak, or over-excited, maybe two. She felt so much better after them that she was able to put on her specs again and have a look in the *Sporting Chronicle* for tomorrow's starters at Leopardstown; an old County Kildare woman, she had never lost her interest in the nags.

The Monica regimen went on for about three months. During all that time she never said a single word of reproach to him. Every morning she said good-bye to him with a sad smile. She welcomed him home every evening with a fond, pathetic kiss, going down then on her knees, in spite of all his protests, to remove his galoshes. He was never so well looked after. She used to heat the seat of his trousers by the fire every morning before letting him put them on. But she stopped going to the pictures. She said she had no heart for them. Instead she would sit opposite him saying the Rosary. If he said anything cheerful she would let out a deep sigh. He found it hard to concentrate on the *Sporting Chronicle*.

After about three months of this both their nerves were so shaken that when he was going to Biarritz for his summer holidays he gave himself away to her by assuring her three times that he was going alone. She decided to call in the help of the bank manager.

'But, my dear Mrs Spillane', he said to her, when she had finished her extraordinary story, 'what on earth can I do? The private lives of my staff are no concern of mine – provided, of course, that there isn't any public scandal, and that it doesn't interfere with the affairs of the bank. I can assure you that your son is an exemplary official. In fact, what you tell me astonishes me. Have you any proof of it?'

She couldn't mention that she had been opening his letters, so she side-stepped that one. What she did say was:

'Amn't I his mother? And let me tell you that if you're astonished I'm more astonished to think you'd allow lassies like that one to be working in a respectable bank like this. 'Tis against nature to have women in banks. 'Tis against God! Banks, indeed! I know another name some people would give them with straps like that one waiting to put their claws into the first poor innocent boy they can capture!'

This rattled him. He had married a lady bank clerk himself and had lived to regret it.

'Mrs Spillane, your son is not a boy. He's a grown man. And you're doing him no good at all with this kind of talk. Your son will probably become a manager himself one day, but it's unlikely unless he gets married. Now, wouldn't the very best solution to all this be if your *boy* were to marry this young lady?'

She rose up before him to her full height, a small, humpty-dumpty old woman, and with misery in her pale-blue eyes and hatred in her voice she said:

'I'd rather see him in his pools of blood at my feet than see him married to that Jezebel!'

The day after he came back from Biarritz he fell down at her feet spouting blood from a burst ulcer, and was rushed off to hospital. Before they started to operate they brought in the priest to him, and by then Benjy was in no state – moral, physical, or strategical – to resist his administrations. It was a close shave; they barely pulled him through; and by the time he was recuperating he was a changed man. The day Mrs Spillane passed a bold-looking strap on the stairs of the nursing home, her eyes as red as her painted lips from crying, and walked in to find Benjy reading *The Life of the Curé d'Ars* of his own free will, she knew that mother love had triumphed at last.

After that Benjy developed a great regard for Saint Augustine. Every evening, now, side by side, he and his mother sat in the bay window of their little villa watching the sun slowly draw its light away from the bay. He never went out of evenings except on works of charity with the Saint Vincent de Pauls. He gave up the liquor. He banned the *Sporting Chronicle*. The only visitors were other fellows from the S. V. de P.'s, or Father Benignus from the Capuchin priory, or Father Semple from the South Chapel, or the curate who had salvaged him in the nursing home. One night when he saw his mother reading a novel called *Her Scarlet Lover* he got up, went to his shelves, and with a sad little smile he handed her a new biography of a Peruvian Jesuit who used to flagellate himself with whips made of old safety-razor blades. There was an embarrassing moment another night when he came home a bit early from his charitable rounds, moved a cushion, found a half-empty bottle of Hennessy's Three Star, and got a definite smell of brandy in the air. Not that he said anything. Nor did he a few evenings later when, with a wry memory of his past follies, he took up that morning's paper to have a look at the racing page and found that day's starters at Hurst Park all checked off pro and con in pencil, with the odds written in beside them. But he began to remember things; he even began to brood – the steak that night had been a bit tough and she had brought him Bordeaux instead of Burgundy. He remembered how, about a year back, he had come one morning on a little heap of coloured betting slips behind D'Alton's six-volume *History of Ireland* on his bookshelves, and hastily and fearfully burned them as his own. He became aware that she was backbiting Ma Looney:

'God forgive me,' she was saying, 'I ran into that ould jade Ma Looney this morning after Mass, and it didn't do me a hap'orth of good. That one is always detracting and backbiting. Oh, an envious jade! Do you remember the time she wanted to persuade me, right or wrong, that you were getting married? Pure jealousy, that's what it was! She's eaten up with it. Do you know now what that one is . . .'

In his years of wickedness Benjy would have listened to her with an indulgent smile. She saw him looking at her now as coldly as if she were a strange woman in a bus. She faltered, shuffled, petered out, and suggested humbly to him that he might like to take the dog for a walk. He did. She profited by his absence: two quick ones. The next night he profited by hers when she toddled off to confession: he rooted the house upside down. He found two empty brandy bottles, eight more betting tickets, her grocer's bills with several incriminating items, and the three anonymous letters. With a sad heart he put them all back where he found them.

'The poor old divil,' he was saying to himself. 'What a lousy, lonely, empty life I've driven her to! God! I've been a bastard to her!'

That night when she came home he had a new bottle of Three Star ready for her. She took a great deal of persuading before she would accept a teeny, little nightcap. She took less and less persuading every night after, but always she took the nip from him humbly, cringingly. He began to collect racing tips for her at the bank.

'You should put a bob on, now and again,' he would say, with his cheery hoot of laughter. 'There's no harm in it, Mammy! 'Twill only amuse you.'

After that it was a joy to him to see her handing out her shilling to him every morning with a cackle of laughter at her own folly – until the day she won at ten to one on an outsider. In her excitement she let out a wail:

'Oh, what misfortune I had that I didn't put ten bob on him!'

With a shock he thought that maybe she always used to put half a crown on her fancy before. He cursed his meanness.

'Never mind,' he comforted her. 'Sure, 'tis only fun. I mean, what do you want the money for?'

'Oho, then, and oho, then,' she said fretfully, 'we could all do with the money. 'Tis all right for you; you don't have to worry about it. Housekeeping isn't what it was when you were a boy.'

'Mammy, are the accounts a worry to you? Would you prefer me to take them off your chest?'

'No, no, no!' she cried at once. 'No worry at all! What would the worry be? Chuchuchu! For goodness' sake, what worry?'

All the same he dropped in to the grocer the next morning on his way to the bank. He came out trembling. Not a bill paid for six months. The butcher had the same story for him. All that morning at the bank he was distracted by misery at the thought of the poor old creature crimping for money while he had been gallivanting with her ladyship in Paris and Biarritz and Cannes. At his lunch hour he went sadly into Joe Rosenberg's betting office to put her shilling on a horse called Silver Lining. It was Joe who took the bob. He looked at it, looked at Benjy, and said:

'Mr Spillane, could I have a word with you for a minute?'

Much surprised at being addressed by name, Benjy passed the lifted lid of the counter to where Joe's big fat hand was already slowly turning the pages of a ledger. Benjy's stomach was slowly turning over with it. Sure enough, when Joe had smoothened out a page with his big fingers that looked as if they had been worn flat by delving in his money satchel, Benjy saw her name at the top of the page. His eye raced down to the foot of the page. A total, in the red, of £125.17.6.

'I thought you didn't know,' said Joe, seeing the look in his face. Then, slowly tapping out 'The Dead March' with his fingers across the total: 'I suppose my money is safe with you?'

'You'll get it,' said Benjy, knowing well that Joe knew well that it was as much as his job was worth to plead the Gaming Act and disown it. He saw that there was no bet under two pounds, several for a fiver, and there was one wild splurge of a tenner.

'What did she back that day?' he asked. Joe had to laugh.

'Do you remember that old four-year-old mare of Billy Morgan's at Punchestown last year?'

'Jasus!' Benjy moaned. 'Sure they're looking for her yet. You'll have to take it in instalments, Joe. Give her no more credit.'

When he got back to the bank he had to sit down. When he saw Angela's legs as she sailed down the aisle, the seam of her black nylons as straight and swelling as the line of a yacht, he thought his ulcer was going to burst all over again. Twice during that afternoon he caught her flirting gaily with the teller in the next cubicle and he got so dizzy that he had to hold on to the desk.

That night as he ate his dinner opposite his mother the silence lay heavy between them like a gramophone record that has not been started. He waited until they were by the fire to let it go.

'Mammy,' he said, leading with his left and ready with the right for her answer, 'would it upset you very much if I got married?'

She turned joyfully to him.

'Oh, Benjy! Isn't that great news? Who is the lucky girl?'

'A young lady I know at the bank,' said Benjy, giving her the right, and waiting with the left for the knockout. 'Her name is Angela.'

He found his two hands being grasped and kissed.

'Childybawn, I'm simply delighted. How soon will it be?'

'You seem,' he said, taken aback, 'to be bloody anxious to get rid of me?'

'No! No, Benjy love! No!' And she began to sniffle. 'Only you've been so cross with me this last six months. There's no pleasing you.'

'Cross?' he roared. 'Cross? Am I hearing things? Was I cross about the brandy? Was I cross about the grocer's bills? Or about the butcher? And what about your hundred and twenty-five pounds, seventeen shillings and sixpence that you owe Joe Rosenberg?'

She crouched down in her chair, her two withered hands clasped before her, and stared at him in horror.

'Oh, Benjy!' she fluttered. 'Is that all you found out?'

You could have counted out one hundred and twenty-five pounds, seventeen shillings, and six pennies before Benjy could close his mouth and control his wandering paws.

'Sacred Heart!' he whispered at last. 'What else is there?'

Her snuffle rose into a wail:

'There's the bloody old money lenders!'

As Benjy sank back into his armchair and gazed at the ceiling, as helpless as a man in a barber's chair, her wail sirened up into a bawl.

'I only wish to God. You got married years and years ago. Ever since you took to. That old piety of yours. You've made my life a misery. Giving me thimblefuls of brandy like a baby. Making me bet in measly ould bobs. Picking and prying at me. From morning to night. Watching every penny I spend. Go on!' she bawled. 'Go on, and get married! And torment some other misfortunate woman. The way you're tormenting *me*!'

Benjy's eyes roved patiently all over the ceiling as if he were in search of the answer to the mystery of life. Not finding it in any part of the ceiling he looked out at the sky. He sought for it in the grass of the garden. At last he sought for it in her face, at the sight of which, all puckered up comically like a baby with the gripes, he burst into laughter. He laughed and he laughed.

'Honest to God, Mammy,' he howled, 'you ought to be put in the budget. You bloody ould rip of hell you!'

She clutched his two hands and drew him towards her.

'Oh, childybawn, they're the first natural words you've said to me in six months!'

He detached himself from her, got up, and looked down at her, flooding with pity at the thought of what the two of them had been through since the Easter before. He patted her hand and said:

'I'm going for a walk.'

He was back in ten minutes with a new bottle of Hennessy. He got out the tumblers and slapped out two hard ones. He put one in her fist, sat on the arm of her chair, put his arm around her shoulder, and made her clink glasses. She was beginning to protest when his look stopped her. The two of them were soon laughing like children or lovers, and discussing his wedding like any natural mother and son the world over.

An hour later, well fortified, he put on his hat and coat and went down to Angela's digs. She was in slacks, and shapely in them, and only that he was not too sure of his ground he would have loved to squeeze the life out of her. Instead she led him into the back parlour, closed the door, walked over to him, and slapped his face. She called him a creeping rat, a cringing worm, a bloody mammy's darling. She asked him did he think she could be picked up and dropped again at his own sweet will. She told him she wouldn't marry him if he was the last man on earth. She asked him did he think she was a common trollop. She asked him why didn't he go and marry his mother since he was so bloody fond of her. To none of this was Benjy in a position to give a truthful, or indeed any, answer. She slapped his face once more. Then she burst into floods of tears on his shoulder. At a quarter to two in the morning the landlady came down in her dressing-gown and threw him out, battered, exhausted, but affianced.

When his old mother died, about five years later, he did marry Angela. As he said when a bachelor pal teased him at the wedding for marrying so young:

'That's all very fine, but, damn it all, I mean to say, a fellow has to have *some* regard for his mother!'

Lovers of the Lake

'They might wear whites,' she had said, as she stood sipping her tea and looking down at the suburban tennis players in the square. And then, turning her head in that swift movement that always reminded him of a jackdaw: 'By the way, Bobby, will you drive me up to Lough Derg next week?'

He replied amiably from the lazy deeps of her armchair.

'Certainly! What part? Killaloe? But is there a good hotel there?'

'I mean the other Lough Derg. I want to do the pilgrimage.'

For a second he looked at her in surprise and then burst into laughter; then he looked at her peeringly.

'Jenny! Are you serious?'

'Of course.'

'Do you mean that place with the island where they go around on their bare feet on sharp stones, and starve for days, and sit up all night ologroaning and ologoaning?' He got out of the chair, went over to the cigarette box on the bookshelves, and, with his back to her, said coldly, 'Are you going religious on me?'

She walked over to him swiftly, turned him about, smiled her smile that was whiter than the whites of her eyes, and lowered her head appealingly on one side. When this produced no effect she said:

'Bobby! I'm always praising you to my friends as a man who takes things as they come. So few men do. Never looking beyond the day. Doing things on the spur of the moment. It's why I like you so much. Other men are always weighing up, and considering and arguing. I've built you up as a sort of magnificent, wild, brainless tomcat. Are you going to let me down now?'

After a while he had looked at his watch and said:

'All right, then. I'll try and fix up a few days free next week. I must drop into the hospital now. But I warn you, Jenny, I've noticed this Holy Joe streak in you before. You'll do it once too often.'

She patted his cheek, kissed him sedately, said, 'You are a good boy,' and saw him out with a loving smile.

They enjoyed that swift morning drive to the Shannon's shore. He suspected nothing when she refused to join him in a drink at Carrick. Leaning on the counter they had joked with the barmaid like any husband and wife off on a motoring holiday. As they rolled smoothly around the northern shore of Lough Gill he had suddenly felt so happy that he had stroked her purple glove and winked at her. The lough was vacant under the midday sun, its vast expanse of stillness broken only by a jumping fish or by its eyelash fringe of reeds. He did not suspect anything when she sent him off to lunch by himself in Sligo, saying that she had to visit an old nun she knew in the convent. So far the journey had been to him no more than one of her caprices; until a yellow signpost marked TO BUNDORAN made them aware that her destination and their parting was near, for she said:

'What are you proposing to do until Wednesday?'

'I hadn't given it a thought.'

'Don't go off and forget all about me, darling. You know you're to pick me up on Wednesday about midday?'

After a silence he grumbled:

'You're making me feel a hell of a bastard, Jenny.'

'Why on earth?'

'All this penitential stuff is because of me, isn't it?'

'Don't be silly. It's just something I thought up all by myself out of my own clever little head.'

He drove on for several miles without speaking. She looked sideways, with amusement, at his ruddy, healthy, hockey-player face glummering under the peak of his checked cap. The brushes at his temples were getting white. Everything about him bespoke the distinguished Dublin surgeon on holiday: his pale-green shirt, his darker-green tie, his double-breasted waistcoat, his driving gloves with the palms made of woven cord. She looked pensively towards the sea. He growled:

'I may as well tell you this much, Jenny, if you were my wife I wouldn't stand for any of this nonsense.'

So their minds had travelled to the same thought? But if she were his wife the question would never have arisen. She knew by the sudden rise of speed that he was in one of his tempers, so that when he pulled into the grass verge, switched off, and turned towards her she was not taken by surprise. A sea gull moaned high overhead. She lifted her grey eyes to his, and smiled, waiting for the attack.

'Jenny, would you mind telling me exactly what all this is about? I mean, why are you doing this fal-lal at this particular time?'

'I always wanted to do this pilgrimage. So it naturally follows that I would do it sometime, doesn't it?'

'Perhaps. But why, for instance, this month and not last month?'

'The island wasn't open to pilgrims last month.'

'Why didn't you go last year instead of this year?'

'You know we went to Austria last year.'

'Why not the year before last?'

'I don't know. And stop bullying me. It is just a thing that everybody wants to do sometime. It is a special sort of Irish thing, like Lourdes, or Fatima, or Lisieux. Everybody who knows about it feels drawn to it. If you were a practising Catholic you'd understand.'

'I understand quite well,' he snapped. 'I know perfectly well that people go on pilgrimages all over the world. Spain. France. Mexico. I shouldn't be surprised if they go on them in Russia. What I am asking you is what has cropped up to produce this extra-special performance just *now*?'

'And I tell you I don't know. The impulse came over me suddenly last Sunday looking at those boys and girls playing tennis. For no reason. It just came. I said to myself, "All right, go now!" I felt that if I didn't do it on the impulse I'd never do it at all. Are you asking me for a rational explanation? I haven't got one. I'm not clever and intelligent like you, darling.'

'You're as clever as a bag of cats.'

She laughed at him.

'I do love you, Bobby, when you are cross. Like a small boy.'

'Why didn't you ask George to drive you?'

She sat up straight.

'I don't want my husband to know anything whatever about this. Please don't mention a word of it to him.'

He grinned at his small victory, considered the scythe of her jawbone, looked at the shining darkness of her hair, and restarted the car.

'All the same,' he said after a mile, 'there must be some reason. Or call it a cause if you don't like the word reason. And I'd give a lot to know what it is.'

After another mile:

'Of course, I might as well be talking to that old dolmen over there as be asking a woman why she does anything. And if she knew she wouldn't tell you.'

After another mile:

'Mind you, I believe all this is just a symptom of something else. Never forget, my girl, that I'm a doctor. I'm trained to interpret symptoms. If a woman comes to me with a pain...'

'Oh, yes, if a woman comes to Surgeon Robert James Flannery with a pain he says to her, "Never mind, that's only a pain." My God! If a woman has a pain she has a bloody pain!'

He said quietly:

'Have you a pain?'

'Oh, do shut up! The only pain I have is in my tummy. I'm ravenous.'

'I'm sorry. Didn't they give you a good lunch at the convent?'

'I took no lunch; you have to arrive at the island fasting. That's the rule.'

'Do you mean to say you've had nothing at all to eat since breakfast?'

'I had no breakfast.'

'What will you get to eat when you arrive on the island?'

'Nothing. Or next to nothing. Everybody has to fast on the island the whole time. Sometime before night I might get a cup of black tea, or hot water with pepper and salt in it. I believe it's one of their lighthearted jokes to call it soup.'

Their speed shot up at once to sixty-five. He drove through Bundoran's siesta hour like the chariot of the Apocalypse. Nearing Ballyshannon they slowed down to a pleasant, humming fifty.

'Jenny!'

'Yes?'

'Are you tired of me?'

'Is this more of you and your symptoms?'

He stopped the car again.

'Please answer my question.'

She laid her purple-gloved hand on his clenched fist.

'Look, darling! We've known one another for six years. You know that like any good little Catholic girl I go to my duties every Easter and every Christmas. Once or twice I've told you so. You've growled and grumbled a bit, but you never made any fuss about it. What are you suddenly worrying about now?'

'Because all that was just routine. Like the French or the Italians. Good Lord, I'm not bigoted. There's no harm in going to church now and again. I do it myself on state occasions, or if I'm staying in some house where they'd be upset if I didn't. But this sort of lunacy isn't routine!'

She slewed her head swiftly away from his angry eyes. A child in a pink pinafore with shoulder frills was driving two black cows through a gap.

'It was never routine. It's the one thing I have to hang on to in an otherwise meaningless existence. No children. A husband I'm not in love with. And I can't marry you.'

She slewed back to him. He slewed away to look up the long empty road before them. He slewed back; he made as if to speak; he slewed away impatiently again.

'No?' she interpreted. 'It isn't any use, is it? It's my problem, not yours. Or if it is yours you've solved it long ago by saying it's all a lot of damned nonsense.'

'And how have you solved it?' he asked sardonically.

'Have you any cause to complain of how I've solved it? Oh, I'm not defending myself. I'm a fraud, I'm a crook, I admit it. You are more honest than I am. You don't believe in anything. But it's the truth that all I have is you and . . .'

'And what?'

'It sounds so blasphemous I can't say it.'

'Say it!'

'All I have is you, and God.'

He took out his cigarette case and took one. She took one. When he lit hers their eyes met. He said, very softly, looking up the empty road:

'Poor Jenny! I wish you'd talked like this to me before. It is, after all, as you say, your own affair. But what I can't get over is that this thing you're doing is so utterly extravagant. To go off to an island, in the middle of a lake, in the mountains, with a lot of Crawthumpers of every age and sex, and no sex, and peel off your stockings and your shoes, and go limping about on your bare feet on a lot of sharp stones, and kneel in the mud, psalming and beating your breast like a criminal, and drink nothing for three days but salt water . . . it's not like you. It's a side of you I've never known before. The only possible explanation for it must be that something is happening inside in you that I've never seen happen before!'

She spread her hands in despair. He chucked away his cigarette and restarted the car. They drove on in silence. A mist began to speckle the windscreen. They turned off the main road into sunless hills, all brown as hay. The next time he glanced at her she was making up her face; her mouth rolling the lipstick into her lips; her eyes rolling around the mirror. He said:

'You're going to have a nice picnic if the weather breaks.'

She glanced out apprehensively.

'It won't be fun.'

A sudden flog of rain lashed into the windscreen. The sky had turned its bucket upside down. He said:

'Even if it's raining do you still have to keep walking around on those damn stones?'

'Yes.'

'You'll get double pneumonia.'

'Don't worry, darling. It's called Saint Patrick's Purgatory. He will look after me.'

That remark started a squabble that lasted until they drew up beside the lake. Other cars stood about like stranded boats. Other pilgrims stood by the boat slip, waiting for the ferry, their backs hunched to the wind, their clothes ruffled like the fur of cattle. She looked out across the lough at the creeping worms of foam.

He looked about him sullenly at the waiting pilgrims, a green bus, two taxi-loads of people waiting for the rain to stop. They were not his kind of people at all, and he said so.

'That,' she smiled, 'is what comes of being a surgeon. You don't meet people, you meet organs. Didn't you once tell me that when you are operating you never look at the patient's face?'

He grunted. Confused and hairy-looking clouds combed themselves on the ridges of the hills. The lake was crumpled and grey, except for those yellow worms of foam blown across it in parallel lines. To the south a cold patch of light made it all look far more dreary. She stared out towards the island and said:

'It's not at all like what I expected.'

'And what the hell did you expect? Capri?'

'I thought of an old island, with old grey ruins, and old holly trees and rhododendrons down to the water, a place where old monks would live.'

They saw tall buildings like modern hotels rising by the island's shore, an octagonal basilica big enough for a city, four or five bare, slated houses, a long shed like a ballroom. There was one tree. Another bus drew up beside them and people peered out through the wiped glass.

'Oh, God!' she groaned. 'I hope this isn't going to be like Lourdes.'

'And what, pray, is wrong with Lourdes when it's at home?'

'Commercialized. I simply can't believe that this island was the most famous pilgrimage of the Middle Ages. On the rim of the known world. It must have been like going off to Jerusalem or coming home brown from the sun with a cockle in your hat from Galilee.'

He put on a vulgar Yukon voice:

'Thar's gold somewhere in them thar hills. It looks to me like a damn good financial proposition for somebody.'

She glared at him. The downpour had slackened. Soon it almost ceased. Gurgles of streams. A sound of pervasive drip. From the back seat she took a small red canvas bag marked T.W.A.

'You will collect me on Wednesday about noon, won't you?'

He looked at her grimly. She looked every one of her forty-one years. The skin of her neck was corrugated. In five years' time she would begin to have jowls.

'Have a good time,' he said, and slammed in the gears, and drove away.

The big, lumbering ferryboat was approaching, its prow slapping the corrugated waves. There were three men to each oar. It began to spit rain again. With about a hundred and fifty men and women, of every age and, so far as she could see, of every class, she clambered aboard. They pushed out and slowly they made the crossing, huddling together from the wind and rain. The boat nosed into its cleft and unloaded. She had a sensation of dark water, wet cement, houses, and a great number of people; and that she would have given gold for a cup of hot tea. Beyond the four or five white-washed houses – she guessed that they had been the only buildings on the island before trains and buses made the pilgrimage popular – and beyond the cement paths, she came on the remains of the natural island: a knoll, some warm grass, the tree, and the roots of the old hermits' cells across whose teeth of stone barefooted pilgrims were already treading on one another's heels. Most of these barefooted people wore mackintoshes. They not only stumbled on one another's heels; they kneeled on one another's toes and tails; for the island was crowded – she thought there must be nearly two thousand people on it. They were packed between the two modern hostels and the big church. She saw a priest in sou'wester and gum boots. A nun waiting for the new arrivals at the door of the women's hostel took her name and address, and gave her the number of her cubicle. She went upstairs to it, laid her red bag on the cot, sat beside it, unfastened her garters, took off her shoes, unpeeled her nylons, and without transition became yet another anonymous pilgrim. As she went out among the pilgrims already praying in the rain she felt only a sense of shame as if she were specially singled out under the microscope of the sky. The wet ground was cold.

A fat old woman in black, rich-breasted, grey-haired, took her kindly by the arm and said in a warm, Kerry voice: 'You're shivering, you poor creature! Hould hard now. Sure, when we have the first station done they'll be giving us the ould cup of black tay.'

And laughed at the folly of this longing for the tea. She winced when she stepped on the gritty concrete of the terrace surrounding the basilica, built out on piles over the lake. A young man smiled sympathetically, seeing that she was a delicate subject for the rigours before her: he was dressed like a clerk, with three pens in his breast pocket, and he wore a Total Abstinence badge.

'Saint's Island they call it,' he smiled. 'Some people think it should be called Divil's Island.'

She disliked his kindness – she had never in her life asked for pity from anybody, but she soon found that the island floated on kindness. Everything and everybody about her seemed to say, 'We are all sinners here, wretched creatures barely worthy of mercy.' She felt the abasement of the doomed. She was among people who had surrendered all personal identity, all pride. It was like being in a concentration camp.

The fat old Kerrywoman was explaining to her what the routine was, and as she listened she realized how long her stay would really be. In prospect it had seemed so short: come on Monday afternoon, leave on Wednesday at noon; it had seemed no more than one complete day and two bits of nights. She had not foreseen that immediately after arriving she must remain out of doors until the darkness fell, walking the rounds of the stones, praying, kneeling, for about five hours. And even then she would get no respite, for she must stay awake all night praying in the basilica. It was then that she would begin the second long day, as long and slow as the night; and on the third day she would still be walking those rounds until mid-day. She would be without food, even when she would have left the island, until the midnight of that third day.

'Yerrah, but sure,' the old woman cackled happily,'they say that fasting is good for the stomach.'

She began to think of 'they'.

They had thought all this up. They had seen how much could be done with simple prayers. For when she began to tot up the number of Paternosters and Aves that she must say she had to stop at the two thousandth. And these reiterated prayers must be said while walking on the stones, or kneeling in the mud, or standing upright with her two arms extended. This was the posture she disliked most. Every time she came to do it, her face to the lake, her arms spread, the queue listening to her renouncing her sins, she had to force herself to the posture and the words. The first time she did it, with the mist blowing into her eyes, her arms out like a crucifix, her lips said the words but her heart cursed herself for coming so unprepared, for coming at all. Before she had completed her first circuit – four times around each one of six cells – one ankle and one toe was bleeding. She was then permitted to ask for the cup of black tea. She received it sullenly, as a prisoner might receive his bread and water.

She wished after that first circuit to start again and complete a second – the six cells, and the seven other ordeals at other points of the island – and so be done for the day. But she found that 'they' had invented something else: she must merge with the whole anonymous mass of pilgrims for mass prayer in the church.

A slur of wet feet; patter of rain on leaded windows; smells of bog water and damp clothing; the thousand voices responding to the incantations. At her right a young girl of about seventeen was uttering heartfelt responses. On her left an old man in his sixties gave them out loudly. On all sides, before her, behind her, the same passionate exchange of energy, while all she felt was a crust hardening about her heart, and she thought, in despair,'I have no more feeling than a stone!' And she thought, looking about her, that tonight this vigil would go on for hour after hour until the dark, leaded windows coloured again in the morning light. She leaned her face in her palms and whispered, 'O God, please let me out of myself!' The waves of voices beat and rumbled in her ears as in an empty shell.

She was carried out on the general sliding whispering of the bare feet into the last gleanings of the daylight to begin her second circuit. In the porch she cowered back from the rain. It was settling into a filthy night. She was thrust forward by the crowd, flowed with its force to the iron cross by the shingle's edge. She took her place in the queue and then with the night wind pasting her hair across her face she raised her arms and once again renounced the world, the flesh, and the Devil. She did four circles of the church on the gritty concrete. She circled the first cell's stones. She completed the second circle. Her prayers were become numb by now. She stumbled, muttering them, up and down the third steeply sloped cell, or bed. She was a drowned cat and one knee was bleeding. At the fourth cell she saw him.

He was standing about six yards away looking at her. He wore a white raincoat buttoned tight about his throat. His feet were bare. His hair was streaked down his forehead as if he had been swimming. She stumbled towards him and dragged him by the arm down to the edge of the boat slip.

'What are you doing here?' she cried furiously. 'Why did you follow me?'

He looked down at her calmly:

'Why shouldn't I be here?'

'Because you don't believe in it! You've just followed me to sneer at me, to mock at me! Or from sheer vulgar curiosity!'

'No,' he said, without raising his voice. 'I've come to see just what it is that you believe in. I want to know all about you. I want to know why you came here. I don't want you to do anything or have anything that I can't do or can't know. And as for believing – we all believe in something.'

Dusk was closing in on the island and the lake. She had to peer into his face to catch his expression.

'But I've known you for years and you've never shown any sign of believing in anything but microscopes and microbes and symptoms. It's absurd, you couldn't be serious about anything like this. I'm beginning to hate you!'

'Are you?' he said, so softly that she had to lean near him to hear him over the slapping of the waves against the boat slip. A slow rift in the clouds let down a star; by its light she saw his smile.

'Yes!' she cried, so loudly that he swept out a hand and gripped her by the arm. Then he took her other arm and said gently:

'I don't think you should have come here, Jenny. You're only tearing yourself to bits. There are some places where some people should never go, things some people should never try to do – however good they may be for others. I know why you came here. You feel you ought to get rid of me, but you haven't the guts to do it, so you come up here into the mountains to get your druids to work it by magic. All right! I'm going to ask them to help you.'

He laughed and let her go, giving her a slight impulse away from him.

'Ask? You will *ask*? Do you mean to tell me that you have said as much as one single, solitary prayer on this island?'

'Yes,' he said casually, 'I have.'

She scorned him.

'Are you trying to tell me, Bobby, that you are doing this pilgrimage?'

'I haven't fasted. I didn't know about that. And, anyway, I probably won't. I've got my pockets stuffed with two pounds of the best chocolates I could buy in Bundoran. I don't suppose I'll even stay up all night like the rest of you. The place is so crowded that I don't suppose anybody will notice me if I curl up in some corner of the boathouse. I heard somebody saying that people had to sleep there last night. But you never know – I might – I just might stay awake. If I do, it will remind me of going to midnight Mass with my father when I was a kid. Or going to retreats, when we used all hold up a lighted candle and renounce the Devil.

'It was a queer sensation standing up there by the lake and saying those words all over again. Do you know, I thought I'd completely forgotten them!'

'The next thing you're going to say is that you believe in the Devil! You fraud!'

'Oh, there's no trouble about believing in that old gentleman. There isn't a doctor in the world who doesn't, though he will give him another name. And on a wet night, in a place like this, you could believe in a lot of things. No, my girl, what I find it hard to believe in is the flesh and the world. They are good things. Do you think I'm ever going to believe that your body and my body are evil? And you don't either! And you are certainly never going to renounce the world, because you are tied to it hand and foot!'

'That's not true!'

His voice cut her like a whip:

'Then why do you go on living with your husband?'

She stammered feebly. He cut at her again:

'You do it because he's rich, and you like comfort, and you like being a "somebody".'

With a switch of her head she brushed past him. She did not see him again that night.

The night world turned imperceptibly. In the church, for hour after hour, the voices obstinately beat back the responses. She sank under the hum of the prayer wheel, the lust for sleep, her own despairs. Was he among the crowd? Or asleep in a corner of the boatshed? She saw his flatly domed fingers, a surgeon's hand, so strong, so sensitive. She gasped at the sensual image she had evoked.

The moon touched a black window with colour. After an age it had stolen to another. Heads drooped. Neighbours poked one another awake with a smile. Many of them had risen from the benches in order to keep themselves awake and were circling the aisles in a loose procession of slurring feet, responding as they moved. Exhaustion began to work on her mind. Objects began to disconnect, become isolated each within its own outline – now it was the pulpit, now a statue, now a crucifix. Each object took on the vividness of a hallucination. The crucifix detached itself from the wall and leaned towards her, and for a long while she saw nothing but the heavy pendent body, the staring eyes, so that when the old man at her side let his head sink over on her shoulder and then woke up with a start she felt him no more than if they were two fishes touching in the sea. Bit by bit the incantations drew her in; sounds came from her mouth; prayers flowed between her and those troubled eyes that fixed hers. She swam into an ecstasy as rare as one of those perfect dances of her youth when she used to swing in a whirl of music, a swirl of bodies, a circling of lights, floated out of her mortal frame, alone in the arms that embraced her.

Suddenly it all exploded. One of the four respites of the night had halted the prayers. The massed pilgrims relaxed. She looked blearily about her, no longer disjunct. Her guts rumbled. She looked at the old man beside her. She smiled at him and he at her.

'My poor old knees are crucified,' he grinned.

'You should have the skirts,' she grinned back.

They were all going out to stretch in the cool, and now dry, air, or to snatch a smoke. The amber windows of the church shivered in a pool of water. A hearty-voiced young woman leaning on the balustrade lit a match for her. The match hissed into the invisible lake lapping below.

'The ould fag,' said the young woman, dragging deep on her cigarette, 'is a great comfort. 'Tis as good as a man.'

'I wonder,' she said, 'what would Saint Patrick think if he saw women smoking on his island?'

'He'd beat the living lights out of the lot of us.'

She laughed aloud. She must tell him that . . . . She began to wander through the dark crowds in search of him. He had said something that wasn't true and she would answer him. She went through the crowds down to the boat slip. He was standing there, looking out into the dark as if he had not stirred since she saw him there before midnight. For a moment she regarded him, frightened by the force of the love that gushed into her. Then she approached him.

'Well, Mr Worldly Wiseman? Enjoying your boathouse bed?'

'I'm doing the vigil,' he said smugly.

'You sound almighty pleased with yourself.'

He spoke eagerly now:

'Jenny, we mustn't quarrel. We must understand one another. And understand this place. I'm just beginning to. An island. In a remote lake. Among the mountains. Nighttime. No sleep. Hunger. The conditions of the desert. I was right in what I said to you. Can't you see how the old hermits who used to live here could swim off into a trance in which nothing existed but themselves and their visions? I told you a man can renounce what he calls the Devil, but not the flesh, not the world. They thought, like you, that they could throw away the flesh and the world, but they were using the flesh to achieve one of the rarest experiences in the world! Don't you see it?'

'Experiences! The next thing you'll be talking about is symptoms.'

'Well, surely, you must have observed?' He peered at the luminous dial of his watch. 'I should say that about four o'clock we will probably begin to experience a definite sense of dissociation. After that a positive alienation . . .'

She turned furiously from him. She came back to say:

'I would much prefer, Bobby, if you would have the decency to go away in the morning. I can find my own way home. I hope we don't meet again on this island. Or out of it!'

'The magic working?' he laughed.

After that she made a deliberate effort of the mind to mean and to feel every separate word of the prayers – which is a great foolishness since prayers are not poems to be read or even understood; they are an instinct; to dance would be as wise. She thought that if she could not feel what she said how could she mean it, and so she tried to savour every word, and, from trying to mean each word, lagged behind the rest, sank into herself, and ceased to pray. After the second respite she prayed only to keep awake. As the first cold pallor of morning came into the windows her heart rose again. But the eastern hills are high here and the morning holds off stubbornly. It is the worst hour of the vigil, when the body ebbs, the prayers sink to a drone, and the night seems to have begun all over again.

At the last respite she emerged to see pale tents of blue on the hills. The slow cumulus clouds cast a sheen on the water. There is no sound. No birds sing. At this hour the pilgrims are too awed or too exhausted to speak, so that the island reverts to its ancient silence in spite of the crowds.

By the end of the last bout she was calm like the morning lake. She longed for the cup of black tea. She was unaware of her companions. She did not think of him. She was unaware of herself. She no more thought of God than a slave thinks of his master, and after she had drunk her tea she sat in the morning sun outside the women's hostel like an old blind woman who has nothing in life to wait for but sleep.

The long day expired as dimly as the vapour rising from the water. The heat became morbid. One is said to be free on this second day to converse, to think, to write, to read, to do anything at all that one pleases except the one thing everybody wants to do – to sleep. She did nothing but watch the clouds, or listen to the gentle muttering of the lake. Before noon she heard some departing pilgrims singing a hymn as the great ferryboats pushed off. She heard their voices without longing;

she did not even desire food. When she met him she was without rancour.

'Still here?' she said, and when he nodded: 'Sleepy?'

'Sleepy.'

'Too many chocolates, probably.'

'I didn't eat them. I took them out of my pockets one by one as I leaned over the balustrade and guessed what centre each had – coffee, marshmallow, nut, toffee, cream – and dropped it in with a little splash to the holy fishes.'

She looked up at him gravely.

'Are you really trying to join in this pilgrimage?'

'Botching it. I'm behindhand with my rounds. I have to do five circuits between today and tomorrow. I may never get them done. Still, something is better than nothing.'

'You dear fool!'

If he had not walked away then she would have had to; such a gush of affection came over her at the thought of what he was doing, and why he was doing it – stupidly, just like a man; sceptically, just like a man; not admitting it to himself, just like a man; for all sorts of damn-fool rational reasons, just like a man; and not at all for the only reason that she knew was his real reason: because she was doing it, which meant that he loved her. She sat back, and closed her eyes, and the tears of chagrin oozed between her lids as she felt her womb stir with desire of him.

When they met again it was late afternoon.

'Done four rounds,' he said so cheerfully that he maddened her.

'It's not golf, Bobby, damn you!'

'I should jolly well think not. I may tell you my feet are in such a condition I won't be able to play golf for a week. Look!'

She did not look. She took his arm and led him to the quietest corner she could find.

'Bobby, I am going to confess something to you. I've been thinking about it all day trying to get it clear. I know now why I came here. I came because I know inside in me that some day our apple will have to fall off the tree. I'm forty. You are nearly fifty. It will have to happen. I came here because I thought it right to admit that some day, if it has to be, I am willing to give you up.'

He began to shake all over with laughter.

'What the hell are you laughing at?' she moaned.

'When women begin to reason! Listen, wasn't there a chap one time who said, "O God, please make me chaste, but not just yet"?'

'What I am saying is "now," if it has to be, if it can be, if I can make it be. I suppose,' she said wildly, 'I'm really asking for a miracle, that my husband would die, or that you'd die, or something like that that would make it all come right!'

He burst into such a peal of laughter that she looked around her apprehensively. A few people near them also happened to be laughing over something and looked at them indulgently.

'Do you realize, Bobby, that when I go to confession here I will have to tell all about us, and I will have to promise to give you up?'

'Yes, darling, and you won't mean a single word of it.'

'But I always mean it!'

He stared at her as if he were pushing curtains aside in her.

'Always? Do you mean you've been saying it for six years?'

'I mean it when I say it. Then I get weak. I can't help it, Bobby. You know that!' She saw the contempt in his eyes and began to talk rapidly, twisting her marriage ring madly around her finger. He kept staring into her eyes like a man staring down the long perspective of a railway line waiting for the engine to appear. 'So you see why there wasn't any sense in asking me yesterday why I come now and not at some other time, because with me there isn't any other time, it's always *now*, I meet you *now*, and I love you *now*, and I think it's not right *now*, and then I think, "No, not *now*," and then I say I'll give you up *now*, and I mean it every time until we meet again, and it begins all over again, and there's never any end to it until some day I can say, "Yes, I used to know him once, but not now," and then it will be a *now* where there won't be any other *now* any more because there'll be nothing to live for.'

The tears were leaking down her face. He sighed:

'Dear me! You have got yourself into a mess, haven't you?'

'O God, the promises and the promises! I wish the world would end tonight and we'd both die together!'

He gave her his big damp handkerchief. She wiped her eyes and blew her nose and said:

'You don't mean to go to confession, do you?'

He chuckled sourly.

'And promise? I must go and finish a round of pious golf. I'm afraid, old girl, you just want to get me into the same mess as yourself. No, thank you. You must solve your own problems in your own way, and I in mine.'

That was the last time she spoke to him that day.

She went back to the balustrade where she had smoked with the hearty girl in the early hours of the morning. She was there again. She wore a scarlet beret. She was smoking again. She began to talk, and the talk flowed from her without stop. She had fine broad shoulders, a big mobile mouth, and a pair of wild goat's eyes. After a while it became clear that the woman was beside herself with terror. She suddenly let it all out in a gush of exhaled smoke.

adultery

'Do you know why I'm hanging around here? Because I ought to go into confession and I'm in dread of it. He'll tear me alive. He'll murdher me. It's not easy for a girl like me, I can promise you!'

'You must have terrible sins to tell?' she smiled comfortingly.

'He'll slaughter me, I'm telling you.'

'What is it? Boys?'

The two goat's eyes dilated with fear and joy. Her hands shook like a drunkard's.

'I can't keep away from them. I wish to God I never came here.'

'But how silly! It's only a human thing. I'm sure half the people here have the same tale to tell. It's an old story, child, the priests are sick of hearing it.'

'Oh, don't be talking! Let me alone! I'm criminal, I tell yeh! And there are things you can't explain to a priest. My God, you can hardly explain 'em to a doctor!'

'You're married?' – looking at her ring.

'Poor Tom! I have him wore out. He took me to a doctor one time to know would anything cure me. The old foolah took me temperature and gave me a book like a bus guide about when it's safe and when it isn't safe to make love, the ould eedjut! I was pregnant again before Christmas. Six years married and I have six kids; nobody could stand that gait o' going. And I'm only twenty-four. Am I to have a baby every year of my life? I'd give me right hand this minute for a double whiskey.'

'Look, you poor child! We are all in the same old ferryboat here. What about me?'

'You?'

'It's not men with me, it's worse.'

'Worse? In God's name, what's worse than men?'

The girl looked all over her, followed her arm down to her hand, to her third finger.

'One man.'

The tawny eyes swivelled back to her face and immediately understood.

'Are you very fond of him?' she asked gently, and taking the unspoken answer said, still more pityingly, 'You can't give him up?'

'It's six years now and I haven't been able to give him up.'

The girl's eyes roved sadly over the lake as if she were surveying a lake of human unhappiness. Then she threw her butt into the water and her red beret disappeared into the maw of the church porch.

She saw him twice before the dusk thickened and the day grew cold again with the early sunset. He was sitting directly opposite her before the men's hostel, smoking, staring at the ground between his legs. They sat facing one another. They were separated by their identities, joined by their love. She glimpsed him only once after that, at the hour when the sky and the hills merge, an outline passing across the lake. Soon after she had permission to go to her cubicle. Immediately she lay down she spiralled to the bottom of a deep lake of sleep.

She awoke refreshed and unburthened. She had received the island's gift: its sense of remoteness from the world, almost a sensation of the world's death. It is the source of the island's kindness. Nobody is just matter, poor to be exploited by rich, weak to be exploited by the strong; in mutual generosity each recognizes the other only as a form of soul; it is a brief, harsh Utopia of equality in nakedness. The bare feet are a symbol of that nakedness unknown in the world they have left.

The happiness to which she awoke was dimmed a little by a conversation she had with an Englishman over breakfast – the usual black tea and a piece of oaten bread. He was a city man who had arrived the day before, been up all night while she slept. He had not yet shaved; he was about sixty-two or three; small and tubby, his eyes perpetually wide and unfocusing behind pince-nez glasses.

'That's right,' he said, answering her question. 'I'm from England. Liverpool. I cross by the night boat and get here the next afternoon. Quite convenient, really. I've come here every year for the last twenty-two years, apart from the war years. I come on account of my wife.'

'Is she ill?'

'She died twenty-two years ago. No, it's not what you might think – I'm not praying for her. She was a good woman, but, well, you see, I wasn't very kind to her. I don't mean I quarrelled with her, or drank, or was unfaithful. I never gambled. I've never smoked in my life.' His hands made a faint movement that was meant to express a whole life, all the confusion and trouble of his soul. 'It's just that I wasn't kind. I didn't make her happy.'

'Isn't that,' she said, to comfort him, 'a very private feeling? I mean, it's not in the Ten Commandments that thou shalt make thy wife happy.'

He did not smile. He made the same faint movement with his fingers.

'Oh, I don't know! What's love if it doesn't do that? I mean to say, it is something godly to love another human being, isn't it? I mean, what does "godly" mean if it doesn't mean giving up everything for another? It isn't human to love, you know. It's foolish, it's a folly, a divine folly. It's beyond all reason, all limits. I didn't rise to it,' he concluded sadly.

She looked at him, and thought, 'A little fat man, a clerk in some Liverpool office all his life, married to some mousy little woman, thinking about love as if he were some sort of Greek mystic.'

'It's often,' she said lamely, 'more difficult to love one's husband, or one's wife, as the case may be, than to love one's neighbour.'

'Oh, much!' he agreed without a smile. 'Much! Much more difficult!'

At which she was overcome by the thought that inside ourselves we have no room without a secret door; no solid self that has not a ghost inside it trying to escape. If I leave Bobby I still have George. If I leave George I still have myself, and whatever I find in myself. She patted the little man's hand and left him, fearing that if she let him talk on even his one little piece of sincerity would prove to be a fantasy, and in the room that he had found behind his own room she would open other doors leading to other obsessions. He had told her something true about her own imperfection, and about the nature of love, and she wanted to share it while it was still true. But she could not find him, and there was still one more circuit to do before the ferryboat left. She did meet Goat's Eyes. The girl clutched her with tears magnifying her yellow-and-green irises and gasped joyously:

'I found a lamb of a priest. A saint anointed! He was as gentle! "What's your husband earning?" says he. "Four pounds ten a week, Father," says I. "And six children?" says he. "You poor woman," says he, "you don't need to come here at all. Your Purgatory is at home." He laid all the blame on poor Tom. And, God forgive me, I let him do it. "Bring him here to me," says he, "and I'll cool him for you." God bless the poor innocent priest, I wish I knew as little about marriage as he does. But,' and here she broke into a wail, 'sure he has me ruined altogether now. He's after making me so fond of poor Tommy I think I'll never get home soon enough to go to bed with him.' And in a vast flood of tears of joy, of relief, and of fresh misery: 'I wish I was a bloomin' nun!'

It was not until they were all waiting at the ferryboat that she saw him. She managed to sit beside him in the boat. He touched her hand and winked. She smiled back at him. The bugler blew his bugle. A tardy traveller came racing out of the men's hostel. The boatload cheered him, the bugler helped him aboard with a joke about people who can't be persuaded to stop praying, and there was a general chaff about people who have a lot to pray about, and then somebody raised the parting hymn, and the rowers began to push the heavy oars, and singing they were slowly rowed across the summer lake back to the world.

They were driving back out of the hills by the road they had come, both silent. At last she could hold in her question no longer:

'Did you go, Bobby?'

Meaning: had he, after all his years of silence, of rebellion, of disbelief, made his peace with God at the price of a compact against her. He replied gently:

'Did I probe your secrets all these years?'

She took the rebuke humbly, and for several miles they drove on in silence. They were close, their shoulders touched, but between them there stood that impenetrable wall of identity that segregates every human being in a private world of self. Feeling it she realized at last that it is only in places like the lake-island that the barriers of self break down. The tubby little clerk from Liverpool had been right. Only when love desires nothing but renunciation, total surrender, does self surpass self. Everybody who ever entered the island left the world of self behind for a few hours, exchanged it for what the little man had called a divine folly. It was possible only for a few hours – unless one had the courage, or the folly, to renounce the world altogether. Then another thought came to her. In the world there might also be escape from the world.

'Do you think, Bobby, that when people are in love they can give up everything for one another?'

'No,' he said flatly. 'Except perhaps in the first raptures?'

'If I had a child I think I could sacrifice anything for it. Even my life.'

'Yes,' he agreed. 'It has been known to happen.'

And she looked at him sadly, knowing that they would never be able to marry, and even if she did that she would never have children. And yet, if they could have married, there was a lake . . .

'Do you know what I'm planning at this moment?' he asked breezily.

She asked without interest what it was.

'Well, I'm simply planning the meal we're going to eat tonight in Galway, at midnight.'

'At midnight? Then we're going on with this pilgrimage? Are we?'

'Don't *you* want to? It was your idea in the beginning.'

'All right. And what are we going to do until midnight? I've never known time to be so long.'

'I'm going to spend the day fishing behind Glencar. That will kill the hungry day. After that, until midnight, we'll take the longest possible road around Connemara. Then would you have any objections to mountain trout cooked in milk, stuffed roast kid with fresh peas and spuds in their jackets, apple pie and whipped cream, with a cool Pouilly Fuissé, a cosy 1929 claret, West of Ireland Pont l'Évêque, finishing up with Gaelic coffee and two Otards? Much more in your line, if I know anything about you, than your silly old black tea and hot salt water.'

'I admit I like the things of the flesh.'

'You live for them!'

He had said it so gently, so affectionately that, half in dismay, half with amusement, she could not help remembering Goat's Eyes, racing home as fast as the bus would carry her to make love to her Tommy. After that they hardly spoke at all, and then only of casual things such as a castle beside the road, the sun on the edging sea, a tinker's caravan, an opening view. It was early afternoon as they entered the deep valley at Glencar and he probed in second gear for an attractive length of stream, found one and started eagerly to put his rod together. He began to walk up against the dazzling bubble of water and within an hour was out of sight. She stretched herself out on a rug on the bank and fell sound asleep.

It was nearly four o'clock before she woke up, stiff and thirsty. She drank from a pool in the stream, and for an hour she sat alone by the pool, looking into its peat-brown depth, as vacantly contented as a tinker's wife to live for the moment, to let time wind and unwind everything. It was five o'clock before she saw him approaching, plodding in his flopping waders, with four trout on a rush stalk. He threw the fish at her feet and himself beside them.

'I nearly ate them raw,' he said.

'Let's cook them and eat them,' she said fiercely.

He looked at her for a moment, then got up and began to gather dry twigs, found Monday's newspaper in the car – it looked like a paper of years ago – and started the fire. She watched while he fed it. When it was big enough in its fall to have made a hot bed of embers he roasted two of the trout across the hook of his gaff, and she smelled the crisping flesh and sighed. At last he laid them, browned and crackly, on the grass by her hand. She took one by its crusted tail, smelled it, looked at him, and slung it furiously into the heart of the fire. He gave a sniff-laugh and did the same with his.

'Copy cat!' she said.

'Let's get the hell out of here,' he said, jumping up. 'Carry the kit, will you?'

She rose, collected the gear, and followed him saying:

'I feel like an Arab wife. "Carry the pack. Go here. Go there."'

They climbed out of the glens on to the flat moorland of the Easky peninsula where the evening light was a cold ochre gleaming across green bogland that was streaked with all the weedy colours of a strand at ebb. At Ballina she suggested that they should have tea.

'It will be a pleasant change of diet!' he said.

When they had found a café and she was ordering the tea he said to the waitress:

'And bring lots of hot buttered toast.'

'This,' she said, as she poured out the tea and held up the milk jug questioningly, 'is a new technique of seduction. Milk?'

'Are you having milk?'

'No.'

'No, then.'

'Some nice hot buttered toast?'

'Are you having toast?' he demanded.

'Why the bloody hell should it be up to me to decide?'

'I asked you a polite question,' he said rudely.

'No.'

'No!'

They looked at one another as they sipped the black tea like two people who are falling head over heels into hatred of one another.

'Could you possibly tell me,' he said presently, 'why I bother my head with a fool of a woman like you?'

'I can only suppose, Bobby, that it is because we are in love with one another.'

'I can only suppose so,' he growled. 'Let's get on!'

They took the longest way round he could find on the map, west into County Mayo, across between the lake at Pontoon, over the level bogland to Castlebar. Here the mountains walled in the bogland plain with cobalt air – in the fading light the land was losing all solidity. Clouds like soapsuds rose and rose over the edges of the mountains until they glowed as if there was a fire of embers behind the blue ranges. In Castlebar he pulled up by the post office and telephoned to the hotel at Salthill for dinner and two rooms. When he came out he saw a poster in a shop window and said:

'Why don't we go to the pictures? It will kill a couple of hours.'

'By rights,' she said, 'you ought to be driving me home to Dublin.'

'If you wish me to I will.'

'Would you if I asked you?'

'Do you want me to?'

'I suppose it's rather late now, isn't it?'

'Not at all. Fast going we could be there about one o'clock. Shall we?'

'It wouldn't help. George is away. I'd have to bring you in and give you something to eat, and ... Let's go to the blasted movies!'

The film was *Charley's Aunt*. They watched its slapstick gloomily. When they came out, after nine o'clock, there was still a vestigial light in the sky. They drove on and on, westward still, prolonging the light, prolonging the drive, holding off the night's decision. Before Killary they paused at a black-faced lake, got out, and stood beside its quarried beauty. Nothing along its stony beach but a few wind-torn rushes.

'I could eat you,' he said.

She replied that only lovers and cannibals talk like that.

They dawdled past the long fiord of Killary where young people on holiday sat outside the hotel, their drinks on the trestled tables. In Clifden the street was empty, people already climbing to bed, as the lights in the upper windows showed. They branched off on the long coastal road where the sparse whitewashed cottages were whiter than the foam of waves that barely suggested sea. At another darker strand they halted, but now they saw no foam at all and divined the sea only by its invisible whispering, or when a star touched a wave. Midnight was now only an hour away.

Their headlights sent rocks and rabbits into movement. The heather streamed past them like kangaroos. It was well past eleven as they poured along the lonely land by Galway Bay. Neither of them had spoken for an hour. As they drove into Salthill there was nobody abroad. Galway was dark. Only the porch light of the hotel showed that it was alive. When he turned off the engine the only sound at first was the crinkle of contracting metal as the engine began to cool. Then to their right they heard the lisping bay. The panel button lit the dashboard clock.

'A quarter to,' he said, leaning back. She neither spoke nor stirred. 'Jenny!' he said sharply.

She turned her head slowly and by the dashboard light he saw her white smile.

'Yes, darling?'

'Worn out?' he asked, and patted her knee.

She vibrated her whole body so that the seat shook, and stretched her arms about her head, and lowering them let her head fall on his shoulder, and sighed happily, and said:

'What I want is a good long drink of anything on earth except tea.'

These homing twelve o'clockers from Lough Derg are well known in every hotel all over the west of Ireland. Revelry is the reward of penance. The porter welcomed them as if they were heroes returned from a war. As he led them to their rooms he praised them, he sympathized with them, he patted them up and he patted them down, he assured them that the ritual grill was at that moment sizzling over the fire, he proffered them hot baths, and he told them where to discover the bar. 'Ye will discover it . . . ' was his phrase. The wording was exact, for the bar's gaiety was muffled by dim lighting, drawn blinds, locked doors. In the overheated room he took off his jacket and loosened his tie. They had to win a corner of the counter, and his order was for two highballs with ice in them. Within two minutes they were at home with the crowd. The island might never have existed if the barmaid, who knew where they had come from, had not laughed: 'I suppose ye'll ate like lions?'

After supper they relished the bar once more, sipping slowly now, so refreshed that they could have started on the road again without distaste or regret. As they sipped they gradually became aware of a soft strumming and drumming near at hand, and were told that there was a dance on in the hotel next door. He raised his eyebrows to her. She laughed and nodded.

They gave it up at three o'clock and walked out into the warm-cool of the early summer morning. Gently tipsy, gently tired they walked to the little promenade. They leaned on the railing and he put his arm about her waist, and she put hers around his, and they gazed at the moon silently raking its path across the sea towards Aran. They had come, she knew, to the decisive moment. He said:

'They have a fine night for it tonight on the island.'

'A better night than we had,' she said tremulously.

After another spell of wave fall and silence he said:

'Do you know what I'm thinking, Jenny? I'm thinking that I wouldn't mind going back there again next year. Maybe I might do it properly the next time?'

'The next time?' she whispered, and all her body began to dissolve and, closing her eyes, she leaned against him. He, too, closed his eyes, and all his body became as rigid as a steel girder that flutters in a storm. Slowly they opened their love-drunk eyes, and stood looking long over the brightness and blackness of the sea. Then, gently, ever so gently, with a gentleness that terrified her he said:

'Shall we go in, my sweet?'

She did not stir. She did not speak. Slowly turning to him she lifted her eyes to him pleadingly.

'No, Bobby, please, not yet.'

'Not yet?'

'Not tonight!'

He looked down at her, and drew his arms about her. They kissed passionately. She knew what that kiss implied. Their mouths parted. Hand in hand they walked slowly back to the hotel, to their separate rooms.

The Fur Coat

When Maguire became Parliamentary Secretary to the Minister for Roads and Railways his wife wound her arms around his neck, lifted herself on her toes, gazed into his eyes and said, adoringly:

'Now, Paddy, I must have a fur coat.'

'Of course, of course, me dear,' Maguire cried, holding her out from him admiringly; for she was a handsome little woman still, in spite of the greying hair and the first hint of a stoop. 'Get two fur coats! Switzer's will give us any amount of tick from now on.'

Molly sat back into her chair with her fingers clasped between her knees and said, chidingly:

'You think I'm extravagant!'

'Indeed, then, I do not. We've had some thin times together and it's about time we had a bit of comfort in our old age. I'd like to see my wife in a fur coat. I'd love to see my wife take a shine out of some of those straps in Grafton Street – painted jades that never lifted a finger for God or man, not to as much as mention the word *Ireland*. By all means get a fur coat. Go down to Switzer's tomorrow morning,' he cried with all the innocence of a warm-hearted, inexperienced man, 'and order the best fur coat that money can buy.'

Molly Maguire looked at him with affection and irritation. The years had polished her hard – politics, revolution, husband in and out of prison, children reared with the help of relatives and Prisoners' Dependents' funds. You could see the years on her finger tips, too pink, too coarse, and in her diamond-bright eyes.

'Paddy, you big fool, do you know what you'd pay for a mink coat? Not to mention a sable? And not as much as to whisper the word broadtail?'

'Say a hundred quid,' said Paddy, manfully. 'What's a hundred quid? I'll be handling millions of public money from now on. I have to think big.'

She replied in her warm Limerick singsong; sedately and proudly as befitted a woman who had often, in her father's country store, handled thousands of pound notes.

'Do you know, Paddy Maguire, what a really bang-up fur coat could cost you? It could cost you a thousand guineas, and more.'

'One thousand guineas? For a coat? Sure, that's a whole year's salary.'

'It is.'

Paddy drew into himself. 'And,' he said, in a cautious voice, 'is that the kind of coat you had in mind?'

She laughed, satisfied at having taken him off his perch.

'Yerrah, not at all. I thought I might pick up a nice little coat for, maybe, thirty or forty or, at the outside, fifty quid. Would that be too much?'

'Go down to Switzer's in the morning and bring it home on your back.'

But, even there, she thought she detected a touch of the bravo, as if he was still feeling himself a great fellow. She let it pass. She said she might have a look around. There was no hurry. She did not bring up the matter again for quite fifteen minutes.

'Paddy! About that fur coat. I sincerely hope you don't think I'm being *vulgar*?'

'How could you be vulgar?'

'Oh, sort of *nouveau riche*. I don't want a fur coat for show-off.' She leaned forward eagerly. 'Do you know the reason why I want a fur coat?'

'To keep you warm. What else?'

'Oh, well, that too, I suppose, yes,' she agreed shortly. 'But you must realize that from this on we'll be getting asked out to parties and receptions and so forth. And – well – I haven't a rag to wear!'

'I see,' Paddy agreed; but she knew that he did not see.

'Look,' she explained, 'what I want is something I can wear any old time. I don't want a fur coat for grandeur.' (This very scornfully.) 'I want to be able to throw it on and go off and be as well dressed as anybody. You see, you can wear any old thing under a fur coat.'

'That sounds a good idea.' He considered the matter as judiciously as if he were considering a memorandum for a projected bypass. She leaned back, contented, with the air of a woman who has successfully laid her conscience to rest.

Then he spoiled it all by asking, 'But, tell me, what do all the women do who haven't fur coats?'

'They dress.'

'Dress? Don't ye all dress?'

'Paddy, don't be silly. They think of nothing else but dress. I have no time for dressing. I'm a busy housewife and, anyway, dressing costs a lot of money.' (Here she caught a flicker in his eye which obviously meant that forty quid isn't to be sniffed at either.) 'I mean they have costumes that cost twenty-five pounds. Half a dozen of 'em. They spend a lot of time and thought over it. They live for it. If you were married to one of 'em you'd soon know what it means to dress. The beauty of a fur coat is that you can just throw it on and you're as good as the best of them.'

'Well, that's fine! Get the ould coat.'

He was evidently no longer enthusiastic. A fur coat, he had learned, is not a grand thing – it is just a useful thing. He drew his brief case towards him. There was that pier down in Kerry to be looked at. 'Mind you,' he added, 'it'd be nice and warm, too. Keep you from getting a cold.'

'Oh, grand, yes, naturally, cosy, yes, all that, yes, yes!'

And she crashed out and banged the door after her and put the children to bed as if she were throwing sacks of turf into a cellar. When she came back he was poring over maps and specifications. She began to patch one of the boy's pyjamas. After a while she held it up and looked at it in despair. She let it sink into her lap and looked at the pile of mending beside her.

'I suppose when I'm dead and gone they'll invent plastic pyjamas that you can wash with a dishcloth and mend with a lump of glue.'

She looked into the heart of the turf fire. A dozen pyjamas ... underwear for the whole house ...

'Paddy!'

'Huh?'

'The last thing that I want anybody to start thinking is that I, by any possible chance, could be getting grand notions.'

She watched him hopefully. He was lost in his plans.

'I can assure you, Paddy, that I loathe – I simply loathe all this modern show-off.'

'That's right.'

'Those wives that think they haven't climbed the social ladder until they've got a fur coat!'

He grunted at the map of the pier.

'Because I don't care what you or anybody else says, Paddy, there *is* something vulgar about a fur coat. There's no shape to them. Especially musquash. What I was thinking of was black Indian lamb. Of course, the real thing would be ocelot. But they're much too dear. The real ones. And I wouldn't be seen dead in an imitation ocelot.'

He glanced sideways from the table. 'You seem to know a lot about fur.' He leaned back and smiled benevolently. 'I never knew you were hankering all this time after a fur coat.'

'Who said I'm hankering! I am *not*. What do you mean? Don't be silly. I just want something decent to wear when we go out to a show, or to wear over a dance frock, that's all. What do you mean – hankering?'

'Well, what's wrong with that thing you have with the fur on the sleeves? The shiny thing with the what-do-you-call-'ems – sequins, is it?'

'*That*! Do you mean *that*? For heaven's sake, don't be talking about what you don't know anything about. I've had *that* for fourteen years. It's like something me grandmother wore at her own funeral.'

He laughed. 'You used to like it.'

'Of course, I liked it when I got it. Honestly, Paddy Maguire, there are times when . . .'

'Sorry, sorry, sorry. I was only trying to be helpful. How much is an ocelot?'

'Eighty-five or ninety – at the least.'

'Well, why not?'

'Paddy, tell me honestly. Honestly, now! Do you seriously think that I could put eighty-five pounds on my back?'

With his pencil Maguire frugally drew a line on the map, reducing the pier by five yards, and wondered would the county surveyor let him get away with it.

'Well, the question is: will you be satisfied with the Indian lamb? What colour did you say it is? Black? That's a very queer lamb.'

Irritably he rubbed out the line. The wretched thing would be too shallow at low water if he cut five yards off it.

'It's dyed. You could get it brown, too,' she cried. 'You could get all sorts of lamb. Broadtail is the fur of unborn Persian lambs.'

That woke him up: the good farmer stock in him was shocked.

'Unborn lambs!' he cried. 'Do you mean to say that they . . .'

'Yes, isn't it awful? Honest to Heaven, Paddy, anyone that'd wear broadtail ought to be put in prison. Paddy, I've made up my mind. I just couldn't buy a fur coat. I just won't buy it. That's the end of it.'

She picked up the pyjamas again and looked at them with moist eyes. He turned to devote his full attention to her problem.

'Molly, darling, I'm afraid I don't understand what you're after. I mean, do you or do you not want a fur coat? I mean, supposing you didn't buy a fur coat, what else could you do?'

'Just exactly what do you mean?' – very coldly.

'I mean, it isn't apparently necessary that you should buy a fur coat. I mean, not if you don't really want to. There must be some other way of dressing besides fur coats? If you have a scunner against fur coats, why not buy something else just as good? There's hundreds of millions of other women in the world and they all haven't fur coats.'

'I've told you before that they dress! And I've no time to dress. I've explained all that to you.'

Maguire got up. He put his back to the fire, his hands behind him, a judicial look on him. He addressed the room.

'All the other women in the world can't all have time to dress. There must be some way out of it. For example, next month there'll be a garden party up at the President's house. How many of all these women will be wearing fur coats?' He addressed the armchair. 'Has Mrs de Valera time to dress?' He turned and leaned over the turf basket. 'Has Mrs General Mulcahy time to dress? There's ways and means of doing everything.' (He shot a quick glance at the map of the pier; you could always knock a couple of feet off the width of it.) 'After all, you've told me yourself that you could purchase a black costume for twenty-five guineas. Is that or is that not a fact? Very well then,' triumphantly, 'why not buy a black costume for twenty-five guineas?'

'Because, you big fathead, I'd have to have shoes and a blouse and hat and gloves and a fur and a purse and everything to match it, and I'd spend far more in the heel of the hunt, and I haven't time for that sort of thing and I'd have to have two or three costumes – Heaven above, I can't appear day after day in the same old rig, can I?'

'Good! Good! That's settled. Now, the question is: shall we or shall we not purchase a fur coat? Now! What is to be said for a fur coat?' He marked off the points on his fingers. 'Number one: it is warm. Number two: it will keep you from getting a cold. Number three . . .'

Molly jumped up, let a scream out of her, and hurled the basket of mending at him.

'Stop it! I told you I don't want a fur coat! And you don't want me to get a fur coat! You're too mean, that's what it is! And, like all the Irish, you have the peasant streak in you. You're all alike, every bloody wan of ye. Keep your rotten fur coat. I never wanted it . . .'

And she ran from the room sobbing with fury and disappointment.

'Mean?' gasped Maguire to himself. 'To think that anybody could say that I . . . Mean!'

She burst open the door to sob:

'I'll go to the garden party in a mackintosh. And I hope that'll satisfy you!' and ran out again.

He sat miserably at his table, cold with anger. He murmured the hateful word over and over, and wondered could there be any truth in it. He added ten yards to the pier. He reduced the ten to five, and then, seeing what he had done, swept the whole thing off the table.

It took them three days to make it up. She had hit him below the belt and they both knew it. On the fourth morning she found a cheque for a hundred and fifty pounds on her dressing table. For a moment her heart leaped. The next moment it died in her. She went down and put her arms about his neck and laid the cheque, torn in four, into his hand.

'I'm sorry, Paddy,' she begged, crying like a kid. 'You're not mean. You never were. It's me that's mean.'

'You! Mean?' he said, fondly holding her in his arms.

'No, I'm not mean. It's not that. I just haven't the heart, Paddy. It was knocked out of me donkeys' years ago.' He looked at her sadly. 'You know what I'm trying to say?'

He nodded. But she saw that he didn't. She was not sure that she knew herself. He took a deep, resolving breath, held her out from him by the shoulders, and looked her straight in the eyes. 'Molly, tell me the truth. You want this coat?'

'I do. O God, I do!'

'Then go out and buy it.'

'I couldn't, Paddy. I just couldn't.'

He looked at her for a long time. Then he asked:

'Why?'

She looked straight at him and, shaking her head sadly, she said in a little sobbing voice:

'I don't know.'

Up the Bare Stairs

A pity beyond all telling is hid in the heart of love.

All the way from Dublin my travelling companion had not spoken a dozen words. After a casual interest in the countryside as we left Kingsbridge he had wrapped a rug about his legs, settled into his corner, and dozed.

He was a bull-shouldered man, about sixty, with coarse, sallow skin stippled with pores, furrowed by deep lines on either side of his mouth: I could imagine him dragging these little dikes open when shaving. He was dressed so conventionally that he might be a judge, a diplomat, a shopwalker, a shipowner, or an old-time Shakespearian actor: black coat, striped trousers, grey spats, white slip inside his waistcoat, butterfly collar folded deeply, and a black cravat held by a gold clasp with a tiny diamond.

The backs of his fingers were hairy: he wore an amethyst ring almost as big as a bishop's. His temples were greying and brushed up in two sweeping wings – wherefore the suggestion of the actor. On the rack over his head was a leather hat case with the initials F.J.N. in Gothic lettering. He was obviously an Englishman who had crossed the night before. Even when the steam of the train lifted to show the black January clouds sweeping across the Galtees, and a splash of sleet hit the window by his ear, he did not waken. Just then the ticket checker came in from the corridor and tipped his shoulder. As he received back his ticket he asked, 'What time do we arrive in Cork?' He said the word *Cork* as only a Corkman can say it, giving the *r* its distinctively delicate palatal trill, not saying 'Corrrk,' or 'Cohk.' He was unmistakably a Corkonian.

At Mallow I came back from tea to find him stretching his legs on the platform and taking notice. He had bought the evening paper and was tapping his thigh with it as he watched, with a quizzical smile, two tipsy old countrymen in amiable dispute, nose to nose, outside the bar. A fine man on his feet; at least six foot two. I bought a paper, also, at the bookstall and as we went on our way we both read.

My eye floated from a heading about a licensing case – the usual long verbatim report, two men found hiding under the stairs, six men with bottles in the stable, much laughter in court, and so on – to a headline beside it: CORKMAN IN BIRTHDAY HONOURS LIST. The paragraph referred to 'Francis James Nugent, Baronet: for War Services.' I looked across at him.

'Did you say something?' he asked.

'No, no! Or, rather, I don't think so.'

'Pretty cold,' he said, in a friendly way. 'Though I will say one thing for the G.S.R., they do heat their trains.'

'Yes, it's nice and warm today. They're not, of course, the G.S.R. now, you know. They're called Corus Iompair Eireann.'

'What's that? Irish for G.S.R.?'

'More or less.'

We talked a bit about the revival of the language. Not that he was interested; but he was tolerant, or perhaps the right word is indifferent. After a bit I said:

'I see there's a Corkman in the new honours list.'

'Oh?'

I glanced up at the rack and said, with a grin:

'I see the initials on your hatbox.'

He chuckled, pleased.

'I suppose I'd better plead guilty.'

'Congratulations.'

'Thank you.'

'What does it feel like?'

He glanced out at the wheeling fields, with their lochs of water and cowering cattle, and then looked back at me with a cynical smile.

'It doesn't feel any different. By the time you get it you've pretty well enjoyed everything it stands for. Still, it helps.'

'I see from the paper that you went to the same school as myself.'

'Are you the old Red and Green, too?'

'Up the Abbey!'

He laughed, pleased again.

'Does all that go on just the same as before?'

'It goes on. Perhaps not just the same as before.'

We talked of West Abbey. I knew none of the men he knew, but he thawed out remembering them.

'Are all the old photographs still in the main hall? Chaps in the

Indian Civil, the Canadian Mounted, the Navy, the Indian Police? God, I used to stare at them when I was a kid.'

'They're gone. They've been replaced by Confirmation groups all wearing holy medals.'

He made a bored face.

'I suppose in those days you little thought you'd be coming back to Cork one day as Sir Francis Nugent.'

He peered at me through his cigarette smoke and nodded sagely.

'I knew.'

'You did!'

'I shouldn't have said that. I couldn't know. But I had a pretty good idea.'

Then he leaned forward and let down all his reserves. As he began my heart sank. He was at the favourite theme of every successful man: 'How I Began.' But as he went on I felt mean and rebuked. I doubt if he had ever told anyone, and before he finished I could only guess why he chose to tell me now.

'You know, it's extraordinary the things that set a fellow going. I always knew I'd get somewhere. Not merely that, but I can tell you the very day, the very hour, I made up my mind I was going to get there. I don't think I was more than fourteen or fifteen at the time. Certainly not more than fifteen. It was as simple as that' – clicking his fingers. 'It was all on account of a little man named Angelo – one of the monks who was teaching us. He's gone to God by now. There was a time when I thought he was the nicest little man in the whole school. Very handsome. Cheeks as red as a girl's, black bristly hair, blue eyes, and the most perfect teeth I've ever seen between a man's lips. He was absolutely full of life, bursting with it. He was really just a big boy and that's probably why we got on so well with him. I've seen him get as much fun out of solving a quadratic equation or a problem in Euclid as a kid with a new toy. He had a marvellous trick of flinging his *cappa* over one shoulder, shoving his two wrists out of his sleeves like a conjurer, snapping up a bit of chalk and saying, "Watch what I'm going to do now," that used to make us sit bolt upright in our desks as if . . . well, as if he was going to do a conjuring trick. And if you could only have seen the way he'd kick ball with us in the yard – you know, the old yard at the back of West Abbey – all we had was a lump of paper tied with twine – shouting and racing like any of us. He really was a good chap. We were very fond of him.

'Too fond of him, I've often thought. He knew it, you see, and it made him put too much of himself into everything we did. And the result was that we were next door to helpless without him. He made us depend on him too much. Perhaps he wasn't the best kind of teacher; perhaps he was too good a teacher – I don't know – have it whichever way you like. If he was tired, or had a headache, or sagged, we sagged. If he was away sick and somebody else had to take charge of us we were a set of duffers. They could be just as cross as he was – he was very severe, he'd take no excuses from anybody – or they could be as merry as he was: it just wasn't the same thing. They had a job to do, and they did the best they could, but with him it wasn't a job, it was his life, it was his joy and his pleasure. You could tell how much the fellows liked him by the way they'd crowd around him at play hour, or at the end of the holidays to say good-bye.

'One particularly nice thing about him was that he had no favourites, no pets, as we used to call them. Did you call them that in your time? But he was – what shall I say? – more than a little partial to me. And for a very, if you like to call it, silly reason. In those days, you see, politics were very hot in Cork city; very hot, very passionate. Of course, they were the old Irish Party days, long before your time, when politics were taken much more seriously than I've ever seen them taken anywhere else. John Redmond had one party called the Molly Maguires, and William O'Brien had another party called the All for Irelanders. Mind you, if you asked me now what it was all about I'd find it very hard to tell you, because they were all the one party at Westminster, and they were all agreed about home rule, but once it came to election time they tore one another to pieces. Fights in the street every night, baton charges, clashes between rival bands, instruments smashed on the pavements. One night, with my own eyes. I saw a big six-foot countryman take a running jump down the grand parade and land right on top of a big drum.

'Well, Angelo was a Molly, and I needn't tell you he was just as excited about politics as he was about everything else, and I was also a Molly and a very hot one. Not that I understood anything at all about it, but just that my father was one of the hottest Redmondites in the city of Cork. And, of course, nothing would do Angelo but to bring politics into class. He'd divide the class into Mollies and All Fors and when we'd be doing Euclid or reciting poetry he'd set one team against the other, and he'd work up the excitement until the fellows would be clambering across the desks, and if any fellow let down his side we'd glare at him until he'd want to creep away out of sight, and if he scored a point we'd cheer him as if he'd kicked a goal in an All Ireland Final.

'It was on one of these days that it happened. We were at the Eighth Problem. The Mollies wanted one point to pull even. I was the last man in – and I muffed it. And no wonder, with Angelo shouting at me like a bull, "Come on, now, Frankie. If A.B. be placed on C.D. . . . Up the Mollies! Go on, Frankie. Go on. If A.B. . . ."

'The All Fors won. Angelo laughed it off with, "Very good, very good, back to yeer places now. Work is work. This isn't the Old Market Place. Now for tomorrow," and so on.

'But he kept me in after school. There I sat, alone in the empty classroom upstairs – you know the one, near the ball alley – with the crows outside in the yard picking up the crusts, and the dusk falling over the city, and Angelo, never speaking a word, walking up and down the end of the room reading his office. As a rule we were let out at three. He kept me there until five o'clock rang. Then he told me to go home and went off himself up to the monastery.

'I walked out of the yard behind him, and at that moment if I had had a revolver in my hand I'd have shot him. I wouldn't have cared if he'd beaten me black and blue. I wouldn't have cared if he'd given me extra work to do at home. He deliberately got me into trouble with my father and mother, and what that meant he understood exactly. Perhaps you don't. You don't know my background as he knew it. When I tell you that my father was a tailor and my mother was a seamstress I needn't tell you any more. When a kid's mother has to work as hard as his father to push him through school you can guess the whole picture. I don't seem to remember an hour, except for Sundays, when one or other, or both, of these machines wasn't whirring in that little room where we lived, down by the distillery, sometimes until twelve or one o'clock at night. I remember that day as I walked home I kept saying to myself over and over again, "If only my mummy wasn't sick." All the way. Past the distillery. Around by the tannery. You possibly know the little terrace of houses. They've been there since the eighteenth century. Dark. We had only two rooms. In the hall. I can still get that stuffy smell that had been locked up there for a hundred and fifty years – up the bare stairs. On the landing there was a tap dripping into an old leaden trough that had been there since the year dot. I could hear the machine whirring. I remember I stopped at the window and picked a dead leaf from the geraniums. I went up the last few steps and I lifted the latch. My father was bent over the machine; specs on his forehead, black skeins of thread around his neck, bare arms. My mother was wrapped in shawls in the old basket chair before the fire. I could draw that room; the two machines, my bed in one corner, my dinner waiting on the table, the tailor's goose heating on the grate. The machine stopped.

"'In the name of God what happened to you, boy?" says my father. "Is there anything wrong? What kept you? Your poor mother there is out of her head worrying about you."

"'Ah, I was just kept in, sir," says I, passing it off as airily as I could. "How are you, Mummy?"

'The old man caught me by the arm.

"'Kept in?" says he, and the way he said it you'd think I was after coming out of the lockup. "Why were you kept in?"

"'Ah, 'twas just a bit of Euclid I didn't know, that's all."

'It was only then I noticed that the mother was asleep. I put my hand to my lips begging him not to waken her. He let a roar out of him.

"'A nice disgrace! Kept in because you didn't know your Euclid!"

"'What is it, what is it, Frankie?" she says, waking up in a fright. "What did they do to you, boy?"

"''Twas nothing at all, Mummy, just that I didn't know a bit of Euclid. I had to stay back to learn it."

"'A nice how d'ye do! And why didn't you know your Euclid?" – and he had me up against the wall and his fist raised.

"'It wasn't really Euclid at all, Father. It was all Angelo's fault. It was all politics. He divided the class into All Fors and Mollies and because the All Fors won he kept me in out of spite. Honestly, that's all it was, Mummy, there was nothing else to it."

"'Holy God," whispers the old man. "So it wasn't only the Euclid, but lettin' down John Redmond in front of the whole class. That's what you did, is it?"

"'Oh, for God's sake, Billy," says the mother, "don't mind John Redmond. 'Tis little John Redmond or any other John Redmond cares about us, but 'tis the work, the work. What are we slaving for, boy, day and night, and all the rest of it? There's your poor father working himself to the bone to send you through school. And so on. Nothing matters, boy, but the work! The work!"

"''Tisn't only the work," says the old man. "'Tisn't only the work," and he was sobbing over it. "But to think of poor John Redmond fighting night after night for Ireland, standing up there in the House of Commons, and you – you brat – couldn't even do a sum in Euclid to stand by him! In your own school! Before everybody! Look at him," he wails, with his arm up to the picture of John Redmond on the wall, with his hooked nose and his jowls like an old countrywoman. "Look at the dacent gentleman. A man that never let down his side. A gentleman to the tips of his toes if there ever was one. And you couldn't do a simple sum in Euclid to help him! Th'other fellows could do it. The All Fors could do it. But my son couldn't do it!"

'And with that he gave me a crack that nearly sent me into the fire.

'The end of it was that I was on my knees with my head on the mother's lap, blubbering, and the old man with his two hands up to John Redmond, and the tears flowing down his face like rain, and the mother wailing, "Won't you promise, Frankie, won't you promise to work, boy?" and I promising and promising anything if she'd only stop crying.

'That was the moment that I swore to myself to get on. But wait! You won't understand why until I've finished.

'The next day Angelo took the same problem, at the same hour, and he asked me to do it again. Now, kids are no fools. I knew by the look on his face why he asked me to do it. He wanted to make friends with me, to have everything the same as if yesterday had never happened. But he didn't know what had happened inside in me the night before. I went through the problem, step by step – I knew it perfectly – down to the Q.E.D.

'"Now, isn't it a pity, Frankie," he says, smiling at me, "that you wouldn't do that yesterday?"

'"Oh," I said, in a very lordly, tired voice, "I just didn't feel like it."

'I knew what was coming to me, and I wanted it, and to make sure that I got it I gave him that sort of insolent smile that drives grownups mad with children. I've seen that smile on my own children's faces now and again, and when I see it I have to go outside the door for fear I'd knock them the length of the room. That is what Angelo did to me. I got up off the floor and I sat back in my place and I had the same insolent smile on my face.

'"Now, if you please," says Angelo, reaching for his cane, and he was as white as his teeth, "will you kindly do the next problem?"

'I did it, step by step, calm as a breeze, down to the Q.E.D. I'd prepared it the night before.

'"Right," says Angelo, and his voice was trembling with rage. "Do the next problem."

'I had him where I wanted him. He was acting unfairly, and he knew it, and the class knew it. I had that problem prepared too. Just to tease him I made a couple of slips, but just as he'd be reaching for the cane I'd correct them. I was a beast, but he'd made me a beast. I did it, down to the Q.E.D., and I smiled at him, and he looked at me. We both knew that from that moment it was war to the knife.

'I worked that night until twelve o'clock; and I worked every night until I left school until twelve o'clock. I never gave him a chance. I had to, because until the day I left that place he followed me. He followed me into the fifth form. And into the sixth. He made several efforts to make it up with me, but I wouldn't let him. He was too useful to me the other way. I sat for the Civil Service and I got first place in the British Isles in three subjects out of five, geometry, chemistry, and history, third in mathematics, fifth in German. I did worst in German because I didn't have Angelo for German. I think I can say without arrogance that I was the most brilliant student that ever passed out of West Abbey School.'

Sir Francis leaned back.

'You must have worked like a black.'

'I did.'

'Well, it was worth it!'

He looked out over the fields which were now becoming colourless in the falling dusk and his voice sank to a murmur, as if he were thinking aloud.

'I don't know. For me? Yes, perhaps. I had no youth. For them? I don't know. I didn't work to get on, I worked to get out. I didn't work to please my mother or my father. I hated my mother and I hated my father from the day they made me cry. They did the one thing to me that I couldn't stand up against. They did what that little cur Angelo planned they'd do. They broke my spirit with pity. They made me cry with pity. Oh, I needn't say I didn't go on hating them. A boy doesn't nourish hatred. He has his life before him. I was too sorry for them. But that's where they lost everything. A boy can be sorry for people who are weak and pitiable, but he can't respect them. And you can't love people if you don't respect them. I pitied them and I despised them. That's the truth.'

He leaned back again.

'You don't look like a man whose spirit was ever broken,' I laughed, a little embarrassed.

'The spirit is always broken by pity. Oh, I patched it up pretty well. I made a man of myself. Or, rather,' he said with passion, 'with what was left of myself after they'd robbed me of my youth that I spent slaving to get away from them.'

'You'd have slaved anyway. You were full of ambition.'

'If I did I'd have done it for ambition alone. I tell you I did it for pity and hate and pride and contempt and God knows what other reason. No. They broke my spirit all right. I know it. The thing I've put in its place is a very different thing. I know it. I've met plenty of men who've got along on ambition and they're whole men. I know it. I'm full of what they put into me – pity and hate and rage and pride and contempt for the weak and anger against all bullying, but, above all, pity, chock-a-block with it. I know it. Pity is the most disintegrating of all human emotions. It's the most disgusting of all human emotions. I know it.'

'What happened to Angelo?'

'I don't know. Nor care. Died, I suppose.'

'And . . . your father?'

'Fifteen years after I left Cork he died. I never saw him. I brought my mother to live with me in London.'

'That was good. You were fond of her.'

'I was sorry for her. That's what she asked me for when I was a boy. I've been sorry for her all my life. Ah!'

His eyes lit up. I looked sideways to see what had arrested him. It was the first lights of Cork, and, mingling with the smoke over the roofs, the January night. Behind the violet hills the last cinder of the sun made a saffron horizon. As the train roared into the tunnel we could see children playing in the streets below the steep embankment, and he was staring at them thirstily, and I must have imagined that I heard their happy shouts. Then the tunnel opened and swallowed us.

There were no lights in the carriage. All I could see was the occasional glow of his cigarette. Presently the glow moved and my knee was touched. His voice said:

'She's with me on this train. My mother. I'm bringing her back to Cork.'

'Will she like that?'

'She's dead.'

The train roared on through the tunnel. As we passed under the first tunnel vent a drip of water fell on the roof. The tiny glow swelled and ebbed softly.

'I'm very sorry.'

His voice said, in the darkness:

'I meant to bury her in London. But I couldn't do it. Silly, wasn't it?'

After a while another drip of water splashed on the roof. The windows were grey.

'You did the kind thing.'

His voice was so low that I barely heard it.

'Kind!'

In a few more minutes we were drawing up in steam alongside the lighted platform. He was standing up, leaning over his hatbox. From it he lifted a silk topper and a dark scarf. He put on his black frock coat. 'Good-bye,' he said politely, and beckoned for a porter.

From the platform I watched him walk down towards the luggage van where a tiny group already stood waiting. They were all poor people. There was a bent old woman there in a black shawl, and three or four humble-looking men in bowler hats and caps. As I watched him bow to them and doff his hat to the old woman and introduce himself, the yellow pine-and-brass of the coffin was already emerging from the van and the undertaker's men in their brass-buttoned coats were taking it from the porters. Among his poor relations he walked reverently, bareheaded, out into the dark stationyard.

They slid the coffin into the motor hearse; he showed his relatives into the carriages, and, stooping, he went in after them. Then the little procession moved slowly out into the streets on its way to whatever chapel would take her for the night into its mortuary.

One True Friend

The lonely woman was as big a ... No! I won't say it. 'T wasn't a very kind thing I was going to say. And I suppose that's the way God made her. And, as the old joker said, we're all as God made us – and some of us worse. But I will say this about her, and her own sons often said it – and 'twas they gave her the name of the lonely woman – she was (if you will pardon my saying so) a damn nuisance. Mind you, she was a good soul – a good, pious, kindly, Christian soul. But she was a nuisance. Her trouble was that she really was lonely, and she was always complaining about how lonely she was, but she would never do anything about it because, so I firmly believe, she liked being lonely.

Where she lived, of course, was no fit place for any Christian to live. She lived in her old rooky-rawky of a house over a tinsmith's shop, where she'd lived since she was first married, and where she'd brought up her family, and where her husband was carried out on the flat of his back, but where now – for she had let her extra rooms, one by one, to the tinsmith downstairs – you heard nothing all day long but the tinny hammering, a *tic-tac-too, tic-tac-too* that would drive anybody mad. And what kind of a house was it, where you smelled nothing but boiling solder from morning to night?

Her sons were always at her to leave it and she'd say, 'I know I ought to leave it. I know it's no place for a lonely woman like me. Nobody to hand me as much as a drop of cold water if I got a stitch in the middle of the night, or maybe an appendicitis. But sure where can I go?'

'But,' they'd say then, 'Mother, come and live with us!'

'Oh, no!' she'd say then. 'Oh, no! Is it go and live with a daughter-in-law? Ha! Cock 'em up with comfort. Tisn't mother-in-laws they want. Oh, no! Nobody wants a poor lonely old woman like me.'

And then her sons would persuade her, and their wives would persuade her, and perhaps, after a lot of persuading, she would agree, and they would go home and get a room ready for her. She would change her mind during the night. Not that they blamed her. Her little kitchen was her palace, and she was the queen of it. She had her cup and her saucer, and her knife and her fork, and she could come when she liked and go when she liked. And if it was a bit silent there at night, when there wasn't a sound from the city, and not a sound in the house but the mice scrabbling downstairs in the dustbin, or the tap dripping, well, she had other things. She had company of her own kind. She would sit looking into the fire in the range, her eyes lost in the great distance of her love for her dead husband, her dead sisters, or the saints. Her sons had each, at one time or another, seen her like that, and as they would look about them at their childhood home picked to the bone, they would find that even in the middle of the day the busy, hammering house would cease to exist, and the little city streets would drop away. Looking at her, and hearing her gentle sigh, how could anyone say to her then, as they so often said on other occasions, 'Mother, why the blazes don't you try to make some friends?' – not seeing her glance up with a smile at Saint Francis, and Saint Francis smiling back.

Then one day, one August second, to be precise, out of the blue, lo and behold, she wrote to one of her sons that she had just met a very nice woman. It had apparently happened when she was doing the Ins and Outs. The Ins and Outs is a devotion where you pay as many visits as possible to a church on the feast called Portiuncula. You go in one door, and say a prayer, and come out another, and that counts as a visit. Then you go back, say another prayer, come out, and that is a second visit, and so on until weariness defeats the pious heart. Mrs Moore was doing this, very contentedly, when she suddenly noticed a young girl in a red beret passing quietly from one Station of the Cross to another. She smiled happily, and went on with her prayers. The church was warm with imprisoned sunlight and the candles on the altar drank in the air. The hot gladioli consumed themselves among the consuming lights. Peace and comfort fell on the old lady, and when the girl slipped in beside her on the bench she was about to put out her hand to stroke the child's head when she saw the girl's fingers creep along the bench, take her purse, and disappear. The next thing was the girl running up the aisle. Mrs Moore ran after her. The girl ran faster. The old woman called on her to stop. The worshippers stood up and looked at them. The girl dropped the purse in the hall and ran across the street – where she was nearly killed by a bus – and the lonely woman fainted. When she woke up she was in the sacristy, and a lady whom she had often seen before was giving her a glass of water.

'You're all right now, Mrs Moore,' said the lady.

'How well you know my name,' she whispered.

'Oh, sure, we all know Mrs Moore,' said the lady. 'Is there a church in the city that doesn't know you? Sure, you live in the churches.'

‚ 'It's my only company,' she sighed.

'A holy woman,' said the lady. 'We know you as well as we know the priests. My name is Mrs Calvert.'

'What a shocking thing to happen!'

'Frightful,' said Mrs Calvert. 'Especially when you think the girl was so young. Think of the condition of her soul!'

'We must do something about it,' said the lonely woman.

At once the two old ladies became as friendly in that common cause as if they had been friends all their lives. They toddled across the street to the dairy where Mrs Calvert lived, and each had a glass of milk. If anybody had looked in through the open door and seen them or if anybody had heard them, he would have said that they were sisters. It turned out that they were alike in everything except what didn't matter. They were both widows. Their families were scattered. They both lived alone. Each was the kind of woman who tells the time by the tolling of the church bells. Mrs Moore hated the noise of the tinsmith. Mrs Calvert was waked every morning by the clank of churns. And if the smell of boiling solder is not nice, neither is the smell of sour milk and cow manure. Nothing distinguished them except that, as they laughingly said, one of them swore by Saint Francis and the other swore by Saint Peter in Chains. After a while, when they were getting up to go, it was a case of:

'And now, Mrs Moore, that we know each other, won't you pray for me?'

'Oh, Mrs Calvert, how can you say that? It is you who must pray for me.'

'Now, now, Mrs Moore, you know you're a saint anointed.'

'Ah, Mrs Calvert, that's all you know. I'm a sinner. A wicked sinner. But when I look at you, I say to myself, "If there was ever a soul with the mark of salvation on her, it's Mrs Calvert."'

'Now, Mrs Moore, it's not kind of you to flatter a wicked person. You must pray for me every day. I need it badly.'

'Mrs Calvert, we'll pray for one another.'

When she had come home from this happy adventure the lonely woman met a strange man on her doorstep.

'Am I speaking to Mrs Moore?' he said politely.

'How well you know my name,' she said.

'Oh,' he smiled, 'sure, we all know Mrs Moore.'

'Really?' she said, very pleased, very grand, but very humble. 'A poor lonely woman like me that I thought nobody knew!'

He laughed at that.

'Now,' he said, 'I believe you had a purse snatched from you this morning?'

'Oh? And who told you that?'

'A friend of yours.'

'A friend of mine? Who on earth can that be?'

'She gave her name as Mrs Calvert. She rang up the police station a quarter of an hour ago. I'm a police detective, and I must investigate the matter. We've had a lot of these complaints recently. Mrs Calvert said you'd recognize this girl. Is that right?'

'You mean would I know her again? I'd know her painted.'

'Fine! Now, I'll tell you what I'll do. If I have a motor car here at your very door, tomorrow morning, will you come down to the Bridewell, and if we have that girl there will you recognize her?'

'O-o-oh, n-o-o-o!' said Mrs Moore. 'I couldn't do *that*!'

And she began a long, long rigmarole that went on for half an hour about how she never went out except to go to the church, and how she could never go down there, behind the old-clothes' market, to the Bridewell, where all the drunks are put every night, and how she really never did go anywhere, and how her sons were always at her to go out more and make friends, and what a lonely life she had, and how it would be far better if she did go out, and all about how she used to go out long ago with her husband, and all about her sisters, and her daughters-in-law, and he listened with the endless curiosity of the born detective, and the endless patience of a man whose spirit is broken from dealing with women, and he kept on talking about that motor car, and how she would drive across the city, and be driven back again, until, gradually, his tempting began to win out. She began to see herself in the car. She thought how she would tell her sons about it. She yielded. Off he went, wiping his brow, exhausted but victorious.

But she did not yield in her mind. At the back of her head, there was a feeling that everything was not quite right. However, her sons had always told her that she was much too suspicious, and that she would make many more friends if she were less suspicious, so she shoved it down and tried to forget all about it.

The following morning she went to the Bridewell in the car, and though her old heart began thumping at the sight of the room the detective took her to, and the handcuffs hanging up, and all the police with their collars open, she did exactly as she was told. She went in and looked at the line-up and came out and said, 'Yes. She was there. The fifth girl from the end, in the red beret.' She was so happy at having done this that she did not pay a great deal of attention to what else they told her, and she was home, after a ride again in the car, before it dawned on her what exactly they had told her. Then she realized that she would have to go to the district court, and get up, before everybody, in the witness box and swear that this was the girl. At that she sat down and shook all over. The girl's relatives would see her. Rough lane people. Her father, her brother, her mother would accost her in the street and abuse her.

'Oh!' she gasped. 'The clever woman! She knew that she might be called on to identify the girl. That was why she sent the detective to me. Oh, the guile! The guile and cleverness of some people! And me, a poor, lonely old woman! What a thing to do to a poor, simple old woman the like of me!'

Whereupon she clapped her hat on her head, and with her white hair flying in the wind she went back to the Bridewell, and sought out the detective and said to him:

'I made a mistake. It was the wrong girl. I remember now. My head is getting addled. I'm so old I don't know what I do be saying. You must forget all about it.'

And even though that man was a patient man, and knew how to handle women, he could not budge her; not with pleading, begging, imploring, even threatening, not even when he sat down on one of the iron-legged stools and growled at her like a tiger.

'Oh, no!' said the lonely woman. 'I'm not able for the world at all. I'm all alone by myself, and I can't be up to the clever and calculating people that are in it. Let the wise and clever Mrs Calvert do it this time – the brave and gallant Mrs Calvert with her Saint Peter in Chains, and her "Pray for me, Mrs Moore!"'

And she told him about her lonely life, and her sisters, and her dead husband, and her sons, and her daughters-in-law, and he listened, and then he said:

'You know! Mrs Calvert *is* going to identify the girl for us. She promised me today that she would. You're wronging her. It's just that she wants you to keep her company. As she says herself, she is of a very nervous disposition and a melancholy turn of mind.'

'Nervous?' cried Mrs Moore. 'I'm five and forty times as nervous as her! What right has she to be nervous and she living over a dairy? Not like a poor, wretched, abandoned creature like me, living with a hammering in my ears all day long – a boozing and a woozing would addle a saint.'

And off she went again about her sons and her sisters and her husband and her daughters-in-law, but it was all to blind herself against the fact that she *had* been wronging Mrs Calvert, and that her suspicious mind – against which her sons so often warned her – had led her astray. At the same time, the detective, in his ingratiating country brogue, kept talking about the car and the drive, and once more, before she rightly knew what she was doing, she yielded, and before she could change her mind, he fled from her and took two double whiskeys at his own expense.

Next morning there was Mrs Calvert smiling sweetly down at her, as if it was *her* bag that was snatched, and as if it was *she* owned the car, and as if the detective was *her* chauffeur, and as if it was *she* who had planned it all. They started off, and the two old ladies chatted the whole way. They enjoyed the sun, and the crowds, and the traffic, and whenever they saw anybody they knew walking along the streets they waved whether the people saw them or not. They said they were doing the right thing, and the girl would be thankful in the end, and the church would be thankful, and the city ought to be thankful, and by the time they had said all that, they were being ushered together into the room with the handcuffs hanging on the wall and the bare stools and the policemen with their collars open as always.

They went in together. Side by side, very pale, Mrs Moore and Mrs Calvert walked up and down before the row of suspects, and sure enough, they saw the bag snatcher staring up at them as bold as brass. They said nothing; they were not supposed to until they came out; but when they came out they said nothing either. At this, the detective, very much surprised, challenged them:

'Well? Ye *did* recognize her! I saw ye did!'

The two pious old ladies gave one another short glances, and the lonely woman whispered:

'What would you say, Mrs Calvert?'

'Did *you* recognize her, Mrs Moore?' murmured the other, shaking from head to foot, and with her mouth in a twisty smile like a woman with palsy.

'I was wondering, Mrs Calvert, what *you* would say,' the lonely woman replied, her two little fists tightly clutched.

'Look here!' put in the detective. 'After all my trouble, don't tell me ye're going to let me down again?'

'Oho! You can't be up to the cleverness of the world nowadays!' said the lonely woman.

'*You* have been very nice about everything,' Mrs Calvert said, turning to him. 'It was a lovely motor drive. I enjoyed it very much.'

The detective gazed at them, first the one shut mouth, and then the other. He saw them looking at him pityingly.

He let them walk home. It was a hot day, and the two ladies were soon tired. They did not speak to each other as they walked across the city. They were so exhausted that they passed two churches without stopping to go in. At last, they came to their own parish church, and at the entrance they separated, bowing to each other without a look or a word. They went into the cool dimness of the church, each to her separate corner, and presently the two grey heads were drooping piously and the familiar beads of prayer dropped from their lips. The lonely woman looked up at Saint Francis, and the other looked up at Saint Peter in Chains. Cautiously, now and again, each looked across the nave when the other was not looking, and then she would turn back, with a sigh of trust and happiness, to look up again at her one true friend.

Persecution Mania

There are two types of Irishman I cannot stand. The first is always trying to behave the way he thinks the English behave. The second is always trying to behave the way he thinks the Irish behave. That sort is a roaring bore. Ike Dignam is like that. He believes that the Irish are witty, so he is forever making laborious jokes. He has a notion that the Irish have a gift for fantasy, so he is constantly talking fey. He also has a notion that the Irish have a magnificent gift for malice, mixed up with another idea of the Irish as great realists, so he loves to abuse everybody for not having more common sense. But as he also believes that the Irish are the most kind and charitable people in the world he ends up every tirade with, 'Ah, sure, God help us, maybe the poor fellow is good at heart.' The result is that you do not know, from one moment to the next, whom you are talking to – Ike the fey or Ike the realist, Ike the malicious or Ike the kind.

I am sure he has no clear idea of himself. He is a political journalist. I have seen him tear the vitals out of a man, and then, over a beer, say, with a shocked guffaw:

'I'm after doin' a terrible thing. Do you know what I said in my column this morning about Harry Lombard? I said, "There is no subject under the sun on which the eloquence does not pour from his lips with the thin fluidity of ass's milk." Honest to God, we're a terrible race. Of course, the man will never talk to me again.'

All as if right hand had no responsibility for left hand. But the exasperating thing is that his victims do talk to him again, and in the most friendly way, though why they do it I do not know considering some of the things he says and writes about them. He is the man who said of a certain woman who is in the habit of writing letters to the press in defense of the Department of Roads and Railways, 'Ah, sure, she wrote that with the minister's tongue in her cheek.' Yet the Minister for Roads and Railways is one of his best friends, and he says, 'Ike Dignam? Ah, sure! He's all right. The poor divil is good at heart.' And the cursed thing is that Ike *is* good at heart. I have long since given up trying to understand what this means. Something vaguely connected with hope, and consolation, and despair, and the endless mercy of God.

Ike naturally has as many enemies as friends, and this is something that *he* cannot understand. Somebody may say:

'But you're forgetting, Ike, what you said about him last year. You said every time he sings "Galway Bay" he turns it into a street puddle.'

Ike will laugh delightedly.

'That was only a bit o' fun. Who'd mind that?'

'How would you like to have things like that said about yourself?'

He will reply, valiantly:

'I wouldn't mind one bit. Not one bit in the world. I'd know 'twas all part of the game. I'd know the poor fellow was really good at heart.'

A few weeks ago he got a taste of his own medicine. He committed the folly of granting to his rivals the ancient wish of all rivals, 'That mine enemy would write a book.' The subject of his book – it was a pamphlet rather than a book – was *The Irish Horse in Irish History*, and it was savagely disembowelled in an anonymous review in one of the popular weeklies. The sentence that wounded him, as it was intended to do, said, 'Mr Dignam's knowledge of hunters is weak, of hacks most profound.'

That very afternoon I met him in Mooney's pub, on the quay. He was staring into the bog-hole deeps of a pint of porter. Seeing me he turned such a morose eye on me that I could tell he had been badly hit.

'You saw what the *Sun* said about my book?' he asked, and when I nodded: 'That's a low paper. A low rag. A vicious-minded rag. That's what it is. Full of venom and hate and the lust for power. And,' he added, slapping the counter, 'destruction!'

'Somebody getting his own back, I suppose?'

'What did I ever do to anybody? Only a bit of give and take. What's done every day of the week in journalism. Surely to Gawd, nobody takes me as seriously as all that!'

'Well, that's more or less all your reviewer did with your book.'

Again the indignant palm slapped the mahogany.

'That's exactly what I dislike about that review. The mean implication. The dirty innuendo. Why couldn't he come out and say it in the open like a man? It's the anonymity of the thing that's so despicable.' Here he fixed me with a cunning eye. 'Who do ye think wrote it?'

I spread my hands.

'I think,' he said sourly, 'that it was Mulvaney wrote it. I made a hare of him one time in my column. But I'm not sure. That's the curse of it. He hasn't enough brains to write it.' He gazed at me for a moment through his eyelashes. 'You didn't write it yourself by any chance?'

I laughed and told him I hadn't read his book. I'd bought it, of course (which I had not), and had every intention of reading it (which was also untrue).

'Or it could be that drunk Cassidy,' he said. 'That fellow has it in for me ever since I said that he spoke in the Dail with the greatest sobriety.' He laughed feebly. 'Everyone knew what I meant. Do you think it might be Cassidy?'

'Ikey, it might be a dozen people.'

'It could be anybody,' he snarled. 'Anybody! Damn it all, if I ever say a thing I say it straight out from the shoulder. Why can't they come into the open?' He leaned nearer and dropped to a whisper. 'I was thinking it might be that redheaded bastard from the All Souls Club. That fellow thinks I'm anticlerical. And,' he guffawed, 'I'm not! That's the joke of it, I'm not!'

'What in the name of all that's holy,' I asked crossly, 'has anti-clericalism got to do with horses?'

He scratched his head fiercely and moaned and shook it.

'Ye never know. The people in this country have as much sense when it comes to religion ... Tell me, did ye ever hear of a thing called Discovery of Documents?'

It was only then I fully realized how badly he had been hit.

'You're not being such an idiot as to be thinking of taking this thing to law?'

'Look't! I don't give one tinker's curse about what anybody says against me, but the one thing I *must* know is who wrote it! If I don't find out who wrote it I'll be suspecting my best friends for the rest of my born days.'

'Well,' I said, finishing my drink and leaving him, 'happy hunting to you.'

A couple of days later I saw him cruising towards me along O'Connell Street glowing like a sunrise.

'I'm on the track of that,' he shouted at me from fifteen yards off. 'I'm on the right scent,' he babbled, and I had time to remember what he was talking about while he explained how he had worked up a friendship with a girl in the office of the *Sun*. ''Tis none of the people I suspected at all. Do you know who I think wrote it now?'

'God knows, maybe you wrote it yourself.'

He shook with laughter.

''Twould be great publicity if I could say I did.' Then he glowered. 'They're entirely capable of saying I did. If they thought anybody would believe 'em. No!' He gripped my arm. ''Twas a woman did it. I should have guessed it from the word "Go."'

'Who is she?'

'I don't know,' he said, sadly.

'Then why did you say . . .?'

'I had a dhream about it. Didn't I see the long, lean, bony hand holding the pen, coming out like a snake from behind a red curtain? Didn't I see the gold bangle on the wrist and all?'

'Did you pull the curtain to see who it was?'

'I pulled and I pulled,' Ikey assured me enthusiastically. 'Dear Gawd, I was all the night pullin'!'

'And,' I suggested bitterly, 'I suppose the curtain was made of iron? You know, Ikey, you'll go crackers if you go on like this.'

With his two hands he dragged his hat down on his head as if he wanted to extinguish himself.

'I will!' he cried, so loudly that passers-by turned to look at the pair of us. 'I'll go stark, staring, roaring mad if I don't find out who wrote that dirty thing about me.'

'Look,' I pleaded. 'What does it all matter? The whole thing is gone completely out of everybody's head but your own. It's all over and done with. And even supposing you did find out who wrote it, what could you do then?'

He folded his arms and gazed down O'Connell Street like Napoleon looking over the Atlantic from St Helena.

'I'd write a Limerick on him. I'd *shrivel* him. I wouldn't leave a peck on his bones. As a matter of fact – cocking an eye on me – 'I've done it already. I wrote ten Limericks the other night on ten different people who might have written that review. I'm thinking of publishing the whole lot of 'em, and if the cap fits they can share it and wear it.'

And before I could stop him he recited to the sky four blistering quatrains on 'Irish Bards and Botch Reviewers'. I took his arm.

'Ikey, that'll be ten enemies you'll make instead of one! Come in here, Ikey, and let me talk to you like a father.'

We went across to Mooney's and I talked for half an hour. I told him we had all been through this sort of thing. I told him that no man who cannot grow an epidermis against malice should try to live in small countries like ours. I said that all that matters is a man's work. I assured him, Heaven forgive me, that he had written a masterly record of *The Irish Horse in Irish History* and that that was the main thing. I developed this soundly into the theory that everything is grist to the mill, and that instead of worrying about this silly review he should go home and write a comic piece about it for *Dublin Opinion*, which, indeed, he could do very well. I built him up as *Dignam solus contra mundum*. He agreed to every word of it. We parted cordially. He was in the happiest temper.

Three days later he came striding towards me, beaming. From afar he hailed my passing ship, roaring like a bosun:

'I found out that bastard! Mulvaney! A friend of mine charged him with it and he didn't deny it.'

'Good. You're satisfied now.'

'I am. I don't give a damn about it now. Sure that fellow's brains are all in his behind. Who'd mind anything he'd say?'

'The whole thing is of no importance.'

'None whatsoever.'

'Splendid. It's all over now.'

'Finished. And done with!'

'Grand!'

'I sent him a hell of a postcard!'

'No?'

'I did,' he chortled, 'I did. All I wrote on it was what I said to yourself: "Your second front is your behind." An open postcard. It was a terrible thing to do,' he beamed. 'Oh, shocking!'

His laughter gusted.

'And you put your name to that?'

'I did not. What a fool I'd be! That'll keep him guessing for a while. 'Twill do him no harm in the world. He's not a bad poor gom. Ah! Sure! The poor divil is good at heart.'

Off he went, striding along, as happy as a child. I went into

Mooney's. There at the counter was Mulvaney, sucking his empty pipe, staring in front of him, his bushy eyebrows as black as night. I wheeled quickly, but he caught the movement and called me. His hand strayed to his breast pocket.

'I'm after receiving a very myst-e-e-rious communication,' he said sombrely.

I did not hear what else he said. I realized that you could do nothing with these people. I realized that the only sensible thing to do was to write a satire on the whole lot of them. I began to wonder could I get any editor anywhere to publish it anonymously.

The Judas Touch

'Mummy!' he screamed from the doorstep as she raced up the path for the bus.

'What is it?' she shouted back, halting, fumbling in her handbag to see if she had her compact. She heard the hum of the starting bus and raced again for the gate.

'Mummy!' he shouted again, and went racing up the path after her.

'Well?' she yelled, looking out the gate, and then looking back, and then looking out again and putting up her hand to stop the bus.

'Can't I go to *The Bandits of Sherwood Forest?*'

'No!' and she was out through the gate and the gate went *bang*!

He raced madly up the path and out after her, and clutched her skirt as the brakes whined and the driver glared at her.

'Mummy, you promised!'

She swept his hand away, furious at the public scene, and climbed on the bus. Then, remembering that she had promised and that she must make some excuse, she added from the step of the bus:

'It's Lent. Nobody goes to the pictures in Lent!'

And the bus went on its way. He raced, bawling, after it until her promise and his hopes were swept around the corner. The road was empty. He collapsed sobbing on the footpath. With the sobs his tummy went in and out like an engine. He tore penny-leaves from the wall. He said all the bad words he knew, which are the same bad words we all know only that he did not know what they meant. Lent was *foutu*! He had already given up sweets for Lent. Sweets were *foutus*! He had given them up to be a good little boy. Good little boys were all *foutus*! He dragged himself up and with one hand he played harp strings of misery along the wall back to the gate. He dragged his feet through the gravel of the path to make tram lines. He scraped with a rusty nail on the new paint of the door. Then he went slowly into the breakfast room, where the morning paper stood up like a tent. Upstairs the vacuum cleaner moaned. A sputter of March rain hit the windows briefly. He saw an aged fly make a smooth landing on the marmalade. His five fingers stole up over it and squashed it into the marmalade. He wiped his fingers all across the tablecloth. Then he surveyed the table in search of something else to do that he ought not to do. The maid stood at the door.

'Did she let you go?'

'No.'

'Did you do what I told you and ask God in your prayers last night to make her let you go?'

'No.'

'You couldn't have luck.' And she went off for the dustpan.

He waited until she had gone upstairs and he heard her *swish-swish*. Then he said, 'God is no blooming good!' with a quick look at the door to be sure that nobody heard that one. His eye caught the shine of the ould jug on the sideboard. His daddy always called it an ould jug; he would say to Mummy, 'I might as well be talking to that ould jug.' He surveyed the jug for a bit out of the corners of his eyes. Then he looked at the door again, up at the ceiling, back to the door, back to the ould jug. His heart thumped fiercely. He took down the jug – it was pink lustre outside, gold inside – and he put it on the chair. He flopped down on his knees before it, joined his two sweaty palms, and said, staring earnestly at the pink belly of the jug:

'O Jug, I adore thee and bless thee. Please, O my good Jug, send me to *The Bandits of Sherwood Forest* at the Plaza.'

He looked up at the ceiling and stuck out his tongue. He looked at the jug. He wagged his palms at it swiftly, a dozen times.

'Jug, gimme half a dollar.'

Not a sound but the upstairs *swish-swish*. He sat back on his heels and considered the jug. He put his nose up to the jug to see himself round and fat; and he blew out a big face to see himself twice as round and fat. Then he bethought himself and kneeled up reverently. He cocked his head on one side and said:

'Jug?'

Nothing happened. He grabbed it and shook it and shouted furiously:

'JUG!'

The next moment he had his fist in the jug, grubbing excitedly. He pulled out two raffle tickets, a bottle of red pills, a foreign coin, a champagne cork, and a half-crown piece. In two shakes of a lamb's tail he was in the hall, dragging on his blue gaberdine, and out the gate with his skullcap down over one eye, pelting up to the village. Billy Busher was there, floating a tin motorboat in a puddle of water. He yelled, 'Busher, I got half a dollar.' And he hunched up to him, swaggering the silver half crown forward guardedly in his palm. Busher's eyes became as big as half crowns and at once he shouted: *'Bandits of Sherwood Forest?'*

'No!'

The tin motorboat meant sea, and sand, and roundabouts, and ice cream, and swimming, and holidays.

'Busher, come on and we'll go down to the seaside.'

They marched off down the hill to the station. A cab driver's erect whip floated over his shoulder like a single strand of hair. The station was empty; there would not be a train for an hour and five minutes. They were content wandering about the platforms, watching a goods train shunting, its steam blowing about them, or they jumped up and down on the weighing machine, and they played with an idle truck. Their tickets cost tenpence each, which left tenpence for grub. They worked it out that they could spend fourpence on ice cream and sixpence on lemonade, cakes, and sweets. They tried to buy ice cream at the bookstall, but the woman gave them a sour look, pulled her scarf more tightly around her chest, and sold them a packet of cough lozenges for twopence: coffee-coloured things, hexagonal, flat, stamped *Mother Markey's Marvels*. They had a rotten taste, like bad liquorice. They stuck them with a quick suck to the windows of the carriage.

Long before they came within sight of the sea they said they could smell it – cool, damp, deep, salty, spumy, windy, roaring; the big green animal of the sea that opens up long white jaws to swallow you up with a swoosh and a roar, but you always run away from it just in time, jumping on the wet sand, shrieking and laughing, and then you run in after it until another long white mouth curls up its jaws to eat you up and spit you out and you run away shrieking again. In their joy and terror of the millions of long white mouths they climbed on the dusty seats of the carriage, and clawed the glass, and hunched their shoulders and hissed at one another like geese. They clung their cheeks sideways to the windows in order to be, each, the first one to shout, 'I see it!'

When the train stopped they were jolted on to the floor. They scrambled up and out, and galloped ahead of the only two other travellers, who drove off into the town on a sidecar, collars up. When they reached the embankment above the station they were blown back on their heels by the wind. They held on to their caps, coats flapping, bodies bumping, looking at the waves thundering on the groaning gravel, and the dust of the waves in the wind, and every cement-fronted villa boarded up and shiny in the spume and the sun.

'Come on away up to the merry-go-rounds,' he screamed, and they ran for the end of the prom and the hillock beyond it where the roundabouts always stood. All they found was a circle of cinders and big pools of water snaked with petrol. When his cap blew into one of those greasy pools he laughed loudly, and Busher laughed loudly, and for fun threw his own cap into another pool. At that they both laughed like mad.

'Come on away up to the ould Crystal Café,' Busher shouted into his ear, 'and we'll buy the ould lemonade.'

They raced one another around the broken wall and up the steps to the upper road, shoving, falling over one another. In the window of the café was a big yellow-and-black notice: TO LET. A rain squall blasted down on them out of the purple sky. For a while they hugged back into the shelter of the café porch. Then Busher said in a flat voice:

'It's all a blooming suck-in.'

When the rain stopped they went slowly to the big tin shelter beside the railway restaurant; it was wide open to the front so that halfway in across its concrete was wet with the rain. They bought one bottle of lemonade in the restaurant and took it out to the long bench of the shelter, and had every second slug out of the bottle. They got one laugh out of that, when the fizz choked Busher's nose. Every few seconds the tin roofs squeaked above the kettledrums of another downpour. At last Busher said:

'You and your shaggin' ould cough lozenges!'

Calvert did not say anything.

'If we had that tuppence now we could buy a cake.'

Calvert did not reply.

'You and your swimming!' Busher snarled. 'You and your merry-go-rounds! Why didn't you come to *The Bandits of Sherwood Forest* when I asked you?'

Calvert said nothing to that either.

'I'm going home,' said Busher and walked off to the station.

Calvert watched him go away. After a few minutes his heart rose – Busher was coming back.

'There's no train,' Busher started to wail, 'until nine o'clock. There's only two trains a day in the winter.' His wail broke into a shameless bawling. 'You're after getting me into a nice fix. My da will leather hell out of me when he catches me home.'

Calvert looked at him in silence.

'And where did you get that half dollar anyway?' Busher charged. 'I bet you stole it from your ma.'

Calvert told him. Busher stopped snivelling.

'Gawd! Calvert! You're after praying to the divil. You'll be damned for a-a-all E-eturnity!'

And he tore out his railway ticket and flung it in terror on the concrete and ran bawling out into the rain. He ran and ran, down into the streets of the town, where, taking thought in his desperation, he made his way to the bus stop, told a sad yarn to the driver and the conductor, and got carried home, gratis and in good time.

The rain hammered the convex roof; the wind rattled its bones; bits of paper went whispering around the corners like mice; the gutters spilled; the light faded. He heard the drums of the high tide pounding the beach. Twice he went out looking for Busher. He returned each time with his hair plastered down his forehead. At six o'clock the woman in charge of the restaurant came out, locked up, and saw him in the dim corner of the shelter. She came over to him, found him shivering, and told him to take shelter in the waiting room of the station.

Nobody had bothered to light the room. There was nothing there but a pine table, two benches, an empty grate, and a poster showing the Bay of Naples. It was so dark that he saw only the table and the poster whenever the eye of the lighthouse beam from Pitch Point looked in through the misted window. He sat there until nearly nine o'clock, not daring to stir, watching and watching for that peering eye.

When he got home his father rushed at him and shouted at him to know where the blazes he had been, and his mother was crying, but when they saw the cut of him they stopped. His mummy and the maid got a hot bath ready for him before the fire, and his da called him 'old man' and undressed him on the warm hearthrug, and his mummy brought him in hot chocolate, and for the first time that day he suddenly began to cry. As he sat in the hot bath and his mummy soaped him they asked him again what had happened to him, and they were so nice about it that he began to bawl and he told them all about the ould jug. His daddy, first, and then his mummy and the maid burst into peal upon peal of laughter, while he sat there in the hot water, holding his mug of chocolate, bawling at the cruelty of everything and everybody who ever had anything to do with him since the day he was born.

The End of the Record

The news went around the poorhouse that there was a man with a recording van in the grounds. He was picking up old stories and songs.

'And they say that he would give you a five-shilling piece into your hand for two verses of an old song,' said Thomas Hunter, an old man from Coomacoppal, in West Kerry, forgetting that five-shilling pieces were no longer in fashion. 'Or for a story, if you have a good one.'

'What sort of stories would them be?' Michael Kivlehan asked sceptically. He was from the barony of Forth and Bargy, in County Wexford, and had been in the poorhouse for eleven years.

'Any story at all only it is to be an old story and a good story. A story about the fairies, or about ghosts, or about the way people lived long ago.'

'And what do he do with 'um when he have 'um?'

'Hasn't he a phonograph? And doesn't he give them out over the wireless? And doesn't everyone in Ireland be listening to them?'

'I wonder now,' said Michael Kivlehan, 'would he give me five shillings for the "Headless Horseman and the Coacha Bowr"?'

Thomas Hunter sighed.

'One time I had a grand story about Finn MacCool and the Scotch giant. But it is gone from me. And I'd be getting my fine five-shilling piece into my fist this minute if I could only announce it to him.'

The two old men sat on the sides of their beds and tried to remember stories. But it was other things they remembered and they forgot all about the man outside who had set them thinking of their childhood.

The doctor had taken the collector into the women's ward to meet Mary Creegan. She was sitting up in bed, alone in the long room; all the other women were out in the warm sun. As the two men walked up the bare floor the collector was trailing a long black cable from a microphone in his hand, and the doctor was telling him that she came from a place called Faill-a-ghleanna in West Cork.

'She should have lots of stories because her husband was famous for them. After he died she went a bit airy so they had to bring her to us. 'Twas a bit tough on her at first. Sixty years in the one cottage – and then to finish up here.' They stood beside her bed. 'I brought a visitor to see you, Mary,' he said in a loud voice.

She did not appear to see them. She was humming happily to herself. Her bony fingers were wound about an ancient rosary beads. Her white hair floated up above a face as tiny and as wrinkled as a forgotten crab apple. All her teeth were gone so that her face was as broad as it was long: it was as if the midwife had pressed the baby's chin and forehead between thumb and forefinger. The doctor gently laid his hand under the tiny chin and turned her face towards him. She smiled.

'Put down the kettle and wet the tay,' she ordered.

The doctor sat on the bed; so did the collector.

''Tis down, Mary, and two eggs in the pot. This poor man here is after coming a long way to talk to you. He's tired out.'

She turned and looked at the stranger. Encouraged by a brightening spark in the depths of her eyes he turned aside and murmured quietly into the microphone, 'Reggy? Recording ten seconds from . . . now.'

'It's a bad road,' she said. 'Ask Jamesy is he keeping that divil of a cow out of the cabbage.'

'She's all right,' the doctor cried into her ear. 'Jamesy is watching her. Be talking to us while we're waiting for the tay. You told me one time you saw a ghost. Is that true?'

She looked out of the window and her eyes opened and narrowed like a fish's gills as if they were sucking something in from the blue sky outside. The collector stealthily approached her chin with the microphone.

'Ghosts? Ayeh! Ha! My ould divil of a tailor is forever and always talkin' about 'um. But, sure, I wouldn't heed him. Bummin' and boashtin' he is from morning to night and never a needle to be shtuck in the shtuff. Where is he? Why don't you ask him to be talking to you about ghoshts?'

The doctor looked across the bed at the collector and raised his eyebrows.

'Maybe you don't believe in them yourself?' he mocked.

'I do *not* believe in 'um. But they're there. Didn't I hear tell of 'um from them that saw 'um? Aye, and often. And often! Aye' – still collecting her thoughts from the sky above the bakehouse chimney –

'wasn't it that way the night Father Regan died? Huh! They called him Father Regan, but he was not a right priest. He was silenced for some wrong thing he did when he was a young priest, and they sent him to Faill-a-ghleanna to be doing penance for it. When his time came to die it was a bad, shtormy night. And when he sent for the parish priest to hear his confession the priest said he could not come. And that was a hard thing to do, for no man should refuse the dying. And they sent another messenger for the priest, and still the priest could not come. "Oh," said Father Regan, "I'm lost now." So they sent a third messenger. And for the third time the priest could not come. And on his way back wasn't the messenger shtopped on the road by a woman? It was Father Regan's own mother. "Go back," says she, "and if the candles by his bed light up," says she, "of their own accord," says she, "he is saved." And the messenger went back, and Father Regan gave wan look at him and he closed his eyes for the last time. With that all the people went on their knees. And they began to pray. If they did, there were three candles at the head of the dead priest. And didn't the one beside the window light up? And after a little while the candle beside the fire clevy lit up. And they went on praying. And the wind and the shtorm screaming about the house, and they watching the wick of the last candle. And, bit by bit, the way you'd blow up a fire with a bellows, didn't the candle over the priest's head light up until the whole room was like broad daylight.'

The old woman's voice suddenly became bright and hard.

'Isn't that tay ready a-yet? Domn and blosht it, ye'll have them eggs like bullets.' She looked alertly at the two men. 'Where am I? Where's Jamesy? What are ye doing to me?'

The doctor held her wrist. Her eyes faded. She sank back heavily.

'I thought,' she wailed, 'that it was how I saw a great brightness.'

The collector spoke one word into the microphone. The old woman had fainted. Overcome with regrets he began to apologize, but the doctor waved his hand at him.

'Excited. I'll send up the sister to give her an injection. Sometimes she loves to talk about old times. It does her good.'

They went out of the empty ward, the cable trailing softly. They passed the male ward. Michael Kivlehan and Thomas Hunter were sitting on their beds. As the doctor led the way downstairs, he said, 'When that generation goes it will be all over. Wait for me outside. There are a couple more. You might get bits and scraps from them.'

The engineer put his head out of the van and said, in the gloomy voice of all engineers, 'That might come through all right.'

When the doctor came out again they sat with a middle-aged man from Wicklow, named Fenelon. He had been on the roads until arthritis crippled him. When he counted the years he spoke in Urdu. He had scraps of the tinker's language which is called Shelta. He said:

'I often walked from Dublin to Puck, and that's a hundred miles, without ever disturbing anything but a hare or a snipe. I'd make for Ross, and then cross to Callan, and by Slievenamon west to the Galtees.'

He did not see the microphone; he did not see his visitors; as the needle softly cut the disc he was seeing only the mountainy sheep that looked at him with slitted eyes, a thing as shaggy as themselves.

They moved on to an old woman who sang a love song for them in a cracked voice. She said she had learned it in Chicago. She gave them a poem of twelve verses about a voyage to the South Seas. They were finishing a disc with a very old man from Carlow when the sister came out and hastily beckoned to the doctor. As they folded up the cable he came back. He said, with a slow shake of the head:

'It's old Mary. I must leave ye. But ye have the best of them. The rest is only the shakings of the bag.'

When they had thanked him and were driving away, the collector said, eagerly:

'Pull up when we're out of the town. I want to play back those discs.'

They circled up and out of the town until its murmur was so faint that they could hear only the loudest cries of the playing children. There they played back the discs, and as they leaned towards the loud-speaker and the black record circled smoothly they could see, sideways through the window, the smoke of the hollow town. The last voice was Mary Creegan's.

' ... *and after a little while the candle beside the fire clevy lit up. And they went on praying. And the wind and the shtorm screaming about the house, and they watching the wick of the last candle. And, bit by bit, the way you'd blow up a fire with a bellows, didn't the candle over the priest's head light up until the whole room was like broad daylight.* ... *Isn't that tay ready a-yet? Domn and blosht it, ye'll have them eggs like bullets.* ... *Where am I? Where's Jamesy? What are ye doing to me?* ... *I thought that it was how I saw a great brightness.*'

The listeners relaxed. Then from the record came a low, lonely cry. It was the fluting of a bittern over moorland. It fluted sadly once again, farther away; and for a third time, almost too faint to be heard. Many times the two men played back those last few inches of disc. Every time they heard the bittern wailing over the mountains.

It was dusk. They laid the voices in a black box and drove away. Then they topped the hill, and the antennae of their headlamps began to probe the winding descent to the next valley.

Lord and Master

Every time Master Kennedy and his wife passed the gates of Carews-court House, and the round little gate lodge and smooth pond, he said that when he retired he would rent that cottage. The summer he retired he did rent it. He was sad that his wife had not lived to share it with him, but he was as happy, otherwise, as a Chinese philosopher, with his books, and his cat, and his tiny garden with its four standard roses, its six gooseberry bushes and its single pear tree.

Around Christmas he fell ill with a cold that nearly finished him, and it was as he lay in bed that he first noticed the patches of damp on the walls. He did not pay much attention until February, when his foot went through the floor of the front room and his boot sole came up green with mildew. He took his stick, put on his hat, and sought out Paddy Markham, the mason, whom he found plastering the base of the wall of Neville's pub in the Main Street.

'Paddy,' he said, 'I have a little job for you.'

Paddy had a hump and a squint and was half the height of the teacher. He had the trowel in one hand and the hawk in the other, and as he listened he kept mixing the bit of mortar on the hawk with the point of the trowel. In the end he chucked the trowel into the mortar and looked up at his old teacher.

'Masther! I'll tell you no lie. I've been tinkerin' with that ould cottage for the last thirty-five years. I made people spend hundreds of pounds on the cottage trying to get the damp out of it. And,' he said triumphantly, 'it's as soppin' as if they never spent a penny on it. I put a damp course under it. I waterproofed it. I plastered it with Pluvex and Supex and Pudlo and Cudlo and Dudlo and the divil knows whato. And you might as well be tryin' to plaster up th' Atlantic Ocean. Oh, mind you,' Paddy went on comfortingly as the master stared down gloomily at his enthusiastic, stupid face, 'It's a nate little house. The house is all right. 'Tis well built, 'tis solid as the Rock o'Gibraltar. But there's wan thing wrong with it.'

'And what the devil is that, pray?'

''Tis the pond that you have in front of you that's seeping onderneath your foundations. There'll be days, Masther, and if you were to take up a floor board in the front room you'd find a lake of wather onderneath it!'

'Oh, well, in that case,' cried the master happily, 'all I have to do is get rid of the pond!'

Paddy cocked his quizzical crooked eye up at him.

'How?' he asked.

'Where does the water in the pond come from?'

Paddy drew back and looked sideways at him.

'It comes in a stream from the big lake in front of Carewscourt House, where else? Or are you coddin' me? As if you didn't know! Do you mean to say you don't know the ould gully with the wooden dam beside Beechmount crossroads? Sure all the water in the town comes down there. Down through the channel from the River Villy that the Carews cut hundreds and hundreds of years ago.'

The master touched his beard.

'And flows into their lake? And out of the lake into my pond? And from my pond in front of all the cottages? And from . . .'

He stopped. He saw a small boy throwing stones into the stream that runs down the middle of the main street of Rathvilly between two low walls and two lines of lime trees. The child stood on the far pavement, which is three steps above the street on that side. The master looked down at the base of the wall that Paddy had been plastering.

'Then that stream must be seeping under every shop along this side of the street? And under every cottage back along the road? As well as under my cottage?'

'To be sure it does,' the mason agreed placidly.

'Then I have no job at all for you, Paddy. The County Council must wall up the dam at Beechmount crossroads.'

And off with the Master back down the street, past the last line of cabins, each with its own little wooden bridge, to his cottage by the pond. There he sat down and wrote a long letter to the secretary of the County Council requesting that the dam at Beechmount be permanently closed.

'But sure, my dear Michael,' laughed the county engineer, Corny Cosgrave, when he called on the master (who had taught him his first pothooks in the national school), 'if we did what you want us to do we'd dry up the bloody lake in Carewscourt.'

'And why not, Cornelius?' the master asked calmly.

'But, it's *their* lake!'

'Is that a fact, Cornelius?' The master smiled patiently. 'And who gave them the right, Cornelius, to deflect the water to make the lake? Did they ask permission of the town of Rathvilly to make the lake? Did they get permission from the County Council to make the lake?'

'You know damn well,' cried Corny testily, 'that there was no such a thing as asking permission in those days. Are ye daft? Sure, if there was even such a thing as a County Council in those days they *were* the County Council. And as for asking permission from the town, sure they made, owned, and ran the bloody town.'

'And do they still own the town, Cornelius?' asked the master, glaring at his pupil like Moses at a backsliding Israelite. 'Is this all our much-vaunted liberty has brought us? You,' persisted the master, in his slow Biblical voice, 'were one of the first young men in this county to take up arms for the independence of your country. You fought...'

Corny held the master's arm.

'Look, Master! For God's sake, leave politics out of this. You'd drag politics into the sale of a wheelbarrow. This question is not a political question. It is a legal question.'

'And is the law of Ireland,' asked the master fiercely, 'for the Saxon or is it for the Gael?'

'The law,' said Cornelius, throwing his arms as wide as possible as if to throw the whole matter as far away from himself as possible, 'is for everybody. Rich and poor. Gentle and simple. Christian and Jew. Young and old. Male and female. Without the slightest distinction of class *or* creed.'

The master smiled at his pupil. Then, as if he had a cane behind his back and was saying, 'Kindly tell me what is the capital of Arakan,' he said:

'Kindly tell me, Cornelius, what is the law in this matter?'

'That will be for the courts to decide.'

At that the master let such a roar out of him that Corny, from old habit, half raised a protective arm.

'So!' the master cried. 'Your decision is that I must go behind the County Council to the courts?'

Corny saw that he had fallen into a trap.

'Now! Now! Don't take me up on a word! How do I know what the council will decide to do?'

'You know damn well that you've decided already what you're going to tell them to do!'

Corny took the master by the arm again. He spoke like a fluting pigeon to him.

'Listen to me, Mr Kennedy.' (The old man did not fail to notice the change from 'My dear Michael' to 'Master' and from 'Master' to 'Mister,' together with the increasing amiability.) 'You and I were old campaigners together. You were a Fenian, and the son of a Fenian. You were the first man to open my eyes to the true facts of the national question. Sure, the way you taught Irish history was a marvel! A positive marvel! And you know that I'm as sound an Irishman as you'll get in the four quarters of Ireland. You know me. I know you. And the two of us understand one another's lingo. But what you forget, and a lot of other people forget, and I say this, now, with the greatest respect for you and in the highest possible regard, is that the people of Ireland can't be going back over old sores forever and ever. There are such things, you know, as what they call *fate accomplee*.' He slapped the master on the shoulder as if it were he who was the ex-teacher and the master the ex-pupil. 'I often heard of people wanting to turn back the clock, but this is the first time I heard of a man wanting to turn back a blooming river!'

The master listened sourly to his peals of laughter.

'Are you telling me, Mr Cosgrave, that you're not able to dam a little stream no bigger than a dog's piddle for the sake of the health of your own town?'

'My dear sir, give me one man with a shovel and I'll do it for you in five minutes.'

'Then why don't you do it in five minutes?'

'Because, dammit, certain people have certain rights, and that's why.'

'It's not by any chance because certain people are afraid oï certain people, and that's why?'

Corny went pink. He seized his hat.

'I will make my report directly to the County Council,' he said coldly. He paused at the door. 'You were always a cantankerous ould divil.'

'And,' the master shouted after him, 'I never gave you enough of the stick on your backside when I had you!'

The clang of the motor-car door and the bang of the cottage door were simultaneous.

Within a week the master's pond had the whole town turned upside down. If a child's cap blew into the stream in the middle of the street, or if he got his feet wet beside the cottages, or if a woman as much as sneezed, or if some old fellow who had never done a day's work in his life got a twinge of rheumatism, somebody would start cursing the stream. He might even strike an attitude and say, 'Is it for this we bled and died?' There was nothing that couldn't be and wasn't connected with the stream. When the price of coal went up, somebody was heard to say:

'And timber galore in the demesne! How fair they wouldn't give it out to the poor? Oho no! All they ever gave us to warm us was their dirty ould wather!'

It wasn't only the Carews. Their relations all over the county came in for it, the Eustaces, the Brodricks, the Connollys, and the Suttons, until, as one of the opposition said, you'd think the stream had as many tributaries as the Ganges. And then there was an ex-soldier who told a whole pub how he once met an Englishman in Burma who said, 'Rathvilly? Isn't that the place where the river runs down the middle of the street?' Hammering the counter this traveller shouted, 'Are we to deshtroy a shtrame that have us made famous the world over?'

'I agree,' the doctor said in the lounge of the Royal Hibernian Hotel, 'that, ideally, the stream ought to be closed. But you know very well that if you close up the stream they'll simply throw their rubbish into the street. And if you block up the stream the cottages will have no running water to wash their clothes in.'

Nobody said anything to that. But the vet winked at the ceiling. They all knew that the doctor attended the Carews.

'Aesthetically speaking,' said the bank clerk, 'it would be a pity to dry up the stream. It's a very pleasant feature in the town. I grant you there's a bit of a niff off it in the summer, but . . .'

'Am I wrong,' the town's cryptosocialist said, 'in thinking that your bank handles the Carews' account?'

'Aha!' from the bank clerk. 'There's Russia talking! You don't mind having your own sister working as a parlourmaid in Carewscourt?'

'A perfect example,' the cryptosocialist cried, 'of the evil network of feudalism.'

'Why the hell's blazes,' said John Jo Sullivan, who owned the garage, and used to be a commandant of the I.R.A. thirty-two years ago, before he got paunchy and balding, 'don't we go out some night and settle the whole bloody thing with one good stick o' dynamite under the ould dam?'

'Well, why don't you, John Jo?' smiled the inspector of the guards, who used to be John Jo's adjutant in those good old days when every question was 'settled with one good stick of dynamite.'

'Because I don't trust you, you bastard,' said John Jo bitterly.

'There was a time when you'd have taken a chance, John Jo,' said the inspector easily. And he added, by way of no harm, from the depths of his armchair, 'By the way, did Carew order that new Humber Hawk from you yet?'

The master thus found support on all sides.

He was all the more dumbfounded when he got a letter a week later from Corny Cosgrave saying that 'in view of the enclosed document no action can be taken in the matter until the next meeting of the County Council.' The document was 'A Grand Petition,' pleading for the preservation of the stream, signed by 279 out of Rathvilly's total of 395 inhabitants. When he had read down the list of names he hurled the paper on the floor and cursed Rathvilly, man, woman, and child, lock, stock, and barrel, back to their seventy-seven generations, for a pack of cowards, liars, and cringing slaves.

Not that he did not know perfectly well the pressure that lay behind every signature on the list. The first name on it was Paddy Markham's. Paddy's brother worked in the Carewscourt sawmills. Every shopkeeper in the town was there: which meant that the Carews owed hundreds of pounds all over the place, and everybody knows there is only one way to treat creditors and that is to make them hop or they'll walk on you. As he examined the list he could find only two names that had not been extracted by force: they were two old women who, to his knowledge, were dead and buried for at least three years. When he saw the two names the master cursed Rathvilly more bitterly than ever.

'My god!' he ground out. 'All we've taught the Carews is how to beat us at our own game!'

It was three weeks to the next meeting of the council. He spent every day of it canvassing the members. Not one man of them refused him support, none promised it. What maddened him above all was the way somebody who had signed the 'Grand Petition' would accost him and congratulate him on the fight he was making.

'But,' he would say coldly, 'your own name is on the petition, signed there in black and white!'

The man would say something like:

'Yerrah, Master, what signify that? Sure all I told them was to throw me name on the ould paper if it gave them any satisfaction. I can assure you, Master, that I'm *one hundred per cent* with you for getting rid of that old stream. 'Tis destroying the health of the town. Fight them, Master! We're behind you to the last ditch.'

At the next meeting of the council he sat at the rear of the room. To his delight one man stood up to support him. He was the Labour member.

'I maintain, Mr Chairman,' the Labour member declared, 'that it would be a most progressive action, which, as well as giving much-needed employment to the town and borough, would benefit the health and sanitation of the working classes, if it was a thing that the stream at present pursuing its noxious course through the main street was to be filled up. It would, for one thing, widen the street.'

'That's right,' put in the Ratepayers' member. 'The unemployed could park their motor cars there.'

'That,' shouted the Labour member, 'is an unworthy remark, but no more than I would expect from the low quarter from whence it came.'

'Your own brother,' shouted the Ratepayers' member, 'signed the petition for to keep it.'

'The brother,' roared the Labour member, 'is as good an Irishman as anybody in this room. And he was never before the courts for keeping his pub open after hours!'

'No, nor for poaching salmon either, I suppose?' taunted the Ratepayers' member.

The chairman banged the table for three solid minutes, during which the two speakers investigated the history of their respective families between the years 1810 and 1952.

'May I ask,' he said, when he had restored order, 'where the sewage would go if we were to fill up the stream?'

'That, Mr Chairman,' declared the Labour member, 'is the whole point. It is high time that the sewage system of this town was put into a proper condition.'

'Aha!' the Farmers' member shouted. 'Now we're getting at it! And your own uncle a contractor!'

This time it took the chairman five minutes to restore order. He gave the floor to John Jo Sullivan, who, they all knew, was going to stand at the next general election for the Dail.

'Mr Chairman,' John Jo said, 'I do not think that I need to make any excuses for what I am going to say here today. I do not think I need to blow my own trumpet. I have no wish nor desire to boast of my national record, nor of those far-off days when Ireland lit a torch that shone around the world. Be that as it may, today, thanks be to God, we have a free country (all but the six northern counties, I hasten to say) in which every man is guaranteed his rights under a free constitution, equally approved by church and state. We have a country, moreover, where any man who may have any doubts as to his rights can have free recourse to the courts of law, where all such little disputes can be amicably settled in honesty and in friendship. Our people,' he intoned, 'have made themselves – and our dear little island – famous all over the world for their long fight down the ages for liberty, and for Christianity. In these dark and troubled days, Mr Chairman, that surround us, with the spectres of war . . .'

At the rear of the room the master rose and walked out so quietly that nobody noticed his going. On his way home he almost admired Carew. Outnumbered four hundred to one he could still keep the rabble under his heels.

On the next morning he went into Limerick city to a solicitor. The solicitor listened to him patiently. Then he said, in the sad, tired voice of a man who is sick to death of all litigation:

'I'm afraid, Mr Kennedy, you have a case. I'm sorry to say I think you have a case.'

'Afraid? Sorry? What do you mean?'

'I mean that you'll go ahead with it. And you won't win it. I know Carew, Mr Kennedy. He is a determined man. If you beat him in the lower courts he'll take you up to the Four Courts, and he won't stop until he ruins you. And if you should, by some miracle, beat him in law he won't stop until he runs you out of the town. He'll fight you to the last ditch, and beyond it. And I must confess, Mr Kennedy, I don't blame him.'

The master rose in his chair.

'That's queer kind of talk to be going on with to your own client. Are you on his side or are you on mine?'

'Sit down there and listen to me! I'm not on his side. But I can put myself in his position. And if you could do the same you'd see that if you were Lord Carew you'd do to him exactly what he is doing to you. Tell the truth, Mr Kennedy. If somebody tried to take away from you something that you and your people had owned for going on two hundred and fifty years, something that you'd looked at every day of your life, ever since you were a boy, something that all your memories were wrapped up in, and your father's and your mother's before you, and back behind them for the seven generations – something you were very, very fond of, Mr Kennedy – wouldn't you fight that man down to the last brass farthing you possessed?'

The master scattered the air with his hands.

'There's no sense nor meaning to this kind of talk! I'm not interested in hypotheses. I'm not Lord Carew, and I don't want to be Lord Carew, and I know nothing about Lord Carew, but I know this, that if I *was* Lord Carew and I wanted to make a lake in front of my house I hope I'd do it some other way than by draining my dirty water past every cottage between my front gate and the gable wall of the chapel.' The old man leaned halfway over the desk. His voice rose. 'If I wanted to make a lake this minute in front of *my* house would I be allowed to run away with half the river to do it? They stole the river!' he shouted. 'They stole the river, and if there's justice in the country they should be made to give it back to the people that owns it. Lord Carew? How could I be ... ' He laughed derisively. 'Do you know,' he ground out hatefully, 'what the Carews did to Rathvilly during the Rebellion of 1798? Do you know that...'

The solicitor listened wearily. When the old man sank back, panting and trembling, he said:

'Very well. You evidently feel strongly about it. And if your mind is made up, your mind is made up. But I warn you that it's going to leave a blister on you to the end of your days. It would be far cheaper for you to leave the cottage altogether.'

'I will *not* leave the cottage. Ever since my wife, God rest her, saw that cottage twenty-five years ago she wanted me to have it. I put the best part of my life's savings into furnishing that cottage. I love the cottage.'

'So be it.'

The master calmed down.

'Why have I a case?'

'If the water is damaging your property somebody must be liable.'

'Good.'

'Mind you, it may not be Carew. It may be the County Council.'

'It *is* Carew. And I'll get him.'

'But Carew will get at the council, you know.'

'How?'

The solicitor parted the air gently with his hands.

All the way back in the train the old teacher kept remembering that gesture. It reminded him of the priest at Mass turning to the people to say *Dominus vobiscum*. He kept murmuring the words to the wet, wheeling fields. They recurred to him many times during the following days, which he spent, often late into the night, writing appealing letters to everybody of position whom he had ever even slightly known. During those nights when he would hear nothing but the swish of the willow outside, or an occasional car driving fast through the town, it seemed to him that, in some way, his desire to go on living in his cottage was linked with his wife's desire to possess it, and that those words, *Dominus vobiscum*, were words of encouragement from her to him. He would seize a new sheet then, and write another long angry letter, to a member of the Dail, to a priest, or to the bishop. He even wrote to the President of Eire. To not one of these letters did he ever receive a reply.

The lawyers were writing more letters. His solicitor quoted against the council a statute from the reign of King John about public waterways. The council's solicitor countered that the lake and its tributaries were Lord Carew's private property. The master's solicitor quoted this against Carew's solicitors. Carew's solicitors replied that they acknowledged responsibility as for the lake, but that once the stream left the demesne it became the public property of the people of Rathvilly. They were sparring all the winter.

Then one afternoon, in late April, the words *Dominus vobiscum* suddenly came to the master with a new meaning. As he murmured the words he looked out of his window. He saw a rainbow that seemed to leap directly from his pond across the sky to the spire on Chapel Hill, and he heard his wife's voice saying, as she had so often said, 'Ah, wisha, Patrick, why do you be always growling against the Church? 'Tis our only friend.' He took his hat and stick and stumped down into the town, and up Chapel Hill to the presbytery. Painfully he climbed the long steps. Puffed, he pulled the china handle of the bell and asked the housekeeper for the monsignor. She put him to wait in the small side parlour.

As he stood and looked over the woven reed of the half screen across the smoky thatch of the little town he saw something he had not noticed before: a big motor car below at the presbytery gate. It was the Carewscourt car.

At the same moment, across the hall, he became aware of a murmur of voices and the sound of somebody laughing. He opened his door a crack. It was the delicate laugh of the monsignor, and he could imagine the dainty little figure, the white hair, the rosy cheeks, the jigging hand, and the touches of red on his vest and his biretta. He felt his heart thrusting against his breastbones. The blood pumped up under his eyes. He crossed the hall and flung open the parlour door. There was Lord Carew, as sallow as an old spoon, long-faced, smiling; and the monsignor seated opposite him, with his pale-pink hand on the big ordnance map spread on the plush-covered table between them. The master lashed the table with his stick so that the papers flew.

'I knew it,' the old man whispered, glaring from one astonished face to the other. 'For forty-five years,' he gasped, 'I've taught in this town, and my poor wife with me. I served you' – he pointed his trembling stick at the monsignor – 'since I was a boy serving Mass at the altar, and now I find you conspiring against me with the gentry!' The monsignor had risen, fluttering his two palms. 'I hoped,' the master sobbed, 'I hoped to find the Church on my side and on the side of my poor wife. But the Church is against us! As the Church was always against us. Against the Fenians. The men of forty-eight. Parnell. Sinn Fein. In the fight for the Republic....'

At that he collapsed. After they had partly revived him, they helped him out between them, down the long steps, and into Carew's car. The cries of the children at play did not pause.

On the way, Carew remembered that the old chap lived alone and instead of pausing at the lodge gates he went on into the avenue to his own front steps. There the butler, hearing him come, was already waiting to open the door of the car. By this time the master had recovered. He looked out at the butler, an old pupil of his, one Timsy Twomey, realized where he was, and scrambled out in angry disdain.

'You'd better have a brandy, Mr Kennedy,' Carew suggested and nodded to Twomey.

'I want nothing from you but the one thing,' the master began haughtily, 'and that . . .'

He stopped. Behind the haze of fishing flies on Carew's tweed hat he saw an oblong sheet of water burning below its low granite coping, fiery in the sun that was sinking between a rosy scallop of clouds and the flowing hills of Villy, now as hard as jewels in the cold April air. Its long smooth glow was broken only by a row of cypresses at its far end, the reflection of whose black plumes plunged into the burning pool to spear the light again. Beneath them were two wrestling Tritons from whose mouths two fountains rose, and crossed and fell with a soft splash. Carew watched the old man's eyes for a moment or two. They were a play of astonishment, delight, and hate.

'Well, Mr Kennedy, there's the cause of it all. And you're looking at it, I think, for the first time? And, probably, for the last time.'

The master looked quickly at him, arrested by his tone.

'I mean,' Carew said, with a little crooked smile on his long sallow face, 'the lake is going to be drained.'

'You're closing the dam?' the master asked, unbelievingly, and looked back at the water which, already, was growing dark and cold.

'You may as well know, if it gives you any pleasure, I'm selling Carewscourt. I've sold it to a teaching order of nuns. Good teachers, I believe. Or so the monsignor tells me. One of the first things they're going to do is to drain the lake. And I'm not much surprised, for it has damn near drained me.'

And he began to explain how badly it had been constructed, with somebody always having to empty it and mend the bottom, or grout the sides, or repair the plumbing of the fountain, or dredge the channels down through the town.

'The sisters are going to plant a sunken garden in it. I'm sorry, but . . . Oh, well! They haven't sat here of summer evenings as I have, watching the sun go down.'

The splash of the fountains had become more distinct. The hills were dark when Twomey opened the glass doors behind them, and stood waiting for his old teacher.

'It'll be a hard frost tonight,' said Carew. 'Do come in. We use the hall now for a dining room,' he said, and he and the master went up the three shallow steps into the house. Twomey held out the glasses on a salver. Each took one. 'I've emptied nearly every room in the house,' Carew said. 'I'll sell everything except those books.'

They walked across the hall to the big bookcase. The master looked into them with interest.

'Mostly Irish books,' Carew said. 'Family history. I'll keep these.'

'And where,' asked the master, speaking for the first time since he asked who would dam the lake, 'where are you going to live, Lord Carew?'

Carew tapped his chest.

'I haven't long to run.' He drained his brandy. 'Can I drive you as far as the gates?'

It took the master a long time to reply. Then he said:

'Thank you. I'd be obliged to you.'

They drove circuitously, around the far end of the lake. There Carew halted the car for a few seconds to look. One star shone greenly in the water. At the far end the hallway made a brief dagger of light. The house rose square, and straight and clear-cut in the last of the sun.

'It is a fine house,' said the master grudgingly.

'It was,' said Carew.

They drove on over the gravel to the gates, the cottage, and the pool.

'Good night, Mr Kennedy. Take care of yourself.'

'Good night, Lord Carew. I suppose the sisters will want this cottage?'

Carew lifted an uncertain hand, meshed his gears, drove away.

When the car lights vanished down the road the master walked towards his cottage. In his willow pool he saw the evening star. He stood looking at it for a long time, serene in the water. As he looked it began to fade. Clouds were coming across the sky. It gleamed again, more brilliantly than before. Then it went out.

He went into his cottage and closed the door. From where he sat inside he could hear the willow whispering to the water and the wall. He would miss his little pool.

An Enduring Friendship

When Georgie Canty saw Louis Golden at the customs counter of the airport he muttered 'Bastard!' under his breath: which was what he hoped most people in Ireland thought of Mr Louis Bloody Well Golden, editor of the *Daily Crucifix*, 'Ireland's One and Only Catholic Daily' – and one too many at that!

Georgie's eyes closed, his mouth zipped tight. His duodenum walked slowly all round his waist with spiked boots. It stuck a redhot sword in through his navel. It pulled his liver out through his ribs. His eyes closed in agony. . . .

He lifted his lids and his eyes swivelled down the counter length at Golden – at his long neck like a heron, his little rabbit's puss with the two white teeth like a nutria, the hunched shoulders of a constipated stork, and the same soapy grin for the customs officer that he probably switched on whenever he'd be talking to a bishop. As he looked at him Georgie wondered if there ever had been a plane crash in which everybody was saved, except one man.

That night at the United Bankers! With himself and Golden, two of a platform of four, debating the motion *That the Irish Are the Most Tolerant Race in the World*. Three sentences. Three not too lengthy sentences about how silly it is for Irishmen to be chasing Freemasons as if they had four horns and two tails; and there he was, the next morning, crucified in the *Crucifix* under a three-column headline – BANKERS DEFEND MASONS – and, on page four, a leading article entitled, 'So This Is Holy Ireland?' signed *Louis Paul Golden*. Naturally he was barely inside the door of the bank before he was called into the parlour.

'I understand, Mr Canty,' old Plummer smiled at him across the carpet with teeth that would clip a hedge, 'I understand that you saw fit to defend Freemasonry in public last night? Is that correct?'

Now, of course every man in the bank knows perfectly well that there isn't a month that old Plumtree Gum doesn't toddle off to the Masonic

Hall with his little apron and all the rest of his regalia; and, for all anybody knows, he might be the great Mah Jong of Molesworth Street, he might be the Prince Mason of the Western World. So, what could Georgie do but rub his palms, smile a man-of-the-world smile, and utter these famous last words:

'Irishmen are in many ways absurd . . .'

They heard Plummer's roar outside in the Foreign Exchange Department. After that it was ding-dong bell for five minutes . . . . Who – would somebody please, *please*, tell him – who ever asked anybody to defend anybody in private or in public? And if, by any possible chance, however remote, anybody ever did happen to require the kind services of anybody why should anybody think that *his* brilliant services were what was specifically demanded by the occasion? And, furthermore, there were people in this city who were very well equipped to defend themselves for themselves. And, furthermore, he himself had lived in this city for fifty-odd years and he had never made any secret of the fact that he was a member of the Worshipful Grand Order, and if he was ever required to defend himself he could do it very well indeed thank you without anybody's assistance! And, further- more, and especially, he would be greatly obliged if people would have the goodness to remember that their job, first, foremost, and before all, was to consider the interests of the institution that paid them and made them, which would be a jolly sight better thing for all concerned than to be going out and opening their bloody gobs to make roaring asses of themselves in the bloody press, and he would be infinitely obliged to Mr Canty if he would remember *that*. And furthermore . . .

Not a peep out of Georgie. He sat dumb as a goldfish until he heard the voice of God Almighty bidding him good morning in a voice like a hangman's chaplain, followed by the words: 'I will consider later, Mr Canty, what disciplinary action may be most appropriate to the occasion.' As Georgie walked back over the two and a half miles of marble floor to his cubbyhole not a sound was heard, not a funeral note, except for some scut softly whistling 'Will Ye No' Come Back Again?' He had not done much work in his cubbyhole that day, waiting to be packed off to some back-of-beyond like Killorglin or Cahirciveen. After six weeks without one good night's sleep, he had applied for a week's leave of absence, on a doctor's certificate.

The loud-speaker retailed a female voice in Irish, of which he understood only the word *Gurrabbulluballoo*, which means, 'Thanks.'

He opened his eyes to see the queue trailing out. He was the last man on the plane. He took the last seat. He found himself sitting beside the last man in the world he had wanted to see again. Their safety belts got entangled. Golden looked up and at once shot out his paw.

'Georgie Canty, for all the world! Well, isn't this the real McCoy! This is great luck.'

Georgie shook his hand warmly.

'Louis Golden. Well, I'm delighted, simply delighted to see you. Travelling far?'

'Let me help you with that belt,' said Golden, and he tucked Canty in like a baby in its pram. Then he patted his thigh. 'How's tricks? I heard you weren't too well.'

'Not bad, not bad. And yourself? And the missus? All the care doing well?'

As they roared down the runway for the take-off Golden blessed himself piously. Canty thought it just as well to do a fiddle, also, around his third vest button.

'I suppose,' he said presently, trying to suggest (but only suggest) a faint sneer, 'you're off to some ecclesiastical conference?'

Golden leaned over with a confidential, crooked grin and nudged Canty.

'Mattherofact, d'ye know what I was doing the last time I was in Paris? I was touring an Australian Jesuit around the night clubs. He was very agreeably surprised.'

'In which sense?' asked Georgie, modulating between innocence and insinuation. Golden only laughed and waved a tolerant claw.

'Harmless. A bit of leg. Nothing more. The usual routine. We did about five or six of them. Folies Bergère. Bal Tabarin. Chin-Chin. Eve. The Blue Angel. Nothing at all to it.'

Georgie squinted sideways at him, thinking of the moths in the Bal Tabarin coming out in the altogether.

'Did *you* approve?' he inquired.

'It's not a question of approving.' When he said 'question' his two white teeth went bare. 'It's all a matter of atmosphere. When in Rome, and so on.'

He grabbed the hostess by the hip and ordered two double brandies. This, mind you, at nine-thirty in the morning!

'Morals,' he explained to Georgie, 'morals in the sense of *mores* are always affected by time and place. For example, would you walk down

O'Connell Street in the middle of the noonday with nothing on but a Lastex slip?'

'The Guards'd have me in the Bridewell in two ticks.'

'There was a fella walked down the Rue Royale last year with nothin'' at all on. He was only fined five francs. Betty Grable could walk down the beach at Biarritz in a G-string and a smile and nobody would look twice at her.'

The brandy was going to Georgie's head. He leaned over and laughed.

'I believe Lady Godiva rode down Broadway wan time in her skin and everybody ran out in wild excitement to see the white horse. But if that be so what's this I hear about the bishops not wanting to see girls wearing cycling shorts?'

'Who would?' cackled Golden, and they went hard at it.

They were still arguing the toss over the Channel, and whether it was the six double brandies, or the elevating sensation of being up in the air, Georgie began, in spite of himself, to find the little runt almost bearable. It was not until the Eiffel Tower appeared out of the smoke that he brought down the question of Freemasons.

'You knew blooming well that night that I wasn't defending Freemasonry. But in spite of that, you bastard, you came out in your rotten rag and tore the guts out of me.'

'Editorial policy.' Blandly.

'Do you realize that you nearly cost me my job?' And he told him all about it.

'Ah! No!' cried Louis, genuinely distressed. 'For God's sake! Is that true? Well, now, doesn't that show ye what Freemasons are!'

All the same he stuck to his guns. Georgie had to grant him that he stuck to his guns.

They were still at it as they whirled around the Undying Flame in the bus; and as Georgie had not booked a hotel he went off with Louis; and by the time they were finishing lunch, and two bottles of Nuits Saint Georges, they had arrived at the Arian heresy – about which they both knew sweet damn-all – and were still at Homoiousian and Homoousian at half past four in front of two Otards and the Café de Paris in the blazing sun.

'Now, look, Louis, you flaming scoundrel,' Georgie was saying, 'your trouble is you're a moralist. All you want is an autocratic, oligarchic church laying down the law about everything from cremation to contraceptives. You're a Puritan! That's what you are!'

Louis leaned a gentle hand on Georgie's arm and breathed on him like a father confessor.

'Georgie! I'll tell you something. Here in Paris. As bloke to bloke. I have exactly the same pashuns as you have. But I *know* me pashuns! I *know* them – and they're dynamite! And what's more, the pashuns of every Irishman are dynamite! And double dynamite! And triple dynamite! And if the priests of Ireland are hard on their own people, it's because they know that if they once took the lid off the pashuns of Irish men and Irish women, ayé and of Irish children, the country would *blow up*! Look at Saint Paul!'

Georgie looked and saw a smashing blonde. Louis dragged him ashore, and the pair of them took Saint Paul down to the Rue Donau where Golden knew a little bar called, of all things, *Le Crucifix*; and then they took Saint Augustine, who was a bloke Georgie said he never liked – and he didn't care *who* knew it! – across to a bar on the Quatre Septembre where they had four flat Guinnesses for ould Ireland's sake; and then they took the Manichees, and the Jansenists, and Pascal, up to the bar at the Gare du Nord; and then they went up to Sacré Coeur to say a prayer, and lean on the balustrade, and Louis explained all about Modernism to Georgie, and Georgie said it was his cup of tea, and to hell with the Council of Trent anyway for jiggering up everything; and then they had dinner near the old Pigalle, with two more bottles of Nuits Saint Georges; and then nothing would do Louis but to prove he wasn't a Puritan by going off to the Bal Tabarin, where they had two bottles of *champagne obligatoire* at three thousand francs a nose.

All Georgie could remember after that was seeing twelve girls coming out on the platform, with about as much on them, if it was all sewn together, as would make a fair-sized loincloth for one Zulu, and telling Louis, with his arm out to the twelve girls:

'There y'are! Janshenist'd shay thatsh shinful! And you – and you're a fellow I never liked, and I don't care what you think! – *you* agree with them!'

'No! Exhplain to ye! Nothing that God made is shinful. Couldn't be. Shin is in us. Those girls aren't even an occashun of shin. And why? 'Cos they don't bother us.'

'Bother me,' said Georgie. 'Bother me a helluva lot. That little wan with the green hair would bother Saint Augustine!'

'God's truth?' asked Louis.

'Struth,' said Georgie.

'Come on out,' said Louis, getting up.

'Sit down,' shouted Georgie, dragging him back.

'C'mout,' said Louis, getting up again.

'Down!' shouts Georgie, hauling him down again.

'Out!' shouts Louis.

'Be quiet!' shouts everybody, and your two men began to shout at everybody else, and to fight one another, and a table gets knocked over, and champagne gets spilled on a girl's dress, and the twelve girls pay no attention at all, only kicking away up in the air like galvanized geese, and the two of them get hauled out and slung out on their backs on the pavement. Like one man they rush back. Like one man they get slung out again. At that they get up and they look into one another's faces, their noses one inch apart.

'You dirty little Freemason!' says Golden, baring his two teeth, and his lips glistening in the moonlight.

'You rotten little Puritan!' says Georgie with the hate of hell in his voice.

At that the two of them stopped dead as if they were a pair of waxworks out of the Musée Grevin, horrified by the sight of the hate in one another's faces. They were so horrified that they burst into a wild fit of laughing. They rocked there in one another's arms, falling over one another with the bitterness of the laughing and the hatred and the shame.

A taxi drew up beside them. They tumbled into it. And the next place they were was in the square in front of Nôtre Dame because Georgie said he wanted to see if the moon could laugh at them as much as it laughed at the gargoyles. The square was empty – it was after one in the morning. The two of them linked arms and began to stroll along the river singing the saddest Irish dirges they knew. Georgie used to say afterwards that he often thought of the poor women inside in the Hôtel Dieu enduring the pangs of childbirth while the two of them were bawling away about their Wild Irish Rose, and wouldn't she come home again, Kathl-e-e-en!

For the rest of the week they were inseparable.

When Georgie and Louis meet nowadays in the street, they always greet one another warmly. They ask after one another's health. They send their regards to one another's wives. If a companion asks either of them, 'Who was that?' he will say the name, add, 'Not a bad sort of chap,' and feel the shame of that night burning in him all over again. For, of course, the truth of the whole matter is that once you go on a drunk with a fellow you're stuck with him for life; and in Ireland every bitter word we say has to be paid for sooner or later in shame, in pity, in kindness, and perhaps even in some queer sort of perverted love.

I Remember! I Remember!

I believe that in every decisive moment of our lives the spur to action comes from that part of the memory where desire lies dozing, awaiting the call to arms. We say to ourselves, 'Now I have decided to do so-and-so,' and straightway we remember that for years and years we have been wanting to do this very thing. There it is, already fully created, clear on the horizon, our longed-for island, its palm tree waving, its white hut gleaming, a brown figure standing on the beach, smiling patiently.

I am remembering Sarah Cotter and her infallible memory. If she were not so childlike, so modest, so meekly and sweetly resigned, she could be a Great Bore, as oppressively looming as the Great Bear. She can remember every least thing she ever heard, down to the last detail, even to the hour of the day when it happened. She is a Domesday Book of total recall for the whole of the little town of Ardagh, where she has lived for some twenty-five years in, you might almost say, the same corner of the same room of the same house, ever since an accident to her spine imprisoned her in a Bath chair at the age of eleven. This accident absolved her from all but the simplest decisions: there was no far-off island for her to dream of. It also meant that all she can now know of the world outside is what she reads, or what she is told by her friends, so that if her friends have told her fibs their consciences should prick them when she trustingly retails something that did not happen, or not quite in that way.

She is a little hunched-up woman with a face like a bit of burnt cork, whose plainness, some might say whose ugliness, you forget immediately you notice her gentle expression, her fluent lips, her warm brown eyes. Remember that, because of her ailment, she is always looking upwards at you when you meet her, so that her eyes have the pleading look of a spaniel, as if she were excusing herself for so much as existing. Her only handsome feature, apart from her doggy eyes, is her hair, long and rich and fair, on which she spends hours every morning, brushing it down into her lap over her shoulder, then brushing and pinning it up in a soft cloud, so overflowing that it makes her agile monkey-face seem about the size of a hazelnut. She lives in almost constant pain. She never complains of it. I have met nobody who does not admire her, nobody who has the least fault to find with her, apart from her invulnerable memory, which all Ardagh both enjoys and fears, and whose insistence can kill like the sirocco.

The only grumbles ever heard from her are two, as constant and soft as the leaves of a bamboo grove. The first is that she wishes she could see more of her sister Mary, a tall, slim, pretty, volatile girl, who twelve years ago married an American businessman, Richard Carton, a Continental buyer for one of New York's biggest stores.

'Not,' she always adds, 'that I don't realize how lucky the pair of us are. We mightn't be seeing one another at all only for Richard having that wonderful job.'

Because of this job, a cablegram or a letter has come twice a year from Mary saying that Richard is off to Europe on another buying spree, which means that Mary will presently stop off at Shannon and drive over to Ardagh for a week of heavenly gossip. Sarah at once announces the news to the whole of Ardagh, with burning cheeks and sparkling eyes. Then she may murmur her other grumble:

'Imagine it! I've seen Richard only once in my life. If he wasn't so busy! If only he could come with Mary for a real long holiday! Then she wouldn't have to go away after one little week. But, of course, she's indispensable to him.'

What she does not know, and what Mary intends that she never shall know, though she fears sometimes that one or two people in Ardagh may know it, or at least suspect it – such as Joe Shorthall, who picks her up at Shannon in his taxi, or the postmistress, who has sent off an occasional telegram for her – is that for the last six years Richard and she have been living partly in New York and partly in their small, elegant house in Zurich, near which their three children are at an English boarding school – so that, all unknown to Sarah, her sister passes between Switzerland and New York about six times a year. As for being indispensable to Richard in his work, the only time she ever ventured to advise him was in Rome. He looked at the object, a large, handsome blue fruit dish, turned it over and showed her the mark of its Californian manufacturer. What keeps her from visiting Sarah more often is the tireless whisper of the Recording Angel's Dictaphone playing back every lightest word that has passed between the two of them since they could begin to talk. She once incautiously wailed to Richard about it:

'It's not just that it's disconcerting to be reminded about things you've said, or discarded or forgotten years and years ago. Oh, if it was only that! She brings out these bits and scraps of things I've forgotten since I was ten, like a dog digging up some old thing you've thrown out on the ash heap and laying it lovingly at your feet – grubby, pointless, silly, worn, stupid things – and she says, "That's you." And I don't recognize them. Or don't want to see them. Old toys, old hats, old buried bones. Sometimes she has to remind me and remind me before I can even know what she's talking about. And, anyway, by this time they're no longer bits of me, they're bits of her. She knows more about me than I know myself. I keep on wondering what else does she know about me that I don't know. What's she going to produce next? Isn't my life my own, goddammit, to keep or to lose or to throw away if I want to? Am I me? Or am I her? I sometimes think I'm possessed by that old Chucklepuss the way some people are possessed by the devil!'

Richard had laughed heartily, and she, remembering too late his first, famous, fatal and final session with Sarah, could have bitten her tongue off. She stuck it out at him. Remembering again, he laughed all the more. Because Richard's memory is just as unerring as Sarah's; and his interest in Mary's past just as avid, or it used to be during the first years of their marriage. He wanted to know everybody she ever knew before he met her, every single thing she had ever done, every thought she had ever thought, every place she had ever been. So, at that first and last meeting between him and Sarah, she had to sit listening, apprehensive or embarrassed, while those two laid out the days of her youth before them like precious things that a pair of antiquaries might love to display to one another but would never part with. As they went on and on she got more and more furious with them:

'Ye make me feel like baby's first shoe. Or a photograph of a First Communion group. Or me aunt's wedding veil. Ye make me feel ninety. Ye make me feel dead!'

Richard only laughed his jolly, buyer's laugh, hangjawed like a pelican – worth thousands to him in his job – and roared at her to go away and leave them to it.

'This Sally girl knows tons more than you ever told me.'

But how could she go? She was as fascinated as she was furious. She was also frightened. For, while Sarah did know, or remember, 'tons more', it was all untrue in the way that a police report is untrue, because it leaves out everything except the facts. As she listened, transfixed as a rabbit is by a dazzling light that hides anything behind it, she remembered a wonderful thing she had once read in Stendhal's diaries – that 'True feeling leaves no memory': meaning that every deep feeling is like a peach, to be eaten straight from the tree of life, not spoiled by pawing and pressing. She swore afterwards that she lost pounds in perspiration while listening to them. The worst sequence was when they started talking about Corney Canty:

'Sally!' she heard Richard saying suddenly. 'Tell me about this young Corney Canty of Mary's. She's told me a lot about that wild boyo. As a matter of fact, why don't we meet him?'

'But, darling,' Mary protested, 'I've told you a dozen times over all that there is...'

'Now, Mary! Now! Let Sally tell me. Go on, Sally! Mary's told me about how they used to go riding to hounds together. And all the other adventures they had. That must have been a wonderful day – As I recall, Mary, it was the May of nineteen-thirty-seven? – when the two of you, alone with three hounds, flushed a fox out of Ballycoole woods and ran him to the edge of Gaunt's Quarry. And the brave Corney – He must really be a marvellous horseman, Sally – just slid after him down the gravel face of that quarry without a moment's hesitation. And poor little Mary here – Look at her, she's pale again at the thought of it! – God, how I admire you, darling! – terrified out of her wits though she was, slid down after him. And they cornered the fox in that quarry! I'd really love to meet this fellow. Why don't we ask him in for a drink tonight?'

Sarah's eyes dropped.

'God rest him!' she murmured.

'Not dead? Killed on the hunting field? A fine young man like that killed in the prime of life! Did you know this, Mary?'

'Did you say "young," Richard?' Sarah soothed him. 'Sure when he died of the drink there a few years back he was seventy-two to the month.'

'Seventy-two?' – looking wide-eyed at Mary, who was crying out desperately:

'Sarah, you're thinking of Corney's uncle. Or his father. He wasn't a year over forty, and as limber as twenty-five. Of course,' gushing to

Richard, 'he was a great rascal, you couldn't trust a word he said, didn't I tell ye the time he deliberately made me fall off that grey mare of his, setting me to a stone wall he knew damn well she couldn't take, so that he could come around and kneel over me on the grass, feeling me here and feeling me there with "Does it hurt here, ducky?" and "Does it hurt there, ducky?," and me with the wind gone out of me so that I couldn't say a bloody worrrd!'

Richard laughed at the familiar story, one of his favourites that he liked to make her tell at every second party, because it brought out the brogue in her voice. Sarah was not to be silenced.

'He was,' she said primly, even a little severely, 'seventy-two years old to the month when he died. No more. No less. I myself witnessed his cross – he couldn't read or write – on the Old Age Pension form on December the first, nineteen hundred and forty-three. He was wearing that old red-flannel-lined raincoat your daddy gave him in thirty-seven when . . .'

'But,' Richard put in, 'that was the year of the quarry hunt.'

'That's right. "I have this coat," said Corney to me, "for six years, and your poor father had it for six years before that, and . . ."'

Mary could see by Richard's face – he could multiply 113 by 113 in his head – that he had already established for himself that 'young Corney' had been an old lad in his middle sixties when she knew him. Sure enough, when Sarah paused, there was a brief silence, suspenseful and decisive, and then he broke into a series of monster guffaws, beating his palms together with delight, relishing with loving malice his wife's scarlet embarrassment. Through his guffaws he managed to utter:

'Mary, you little divil, I always knew you exaggerate a bit, but this . . .'

Wildly she fought for her hour as she had lived it:

'I didn't exaggerate. That was typical of Corney to exaggerate his age to get the pension. He fooled you up to the eyes, Sarah; when we hunted that fox he was forty, forty-two at the very most, forty-two at the outside limit, not a minute over it.'

One glance from Richard's bubbling shoulders and wrinkled-up eyes to Sarah's prim mouth told her that the battle was hopeless. There Sarah sat, erect in her chair, too nice to contradict further, too honest to compound a felony, giving her head short little shakes that said as plainly as speech, 'Seventy-two. To the month. No more. No less.'

Neither then nor at any time after could Mary have understood that Richard was just as happy with her as a splendid Teller of Tales as he had been with her as his Wild Irish Girl. Blinded by love, he drew out the session for hour after hour. He only realized his folly that night, in the hour of tenderness, in bed.

'Dammit,' she said, as they lay side by side, in her parents' old room upstairs, the heavy mirror in the coffinlike wardrobe catching the last of the summer daylight, the faint baa-ing of sheep coming from the Fair Green, 'I did slide down that old quarry. I wasn't codding about it. And he wasn't an old man. And even if he was I think that makes it a hell of a sight more exciting than the sentimental way you want it. Handsome young Irish huntsman. Brave young Irish girl. It makes me sick the way you always want to romanticize everything about me.'

His hands behind his poll, he began to shake all over again until she started to hammer him with her fists on his chest, and he to embrace and fondle her with a new love, a new admiration – he said the words, just so, explicitly – which, she declared, turning her behind to him huffily, was entirely beyond her modest intelligence. She whirled, and sat up and shouted:

'Are you trying to say that you prefer me as a liar?'

'Husssh! My wild little girleen! Sarah will hear you.'

'I don't give a damn if she does hear me. What does she know about it? She wasn't there. It was she started all this, and you kept at her and at her to make me seem more of a liar.'

'Nonsense, darling. It's just that you have this wonderful Irish gift for fantasy.'

'It's not fantasy. It's true, true, true. Every word of it is true. There may be some detail here or there, some trivial, irrelevant thing, some small thing slipped up, but it's all true. And I am not going to have you and old Sarah Sucklepuss down there stealing my life from me with her bloody old . . .'

And, to his pitying astonishment, she burst into a long, low wail of weeping, sobbing into the pillow like, he thought, as he laid his palm on her wet cheek, a child whose dog has been rolled over by a bus before her eyes.

'You don't understand, Dicky,' she wailed into his armpit. 'It's torture to hear her digging up my life and turning it all into lies that never happened the way she says they happened.'

'But you must have told her they happened that way?'

'I told her the bones. And all she has of anything now is the bones. I can't remember the bones. All I have is the feeling I had at the time. Or else I can't remember at all.'

'Tell her so. Say you forget.'

'It would be like taking her life away from her. All the poor old Sucklepuss has is my bones.'

She wept herself asleep on his shoulder. It is the measure of his distress at what he had done to her, of his natural shrewdness, and of his sensitiveness hidden behind his cocktail-bar laugh that as he lay there, listening to the dim, distant, ceaseless baa-ing, he decided never again to visit Ardagh.

But this was years ago, and since then Mary's life has stopped being the flowing, straightforward river it once was. Not that life ever is like a river that starts from many tributaries and flows at the end straight to the sea; it is more like the line of life on my palm that starts firmly and frays over the edge in a cataract of little streams of which it is impossible to say where each began. Richard has small interest now in her youth. He is rarely amused by her exaggerations: the wind that blew the legs off her, or the bus that went down Fifth Avenue at a hundred miles per hour. Her lovely, lighthearted, featherheaded ways are now her usual scattiness. She finds it more and more difficult to follow Sarah's letters about the latest doings of Ardagh. And the only way Sarah can form any clear pictures of Mary's life in New York is by those intimate gossips, prolonged into the silence of the night, during Mary's precious half-yearly visits to the little house near the end of the Main Street of Ardagh. Yet, it was just when, for this very reason, one might have expected the visits to become either more frequent or longer that they suddenly became so curt that everybody but Sarah foresaw their end.

It all started out of a ridiculous little incident that occurred during Mary's March visit last year. Over the years she had been trying in vain to free herself from Sarah's memory by catching her out in an error of fact. On this wet, March night she suddenly became aware that Sarah was talking of a German air raid on a part of the Irish coast where some old friends of Richard's, working in the American diplomatic service during the war, had had a summer house. Knowing well that no German bombs had dropped on this part of the coast, she felt an overwhelming sense of relief. She did not contradict the Recording

Angel. She did not crow over her. She stayed as quiet as a cat watching a mouse. The whole glorious value of the error was that Sarah must never become aware of it. The night passed with the error uncorrected. At about two o'clock in the morning. Mary woke up as if to the sound of a shot, remembering clearly that a floating sea-mine had exploded on that part of the coast and damaged a summer house. She left Ardagh the next day, only three days after she had arrived, to Sarah's dumb dismay, on the feeble excuse of being worried about Richard's health. 'Oh, Sarah, I live in terror that he'll have to give up the job altogether, he's driven *so* hard!'

Six months later, in September, Mary came again, and left after two days.

They were having afternoon tea on the second day of this visit – it was a Sunday afternoon – in the bay of the front room, looking out on the empty autumn street, with Sarah happily squeezing the last drops out of a long, lightly amusing recollection of the famous night seventeen years before when Mary, still at school, organized a secret Midsummer Eve party to hail the sun rising over the Galtee Mountains. She had rowed her party, five in all, across the river in the dark and lit a pagan midsummer-fire in, of all places, the playing fields adjoining the Mercy Convent. The nuns, rising to sing their Matins, had heard the singing and seen the fire, and raised a terrible row about it, which set the whole town talking for weeks after. Sarah happily followed the history of everybody even distantly connected with the affair down to the hour of that afternoon tea. Her comments were largely a string of *Requiescats*, a ritual habit which always secretly tickled Mary: it was as if the Recording Angel had a secondary job as Lady High Executioner. ('Anna Grey? Died nine years back, Mary. Tommy Morgan? Failing. Failing before his people's eyes. Joe Fenelon took to the bottle, poor boy. Molly Cardew? Ah, God rest her . . .')

Without a pause Sarah suddenly leaned forward and said:

'Mary, tell me! How is Nathan Cash these days?'

'Nathan who?' Mary had said, parrying wildly at the unexpected transition. This sort of thing was always happening – Sarah suddenly producing some name or event about which she was supposed to know nothing.

'Cash!' Sarah said loudly, rather like people who raise their voices when talking to foreigners in order to be better understood. 'Your friend Nathan Cash. The man who was a director of the Bell Telephone

Company in Newark, New Jersey. He married that Jane Barter whose uncle was a partner in Chuck Full O'Nuts before he divorced her last year after playing around, I think I gathered from you, with some other woman, you-never-said-who. And, after all, he didn't marry her either.'

'Didn't he?' Mary said dully, choked with rage against herself for having as much as mentioned Nathan to Sarah.

'When you came last March you told me he was after marrying Carrie Brindle, a rich Jewish girl from Buffalo. Surely you remember?'

Mary could only give a miserable little laugh.

'You told me about it last March! When you came off the *Liberté*. You told me,' Sarah smiled lovingly and admiringly, 'how he gave yourself orchids for your birthday in January.'

'Why, and so he did!' Mary laughed gaily, her anger with herself mounting and spilling. Last March, coming off that damned six-days boat of loneliness, she had had to talk to somebody about him.

'He is a very handsome man,' Sarah smiled gently. Mary stared at her. 'You showed me his photograph.'

'Did I really?' Mary gurgled, and spread her ringed fingers indifferently. 'Richard and I meet so many people.'

Sarah sighed.

'It must be grand to be getting orchids. That was the only time in my life I saw orchids. She laughed at her own ignorance. 'I thought they were passion flowers. I forgot to ask you,' with a happy smile, 'was it Mr Cash gave them to you before you sailed?'

Mary looked swiftly at her, but it was plain that she was not probing. Sarah's questions were always innocent, pointless, without guile. She looked out, frowningly, at the granite brown of the old North Gate, under whose arch the almost-silent Main Street of Ardagh flows into the completely silent countryside. She heard the soft *cric-croc* of a cart entering slowly under the arch from the farther side. The little cart slowly emerged from under the arch, salmonpink, bearing its pyramid of black peat, drawn by a tiny, grey donkey. It *cric-crocked* slowly past her vision. She found herself murmuring as softly and slowly, feeling as she did so that this was exactly how she had been wheedled last March into talking about Nathan:

'I bought those orchids last March. I just had to have them.'

'Why, Mary?' – gently.

'I was feeling very down.'

'What happened to you?' – sympathetically.

'I'd had a terrible quarrel with a friend.'

'Who, Mary?' – tenderly.

'A friend. Nobody you know. A woman. A woman called Gold. Nancy Gold. There was nobody to see me off on the boat. Richard had gone by plane direct to Berne. The cabin looked empty. No flowers. No bottle of champagne. No basket of fruit. When I went down to lunch I stood at the turn of the staircase and saw all those men and women chattering around all those white tables and all the women wearing corsages. I turned back and went up to the florist and I bought me two orchids.'

Neither of them spoke for a while.

'Well, well,' Sarah concluded. 'And so he married the Jewish woman in the heel of the hunt. Is he happy with her, would you say?'

'How should I know? We never meet. I'm not sure that I like him very much really.'

Sarah smiled in loyal admiration.

'He liked you once, though. Enough anyway to give you orchids.'

'That was just one night going to the opera. I thought at the time it was a little plush of him. Still, a woman likes those little attentions.'

'You always liked nice things. You always like those little attentions. I can see why you bought them for yourself on the boat.'

'It was just that I was down in the mouth.'

'And then there was Richard on your mind, too.'

'Richard?' Mary stared at her as if she was a witch or a fortune-teller.

'I mean you were worried about him.'

'Was I?'

'He was ill. You left here after three days to be with him. I knew the minute you came in the door, Mary, off that old boat, that you weren't your old self.'

Mary gave her a desperate look. She got up.

'I think I'll go for a stroll. I have a bit of a headache.'

She went out, under the arch, so unmistakably a foreigner in her high-collared mink coat, her furry hat and her spiked heels that the few townsfolk who were in the Sunday street stared at her, but sideways so as not to be seen staring. She saw none of them, nothing, none of the familiar names over the shuttered shops, unchanged for as long as she could remember – Fenelon the grocer, Ryan the draper, Shorthall's

Garage, Morgan and Corneille, Furnishers, Upholsterers and Under-
takers, Saint Anne's Nursing Home and old Dr Freeman's brass plate
polished into holes at the corners. The street petered out where a bright
yellow signpost directed her across the bridge to the dark yellow furze
on the rising foothills.

She leaned over the limestone parapet, lit a cigarette, and glared
along the barely flowing river with its shallow autumn pools and its
dry beaches. She pounded the parapet with her gloved fist and said,
aloud: 'It's intolerable!' Her cigarette ash floated down into the river.
On one side of the river were the long gardens at the back of the Main
Street's houses, coming right down to the riverbank; and, farther on,
plumb with the river, the backs of old donkey-grey warehouses,
decaying now, eyeless, little used since the river silted up and ceased
to be navigable. The Franciscan belfry was reflected in an islanded pool
among the gravel at the bend of the river, and in the pool a sweep of
yellow from the far hills that rose to the farther mountains over whose
rounded backs the sailing clouds had long ago seemed so often to call
her to come away, to come away. Today the clouds were one solid,
frozen mass, tomblike, so that if they moved they moved massively,
and she could not tell if they moved at all.

She had rowed across the river down there, that Midsummer Eve,
with Annie Grey, and Tommy Morgan, and Joe Fenelon and Molly
Cardew. She had borrowed her daddy's gramophone and twelve of his
gayest Italian records, and halfway across, the records, which she had
placed on top of the gramophone, began to slide one by one into the
water with gentle plops. Midsummer heat, and a great sky of stars and
the whole of Ardagh sound asleep. While waiting for the sun to rise they
swam in one of the pools, and then, at the first ghost of light, not light,
a hint of morning, they lit the fire and played a muffled '*O Sole Mio*'
and a wind blew the wood ash into the cups of wine that Joe Fenelon
had stolen from his father's shop. She had not thought of that grey dust
in the wine for seventeen years. It was, she thought savagely, the sort
of thing that Sarah's memories never remembered, along with the
gaiety of Corney Canty, and the way redheaded Molly Cardew used to
tickle the back of Tommy Morgan's neck so that he would hunch up
his shoulders and say, affectionately-irritably, 'Go away, you green
frog you!' and poor weak-minded Joe Fenelon's lovely tenor voice
singing 'I'll Take Ye Home Again, Kathleen' at every party. The ash in
the wine was just another piece of her real life immured, with the bones

of everything she had ever done or said, in the vaults of Sarah's infallible memoirs. Would Nathan Cash one day join these dead bones? Had he already gone there, with all she had been through because of him? Would all her life, unless she really went away and left her past behind her?

She blew out a long breath of smoke and threw her cigarette into the river. She would call in to Shorthall's Garage on the way home. The car would come for her at nine in the morning. By evening she would be floating down over the pinewoods on the little hills about the airstrip at Zurich. Blonde hostesses. Pure-white washrooms. ('Just like Newark,' Richard had once laughed.) And her ritual first cup of *café au lait* at the tall counter, while Richard waited with Donna, and Biddy and Patrick. But she did not stir until a soft rain began to fall, a dew, a mist, and she was aware that it was dusk. The streets were empty, the slates shone purple. The turf smoke medicinal in the air. She stopped by the garage, passed on, stopped again, hesitated again, half turned back and then, with a groan, went on to the house. She went upstairs to her room and lay there, with the last pallor of the day in the dark mirror of the wardrobe, until dinnertime.

For their coffee they sat in the bay window. They gossiped amiably, Mary half listening, her head half turned to the footfalls passing down the street to evening Benediction at the Franciscan priory. Sarah said:

'By the way, Mary, wasn't it very sad about your poor friend, Mrs Henry Beirne!'

Mary turned her head a little farther towards the window as if she were trying to hear something out there, but really to hide the look of blank fear that she could feel coming into her eyes. She knew no Mrs Henry Beirne. Her frightened efforts to recall the woman produced nothing clearer than the vague cloud that a drop of absinthe forms in a glass of water, a fume like smoke, a wavering embryo without a face. The last ghostly footstep faded. She whispered, groping for information:

'Yes. It was very sad. How did you know about it?'

'The Dublin papers had it on account of the other woman being related to the Bishop of Kilkenny. I don't think she could be more than thirty-two. Would you say so?'

'Surely more?' – groping still. Could it be a divorce? Or an accident?

Why couldn't Sarah say what happened? Was the woman dead? The wraith in the water began to curl into another as yet undecipherable shape. She said gently: 'Was her age given in the papers?'

'Not at all, but, sure, 'tis easy to work it out. We know she was the Class of Forty-one. Give her twenty or twenty-one at the Commencement, and wasn't it then she first met Henry Beirne? He proposed to her that very evening on the Common. You danced with him at the Ritz that night. You had the gold dress with the cream insets. How many children was it you said they had?'

As the white shape in the water took on a remembered face, Mary barely stopped herself from saying, 'My God, it must be nine years since I saw that bitch Lucy Burbank.' She said, dully:

'Children? Four' – and immediately regretted it, realizing that to say anything precise to Sarah about anything was only laying the ground for more questions next year, or in three or five years' time, when she would have completely forgotten what she had earlier said. They talked a little more about Lucy Burbank-Beirne. Mary never did find out what exactly happened to the woman that was so very sad.

'It's time we lit the lamp,' Sarah said.

It was dark. The rain had stopped and restarted. The footsteps had all returned the way they had come. In another hour the only sound in the long, winding street would be the drip of rain. Not a ground-floor window would be lit. There would not even be a Civic Guard out on a wet night like this. She gathered up the coffee cups and took them out to the kitchen on the old silver-plated salver, with the copper showing through, that her father had won at a golf tournament forty years ago. She returned and lifted off the pink globe of the oil lamp, her back to Sarah, and then lifted off the glass chimney, and put a match to the two charred wicks and watched the flame creep across their ridged edges. She replaced the glass chimney. Still with her back to Sarah, she said:

'I have bad news to break to you, Sarah.'

'Oh, Mary, don't frighten me.'

'I've been trying to get myself to tell you since I came.'

'What is it, love?'

Carefully she replaced the pink globe, aware of its warm light under her chin.

'Richard has given up his job. I came alone this time. I came only to tell you. I must go away tomorrow morning.'

She slowly raised the first wick, and then the second wick, and felt the room behind her fill with light. She heard a noise like a drip of rain, or melting snow, or oozing blood.

'Oh, Mary, don't go away from me!'

She turned. For the first time, Sarah was pleading with her, her little brown face smaller than ever under the great cloud of hair, her two brown spaniel's eyes brimming with tears.

'I must go!' Mary cried, her two fists trembling by her side. 'I must go!'

'I'll never see you again!'

Mary sank on her knees and looped her arms lovingly about her waist.

'Of course you will, you silly-billy,' she laughed. 'You'll see me lots of times.'

They gazed at one another fondly for a long while. Then Mary rose and went to the dark window and drew the curtains together with a swish. Arranging the folds of the curtains, she said, reassuringly, like a mother to a child:

'You'll see me lots of times. Lots and lots of times.'

Behind her, Sarah said resignedly:

'Will I, Mary?'

The Sugawn Chair

Every autumn I am reminded of an abandoned sugawn chair that languished for years, without a seat, in the attic of my old home. It is associated in my mind with an enormous sack which the carter used to dump with a thud on the kitchen floor around every October. I was a small kid then, and it was as high as myself. This sack had come 'up from the country', a sort of diplomatic messenger from the fields to the city. It smelled of dust and hay and apples, for the top half of it always bulged with potatoes, and, under a layer of hay, the bottom half bulged with apples. Its arrival always gave my mother great joy and a little sorrow, because it came from the farm where she had been born. Immediately she saw it she glowed with pride in having a 'back', as she called it – meaning something behind her more solid and permanent than city streets, though she was also saddened by the memories that choked her with this smell of hay and potatoes from the home farm, and apples from the little orchard near the farmhouse. My father, who had also been born on a farm, also took great pleasure in these country fruits, and as the two of them stood over the sack, in the kitchen, in the middle of the humming city, everything that their youth had meant to them used to make them smile and laugh and use words that they had never used during the rest of the year, and which I thought magical: words like *late sowing*, *clover crop*, *inch field*, *marl bottom*, *headlands*, *tubers*, and the names of potatoes, British Queens or Arran Banners, that sounded to me like the names of regiments. For those moments my father and mother became a young, courting couple again. As they stood over that sack, as you might say warming their hands to it, they were intensely happy, close to each other, in love again. To me they were two very old people. Counting back now, I reckon that they were about forty-two or forty-three.

One autumn evening after the sack arrived, my father went up to the attic and brought down the old sugawn chair. I suppose he had had it sent up from his home farm. It was the only thing of its kind in our house, which they had filled – in the usual peasants' idea of what constitutes elegance – with plush chairs, gold-framed pictures of Stags at Bay, and exotic tropical birds, pelmets on the mantelpieces, Delft shepherdesses, Chinese mandarins with nodding heads, brass bedsteads with mighty knobs and mother-of-pearl escutcheons set with bits of mirror, vast mahogany chiffoniers, and so on. But the plush-bottomed chairs, with their turned legs and their stiff backs, were for show, not for comfort, whereas in the old country sugawn chair my da could tilt and squeak and rock to his behind's content.

It had been in the place for years, rockety, bockety, chipped and well-polished, and known simply as 'your father's chair', until the night when, as he was reading the *Evening Echo* with his legs up on the kitchen range, there was a sudden rending noise, and down he went through the seat of it. There he was then, bending over, with the chair stuck on to him, and my mother and myself in the splits of laughter, pulling it from him while he cursed like a trooper. This was the wreck that he now suddenly brought down from the dusty attic.

The next day, he brought in a great sack of straw from the Cornmarket, a half-gallon of porter and two old buddies from the street – an ex-soldier known to the kids around as 'Tear-'em-and-ate-'em' and a little dwarf of a man who guarded the stage door at the Opera House when he was not being the sacristan at the chapel. I was enchanted when I heard what they were going to do. They were going to make ropes of straw – a miracle I had never heard of – and reseat the chair. Bursting with pride in my da, I ran out and brought in my best pal, and the two of us sat as quiet as cats on the kitchen table, watching the three men filling the place with dust, straw, and loud arguments as they began to twist the ropes for the bottom of the chair.

More strange words began to float in the air with the dust: *scallops, flat tops, bulrushes, cipeens, fields in great heart* . . . And when the three sat down for a swig of porter, and looked at the old polished skeleton in the middle of the floor, they began to rub the insides of their thighs and say how there was no life at all like the country life, and my mother poured out more porter for them, and laughed happily when my da began to talk about horses, and harrows, and a day after the plough, and how, for *that* much, he'd throw up this blooming city life altogether and settle down on a bit of a farm for the heel of his days.

This was a game of which he, she and I never got tired, a fairy tale that was so alluring it did not matter a damn that they had not enough money to buy a window box, let alone a farm of land.

'Do you remember that little place,' she would say, 'that was going last year down at Nantenan?'

When she said that, I could see the little reedy fields of Limerick that I knew from holidays with my uncle, and the crumbling stone walls of old demesnes with the moss and saffron lichen on them, and the willow sighing softly by the Deel, and I could smell the wet turf rising in the damp air, and, above all, the tall wildflowers of the mallow, at first cabbage-leaved, then pink and coarse, then gossamery, then breaking into cakes that I used to eat – a rank weed that is the mark of ruin in so many Irish villages, and whose profusion and colour is for me the sublime emblem of Limerick's loneliness, loveliness and decay.

'Ah!' my da would roar. 'You and your blooming ould Limerick! That bog of a place! Oh, but, God blast it, why didn't I grab that little farm I was looking at two years ago there below Emo!'

'Oho, ho, ho!' she would scoff. 'The Queen's! The Lousy Queen's! God, I'd live like a tiger and die like a Turk for Limerick. For one patch of good old Limerick. Oh, Limerick, my love, and it isn't alike! Where would you get spuds and apples the like of them in the length and breadth of the Queen's County?'

And she grabbed a fist of hay from the bag and buried her face in it, and the tears began to stream down her face, and me and my pal screaming with laughter at her, and the sacristan lauding Tipperary, and the voices rose as Tear-'em-and-ate-'em brought up the River Barrow and the fields of Carlow, until my da jumped up with:

'Come on, lads, the day is dyin' and acres wide before us!'

For all that, the straw rope was slow in emerging. Their arguments about it got louder and their voices sharper. At first all their worry had been whether the kitchen was long enough for the rope; but so far, only a few, brief worms of straw lay on the red tiles. The sacristan said: 'That bloody straw is too moist.' When he was a boy in Tipp he never seen straw the like o' that. Tear-'em-and-ate-'em said that straw was old straw. When he was a lad in Carlow they never used old straw. Never! Under no possible circumstances! My dad said: 'What's wrong with that straw is it's too bloomin' short!' And they began to kick the bits with their toes, and grimace at the heap on the floor, and pick up bits and fray them apart and throw them aside until the whole floor was like a stable. At last they put on their coats, and gave the straw a final few kicks, and my pal jumped down and said he was going back to his handball and, in my heart, I knew that they were three impostors.

The kitchen was tidy that evening when I came back with the *Evening Echo*. My da was standing by the sack of potatoes. He had a spud in his fist, rubbing off the dust of its clay with his thumb. When he saw me he tossed it back in the sack, took the paper, took one of the plush-bottom chairs and sat on it with a little grimace. I did not say anything, but young as I was, I could see that he was not reading what he was looking at. God knows what he was seeing at that moment.

For years the anatomy of the chair stood in one of the empty attics. It was there for many years after my father died. When my mother died and I had to sell out the few bits of junk that still remained from their lives, the dealer would not bother to take the useless frame, so that when, for the last time, I walked about the echoing house, I found it standing alone in the middle of the bare attic. As I looked at it I smelled apples, and the musk of Limerick's dust, and the turf-tang from its cottages, and the mallows among the limestone ruins, and I saw my mother and my father again as they were that morning – standing over the autumn sack, their arms about one another, laughing foolishly, and madly in love again.

A Shadow, Silent as a Cloud

In the empty dining room, lit by a single electric bulb hanging from the rosette in the ceiling, the black-marble clock chimed slowly seven times and a sputter of rain tapped at the windows. The three tables, long, white and narrow, arranged like the letter U, looked very white under that single bulb. At one end of the top table there was a waitress, moving slowly from chair to chair, looking at the cards bearing the names of the guests she would have to serve. She was about fifty, but still handsome and well-shaped though a bit on the dumpy side. She murmured the names in different voices to suit her notion of what they might look like. She said *Miss Olive Harold* in a thin-lipped and prim voice. It was a Protestant sort of name, a hard-faced name. She made *Mr Condon Larkin* into a soft, round-faced man. She said *Miss Stella Shannon* twice, it was such a nice name, young, and lovely, and a bit lost. *Mr Kevin Lowry* could be a gloomy sort of fellow, or he could be a jolly, laughing fellow. *Monsignor O'Connell* ... A bit of wood ash fell from the fire, which was quietly oozing wet sap. She made a crooked mouth at the initials of *Professor J. T. G. Quigley's* name. The next card was at the centre of the table, the chairman's place. *Jeremiah J. Collis.*

She looked over at the fire and saw a gate lodge with a thick laurel copse around it, almost a quarter-acre of close-planted laurels, trimmed level at about four feet from the ground, a miniature forest into which she used to crawl on the crinkling brown leaves. There was a bay tree. She looked up across the wide, spreading pasture to the white door pillars of the Big House. Behind it there were the rolling mountains. On quiet days you could hear the tramcars at Rathfarnham village jolting over the junction points. Her lips, without speaking it, shaped the single word, *Templeogue.* She did not notice that the piece of fallen wood was giving out a pungent smell, like laurel burning. She was still there, with one hand on the chair back, smiling at the fire, when the headwaiter came in and switched on all the lights, and then all the other waiters and hired waitresses like herself came in after him in a chattering gaggle. The headwaiter directed them to their stations, and there they stood, as straight as statues, until the first group of guests came hesitantly to the big doorway and began to cluster around the seating plan on the easel beside it.

She recognized him immediately he came in. He was after getting terribly loguey; his hair was grey at the sides; his chin bulged over his white tie; but he was a fine figure of a man still. He passed to his place, talking and laughing with a soft, pretty young woman with coils of fair hair on top of her head. She had a pale face, red lips and a wrinkled forehead. He called her Stella and it was as plain as a pikestaff that he was gone about her. When he sat down she saw the thin patch on top of his head, but when he said over his shoulder, 'The wine list, please,' she thought his voice was just the same voice, only grown older. When she got the wine list and put it into his backward-stretching hand, the professor beside him was saying, 'All right, Jerry, but I warn you that if you don't phrase it very carefully they will misunderstand your motives.' At that he laughed, and his laugh was a boy's laugh.

From that on she was much too busy to look at him again, until he got up to give the toast of 'Ireland', and said, 'You may smoke, gentlemen'. After a while he laid down his cigar and tapped his coffee cup with his spoon, and stood up to give his speech. She moved over by the left-hand table to take a good stock of him. His waistcoat had burst its bottom button, his jowls were flushed from the wine and the heat, but still and all he really was a fine figure of a man.

During the first few minutes she did not take in one word he said, she felt so nervous for him, but she soon became aware that he was entirely at his ease and she started to listen with interest.

'And so, I hope you can now see, ladies and gentlemen, why I have called my address by the slightly sentimental title "Lest We Forget". Because it does seem to me that we architects forget far too much and far too easily in our eagerness to invent, to innovate, to be modern and progressive. Instead, my feeling is that we should encourage our memories to interrupt us in our haste, to pursue us as we run away from them, to surprise and halt us by the richness of the message that the past can lay in our hands, warning us to go easy when we are going too fast and too far. After all, when you come to think of it, what else is memory but the recognition of experience? And' – he held out his hands appealingly and smiled around the tables – 'let's be honest, what else, all too often, is this famous experience of ours – about which we are always boasting to our juniors – what else is it but the lamentable record of our carefully concealed mistakes?'

For that he got a little laughter and ironic applause.

'Now, I don't pretend to any special wisdom, and I am not yet quite as old as the Methuselah of George Bernard Shaw, or,' with a deferential little bow and a smile towards the Monsignor, 'should I have said the Methuselah of that somewhat more famous author, Genesis?'

They all craned to look at the Monsignor. Seeing him smile indulgently, they crackled into a light laughter. At the next sentence she saw, with amusement, the wry way he touched his thin poll.

'Yet even I sometimes become aware of mortal dissolution and feel the falling of the leaves.'

The words and the gesture evoked more laughter. As if he knew that he had their full attention now he leaned forward on his ten finger tips and let his voice become warm and serious.

'Perhaps that is why I feel so certain that I know what we are all afraid of? We are afraid of being thought old-fashioned. And yet can there be any single one of us, whether young or old, who will dare to deny that our profession is as much concerned with the passing away of old things as with their replacement by new things? That we have something to learn from the very things that we are destroying? For is it not true that to create is in some sense to change, and to change is in some sense to destroy? All creative work is a form of destruction.'

He leaned up and held a longer pause of silence than he had dared before, and, for a while after, he spoke quite conversationally, almost carelessly:

'It's very hard, whenever I drive out of Dublin, not to feel a bit sorry when I look around me at the ranks of new and shining houses stretching out and out all around the old battered centre I've left behind me. I naturally feel a sense of professional pride in these new homes, but I feel sad because those new settlements – it is the only word for them – have no tradition, no feel of the past, no memories, and they have been built on fields that, for generations upon generations, were full of associations and memories. In all these building schemes of ours let us never forget that we are bartering something that is as eloquent as it is old for something that, however good and necessary, is as mute and dumb as it is unappeasably strange and new.'

He paused briefly, and in that moment she heard the young man at her elbow whispering across the table to another young man: 'Clever bastard! Here comes the Templeogue job.' Alerted and annoyed, she began to listen more carefully. He was still speaking quite easily, without any flourish of any kind, voice or hands:

'It would be insulting to this Institute of ours to suggest for a moment that anybody here thinks that architecture is just so much mute stone. Every city is the richer for having absorbed something of the vibrations of the living and the dead. It is not merely that we like to know that somebody famous spoke from this loggia or died on those steps; that in our own capital such noble spirits as Edmund Burke, or Oliver Goldsmith, or Tom Moore, or Charles Stewart Parnell, or Patrick Pearse walked these streets or died within the sounds of their traffic – it makes architecture more living that countless humble citizens have hollowed the steps of a church or sat in the benches of some old school. Must we always barter away that livingness of the dead for the weaker pulsations and meaner associations of the passing day?'

With that one passionate question he picked up and tossed away his card of jottings. Then he smiled and was casual again:

'You know, you could evoke a whole century with one glance at Sheridan the playwright's house in Dorset Street. But I challenge even the most pugnacious gentleman among ye to say that he feels his dander rise today as he changes gear among the red-roofed bungalows of modern Donnybrook.'

He let the ripple of chuckles die away. As he went on she thought he threw a glance at Miss Shannon.

'Or could even the youngest and most romantic lady present confess that she ever thinks of poor Pamela, Lord Edward's unhappy widow, as she whirls in the number eight bus past the Frascati of modern Blackrock? It is the same everywhere. It is right and proper to build new homes. Do we have to do it by knocking down the bridges of history?'

At this, the young man near her who had whispered across the table leaned back in his chair and sighed audibly at the ceiling.

'Yet even in my boyhood places like Rathfarnham were still the haunts of wandering tinkers, wild birds and strolling lovers. The rural charm of Templeogue still had that air of seclusion which once drew Charles Lever and his young bride to live and love there among the fields and hedgerows, within view of the rolling drums of the Dublin mountains topped by the Hell Fire Club and the cairns of the Three

Rock. Must this too, this latest place to be threatened by what we grandiosely call Urban Development, also be utterly destroyed? Must we lose entirely the inheritance of our Irish past?'

The earnestness of this sentence won him a clatter of applause. Even she joined in, and all the louder because the contemptuous young man in front of her was now groaning in audible pain into his two fists. Jerry was now racing on eloquently, but she no longer heard him. With bright, moist eyes she saw only the old gate lodge, the laurel copse, the motionless swing hanging from the beech, and under it the oily celandines and the yellow aconites. Besides, her eyes had wandered to Miss Shannon and Mr Condon Larkin. Miss Shannon's left hand hung down by the side of her chair, Mr Larkin's right hand hung by the side of his, and the two hands gently fondled one another. She was leaning forward, chin on elbowed palm; he was leaning back; both were looking up at the speaker. Anyone could tell that they were not paying the slightest attention to his words.

By the time she had done her part in clearing the tables the bar was packed out, but she saw him, taller than all the rest, in the middle of the crush, arguing with Miss Shannon, Mr Condon Larkin, Professor Quigley, and two or three of the younger men, including the contemptuous young man, who had, she now saw, a beaky nose, tousled fair hair and a slight tuft of fair beard, two prominent teeth and fierce, small blue eyes. He was very angry, and as she pushed nearer she heard him saying in a voice loud enough to be heard above the general babble:

'It's all a damned lot of sentimentality. And I don't believe you mean a bloody word of it. And as for dragging in Tommy Moore, may God forgive you! Now, Edmund Burke I'll grant ye! Dammit, I'll even give you Parnell! But, God Almighty, not Tommy Moore!'

Jerry was also angry.

'And what,' he demanded from the heights, 'what, pray, is wrong with Tom Moore?'

The professor looked as if he was trying to calm them both. The toothy young man spat back in an insulting voice:

'He was a sentimentalist, and wurrse than a sentimentalist. He was a calculating sentimentalist. That thing on his sleeve ∴.. What was it but the price ticket of a turn-coat?'

'Now, now,' the professor intervened, 'it was a heart all the same.

A song like 'Oft in the Stilly Night could not have been composed by a man without real feeling.'

'Feeling! To conceal what? Ambition! Like all sentimentalists he...'

The professor shot a frightened look around the bar – they were all talking at the tops of their voices – and laid a hand on the young man's shoulder, saying:

'Nevertheless, Mr Collyer, it is a lovely song. Jerry, raise it for us. Give us a bar.'

'I will, then,' Jerry said. She withdrew as he laid his glass on the counter, crying, 'And if I maul it itself it'll still be a fine song. Silence for your president!' he shouted, and although a few of them gave a mock-serious cheer, gradually the whole bar fell silent. He cleared his throat and began to sing with feeling. As she stood by the door, half in the corridor, listening, others came along from the lounge to listen. She thought it was splendid the way he put his heart into it, in his fine, deep bass voice, especially when he came to the low, vibrating notes of:

> The smiles, the tears of boyhood years,
> The words of love then spoken...

He was looking all the time at Stella Shannon, who kept looking from under her worried brows at Condon Larkin, whose eyes kept expanding and contracting nervously in an evident effort to keep sober.

When the clapping ended, Jerry took back his glass with a sweep and winked triumphantly at young Collyer. Before they could resume their argument she sent in the Boots to him. She watched the Boots touch his arm and whisper, and Jerry look out at her over the heads of the crowd. He came towards her, turning to wag a smug finger at the young man, crying, 'When I've squared up for the wine I'll be back. I won't let you get away with it as easily as all that, my young boyo!' He was groping in his tails for his wallet as he crushed through the door out to her. She moved a few feet up the corridor away from the bar and the noise.

'The wine?' he said. 'How much?'

'It's not the wine, Jerry.' She smiled when he opened his eyes haughtily at her use of his first name. 'I see you don't remember me?'

'I'm very sorry,' he apologized. 'I gather I ought to remember you. But as a matter of fact I just don't.'

She laughed and felt herself blushing.

'You once asked me to marry you. I was twelve at the time. My name is Lily Collis now but I used to be Lily Braden when you knew me long ago. I married a cousin of your own – Victor Collis. He was Uncle Mel's son. We used all be playing together by Uncle Mel's lodge at Templeogue. Do you forget?'

He saw a red plush divan beside him.

'Won't you sit down?' he said to her gently.

'Ah, no, it wouldn't be right, I should really be in the lounge now, I'm on duty there, and at the dance afterwards. Am I embarrassing you?'

'Good Lord, no, not in the least. But I am going to sit down.'

He sat, and looked up at her and laughed.

'You used to have long fair plaits of hair down your back. I was gone about you. I used to swing you on the old beech tree. Twenty swings for a kiss. Wasn't that the tariff?' She laughed happily. 'So you married Uncle Mel's boy. There were such a lot of Collises. From Glasnevin, the North Circular Road, Howth, Raheny, and a few on the south side at Cabinteely, and old Templeogue. Do you realize, Lily, that it must be nearly thirty years since I last laid eyes on you?'

'It is, and thirty-seven years ago. I was thirteen when we last saw one another and you were sixteen. You're every bit of fifty-three, Jerry.'

He raised mock-pleading palms, laughing again.

'Spare my last remaining grey hairs.'

'I simply had to speak to you when I heard you talking about the old place tonight. It's marvellous the way you remember it so well. The path through the wood, and the pond behind the lodge, and the old swing and all.'

'And the smell of the wood-smoke,' he said.

'And the geese pickin' in the grass.'

'And the old avenue all weeds,' he laughed.

'And the old stables falling down,' she cried.

'Do you remember the day the hunt chased a fox across the avenue?'

'I see you have it all!' she cried.

They were silent, looking at one another. In the bar a woman's voice had begun to sing 'Has Sorrow Thy Young Days Shaded?'

'They're still at it about Tom Moore,' he said.

In a mirror facing into the bar she saw that the singer was Miss Shannon.

'Uncle Mel!' Jerry was saying, staring up at her. 'He ran away to sea when he was a boy, and came back, and married into the gate lodge. He had a four-master in a bottle in the fanlight.'

'You know that he killed himself in the heel of the hunt?'

'Ah, no! For God's sake!'

'He was left alone in the lodge after Victor married me. One winter he got raging pneumonia and he wouldn't give in to it. They picked him up one night off the steps of the Parnell monument and took him across to the Rotunda hospital. He'd tell nobody who he was or where he lived, so they took him up to the Workhouse and he died there. It was only after he was buried, in the paupers' graveyard, that we heard about it. I think it was a sort of wild revenge he took on Victor for marrying me. But the Collises were always like that – wild and obstinate and vengeful.'

He shook his head, half sadly, half proudly.

'God knows, Lily, and that's a true bill. Do you know that I didn't speak to my father for seven years before he died? And all over nothing but politics. I pushed myself through college under my own steam. When he was gone I had to support my mother and my two sisters. I climbed to the top of the tree with my two bare hands. But, by God, I did it. Nothing stopped me and nothing ever will stop me from getting what I want. Oho! We're an obstinate set all right. Tell me, what happened at all to Uncle Ned Collis?'

She threw her head sideways to laugh again, but this time her laugh was a half groan.

'There was a wild divil o' hell for you. Always hitting the bottle. Once when he was on a batter didn't he lose his ship at the North Wall, and what did he do but dive into the Liffey and swim after it to the Poolbeg lighthouse, where he knew it would be halting. He died raving in New Orleans.'

He had once been in New Orleans. He saw the mists and the lights on the Mississippi. His eyes blazed:

'Divils o' hell, every one of them! My mother often told me about a Collis woman who swam from Ireland's Eye to the Bailey lighthouse around by Balscadden, a swim no man ever did before or since.' He got up and took her hand in his two hands. 'Lily, there's nobody like the old stock. There was always great stuff in us.' He felt her ring, looked at it and back at her. 'Family?'

'Three, two boys and a girl. Not that they're boys any longer. The eldest is married. He went off to England last month. He's a doctor. The second is on a ship; he's a radio officer. Annie's at home; she's a radiologist.' She paused, saw him look over her uniform, smiled proudly. 'You know Victor well – he's the headwaiter at the Oyster.'

'Good Lord, I must have seen him every week of my life for the last ten years. Why didn't he talk to me and say who he was?'

'It wouldn't be right. But leave you talk to him the next time you go into the Oyster.'

'I will.'

But he had the premonition that he would never dine at the Oyster again. She went on:

'Now that the children are grown up I take a relief job like this now and again. For a night, for a week. What do I want sitting at home in Ringsend doing nothing? I'm here just for tonight. Tomorrow, now, I'll go around and see the lakes.'

'So you married and lived happy ever afterwards.'

'Since you wouldn't have me,' she laughed coyly. 'But what about yourself?'

He released her hand.

'I'm an old dyed-in-the-wool bachelor, Lily. I was too busy and ambitious for that sort of thing when I was young, and now that I'm an old codger nobody wants me.'

'Nonsense, Jerry,' she said maternally. 'I saw you throwing great sheep's eyes at Miss Shannon. You'll get married one of these days. But I'm keeping you from your friends, and I ought to be on the job. It was grand talking about old times, Jerry. I'm glad one Collis anyway made a success of his life. You gave a great speech. They're all talking about it in the lounge. They say you're sure to be given the job. What is it?'

He made a little grimace.

'Just a big housing scheme. But all I'm interested in is that whoever gets it should do it properly. Old things are precious, Lily. The older I grow the more I feel it.'

'Of course you should get it,' she declared loyally. 'Who better? And I hope you'll make a packet of money out of it.'

They shook hands warmly. He watched her walking away from him down the corridor. A tidy figure. Handsome. Full of courage. And damned intelligent. In the bar Stella's song was dying sweetly and sadly.

> If thus the cold world now wither
> Each feeling that once was dear . . .

He hesitated, saw a French window beside him, opened it and stepped out into the night.

The darkness was moist but warm. The whole sky one basketful of stars. Feeling a gravel path under his shoes, he walked slowly along it until he heard the lake lapping the shore like a cat, and, as he grew accustomed to the dark, he made out a small wooden wharf jutting into the waves in the lee of a boathouse. He smelled laurels, and rotting wrack and reeds. He leaned against the shed, and half saw the wide lakes stretching all around, with their black islands, and their peaked mountains cutting off the stars. The south wind flowed gently and indifferently over it all.

Afterwards he would say, 'She gave me a bit of a shake, I can tell you.' Yet what it was in their brief encounter that disturbed him he could never say. All he knew was that he had felt a shadow, silent as a cloud, that he had not heeded for many years, and a sudden wish to be alone with it. He stayed by the lake for the length of three cigarettes.

They had lived recklessly, some of them wildly, all of them devil-may-cares who took life in both hands and squandered it without calculation. But because they had lived like that they did not need pity. Old Ned, diving drunk off the side of the quay and swimming after his ship? He'd have spat on pity! 'Died raving in New Orleans . . . ' They had refused, rejected, despised something precious, and powerful and real, but they were not failures. Failures were another kind of drunk altogether, fellows like Condon Larkin, hanging around waiting for somebody's pity to pick them out of the gutter. He whipped his second cigarette out of his case and lit it with an angry click of his lighter. Failures are ambitious, calculating people, men who feel disaster in the softest wind. It was not that they were just reckless. Lily was a Collis. With her eyes that could skiver you, and her hard little body like a pony, and her hands like plates, and her three children she'd slaved for, made one a doctor, one a radiologist, sent one to sea, as she sent old Victor padding off every morning and evening to the Oyster in his black tie and his tails. He saw their box of a house in Ringsend, red brick, three windows, a green door with an iron knocker, one of hundreds like it, near the sooty church by the canal basin, never free of the rattle of the trams, car lights flashing across the ceilings, ships' sirens on the Liffey. He laughed admiringly. Just the sort of woman who would have swum from Ireland's Eye to the Bailey lighthouse and back again. With a gasp of anger he had flicked his cigarette in an arc into the water. 'She knocked me off my stilts somehow,' he would say afterwards. But he would never admit that she had left him with a sense of smallness and shame.

Lighting his third cigarette, he turned in the direction of the hotel and the faint throb of dance music. Young Collyer would probably say that he was slobbering now about the small homes of the living as before about the big houses of the dead. He went on slowly beside a stony piece of beach and the slopping water until he saw to his left the bright windows beaming light down over the lawn to a white garden seat at the edge of the lake. One window was open. Through it he could see the dancers when they moved past it.

Halted, he was looking irresolutely at the window when he heard his name called from somewhere nearby. He made out a rustic summer house with a conical, thatched roof, at the end of a tiny side path. He walked towards it, peered in, and saw two cigarettes glowing in the dark.

'Who's there?' he asked.

'Us,' said Stella's voice, softly.

He flicked on his cigarette lighter and held it like a torch over his head.

'The Statue of Liberty?' Stella's voice asked.

He made out Condon Larkin sitting beside her. Her shoulders were bare, her face pale, her neck as straight as a swan's, and he thought that she was looking at him quizzically. Just before he put out the flame he saw on the table between them a bottle of brandy. He stopped and entered and sat beside her, and, gradually, by the reflected sheen of the lights and the stars, he saw her better, and that her two hands were clasping a brandy glass as if it were a chalice. He felt a great knot of anger against Larkin bulging in his chest but he managed to say quietly:

'Stella, dear, don't you think it would be more prudent for you to sit indoors? Or at least to wear a wrap?'

Her head swayed feebly on her long neck like a daffodil in a slight wind, and she said in a kind parody of his voice:

'Dear Jerry. Prudent Jerry. Surely you ought to be indoors promoting your cause?'

Larkin leaned across her towards him and began to speak in the overslow, overcareful enunciation of all drunks.

'Mis-ter Pres-i-dent, we were discuss-ing you. I want to con-grat-ulate you, most sincerely. On a very subtle speech. Especially that part of your speech that dealt with Templeogue. I sincere-ly hope they will put you in charge of the entire scheme. I sincerely mean that.'

'Shut up, Larkin,' he said crossly.

'Stella! Our Pres-i-dent tells me to shut up. But I won't shut up. Why should I shut up? It was a very fine speech. And I repeat that.'

'All right, Larkin! What you are trying to say, only you haven't the guts to say it straight out, is that all I care about is getting the Templeogue job. Thank you kindly.'

Stella laid her hand on his, softly.

'Jerry! Condy and I have often talked about this. We believe that what you said about creating and destroying being very close to one another is true. Terribly true.'

He realized from her touch and her tone that they were not mocking him: they really had liked his speech. Larkin leaned over again, crushing Stella against him in a blended waft of jasmine and brandy.

'She's right. It's terribly true! "To create," you said, "is to change. And to change is to de-stroy." And why is it true? It's true because every man who creates is a god-damned, flame-ing, bloody ego-tist. That's why I'll always be a dud. No, Stella!' he snarled querulously, shoving her hand away from him. 'You've rubbed it into me often enough. I'm too diffident. I've no ambition. I'm a dud!'

She sighed at Jerry.

'It's why Condy and I liked your speech so much, Jerry. We feel that everybody should be more diffident. Let things grow naturally, like leaves. You know – the lilies of the field and all that. Condy says why should anybody impose his hand on the handiwork of God?'

His anger burst from him.

'But that isn't what I meant at all. We have to create whether we like it or not. People have to live in houses. We have to build for them, and go on building, even if it's only a road, a bridge, a culvert over a stream. We have to go on into the future. What I'd like to do is to manoeuvre vast schemes for living people about these old towns and villages, spread on and on and out and out, like an army of tanks sweeping in wide arcs about some country they want to conquer. We have to do it. Even if we don't want to do it life will make us do it, shoving us on behind. We can't help it!'

Larkin started to say something, and then gave up the ghost, his head sinking into his arms, his glass rolling over to the ground. Almost at once his heavy breathing showed that he had fallen asleep. For a moment Stella's hand hovered towards his head, and then slowly returned to her glass. She whispered:

'I'm afraid he's a weak argument against you. Actually he is a very good architect. He just hasn't got your drive.'

He said irritably:

'This gazebo is as damp as a fungus. Let's get out of here for a minute for a breath of clean air.'

She rose, and teetered a little. When he held her arm to steady her it was like taking a bird by the wing. Outside she lifted her furrowed forehead to the sky and murmured, 'The stars of heaven.' She had a strangely worn face for so young a woman. The pose had tautened her small breasts. He wanted to touch her bare shoulders.

'Stella! You'll never be able to do anything with him. He's not a good architect. He's not a good anything. He's just a drunk.'

Still upward-looking, she waved a hand in weak deprecation.

'Please, don't bring all that up again.'

'Stella! Is the real reason why you won't have me that I'm too old?'

She did not so much shake her head as let it roll from side to side, and then it rolled downward of its own weight so that she was looking out under her wrinkled forehead to where the light from the hotel touched the water's edge. He asked passionately:

'Why must you always go around picking people up out of the gutter? Lame dogs. Weaklings. Fellows who . . .'

She silenced him with a hand on his arm, and a backward look at the summer hut.

'Poor Condy!' she protested softly.

'And why not poor Jerry? Don't I deserve anything? Haven't I worked for it? Don't I deserve a wife, and a home, and children?'

'Poor Jerry,' she placated with an appealing smile. 'I'm sure you deserve a lot of things.'

'But not from you?'

'I wouldn't be any use to you, Jerry. I'd always want to be whatever I am, and you would always be wanting to change me. Oh, I know you'd be kind to me, proud of me, preserve one little corner of me to show your friends, but you'd surround me, encircle me, swallow me up the way you would like to swallow up Templeogue.'

They were silent for a moment, both looking out at the dark lake that slopped endlessly.

'So you really didn't believe a word I said tonight?'

'I believed it. But you did not. You are very ambitious, aren't you, Jerry?'

He did not answer her. He became so excited by the hope that she was asking a question about whose answer she was still in doubt that his fists in his pockets began to tremble, and he was made almost drunk by the scent of her body beside him, and the smells of the lake and the shore and the whispering waves. He did not look at her, but he knew that she was swaying gently by his side, looking up at him.

'All I want is you. You'd be my inspiration in everything I did.'

'What a role!'

'I want nothing in the world but you.'

'Not even Templeogue?'

'If I give up Templeogue will you marry me?'

'Yes! Like a shot!'

He said nothing. She lifted her head to the stars and began to laugh mockingly. She stopped suddenly. From inside the hut the sleepy voice groaned her name. She turned and faced the dark opening. She laid a hand on Jerry's arm.

'He's not a bad architect. He should have a job in the Board of Works, looking after old Georgian houses, old churches, old monuments. He has great taste, great reverence. There is a job vacant in the Board of Works. It would suit him perfectly. Could you say a word for him there, Jerry?'

He looked down at her delicate, worried, tiny face.

'Supposing I took that job myself, would you marry me?'

She shook her head drunkenly.

'Jerry! You might as well try to walk on the lake. We are what we are.'

He took her forcibly by her bare shoulders.

'Stella! Stay with me, come away with me.'

She released herself gently, went into the hut and composedly sat down. He saw her hand stroke the tousled head on the table, and he knew in that instant that in trying to save Larkin she would ruin her own life, and all sorts of ideas jumbled wildly into him, such as that there is no such thing as saving your life or squandering your life because nobody knows what life is until he has lived out so much of it that it is too late then to do anything but go on the way you have gone on, or been driven on, from the beginning. We are free to be, to act, to live, to create, to imagine, call it whatever you like, only inside our own destiny, or else to spit in the face of destiny and be destroyed by it. If a man won't do that all he can do is to bake his bread and throw it on the waters, and hope to God that what he is doing – he gazed up and around him – is the will of the night, the stars, the god of this whole flaming bloody unintelligible universe.

He turned and strode towards the lighted windows. The central window of the middle three was a French window, opening on to steps leading to the lawn. He went up there, and stood in the opening, his hands in his pockets, his shoulders back, watching the couples floating by, smiling benevolently whenever his eye caught somebody he knew. Presently he saw, on a settee in a corner, young Collyer and Kevin Lowry with two young women. He advanced towards them jauntily, swaying his shoulders and his tails, beaming at them.

'Well, now!' he laughed, sitting between the two young women and putting his arms around their shoulders. 'Boys, I see, will be boyos, and it follows that girls will be girlos! Here, what are we drinking? Where are the bloody waiters?'

He raised an arm, clicked his fingers, and Lily Collis came forward smiling. He winked at her.

'Tell the wine waiter to bring me two bottles of fizz, Lily. The best in the house.'

She cast a quick eye at the two young women, smiled at him and went off.

He had already turned eagerly to the young men, talking to them rapidly and forcefully. Between them was a low table with a white marble top. From his waistcoat pocket he produced a gold pencil and with vigorous strokes he slashed lines across it to mark roads, avenues, fields, houses. At first they listened to him quizzically, giving one another long impassive looks, but by degrees his energy and his enthusiasm flooded them into the net of the discussion, so that when the champagne came they ignored it, leaning absorbedly over the table, pointing, arguing, laughing excitedly. The dancers floated by, the music drummed. Once he leaned back and glanced through the French window. The stars glinted. The dark lake lapped the shore.

A Touch of Autumn in the Air

It was, of all people, Daniel Cashen of Roscommon who first made me realize that the fragments of any experience that remain in a man's memory, like bits and scraps of a ruined temple, are preserved from time not at random but by the inmost desires of his personality.

Cashen was neither sensitive nor intelligent. He was a caricature of the self-made, self-educated, nineteenth-century businessman. Some seventy years ago he had set up a small woollen factory in County Roscommon which, by hard work from early morning to late at night, and by making everybody around him work at the same pace, he developed into a thriving industry which he personally owned. His Swansdown Blankets, for example, were the only kind of blankets my mother ever bought. Though old when I made his acquaintance, he was still a powerful horse of a man, always dressed in well-pressed Irish tweeds, heavy countryman's boots, and a fawn, flat-topped bowler hat set squat above a big, red, square face, heavy handle-bar moustaches and pale blue, staring eyes of which one always saw the complete circle of the iris, challenging, concentrated, slightly mad.

One would not expect such a man to say anything very profound about the workings of the memory, and he did not. All he did was to indulge in a brief burst of reminiscence in a hotel foyer, induced by my casual remark that it was a lovely, sunny day outside but that there was a touch of autumn in the air. The illuminating thing was the bewildered look that came into those pale, staring eyes as he talked. It revealed that he was much more touched and troubled by the Why of memory than by the Fact of memory. He was saying, in effect: Why do I remember that? Why do I not remember the other thing? For the first time in his life something within him had gone out of control.

What he started to talk about was a holiday he spent when just under fifteen, in what was at that time called the Queen's County. It had lasted two months, September and October. 'Lovely, sunny weather, just like today.' What had begun to bother him was not so much that the days had merged and melted together in his memory – after so many years that was only natural – but that here and there, from a few days of no more evident importance than any other days, a few trivial things stuck up above the tides of forgetfulness. And as he mentioned them I could see that he was fumbling, a little fearfully, towards the notion that there might be some meaning in the pattern of those indestructible bits of the jigsaw of his youth, perhaps even some sort of revelation in their obstinacy after so much else had dropped down the crevices of time.

He did not come directly to the major memory that had set his mind working in this way. He mentioned a few lesser memories first, staring out through the revolving glass doors at the sunny street. There was the afternoon when, by idle chance, he leaned over a small stone bridge near his Uncle Bartle's farm and became held for an hour by the mesmerism of the stream flickering through the chickweed. As could happen likewise to a great number of busy men, who normally never think at all about the subjective side of themselves, and are overwhelmed by the mystery of it if once they do advert to it, he attached an almost magical import to the discovery that he had never forgotten the bright pleasure of that casual hour.

'No, John! Although it must be near sixty years ago. And I don't believe I ever will forget it. Why is that?'

Of course, he admitted modestly, he had a phenomenal memory, and to prove it he invited me to ask him the telephone numbers of any half-dozen shops in town. But, yet, there was that red hay barn where he and his cousin, Kitty Bergin, played and tumbled a score of times – it was a blur.

'I can't even remember whether the damn thing was made of timber or corrugated iron!'

Or there was the sunken river, away back on the level leas, a stream rather than a river, where one warm September Sunday after Mass he saw, with distasteful pleasure, the men splashing around naked, roughly ducking a boy who had joined them, laughing at his screams. But, whereas he also still possessed the soft, surrounding fields, the imperceptibly moving clouds, the crunch of a jolting cart far away, the silence so deep that you could have heard an apple falling, he had lost every detail of the walk to and from the river, and every hour before and after it. A less arrogant man might have accepted the simple explanation that the mind wavers in and out of alertness, is bright at one moment, dim at the next. Those mad, round irises glared at the suggestion that his mind could at any time be dim.

He pointed out that he knew the country for miles around, intimately, walking it and cycling it day after day: what clung to him of it all, like burrs, were mere spots – a rusty iron gate falling apart, a crossroads tree with a black patch burnt at its base, an uneventful turn off the main road, a few undistinguished yards of the three miles of wall around the local demesne. He laughed scornfully at my idea that his mind became bright only for those few yards of wall.

'Well, perhaps it became dim then? You were thinking hard about other things up to that point in your walk?'

Here he allowed his real trouble to expose itself. He had not only remembered pointless scraps, but, I found, those scraps had been coming back to him repeatedly during the last few days with a tormenting joy, so that here he was, an old man, fondling nothings as lovingly as if he were fondling a lock of a dead woman's hair. It was plain, at last, that he was thinking of all those fragments of his boyhood as the fish scales of some wonderful fish, never-to-be-seen, sinuous and shining, that had escaped from his net into the ocean.

What had started him off was simple. (I reconstruct it as well as I can, intuiting and enlarging from his own brief, blunt words.) A few mornings before our meeting, fine and sunny also, he had happened to go into a toyshop where they also sold sweets. He was suddenly transfixed by the smell peculiar to these shops – scented soaps, the paint on the tin toys and the sprayed wooden trucks, the smell of the children's gift books, the sweetness of the sweets. At once he was back in that holiday, with his cousin Kitty Bergin, on the leas behind her father's farmhouse (his Uncle Bartle's), one sunny, mistified October morning, driving in a donkey cart down to where his uncle and his cousin Jack were ditching a small meadow that they had retrieved from the rushes and the bog water.

As Kitty and he slowly jolted along the rutted track deeper and deeper into this wide, flat river basin of the Barrow, whose hundreds of streams and dykes feed into what, by a gradual addition, becomes a river some twenty miles away, the two men whom they were approaching looked so minute on the level bog, under the vast sky, that Dan got a queer feeling of his own smallness in observing theirs. As he looked back, the white, thatched farmhouse nestling into the earth had never seemed so homely, cosy and comforting.

Ferns crackled at the hub. When he clutched one its fronds were warm but wet. It was the season when webs are flung with a wild energy across chasms. He wiped his face several times. He saw dew drops in a row in mid-air, invisibly supported between frond and frond. A lean swathe of mist, or was it low cloud, floated beneath far hills. Presently they saw behind the two men a pond with a fringe of reeds. Against an outcrop of delicately decayed limestone was a bent hawthorn in a cloud of ruby berries. Or could it have been a rowan tree? The sky was a pale green. The little shaven meadow was as lemon-bright as fallen ash leaves before the dew dries on their drifts, so that it would have been hard to say whether the liquid lemon of the meadow was evaporating into the sky or the sky melting down into the field.

They were on a happy mission. Mulvaney the postman had brought two letters to the farmhouse from two other sons: Owen, who was a pit manager in the mines at Castlecomer, and Christopher (who, out of respect, was never referred to as Christy), then studying for the priesthood in a Dublin seminary. Aunt Molly had sent them off with the letters, a jug of hot tea and thick rounds of fresh, homemade bread and homemade apple jam smelling of cloves, a great favourite of Uncle Bartle's. They duly reached the two men, relieved the donkey of bridle, bit and winkers so that he could graze in the meadow, spread sacks to sit on, and while Kitty poured the tea into mugs Bartle reverently wiped his clayey hands on the sides of his trousers and took the letters. As he read them aloud in a slow, singsong voice, like a man intoning his prayers, it was clear that those two sons had gone so far outside his own experience of the big world that he stood a little in awe of them both. It was a picture to be remembered for years: the meadow, the old man, the smoke of the distant farmhouse, patriarchal. sheltered, simple.

When he laid down the letter from the priest-to-be he said:

'He's doing well. A steady lad.'

When he had read the letter from the mines he said:

'He's doing fine. If he escapes the danger he will go far.'

While Jack was reading the letters Kitty whispered to Danny, thumbing the moon's faint crescent:

'Look! It says D for Danny.'

'Or,' he murmured to her boldly, 'it could be D for Dear?'

Her warning glare towards her father was an admission.

'I see here,' Jack commented, while his father sucked at the tea, 'that

Christopher is after visiting Fanny Emphie. Her name in religion is Sister Fidelia.'

Dan had seen this girl at the Curragh Races during the first week of his holidays, a neighbour's daughter who, a few weeks later, entered the convent. He had heard them joking one night about how she and Christopher had at one time been 'great' with one another. He remembered a slight, skinny girl with a cocked nose, laughing moist lips and shining white teeth.

'Read me out that bit,' Bartle ordered. 'I didn't note that.'

'"I got special leave from the President to visit Sister Fidelia, last week, at Saint Joachim's. She is well and happy but looked pale. She asked after you all. Saint Joachim's has nice grounds, but the trams pass outside the wall and she said that for the first couple of weeks she could hardly sleep at all."'

The two men went on drinking their tea. It occurred to Dan that they did not care much for Fanny Emphie. He saw her now in her black robes walking along a gravelled path under the high walls of the convent, outside which the trams at night drew their glow in the air overhead. It also occurred to him, for no reason, that Kitty Bergin might one day think of becoming a nun, and he looked at her with a pang of premonitory loss. Why should any of them leave this quiet place?

'Ha!' said old Bartle suddenly, and winked at Danny, and rubbed his dusty hands and drew out his pipe. This meant that they must all get back to work.

Kitty gathered up the utensils, Danny tackled the donkey, the others went back to their ditching and she and Danny drove back to where the fern was plentiful for bedding. Taking two sickles, they began to rasp through the stalks. After a while she straightened up, so did he, and they regarded one another, waist-deep in the fern.

'Do you think,' she asked him pertly, 'would I make a nice nun?'

'You!' he said, startled that the same thought had entered their heads at the same time.

She came across to him, slipped from his pocket the big blue handkerchief in which the bread had been wrapped, cast it in an arc about her fair head, drew it tightly under her chin with her left hand, and then with a deft peck of her right finger and thumb cowled it forward over her forehead and her up-looking blue eyes.

'Sister Fidelia, sir,' she curtsied, provokingly.

He grappled with her as awkwardly as any country boy, paying the sort of homage he expected was expected of him, and she, laughing, wrestled strongly with him. They swayed in one another's arms, aware of each other's bodies, until she cried, 'Here's Daddy,' and when he let her go mocked him from a safe distance for his innocence. But as they cut the fern again her sidelong glances made him happy.

They piled the cut fern into the cart, climbed on top of it, and lay face down on it, feeling the wind so cold that they instinctively pressed closer together. They jolted out to the main road, and as they ambled along they talked, and it seemed to him that it was very serious talk, but he forgot every word of it. When they came near the crossroads with its little sweetshop, they decided to buy a half-penny-worth of their favourite sweets, those flat, odd-shaped sweets – diamonds, hearts, hexagonals – called Conversation Lozenges because each sweet bore on its coarse surface a ring-posy in coloured ink, such as Mizpah, Truth Tries Troth, Do You Care? or All for Love. Some bore girls' names, such as Gladys or Alice. His first sweet said, Yours in Heart. He handed it to her with a smile; she at once popped it into her mouth, laughing at his folly. As they ambled along so, slowly, chatting and chewing, the donkey's hooves whispering through the fallen beech leaves, they heard high above the bare arches of the trees the faint honking of the wild geese called down from the north by the October moon.

It was to those two or three hours of that October morning many years ago that he was whirled back as he stood transfixed by the smells of the sweets-and-toys-shop. Forgetting what he had come there to buy, he asked them if they sold Conversation Lozenges. They had never heard of them. As he turned to go he saw a nun leafing through the children's gift books. He went near her and, pretending to look at a book, peered under her cowl. To his surprise she was a very old nun. On the pavement he glanced up at the sky and was startled to see there the faint crescent moon. He was startled because he remembered that he had seen it earlier in the morning, and had quite forgotten the fact.

He at once distrusted the message of his memory. Perhaps it was not that the smells had reminded him of little Kitty Bergin eating Yours in Heart, or pretending to be a nun, or wrestling with him in the fern? Perhaps what had called him back was the indifference of those two men to the fate of the nun? Or was there some special meaning for him in those arrowing geese? Or in the cosy, sheltered farmhouse? Maybe the important thing that day had been the old man humbly reading the letters? Why had the two men looked so small under the open sky of the bogland? D, she had said, for Danny . . .

As he stared at me there in the hotel foyer, my heart softened towards him. The pain in his eyes was the pain of a man who has begun to lose one of the great pleasures of life in the discovery that we can never truly remember anything at all, that we are for a great part of our lives at the mercy of uncharted currents of the heart. It would have been futile to try to comfort him by saying that those currents may be charted elsewhere, that even when those revolving glass doors in front of us flashed in the October sun the whole movement of the universe since time began was involved in that coincidence of light. Daniel Cashen of Roscommon would get small comfort out of thinking of himself as a little blob of phosphorescence running along the curl of a wave at night.

And then, by chance, I did say something that comforted him, because as he shook hands with me and said he must be off, I said, without thinking:

'I hope the blankets are doing well?'

'Aha!' he cried triumphantly. 'Better than ever.'

And tapped his flat-topped hat more firmly on his head and whirled the doors before him out into the sunny street as imperiously as any man accustomed to ordering everything that comes his way.

Through the slowing doors I watched him halt on the pavement. He looked slowly to the right, and then he looked towards his left, and then, slowly, he looked up around the sky until he found what he was looking for. After a few moments he shivered up his shoulders around his neck, looked at the ground at his feet, put his two hands into his pockets, and moved very slowly away, still down-looking, out of sight.

Poor man, I thought when he was gone; rash, blunt, undevious; yet, in his own crude way, more true to life than his famous French contemporary who recaptured lost time only by dilating, inventing, suppressing, merging such of its realities as he could recall, and inventing whatever he could not. Cashen was playing archaeology with his boyhood, trying to deduce a whole self out of a few dusty shards. It was, of course, far too late. My guess was that of the few scraps that he now held in his hands the clue lay not so much in the offer of love and the images of retirement, the girl's courtship, the white farmhouse snuggling down cosily into the earth under the vast dome of the sky, and the old man left behind by his sons, as in the challenging sight of his own littleness on that aqueous plain whose streams barely trickled to the open sea. He said he hadn't thought of it for sixty years. Perhaps not? But he was thinking of it now, when the adventure was pretty well over. As it was. A week later a friend rang me up and said, 'Did you hear who's died?' I knew at once, but I asked the question.

He left nearly a hundred and fifty thousand pounds – a lot of money in our country – and, since he never married, he divided it all up among his relatives by birth, most of them comparatively poor people and most of them living in what used to be called, in his boyhood, the Queen's County.

The Younger Generation

When the door closed behind Count Toby the bishop's eyebrows soared. He swivelled back to his desk with a groan, took up his pen, and read the last sentence that he had written an hour ago. Then he shook his head like a dog just come out of a river. The finger with the great amethyst ring began to tap the mahogany. He lifted the edge of his cuff, glanced at his wristlet watch, and said aloud, 'Oh, dear, dear!' When he heard the door opening once more he lifted the eyes of a martyr to the ceiling.

'I'm sorry for interrupting you again, my lord,' palpitated Count Toby. 'I just came back to beg you not to say a word about all this to my wife. And I'm very sorry to have occupied so much of your time. I've talked much too much about my unfortunate affairs. You didn't come to Aughty Castle for *that*. And I'm just sending in Bridie with your egg flip.'

He backed out, bumped the jamb, said, 'Sorry, sorry,' as if he were apologizing to the door. He closed it with a tiny click.

'Ninny!' the bishop grunted, swivelled back, gripped his pen in his fist like a dagger, glared again at what he had written, read it twice, read it three times, exhaled groaningly, and tossed down the pen.

He made yet another effort to concentrate on his pastoral. ' . . . and so guide them,' he intoned, 'to a happy union where their own lives shall repeat this same wonderful cycle of love, marriage and parenthood.'

He leaned back and let his eyes wander to the ocean's vast dishes of sunlight. A yacht, miles out, was becalmed in the dead centre of one of those circles of sun. His eyes sank to the rocks offshore, pale as pearls. On the second terrace the gardener was softly raking the gravel.

'Such a lovely place!'

He took out his pouch and his pipe and began, pensively, to fill it. The raking stopped. The only sound then was a thrush cracking a snail against a stone, and the bishop chuckling softly and sardonically into his pouch.

'Poor Toby!' he said.

His finger deftly coaxed the shreds into the bowl.

'Still, gentleman,' he murmured into his pouch, 'this is going just a little bit too far. I suppose it's fair enough for the laity to treat us as their spiritual doctors. As we are, there's no getting away from it, as we are. But really and truly! And yet, gentlemen, we're told that the first ten years of marriage are the worst? Well, we make many sacrifices, gentlemen, but . . . ' He let pouch and pipe sink into his lap and looked out to sea again. 'How long can they be . . . It must be twenty years . . .'

Tut-tutting, he resumed the filling of his pipe.

'You know what it is, gentlemen? There's a good deal of truth in the old country saying that the best of wives needs a dose of ashplant medicine now and again. Externally applied, gentlemen. Well laid on, gentlemen. As my old gardener, Philly Cashman, used to say – God be good to him, many a dewy head o' cabbage he stole from me back in County Cavan – "There's only the wan cure, me lord, for shlow horses and fasht women and that's the shtick!"'

As he lit his pipe he looked through the smoke at his unfinished pastoral. Hurling away the match, he puffed fiercely, seized the pen, and with concentration wrote a new heading: 'Duties of Married People Towards Each Other'. He drove on heavily for about five minutes, but it was like pushing a wheelbarrow through mud. There was a knock at the door. The egg flip?

'Come in!'

He achieved another sentence.

'My lord, am I disturbing you?'

He swivelled, and rose.

'Good morning, Miss Burke! I thought it was the maid with my egg flip.' He held out his hand. He noticed that she did not kiss the ring. 'You weren't down to breakfast? Ah, I see you were out riding.'

She might have changed out of her jodhpurs. He admired the handsome, sullen face, the bold wings to the eyebrows; very like the mother; a divil at a point-to-point. She twirled her crop nervously between her fingers.

'My lord, I want to apologize. I mean for last night. It's dreadful that this sort of thing should happen the very first night you stay with us. And you came for rest and – '

She indicated his pastoral with a glance.

'Say nothing at all about it, child. A thing of nothing. These little upsets occur in the best of households. You were just a little upset last night. A bit out of sorts.'

The dark head tilted like a frightened race horse. The eyes, dilated, caught the blue of the sky.

'I wasn't apologizing for myself. Mummy has been like that for months past. You must excuse her.'

'Your mother is a great credit to your rearing,' he said dryly.

She reddened and cried:

'Daddy is a martyr to her; nobody else would stand her for a week.'

'My child! My child!'

'But it's perfectly true. I know my own mother. This has been going on for years.'

'Miss Anne,' he took her trembling hand, 'sit down there and listen to me'. She took the edge of a chair. 'I've known you since you were that high.' He smiled at her paternally. 'I've known ye all since I was a simple curate in this parish thirty-one years ago. Look now, I'm not going to talk to you like a bishop at all but like an old friend of the family. You're not being quite fair to your mother. She's worried about this marriage of yours.'

'Oh, it's natural that you'd take Mummy's side. I quite understand that. It's natural you wouldn't want me to marry a Protestant but...'

'Now, that's where you're wrong. It's not at all natural. On the contrary. It's the most natural thing in the wide world for you to fall in love with this young man, why wouldn't you? When a girl is attracted by the twinkle in a young man's eye, or the cock of his head, or whatever else it is that attracts ye in young men' – he invited her smile; she yielded it perfunctorily – 'it isn't of his religion she does be thinking. And if a girl does fall in love with a young man, what is more natural than that she should want to marry him? What is more proper, in fact? And, then, Miss Anne, what would be more natural than that I, or any other priest, would want to see that young girl married to the man she loves?'

She stared at him, darting from one eye to the other, in search of the snare.

'But, Miss Anne, we can't live by nature alone.'

As he waited for her to appreciate his point, he heard the thrush cracking another snail. In a faint impulse of irritation he remembered the Persian fable about the holy man whose first impulsive desires were all fulfilled, disastrously.

'What I mean is, we sometimes have to resist our natural impulses.'

'But,' she almost sobbed, 'Mummy isn't thinking of anything like that. She wouldn't care if he was a Turk. It's just that she doesn't want me to be married to anybody. She's jealous of me, she always was jealous of me, she hates me, and I hate her, I *do*, I hate her!'

'Oh, dear, dear! You know, Miss Anne . . . The present generation . . . When I was a boy in County Cavan . . . Listen to me! A mother is the best guide any girl could possibly . . . She is wiser in the ways of the world than you are. She's . . .'

She laughed harshly.

'But it isn't true, my lord. Mummy isn't in the least wise. She's got no sense at all. What's the use of pretending? Oh, I do wish, my lord – I'm not being rude or disrespectful – that priests wouldn't always talk to me as if I were a girl of fifteen or a servant in the kitchen. I'm a grown woman. And as for Mummy being better than me, well, the fact of the matter is, you must have seen it for yourself last night, she drinks like a fish. She's tight half the day.'

He leaned back and stroked his cheek heavily. He surveyed her coldly.

'Do you love this man very much?'

'Yes.'

He detected a shadow of a pause, and peered at her.

'My lord, I hope you won't mind my saying this. It often seems to me that there is . . . that the Church in Ireland . . . that it caters only to the poor and ignorant and there's no place in it for educated people.'

'Well, Miss Anne, it may be, it may be. But if there is no room in the Church for educated people, what is going to happen to poor me?'

She collapsed. He could see her knees trembling. He raised his hand.

'Tell me, my child, do you belong to any club anywhere? Any club? A tennis club? Anything?'

She was on guard again.

'I belong to the Automobile Club in Dublin. It's useful when I go up for a dance and want to change my frock.'

'All right. Very well. Now, there are rules in that club, aren't there?'

'Yes. Of course.' Watching him carefully.

'And in any other club there are rules? And if you don't like those rules you have to leave the club – or they'll throw you out on your neck. Isn't that so?'

'Ye-e-es. I suppose so.'

'And you may go from club to club, but no matter where you halt there are still rules? Aren't there? And,' leaning close to her and speaking with all the solemnity in his power, 'if you aren't satisfied to obey the rules of any club all you can do is go wandering around the streets like a lost soul. Isn't that so?'

She saw his point. Her eyes fell.

'Isn't that so?' he insisted, almost bullying her.

'In a way . . .'

'Isn't that the whole thing in a nutshell? You want to dodge the rules. Isn't that the holy all of it?'

'I could go to a hotel,' she said wildly.

He had to laugh at that.

'Even in a hotel there are rules. I live in a palace. A palace, God help us! Do you think I don't have to toe the line? All you want is your own will and your own way, without regard to the commands of the Church. Be honest, now. Admit it like a brave girl. Isn't that the beginning and end of it?'

'But there are rules and rules, there are sensible rules, in England Catholics are allowed to marry Protestants under dispensation, why should an absolute rule be laid down here?'

'Because I say so,' he said severely, and felt his back to the wall. 'It is the rule of this diocese. It is *my* rule.'

He looked hastily at his desk to indicate that there was no more to be said. He knew what she would try next if he gave her half a chance, and his face darkened as a hundred unpleasant ideas poured into his mind – Gallicanism, *cuius regio*, Modernism, Loisy and Tyrrell and old von Hügel, who barely escaped by the skin of his teeth, the Tutiorists, centuries of dispute, the souls who were lost in heresy, the souls that were barely saved . . .

She made one last effort, her lovely features buttoned up with anger and despair and humiliation.

'But, my lord, if I lived in another diocese this silly rule wouldn't apply to me.'

'Silly? Thank you very much, Miss Burke.'

'I'm sorry. I'm being rude. I beg your pardon. Our guest. Peace and quietness. The first night...'

'No apologies, Miss Anne. We're old friends. Come to me, child, if you are in trouble at any time. I'll pray for you. Now, God help me, I must write my pastoral.'

When she shut the door, he sat to his desk, took a new sheet and wrote fast: 'Duties of Children to Parents and Superiors.' He jotted down guide words. 'Obedience. Respect. Discipline. Changing times. Young generation. Church as Wise Guardian. Patience and Understanding.' He wrote easily on the last theme.

' ... warm young blood ... In misunderstanding their own true motives ... Yet this spirit of rebellion is sometimes no more than the headstrong impatience of youth, and the Church will gently and kindly guide them from this wayward path back to those sane and wise precepts which the experience of centuries has tested and not found wanting.'

He read it aloud, crumpled the page and hurled it into the wastepaper basket.

The yacht was still becalmed in the centre of an unruffled circle. The door opened after a faint knock and the maid came in with the egg flip. He relaxed.

'Thanks, Bridie. You *are* Bridie?'

'Yes, Father, I mean my lord.' Curtsying.

'Bridie what?'

'Bridie Lynam, my lord.' Curtsying.

'That's a familiar name. Where do you come from?'

'West of Cootehill, my lord.' Curtsying.

'Ah, no?' In huge, boyish delight. 'So you're a Cavan girl? Well, well, isn't that a coincidence! Cootehill? Ah, glory be to God, Cootehill! Well, to be sure and to be sorry.' He beamed at her. 'Bridie Lynam from Cootehill in the County Cavan. I'm delighted to hear that. Tell me, is it long now since you left Cootehill?'

'Only the two weeks, my lord.'

'Only two weeks! Listen – wallowing back into his chair for a chat. 'Is that ould bakery of Haffigan's still at the end of the Main Street?'

'Indeed it is, my lord.'

He stared and stared at her, or, rather, at the cerise wall of Haffigan's Steam Bakery, and then he burst out into a peal of laughter, while the girl smiled and squirmed shyly to see the bishop laughing over such a simple thing.

'Well, Bridie Lynam, if I got a pound for every time I bought a steaming currant loaf at Haffigan's on my way to school! Dear me.' He took a sip of his egg flip. 'I don't think they put sugar in this, Bridie?'

'Oh, my lord' – red with confusion. 'I'll get it, my lord.'

'Do, do, and come back and we'll have a little gosther about old times. Haffigan's Steam Bakery!'

Smiling broadly, he went back to his desk, and to his first page, and began to punctuate. Then he began to alter words. He was straightway writing in his best vein on the joy of parents in their first child. A knock.

'Come in, come in,' he welcomed and wrote on. He became aware that the countess was speaking to him:

'I'm afraid the egg flip was a bit late, my lord. Anne never told me. She forgets so many things. This room is very close. Let me close the blinds. Where you ever in Venice, my lord?'

'Let them be, please. I like the sun.'

As she kept wandering around, patting a pillow, changing the position of a book, tipping a curtain, peering into the garden, he wondered whether her auburn mop was dyed or false.

'Yes! The sun. The sunflower to the sun.' She looked around her distractedly. 'Anne adores the sun. She lies in it all day long. Strange girl. I do hope everything is all right? I simply cannot get trained servants nowadays. I often long for the old days when one whipped one's serfs.'

Suddenly she swooped on her knees before him, and burst into a loud sobbing wail:

'Oh, my lord, help me! Everybody in this house hates me. Everybody is plotting against me. My daughter hates me. I haven't a friend in the world. What will I do? What will I do?' The bishop looked wildly around him. Her wail became piercing. She clawed at his coat-tails. 'They all think I'm just a stupid, blowzy old woman! Day and night, my lord, they are at me!'

Count Toby opened the door and with a look of shame and agony he said, very gently, 'Mary, dear?' The bishop helped her to her feet. With sudden, monstrous dignity she walked out. The count looked miserably at the bishop and closed the door.

The bishop stared at the door until Bridie Lynam came in with the sugar bowl, pale and flustered.

'Thank you, Bridie,' he whispered. As she was about to go, he decided to add: 'I hope you'll be happy here. Nice place. The count is a grand man. One of the old stock.'

'Yes, my lord.' She added: 'I'm leaving next week, my lord. I'm goin' to England.'

He turned his back on her. The yacht was still there.

'That's a long way away. Have you friends there?'

'Yes, my lord' – softly.

He kept his back to her so that she might not feel shy and asked:

'Is there a boy there?'

Her 'Yes, my lord' was so soft he hardly heard it.

'Irish boy?'

'From Cootehill, my lord.'

He sighed.

'They're all going,' he murmured to himself.

He remained for so long looking out at the scallop of clouds along the horizon that when he turned the room was empty. He sat to his desk again. He moved his papers aside. Drawing another clean sheet towards him, he leaned his head on his hand and began to write a letter.

'My Dearest Darling Mother, I often think how kind the good God has been to me to have given me so good a mother. Since I first knelt at your lap to say my prayers . . . ' He wrote on quietly. 'And as it was you who welcomed me home from school so it was to you that I returned every year from college . . . ' He wrote on, finished the page and signed it, 'Your loving son, Danny.' Then he took the sheet and very carefully, very deliberately, tore it into tiny fragments and let them flutter like snow into the basket.

Then he cupped his face in his hands and whispered, like a prayer, 'Tomorrow I'll say Mass for the respose of your dear soul.' Wearily he resumed his pastoral letter, and now it wrote itself quietly and simply. But as he wrote he felt no joy or pride in it, no more than if this, too, were a letter not to the living but to the dying and the dead. He was not interrupted agai. . By lunchtime he had finished the first draft.

Only Count Toby came to lunch. They talked of old friends and old times. After a while the bishop said, gently, 'Perhaps, Toby, do you think it might be better, conceivably, if I were to leave this afternoon?'

Toby glanced up at him under his sad spaniel's eyebrows.

'Perhaps so, Danny.'

The bishop nodded and began to talk, at random, about the cemetery of Père Lachaise and the wildfire that runs at night along the cemetery paths. The count stirred his coffee in silence: he was remembering how he had taken Anne there when she was fifteen, and how lovely she had looked as she threw herself into his arms at the sight of a little leaping tongue of blue fire among the immortelles on a grave.

'Anne,' he said after a long time, 'has just told me that she is going to take a flat in Dublin.'

'Ha!' said the bishop. 'So she's trying a new club?'

'How is that?' asked Count Toby.

'Ah, nothing! Nothing.'

Love's Young Dream

I don't remember my first visits to that part of Ireland, although my father often told me that since I was four years old I used to be sent there every year, sometimes twice a year. He was a ship's captain, my mother had died when I was three, and whenever he was at sea and no nearer relative could have me I would be sent off for safekeeping to the County Kildare.

The first visit I remember at all clearly was when I was ten, to my Uncle Gerry's farm near the town of Newbridge. I remember it because it was during this visit that Noreen Coogan pushed me into the Liffey. (Noreen was the only child of my aunt's servant, Nancy Coogan; that year she must have been about twelve or thirteen.) I can still see myself standing dripping on the bank, crying miserably, and my uncle assuring me that Noreen – 'The bold, bad slut!' – would be kept far away from me for the rest of the holidays; at which I began to wail more loudly than before, and he, guessing the state of my heart, began to laugh so loudly at me that I fairly bawled.

I have no clear image of what Noreen looked like at the time, or, indeed, at any later time. All I have clearly in my memory is a vision of a cloud of corn-fair hair, and two large cornflower eyes, and for some reason or other, I always want to say that she had a complexion like sweet peas. Perhaps I saw her at some time with a big bunch of cream-and-pink sweet peas in her arms, or standing in a garden with a lot of sweet peas in it, and felt that the delicate blend of colours and scents was a perfect setting for her. But all my memories of those early visits are like that – both actual and dim, like the haze of heat that used to soften the fair surface of the far meadows across the river, or the swarms of gnats rising and sinking hazily over the reeds below the bridge. I am sure I saw my uncle's stableman, Marky Fenelon, quite clearly, a little man with a face all composed of marbles, from his blackberry eyes to his crumpled chin or his tightly wound ears; but when I heard that he was a Palatine I never asked what it meant and did not care. I was very clearly aware of Nancy Coogan, big, bustling, bosomy, bare-armed and with a laugh like a thunderclap, but when I gathered somehow that she and Marky were courting and would marry some day all that this *some day* meant to me was Never. Is all childhood made up of facts of nature that are accepted beyond questioning? Perhaps mine was prolonged. When I was thirteen I was so vague as to what marrying meant that I much amused Nancy by asking her why some ladies are called Miss and some Mrs. She laughed and said the misses are the ones that miss, which I thought very clever indeed.

One reason why Noreen and my clearer memories of Newbridge go together is that she focused my holidays for me. She was their one clear centre from which everything went outward and to which everything returned. For after I was ten she became as certain and fixed a part of those visits as my first sight of the elongated Main Street of Newbridge, with the walls of the cavalry barracks all along one side of it and the sutlers' shops all along the other; or the peaceful sound of the gun wagons jingling along the dusty roads – they suddenly sounded less peaceful the year the Great War broke out; or the happy moment of arrival at the farm when I would run to meet Marky Fenelon in the wide, cobbled yard and at once hand him his ritual present of a pound of sailor's twist, bought for him by my father; or – one of the happiest moments of all – when I would run into the flagged kitchen to Nancy with her ritual present, which was always a lacy blouse bought in some port like Gibraltar, or Naples or Genoa. At the sight of me she would let out a welcoming roar of laughter, squash me up against her great, soft, bulging bosom, give me a smacking kiss and lift me, laughing and shrieking, high in the air until my head nearly touched the ceiling.

It was the year in which I asked my famous question about the difference between misses and missuses that I also felt the first faintest, least stir of questioning interest in Nancy's and Marky's marathon courtship. It was really no more than an idle question and I had only a small interest in the answer. That day she was making soda bread on the kitchen table and I was sitting up on the end of the table watching her knead and pound the dough.

'Nancy!' I said pertly. 'What's up with you at all that you're not marrying Marky? When are you going to marry him? Marry him tomorrow, Nancy! Go on, Nancy! Will you marry him tomorrow?'

She let out one of her wild laughs and began to scrape the dough from her fingers and fling the scrapings down on the kneading board, saying gaily with each flap of her hands:

'This year! Next year! Sometime! Never!'

'Is it the way, Nancy, that you're not in love with Marky?'

This time her laughter was a quarry blast.

'God love you, you poor child, that has nothing at all to do with it. It's just that he doesn't like having Noreen living with us. Now, go off and play with the cat,' she added crossly, and began to carve a deep cross into the flattened loaf. At once I wanted to stab her cake myself and began begging her for the knife. Anyway, this talk about Noreen and Marky merely meant what I had always known, that they would all be always there waiting for me at the start of every holiday.

One reason why I know I was thirteen that year was that the next time I went to stay with Uncle Gerry I was fifteen, and this I know because I very soon found out that those two extra years made a great difference to all of us. What made the difference was that in my fourteenth year I spent a long summer spell with my three Feehan cousins, some seven or eight miles away from the Newbridge farm over on the plain of the Curragh. There I had another uncle, Ken Feehan, who had some sort of job in connection with the racecourse.

The Curragh is famous for two things, its racecourse on one side of the plain and on the other the extended military settlement, which seems to outline the farthest edge of green with the long faint stroke of a red pencil. This settlement is still known as the Camp, long after its original tent canvas has been transformed into barrack squares in red brick, wooden huts, tin chapels and tin shops. Sheltering belts of stunted firs have now been planted along its entire length to protect it from the bitter winds blowing down from the mountains, whose slow drum roll closes the view to the southeast. From the door of my Uncle Ken's house, a long, whitewashed cottage or bungalow near the grandstand, we looked southeast at the far-off red pencil-line across a rolling expanse of short grass, empty except for a few cropping sheep, scattered tufts of furze and an occasional car slowly beetling along the road that crosses the Curragh from Newbridge to the south.

It was an empty place for three girls to live in. It is also to the point that the plain is of great age. The couple of roads that cross it are the old woolpack roads into Danish Dublin. It is known that the distant finger of the round tower of Kildare, to the west, was grey with age in the twelfth century. There was a racecourse here some two thousand years ago. Weapons of the Stone Age have been dug up in various parts of the plain. I like to think of this silent antiquity whenever I think of Philly, the eldest of my three cousins, standing at night at the door of the cottage – it is the way I always remember her now – staring across the plain at the only thing there that really interested her, the remote lights of the military camp. Whether the Camp had always excited her or not I do not know, but when I first met her, after the outbreak of the war, everything about it did – the news of departing or arriving regiments, the crackle of gunfire from the pits, the distant flash of a heliograph on bright days, the faint sound of regimental bands borne to us on the south-easterly wind. Standing there at the cottage door, she would talk endlessly of all the handsome and brave poor boys fighting and falling at that very moment on the plains of Flanders. She inferred the whole war from the flash of a mirror, the short rattle of rifle fire, the faint beating of drums, a wavering bugle call. She was eighteen.

I have no doubts at all about Philly's looks. She was not pretty but she was not plain. I grant that her nose was a bit peaky, her teeth slightly prominent, her figure almost skinny; but she had two lively brown eyes like an Italian girl, and her dark, shining hair was combed slick back from her prominent profile with the effect of a figurehead on a ship's prow. Her lower lip was always moistened by her upper teeth, her hands were nervous, her laughter on a hair trigger, her moods unpredictable and turning as rapidly as a trout in a stream; and she was a magnificent liar. This, I see, is as much an implication of her nature as a description of her appearance, but it is how she struck everybody who met her – an unflattering impression dispelled completely in one second.

That I have no wish to do more than mention her two sisters, Moll and Una, may suggest further the force of her personality. She overshadowed them completely, although both of them were capable and pleasing girls. She bullied Moll all the time and she forced all the housework on her simply by refusing to do her own share of it. Poor Moll, a soft, rotund, pouting girl, was no match for her and never did anything in self-defence except complain feebly, weep a little, then laugh despairingly and with a wag of her bottom go on cheerfully with her double chores. Philly did not need to bully Una, a gentle, fair-flaxen girl of about my own age – she was too young and delicate for bullying, cycled into Newbridge every day to school at the local convent, and studied endlessly when at home. I think she had realized very early that the cottage was a place to get out of as quickly as possible.

I liked the three of them, but I far preferred Philly. She was more fun, and I liked the streak of boyish devilment in her that always made her ready for any escapade. I suppose she suffered me as being better company than none, and I also suppose that the main thing in my favour was that although a child to her eyes I was at least male. This is not merely an unkind remark. Her reputation had preceded my meeting with her. Back in Newbridge the general attitude to her was that she was a foolish virgin. At the mention of her name my Uncle Gerry had just phewed out a long, contemptuously good-humoured breath. My aunt laughed at her. Once she made the witty and shrewd remark: 'That girl has far too many beaus to her string.' Nancy sniffed mockingly, 'That featherhead!'; but she may have jealously compared her to her own adored Noreen. Marky said, 'Aha! A bold lassie!' Noreen was, by turns, respectfully and scornfully silent, but, young as I was, I smelled envy.

As for her own sisters, they admired her and feared her and did not love her. They assured me privately that her list of boys was as long as my arm. ('Boys' was a popular word at that time – the 'boys' at the Front, our 'boys' in Flanders, and so on.) Their list included a rich trainer from the County Meath, a subaltern from the Camp, a jockey, a farmer from behind Kildare, a publican's son in Newbridge, a young lawyer from Dublin, even a stableboy from the stables of one of the wealthy trainers who, then as now, lived in half-timbered houses all around the edge of the plain behind white rails and clipped privet hedges. I gathered that all of these beaus were met on race days, in the enclosure, on the members' stand, in the restaurant, to all of which places, because of her father, she had complete access. There was more than a suggestion that she met her admirers on varying terms, playing whatever role pleased her fancy and suited their class. Certainly, those days when everybody of her own class swarmed on the open plain outside the rails and only the comparatively few paid to go inside them, the daughter of an employee of the Turf Club would have had to present herself very well indeed to be accepted by a lieutenant, a lawyer or a trainer.

I was torn this way and that by her. In loyalty to Newbridge I knew I should think her a figure of fun, and I could see that she was a little bully and a shrew, but she would sweep me off my feet whenever she started to talk about that Camp, whose lights flickered at night across an empty plain. She turned it into a magic doorway to the world. In Newbridge, everything, I have said, had been actual but hazy. When she talked to me about the real world I heard Life begin to paw its stable floor.

'Listen, lad! When you grow up take the King's shilling! Be a soldier! See the world!' And then, with her wide, wild, white-toothed laugh: 'Or, if it has to be, see the next world!'

I shall never have a dim or hazy notion of Philly Feehan as long as I remember the baking day when the four of us stood at the door of the cottage, the racecourse behind us as empty as a ballroom on the morning after a dance, the plain before us as empty as a bed at noon, and watched a small, slow cloud of dust move at marching pace from the Camp towards the railway station at Kildare, and heard the clear rattle of the parting snare drums. She shocked us all by suddenly crying out with passion, her brown eyes fixed on the little creeping dust cloud, her face pale under her shiny, black coif:

'I wish to God Almighty I was a bloody hussar!'

She taught me how to smoke. I drank my first beer with her in a hotel bar across the plain in Kilcullen. She gave me my first lesson in dancing. Looking back at her now, I see why her type of girl was the ideal of the soldiers of the Nineteen-fourteen War. They had been made to think of themselves as 'boys'. Their ideal woman was the young virgin, still with her hair down, the Flapper, a blend of devilment and innocence – their most highly desired antithesis to rain-filled trenches, mud above their puttees, and shells whining and exploding over their heads all day long.

So, you can guess why my next visit to Newbridge was different from any that went before. I was now turned fifteen. Noreen was eighteen. The others were beyond the years. They behaved to me as always, but I was not the same with them. I had become wary. It began the minute I arrived. When my Uncle Gerry drove the old tub-trap into the cobbled yard through the big tarred gates opened by Marky immediately he heard the familiar clop of the pony coming along the road, I handed the ritual pound of twist over the side to Marky, alighted, asked the usual questions, said 'I suppose ye're not married yet?' and then, as if on an afterthought, 'Oh, and how's our little Noreen these days?'

She must have done something to annoy him specially that day because he said grimly and shortly:

'Oh, very well, I believe! A bit rakish, now and again! But very well. In the best of health.'

I was alert at once.

'In what way rakish, Marky?' I laughed innocently.

'Ah!' He shook his head upward. If he had been a horse I would have heard the rattle of the bit and seen the yellow teeth. 'I suppose it might be through having no father to keep her in order.'

I nodded in sage agreement.

'How long is it now, Marky, since he died?'

He was untackling the pony, detaching the traces from the hames, his face against the pony's neck, but though I could not see him I knew from his voice that he was not going to pursue the subject.

'Well!' he growled into the pony's back. 'It was all a long time ago. Nancy's inside expecting you.'

He could hardly have said it plainer. I went indoors to her and produced the usual Italian blouse. She hugged me and kissed me, but I was too grown-up now to be lifted to the ceiling, and I hugged her back hard and thought she had fine eyes and was a damn handsome woman yet. Finally I said it:

'And how's Noreen these days?'

She turned back to the table and gently lifted the white silk blouse and said in a thick, cosy voice:

''Tis lovely. 'Twill suit Noreen down to the ground.'

'But,' I protested, 'it's for you! My father sent it for you.'

'Tshah! What do I want with finery? I'm gone beyond fineries. But,' smiling fondly, and lifting up the blouse again by the points of the shoulders to look it all over, 'Noreen will look a masher in that.'

No age is at once so insensitive and so sensitive as adolescence. It is one reason why young people are so exasperating to adults. I looked at her with curiosity, oblivious of her maternal devotion, and elegantly leaning against the table I ventured:

'Nancy! If you were married the three of ye would be as happy as three kittens in a basket. And Marky would be a father to Noreen.'

She dropped the blouse in a silken heap, gave me a sharp look and flounced to the fireplace.

'Noreen,' she said to the range, banging in the damper, 'doesn't want him as long as she has me! Anyway, since he won't have both of us he can have neither of us. Have you seen your aunt yet? She'll be expecting you.'

The flick of her skirt frightened me. I did not know what I had touched, but it felt red-hot. All I knew was that this prolonged courtship of theirs was going, if not gone, on the rocks.

That first day I did not run down the road in search of Noreen as I would have done two years before. I walked down to where Coshea's Boreen comes out on River Road and I came on her there, beyond the laundry, leaning over the wall, showing the hollow backs of her knees, chewing a bit of straw, looking across the river at the meadows and the Dublin road beyond them. I stole up behind her, slipped my arm about her waist and said gaily, 'Hello, Sis!'

She just glanced at me and said:

'Do you mind removing your arm?'

'Oho!' Very loftily. 'Touch me not, eh?'

I was so mad I could have spat in her eye, but I pretended nothing – I would not give her that much satisfaction. Instead, I started chatting away about what I had been doing since I saw her two summers ago. She kept chewing the straw and looking idly across the river. I do not remember what precisely I said that made her begin to pay heed to me except that it was my idea of a gentle probe about Marky and her mother, but it made her give me a slow, mocking smile that said, as plainly and scornfully as if she had spoken the actual words of an American phrase that was beginning to be current at the time: 'Well, and what do you know?' – meaning that I had surprised her, and that I knew nothing, not only about Marky and her mammy but about Everything in General, and that I could bloody-well stop pumping her and go away and find it all out for myself the way she had done. I expected her to say at any moment, 'Hump off, kid!' She conveyed it silently. Women do not talk to small boys.

If I had had any pride I would have walked away from her. But at fifteen years and a couple of months you are so frantic to know all about Everything in General that you have no pride, only lots of cunning. I said, very sadly:

'I suppose, Noreen, you think I'm only a kid?'

'How old are you?' she asked, with just a faint touch of sympathy in her voice.

'Going on to sixteen. But everybody,' I said bitterly, 'talks to me as if I were still ten. Have a fag?'

I flashed out my new mock-silver cigarette case. I observed with satisfaction the way she glanced down the road towards the bridge and the end of the Main Street, and then turned and leaned her back on the wall and glanced idly up Cat Lane before saying, in a bored voice:

'I suppose, really, I might as well.'

I noted also that she smoked the way all girls smoke who are not smokers, continually corking and uncorking her mouth. I kept up the role of downtrodden youth:

"Tis well for you, Noreen. I only wish I was eighteen. You can do what you like. My da would leather hell out of me if he caught me smoking. The way he talks to me about my stamina and my muscles you'd think he wants me to be another Jack Johnson. Would Nancy be cross with you?'

'I'd like to see her!' she boasted.

'I know a girl in Dublin who smokes thirty a day.'

This was too much for her.

'You know nothing about girls!'

'Oho! We grow up fast in Dublin!'

I blew smoke down my nose and turned around and leaned over the river wall and spat in the river. She also turned and blew smoke down her nose and spat in the river. For a moment or two she looked across at the golden meadows. Then:

'I'm engaged to be married.'

I was shocked upright.

'You can't be! Not at eighteen! You're too young!'

'I won't get married for a year or two, of course. But I'll get married when I'm twenty. You don't think I'm going to hang around here tied to my ma's apron strings all my bloomin' life?'

'Where's your engagement ring?'

'It's a secret yet,' she said, with another slow, hot look.

I looked at her for a while, torn between disbelief and a disappointment that had something in it of despair. Then I let my cigarette fall into the river. It was like a fellow throwing down his gun. She said:

'Come on and we'll walk down by the weirs.'

I walked by her side until we came to a hawthorn in full spate, listening to her telling me all about her boy. He was a sergeant on the Curragh. He cycled over from the Camp whenever he was off duty and she went out to meet him halfway. He was not going to remain a sergeant for long; he was 'going for an officer', and when he got his commission they would live in London. I asked her if Nancy knew about all this. It was the only thing I said that upset her.

'If you say one word to her,' she threatened, 'I'll cut the thripes out of you.'

After a bit I risked saying:

'If he saw us together now would he be jealous?'

She was pleased to laugh, condescendingly.

'I'd love to see him jealous. He's simply mad about me.'

And she drowned me with talk of the life she was having now as his 'belle', and the life she would have after she was married, until it was I who became mad with jealousy. Do you doubt it? Even if I *was* only fifteen and three months? Dear Heaven! Does nobody in the world know how old it is to be fifteen and three months? Whenever now I see a group of boys returning, say after holidays, to school, of any age between twelve and eighteen, I look most carefully into their faces in search of eyes that correspond to my unalterable concept of fifteen and three months. I look at myself through those eyes. I see my own frustration in them. For how can anybody who has to come close to them not feel their helplessness? Each of them is imprisoned in childhood and no one can tell him how to escape. Each of them must, blind-eyed, gnaw his way out, secretly and unaided. That they may be the eyes of boys who are mathematically fourteen, seventeen, even (I have met them) nineteen does not matter. All that matters is the fear of being on a brink and not knowing what is beyond it. At certain moments all through our lives we touch a point where ignorance is teetering on the brink of some essential revelation which we fear as much as we need it. These brinks, these barriers, these *No Road* signs recur and recur. They produce our most exhausting and hateful dreams. They tell us every time that we have to be born all over again, grow, change, free ourselves yet once again. Each teetering moment is as terrible as the imaginary point of time in Eastern philosophy when a dying man, who knows that within a few seconds he will be reincarnated, clings to life in terror of his next shape or dies in the desire to know it. The particular tenderness attaching to the age which I call fifteen-and-three-months is that it is the first of many such steps and trials and must affect the nature of all that follow.

Since that July I have been in love half a dozen times, but I have never felt anything since like the tearing torment of those few weeks of summer. How I used to fawn on this creature, whose beauty, I now know, was an illusion! How I used to flatter this girl, whom, I was so soon to realize, I should never have trusted, merely to be allowed to sit beside her and secretly feel the edge of her skirt!

'And does he take you to many dances in the Camp, Noreen? But where do you get the dance dresses? I'd love to see you dressed for a dance! You must look smashing! But where do you get this little card that you write the dances on? Did you say that it is a pink pencil that's attached to it? By a pink thread? You didn't *really* mean, did you, Noreen, that they have *six* wineglasses?'

Her least word could crush me like a moth. But from that summer on she had a power over all of us that was like a tyrant's. One night when Nancy flounced in with the supper and banged down the teapot, and whisked out again with a flick of her tail, my uncle said crossly, 'What's up with that one now?' – implying that things had been 'up with' her before now; my aunt shot a glance at me and said, 'Our ladyship is gone to the pictures without taking Nancy. And Marky is gone off to a whist drive.' I wonder they didn't notice me. Cinema, indeed! I saw the road to the Curragh, dark, secret, scented. Thinking of that sergeant, I must have had eyes like two revolvers. Yet I never realized the extent of Nancy's miseries and suspicions until, one day, she frightened me by saying:

'What are you always mooning about for by yourself? You have no life in you at all this year. Was it you I saw wandering out the road by yourself the other night?'

I knew then that she also had been wandering along the roads at dark, searching for her lamb.

For three whole despairing weeks I did not see Noreen at all. Then, quite suddenly, one Sunday morning I collapsed at Mass. My uncle's doctor diagnosed my illness as acute anaemia, but I am satisfied now that it was a traumatic illness. On August the ninth I was sent home. My father got three months' leave to be near me, and I remained at home under his care for the rest of the summer and most of the autumn. Then, towards the end of October, I began to get a bit brighter in myself when he said that I should go to the Feehans and he would join me there for Christmas with his brother Kenneth, whom he had not seen for some years. I argued to myself that Newbridge would be only a few miles away and that I could more tactfully spy out the land from the slopes of the Curragh. As it happened, things turned out very differently from the way I expected.

I had not reckoned with the weather. To understand this, you should see the place as I did that November. In the winter the Curragh seems older and wider. The foggy air extends its size by concealing its boundaries. The grass is amber, as if from the great age of the plain. For one week that November a sprinkle of snow fell almost every day, so that all the bottoms were white and the crowns of their slopes were melted green. At dusk the whole plain seemed to surge against the glimmering cliffs of the distant Camp and only the lights of a travelling car would then restore the earth to its natural solidity. In the cottage life became as restricted as aboard a ship. Only easygoing Moll was content, her tubby figure always moving busily through the pale glow of the house.

On most days there was little to do but watch the horses at the morning workouts – whenever a horse halted steam enveloped its jockey – or, if the air cleared, walk across to the Camp. It was always Philly who proposed this expedition – no other walk appealed to her – even if we did nothing when we got there except buy some trifle at the stores, such as the latest copy of the *Strand* or the *Red Magazine*, or, if she had the money, she might treat herself to a small bottle of scent. Her favourite, I remember, was some allegedly Oriental perfume called Phul-Nana. We might go into the red-painted tin chapel to say a prayer for the boys. Its candles were as calm as light that had gone to sleep, its tin roof creaking faintly in the wind.

I had always thought the Camp a bleak and empty place. During the winter it was as blank and cold as a plate of sheet iron, and as silent as an abandoned factory building. One wondered where all the soldiers were. It was so silent that it was startling to hear a lorry zooming up the hill towards the tower with its Union Jack hanging soggily from the flagstaff. After the lorry had passed into the Camp there was a ghostliness about the long tracks that it had left behind it on the slight snow. Noreen had talked about 'all the fun' that took place here in the winter. When I asked Philly where all the fun was, she said crossly that it all took place at night. I could only imagine, or over-imagine, its supposed liveliness at those hours when she and I would stand in the porch of the cottage gazing fixedly at its flickering until the cold defeated her curiosity and desire.

After about three weeks I suddenly began to feel one night that something had happened between us, standing there under the porch, watching those distant fireflies, sometimes talking, sometimes hardly speaking at all. At first it had the feeling of some form of complicity or collusion. I even wondered whether it might not be that the years between us had dwindled since I last stayed in the cottage. She had been eighteen then. I had been fourteen, divided from her by childhood. Now that she was twenty and I on the brink of sixteen there was barely a rivulet between us. I noted too that she had recently begun to converse more seriously with me. Perhaps that was merely because she was bored, or perhaps it was because I no longer felt obliged by loyalty to Newbridge to think of her as a comic figure, and so felt a greater sympathy with her. She continued to impress me in other ways. The season induced her to do something else that she had never done during the summer: to practise on the old upright Collard and Collard, with its pale-green, fluted satin shining behind its mahogany fretwork. Its strings sounded very tinkly during that snowy week. During the thaw they jangled. One night I found her reading, pencil in hand, and asked, 'What's the book?' It was Moran's *French Grammar*. She was trying unaided to learn the language. I noted the books she was reading – histories, travel books, famous biographies. She borrowed most of these from a widow, much older than herself, living in Kildare, a colonel's widow, whom she had met by chance at one of the meetings on the Curragh.

After I had heard about the colonel's widow I guessed the truth. With the diabolical shrewdness of my age I saw that she was playing, for me, the part of a woman of a certain age with nothing left for her to do but to encourage a young man who still had the world before him. She once said, 'Ah! If I only had my life to live over again!' But, in the end, this pretending to be so much older than she was worked directly opposite to her intentions. In her sense of the dramatic difference between our ages she let down all her defences, as if she were a very, very old lady thinking, 'Nothing that I can say can possibly matter from one so old to one so tender.' The result was inevitable. When a passionate sigh or a deliberate profanity led her to expose her hand I, quietly, read her hand and excited by what I saw encouraged her without guile. In proportion as she responded to the rising sap of my wonder she lapsed into sincerity and I achieved equality. It was for this unguarded moment that I was lying in wait, as my earlier experience with Noreen had taught me that I must if I wished to be treated as an equal.

I think she first realized how far she had lowered her defences the night when, as we sat alone over the parlour fire – Moll was singing in the kitchen, Uncle Ken in bed with his rheumatics and Una studying in her bedroom – I looked at her after she had told some wildly romantic story of army life in India and said, in a tone of voice with which I hoped her older admirers had made her familiar:

'Philly, you have lovely hair. I'm sorry you put it up since I was here before. I'd love to see you letting it all ripple down your back.'

I knew by the start she gave and the abrupt way she said, 'My hair is all right,' that she had recognized the tone. When I kept looking at her with a curved smile and lowering eyes, I was gratified to see the frightened look in her eyes. It meant that I was able to interest her not as a boy but as a man, so that I was merely amused to see her trying to flounder back quickly to the role of the grown woman talking graciously to the young boy.

I was content with this new situation for about a week: that is to say, I played the role of the sixteen-year-old pupil with a twenty-year-old teacher who knows that he is attracted by her, but who feels that it is as much her duty to keep him in his place as it is her pleasure to hold his admiration. Suddenly, I got tired of it. One night, in a temper at some correction she had made, I shut the book with a bang, glared at her, and said that I preferred to work alone.

'But,' she smiled sweetly, 'I only want to *help* you!'

'I don't want you to *help* me!' I cried haughtily.

'Believe me, my child,' she said sarcastically, 'you need a great deal of help.'

'Not from you!' I retorted.

'Master Know-all!'

'And I'm not a child!'

'You are a schoolboy.'

I screamed at her:

'I'm not. I'm not. I'm not.'

She flew into a rage herself.

'Be quiet! Remember that if you can't behave yourself you can't stay here!'

I swept the books from the table, and raced out of the parlour, and the cottage, into the garden, and so through the wicket gate straight on to the darkness and emptiness of the plain.

The night was frosty. Not only the Camp but the whole hollow plain was an iron dish. But I was not aware of the cold as I walked straight ahead, as hot with anger as a man might be with alcohol – that anger of resentment which makes young people cry at the very injustice of being born. It began to die in me only as the exhaustion induced by constant stumbling in the dark, the splendour of the sky, the magnitude of the plain and the cold night air worked on me to cool my rage and fan my desire.

I lay down under the shelter of a furze clump, between the Camp lights and the cottage lights. Once I thought I heard the coughing of a sheep. Then I realized that I was hearing only the wind rattling through some withered thistles near my feet. The wind, the darkness, the stars, the lights, the size of the plain dwindled me and isolated me. My isolation turned all these human and sky-borne lights into my guides and companions. When my head rolled to the north to the lone cottage, to the south to the windwashed campfires, and looked straight up to the stars of the Charioteer, I remember shouting out in my excitement, without knowing what I meant, 'The lights! The lights!' – as if I wanted some pyrotechnic convulsion in nature to occur, some flashing voice to speak. Only the wind whispered. Only the dried thistles coughed.

It was long after midnight when I re-entered the garden. The cottage was quiet. She would have heard the sweetbriar squeaking over the porch, the soft snoring of her daddy, and after a little while, her bedroom door being opened. She must have thought it was Moll, because she said nothing. I heard her gasp when my hand fell on her bare arm, and I whispered:

'It's me, Philly.'

She sat up, whispering, 'What's wrong?' and I heard her fumbling with the matches.

'Don't light a light!' I begged.

'What is wrong?' she whispered again, and the rest of our talk was carried on in whispering in the dark.

'Philly, I don't want to fight with you.'

'That's all right, we both lost our tempers.'

'I'm very fond of you, Philly.'

'So am I, of you. Good night, now.'

'But I'm not a schoolboy.'

'Yes, yes. Go to your room now. Daddy will be raging if he hears you.'

'Philly! You are a grown woman. And I am *not* a boy.'

'I only said it to tease you.'

'Philly!' I could feel my heart pounding.

'Yes?'

'Kiss me!'

'If you don't go back to bed at once I will call Molly.'

'If you don't kiss me I'll run out of the house and never come back again. Never! Never again!'

(She said that my voice rose: 'You were sort of gasping. You were threatening me. I was sure daddy would hear.')

'If I give you one kiss will you go right back to bed?'

I still feel that first kiss, her parted lips, the gateways of the world opening, the stars over the plain shivering, the wind blowing, and her terror as she said:

'Now go!'

'Another!'

She struck a match, lit her candle, and saw me in my trousers, shirt and bare feet. She started to upbraid me, but I saw that she saw at a glance that she was no longer dealing with a boy. I sat on the side of her bed, filled with wonder and delight at her bare shoulders and her dark, shining hair down about them, and the knowledge that she was not looking at me as a boy nor speaking to me as a boy. She gripped my hand and she assured me that in future I would have to keep to myself or leave the house, that she knew now that she had been stupid and foolish to have treated me as a boy, because any woman should have known better, but that she understood now and she hoped I understood, so would I please realize that I was a man and behave like a man? And as she whispered, like this, so seriously, I stroked her bare forearm, and felt the trembling of it and the weakness entering into it, and so must she because she stretched out her clenched knuckles to the wall.

'I am going to call Molly!'

'Just one last kiss?' I begged, staring at the whiteness of her neck and bosom.

Still holding her knuckles to the wall:

'On your word of honour, you will go then?'

'On my word of honour.'

When we parted, two hours later, she upbraided me with a gentleness that affected me far more than anything else that had happened since our quarrel in the parlour.

I lay awake until I heard the cock crowing. I felt no triumph. My delight was chastened by its own wonder. If she thought that I was in love with her she was deluded. I was too supremely astonished by my adventure to be fully aware of her, and when we met in the morning and I looked at her as if she were a mirror I did not recognize myself. Totally unaware that what appealed to her in me was my utter innocence, taking her to be a woman who had seen strange places, known strange people, heard strange things that I had never seen, known or heard, fearing that she was aware only of my utter inexperience, I behaved unnaturally and self-consciously, hurting her cruelly by what I considered were the proper airs of any man of the world on such occasions. I spoke coolly to her, smiled cynically, once I even winked at her. Whatever I did I knew that I must conceal my ignorance from her; for during those two hours, lying close together, we had been as harmless as doves, as innocent as lambs, simply because I – as I thought then, but as I see now both of us – had not known what else to do.

Besides, I now needed above everything else a retirement into silence, secrecy, self-contemplation, spiritual digestion, a summoning of shocked resources. I put on my cap after breakfast, borrowed one of my uncle's walking sticks, put a cigarette into the side of my mouth, waved a 'Tol-lol' to the three girls, and spent the whole day wandering, blind and lost, about the back roads that lead into the great central bogland of Ireland, an earth-lake of purple heather, where you might tramp all day and see nothing stir except a snipe rising with a whir or, far away, a sloping pillar of blue peat-smoke from a turf-cutter's fire. Its emptiness suited my sense of lostness. I had no wish to arrive anywhere. I wanted to remain undestined. All I wanted was that my other lost self should come back to me. In much the same spirit I so obviously avoided every chance of being alone with her that she must, surely, have begun to ask herself, 'Does he loathe the sight of me?' just as I kept saying to myself, 'Does she despise me now? Did it really happen at all? Did she upbraid me, and push me away and draw me towards her again and again?' At last my awe began to defog. Passing her in the little corridor one afternoon, I gripped her hand and said, 'Tonight?' She nodded, then to my astonishment burst into tears, and slipped from me into her room.

That night the barriers rose between us at once. I was frightened by her silence into silence. I was repelled, even disgusted, by the stuffiness of the room, the smelly candle, the tousled bed, our humiliating stealth. We gripped one another at every creak, lying rigid to listen. I could have cried for rage when I was alone again. Our public behaviour became correspondingly gracious. It was of what I would now call a Byzantine formality, a Mandarin formality. My manner would not have shamed a grand seigneur; hers a princess. There also began between us a series of long, maundering talks about love and marriage which could come to no conclusion, which indeed could hardly have made sense since each of us was trying to instruct the other without exposing the fact that neither of us had anything to reveal.

The fact is only too obvious, we both had within us the same monstrous weapon of destruction. She had imagined too many romantic stories; I had imagined too luxuriantly; both of us had imagined outside ourselves. Fountains and flags and flowers were elsewhere, always elsewhere, under the Himalayas, on the plains of France, an eye-cast across the plain. So, when I asked her about those wonderful winter dances in the Camp and she admitted that she had not yet been to one, the thought had no sequence unfavourable to her because, after all, she *had* met a real lieutenant at the races. Still, her nature's lighthouse was not roving as it used to rove for me at the pier's end. What had attracted me in her had been the flare that said, 'This way to the open sea!' I could not avoid seeing that we had both suddenly become dependent: on this cottage (to which we had once turned our backs to look at the lights across the plain), on my uncle, on my father, on the few shillings that they yielded us for pocket money, on the stuffy little timber-lined room with the chamber pot under the bed, and the varnish blistered from the summer heat and one corner of the ceiling damp. The day she clutched me and said, miserably, 'Do you love me at all?' I realized that she had become dependent on me. My father came next day. I immediately asked him if I might go to the farm at Newbridge for Christmas, and I went there that very evening.

It was like going out of a dim room into full sunshine. I saw everything clearly. They had all been right about Philly; she was a silly featherhead, full of vapourings and nonsense. I no sooner mentioned the Camp to Noreen than she at once made me see it for what it was. Even during the two months while I had been at the cottage looking across at the Camp, she had cycled across there to three dances and she described them to me fully and simply. There was nothing now about pink cards, and pink pencils and six wineglasses; and when I cried, 'But you *told* me!' she only laughed and said she had been making fun of me. That sort of thing might happen in the officers' mess on a special occasion, such as a big dinner dance – she was not certain because she had never been to such an event – but I surely did not think that it was the form at the sergeants' mess? She said that if I wanted badly to take her to a dance there her man would arrange it. And it was clear that she meant this, and that she was now in the habit of going wherever she liked, and in every other way behaving like a grown young woman.

Within an hour I was under her spell again. She seemed to be more beautiful than ever. She was the actuality of all I had imagined Philly to be. But it was not only her beauty that held me now – that mane of sunlight about her head, her full lips the colour of a pale tea rose, her body that was just beginning to take on her mother's plump strength. Her real attraction for me now was her blunt matter-of-factness, her wilfulness, which produced more and more sighs from my aunt, and frowns from my uncle and growls from Marky, and – a thing I could never have expected – a sudden flood of tears from Nancy on the only occasion that she talked about her.

'But why?' I asked my uncle. 'Why?'

The solemnly pitying look he gave me said more than his words:

'Nancy gave up a great deal for that girl. I warned her! But nobody can save a mother from herself.'

I discussed it with Marky:

'People have to grow up!' I protested to him. 'Noreen must be near twenty.'

'I foresaw it,' he growled. 'And I was right.'

None of them understood her. And yet I could sympathise with them. There were times when I almost hated her myself, so greatly did I need her, and so well did she know it, and so ruthlessly did she exact the price of my need, day after day. When she started again to dodge me for days it was solely, I knew well, for the pleasure of making me realize how essential she was to me. I realized it only too well. Within two weeks the pattern of the previous summer began to repeat itself – one day made radiant by her company followed by three without her, so miserably blank by comparison that I could imagine that she had plotted the contrast; appointments made only to be broken, or kept briefly and summarily interrupted. It would not have been so humiliating if she had made it clear to me that I was only a foil or a fill-in for her sergeant; but there were days when she treated me as much more than that, and then, without warning, she would slap me down with those damned three years between us.

The end came after I had spent six whole, empty days cycling around the country desperately searching for her. On the afternoon of that fateful seventh day, just as the first suggestion of twilight was entering the chilly air, I turned down one of those aimless side lanes that lead under the railway towards the level bog. I had come there across the Curragh. After the plain, open as a giant lawn, this hollowed lane, deep under trees slung like hammocks from ditch to ditch, gave me a queer feeling of enclosure, secrecy and remoteness. I had been there once before during the summer, also in search of her, and I had then got exactly the same labyrinthine feeling that I was going underground. That summer day the lane had been a pool of tropical heat, a clot of mingled smells from the overgrown ditches teeming thickly with devil's bread, meadowsweet, loosestrife, cow-eyed daisies, greasy buttercups, purple scabious, great rusty stalks of dock, briars hooped like barbed wire, drooping hawks-beard. This winter evening these flowers and weeds were a damp catacomb of shrunken bones. The fallen leaves were squashy. The arms of the trees were darkly shrunken against the lowering sky. Once a bird scrabbled. Otherwise there was not the least sound. It became almost dark where the lane descended under a stone railway bridge before emerging to end at a wooden gate, grey and worm-eaten, leading out to the bog, now so vague in the half-light that all I saw of it clearly was the occasional eye of a pool catching the last gleams from the watery sky.

She stood with her back to me, leaning over the old gate, gazing out over the bog. She started when she heard my step. My heart was battering, but I managed to say, with a pretence of gaiety:

'Hello, Noreen! Waiting for your beau?'

'And what if I am, nosy?'

'Oho! Nothing at all! Is he letting you down tonight?'

For a second she seemed to bend and slacken, and I relished the sight. She recovered herself, with a wicked grin.

'You can be my beau tonight. You're not so awful-looking. You'd pass in a crowd, I suppose.'

I had leaned idly against the gate. I was wearing my school cap. She took it off, threw it on the ground and brushed back my hair with her palm. A brighter gleam flitted through the clouds. A bog pool glinted greenly behind her shoulder. The smells of the dank vegetation grew thicker. My breath came faster.

'You know, kid, if you did your hair properly . . . Have you no sweetie of your own?'

'Yes!' I said. 'Up in Dublin.'

'What's she like?'

I could only think of Philly, red-eyed from weeping. I could not talk about that goose to a girl who was going to marry a sergeant who would soon take his commission as an officer and carry her off to England, a married woman. I shook my head dumbly and gazed into her blue eyes.

'Well,' she said impatiently, 'what does *she* say to you when you walk her out? What do you say to her?' She suddenly dragged my arm behind her waist. 'Here! Suppose I was her, what would I be saying to you now?' I shivered at her touch. 'Go on!' she mocked.

'I don't think you'd say anything. You'd just look at me.'

She looked at me sidewards and upwards from under droopy lids.

'This way?'

'No!' I said furiously. 'More like . . . I dunno how! More like a sheep?'

She detached my arm irritably. Then she laughed at me pitilessly. Peremptorily she put my arm back again around her waist.

'You're a very timid courter. Say something to me. As if I was your girl.'

I whispered, seeing her cloud of flaxen hair against a pale star:

'You're like an angel, Noreen.'

She sighed a happy sigh that was almost a groan. She looked past me up the dark tunnel with heavy eyelids.

''Tis like the pictures,' she said sleepily. 'Go on.'

'I could pray to you, Noreen.'

'Go on,' she murmured, throatily, leaning against me.

'When I see the sun through the window in the priory I think of you, Noreen.'

Her eyes were closed. She muttered, as if barely awake:

'Why does nobody talk to me like that?'

'Doesn't your sergeant?'

She opened her eyes wide, blue-sky-wide, and stared at me enormously:

'What window?'

'The window of Mary Magdalen with the long golden hair.'

She pushed me away and roared laughing at me; perhaps, I now think, at the pair of us; and was there, I have sometimes wondered, a bitterness in her laughing?

'Honest to God you're a scream!' She quietened and looked seriously at me. 'You poor little bastard!' she said. 'I don't know what I'm going to do with you.'

She really did seem to be considering the problem, so that I felt a great warmth of happiness that she should be thinking kindly about me even if she was a grown woman and even if she still thought I was only a boy. Then she stiffened suddenly, and shoved me away. She had lifted her head like a bird that hears a warning screech from its mate.

'Hop it!' she rapped at me. 'Clear out!' – and began to clamber over the gate into the field beyond.

It did not occur to me to disobey. In a daze of shame I went slowly back up the lane to where I had thrown my bicycle against the ditch. Only when I was on the road did I remember my cap, and laying the bicycle aside I went back for it, thinking she had run off into the field beyond the gate. As I came to the bridge I saw them on the other side of the gate, framed by the stone arch, in one another's arms, their mouths locked. Knowledge turned me into a statue. He was not a sergeant. He was not even a private soldier. He was a little buttoned-up lump of a fellow with a coarse cap on his head, peaked upward so that what there was left of salvaged daylight on his little, wizened horse's face made me realize that he could only be a stableman like Marky Fenelon. As I stood there, petrified, his fist clutched her yellow mop and slowly dragged her head backward. Her mouth fell open like the red gullet of a cat.

I slunk into the ditch. Then I crept away up the lane, jumped on my bicycle and rode off like a madman. I was aware of stars through black branches. Behind me, far away, across the plain, a bugle began to unfold its gay elaborate call. As it came and died away I imaged the illusory lights of the Camp flickering in the wind that had silenced the wavering notes, and I thought of that flickering line not as lights but as lies. Yet I did not feel anger, or disgust, I did not feel deceived, or betrayed, or derided. I felt only a hollow in me full of defeat, now and forever after. It was a secret moment. Nobody knew it. Nobody would ever know it. But as I rode through the Main Street of Newbridge, along one side of which the shops were now lighted, and the girls already parading the pavement, and the soldiers coming out of the barracks across the street, in twos and threes, for a night's pleasure, I kept my head lowered over the handle bars, as if I was afraid that somebody would guess my shame in my knowledge of my defeat.

I had wanted to know what there is to know; to possess life and be its master. The moment I found out that nobody knows, I had exposed myself to myself. I would never do it again. The shame of it was too much to bear. Like everybody else I would pretend for the rest of my life. I would compound; I would invent – poetry, religion, common sense, kindness, good cheer, the sigh, the laugh, the shrug, everything that saves us from having to admit that beauty and goodness exist here only for as long as we create and nourish them by the force of our dreams, that there is nothing outside ourselves apart from our imaginings.

I rode home. I was in nice time for supper. My uncle said:

'That's a fine complexion you have. Been cycling?'

'It was a grand day for it!' I smiled. 'And a grand night of stars.'

He winked at me and began mockingly to hum the barcarole from *Hoffman*.

The next morning as I passed the gate lodge Noreen came out, and with one of her slow, smiling looks, as of a fellow conspirator, she handed me my cap, wet, crumpled and muddy. When I unfolded it I found the silver track of a snail across the lining. I let it fall into the Liffey, where it slowly floated away.

I did not go down there again for a couple of years. By then I was doing medicine at the university. When my Uncle Gerry met me at the station he laughed loudly:

'By Gor, John, I hardly recognized you. They're after making a grand straight fellow out of you. You'd better stop growing up now and start growing out for a change.'

As I watched him lumbering into the old tub-trap I said:

'You're after getting a bit on the heavy side yourself, Uncle Gerry.'

'Anno Domini!' he said, flicking up the pony, who had also got so fat that he had rubbed the paint off the insides of the shafts.

As we trotted along the road I asked after my aunt, and Marky, and Nancy, and the farm, but what I wanted to get on to as quickly as I decently could was whether he had any tips for the July races. It was not until I was unpacking and came on my father's usual presents for Marky and Nancy that I remembered that Noreen had got married a few months back; for there were two Italian blouses this time, one white blouse for Nancy, and one pale-blue marked *For Noreen*, which I took to be a wedding token. I found Nancy in the kitchen, and I could see no great change in her, apart from a few grey streaks of hair, and that she was getting 'right loguey' too. She shouted with delight when she saw me:

'Aha! You're not a child any more! God be with the days when I used to throw you up to the ceiling. But I'm going to kiss you all the same.'

And we kissed with double-hearty smacks and laughs. Then I handed over the two blouses with a mock bow.

'With my papa's compliments, madame!'

'They're gorgeous!' she said, laying the two of them side by side. The arm of the blue fell on the arm of the white. Gently she lifted the blue sleeve and let it sink on its own blouse. 'I'll post it to her. You heard she went off from me in the heel of the hunt? Aye! She fell in with a soldier here in the barracks and followed him to London. It wouldn't surprise me to hear one of these days that his regiment was posted overseas, to India, or Africa or Egypt. Then she'll be gone from me entirely.'

She smiled, but it was a sad smile.

'I'm sorry, Nancy. You'll surely miss her.'

Her smile went. She said vehemently:

'I will not! There was a time when I'd have laid down my life for that girl. I don't care no more about her now than the child unborn.' She smiled sadly again. 'Ye used to be great pals at one time.'

'Yes,' I agreed shortly, and I was glad to turn round and see Marky darkening the doorway.

We greeted one another warmly. I handed him the sailor's twist. As we were flattering one another I wondered if I was expected to make the old joke about his getting married to Nancy, but that year I was in love with a girl at the university and he looked so grey and wizened and she looked so fat that the joke seemed rather stale and even a little unseemly. I got him to talk about the July races, because my uncle had said that he was interested in a horse called Flyaway, and he started to tell me all about it.

Suddenly, as we talked, there was a noise behind us, like a clatter of pigeons rising. It was Nancy rending the blue blouse from the top to bottom, tearing at it savagely again and again, her teeth bared, her eyes out on pins. Marky, undeflected, merely glanced at her and went on talking in his slow steady voice about Flyaway. We heard the bang of the range lid. Staring at him, I got the smell of burning silk. Marky, seeing that I was too dazed to listen, took me by the arm and, still talking about the horse, guided me out into the hot sun of the cobbled yard. I looked back at the kitchen door.

'Never heed her,' he said. 'She's upset. She feels very lonely in herself this long time.'

'Marky! Did Noreen get into trouble or something?'

'No! She just hoisted her sails, and off with her. It was just as well! Seeing her going off there every night with common fellows around the town, and poor Nancy in that kitchen sitting looking at the fire in the range...'

'Wasn't it a pity yourself and Nancy didn't make a match of it?'

He looked at me from under his grey eyebrows and said, quietly:

'And give it to say to everyone that I had another man's child under my roof?'

'What matter?' I cried. 'What matter?'

He shook his little bullet head slowly and slowly pronounced judgment:

'It does matter. I heard it said too often that no man nor beast ever loved their young with the fierce love of a woman for her by-child.' He tapped me lightly on the arm with the twist tobacco. 'If I was you I'd put ten shillings on Flyaway,' and he limped away about his affairs.

The natural way back into the house was through the kitchen. Nancy was standing by the range, with the poker in her fist and her greying head to the door. I knew she had heard the lifted latch, but she held her rounded back rigidly against me. I waited. She turned, looked at me and said coldly:

'Well? Do you want something?'

As I looked at her a bugle began to unfold its far-carrying notes from the distant barracks. Then its convoluted call wavered on the changing wind and died away. Did I hear the sparrows chirruping in the walled orchard? Did the ivy at the window rustle? I saw the evening star and the west was already a cold green. Did I smell decaying vegetation? It was the hour when the soldiers would soon be coming out to meet their girls. I made a feeble gesture with my hands, and walked off to another part of the house. I wanted badly to read about Flyaway.

All that happened over forty years ago. I have three children of my own now. One is fourteen, one is nearly sixteen, and the eldest is a few months over eighteen. The middle one is my son. When I happened to look at him the other night across the fire I saw what I felt to be a familiar look in his eyes and all this came back to me. After all, I have now come to the age when memories are meaningful – the age when a man knows that he has lived. The farm has descended to a second cousin, but my family goes down there now and again for a holiday. They tell me that the cottage on the Curragh is completely disappeared, knocked down to make room for a car park. When I talk to them about bugle calls they laugh at me and say: 'Daddy! Buglers, and drummer boys, and gun wagons and semaphores and all that sort of thing belong to the time of the Boer War.' They say you cannot see the lights of the Camp anymore because of the spruce and firs that have been planted there as a shelter belt. But I could always go to the Curragh for the races.

Neither trained horses nor wild horses would drag me down there. The only thing that would tempt me there would be to feel and smell the night over the plain. I daren't do it. I would still see the flickering lights. I would hear the wavering sound of a far-off bugle. And I would know that these things that I could neither see nor hear are the only reality.

Two of a Kind

Maxer Creedon was not drunk, but he was melancholy-drunk, and he knew it and he was afraid of it.

At first he had loved being there in the jammed streets, with everybody who passed him carrying parcels wrapped in green or gold, tied with big red ribbons and fixed with berried holly sprigs. Whenever he bumped into someone, parcels toppled and they both cried 'Ooops!' or 'Sorree!' and laughed at one another. A star of snow sank nestling into a woman's hair. He smelled pine and balsam. He saw twelve golden angels blaring silently from twelve golden trumpets in Rockefeller Plaza. He pointed out to a cop that when the traffic lights down Park Avenue changed from red to green the row of white Christmas trees away down the line changed colour by reflection. The cop was very grateful to him. The haze of light on the tops of the buildings made a halo over Fifth Avenue. It was all just the way he knew it would be, and he slopping down from Halifax in that damned old tanker. Then, suddenly, he swung his right arm in a wild arc of disgust.

'To hell with 'em! To hell with everybody!'

'Ooops! Hoho, there! Sorree!'

He refused to laugh back.

'Poor Creedon!' he said to himself. 'All alone in New York, on Christmas-bloody-well-Eve, with nobody to talk to, and nowhere to go only back to the bloody old ship. New York all lit up. Everybody all lit up. Except poor old Creedon.'

He began to cry for poor old Creedon. Crying, he reeled through the passing feet. The next thing he knew he was sitting up at the counter of an Eighth Avenue drugstore sucking black coffee, with one eye screwed-up to look out at the changing traffic lights, chuckling happily over a yarn his mother used to tell him long ago about a place called Ballyroche. He had been there only once, nine years ago, for her funeral. Beaming into his coffee cup, or looking out at the changing traffic lights, he went through his favourite yarn about Poor Lily:

'Ah, wisha! Poor Lily! I wonder where is she atall, atall now. Is she dead or alive. It all happened through an Italian who used to be going from one farm to another selling painted statues. Bandello his name was, a handsome black divil o' hell! I never in all my born days saw a more handsome divil. Well, one wet, wild, windy October morning what did she do but creep out of her bed and we all sound asleep and go off with him. Often and often I heard my father say that the last seen of her was standing under the big tree at Ballyroche Cross, sheltering from the rain, at about eight o'clock in the morning. It was Mikey Clancy the postman saw her. "Yerrah, Lily girl," says he, "what are you doing here at this hour of the morning?" "I'm waiting," says she, "for to go into Fareens on the milk cart." And from that day to this not a sight nor a sound of her no more than if the earth had swallowed her. Except for the one letter from a priest in America to say she was happily married in Brooklyn, New York.'

Maxer chuckled again. The yarn always ended up with the count of the years. The last time he heard it the count had reached forty-one. By this year it would have been fifty.

Maxer put down his cup. For the first time in his life it came to him that the yarn was a true story about a real woman. For as long as four traffic-light changes he fumbled with this fact. Then, like a man hearing a fog signal come again and again from an approaching ship, and at last hearing it close at hand, and then seeing an actual if dim shape, wrapped in a cocoon of haze, the great idea revealed itself.

He lumbered down from his stool and went over to the telephones. His lumpish finger began to trace its way down the grey pages among the Brooklyn *Ban's*. His finger stopped. He read the name aloud. *Bandello, Mrs Lily*. He found a dime, tinkled it home, and dialled the number slowly. On the third ring he heard an old woman's voice. Knowing that she would be very old and might be deaf, he said very loudly and with the extra-meticulous enunciation of all drunks:

'My name is Matthew Creedon. Only my friends all call me Maxer. I come from Limerick, Ireland. My mother came from the townland of Ballyroche. Are you by any chance my Auntie Lily?'

Her reply was a bark:

'What do you want?'

'Nothing at all! Only I thought, if you are the lady in question, that we might have a bit of an ould gosther. I'm a sailor. Docked this morning in the Hudson.'

The voice was still hard and cold:

'Did somebody tell you to call me?'

He began to get cross with her.

'Naw! Just by a fluke I happened to look up your name in the directory. I often heard my mother talking about you. I just felt I'd like to talk to somebody. Being Christmas and all to that. And knowing nobody in New York. But if you don't like the idea, it's okay with me. I don't want to butt in on anybody. Good-bye.'

'Wait! You're sure nobody sent you?'

'Inspiration sent me! Father Christmas sent me!' (She could take that any way she bloody-well liked!) 'Look! It seems to me I'm buttin' in. Let's skip it.'

'No. Why don't you come over and see me?'

Suspiciously he said:

'This minute?'

'Right away!'

At the sudden welcome of her voice all his annoyance vanished.

'Sure, Auntie Lily! I'll be right over. But, listen, I sincerely hope you're not thinking I'm buttin' in. Because if you are . . .'

'It was very nice of you to call me, Matty, very nice indeed. I'll be glad to see you.'

He hung up, grinning. She was just like his mother – the same old Limerick accent. After fifty years. And the same bossy voice. If she was a day she'd be seventy. She'd be tall, and thin, and handsome, and the real lawdy-daw, doing the grand lady, and under it all she'd be as soft as mountain moss. She'd be tidying the house now like a divil. And giving jaw to ould Bandello. If he was still alive.

He got lost on the subway, so that when he came up it was dark. He paused to have another black coffee. Then he paused to buy a bottle of Jamaica rum as a present for her. And then he had to walk five blocks before he found the house where she lived. The automobiles parked under the lights were all snow-covered. She lived in a brownstone house with high steps. Six other families had rooms in it.

The minute he saw her on top of the not brightly lit landing, looking down at him, he saw something he had completely forgotten. She had his mother's height, and slimness, and her wide mouth, but he had forgotten the pale, liquid blue of the eyes and they stopped him dead on the stairs, his hand tight on the banister. At the sight of them he heard the soft wind sighing over the level Limerick plain and his whole body shivered. For miles and miles not a sound but that soughing wind that makes the meadows and the wheat fields flow like water. All over that plain, where a crossroads is an event, where a little, sleepy lake is an excitement. Where their streams are rivers to them. Where their villages are towns. The resting cows look at you out of owls' eyes over the greasy tips of the buttercups. The meadow grass is up to their bellies. Those two pale eyes looking down at him were bits of the pale albino sky stretched tightly over the Shannon plain.

Slowly he climbed up to meet her, but even when they stood side by side she was still able to look down at him, searching his face with her pallid eyes. He knew what she was looking for, and he knew she had found it when she threw her bony arms around his neck and broke into a low, soft wailing just like that Shannon wind.

'Auntie! You're the living image of her!'

On the click of a finger she became bossy and cross with him, hauling him by his two hands into her room:

'You've been drinking! And what delayed you? And I suppose not a scrap of solid food in your stomach since morning?'

He smiled humbly.

'I'm sorry, Auntie. 'Twas just on account of being all alone, you know. And everybody else making whoopee.' He hauled out the peace offering of the rum. 'Let's have a drink!'

She was fussing all over him immediately.

'You gotta eat something first. Drinking like that all day, I'm ashamed of you! Sit down, boy. Take off your jacket. I got coffee, and cookies, and hamburgers, and a pie, I always lay in a stock for Christmas. All of the neighbours visit me. Everybody knows that Lily Bandello keeps an open house for Christmas, nobody is ever going to say Lily Bandello didn't have a welcome for all her friends and relations at Christmastime . . .'

She bustled in and out of the kitchenette, talking back to him without stop.

It was a big, dusky room, himself looking at himself out of a tall, mirrored wardrobe piled on top with cardboard boxes. There was a divan in one corner as high as a bed, and he guessed that there was a washbasin behind the old peacock-screen. A single bulb hung in the centre of the ceiling, in a fluted glass bell with pink frilly edges. The pope over the bed was Leo XIII. The snowflakes kept touching the bare windowpanes like kittens' paws trying to get in. When she began on the questions, he wished he had not come.

'How's Bid?' she called out from the kitchen.

'Bid? My mother? Oh, well, of course, I mean to say . . . My mother? Oh, she's grand, Auntie! Never better. For her age, of course, that is. Fine, fine out! Just like yourself. Only for the touch of the old rheumatism now and again.'

'Go on, tell me about all of them. How's Uncle Matty? And how's Cis? When were you down in Ballyroche last? But, sure, it's all changed now I suppose, with electric light and everything up to date? And I suppose the old pony and trap is gone years ago? It was only last night I was thinking of Mikey Clancy the postman.' She came in, planking down the plates, an iced Christmas cake, the coffeepot: 'Go on! You're telling me nothing.'

She stood over him, waiting, her pale eyes wide, her mouth stretched. He said:

'My Uncle Matty? Oh well, of course, now, he's not as young as he was. But I saw him there last year. He was looking fine. Fine out. I'd be inclined to say he'd be a bit stooped. But in great form. For his age, that is.'

'Sit in. Eat up. Eat up. Don't mind me. He has a big family now, no doubt?'

'A family? Naturally! There's Tom. And there's Kitty, that's my Aunt Kitty, it *is* Kitty, isn't it, yes, my Auntie Kitty. And . . . God, I can't remember the half of them.'

She shoved the hamburgers towards him. She made him pour the coffee and tell her if he liked it. She told him he was a bad reporter.

'Tell me all about the old place!'

He stuffed his mouth to give him time to think.

'They have twenty-one cows. Holsteins. The black and white chaps. And a red barn. And a shelter belt of pines. 'Tis lovely there now to see the wind in the trees, and when the night falls the way the lighthouse starts winking at you, and . . .'

'What lighthouse?' She glared at him. She drew back from him. 'Are ye daft? What are you dreaming about? Is it a lighthouse in the middle of the County Limerick?'

'There is a lighthouse! I saw it in the harbour!'

But he suddenly remembered that where he had seen it was in a toyshop on Eighth Avenue, with a farm beyond it and a red barn and small cows, and a train going round and round it all.

'Harbour, Matty? Are ye out of your senses?'

'I saw it with my own two eyes.'

Her eyes were like marbles. Suddenly she leaned over like a willow – just the way his mother used to lean over – and laughed and laughed.

'I know what you're talking about now. The lighthouse on the Shannon! Lord save us, how many times did I see it at night from the hill of Ballingarry! But there's no harbour, Matty.'

'There's the harbour at Foynes!'

'Oh, for God's sake!' she cried. 'That's miles and miles and miles away. 'Tis and twenty miles away! And where could you see any train, day or night, from anywhere at all near Ballyroche?'

They argued it hither and over until she suddenly found that the coffee was gone cold and rushed away with the pot to the kitchen. Even there she kept up the argument, calling out that certainly, you could see Moneygay Castle, and the turn of the River Deel on a fine day, but no train, and then she went on about the stepping-stones over the river, and came back babbling about Normoyle's bull that chased them across the dry river, one hot summer's day . . .

He said:

'Auntie! Why the hell did you never write home?'

'Not even once?' she said, with a crooked smile like a bold child.

'Not a sight nor a sound of you from the day you left Ballyroche, as my mother used to say, no more than if the earth swallowed you. You're a nice one!'

'Eat up!' she commanded him, with a little laugh and a tap on his wrist.

'Did you always live here, Auntie Lily?'

She sat down and put her face between her palms with her elbows on the table and looked at him.

'Here? Well, no . . . That is to say, no! My husband and me had a house of our very own over in East Fifty-eighth. He did very well for himself. He was quite a rich man when he died. A big jeweller. When he was killed in an airplane crash five years ago he left me very well off. But sure I didn't need a house of my own and I had lots of friends in Brooklyn, so I came to live here.'

'Fine! What more do you want, that is for a lone woman! No family?'

'I have my son. But he's married, to a Pole, they'll be over here first thing tomorrow morning to take me off to spend Christmas with them. They have an apartment on Riverside Drive. He is the manager of a big department store, Macy's on Flatbush Avenue. But tell me about Bid's children. You must have lots of brothers and sisters. Where are you going from here? Back to Ireland? To Limerick? To Ballyroche?'

He laughed.

'Where else would I go? Our next trip we hit the port of London. I'll be back like an arrow to Ballyroche. They'll be delighted to hear I met you. They'll be asking me all sorts of questions about you. Tell me more about your son, Auntie. Has he a family?'

'My son? Well, my son's name is Thomas. His wife's name is Catherine. She is very beautiful. She has means of her own. They are very happy. He is very well off. He's in charge of a big store, Sears Roebuck on Bedford Avenue. Oh, a fine boy. Fine out! As you say. Fine out. He has three children. There's Cissy, and Matty. And . . .'

Her voice faltered. When she closed her eyes he saw how old she was. She rose and from the bottom drawer of a chest of drawers she pulled out a photograph album. She laid it in front of him and sat back opposite him.

'That is my boy.'

When he said he was like her she said he was very like his father. Maxer said that he often heard that her husband was a most handsome man.

'Have you a picture of him?'

She drew the picture of her son towards her and looked down at it.

'Tell me more about Ballyroche,' she cried.

As he started into a long description of a harvest home he saw her eyes close again, and her breath came more heavily and he felt that she was not hearing a word he said. Then, suddenly, her palm slapped down on the picture of the young man, and he knew that she was not heeding him any more than if he wasn't there. Her fingers closed on the pasteboard. She shied it wildly across the room, where it struck the glass of the window flat on, hesitated and slid to the ground. Maxer saw snowflakes melting as often as they touched the pane. When he looked back at her she was leaning across the table, one white lock down over one eye, her yellow teeth bared.

'You spy!' she spat at him. 'You came from *them!* To spy on me!'

'I came from friendliness.'

'Or was it for a ha'porth of look-about? Well, you can go back to Ballyroche and tell 'em whatever you like. Tell 'em I'm starving if that'll please 'em, the mean, miserable, lousy set that never gave a damn about me from the day I left 'em. For forty years my own sister, your mother, never wrote one line to say . . .'

'You know damn well she'd have done anything for you if she only knew where you were. Her heart was stuck in you. The two of you were inside one another's pockets. My God, she was forever talking and talking about you. Morning noon and night . . .'

She shouted at him across the table.

'I wrote six letters . . .'

'She never got them.'

'I registered two of them.'

'Nobody ever got a line from you, or about you, only for the one letter from the priest that married you to say you were well and happy.'

'What he wrote was that I was down and out. I saw the letter. I let him send it. That Wop left me flat in this city with my baby. I wrote to everybody – my mother, my father, to Bid after she was your mother and had a home of her own. I had to work every day of my life. I worked today. I'll work tomorrow. If you want to know what I do I clean out offices. I worked to bring up my son, and what did he do? Walked out on me with that Polack of his and that was the last I saw of him, or her, or any human being belonging to me until I saw you. Tell them every word of it. They'll love it!'

Maxer got up and went over slowly to the bed for his jacket. As he buttoned it he looked at her glaring at him across the table. Then he looked away from her at the snowflakes feeling the windowpane and dying there. He said, quietly:

'They're all dead. As for Limerick – I haven't been back to Ireland for eight years. When my mum died my father got married again. I ran away to sea when I was sixteen.'

He took his cap. When he was at the door he heard a chair fall and then she was at his side, holding his arm, whispering gently to him:

'Don't go away, Matty.' Her pallid eyes were flooded. 'For God's sake, don't leave me alone with *them* on Christmas Eve!'

Maxer stared at her. Her lips were wavering as if a wind were blowing over them. She had the face of a frightened girl. He threw his cap on the bed and went over and sat down beside it. While he sat there like a big baboon, with his hands between his knees, looking at the snowflakes, she raced into the kitchen to put on the kettle for rum punch. It was a long while before she brought in the two big glasses of punch, with orange sliced in them, and brown sugar like drowned sand at the base of them. When she held them out to him he looked first at them, and then at her, so timid, so pleading, and he began to laugh and laugh – a laugh that he choked by covering his eyes with his hands.

'Damn ye!' he groaned into his hands. 'I was better off drunk.'

She sat beside him on the bed. He looked up. He took one of the glasses and touched hers with it.

'Here's to poor Lily!' he smiled.

She fondled his free hand.

'Lovie, tell me this one thing and tell me true. Did she really and truly talk about me? Or was that all lies too?'

'She'd be crying rain down when she'd be talking about you. She was always and ever talking about you. She was mad about you.'

She sighed a long sigh.

'For years I couldn't understand it. But when my boy left me for that Polack I understood it. I guess Bid had a tough time bringing you all up. And there's no one more hard in all the world than a mother when she's thinking of her own. I'm glad she talked about me. It's better than nothing.'

They sat there on the bed talking and talking. She made more punch, and then more, and in the end they finished the bottle between them, talking about everybody either of them had known in or within miles of the County Limerick. They fixed to spend Christmas Day together, and have Christmas dinner downtown, and maybe go to a picture and then come back and talk some more.

Every time Maxer comes to New York he rings her number. He can hardly breathe until he hears her voice saying, 'Hello, Matty.' They go on the town then and have dinner, always at some place with an Irish name, or a green neon shamrock above the door, and then they go to a movie or a show, and then come back to her room to have a drink and a talk about his last voyage, or the picture post cards he sent her, his latest bits and scraps of news about the Shannon shore. They always get first-class service in restaurants, although Maxer never noticed it until the night a waiter said, 'And what's mom having?' at which she gave him a slow wink out of her pale Limerick eyes and a slow, lover's smile.

Angels and Ministers of Grace

'You can dress now, Mr Neason,' the doctor said. He went back slowly to his desk and began to write.

Jacky, still holding his shirt in his palms, looked hard at him and he didn't like the look of him at all.

'Well, Doc?' he got out in a kind of choke between the rise and fall of his Adam's apple. 'What's the verdict?'

'The verdict is that your heart is a bit dicky, and your blood pressure is high, but otherwise you're all right.'

'A bit dicky?' said Jacky, suddenly crumpling up the shirt in his fists. Still clutching the shirt he sat down. His heart was fluttering like a slack sail. 'What do you mean, dicky?'

'Well, without going into technical details, the fact is you've been overdoing it and your old ticker has got a bit tired, that's all. If you go to bed and rest up for a couple of months and take things easy from this on you'll probably live to be a hundred. If you don't it could become very serious.'

Jacky forgot his fright.

'Rest? In bed? Sure, flat racing begins next weekend!'

'Mr Neason, you are not going to see a racecourse for another two months. If you do you must get another doctor.'

'But, sure, Holy God, I was never in bed for more than four hours any night o' me life! What'll I be doing in bed for two months?'

'You can listen to the radio. And you can read. And, well, you can be listening to the radio. And you can read.'

'Read what?'

'Anything not too exciting. Someone once told me that whenever H. G. Wells went on a long journey he used to take a volume of the *Encyclopedia Britannica* with him. I'll come and visit you now and again.'

'Can't I come and see you?' Jacky asked feebly.

'It'll be safer the other way,' said the doctor, and it was then that Jacky knew he was really bad.

'Can I take e'er a drink?' he asked, now sagging on the ropes.

'A little glass of malt, or a bottle of stout, whenever you feel like it will do you no harm in the world. But keep off women. It takes the blood away from the head.'

'I never had much to do with them,' said Jacky sourly, putting his head into his shirt.

He went home, took a stiff whiskey, told his wife the news and got into bed. When she saw him in bed she began to cry, and she went on crying so long that he had to tell her he wasn't dead yet. At that she buttoned her lips to keep from crying more than ever. She managed to ask him was there anything special he wanted.

'Is there such a thing in the house as an encyclopedia?' he asked.

'Such a thing as a what?'

'An encyclopedia. The doctor said I must read.'

She looked sadly at him and the tears came again.

'Poor Jacky,' she sobbed, 'I never thought I'd see you reduced to this,' and she went away to look.

It did not take her long – there were not twenty books in the house; bookmakers don't collect that sort of book – so she went around next door to Noreen Mulvey, the schoolmaster's wife. She was soon back with a big black book with red edges called *A Catholic Dictionary*.

'Where the hell did I buy that?' Jacky asked.

'You didn't. I got it from Noreen Mulvey. She said 'tis as good as an encyclopedia.'

Jacky looked gloomily through the funereal volume. He found a green rubber stamp inside the cover. *Saint Jacob's College, Putney Green, Middlesex, London*. There were a lot of queer words in black type, of which the first was *Abbacomites*.

''Twill last me out,' he said mumpishly and settled himself to read.

The first article informed him that abbacomites were noble abbots, or count abbots, to whom the courts of the time gave abbacies for pecuniary profit. He was further informed that these abbots included not only the sons of nobles but their daughters, and even their wives.

'Nice blackguarding!' Jacky muttered and settled himself more comfortably to read the next article, which was headed *Abbess*. He read the brief paragraph with interest, especially the part that informed him that in the Brigittine Order and in the Order of Fontevrault, where there were monasteries for both nuns and monks side by side, 'the monks were bound to obey the abbess of the related monastery.'

'My ladies!' he growled sardonically and went on to *Abbots*.

He began to wilt a little here – the article was long and technical – though he rallied at the paragraph describing the bright young abbés, 'fluttering around the Court of Versailles,' who never so much as saw the abbeys from which they drew their incomes. He weakened again at *Abbreviations* and he nearly gave up at *Abjuration of Heresy*, but he was arrested by the *Abrahamites* because it struck him that these fellows were not far wrong when they declared that 'the good God had created men's souls, but the wicked power, or demiurge, had created their bodies'. However, at the end of this article there was a reference to a later entry on Manicheanism, of which Jacky read enough to decide that they were a lot of bloody foolahs and that the writer on Abrahamitism had been right to give them hell.

Abraxas bored him. *Absolution* was full of *a*'s, and *b*'s and *c*'s. As for the *Acaeometi* or Sleepless Monks, it was plain that they were another set of born eedjuts. It was then, as he began to ruffle the pages impatiently, that his eye fell on *Adam*. He read this article not only once but three times. When his wife came in with an eggnog she found him leaning back and staring pensively out of the window.

'Come here to me, Eileen,' he said, taking the eggnog with an absent hand. 'Did it ever occur to you that Adam and Eve made nothing at all of going around in their pelts?'

'Everyone knows that,' she said, tucking in the bedclothes.

'What I mean is did it ever occur to you that they didn't mind one bit?'

'I suppose the poor things were innocent until the devil tempted them.'

He cocked his head cutely at her.

'I'll go so far with you,' he agreed. 'But did it ever occur to you to ask how did the devil manage it if they were all that innocent?'

'Why wouldn't he?' she scoffed. 'Isn't it the innocent ones that always fall?'

'Fair enough,' he agreed again, and then in the smug voice of a chess player saying 'Checkmate,' he said: 'But what you're forgettin' is that this was in the Garden of Eden where sin didn't exist.'

'The devil invented it,' she said hurriedly.

'Heresy!' he pronounced and tapped the book. 'I'm after reading it here under *Abrahamites.*'

'Will you have chops for your supper?' she asked.

He nodded without interest.

'It only stands to reason,' he pointed out. 'You can't tempt a man who is so innocent he doesn't mind seeing a woman going around in her pelt.'

'But what about the apple?' she cried.

'Aha! But what *was* the apple?'

''Twas just an apple. Anyway it was something they weren't allowed to have,' she declared with all the vehemence of a woman who knows that she does not understand what she is saying and must therefore say it as emphatically as she can. But Jacky was, by now, beyond arguing along these lines. He said loftily that the Council of Trent left the matter entirely open. She whisked her head in the air, and at the door she turned to remark with proper feminine unfairness, and irrelevance, that it would be better for him to be saying his prayers.

By suppertime he had moved farther on. Conquering all the territory that he touched, he learned much that he had not previously even thought it possible to know about the subject of *Adultery*. It was an article with cross-references to *Marriage* and *Affinity*. When Eileen came back with the supper tray, bearing two fine chops and a glass of Guinness with a one-inch froth on it, she again found him looking thoughtfully out of the window. As she laid the tray on his unheeding lap he said:

'Did you know that a man can't marry his own mother-in-law?'

'Your mother-in-law,' she informed him coldly, 'is in her grave this seven years. And when she was alive you hadn't as much as a good word to throw her no more than to the cat.'

'I am not,' he told her with a nice and infuriating blend of courtesy and condescension, 'discussing your mother. It is a question of canon law.'

Her breath went up her nose like the whistle of a train.

'Eat your chops while they're hot,' she said, and went out with prim lips.

Milo Mulvey called in about ten o'clock to offer his condolences to the patient. Eileen told him to save his sympathy because her hero (her own term) was full of buck and guff. She led him upstairs and while he sat on a canebottomed chair by the bed she leaned over the end of it. Milo adopted the false-jolly manner of all visitors to sickrooms.

'Well, Jacky my ould tar,' he cried jovially, 'so this is what slow horses and fast women did to you?' – with a wink at Eileen to take the harm out of it.

'Milo!' Jacky addressed him seriously. 'Do you really believe that a thousand angels can stand on the point of a needle?'

Milo looked at him, and then he looked a question at Eileen.

'He's that way all day,' she said. ''Tis all on account of that book you gave him.'

'Is that mine?' Milo asked, leaning over to glance at the sombre volume. 'Where did you get it?'

'I borrowed it from Noreen today. Worse luck. The professor here said he wanted to read something.'

'You poor man,' Milo said, 'I'll bring you around half a dozen detective stories.'

'Thanks,' said Jacky, 'but I don't want them. This is the most interesting book I ever read in my life. Barring that book of famous crimes you lent me last year when I had the flu. But do you – and this is a serious question now mind you – do you really and truly believe that a thousand angels can stand on the point of a needle?'

'You're very interested in religion all of a sudden,' Milo said suspiciously.

'For a man,' Eileen agreed dryly, 'who wasn't to church, chapel or meeting for the last five years.'

Jacky leaned out of bed and tapped Milo's knee.

'Milo! Will you tell me how the hell's blazes could even one angel stand on the point of a needle, let alone a thousand of 'em?'

'Answer the professor,' Eileen said wearily to Milo.

'Well,' Milo began, a bit embarrassed and not sure he was not being chaffed by the two of them, 'if you are serious about this the answer is, of course, that angels are pure spirits. I mean they can pass through walls and floors and ceilings. I mean they have neither length, nor breadth, nor depth. I mean they are pure intelligences.'

'What you mean,' Eileen said flatly, 'is that angels have no legs.'

'Well,' Milo conceded unwillingly, 'that is more or less what it comes to.'

'The professor,' she said in a long sigh, 'is now about to ask you how they can stand if they have no legs.'

Milo laughed easily. He turned to Jacky. He was a man who loved explaining things, which was why he was a teacher.

'That's very simple, Jacky. Let me explain it to you. You see, when you say "stand" you don't really mean "stand". You mustn't take these things literally. You know very well, for instance, that when you say "going up to heaven" or "going down to hell," you don't mean "up" and "down" the way we mean upstairs and downstairs. It's the same with everything else. I mean you don't think God has whiskers, do you? You follow me?'

He found himself faltering. Jacky was looking at him rather coldly, something like the way a boss-gangster might look at one of his gang who is explaining volubly how he happened to be seen coming out of the headquarters of the police precinct the previous night at half past eleven arm in arm with the district prosecutor. Milo turned to Eileen:

'*You* understand me, Eileen, don't you? I mean it's impossible for us to as much as talk of things of this kind without forming misleading pictures of them. But, of course,' with a fluent wave of his hand, 'that doesn't mean that our pictures bear any relation to actuality. I mean we don't think that angels have actual wings and all to that, do we?'

He laughed cajolingly, anticipating her answering smile of approval.

She did not smile. She looked sadly at him. Then she looked at Jacky.

'Go on, professor!'

'All the same, Milo,' Jacky said, 'I believe it is a fact that the angels can commit sin?'

'Well, they certainly did once,' Milo agreed, but his eyes were beginning to get shifty. 'The fallen angels and all that. Milton,' he added absently. '*Paradise Lost*.'

'And what,' Jacky asked with a polite interest, 'do you suppose they did it with? Having no legs and so on?'

'With their minds!' said Milo wildly.

'I see,' said Jacky. 'With their minds.'

There was a long pause. Eileen came to the rescue with 'Would you like a bottle of stout, Milo?', very much like a boxer's second at the end of the tenth round saying to a man whose only wish on God's earth is that he had never come into the ring, 'Would ye care for a small brandy?'

Milo said that he would, yes, thanks, he would, thanks very much, take a, in fact, yes a bottle of stout if she had one handy. As she leaned up and went for the stout she heard Milo acceding to her hero that a lot of these things are difficult to our mortal understanding, and Jacky magnanimously agreeing that he could see that, and:

'Take the Garden of Eden, now, for example!'

When she came back with the tray she found the two heads together, going word for word through a page of the black book. She observed that Milo looked much less jovial than when he sailed into the room a quarter of an hour before.

Milo did not call in again until several nights later. He had not been in the bedroom for ten minutes, chatting about this and that, when the doorbell rang. Eileen went down and came back accompanied by Father Milvey. She showed his Reverence in, and when he and Milo greeted one another with as much astonishment as if they had not met for six months, she looked over at Jacky, caught his eye and gave him a moth-wink out of a porcelain face. (The parish joke about the firm of Mulvey and Milvey had moss on it.) Father Milvey was a tidy little man, always as neat as a cuff straight from the laundry; and he might have been thought of as a tidy, cheerful little man if he had not had a slight squint which gave him a somewhat distant look. He greeted the patient with the usual sickroom cordiality. Eileen went downstairs for the bottle of whiskey, and after she had come back and helped them all round, and helped herself, she took up her usual position leaning over the end of the bed, waiting for his Reverence to mention the Garden of Eden. He did it very simply.

'Yerrah, what's the big book, Jacky? Oh? I hope it's not one of those American things, all written in words of one syllable and as full of pictures as if the Vatican was in Hollywood. Well, the Lord knows 'tis high time you took a bit of interest in something else besides horses.'

Jacky fended him off just as simply. He pushed the book aside with a casual:

'Ach, it passes the time, Father.'

There was a short silence. Then Milo made the approach direct.

'He had a bit of difficulty there the other night, Father, with the Garden of Eden. As a matter of fact it stumped myself.'

'Oho, is that so?' said the little priest with a cheerful laugh. 'Nothing like beginning at the beginning, is there? And what was that now?' he asked Jacky, and Eileen saw his hand moving slowly to his pocket, and protruding therefrom the corner of a pale-green pamphlet. She foresaw the look of surprise, could already hear the words, 'extraordinary coincidence . . .'

'Ah, nothing much,' said Jacky.

'What was it, though?'

'Hell!' said Jacky.

Father Milvey's eyes strayed towards Milo's. The look plainly meant: 'I thought you said angels?' His hand came back to his glass. He smiled at Jacky.

'No better subject for a man in your position, Jacky. Did you ever hear the one about the old lad who was dying, and the priest said, "Now, Michael, you renounce the devil, don't you?" Do you know what the old chap said? "Ah, wisha, Father," says he, in a very troubled sort of voice, "I don't think this is any time for me to be antagonizing *anybody*!"' He let the laughter pass, and then he said easily: 'Well, what about hell?'

'Fire!' said Jacky. 'I don't believe a word of it.'

His Reverence's face darkened. Help for the humble was one thing, the proud were another matter altogether. He adopted a sarcastic tone.

'I think,' he said, 'the old man I was just telling you about was a little more prudent in his approach to the question of hell-fire.'

Jacky took umbrage at his tone.

'There's no such a thing as hell-fire,' he said roundly.

'Oh, well, of course, Mr Neason, if you want to go against the general consensus of theological opinion! What do you choose, in your wisdom, to make, for example, of those words: "Depart from me ye accursed into everlasting fire prepared for the devil and his angels?"'

'Angels?' asked Jacky, lifting his eyebrows.

Milo intervened hastily:

'I think, Father, what was troubling Jacky there was the question of angels being pure spirits.'

'What of it?'

Jacky, a man of infinite delicacy, lowered his eyes to his glass.

'I must say I fail to see your difficulty,' his Reverence pursued, and put out his palm when Milo restlessly started to intervene again. 'No, Milo! I *like* to hear these lay theologians talking.'

'Ach, 'tis nothing at all, Father,' Jacky said shyly. 'I'm sure 'tis a very simple thing if I only understood it. Only. Well. Pure spirits, you see? And real fire? I mean, could they, so to speak, feel it?'

'Tshah!' cried Father Milvey. 'Suarez ... ' He halted. It was a long time since he had read his Suarez. 'Origen,' he began. He stopped again. It was even longer since he had read his Origen. He wavered for a moment or two, and then he became a nice little man again. He expanded into a benevolent smile. 'Wisha, tell me, Jacky, why does all this interest you anyway?'

'It just passes the time, Father.'

Father Milvey laughed.

'You know, you remind me of a man – this is a good one, I only heard it the other day...'

Eileen leaned up. She knew that the rest of the visit would pass off swimmingly.

It was four days before Milo called in again. Jacky thought he looked a bit dark under the eyes, but he decided not to remark on it. Anyway Milo did not give him time; he threw his hat on the bed, sat on the chair, leaned forward with his two hands on his knees, and stared at Jacky with a fierce intensity. Normally, Milo was a rotund, assured sort of man; his tiny mouth, like a child whistling, pursed complacently; a man as resolutely tidy-minded as the row of three pens in his breast pocket, each with a little coloured dot to indicate the colour of the ink. He did not look like that at all tonight. Jacky looked at his furrowed brow and the deep, forked lines from his nose to his button-mouth, and wondered could he be on a batter.

'Jacky!' he said harshly. 'All this about hell!'

'Yerrah,' Jacky waved airily, 'that's only chicken feed. You explained all that to me. 'Tis all figurative.' To change the subject, he leaned over and tapped Milo's taut knee. 'But, come here to me, Milo, did it ever occur to you that the antipopes...'

Milo choked. He sat back.

'Look!' he almost sobbed. 'First it was angels. Then it was fallen angels. Then it was hell. Now it's antipopes. Will ye, for God's sake, keep to one thing. I'm bothered to blazes about this question of hell.'

'Don't give it a thought,' Jacky soothed him. 'You mustn't take these things too literally. I mean fire and flame and all that!'

'But Father Milvey says, and he's been reading it up, that you must take it literally. My God, 'tis the cornerstone of Christianity. All the eschatological conceptions of the postexilic writings...'

'You're thinking too much about these things,' Jacky said crossly.

'Thinking?' Milo gasped and his round eyes flamed bloodshot. 'I've done nothing for four days and four nights but think about it! My head is addled with thinking!'

'I'll tell you my idea about all that,' Jacky confided. 'I believe there's a hell there all right but there's no one in it.'

'That's what Father Conroy says!'

'Who's he?'

Milo's voice became sullen. He explained unwillingly:

'He's the Jesuit that Father Milvey's consulting about it. But Father Saturninus says...'

'I never heard of him. Where'd you dig *him* up?'

'He's the Capuchin who's conducting the mission this week in Saint Gabriel's. The three of them are at it every night inside in the presbytery. You know very well that the sermon on hell is the lynchpin of every mission. Fire coming out of the noses of the damned, fire out of their ears, fire out of their eyeballs, their hands up for one half-cup of cold water – you know the line! Mind you, not that I approve of it! But it always gets the hard chaws, it gets the fellows that nobody else and nothing else can get. Well, Father Saturninus says all this talk and discussion has him off his stroke. Think of it! Every night people waiting for the sermon on hell and Saturninus climbing up in the pulpit knowing they're waiting for it, and knowing he won't be able to do it. Of course, he could easily talk about hell as a lonely, miserable, desolate place where everybody was always groaning and moaning for the sight of heaven and having no hope of ever seeing it, but you know as well as I do that a hell without fire, and lots and lots of it, isn't worth a tinker's curse to anybody.'

'Well,' said Jacky impatiently, 'I don't see how I can help you. If you want to believe in fire and brimstone...'

Milo grasped his wrist. His voice became a whisper.

'Jacky,' he whispered. 'I don't believe one single bloody word of it.'

'Then what are you worrying about?'

'I'm worrying because I *can't* believe in it! I was happy as long as I *did* believe in it! I *want* to believe in it!'

Jacky threw his hands up in total disgust.

'But, don't you see, Jacky, if you don't believe in hell you don't believe in divils, and if you don't believe in divils you don't believe in the Garden of Eden.' His voice sank to a frightened whisper again. He seized Jacky by the arm. Jacky drew back his chin into his chest, and crushed back into the pillows to get away from the two wild bullet eyes coming closer and closer to him. 'Jacky!' whispered Milo. 'What *was* the apple?'

'A figure of speech!'

Milo dashed his arm away, jumped to his feet, gripped his head in his hands and uttered a hollow and unlikely 'Ha! Ha! Ha!' in three descending notes like a stage villain. His voice became quite normal and casual.

'Can *you eat* a figure of speech?' he asked very politely.

'There was no eatin'. That was another figure of speech, like the angels that have no legs.'

'You mean, I presume,' Milo asked, with a gentle and courteous smile, and a delicate shrug of his Rugby-player's shoulders, 'that Adam had no mouth?'

'Adam was a figure of speech,' Jacky said stolidly.

'I'm going mad!' Milo screamed, so loud that Jacky had one leg out of bed to call Eileen before Milo subsided as quickly and utterly as he had soared. He smiled wanly. 'Sorry, old boy,' he said in the stiff-upper-lip voice of an old Bedalian on the Amazon who has rudely trod on the tail of an anaconda. 'A bit on edge these days. Bad show. I only wish I could see the end of it. The worst of it is Father Milvey says it's all my fault keeping such books in the house. And lending them to you. I wish to God I never gave you that book! I wish to God I never laid eyes on it!'

Jacky fished it out of the eiderdown and handed it to him.

'Take it,' he said. 'I'm sick of it. 'Tis all full of "This one says" and "That one says." Have you er'er an ould detective story?'

'But, Jacky! About *hell?*'

'Forget it!' said Jacky. 'Eileen!' he roared. 'Bring up the bottle of whiskey.'

'No thanks,' said Milo, getting up gloomily and putting the obscure volume under his arm. 'Father Milvey is coming around to my place tonight and I'll have to have a jar with him.' He looked down miserably at Jacky. 'You're looking fine!'

'Why wouldn't I, and I living like a lord?'

''Tis well for you,' Milo grumbled sourly, and went out slowly.

After a while Eileen came upstairs to him bearing the whiskey bottle, two glasses and a big red book.

'What's that book?' he asked suspiciously.

'Milo gave it to me for you. 'Tis *The Arabian Nights*. He said not to let Father Milvey see it. Some of the pictures in it will raise your blood pressure.'

Jacky grunted. He was watching her pouring out the liquor.

'Come here to me, Eileen,' he said, his eye fixed thoughtfully on the glass. 'Did it ever, by any chance, occur to you that...'

'What is it now?' she asked threateningly, withholding the glass from him.

'I was only going to say,' he went on humbly, 'did it ever occur to you that the bottom of a whiskey bottle is much too near the top?'

She gave him one of those coldly affectionate looks of which only wives are capable, added a half-inch to his glass, and handed it over to him.

'You ould savage,' she said fondly, and began to tuck him in for the night. To show her approval of him she left the bottle by his side.

Left to himself he opened the big red book. He savoured it. He began to relish it. He was soon enjoying it. He snuggled into his pillow and, with one hand for the page and one for his glass, he entered the Thousand and One Nights. Thanks be to God, here at least there were lots and lots of legs. Towards midnight he gently let the blind roll up to see what sort of a night it was. His eye fell on the light streaming out from Milo Mulvey's sitting room across the grass of his back garden: the theological session in full swing. He raised his eyes to the night sky. It was a fine, sweet, open-faced night in May. A star among the many stars beamed at him. There are more things in heaven... With renewed relish he returned to the Grand Vizier's daughter. His glass was full.

One Night in Turin

1

One robin-singing, cloud-racing, wet-grassed Monday morning last April, Walter Hunter came down to breakfast as usual at half past eight – nice time to let him drive at his ease to his office in Cork city for ten, a gentlemanly hour – picked up his neatly folded *Irish Times* from the hall table and roared into the rear of the house, 'Devilled kidneys forward, Mrs Canty.' He glanced at the headlines as he passed out on to his lawn. The glass door flashed sunlight, greenery, and cloudland about his head. He surveyed with pleasure the host of daffodils on his dew-wet fields stretching down to the low tide, the cloud-castles over the harbour, but on crackling the paper wide open forgot all about them, breakfast, his office and work. The first entry in the *Social and Personal* column read: 'The Countess Maria Rinaldi has arrived in Dublin and is staying for a few days at the Russell Hotel.' He lifted his head, looked here, there and everywhere among the racing clouds as if he had suddenly heard the twittering of a flock of duck, turned and walked quickly back into his study to telephone her. Just as his fist closed on the receiver he paused, like a stopped film. For one minute he was immobile. In that minute he remembered the seven occasions – especially the first and last – on which he had seen her since she left Ireland, sixteen years ago.

The first occasion was now part of his blood stream. It had occurred in 'Forty-six. He had gone with Betsy Cotman to Cervinia, ostensibly for the skiing. It was his first trip abroad since the war, that event whose prolongation so insensibly aged us all. Two years before it began he had gone back to study at the King's Inns, belatedly finishing his law studies, feeling himself still a student among students. By 'Forty-six he was coming down the straight to forty; still handsome, with a few interesting flecks of grey on his temples, in perfect physical trim, having already put half of a good life behind him – he knew it all, he would tell you, with a gay wave of his long fingers – and with the clearest intention of holding on to his good fortune as long as possible.

Cervinia, however, had not been entirely a success. Betsy had stayed with him for only three days – she then had to hurry on to St Moritz to establish herself there before her husband came out – but he had seen her go with relief. In those three days and nights he had discovered that she had no interest in anything that she could not manhandle as a form of healthy sport. Her whole life seemed like a long and rich dinner where every course was a repetition of the pleasure of the last course under a different name. Whether she was skiing, tobogganing, mountain climbing, figure skating, or making love, she never altered her tone one jot, never abated her voice by as much as a quarter tone. She had leaped like a chamois from the snow to the bed, from the bed to the snow, oblivious of the chasms that yawned between her inexhaustible store of hearty Anglo-Saxon good cheer and his Irish sensibilities. He waved her good-bye between a sigh of satisfaction and a breath of nausea, and returned deep-breathing to the pure white mountains. He got in four days of middling-to-good skiing, and then the threatened wet snow fell. He came down into Torino to eke out there the last forty-eight hours of his brief holiday. (His father had died during the war, he was in charge of the family business of Hunter and Hunter, so that all his escapes now had to be intense and brief.)

He was delighted to be alone in snow-covered Turin. Never having stayed before in any Lombard or Swiss city in bad weather, he discovered for the first time the merits of those northern arcades which both allow and tempt one to pass sociably and in comfort from café to café. He was excited by the contrast between these crowded cafés and the sense of isolation that he got from the warnings of the white heaps of bomb rubble, the silent white ruins of crumbled houses, the brown desolation of the swollen Po, the great white, empty squares bluishly lit at night by lean streaks of light from lower-floor windows. As he wandered about, he recalled the many trestle bridges over which his train from Paris had so cautiously crawled. He felt like a pioneer postwar explorer. How wonderful, he thought, it could be to be completely cut off here for a couple of months. He would pass his days in one café after another, hot and steamy, smelling of coffee and *nazionales*. He would make the acquaintance of a few intelligent and interesting men in whose company he would forget all about his stupid and slightly humiliating adventure with that fool of a woman.

His first night was not a success. He spent it in a big, chattering café in the Piazza Carlo Felice. There was no trouble at all about making acquaintances – tourists were still few enough to be interesting novelties in 'Forty-six. But he got buttonholed by one old, bearded character who talked with the same inexhaustible and unprofitable energy about war and politics in Italy as Betsy had about hunting and fishing in England and Ireland. Also, that night he had an unpleasant dream. He dreamed of being squashed (right across his smooth, soft belly) by some great collapsing weight – like an ant one crushed underfoot. He awoke and lit the light to drive away the image. Would he feel terrible agony? Or would it be immediate death? Would he, dead or alive or unconscious, wriggle galvanically like a fly in a candle-flame for a second? He thought of brutal writers and painters who have painted such cruel things. Faulkner? Describing a man burned in a plane crash. Hemingway, describing a man thumbing out another man's eye and then biting off the dangling eyeball. Algren. Why do they do it? Exorcising, or indulging their egos?

There was not a sound from the street. The snow silenced every outer noise. We drag our ego with us through life, chained to it, in its power, not it in ours. We are free of it, or seem to be free of it, only in rare hours – relaxed by the achievement of climbing a mountain peak, elevated by the speed of a dangerous ski run, in the quiet hour after love, calmed by the wonder of some splendid view, asleep, when slightly drunk, listening to music. Where had he heard or read of a man of the most strict behaviour who came within an inch of being killed by a falling beam, who said to himself, 'I was as good as killed! Well, then, my past is finished,' and proceeded to spend the rest of his life in the pursuit of pleasure? He thought, for no apparent reason, of Betsy Cotman – and groaned with displeasure. When he awoke, his light was still lighted. The grimness of his dream remained with him for several hours – an unpleasant wash of grey colour across the sunny morning.

He spent the forenoon shopping: a trifle for his cook, she was worth the attention; a trifle for his secretary, poor thing; an expensive pair of gold earrings for Betsy, these affairs had to be finished off in style. The afternoon and evening he spent in three different cafés, where, again, the talk was easy, amiable, and unimportant. He dined well, went to an American film, and on the way home was accosted at a dark corner by a young man who tried to sell him a fake Parker 51 fountain pen. Walter took the pen in his hand, it came apart immediately and the young man burst into tears. Walter took him to a bar for a drink and the young man revealed his misery. He had spent his only five hundred lire on ten of these fake pens, expecting to resell them for two thousand five hundred. He laid them on the marble table – they were all defective. He had been cruelly defrauded. Walter watched him take one apart and fiddle with it, passionately, despairingly. When the top half of the casing would not screw into the bottom half, he burst into tears once more. Walter gave him a thousand lire and they parted like old friends. But as Walter went out he looked back. The young man was again tearing at the pen. He never forgot that image of the young man's despairing efforts to undo his disaster. He often told his friends about it. 'It brought', he would say, 'the whole war, the whole of Turin, down to the point of a pen'.

His second, and last, day passed just as pleasantly. He went to see the alleged Veil of Veronica in the cathedral. He was not impressed. At lunch he met a man with one arm, an unrepentant Fascist who knew, as a certain fact, that Mussolini had never been shot – it was his double who had been shot – was hiding in Switzerland and would return again to lead a resurgent Italy. He listened to some more vague talk in two more cafés, content to sit on there, slowly filling up his cooling-tank with the ice water of their new-found patriotic ideals and his own moral resolutions. By the time he had again dined and wined himself well he was in an entirely pleasant state of mental and emotional euphoria. It was at this moment that his great adventure began.

His eye fell on a poster – they were playing *La Sonnambula* that night at the opera. He hastened around to the theatre, managed to procure a ticket, took his seat just as the lights dimmed, and within minutes he was leaning forward, rigid with excitement. Molly O'Sullivan had walked on to the stage as the miller's daughter, Amina. At once there grew in him the strangest and sweetest sense of secret complicity with her life – the only man in the whole theatre who had known her as a girl, indeed almost as a child, in Ireland. This feeling was so sweet and strong that he immediately resolved never to tell anybody at home in Ireland that he had been in the theatre that night. He resolved not even to send his card around to her. If he did, he would have to meet her in the company of other admirers behind the scenes, where she would simply become public property – the wonderful new soprano who had been discovered in a wayside *taverna* in the wilds of Ireland. She would no longer be the charming young girl on whom he first laid eyes behind the counter of old Katy O'Sullivan's pub in Coomagara – a pub well known to all late travellers between Cork and Kinsale for being open at all hours, for bad whiskey, poor measure, and the blond charms of the daughter of the house – good-looking in a saucy way, he had thought her the first time he saw her, as vain as a peacock, an outrageous flirt, almost too obviously nobody's fool, but, just as obviously, as innocent and (he had quoted Yeats to himself on their first encounter) 'as ignorant as the dawn'. In her crowded dressing room she would neither be that enchanting apparition emerging, in pure white, under pale, cold, greeny moonlight to mourn her lost love, nor the young girl he used to secretly admire in Dublin during the couple of years after her discovery, whom he used to ambush casually in dusty teashops, in the distempered corridors of the Academy of Music, or walking with her fellow students across Saint Stephen's Green, past the old bandstand, the great beds of geraniums, and the statue of George the Third facing the humped bridge over the ponds. He left the theatre as furtively as a kidnapper. He would write to her when he got home. He would come out again in the summer and confess everything to her.

When he got back home to Hunterscourt he bought recordings of the opera, and, that winter, whenever he put them on for his friends he felt again the secret bond that he had formed with her in Turin, so that if one of his guests asked some such simple question as, 'Is this by Verdi?' or, 'Wally, is this the opera with the song that Joyce's ould father used to love?' he would not correct them, he would not hear them, he would say, in the detached voice of the president of the Cork Grand Opera Society, 'There's a rather nice little aria coming up now.' Then, hearing once more the '*Ah, non credea mirarti*' or the '*Ah, non giunge,*' he would lean back in his armchair by the fire to see her again, gleaming like a snow maiden under a canopy of light and music; or see himself, after the performance, half stunned by delight and wonder, sipping brandy after brandy in a mirrored café by the railway station, with his packed bags and his oiled skis on the floor beside him, waiting, long after the crowd had thinned away, for the Rome-Paris Express to pass at two in the morning, drunkenly watching the wet snowflakes melting on the panes, sinking heavily into the palms outside, floating in a white fuzz around the cloudy electric lights, and now and again a soft thunder rolling dully down from the mountains along the tawny valley of the swollen Po. He had no clear recollection of the journey home.

He remembered only her gleaming image, the music, the falling snow, the heavy, silent streets.

One thing about her soon began to disturb him. At first her image came obediently when he called her. Presently he ceased to control her. Now it was she who ambushed him. Her image became so merged with his own being that any least disturbance in any corner of his senses could awaken her from her coiled sleep, until he came to realize that he had had his greatest illusion of power over his thoughts of her when he was most subject to them. He did not write to her. He did not go to Italy that summer. It was as if he feared to meet her. After that it even seemed to him that she spied on him. Whenever the thought of her visited him among his legal cronies, or among his Bohemian-theatrical friends up in Dublin, he became terrified that some day he would talk to them of her, and he went among them no more. More than that – his affairs with women became infrequent, casual and coarse. 'The worse the better,' he said to himself – though not excusing himself, for it was his self-boast that he never deceived himself about anything.

Being a lawyer accustomed to examining other people's motives, he naturally spent many hours trying to understand why he kept on postponing an avowal of his passion for her. After long consideration, he decided that she was like certain lights that can be discerned only by not looking straight at them – a dim star, a remote airport beacon in a fog, a lamp in a distant cottage window. She represented something in himself that he could only approach obliquely and slowly. 'After all, you don't change your politics or your religion all of a sudden,' he caught himself saying aloud to himself one night. Besides, he knew that nobody really lives entirely by what he professes. She was his illogical goddess. He remembered a Catholic friend of his who was always good-humouredly teasing him for being a Protestant – 'next door to an atheist' – meaning a man for whom nothing existed beyond the earth, the body and the understanding. Yet this pious man, he found out, always carried a four-leafed clover in his cigarette case as a luck charm. 'Against what, in your good God's name?' Walter had asked him with a grin. 'Destiny!' said his friend, with a fierce glare.

He did not blame his friend for teasing him. It must have seemed to many that he had indeed lived all his life by the law of passionate pleasure. He had loved sport – hunting, shooting, fishing. Hunters-court, his father's and his grandfather's home before him, was ideal for any man who enjoyed the open-air life: an old Georgian house

(originally the dower house of Lord Boyne's estate across the fields)
situated twelve and a quarter miles out of town on a hundred and fifty
acres of mixed land ranging from rich alluvial soil down to the kind of
reedy-quaggy fields that you find so often along the lower Lee. On any
fine morning, before driving into his office in his Mercedes-Benz, he
could hack about for an hour on his little demesne, or wander with his
gun, or if it is high tide sail down the creek into Cork Harbour to cast
a line, or swim in his pelt, completely unobserved, or merely lie on his
back gazing up at the harbour sky, vast, always cloud-packed, faintly
mobile. The house had half a dozen modern loose-boxes. He had plenty
of friends glad to come down for a few days' sailing or for rough-shooting on another hundred acres that he had rented and preserved around
the hills of Fermoy. As for other pleasures, where could a man be better
situated than within a bare twenty minutes of a modern airport with
planes for Dublin, and from that onward to any city on the Continent
that he cares to choose? He had several times taken off from Cork after
a leisurely lunch on Friday, enjoyed two crowded days in Paris, and on
Monday morning walked into Hunter and Hunter's on the South Mall,
and hung up his bowler hat and his umbrella with as staid and
contented a 'Good morning, Miss O' and a 'Morning, Mr Dooley' as if
he had spent the weekend reading *Sense and Sensibility*. What his good
friends did not realize, of course, was that it palls. After forty, it begins
to pall. He had not realized it himself until that night in Turin. Those
hesitations ever since, all those oblique and sidelong efforts to see the
dim star, the cottage window, the airport beacon in the fog, were – he
now knew – his efforts to understand what it was that he had desired
and not found in the hunt, the shoot, on the wind-pocked sea, all these
casual women.

Having settled on one explanation for his prolonged hesitations and
his frightened secrecy about her, he at once decided on two more – that
the real reasons he was being cautious were (a) that he was so much
older than she and (b) that he really did not know anything about her
as a woman. (His great motto about women had always been a
minatory, 'They change, you know, they change!') Accordingly, he
kept on making and remaking decisions about her, until he suddenly
realized that he had, as it were overnight, become two years older, and
so had she, which made both his reasons still more cogent. He
thereupon wrote several letters to her – and did not send them. He
booked train and plane reservations to go out and meet her, and did not

go. One morning his paper announced that she had married Count Giorgio Rinaldi, a landowner with some undefined industrial interests near Bergamo. He wrote to her at once, to congratulate her, assuring her that this was what she both deserved and needed. His second and third encounters with her occurred soon after.

These were the years when his holidays happened to take him to the Dolomites: he visited her and Giorgio in their home outside Bergamo. He made these visits nervously, and after much hesitation. They established only that she had ceased to be an opera singer, that she was living in the grand manner, and that she was a beautiful woman of skill and taste, with a high, marble-white forehead, delicately veined, big grey eyes, globular as a Pekinese's, a poreless skin, exquisitely carved lips and a great pile of braided, blonde hair – a rich, mature beauty, with an Italian-style figure. Anybody who had not known her as Molly O'Sullivan of Coomagara could easily have thought she had always been a *contessa*. She was, he reckoned, thirty or thirty-one. He was nearly forty-three.

The next winter he met them twice in Milan; once for dinner before the opera at Crispi's; the second time, after the opera, when the three of them walked, chatting happily arm in arm, across the foggy piazza and through the arcade for late supper at Savini's. It was a gay night, as gay and warm in feeling as the little red table lamps and the chatter of the crowded arcade. She was completely real to him that night, both as Molly O'Sullivan and as the Contessa Rinaldi.

The next summer, when he happened to be motoring along the lakes from Berne to Venice, he called on them one afternoon where they were in *villeggiatura* in a small cottage above Lecco. High up there it was cool. They drank cold white wine. The lake below was a dark blue. They could see the snowy Alps. He noted, with satisfaction, that the marriage was a childless one.

It was on their last, entirely unplanned, meeting, seven months ago, in Rome, that his swift thoughts converged as he stood immobile over the black telephone. That night, he very nearly told her his secret about the snowy night in Turin. Unfortunately, neither the place nor the occasion encouraged the exchange of memories, least of all that kind of memory. She had come to Rome because Giorgio had come there to consult a specialist. He had met her so unexpectedly, with such a shock of delight, that for a moment he could not talk to her, at a diplomatic cocktail party in the Palazzo Farnese. Since she could not dine with him – she had to go back to the nursing home to dine with Giorgio – he persuaded her to meet him afterwards at Doney's for a nightcap.

She came, late, so that his nerves were all on edge before she entered, dressed as she had been at the Embassy, in a costume of raw silk the colour of alder-flowers, not much lighter in hue than her hair, and even her wide floppy hat of openwork straw was covered in cream lace, its white brim fringed about her sun-tanned face. She looked so lovely, though so troubled, that he regretted he had not selected a more secluded place than a Via Veneto café. He was relieved that he had at least chosen to meet her indoors at Doney's, where it is usually quiet enough in warm weather, when the crowds prefer to sit outside, three deep on the pavement under the coloured canopies. By ill luck, just as they sat to a table in a quiet corner indoors, a sudden September cloudburst fell on the city, and at once the hundreds of gossippers on the pavement came rushing indoors, laughing noisily at the unexpected disaster, carrying their drinks, obtruding everywhere in the *salon*, with waiters racing in and out, holding chairs aloft as if they were going to brain everybody. Even so, as he listened to her telling him Giorgio's symptoms – she feared the usual malignancy – he was sure he could detect certain resonances, conveyed by the tone of her voice rather than by the words, certain undertones not connected with her fears for his bodily health, taut, nervous, accentuated perhaps by the rattling rain, the low peals of summer thunder, the gabbling crowd.

He stared at her, crouching, shaking his head in sad condolence, smiling with affectionate pity across the brown table, his bat's ears sharpened by his amorous feeling for her. He became aware that her beauty, tonight, was not only rich but sad, and, on an instant, he was transfixed by the true meaning of her melancholy and moritural loveliness. It came to him when the brilliant lights of the chandeliers suddenly dimmed as if they had all been lowered into the sea, a loud peal of thunder reverberated over the rain-torn city, and the *salon* sent up a laughing, cheering scream of mock fright. In that second he saw her exactly as he had seen her seven years before in the pallid moonlight of *The Sleepwalker*, her eyelids drooping not for Rinaldi but for herself. He cunningly threw out a casual remark about the happiness of Bergamo and coupled it with that gay night in Milan when they all three had hurried arm in arm across the foggy piazza to the warmth of Savini's and the cheery vulgarity of French champagne with the ritual *risotto al salto*. She replied to his remark – he had trembled while he waited for her reply – with an all but imperceptible lifting of one shoulder. In that instant he knew that they had ceased to love.

He had been about to win all her trust when the dimmed lights rose again into a full white blaze and the crowd cheered and applauded as if they were at the end of an opera. He had turned and glared at the laughing gabblers as if to shout, 'Silence in the court!' When he turned back he found that she was looking intensely at a young couple beside them, bantering one another loudly and happily, hands clasped across the table. Walter gazed, just as enviously, at her exquisitely curved mouth. As if she felt his look she turned swiftly to him, said brightly in a comic, stage-Irish brogue, 'Well, is there e'er a dhrop left in our ould bottle o' fizz?' – and the sole propitious moment of the night was gone.

The storm passed over. The night was warm and bland again. The *salon* emptied. They talked for a while about what they called their past lives. Since they had not talked alone for many years, this was his first real opportunity to observe how her mind had developed in the meantime. As they talked she became so heated about a couple of remembered (or imagined) insults from her early critics that he began at first to fear that she was a blend – not unfamiliar and very displeasing to him – of the wilful and the unworldly. She conveyed a sense of something wanton, something wild, forcibly bearing off a nature entirely simple and innocent like a strong tide carrying a child's boat out to sea. It fitted in with his first impression of her long ago, in that pub at Coomagara, as a proud, flirtatious girl, 'ignorant as the dawn'; as it fitted also with his vision of her at the opera, a sleepwalking snow maiden wrapped in a canopy of cold light and passionate music. Not that he would have minded her being wilful or unworldly; but he was always disturbed by the wilful who are also unworldly. He had met them only too often in his business – the Irish are a litigious people – unpersuadable, passionate men and women coming into his office, saying fiercely, 'I want justice!' or 'I'll fight to my last penny for my rights!' As he saw things, the unworldly man (unless he had abandoned the wilful life struggle altogether, like the priest or the professor) was no man. He was unsexed, weak and womanish. Likewise, the unworldly woman (unless she had left the world to become a nun) was no woman. She was a childlike, retarded, silly creature of no interest to any grown man. In fact to him the words man, woman, wilful and unworldly were mutually destructive. He could not even enjoy novels about unworldly women living in the active world, not even satires about them, such as Jane Austen wrote; they were not grown up, they were not nubile, they were not playing their proper role in life.

They strolled arm in arm to the Piazza Barberini. By this time he was more eager than ever to be certain whether she had or had not been unhappy with Rinaldi; a thousand times more eager to find out why she had been unhappy – if she had been; ten thousand times still more eager to know if she had been worldly enough to have taken a lover. The lights shivered over the fountaining spume of Triton. A *carrozza* and two taxis stood waiting. He simply had to dare ask the question uppermost in his mind:

'Molly, we've known one another for so long you won't be angry at my asking you something. You have been unhappy with Rinaldi, haven't you?'

She did not answer. She shook her head so slowly that she might have meant anything by it, such as, 'Who is not unhappy?' or 'How impossible it is to talk of such things now!' It might have been meant as a rebuff. It was a poor evasion, since by not denying it she had virtually admitted it. Nevertheless, a slight doubt remained. He tried another approach:

'Is it very lively in Bergamo?'

'It is intensely boring. The place is so small. So conservative. So clannish. You can imagine it. You live in a small city yourself, or is it a large town? We both know what Cork city is like. Rainy, too, like Bergamo. If Milan were not so near Bergamo, it would be unbearable. They all go to Milan for their pleasures as people from Cork go to Dublin, or to London. Or,' she smiled, looking crookedly at him, 'to Rome. At first this used to upset me. It seemed so cowardly. Why on earth, I used to ask myself, don't people lead whatever life they want to lead? Rinaldi explained to me that it is universal practice not to. Half the tourists, he pointed out to me, are provincials on the loose. We have some American business acquaintances. One of them is a very intelligent and amusing man from the Middle West. He once said to us that all over the United States, even in the most puritanical parts, certain cities are specially protected or preserved for this purpose. He once described to us what night life is like in Kansas City. I was fascinated and appalled.'

He pressed her arm.

'In so boring a city you must be pestered by would-be lovers?'

'Bergamo is full of feelings of honour.'

Her answers enchanted him: intelligent, evasive, delicately ambiguous, a true woman of the world out of another age.

Her taxi drew up. He lifted her hand to his moustache.

'I'll see you in the spring!' he cried. 'If not sooner.'

Since then he had written to her several times. She had told him in her Christmas letter that Rinaldi had died. He had written his condolences. In March he had asked if he might visit her in April.

Two birds, black as the telephone, darted past his window in a flurry of wings and love song. He slowly lifted the receiver, saying to himself, 'If she will lunch with me today, I will tell her about that night in Turin. If the fact that I have kept that secret all these years doesn't convince her . . . ' He finished it aloud: 'I'll be back here tonight.'

2

All the way up to Dublin he made and remade plans. He would blurt out nothing. There were still one or two things about her that he must probe. Had she really been unhappy with Rinaldi? Had he been unhappy with her? If so, whose fault was it? That possible lover? Would she want to marry again? He counted her years in Italy. Bergamo. Milan. Rome. Venice. What would she now think of Cork city, of Hunterscourt! It could be as fine a setting for her, by God, as Castle Boyne next door to him. At once he abandoned the idea – nobody must know until everything was certain. If he failed, they would call him an old fool, an old goat, an old ram.

He passed thirty or forty miles seeing her in his home. She would sing every year, at their opera. Sometimes it lasted a full week. She could be the queen of the whole county. Of the whole country! They would travel, following the opera to Covent Garden, Paris, Salzburg, the Scala, the San Carlo, Rome, the Fenice. Then, just as he was imagining them walking arm in arm from the Hotel Danieli across the Piazza San Marco into the lanes leading to the Fenice, there jumped into his head a remark made to him by a kind friend in Cork only two weeks before in the Yacht Club – it was actually young Boyne, Lord Boyne's eldest brat – 'You know what it is, Wally? You must be by now the oldest established bachelor in the whole of the County Cork! And, by God, you're *still* eligible.' At the sting of that *still*, he almost doubled his speed. Then he slackened it. He was soothed by the recollection of the image he had formed of her at that midnight farewell by the fountain of Triton: a woman of the world out of another age.

Across the table she looked as beautiful and elegant as ever – those lamplike eyes, the corn-fair hair, poreless skin, tinted eyelids, pallid lipstick, paler nails, Via Monte Napoleone frock (she admitted it), tinkling wrist. But where he had expected a *contessa*, he found a young student She behaved exactly as she had the first time he had seen her in Dublin in her student days, crossing the Green from the Academy with two other girls, laughing aloud, white-mouthed, red-lipped, tongue-showing like a cat. When he mentioned it now, she laughed in the same way, and her strong arm across the lunch table grasped his hand like a boy.

'Isn't it wonderful?' she cried, so loudly that people nearby turned to frown, and remained looking, transfixed by her beauty.

'What,' he asked hopefully, 'is wonderful?'

'My being here, of course! Back where my life began. I've done so much, I've travelled, I've made so many friends, I've been flattered and fêted wherever I've gone, and nothing, nothing, nothing has been so marvellous as this coming back, not just to Ireland only, not just only to Dublin – though it's so beauuuuutiful! – but to this very hotel, on this same old Green, that I used to cross every day on my way to the Academy. Do you remember when we were young, Walter? We used to think this hotel was only for the big nobs? Now I have a suite in it. My bathroom is in pale green, even down to the bidet. My bath is sunk in the floor like a Roman bath. Me! Molly O'Sullivan!' She laughed at her folly. 'What are you doing in Dublin, Walter?'

'I'm on a secret mission.'

'Big business?' – with big eyes.

The waiter, bringing the champagne bottle to show, gave him time to command himself.

'If you must know, I'm here because of a woman.'

She again seized his hand in her boyish grip.

'Who is she? Do I know her? Tell me at once. What fun! Are you thinking of marrying? It's not too late.'

'I'm not young,' he confessed wryly. 'I'm forty-six.'

'If the heart is young! How long has this been going on?'

'For quite a number of years.'

She drew back.

'Then it can't be secret? You said, "a *secret* mission".'

Caught by her great eyes, he felt his chest tighten. He was on the point of confessing everything to her when the bottle popped. While the waiter poured for him to taste he formulated a new plan. When the waiter had poured for both of them, and gone, he said:

'Molly! I'll go to confession to you. The reason I rang you was because I want your help. I'm going to spend three days on my secret mission. Within these three days I'm going to decide. Advise me. It's true you are much younger than I am. But you have been married and I have not. Am I being foolish? Marriage is no joke at forty-six.'

He observed her intently. Her eyes sank slowly to her plate. With her fork she began slowly to divide the orange salmon. Was she guessing? Then she lifted her glass, and her eyes were full of kindness.

'Success!' she smiled. 'Tell me about your ladylove.'

'She is about your age. Your colouring, too. She was married. Her husband died. I'd have married her long ago if I hadn't let her slip through my fingers when I was young. Besides, she was engaged, and I didn't want to upset her.'

He believed he had always been drawn to her, but that she had been always dedicated. He was merely interpreting her vocation as a form of engagement. If he were to explain his meaning to her in this way she would understand immediately. He went on telling her of his long devotion and his long restraint.

'And so,' he finished, 'when she became free again I found all my old feelings lighting up as warm as ever after all these years.'

'I would never,' she said warmly, 'have thought it of you, Walter. I had always thought of you as more interested in your career than in anything or anybody else. Tell me more about her.'

His ladylove – so she had called her – lived in Ireland until she was about twenty-one. She had taken a degree in arts at Dublin University. Then she had gone abroad. To Spain. As a governess. After a year of this an uncle died and left her a small legacy. She immediately went to London. To a school of acting. During the war she fell in with one of the Free French. A young aristocrat. Interested in play production. For four years she did all sorts of acting, including provincial repertory. She twice got small parts in the West End, but she never really succeeded on the London stage, probably because, immediately the war ended, she married her Frenchman. They went to live abroad. In Bordeaux.

She was staring out at the Green. He added that there had been no children. She went on looking out at the Green, slowly turning her champagne glass. He said he had an idea that the marriage had not been entirely happy.

'I,' she said, without turning her head, and stopped.

He leaned forward.

'I,' she said, 'you might say, could have made Rome. Even,' a little less assuredly, 'Naples?' Still less assuredly, 'Even Milan? Instead, I married. I am back,' and she stopped again. She finished, speaking with sudden bitterness, 'where I began. She sounds very interesting.' she said without interest. 'I suppose it was because of her you didn't take any interest in me when I was at the Academy. What is her name?'

'I will tell you her name on Wednesday night, my last night, if you will dine with me.'

She smiled warmly, laying her hand on the back of his hand.

'Very well. But if you have not succeeded in your great adventure it won't be a very happy occasion? And if you have succeeded it won't be with *me* you'll be wanting to dine?'

He laid his free palm on the back of her hand. She castled her free palm on the back of his.

'That,' he said, 'is all you know! I'll be so happy if I succeed that there's nobody on earth I'll want to tell everything to sooner than you – where we will live, and what we will be doing for the rest of our lives.'

She gave him a curious look.

'Tell me where you live. I ought to know your house from the old days. Isn't it called Hunterscourt? Where exactly is it?'

He told her all about his house. She asked him so many questions about the life he led, about the people around him, about his neighbours and friends that he wondered if she had already guessed what he was after. Her questions were a bewildering blend of ignorance and shrewdness, as when she asked, with a knowing air, if all fillies ran faster than colts, or, 'Is it a fact that the Shannon is the widest river in the whole world?' But then, when he would be feeling completely dismayed by her folly, he would find himself being asked some coldly sensible question about current land values in Cork County. Was she a grown woman only by fits and starts? They talked for so long that he suddenly noticed that they were the only two people in the restaurant. He immediately became terrified – he had established nothing, found out nothing, asked nothing to the point of his quest, and here she was collecting her gloves. He said wildly:

'But you should see Cork again yourself. It is really a little Bergamo. With the hills, too! But not the antiquities. Or the sun. We haven't the same food. Or the wine. Why don't you pay us a visit? I have a whole big house eating its head off.'

'As a matter of fact I was half thinking of visiting some friends there.'

He felt a twinge of dismay. He knew nobody in County Cork who could have met her since she became famous.

'Who are these friends?' he asked crossly.

'Old Lord Boyne.'

He felt the bite of jealousy. He had gone across his fields to Castle Boyne twice to dine and had had the Boynes back twice to dinner at Hunterscourt: they had talked of Italy, but never mentioned the Rinaldis. Old Boyne's crumbling demesne wall shut out the world.

'I did not know,' he said coldly, 'that you knew the Boynes.'

'We met them last year. We were all staying at the Villa d'Este. In May.'

'In May.'

How childish! In May, before the tourists came. Then you retired to the mountains, then you might look at the sea, turn up later in Venice, go to Egypt if you had the money, then try the skiing, then return to Milan for the gossip and the season. It was a little common of her, really. He drew the lunch to an abrupt close.

As she walked ahead of him past the cocktail lounge she glanced in and casually waved to somebody in there. As he passed he also looked into its artificial dusk. It was young Boyne, his long legs hooped up at the counter. They raised friendly hands in mutual salute. He got the unpleasant feeling of being spied on. In the foyer she thanked him for the wonderful lunch and half turned to the stairs. In sudden despair he held her hand.

'How long are you staying here?'

'Three days.'

'Let's dine tonight!' he begged. 'You haven't given me any advice at all!'

'*Magari!*'

She had a dinner date. Lunch tomorrow? She was going out of town for lunch tomorrow. He had to be content with dinner tomorrow night – his second day otherwise wasted.

'I know so little about you,' he said plaintively, still holding her hand, looking at her. 'Have you relatives out of town? I mean, that you are lunching with tomorrow?'

'We are lunching at Killeen Castle.'

'We?' he smiled, apprehensively.

'I'm going with young George Boyne, he wants to buy a filly from the Sassoon stables.' She shook his hand. '*A domani!*' she beamed at him. 'And, *caro*, best of luck in your secret mission. *Ciaou!*'

Two steps up, she laid her hand on the newel post, turned gracefully and to his amazement winked at him. As if his secret love were some sort of jolly joke! He followed her with lifting eyes and chin. He frowned at the faint ridge of corset across her taut Italianate bottom. The calves of a peasant. He called to her just as she was about to disappear at the turn of the stairs:

'Molly! I'm being around town. Is there any little thing I can do for you?'

She glowed. Yes, there was a small thing. To collect a package from the cleaners, who, she laughed, do express cleaning but not express delivery.

'It will be a pleasure.'

He turned away, bewildered. Definitely not quite a woman, much more than a girl, yet with all the mature beauty of a desirable woman. He wondered how Rinaldi had handled her. Not easily, he guessed, remembering having read somewhere (he had wondered how the fellow knew it) that no women in the world are more passionate than the Irish and less erotic. The thought explained her. He smiled happily and slyly as he moved towards the desk where the hotel register still lay open after the last arrival. She was still unspoiled. And undespoiled. His smile vanished as his eye fell on George Boyne's signature. He stood in the doorway, glaring moodily at the sunlit Green. He turned back and, from the desk, rang her cleaners.

'Yes!' a girlish voice cried, gleefully and proudly. 'Countess Rinaldi's dresses are all ready.'

Dresses? Yes. Two frocks, one costume and an overcoat. He became scarlet at the idea of her expecting him to carry all that load of stuff through the city's streets. He gave the doorman half crown, bade him have the parcel collected, and went across the street into the Green, whirling his stick with annoyance. Really, he thought, the woman is completely juvenile.

Very different, *very* different, to what she had led him to expect.

3

She stood by the window, the lace curtain in her hand, and watched him cross the street and enter the Green, gaily twirling his walking stick. Dear Walter, always fancying himself the lady-killer. I sometimes wonder is he a homosexual, with all that pomade, and the wavy hair, and the smell of *eau verte*, and the tight waist, and the flower in the buttonhole and the dandy's walking stick.

It's wonderful to be back. A lunch like that now with an Italian and he'd be playing footy with you all the time, pressing your knee, paying you sugary compliments. All poor old Walter wants to do is to talk about himself and amuse you. Just the same, even one little compliment would be appreciated. Such as, I heard about your singing, or, I hope you're going to sing for us in Ireland. I said, So that's why you didn't take any interest in me when I was at the Academy, and he just opened his mouth like a fish. But that is the one great drawback in Ireland – they never ask you about yourself. So you're back? they say. That is achievement enough for them.

She drew a deep, slow breath as if she were about to break into song.

And God knows they are right to have a good opinion of themselves, the kindest people on earth. Look at him there now trotting off so nicely to collect my things for me.

He can't be serious about that woman. Or did he make her up? There never was any such a girl in Dublin in my time or I'd have heard of her. It's another one of his jokes, like Cork being a little Bergamo, with the hills, but without the sun, or the monuments, or the food, or the drink. I must tell that one to George. He'd have made it sound perfect if he'd said, And without the mothers, and the grandmothers, and the aunts, and the great-aunts, and the great-grandmothers. But he couldn't be serious, he'd be crazy, he's bald at the top, fifty if he's a day, and when we were at the Academy we thought he was ages. I well remember that first morning I saw him on the Green, with Lil Boylan and Judy Helen. Judy nudged me and said, Here's the college Don Juan, so I put on a great laugh, pretending not to see him at all, doing the innocent young girl up from the country. His eyes nearly fell out of his head. God help me, I didn't need to do much pretending. Sweet seventeen, and now I'm twice as old and with not much more sense. If it's crazy for him, what about me?

He went out of sight among the trees. She let the curtain fall. She looked at herself in the full-length mirror between the windows. She lifted her chin, pulled in her waist and jerked up the corners of her lips.

Thirty-four, and still thinking of *l'amore*? The last word of the famous first act. I never sang Mimi. I haven't the range. It would be another story if I was an actress like his friend. They can go on forever, like men, but not a singer, or not at my age.

She slowly ran her palm up under her chin to see the crepe gather.

That Fratella woman who cracked in the top C in Foggia! The way they whistled at her! Imagine having to take to the road again. Bari. Taranto. Reggio. Catania. What a night! *Carmen.* The rain and the wind howling in from the sea, and an old chipped enamel bucket plonking like a double bass in the corner of the dressing room at every drop from the ceiling. I got six encores.

She smoothed down her hips, turned to laugh sideways at herself, jacket open, hands on hips, wrenched-back shoulders, tilted chin. *L'amour est l'enfant de Bohème qui n'a jamais, jamais connu de loi. Si tu ne m'aime pas je t'aime, prends garde à toi.*

I suppose I ought to be out in that lovely green sun.

What is keeping him down there? I don't even know for certain how old he is. He says twenty-five but all young men add it on, or grow beards like Aldiberti – but he says it sells his *tessuti* better. All I get out of him is compliments, flattery galore, the old Irish plamaus, but always dodging off like a trout just when I think, He's going to ask me now. Like a little fox. Sly. A darling, dear, furry little fox, with a long brush. Giorgio! He's only a boy. If he was an Italian I'd know he was only after the one thing. Dear God, if he is, what must he think of me?

She jangled her wrist loudly. She went to the window. Two girls, carrying books, passed along the rails. She shook her head over them littley-bittley. She chuckled fondly as they passed away gossiping.

Was I innocent when I went to Italy? I was a total fool. And *still* am! Like saying, I'm back where I began. Letting myself down opposite him.

And even then he didn't pay me a compliment. Does that damn bar never close? *Sono la Contessa Maria Maddalena Rinaldi.* And what is it to the Contessa Rinaldi to be the Countess of Boyne? And anyway old Boyne will live to be a hundred. A little Bergamo? I want a big Bergamo, Rome, Paris, London, New York. God in heaven, do I want the same thing all over again? I was mad to have come. It was God sent him, there's no fool like an old fool, I must be mad, I'll finish off the whole thing, I'll have nothing more to do with him, when that telephone rings I'll just say, very, very quietly, a bit sad, to make it real, there's no need to hurt him, I'll say, Giorgio, a terrible thing has happened, I have just received a telegram from Coomagara where my grandfather lies seriously ill.

The telephone buzzed.

I'm independent of him. I could always live in Dublin. They'd jump at me for the Dublin Grand Opera. I could sing for the Rathmines and Rathgar. I could sing on the radio.

The telephone buzzed.

It couldn't be Aldiberti. He doesn't know where I'm staying. But if I say Coomagara he'll say, I'll drive you down. I.

The telephone buzzed.

She put her handkerchief to her mouth and ran to the window, and then ran back to the telephone, and snatched it up.

'Giorgio! What on earth are you doing down there? No, *caro*, you will *not* come up here. Yes, yes, and I might too if it were Milano again. But this isn't Milano. I will meet you in the foyer. Oh! I have had such an amusing lunch. I must tell you all about it. Such an amusing lunch! Such fun!'

4

Halfway across the Green he stopped dead. He felt that triple pain of emptiness, inertia and frustration which man calls loneliness. He crossed over to the Club. The bar was closed, the library was empty, the billiard table lay under a grey shroud. He walked slowly, killing time, twirling his stick, down the quays to Farquharson and Murphy's about a conveyance that, he knew, could as well be settled in a month's time by a post card. He walked back, slowly, across the Liffey, over Capel Street bridge, along the quays, along Grafton Street, into Knowles's, where he ordered two dozen red roses to be sent at once to her room. On the card he wrote: *Carissima, Red Roses for Thee*. He walked slowly on to Prost's, where he had a shampoo and a hot towel. He walked out to the Shelbourne. He had a word with Leo at the door. He had a word with Christy O'Connor at the bar, and a prolonged Tio Pepe. He then decided to have tea in the lounge. He stood at the door and recognized three old regulars. His breath stopped. She was seated in a corner, laughing gaily with young Boyne. He withdrew quickly and went out. Outside, he bought the *Evening Mail*. He saw, with a groan, that the Rathmines and Rathgar were once again, yet once again, doing *The Mikado* at the Gaiety. There was not a damn thing that he wanted to see, not even a film. He looked aimlessly all about him. He walked to the hotel. He undressed. He went to bed.

He awoke at six. He had a bath. He shaved. He changed. He went down to the front door. He selected Davy Byrne's for his *apéritif* and strolled, with pleasant anticipation, across the Green. The public part of the bar was full of what he called up-from-the-countrys, men and women with felt hats and paper parcels. He was about to persist into the rear lounge when he thought, though he was not certain of it, that he saw, through the ornamental wrought-iron gate, young Boyne's poll, and thought, again uncertainly, that the poll turned and a cold eye glimpsed him. He turned to go, and then, because he had to be certain, turned again and entered through the gate into the lounge bar. There was nobody sitting at the table by the gate. On the small black-topped table he saw two glasses, one half filled. She had not told him who she was dining with. He went swiftly through the bar and out through the rear door, and by the side lane back to the street. He saw nobody there whom he knew. He walked across the street to the Bailey. There he found a red beard talking about vintage cars in a loud haw-haw voice to a black R.A.F. moustache a foot wide. He went down to the Buttery. It was crowded, but there were a few two-splits-behind and a few fast fillies, so he sat up at the bar. He had a word with George and a prolonged Tio Pepe. He was afraid to dine at any city restaurant, so he walked back to the hotel. He got out the Mercedes and drove out of town to the Yacht Club. He parked, reserved a table, and went for a stroll along the East Pier.

He always liked the force of that stony white arm curved against the ponderous sea. Dublin smoked faintly to the west, low-lying as an encampment, sharp-edged as a saw, pensive as Sunday. Great pink clouds lay like overblown roses strewn along the bruise-blue horizon. Inch by inch the calm evening began to fade into a dusk the colour of cigarette smoke. Some townspeople, lured by the calm weather, were walking on the pier, taking the air, inspecting one another. A few early yachts, anchored to their reflections, pointed their noses eastward – the town's best weather vanes. For a few moments he paused to watch the gulls soaring and sinking about the funnel of the mailboat steaming gently at its pier. At first he passed many strollers, in pairs and fours, chatting companionably, but they became fewer the farther out he walked towards the pier's end with its lighthouse lantern blank and unrevolving.

Gradually he felt the wide sky, the wide bay and the oncoming dusk begin to envelop and isolate him. Now there were no strollers at all. The white tower and the glass of the many-windowed lantern rose coldly above him. When he looked back he saw a few lighted windows along the front. He barely made out the seagulls circling above the mailboat, blue blobs, but he did not hear their cries. The tall windows of his club were greenly lit. Behind the town the Dublin mountains rolled, empty and opaque, as if he were looking at them through smoked glass. Suddenly a yellow finger of light touched the dusty water of the harbour, moved across it, and then the electric string of lamps along the front and down the pier were lit. He climbed the stone steps up the side of the sea wall and went out through the embrasure. There was the night sea, the cold east wind, the sullen wash and slop of waves, one star.

How wonderful it would be now to have her, here, by his side, about to dine with him, hostess of a big dinner party in the club, at the head of the table, admired, glancing lovingly down its length at him. They would have lots of parties. How wonderful it would be to turn from this sea and wind and find her coming towards him now through the dusk, his phantom, seagull-white, smiling with winged lips. They would walk back along the stony arm, her soft arm in his. They would dine in the club, alone, make plans for travel, talk about opera, return to the city, not needing anybody, together, alone. The chilly wind said, But she isn't. Away out in the darkness the Kish lightship blinked. The chill wind said, Aren't you a fool to dream like this? What would one of your clients, what would Farquharson or Murphy think of you? He replied, self-mocking, This is another department, and remembered that somebody (and with a start he remembered that it had been old

Lord Boyne) once said to him, We are rational about everything except our passions and our children. The wind said, It is cold. His shiver admitted it. He descended the steps and walked swiftly back along the dark and empty monolith. It was like some big public building closing for the night.

He was glad to see a fire alight in the club. His table was marked *Reserved*, unnecessarily – it was early in the season for diners. There was nobody in the silent dining room with its empty white tables; its portraits of bearded commodores, its enormous Victorian seascapes bloomed like grapes. Once a man's head appeared around the door, said a cheery good night, and vanished. He heard the voice of a young man bantering the waitress in the kitchen, and her repeated laughter. He had often seen her smile, never heard her laugh. Once he thought how, more than once during the day, he had had half a notion to throw up the whole thing and go back to Cork. Not now! He drank off his claret with determination. Tomorrow night he would put her to the test. Finally.

The lighthouse swept at intervals. He prolonged his brandy, carefully shaping the words he would say to her. His blood thickened. The dark thickened. He dared not look at his watch. There were no hands on its face. The mailboat hooted before departure. Only nine? He called for a cigar. He ordered another brandy and took it into the reading room so that the waitress could be finished with him. He sat in the empty reading room, on the long leather-covered settee, facing the harbour and the beam that slowly circled and recircled the compass of the night. Slowly his courage oozed. She was at this moment dining with George Boyne.

He surrendered, went to his Mercedes, and drove into the bright city, and through it, and out of it, for home, driven by the furies of his own folly, contempt for his indecision, worked-up hate, bitter pride, cruel reason. It was after two when he pulled up at the gate to Hunterscourt. The house was dark. Here, together, when dark came, after dinner, they would not hear a sound unless it would be Mrs Canty in the kitchen rattling cutlery, or the fire puttering at their feet; later they might hear cows munching, or a plane facing out over the sea; latest of all, lying together in the darkness, they would hear nothing at all.

He turned and drove hell-for-leather back to Dublin, chasing his shivering headlights, passing sleeping cottages, dark villages, echoing through empty towns. He would insist on seeing her at breakfast.

5

George was laughing at her across the small, red table lamp. Over its upthrown light his handsome young face, pointed like a fox, his wide, mocking mouth, his madcap eyes, gleamed like a teenage Mephistopheles.

'Tell him at breakfast,' he said. 'Why keep the poor old fathead in misery until dinner?'

When he drew back she had to peer around the red lamp to see him. Usually when he was in this crazy mood she wanted to devour him the way a mother wants to devour a baby. Through her tears she was aware how his air of wickedness suited him.

'I can't believe it,' she protested. 'Old Walter!'

'He's not as old as all that,' he said crossly. 'Be realistic. He's not much older than you than you are than me. He is still considered one of the most eligible bachelors in County Cork.'

'But I assure you – he never uttered one word to me about marriage.'

'Molly! For the last time! He told you he was in love with an Irishwoman. Whom he met when he was a student. Who studied abroad. Who went on the stage, married a foreigner, lived abroad, is now a widow, has your colouring, is about your age. And he said he is in Dublin to try his fortune with her. Isn't that enough? Without the two dozen red roses – and the *carissima?* What more do you want? Unless,' his voice hardened as he again leaned over the little lamp-glow and peered at her with suspicion, 'you've been making it up. *Pour encourager les autres?'*

She leaned back, twisting her rings, surveying his under-lighted face.

Earlier they had strolled around the Green, had tea at the Shelbourne, strolled again, just barely dodged him in Davy Byrne's. They dined happily at Jammet's until the wine and the brandy began to go to his head and he had begun groping under the table.

'I don't want that, Giorgio!'

'Liar!'

'Well, not only that!'

'Then what else do you want? A title?'

'I have a title.'

'Haw-haw! Wop title!'

She made him apologize; he fell into a dark mood, and would not talk. Embarrassed by the waiters' glances – she suspected that they were not unacquainted with his moods – she had quietly proposed that they bring the evening to an end, whereupon he suddenly became plaintive and begged her not to break off on this note. So they drove, in his car, out of the city up into the hills to the turn of the road at Killakee from which all Dublin lies below, a half-dish of lights encircling the dark bay. Far away a lighthouse slowly circled.

She had been afraid there might be more demands for caresses here. Instead, when she withdrew to her end of the seat, leaning against the window, looking down at the lighted plain, he withdrew to his corner. He did not even once touch her hand. They were silent for a long time. Then he said, reverting to an earlier run of talk at the Shelbourne:

'Tell me more about your lunch today. It fascinates me. What exactly, tell me again, did old Hunter say about this woman of his?'

She humoured him, let him lead her through the whole conversation, back and forth, as if she were a witness in the box. When he had exhausted her memory he fell silent. Whenever the wind whispered the lights far below seemed to flicker. In his dark corner he chuckled to himself, his only comment, at that stage, a contemptuous:

'He has no such woman.'

'Poor Walter! He has to pretend.'

'The man is a goose. Dammit, he ought to know the world better by now. He's old enough!'

'You don't need to be so cruel.'

She was the goose. She should not have come. Sullenly from his corner he had said:

'So you have allotted two dinners to him and only one to me?'

If he had said it in simple disappointment she might have presumed affection – not when he said it sulkily, superbly self-concerned, out of the hurt vanity of a young man. She had drawn her coat around her neck, felt all her years, asked him quietly:

'How old are you, Giorgio?'

'I told you.' Crossly. 'Twenty-five. Why?'

'Does one dinner more or less with me mean so very much to you?'

'It could be a test of how much you love me.'

'And how much do you love me, Giorgio? And in what sense, Giorgio, do you love me?'

From his corner, in a very loud voice, as if he had been asked if he liked *risotto*:

'Very much. In every sense. After Milano you should know that.' Then his tone had suddenly changed, softened, deepened: 'I don't know when I met anybody I liked more than you. I'd marry you like a shot if I could.'

'And are you married, Giorgio?' – wanly.

In a furious, sarcastic mutter:

'My mother has other plans for me.'

'So the Contessa Rinaldi is not good enough for the Countess of Boyne!'

At this he had laughed gaily. It was one reason why she liked him so much: his moods could change like the wind scurrying over the surface of a lake. He said:

'I do wish you would understand the way things really happen in this world. It's got nothing to do with your not being good enough. It's simply that you are broke. As a matter of fact my mother has a great admiration for you. From her point of view it's wholly to your credit that you should have been born in that filthy old pub at Coomagara. Why, she holds you up to me as a model of what *can* be done with nothing. She says you are a spirited and clever woman. But you don't know how tough she is. And she's inquisitive as a hen. That time we met you on the Lakes she went snooping all around the hotel trying to find out about you and Rinaldi. It wasn't difficult. One night at dinner, on the terrace – all those little lamps, the full moon on the lake, the little steamer floating by with its dance music – after the three of us had passed your table, bowing, she shook out her napkin, and whispered to my father and me, like the damned old witch she is, "My dears, I've just had the most interesting talk with that tall old lady from Milan. She knows the Rinaldis intimately. They are completely on the rocks, just as poor as we are."'

'Why did she spy on us?'

'Because she saw I was keen on you, of course. Why else?'

'And are you really so poor?' she had asked dully.

'My mother says she's going to turn Castle Boyne into a guesthouse for rich Americans.'

'So that's that?'

'That's that, my dear!'

She had looked across at him, immobile, glaring out over the lighted dashboard at the lights of Dublin.

'Giorgio, are you wondering if I'm wondering whether your story is true or not?'

'It's all too true!'

'Giorgio, tell me. What is your chosen bride like? My colouring? A bit younger? My figure? Lived abroad? Went to – '

'Stop it! She's no age, no figure, no colouring. We have never seen her. My mother says she will be one of the rich Americans.'

She had shivered with pity for him, and said:

'Let's go and dance somewhere. The cold of death is in my bones.'

So they had come down here to this obscure little supper-and-dancing place, somewhere off the windy quays, so dimly lit she could not decipher the travel posters on the walls. They could barely see one another. Now and again other couples would appear out of the dusk on the tiny floor, but there was no telling how few or how many other people were there. They danced to the radiogram. Once she said, 'Do you like this place?' He said, 'No, but what else is there to do?' They ordered *risotto*. He had brandies; to save his pocket she drank beer. She knew he was in his wicked mood when he said, 'These are Italian travel posters. I believe one of them invites us all to come to Bergamo.'

It was after his third brandy that he had leaned over the lamp and cackled:

'Molly, are you really so utterly innocent that you don't know what Walter Hunter is after?'

And then he told her, and she refused to believe him until he beat her down and down. When he saw her in tears he bade her airily not to cry – she could still accept her old beau. Her protestations became feebler and feebler. She surrendered only when he asked her if she had been making it all up, 'to encourage the others'.

She leaned back to survey him, in all three of them, the ridiculous lurches of love.

'I suppose', she said sadly, 'you don't realize that you are trying to bully me, Giorgio. But why should you care? You're as good as betrothed to an American from Minneapolis.'

'I do care!' he cried back at her.

'Yet you want me to marry Walter Hunter?'

'I want you to marry nobody but me.'

She was so astonished by his tone that she snatched the red shade off the lamp. In the naked light his face was transformed. He looked about seventeen, his mouth melting, his eyes misted. Furiously he snatched the shade from her and restored the ruby dusk. There was a prolonged silence, except for the slither of dance shoes and the staccato hiss of a gourd in a Cuban thrum. She collected her bag and gloves:

'I wish I were rich. Innocent child that you are! Let's go. The night is finished.'

'One more dance?'

They did not dance it Cuban-way. They held one another very tight. He made her feel like a mother with a child. Then he called the waiter, fumbled with the bill and his wallet, said brusquely to her, 'I haven't enough, can you lend me a quid?' She did not dare not take the change from him. They walked back arm in arm across the river, around the locked-up Green. Down here in the plain the wind was slight. The stars were out in their legions. In the empty foyer of the hotel he said:

'I suppose I've cooked my goose with you now?'

'There wasn't any goose, Giorgio,' she said fondly, and bent her cheek to be kissed. 'Only a little *poussin*. Sleep well.'

'I'm not going to sleep. It's a fine night for driving. I'll be home in time to see the morning coming up over your little Bergamo. Have a nice breakfast with old Wally.'

She did not sleep until late morning. Her shame kept her awake, and the image of that young face, lean, sensitive, cruel, greedy, madcap, enchanting, lovable, staring through the headlights fleeing before him. She kept turning and twisting in her bed and in her mind away from thoughts of Walter Hunter. It would be a refuge. All her worldly wisdom told her it would be a sensible and interesting and dangerous refuge. So close to George. With his rich American wife? Poor Giorgio!

6

Tired from his long drive, he did not wake until late morning. When he was about to go downstairs he found an envelope angled under his door. It contained a sheet of hotel note-paper bearing a message from her. *Dear Walter, If you are free for lunch do join me in the foyer at noon. I shall be alone. Molly.* He hastened down. She looked up at him with a wan smile.

'This is delightful, Molly! But you said you were lunching with the Killeens?'

'I decided not to go.'

'Our dinner tonight is all right?' he asked.

'We must make it lunch instead, Walter. I cannot dine with you tonight, I am flying to Milan. Let's go into lunch at once, shall we?'

He followed her, aghast. He sat on the edge of his chair, he fiddled with his knife, he stared at her, he told the waiter they did not wish to drink, he called him back.

'Yes, drinks, please,' he panted. 'Molly? Champagne?'

'Please, Walter!' she groaned. 'Not champagne!'

'Two Martinis.'

He glared at her blankly. All his carefully prepared words had flown away like escaped pigeons.

'And tomorrow night, too? Is that dinner gone, too?' He was getting more and more angry. 'Really, this is too bad of you, Molly!'

She could only open her palms and smile sadly. She saw that he was so upset that he was liable to say the first thing that came into his head, and to her dismay, she found that his anger and his misery made him more *simpatico* than she had ever found him before.

'Molly!' he barked. At once he said, 'Sorry!' and laughed, and then coughed, and said, 'I had a wonderful night last night. I dined alone. At the Yacht Club.'

She looked at her hands. Was she expected to ask, Why wonderful? She looked up. He became aware of her pallor. Her eyes were tired, as if she, too, had not slept. It gave her, as on that night of summer rain in Rome, the vanishing beauty of a peach ripened to the full point when it ought to be picked and eaten at once. He said, in a little voice – strange and rather touching to her in a man so broad, big and ruddy:

'You are pale, Molly. It makes you even more beautiful.'

She smiled feebly at the compliment.

'I didn't sleep very well.'

'I did not sleep at all. I drove all the way down to Cork after dinner. And back again.'

She closed her eyes. He too? This, she thought, is one of those things I will laugh at when I am an old woman.

'Rather a long drive,' she said flatly.

'It was after six before I got back. But I didn't mind. I was thinking of the woman I love. From the hill above Saggart I saw the morning sun spreading over Dublin. I was thinking of her, asleep. Her hair strewn on the pillow.'

His pigeons were circling, sinking, coming back to him. His eyes began to glow. Any minute now, she felt, he will come to it. They picked at random from the outsize menu. He lifted his glass.

'You know,' he said, more at his ease now, 'the only times I ever saw you alone you looked pale, lovely, and unhappy.'

'Alone?' she asked, startled.

'Alone, I mean, since we were students. Yesterday. Now. That wet night in Rome. The first time was in Turin.'

'We never met in Turin.'

He leaned forward.

'I did not say met, I said saw. It was in 'Forty-six. Just after the war. I had gone up to Cervinia for the skiing...'

He went bit by bit through his story. With apprehension he noted that she paid no attention to the omelette that had been placed before her. She was staring fixedly through the muslin curtains at the Green. By the time he said, 'They were playing *La Sonnambula*,' he saw, with puzzlement, that her eyes were tear-covered. At the end, when he said, 'You walked out on the stage and I nearly died,' she looked straight at him through the water of her tears.

'And you were actually there all the time! Why on earth didn't you come around afterwards?'

They stared at one another; she waiting for his answer, he gaping at her because he no longer knew the answer. His secret image of her had vanished. Rapidly, as if he were racing backwards after it, he tried to re-create the night, talked of the music act by act, of her songs, of her singing, the lighting, the last falling curtain.

'Walter, you know it so well! And you are so right about that night in Turin. It was one of the best performances I ever gave. As I have good reason to know. But why did you never tell me all this?'

He saw himself in that café, waiting for the train at two in the morning.

'I don't know,' he gasped. 'I was so lonely! And I was so happy!'

She threw up her chin and she laughed the strangest laugh, a laugh like a breaking wave, curling and breaking between pride and regret.

'I was happy too. If you only knew! I often wonder was I ever quite so happy since. It was that very night, between the acts, in my dressing room, that Rinaldi came in and first told me he was in love with me.

Do you remember that enormous bouquet I got at the curtain? Great *reine de joie* roses, straight up from Africa, he had telephoned for them that morning to Milan. They came only just in time, the boy ran with them in his arms, from the taxi, right on to the stage. There were snowflakes on them. They must have cost him the earth. But he was always a spendthrift. No wonder we went broke!' She drew in a deep, passionate, hissing, sobbing breath between her clenched teeth, her eyes swimming, her fists crunched together. 'I'm glad we were broke. I'd do it again. It's the only way to live. Not giving a damn.'

'And I,' he said, 'was sitting for hour after hour after the show in a café, drinking, thinking of you, lost in you!'

'Do you know,' she raced on, lost in herself, 'what we did after the show? You should have been there. Rinaldi invited the whole company to a party at his hotel. He whistled up such a party as you've never seen. Dancing, singing, champagne. And when it was all over, and they were all gone, and now that it's all over forever and all gone forever, I can tell you, Rinaldi and I, left alone . . .'

She hid her screwed-up face in her hands. The sensual picture she evoked sent the blood to his eyes. He stared at her, feeling the first pangs of jealousy, loss, creeping lust. He waited until she was blowing her nose, looking at him self-mockingly, fishing for her compact in her bag, glancing about the restaurant to see if anybody had observed her. She said:

'For two years I kept refusing him. Then I decided that I never would be a great singer.' She shrugged. She looked up at him with sudden recollection: 'What did you say you did that night?'

He told her again, with bitter feeling. She shook her head.

'What a *salade* we make of our lives!' she sighed.

'So you were unhappy with Rinaldi.'

'Unhappy? Who said I was unhappy?'

'You have conveyed it to me in a dozen ways. Molly!' he said intensely, leaning over to her. 'Don't try to deceive me. You can't. Don't try to deceive yourself by idealizing him now. You are in the prime of life, your whole life is before you, you can't stop living.' He paused. He asked it quietly, but unmistakably: 'Would you dare look for happiness again?'

She looked at him for a long while. He hid his trembling hands under the table. She lowered her face in her hands and he saw that her hands, too, were trembling. He leaned back and waited for his fate. When she raised her head and he saw the tears in her eyes again, he knew that he had evoked the one night of all her life that he could never defeat. She said, so softly that he had to lean forward to hear her:

'Walter! Nobody ever finds happiness. We make it, the way people mean when they say, "Let's make love". We create it. For all I know we imagine it. We make happiness easily when we are young, because we are full of dreams, and ideals, and visions, and courage. We make our own world that pushes away the other world – your world, and my world, old people's worlds. The young despise the world. Didn't you ever say it when you were young? I'll conquer the world! But you know what happens to us. That little flame in us that could burn up the world when we're young – we sell a little bit of it here, and a little bit of it there, until, in the end, we haven't as much of it left in us as would light a cigarette. And yet,' she said, frowning through him, 'it is there, to the end. You feel always you might blow on it, make it big again, go on to the very end, without giving up, find the thing, discover the thing, invent the thing, call it anything you like, that you'd always been wanting. Walter, I am not your thing. You are not my thing. I have very little courage left in me, Walter. In fact,' she moaned, 'I have hardly any left in me at all. That's why I'm flying to Milan tonight. My bags are packed and ready in the hall. Don't come with me.'

She grabbed her gloves and her handbag, shook hands with him strongly, and quickly left the restaurant.

In the hotel porch, while her suitcases were being loaded on a taxi, she picked up a coloured post card of Saint Stephen's Green, addressed it to The Honourable George Boyne, Ringaskiddy, Co. Cork, and scrawled on it: *I did it well, nobly and virtuously, and you would have thought me a damn fool. I have all my life to wonder if I was. M.* As she stepped into the taxi she saw, down along the wine-red line of Georgian buildings, a gathering of students, girls and boys, outside the University Club, chattering and laughing gaily. She looked at them without envy, slammed the door of the taxi, and drove away.

He let the lace curtain fall. He sat on, sipping a brandy. For the first time in his life he felt the agony that a man suffers in the full awareness of loss. All his senses are alerted a millionfold. His brain burns like a forest fire. And he feels as if the essential parts of his body have been cut out. He saw her hands, her dilated eyes, her convoluted smile. They were not only her hands, eyes and smile but the beauty and desirability of everything unattainable in life. From his pocket he drew out her letter of an hour ago and read it. He saw only the force of her wrist, the strength of her body. He saw her as he had never dared to see her before: those firm calves, the breadth of her hips, her narrow waist, her rich breasts, her yellow pile of hair falling down over her bare body. All this he had lost, as a duellist can lose, forever, as a boxer can lose, forever, as a damned soul loses, forever. This, he knew, he had always wanted. He ordered a brandy, and another, and another, until he was left there alone, seeking for her other image in the round, shining snifter, as one seeks in those toy, round globes that when you shake them give the illusion of falling snow, a tiny figure, remote as a fairy tale, white and virginal, smiling out at him. If he could see her like that, the snow falling silently, the arc lamps fogged by it, the soft thunder in his veins, the music weaving in his memory, he would be happy even though he knew that he would never see her otherwise again. Always the proud, rich, sensual image came before him, smiling, full of love, but not for him.

He gave the young waiter who had been patiently attending him a heavy tip, and went out hatless across the Green to the record shop on Dawson Street. An April shower spattered the shopwindow as he sat in the little booth listening to the '*Ah, non credea mirarti,*' looking out at the falling shower, at the passers-by. The song was as pure as a lark in the clear air. It evoked only the image of a naked Venus. He bought it, went across the street to Doran's pub, from Doran's to the gentle dimness of the empty Buttery, from there to Davy's and from there across to the Bailey. All that afternoon and evening and night he ate nothing. There are in Dublin occasions of vice more squalid by far than in cities that have not been cleaned up. When he reeled out of his last pub late that night, he sought out one of these places, and entered his little season of hell.

He woke up about four in the morning, lying in a lane along the garages and stables at the backs of some houses. He felt a cold mist falling on him. There was congealed blood on his forehead. His pockets were emptied of money. Unheeded, he got back through the empty city to his car outside the hotel, and managed to drive out of the city. He pulled up on the hill above Saggart and got out to wash himself in a stream.

The rain had stopped. There was Dublin's dish of coloured lights below him on the still-dark plain. A cold light touched the underside of the clouds over the Irish Sea. Far away the Bailey lighthouse circled slowly through the pre-morning dusk. He stayed looking over the city and the sea for a long while, watching them slowly become cold and clear, until two sunbeams leaped from below the horizon, a bird threw out a pillar of song, and, as if to its conductor's baton, all the birds at once began to sing like blazes. He closed his eyes and whispered 'Christ!' out of the depths of his delight and misery. Then he went back to the car and drove away into the cold wetness of the morning.

A dream? Ah, well! It wasn't such a bad dream. If only I hadn't tried to make it become real. Still, isn't this the way most of us spend our lives, waiting for some island or another to rise out of the mist, become cold and clear, and . . . so . . .

Miracles Don't Happen Twice

I met Giancarlo on the seafront of Bari late one dank night in October. The Adriatic wind was cold. The waves slapped drearily along the Lungomare. Because of the chilly wind and the gusts of rain only a few people were out of doors, although all Bari loves to gravitate every night to the seafront, enjoying the lights of the cinemas, the big hotels, the fish-vendors' flares, and an occasional boat offshore luring the fish to the spear with white, down-thrown lamps. I had paused to look with amusement at a travel poster showing the Tower of London as red as wine under an improbably blue English sky. The lights glistened on the raindrops sliding down it. 'Yes!' I was thinking. 'And I suppose outside Victoria Station the rain is pelting posters of sunny Italy.' A voice at my side said:

'*E freddo stasera, signore.*'

He was a little man, with pansy-dark eyes. He was smiling an engaging smile. He wore a raincoat but no hat and he carried a briefcase. One glance at him and I was in no doubt that he belonged to a large and ancient Italian profession. Then, instead of asking me if I wanted a nice girl, he said comfortingly that the sun would shine again tomorrow, and then, in English:

'You are English, *signore?*'

I said 'Yes,' because I have found in Italy that if I say I come from Ireland either they say, 'Ah, yes! The dykes and the windmills!' or else a haze comes over their eyes and I have to explain that Ireland is an island near England – which I find a little humiliating and they find disappointing. Sometimes, when I really want to please them, I choose to be an American and invent a home in Chicago or Minneapolis.

'I also have been in England,' said the little man eagerly. 'My sister lives in England. Near Bournemouth. Do you know Bournemouth, *signore?* I know it very well. And Poole. And Eastbourne.'

As he chattered on I began to wonder if he were a real professional. Perhaps he was merely an amateur who would presently produce picture post cards, cheap coral brooches or American cigarettes from his little bag, and would mention girls only if all else failed. I fell into talk with him willingly. Bari is not an exciting city; the hours after dinner are the most lonely hours for a traveller; and, anyway, I have a sympathetic feeling for Italian pimps. They are not bad fellows. They are a race outside our world. They do not tempt us. We tempt them. They have no wish to harm us. They will merely assist us to harm ourselves if we so desire.

After a while I said, 'Let's get out of this beastly wind and have a drink somewhere,' and we began to walk past the Old Port towards the Corso, talking about Dorset. But he did not pause at the Corso, for he said kindly: 'It is too expensive here. I know a good place,' and led me onward in o the dark and winding streets of the old town away behind the docks, until, in a particularly dark and narrow alley, we came to a hole in a wall. It was a wineshop, arched, empty, brightly lit. There we sat to a trestled table, over a flask of acrid wine. We were alone.

'And what is your sister working at in England?' I asked.

'Oh! She is not working,' he said proudly. 'She is married to a wealthy paper manufacturer.'

'Really?' I said, deciding that for tonight I would have to be at least a Sheffield steel king.

'But it is true!' he assured me, instantly interpreting my look. 'Veritably true! She went there when she was eleven. Her name then was Federica Peruzzi. Now her name is Mrs Philpot.'

He produced an envelope bearing an English stamp. The dove-grey paper was deckled, embossed with an address in Bournemouth, and signed Federica.

'It happened so,' he explained. 'After the first war I and my sister were only small children. We lived in Altamura, up in the hills. We had nothing to eat. We came down to Bari because we heard the British navy was in the port.' He shrugged and made a face of shame. 'We were begging outside the big hotels on the seafront. What else could we do? All I had to sell was one double-almond. As you know, the double-almond brings luck. And,' he cried, with a vast, baby-faced smile, 'mine brought luck to me. For one night when a sea captain came out of the Grand Hotel I offered him my double-almond. He took it. He looked at me. He looked at my sister. He looked and looked at her. And suddenly he began to weep. "*Signore*," I said, "why are you crying?" He took me aside and he began to ask me questions, but he could not take his eyes from my sister. I was very troubled for her. I was only fourteen, and in Altamura they had said that we should find the big world in the valley a very wicked place.'

Giancarlo wriggled apologetically with his whole body.

'You see, I loved my little sister, and she was only eleven. But the captain soon explained. His name was Captain Edgeworth. He had lost his only child during the war, and he said that Federica was the living image of his Gladys who had died. And as he said this he became sad and wept again. I knew then that he was an honest man.

'The captain gave me fifty lire and told us both to be at the hotel again the next morning at ten o'clock. Oh! What a meal we had that night! It is thirty-four years ago and never since have I eaten a better meal. Never, never, never as long as I live will I forget that meal. All night Federica could not sleep. She kept waking me up and crying out, "Giancarlo! Our fortunes are made! The rich Englishman will take care of us for the rest of our lives." But I said, "Sleep, little one. We shall never see the captain again. Let us be content with our fifty lire."'

Clearly, so far, a true story. Those cries of hope were not invented. They could only have come out of the old Italian belief in magic, miracles, the wheel of fortune, the *Totocalcio* (their football pools), in short, some *deus ex machina* who alone can change the hopeless reality of life.

'But I was wrong, *signore*. The captain was waiting for us the next morning. He said, "Now we go to Altamura". We took the train into the hills. He slept that night in the one bed between me and my father, with Federica asleep at the tail of it. He ate our poor food, roasted herrings and dry bread. He trusted me with all his money. I could have run away with it all, but I did not touch one lire of it. He arranged between my father and a lawyer to adopt Federica, and to change her name to Edgeworth. The next day we returned to Bari and he took Federica with him to England. When he died he left her all his money. She met a Mr Philpot and married him. Now she has two sons. One of them was fighting here in Italy during the war.'

He drew out his wallet and showed me a crumpled family photograph: two youths, a very lean, English-looking papa and a middle-aged woman full of Italian fat.

'And you?' I asked. 'Did the captain do anything for you?'

'Had I not given up my sister whom I loved? Of course, he gave me money. I travelled a little. I have even been to Rome. I became a valet to a rich American lady in Rome. But I was not happy with her. She was not young and she was not beautiful and she was always trying to make love to me. I could have married her and had all her money, but I was young and romantic, and I wanted real love. Once Federica brought me to Bournemouth. I was unhappy there too. I saw that she did not want me any more. I came back to Bari. I fell in love. I got married.'

He removed his raincoat and showed me the tab. It bore the name and address of Burton's in Piccadilly.

'Federica sent me this coat. Sometimes she sends me shirts and shoes. But never any money.'

We had some more wine. He asked me about my life. I described to him my two steel factories near Sheffield. He said he was gratified and honoured to know me. We talked of his life and with a shrug of self-contempt he gave me a glimpse into his briefcase: brooches of orange-pale coral, picture post cards, American cigarettes. I found that he sometimes gets jobs as a waiter. We talked of the *Totocalcio*. I bought a ticket for him from the *padrone*, and selected the teams, and wrote in his name. As I wrote in his name the sound of the wintry wind outside was one with his deep breathing into my ear.

'It will be lucky,' he cried. 'I know it! It will win a prize! Will it not, Giacomo?' – turning to the *padrone*, who merely lifted his shoulders and let them fall again. We had some more wine. It was half past eleven before we rose and went out into the wind and the darkness. As he walked down the lane Giancarlo stopped and turned. I was afraid that he was going, at last, to ask me if I wanted a nice girl, and I dearly hoped he would not. When he did not I hoped that I understood why. We had drunk wine together, we had exchanged confidences, we were friends.

Just then the yellow light from a window fell on a dark-haired little girl of about eleven who had come dashing up to him, clasping him about the knees, saying, 'Momma is looking for you!' He lifted her into his arms, and kissed her passionately. Then he turned slowly towards me, gazed at me in awe, and whispered:

'This is Federica!' And to her, as if he were showing her the statue of a saint in church: 'Little one! This is a rich Englishman who has just arrived in Bari.'

For one entranced moment the two of them gazed at me. By the child's wide eyes I knew that she had often heard poppa's fairy tale. For that one moment, in that dark wind-swept alley, I knew what it feels like to be a god in a machine. Then a gust of rain came blasting down on us. I groped in my hip pocket for a note and crumpled it into Giancarlo's fist, gripped his arm, said the hour was late, said my family was waiting for me at my hotel, cried, '*Arivederci!*'

Half an hour later I was lying in the warmth of my bed in the Grand Hotel delle Nazioni. Outside I could hear the slapping waves and the wind moaning down from Altamura.

No Country for Old Men

1

One morning last September, all the Dublin papers carried headlines like these:

END OF CARNDUFF TRIAL

ONE YEAR FOR COMPANY DIRECTOR

This is how one daily paper reported the conclusion of the odd affair:

> At the Belfast Assizes yesterday, sentences of one year and of six months respectively were passed on Joseph Peter Cassidy (sixty-three), described as a manufacturer and company director, and Frederick Robert Wilson (fifty-seven), described as accountant and secretary. Both men gave their address as Boyne Close, County Louth. Cassidy had been charged with the illegal possession of a revolver and six rounds of ammunition, with being a member of an illegal organization, and with entering Northern Ireland by an unrecognized road on the night of July 15th last. Wilson had been charged with membership in an illegal organization and entering Northern Ireland by an unrecognized road on the same date.
>
> In sentencing the accused, Mr Justice Cantwell said that on the night in question an attack had been made on Carnduff Police Barracks, in the course of which a policeman had been shot dead, and that, after the attack a motor van, the admitted property of Cassidy, had been found only two miles away from Carnduff, its interior heavily stained with blood.
>
> During the trial both defendants insisted that they had no connection whatever with the attack on Carnduff Barracks and that they had entered Northern Ireland on the night in question solely in search of the motor van, which had been removed without permission from the premises of Celtic Corsets Ltd, of Boyne Close,

Drogheda. Cassidy said that he had carried the revolver solely for his own protection.

Mr Cassidy is a well-known Dublin businessman, a widower with one son, managing director of Celtic Corsets Ltd, and of Gaelic Gowns Ltd. Mr Wilson is secretary to the firm of Celtic Corsets Ltd, and is unmarried. Both men took part in the 1916 Rising and served side by side in the First Dublin Brigade during the War of Independence.

Both accused have been removed to Crumlin Road Prison, Belfast, to serve their sentences.

The reports in all the other papers were equally short, not to say meagre. And yet none of us considered that they should have been more informative. The fact is that whenever perfunctory reports like this appear in the Irish papers we all understand at once that the press is laying a finger on its lips either for political reasons or religious reasons or through a sense of personal delicacy. We guess that some decent man is in trouble, or that some unfortunate priest has gone off the rails, or that some public man has been caught, as the Americans say so vulgarly, with his pants down. We approve of this reserve, this proper regard for human feelings, this *gentillesse* (as the French say), because we Irish have a certain hidalgo quality about us. And, anyway, it might be our turn tomorrow. So we draw a seemly cloak of public reticence over the matter, and then – in whatever golf club, or yacht club, or restaurant or pub the characters in question have been accustomed to frequent – we tap the old grapevine to find out what these fellows have been up to. Over the malt we pass our own judgment on them in seemly privacy.

We certainly had to pursue this Carnduff affair beyond public report and private rumour. We all knew quite well that Joe Cassidy is far too cagey to become a member of any illegal organization at his age and with his income. We know him for a sound, law-abiding citizen who has not carried a gun, let alone killed anybody, for at least thirty-five years. We know Freddy Wilson less well, because he left the country nearly thirty years ago, immediately after the Troubles. Nevertheless, those of us who had known him then, or met him since his return to Ireland to work for Joe Cassidy, assured us that if he actually was doing anything illegal in Northern Ireland it was unthinkable that any policeman would catch him doing it.

We found that Joe's only son, Frank, was a member of the Irish Republican Army, and that on that July night it was he who had borrowed the firm's van to take part in a raid across the border. It so happened that when Joe heard about the van he was at a dinner of the Drogheda chapel of the Irish Manufacturers' Social and Patriotic, and his guts being rich of wine, he had become, not unnaturally, incensed against the boy. After all, Frank could just as easily have stolen somebody else's van. Still in his white tie and tails, and full of fire, Joe had jumped into his Jaguar, and with – or so we presumed – Freddy Wilson, he had torn hell-for-leather after the blue van with the pink corset painted on each side of it. Aided by various sympathetic souls along the road, he had picked up the trail and had the good luck to come up with Frank, a bare ten minutes after the raid, across the border, still with the van, trying to get one of his wounded men back to safety. The wounded youth died under their eyes on the side of the road. The rest was easy to imagine.

Joe and Freddy had sent the son racing back across the border in the Jaguar. They then took over the van and the dead boy. We took off our hats to Joe Cassidy and Freddy Wilson and we let it be known to them both that there would be a public dinner at the Dolphin waiting for them when they came out of gaol.

But as the months went by some more details leaked out. For one thing, Freddy had not been with Joe in the Jaguar. Freddy had been in the van with Frank. He had forced Joe's son to take him with him on the raid across the border because he was taking French leave of Celtic Corsets Ltd, with four thousand pounds' worth of bearer bonds belonging to his old comrade-in-arms in his breast pocket. And he might have got away with them if he had not had the bravado to leave a taunting farewell message to Joe behind him.

The rest was true enough. Joe and Freddy had persuaded Frank to take the Jaguar while they stayed with the van. There they were, then, with a dead youth on their hands, at about one o'clock in the morning, only a mile away from a police barracks that had been attacked by bomb and machine-gun fire ten minutes before...

2

Joe waited until he heard the Jaguar driving rapidly away. Then he ran back to the fork of the road as fast as his great bulk and the thin pumps he was wearing would allow. As he ran he could hear nothing but the sound of his own panting and the patter of his pumps on the road. He had no torch, so when he came to the fork he snapped on his petrol lighter and by its fitful light he began shuffling through the long grass, bending, peering, groping, and cursing. He could see nothing except the grass until a beam of light from behind his back showed him the staring face of the dead young man at his feet.

'Found him?' Freddy's voice said from behind the beam.

'The bastards!' Joe said. 'We've got to get him into the van and across the border at once. Bring up the van!'

Freddy turned and ran for the van. While he waited for him to return, Joe clambered up on the ditch and saw, a mile away, the kangaroo jumps of the Jaguar's lights making towards the south. He looked left and saw Freddy's lights coming up the road. Then, still farther left, or northward, he saw a third set of lights moving towards the east. The moon was rising and it made the trees against it look very black. Then they were lifting the dead youth, laying him into the back of the van, and Freddy was driving back the way they had come. As he drove Freddy said:

'Did you see the lights of a car away there to the north? It may only be a private car on the main road from Newtown Butler to Clones, but if we are still in the North they may be police or B Specials trying to cut us off. Damnation! I wish I knew to hell where exactly our wandering border is tonight.'

They took a right turn. The headlights likewise turned and moved parallel to them on their left.

'I don't like this at all,' Freddy said. 'See that?' he shouted, and Joe saw what he meant.

It was a letter box inset into a wall, painted in English red. They were still in the North.

When they came to a T-sign they were aware of the other car's lights, now not more than a quarter of a mile to the east. Freddy whirled west, curved under a railway bridge, tore into sixty on the straight, and let out a cry of joy. His headlights had picked up a tattered Southern tricolour hanging from the branch of a tree: they had crossed the border already. He came to a fork, pulled up, turned off his engine, and they both looked back and listened. The lights of the pursuing car were halted about half a mile behind them. They could hear its engine humming in the still summer night.

'This is all very well,' Joe said. 'We're in the South now. But this bloody border loops all over the place. Any road we take, if we take it far enough, might take us back into trouble again. We had better go very carefully, Freddy-boy!'

Freddy let in the gears and sneaked slowly along the road. The lights behind them moved slowly against distant treetops. Freddy pulled up. The lights whirled and vanished.

'I'm afraid to go on. I expect they have a transmitter.'

He got out and climbed the ditch, followed by Joe. He pointed:

'See that? They're going south! I know what's happened. This road must cross a pocket of the South enclosed by two pincers of the North. They're going down the eastern leg of the pocket to cut us off there if we try to cross it.'

'Then,' Joe said, 'let's run across the western leg and get out that way.'

'You can bet your last bullet they have a patrol down that way already.'

'Then we're boxed!' said Joe. 'Have we a map?'

'No! But I see a cottage. I'm going to take a chance on it. We must have a guide.'

'What the hell is the good of a guide if there's no road out of this pocket?'

'We can walk across the fields, can't we? But – and Freddy nodded his head towards the back of the van, questioningly.

Joe looked into the dark maw behind him.

'We'll carry him. I'm not going to let those bastards get him. Once they identify him, all his relations up here will be in the soup.'

They got out and knocked at the door of the long, slateroofed cottage. There was no sound from inside it. They knocked again several times, but they could not hear as much as the sound of breathing from inside. To Joe's surprise, a gun appeared in Freddy's hand. It was that rather old-fashioned type of long-nosed automatic known as a Peter the Painter. Joe knew this type of gun well; he had always carried a Peter the Painter in the old days. As his eye fell on it he remembered in a flash one night when it jammed during a raid in Clanbrassil Street and he would have been a gone man if Freddy had not shot the Black and Tan who was firing at him. Before he could say anything, Freddy had pushed in a pane of glass with the point of his gun and shouted through the hole:

'This is the I.R.A. There's six of us. If you don't come out we'll burn you out. We'll give you one minute.'

After a few seconds they heard a slight noise, and then a man's voice said:

'Come to the door.'

'No tricks!' Freddy shouted. 'We'll shoot!'

They heard a sound of footsteps, and something like a tin basin falling on a stone floor and rotating noisily to rest. A pale glimmer of light appeared to pass the window. A chain rattled and the door opened on the chain, a device Freddy had never in his life seen in any part of the country, even during the Troubles years ago, when he had often been out at all hours of the night in the loneliest mountainy places behind Dublin. His torch showed the face of a pale but unfrightened middle-aged man looking out through the three-inch opening. Impressed by the man's steady look, he said more quietly than he had intended:

'All we want is a guide. We've lost our way and we want to get back on foot across the border.'

'No!' the man said sturdily. 'I'm not going to help you. This may be the South, but a heap of my neighbours are Orangemen. I do a lot of work with folk across the border.' His eye fell on the long-nosed gun. 'Of course,' he went on amiably, 'if you were to as much as point your gun at me . . .'

Freddy grinned with relief. 'Consider it done,' he said.

'You must do it so that I can honestly swear that you did do it.'

Freddy raised the revolver. For good measure he said cheerfully:

'If you don't help us I'll shoot you where you stand.'

'Wait until I tell the missus and get me boots on. And put out the lights of yon car. We can take no chances.'

Three minutes later the three of them were back in the van. Their guide made no comment on the fact that they were only two and that one of them was in evening clothes. He did observe dryly that they were mighty old to be in the I.R.A. To this Freddy replied:

'We're two brigadier generals. Did you hear the racket our lads made tonight?'

'I heard something like firing in the direction of Carnduff about half an hour ago. And I saw a rocket going up from over thereabouts about twenty minutes back.'

'Twenty minutes! No wonder the patrols are out.'

They drove slowly, in silence and moonlit darkness, until they came to a fork where they turned south and came to a railway bridge. Freddy was silent because he was aware of the presence of danger; the man was silent because he was a Northerner; and Joe was silent because he was thinking about the gun. After driving for what seemed to Freddy like a long mile, the man at his side told him they must now abandon the van and walk the rest. Even when they opened the van doors and lifted out the dead young man he said nothing, only stooping to look into the blankly staring eyes, shaking his head partly from pity and partly to indicate that he did not recognize him. The three of them carried the body south along the track. It was slow walking, and when he halted them and assured them they had not covered a quarter-mile their aging bones could not believe him. He whispered:

'I'm going to leave ye now. If ye followed this road or yon railway line any farther ye'd find yeerselves back inside the border. From this on ye'll have to take to the fields. Go in a straight line with yon red star foreninst ye. After about half a mile or so ye'll pass out through our Gap o' the North. The Gap's not much more than a quarter-mile wide down there, but ye can't miss it if ye remark that it lies between a wide copse of beeches on the west and a low grassy hill on the east. Carry on then and it'll maybe be another half-mile before you come to a wee road. Ye'll be well into the South by then. That road will take ye fair and free anywhere ye like in the Republic.'

They looked ahead of them into the level darkness. The sky was white with stars. In the clear summer sky the moon was now as big and bright as a tin basin. They saw no lights on the plain. They heard no least sound. Freddy whispered:

'Is there any danger that the Specials, if they're out, would cross the Gap to stop us?'

'Every danger! They'd follow a man twenty miles into the Republic if their blood was up. And it'll be up the night. Ye'll have to move slowly and quietly and take no chances. I can do no more for ye. God bless ye! And don't make a sound. D'ye hear that dog?'

They heard a dog barking.

'That dog must be three miles away.'

When they looked around again he had vanished as if he had been a ghost or a leprechaun.

When he had vanished they sat to rest with the dead youth between them on the grass. Joe whispered that that was a fine Irishman and when, if ever, they got safe home he'd send his wife a present of half a dozen Celtic Corsets. They dared not smoke. On a clear night like this the glow of a cigarette would be seen a mile off. The low barking of the distant dog went on baying the moon. Freddy was bending over the nameless youth, looking at him by the light of the moon. The blank eyes stared at the sky. The hair was dark and glossy. The nose was broad with wide nostrils. The open mouth showed fine white teeth smiling at them.

'Do you remember Harry de Lacey?' he whispered back to Joe. 'He was killed in that ambush at Finglas in Nineteen-twenty. This lad is very like him.'

Joe leaned over to look.

'He's not unlike,' he whispered. 'I met Harry's brother Tony only the other day. He has a job in the Dublin Corporation.'

'We don't even know this lad's name,' Freddy whispered. 'We ought to search him. If we're caught or have to run for it we don't want to leave anything on him that would identify him.'

They went through the youth's pockets. He was carrying a heavy Webley forty-five and six spare rounds. Joe thought of Freddy's Peter the Painter and quickly pocketed the Webley and the bullets. Between them they collected a cheap pocketbook, some papers, a pale-blue handkerchief, a full packet of cigarettes, matches, a few coins, a door key, a hair comb, a fountain pen, a gardener's pruning knife, rosary beads and his wristlet watch. Since they dared not light a match to look at the papers or the pocketbook, and the moonlight was not bright enough to read them, they wrapped the lot in the blue handkerchief and buried it carefully under some loose stones directly at the foot of a stanchion wire from one of the telegraph poles along the railway embankment. Then Freddy took a line between a near, lone tree, a copse beyond it, and the red star, and they staggered off, carrying the corpse between them by the armpits and the legs.

It was heavy going, and they advanced very slowly, listening carefully, breathing heavily, resting many times – they were not young and a body is dead weight – and always laying the corpse between them on the dew-wet ground. During the first panting pause Joe tore off his stiff collar and black tie and whispered from where he lay on his back to Freddy, also strewn supine beside him on the grass:

'Where did you get that Peter the Painter?'

'I've had it by me for thirty-five years.'

'If we're challenged will you fire?'

'To the last bullet, damn them!'

'Good man!' Joe whispered.

Freddy was sitting up in angry surprise.

'Did you doubt it? You don't think I'm going to do five years in gaol in Belfast for this?'

Joe hesitated and then said apologetically: 'I wouldn't have asked you in the old days. But we're not as young as we were.'

Freddy lay back. He was silent for a while. Then, softly, he uttered his thoughts, not so much to the ear beside him as to the stars above him:

'I don't blame you. When a man starts to grow away from his youth he gets fond of the world. But you forget that when we grow older still we begin to get sick of it! Dying would be easy now, Joe!'

'Yes?'

'Did you ever read Faust?' Freddy whispered.

'I saw the opera once or twice, at the Gaiety.'

'The opera is no good! They always make Faust an old fellow with white whiskers. That's not true to life. An old bucko like that wouldn't give a damn about being young again. Not after philosophic wisdom came to him. I've read everything about Faust I could lay my hands on. I used to think one time that it was wrong for Goethe to make Faust ruin that girl. I used to think that if Faust was a magician and had all that magical power he should have been able to have any girl without ruining her. As I got older I realized how true it was. It's the whole point of the story. There's no magic strong enough to cheat the world. It was right to make the world, the flesh, and the devil cheat him in the end.'

'There's no such thing as magic!' Joe murmured smugly.

Freddy laughed softly and bitterly.

'I studied that subject very carefully the time I had a tricks and jokes shop in Manchester. I studied white magic and black magic. I studied telepathy, and hypnotism, and spiritualism. I even studied the Black Mass.' He chuckled quietly. 'One time during the war I drew circles on the floor of the shop with chalk, late at night. All the city was under the blackout, and nobody in the streets but the firewardens. Suddenly all the air-raid sirens began to wail. Then the only sound was the bombs and the ack-ack. I raised my voice and I called up the devil. The next second the whole block next to ours went up with a bang. Do *you* believe in the devil?'

'Oh, well!' Joe laughed, evading carefully, as if he did not wish to antagonize anybody. 'But not with horns and a tail, of course!'

'He's there,' Freddy whispered. 'The whole world's a juke box full of his little whiney tunes. You can buy them from him the way you could have bought my tricks and jokes from me. You don't know what I'm talking about! You're too bloody stupid.' He paused and said apologetically: 'I'm trying to explain to you why I tried to steal your bearer bonds tonight.'

'Forget it,' said Joe. 'For the time being,' he added hastily.

'I wasn't able to do it,' Freddy said, 'because you are a better gangster than me.'

He sat straight up and looked down at the youth's face staring at the stars. Joe sat up too. As if still thinking of the devil he whispered:

'I never did any harm to anyone.'

'Apart from existing!'

'I go to confession and Communion every first Friday of the month. I go every year of my life to Lough Derg. That's no joke of a pilgrimage. Three nights fasting and walking on the cold stones. I was often wet to the skin, kneeling in the rain. That ought to help me when my hour comes.'

'I'm a poor sort of Christian,' Freddy said. 'If I ever was one.'

'You ought to do Lough Derg,' Joe advised him fraternally. 'I'm going to do Lough Derg if I get safe out of this bloody kip-o'-the-reel.' He took out the Webley and broke it open. 'Begod,' he whispered, 'he's after firing every bloody round in this!'

He started to eject the spent rounds and reload the chambers.

'That's the ticket,' Freddy murmured, watching him. 'Always back for a win or a place. Put your trust in God but keep your powder dry. Leave us be going. It's near two o'clock. The sun will be up soon after four.'

All over the land there were long, thick swaths of moonlit mist, so that when each took his turn at carrying the dead youth on his back he looked like a giant walking through milk. In this way they moved a bit faster, but Freddy had to halt many times because Joe's knee began to pain him badly, so that he limped and groaned even when he was walking unburthened. His stiff shirt was crumpled like an old sail. His thin streaks of grey hair halved his big rosy turnip of a head. His ruddy face was wet with perspiration. His light shoes were soon soaked with the heavy dew and muddy from a swampy patch on which they chanced in the darkness. During one of their pauses to rest he whispered, looking at the anonymous face looking up beyond him at the studded sky:

'Was it all a waste?'

'He died young,' Freddy said enviously. 'Bliss was it in that dawn . . . People envy us, too. They say we had the dawn, and the whole day after it. Now every day is either a year long or it has only a couple of hours in it.'

And he suddenly thought, in fright, of all the hosts of young men who were killed in the wars of Europe, more of them than the hosts of visible and invisible stars overhead, and he felt that death is always a waste.

'I wasn't thinking of him,' Joe whispered. 'I was thinking of us and all we did in our time.'

'Yah!' Freddy mocked, mocking his own last thought. 'Time is an old man's thought. When you're young you don't need clocks or watches. You measure things by Now. For dogs and boys it's always Now. A Now that lasts forever. Do you remember the long summer days when you were young? Endless! That's because when you're young you're not killing yourself by thinking. You're just doing and living, without an atom of consciousness of the wonder of what you're squandering. "That is no country for old men. The young in one another's arms . . . " Even death is lovely when you're young. But it's a terrible and lonely thing to look at the face of death when you're young. It unfits you for the long humiliation of life. Aye! When a man stops living he starts watching the end of the sandglass dripping to tell him that his egg is cooked. Did you ever examine your conscience, Joe?'

Joe started.

'My conscience? I examine it every month when I go to confession.'

'That's where time and age get a hold of you. They remind you that sooner or later you'll have to set your sail and float out to sea. But you don't know what I'm talking about – you haven't got a conscience.'

'I know right form wrong,' Joe said warmly. 'More than you do! What were you trying to do tonight with my bearer bonds?'

Freddy ignored him. He said coldly:

'We are a childish people. As childish as a boy with his first catapult, or an old stone in a river-bed.'

Joe said, 'Aye!' indifferently and placatingly. He was thinking what a lunatic he had been to bring this lunatic back to Ireland to work for him.

'You know something, Joe? This country was made for young people. Nobody else but them can live in it, or die in it. Look at you and me! We can neither live in it nor die in it. This country is a cheat of a country for old men, that's why all the old men in this country are cheats – cheating the cheat! Look at us tonight. Why don't the bloody British military or the bloody black-coated bobbies or the flaming B Specials come and give us a chance now to fight them and die decent? But – no! They won't. Another bloody cheat! We're not even allowed to die! All we can do is go creeping around eating, and drinking, and blathering and cheating, and making money, and getting old and withered, and beating our breasts like you, you dying sow, up in Lough Derg.' His voice had been rising all the time. Now he suddenly lifted his head like a dog baying the moon and lifted his two fists to the night and screamed at the top of his voice: 'I want to fight! Come out, ye bastards, and fight!'

Joe grabbed him and clasped a hand over his mouth.

'For Christ's sake!' he growled. 'Are ye mad? Do you want them to catch *him?*'

Freddy bowed his head. Then he lifted it and shook it sadly. His calm was as sudden as his storm. He whispered:

'You see? You're caught, even through the dead. I tell you it's only the young who can die well, because they're proud and ignorant and lovely.' He leaned over and brushed away a tender-legged spider from the young man's pallid brow. 'We lost his hat,' he observed. 'Some ould lad will find it and wear it. Like a crown. Do I see the light of a car? Or a window?'

'If you do, you might be seeing the road we're looking for.'

'Come on!'

They struggled on again. Freddy had to do all the carrying now, with the corpse slung backwards loosely over one shoulder in a sort of fireman's lift. He was wet to his knees. He squelched at every step. The corpse's head rolled at every stumble, and its two hanging hands swayed. At the next pause, after Freddy had laid him softly down, Joe said, wiping his face and neck:

'Freddy, would you explain one thing to me? Why was I such a fool as to bring you back here from Manchester?'

Freddy looked ironically at him.

'Because I'm your lost youth. I'm your lost faith. You can never stop remembering the time when you were young and slim, like this poor devil here, when you felt immortal, when you felt grand, when you felt the lord of the world. And you can never understand why you stopped feeling like that. So you wanted to have me around to see how was I handling your problem.'

'Freddy, why was it that when we were young and trying to die for Ireland we all felt immortal?'

'Because time meant nothing to us. I've explained all that to you, you big ballox!'

'We were like angels,' Joe whispered, filled with awe.

'With flaming swords!'

'And now,' said Joe, bitterly, 'I'm selling women's corsets'.

They lay on the grass, the dead boy between them, all three staring up. A star streaked across the sky, exploded and vanished. At long last Joe said, so gently that Freddy barely heard him: 'You called me a gangster a minute ago. Well, I was one, and I'm not ashamed of it.'

Freddy, supine and silent, stared upward at the lofty white ball of the moon. After a while:

'That isn't correct. We *are* gangsters now. But we weren't always. We were killers. In every revolution there have to be killers. But there also have to be men who sanctify the killing. They make it holy, and beautiful, and splendid and glorious. We had a lot of men like that in Ireland once, and as long as we had them life was worth killing. They gave us a faith. Now we're killers still, but there's nobody to kill now so we've gone into business. We use the word in business – "A wonderful killing".'

His eyes focused away from the moon towards the pale blue flowers beside him that were bright even in death. He went on:

'Joe! I'm sick of hearing you talking about all you're trying to do now for Ireland. It won't work. Nothing on God's earth could make corsets holy, or beautiful, or splendid or glorious.'

After a while he became aware that Joe was crying. After another while Joe said:

'If any of the fellows in the Dolphin saw me now they'd think me mad.'

'They're usually mad enough to think you're sane,' Freddy said, and they scrambled up again.

The next time they rested they were sitting back to back by a mossy rock protruding from the stubble of a cut meadow. Joe said sourly:

'A bloody tricks and jokes shop! So that's what you were doing all those years in Manchester? Were you down to that?'

Freddy snorted.

'When I left Ireland in 'Twenty-two I hadn't as much as a penny piece. I was the dis-bloody-well-illusioned revolutionary. Even to think of Ireland made me puke what I never ate. I was so low that first year in Manchester that if I took one step up I'd be in the gutter. I had no skill. I was just a smarty. I met a widow whose husband used to run a tricks and jokes shop; you know the sort of thing – false noses, imitation ink blobs, stink bombs, card tricks, little Celluloid babies that squirt water when you squash 'em, nutcrackers in the shape of a woman's legs, drinking glasses that leak down your shirt front when you use them, cockroaches to drop in a fellow's beer. A cosy little place. With a cosy little room behind the shop. On winter nights, after we put up the shuts, with the soft pink web of Lancashire mist down over the city, we'd sit on each side of the little red eye of the cooking range. Liz would be reading the *Evening Chronicle* – she always preferred it to the *News* for some reason. She'd say, "Freddy wot abaht comin' to see Clark Guyble in *Hearts Aflyme?*" I wouldn't go. I'd be reading a book about Irish history, or thinking, "What is it like tonight in Dublin?" She never knew what I was thinking. She'd say, "Wot are you thinking abaht?" I'd say, "Some new trick". I used to deceive her nearly every night of the year. We lived together for eighteen years. She was killed in the blitz. I found her stark naked in the rubble, sliced in two.'

He half slewed around to Joe. Joe turned to him. He went on:

'While you, you big sow, were here in Ireland, getting fatter and fatter, making corsets with designs from the Lindisfarne Gospels on 'em. I wrote to you for help twice. Did you answer me? Did you, you cur?'

'I was working for Ireland,' Joe protested. 'Building up the country we fought for.'

Freddy took out his Peter the Painter and began to wipe it in his handkerchief. Joe felt in his tails for the Webley.

'That looks very like my old Peter the Painter,' he said.

'It is! I took it with me to Manchester after the Troubles and the Treaty. In memory of the old days when we were all boys together.'

Joe faced him, full of joy.

'Did you really? All those years?'

Freddy slipped off the safety catch of the Peter the Painter. His forefinger padded gently on the trigger. His left hand felt for the bulk of the bearer bonds in his breast pocket. Joe gripped the butt of the Webley. Smiling, they faced one another.

'Freddy!' Joe said quickly. 'After you left Ireland in 'Twenty-two it was the Civil War, when every man had to choose his side, for the Free State or for the Republic, for De Valera or for Mick Collins. I followed Mick.'

'I know it,' Freddy smiled. 'And it was as well for me that I went to England, for if I'd stayed at home I'd have been for Dev. And you'd have plugged me for it!' he added savagely.

Joe gripped his arm. His voice rose.

'I never killed no Irishman!'

'Maybe you didn't,' Freddy agreed, and swayed the gun a little. 'All you had to do was to give the orders. "Is that bastard de Lacey alive yet?" you'd say to one of your pals. And you wouldn't have to say it twice.'

He pointed the gun at Joe as if he merely wanted to emphasize the 'you'.

'Why do you mention that name?' Joe asked in a cold whisper.

'We mentioned it a while ago. But you only mentioned his brother Tony. How well you never mentioned his brother Marky? Marky de Lacey was my best friend, Joe,' he said, and stuck the gun into Joe's side. 'My best friend! And he was found up on the Three Rock Mountain with a hole in his skull. Don't you ever think of him, Joe, when you're up in Lough Derg praying for your rotten carcass? Don't you ever once think of Marky de Lacey?'

Joe's hand made a backward movement, but Freddy stuck his gun barrel deeper into his fat. Joe's voice rose higher still.

'I never laid a wet finger on Marky de Lacey!'

'Oho!' Freddy sighed. 'Wasn't it well for me I went to England!'

Joe's voice rose to a bat's squeak in the warmth of his protestation: 'Not you, Freddy! Not you! Not you!'

Freddy peered at the dark outline of his turnip head and saw the faint starlit shine on the sweat of his temples and he saw the two eyes glowing like a cat's at him. He withdrew the gun.

'Hell roast yeh,' he said exhaustedly. 'If you say so I have to believe you.'

'I do say so, Freddy. I swear it before God Almighty.'

'All right,' Freddy agreed wearily. 'If you swear it before God Almighty. I suppose I really am your last remaining bit of honesty.'

He leaned down and began to brush a stalk of unmown meadowsweet with the long tip of the automatic. He wondered if he should tell Joe why he had really kept it all those years. He decided not to tell, because he did not care any more. He suddenly felt the way a man must feel when he realizes that he has at last become impotent from old age. He clicked on the safety catch. Joe leaned closer to him:

'Freddy, it's what I often wanted to tell you. The real reason why I brought you home was that I wanted to clear up everything with everybody. They say I did things I never did, they put all the blame on me for things other men did, and because I was the boss I had to take the knock, but I never did them. I'd have told you all this years ago only I thought you were another that didn't trust me. It was only when I saw tonight how you kept my old Peter the Painter for old times' sake – and when we're here together helping the young fellows – handing on the torch as you might say – keeping the old flag flyin' – that I knew you'd believe your old pal in the heel of it all.'

Freddy looked at the smooth, young face on the grass. He clicked the safety catch off again. He looked at the great, ugly, sweating head leaning over and down to him, and he smelled the smell of fear. In disgust he clicked the safety catch on again. All his hate was gone.

'Oh, well,' he said, 'if you even only did a tenth of the things they say you did, Lough Derg won't save you. Nor all the fivers you ever gave to old beggarwomen for winter coal. Come on! It'll soon be a new day. Leave us bury him. Leave us bury everything we ever believed in and be shut of them forever.'

They got up once more. Lugging the dead boy between them, they struggled on.

The invisible sun was now glowing beyond the level land to their left. Soon the sky over there became a faint fringe of apricot merging into the mauve night retreating across the sky. They crossed another mist-swathed field and came to a low wall which, they found, edged a little road near the junction of three roads. When they climbed over the low wall and laid their burthen on the dew-wet verge, they both tumbled exhausted on the grass.

'We made it,' Joe said aloud.

'I'm sorry we did,' said Freddy, strewn on his back.

He woke a quarter of an hour later, sat up, and saw a building about five hundred yards up the road, its chimneys standing dark against the bright portion of the sky. In the raw morning light it looked cold and unfriendly. As he got up and walked towards it he suffered a gently pricking pang of realization that he was back in a world so long forgotten that, seen again, it was as unreal as a half-remembered dream. He was looking at a schoolhouse, stone-cut, slated, at least seventy-five years old. He went in through the little iron gate and looked up at the carved plaque on the wall. It was in Irish. They were safely in the South.

Turning around, he saw a cement-faced dwelling house facing the school, all its tawny holland blinds drawn on sleep, its shaggy lawn and draggled flower beds grey with dew. The teacher's house. He looked wider still, oppressed by the intense silence, by the suspension of life, by the half-light; the spread of empty sky and land entered him as an image of Death waiting to enfold his own slight figure alone at its morning edge. He might have been a bather naked by the edge of the sea about to commit himself, to swim out until he could swim no farther. As a youth he would have held out his arms joyously to it, exulting in the adventure. Now, it was not an ocean that invited him; it was just another day. Yet it was also the hour when a man can no longer evade whatever truth he has collected through his life. He felt for his gun again, and as he touched it he felt like a gambler rubbing his last ivory chip between his fingers.

He turned and ran back quickly along the little dusty road to Joe and he kicked him hard on the rump. Joe started awake and groaned with stiffness and pain. Freddy knelt beside him on one knee.

'Joe!' he besought him.

'I'll get rheumatics outa this. I know I will!' Joe said.

'Joe! Leave us go up North for God's sake and let off a couple of rounds at somebody. We don't want to go home now, do we? Joe! You bastard! It's our last chance to do something decent before we die.'

'Die?' said Joe, and let out a gasp of pain as the night scrawled its first revenge on his lumbar regions. 'Begod and I can tell you it would give me the greatest satisfaction to have a crack at those bastards.'

Meaning, Freddy understood miserably, that it would, in other, more suitable, entirely hypothetical and now quite historical times and circumstances, have given him the greatest satisfaction. Freddy clutched his arm.

'Joe!' he sobbed. 'For God's sake, Joe!'

'At night sometime?' Joe temporized. 'That'd be the ticket! Eh?'

'Now!' Freddy wailed. 'You know damn well that once you get back to your office and your desk and your appointments book, and all the photographs of yourself all over the mantelpiece, you'll never do another decent thing to your dying day.'

'It's a pipe dream,' Joe sighed, and felt his hip tenderly. 'Our dancing days are done.'

Freddy rose up slowly and looked down at him. He threw his Peter the Painter into a green-coated pool beside the road. He felt his breast pocket and pulled out the fat, folded envelope containing the bearer bonds. After a second's hesitation he threw the package into Joe's lap. Joe put the package in his breast pocket, took out the Webley, looked at it, glanced mistrustfully at Freddy, and put it back in his pocket. Freddy sniffed sarcastically. Then he jerked his head towards the schoolhouse.

'That's the schoolteacher's house up the road. We'll carry him up there and hide him there under the fuchsia bushes. Your Frankie can come back tonight and bury him. Then we'll walk on until we meet a car. I could do with a whiskey.'

Joe was still sitting on the grey-wet grass, his two hands splayed out on either side of him. As he looked up the road his voice took on a touch of its normal daytime hectoring tone:

'Are you quite sure we're in the South?'

'I'm afraid so,' Freddy said, as impersonally as any secretary to any manager.

Joe, spread-handed, spread-legged, looked up the road, and sank back even more heavily on his behind. He shook his fat head miserably and clutched his sore knee.

'I'm played out.'

'All right. Lie down and rest, you sod! I'll carry it.'

'No,' Joe snarled. 'We carried it together so far. We'll carry it to the end together.'

Once more they struggled up the road, bearing the youth between them, Freddy holding him under the knees, Joe holding him under the armpits; a small man in a grey alpaca coat and a big, burly man in tails, white shirt front, no collar. They laid the youth as far in as they could under the fuchsia hedge of the teacher's garden. Two trushes hopped on the shaggy lawn. The holland blinds did not stir. As Freddy crossed the arms on the chest, a red petal fell on one of the hands and drops of dew sprinkled one cheek. They arranged the branches to hide the body; Joe knelt and recited three Hail Marys, and Freddy, standing, heard himself murmuring the responses as if somebody else were saying them. He was much impressed by the intercession for all sinners at the hour of death. It made him realize that the figure hidden under the flowering shrub was dead. They threw a last glance at the holland blinds and quietly left the garden. Foot-weary, they walked away up the dusty road, heads lowered, a little at a loss at having no burthen to carry, so tired out that they did not advert to the fact that the sunrise was on their right.

Less than half an hour later they were back in the North, facing the guns of a Northern patrol.

Freddy is out now, and back on his job with Celtic Corsets Ltd. After all, as he says to Joe every week when he visits him in Crumlin Road Prison, Belfast, where else can he go? And who else, as Joe replies, would be fool enough to have him? These weekly visits are ostensibly to discuss business, but the part that Joe really loves – though he pretends modestly to wave it away – is when Freddy draws from his portfolio what they call the Manuscript. it is Joe's biography, which Freddy is composing very carefully and very, very slowly. As he reads the latest couple of pages, the prison walls fade, and Death flowers exquisitely again.

In the Bosom of the Country

Then, suddenly, after all their years of love, ten of them, five a-growing and five a-dying, death came. They were lying side by side in the big, bridal bed under its looped-up canopy of pink silk on whose slope the sunset gently laid the twig-pattern of the elms in her drive. She had tossed aside her fair hair so that it lay in a heavy tangle on her left shoulder, and was pensively watching him brushing up his greying, military moustaches with the knuckle of his forefinger. She started to scratch his shoulder with her nails, gently at first, then a little more wickedly until he turned to look at her. The sunset revealed the dark roots at the parting of her hair and caught a wrinkle at the corner of her eye. Recognizing a familiar mood he smiled nervously at her curl-at-the-corner smile, slightly mocking, shy, minxish, naughty. A prelude to another pretty quarrel? He soon stopped smiling; this time there was substance to her fret.

'Well, my dashing Major? Are you betraying me with one of your great galumphing horsey wenches from the Hunt? Account for yourself. Two months all but a week? And before that how long was it? Keene by name but not so keen by nature? Is this your idea of devotion? Are you getting tired of me?'

'Anna!' he protested.

He wanted to glance at his watch but his left arm still lay under her waist. He glanced at the ruddy sun behind the elm-boles. Half past four? With a sudden blare the telephone rang. 'Botheration!' she snapped, and reached out her long, bare arm for the receiver. He noticed the little purse of skin hanging from her elbow. Poor dear! He really did love her, but, dammit, they weren't either of them as young as they . . . She sat straight up, crying out, 'No! Oh, no!' He heard a few more squawkings from the receiver and her 'I'll be right over!' She hung up and leaped out of bed, scrambling all over the floor for her clothes.

'It's the hospital. Arty's dead. I've lost my poor husband.'

Something there had kept bothering him for days, something out of tune that alerted him, something that did not seem right. It was not the time and the place. Although, dammit, if, instead of the telephone ringing to say that Arty had gone, Arty had opened the door and peeped in he could not have chosen a more awkward moment to impose himself. Nor could it have been guilt – not after all these years. It could not have been anything they said – so little had been said in their haste to dress. It could only be something tiny, like an eye glancing over a bare shoulder or some single word or gesture that was not meant to mean anything but did. Not that he ever got down to thinking it out properly. 'Am I,' he wondered, 'shying off it for fear of finding out?'

A modest man, he knew his worth. She was not the only person who joked about his name. He did it himself. It was inevitable – F.L. Keene. In the army they used to call him old Festina Lente and kept him to the rank of Major. A good old dobbin. Sure and steady. But, at least, he tried to be honest, and he had flashes, dammit. Once, long ago, Anna had asked him how many women he had loved, and he truly replied, 'Only you.' 'You seem very adept?' she had said sceptically, at which he had asked her the same question about herself and she had answered, 'Only you! Oh, of course, I thought I loved Arty when I married him. But I was very young. I soon found out.' Considering him she had said, 'We get on well for a pair of ignoramuses.' He had thought about this for a while and then, to his own surprise, came up with, 'Love is like jungle warfare at night, it keys you up, you feel things you can't see.' (Like now, when that indefinable something passed in the air between them.)

For her part, when he said that about love and the jungle, she had laughed merrily, sensitive enough to respond to his doleful humour, not intelligent enough to define it. It was his great attraction of which he was quite unaware, always to expect the worst – it made him infinitely tender and pitiful towards everybody. 'I am a dull dog,' he used to say to her sometimes and it used to make her throw her arms around him. Her big, stupid, dull, loyal dog would look at her in astonishment and love. She was his opposite, endlessly hoping for the best, and better. Had she been smarter she would have realized that pessimists are usually kind. The gay, bubbling over, have no time for the pitiful. Love lives in sealed bottles of regret.

He went to the funeral, hoping to have a chat with Mabel Tallant, the only person, he hoped, who knew all about the pair of them. There were so many people there that he decided to keep discreetly to the rear of the crowd. He was surprised at the size of the turn-out but supposed that a man cannot be a District Justice without making a pack of friends. Anyway, the Irish have a great gift for death, wakes and funerals. They are really at their best in misfortune. Used to it, I suppose? And sport. Quid pro quo, what? The thing that surprised him most, as he stood watching the mourners file in and out of the church was that while he knew many of them by sight, and perhaps a dozen by name – the vet, the Guards' Inspector, a couple of doctors, shopkeepers from the town, two or three fellows he had hunted with, and those well enough to nod to – he did not know one of them intimately, apart from Mabel Tallant. With her he just managed to get a word: she said she was taking Anna home with her for a couple of days after the relatives left. 'Give her my love,' he whispered hastily. Mabel had smiled sadly and whispered back, 'Everybody can sleep in peace now.'

He drove away, unaccosted by anybody, wondering what the devil she meant, wondering also why the devil it was that ever since he came to live in Ireland he was always wondering what somebody meant about some damn thing or another. He decided yet once more that they had to talk roundabout because they never had anything to say that was worth saying directly. The yews of his drive were dripping as he drove up to his empty house: nothing would do old Mrs Mac but to go to the funeral. The fire was out. Why had he ever come here? But he had been over all that, too. If his uncle had not left him this place he might never have come back from Kenya; and he might have left after the first year if he had not met Anna Mohan. But now? With Africa gone to hell? Package-safaris all over the place. You might as well think of living in Piccadilly Circus.

The week after the funeral, as he was hacking home from the hunt, Mabel rode up beside him. She was red as a turnip from the wind, mud-spattered to her stock, a grey hair drooping from under her hat, and on her right jaw a streak of dried blood.

'Hello, Mabel? Fall? No bones broken, I hope? You know, you are looking younger every day. But, then, we all know you are a marvel!'

'My dear Frank,' she laughed in her jolly, mannish way; she always laughed at everything, 'if you're referring to my great age I assure you I'm not giving up for a long time yet. Even if I am fifty I'm not decrepit. And I don't think you can give me many years, can you? I wasn't tossed, I'm more wet than muddy. I stayed behind with the Master to put back a few poles that we knocked at the Stameen. I've got half the stream in my boots this minute.'

They ambled along for a quarter of a mile with no more than a few tired words about the hunt. They had had three good runs. The Master was digging out the last fox. You have to give the farmers some satisfaction. After another silence he said, 'How is Anna?'

'You ask me?'

'I suppose I should call on her soon. I don't want to be indiscreet, you know,'

'You could be a bit too discreet.'

'I was always discreet about Anna. I owed it to her. Nobody but you ever knew about Anna and me.'

'Knew? Knows? Maybe not, but you've lived long enough in these parts to know that there's damn little goes on here that everybody doesn't suspect.' She hooted gaily, 'Sometimes a lot more than they've any reason to suspect. It fills their lives, I suppose.'

'Anna and I used always say that they might suspect but they couldn't be sure, and that was what really counted.'

'Past history?'

She laughed. He frowned. Not because her laugh suggested some unspoken blame of him but that it echoed certain spoken, and unspoken prophecies about Anna: her unbridled tongue, as of a woman who had been spoiled as a too-pretty girl, her temper, her tears, her enthusiasms, her wanting always to be smarter than she was, her melancholy days that went on and on, her warm days that were too warm to last, like a hot day in summer, her sudden bursts of generosity towards some women and her sudden bursts of jealousy towards other women – always young, pretty women. One by one Mabel had shaken her head over Anna's 'ways', and he had liked her all the more for it because in spite of everything she seemed to love her. Or was it that she, too, felt sorry for her?

It was growing dusk when they got to Bardy Hill. Fumes of fog were lying over the reedy plain. The tired horses slowed to a walk. She tapped his thigh with her crop.

'Frank! You're fooling yourself. I heard a bit of gossip at the meet this morning.'

'What did you hear?'

'Not much. Somebody said, "I wonder is Major Keene going to marry her now."'

He suddenly realized what that 'something' had been. She had said, 'Arty's dead, I've lost my poor husband.' Lost? Or was that the word they said to her on the phone? Dammit, she had lost him ten years ago.

'Mabel! If Arty had died ten years ago, even five, even three, I'd have married her like a shot. We dreamed of it. We lived on the dream of it. Not on the hope, dammit, no! We never said "die". We said, "if anything happened to him". Always talking about how happy we could be together. Just the two of us. Morning, noon and night. Lovers' talk! But, ye know, hope deferred maketh the heart sick. Anna being a Catholic there was no hope of a divorce. And, anyway, she was fond of him. In the end I gave up hope. I'll tell ye something else, Mabel. I was with her the day Arty died. I hadn't been with her for two months before that. And before that I dunno when. That day, I knew it was all over.'

He frowned again when Mabel said nothing. Venus shone, alone, in a green sky above a low spear of clouds. The horses, smelling home, began to trot downhill. They pulled up at Ballymeen Cross – they had each about half a mile to go.

'Do you think she really expects me to marry her?' he asked unhappily.

'I can only give you the woman's point of view. I'd think it damn cheap of you if you didn't make an honest woman of her. It will be pretty lonely for her in·that old house at Culadrum. To put it at its lowest a husband is a handy thing to have about a house.' She laughed sourly. 'I should know.'

She jerked the head of her horse, and cantered away. He did the same. Once, and he regretted it, he took out his anger on the animal with his crop. Twice he uttered the word 'Damnation!' A pool of water gleamed coldly on his drive. A blank window held the last of the day. Culadrum would not be much of a home for Anna from now on. He should know.

He ate little, drank too much wine, slept badly, and immediately after breakfast he drove over to Culadrum. He found her in her drawing-room reading *The Irish Times* before the fire, slim-looking in proper black, very becoming, with a tiny white ruff under her chin, and hanging beneath it one of those little pendants called a Lavallière, a small, coloured miniature of Arty as a young man. With her tightbusted dress, and her fair hair done in a coil on the top of her head

she had a Victorian look, like a queen in mourning. His heart went out
to her. He kissed her and said gallantly, 'Now, my darling, before the
whole world you can be all mine!' To his delight she blushed, a thing
he had not seen her do for years. They sat in armchairs on either side
of the fire.

'Frank! We have waited so long you won't mind waiting another
while, will you?'

'As long as you like, Anna.'

'There is a special reason why we must wait a bit. It has to do with
local opinion. I want to be married in a Catholic church.'

So, she *had* been thinking about it!

'By all means. I'm not bigoted. In for a penny in for a pound.'

'I want everything to be done regularly. I want to clear up
everything. We will live here. In this house our life is before us. All my
friends and all Arty's old friends are Catholics. They move in their own
circle, just as people do everywhere. I'm not one of the hunting set, as
they aren't either, except for one or two maybe. So it is frightfully
important that they should all become your friends too. Oh, my
darling, it would make all the difference in the world if you were a
Catholic!'

He sat back slowly.

'Well, unfortunately, I'm not.'

'Frank! For me? It would make all the difference for me if you became
a Catholic. Oh, if you could only become a Catholic, Frank! Won't you?
We'd be all together then. And I'd be so happy!'

'But, dammit, Anna, you're not seriously suggesting that they'd look
down on you in some way if you married a Protestant?'

'A mixed marriage? They won't have it in this diocese. Anyway we
never did it in our family. Even where they do allow it it's a hole and
corner affair. It's not the same thing at all. Documents. Guarantees.
Back-door stuff. Ugh!'

'It's beyond me.'

She laughed her little curl-at-the-corners Anna-laugh.

'You've lived in Ireland, Frank, for ten years, and I honestly don't
believe you still understand the Irish.'

'Is there anything to understand?'

'Besides, there is something else we have to face.'

'Something else? What else, for God's sake?'

'We always said they didn't know. But in our hearts we always knew that they did know. They always do know. Bother them! Oh, they mightn't have known *exactly*, but they must have known that there was *something* between us. Of course, there is one way out of it. If you don't marry me now they will say they were wrong.'

'But I don't want a way out of it. I want you!'

'But, Frank, if we do marry, you see, then they will know for certain that they were right all along. They'd never feel happy about us. They'd always be whispering about our past. We'd see it in their eyes. They might never visit us at all! And you couldn't blame them, could you? But if you became a Catholic, Frank, they'd be so happy about it that they'd forget and forgive everything. Besides, it was always the one thing – I mean if there ever was any teeny, little thing at all – that stood between us now and again. Now when we can be married, if we do marry, at last, at long last – Oh, my darling! – I want us to be one in everything before the world!'

'It never seemed to bother you before?'

'Of course it bothered me. I often cried about it when you left me.'

'Why did you never speak to me about it?'

'I was afraid of losing you,' she said sombrely.

He stood up, went to the window and looked glumly out through the frosty leaf-tracery on the glass. Accustomed to his ways she kept looking at his back under her eyebrows, waiting on his digestion. Presently he did a smart rightabout turn.

'This,' he declared, 'is a bomb-shell. Dammit, it's an absolute bomb-shell. When we couldn't marry you were so afraid to lose me that you never uttered a word about religion, and now, when we can marry, you give me the choice of being a cad if I don't and a Catholic if I do.'

'Darling, if you can't I shan't blame you. And if you can't I am not going to lose you. No matter what it costs me. Unless you want to ditch me, of course?'

'That I shall never do.'

She joined him at the window, and with one coaxing, pussy-cat finger she stroked his moustaches right and left, and kissed his lips.

'Think about it, darling.'

He stared at her, snatched his cap and left abruptly. After driving in circles for an hour he found himself outside Mabel Tallant's house at Bunahown. She was in the stables watching her groom combing her grey hunter. When he told her she laughed so loudly that he saw her gold-tipped molars.

'You're stuck, my boy!'

'But she might just as well ask me to become a Muslim or a Parsee! It isn't fair!'

She laughed gleefully again, then became solemn.

'Frank?'

'Well?'

'Suppose this happened ten years ago when you first fell in love with Anna? Suppose she wasn't married then? Suppose she asked you then to do this for her, would you have done it? Would you have said it wasn't fair?'

He glared at her, shuffled a bit, strode away.

After a week of torture, sitting for hours alone over his fire, or stalking alone about the leafless roads, he drove into town, stiffened himself with a glass of whiskey at The Royal Hotel and asked the waitress where the Catholic presbytery was. She directed him to Pearse Square with an enthusiasm that he found nauseating. The presbytery looked like a home for orphans, tall, Victorian, redbrick, with imitation stone quoins in grey plaster, pointed in black. Every window looked up at the wet February sky over brass-tipped half-screens. He hauled stoutly at the brass bell-handle and stood to attention glaring at the door. He asked the scrubby boy who opened it for the Parish Priest and was shown into a chilly front room. Drawing? Waiting? Committee? Dining? He found himself faced by a lifesize statue of Christ pointedly exhibiting His rosy heart. He turned his back to it. He did not sit down. This was a thing a man met on his two feet.

The door opened, very slowly. The priest who entered was an old man of at least sixty-five or more. He wore a monsignor's russet vest beneath a celluloid Roman collar that brushed the cincture of white hair about his roped neck. His voice was as mild as milk, his manner as courteous as a glass of port. When he told his visitor that he had been a chaplain with the Royal Inniskillings towards the end of the 1914 war, they were both only too happy to sit, smoke and chat about Château Thierry, the Sambre, the Somme, places known to the younger warrior of the two with the reverence proper to ancient history. Then they retired upstairs to the monsignor's sitting-room, the fireside and a whiskey bottle. An old Alsatian bitch lay strewn on the hearthrug between them.

By the time they got down to business the major felt as relaxed in his armchair, prickly with horsehair, as if they had just met in a club. All went well until he uttered the name, Mrs Anna Mohan. The monsignor's eyelids fell.

'Mrs Mohan? Ah, yes! Lives over at Culadrum House. I knew her father and mother very well. I wouldn't say they were exactly zealous Catholics. But they were good people. Hm! Well, well! Anna Carty, that was. A handsome girl when she was a child. I remember now, they sent her to some convent school in Kent. And after that to some place in Switzerland – Lausanne, I believe – to a finishing school. Rather a mistake that. Risky.'

'Risky?'

The word could have connotations.

'Oh, I am not criticizing them. It is simply that I always feel that if a girl is going to live in Ireland it's wiser to bring her up here. She must have been very young when she married Mohan. Why, we buried him only two, three weeks ago. Hm! I see!'

He looked at the major without expression, but it was plain enough that he did see.

'Well, Major? Tell me this. Would I be wrong in surmising that you are doing this chiefly, if not wholly, to please Mrs Mohan?'

'A fair question, padre. Yes, you've got it. That's about the run of it.'

'I mean, you are not being drawn to the Catholic Church entirely for its own sake, are you?'

'I'll be perfectly straight with you, padre, I don't know anything at all about the Catholic Church. I'll go further. I'm not going to become a Catholic, or anything like it, until I know a lot more about the whole thing.'

'Very wise. In other words, you are not asking me to give you a course of instruction. You are just asking me for some preliminary information.'

'Yes! Yes, that's about the run of it.'

'Is there, then, something that particularly interests you, or shall I say that bothers you, about our Church?'

'Why, dammit, everything about the Catholic Church bothers me. Not that I ever thought about it. But I suppose if you ask me a straight question I might say, well, for example, I might say what's all this about the infallibility of the Pope? It's a tall order, ye know, if somebody comes out every day of the week about something and says "That's it! You've got to take it because I'm infallible!" I mean, supposing the Pope came out tomorrow and said Napoleon was a woman, or that a line isn't the shortest distance between two points, or that the Law of Gravitation is all nonsense, you can't deny it, padre, that that'd be a hell of a tall order. You don't mind my being frank about this, I hope?'

The monsignor patted down the glowing tobacco in his pipe with an asbestos finger and said mildly that no, he did not mind at all.

'Not, of course, that what you suggest bears any relation to reality. But I don't mind. I mean, the examples you have chosen are not the very best in the world.' Here he waved his mottled hand. 'Since Mr Einstein, as the old song says, fings ain't wot they used ter be.' He wandered off a bit about Tycho Brahe and the mathematics of planetary attraction until he saw a glaze gathering over his visitor's eyes. 'In fact, His Holiness hardly ever speaks infallibly. The doctrine of Infallibility was pronounced in 1870.' He halted, thinking of such names as Newman and Lord Acton, and went on hastily. 'Since then I don't think the Pope has spoken *ex cathedra* more than . . . Is it twice, or three times? And if I may say so, quite enough, too! Though some people might think even that much was excessive. Things change.' He fell into a private thought. 'Change and expand.'

'Only twice or three times? Is this a fact? Dammit, I never knew this! But,' he pounced, 'when he does we have to believe him, eh?'

'Major Keene, I think all this would seem much simpler to us if we were to think of the whole matter as one of obedience rather than of conviction. You are a soldier. You know about obedience. During the war if your colonel told you to advance on Hill 22 with three men and that old Alsatian there and take Objective 46, which you knew quite well was held by a thousand men, what would you do about it?'

'I'd obey at once.'

'Yes. You would obey. Somebody's got to give the orders.'

Keene stared at him out of his two great, blue eyes like a horse facing a jump.

'By George, you're a hundred per cent right, padre! Somebody's got to be boss. Not like all this damned, modern Whiggery we've got now. When everybody wants to be the boss. All those Trade Unions . . . But, mind you, you've touched on another question there. Only last Sunday my housekeeper, Mrs MacCarthy, told me that, when she was at Mass, right here in town, one of your curates . . . You won't mind my saying this?'

'Fire away, Major. Fire away.'

'She told me . . . Mind you, she's a bit of an old exaggerator, but I wouldn't say she's a liar, just Irish ye know, she told me that one of your curates said from the pulpit that any girl going around this town in tight jeans was walking straight on the road to hell. Now, that's a bit of a tall order, padre! What do you say to that?'

The monsignor sighed wheezily.

'Yes. Well. We do seem to have wandered a bit from papal infallibility. But, since you raise the question . . . You, again as an old soldier, must know what happens to orders by the time they pass down to the lower ranks. It's a case of the sergeants' mess, my dear Major. The sergeants' mess in every sense of the word, and you know what I'm talking about.'

'By George! Don't I? Ye know, padre, it's a downright pleasure to talk to a man like you who knows the ways of the big world. You make me feel quite homesick for it.'

'So? Obedience! And order. And authority. You revere your Queen. The proud symbol of the power of your Empire. We Catholics revere the Pope. The proud symbol of our Empire. The Roman Empire. You and I, each in his own way, respect authority, desire order and uphold power.'

'Splendid! I can see that. In fact I begin to see a lot of daylight. Ye know, if we had a couple of chats I shouldn't be at all surprised if we found we had a good deal of ground in common. Mind you, I'm not going to be rushed into this. I'm sure that when I start thinking about it I'll come up with a lot of things that bother me. Mixed marriages, for instance. There's another tall order. And, let me see, hasn't there been some difficulty about the Virgin? And then, of course, there's contraception – ran into that a lot in India. I need hardly say my interest in the matter is purely academic.'

'So is mine.'

He rose.

'Why don't you come to dinner next week, Major, when as you say you will have thought some more about it, and we can combine business, if I may so call it, with pleasure. I've got quite a sound port.'

'Aha! I know something about port.'

The monsignor warmed.

'Do you now? Tell me, did you ever take port for breakfast?'

The major guffawed.

'Oh dammit no! No! Not for breakfast, padre!'

The monsignor chuckled.

'Then I am afraid you don't know anything at all about port. Wait until you taste mine. But I'm afraid if you are a connoisseur in wine you had better bring your own. Ah! The great wines of France. 1917. Spoiled my palate. I can't afford vintage wine any longer.'

'I've got a dozen of Forty-nine Beaunes-Villages at home. I'll bring a couple of bottles with me. By God, this is a splendid idea! I beg your pardon, monsignor, here I am cursing like a trooper in the presence of your reverence.'

'Pshaw! I'm inured to it. I remember one morning outside Ypres. Just before we went into battle. Two dragoons fighting, one of them an Orangeman and the other a Catholic, shouting like troopers. They had to be heard – the barrage going right over our heads, hell open to Christians, the captain staring at his wristwatch waiting for the second to go over the top. Do you remember – Ah, no, you're too young! – those old wristwatches with little metal grilles over them? I never heard such language in all my life as that Orangeman was giving out of him. In the end the other fellow, he was a Corkman, shoved his bayonet up within an inch of the other fellow's throat and he shouts, "Look, Sammy! I'm in the state of grace now before the battle, but with the help of God I won't be so handicapped before the day is out, and I tell you if I meet you then I'll shove this blank blank..."'

He clasped Keene by the arm for support as he bent over and laughed at the memory of it. Then he straightened and sighed.

'Poor chaps, neither of 'em came back. And I'm sure the good Lord was equally kind to the pair of them. Next Thursday, Major. At nineteen hours. Goodness me, I haven't used that phrase for it must be forty years. We'll be talking of old times together.'

Keene clasped his hand. He left the presbytery, glancing in respectfully at the impassive eyes of the Sacred Heart.

Those Thursday dinners became such a solemn, as well as delightful opening of hearts that within two months the monsignor was straining hard to hold his neophyte from declaring himself a Catholic on the spot. Indeed, one silent April night, during their third month, as he was showing his guest out into the moist emptiness of Pearse Square he said,

'I shall bless the day, Frank, when you become, if you do become, a Catholic, but I confess I shall have one small regret. The end of our little dinners.'

'Nonsense! Why should they end?'

'They will end.'

By the end of April the major was coming up aginst the hard stuff: the one sector of the battlefield to whose ground he returned obstinately, uncomfortably, scarred a little, sometimes approaching it as quietly as if he were on a lone night-raid. They might be talking about books – say, *Adam Bede* or *The Three Musketeers* and he might slip in:

'Padre! Can one never, simply never say that there are times when love conquers all? I mean, is that kind of love always, simply always, a sin?'

'I'm afraid, Frank, it is. Always a sin. I'm afraid there just isn't any way around that one. Nor, I fear, could any clergyman of any persuasion say anything else.' He allowed himself a slim smile. 'You remind me of old Professor Mahaffy of Trinity College in Dublin. He was a great wag, you know. One time he confided, or pretended to confide in a fashionable Dublin Jesuit, a close friend of his, that he felt drawn to the Catholic Church. Very naturally his Jesuit friend was only too eager to pluck the plum. Another glass? "Not a drop is sold till it's seven years old." Well, it appeared that there was just one small obstacle. Just one tiny, little problem. "If you can only allow me," Mahaffy said, and I am sure he said it with a poker-face, "to believe that Christ was not God I will join your Church tomorrow morning." His Jesuit friend is said to have paused for a long time. And at last he said, very regretfully, as I say to you now about adultery, "I'm afraid there isn't any way around that one." There are some things nobody can get around. Not even the Pope. Let alone me.'

Finally, one night, Frank said, plump out:

'Padre! When, and if, you consider me worthy to be received into the Church shall I have to go to Confession?'

'We will, naturally, have to clear up your past. Not that I think it will bother you very much. There are so few sins, and they repeat themselves endlessly. Even boringly. It is only the circumstances that change.'

'I was coming to exactly that. There is a bit of my past that I would like to clear up right away. I want to tell you that I have been in love with Anna Mohan for some ten years. I mean, we have been lovers in the full sense of the word. And I have never felt guilty about it. My fault, no doubt, but there it is. After all, she was only married to him in theory as you might say. He's gone now and words cannot harm him, everybody knows that he was a roaring alcoholic. Don't those circumstances you speak of alter such cases as mine?'

'He was addicted,' the monsignor agreed sadly. 'As for your case, that he was addicted is sad but it is not relevant to the law. Hard cases make bad laws. Nor is it relevant that you did not feel a sense of guilt. A stern moralist might speak to you of an atrophied conscience. I think it is enough for me to remind you that many men, known to history, men like Hitler or Stalin, committed the greatest crimes without feeling any sense of guilt. I can only repeat to you that adultery is a very grave sin. It is even two sins, for it also sins against the law that thou shalt not steal. She was his wife. I do not wish to overstress the point, but it does arise. Furthermore, chastity is not only of the body. In what is commonly called sex the body and the soul are one. You simply have to accept what I say.'

'She did lose something when he died. I have realized that.'

'I think,' the monsignor added, gravely, 'that this is something that it is your duty to clarify.' He paused and then added, pointedly, 'All round.'

'I accept what you say,' his neophyte sighed. 'It is most troubling.'

The monsignor quietly refilled his glass, wondering a little whether his pupil had some extra reason to be troubled.

He had. By now he was also receiving intermittent instruction from Anna, and on those occasions the tender feelings that she aroused in him were at times more than he could control. On one such occasion, looking up at her pink canopy, he said to her, 'Poor Anna! I can see now why you used sometimes to cry. It was a sin.' She smiled her curl-smile and whispered, 'But, sure, it no longer is.'

'Anna! We must not deceive ourselves. We're not married yet, ye know.'

'We are married in the sight of God,' she said and scratched him a little. 'The Church will bless us.'

'The Church must bless us first.'

'Ah, but sure,' she wheedled, 'it's so much nicer before.'

'It will be much, much nicer when you will lawfully be mine before man and God.'

'Darling!' she cried, and scratched wickedly. 'Don't be a bore! Are you a lawyer or a lover?'

'But the monsignor says...'

At this she flew into a rage.

'For Heaven's sake, who are you marrying? Me or the monsignor?'

He forbore to reply. He was troubled, and not for the first time, by the thought, 'Is she in more need of instruction than me?' This, however, was something that, in delicacy, he could not broach to her, or, in loyalty, to the monsignor – unless he might, perhaps, act as a go-between?

'Monsignor! I have one last question. To revert once more to my old problem, I do see, now, that I have indeed been guilty of a grave sin. I no longer contest it. It is undeniable. I cannot understand how I ever doubted it. But, supposing I had lain not with a married woman but with an unmarried woman, may I ask, is it in that case permissible for either party to feel just a little bit less guilty?'

'In such a hypothetical case,' his friend said dryly, 'either party would merely have been breaking one commandment at a time.'

'How stupid of me! How is it that everything becomes so simple when you explain it?'

The occasion to relay the consequences of his question was not long in coming. Under the canopy, he gently pointed out to Anna that they would both have to confess all this sooner or later, as one sin on her part, of two on his. She declared at once, and with passion, that she had no intention of doing anything of the sort.

'Do you think,' she cried, drawing blood from him this time, 'that I am going to spoil all our years and years of love by saying now that they were beastly and horrible?' Then seeing in his terrified horse-eyes how deeply she had shocked him, she added, easily, 'One could of course go through the *formality*.'

'Of course!' he agreed, profoundly relieved to find that she really was, after all a Catholic. She went on:

'Why not? One will say that one has transgressed. That's it. Transgressed. To pass over. To step beyond. Beyond the red line. A little.'

'Indeed,' he agreed happily, 'so we will! I'm so relieved! I'm so glad!'

'But, sure, Frank we'll know in our hearts, of course, that we didn't really do anything very bad at all'

'But, my dear Anna, there is the law! *Thou shalt not commit adultery.*'

At this she sat up, seized him by the hair and shook him like a dog.

'Are you calling me an adulteress?'

He sat up, waved his arms despairingly and wailed at her.

'My darling! I sit in judgement on nobody. But,' he said miserably. 'I *have* been an adulterer.'

She stroked his moustaches and kissed him tenderly.

'Not really, darling. That's just an old afterthought you are having now. You were as innocent as a child at the time.'

He sank back and rolled his tousled head sadly on the pillow.

'I'm such a simple sort of chap, Anna, and it's all such a simple thing, and I understand it so simply, and I do wish that you didn't make it all so damned complicated.'

She laughed and laughed.

'I make it complicated? It is I who am simple about it – your new friends who are tying everything up in knots with their laws, and rules, and regulations, and definitions, and sub-definitions that nobody can make head or tail of. I was brought up on all that stuff. I know it. You don't. They are at it all the time. So many ounces you may eat during Lent in France, so many in Spain. You can't eat meat on Fridays but it's no harm to eat frogs, and snakes and snails. I suppose you could even eat tripe! How much interest may one businessman draw on his deal. How much may another draw on another. Do you think anybody can really measure things like that? A baby who dies without being baptized must go to some place called Limbo that nobody ever knew what it is or in what corner of creation to put it. All that stuff has nothing to do with religion. How could it? Do you know that Saint Augustine said that all unbaptized children are condemned to suffer in eternal fire? Is *that* religion?'

'Are you sure Saint Augustine said this?'

'I was educated in Lausanne,' she said proudly. 'It's the home of Saint Augustine. All those stinking Calvinists.' She began to sob into the pillow. 'I wish I'd never asked you to become a Catholic. I wouldn't have if I knew you were going to take it as seriously as all this.'

'Don't cry, my daffodil! In a few months it will all be over and we will never need to talk of these terrible things again.'

She flew at once into a state of total happiness; she clapped her hands gaily.

'Oh, what fun it will be! In a couple of months you will be my loving husband. We'll be welcomed by everybody with open arms, we'll be known as the greatest lovers in all Ireland, the women will envy me and the men will smile at you and clap you on the back. I can't wait for it.'

'God speed the day when I shall at last be received.'

'And I shall be married!'

For six days and six nights he kept away from the monsignor, thinking of all those millions of babies burning in eternal fire, until his whole soul felt beaten all over by devils armed with sticks, and shovels, and red-hot tongs. On the seventh night he invited the monsignor to dinner. Like a good host he kept from his troubles until the port passed. Then, unsteadily, he said, 'Monsignor, I have another question, a small, tiny little problem. Tell me, where is Limbo?'

The old man paused in the act of raising his glass to his lips and looked at him apprehensively. He had dealt with Transubstantiation, Miracles, the Resurrection, Indulgences, Galileo, the Virgin Birth, the Immaculate Conception, Grace, Predestination, the Will, Mixed Marriages, even Adultery. These great mysteries and problems had presented no lasting difficulty either to him or to his dear friend. But Limbo? He knew from long experience how easily the small things, rather than the big ones, can shatter a man's faith.

'Why did you ask me that question?' he said sadly.

'It just occurred to me,' the major said loyally and curled a little at his lack of frankness to his friend.

'I see!'

'Is it true, monsignor, as I have read, that Saint Augustine said that all babies who have not been baptized must burn in eternal fire?'

With a whole movement of his arm the monsignor pushed his glass slowly to one side. His night was in ruins.

'I believe so,' he said, and thrust gallantly on. 'Still, there are other and more benignant views. It all arose, I presume, out of the problem of where to place those unbaptized souls who died before Christ, and those others who died after Him without ever hearing of Him. I believe it was the Council of Florence that decreed it.' He faltered. 'It was a rather confused Council. So confused that I gather that its Acts have perished. It laid down, it was in the fifteenth century, that nobody who is unbaptized may enter heaven. Since then many thinkers have, in their mercy, felt a repugnance to the idea. Many theologians have sought out ways of accepting the doctrine while, as you might say, circumventing, or anyway softening, its melancholy implications. Major! Do you really want me to go into this matter of Limbo? It is not a primal question.'

'It bothers me, monsignor.'

'I see. Well. I do know that one Italian theologian, whose name escapes me at the moment, felt that God might instruct the angels to confer baptism on those children – who might otherwise perish without it. Another theologian felt that the sincere wish of the parent that the child might have been baptized could be a fair equivalent. Saint Thomas felt, humanely, that those children suffer no pain of the body, although they must, indeed, always grieve that they can never see God. Just as a bird, or a mouse, might grieve that it can never be a man, or speak to an emperor or king.'

'How sad!'

'Of course, Major,' the monsignor whispered, 'we have to recognize that we have no purely human right to Heaven. Heaven is a gift God could, without injustice, deny it to us. I suggest it was originally a rabbinical idea.'

The priest looked into the glowing ashes of the fire. The major looked out at the darkness of the night. Through the open window the invisible fields sent in the sweetness of the May-blossom. After a long while the monsignor said, 'There are many mysteries in life that we have to accept in humility without understanding them. Indeed, it is because we do not understand the mystery that we do accept it – and live with it.'

As he drove away the major watched the beams of his car until they touched the last of his yews, and stood there until the smell of his petrol faded in the pure air. He walked up and down his avenue many times. Afterwards he sat before his dying fire until sleep came to him, where he slouched by its ashes.

It was quite early, a bird-singing May morning, gleaming after a light shower of rain, when he faced her fresh and handsome, breakfasting beside her cheerful morning fire. He said firmly, 'Anna, I can never become a Catholic.'

Her cup clattered into its saucer.

'But, Frank, you must! Do you expect me to marry you like a

Protestant in a registry office? Or to live with you for the rest of my life with you in what you now think of as a cesspool of sin?'

'I am proposing nothing. I can think of nothing. It is just that I am too old, or too stupid, to be able to follow you both.'

'You just want to be shut of me.' She raised her tear-filled eyes. 'Or is it that it is I who am too old and too stupid? Why can't you be as I am? After all I am a Catholic!'

'I have sometimes wondered, Anna, what you are.'

Her fury burst about him like shrapnel. She dashed down *The Irish Times*.

'How dare you? Of course I am a Catholic. What's wrong with you is that you want everything to be perfect. As clean, and bare and tidy as a barrack square. That's it! All you are is a bloody English major who wants everybody's buttons to be polished and everybody's cap to be as straight as a plate.'

'But it wasn't I who raised the question of Limbo!'

'To hell with Limbo! If there is a hell! Or a Limbo! What's wrong with you is you're too conceited. You want to cross every I and dot every T. Why do you want to understand everything? Why can't you just accept things the way I do?'

'Do you accept Limbo?'

'I never think about Limbo. I never think about stupid things like that. I think only of God, and the stars, and of Heaven, and of love, and of you.'

'You put me to a great test, Anna. As the monsignor says I must also think of the cross and the nails. Just as he says that in love the soul and the body are one.'

'You're a liar! All this is just a cute device to get out of marrying me. I see through you. I see through your cheap trickery. I see through your dirty Saxon guile. If you were the last man on earth this minute, Frank Keene, I wouldn't marry you now. Please don't come near me ever again!'

She swept out and crashed the door. He retrieved *The Irish Times* from the fire, beat out its flames and went away.

He had no one left to talk to. He had pestered the monsignor beyond endurance. He had never attended the Church of Ireland. Anyway he doubted if they knew very much about Limbo or the Council of Naples. Mabel Tallant would only laugh at him. He had devoted so many years of his life to Anna that he had made no friends. And now she neither loved him nor respected him, and he did not . . . He crushed down the bleak admission.

After three weeks of the blackest misery, he dashed off a letter:

Monseigneur, Mon General, Mon ami,

If I may be allowed to declare my belief in things that I do not understand and to accept in humility things that I do not approve I am ready, at your command, to take Mount Sion, even unaccompanied by your Alsatian bitch. Give me your order. I will obey.

Your obedient servant,

Francis Lancelot Keene,

Major,

LRCPE and LM,

Late RAMC,

Dunkirk, Tunisia, Libya, Egypt, Italy,

Dispatches, medal and clasp, DSO,

1940-1945.

Retired.

The reply came by telegram the next day. At the sight of the single word of command a sudden rage boiled up in him. Who did he think he was? A bloody general? One man? And no dog? Against an army of doubts . . .

He chose July 9th for it, the feast day of two English saints, John Fisher, bishop, and Thomas More, chancellor, both martyrs.

It was raining as he entered the presbytery. In the monsignor's parlour the old Alsatian half looked up at him and sank back into its doze. The two men walked silently across to the church where the monsignor invested himself in his surplice and stole, and the major knelt by the rails of a sidechapel, feeling nothing whatsoever as he repeated the words of recantation and of belief. They then retired to the presbytery where the major knelt by the monsignor's chair for his first confession. During the previous days he had been girding himself for his complete life-story. The monsignor truncated even that piece of the ceremony, saying, 'I imagine I know it all. Women, and drink, and I suppose swearing like a trooper. Unless there is some special sin of your past life that you want to mention?'

Humbly, the major said, 'Sloth,' and got a faint satisfaction from the painful admission.

Then sunshine flooded his heart when the monsignor told him that his penance would be to say, that night, three Ave Marias.

'So little? After so long?'

'God loves you,' the monsignor said, and bade him to say his Act of Contrition.

The major's eyes filled with tears as he heard the murmuring words of absolution mingle with his own. The monsignor then raised him to his feet and warmly shook both his hands.

'My dear friend in Christ. Now you are one of us. Do your best. In the bosom of the Church. And,' briskly removing his vestments, 'let's go back now and have a good dollop of malt.'

Over the glass the major said happily, 'I was afraid I was going to feel nothing at all. Wouldn't that have been awful?'

'My dear Frank, we are strange cattle. Often, even when I say Mass, I don't feel that it is doing me a bit of good. But I know it is, so I do not worry. The heart may be the centre of all things but in the end it's not our feelings that matter but our good works. As you and I know well, more men go weak in battle from feeling too much than from feeling too little.' He chuckled. 'I remember one time we had a Colonel Home-Crean in the Inniskillings who was always carrying on about the martial spirit. He meant well. But the troops called him Old Carry On. It wasn't a bad pun, because whenever he finished one of his speeches he always said, "Carry on, Sergeant."'

The major laughed wryly.

'Pass the buck.'

'I say it still. I say it now, Frank, to you.'

He tore back at sixty miles an hour to Culadrum to meet her, singing all the way at the top of his voice *When the Saints go marching in*. There was a shower, the sun ebbed and flowed, and 'Blow me,' he cheered, 'if they haven't sent me a rainbow!' He hooted his horn along her drive, and there she was running down the steps on to the gravel to embrace him.

''Tis done,' he laughed, and she said, 'You look about seventeen!'

'God loves me!' he said.

'Did you fix up about the marriage?'

'Good Lord! I forgot all about it!'

'You immense dope!' she laughed. 'That was the whole point. Go back tonight and fix it. And do remember – the tenth of August. We've got all the tickets, darling! Promise?'

'You're still sure it's not a bit too soon? I mean that people may think that . . .'

She laughed triumphantly.

'I want them to think! I'll blame it all on my impetuous lover. And, now, you must come and see my new dresses and hats, a whole crateful of them came this morning from Dublin.'

She took him by the hand, and galloped him upstairs to her room's litter of hillocked tissue and coloured cardboard boxes.

'Sit there. And don't dare stir.' She tore off her frock; he sat and beamed at her, in her panties and bra, circling, preening, glaring in the long mirror at herself in pale toques, straw-hats in white, in mauve, in liver-pink, and he was so happy at her childish happiness that for a moment he was terrified that she would next want him to go to bed with her. Thank heaven, she was too excited to think about it. Once as she posed a pale-blue pillbox on the back of her poll, saying, 'Or this one?' he wondered whether she had gone, or when she would go to Confession, and decided that he would not press her about it just now. Perhaps never at all.

They were married before a large congregation in the cathedral. He recognized many whom he had seen six months before at the funeral. He felt a bit self-conscious about his age, and hers, and several times, when it was over, he had to stop himself from interpreting their broad smiles and their hearty congratulations. Still, whether confetti-speck-led in his grey topper and tails outside the church door, or mingling with the crowd in his new pin-stripe at the champagne reception in the Royal Hotel, he felt he had carried it all off like a soldier and a gentleman, talking now with the Inspector about tinkers, now with a very serious young librarian about the publications of the Irish Manuscripts Commission, now with Mulcahy the chemist, about the 'extraordinary' number of women in the town who took barbiturates for 'the narves', or listening in polite astonishment to a curate whom he had never met before weighing the comparative merits of President Salazar and General Franco. Then they were in his car driving off amid huzzas and laughter, down along the Main Street, out into the country for Dublin, for London and Lausanne. They were both tipsy. She was weeping softly. He filled with pity and love.

'You're not upset, darling?'

'It's just my nerves,' she smiled bravely, took a pill from her bag, and was soon chortling once more.

Everything turned out afterwards just as she had foretold. They set up house together in Culadrum. All her old friends, and her late husband's friends, came often and regularly to visit them. They played bridge with them at least twice a week. In the season he hunted three times a week. He took complete charge of her garden. He developed an interest in local archaeology. She was entirely happy, scratched him no longer and wept no more. He enjoyed all the quiet self-satisfaction of a man who, at some cost to himself, has done the right thing and found everything turning out splendidly. As he marched the roads erect, chest out, with his stick and his dog, he was admired, liked and envied by all.

Winter came. The rains and the barometer fell. She began to make excuses about going to Mass on account of the awful weather and her health. At first he found, to his regret, that he was often going to Mass alone. Then he found that he was always going alone. He began to wonder at this, ask questions about it, become testy about it, and at last they argued crossly over it every Sunday morning. There were long silences because of it. Once a whole week passed without a word spoken. He finally realized that she had no interest at all in religion, and had never had. There he felt a great hole opening in his belly, crawling like fear, recurrent as a fever, painful as betrayal, until he could no longer bear his misery alone.

'But, monsignor,' he wailed, 'why did the woman insist on my becoming a Catholic if she doesn't believe in it herself? Why in God's name did she do this to me?'

His friend did not hesitate – he never had hesitated.

'Superstition. Fear perhaps? She has memories of childhood. Of the dark. The thin red line that may not be crossed.'

'But we crossed it over and over again, for years!'

'That was not for ever.'

'Could we not have had a mixed marriage?'

'It could have been managed. Somehow. Somewhere. She wanted the Real Thing. The laying on of hands. The propitiation. The magic touch. I suspect, Frank, that your wife is a very simple woman. We have millions of them in the Church. Full of what I call ignorant innocence.

They don't do much harm to anybody, except themselves. Or if they become vain, or proud, or we press them too hard, then they turn on us like a knife. Don't force her. You have a problem. You took a chance and now you must find some way of living with it, in faith, and courage and trust. Just remember that your wife is a little vain, rather spoiled I imagine, possibly a trifle conceited, too. And, or so I feel, very unsure of herself. Hence her superstition. African missionaries tell me that they are very familiar with it.'

The major stared at him, containing the urge to say, 'Why the hell didn't you tell me all this before?'

'And what is my superstition?' he asked curtly.

'You are different. You worked your passage. Only . . .'

Here he did hesitate.

'Only?'

'Only do not expect miracles. You may, of course, pray for one. I suppose it is what we all pray for really.'

He took to going to early Mass every morning, much to her annoyance because no matter how quietly he stole out of her bed she always woke up, turning over and muttering things like, 'For God's sake isn't Sunday enough for you?' or 'My nerves are shot to bits with you and your blooming piety!' By Christmas he had taken to sleeping alone. By February he was praying for the gift of silence and drinking like a fish. In spite of that he had lost eleven pounds weight by March and was thinking of running away to Malaysia. By April he could no longer keep his food down. And then their war suddenly ended, in an explosion of light. He had gone out one morning into her walled garden to jab, stoically, at the grass and the pearlwort between the cracks of her crazy-pavement. The night had been a blur of wet trees; now a skyload of sun warmed his stooped back. He smelled the cosseted earth, glanced at her ancient espaliers, became aware of a thrush's throat, blackbirds skirling, the chaffinches' in-and-out, the powerful robin, two loving tits that flicked into the gleaming cloud of an old cherry tree propped over his head. As he picked on and on, patiently and humbly, his memory slowly expanded in widening circles out to the covert of Easter Hill, out beyond the furze-yellow slopes of the Stameen river, away out after that great wheeling run of a month ago across the reedy plain, past its fallen dolmen and its ruined abbey, losing the scent, finding it again, five glorious, nonstop, hammering miles of it. As he shifted the kneeler he noticed the first tiny bells of her white rhododendron. Christ was risen. Steaming roads stretched like wet rulers across the bog, past a pub, a garage, a grey National School, under a procession of elms against a foam-bath of clouds. At his toe he saw a blue eggshell.

At that moment a window in the house was lifted. Looking up, he saw her, in her pink morning-dress, leaning on the sill with both hands, staring over the countryside. He had a vision and in a flash it burst on him that everything she saw and he remembered came out of one eggshell. She waved to him, casually. He waved back wildly with his weeder. She retired.

'Monsignor! It was something that could only happen in Lourdes! How right you were! Never force things. Change and expand. Move slowly. Live with your problems. There are no laws for hard cases. Trust and courage solves everything. And, as you say, most of those laws are just so many old-fashioned rabbinical ideas. And the decrees of the Councils all lost! Heaven is a gift. The heart is the centre. Carry on. We can only all do our best. God loves us. Not a single cross word for two weeks! Everything absolutely ticketyboo. Monsignor, you should be a cardinal!'

They had met in the street. The old man had heard him impassively. Leaning forward on his umbrella he lifted his head from his toes for one quick glance, almost it occurred to the major in his excitement, as if he were not a cardinal but an African missionary.

'You say nothing?' he asked anxiously.

'I was just thinking. Frank. An odd thing! When we were in the Connaught Rangers we never said "Ticketyboo". What we used to say was "All kiff!" Hindustani, do you suppose? That's good news.' He shook hands limply, turned to go, turned back, said, 'Carry on, Frank,' and went on his slow way down the street, followed by his friend's wide-eyed stare of puzzlement, annoyance, affection and undiminished admiration. Two days later he attended his funeral. It was a damp day, and it did not do his rheumatism any good.

The next morning was a Sunday. The storm woke him. Through the corner of his blind he saw spilling rain, waving treetops and Noreen the maid, wrapped up in yellow cellophane like a lifeboat captain, wobbling on her bicycle down the avenue to Mass. He felt a twinge in his shoulder. He said, 'Well, I was at Mass yesterday,' lay back and dozed for an hour. He heard the soft boom of the breakfast gong, and

Anna's door open and close. As he went downstairs in his dressing-gown he smelled bacon and coffee. She was sitting by the breakfast table in her morning-gown. The fire blazed cosily. 'Good morning, love,' he said and kissed her forehead.

'Are you going out?' she asked and looked at the overspilling gutters dropping great glass beads of water past the window.

'Arthritis,' he said sheepishly.

'Why, in God's name,' she groaned, 'do we live in this climate?'

'We live where we are fated to live, in the bosom of the country,' and he lifted the chased lid of the breakfast dish.

She frowned. They munched silently. To cheer her he suggested that they might go to Italy in May, to Venice, to Rome, and he began to plan how they could go and what they could see there together. Far away a church bell tolled, on the wet wind, like a bell for the dead. He went on talking very gaily, very rapidly, very loudly. She smiled her curl-smile and said, 'Why not Lausanne?'

'Indeed, indeed! Anywhere! To get away!'

Dividends

1

As far as Mel Meldrum was concerned *l'affaire Anna*, as he was to call it, began one wet and windy April morning in 1944 when his chief clerk, Mooney, knocked at the door of his sanctum, handed him my letter, marked *Personal* and *By Hand*, and said that the bearer was an old lady in a black bonnet sitting outside in the main office 'shaking her blooming umbrella all over your new Turkish carpet'. I can see Mel glancing at my signature, smiling at his memories of our college days together twenty years before, rapidly taking the point of the letter and ordering Miss Whelan to be shown in to him at once. He rises courteously, begs her to be seated, watches amusedly while she fumbles in her woven shopping-bag, and produces, proudly I have no doubt, a fat, wrinkled envelope containing the £350 in thirty-five white Bank of England notes. He receives it from her with a small bow. It was why I sent her to him; he was always affable, almost unctuous, with old ladies.

My Aunty Anna Maria was my mother's sister. Until she got this small legacy from another sister, who had recently died in a place called Toogong in New South Wales, she had never before possessed such a lump sum. She had existed for thirty-odd years on a modest salary as cook-housekeeper to a highly successful horse-trainer in County Kildare; and then on the small pension he kindly gave her, supplemented occasionally by minute subventions from a nephew here and a niece there whenever we had the decency to remember how she used to stuff us with cakes and lemonade during our summer holidays on the edge of the Curragh where we loved to visit her in the staff quarters of the trainer's house. My father died, in Cork, so she came down there when she was about fifty-five, to live with my mother; and when my mother died she had stayed on, alone, in the city, living in a single room in a battered old fabric of a tenement overlooking one of Cork's many abandoned quaysides – silent except for the poor kids from the lanes around playing and screaming in the street, or the gulls swooping over the bits of floating orange-skin, breadcrusts or potato peelings backing slowly up-river on the high tide. When Mel saw her she was turned seventy. To my shame I had not seen her for twelve years. I had left Cork before she came there, and returned only once, for my mother's funeral. I was now married and living in Dublin.

It had taken me weeks of letter-writing, back and forth, to persuade her to invest her legacy, and I was delighted when she agreed, because I knew that if she did not she would either scatter it in dribs and drabs, or lose it in the street some day, or hide it in some corner of her room and not remember where before the mice had eaten it into confetti.

Mel described in a long, amusing letter how he had accepted the envelope 'with measured ceremony'. He had given her his best advice 'like a pontiff'. He explained to her that the sum was too small for an annuity, and she was too old for growth-shares, so he must advise her to buy 8% Preference shares in Sunbeam-Wolsey. He refused to charge her his usual stockbroker's fee, and, kindest act of all, told her that instead of waiting from one six-month period to the next for her modest dividends (£28 a year) she might, if she so wished, come into the office on the first of every month, and his chief clerk would there pay her the equivalent of her £28 per annum in twelve equal portions. She accepted his offer 'like a queen'. I could henceforth be happy to think of her toddling on the first of every month into Meldrum, Guy and Meldrum, smiling and bobbing under her black, spangled bonnet, and departing, amid the pleased smiles of everybody in the office, with her six shillings and eight pennies, wrapped in two single pound notes, clasped in the heel of her gloved fist.

I sent him my cordial thanks and thought no more about her until exactly one year later when he wrote to me that she had ordered him to sell her shares. It appeared that she had become smitten by a sudden longing to possess a blue, brocaded, saddle-back armchair that she had seen one morning in the window of Cash's in Patrick Steet. It appeared further that for months past 'a certain Mrs Bastable and a certain Mrs Sealy', two cronies as doddering as herself, also in her tenement on Lavitt's Quay, had been telling her that nobody but 'a born foolah' would leave 'all that lovely money' lying idle in Mister Meldrum's fine office on the South Mall.

It was easy enough to hear these two tempters at work on her:

'Sure, Miss Whalen, you could buy all the armchairs in Cork with that much money! And look at your poor ould room with the paint falling off the ceiling like snow! And your poor ould curtains in tatthers on yer winda! Why don't you buy an electric fire that would keep you warm all the winter? And two grand, soft Blarney blankets for your bed? And a pink, quilted eiderdown? And, anyway, sure that measley ould two quid that Meldrum gives you wouldn't buy a dead cat! And supposing yeh die? What'll happen it then? Get a hold of your money, girl, and *spend it*!'

Mel counter-argued and counter-pleaded. I pleaded. I got her parish priest to plead with her. I even offered to buy her the brocaded armchair as a present. It was no use. Mel sold her shares, gave her a cheque for £350, wished her well, and we both washed our hands of her.

I next got a long and slightly testy letter from Mel, written on the first day of the following month of May. It began, 'Your good Aunty Anna has this morning turned up again in my office, bright as a new-born smile, bowing and bobbing as usual, calmly asking my chief clerk Mooney for what she calls, if you please, *her* little divvies...'

In dismay he had come out to her.

'But, Miss Whelan, you've sold your shares! Don't you remember?'

Aunt Maria smiled cunningly at him.

'Ah, yes!' she agreed. 'But I didn't sell my little divvies!'

'But,' Mel laughed, 'your dividends accrued from the capital sum you invested. Once a client sells his shares he withdraws the capital and there can be no more dividends. Surely you understand that?'

At once Aunty Anna's smile vanished. A dark fright started at the bottom of her chin and climbed slowly up to her eyes.

'Mister Meldrum, you know well that I didn't sell me little divvies. I want me little divvies. You always gave me them. They belong to me. Why can't you give them to me now the way you always gave me them at the first of every month? Why are you keeping them back from me now?'

'Miss Whelan, when a client sells his shares they are gone. And when they are gone the dividends naturally cease forthwith. You instructed me to sell. I did so. I gave you back your money in a lump sum. If you now wish to give me back that lump sum I shall be most happy to buy you more shares and your dividends will begin again. Otherwise we have nothing for you.'

Aunty Anna had burst into floods of tears, and she began to wail, with the whole office staring at the pair of them.

'What do I want with shares? I don't want any more ould shares. I gave you back me shares. Keep 'em! I don't want 'em. All I want is me little divvies. And anyway I haven't the money you gave me, I bought an armchair with it, and an electric fire from the ESB, and a costume from Dowden's, and I gave fifty pounds to the Canon to say Masses for my poor soul when I'm dead, and I loaned ten quid to Mrs Bastable on the ground-floor, and ten quid to Mrs Sealy on the third floor back, and what with this and that and the other all I have left is a few quid, and I don't know where I put 'em, I'd lay down me life I put 'em in the brown teapot on the top shelf but when I went looking for them yesterday I couldn't find them high nor low. Mrs Sealy says I must have made tea with them, but I tell you, Mister Meldrum, I wouldn't trust that one as far as I'd throw her. Mister Meldrum, give me me little divvies. They're all I have to live on bar that mangy old pension. I want me divvies here and now, if you please, or I'll go out there in the street and call a policeman!'

Mel led her gently into his inner sanctum, together with his book-keeper, and the two of them spent an hour explaining to her, in every way they could think of, the difference between shares and dividends. They showed her the receipt for the purchase of the shares, for the dividends they had earned over the year, the notation of the re-sale of the shares, and the red line drawn clearly at the end of her account to show that it was now closed for ever. They might as well have been talking to the carpet. Aunty Anna just could not understand that he who does not speculate cannot accumulate. The upshot of it was that she became so upset, and Mel became so angry with her, and then so upset because he had upset her that, to comfort her, he took £2 6s. 8d. out of his pocket, the equivalent of what she had hitherto lawfully drawn every month, told her that this was the end, the very end, and that she must now reconcile herself, firmly and finally, if she would be so very kind, to the plain fact that she was no longer in the market for anything. And so he showed her out, bobbing and smiling, and happy, and (he hoped), convinced. He was most forbearing about it all. Three pages he wrote about it to me. All I could do was to write him a properly apologetic and deeply grateful reply, enclosing my cheque for £2 6s. 8d., which, I noted, in some surprise, he duly cashed.

On the morning of the first of the following month of June he was on the telephone. His voice over the wire sounded rather strangled.

'Your good aunt is back here in my office again. She is sitting directly opposite me. She seems to be in very good health. And in good spirits to boot. In fact she is beaming at me. Nevertheless she is once more demanding dividends on shares which she does not possess. Will you kindly tell me at once what you wish me to do with, for, or to her?'

'Oh, Lord, Mel! This is too bad! I'm very sorry! I'm awfully sorry. Look, Mel, couldn't you just explain firmly to the old lady that ...'

At this his voice rose to a squeak of utter exasperation.

'Miss Whelan has been in my private office for the past three-quarters of a bloody hour with my book-keeper, my assistant book-keeper, my chief clerk ...'

'Mel! I'll tell you what to do. Just give her the two quid six and eight and I'll send you a cheque for it this minute, and then tell her never, just simply never, to darken your doors again.'

Mel's voice became precise, piercing, priggish and prim in a way that suddenly recalled to me a familiar side of his nature that I had completely forgotten until that moment.

'I have no hope what-so-ever of achieve-ing the entire-ly de-sirable state of affairs that you so blandly de-pict. I am afraid the time has arrived for you to come down to Cork in person and talk in person to your good aunt. Furthermore, I must tell you that your proposal about a cheque is totally contrary to my principles as a man and as a stockbroker. It is contrary to the whole ethics, and the whole philosophy, the whole morality of stockbroking. It is inconsistent, unrealistic, unprofessional and absurd. As I have explained to Miss Whelan, he who saves may invest, he who invests may accumulate, he who does not save may not ...'

'Mel, for God's sake come off it! How the hell can she save anything at all on that measley old pension of hers? Who do you think she is? Bernard Baruch? Henry Ford? John D. Rockefeller? Gulbenkian?'

'In that case,' he retorted, 'it is as absurd for her to expect as it would be unrealistic for me to pretend that she is entitled to returns on non-existent capital. In the name of justice, equity and realism, above all in the name of realism, I will not and I cannot pretend to pay any client dividends that simply do not exist ... Excuse me one moment.'

Here I could hear a confused babble of voices as of four or five people engaged in passionate argument, 161 blessed miles away from my study in Dublin.

'Hello!' he roared. 'How soon, for God Almighty's sake, can you come down to Cork and settle this matter with your aunt?'

I saw that there was no way out of it. It was a Friday. I said that I would take the morning train on Saturday.

'I will meet you at the station.'

'Is this an order?' I asked wryly.

His answer was clipped. He recovered himself sufficiently to add 'Please!' and even to mention that I could get some sort of ragtime lunch on the train. When I said I would be there, he calmed down. He expanded. He even became amiable. When he broke into French I remembered how, in his student days, he used to go to France every summer and Easter with his widowed mother.

'Bon! Nous causerons de beaucoup de choses. Et nous donnerons le coup-de-grace à l'affaire Anna, et à ses actions imaginaires' – and hung up.

Actions? My dictionary told me that the word means *acts, actions, performances, battles, postures, stocks, shares.* As I put back the volume on its shelf I remembered how good he always used to be at social work among the poor of Cork. I also wondered a little how such a man could see nothing wrong with giving charity outside his office in the name of Saint Vincent de Paul but everything wrong with the idea of bestowing largesse inside it in the name of pity. I also realized that I had not met him for some twenty years.

2

It was a perfect June morning. All the way down from Dublin to Cork the country looked so soft and fresh, so green and young, and I lunched so well that my heart gradually warmed both to Aunty Anna and to Mel, the dual cause of this pleasant excursion back to my homeground. As the fields floated past and the waves of the telegraph wires rolled and sank I started to recall the Mel I used to know. Indeed if anybody at that moment had asked me about him – say, that old priest half dozing on the seat opposite me – I would have launched on a eulogy as long as an elegy.

Stout fellow! Salt of the earth! As fine a chap as you could hope to meet in a day's march. Honest, kind and absolutely reliable. The sort of man who would never, simply never let you down. A worthy inheritor of his father's and his grandfather's business. Handsome, strong, tall, always well dressed – in the old days, we all thought him a bit of a dandy. And so easy! As smooth and easy as that bog-stream outside there. Oh, now and again he could be gruff if you rubbed him the wrong way, and he was sometimes given a bit to playing the big shot. And by that same token he always boasted that he was a first class shot. A real, clean-living, open-air man. What else? Well informed about music. And the opera. Spoke French well – those visits abroad with his mother. A strong civic sense, always proud of his native city. Who was it that told me a few years ago that he is up to his neck nowadays in all sorts of worthy societies in Cork? The Old Folks Association, the Safety First Association, Saint Vincent de Paul, the Archaeological Society, the Society for the Prevention of Cruelty to Animals, the African Mission Brotherhood...

I glanced across at my old priest. He was looking at me as if I had been talking aloud to myself. I turned to the fields.

'Well ... Not exactly sociable, I suppose. Unless a committee meeting in a hotel room can be called a jolly sociable occasion.'

Come to think of it, he always did keep a bit to himself. Not stand-offishly, more of a class thing, being so much richer than the rest of us. Or was he a little shy? And I did hear recently that he has given up shooting and taken to bird-watching – from a weekend cottage he has outside Cork, some place along the valley of the Lee beyond Inniscarra. His private hide-out where he can 'get away from it all'.

The old priest was still looking at me. I turned to watch a racing horse.

'All? I suppose he means the roaring traffic of Cork, which, when I was a student, chiefly meant jarvey-cars, bullocks, dray-horses and bicycles. It is a quiet place. Not really a city at all. And then, of course, we mustn't forget Cork's famous social whirl. Bridge every night, golf every Saturday, and, for the happy few, a spot of sailing in the harbour over the weekend. And tubs of secret drinking in hotel lounges for the happy many, stealing in discreetly by the back door. Or were they the unhappy many? Cork can be a pretty grim place in the winter. As I well know! Lord! don't I know!'

A sunshot shower of rain flecked the windows of the train.

'We may as well face it. Cork is a place where it rains, and rains, and rains, with an implacable and persistent slowness. A frightful place, really, in the winter! Of course, if you have enough piastres you can knock out a good time even in Cork. But you have to have the piastres. And I never did. Mel did. And lots of 'em. Rich? Very. At least by Cork standards. A tight, bloody hole, full to the butt of the lugs with old family businesses that keep a firm grip on their miserly homesteads.'

Was that priest raising his eyebrows at me?

'Naturally, he's a Catholic! A most devoted Catholic. No! A baptized, confirmed and unmarried bachelor. That is odd – because he always had a great eye for the girls. Funny I never thought of it before. In Ireland you don't, somehow. You get so used to the widowed mother in the background, or the uncle who is a bishop, or the two brothers who are priests, or the three sisters who are nuns. The tradition of celibacy. But, by God, he did have that roving eye! Why didn't he marry? And he was quite good-looking. Even if he has slightly prominent teeth, and a rather silly, affected way of shaving that leaves a tuft of hair on each cheekbone.'

I closed my eyes to see him better. I wondered why the hell I was coming down here at all.

'He must be forty-six or forty-seven by now. If his taste in clothes is what it used to be he will be wearing a check sports coat with two splits behind and a check cap slightly yawed over his gamesome eye. The country squire's weekend costume.

'Is there,' I asked the priest, 'a train back out of Cork tonight?'

He smiled crookedly.

'There is. A slow one. You're not staying long with us, I see?'

'I have to get back tonight.'

I felt my face flushing. My wife is not well. My youngest daughter has a fever. I am in a bad shape myself, Mel. In fact I am running a temperature of 102°. My brother is arriving from London on Sunday morning. My best friend is dying. My uncle died yesterday. I simply have to go to his funeral.

'Are you sure, Father, there is a train out of Cork tonight?'

'There is. One of these days they say we are going to have our own airport. With aeroplanes.'

The rain stopped and the sun burst out, but I did not trust it one inch. I recognized familiar fields. Poor-looking fields. The rain. The cold. My poverty-stricken youth in Cork. We passed Blarney. Then we were in the tunnel, and though I knew there is this long tunnel into Cork I had forgotten how long it was, how smelly and how dark.

He was the first person I saw on the platform, in his tweeds and his sporty cap. The wings of his hair were turning white. His teeth were much too white to be his own. He wore spectacles. We greeted one another warmly.

People talk of well-remembered voices. I recognized his slightly hectoring Oxford-cum-Cork accent only when he said, 'Well. So we got Your Highness down to Cork at last?' I laughed, 'Why do Cork people always say "up to Dublin" and "down to Cork"? Here I am, like Orpheus.' He sniffed by way of reply, and we went out of the station yard teasing one another amiably about our advancing years, sat into his white sports Jaguar and shot across the station yard like a bullet.

3

'Well?' I said. 'And how did you finish up yesterday with my dear old Aunty Anna?'

He pretended to be coping with the traffic – at that point a dozen bullocks lurching wild-eyed all over the street before the howls and waving arms of two equally wild-eyed drovers. Then, with a sheepish side glance and a grin that was clearly meant to involve me in his illogicality, he said:

'I gave her the odd two quid again. She will obviously be back in a month. And every month for the rest of her life. Unless we do something drastic about her.'

'I see. Are we going to beard her now?'

'No! I don't work on Saturdays. And I'm not going to break my rule of life for that accursed old hairpin. I'm driving you out to my Sabine farm. We've got the whole weekend. We'll talk about her tonight after dinner. And not one minute before!'

I bridled. After all, I was very fond of my Aunty Anna, even if I had not visited her for the last twelve years, and I objected to being shanghaied like this without as much as a 'If you'd like it', or 'If you can spare the time', or 'By your leave'. Was he at his old game of playing the big shot? The bossy businessman? At close quarters, over a whole weekend, was he going to turn out to be an awful bore? However, he had been very kind to Aunty Anna, and I had got him into this mess, and I was under an obligation to him, so I said, as pleasantly as I could, 'That's very kind of you, Mel. I can see my aunt tomorrow morning, and I'm sure there must be an afternoon train home.'

'If that's what you want,' he said, rather huffily. Then he said, cheerfully, 'If there is a train to Dublin on Sundays I'm sure it takes about ten hours.' Then he said, so smugly that anybody who did not know him could well have taken an immediate dislike to him, 'You're going to like my cottage – it's a real beauty. Nobody in Cork has anything like it!'

I did not talk much during the drive into and out of the city. It reminded me too much of my father and mother, of my lost youth. He blathered on and on about its great future, its economic development, the airport they were sure to have some day, as if he were the Lord Mayor of the damn place. Then we were out of it and in the country again, and presently – it cannot have been more than twenty minutes at his mad speed – he said, 'Behold my Sabine farm!'

At first glance, through the trees, it looked like the sort of cottage that would make any estate-agent start pouring out words like 'rustic', 'picturesque', 'antique', 'venerable', 'traditional', 'old-world' and every other kind of pin-headed euphemism for damp, dirty, crumbling, phoney, half ruined, fourth-hand and thoroughly uncomfortable. When we drew up by its little wooden gate, it turned out to be the sort of dream-cottage you meet in English detective stories, or on the travel posters of British Railways. It stood under its trim roof of thatch on a sunbathed sideroad, in about two acres of orchard, kitchen garden and lawn, facing a small, old church with a not ungraceful spire in brownstone directly above the Lee murmuring far below in a valley scooped aeons ago out of the surrounding hills and covered now with young pine-woods. It was long, low and pink-washed, with diamond panes in its small windows, and its walls were covered by a thick curtain of Albertine roses that would be a mellow blaze within a week or two. The door, painted in William Morris blue, was opened by a brown-eyed young woman whom he introduced as, 'My housekeeper. My invaluable Sheila.' The living-room was long and low-ceilinged, furnished in elegant Adams and Chippendale, carpeted in pale green from wall to wall, with an unnecessary but welcoming wood fire sizzling softly in an old brick fireplace. Later I found that he had put in central heating, electric light and an American-style kitchen. His Sheila brought us Scotch, water and ice-cubes, and we sank into two deep armchairs beside the fire.

'You seem to live pretty well, friend,' I admitted grudgingly.

'I like the simple life,' he breezed. 'But I'm not simple-minded about it, I'm a realist.'

I humphed internally. I recognized the common illusion of most businessmen that writers are all mental defectives, dreamy romancers with about as much commonsense as would fit in one of their small toes. Really, I thought again, all this might well turn out to be a frightful bore.

I became aware that his housekeeper was still standing beside us. Her brown eyes reminded me of two shining chestnuts. If her chin had not been a shadow overshot she would have been a beauty. What struck me most about her was not, however, her face, her trim figure or her straight back, but her air of calm self-possession. He gave her a quick, all-over glance.

'Well, my dear? What are you giving us for dinner tonight?'

'Two roast chickens. Parsley potatoes. New. Your own. And fresh peas from the garden.'

'And for sweet? Apart from yourself?' he asked, with that kind of gawky smile with which elderly men try to curry favour with scowling children, and that celibates overdo for handsome young women.

'Apart from myself,' she replied calmly, 'there will be an apple pie. They are the last apples left in your loft.'

'With cream?'

'Naturally.'

'And the wine?'

She nodded to two bottles standing at a discreet distance from the brickwork of the fireplace. Gevrey Chambertin: 1949.

'Excellent. We will dine at seven-thirty.' He turned away from her. 'Drink up! I saw two kingfishers flashing along the river last week and I want to check whether they are still there. They've just got married,' he added, with a raise-your-eyebrows grin at Sheila, who tossed her head and went off about her business.

'And where did that treasure come from?' I asked, carefully keeping the note of suspicion out of my voice, and noting inwardly that twenty years ago I would have started to pull his leg about her.

'Pure luck. She is a typist in my office. I used to have a dreadful old hairpin, as old and almost as doddery as your mad aunt. Then I suddenly found out that Sheila lives halfway between here and Cork, in a labourer's cottage on the side of the road. When I suggested to her that she might lend a hand and make some extra cash she jumped at it. Every Friday night I drive her home from the office on my way here, collect her on Saturday morning, and Bob's-your-uncle.'

He gathered up his binoculars, notebooks and camera, and we went off after the kingfishers. I enjoyed every minute of it, tramping for about three hours up and down the river bed. He found his kingfishers, a nesting heron, and became madly excited when he picked out through his binoculars, and let me also see, a buff-coloured bird about the size of a thrush but with a long beak, a crest and black and white stripes on its wings, perched on a tall beech tree.

'Can it,' he kept saying in a shouting whisper, 'but it can't be, can it *possibly* be a hoopoe?'

He entered every detail in his field notebook, date, hour, temperature, compass bearings and heaven only knows what else, and he became so boyish about it all that my earlier annoyance with him vanished completely. When, on the way home, I asked him casually how old he was, and he said 'Forty-seven', my earlier suspicions also vanished. He was at least twice her age. By the time we got back to his cottage I felt not only so pleasantly tired but so pleasantly relaxed that I told him I had decided not to return home until the Monday morning.

The wood fire, now that the evening chill had come, was welcoming. I found that there were two baths, and lots of hot water. I wallowed in mine for twenty minutes. When we both emerged his Sheila made us a shaker of martinis, and through them we moved leisurely into a perfect dinner. She had not roasted the chickens, she had broiled them *en papilottes*. She must have spent an hour on the apple pie alone – my wife, who is a first-rate cook, could not have improved on its delicate crust.

'Did you teach her all this cooking, Mel?'

'I confess I have tried to play Professor Higgins to her Pygmalion. But only,' he winked, 'as to her cooking. So far.'

By the time we had finished off the two bottles of Burgundy and retired to our armchairs before the fire we were the old – that is the young – Mel and Sean. She lit two shaded lamps, brought us Italian coffee, a bottle of Hine, two warmed glasses, the cigar-box and our slippers.

'Wonderful woman!' I murmured. 'I hope you never lose her.'

'She is useful,' he agreed shortly, poured the brandy and, like me, stretched out his long legs to the fire.

For a while there was not a sound except the sizzle of the logs and an occasional slight tinkle from the direction of the kitchen. The deep, darkening country closed around us in such utter silence that when I strained my ears to listen I could hear, deep in the valley, the whisper of the river. Did I hear a pheasant coughing? Drowsily I remembered that he had said that we would talk tonight of Aunty Anna. I had no wish to talk about Aunty Anna, and by the sleepy way he was regarding the fire through his brandy glass I hoped he felt the same. Then I heard his voice, and with something sharper than regret I gathered that he had begun to talk about himself.

4

'Sean, I'm very glad you came. For a long time now I've been working out a certain idea, something rather important, and I want to try it out on you, just as a sort of test.'

Just barely holding off the sleep of bliss, I nodded easily.

'Did it ever strike you that every man – which includes every woman – is his own potter? I mean, that sooner or later every man takes up what you might call the clay, or the plasticine, or the mud, call it what you like, of his experience of life, and throws it down on his potter's wheel, and starts the pedal going, and rounds it up into a shape? Into what I call his idea of the shape of his whole life? Are you following me?'

I nodded myself awake.

'Good! Now for the big snag. It is, why do we do this? I can't say we do it to please ourselves, because we can *have* no selves – can we? We can't *see* ourselves – can we? – or *know* ourselves – can we? – and therefore we cannot *be* ourselves – can we? – until we have made this shape, and looked at it, as one would look in a mirror, and said to ourselves, "That's me! That's my vocation. My ambition. My politics. My faith. My whole life." I mean,' he pounded on, with a force of energy that made me even more tired and sleepy than before, 'I cannot say "That's me" until I have made my shape, because there is no *me* until I have made my shape. Therefore I can get no real pleasure of it all until the job is actually done. That's a pretty disturbing thought, what-what?'

I pulled myself awake. What had I walked into? Two nights of this twaddle? There simply had to be an afternoon train tomorrow!

'And when the job is done, Mel?'

He gave me a powerful slap on the thigh.

'Then I begin to live. When I at last know exactly what I am, I at last know exactly what I want to do, because my shape, my image, now tells me what I do want to do.'

I sighed and stretched.

'And then, Mel, some other fellow comes along and he looks at your portrait of the artist as a young dog, and he says, "No! This may be some crazy dream Mel has of himself, or some crazy dream he has of the world as he would like it to be, but it's not our Mel, and it's not our world."'

'Ha-ha, and I might say the same to him, and to his world?'

'You certainly might. But, of course, I hope you're not so daft as to deny that all the time there must be a real objective world outside there? Made up of stockbrokers and tax-collectors, and physicists, and isoprene, and polmerization . . .'

'By the way, rubber is going up.'

' . . . and gravitation, electricity, atomic weight, blood pressure, measles, kids getting sick, old people dying and kingfishers mating, and so on and so on. And a real, objective you, me, and Tom, Dick and Harry inside in each one of us, and no fancies and no fooling.' I laughed. 'Mel, you're a joy! I'm glad to inform you that you haven't changed one iota since the days when we used to come out from old Father Abstractibus's philosophy lectures, long ago in University College, Cork, and lie on the grass of the quadrangle, and talk for hours about the Object and the Subject and "What is Reality?", and "What is the stars?", and never got one inch beyond chasing our own tails. And here you are, still at it! It's a pointless pursuit, and I'm in no mood for it. Mel! If we have to talk about anything at all on top of that wonderful dinner, and that marvellous Gevrey Chambertin, and this perfect brandy, let's talk about a painfully real subject. Let's talk about my Aunty Anna.'

'That,' he said calmly, 'is what I am talking about. About people who live in imaginations, and fantasies, and illusions about themselves. What, so far as I can see, the whole blessed world is doing all the time. Including your dear Auntie Anna Maria Whelan.' He stretched out his foot and touched my ankle with the toe of his slipper. 'Do you know what your dear Auntie Anna did with that three hundred and fifty quid?'

'You told me. She bought an armchair, and an electric fire, and an eiderdown, and curtains, and Masses for her soul, and she gave loans to...'

'Rubbish! That's what she said. She bought a fur coat with the three-fifty quid.'

'You're a liar!'

'She is the liar.'

'Then you're joking.'

'It's no joke, my friend. The old divil had the cheek to have it on her back when she came into my office yesterday. When she went out I had a brain-wave. I rang up a friend of mine who works with the Saint Vincent de Paul's in her part of the city and I asked him to drop around and have a look at her place. No armchair, no electric fire, no eiderdown, no new curtains, no nothing. And as for those loans that she invented, as he pointed out to me, the poor don't give anybody loans of ten quid a time. Ten shillings would be more like it. If that! You talk very glibly about the "real, objective world outside there". You don't seem to know so very much about it, after all, do you?'

His air of condescension infuriated me.

'It was probably a cheap, second-hand coat!'

'I checked up on that too. Cork is a small place, and there aren't many shops where you can buy new fur coats for a sum as large as that. I rang up Bob Rohu and I told him the whole yarn. I hit a bull's eye at once. He sold it to her himself. He remembered the transaction very well – as you might expect. A poor old woman like her doesn't come in every day to buy a bang-up fur coat. She paid him two hundred and seventy-five pounds for that fur coat. In notes.' He paused. He concluded with sardonic formality, 'You perceive my trend?'

I was furious, chastened and filled with pity for my Aunty Anna. I saw also that whatever picture Mel had made of himself it would not show him as anybody's fool. I could have choked him. Here was I, who had known Aunty Anna all my life, a man who was supposed to know something about human nature, and here was this fellow who had only met Aunty Anna three or four times in his life, pitilessly exposing her to me as a woman perched out there for thirty years on that big, grassy, empty plain of the Curragh of Kildare, working, since she was twenty, for a wealthy trainer, seeing his rich, horsy clients coming and going in all their finery, and thinking, as she grew older and older, with no man ever asking her to marry him – Why the hell had I never realized that she would think it? – that she would never possess anything even dimly like what they possessed. Until, by pure chance, at the age of seventy-odd, she finds herself drawing dividends like the best of them, trading in the stock-market just like the best of them, being received like a lady by the best stockbroker in Cork – and sees that fur coat in a shop window.

Mel was slowly rolling his brandy around in his brandy glass and watching me slyly.

'Interesting, isn't it?' he said.

'Very,' I said bitterly. After a while of silence I said, 'And this is why she won't get any more of what she thinks are her little divvies? Even if I agreed to pay you for them?'

He answered with anger, almost with passion:

'It is. The woman is fooling herself, and I refuse to encourage her. She is trying to make nonsense of everything I believe in. And I won't let her do it. Would you, as a writer, write something you didn't believe to be true?'

'Don't be silly! I'm pleased and proud any time I think I'm able to tell even one tenth of the truth.'

'Would you, if you were a doctor, tell lies to a patient?'

'Doctors have to do it all the time. To help them to live. To make it easier for them to die.'

'Well, I don't and won't tell lies. Facts are facts in my profession, and I have to live by them.'

'You gamble.'

'I do not.'

'You encourage your clients to gamble.'

'I do not.'

'Then what do you do for a living?'

'I hope.'

We laughed. We calmed down.

'What about charity, Mel?'

'I would have no objection to giving your aunt charity. I like the old thing. She is a nice poor soul. And my friend in the Vincent de Paul assures me that she is a very worthy creature. In fact I'd be quite happy to pay the old hairpin ... ' Here the chill caution of the trained businessman entered his voice, 'I'd be quite happy to go halves with you in paying her the equivalent of her blasted divvies every year. But not as dividends! Strictly as a gift from the pair of us.'

'Mel, that's kind of you! Our whole problem is solved. Let's give her the £28 a year as a present. What are you looking at me like that for?'

'She won't take it.'

'Why won't she take it?'

'Because it's charity. And she doesn't want charity. The poor never want charity. They hate it because it makes them feel their poverty. Any of them that have any pride left in them. And that old lady is stiff with pride. You could take a gift from me, I could take a gift from you, Queen Victoria would have taken all India and hung it on her charm bracelet without as much as a thank you. But not the poor! However, try her. Take the Jaguar tomorrow morning and drive into town and take her out to lunch. I bet you a tenner to a bob she'll refuse.' He rose. 'Ah! Here we are!'

This was for our housekeeper, waiting, ready to be driven home. She was wearing a small fur hat and a neat, belted tweed coat. From under her hat her dark hair crooked around each cheek. Now that she was wearing high-heeled shoes I noticed how long and elegant her legs were.

'That,' said Mel, surveying her, 'is a darling little hat you have.'

'I had it on this morning,' she said quietly. 'But men never notice anything.'

'Where did you get it?'

'I bought it of course. It's wild mink. I've been saving up for it for years. I got it at Rohu's.'

'Good girl!' he said enthusiastically, and looked at me in approval of his pupil, while I wondered if he knew how much even that little dream of wild mink cost her. She might well have been saving up for it for years. 'I'll bring around the car. I won't be long,' he said to me. 'Play yourself some music while we're away. I've got some good records.'

When he had gone out I said to her, 'Won't you sit down while you are waiting?' and she sat sedately on the arm of his vacated chair and crossed her pretty heron's legs.

'Do you like music, Sheila?'

'I used to like only jazz. Recently I've come to prefer classical music. Mr Meldrum has been introducing me to it. Shall I show you how to work the machine? It's new and he is very particular about it. It has two extensions. They give you the impression that you are surrounded by an orchestra. Oh!' lifting the lid and looking in. 'There's a record on it. Yes, here is the jacket – it's *The Siegfried Idyll*. Would you like to play this one. Or would you perhaps prefer something more modern?'

(I thought, 'You may only be a typist in his office but you have the manners of a woman of the world.')

'Yes, I'd like to hear that again. It's years since I heard any Wagner. Do *you* like it?'

'We've played it so often now that I'm just beginning to understand what it's all about.'

'And what is it all about?' I smiled.

She switched on the machine and closed the lid.

'I suppose it's about happiness through love. It takes a little time to warm up. Then it works automatically.'

I glanced at her. Was she a deep one? His horn hooted from the road. For the first time she smiled. She had perfect teeth.

'I must be off. Don't let the fire die down. He sometimes sits up late. There are plenty of logs. And I've fixed the electric blankets at Number Two heat, so they will be nice and cosy before you have finished your last nightcaps. Goodnight.'

When she was gone I walked to the window to look after her and saw that a vast moon had risen over the dark hills surrounding the valley, touching their round breasts as softly as a kiss. He and she stood arm in arm looking at it, he leaning a little over her, pointing up to the moon as if he were showing it to an infant, and saying something that, for once, must have not been off the mark, because she swiftly turned her face up to him and laughed gloriously. Just as he touched her furry cap with his finger the record behind me fell into place and a score of violins began whispering, pulsing and swelling around me as power-fully as the immense moon. In that second I had no more doubts about the pair of them. He released her arm, opened the door of the car for her so that its carriage light fell for a second on her radiant smile. He banged her door, got in on his side and shot away. I returned slowly to my armchair, my brandy and cigar, and stared into the flickering fire.

Gradually the idyll rose in wave after wave to its first crescendo until the bows of the violins were so many lashing whips of passionate sound. The lunatic! Sitting here, of nights, in this silent valley, with her opposite him, listening to music like this Christmas morning music, composed by a lover for his sleeping beloved. If it made me wish to God I was at home in bed with my wife what, in heaven's name, must it do to him? I suddenly remembered something that made me snatch up the jacket of the record. I was right. Wagner wrote that love idyll when he was fifty-seven, having fallen in love with Cosima Liszt when he was in his forties and she in her twenties, and I began to think of other elderly men who had married young women, finding them even in that tight little city a few miles away. Wintering men plucking their budding roses. Old Robert Cottrell, the ship-owner, who married a barmaid out of the Victoria Hotel. Frank Lane, the distiller, who at sixty picked a pretty waitress out of The Golden Tavern. And who was that miller who, after being a widower for twenty-five years, fell in love with one of his mill-girls and had children by her, younger than his grandchildren? It is the sort of thing that can easily happen to men who have lived all their lives by the most rigid conventions, and then suddenly get sick of it all and throw their hats over the moon.

I became more calm as the music slowly died in exhaustion of its own surfeit. He was as open as a book – all that talk of his about men taking the clay of life and making a self-shape of it. Of her I knew nothing except that he had said she lived in a roadside cottage and, as he must know well – and he would be the first to say it – that a rich stockbroker would be a wonderful catch for her. I started to walk restlessly about the house. By error I entered his bedroom. I shut the door quickly, feeling that I was floundering in deep and dangerous tides. The covers of his bed had been neatly turned down at an angle of forty-five degrees and on his pillow there lay a red rosebud. I went to bed and fell into such a sound sleep that I did not hear him return.

When I woke up it was blazing sun outside and the cottage was empty: he had presumably gone to Mass and to collect her. When they came in he was wearing the rosebud in his lapel. After breakfast I took the Jaguar and drove into town to meet my Aunty Anna.

5

The city was full of the sound of church bells but there was hardly a soul out along the quay where she lived. Even the gulls were silent, floating on the river or perched along the quayside walls. I drew up outside her old fabric of a house, its railings crooked, its fanlight cracked, its traditional eight-panelled door clotted with years of paint asking only for a blowlamp and a week's scraping to reveal chiselled mouldings and fine mahogany. I sat for a while in the car thinking of the Aunty Anna I knew and the best way to handle her.

She had always been a soft, slack, complaining creature with, so far as I knew, no keener interests in life than backing horses, telling fortunes on the cups and cards, eating boiled sweets and reading violet-coloured penny novelettes. I should have brought her a box of chocolates. I drove off and managed to find a shop open that sold them. It may have been, it occurred to me, this love of boiled sweets that used to give her so much trouble with her teeth; they used to pain her a great deal and several of them were decayed in the front of her mouth. At that time there was some kind of pulp, paste or malleable wafer that poor country folk used as a dental stopgap to hide these marks of decay on special occasions. Or perhaps it was only white paper chewed-up? She used it constantly and it made her teeth look like putty. The poor woman had also had an operation performed, unskilfully, on her left elbow, which had a moist hollow, like a navel, where the point of the ulna ought to have been; she used to nurse it all the time with her fondling right hand, especially on cold or windy days. Would the poor old thing respond to the idea of going to a good surgeon? Or I could, perhaps, tempt her with some good, stout, comfortable dresses: my wife could easily get those for her. Not that I feared, looking up at the crumbling bricks of her tenement, that I would have any difficulty in persuading her to accept an annual gift, and I thought back to those days on the rolling, green Curragh when she had at least had every comfort, the best of food and healthy, country air, and I realized that she should never have left her base, and that the ideal, but now impossible, thing for her to do would be to go back and live in the country where she belonged.

A few minutes later I was holding her weeping in my arms in her one room where she had cooked slept and sat day after day for so many years, and as I smelled the familiar, indefinable musk of urban poverty, suggestive mainly of sour clothes, bad sewage and fried onions, I was overcome with shame that I had not visited her once during the twelve years since I left Cork to be married. I kissed her, and she kissed me, as maternally as if I were still a small boy. Then I stood back, looked at her and got a shock of memory. She had a face like an old turtle, she was humped like a heron and she was rouged. Long ago, my mother had laughed one day and said she did it with geranium petals rubbed lightly in pale-brown boot polish. I noted, too, that all her decayed teeth were replaced by a good denture, and that her hair was tinted and blued. Like a boy I endured the reproaches that she poured over me, and then, eager to be out of that jumbled, stuffy room, I bustled her to get ready and come out to lunch at the Victoria Hotel.

She put on her fur coat, and a small, ancient straw hat, gay with white daisies. Once she was dressed she became rigid with what Cork calls grandeur, as when she said: 'This is quite a nice little car,' and started talking about all the much grander cars she used to drive in at the Curragh Races. At lunch she held her knife and fork at right-angles to her plate, sipped her wine like a bird, drank her coffee with the little finger crooked, hem-hemmed into her napkin like a nun and small-talked as if she were royalty giving me an audience, all of it gossip and chit-chat about the gentry of the Curragh and their fine ladies and great houses. At the end of the lunch she produced a compact, powdered her nose, examined her face intently all over and delicately applied a pink lipstick. She evaded all my efforts to talk of old times until we moved into the empty lounge where I had a stout brandy. She preferred a gin-and-lime. At last I did lure her out of her glorious past to my proposal that I should give her twenty-eight pounds a year (I carefully left Mel out of it) as a little gesture, 'For old times' sake, *Aunty*?' – trying to make her stop being Her Majesty, and become my Aunty Anna again.

She made short work of me.

'No! Thank you very much. Now that I have my divvies I don't need it.'

From there we went back and forth over the whole thing, over more brandy and gin, for two fruitless hours. Gifts she would ('of course') not accept. Her divvies she would ('of course') not renounce. By the end of it I had gained only one point. She said, coldly but with spirit, that if 'that man' denied her her rights she would never darken his door again.

'I will have nothing more to do with this so-called Mister Meldrum. I am finished with all fraudulent stockbrokers for ever.'

It was four o'clock before I surrendered, furious, rejected, humiliated and exhausted. I drove her around the city, slowly at her queenly request, in my white Jaguar (in which, I told her, I had arrived from Dublin that morning), and ended up at her door amid a crowd of lane kids oohing and aahing at what one of them called Snow White's car. I promised faithfully to visit her again next summer, kissed her goodbye, excused my haste by saying that I had to be back in Dublin before nightfall and drove away amid the huzzas of the tiny mob. As soon as I got around a corner I paused to rub off her lipstick. I felt very proud of her, I despised myself, and I hated Mel and all that he and his kind stood for – by which I do not now know what I meant then, unless it had something to do with the corrupting power of money over us all.

I was in no mood to face his guffaws of triumph. I parked the Jaguar on the empty South Mall and went wandering through the silent, Sunday streets of this city of my youth, seeing little of it. I was too angry, and too absorbed in trying to devise some means of helping her, and at every turn bothered by unhappy thoughts about Mel and myself, and about whatever it was that the years had done to us both. Was he right in saying that I knew nothing about poor people like Aunty Anna? His Sheila was a young, pretty Aunty Anna, poor like her, being drawn now, as she had been, close to the world of wealth. What did he really know about her? The question brought me to the point – I was then leaning over the old South Gate Bridge, looking down into the River Lee, far from sweet-smelling at low tide – thinking again not of him alone but of myself and him, as we were when we were here, at college together, years ago. What did I really ever know about him? My Aunty Anna was dead, replaced by what would have been described in one of her violet-covered novelettes as 'Miss Anna Whelan, A Country Lady in reduced circumstances', with nothing left to her from her better days but her memories and her fur coat; defrauded and impoverished of thousands of pounds – her lost fortune would be at least that much within a matter of weeks – by a slick stockbroker. Had my Mel ever existed?

We are not one person. We pass through several lives of faith, ambition, sometimes love, often friendship. We change, die and live again. In that cosy cottage of his had I been the guest of a ghost? Myself a ghost? If he was a new man his Sheila might know him. I did not. For all I knew, she was creating him. All I knew, as I rose from the parapet and walked back to the car, was that I must return to his cottage, as I must leave it, in the most careful silence.

I got back in time to join him and the local curate in another of Sheila's cool five-to-one martinis. Over the dinner, which was just as good as the one the night before, I left the talk to Mel and his guest, all about archaeology, birds, the proposed airport, Cork's current political gossip. I envied the pair of them. Nobody in a capital city can ever be so intimately and intensely absorbed about local matters as provincials always are about the doings and the characters of their city-states. The curate left early. Mel drove Sheila home immediately after. He returned, within twenty minutes.

I was standing with my hand on the high mantelpiece of the fireplace listening to the *verso* of the *Siegfried Idyll*, the end of the last act of *Die Walküre*. As he came in I raised a silencing hand, excited as I was by the heroic loveliness of this music that lays Brünhilde on the mountainside in Valhalla, at the centre of encircling fires through which a young man, who will be Siegfried, will one day break to deliver her with a kiss. Mel threw himself into his armchair, his hands behind his head, and we both listened until the music ended and the silence and the dark of the country began to hum again in our ears. For a while we said nothing. Then I did what I had promised not to do.

'Well?' I asked, looking down at him.

'Well?' he said, looking up at me.

'Do I congratulate you?'

'On what?'

'On your Brünhilde.'

Lazily he rolled his head on the back of his chair.

'Meaning no? Or that you don't know?'

Again he slowly rolled his head.

'Giving nothing away? Mel, you used not to be so damn cautious. What has happened to you? Come on, Mel, take a chance on life. Begin by giving Aunty Anna her divvies.'

'Aha? So she refused our gift?'

'She refused. Also she will trouble you no more. She is now convinced that you are a fraudulent stockbroker who has robbed her of a fortune. Come on, man! Gamble for once in your cautious life. Stop being a fraudulent broker.'

'Are you suggesting that I should let your aunt blackmail me?'

'I'm suggesting that you forget the idol you have made outside in the woodshed. It's not you. It can't be you. The Mel I knew can't be that fancy portrait of an unbreakable, incorruptible, crusty, self-absorbed old man, stiff-necked with principles and pride and priggishness. It is a false god. Kick it out on the rubbish heap. When you have made yourself a real image of yourself you'll find there is nothing so terribly frightening about giving Aunty Anna her divvies – or marrying Sheila.'

I had said 'frightening' because immediately I started suggesting that he was different to whatever he wanted to be I had seen his eyes under his blond eyelashes contract, a blush appear on his cheekbones under their grey outcrops of hair, his mouth begin to melt. With a flick he threw away the sudden fear.

'I haven't changed. I am what I am, always was and intend always to be. And if I am a prig, as you so kindly call me, I'm content to be a prig. It's better than being a cockeyed dreamer like you and your mad aunt.'

'Then why are you playing with the girl?'

'I am not.'

'In that case you might wipe that lipstick off your cheek.'

'You know nothing about her.' He paused. 'She has a boyfriend. He was waiting for her again at her cottage tonight.'

'I shouldn't be surprised if she had a dozen boy-friends. A girl as pretty as that! You have seen him often?'

'I have. He comes around here on his motor-bicycle whenever she stays a bit later than usual. Just to offer her a lift home. Just by way of no harm. Each time, she goes off with him at once. I followed them one night. I saw them kissing and hugging under a tree. If she can deceive him she could deceive me. If I married her I might be unhappy all my life, I'd be jealous and suspicious of her all my life.'

'You make me sick! *You* might not be happy? Why don't you say she might not be happy? What sort of a thing do you think marriage is? One long honeymoon? Happiness is a bonus. You smuggle it. You work for it. It comes and goes. You have to be in the market to snatch it. Where's your realism? He who does not speculate cannot accumulate. Stop being such a coward! Live, man, live!'

'I prefer to be logical.'

'Then you certainly will not give Aunty Anna her imaginary divvies, and you will have to sack your imaginary Sheila, and then you will be very unhappy indeed.'

'I may be. It will wear off. And, anyway, it's none of your damn business.'

For a couple of moments we looked at one another hatefully. Then I turned and without saying goodnight went to my room. Almost immediately I heard the front door slam. Parting the curtains I saw him stride down the path, out into the moonlit road and around the corner under the deep shadows of the trees towards where we had gone yesterday to watch the kingfishers, the nesting heron and that unlikely, crested, exotic bird. For a second my heart went out to him. Then I shrugged him off in despair. I was awakened – my watch said it was two o'clock – by the sound of the Brünhildeian flames wavering, leaping, pulsing from their mountaintop among the gods. I, in bed, he, by the ashen fire, listened to it together. After it died away I heard his door click.

In the morning I rose to find him already up and in his spotless yellow-and-white kitchen making coffee and toast.

'Morning, Mel!'

'Hello! Sleep well? I'm the cook on Monday mornings. She leaves everything ready, as you see,' nodding to the napery, china and silverware on the table.

She had even left a tiny bouquet of polyanthuses, alyssum and cowslips in a vase.

He was dressed for the city in his black jacket, with black and grey-striped trousers, grey Suède waistctoat, stiff white collar and striped shirt, a small pearl tie-pin in his grey tie. Over the coffee he talked about birds, and for that while, as on the Saturday, he was again his old attractive, youthful, zestful self. He talked of the hoopoe, saying, 'It cannot have been one – they pass us by in the spring.' He talked about night-jars. He sounded knowledgeable about owls. When we were ready to go he saw to it that every curtain was drawn ('The sun fades the mahogany') and every window carefully fastened, took down his bowler hat and umbrella, double-locked the door, felt it twice, looked all over the front of the cottage, and we drove off into another sunbathed morning.

On the way into town we picked up Sheila outside her roadside cottage, and after that we did not speak at all until he dropped her at his office. There I tried to insist on his not seeing me off at the station – he was a busy man, Monday morning and all that, he must have lots to attend to – and he insisted against my insisting, and we almost squabbled again before he gave in so far as to go into his office to ask if there was anything urgent. He brought me in with him, and formally introduced me to his chief accountant and his book-keeper. While he ruffled through his mail, I chatted with them, and noted the Turkish carpet, and all his modern gadgets, and thought that this was the place where Aunty Anna began to change. At the station he insisted on buying me the morning papers, and on waiting by my carriage door until the train should carry me away. I thanked him for our enjoyable weekend, assured him I meant it, praised his cottage, remembered the food and the wine, promised that we would meet again, to which he nodded, and exchanged a few polite, parting words. As the porters started to slam the last doors, and pull up the windows against the rank smells of the tunnel at the platform's end, he said, his pointed face lifted below my window, his eyes sullen above the two little tufts of greying hair on his cheekbones:

'You will be pleased to hear, by the way, that I have decided to give your aunt her dividends, as usual. Naturally, we go halves in that.'

I leaned down and grasped his shoulder.

'And marry Sheila?'

'I know when I'm licked. I'm going to give her the sack this morning. I'll have to get a new housekeeper. I am going to ask your Aunty Anna.'

'But she's seventy! And a lady in reduced circumstances. She will refuse.'

'Not when she sees my cottage,' he said arrogantly. 'I'm only there on weekends. She can imagine she is a real lady for five days in the week. Not bad! And she has been a cook. And she won't tempt my flesh. Hail! And Farewell!'

The train started to puff and chug and he and the platform slid slowly away.

Seconds later I was in the tunnel. My window went opaque. I got the rancid smell of the underworld. 'And Farewell?' Evidently I was not, it was a just judgement on my presumption, to meet him ever again. I had probed, I had interfered, I had uncovered his most secret dream and destroyed it by forcing him to bring it to the test of reality. I had been tiresome in every way. I had counted on finding the Mel I had thought I had always known, felt affronted at finding him rather different, tried to make him more different, and yet at the same time have my old Mel, and was furious when he insisted on remaining whatever he thought he always had been. In such irreducibly plenary moments of total mess, shame and embarrassment the truth can only be trite, though none the less the truth for that. Youth only knows embryos. Life is equivocal. Life is a gamble. Friendship is frail. Love is a risk. All any man can do when fate sends some shining dream his way is to embrace it and fight for it without rest or reason because we do all the important things of life for reasons (It *has* been said!) of which reason knows nothing – until about twenty years after.

For that mile of tunnel I had them all there together with me in that dark carriage, with the cold smell of steam, and an occasional splash of water on the roof from the ventilation shafts to the upper air. Abruptly, the tunnel shot away and I felt like a skin-diver soaring from the sea to the light of day. Green country exploded around me on all sides in universal sunlight. Small, pink cars went ambling below me along dusty side-roads to the creamery. Black-and-white cows munched. Everywhere in the fields men were at their morning work. I opened the window to let in the fresh air. Then, with only occasional glances out at the fields floating away behind me, and at certain images and thoughts that became fainter and fewer with the passing miles, I settled down to my newspapers and the gathering thoughts of my home and my work.

I have never seen him since, although we are both now ageing men, but, perhaps three times, it could be four, as if a little switch went click in my memory he has revisited me – a dubious shadow, with two grey tufts on his cheeks and a long nose like Sherlock Holmes . . . No more. He did write to me once, after – not, I observed, *when* – Aunty Anna died, in his service, aged eighty-one. Piously, he had attended to everything. He enclosed some snapshots that he had found in her bag: herself as a young woman, horses on the Curragh, myself as a young boy. In her will, he mentioned, she had bequeathed her dividends to him.

The Heat of the Sun

They never said, 'Let's go down to Rodgers', although it was old Rodgers who owned the pub; they said, 'Let's go down to Uncle Alfie.' A good pub is like that, it is the barman who makes it, not the boss. They gave their custom to Rodgers, they gave their confidence to Alfie. He knew them all, some of them ever since they were old enough to drink their first pint in a pub. He knew their fathers, mothers, brothers, sisters, girls, prospects, wages, hopes, fears and what they were always calling their ideas and their ideals and that he called their ould guff. Always their friend, sometimes their philosopher, he was rarely their guide. Your da gave you money (sometimes) and you hardly thanked him for it. Alfie loaned it. You da gave you advice and you resented it. Alfie could give you a rap as sharp as lightning, and you accepted it because he gave it as your equal. Your da never had any news. Alfie knew everything. He was your postman, passing on bits of paper with messages in pencil: 'Deirdre was asking after you, try 803222, Hughesy.' Or, 'For Jay's sake leave a half-note for me, Paddywhack.' He might hand you out a coloured postcard with a foreign stamp, taken from the little sheaf stuck behind the cash register. The sheeting around the register was as wall-papered as a Travel Bureau with coloured postcards from all over the world. Best of all, he was there always: his coat off, his shirtsleeves rolled up, his bowler hat always on his balding red head, a monument in a white apron, with a brogue like an echo in an empty barrel.

You pushed the two glass doors in like a king.

'Hi, Alfie!'

'Jakus, Johnny, is that yourself?' With a slap on the shoulder and your drink slid in front of you unasked. 'Fwhere were you this time? Did yoo have a good voyage?'

'Not bad. Same old thing – Black Sea, the Piraeus, Palermo, Naples, Genoa. Crumby dumps!' Your half pint aloft. 'What's the best port in all creation, Alfie?'

'As if yoo needed to ask me!'

'Here's to it, and God bless it. *Dublin town, O Dublin town / That's where I long to be, / With the friends so dear to me, / Grafton Street where it's all so gay. / And the lights of Scotsman's Bay.* Theme-song of every poor bloody exile of Erin. Up the rebels. Long live the Queen of Sheba. How's Tommy? How's Angela? How's Casey, Joanna, Hughesy, Paddywhack? Does my little black-eyed Deirdre still love me?'

'Paddy was in on Chuesday night. He's working with the Gas Company now.'

'Poor old Paddywhack! Has he the gold wristlet still? And the signet ring? Will the poor bugger never get a decent job?'

'His wife had another child. That's six he has now.'

'Sacred Heart!'

'Hughesy is going strong with Flossie.'

(He noticed that Deirdre was being passed over.)

'Sure that line is four years old. When is the bastard going to make an honest woman of her?'

'Is it a busman? She's aiming higher than that. The trouble with yoo young fellows is ye pick gurls beyond yeer means. Yeer eyes are bigger than yeer balls. Leave them their youth. Wedded, bedded and deaded, the world knows it.'

He was anti-woman. Everybody knew he had a wife somewhere, and three kids, separated five years ago. She was before their time – none of them had ever seen her. Poor old Alfie! In hope and in dreams and in insecurity is life. In home and in safety is . . . He should know, he had it every time he came home. Like tonight:

'Oh, no! Johnny! You're not going out from us on your first night home? We haven't seen you for four months! And your father and me looking forward to a nice bit of a chat. About your future, Johnny. About your plans, Johnny. About your prospects. Sit down there now and be talking to us.'

You sat back. They talked. You mumbled. The end of it was always the same. After another half-hour of twitching you said it again.

'I think I'll drop down to Uncle Alfie for an hour to see the boys. I won't be late, Mum. But leave the key under the mat. Don't wait up for me, I'll creep in like a mouse.'

Hating the way they looked at one another, knowing well that you wouldn't be in before one in the morning – if then – shoes in hand, head cocked for the slightest tweak of a bedspring upstairs, feeling a right bastard or, if with God's help, you were tight enough, feeling nothing but your way. Hell roast 'em! Why couldn't they understand that when you cabled, 'Coming home Thursday stop love stop Johnny,' it meant you wanted to see them okay, and you were bringing presents for them, okay, and it would be nice to have your own old room, okay, but what you were really seeing was the gleam of the bottles, and the wet mahogany, and the slow, floating layers of smoke, shoulders pushing, hands shooting, everybody talking at the top of his voice to be heard and old Alfie grinning at ye all like an ape. God Almighty! When a fellow has only seven lousy days shore leave . . .

It was dry October, the softest twinge of faintest fog, the streets empty, a halo around every light, a right night for a landfall. Tramping downhill, peaked cap slanted, whistling, he foresaw it all. A dollar to a dime on it – Alfie would resume exactly where they left off four months ago:

'Johnny! It is high time yoo thought of settling down.'

'Gimme a chance, Alfie. I'm only twenty-three. I'll settle down some day. Why don't you say that to Loftus or Casey?'

'Loftus will find it hard. With that short leg. Anyway I mean settle down ashore. That wandering life you're leading! It's no life!'

'I'm not ready, Alfie. I want to meet the right girl. I'm mad about Deirdre, but she's always talking about motorcars, and houses in Foxrock, and Sunday morning sherry parties. I'm not sure of her. The right girl is damn hard to find. It's a funny thing, Alfie, all the nice women I meet are married women.'

'An ould shtory. And the ladies tell me all the nice men are married men. I think the truth is that no wan is ready until they know by heart the music that tames the wild bashte – know it and are beginning to forget it. I don't think Deirdre is the right sawrt for you at all, Johnny. She's too expensive for you. She's too ambitious. She's like Flossie – playing with Hughesy, trying to learn the chune on the cheap, as you might say. Johnny! If I were you, I'd choose a woman of experience. What'd suit you, now, down to the ground would be a nice, soft, cosy, widow-woman that knows every chune in the piper's bag.'

'Oh, for God's sake, Alfie! With a wooden leg? And a yellow wig? And a blue bank-book? I'm young, Alfie. What I dream about, in the middle watch, looking up at the stars, is a young, beautiful, exquisite, lovely, fond, right-dimensional Irish girl of eighteen. Like my little Deirdre.

Pure as the driven snow. Loyal and true. Gentle as the dawn. Deirdre, without the motor-car!'

Alfie would draw up from the counter and make a face as if he was sucking alum.

'You could sing it if yoo had the voice for it. *"She was luvely and fair, as the roase of the Summer, But it was not her beauutye aloane tha-at won me . . ."'*

He would snatch it from him tonight:

'"*Oh no! 'Twas the truth in her eyes ever dawning, That made me love Mary, the Rose of Tra-a-leee.*" A hundred per cent right, Alfie. Lead me to her.'

'I wouldn't give you two pinnies for a gurl of eighteen – she couldn't cook an egg for you. And dimensions are all very fine and dandy, but they don't lasht, boy. They don't lasht! Did I ever tell yoo about the fellow that married the opera singer? She was like an angel out of heaven on the stage. In the bed she was no better to him than an ould shweeping brush. He used to wake her up in the middle of the night and say, "Sing, damn yoor sowl!"'

Aboard ship he had told them that one many times. Always the old deck-hands would nod solemnly and say, 'And e's dead right, chum! Feed me and love me, what more can a man ask for?' Well, if he said it tonight he would be ready for him; drawing himself up, with one hand flat on his top, left, brass button:

'Alfie! In this rotten, cheating, stinking, lousy, modern world my generation is going to *fight* for our ideals!'

Four miles out over the shadow sea the light on the Kish bank winked drowsily. Fog? It was so quiet along the promenade that he could hear the small waves below him sucking into the rocks. Wind soft from the south. The only person he passed was a Civic Guard in a cape. He turned right, then left, passed the Coal Harbour, wheeled right again, left, and there were the lights flowing out on the pavement. He pushed the two glass doors in like a king.

'Hi! . . .'

He stopped. The young barman was staring at him with uplifted eyebrows. He looked around. The place was like a morgue. He recognized old Molly Goosegog, her fat legs spread, soaking it up as usual with the one-armed colonel. Three business types, their hats on, hunched over a table, talking low. In the farthest corner two middle-aged women were drinking gins and bitters. Dyed, dried, skewered and skivered, two old boiling hens, cigarettes dangled from their red beaks. He moved slowly to the counter.

'Where's Alfie?' he asked quietly.

'On leave.'

'Alfie never took leave in his life unless he took leave of his senses.'

'Well, he's on leave now. What can I get you, sir?'

Sir! Sullenly he said, 'A large whiskey,' although he had been planning a night of draught porter. Alfie would have said, 'Johnny! There is no such thing on earth as a *large* whiskey.' Or he might have said nothing but come back with a half pint of draught and said, 'That'll be better for you.'

Was it because it was Thursday night? Nobody much ever came on Thursday night: less even than came on Friday night. Everyone stony. Behold my beeves and fatlings are all killed, and nobody cometh to eat them. Seven lousy nights and the first a flop? Go forth into the highways and by-ways. From pub to pub? The whiskey appeared before him. The barman stood waiting. He looked up.

'Four and sixpence, sir.'

With Alfie, you let it run for a week, for two, for three, for as long as you liked. Then you asked, 'What's on the slate, Alfie?' and, if you were flush, you paid a half-note over and above for future credit. Man knoweth not the hour nor the night. He paid out four shillings and a sixpenny bit. The barman rang it up and retired down the counter to lean over his *Herald*.

'How long is Alfie going to be on leave?'

The fellow barely glanced up.

'I don't know, I'm only here this past two weeks.'

'Is the boss in?'

'He's gone down to the chapel. The October Devotions.'

Thinking of his latter end. *Dies irae, dies illae.* Back in Newbridge with the Dominicans. All Souls Night. He glanced at the door. Would there be anyone down at The Blue Peter? Or in Mooney's? Maybe in The Purty Kitchen?'

'Any message for me there behind the old cashbox?'

'Name?'

'Kendrick.'

The barman, his back to him, went through the light sheaf. Without turning he said, 'Nothing,' shoved it back and returned to his *Herald*.

Out of sight out of mind. Bugger the whole lousy lot of them! And Deirdre along with them! The glass doors swished open and there were Paddywhack and Loftus. He leaped from his stool.

'Hi, scouts!'

'Johnny!'

Handshakes all round. Paddy was as hungry-looking as a displaced Arab. His shirtsleeves too long. The gold wristlet. The signet ring. Loftus, as always, as lean and yellow as a Dane. Hoppity Loftus with his short leg. He never worked. He was a Prod and had an English accent, and he lived off his mother. All he did was to get her breakfast in the morning and have her supper ready for her at night. She worked in the Sweep.

'Name it, boys! I'm standing!'

Paddy looked thirstily at the glass of whiskey.

'Are you on the hard tack?'

'Naw! Just this bloody place gave me the willies. The usual?' He commanded the barman. 'Two halfpints. Make it three and I'll use this as a chaser. God, it's marvellous to see ye! Come on, come on! Give! Give! Gimme all the dirt. Tell me more, tell me all. Are you still with the Gas Company, Paddy?'

'I'm with a house-agent now. Looney and Cassidy. In Dame Street.' He made a fish-face. 'NBG Paid on commission. Just to tide me over a bad patch.' He laughed cheerfully. 'The wife is preggers again.'

'Paddy! I dunno how you do it.'

'I'm told,' said Loftus lightly, 'that it's a very simple matter, really.'

'How's your mother, Loftus?'

A rude question. Loftus shrugged it away. They took their drinks to one of the round tables. Paddy lifted his glass.

'Johnny! You don't know how lucky you are. A steady job, cash in your pocket, a girl in every port.'

'And as brown,' said Loftus lifting his glass, 'and as round as a football.'

'Me round?' he shouted, ripped open the jacket of his uniform and banged his narrow waist. 'Feel that, go on, feel it! Hard as iron, boy! Eight stone ten. You,' he said condescendingly, rebuttoning, 'must be about ten stone eight.' He paused. Then he had to say it: 'Does Deirdre still love me?'

Loftus's eyes glinted as he proffered the sponge on the spear.

'I saw her two weeks ago in a red Triumph. A medical student from Trinity, I believe. She looked smashing.'

His heart curdled, his throat tightened, he laughed loudly.

'So the little bitch is betraying me, eh?'

He could see her, with her dark hair curled down on one shoulder as if she had a monkey on her head. The red lips. The high bosoms.

'It's just because you're not around much,' Paddy said comfortingly. 'Wait until she hears you're home!'

'How are all those girls of yours?' Loftus smiled. 'In foreign parts.'

Paddy poured sad oil.

'Too bad about poor Alfie?'

'I heard nothing,' he said sourly. 'Nobody writes to me. Where *is* the ould devil!'

'You didn't know! Hospice for the Dying. Cancer. These last three months. It'll be any day now.'

It gagged him. There was a long silence. His first death. The double doors let in Hughesy and Flossie; their oldest and youngest – a blonde mop, black lashes, a good looker, but not a patch on his D. Their welcomes were muted. They sat down stiffly like people who did not mean to stay.

'"Here,"' he chanted mournfully, '"here, the gang's all here."'

'Not all of us,' Paddy said.

'This is a committee meeting, really,' Hughesy said, taking charge of it at once. 'Well?' he asked Paddywhack and Loftus. 'How much can we raise?'

'We're gathering for Mrs Alfie,' Paddywhack explained. 'She hadn't a sou.'

'I managed to borrow five bob,' Flossie said, taking two half-crowns from inside her glove and laying them on the table.

'That,' said Hughesy, putting down half a crown, 'is all I can manage.'

Paddywhack squirmed and said, 'Six kids and another coming, and Thursday night.'

Loftus showed empty palms. 'Unless I could pop something?'

He felt worse than a wanderer – a stranger.

'Mrs Alfie? How in God's name did ye meet *her*?' he asked Hughesy.

'It was Alfie asked us to keep an eye on her and the kids. I saw him again today,' he told the others.

'How is he?' he asked.

Hughesy looked away.

'Alas, poor Yorick,' Loftus said. 'A skull!'

Flossie began to cry.

'But where's the rest of the gang? Joanna, and Tommy, and Angela and Casey.'

He stopped short of Deirdre. Paddywhack shook his head and made faint gestures.

'I nearly didn't come myself. Can you manage anything, Johnny?'

He took out his pocketbook and planked down a pound note.

'Good man!' said Hughesy, and looked up at the barman standing over them, and down at the pound note. He smiled apologetically at Johnny. 'Any more of that nice stuff?'

'Come on, scouts, I'm standing. If it's to be a wake, for Christ's sake let it be a wake. What's yours, Flossie? Still sticking to the dry sherry? Hughesy? The old pint?' He nodded to the barman, who departed silently. 'Let me in on this. Tell me all about Alfie.'

As the drinks warmed them they talked. A man, by God! A true friend if there ever was one. They don't often come like that nowadays. True from his bald head to the soles of his feet. Tried and true. A son of the soil. A bit of old Ireland. Vanishing down the drain. Not one bit of cod about him. His jokes . . . We shall not look upon his like again. The pound note melted. Paddywhack said, 'Life is a mystery all right. She looks such a nice woman, and she *is* a nice woman, and full of guts, not one word of complaint, and three kids. What in God's name happened to them?' They told him, asking how she lived, that she used to work as a dressmaker. 'Yes, he did!' Loftus answered him. 'After a fashion, he did. He supported her. After a fashion.' Flossie said she would never come to this pub again. They agreed with Hughesy that Dublin wouldn't be the same without him. She said the fact was he had nothing to do with all those . . . They followed her eyes down to Molly Goosegog and the one-armed colonel, and the three business types, and the two boiled hakes with the gins and bitters. Hughesy slapped the table. 'And that's a true bill, Flossie! He was one of us. Old in body but young in heart. You agree, Johnny?' He agreed that Alfie was the only man he ever met who understood them. 'He fought for his ideals.' They talked of understanding, and ideals, and truth, and true love, and how well Alfie understood what it means to be young, and to believe in things, that was it – to believe in things. A second pound was melting, and it was after ten, when Flossie said to Hughesy that she must go home soon.

'Mind your few quid, Johnny,' Hughesy said. 'What's left there will be enough. A dozen bottles of stout, say a dozen and a half. Just to cheer her up. We'll drop around for a minute, Flossie. Just to cheer her up.'

'One for the road,' he insisted, and held them. They leaned back.

It was nearly eleven when they left in a bunch, carrying the three brown-paper bags of stout, out into the dry streets, the nebulous night, under the dim stars and the gathering clouds that were lit by the city's glow. Loftus said it was a fine night for a ramble. Hughesy laughed and said, 'Or for courting.' Two by two, hooting merrily backwards and forwards at one another, they wound up among shaggy, dim-lit squares with names like Albert Gardens, Aldershot Place or Portland Square, all marked on green and white tablets in Irish and English, until they came to a basement door and, stepping down to it, rang and waited in a bunch under a stone arch. In the dark they were suddenly silent, listening. A light went on over the door. She opened it.

Alfie's youth. She was soft and welcoming. All the parts of her face seemed to be running into one another, dissolving like ice-cream in the sun, her mouth melting, her blue-blue eyes swimming. A loose tress of her grey-fair hair flowed over a high forehead. Her voice was as timid as butter. She was not a bad-looking woman, and for a moment a little flame of youth flared up in her when they introduced him to her, and she laughed softly and said, 'So this is Johnny! He said you were the baby of the lot.' She held his hand in her two hands, moist and warm as if she had been washing something, and he remembered a line from a poem they used to read at school, long forgotten, never understood. *Fear no more the heat of the sun . . .*

'Glad to meet you, Mrs Alfie,' he said and realized for the first time that he did not know Alfie's name.

'We brought a few drinks,' Hughesy explained. 'Just to brighten the night.'

'Come in, boys, come in. Talk low,' she begged. 'Jenny is only just gone to sleep.'

The low room was small and untidy, and smelled of soap. The fire was ashen. She had only two glasses. They sat in a circle and drank out of cups, or from the bottle-necks. Moist cloths hung drooping and wet on a line; the stuffing of the chairs tufted out, he saw a toy horse with three legs, torn green paperbacks, a house-of-cards half collapsed on a tray. Staring at her, he heard nothing of their whispering; both surprised and pleased to hear her laugh so often. He became aware that Hughesy and Flossie were fading out, for the last bus. Around midnight Paddywhack said he must give the wife a hand with the kids, and slid away. She put a few bits of sticks in the grate and tried ineffectually to remake the fire. Then Loftus clumped off home to his mother and there were only the two of them in the room, stooping over one flicker in the ashes, whispering, heads together.

Only once again did she mention Alfie; when she said, 'They're a grand bunch. Ye are all good boys. Decent young men. It was what he always said about ye.'

'Did you see him often?'

'Hardly at all. He might drop in after he shut the pub. To see the children. He told me he was always at ye to settle down. Hughesy, and Flossie, and Casey, and Loftus and you. Do you like Loftus?'

'He's cold. And bitter.'

'Is Deirdre your girl?'

'Yes. But I think she's letting me down. Did you meet her? She's a smasher.'

'She is a beautiful girl. I don't want to interfere in your life, Johnny, but I would be inclined to think that I would nearly say that she might have a hard streak in her.'

'Not like you?' he smiled.

'I'm not faulting her. A woman must think of her own good.'

There he was off, full-cock, about youth, ideals, loyalty, truth, honesty, love, things that only the gang understood, everybody else talking to you about your future, and good jobs, and making money. 'Ireland is the last fortress. The Noah's Ark of the world. No place like it.' And he should know, an exile! She agreed, she agreed. She said, 'The people here are warm and natural still in spite of all.' He was with her, all the way with her. 'We are not materialists. Not the best of us.' At that they were both off, whispering breaking into louder talk, hushing, glancing fearfully at the door of the bedroom.

The last flicker of the fire died away. They drank the last bottle of stout between them, passing it from mouth to mouth. Her voice grew softer, her hand when she held his was padded like a cat's. The night became a fugitive. Faintly a foghorn in the bay moaned through a muffled blanket. He looked out and up through the window and saw a yellow blur of street light, and the mist that clung wetly to a fogged tree. She got up to make tea. He followed her into the messy kitchen to help and talk. They came back and she put a few more futile chips of sticks on the warm ashes. She laughed at the slightest thing – when the toy horse toppled, or when he told her about the dog, kicked, and beaten, and mangy, that he bought in Palermo, and how it swam ashore back to its Moorish slum. Or that night in Odessa in the YMCA when he got into a fight by pretending the C stood for Communist.

When it was two o'clock he said, 'You must send me away.' She said, 'Listen to the dripping outside. Oh, don't go away, Johnny!' He said, 'You must sleep.' She said, 'I don't know what sleep is,' and held him by his wrist, frightened to be left alone. 'Listen to the drip-drop,' she wheedled. 'And look! It's yellow as mustard outside. Sleep here. Sleep in my bed. We're friends, aren't we? Just lie and sleep. You're a good boy. I know you. Go in there and lie down.' She led him into the bedroom with its unmade bed. He barely made out the child asleep on a camp-bed, one arm hooped around its head. She took her nightgown from a chair and went out.

He hung up his jacket, removed his shoes and lay down, gazing out the door at the yellow blur of the street lamp. It was as cold as the grave in the bed. She came back in her rumpled nightdress, her hair about her shoulders, got in under the clothes beside him and put out the light. The yellow street lamp bleared in through the bedroom door.

'It's bloody cold,' he said.

'We'll soon warm up. You should have taken your clothes off and got under the blankets, sure what does it matter?'

They lay in silence for a while, hearing nothing but their breathing and the faint, far fog-horn. He moved closer and began to whisper into her ear about what it means to be homeless, and she whispered to him about the time she came up to Dublin for the first time from County Cavan, for her honeymoon. She never once went back there. He whispered to her, 'You are a heroine.' She said, 'You're a good lad, Johnny.'

After a while more she said, 'We must sleep,' and he lay on his back, his hands clasped behind his head. After a long while he said, 'Deirdre is a bitch,' and she said, 'She is very young.' After another while he whispered, 'Try to sleep,' and she whispered, 'Yes.' After another long time he said, 'You're not sleeping. You are thinking of him. When will you know?' She said, 'It might be any minute. Then I'll sleep. And sleep. And sleep.'

Sleep stole on him. He woke abruptly, at five o'clock. She was no longer in the bed. He saw her in the front room, a man's overcoat on her shoulders, leaning her elbows on the window-sill staring out. In his stockinged feet he went to her and put his arm around her shoulder.

'You can't sleep?'

She did not stir. Her face had melted completely, her two cheeks were wet. He did not know what to say to her. By the cleansed lamplight outside he saw that the fog had lifted. She whispered. 'It's all over.'

'You can't tell!'

'I know it. I'll go out and ring the hospital at six o'clock. But I know it.' Her face screwed up and more tears oozed from her closed eyes. 'You'd better go, Johnny. Your people may be worrying.'

He dressed, shivering, among the empty bottles of stout on the floor, some of them standing to attention, some of them rolled on their sides. He put on his peaked cap with the white top, patted her hooped back, said, 'God help you,' and went out up the steps to the street level. It was black as night. From the pavement he looked down at the shadow of her face behind the misty glass, lifted a hand and walked away.

When he came to the Coal Harbour he halted on the centre of the railway bridge and leaned his hands on the wet parapet. Six miles across the level bay the string of orange lights flickered along the shoreline, and farther west the city's night-glow underlit its mirror of cloud. The harbour water, dark as oil, held the riding-light of a coaltub. He drew in deep breaths of the raw air and blinked his sanded eyes. He said quietly, 'I still love you, you bitch.' Then he lifted his head, put his two palms about his mouth like a megaphone, and howled in a long, wild howl across the bay, 'Do you love me?'

The city lay remote under its dull mirror.

He rubbed the stone and remembered, 'Quiet consummation have; and renowned be thy grave' – and marched homewards, arms swinging, chin up, white cap slanted. The water of the main harbour was inscribed by a slow wheel of light. Far out from the Kish bank a flight of light beamed and died at regular intervals. The whole way home the only sound he heard was a faint, faraway humming like a bee, a dawn-flight out of Dublin across the sea.

As he stole indoors a voice whispered, upstairs, 'Are you all right, darling?'

'Okay, Mum!'

'Daddy's asleep.'

'Okay, Mum.'
'Sleep well, love.'
'Okay, Mum. I'll sleep. And sleep. And sleep.'

The Human Thing

It is not always cold in the Basses-Alpes – but on that late September evening (was it as long as ten years ago?) when I rang his presbytery bell it was very cold. The only answer to my call was the wind funnelling down that tiny, flagged street of his, narrow as a bedspread and smelly as a bedpan. It was like aerial gunnery aimed over thirty miles of forests and ravines to strike the sea five miles out beyond the warm beaches of Nice where I had toasted myself that morning in the Riviera sun. Was I to have to spend the night alone up here in Argons? And, if so, was there even a half-decent hotel in Argons? It would be dusk within an hour. I rang again and pressed for shelter against his studded door. Suddenly it opened and a woman passed hastily out into the narrow street. All I saw was a snapshot glimpse of a brightly made-up mouth in a dark face, a stocky figure, well dressed, a bit over-blown in the Italian way that you so often see along this border. Afterwards I wondered if she had been wearing a long black veil like a war-widow. The old housekeeper all but closed the door after her, glared at me with two sooty eyes from under a top-knot like the ace of spades, accepted my card and my tiny letter of introduction, closed the door within an inch of its jamb and backed into the house. This meant at least that he was at home, and I straightway forgot everything except what the Abbé de Saint Laurent had told me about him a few days before in his sunbathed little study in Nice.

'Argons?' he had said. 'In that case I know the very man for you. You must call on my good confrère the Abbé Morfé. He will tell you everything you want to know about the traditional life of the Basses-Alpes.'

And straightway sat to his desk and began to write on a small sheet of paper, murmuring over one sunlit shoulder as he wrote:

'He is not French, of course. Although you would never suspect it he has been with us so long – for at least twenty years. He is an Irishman. One of several who volunteered for the French mission after the War, when we were badly in need of priests. As we still are! You may talk to him freely. Not,' he smiled back at me around the corner of his glasses, 'that you will need to. He will do the talking. How do you spell your name? Thank you. A very outspoken man. Sometimes, I think, a little too outspoken. But,' and here he turned right around to me, 'zealous! Beyond my vocabulary. A downright man. And absolutely fearless.' He turned back to his desk to inscribe the tiny envelope. 'The perfect priest for the mountains. Ireland, as you must know, was never Romanized. So you, as an Englishman . . . ' (He did not observe my sigh; I am always being mistaken for an Englishman.) ' . . . will understand readily what I mean when I say that he represents the best, the very best of *l'église des barbares.*'

He folded his small letter into its small envelope, handed it to me courteously, and wafted me upwards and onwards towards nether Gaul.

As if under another wild blast of wind the door was flung open. I saw a powerful-looking countryman. His face was the colour of raw bacon cured by the sun and the wind. In his left hand he held my card, in his right a fat claw-hammer which he flung behind the door with such a clatter that for a second I was taken aback by the violence of the gesture; all the more so because he was shouting back into the house, '*Mais, je vous ai dis que je ne la connais pas!*' He turned back to me, warmly welcoming, cried, 'Come in, Sean! Come in!' and I was straightway back in the County Mayo; though in Ireland only a Protestant clergyman would have looked so indigent. His soutane was old and dusty, his boots were unlaced, he wore an old, fraying straw hat on the back of his balding poll, he was smoking a pipe mended with twine.

'I was making a coop for the hens!' he said.

'I'm interrupting you?'

'The most pleasant interruption in the world!' he laughed, and with one big hand on my shoulder he drew me in and invited me to stay not only for the night but for as long as I pleased: to which I cautiously replied that it could, alas, only be for one night. When we were in his living-room – oh! the joy of that sizzling log fire! – he at once produced a full bottle of Tullamore Dew, which, I noticed, was not only dusty but had never been opened. He sank as slowly as an elephant into his leather-covered armchair and began to talk non-stop about Ireland.

Everything in the room was of the region, and it was all as darkly impersonal as a convent: the hand-wrought firedogs, the heavy furniture that had obviously been made on the spot a long time ago, the greying, pious prints, the brown tiles, the adze-marked beams under a ceiling that had once been white plaster and was now tea-coloured from years of wood smoke and nicotine. As my feet thawed my heart rose – all this was exactly the sort of thing I needed for my article. But for well over an hour he did not give me a chance to ask him any of the questions that had brought me to his door – he asked all the questions, and rarely waited for my answers. I could see only three tokens of our common country: the until-now unopened bottle of whiskey; the corner of *The Sunday Independent*, still in its folder, still bearing its green Irish stamp, edging out from under the papers of the *midi*; and a small cushion embroidered with green and red leprechauns bulging from under his fat elbow. I could imagine it coming to him, with 'Merry Christmas', from some distant Deirdre or Mary.

At long last he let Ireland drop. Touching the Abbé's note (a little frigidly?) he said:

'Well, so you are going to write about us? And what have you discovered so far, pray?'

'More or less what you'd expect.'

'And,' a little guardedly, 'what would I expect?'

'What every traveller in a strange place expects, that the truth about every place is the sum of everybody's contradictions.'

'Such as?'

'Well, for example, everybody I meet east of the Var tells me that the old, traditional life now exists nowhere except west of the Var, and everybody west of the Var tells me that if I want to see the old ways I must come up here into the mountains. What would you say to that?'

He sniffed, and at once struck the chord that dominated everything else that was to follow.

'Do you know phwat it is?' he said in a buttermilk brogue, with a buttermilk smile, 'I'm not sure that I'm fit to tawlk about this ould counthry at all, at all. 'Tis a quare counthry. To tell you the honest truth, Sean, I'm gettin' a bit fed up with the Frinch. I have to live with them you know.'

Meaning that I was just a tourist? The jab and the brogue delighted and alerted me. A false brogue, as every Irishman knows, is a sure sign that the speaker is about to say something so true that he wants to blunt the edge of it by presenting it as a kind of family joke. I said, adopting the same sword-in-the-scabbard technique:

'Shure and all, isn't it a bit late in the day for you to be feeling that way now, Father? After all your thirty-odd years shepherding thim?'

He looked at me unamiably. A point apiece. We were playing that ancient Irish game known as conversational poker, a game which nobody can win and nobody can lose because nobody may utter the open truth but everybody must give and take a few sharp little smacks of it or the game is no good at all.

'Better late than never,' he said sourly. 'As is the way with most of us?'

He began to talk slowly. Was he feeling his way into my mind? Or into his own? He casually refreshed my glass. But as we progressed I thought I noticed a difference in his way of playing the Game: if we were playing the Game. After all he was a priest, and a French priest, and a French priest of the mountains – a man, that is, for whom the stakes in every game are infinite.

'The Basses-Alpes? Mind you, Sean, the Basses-Alpes aren't such a bad country. Not rich, of course. Anyway not rich the way the coast is rich. But it has things the coast never had and never will have. There are people who like to bask on the Riviera, who like to have Nice sunny apartments and Nice sunny congregations. But, sure, the Riviera isn't country at all! What is the Riviera but one blooming esplanade forty miles long? A string of international resorts without a stem of local character? Without any character! Without any values except cold, commercial cash values. But we aren't poor either. The land down there, you've seen it, is all ravined and gorged. Hard, stony uplands. With their olive groves abandoned, and their villages crumbling, or turned into tourist traps, and their farmhouses for sale to foreigners. And all the young people going. Gone! Lured away down to the bright lights along the coast. All of them wanting to be croupiers, or traffic cops in white helmets, or factory workers in white overalls. When I think of places like St Paul! A sink of iniquity I call it. For all I know it may be a place that you like to visit. And for good reasons, comfortable hotels, good food. But fifty years ago that was a decent, little country hill village. What is it today? Packed to the last corner with what, with who? The *haut monde*! Paahrisians! In bikinis and beach pyjamas! Do you know who the organist in that little church is today? A Protestant! And glad to have him. And now don't start talking to me about arty-arty chapels like that one by Matisse up in Vence. A chapel? It's a bathroom designed by a freethinker.'

'Was Matisse a freethinker?'

'You can have him! Listen! There's one thing on earth that I can't stand and that's milk and water Catholics.'

His eyes glinted. If this was, by any chance, a jab at me, maybe we were still playing the Game. He went on:

'Up here it is different. Up here the forests mean – well, you might call it comparative wealth for some and a good living for all. So our people have stayed on. The bright lights are farther away.' His voice slowed. 'Yes, our people have stayed on.'

'And,' I leaned forward eagerly, 'kept the old life ways?'

He knocked his pipe out with slow, careful taps on the head of a firedog. I had the feeling that the Game was over.

'I'll explain to you what I mean by milk and water religion. I know of instances of women in these parts deliberately going off and having affairs – and I mean respectable, married women with families – for no reason but because it is the modern fashion. Women born and reared in these parts, copying, that's all it is, the ways of places they think better than their own. To be as smart as the best. To be in the fashion. I find that utterly contemptible.'

He was so passionate about it that I demurred, though cautiously since he felt so strongly about it.

'Surely,' I proposed gently, 'one must go by cases? I mean a woman might be terribly unhappy. Her husband might be a boor, or a bore, or even a drunk. She might have met with some man whom she wished she had married, some man she loved or thought she loved . . .'

'That has nothing whatever to do with it! I could understand it if there was a bit of real passion in it. I could make allowances. I could even forgive it. It is my job to forgive. But they do it for the most vulgar of all reasons, just to be up to the minute. To be *à la page*. They do it simply to have something to boast about at the tea-table.'

'And the men?'

'The same! People like that have no religion, no character. They have nothing. That's what I mean by milk and water religion.'

'And for this you blame the gentry?'

'I never mentioned the gentry.'

'You said they want to be as smart as the best. To be in the fashion. Which best? Whose fashion? The nobs'?'

'You never get this sort of thing among the gentry, certainly not among the real noblesse. Oh, of course, you will find sinners among them, as you will everywhere. The flesh is the flesh, high or low. We are all creatures of the flesh. But this thing doesn't come from the flesh. It isn't even honest sensuality. It comes from the corruption of the mind. It comes from meanness of the mind. It's plain, vulgar, bloody tomfoolery. It is indifference. It is spiritual death. It is apostasy.'

He slapped the side of his armchair. An uncomfortable silence fell on us. Was he always as irascible as this?

'Maybe I'm in a pessimistic mood,' he grumbled. 'Gimme your glass. I'm a bad host. Maybe what I need is a week after the grouse in County Mayo.'

'Aye,' I said, more than willing to return to the Game. 'They say there's nothing like a good grouse for a bad theologian.'

'Why is it bad theology, pray?'

'Well, after all, "the greatest of these is charity".'

'Oho! There is always charity.'

(He sounded as if he was a bit sick of charity.)

'This couldn't be a long backwash from the French Revolution? I notice your little street here is called the Rue Carnot.'

'There is also,' he parried back, 'A Rue Saint Roch. That's San Rocco. The good Italian influence. The bond with Rome.'

'Yes!' I said dryly. 'I noticed that Italian influence. In the Place Garibaldi.'

He snarled it:

'That crew!'

We both laughed. (There really is a lot to be said for the urbanity of the Game.) Just then old Ace of Spades came in to say in her sullen voice:

'Dinner is served, Father. And that lady telephoned to say the funeral will be tomorrow at nine o'clock.'

He looked hard at her.

'Anastasia, do you know this Madame Bailly?'

'She has been living in Alberon this five years.'

'Funny that I can't remember her. I'll just ring Father Benoit.' He turned to me. 'He is one of my curates. We have a big parish. We divide it among the three of us.'

I had driven up through Alberon: one of those small places with a couple of sawmills, and with more garages than hotels, which means that everything goes stone-dead after October when the big passes get clogged with snow.

'Let's eat!'

We went into his dining-room. As he flung out his serviette, tucked it under his jaw and began to pour the wine, he said:

'The poor woman's husband was killed this afternoon in an accident. A tree fell right across his back. He owned a hotel, a garage and a sawmill in Alberon. She came about the funeral.' He paused in the act of filling his own glass. 'Bailly?' I know a couple of Baillys around Grasse. And,' he growled, 'nothing much good about any of them'.

'Liberals?' I teased.

'Puh! You mentioned Garibaldi. And Carnot. It would be very interesting study for you to find out at what date these names came in . . . and at what date a lot of other things began to come in.'

We talked at random. Presently he said:

'I don't want you to misunderstand me about the gentry. When all is said and done they are still the best people in France. They're on the way out, of course. They have no political gumption. And no money. And no influence. Your Liberals, as you choose to call them, are pushing them over the last edge of the ravines. What's left of them.' He sipped his wine and frowned. 'Bailly? Somehow or other that name keeps ringing a bell somewhere in what's left of my poor old head.'

'Haven't you the Liber Animarum?' I asked, meaning the thick, black notebook I had been shown once in an Irish presbytery by an old priest who had once been a dear friend of mine. These stubby books have a page to every parishioner: name, business, address, married or single, whether he practises his religion or not, and sometimes, though rarely, a more intimate comment if the priest considers it necessary to probe more deeply. He snorted.

'Ha! Liber Animarium, how are you? 'Tis easy seen that you come from Holy Ireland. Themselves and their card-indexes. What I call IBM Catholicism. It's as much as my two curates and myself can do to get around to visiting our parishioners once every two years. If that! And sometimes none too welcome at that! Have you any idea at all of the size of our parishes? If it wasn't for our housekeepers . . .' He stopped dead. He sighed. 'I must be getting old. I'm losing my grip.'

He rang the little brass bell on the table and waited for her to appear at the door.

'Tell me,' he said. 'Do you really know this Madame Bailly?'

'Everybody in Alberon knows her.'

'Yes, yes, you told me she is from Alberon.'

'I said she lives in Alberon.'

He pushed his chair back and faced her.

'Anastasia! What are you trying to say exactly? Where did she come from?'

'Cannes.'

'And Bailly married her and brought her to Alberon five years ago?'

'M. Bailly's wife and four children are living in Grasse with his mother.'

There was a long silence. He said, 'Bailly sent them away?'

Her sooty eyes stared at him. Her shoulders barely moved. He thanked her and nodded her out. He pushed his dinner away and his face was pale about his tightly clenched lips – the only part of that ruddy face that could grow pale.

'Five years! What sort of a priest am I? What sort of a parish do I run? Under my very nose! And now this person has the insolence to come here and ask me to give him a Christian burial! I'll soon put a stop to that!'

'My God! You can't refuse to bury the man? You can't let him be put into a hole in the ground like an animal?'

'And do you think that after leading this kind of life, giving public scandal for five years, openly and brazenly, that I am going to give him public burial now as a good Catholic? What would my parishioners say? What would they think? Do you think that it's for this I came here thirty-three years ago, to bless scandalmongers like those two apostates?'

'Isn't that a bit extreme? Sinners, yes. Call them that if you like. That, of course. But in mere charity...'

'Charity! Everybody always talks to me about charity! What is charity?'

'Love, I suppose. I suppose those two unfortunate people loved one another.'

'And his wife? And his four children? Did he love *them*?'

'But he may, even at the last minute, have hoped for forgiveness. If you had been there when that tree fell on him would you not have given him Extreme Unction? Anointed his eyes, and hands, and mouth, and prayed for his forgiveness?'

Outside, a wild rush of wind rattled leaves against the pane like a million clamouring fingers.

'Well, I was *not* there,' he said heavily. 'He died as he lived, struck down by the hand of God. I'm going to phone Father Benoit.'

Alone in the room I tried to visualize that stocky Italianate woman I had seen hurrying away from his door. I tried to see her and her dead lover in their hotel in Alberon, and I realized that this was one life story that I would never know. All I could imagine was a hundred spade-heads like old Anastasia in that little hill town besieging her with their cruel silence and their bitter eyes. He came back and slumped into his chair.

'He is out.'

I sat opposite him and I thought: 'And here is another life-story that I will never know!' After a few moments he said, quietly:

'Charity, Sean, is a virtue. It is, as you say, love – the love of all things through God, the love of God in all things. As for your love, human love? It is that, too. As Saint Bonaventure said, it is the life that couples the lover to the beloved. *Vita copulans amantem cum amato.* But it is that in the name of God, for God and by God. One act of love in a lifetime is an immensity. But one mortal sin can of itself destroy all love, and all life, as that man destroyed two lives over and over again before the eyes of the world.' He stopped and got up again. 'This thing must be ended publicly! As it was begun publicly. I must go down there at once.'

'Tonight?'

We both looked at the window. The mistral was at its full force. A wild sheaf of leaves whirled horizontally past the window.

'Let me drive you,' I offered, miserably.

'I'd be glad if you did. I'm in no fit state to drive.'

We buttoned ourselves up in our overcoats, pulled on our berets, and crushed into my little Dauphine. He directed me on the long, winding road where the woods on each side waved in one solid mass like a turbulent sea. I was too busy watching the road to talk. All the way he never spoke except to say 'Fork left', or 'Right here'. I felt like a man driving an executioner to the place of execution and I did not know which of the two of us I disliked the more at that moment. When we entered Alberon the streets were empty and dark. Two cafés were lighted, their windows opaque with condensed moisture. He suddenly said, revealing that he had been thinking in that language:

'*C'est dans la Place . II s'appelle Le Chamois.*'

It was a three-storey house with the usual Alpine roof pitched to a peak and smoothing out at the base to let the great weight of snow slide down and melt on the gutters. On the ground floor there was a café, all dark and buttoned-up. Two windows on the storey above it were lighted. When he got out and was ringing at the door I withdrew to the centre of the little Place to park and wait. It took a couple of rings to produce an answer. When the door opened I saw, against the light inside, the dark outline of the woman who called herself Madame Bailly. He stepped inside at once, the door closed. I was alone with the mistral, the darkness and the empty Place.

The perfect priest for the mountains. Getting a bit fed-up with the Frinch. Nice people and Nice apartments. Absolutely fearless. Down-right. A finger on a switch lit up two more windows upstairs. *Vita copulans amantem cum amato.* Would he be laid out in there on his bed of love? Zealous beyond my vocabulary. The mistral blew around and around me in moaning circles. Two men, an older and a younger, came, heads down, into the square from the left. I saw them pause at the closed-up Café le Chamois, look at its dark window, making some gestures that could only mean, 'Ah yes! I heard that . . . ' Then one of them stretched his arm forward and they went on again, heads down, to, I presumed, one of the other cafés, where no doubt as in every house in the town . . . I started the engine and turned on the heat.

After another long wait those two extra windows went dark. Still he did not come out. One mortal act of love in a lifetime is an immensity. One mortal sin can destroy the whole of that love and of that life for ever. Damn it, why doesn't he finish her off quickly? That, at least, would be a small act of Charity! A big truck and trailer laden with long baulks of timber trundled into the square and out at the other end. Then only the wind and the darkness again.

At last a flood of light beamed out on the pavement as the door opened and I saw his great bulky outline. He was shaking hands with the woman in black. As I peered forward I saw that it was not the same woman. He bowed to her and looked around for me. I drove over to meet him. She slowly closed the door, he clambered in, and silently waved me onward.

I could not see his face in the darkness but by the dashboard light I saw his hand, lying loosely on his thigh, shaking like a man with the palsy.

'Well?' I asked.

He spoke so softly I could barely hear him.

'I could not believe such love existed on this earth.'

'Madame Bailly?'

'She came down from Grasse. With her four children. For the funeral.'

'There will be a funeral?'

'Could I refuse his wife?'

'And the other?'

'The two of them are there together. Comforting one another.'

No more was said until we were back in his living-room, in his dark presbytery, in his tiny, smelly street. There, standing by the grey ash of his dying fire, still in his beret and his long overcoat, he turned on me a face twisted by agony and cried:

'Did I do right?'

'You did the human thing, Father.'

'Ah! The human thing?' He shook his head, uncomforted. He laid his hand in a kindly way on my shoulder. 'Sleep well, you!' – as one who would not. 'And I never told you anything at all, at all, about the ould Basses-Alpes!'

I hardly slept at all. All night the wind moaned through his narrow street, down over every forest, village and black ravine. Were those two women awake? I wished I was down where the bright lights of the esplanades glinted in the whispering sea.

One Man, One Boat, One Girl

1

The first time I met Olly Carson I was sitting on a crate with T. J. Mooney in the Despatch Yard of the factory during the lunch break, each of us holding a bottle of Guinness in each fist. We were celebrating two famous birthdays, my twenty-first and his thirtieth, and T.J. was giving out the score about *Man and Superman*, his favourite anti-female tract. Olly came by, stopped, looked at the two of us out of his comical gooseberry eyes, winked, pulled another bottle of Guinness out of his lunch-bag, sat up beside us without being asked, and started at once on a bawdy story about a barmaid and a champagne cork. From that moment we were a cabal. When he told us that he had only just come over from Sheffield and did not know a soul in Cork I nudged T.J., he looked at me, I raised my eyebrows, and he nodded. Straightway we introduced Olly to the Rules of the River. One man, One boat, One girl.

The next Sunday, by way of initiating him, we sent him off down the Marina while we were getting out the boats from the rowing club. In those days, before cars started ruining the roads, before outboard-motors, and caravans, and cinemas, and Telly, and touring buses, and Teddy Boys and all this bloody modern fal-lal, the Lee used to be full of boats every Saturday and Sunday, and the Marina full of strolling couples from dawn to dark. As T.J. once said there were as many marriages made on the Marina as were ever made in Heaven.

'Why don't we fix up with the girls beforehand?' Olly asked.

'That,' T.J. explained, 'is on account of Rules four, five and six. Adventure. No attachments. And no regrets.'

'Suits me!' says Olly and off he went.

Within fifteen minutes he was back leading two of them by the grin.

He trotted off again and he was back almost as quickly with a real dazzler for himself. After that he became the official Club Decoy. God knows what he had for the girls. He was no beauty. He had a pug nose and hobby-horse nostrils. He was strong and powerful but in a bathing dress he had stubby thighs and legs like a grown-up circus dwarf. He had no least idea how to dress – he always wore brown shoes with a dark suit, and on the river he wore his bowler hat even with his coat off. His pay packet was no fatter than Jim's or mine or anybody else's at the works. If it was not for his two rakehell eyes I do not know what he had for the women. Whatever he had they used to swing out of his arm, gazing adoringly and uncertainly into his two pop-eyes as if he was Rudolph Valentino in person.

'What's the trick, Olly?' I once asked him. 'Do you spray 'em with Secrets of Venus out of your cuff? Or drop cigarette-ash into their lemonade?'

Olly was very serious, very English, no matter what you asked him.

'I ain't got no tricks, Alphonsus,' he said. 'I think maybe the fack o' the matter is I've got a kind heart for the girls. They trust me, see? Or maybe the fack o' the matter is I'm not afraid of 'em, like all you bloomin' Irish.'

'That,' said T.J., prophetically as I now see, 'is where the ferry-boat will leave you some day. You'd be wiser to be afraid of 'em. As Shaw says...'

'Oh, F. Shaw!' says Olly.

'I beg your pardon,' says T.J. 'G. B. Shaw.'

In the end T.J. decided that they trusted him but that they thought he was a bit of a mug; but then, as he said, regarding me pityingly:

'You are a bit of a mug, too, Al, so the mystery remains.'

Will somebody tell me what has happened to time? There were a hundred hours in every one of those long Saturdays and Sundays on the river. And is it only in memory that it never rains, and that all girls are gamesome? Inside one month of that first season with us Olly knew every creek on the river, every stream on every creek, every field on every stream where you could tie up and get down to business, as cosy as a squawl of kittens in a basket, full of peace and joy and contentment the livelong day. In the late evening – lightsome until eleven o'clock in June – we would foregather and row home, tail to prow, like a little musical armada, T.J. swinging his old roundy concertina, me with my trumpet and Olly had a voice that made Caruso sound like a tomtit. When we came to the lights of Montenotte we used to wake the echoes in the hills.

I will never forget one late August night, it was our second season together, when we drew up for a rest opposite the old Shandon Rowing Club on the Marina. Before you could sing A to a tuning fork we had the boys and girls creeping out of the shadows of the avenue two by two down to the edge of the quay, sitting on the limestone wall, legs dangling, chiming in harmony all the songs you ever heard out of Grand Opera, Victor Herbert, G. and S., all those nice, sentimental, happy, pre-bloody-jazz-age songs like *By the Light of the Silvery Moon*, or *Farewell My Own*, *Light of My Life*, *Farewell*, or *Home to Our Mountains*, or

> *The moon hath raised her lamp above*
> *To light the way to thee, my love . . .*

The night came down like a curtain over the elm trees. Across the river the engine of the last excursion train from Youghal was blowing sparks up to the stars. The excursionists were waving their handkerchiefs out of the windows like mad, and the lights in the hundreds of houses up on the hill were dancing like fireflies. It was near two in the morning before we got home. We had to hire a sidecar and dump the girls on tip-toe, one by one, fifty yards from their doorsteps and their frothing fathers. We never saw them again. 'No attachments. No regrets.' No wonder you get all those angry young bums nowadays. They never knew how happy the world was between the two wars. Sheer heaven!

2

We had three good summers of it – and then the inevitable *femme fatale*!

It was a Sunday morning, blue sky, wind from the SW, boats almost ready – rugs, grub, cushions, concertina, trumpet – and T.J. was just about to say to Olly, 'Off you go, boy, collect the flesh!' when Janey

Anne Breen hove into view. I knew her slightly through a third cousin of mine, a very pretty girl named Fan Looney; the two of them used to go off together once a week saving sinners with the Ladies' Saint Vincent de Paul. Without thinking, I said:

'Hello, Janey Anne!'

'Good morning, Alphonsus,' says she. 'Off for a little row? Very good. Very healthy.'

I introduced the boys, we chatted for a bit, and before I could warn Olly he did it. It must have been pure reflex action because she had, and still has, a thin hardbeak smile, mousy hair, as dry as a Temperance Club cat and crimped like corrugated iron, two peg legs the same width all the way up stuck into size eight shoes, black and squat-heeled, with big, black bow-knots, and she was wearing, as she always did, and when I saw her the other day she still was wearing it, an electric-blue frock that T.J. said always made him think of methylated spirits. If she had anything at all that you could look at it they were her two goofy eyes, sweety, softy, eyes, twice their natural size behind her thick, rimless spectacles, and two big front teeth lying white and wet on her lower lip as if she was always saying fuf-fuf. Whatever made him do it, Olly slips his arm around her waist and says, in his best Harry Lauder accent, 'Coom on, lass, what about a kiss and a squeeze for poor old Olly, eh?' She gave him a crack across the puss that you could hear echoing across the Marina half an hour after, and off she stalked, nose and specs in the air, her heels digging holes of anger in the ground, and Olly picking up his bowler hat off the grass and gazing after her with his mouth open and T.J. in the splits of laughter.

T.J. always had a very strange way of laughing. He used to bend over as if he was trying to kiss his knees, his hands trailing the ground, for all the world like a cow laughing at a pound of butter. That was the way he was now, and me leaning across his back, patting him like a baby with the hiccups. As soon as he could talk he explained matters to Olly.

'No, Olly! No, boy! Not with black shoes and bow-ties to them. Not with specs. Not with a Child of Mary medal around her neck. Not with no mother, a brother a priest, and a sister a nun.'

'Nun?' he says. 'You mean locked up for life in a bloomin' convent?'

'That's the idea,' I said. 'And if somebody doesn't pick Janey Anne up very soon she'll be locked up too in about a hundred yards of nun's veiling. She's a good girl, Olly. G-O-O-D. One of those girls you read about in ancient books.'

He stared after her, gargling.

'Pure,' says T.J., 'as the driven snow. Now off you go, Olly, like a good boy, and find us a couple of nice bad girls like you always do. Young, and tender and jumping like April lambs.'

He trotted off after her, caught up with her, and took off his hat and began adulating in front of her.

'For God's sake,' says T.J. watching him, 'surely he's not trying to persuade that stick to come on the river with him? She must be turned thirty if she's a day.'

We watched the two of them walking away from us along the path, Olly with his hat in his hand, angled sideways towards her, bowing like a shop-walker, and her ladyship talking down the side of her arm at him as if she was ticking off a bold, bad doggie. They went on, and they went on, along the path, under the trees, around the bend of the Marina, out of sight. We sat down to wait. After half an hour T.J. jumped up and said, angrily, 'Come on. We'll take one boat between us.'

We rowed down the river, not speaking, until we passed the end of the Marina. I was stroke. I said over my shoulder:

'Do you see what I see?'

The two of them were sitting on the last bench of the Marina and they were laughing.

'So be it!' says T.J. 'He can have his attachment. And his regrets.'

'We might have a few regrets, too.'

'You're young, boy, you'll find you get over these things.'

I could not see his face but I did not like his tone. He sounded like a bitter old man.

3

They were married that July, and I had to drag T.J. to the wedding, the usual hole and corner affair in the presbytery, Olly being a Baptist and sticking to it; and after the honeymoon I had to drag him with me to visit them in their little garden flat on the Lower Road, a bare hundred yards from the river. I think T.J. came only because it was a damp night and he had nowhere else to go.

'Anyway,' I said, as I squeaked open the garden gate, 'it's only polite. This looks like a cosy little love-nest.'

'Says the setter to the snipe.'

He was just after buying a pure bred, golden setter pup, named Babs, spayed.

'I bet you tuppence we'll have to leave Babs outside,' he said. And I bet you we won't get a drink either.'

She opened the door. Specs, bird's eyes, wet teeth, electric-blue dress. An old black mongrel cocker ran out and in a second the two dogs were at it. She retrieved the mongrel.

'Come to mumsy-wumsy,' she says, almost suckling him. 'Poor little Charlie-Barlie. Bold, bad, foxy dog! Boo!'

'Bitch,' says T.J. coldly.

Olly was behind her, grinning.

'Charlie's a present from an old admirer,' he says, with a lewd wink.

'Oliver!' she upbraided. 'He is not. Charlie-Barlie,' she explained primly, 'was left in my care a year ago by an old friend who had to go to sea.'

Olly pinched her behind.

'Old friend? Ha-ha!' and he winked at us again.

We had to leave Babs outside, tied to the railings.

'Won't you wipe your feet?' she begged. 'I did the lino today.'

We could smell it. Brand new, red roses climbing all over golden lattice-work. She had the Infant of Prague on the wall with an electric bulb glowing in front of it. She had a holy-water font on the wall, too. For spite T.J. dropped his cigarette ash into it. The little parlour was as neat as an altar. They sat on each side of the fire, and T.J. and me sat on a new settee against the opposite wall. Olly produced two bottles of Guinness and poured them for us. She took away the bottles and the corkscrew and we knew that was that.

'Well,' I said, friendly-like, 'and how did the honeymoon go?'

'Guess where we went?' Olly grinned.

'London? Isle of Man? Killarney? Southend? Brighton?' Olly grinned a No to all of them.

'We took a rowboat and set off to explore the river. Lots of nice little cosy corners down there, eh?'

He clicked his tongue and raised shocked eyebrows.

'Oliver!' said Janey Anne, and we knew that he had told her all.

If T.J.'s slow smile was a knife it would have cut his jaw off.

'Nice time?' I asked Olly, and his tone changed.

'So-so!'

'It rained,' she grimaced.

'A little accident,' he gestured.

'Oliver rocked the boat,' she said and glared at him.

'As a matter o' fack, poor little Janey fell into the river. She got a bad cold. She lost her glasses. So we came home.'

Jim made a very sad face and looked very happy. Then he slowly began to go as white as cheese because Olly had started in on the story of the blind salesman who met the deaf whore. This was always a thing about T.J. Any story you liked among men, but a single off-colour word in the presence of women made him go white with anger. I looked at Janey Anne. She was chuckling. Olly finished his yarn, winked at me, and looked expectantly at Janey. Her face at once did a quick curtain and she said severely:

'Oliver!'

He guffawed. His gooseberry eyes rolled in their sockets. He said:

'Did I ever tell you the one about the barmaid and the champagne cork?'

'Yes,' said Jim like a bullet.

That did not stop Olly. Janey Anne gurgled. Olly finished, winked, waited, got his 'Oliver!' and guffawed happily. He then started in, at length and detail, on our river days. T.J. looked four times at his watch. He held his empty glass between his clasped hands as if he was trying to press it to bits. Janey listened, radiant until it was all finished with Olly singing our Barcarolle, *River girls, O river girls, How we love your dancing curls*. Then she snapped down the black curtain and said to T.J.:

'I think you have been a bunch of very bad boys, Mister Mooney. I am really shocked at you. After all you are older than Oliver. Not to mention poor Alphonsus there, and he's only a boy.'

Oliver, lolling in his armchair, beamed at us both. His beaming face said it for him:

'Did you ever in all your life see such a sweet, innocent little girl as I found?'

When we at last got out of that flat Jim untied the setter without a word, and he did not say a word until we were back in our digs, him sitting on his bed, and me on mine looking at the rain flecking the window, thinking of one wet Sunday, a couple of years back, when I was on the river with that pretty girl Fan Looney.

'Well?' he said at last. 'What are you thinking about?'

'Me?' I said, looking away from the rain on the window. 'Nothing!'

'Damn it,' he snarled, 'you must be thinking about something.'

'Very well,' I laughed. 'In that case tell me what was I thinking?'

'How the hell do I know what you were thinking?'

'Then I don't know what I was thinking either.'

'So you admit you were thinking?'

'T.J.,' I pleaded. 'Come off it.'

'And you were looking at me!' he growled.

'I was not looking at you, I'm sick of looking at you, do you think I'm in love with you?'

'Oh! So you were thinking about love?'

'Are you going slightly daft?'

'I got over that stage years ago. But *I'll* tell *you* what *I* was thinking. I was thinking, why is it in the name of all that's holy that fellows see things in girls that simply aren't there? And that's what you were thinking, too, whether you know it or not.'

'Tell me,' I said, to pacify him. 'Why *do* we see things in girls that aren't there?'

He whispered across to me:

'Because they aren't there.'

I began to think that maybe he really was going a bit daft. I started looking again at the drops of rain on the pane.

'Well?' he said, after another while. 'Why don't you say it straight out?'

'Say what straight out?'

'What you're thinking.'

'I'm not thinking! Unless,' I said, on an inspiration-like, 'maybe I was thinking, why do girls see things in fellows that aren't there?'

'You're a flaming liar! You were thinking no such a thing! You were thinking when will I start seeing things in some girl that aren't there. And that's why you were looking at me.'

I laughed very loudly at that, because it had crossed my mind that it was a funny thing that he had never married.

'And,' he said, very solemn-like, 'I'll tell you another thing I was thinking. It won't be long before I see you starting to see things in some girl that aren't there. If you haven't started doing it already.'

At that I peeled off and went to bed. So did he. I stayed awake for hours listening to the rain, and I could tell he wasn't asleep either.

4

After that night we could not be kept away from Olly and Janey. Once a week, at least, we would tie Babs to the railings, ring the bell, wipe our feet, sit on the settee, accept our glass of stout, and, as T.J. put it, wait for Olly to start unveiling. He was right – it was just like the quick-change-artist act in an old-time Music Hall. Enter Olly as Cork's Casanova, the historian of the river and all its wily ways. Loud guffaws. Black curtains. Enter Professor Oliver Carson as the warm admirer of Little Tich, George Robey, Lord Beaverbrook, Chief Scout Baron Baden-Powell, Marie Stopes, Stanley Baldwin and Eamonn de Valera. Black-out. Bright lights. Drum-rolls. Enter Olly in a check suit, straw hat, white bowler and malacca: 'Did I ever tell you the one about the absent-minded Professor who took his dog down to the garage to be oiled and greased?' Guffaws. Black curtains. Enter the Confirmed Pacifist: 'Let me ask you a question, sir. If you was to say to me, "What would you do if you saw your poor, dumb sister being raped by a German?" what would I answer you? I would answer you, "I ain't got no dumb sister! That's my wife!" Hahaha!' Oliver! Black curtains. Enter Olly, very serious, as John Calvin, announcing the doctrine of the salvation of the elect; which, so far as I could make out, included everybody in the world except the foreman of the works and the population of Germany. To that particular shebang Janey Anne could only respond with small, gasping noises.

Every night T.J. would come away either in a daze of silence, or asking the same question in a variety of ways: What did I think of *that* performance? I answered him once and only once. I said that I thought Olly was being very honest with her, that he was laying his soul open at her feet, and that it was very noble of him. I thought T.J. would strike me with the setter.

'Honest?' he roared at me. 'Noble? Do you want to drive me mad? Well, that's the end of it. I'm finished with him. If that's what you think he's doing I'm never going to put my head inside that madhouse again. For the first time in my life I'm actually beginning to sympathize with that eedjut of a woman. I'm honestly beginning to conclude that the unfortunate woman is too bewildered at finding herself married to that roaring lunatic that she'll either sink an axe in his head or end up raving in a padded cell.'

The week after that Olly unveiled in a way that dumb-founded the three of us. He revealed that he was a Freemason, that his father was a Freemason, and that not only had he been a member of a Sheffield Lodge but that the first thing he did when he landed in Cork was to join the local Lodge. I looked over at Janey Anne, and by the fright in her face I saw that, like us, this was the first she had heard of it. As if I was sitting inside in her head I could feel the rats running around in her brain. Secret society, condemned by the Church, enemies of the Vatican, Grand Orient, goats, devils, Carbonaries, Black Magic, passwords, handgrips, tip-the-wink, never-know-who-you're-talking-to, red fire, dark rooms, the-Lord-save-us-or-we-perish – all this time, unbeknownst to her, in her own house, from her Olly whose jokes she laughed at, whose life she thought was an open book to her, whom she had by this seen night after night padding around on his stubby legs in his nightshirt, now looking at her as mild as milk saying:
'Very fine body of men. Very philantropophic. Philantropophic to everybody. Without respect to class or creed.'
T.J. got me out as fast as he decently could. As we untied Babs we could hear the voices rising inside the window of the little parlour. When we taxed Olly the next day about never telling us he was a Mason he said, shortly, that he did not want to upset us.
'But what about Janey Anne?' T.J. asked.
'Well, I've told her, haven't I?'
'You didn't tell beforehand,' I charged him.
'She wouldn't have had me.'
At that T.J. said one of those daft things he was always saying:
'She'd have had you double-quick. A brand from the burning, Olly. A brand from the burning.'

We did not go down so often to the flat after that. The atmosphere, if I might make so bold as to borrow the vivid image, had changed. For one thing the Troubles were starting, and Olly was English and she was Irish. For another thing they could not talk about anything now without her dragging the Masons into it. A sign of it was that Olly had got hold of a little-toy Union Jack, the sort you might put up in front of your motor-car if you were daft enough; and she had brought a little toy papal-flag, yellow and white; and they had stuck the two flags into vases on each side of the mantelpiece, so that all they had to do then was to look at one flag or the other and off they were, hammer and tongs. If we walked into the middle of one of these arguments they barely took time off to greet us, and as Olly drew the two bottles of stout he would hardly look at what he was doing.

'England,' he would say to her, hauling at the cork, 'is my! Country! Right! Or! Wrong!'

'Then why didn't you fight for your country during the war?' from Janey Anne, never afraid to hit below the belt.

'I 'ave my convictions,' he said. 'And I stand by 'em.'

'Ha!' she said. 'Locked up in your bedroom drawer in tissue-paper, your little green and gold apron, with your sash, and your trowel and your secret book of the devil's rules!'

When she talked that way, T.J. said afterwards, she looked like Bluebeard's wife talking about the locked chamber.

'Are we discussing the Empire or the Freemasons?' Olly asked politely.

'How any men,' she sailed on, 'can be so ignorant, so misled, so benighted, so superstitious as to be riding a goat around a room...'

'Janey Anne,' Olly protested, 'we don't go riding no goats around no rooms. You're not allowed to keep a goat in a room. The RSPCA would be after you like a shot.'

'Ye call up the devil!'

'Janey Anne! Do you really and truly think I'm the kind of man who...'

'Then why don't you tell me what goes on there?'

Very quietly he explained all over again that Freemasonry is a purely philanthropic society.

'Good works. Helping poor boys who are afflicted in any way. Orphans. Polios. Bastards. All the same to us. Each for all. All for each. Assisting one another in our private or commercial difficulties. Naturally these are things we don't wish to be discussed in public. You can see that, darlingkins, can't you?'

She looked at him, doubtfully, tight-mouthed, teeth buried, eyes big as plates, and started muttering about secret societies condemned by the Pope.

'Janey Anne! Don't you trust your own Ollykins?'

We could see her wavering. Then she cracked her beak on a hard, hempseed 'No!'

'I think it's wicked, and sinful and evil. I don't know why I ever married a man who keeps secrets from his wife. A man with a double life. Not like other men I've known. Carol Costigan wouldn't have deceived me like this. Johnny Hartigan wouldn't have done it. Georgie Conlon wouldn't have done it. But you . . . Come to mumsy, my own Charlie-Barlie,' she says picking up the old mongrel and putting her nose down to his nose. 'You wouldn't deceive me like that, would you?'

'No,' says Olly sourly. 'Not unless he went riding a goat around a room.'

'Oliver!'

'Or started wearing a little green apron like a nancyboy. Go on, kiss him, do!'

'Don't you dare say one word against a woman's best friend! You Mason! You!'

T.J. would always leave the flat whistling after one of these hot nights; or saying something cheerful like, 'It's on the rocks! We'll all be back on the river next June.'

5

Just before Christmas Olly came up to me in the works one Monday morning red with pride and excitement.

'Know what's happened? I've been made Master of my Lodge. Elected last Friday night.'

'Here?'

'Here in Cork. Wot an 'onour! My old man'll be tickled to death.'

'What about Janey Anne?'

'Delighted. She'll be at the Banquet. She's gone into town to buy a frock. She's thinking of blue.'

When I told T.J. he said he did not believe it. I assured him that Olly himself told me. He said he meant about Janey being delighted. After supper he said we must go down to the flat at once. Olly was not at home but she brought us in, gave us the two bottles of stout, so far forgot herself as to bring out two more, and started in to tell us all about it, as excited as a girl going to her first dance.

'Of *course* I'm going to the Banquet! It really is a great honour for Oliver. And as his wife I shall be the First Lady.'

'But what about the Church?' T.J. goaded.

'Well,' she said primly, 'at first, when he asked me would I sit beside him in the place of honour at the Banquet I didn't know what to say. So I went around on Saturday morning to Saint Anne's to consult Father Butts. It was he married us. He said he would have to think about it and to come back that night. When I went back that night he asked me why I wanted to go to the Banquet. I said I wanted to stand by my marriage vows to love, honour and obey. He said he must think some more about it and to come back on Sunday afternoon. So I went back on Sunday afternoon and he said: "Where will this Banquet be held?" I said, "In the Imperial Hotel." He said, "Very well, Mrs Carson, you may attend the Banquet. The place is neutral. And the intention is to avoid domestic friction. But, after this, you must try to wean him away from his ungodly ways." I thought he was very understanding. Even when I asked him should I tell Oliver that I had consulted him he said, "It would be tactless and unnecessary." I was thinking of blue.'

'Your taste is perfect,' T.J. said. 'And you are very loyal.'

On our way home I told him I was surprised at his paying her the compliment of being loyal. He explained to me that he did not mean that she was being loyal to Olly.

6

I think it was in the end of January that Olly came over to us one morning waving a telegram. It was a radiogram for Janey that her father had sent down to them the night before. It said: *Arriving Cork Thursday night for three days stop hospitality welcome if available stop three cheers and what-ho Carol.*

'It's from her old boy-friend Carol Costigan. A radio-officer with P. and O. Wonderful man. Salt of the earth. Janey wants the two of you to come to supper on Thursday night and view my defeated rival.' He began to laugh like a zany. 'The joke of the whole thing is Janey's like a cat on hot bricks. She never told him she's married. He's going to get a right land when he sees me.'

We went down, we tied Babs to the railings, rang, were let in by Olly, who gave us a rather watery wink, wiped our feet and went into the parlour. The first person I saw was Mrs Charles Costigan, a luscious blonde. Then I saw Mr Salt-of-the Earth Costigan. He was about the size of a jockey, false teeth, hair going thin, and he had a bulge under each eye like a blue moon in its last quarter. Mrs Costigan turned out to be Yorkshire, and a non-stop talker, with all of Olly's sense of humour, who roared at his roughest jokes, told a few blue ones of her own, and lowered her liquor like a man – whiskey, in honour of the double marriage. I will say this for Janey Anne, that she carried the whole thing off like a good sport: loud jokes and laughter about secret marriages, and 'I-only-had-to-turn-my-back', and 'We-both-seem-to-like-the-English-don't-we?' But Olly was not taking it so well. He kept looking at Costigan, and then glancing over at Janey Anne, and it was as plain as a pikestaff that he was wondering what she had ever seen in the fellow. All the same, the man was his guest, so after the supper was over he had no option when Costigan said, probably because he saw there was no more liquor coming up, 'Say, chaps. Why don't we leave the girls alone for a bit to get acquainted and drop around the corner for a little bit of manly pow-wow and a night-cap? What-ho?'

We went down the road to the old *Internationale*, just where the houses stop and the river is wide open. It was a lovely calm night, with a tingle of frost in the air. The buses were like stars, and the stars were like buses. A ship went slowly chugging down the river on the high tide. For an hour it was just like the good old days, boozing there together, swopping yarns – if Olly was being a bit quiet, for him – so that I was disappointed when T.J. said it was getting late and we must push off for home. On the way I said:

'Did you remark how quiet Olly was? I think he's feeling sorry for poor Janey. That fellow Costigan was a terrible let down for her opposite us all.'

T.J. snorted at me.

'Simple Simon,' he said.

'What do you mean, Simple Simon?'

'Don't you know a Woolworth's wedding-ring when you see it?'

The following morning Olly stepped into line with us and came right out with it.

'I told that fellow this morning that if he and his floosy aren't out of my house when I come back tonight I'll throw the pair of 'em out on their necks in the middle of the road.'

'How did you find out?' T.J. asked.

'He had the cool, brazen brass to tell me. He had the gall to think that I'm his kind of a man. I didn't sleep a wink. I could hear Janey crying all night. Do you know what? Her pillow was as wet this morning as if you'd thrown a bucket of water on it.'

At that T.J. stopped dead, and doubled over, pawing the ground, and all the fellows passing by looking at him and smiling to see him laughing. Olly dragged him up and around by the shoulder, and I thought he was going to hit him.

'What the 'ell are you laughing at?' he bellowed, and all the fellows stopped to look.

'Jealous!' Jim wails, between his laughs. 'Jealous!'

'Janey! Of that floosy? For that rat?' he roared. T.J. quietened. He stared at Olly as if he had been struck dumb. He shook him off.

'Did I say *she* was jealous?' he sneered, and walked away.

7

We never visited the flat again. We did not talk to Olly for the best part of two months. I did not see much of T.J. either, outside the digs, and not very much in them – I had seen a streak of cruelty in him that I did not like. Besides, that winter I was in the IRA and I was doing a special night course three times a week at the Tech, and I may as well also mention that once or twice I tried courting Fan Looney. And if I must tell the whole truth of it she would have nothing to do with me. She said she had heard too much about my goings-on from Janey Anne. In the end it was Olly who talked to us. He came and sat down beside us one day in the canteen. He was his old, cheery self.

'Boys!' he said right off the reel, 'my Janey Anne is one of the great women of all time. As Father Butts said to me last night when I was seeing him off at the door, "Your wife, Mr Carson, is a credit to Faith and Fatherland." I never before realized wot comfort a troubled soul can get out of religion. It's made me think, let me tell you that. It made me ponder very seriously on a lot o' things.'

'Coming over?' asks T.J. 'And, if so, what about the Freemasons?'

'As a matter o' fack,' says Olly, obviously dying to talk about it, 'Father Butts is very understanding about that particular question. He opened my eyes to a lot of things I never knew about the Masons. And he opened Janey Anne's eyes too. He lent us a very interesting book on the subjeck there last month. The two of us are reading it every night over the fire. It's these bleeding Continentals that gave us a bad name. The fack is English Freemasonry is away out on its own. British to the backbone! Not that I'm entirely convinced, mind you. But historically speaking...'

And off he went about the Scotch Rite, and some crowd called the Knights Templar, and the French Revolution came into it, and six Papal bulls, and only the siren stopped him.

'Hooked,' said T.J., as we walked back to the bench, 'booked and cooked to a cinder. He'll be dripping holy medals by Easter!'

Jim was wrong. That Easter, Olly got the 'flu and died as he had lived, a true-born English Baptist. T.J. and me went down to the house for the funeral and she brought us in to see him in the coffin. When I saw what I saw the tears started rolling down my face. She had him laid out in the Franciscan habit, and at his head she had laid his little Papal flag that used to stand in the vase on her side of the mantelpiece. I never saw any woman look so happy.

'He was a bad, bad boy,' she smiled. 'But God will forgive him. As He will forgive ye, too. Praise and glory be to His name.'

That afternoon we walked away from the graveside as silent as the grave. It started to rain and we halted under a yew. The funeral was very largely attended, Catholics, Masons, Baptists, Boys' Brigade, all sorts and sizes of people, workers from the factory, every class and creed, scattered under yews all over the place sheltering from the rain.

'I suppose,' says T.J., after a while, 'we know what we're thinking?'

'T.J.!' says I, and I was wiping my face with my handkerchief. 'I'm not thinking anything at all, no more than that pile of ould yellow bones there. And I don't want to think, because all I want to do is to forget.'

'Well, I'll tell you what I'm thinking. That woman fattens on guilt like a cemetery worm.'

'Guilt? What has she to feel guilty about?'

'Nothing!' he shouted at me, forgetting where we were. 'That's why she loves it.'

'Daft!' I said and I threw the back of my hand to him and walked away down the path. He came raging after me, he shoved me up against a Celtic cross, he put his long nose into my face and he started haranguing me as if I was a public meeting, one hand on my chest, the other pointing like a politician's statue across the white headstones.

'Do we or do we not know what she did to that poor sucker lying there in his fancy dress under five feet of ground? Did she or did she not hypnotize him into thinking she was the incarnation of all goodness and virtue and that he was nothing but a Sheffield orang-outang?'

'Well, Olly, certainly, had a very high opinion of his wife.'

'And why? Why? Isn't this the question that's been tormenting you and me from the first day they laid eyes on one another?'

'Look,' I said, 'all I know is that the cold of his ould cross is going in through the small of my back.'

He held me gripped tighter than ever.

'I have decided,' he said, and his eyes were like two gimlets, 'that in what is commonly called love·man creates woman after his own unlikeness. In love woman is man's image of what he is not. In love man is his own creator, midwife and gravedigger, awake, asleep, dreaming or hypnotized the way you are at this very moment into thinking what I damn well know you are thinking only you haven't the guts to say it.'

I threw him off, and graveyard or no graveyard I let a roar out of me:

'I'm thinking of nothing! And I'm proud to say I'm thinking of nothing! And I'll give you a sock in your greyhound's puss if you don't stop thinking for me. Aye, and tormenting me in the middle of my sorrow for my poor dead friend Olly Carson lying over there under a ton of wet earth and a pile of glass flowers.'

He leaned one hand against the Celtic cross and he sneered at me:

'You're thinking of your lousy soul and of your latter end.'

I can still hear the whistling of the blackbirds. I can see the sun on the raindrops of the yews, and the mourners fluffing themselves out, and the long black cloud moving like a black pot lid away over the city. I knew somehow that this was going to be the most wonderful night of my life and I began to cry rain down into the ould cross at the thought of it. At that the kindness broke out in him, and I was never more touched by anything he ever said to me as by what he said then. He put his arm around my shoulder and he said:

'Aly, boy,' says he, 'will you wipe your face, yoh slobbering eedjut? And stop disgracing me in the public graveyard? Come on out here to *The Last Post* and I'll stand you a pint of the best.' The pub was full. Of mourners. We leaned on the counter looking down into our two pints. Someone lit the gas-mantle. It was like the green sea. I started thinking to myself that no man can do without a friend. And I was thinking, wouldn't it be sort of nice, when all is said and done, to have somebody to look after me when I got old, and to lay me out when I'd be dead, with the tricolour over my coffin, and my IRA gun lying on top of it, and the band after the hearse playing *The Flowers of the Forest*, or the Dead March from *Saul*. I looked up at T.J. smoking his pipe and pondering on his pint, and I confessed it to him. I expected him to bawl me out. He looked at me a bit sadly, but kindly too, like some old priest after listening to you telling him your sins. He patted me on the shoulder, and he began at me, soft and warm, kind of pleased, I suppose, that I had confided in him:

'Al! There is no doubt whatever about it, you are a gom. And you always were a gom. And you always will be a gom. And it's a good job for you that you have somebody like me to advise you. A babe in arms, a poor, young fellow up from the country that knows nothing about the ways of the world or the wiles of women. If it wasn't for me looking after you you might have been hooked long ago by some vampire like that wan,' with a jerk of his head to the cemetery. 'Sucking your blood. Leeching you like a succubus. Turning you into a poppet. Let me tell you this one thing, and mark it once and for all. All every woman is waiting for is the day she can lay you out and be praying for you, and feeling good about you. They keep you out of their bed when you're alive, and they sleep with you when you're dead. The war of the sexes is declared by women on the weaker sex, and entered into by men because we are the weaker sex. And when we're beaten to the bed, that is to say when we think we have conquered our woman, what do we do but put her up on an altar and grovel before her, and work ourselves to a lather for her into an early grave?'

'But, T.J., what about love?'

'Love, my dear, poor boy, is a sedative disguised as a stimulant. It's a mirror where man sees himself as a monster, and woman as a thing of untarnished beauty. If it wasn't for that all men would otherwise, and normally fear all women. You fear women. I fear women. But because we need them we have to have them. And that's where they have us, in the great and final triumph of women over men, called – by them, not by us, and well-called – Happy Wedlock. Love is a prison staffed by female warders. Let me tell you . . .'

It went on for an hour, non-stop, pouring into me, pint after pint, like the sea into a cave. I did not understand one hundredth part of it. But I understood enough of it. I understood that he was advising me to look into the mirror of my own heart and there I would see Love smiling sweetly out at me. I went down to Fan Looney that night, and I told her all about it. When I was finished she said in her nice, sweet way that she always knew that Jim Mooney was no proper company for a nice young man like me, and if I had found him out she was very glad.

'Maybe,' I said, daringly, ''tis the way I found you? Have I a chance, Fan?'

She looked at me, and her eyes filled and her voice broke.

'Oh, Alphonsus!' she says. 'What are you after doing to me? I was a happy girl without a thought of anything in the world until you came talking to me and now you're after turning me into a grown woman. And,' she said, sobbing into my shoulder, 'now we'll have to start planning.'

'We will, Fan,' I said and I felt just as miserable as herself, and she made me feel an awful brute.

'You'll have to give up the drink,' she wailed.

'I will, I will,' I promised.

'And cut down on smoking,' she wept.

'Anything in the world you say, Fan! If you'll only stop crying.'

We are settled down now. We have five lovely children. Cherubs! I'm foreman of the works. And I can assure you I keep a sharp eye on the young fellows. After all, I know the ways of the world. T.J. got another job. For years I did not lay eyes on him until there last month when I was walking down the Marina one Sunday with Fan pushing little Sean in the gocart, and I had Deirdre on my shoulder. Suddenly I stopped dead. I saw the grey-haired man on the river, pulling along at his ease. In the prow with her nose up was a red setter, and it was that made me recognize him.

'Fan!' I said. 'That's T.J.'

She looked and she laughed sharp-like.

'The Rule of the River,' she said.

It was a lovely June morning, wind from the southwest, and the ebb with him. Very nice. He would come back on the tide. As late as he liked.

'Well?' Fan asked. 'What are you thinking?'

'Ach! Nothing!'

'You were smiling,' she said suspiciously.

'Was I?'

'Yes, you were!' she said and she gave me a dark look.

'I was just smiling sad-like. Thinking what a lonely poor divil he is.'

We walked on. I watched him slowly pull away from us. I could not get the old Barcarolle out of my head. *River girls, O river girls. How we love your dancing curls . . .*

I was careful not to smile.

Charlie's Greek

It was twenty-odd years before I saw Rika Prevelakis again, encouraged to visit her by, of all people Charlie, for, of all things fun, in, of all places Athens. 'You will have no trouble in finding her,' he assured me. 'Everybody in the university knows her well.'

She did not look her forty-five years, though she had grown stout, motherly and quizzical. Her hair was still black but not so oily. Her skin looked so delicately soft and pink that I at once remembered our old Dublin joke: 'Charlie, does her face-powder taste of Turkish Delight?', and his cheerful wink in reply. Nothing really betrayed her age except those Swiss rings she wore, too tight on her plump fingers, the faint necklace of Venus on her throat, and the hard ball of her calf. I gathered that her husband, whom I did not meet, was an exporter of fruit, and judging by her charming house, with its modern paintings and pieces of modern sculpture, he was a highly successful one. She told me that her eldest son – she had three – was nineteen, a figure that startled me by taking me back directly to the year after her famous visit to Dublin. So she had made up her mind about Charlie as rapidly as that!

She was delighted to get first-hand news of him, asked many questions about him, and although she now clearly thought of him with a certain good-humoured self-mockery it was plain that she still remembered him with a warm and grateful affection.

'He made me come alive,' she said so simply that the hackneyed words sounded as fresh as truth.

We chatted for nearly an hour; at the end, just as I was leaving her, I said:

'I'd be interested to know how you would sum up Charlie at the end of it all?'

She laughed and put on a stage Anglo-Greek accent:

'My husband always say, and my husband ees a wise man, that whenever he ees asked hees opinion of any man he avoids the opeenion and sketches the leetle portrait.'

Wise man, indeed I thought as I walked away from her delightful house whose garden overlooked the winking blue of the Piraeus. 'Opeenions?' If I asked any dozen men who knew Charlie in his heyday I could guess the sort of juryman's anthology I would collect:

1. Charlie Carton? I'd trust him with my wife! For five minutes.
2. You know, I honestly and truly believe that he was the most outgoing, warmhearted, affectionate young fellow I ever met.
3. A cold, self-indulgent, self-centred, unprincipled hedonist!
4. A genuine lover of mankind, a born reformer and a natural revolutionary. Damn few people like him left in Ireland today.
5. What an orator! Brilliant! And so gay. A most amusing chap. A dreamer and a rebel. The essence of everything that is fine in the Irish nature.
6. Charlie Carton? That Big Mouth!
7. Would you not agree with me that he was rather a nice blend of Don Juan and Saint Francis? I mean, it was a toss of a coin which side of him would win out in the end. By the way, which has won out?
8. Had he any principles at all? I've seen him weep over a sick child in the slums one minute and the next minute deceive a woman, pitilessly.
9. No, I don't think I'd say that Charlie ever had many principles. A few? Perhaps? They certainly didn't lie too heavily on him. Do you remember what Aristide Briand said one time about principles? *Il faut toujours s'appuyer sur les principes; ils finissent par en céder.* Always lean hard on your principles – sooner or later they will give way. One thing about Charlie, though – he was a damn good sport. A real man's man. I liked him.
10. If you want my frank opinion of him he was a flaming bloody humbug.
11. I only knew him in his college days. He'd give you the shirt off his back. You have to forgive a lot to a youngster like that.
12. Soft. To the marrow of his bones. Mush. Incapable of tenderness because incapable of fierceness. Ask any woman. The only good thing they could all say for him would be that if he deceived them he damn soon undeceived them.

There was that night he loaned me his bed-sitter in London. The telephone rang every half-hour from midnight on. Always the same woman or girl.

'No,' I would reply. 'Mr Carton isn't here. I'm only a guest, occupying his room for the night.' Or: 'I assure you Charlie isn't here. For God's sake do you realize it's one o'clock in the morning, and I'm trying to sleep!' Each time she said the same forlorn thing: 'Well, just tell him I just rang up just to say goodbye.' After half an hour back she would come again, and again, and again, until, between fury and pity, I began to wonder whether he had not been expecting exactly this when he so generously offered me the loan of his room. In the end I appealed to the operator. In a tired, polite, English, three-o'clock-in-the-morning voice he said: 'I'm very sorry, sir, I've explained to the lady that Mr Carton isn't there. It does no good, poor thing. Besides, I'm obliged to put the calls through. And mark you, this is costing her a pretty penny – she's on long distance from Strasbourg.'

A Salvador Dali would have painted him with a woman looking out of each eye. His handsome boyish face would have delighted any painter of the high Renaissance in search of the epitome of the power and prime of youth; though it would have been a Florentine painter rather than a Venetian, because of his colourless skin, his buttercup hair, his teeth so small and perfect, his heavy-lidded eyes and because in spite of his bulk he suggested surface rather than roundness, depth or solidity. Neither his face nor his body ever made you conscious of his bones. Stripped for the boxing ring his body looked so soft, almost so feminine that nobody who had not already seen him box would have taken him for a stayer. But he was a stayer, and a frequent winner, obstinate, agile as a boy, a fender rather than a fighter, winning always on points of skill. He outboxed his men and outflirted his women. His boyishness was a fake. At forty-one he was still eager, laughing, garrulous, completely indifferent to appearance, uncombed, almost unkempt, genuinely feckless – he never gave a tuppenny damn about money or possessions and he was generally broke; which may have been the main reason why, even in his schooldays, women wanted to mother him and love him. It must have come as a shock to them to discover that his fecklessness was all-embracing, in every sense of the word. Their pretty boy was as hard as nails. I thought of him the first time I saw that well-known portrait of Lodovico Capponi by Bronzino in the Frick museum – an elegant young ephebe as you might think until you looked into his cool, grey X-ray eyes, and they make you jump like a drop of boiling water on your hand.

One of our jurymen remembers him as a natural revolutionary; another as a rebel. He was born in the wrong place and the wrong age to be either, to the full – in Ireland after the Troubles. How happy he would have been in the thick of them! If he had been shot then (though I have the feeling that he would have outboxed them too) he would now be one of our best-loved boy-heroes. He was born too soon for the war against the Nazis, and the Spanish Civil War was almost over when he was leaving school – together with the not-all-that-young school-mother who took him camping in a pup-tent all around England for the whole of that summer.

'She completed my education,' he used to say, with his usual happy grin. 'What happened to her? I don't know. She got sacked, of course. Oh, yes, she wrote to me. But,' with a graceful circle of his slender strong hand, 'we had completed the medallion of our love.'

That was the way he always talked, romantically; and behaved, ruthlessly. He used to say:

'I'm not really all that Irish, you know! The Cartons were always Cromwellian settlers. And you know how it is with these colonials. One moves on.'

'Would you,' I asked Rika Prevelakis, 'say he was ruthless?'

By way of reply she recalled their last encounter. I already knew (we all knew) something about it. She frankly filled in the details.

It happened at the time of his famous Monster Public Protest Meeting in Forty-one. He was then one of Ireland's active Communists (had we twelve?); in public calling himself a member of the Irish Labour Party which, as everybody knows, was and is about as left as my right foot; calling himself a socialist in private; and (his own confession) in his bed or his bath loudly declaring himself a Marxist. The date is vital. Forty-one was a tough time anywhere in these islands for anyone to be a Communist. The Russians were still holding to their non-aggression pact with Hitler. The many thousands of Irish in the British army felt they were there to fight Communism as well as Nazism. Dunkirk was over. So was the Battle of Britain. But when Spain invaded Tangier, which reminded us all of the existence of General Franco, and the Germans entered Athens, which reminded Charlie of Lord Byron, it seemed the perfect moment to appeal to Ireland about the rights of small nations. Accordingly, Charlie and his friends boldly announced a Monster Public Meeting 'in honour of Greece' for the night of May 4th. The timing could not have been more awkward for all concerned. Had they waited until June Russia would by then be fighting Germany. And four days before the meeting this old flame of Charlie's turned up in Dublin.

She was about twenty-five then; small, dark, reasonably pretty, and so enchanted to find Charlie up in arms in defence of her country that her prettiness bloomed out in a sort of fiery beauty. In every way but one she was a most appealing young woman, as all who met her agreed; and most of us did meet her because from the minute she arrived he was madly trying to fob her off on his friends. (With her, also, it appeared, he had completed the medallion of their love – anyway of his love.) Her one unappealing characteristic was that although she was highly educated – she was then teaching Greek and Greek history in London to Foreign Office chaps – and well informed about most things, shrewd, hard-headed and clear-eyed, she was pathetically unable to perceive that Charlie detested her in proportion as her pursuit of him and his flight from her made them both look ridiculous.

'It's awful!' he sweated. 'It's like a blooming honeymoon! She never lets up for one minute. Can we have breakfast together? What am I doing for lunch? Where am I going for dinner? What about tonight, tomorrow night, the day after tomorrow! Listen – be a sport for God's sake; take her out to lunch for me and lose her somewhere in the mountains.'

One immediate result during those days before the Meeting was that we all had her on the telephone:

'Can I speak to Mr Carton, please?'

'Hello! Is that Rika? I'm afraid Charlie isn't here. He's never here. He doesn't live here, you know.'

'But he must be there! He told me to ring this number if he didn't turn up!'

'Turn up where?'

'In Stephen's Green. At three o'clock. Beside the bust of James Clarence Mangan.'

In the soft Spring rain? Now four o'clock! With a drop on the tip of James Clarence Mangan's green nose? What a good idea for getting shut of a girl! But it was not good enough for Rika.

'Well, he just isn't here.'

'I will ring again.'

'It isn't any good. He never is here.'

'I will ring again. He told me to keep on trying. When he comes please tell him to wait until I ring again.'

We kept asking ourselves, and asking one another why he was so devious with her. Why, if only in sheer kindness of heart didn't he give her the straight uppercut? Was this the soft streak in him? She revealed that whenever he could not avoid meeting her he would sit by her side, hold her hand, gaze into her eyes and in his rich Irish voice recite poetry to her, Byron for preference:

> *Eternal spirit of the chainless Mind!*
> *Brightest in dungeons, Liberty, thou art,*
> *For there thy habitation is the heart –*
> *The heart which love of thee alone can bind . . .*

If she raged at him he would say, soothingly and softly, 'Let the doves settle, Rika! Let the doves settle on your looovely head!' Once, being still as tempestuous as (in his admiring phrase) the stormy Aegean she found him gripping her hand and asking, 'Do I hold the hand of Queen Maeve?' to which she unwisely replied, 'Who is Queen Maeve?' only to find herself at once bewildered, delighted, infuriated and irrecoverably lost in a golden-and-purple tapestry of Celtic myth and legend:

'Our past, Rika, is so old and rich, like your great past, out of which you have come to us, so filled with wonder and mystery that it surrounds us like the murmuring night-sea, crowded with the dim faces and the lost voices of our dead, whose whispering words we never cease to hear and can never hope to understand. In that dark night of the Irish memory there looms always our bull-goddess Queen Maeve, surrounded by the tossing heads of the eternal sea, her herd of white bulls, up to their bellies in the green pastures of the ocean, her spear aloft, her great eyes roolling . . .'

She was never to know how that story ended. Dazed and mesmerised, in the very heat, heart and height of it, she saw him leap up and cry: 'My comrades await me! The battle approaches. Meet me in Davy Byrne's back in an hour's time.'

And there he was pounding down the stairs with her shouting over the banisters, 'But if you aren't there?', and him shouting up from the bottom of the well 'Ring 707070!' She had waited for the length of four whiskeys in Davy Byrne's. She had then found that there is no such telephone number as 707070, and decided that she had misunderstood him: until she saw it the next day in a bookshop window. *I Did Penal Servitude*. By 707070.

By the morning of the Meeting she was beside herself. Up to then she had grudgingly accepted that his secret preparations for the Meeting were a reasonable explanation for his disappearances and non-appearances. But when the Meeting would be over and done with? She knew that that would be either the end or the beginning of everything. Early that morning, so early that the gulls were still screaming down on the garbage bins, she found herself awakened by a knocking on the door of her hotel bedroom. He was standing in the corridor carrying a suitcase, his collar up, his buttercup hair in his eyes, and his eyes staring. He laid the suitcase at her feet and said with a terrible earnestness:

'Rika, when, perhaps even before, the Meeting ends tonight the whole city will be a cauldron of excitement. There may be riots. Blood may flow in the streets. Unless I am in jail, or dead, I will come to this hotel at twelve o'clock tonight with a motor-car. I know the night porter. A grand young fellow from Kerry. One of us. Absolutely reliable. He will let me in by the back door. We will fly together into the mountains where a friend of mine has a lime-white cottage with a roof of golden thatch beside a dark lake where the ripples are for ever washing in the reeds and the wild water for ever lapping on the crags, and there at last we will be alone.'

'But,' she had asked, clutching her dressing-gown to her neck, 'how do I really know that I can really trust you to come?'

He had glared at her.

'Trust? It is I who trust you. This case,' down-pointing, 'contains everything I possess – papers, books, letters, plans, maps. Enough to ruin me for life! Is this hand I grasp the hand of a weakling or the hand of Queen Maeve?'

('Idiot that I was,' she sighed, 'I said "Queen Maeve".')

'At midnight! Be ready! Be waiting! My Grecian bride!'

(Throwing out her arms like a pope she cried: 'And he was gone!')

She went to the Monster Meeting. ('I *attended* it,' she said mockingly.) The evening was a trifle damp. Charlie had said that College Green would be thronged from end to end. Rika found a gathering of about three hundred people most of whom looked like evening strollers, invited by a loudspeaker – and gently shepherded by an Inspector and six guards – off the main thoroughfare of College

Green into a piazzetta called Foster Place. This broad brief cul-de-sac, mainly occupied by banks, is used during the day as a parking space, and commonly used by night for smaller public gatherings such as this. She soon observed that the organizers of the Meeting (old campaigners), having placed their decoy speaker at the farther or inner end of the cul-de-sac, then drew up a convertible motor-car at the other or open end for their main speakers, with the evident intention of leaving themselves a ready line of retreat into College Green if things turned nasty. Across the backs of the convertible's seats they had laid the kind of shallow packing-case which is used for transporting such flat objects as sheets of glass, wall-boards or pictures, a platform just wide enough to support and display one speaker at a time.

The pilot-speaker – a young Trinity College student named Phil Clune, who was later to become chief financial adviser to one of the new African nations – was both careful and lucky enough not to provoke his audience to anything more serious than a few sarcastic interruptions on the lines of 'Lord Byron was a dirty scut!', or 'And what did Greece do for us when we wor fightin' the Black and Tans?', or, in bland disregard for Phil's age, 'And where wor you in Nineteen Sixteen?' She found it all deflating and confusing until the crowd had to turn right around to face the main speakers. Then things began to warm up a bit while still remaining confusing, especially when what she called 'a butchy-looking woman with cropped grey hair like Gertrude Stein' started to speak of the Greek church as a citadel of truth, liberty and outstanding moral courage. This produced shouts of 'What Greek church?', and 'We don't recognize no Greek Church', which made her feel that it was her duty to explain to those near her what the Greek church really was; the main effect of which was to break up the opposition into small growling groups arguing among themselves about which Greek church recognized Rome and which recognized Constantinople. These arguments subsided when the butchy woman started talking about 'the deplorable silence of the Prisoner of the Vatican', whom she referred to, rather over-familiarly, as 'Papa Pacelli'. The result was such angry cries as, 'His Holiness the Pope to you, ma'am!' and, 'Hey! Are you from Belfast?'

At this point, if Rika had known her Dublin properly she would have realized that it would only be a matter of minutes before somebody would start singing *Faith of Our Fathers*, and then it would be high time for all prudent men and women to start edging off to the shelter of the nearest bank-doorway. Instead she started elbowing to the front where she saw Charlie insistently plucking at the tail of Gertrude Stein's skirt and madly whispering something to her that made her quickly wind up whatever she was saying about the Red Dean of Saint Paul's and lumber down off the packing-case.

Charlie at once leaped to the rostrum, his arms spread, his yellow hair blowing in the wet wind, his splendid voice ringing out:

> '*"Eternal spirit of the chainless mind!*
> *Brightest in dungeons, Liberty, thou art,*
> *For there thy habitation is the heart –*
> *The heart which love of thee alone can bind . . ."*

'My friends! I give you a clarion-call that I believe no man or woman listening to me can fail to answer. Up the Republic!'

The crowd did not say a word in answer to this clarion call – which was probably exactly what he wanted since they at once fell silent to listen, though possibly more dominated by his fine orator's voice and his burly lithe boxer's body than by the actual words he said:

('Oh!' she recalled. 'He looked superb. I fell in love with him all over again. Say what you like about him, he had presence. He had guts.')

'My friends!' he shouted. 'We are an old and ancient race whose past is so old and so rich, so filled with wonder and mystery that it surrounds us like the murmuring night-sea that defends our green shores, like the whispering Aegean whose antique memories for ever ripple among the reeds and lap upon the crags of ancient Greece. That darkness of Ireland's primordial memories is crowded tonight with the dim faces and the murmuring voices of our beloved and rebellious dead, whose words we never cease to hear and every syllable of which we fully and clearly understand – whether it be Queen Maeve of Connaught among her herds of milk-white bulls, the tossing foam of the sea, her great spear aloft, her thunderous voice calling to us to remember our birthright, or the quiet, sad figure of Cathleen the daughter of Houlihan passing through the shadows like an uncrowned queen.'

(Rika shrugged. 'Yes! He had only been practising on me. But I felt it made me his colleague! And I was proud of it!')

'My friends!' Charlie was bellowing. 'What do those voices say to us tonight? They say to us: "As we are free and as we will remain free, so must all mankind be free and for ever so remain."'

At which point he whipped a small tricolour from his left-hand inside pocket and waved it over his head – a gesture that actually produced a few approving cheers.

'But, my friends, I said "*all* mankind!"'

At which he whipped from his right-hand inside pocket the blue and white flag of Greece.

'This is the flag of fighting Greece! Tonight we fight under two flags in Freedom's name. Long live Liberty!'

He got a few more cheers. He now produced from his left-hand outside pocket the black swastika on a red ground.

'Does this flag stand for that Liberty? For your liberty, or for the liberty of your children? What can you say, what think, what feel? I will tell you what I think of it.'

And like a conjurer he produced half a dozen matches from his vest pocket, struck them alight on the seat of his trousers, and the Nazi emblem burst into flames. ('I had it well soaked in petrol!' he explained to us afterwards.)

'A sign!' he roared, as the emblem flamed and fell. 'A sign as black as treachery and as red as blood. And only in blood can all its cruelties be avenged!'

At this the Inspector and his six guards began to edge forward. After all, Ireland was officially a neutral country, even if we were more neutral against Germany than for it, and he had issued stern warnings before the meeting began that no word should be said that night contrary to Irish neutrality. But Charlie's next words made him pause, indecisively:

'I mean, my friends, the blood coursing through your veins, pulsing in your hearts with pity for the children in our slums, our unemployed wailing for bread, our aged sick neglected and dying all about us, the thousands of our young men, aye and our young maidens, mounting the gangways day and night to emigrate to foreign shores. Your warm Irish blood can remind you only of the triple cry of Liberty, Equality and Fraternity that led so many of our young men in every age to die for the Republic. That blood is the Rights of Man! That blood is the colour of universal brotherhood!'

Reaching behind him he received, unfurled and waved, blazing in the electric light of the street lamps, the red flag.

At one and the same moment a collective howl of rage burst from the crowd, a female voice began to sing *Faith of Our Fathers*, the Inspector and the guards breasted towards the car, the mob surged forwards, the car rocked and Charlie, to prevent himself from being thrown down among the lions, grasped the lamp-post beside him, and clambered up it like a monkey, still waving the red flag, still shouting 'Long live Liberty!'

(I could see it all in Rika's eyes, immense as two coloured television screens.)

'You know, those Irish policemen were marvellous! They got in a circle around the car and the lamp-post. One of them climbed up and pulled Charlie down by the legs, and the Inspector said, "Run, you bastard!" And, my God, how he ran! Some of the crowd ran after him, but he was too fast for them. I kept clawing at the Inspector and shouting, "I am a Greek girl!" He caught me and threw me head first into the car, my legs up in the air, just as the car started and ran away with me, the butchy woman, four or five men, and the red flag streaming behind them. They stopped in a long, quiet street, pulled me out and dumped me on the pavement, and drove away off down that long street into the fog.

'My face was bleeding. My stockings were torn. I was a sight. When I got up I saw I was opposite the Abbey Theatre and I will always remember the play they were playing that night. It was called *The Whiteheaded boy*. When I saw it I thought of Charlie. My God! I said to myself. He may want to hide in my hotel, and I ran all the way to it. I cleaned myself up to look my best for him when he would come at twelve o'clock. I packed my bags though I was shaking so much I could hardly do it, and then I threw myself on the bed and I cried for my whiteheaded boy. I cried that he knew I had seen him run, that he had been shamed into running for his life, that he was homeless and an outcast. Then suddenly I saw his suitcase and I thought, my God, the police may come here searching for him and find all his papers, and letters, and plans. I managed to lug it to the window-sill – it was very heavy – and I stood it up there outside the window and I drew the blind and the curtains, and I lay down again to cry and to wait.'

'I woke up at half-past one. I ran down to consult with the night porter, Charlie's friend. He was a nice, sweet boy, about seventeen or eighteen. He told me he had never heard of Charlie Carton. I knew then that Charlie would never come. But what was I to do with the suitcase? I decided to take this boy into my confidence. I told him that Charlie was a patriot and a hunted man. I shall never forget what he said to me. He said, "Miss, if he's for Ireland, I'll do anything for him." I cried when he said that, it was so warm, so Greek. When I told him about the suitcase that I must protect with my life, he got a bunch of keys and a screwdriver and we went upstairs together to see what we should do with this terrible suitcase. Between us, this boy and me, we dragged it in from the windowsill – it was by this time soaked with the rain – and we laid it on the ground and we worked on it and at last we managed to open it.'

(I shook my head. Not because I did not know what was in it – Charlie had told me – but in pity for her. Rika looked out of her window down at the waters of the port.)

'I suppose,' she said, 'in everybody's life there is one moment of shame that he never forgets. This was my moment – when that boy opened that suitcase, that nice boy who would have done anything for Ireland. It contained two bags of sand. Nothing else.' She laughed merrily. 'He really was a rascal! I told the boy, "This is probably dynamite." All he said was, "Yes, miss." I stayed in my room until the morning broke. Then I took the boat for London.'

I think if Charlie were with us at that moment I would have struck him. I said:

'Some people would be less kind about him than you. They would say he was a poseur, a sham, an actor.'

'Oh, no! He was much more than that! Much more! He was actor, dramatist, producer and play all in one. And we were his audience. He was always trying to play out some play of life that was real to him for as long as he imagined it, though it was always only real in the way a child's soap bubble is real. A dream full of swirling colours, in the end floating away, exploding silently.'

'Wasn't that a bit hard on the people who had to be his co-actors?'

'You mean people like me? Very hard. If we were foolish enough to think that any of his plays would last. Not hard if we knew that at any moment he would ring down the curtain and start another romantic play in some other theatre, in some other city, in some other country. Even then, of course, it was hard on his fellow-actors whom he left behind out of a job. He was inexpressibly selfish because he was *so* hopelessly romantic. Always dashing away. An artist whose only art was his life. Not a very good artist, I grant you, but, still, an artist.'

'Some people would say he was just a Don Juan.'

'I hope not! That most unhappy race of men. Always chasing shadows. Always hoping. Never sure. He is married.'

Was it a statement or a question?

'How did you know?'

She smiled:

'We all marry. If it comes to that Don Juans – and Donna Juanitas too – are of all people the most certain to marry, in order to be sure at least once before they die, or become impotent. To feel sure that their search was ... Oh, well, it's too difficult. It took me a long time to work it out. Until I did I hated him more than I have hated anyone else in my whole life. And,' she grinned, 'I'm very good at hating. When I realized that he just had to be what he is I no longer cared.'

'Have you ever written to him?'

She looked at me coldly.

'I am a happily married woman, with three sons. I am a professor. I have an adoring husband. I have a lovely home. Why should I write to him?'

'He has not forgotten you.'

She smiled a gratified smile and we shook hands.

'Give him my affectionate greetings. And all my sympathy.'

I glanced at her, startled until I saw that she did not mean it derisively. Her last question was to ask what he was doing now. I told her: a salesman for sanitary equipment. She was still laughing as she closed the door.

As I walked down through the narrow streets about the port I wondered for a long time what I would say if somebody asked me for my opinion of her. Like all experienced women, sensible, practical, and absolutely without illusions, despising above all those fantasies of which even the oldest men are never entirely free? Or would even she sometimes remember, with a tiny, secret, happy smile, certain earlier days when she had been a little otherwise?

I was amused when I told Charlie of our meeting in Athens, and he at once asked, eagerly, if she remembered him.

'Indelibly!'

'And is she still beautiful?'

'More so than ever!'

I watched his blue X-ray eyes narrow with penetration, widen with the lovely image they received, and then, ever so slowly, relinquish another dream. He had little bags under his eyes. His hair was thin as dust. He said, 'Oh, well! We had completed the medallion of our love!' – and made a graceful circle with his slender hand.

Billy Billee

'Charms, omens and dreams . . . ' He came on the phrase while ruffling through some sixty-year-old papers. It was in his first penny Catechism, salmon-pink, ear-crumpled, tattered. '*Question:* What else is forbidden by the first commandment? *Answer:* All dealings with the devil, all superstitious practices, such as consulting fortune-tellers or trusting in charms, omens and dreams.' He grunted. He said aloud, 'Oh, yes! Oh, yes, indeed!' He lit his pipe. He gazed out over the harbour. What was her name? He sniff-grinned. Presently the old man was scribbling on the back pages of the Catechism. It finally came out as, and he gave it the title of, *The Ballad of Billy Billee.*

> *Dear Blackie, dear Lottie, Billy Billee,*
> *Star of my morning's simplicity,*
> *Whispering low that love's sorcery*
> *Is hidden in charms, omens and dreams,*
> *That love, ever true to her faithful few,*
> *Like me and like you, gives us our due*
> *Fullness of bliss, eventually.*
> *Did you lie? Once again, my old query!*
> *Did you really dance that night for me?*
> *That November night when I thrilled to see*
> *You leap on the stage of an earlier age*
> *To the whistles and wolf-calls*
> *Of the boys in the front stalls*
> *Immediately under Box B, and me.*

Wearing his best Sunday suit, short trousers, with bare knees, a red bow tie in his celluloid Eton collar, fawn-edged, hot palms clung to the purple carton of Rowntree's Cream-filled Chocolates that, to crown his night, she had put for him on the velvet ledge of Box B. His face felt underlit by the blaze of the footlights.

Barely fourteen, the first time I'd seen
The frilly high kick, the round of a knee,
The entrechat flick, splits done to a T,
Full of pride as a bride 'till I damn near died
When, tier upon tier, they started to cheer,
You made it so clear, every wink, every leer,
You were dancing for me, for me, in Box B.

Not even barely fourteen. Thirteen and ten months. And she? Thirty-five, Thirty-six? Thirty-seven? Her red, toy-soldier cheeks hopping, her breasts jumping, her shoulders powder-white, her strong legs tightly cross-gartered. Had she ever been slimmer? Or in those days did men like their women plump? They certainly did not two years later when the stalls were half-filled at every matinée by wounded soldiers in hospital cream-and-blue, smilingly lifting their crutches to the applause of the audience as they faltered to their seats. Their ideal was the teenager, hair shingled, her eyes vast and unrevealing, a slim illusion of innocence.

Your Bolero brought the gallery
Up on their feet in a roar like the sea
For you, for me, crouched like a flea,
Caught by a spotlight, held by your glare,
Your whirligigs, your stamping rages,
Cursing like blazes, wishing to Jaysus
I was dead in the bed of the old River Lee.

And he really was praying: 'O dear, kind Jesus, please make them believe I'm her byechild. Brought over from London specially to see mamma dancing on the stage of the Cork Opera House.' (Only the week before she had put him in Box B to see *East Lynne*.)

Not that her figure was news to him. He knew all about it from certain damp afternoons when she showed him photographs of herself on her world-wide tours with The Dainty Delamare Dancers.

'That's me in Singapore, dearie. What fun that was! That's me in Toronto. Look at that snow! Seventy-two inches it was! Me in Auckland. Here's me in Jo'burg. Me and Molly Marples in Bombay. O how I love you! Roll on you rolling rivah! Where the dawn comes up like thundah outa Chiner 'cross the biy.'

She absently stroked his bare knee.

'Across wot biy, Mrs Black?' (In her company he used always talk the way she talked.)

'The Biy o' Chiner! Doncherknow no geography, Jacky dearie?'

She was their star lodger. She had stayed with them for three out of the four years that Jimmy J. Black spent in Cork as manager of the Opera House.

It was upstairs, in their sitting-room, that she used to show him those albums of her youth, one plump hand about his shoulder and the other turning the pages, her armpits exuding a scent that he knew was called Phul Nana because she once bedewed his crumpled handkerchief and his hair with it. Much to the annoyance of his mother who said that he must have been secretly creeping into her sitting-room, which was true, or else that she was 'up to no good' – a remark that inflamed him with enchanting possibilities.

'Up to no good?' Or just that she wanted somebody to talk to? Even if it was only a kid of thirteen, about her days of glory.

> *So long ago, yet I still want to know,*
> *After we parted where did you go,*
> *With what Jimmy or Jack, Tommy or Joe,*
> *To what house on the hill, what toff for a thrill,*
> *What military swell, tight as a kite,*
> *Laughing like hell, well out of sight –*
> *At the back, maybe, of Box A below?*

Face it! Give her thirty-seven. Hot as hell. Common as Get Out. A lecherous, treacherous old bitch. Only a boy would have thought her any better. English, of course. Maiden name, Carlotta Tottle. Born in Highgate, London. Father, a barber. Mother, a dresser in the Palace Music Hall, on King's Road. Pomade, patchouli and poverty.

(Across the bay the lighthouse gleamed, and was gone.)

What a throaty voice she had that day!

'You do know 'Ighget, Jacky dearie, or don't you? I mean, you must at least 'ave 'eard of 'Ighget?'

'No! Ah, no, Mrs Black, I don't know about Ighget at all, at all.'

'Not even 'eard of 'Ihget? My Gawd! Where 'ave you been all these years? 'Ighget's near 'Ampstead. Come on, Jacky! Surely you 'ave 'eard of 'Ampstead 'Eath?'

'Oh yes, Mrs Black, I do know about Ampstead Eath. I've read *The Woman in White*, and that begins at midnight on Ampstead Eath. Remember, Mrs Black?'

'Call me Lottie.'

'As a matter of fact, Mrs Black, Lottie, I know an awful lot about London. I've read all about Sherlock Holmes and I know all about Baker's Street, and the great detective Nelson Lee, and Sexton Blake, and Pedro and Tinker, and I've read Fergus Hume's *The Mystery of a Hansom Cab*. And I know about Paris, too, *The Three Musketeers*, and *The Hunchback of Notre Dame*, and *The Murders in the Rue Morgue*, and *The Scarlet Pimpernel*. And Rome. That's in *Fabiola* by Cardinal John Henry Nicholas Patrick Stephen Wiseman. He was called Patrick because his father was from Waterford. Lots of English cardinals were Irish, you know. That's why we always say that Ireland is the brightest jewel in the crown of Rome. I got *Fabiola* for a present at my First Communion. I read it four times.'

'Fancy that now!' she had laughed – she always made two chins when she laughed. She stroked his head. Then she breathed out a deep sigh.

'See wot comes of reading books. Now, before Jimmy J. brought me to Ireland I'd never read any book at all about this plice. If anyone had told me that one day I'd be living in Cork I wouldn't 'ave as much as known what country they meant. At your age I was dreaming of the wide, wide world.'

At which she looked glumly out of the window at the empty, Sunday afternoon square. There the only noise was a sparrow squeaking in the damp gardens of the Cork School of Art, whose tall, red railings swept around to the front of the Opera House.

It was his clearest image of her, leaning her elbows on the window-sill between the blowing lace curtains, her round, rosy face in her hands, gazing down into the square, or up the lean length of Academy Street at whose distant end she could see a trickle of traffic passing silently along Patrick Street. On fine days she used to spend hours that way. Like a wax statue. Sometimes talking, dreamily. Sometimes, then, her hand would touch his bare knee. A padded hand, not young.

> *Whenever my hand knocks out my dottle,*
> *Cowslip-freckled all over with mottle,*
> *Whenever I pluck the strings of my throttle,*

> *I understand your hand on my knee*
> *As you talked of Rio or Singapore,*
> *And why, with a sigh, more and more,*
> *As I do now, you groped for the bottle.*

When they were in their cups the rows she and Black used to have! Shouting and throwing things at one another, making so much noise that one night his father had to go upstairs and beg them to pipe down for God's sake and the honour of his house.

Black could not complain if she took to the bottle. A convivial fellow who belonged to two boozing clubs and never came home before two in the morning. A fine figure of a man, though! Tall, straight, florid. At his best standing every night in the brilliant front of the Opera House, in his white tie, tails and high choker, ready to click his fingers to an usher, wink at a club crony, bow over a city merchant and his wife, hover about a bunch of English officers down from the barracks. A solid Londoner, mounting guard, like them, over his far-flung outpost of the Empire.

That was her finest hour, too, in a feather boa and a picture-hat two feet wide, in her regular place in Box B, second-up, right-hand side, drinking in the smells of canvas-glue, grease-paint, stale dust, old ropes, faded scent.

One night after a Rugby Final the University students started a small riot in the Pit, and Jimmy came before the curtain. (The Bay of Naples in blue, Vesuvius in scarlet eruption, acres and acres of purple bougainvillaea.) They boohed him. He threatened to call in the police if they didn't stop it. They boohed louder. He retired in disdain and defeat.

'Oooh!' Lottie said afterwards. 'He looked so brive. Standing up there behind the footlights. Ficing them all.'

Sun-bronzed, gun in hand, topee over his left eye?

But Jimmy was smart. When the students started writing furious letters to *The Cork Examiner* he invited the whole team and their followers to be the free guests of the Opera House the next Monday night, and before the play began he came out again before the billowing Bay of Naples and made such a fine, manly, chummy speech about fair play and goodwill between fellow-sportsmen that they cheered him to the roof and sang *For He's a Jolly Good Fellow* . . .

'I tell you straight! I nearly cried up there in my box, I was so proud of my man!'

Jimmy J. must have made lots of good friends during his four years in Cork city; not one of them ever visited her. You could see it by the bareness of her mantelpiece. Every other coming-and-going lodger, actor and actresses all, used to crowd their mantelpiece with photographs in silver frames and leather frames, smiling relatives and friends, always signed. She had only two pictures to show: one of Jimmy, in his choker; the other of herself – brief frock, bare shoulders, fat, gartered legs, standing against a photographer's woodland scene, ferns to her right, ferns to her left, her plump arms poised as if she were about to rise with a whir out of the heather.

(Directly outside his window a seagull squawked. Alone. He listened. Not a sound.)

He had grown up in Cork, and never known until he left it how utterly alone he had been there, and how little he even still knew about what older people did there. The place was full of rich merchants. Did they have a good time? Did they entertain? Did they throw dinner-parties? Did they have dinner at all? Or did they just have high tea when they returned home at night to their big houses on the hills? Did they have bridge-parties? Travel? Whatever they did they would not have Lottie Black from King's Road, the barber's daughter, among their guests. She was as much outside it all as he was. Two of a kind.

They had no children. Neither of them ever read a book. They read the grey morning paper, the pink *Evening Echo*, the weekly, red-covered *Answers*, the green-covered *Tit Bits*, Horatio Bottomley's yellow-covered *John Bull*, and the black-and-white *London Life*. It was that one that lured him every week into her room to peep at its sepia Art Supplement – always a naked woman, with a figure as plump as her own. After which he might take a deep smell of her Phul Nana, with its label showing a harem-girl dancing in diaphanous trousers. Their whole apartment reeked of Phul Nana. Their lavatory stank of it.

The day she came back unexpectedly to her room and caught him looking at *London Life* . . . When he saw that she saw what he had been looking at he started to bolt.

'Don't run awiy, Jacky,' she ordered, going to the mirror to remove her gloves and her hat, fluff up her hair, and look at him, impaled in the glass, staring at her across the room.

'So soon?' she laughed. 'You know you'll be a 'andsome fellow when you grow up. I shouldn't be surprised if.'

She stopped, turned and surveyed him. Then she sat in her chintz-covered armchair by the open window and with one finger beckoned him over to her. He came and stood by her shoulder and she put her arm around his waist. Her throat whispered it, her eyes looking into his, six inches away:

'I suppose you'd like to see a real woman like that, wouldn't you?'

He hardly had the breath to breathe, let alone to answer, as she undid the top buttons of her blouse, and always looking at him led his hand firmly inside it to the hot blubber of her breast.

'Oooh!' she said. 'Your hand is so bloody cold!'

And threw his hand away, buttoned her blouse and glared into the square. Then she said:

'After I first married Jimmy I used to often wonder wouldn't it be nice if...'

She stopped. She looked back at him for a long while. Then she said gently, 'Poor little bastard!' Then she patted his bottom. Then she said furiously, 'Run off to your bloody mama!' He did not dare return for weeks.

She discovered God during her second year with them, one soft, spring night when every place of entertainment in the city was as dark as her boot for Holy Week, the last in Lent. The Opera House was shut; the music-hall; every cinema; our one *Palais-de-Dance*. The two clubs drew their blinds. Men slipped into the pubs by back alleys. Only the pigeons in the square dared to court openly: the male pigeon puffing himself into a muff of feather, displaying his fantail, following the female around with a piteous *luggudygoo, luggudygoo*, snubbed always by a scornful *so what, so what*? Only the black of the ash trees dared to burgeon. At night the square and streets were like a wake-house until a quarter to eight when the patter of footsteps that usually hastened eastward beneath their windows to the Opera House now hastened westward to the parish church of Saints Peter and Paul.

That Wednesday night his mother and he were getting ready to go out to the chapel when they suddenly saw her standing in the doorway of the kitchen, so pale and frightened that she at once reminded him of Lady Macbeth in the sleep-walking scene. His mother, her arms hooped over her head in the act of shoving her black hatpins into her black straw hat, cried out at her:

'Lord save us, Mrs Black, I thought you were a ghost!'

'I wish to Gawd in 'eaven I was a man!'

'But, Mrs Black, that's flying in the face of God's holy will!'

'Then wot is God's 'oly will! I've been walking the streets of Cork until my feet are dropping off me. Everything shut tight as a tick. Jimmy in his club soaking it up. Wot about me? I awsk you, is it Gawd's 'oly will for me to become a roaring, bloody secret, soaking, stinking alcoholic?'

'Why don't you come out with us to the Devotions?'

'Wotcher mean?'

'I mean,' his mother said piously, 'that we must all pray for the sins of the world. For Jesus in the garden of Gethsemane. Every one of his apostles abandoning Him. And the priests praying on the two sides of the empty altar. Until only the one blessed, holy, white candle is left alight in the whole church.'

'And then,' he had joined in, 'when that last candle is taken away behind the altar the electric lights go out and we all clap our hands in the darkness.'

'For the night of Calvary,' from his mother. 'For the end of the world.'

'The end of the world! Wot end? Wot world?'

'Every Wednesday, Thursday and Friday of Holy Week,' his mother said flatly.

He sat between them in the church. His mother loaned her one of her rosaries, which, on seeing other old ladies do so, she kissed repeatedly. She went with them on the following nights. He went with her alone to the morning devotions on Holy Thursday, where she loved the flower-drowned Altar of Repose. She stood for a long while before the great statue of Calvary, which included Mary Magdalen and the Madonna, and afterwards she had long, pious talks with his mother and father about it all.

> When you said every Magdalen everywhere
> Kneels at the foot of Calvary's stair
> Singing the song of all girls who bear
> The fruit of their ignorant Spring in the Fall,
> Whom did you see, rich with maternity,

Pushing a pram for all eternity –
A planet afloat in the heavenly air?

Summer is a thin time for churches and cities. He and his mother and father went off on their usual summer holidays to the County Limerick, to watch its crops grow brown and its shallow lakes sink lower still. When they came back they found that she had pinned or pasted on the wallpaper of her apartment, pages upon pages cut from art magazines showing plump, vast-limbed nudes: naked Andromeda chained to her rock, Rubens' half-naked Sabine women, Titian's Profane Love. Every week another naked woman smiled from the wall. They curled there in the heat of an Indian summer that filled the square with boys playing football, little girls playing with skipping-ropes, big girls singing, arm-in-arm, three abreast, around the Opera House, shawled women coming out from the lanes to give their babies to the cool of the night.

By September, her nudes clung like snowflakes to her mantelpiece, her washbasin, billowed from her mirrors. They pursued Black into the bedroom. A line of them hung over their double-bed. They adorned the walls of the bathroom.

Every day his mother said disgustedly that her house was not that kind of a house. She announced one afternoon that either the pictures must go or the Blacks must go, and stamped upstairs to give out her ultimatum. She came down as soft as a dewdrop.

'We can only pray for her,' she said. 'That man,' she cried, with womanly passion, 'should be horsewhipped. All he thinks of from morning to night is drink. Is he a man at all? Ah,' she sighed, looking across at the statue of the Virgin in the kitchen-corner, 'may the mother of sorrows look down on the poor mothers of the world.'

Day after day he used to spy on her from a far corner of the square, gazing up at her window where she sat gazing glumly down at the mothers with their babies, and the children playing; or, at dusk, listening to the arm-in-arm girls singing their love-songs from one lamp-post to the next. Then, in the damp of October, the pictures began to slide to the floor, where their slavey, Bridie McCarthy, used to collect them and bring them, with much lewd smirking and winking, to his mother, who would at once seize them and poke them into the red fires of the kitchen range. Not until they were all gone did he dare to start revisiting her in her room. She let him hold her hand.

Then she discovered Magic. One morning, just after breakfast, she appeared in the kitchen, radiant, gurgling with laughter, to tell his mother what had happened the night before. That week there was a conjurer in the Opera House called Chung Ling Soo. He did all the usual tricks, including The Lady Sawn in Half – a shapely, blonde young woman who also stayed with them and who always laughed merrily when his mother said to her each morning, between relief and disappointment, 'So ye're alive still?' Chung Ling Soo also threw cards, magically produced out of the air, down to the people in the stalls, entitling them to have their fortunes told during the interval by a chiromancer sitting in oriental robes in a little coloured tent in the foyer. Billy had got one of these cards, and had her fortune told.

'I let down my veil and I took off my ring so he wouldn't know anything about me. The things he said to me! O, very clever, you know! O, very clever, those orientals! He said "You've got bed-trouble! The third finger of your left hand is lonely. You will cross deep water in the space of Three. You will meet a fair man under the Crown. You will walk with him under the Star between Trees and Water. He will have great Hearts for you. You will touch Gold. You will have three children."'

She burst into peals of laughter.

That was when she first began to show him those albums of her tours, her arm about his shoulder, her plump fingers touching his knee, her eyes wandering down over the square or up the lean street. It was then, too, that she started going to the Turkish Baths on the South Mall to get her weight down; and to Professor Angiolini's Dancing Studio in Cook Street. She was less and less often in the house, especially on weekends, when, so she said, she was able to use the stage of the Opera House for rehearsing. Finally she announced that, for a charity concert, she was going to dance again.

(The fog-horn grunted like a pig across the misting water of the bay. He laid down his pipe and began to scribble some more figures on the pink cover of the Catechism. She danced on the night of November 10th, 1912.)

> *You danced for a dream, for a gleam in your eye*
> *That no one could spy, not even I,*
> *Perched so close, perched so high*
> *That I once saw you spit in the wings.*

At the end I raced down the long corridor,
You winked one eye through your dressing-room door,
And laughed. I turned. I wished I could die.

The next day when he came hurrying home from school she was gone. The only sign of her was one small, lace-edged handkerchief in the fireplace. It smelled of Phul Nana and whiskey. He kept it a long time. Then he stuffed it into a mousehole in his attic bedroom where – he presumed he might now suppose – the mice dreamed on it and had lots of fat little babies.

Come the next July, just as they were all about to go off again on their holidays, Jimmy Black told his father that she had died and was buried in Bombay.

'Very hot,' he said stiffly. 'Very hot in Bombay.'

It was later rumoured around Cork that she had died in childbirth.

Not even a child to dandle.
Charms, Omens and Dreams –
That's a game that's hard to handle,
Though – say it, say it –
You who led me on to play it,
A dream you found well worth the candle?

Before the Daystar

When you come out into the Place Pigalle from its dark side-streets your
first impression is of its brightness, then crowds, then noise, and then
you become one more aimless wanderer around the jammed pavements. Tonight there was a sharp sense of liveliness, even gaiety,
almost like the end of a feast-day, although the streets were cold and
damp and a cobweb of pink mist hung suspended over the roofs. It was
Christmas Eve, about ten minutes short of midnight.

In a corner of the overcrowded terrace of *Le Rêve* five young people,
three young men and two young women, sat crushed about a small
table behind the fogged glass partitions, talking loudly to make
themselves heard above the gabble. The youth who was doing most of
the talking looked like a light-weight boxer. He wore a black
polonecked sweater; his blue-black hair, harsh as metal, peaked over
his forehead like a wound-up watch-spring; his smile was a lighthouse
flash. The others interrupted him only to spur him on. Their
Scherazade? Their pet liar? Indulged. Bantered. Approved.

In a pause in his flow of talk the fair-mousy, pretty girl at his side
tilted her scarlet tarboosh so as to tickle his cheek with its blue, silk
tassel, and said, 'Happy now, Andy? This is better than Dublin, isn't
it? Or isn't it?'

He gave her his white grin, gripped her frail arm and squeezed it.

'As happy, Jenny, as a lamb with two mothers.'

He turned swiftly to the fat youth at his other side. 'Jaysus, Fatso,
I wonder what'd we be all doing this minit if we were back in
Dublin?'

Fatso raised a finger for silence, groped inside his mustard-and-cress
overcoat and slowly, very slowly, drew a vast, silver half-hunter from
the well of his fob-pocket. He clicked it open with the air of an ancient
out of an ancient world, considered its convex face, smooth, shiny and
milk-white as his own; and pronounced in a slow Abbey Theatre
brogue.

'I would be affther thinking, dearly beloved, that at this minit we would all be up in the Lamb Doyle's, or in The Goat, or The Cross Guns, or The Purty Kitchen where George the Fourth had his first glass of Guinness, being thrun out on our ears for the fourth time in succession. Althernatively, Andy, you would be snoring in your little white cot in your little white home in Templeogue.'

'Would I now? Well, then, let me tell you, Mister Laurence-O-bloody-well-Toole, I'd be doing no such a thing. I'd be being hauled off by my ma by the short hairs to Midnight Mass. That is, after the usual couple of preliminary breast-wallopings with the Dominican fathers up in Blackhorse Lane.'

He paused to turn to Biddy.

'Our privileged heathen,' he mocked.

Champagne-blonde, older than Jenny, not pretty, her splendid pigeon's bust straining her white sweater.

'Yes?' she queried, in an English voice so tiny that the first time they met her they had asked her if she had the pip.

'I mean Confession,' he explained, politely flicking two imaginary crumbs, one-two, from her bosoms. 'The annual clear-out. Old Father Berengarius. A mile of hardy sinners queuing up before me. The ould chapel as cold as a vault, and the wind under the slates moaning like a hundred banshees. He's as deaf as a post. Very convenient for yours truly. Doesn't hear a blooming word you say. Did I ever tell ye the night he disgraced me ma?'

He received their quizzical attention.

'There she was, late on Saturday night, inside in the confession box, asking him, if you please, was it a sin for her to believe in spirits and ghosts, and the mile of hardy boys outside all grumbling, and growling and rearing to get in and get out before the pubs closed on them. "Having commerce with ghosts", was what she called it. "What are ye saying to me?" says he, and his hand to his ear. "Is it a sin, Father," says she at the top of her voice, "to have commerce with ghosts?" "Speak up," says he in a roar that you could hear down at O'Connell Bridge. "To have commerce with ghosts, Father," she squawks, and the buckos outside all leaning sideways to hear the pair of them. "You have been having commerce with goats!" he roars at her. "At your age?"'

Once more they gave him the soft accolade of their laughter. Modestly rejecting the honour he turned aside and as suddenly turned back. Crook-necked he gestured to the dark street behind their corner café.

'Will yez look, boys! The foxy-headed whore is back again. Trying to click a GI she is this time. They're brazen tonight. Out in the open. He's twice her height. He'll make pancakes of her.'

They all swayed. The nearest of them to the glass partition was Mackinnon. He peered out under his black Homburg hat, low over the boils on his forehead. She was a small, skinny woman in a sheepskin jacket, a white beret, a white satin bottom as taut as two mushrooms.

'She must be frozen,' said Jenny pityingly.

'Behold the fruits of French logic,' Biddy piped. 'They close the brothels and every woman in Paris gets pneumonia. That foolish man will be streaming at the nose tomorrow morning.'

'I consider it most unseemly,' said Mackinnon. 'On Christmas Eve!'

Andy pointed his index finger at him, pulled the trigger, said, 'Bang, you're dead!' They laughed. They knew their Mac. A tongue of gall. He had never said an original word in his life. He worked at the Irish embassy. He would go far. They called him Mac the Knife.

'Mac!' Andy said, 'I wish you to understand that I am on the side of all rebels, exiles, outcasts and sinners. What Genet called The Saints of the Underworld.'

Biddy calmed his clenched fist with one scarlet-netted palm.

'Easy, Andy! And it was not Genet. Pasolini. And I do trust, dear boy, that you are not going to go all romantic on me tonight. I mean, talking about Dublin. And your mamma. And Midnight Mass. And Confession. And Dominican fathers. And, now, French hoahs.'

He was too fascinated by the comedy in the street to heed her. She enlisted Jenny's help.

'Jenny, is our broth of a boy about to get plawstered on us yet once again?'

'Haven't you observed?' Jenny sniffed, 'whenever he takes to the bottle in a big way it always means the one thing? Some new crisis with his precious Deirdre.'

'Deirdre?' she whispered. 'But that little Irish fool doesn't mean a thing to him. Deirdre is merely the girl he sleeps with.'

At this Jenny laughed so bitterly that Biddy peered one-eyed at her.

'I trust, my dear, that you are not getting soft on him? I mean, as one old harridan to another, you must be hitting twenty. And,' she whispered out of the side of her mouth, 'he is only a poo-o-oodle!'

Jenny considered him seriously. In Paris less than six months, as Dubliny as the first day they met him, light-headed, light-hearted, feckless, a liar, much too fond of his liquor. Nobody was ever going to travel very far on his roundabout. Certainly not Deirdre. As if he felt her looking at him he grinned at her and turned back to the street. She said loftily to Biddy, 'I assure you!'

'There is no need to protest, dawrling. We're all gone about Andy. That irresistible Irish charm. He's even gone about himself. It's his disease.'

Under the table Jenny felt his hand creeping slowly over her knee.

'Andy, why didn't you bring Deirdre tonight?'

His hand withdrew. He sighed, 'Poor little Deirdre.' He burst into a sudden passion. 'Jenny! Do you know what I am? I'm a sink!'

'Tell us, Andy,' she said sympathetically, 'why are you a sink?'

'No! You tell me! Examine me! Have no mercy on me! Tell me what's wrong with me.'

Mac the Knife tapped his arm. His speckled forehead became suffused with venom. He assumed a stage-Cockney's wheeze.

'I'll tell you, chum, wot's wrong with you. You're 'omesick for dear, old, dirty Dublin. Your wrists long for the chains. Your back aches for the lash. Cheer up, chum, this time next year you'll be back there for keeps, with no Pigalle, and no cafés, and no night-clubs, and you'll have your eye on a good job, and be wearing more holy medals than a Lourdes veteran, and you'll be running off like a good little boy to Midnight Mass, and Aurora Mass, and Third Mass, and Fourth Mass, and...'

Andy leaped up. His chair fell. All over the terrace heads turned lazily towards them. A waiter paused in his stride.

'Do you want a sock in the kisser?' he roared.

The two girls dragged him down.

'Andy!' Jenny chided and stroked his arm as if he was a cross dog. 'Aa-a-ndy!'

He retrieved his chair. He sat down glowering. Then he leaned over, seized Mac's hand and shook it warmly, rapidly, hurtingly.

'Mac! My old pal from schoolboys' happy days! As one unconverted and thoroughly corrupted Irish crook to another leave us be honest for one brief moment of our all too long and useless lives. Leave us admit that we've both been emancipated by La Belle France. We've killed Mother Ireland. We're free!' His grin fell dead on the table. His visor sank slowly over his toddy. 'We're emancipated. And disbloodywellillusioned.'

'I knew it,' Biddy piped to the striped awning. 'The Celtic Goat of Pure Romance. I saw it coming. I felt it in my bones. And I warn everybody present that I shall not be able to bear much more of it.'

Andy's head shot up.

'Anyway I gave up all that Holy Joe stuff years ago. I was a converted atheist at the age of seven. I was thrown out of school at fourteen for denying the existence of God. I proved it by logarithms.'

'You don't say so?' Mac jeered.

Andy shot him again on a quick draw, turned to Jenny, put his arm about her narrow waist and confided into her ear for all to hear.

'Jenny, my love, I'll tell you why I'm a sink. This morning Deirdre said to me. "Don't go out from me tonight, love! Don't leave me on Christmas Eve," says she. "Okay," says I, "come along with me." "You'll only get tight again, shéri," shays she. "Don't abandon your own loving, little Deirdre," shays she. "Spend it alone with me," shays she. But I did leave her! And I *am* going to get tight! And to hell with her! God Almighty, does she want to turn me into a monk? Imagine a fellow not having a couple of jars with his pals on a Christmas Eve! The trouble with Deirdre is she's not emancipated. There's one for you, Mac, who'll be back in Dublin in six months. In five years she'll have a squawl of kids around her saying the Rosary every night. Still and all I did ditch her. And there's no getting away from it. I'm a lousy sink!'

She stroked his cheek with one long finger.

'I don't think you're a lousy sink, Andy. I think you're a sweet sink. You just can't hold your liquor, any more than you can hold your conscience.'

He tightened his arm about her waist.

'Jenny! You understand me better than anybody else in the entire, global world. You're the grandest girl in all creation!'

'Better than Deirdre?'

He banged the table and shouted.

'I'm worse than a sink. I'm a flamin', flittherin', filthy, finished-off sink!'

'Jesus help me,' Biddy moaned, and began wearily to powder her nose.

Jenny whispered something into the whorls of his ear, he let his head sink on her shoulder, her blue tassel fell over his eye, he put his arm around her again. Mackinnon twirled a palm of antique boredom at Larry Doyle, who beamed pleadingly at him as if begging indulgence for all young lovers. Suddenly Andy flung up his head with a wild jerk.

'Boys and girls! I have a smashing idea! Why don't we all tumble into a taxi and go off to Midnight Mass in the Irish Church?'

'Here it comes,' said Biddy, brightly snapping her compact. 'Back to our vomit. Cassandra the daughter of Priam, that's me. Often heard, rarely heeded, always right. Never let it be said that I am a spoilsport,' she begged them all, gathering up her handbag and a four-foot-long, peacock-blue umbrella. 'Which is this church you mentioned, Charlie? Church of Ireland? Papish? Celtic synagogue? I'm with you all the way even to the Mosque. Or would it do if I led you to some good, old, solid ten-by-twenty Nonconformist tin chapel somewhere?'

Mackinnon rose, took off his black hat, held it to his chest and spoke with Castilian pride.

'*Mademoiselle, vous oubliez que je suis Catholique.*'

She made a soft noise like a duck getting sick, they all laughed, and while Andy was paying the bill they scrambled out on to the pavement. It was jammed by the crowd outside *Le Jardin d'Eve* looking at lighted photographs of naked women with breasts like udders. Biddy said in annoyance to Jenny. 'I notice they always leave him to pay the bill.'

'The boy is a fool. He loves to play the milord.'

'Tell me, does he always get religion when he starts thinking of Deirdre?'

'You've known him as long as I have. Are you getting soft on him now?'

Biddy shrugged.

'I wouldn't mind having a bash at old Andy.'

'He's not your sort. He is what you said. A poodle. A puppy. He's just a kid. Let him alone.'

The kid rushed out and hooked the pair of them into the crowd. They saw the redheaded whore, her eyes circling slowly about her like a slow waltz, glance at and dismiss Mac and Larry. Andy laughed, 'Business bad tonight.' It occurred miserably to Jenny that her eyeballs would be circling under her green eyelids even in her sleep. Larry called out, 'The Irish Church is miles away, can't we go somewhere else?' The crowd bumped them. The doorman of *Le Jardin d'Eve* barked at them to come and see the most nude women in the whole world. 'Ask him,' Andy suggested, and Larry approached him. While Larry and he were comparing silver half-hunter with gold half-hunter Biddy said he was like Georges Brassens' daddy. Jenny said he was like her own daddy. The barker closed his watch, directed them to the Rue des Martyrs, called after them '*Vite, mes enfants! C'est tard!*' Then, behind them his voice soared, '*Les plus nues du monde . . .*'

They turned from the lights, and the crowds, and the rumbling beat of Pigalle's heart into the narrow street whose prolonged silence gleamed distantly with coloured windows. By the time they were filing into the church the congregation were shuffling erect for the Gospel. Biddy halted inside the door. Mac and Larry stayed with her. Andy probed along the aisle and found two empty places in the front row directly facing a small Christmas manger with the Infant, the Virgin, Saint Joseph, the cow, the ass, the shepherds and the coloured kings huddled about a crib under an amber light and a bald electric star. Whoever had arranged the *crèche* had perched a stuffed robin redbreast on the edge of the cot. Andy nudged her, nodded at it, and winked conspiratorially.

She was back, one frosty morning, four years ago, at home, awakened by a thud on her bedroom window: it was a robin lying stunned on the window-sill. In her nightgown by the open window she had held it, throbbing between her palms, staring at the one big eye staring up at her, and for that one sleepy moment all life was as simple as a captured bird. She opened her palms, the robin flew off into the frosty air, and the morning star gleamed above the hills and the murmuring beach. *In splendoribus sanctorum.* The priest was intoning the psalm. In the brightness of the saints, she remembered from other midnight masses. *Ex utero anti luciferam . . .* From the womb before the day-star, I begot Thee. Did he remember? She touched the hand beside her and they looked at one another. Thereafter, silently from her white shore her bright moment ebbed. It fell as softly as a leaf from a book, a rose petal. Her window empty, her beach dry, she saw, leaning against a pillar beside them, the woman in the sheepskin coat. When the sanctus tinkled everybody else but she knelt. When everyone raised their heads she was still standing there, staring blankly in front of her. Andy was gone. There was no sign of him down the aisle, nor could she see the other three.

Crossly, she made her way back to the doorway, and out to the street. It was so dark that at first she saw nothing; then she made out the four figures on the opposite side of the street clumped like a bunch of gangsters, smoking cigarettes. She crossed over.

'Why did you come out?'

Biddy slowly smoothened her netted fingers and said sullenly, 'It wasn't my show, dawrling.' Larry Doyle looked uncomfortably at Mac the Knife who made a half-moon with his hangdog mouth, performed a high, dissociating shrug, and looked at Andy who let out a zany guffaw and then said sulkily, angrily, 'We should never have gone!

'It was you who proposed it!'

'We shouldn't have done it!'

'I thought they were doing it very nicely?'

He appealed to them, boxer-crouched.

'When you don't believe in a thing what is it but tomfoolery?' He stood back, his claws to his chest. 'I don't believe in anything. It's all kid stuff. I felt indecent inside there.' He shot out his left. 'And that bloody redhead in there finished me off. God Almighty, people have to be honest, don't they? They have to come clean, don't they? When I saw that wan in there I felt, Jaysus, what am I but another dirty bloody hypocrite?'

Jenny slapped his face, stepped back in dread, ran a few yards downhill, he after her, turned, a lean hare, ran faster and faster until he caught her, whirling her against a black wall under a street lamp, gasping, her palms spread against him. They panted.

'What's wrong, girleen?'

'What's wrong is that you *are* a hypocrite. First Deirdre. Then that street-walker. Who are you going to blame yourself on next? Me? Biddy? Why don't you go back to Dublin and rot there? It's what you want, isn't it?'

She turned to the wall and burst into tears. He waited while she sobbed. When she was quiet she turned and asked him for his handkerchief, wiped her eyes, said, 'May I blow?', and blew.

'Why should I want to go back to Dublin? I'm happy here, with you, and Biddy, and all the gang.'

'Are you?' she challenged. She gave him back his handkerchief. 'I

think, Andy,' she said quietly, 'you'd better go back now to Deirdre.
You know she'll be waiting up for you all night.'

He made a noise of disgust.

'She's not the answer.'

'And what is?'

He took her arm and led her back to the group. Sacerdotally, Larry
blessed them with a sweeping arm, '*Benedicat vos. Pax vobiscum.*'
Mackinnon said, with immense bonhomie. 'A Happy Christmas to the
happy pair!' Biddy said, coldly, 'And what does one do now?' Larry
threw his arms around Jenny, and intoned.

> *My beloved, drink the cup that cheers*
> *Today of past regrets and future fears,*
> *For, ah, tomorrow we may be*
> *With yesterday's seven thousand years.*

Nobody commented. The woman was standing alone on the step of
the porch looking across at them. As they looked at her Andy walked
over and spoke with her. Then the two walked off slowly, out of
sight.

Mac gave a beck of his head to Larry, said to the girls, '*Le Rêve*', and
the two of them went off, hunched together, nose to nose, back to
Pigalle. Jenny whirled and stared downhill towards the pink glow over
Paris. For a while, Biddy considered her rigid back. Then she
contemplated her long slim legs. Then she regarded her left thumb,
wiggling it double-jointedly. Then she looked up at the sky and said,
'Andy once told me he spent an entire night discussing the works of Guy
de Maupassant with a hoah in Marseille. He said they were still at it
when the sun rose behind the Château d'If. Odd! Even in Marseille the
sun does not rise in the west. I shouldn't worry about him if I were you,
Jenny. He will be back in *Le Rêve* in half an hour as chaste as the dawn
and without as much as a franc in his pocket. He'll tell us that she has
a grandmother in Provence, or a child in hospital, or that she reads
Pascal every night. The party's over. The night is bitter cold. And I am
sick at heart. We'll get a taxi and I'll drop you at your door.'

'I want to walk,' Jenny said sourly.

Biddy's fledgling's voice took on an edge.

'In this cold? To Saint Germain? Do you want to die for him, like
Mimi?'

'What is he up to? Always expiating for something or other? What's the point of it? Why doesn't he grow up? If he does give that woman all his money he'll only leave Deirdre penniless for a month, and borrow from us, and then borrow from his mamma to pay us back.'

'Unlike us he is young and innocent. It is what makes him so appealing. In his bothered way he's different.'

'Or is it just that all Irish men are different? Look at the other two. My God! What are we *doing* with them?'

Biddy hooted.

'Dear child, you obviously have no idea what Englishmen are like. I know! I've put dozens of them through my little white hands. Full to the gullet of guilt, black silences, sudden glooms, damp despairs, floods of tears and then that awful, manny, British laughter and "Let's have another one, old girl". Paris has been absolute bliss after London. Every Frenchman a swine. It's been such a relief. It's his only trouble – he thinks he's a sink and he isn't. It takes centuries to produce a really first-class sink. Still he shows promise. The right woman could do a lot for him. Not Deirdre, a silly little Dublin chit, just as stupid as himself. Let's get a cab. I'll pay for it and drop you right at your door.'

'I still want to walk,' Jenny said stolidly.

'It's savage. My ears are dangling by a thread. A cab, for God's sake!'

'Are you trying to get rid of me?'

Biddy regarded her with admiration, and shrugged.

'Biddy! What do we see in him?'

'Ignorance? Hopelessness? Eagerness? Terror? Charm?'

'But he is such a fraud!'

'And as you said, such a fool!'

'But, you say, innocent?'

'As a rose!' Biddy sighed.

'Let's go back to *Le Réve* and see if he does come back.'

'He will come back. His type always comes back. One of the lads.'

He came, wildly excited, bustling in, penniless, full to the gullet of lies and boastings – or, if they were not lies, of fantasies, and if they were not boastings, of dreams.

'All our lives,' he pronounced, 'we dream of love, and love eludes us. We have fled, Mac, from the sow that eats its own farrow. And all the time we dream of our childhood and are never free of it. O exiles of Erin, love ye one another. My bloody foot! Two single tickets to Dublin, that's the right ticket. But where shall we find her? Every mis-match Irishman a born matchmaker, and good at it. Saving others who cannot save himself. Sitting in a Dublin pool of drink and dreaming of the Arc de Triomphe. I told her I'd follow any woman to the ends of the earth but not to the end of the world. Nobody would take a fellow up on that! Gimme the Queensberry Rules and be God I'll not complain. I want a loving, lovely, innocent wife!'

'With squads of babies?' Jenny asked and felt his hand start to rove over her knee.

'Squads and squads of them!'

'All chawnting the Rosary?' Biddy piped mockingly, and pressed his other hand.

Their mockery could not halt him. The girls looked at one another with big eyes, shook their heads and made wry mouths of self-astonishment. Mac's eyes kept closing and half opening from sleep and drink. 'What are we waiting for?' he asked dully. Larry Doyle looked at his turnip-watch and sighed, 'It's gone two'clock.' The terrace was empty. The pink haze fell as glistening rain on the street. Nobody stirred. Even their talker was silent.

After a while he spoke, looking around at them sullenly.

'I'm going to take a plane to Dublin in the morning. Who'll lend me the money?'

£1000 for Rosebud

Rosebud met him one summer afternoon in London while she was lying flat on her face on the pavement of St James's Street outside Prunier's restaurant, during an air-raid. 'Suited him down to the ground,' she used to say long afterwards, with a laugh, 'I didn't stand a chance.' When the bomb fell somewhere in Green Park she looked sideways and saw a handsome young fellow in the RAF lying beside her, head on elbow, pensively admiring her. He might well admire her – hair like a wheat-field in September, two big frightened eyes of cornflower-blue, aged, he rightly guessed, about nineteen, and nicely fat. Plump girls were at a premium in London during those years of food rationing. She was happy to let him lead her off to the Ritz for a drink, downstairs in the crowded bar; all present, he assured her, being either spies or counterspies, heroes or whores. He told her that he was in Intelligence, with the effective rank of Wing Commander, and that his father owned a racing stable in Ireland. His name was Mick Donnelly. He had the mouth of a boy, the jaw of a man, and wicked brown eyes. She told him she was Rose Powis, straight off a farm in Wiltshire. Within an hour they were madly in love, within a week she had slept with him, a month later he married her, and the next day he left her, for Sicily and the Italian campaign, promising that when the war was over he would transplant his Rosebud to the finest house in Mayfair where they would live like a king and a queen.

She believed every word he said, and she knew that nothing he could ever do or say all her life long could hurt or surprise her. Within two months of his return, demobbed and jobless, he had surprised her so often and so variously – even though she was by then twenty-two, and those three years in London had taught her a lot – that she never mentioned him afterwards to any old, wartime chum without ending up, 'Say what you like about Clarence, life is never dull with him.'

The 'Clarence' had been her lightest shock.

'You see, Rosebud,' he explained to her, 'it was all mummy's fault.

She christened me Clarence Michael, after the Duke of Clarence, and then, God knows why, always called me Mikey. I hated it but it stuck. Furthermore, the proper spelling of our name is not Donnelly but Dunally. So, from this on I am Captain Clarence Dunally. Much better style! More dash to it! And much more in keeping with the kind of appointment I want, and,' sternly, 'mean to get.'

She had been Mrs Mick Donnelly. Now she was Mrs Clarence Dunally. She thought it great fun. She was game for anything – so long as it was not mean, or calculating, or nasty. Reared on a farm, educated by a war, total and timeless at every moment, she had the simple appetites of a kid-goat and was as innocent of morals as a child. In other circumstances, depending on what wind blew into her eager sails, she could have been anybody, done anything, died in the swamps of Ravenna wearing a red shirt, stabbed Marat in his bath, been a Manon or a Margherita, Lady Macbeth or Lucy Lockit, Judith or Saint Joan.

'Fine!' she said. 'Clarence! And what's my name?' she asked with fond assurance.

'You,' he said throatily, 'will always be my Rosebud, let's go to bed.'

It also surprised her a little, but it did not trouble her, as long as the funds lasted, that he showed no sign either of getting a job or of much wanting to get one. She was merely sad for him when he broke the news to her that his dad's racing stable had gone bankrupt during the war so that, as he put it, he had 'no very large prospects for the future'. She was further surprised, but more angered, for his sake, when he explained that owing to certain, low army intrigues, too complicated for her to follow, he would not enjoy the pension due to a Wing Commander. Only one thing he did really shook her – the place where he took her to live.

On his return to London and civilian life they had gone straight into Claridge's for three gloriously spendthrift nights, and then into a lodging-house in Paddington. They were still there two months later. What with the bombing, and no houses being built, and mobs of extra people in London, they soon found that they would be lucky to get houseroom anywhere. At last, nagged just a tiny bit by her, Clarence solved the problem overnight. He rented a small houseboat, called *Evangeline*, permanently moored to the towpath above Walton-on-Thames.

'Do us for a few months,' he said. 'Just to get over a bad patch. Just long enough to give me time to explore the ground at my ease.'

One glance at *Evangeline* made her eyebrows soar and her heart sink. She felt her first hint of fear. She saw an ancient, waterlogged wreck; everything metal on it was rusty, the glass in the tiny portholes was broken; its woodwork had fed generations of woodlice. It had, obviously, stood, lain or leaned there for so many years that nothing now kept it from keeling over in the mud but its gangplank, its hawsers and its long-settled condition. She foresaw fog, smelled rats, noted that it was a mile from the nearest shop, guessed that it must be twenty from Mayfair, and on dark nights every step of that overgrown towpath would be a menace. She threw her arms about his neck and said, 'Clarence, how clever of you! We'll make it simply lovely. Let's get cracking at it right away!'

It was October and raining. They worked on *Evangeline* like galley-slaves all through that autumn and into the fogs of winter. They caulked the yawning timbers, replaced what they could afford of the rotted woodwork, painted the superstructure in pink and every inch inside in white. Rosebud lined the scuppers with Henry Jacoby geraniums in toffee-tins and hopefully set an Albertine rose in a tub to grow across a trellis above the companion-way.

One afternoon in November, when they had almost finished the job, that is, done about as much to the junk as they could do, a lone passer-by along the towpath paused to watch them, said, 'Looking ahead to the summer? It will be fun,' and winked. They thanked him and said yes, it would be nice for weekends in the summer. When he had passed on they looked at one another shamefacedly. They had come to know from the various words dropped by tradesmen and others that that was about what the river had always rated in those parts, a raffish wink. Clarence said nothing. He had already noted that Rosebud could never mention the name *Evangeline* without an embarrassed flutter of her eyelids. She had already observed that whenever he gave his address to a stranger he let his hands rise and fall feebly like a dying duck, though if the man said encouragingly, as he usually did (with or without a wink), 'Lucky to have anything these days!', Clarence would always gallantly agree, and always add, 'It's not exactly Mayfair, of course.'

That night – they were below, finishing their dinner of sausages and mash, and their one bottle of beer – she said, probing him, 'Clarence, if this isn't exactly Mayfair, what *is* it?'

'It's County,' he said bravely, and then hit his fist a wallop on the deckbeam two feet over his head. 'Rosebud, we've got to get out of it. We're mad to be living in this Chinese sampan. Into the Rialto! Into Mecca! I said Mayfair, and I mean Mayfair! Some people might even settle for a mews off Pont Street, or a mews in Kinnerton Street. They might even settle for NW1 – all those super Nash terraces. But not me! If I could only lay my hand on a thousand quid, if I . . .'

'Here, here, hold on! What's a supernash terrace?'

'Nash? Great English architect. Don't you know? Haven't you heard? Sir Henry Nash. Wonderful houses. Pure seventeenth century.'

'Seventeenth century? That was the time of Queen Elizabeth. They must be as rotten as this junk. And what's wrong with a nice little house in Hampton, or Kingston, or Richmond, or even in Walton-on-Thames?'

He looked at her as coldly as if she were a stranger.

'Did you say Walton-on- . . .? Rosebud, I see I've got to take your education in hand.'

He had placed, she had seen them but never looked into them, three books on a small bulkhead shelf. He shoved aside the plates, the beer-bottle and the bits of holly branches she had stuck in a milk-bottle, took down the three books and lobbed them on the table. Then he stared at her, like a dentist gazing speculatively at a really hopeless tooth.

'Where can I begin? This is *Who's Who*. Observe! A plain statement. No question-mark. Everybody, I mean everybody, is there – who counts. This one is *The Home Lawyer*. I've won a dozen court-martials out of that.'

She ruffled it. It was, in due course, to become her favourite book of the three, so much so that whenever she laid it on the table it opened of its own accord, as softly as a sea-anemone, at the chapter headed 'Divorce'.

'This one is the map of the known world. *The A.1 Atlas of London and Outer Suburbs. Latest, revised edition*. Three and six. This tells us where everybody out of *Who's Who*, who lives in London, lives. Now!'

He opened it. Like a field-marshal he spread his hands above the web of black streets and began.

'Operation Rosebud! Here,' drawing a swift line about Mayfair, 'is our objective. The heart of W1. But don't let that fox you. Soho is also W1. And a damned shame it was to put it there. Good Lord, if it comes to that Tottenham Court Road – and we all know what that means – is W1. But this,' finger on the M of Mayfair, 'is the citadel we shall enter and conquer. There are alternatives? NW1? You've got some really posh places up there. Clarence Gate. Or York Gate. Down here, SW1. Pretty good. Backs on Belgravia. Which, you observe, backs on Buck Palace itself. SW3? Tricky, but not bad. I've been tempted in my time by Cheyne Walk, even Brompton Square. Time was when I wouldn't have sniffed even at Egerton Gardens. Though, God knows, the way the world is going nowadays you never know who might be cowering in some godawful square off dim places like the Fulham Road. Would you believe it, Rosebud, I know a depressed peer who's actually reduced to a boarding house in Bayswater. And a pal of mine told me the other day, it made my hair stand on end, that he knows a retired general who is actually living on a barge beside the gasworks on the Grand Union Canal at Hanwell! Could you ever believe such a thing would happen?'

'If you say so, Clarence!'

'The moral is plain!' he snapped. 'Never give up a major objective for a lesser. I have set my face against that pitfall. Because if you once let yourself think that you might put up with less than the best you'll end up by taking less than the less. And in the end, less than the less than the less! No! A garret in Mayfair, Rosebud, even a simple garret will do us for a first foothold. I know so much. I can teach you so much. If we could only lay our mittens on a thousand quid and a garret in Mayfair I know, I simply know, that with your beauty and my brains we'd be on top of the social tree in six months.'

'But, tell me, Clarence, supposing we did get a garret in Mayfair, what would we do there?'

'Haha! Second stage of Operation Rosebud. It wouldn't really matter a damn what we did, ye know! Infiltrate. First get in. Once in – spread. I could start by making leatherbelts for Fortnum and Mason like that fellow Roskolski who began with five quid in a back-lane off Bruton Street and now has a swank shop in Bond Street. And how did he do it? He got to know the right people! You could sew old school ties for Burlington Arcade like that Polish Countess who came there as a kitchen-maid and now has that posh boutique in Pont Street. Clients, friends, backers! That's the ticket. I could even be a taxi-driver and some day pick up Lord Who's Who, the fellow that started Marks and Spencers on a borrowed five hundred quid. "Where do you live?" he'd say. "Oh," I'd say, casually-like, bowling him over on the spot, "I've got a little hole in Mayfair. Why don't you drop around some night, my lord, and have a good Russian vodka? I could tell you things about London that not even you know." Into my lap in the click of a finger! But supposing I said, "I've got a little hole in Pimlico?" do you think he'd bite? See what I mean? Be around. Have your ear to the ground. Be in the way of luck. Be where the pickings are. Plant your knowledge where it's going to bear juicy fruit. But how in hell can we possibly hope to get to know anybody from a base like this? I tell you, Rosebud, I'd commit the most foul, fiendish, hellborn, stygian, diabolical, unforgivable crime this minute for even a coal-hole on the uttermost edge of Mayfair.'

She laughed fondly at him, patted his head, told him he wouldn't hurt a flea, and went off with the dishes to the galley.

'Little do you know me, my lass!' he called after her. 'Little do you know!'

Rubbing the greasy dishes with her rosy fingers and throwing the scrap out of the porthole into the flowing river she wondered. Three months on the houseboat as a wife had taught her more than her three years in London as a grass-widow. She had foreseen the rats frisking under the floorboards, the fog lying thick as wool on the river. She had not foreseen the savage damp, or how lonely the drip off the poplars could sound on the deck when he was in town, the discreet pawnshops of Kingston and Richmond, or that Clarence was full as a honeycomb of secret places where no woman would ever go. She was often reminded of him by their cat, Rodolphe, squatting by the stove with eyes half-closed in veiled aloofness. On such lonely days and dripping nights she had sometimes got the feeling that *Evangeline*, stuck in the mud, moored by the edge of the flowing river, was an image of her own life in those three years since she left the farm at Tisbury for the blackout, the bombs, the excitement of London. Which was why, on many such nights, silent except for more instructions about Operation Rosebud, more nervy plottings and wonderings about how could they get to Mayfair and where the hell could they get a thousand quid, and the life they were going to have when they got out of this junk on the Upper Amazon, she would silence him with, 'Darling, do you really love me?' and he would simply utter her rosy name from the depths of his throat and she would say, from the depths of hers, 'Let's go to bed,' and, for a while, they would hear only the water muttering past their ears, and, for a long, wild, heavenly while, nothing at all. (She was not a girl to make any bones about that. 'He was *marvellous* in bed!') Then, after he had fallen into a contented sleep, she would lie awake gazing fondly sideways at him who, for all his boastings about all he knew, looked then as helpless as a boy.

All he knew... They were such odd things, and so interesting, and always so mixed up with 'our future', and with 'maintaining us in the manner to which we are accustomed' – not 'his' future, or the manner 'to which "I" am accustomed' – that she could listen to him happily for hours of it.

One night it would be all about food and drink.

'Drink is very important. Vodka, for example, must always be served in paper-thin, ice-cold glasses. And whatever the hell it is always call it Soviet vodka. No real gentleman would drink anything else. Major Grey's Chütney? Sound stuff – but never ask for it, too many people know about it. Gentlemen's Relish is definitely eaten by gentlemen. But Riley's Royal Fishpaste is most certainly not eaten by royalty. Then there's sauces. Very tricky. I once heard about a fellow at a bank luncheon who asked the head-waiter in a loud voice for some stuff called Kutie Katie's Curry. I believe you could have heard a pin drop. Draw a veil! Painful story! Poor slob had to emigrate to Australia.'

Another night it would be clothes.

'A law of life! No matter what depths a fellow may be driven to he must never, simply never, wear a made-up tie. If you're rich you can dress in rags. If you're hard-up – use the best tailor in Savile Row. Last button of the weskit left undone? No, madam! Only grammar-school boys, Africans, – Abyssinians – poor old Haile Selassie always does it – Indians, Italians and Americans trying to be English do that any more. No weskit! Weskits are gone! Absolutely out of date. So are watches with chains. Better have no watch at all. Or a signet-fob on a black ribbon. Did you know that Edward the Seventh creased his pants down the sides?'

Conversation.

'I suppose you think good chat drips from the tongue? No, madam! You make it up the night before. Little casual odds and ends. Such as, "I wonder how many of Edward the Seventh's bastards could I name off-hand?" Or, "How many people know that if Oscar Wilde hadn't rejected the filthy advances of the Marquis of Queensberry he'd never have been hounded by that old sod?" Or somebody happens to say "Trilby". Ha, ha! That's my cue. "Did you know that her real name was Billy O' Farrell? Father a parson in Trinity College, Dublin. Had her by a barmaid in Paris." Oh, we'll keep them gaping, Rosebud! We'll dazzle 'em!'

'We?' Love would gush in her. 'Do you really love me, Clarence?' And the sleeping boyish face on the unwashed pillow-slip of the double-berth, and she, as the winter dragged on, and he still jobless, feeling fear for him or, as the first signs of spring came, jealousy, of certain unknowns, creeping slowly over her love like the lichen scaling the tree trunks on the bank.

Her mamma's letters from Tisbury always ended, 'What's Clarence doing these days?' She never answered the question. She could only have said, 'He goes to town every morning' – having kissed her tenderly, taken his bowler hat, and his rolled umbrella, said, 'Into the breach once more dear friends', stalking then across the gangway, back erect, gamp on shoulder like a gun, along the tow-path for the train to Mecca. If she asked him on his return – she soon ceased to ask – what he had done during the day he would talk volubly about it.

He had met an old pal at the Army and Navy Club. 'A grand chap! He swears he's got a real opening for me. It appears that the latest idea in textiles is plastic lavatory basins. Let me tell you all about them. You see, the great thing about these gadgets is that if you wanted to you could roll 'em up and put them in your pocket. They're made in . . .'

Or he had run into Tommy Lancing at the Union Jack Club.

'Let me tell you, Rosebud, about Tommy Lancing. My bosom friend. Saved his life once outside Catania. He's sitting pretty now, importing furs. He's mad about racing. He persuaded me to put ten bob, ten whole bob, on a horse running at Kempton Park, an absolutely wizard tip he got at the Cavalry Club.'

And that would be a day when he would then either plank down on the table ten single pound notes, or sadly produce Tommy Lancing's carbon copy – careful man – of an IOU for ten shillings. She never asked him how he got entry into those clubs. She was too eager to know what it was like inside such grand places.

On bad days he might have just dropped into the Distressed Gentlefolks' Aid Association, or visited an old chum in the Star and

Garter Home for Disabled Soldiers and Sailors, on Richmond Hill. Once – they were at rock-bottom that week – he had called in, 'just for idle curiosity', to the Army and Navy Labour and Window Cleaning Corps. Her heart leaked for him that night. Now and again, through his 'contacts' he would get a real job, never held for long. ('Bum lot! Pointless! Leads nowhere.') Once it was with the Society for Improving the Condition of the Labouring Classes; once with the Junior Imperial League; once with the Irish Church Missions and Scripture Readers Society, a job he held for two whole weeks. She always asked him what he had for lunch, to which he would always say, 'Beer and a sandwich,' and he would ask what was there for dinner. She would reply, 'The usual – mash and bangers,' or, 'There's a bit of cold meat left,' and produce an excuse for a meal, with branches or wild flowers from the tow-path stuck into the milk-bottle. After it they would always go down to *The Bunch of Grapes* for a half-pint of mild-and-bitter apiece.

The jealousy began over what he called his art gallery, five framed photographs of female nudes fastened to the wall of the cabin. She had never bothered her head about them until the night she heard him hail her from the deck with a joyous cry of 'Lolly!' and come clattering below to throw fifty quid in tenners on the table under her widening eyes.

'Who?' she asked in excitement.

'Haha! I have friends.'

An old chum! Spike Halloran of the Royal Irish. 'Let me tell you about good old Spike . . .'

They had drinks in *The Bunch of Grapes* that night, and went out the next night to celebrate in style. 'As befits our station in life.' They went into Richmond for steaks and wine at Shortt's, and afterwards around to *The Three Crows* on the Green to booze up. There they ran into a young fellow named Milo Doyle – blue eyes, a complexion like a girl, a creamy brogue, a Customs officer somewhere – a simple chap who enchanted Rosebud by seriously believing Clarence's joke that he was Sir Clarence Dunally, and gave Clarence even greater delight by being so obviously taken by Rosebud who, as he well knew, would not have given the trout's eye to a duke. Afterwards when he teased her about the lad, in their double-bunk, she had just laughed and said, 'Nice boys like him shouldn't be left out alone in London.'

'Nicer than me?' he had asked throatily.

'Lots of men are nicer than you, darling. But nobody is so attractive.'

After that they heard no noises in the boat for a long while. Then, as he slept and she lay awake, jealousy burst in her like an aneurysm of rage. Her eyes, wandering around the cabin, had halted where there had always been those five photographs. Now there were only four. For a long time she again heard nothing, neither the occasional rat awake, nor the gurgle of the water, nor the distant sound of the railway. She waited until he left the next morning, unscrewed two of the photographs and carefully took them apart. On the back of the first she read the inscription, 'Belinda – altogether yours'; and on the back of the second, 'Coco to Clarence, with luff.' The other two pictures were also of Belinda and Coco. Staring at their bare haunches she remembered that during their earliest days together he had a camera and had coaxed her into letting him photograph her in the nude. She also remembered certain coy references to a Lady Belinda. She had laughed – she had never taken men's boastings about women seriously. She knew now that a picture like that would be easily worth fifty quid to a real Lady Belinda.

She held her fire – she had too often heard her mamma say, 'I'm not going to dig my grave with my teeth, or my tongue' – until a month later when they were broke again. Coco disappeared and another fifty quid came – he came back with it quite late that night. She had been simmering all day and now she let him have it. She called him names and words she had never known she knew. She finally leaped on him and scrawled his face with her nails.

'What am I married to? A pimp, or a blackmailer, or both? How long has this been going on? How long have you known these women?'

'Hi! Hi! Hi!' was all he could shout, fighting her off, pursued by her from saloon to cabin and back again. 'What's all this about? You gone daft?'

She hit him on the head with the beer-bottle, she threw *Who's Who* at him, she tore his *A.1 Atlas* down the spine, flung it on the floor and kicked it. To his horror she grabbed his ten fivers, tore them across and showered them at him. Then, glaring and panting, she was sitting on the berth, spitting at him when she had the spit, he standing in the farthest corner of the saloon by the companion-way, ready to dash for the deck, dabbing his bleeding face with his handkerchief.

'You second-lieutenant! You were never a captain, you were never a Wing Commander, you were never anything, you ground-force garbage emptier, with your bowler hat, and your rolled gamp, and your two splits behind over your duck's bottom! You toy drum-major! You vain, vapid, muttonheaded, silly, bone-lazy, bloody ass!'

'But, Rosebud,' he said gently, 'I did it for you. Honestly!'

At which appalling statement, patently true, she had to bustle out to the WC and sit there weeping on the can for sheer love of him. When she came back all she said was, 'You do it again, Clarence, and I'm quitting. And for keeps.' She asked no more questions. Unasked, he told her that he took all those silly pictures for fun, during the war, when everybody was a bit crazy, and kept them for fun, and for memories, and anyway, it all happened before he met his own, his only, his dear. 'My darling, loved Rosebud.' Bit by bit he melted her. Then he got throaty. She forgave him. Locked in one another's arms they did not hear a sound until the morning.

The next night he made her come out to dinner on, his own words, 'the wicked lolly'. She only went because he had run into that young Irish fellow Milo Doyle and, for her sake, asked him to join them. They had by then met him several times and become quite friendly with him. He had visited them on the boat, they had met him for drinks at Hammersmith, he had taken them to supper in a little Italian place off the Brompton Road. She liked him, Clarence's pal, a pleasant young fellow, neither handsome nor unhandsome, quiet, a bit dull really, the son of an Irish farmer, always sighing for 'Ioreland'. This night he was in high fettle – he was about to be transferred from Dover to Holyhead. He even sang them an Irish song called, 'One step nearer home!' Clarence was at his deludhering best as the fellow exile. 'Go on,' Clarence kept prodding him, 'tell us more about good old County Roscommon.' She liked him a lot then, talking excitedly about County Roscommon and his boyhood there. She exchanged Wiltshire and her childhood. She even pretended to flirt with him because he blushed so easily. It was a good night.

'All the same, Clarence, it wasn't worth it. Poor but honest – that's me.'

The next morning, as he was sitting up in their berth drinking his morning cuppa, she sitting sideways on it, leaning across his legs, drinking hers, she knew by the way his eyes were half-closed that he was moving around inside his own secret mind. Presently he said:

'Wasn't that interesting, what Milo was saying last night about gold watches?'

'What about them?' she asked, and felt her heart going bang-bang.

'Silly! Or were you too busy flirting with him to notice? Gold watches smuggled out of Ireland. Every one of 'em worth in London, depending on its value, anything from five to ten quid in sheer profit?'

'Clarence! Stop it! For God's sake, if you're thinking . . .'

'Somebody's got to think or we'll never get out of this madhouse!'

From there the argument began. It went on hammer and tongs for an hour. He must have known he had won when she said, 'And anyway, where would you get the money to buy them?' He leaped from the bunk, in his red-and-white spotted pyjamas, seized his striped trousers, emptied the pockets on the blankets and counted his cash. There were forty-five pounds odd, in coins and in notes – now mended across with stamp-selvage.

'See! We've got forty-five. Another fifty-five and we've a hundred quid in capital!'

He began to wash, shave and dress, whistling, fresh as a daisy, pursued by more hopeless pleadings and warnings, even while he was stalking across the gangplank, and vanishing, rolled gamp on shoulder, his bowler hat on his ear, two splits behind, down the towpath for the Rialto.

It came as no surprise to her when he returned that evening triumphant. ('If he had put only one-tenth of the persistence . . .')

'Got it! Fifty-five quid! Tommy Lancing! And it's God's truth this time. The three bottoms are still there on the wall. And there's his carbon of my IOU.'

'You will do this once, Clarence.'

'I'll try it once.'

'If it works you will try it twice.'

'Possibly.'

'You will try it three times, and then you will either be caught or I won't be able to stand it one second longer. But whether you're caught or whether you're not you'll give me whatever rotten money you make, every single penny of it and I'll open a bank account for it in my name. Not that I want to be associated with this swindle, but I can at least try to protect myself and you, and I can stop you from wasting your precious lolly on your usual swank and nonsense.'

He agreed, sulkily. He made his haul. And it was a washout. There had been no hitch in Dublin – no country is much interested in what goes out of it. There had been no hitch in Holyhead. In the Customs hall he had easily picked out Milo along the line of counters, planked his hide suitcase in front of him, said, 'What cheer, Milo!' and opened it with a frank sweep of his honest arm.

'Hello, Clarence! You've been over?'

'Just been vetting a horse for a hunting friend,' Sir Clarence said. 'No dice. Spavined brute. Hoho! Can't trust these Irish. What, what?'

Milo had patted his shirts perfunctorily, chalked his bag, said, 'Give my regards to herself', and Clarence had walked on to the train with his five watches – all he had been able to afford – strapped around his waist under his shirt. It took him a week to sell them, and, when he had deducted his expenses, about £10, he found that all he made was twenty-three quid odd. For half a day he was filled with gloom. At this rate it would take him years to achieve a coalhouse in Pimlico. She did not tease him – she was too happy that it was all over. She even felt sorry for him. By that night he had rallied. The answer was simple: they must go into this thing in a much bigger way. He had about £113. Where would he get another hundred quid?

'What can we sell, Rosebud?'

She laughed at him affectionately. He jumped up.

'I've got it! We'll sell *Evangeline*.'

'Are you out of your mind? It's not ours to sell. We only rent the junk.'

'We can sell it to somebody who wants a houseboat for the summer. Offer them an option for a hundred quid down and the rest on possession. Three months to go until June, they'll never cop on. In June we pay them back the option and if the worst came to the worst we'd be no worse off than we are already. Bob's-your-uncle!'

She closed her eyes in agony and gave him up.

'Surely,' Milo said to her afterwards, 'at the moment you should have known.'

'Known? Known what? Known Clarence? I knew him from the first day he led me to that houseboat. Our home. You saw her when we'd worked at her. Hoo, hoo! If you'd seen her that day! It was October, and raining. That night! Don't remind me of it. I looked around me and I said to myself, "So this is the sort of bloke I'm married to." Oh, I knew Clarence! You never did. He'd charm the birds off the trees. He'd sell

radiators in hell. And aren't you forgetting something? That love is
perfect and the loved one can do no wrong.'

'I meant, "known yourself".'

'And who does, smartie? But there was something I did get to know.
Going away like that he left me alone for the first time in my life. Really
alone, for days at a time locked up in that bloody submarine.'

She had been alone in London when he was off with the Eighth Army,
but she was working then and had friends. The dank tow-path, the
locked-down houseboat, the fogs, the total silence, the rain, the
jet-black nights relieved only by the distant glow of London on the
underbelly of the sky were very different. Forcing herself to go alone
one night into Walton-on-Thames, wandering alone in her white
mackintosh around its streets, she saw it for the first time as it really
was. The pub lights appealed, the Palais de Danse was neon-red, the
cinema lights blazing white, she felt that in every other little
villa-house – red roof, tiny garden, bow-windows, empty garage, people
were playing bridge or listening to the Light Programme. To hell with
Mayfair! She wanted a home, and kids, a pram, going shopping, hearing
the *Daily Mail* flop on the hall every morning, the milkman jangle the
bottles, Clarence yawning and saying, 'I better get up, I suppose, and
get off to the office.'

On his second visit to Ireland he took with him a round two-hundred
quid. On the resale he made fifty. His third haul, she noted with
satisfaction, brought her bank total up to £310. A couple of days after
his return he got a letter, one sentence: 'The chief officer here asked
me on Monday after you left were you a pal of mine.' There was no
signature and no address but the postmark said Holyhead. He did not
hesitate a second. Tommy Lancing was clamouring for the repayment
of his loan. That morning Rosie had put pussy-willows in the
milk-bottle. April.

'They've copped on to me. Now you must go.'

'No!'

'Rosebud!' – appealingly.

'No! And that's flat.'

'Rosebud!' – threateningly.

'No! And now I've said "No" three times and that's three times too
many. I won't do it. I like the money just as much as you do but this
I won't do.'

'Rosebud, you damned fool, do you realize that on two more runs, just two more runs, we'll have five hundred of that thousand quid we've been wanting all our lives. We'll be within sight of a home where we always wanted to have a home.'

'Lives? A home? What do you know about lives? I want a decent home, a real home, kids, a pram, a . . .'

'I want you to have a real life.'

'And I want it! I'd do a lot for it. But not this. I won't do it. You know damn well either one of us will get caught or that poor boy Milo will get into trouble. He'll get the sack. Do you want that to happen? I couldn't live with it.'

'For me, Rosebud? For us? Say just one, just one more run!'

Once more the hammer and tongs began again. She gave in. She had her own dream.

The evening she came back from Dublin and Holyhead she threw the watches on the bed and sat down and stared at him like death.

'For Christ's sake, Rosebud! What happened?'

'Nothing.'

'Then what's wrong?'

'When he chalked my bag he looked at me and he blushed.'

Clarence snatched up the watches. He held them over her head. He clutched them to his chest. He laughed triumphantly.

'Splendid! Perfect! It's in the bag. He'd do anything for you.'

She said quietly that he well might, and that was precisely why this (she screamed it) was the bloody end.

He approached her, hooped, white, trembling, his eyes peering, his hands shaking.

'Then I'm going to do it the next time. And this time if I'm going to chance it I'm going to chance it big. I must get another hundred quid. Another two hundred quid! We'd be over the line, we'd be in the big push. It's your life that's at stake, our lives.'

She caught his glance over her head at the three photographs. She said, 'No!'

They squabbled for two days. Then it was she who got the letter, from Dublin.

Dear Mrs Dunnally,

I am so happy in myself that I must tell you my great news. I've done it at last. I'm back in Ireland. A while ago there I applied for a post with the Irish Customs. Last week they called me for an interview, and the Wednesday you passed through Holyhead, you brought me luck, I went home and there was the letter waiting for me telling me I had been successful. I am in Dublin now stationed at Dunleary Pier. I had to tell you because I knew you would be particularly pleased by my news. Please give my regards to Clarence. I remembered you both at Mass this morning.

Yours sincerely,
Milo Doyle.

She gave the letter to him and went to the porthole. A swallow skimmed the water. She heard him utter a deep and fervent 'Damnation!' After that he was silent for so long that she turned to look at him. His eyes half closed, he was slowly winding the letter about his forefinger. She sat down, and watched him and waited. He tossed the paper tube on the table and glanced over at her. His voice was very soft and very slow.

'So there is a Customs in Dublin . . . Does that suggest something to you? No? It does to me. It means there must be things worth smuggling *in* there. Eh?'

She did not stir. She sat looking at him like a brass idol. He did not say anything until, bowler-hatted, his rolled umbrella in his fist, he was ready to leave the boat. She had not stirred.

'I have to do it. Within a month that fellow will be coming around about the boat.'

She did not answer. He went to the bulkhead, ripped the three photographs from it, slipped them into his pocket and clattered up the companion-way.

She spent the morning and early afternoon cleaning and polishing the boat. She took the brown-paper coverings from her geraniums and pruned them down – there could hardly be any more frosts. She let the Albertine look after itself. She washed herself from head to foot, packed a suitcase, ate a sandwich, drank a beer, wrote 'Goodbye' on the back of Milo's letter and propped it against the bottle of beer. Then she looked about her carefully for the last time, and left. She put the key where they always did under a stone on the bank.

At the ticket office of the Southern Railway she bought her ticket for London. She was turning around to pick up her suitcase when she found him beside her holding it. He took her by the arm and led her firmly to the waiting-room, sat her down, sat beside her and laid the three photographs on her lap.

'I couldn't do it. I did better. I spilled the whole thing to Tommy Lancing. God, what a rocket I got from him! Why the hell hadn't I told him before? Was I a pal or was I not? He rumbled it in one second. Fur coats! That's the real McCoy for Ireland. As you know, he imports them. He's putting five hundred quid into it. He takes a third and we take the rest.' He laid a fat envelope on top of the pictures in her lap. 'There's five hundred Johnny-o-Goblins in that. Now, are you with us?'

She took the lot from her lap and gave them back to him.

'I'm going home to Mum and Dad.'

'Don't do that! Believe me or not, God's truth, I'd be lost without you. I want you. I couldn't live without you.' Furious, she made to get up; he held her down. 'Why don't you just go to London for a couple of days and think it over? Get away from me. We've been too much on top of one another. Go to Bournemouth. Forget me for a while. You could go to Dublin.'

She looked at him.

'Why Dublin?'

'Anywhere, but, for God's sake, not home. Give me a break, lass. Just two or three days. If you come back I'll never raise the question again. We'll go on just as we did before all this began,' and he lobbed the pictures and the five hundred pounds back into her lap and strode out the door. By the time she had thrown the stuff after him he was gone.

She sat beside her suitcase for as long as it took two trains to pull in and out. Then she got up, took the package, and went out on the platform to wait for the next train. She spent the night in a cheap hotel near Waterloo. If there had been a telephone on the boat she would have phoned him. She even thought of going straight back to him. The next day, not thinking, not planning, not deciding, just going, she found herself on a plane for Dublin.

That night, sitting among the Saturday night crowd in Mooney's in Dunleary, over a couple of Guinness, she told Milo about the watches.

'I know I shouldn't have come, Milo, but I've no one to talk to about it all. And I've got to talk to somebody. Well, should I leave him?'

He pondered on it, or on something.

'Does he love you, Rosie?'

'He says he loves me, he says he's doing it all for me. He calls it Operation Rosebud. He doesn't call it Operation Clarence. But I wonder.'

'That's the crux. After all, a fellow has to give proof of his love. Show a woman what he'd do for her. I don't mean he has to go out and kill tigers, or, like the old knights long ago, go out carrying his lady's handkerchief and come back with the Golden Fleece or something. That old houseboat he put you into! I suppose you might think my ideas about love are very dull, and ordinary and, as you might say, homespun. But from the first day I started earning money I started putting a bit aside every week against the day when I might meet a girl and want to marry her. I could see it – the red roof, and the bit of garden, and how we'd have a television.' He laughed at himself. 'And – it's not very romantic I suppose – we'd have a washing-machine. And a pram in the garage. *Very* dull!'

'You're making fun of me. You're mocking me.'

'*Me?* Mocking *you?* Rosie!'

She could not stop herself; she put her hand across the formica table, clasped his hand and pressed it.

'You're a good man, Milo.'

She wrote to Clarence that she was not going back to the *Evangeline* ever again, she did not know if they could ever make a life together, but if they ever did it would have to be in a real home, and she described to him how nice Walton-on-Thames was. If he sent her the address of the man who had taken the option on the boat she would send him a cheque for £100. And he must get a job. She signed it, 'Love, Rosebud', and enclosed a five-pound note. He recognized the address of Milo's lodgings. He wired. 'Send me a tenner. Leaving junk. Will write soon. Have a lovely time. Longing for you. Clarence.' When his letter came, a week later, it was headed '13a Antrobus Street, SW1, Near Buckingham Palace.' It ran:

My Rosebud!
    I've done it at last. SW1 . . .

(It was, indeed, technically in SW1, although the street turned out to be in Pimlico, and on the wrong side of the railway lines radiating out from Victoria Station.)

... And I've got a job. It's not much but it will do for a while. I've left the junk for keeps and as nobody but you know where I am we needn't pay back that option money ... London is absolute heaven, people, people, people. I'm dying for you to see it, and to touch you and give you a thousand smacking kisses and great hugs.

Your own, wicked old Clarence.

The next morning she was outside 13a Antrobus Street, and there was Clarence at the door going off to work in his dungarees, jacket, neckerchief and cap – he was window-cleaning – with a grin as wide as a church door and a hug like a bear.

The room was terrible. She worked on it in a frenzy all day to astonish him when he came back, with half-a-dozen bottles of beer in a bag, and a mouthful of jokes, and then she was sitting beside him in a pub, or arm-in-arm out in the streets, with the crowds, and the traffic and the good old smells of London, until the cosy night opened its arms to them both, and she was utterly certain of him and herself as the noises gradually vanished into their own breathing and his little murmuring words of love.

On the third day, at lunchtime, he said,

'Rosebud! I'm really on to something good at last! I met a man today...'

'Clarence. If you could only get a decent job!'

His brows sank.

'What do you mean, decent job? Do you mean five quid a week? What do you want to do with me? Make me a commissionaire outside Harrod's in a guardsman's coat, with a bandsman's epaulettes, and big brass buttons, tipping me cap to nobs in swank cars? A car-salesman selling dud cars in Paddington? An auctioneer's assistant in a green apron holding up antique chamberpots? Let's face it! I'm not trained for anything. I'm thirty. I can't start at the bottom at thirty. I'm making for the top!'

'But before the war...'

'Before the frigging war I lived in Ireland, I was a young fellow about town, I lived off my people, I hung around Dublin. The only job I ever had was for six months before the war and do you know what that was? In a drapery store selling yards of flowered muslin for women's frocks. Do you expect me to go back to that?'

'But other men...'

'Rosebud! One run. Just one run with two fur coats, another two hundred quid, within yards of the winning-post. One more . . .'

'One more, and one more! I won't do it. I'd be caught. You don't care if I'm caught.'

'You can't be caught, not with Milo there.'

'He wouldn't know. I couldn't tell him. He'd kill me if he found out.'

Clarence peered at her.

'You soft on Milo?' he asked gently.

She stared at him sullenly.

'I like him. So what?'

'Nothing. I was just thinking. An idea. Look! Just one more little run, Rosebud? And this time I mean it. Honest to God, just this once and it's in the bag.'

'Clarence, don't send me back. I beg and implore you, don't send me back.'

'I ask so little.'

She argued no longer. She said sadly, 'You think more of your thousand quid than you do of me.'

'Untrue! I love you, I want you always and I'll never let you down, and if you love me you'll never let me down. Do you love me, Rosebud?'

'I don't think it's me that's the trouble there,' she said, and let it go, and took her mac and her head-scarf and went to the pictures.

It may have been then that she made her decision, or later, wandering about stuffy, smelly streets that had suddenly become hateful to her, thinking of the cool rain of Dublin, a shadow of a mist, so light that the earth was dry under every bush, so faint that you saw it only against dark tree-caves or in hollow archways, or on the windows of Rosita's Fish and Chip Shop where she had eaten with Milo, hearing the evening bells, looking out and up at the long, grey, tented daylight. In early May she went back to Dublin, laden.

All the way across she had wondered, 'What will I feel? Will he suspect? Will I blush when he chalks my bags?' She stood tense on the deck as the morning light slowly touched the mountains, the green hills, the wet houses, the town's church-spires and, at last, they were bumping the black pier with its fenders made of hairy ropes. When she saw him, pink, fresh, so young, absorbed in his job, she was so far from feeling anything but pleasure in his sudden flash of delight – 'Three bags? I see you brought everything!' – that it was she who blushed, forgot all about her contraband and was about to open up her suitcases when he chalked them with a cheerful grin and a 'See you later!' Within hours she was wondering what on earth she had ever seen in Pimlico or why she had ever left Dublin.

They were together all day, and still together late that night at the pier's end, looking at the late Irish sunset – it was nearly eleven o'clock – still red low over distant Dublin.

'Milo,' she said suddenly, 'I'm not going back to London.'

For a second she thought he was going to kiss her: then she realized that he was the sort of fellow to whom a kiss is as good as a promise. Without intent, or the desire that waits on it, she leaned her head on his shoulder in a posture that obliged him to put an arm about her waist.

'You're married to him.'

Slowly she released his arm and stood erect. She turned from the last red-black line over the city and looked eastward across the sea. As she looked creeping horror entered her. Only last week, in that crowded pub outside Victoria Station, talking over their beer with some fellows about marriage and divorce, Clarence had said, 'Funny thing, there's no divorce in Ireland. But any man or woman who was married in a registry-office in England can remarry in Ireland. Catholics don't count that as a real marriage. So, Rosebud here,' he laughed, 'could chuck me any day she liked and marry an Irish Catholic!'

He had looked at her, smiling softly, with half-closing eyes.

'Let's go back,' she said sombrely to Milo, and all the way along the slim lamplit pier she was silent. Why had he brought that up? She halted and gripped Milo's arm, staring at nothing.

'Are you all right, Rosie?'

Could it be possible? Operation Rosebud? Was the bastard thinking that if she married him it would be awfully convenient . . .

'I'm just feeling tired, Milo.'

'Sit down here. You've been having a hard time of it.'

She sat on the bench, still holding his arm. Two could play at that game.

'What you need, Rosie, is a long, long rest.'

'With you around I mean to take a long rest.' She leaned towards him. 'Kiss me, Milo.'

He did so, chastely, on her cheek. She did not press him further. She just said, 'Milo, I'm sure there are lots of men just as attractive as you. But few can be nicer.'

The furs were locked in her wardrobe. Every morning, after Milo went out to work, she took a cab at the pier and drove into Dublin with them. Within a week her bank-book showed a total touching the last quarter of the thousand. After that she dawdled on happily, blind to thought – every day Milo and she seemed to have so much to do, to see, to talk about. She mentioned to him this strange idea that an Irish Catholic could, if he wanted to, marry a woman who was already married legally in England. He had never heard of such a thing. She said, 'It must be a crazy idea I picked up all wrong.' When she wrote to Clarence about the furs he wrote back, 'Wonderful woman! Have a nice time, ducks! I can wait. But don't keep me hanging too long. I'm only human. And I'm mad about my Rosebud. Every day I clean a window I say, "Soon one day I'll be watching some other poor bugger cleaning ours."'

She heard no more from him until, as if he was inside her head, as if he knew every movement of her body, she got a letter headed Tisbury, Wiltshire, in his handwriting. 'Dad is ill. The doctor talks about heart. Do come and see us, even if it's only for a day...' Wavering, she kept it for two days. Then she tore it up, savagely. That night, in Rosita's, she said:

'I've made up my mind, Milo. It's not very ladylike of me to say it, but it's say it or go back. If I stay would you marry me?'

He whispered his answer:

'As a matter of fact I found that I could. I remembered what you said and I inquired about it. There is nothing against it in principle. There have been several cases like it.'

'Well?'

'There's only one thing I'm not sure of.'

'Which is?'

'I'm not sure that you love me.'

'Oh, you great fathead! Milo, you said it yourself – there's only one proof of love, what you'd do for love. Don't you know I'd do anything for you? Anything! Just anything to make you sure?'

She made him sure that night. She was astonished by his wild passion, of which afterwards he was both touchingly ashamed and youthfully proud.

She delayed writing to Clarence. Then she invented an illness and sent him a tenner. When his letters became impatient she replied to them lovingly, sending more money, and telling him that she was now all in favour of his scheme, exploring everywhere for better markets. By late June he was getting angry. She tried to pacify him by telling him that since it would be far better to sell the coats to private customers she had already fixed one and nearly fixed another, that she wanted to bring three or even four coats, that he would be wise to wait. She sent him twenty pounds. When June ended he ordered her to return within three days or he would come over himself. She did not reply. He wired her: 'Am crossing by tomorrow's mailboat.' When she wired back she wrote at first only, 'You may come,' then, with a last vestige of old feeling, chiefly pity, she added, 'But take no chances,' signing it, 'Rose Powis.'

Her time was up. The next morning she went to a doctor; that afternoon she told Milo everything. If she had been confessing to one of his priests she could not have bared herself more completely. She even told him all about the photographs, and the furs she had smuggled. The disgust on his face when she spoke of the nude pictures terrified her. At the furs his rage was as wild as his love had been. From Clarence she would not have minded the words he spat at her; from his mouth they were horrible because he believed them, and from him they were just. When at last he had exhausted himself and was sitting, sobbing into his hands, on the edge of the old, velvet armchair of the sitting-room of their lodging-house, she sat in the farthest corner of the room and stared at him hopelessly. The rest was as quiet as mice talking.

'I did it only for you, Milo. Honestly.'

He raised his head.

'Honestly? That! From you?'

'I loved you. I still love you. I want you always. I'll never let you down, and if you love me you'll never let me down. I'd be lost now without you. I wanted you. I wanted your baby.'

'How do I know it is mine?'

'I know! I'm four weeks gone, and I'm as regular as clockwork.'

'I don't believe you.'

'All right! If you won't have me, I will just have to go back to Clarence. I'll palm it off on him. He'll be mad. But he'll never know. Is that what you want?'

'If you could fool him you could fool me.'

'I wouldn't. There's just that difference, Milo. I love you.'

'Love!

There was a long silence during which they sat and stared at one another.

'Why don't you chance it, Milo? We could be very happy. We could make a go of it.'

He kept staring at her. She got up.

'It's not such a big chance to take,' she said sullenly. 'Well? Finish me off! Do I stay with you? Or do I go back to him?'

'You could do that? Ha! Maybe you love him, too!'

'No, Milo! I don't think that any more.'

'Think! Do you *know*? Do you know anything? Which of us do you love?'

'Isn't that up to you?'

That was their longest silence. The room darkened slowly. She saw seagulls wheeling against a blue-black sky above the mailboat's masts. She went to the door. He stood up.

'Would you swear to God in heaven that it is my child?'

'No! I don't hold with that lark. And I'm not going on my knees to you. If you don't believe me, you don't love me, and I don't want you if you don't love me, and if you don't love me it wouldn't make any bloody difference to you anyway. Let it go, Milo! You've had your fun. Besides, it's not your baby. Or mine! It's ours!'

She opened the door. He banged it to.

'Suppose I did chance it?'

'Why should you?'

'I suppose because I thought you loved me.'

'Why am I in no doubt? Why is it always the man who can't trust?'

He fell, weeping, on her chest.

'I believe you, Rose! Don't let me down!'

She threw her arms about him and gave out a deep triumphant sigh, like a ship sloping into harbour with furling sails. She drew back and looked at him fondly.

'Milo, I won't let you down. You'll see. We will make a go of it! Oh, Milo!' she laughed, and he with her. 'Isn't it just like that picture we saw last week at the Pav!'

She stood back from him, rummaged in the bag on her arm, found the bank-book and gave it to him. He threw it on the floor as if it was a snake. The thunder crashed.

'Why do you give me that thing?'

'Throw it into the sea. Do what you like with it. All I'm worth now is what I'm standing up in. You have me as you see me.'

'It's the way I want to see you,' he laughed, 'Or even in less.'

They stood clasped together, their eyes closed, indifferent to the sudden downpour of rain and the rumble of the thunderstorm as it wandered away to sea, where, miles out, under the vast storm-cloud stretched all across the horizon, a small brush of smoke indicated the mailboat beating its way into the west wind towards their sheltering shore. He sought her mouth.

'My darling!' he muttered throatily through her lips. 'Let's go to bed.'

She seized his hand and they fled, cautiously, through the dusky corridor to her room. They were lost in love for so long that they did not even hear the soft hoot of the mailboat making its careful entry to the pier.

A Sweet Colleen

The stink and smell and dust of this bloody station! And the rudeness
of that fellow in the ticket office. What a fool to come by bus, and an
hour too early. She was exhausted from lugging this old leather suitcase
of Aunt Edie's. She let a parcel fall. A porter came over to her.

'Can I help you, miss?'

'Oh, please do! The Irish Mail.'

'Got a seat reserved?'

'O Lord, I forgot!'

Nice voice, nice kid, nice legs and the real Rossetti neck.

'This way, miss.'

When he had lobbed her case up on the rack of an empty carriage and
she was fumbling for a coin in her purse, he said:

'Forget it.'

She looked up at him. He had the most beautiful eyes she ever saw,
pure cerulean, with long lashes. His temples were grey. Plump apple
cheeks like an old lady.

'I'm Irish, too,' he smiled. 'That's a heavy bag.'

He removed his porter's cap to pad his forehead with a blue
handkerchief. He could be forty. He chucked down his waistcoat, put
away the handkerchief in his back pocket. But she noted that he still
held his peaked cap in his hand. He was so tall that he was able to lean
on one foot with his other hand grasping the rack above him.

'Been on a holiday?' he asked.

'I work in London.'

'Over long?'

'Three months.'

'First time?'

'Yes.'

'I could guess. Like it?'

Was this a bit unusual? But the platform was empty, there was no rush yet and Daddy used always say that once you got on the Irish Mail you were in the friendly climate already.

'I have a nice, quiet job. It's all right. I work in the National Gallery.'

'I'll be blowed!' he laughed, but quietly. 'I worked there for three and a half years. I used to be one of the warders.'

She could imagine him in the gallery in uniform, and knew at once that he had been in the War, and she would take a small bet that he had been a sergeant.

'And what do you do in the Gallery?'

'I work in the bookstall.'

He laughed happily, as if recalling the good old bookstall.

'I'd better drop into the Gallery one of these days and count the pictures. There were a couple there I used to like. The Rokeby Venus.'

She smiled discreetly. He said:

'Actually my favourite painter is Dante Gabriel Rossetti.'

She saw that he would have liked to go on chatting and gave him full marks for not doing it. He stepped back on to the platform, put on his cap, half an inch sideways, swept the grey wing of his hair back over his ear, closed the door and said through the window:

'Give my love to O'Connell Street. And take good care of yourself. You ought to. A girl as pretty as you.'

He went off laughing. Funny little fluting voice she has. He suddenly wheeled and came back to the window.

'Tell old Rutchie I was asking for him. My name is Tom Dalton.' He laughed back mockingly over his shoulder. 'Tell him give my love to Pom Pom.'

Rutchie? She wondered a bit at a Gallery warder becoming a railway porter. Maybe there was more money in railways. The journey sent him out of her head: the sleepless discomfort, the changing to the mailboat at Holyhead in the small hours, meeting her sisters, Dublin, everything.

Then one afternoon about a month later she heard herself being asked for the postcard of the Rossetti *Damozel*, looked up and saw the beautiful blue eyes smiling at her.

'Hello,' he said politely. 'Forgotten me? Tom Dalton. Euston Station. The Irish Mail. Did you have a pleasant holiday?'

'I remember you,' she said, and caught herself blushing and glancing along the counter out of the corner of her eye to see if Lorna Alleyn was listening.

'How is Dublin?'

'Just the same old Dublin,' she laughed, responding to his genial smile. His own teeth; staining; he smoked too much; and a pipe, the way Daddy used to. 'Have you been home this summer?'

'Why, girl, it's fifteen years since I saw Dublin. I wish you'd tell me some time what it's like nowadays. You wouldn't care to join me for lunch? No harm in asking, I hope?'

Her eye wandered to a waiting customer and she excused herself. When she came back to his end of the counter he was still there, leafing the cards. He was wearing a well-cut, grey suit and soft, brown hat with a snap-brim. She wondered what his story might be.

'No?' he asked lightly, yet with such a note of pleading also that she hated to refuse him.

'I'm sorry, I'm not free for lunch.'

'Why not come out and have a bit of dinner with me tonight at a nice little Greek café?'

In her embarrassment she laughed.

'Aren't you working now?'

'I can get a pal to stand in for me. Give him five bob. We often do it on night-shifts.'

'Oh, all right! Thank you. It is very kind of you.'

'Fine. I'll see you outside when you knock off. Now I'm going in to see my favourite picture. He held up the postcard. 'She's very like you.'

During the afternoon she went into the gallery herself to have a look at that picture. She was standing on one leg looking at it, searching for some mirror-likeness when she became aware that two men who had been talking quietly in a corner of the room were parting, and that one of them was approaching her. He was sallow, middle aged, very dark eyed, soldierly, not bad looking. He said amiably:

'Excuse me, you are at the bookstall, aren't you?'

He spoke as softly as befitted the place and the heavy, June afternoon.

'Yes.'

'I noticed you a couple of times. It is pleasant to find that one can go from postcards to pictures as well as from pictures to postcards. I'm in the curator's office. My name is Rucellai. Guido Rucellai.'

'What name did you say?'

'Rucellai.'

'Oh? Did you know a warder named Tom Dalton who used to work here?'

'The mad Irishman?'

'In what way was he mad? By the way I am Irish.'

He raised an apologetic hand and eyebrow. His teeth were white as paper. A strong, hooked nose.

'There is no real harm in being considered a little mad, you know. My English friends consider me a mad Italian. I have several Polish friends and I think them all quite mad. Only the English are never mad. Do you like Rossetti? Of course he was not really English. His father was an Italian. Very nice drawing there.'

'Somebody said that she appears to be a little like me.'

He looked to and fro between her and the picture, so often that she felt herself blushing.

'Nonsense. You are High Renaissance. Parmigianino?' he suggested, looked her all over. 'No, it must be a Florentine. Domenico called Veneziano? No! Pollaiuolo? Or why not Botticelli? The sloping shoulders, the distant look, the firm legs. That's it. As a matter of fact there is a girl very like you in the Villa Lemmi frescoes.'

'Why was Tom Dalton considered mad?'

'Do you know him very well?'

'I do not know him at all. I just met him by chance last month at Euston Station. He is a railway porter now.'

'Hm! He may be more suited to a railway station than an art gallery. I think I may have said that he is mad because he got so excited and cross with me one day. He told me, an Italian – consider my position here – that he hates all Italians. I had to reprimand him. I found out later that he married an Italian girl during or just after the war, and it turned out badly.'

'Oh, well! I must go.'

'Come again, Miss Plunkett?'

'You know my name?'

'I inquired,' he smiled. 'I don't know your first name.'

'Barbara.'

'Come again, Barbara' – and he bowed from the neck sedately. A bit superior? Or was he soapy?

Dalton took her first to a pub called The Cat and Cage off Oxford Street, at the Marble Arch end. It was a quiet street, among flats, mews, office buildings and the backs of hotels. Evening sparrows chirruped in the runnels. One might expect to find near at hand a flower shop, small but elegant houses, a church, an expensive boutique.

'This is a nobby district,' he told her. Watching her looking around at the mahogany and the cut-glass mirrors, he could tell that she had never been in a pub before. There were less than a dozen customers there. 'Anyway it once was a nobby district. We are in what Sidney Smith called the parallelogram – that is the whole district between Oxford Street south to Piccadilly, and from Park Lane over to Regent Street. Cream of the cream when England was an empire and Ireland was her pup.'

'Who is Sidney Smith? A friend of yours?'

'He's dead long ago, a famous English writer.'

'Do you read a lot?'

'It passes the time. What's your poison?'

She did not know what he could afford so she asked him to decide. He brought her a dry sherry and a pint of mild-and-bitter for himself.

'Sherry is always safe,' he advised her gently. 'It is a ladylike drink. And take it dryish, never sweet. Never take Martinis. Two of them could knock you out so you wouldn't know what you were saying or doing. Besides, they are expensive and no lady feels happy if she feels she is drinking beyond the means of her consort. I hope you don't mind my bringing you here for an *apéritif*. I thought it might interest you. Nowadays it is quite a respectable thing to do. Of course, there are some pubs I wouldn't bring you into.'

'It is a lovely pub. It is the nicest pub I have ever been in. Thank you for bringing me to this pub.'

He asked her what he might call her; and if he might call her Barbara; and would she call him Tom; he felt as if she were his own daughter; and did she mind if he smoked his pipe?

'I love a pipe. Daddy always smoked a pipe. It makes me feel quite at home.'

He laughed, a little mockingly, but she plainly did not see his joke. She was as slim as a sapling in the moon of March, with the *Damozel's* waving hair, and eyes blue as speedwell. *The wonder was not yet quite gone from that still look of hers.* No lipstick yet. A bit on the skinny side, in spite of the strong legs.

'How old are you, Barbara?'

'Nineteen and a bit more' – adding one to her eighteen.

'I've got an idea. The next time you go to Dublin I'll get you a "P" Ticket. "P" stands for Privileged. If I say you're my daughter I can get you a ticket for next to nothing.'

'You are awfully kind, Tom,' she said, considering him. 'Are you sure that would be all right? I mean wouldn't they want me to prove my identity and so on? I would not want to get you into trouble.'

He looked hard at her.

'You're not being snobby, are you? Not wanting to say you are a porter's daughter? There are no questions asked, you know. You just present your ticket like everybody else. We're all one in this on the railways. Each for all and all for each as you might say.' He patted her knee paternally a couple of times. 'It's all right, I've upset you now I can see. You're not a bit snobby. What was the journey like this time?'

'Fine. Except for having to change for the mailboat; get out at two in the morning just when you are almost beginning to fall asleep.'

'How I know these night trains! During the war – ooh!'

As he talked on she was pleased to find that he had, indeed, been a sergeant, fought in the desert and right up through Italy. And, as Rucellai said, he had married an Italian girl and it had not worked; in fact he had only lived with her for a year and then sent her back with her child to her people in Italy. He told her this quite calmly, as if it was something he had put well behind him.

'Last time I saw her she was a little bit of a thing. She'll be fifteen now. I've seen her photograph, quite pretty. It was a pity, but what's the use? I couldn't bring up a child on my own in London, and her mother was a wash-out. Her old *nonna* will look after her. If I could have married again . . . But being a Catholic!'

She said he must be lonely, but he waved it away.

'Tell me about dear old dirty Dublin,' he said, with one eye over the rim of his tankard. 'Where do you live there?'

Well . . . She lived with her mamma and her three sisters up in the hills behind Rathfarnham. It was a dear old house, supposed to be eighteenth century, all curls, and corners, and humpty-dumpty roofs. Daddy was dead. He had been a retired army captain. She did not specify British Army, but he knew it. He asked her where exactly in

Rathfarnham, or beyond it, she lived; he wanted to know; he really would like to know.

'Up near Rockbrook. It's lovely there. We can see Dublin miles away below us, on the bay. At night you can see the line of yellow lights strung out along the edge of the water beyond Clontarf. And all the little lights of the city. It's really lovely, Tom! It's like a stage, with footlights. We've always lived there. It's a bit far out, but Donna and Lulu and I went in every day for two years to Alexandra College. Of course since Daddy died we've been hard up and I knew that, sooner or later, I'd have to take a job. I wanted to be an air hostess with Aer Lingus but Mamma was dead against it. She always said, "It's no use, Babs, our sort never earned their living." She thinks what I am doing now is not work, not real work. She lives in a dream. I think she always hoped I'd marry an earl or something.'

She laughed gaily at the folly of their lives. He chuckled.

'All Ireland lives in a dream, bless its heart. I believe I know your house. I used often go up around Rockbrook on Sundays when I was in the cycling-club with a lot of boys and girls out of the factory – Jacobs'. We'd cycle all around through Glencree, on up the Old Long Hill or up the Sally Gap. And so that's where you always lived?'

'Always and always.'

From Oxford Street they could hear, through the open doors, the swishing of tyres. That night below Monte Cassino, looking out of that *cantina*, the bombing up in the hills, he had a letch for Oxford Street; a pipe-dream Oxford Street, with no blitz or black-out and the girls all wearing light cotton frocks.

'What used you do all day up in Rockbrook?'

'I used to love drawing horses. I could sit drawing horses all day long. I'm really quite good at drawing horses. I think that's why I looked for a job in the Gallery. When they asked me what was I good at I said, "Horses", so they gave me the job. You see, it did help. We used to ride a bit when we were able to afford it. Played tennis a bit. The old tennis lawn was full of bumps. We went to a dance once or twice. Nothing much, really. Or went down to town to meet somebody for a coffee. Really, the time just passed. But I did like drawing horses. Bears, too, but I was not so good at bears.'

He put down his tankard. He felt his heart beating. Smoking too much? He looked around the pub. In one corner a small man in a bowler hat was feeling a fat woman's knee and she was shaking in her fat with laughter at whatever he was saying to her.

'Barbara! Have you got any friends here?'

'Not real friends. I have Aunt Edie, of course, but she lives in Hampton Court. She is one of those State widows or whatever they call them. Her husband was governor of the Bahamas. She has arthritis, so she never comes out.'

'Where do you live?'

'In Oakley Street I have a room there.'

'Are you sure you're able to look after yourself in London?'

She opened her speedwell eyes.

'What on earth can you mean? I've been looking after myself all my life. Mamma is sweet but she does not know whether she is coming or going. I've often cooked for the five of us. So there!'

'What can you cook?'

'I can cook a steak. I can cook bacon and eggs. I used to be good at cooking a ragout, but I'm forgetting recently what I used to put into it. I was thinking of it only the other day when I saw onions selling in a shop. Tom! What does go into a stew? Do you put onions in yours? Oh, I can cook when I put my mind to it, I do assure you. You must come to my place one night and I will show you!'

He laid down his pipe. His hand fondled his heart-side.

'I am going to have another beer. Another sherry?'

'Will it make me tight?'

'I don't think so.'

He had intended to take her to a Greek place he knew between Oxford Street and Soho Square; instead he took her to Bertorelli's in Charlotte Street. He ordered for them both, including a half of Chianti.

'It is Italian but it is good. Now and again, for a blow-out on payday, I come down here from my hill fortress.'

She felt sad that he lived on the Harrow Road because she had passed that way once and got an impression of an Irishy quarter with flats over cafés, a bit toughy: he probably could not afford anything better, supporting his wife and daughter in Italy. For no reason she saw him in his room on a Sunday evening, when London can be rather dreary, sitting in his room reading Sidney Smith, looking out at the noisy street. Oakley Street, anyway, was at least quiet. Maybe this was what made him become a railway porter? He could make friends that way.

'Don't you ever want to go back to Ireland, Tom?'

'You ask me that? You know how it is being a misfit in Ireland.'

'True, I do know, don't I?'

They considered one another silently in the noisy, cheerful, crowded hither-and-thither of the restaurant until he wandered out of that island of silence into a winding, wandering discussion about what it is to be an exile and about friendship as an island in an island – 'You know, like Robinson Crusoe and the footprint.

'The Irish are like Jews. It's in our blood. We never belong, not really. Being Catholics, too, cuts us off. We are exiles in the bloody world. Shaw said somewhere, I think it's in *John Bull's Other Island*, that the Irish are hardheaded and realistic. I don't believe a word of it. What makes us get on in the world whenever we do it is the outcast feeling, never knowing when some blow is going to fall. You and me, though, we don't give a damn about the world, do we? Do you?'

'Not really. No! I don't think I do.'

'All we ever want is a couple of drinks and a friend to pass the night.'

That, she was to find, was always his style of talk. He was on now to love and marriage, talking non-stop, even when they went out into the summer-lit evening and took a bus to the Park and were strolling across it, threading their way through the last couples strewn like forgotten dolls on the grass, enjoying the coolness after the hot day. He was telling her about the odd characters he had met in the army, and out of it; 'opening your blue eyes', as he said with his little mocking smile, 'to the ways of the world'; just to show her the queer, dark things that are in men, especially men you would never suspect, and how all but a few confuse their lives in love and marriage. All she said was, 'Yes!' or 'Oh, yes, indeed.' Nobody had ever talked to her like this ever before.

She saw his big hands, pallid in the evening light, and wondered mildly, though only for a second, and for the last time, if she was wise to be with him, alone. They sat, and he talked now about Italy, while the sky over the farthest roofs became masked with silver-grey, the grass grew dusky, the trees grew heavy and dark, and the water darkened; and then, across the park, lights came out in the streets and the booming traffic dulled.

'You loved Italy, really, didn't you, Tom?'

'But not Italians. I don't trust them. And I advise you, if you ever run into any of them here, don't you trust them either. We never trusted them in the army. All the men ever think about is their looks. Combing their hair all day long. Pfu! And all the girls think about is men. I knew lots of men besides me who fell for Italian girls, and it never worked for any of them that I knew.'

She was on the point of mentioning Rucellai. She shied off it.

'Tom, tell me about your wife.'

'She was pretty. I met her in 'forty-three one night in a village called San Vittore. Just below Monte Cassino. Oh, maybe she wasn't all that pretty, maybe I was like a lot of other chaps who fell for Italian girls, maybe we weren't so much in love with the girls as dying for a taste of home. Besides I was only twenty-two when I went into the army, straight from Ireland where twenty-two is equal to about seventeen or eighteen here. I'd had four years of the war. I saw her only twice, then we pushed on to join up with the Yanks from Anzio. It was months before we entered Rome. You know what I mean – absence. I got three days' leave to meet her in Naples. A girl like you couldn't even imagine what Naples was like that time. God! It was filth! She was young, and sweet, and lovely, and O Lord God, innocent as the moon, and I asked her to marry me. I had to wait until 'forty-six. I was thirty and that was the first time I slept with a girl, believe it or not. She gave me a baby.'

Her white throat was the only thing he could see clearly. Like the whisper of leaves, that was her voice. She would have breasts like little white apples. He jumped up.

'I'll see you home,' he said, and led her, arm-in-arm, through the Park, talking incessantly, as if he had not talked to anybody for months, walking the whole way to her door. She politely invited him in for a cup of coffee. He did not seem to hear. There were five bell-pushes on the door-jamb and he was examining them. He laid his finger on one of the tabs and, in a dark, heavy voice, he asked, 'Antonelli. Who is he?'

'I believe he is a musician.' She opened the door. 'He plays the oboe. Listen, I think he is playing now. My landlord says he is a nice man.'

'How do you know he is nice?' he said angrily. 'You think every man you meet is nice. Is he young?'

'Oh, no! About your age, I should think. He is quite an elderly man.'

He gave a sharp laugh, looked abruptly at his watch, said:

'I'll give you a ring some time.'

'Thank you for a delightful evening. I enjoyed it immensely. You were really very kind to ask me, and nobody has ever talked to me before like you. Not even Daddy. And we were great pals.'

He jerked out another laugh, and ran down the steps, waving backwards. She watched him almost race across the street. He seemed a little put out. Perhaps she should have pressed him to come in for a coffee. She closed the door. The hall was stuffy. No letter. Upstairs the oboe had stopped. She regretted the end of the day. The Irish are so nice.

He did ring her again about a week later, and they met again at The Cat and Cage; but not for dinner, because – or so he said – he was on a night-shift. She hoped it was not because he was short of money, and she noted that he was not smoking. She happened to utter the wish that she were going home for the long August weekend, now a month away.

'Go!' he said. 'I'll get you the ticket. Cost you hardly anything.'

He did get her the 'P' ticket, then met her, all smiles, at Euston Station and put her into a First Class carriage, to which – she already felt him an old friend – she did not demur.

'You've squared this up, too, Tom?'

'All the way,' he grinned. 'It gives you a better chance to snatch a sleep before they turf you out at two in the morning in Holyhead.'

Of unkindness she had had no experience, though she knew indifference, yet his attentions made her think, when she was home, that he must be one of the kindest men alive. She had done nothing for him to deserve his kindness; merely met him, twice, at a pub, brought him twice to her room for coffee and a chat, sent him two postcards to cheer him up; so that she was furious when her mamma laughed over the railway porter who got her daughter free travel on British Railways, saying, hootingly, 'There you are! It shows you the depths to which the Socialists have dragged poor old England. Corruption from top to bottom.'

She was so furious at this mean-spirited way of looking at his kindness that she did not bother to explain. All she said even to her sisters was that she had a secret man in her life, but they refused to take it as a joke, probing and probing until they got it out of her that she was talking about a railway porter, at which they said:

'You and your jokes! Now, if you said a Member of Parliament, or a movie actor, or a stockbroker...'

Bored, she listened to them babbling by the hour on the telephone to their boys. She was ashamed for them when she heard them telling Mamma cover-up lies about their meetings with boys in town. (As she said, afterwards, to Tom, 'They seemed such kids to me. And dreadful snobs.')

She never mentioned Rucellai, whom she had now met several times, in the Gallery restaurant, over elevenses, and at tea, and who had twice taken her to lunch outside. She loved listening to him talking about Italy and his experiences during the war when he had known and worked with all the famous partisan leaders, Ada Gobetti in Torino, Dante Livio Bianco in Piedmont, Filippe Beltrame in Val d'Ossela, Bisagno in Liguria – at first mere names to her, then growing, as he talked of them, into real men. What she most liked to hear him talk about was his boyhood and youth outside Turin – the hill villages, the vineyards, the small fields, the screens of reeds, the river in its deep valley, the tiny, far-away passing train, small things that glowed in his mind like bits of an old world slipping away into a legend that had once been his life.

'It is my myth,' he once said, between a smile and a sigh.

Lying on the dandelions of the ragged lawn on her stomach, with one of her daddy's war-histories between her elbows, open at *The Italian Campaign, 1944*, she looked out over Dublin at the clouds moving in a white mass slowly towards England. She sent a postcard to Signor Rucellai, at the Gallery; and another to Mr Thomas Dalton, at his address in the Harrow Road. Apart from their first meeting, that day in the Gallery looking at the Rossetti drawing, she had not mentioned Tom to him. But he had spoken of him.

'Odd your meeting Dalton. Oh, I have no doubt he is a decent chap, as the English say, but he wouldn't know anything about Italy or the Italians because he never knew any of these things. He only saw the war from the sergeant's viewpoint. It is all over now and I am a kind of clerk, if you like, and he is a railway porter, but we are made by our experiences. Twenty-two years ago when I came over here first to help Don Sturzo to explain these things to the stupid British all this was high politics. The things we do pass but the lessons of the things – that is the important matter, that is the real experience.'

Twenty-two years ago? He looks so young, with his dark hair, and his straight back, and his clear eyes. If there was a war tomorrow he could be in the thick of it again. But not poor, nice old Tom!

When she stepped down to the platform off the Irish Mail in the early morning she saw him in his porter's cap and vest. He was limping. He saw her and waved to her. She looked like a child, tousled after her sleepless night. Passengers off night trains always reminded him of soldiers or children, waking up like puppets coming alive.

'I knew you'd be on it,' he said gleefully, 'I got your postcard.'

'Tom, you're limping!'

'Pfu! Just a touch of sciatica.'

'Oh, Tom, you've not been taking care of yourself.'

'Now you're here I will' – taking her bag. 'Have a nice holiday?'

'Not really. It was a failure, really. Really and truly. I must be getting old. Or losing touch. I'm very glad to be back. That is the real truth.'

He chuckled down in his throat.

'Come back to England, mavourneen, mavourneen. I'll tell you this – I'm damn glad to have you back, Barbara.'

It touched her that one person more or less in London could make any difference to such a lonely man. His limp was bad as he led her to a taxi – she had to be at her post in the Gallery that morning. As he closed the door of the taxi he said, 'Tonight we'll have a drink at The Cat and Cage and you must tell me all about it. But right afterwards you go right to bed, my dear, and make up for your lost sleep. Tomorrow night I'll show you a new restaurant I've found. Spanish. Tops. Have a good breakfast.'

She wiggled her fingers to him as she drove out into the morning sunlight of the station yard. A red milk-car by the kerb on Euston Road welcomed her home.

As he watched her go a mate said to him, 'Oye, Paddy! You're picking 'em young.'

'That,' he said with dignity, 'is my little girl, Barbara.'

'Sorry, chum. Didn't know you had a daughter. Got any more as pretty as her?'

'My one and only,' he said, and limped away.

For economy's sake she let breakfast wait until elevenses in the Gallery. Rucellai was there.

'Welcome,' he said. 'I am glad to see you.'

'Do you really mean that?'

'I never say things I do not mean. London has been making *la festa*, and making me feel a stranger. I stayed in my lodgings all Sunday, reading. I felt a little jealous of you, able to go home and be happy. But all my life I have been unhappy.'

'But you know, Rucellai, I wasn't happy.' (Neither then nor at any time did she call him Guido. He preferred to be called Rucellai because it was not his real name: it was his Partisan name. He had, he said, bade farewell to his youthful reality, and he once startled her by saying that she would, soon, bid farewell to hers.) 'I was miserable. Is that awful of me? I ought not to feel that way about my own home.'

At once he lit up, both excited and pleased.

'Exactly the same thing happened to me after the war when I went back to Turin. For years I'd been dreaming of going back home. It was no longer my Torino. All my friends were either scattered, or killed, or married, or interested only in making money. Heroes had become men. I was an exile in my own country. I am also an exile here. You are experiencing the same thing now. And here you, too, you are also an exile, in this Anglo-Saxon city with its queen, and its court, and its rich clubs. What does one do about it? We must talk of this,' he urged. 'Will you dine with me tonight?'

Alas! She was exhausted by the journey, already half asleep on her feet. He need not be surprised if she were found curled up under the counter of the bookstall, snoring.

'Very well,' he ordered, 'tomorrow night we dine. We will go to La Speranza. One of the best Italian restaurants in London.'

He rose, bowed, left her. She would have to tell Tom that she had forgotten that tomorrow night she must go and visit Aunt Edie in Hampton Court, with messages from Mamma. And so she did, fixing to eat with him two nights after. Later, looking at herself in the washroom mirror, she remembered Lulu and Donna deceiving Mamma about their meetings with boys because they thought they were in love.

'Am I,' she asked her mirror, her comb suspended, 'in love?'

She laughed it away. How old was he? Forty? More? It was just that he was interesting to talk to; as she again found him the next night, sitting beside him in the expensive-looking pale cream and green restaurant, with all the waiters dressed like gentlemen at a dance, and all the other diners obviously rotten with money. She said, 'I hope this is not too expensive a restaurant, Rucellai? No lady feels happy, you know, if she is dining beyond the means of her consort.'

He had some profound thoughts (his words) about this.

'Money,' he said, 'does not necessarily make people happy. Happiness comes from the heart. Happiness is freedom. Freedom, to me, is not having bonds. You have no bonds. I have no bonds. This is one of the great merits of being an exile. No ties of relatives. Here I am just me. You are just you. It is a great thing to be oneself. I have never been attracted by an Englishwoman because I could not feel that I possessed her completely. Only the beloved should exist for the beloved. This country which you and I inhabit is a good place for us because it is the land of loneliness.'

Trying to understand his strange and interesting philosophy she asked:

'Are you lonely, Rucellai?'

'I,' he said proudly, 'am always lonely. I am a dreamer of dreams. I am a sad, bad man. *Tristuccio.*'

'But you have been a man who did great things too. A man of action. Those days of the Partisans were not just dreams.'

'My dreams came true – briefly. I was in love in those great days with my country. The land of loneliness – and this is a profound thought – is the land of love where love is unrequited.'

'Poor Rucellai!'

'Do you not,' he asked her seriously, 'ever feel this loneliness?'

'Oh, yes!' she agreed. 'I am often lonely on Sunday afternoons.'

'Tonight,' he smiled at her, 'I will not be lonely. Nor you. Tonight our country of dreams will have a population of two.'

'Will you never go back to Italy?' she asked hastily, fearing that she understood him.

'What should I do in Torino at my age? One day I will go back, as all Italians do, but only when they can *far figura*, cut a dash, as you say, with a lemon-coloured car and a pretty wife. If I went back now I would be competing with men twenty years younger than me, men who have been keeping their eyes on jobs ever since they went up to the university, flattering their professors, carrying his briefcase, opening the door of his car for him, taking his daughter out, with discretion, agreeing with all his rotten political ideas. No! *Sta bene qui.*'

'What does that mean?'

'I'm fine here.'

'You must help me to learn Italian. Whatever else you lose you cannot lose that.'

'I should not want to. I love Italy, there is no country like Italy, but I do not admire her as I used to. I have seen her naked and ashamed. You must come to my flat for lessons. I will give you a lesson every night. But now we must hurry.'

Every night?

He had tickets for a concert of Italian music, mostly of the seventeenth and eighteenth century, Cimarosa, Lully and Tartini. During the *largo* of the Cimarosa Concerto in G he laid his hand on hers and they smiled at one another over the dreamy flutes and the muted strings humming like bees. 'All the tears and gaiety of the south,' he whispered. During the Lully he laid his hand tenderly on her knee. In an interval she delicately pointed to his temple and dared to say that she saw one grey hair.

'Do you mind?' he asked. 'I could dye it if you wish.'

'No. I think, really and truly, I prefer older men. They are more interesting. Usually.'

He made her blush by asking her if she had had great experience of older men. During the Tartini she held his hand, tightly. After the concert she invited him to have coffee with her in her room. As he helped her doff her coat he kissed her, and asked her if she were a Catholic. When she said, 'No! Daddy was a Presbyterian,' he said that he would instruct her, and began to unbutton her blouse, and her heart began to wallop.

'There! The sloping Botticelli shoulders. The wide-eyed look of the air and the sea and the earth.'

'Rucellai,' she whispered, while he was removing her blouse, 'I never let anybody do this before.'

He laughed. 'You prefer to do it yourself?' His arms were around her, groping for the fasteners of her brassiere. She grabbed it to her bosom.

'Rucellai! I'm, really and truly, not that sort of girl. Really and truly I'm not!'

'You have not had lovers?' he demanded, glaring at her.

'Lots!' she said, terrified. 'Dozens!'

'Tell me the truth!' he bullied.

'No!' she squeaked. 'Never!' She paled. 'I mean not really and truly.'

'Which is it in the name of Jesu?' he shouted.

She clasped her arms in front of her and burst into tears of misery and shame.

'Donna e madonna!' he shouted, fell on his knees, clasped her about her thighs and gazed up at her in joy. 'A virgin!' Rising, he gently slipped down one strap, kissed the slope of her breast with reverence, and replaced her blouse. 'We shall be married in the New Year. And we shall live in a flat in Wigmore Street. And drive a yellow M.G. It has been my dream for years.'

He gazed at her voraciously, threw his hand up in the air, and moaned, 'See what England has done to me! I am behaving like a milord. Italian and religion tomorrow night,' and dashed for the door.

O gosh! Tom!

'Not tomorrow night! I have to go to my dear Aunt Edie to Hampton Court Palace with a pair of chickens from Mamma.'

He paused at the door. He said in the cool lofty voice of an old Wykhamist, 'Hampton Court Palace? Really? You have an aunt in the Palace? Can you find your own way to the Palace? Will you be returning late from the Palace? After dark? I'm sure Aunt Edie would disapprove strongly. As do I!'

'I've done it a dozen times. And it will not be late, nor after dark.'

He shook his head dolefully.

'You don't know how attractive you are, or how innocent you are. All those coloureds! I have often thought that young ladies in London should all carry police whistles. I shall buy you one.'

He looked as if he was about to hurl himself on her. Instead he hurled himself down the stairs, thump-thump. Just as it was beginning to soak into her mind, which felt like a flower-bed after a Newfoundland had lolloped over it, that he had talked about marriage, her doorbell rang. Her white blouse flying she ran to the window, lifted it and looked down at the pavement. He started waving, and using his palms as a megaphone he shouted up:

'Cover yourself! No bra! Button up!'

'What is it?' she shouted down, clutching her collar to her neck.

'Those chickens!' he shouted. 'They'll go bad. The heat.'

'The what? I can't hear.'

'The chickens!' he boomed.

'What chickens?' she shouted down.

'For Aunt Edie!' he shouted back.

A window lifted across the street and a man shouted:

'Would you please be quiet, you silly oaf!'

'They are waiting for me at Fortnum and Mason's,' she shouted, astounded at her powers of invention.

He waved and sent her up an immense shrug, threw one arm into the air to the man across the street, uttering some Italian vocable which may have been meaningless but which sounded insulting, and to which the man in the window replied with two uplifted fingers and an English vocable which she knew had no meaning but sounded just as rude, and so – he replying to the man, the man to him, he back to the man, the man to his back – he went away. Then the man, who, she observed, was young and stark naked, waved to her, whereupon she slapped down the window, flicked the curtains together, and threw herself on the bed staring at the mottled ceiling.

'But I couldn't,' she said, and on her fingers started to make calculations.

If he is now twenty years older than his competitors who would be, say, twenty-one, he is forty-one, in which case – forty-one from 1962, one from two, four from six, leaves 1921, and that means when the war broke out, 1939, one from nine leaves eight, two from three leaves one – he was only eighteen then and could not have taken part in high politics with Don Furso and is A Liar! No! He said he came here twenty-two years ago, which is 1940, and was only nineteen, and is still A Liar! Or else he is much older. My God! How old is he? He could be forty-five! Twenty-seven years older than me. Oh! If I had only somebody to talk to! He could have a wife in Italy, too! If only old Tom didn't hate all Italians! I could trust Tom. If he knows anything really about anything. But I know all he would say is that Rucellai is a treacherous Italian. O gosh.

At which she thought how awfully awkward it would be if the two of them ever met, and got up and looked with wide eyes in her mirror at her Botticelli shoulders.

Tom took her to his Spanish restaurant and talked about Socialism, and an American philosopher named George Henry, and loaned her a slightly worn paper-back copy of Shaw's *Intelligent Woman's Guide to Socialism and Capitalism*, which had the mark of a tea-cup on the cover. She took him to Oakley Street for coffee. There, in the hall, she found waiting for her a portable gramophone and a record of the Cimarosa Concerto in G. She deftly hid the card accompanying them – it bore the message, 'Music, Religion, Language and Love, this is Our Lonely Land' – and said to Tom, 'Oh, look at what I bought at lunchtime. I wanted you to hear a record that might remind you of happier days. It contains all the sorrow and gaiety of the South.'

As she played it for him she sat curled on the floor, thinking, while he tapped his foot to the *rondo* and the *allegro*, that he was very like old Sullivan who used to help Daddy in the garden, and to whom she often confided her troubles; which, in turn, reminded her of old Sulky the white Persian into whose belly she used to cry whenever she was sad. When it was over she said, 'Are you a Catholic still, Tom?'

'Yes.'

'Are all Catholics very strict?'

'Some of them are. In Ireland most of 'em are. In Italy they take it in their stride.'

'Are *you* strict?'

The way she was sitting . . . He looked out the window. 'Not as much as I ought to be.'

'Tom, what do Catholic girls in Ireland do about men?'

He chuckled his throat-smile.

'They do their best. Why are you asking?'

'What does "do their best" mean?'

He shuffled in his chair, and coughed a bit, and rubbed his heart, and said, 'Ye're wearing yeer skirts very short this year.' She pulled her skirt over her knees. 'Listen! Didn't you ever have any boy-friends? You know what I mean.'

He got up and went over to sit on the edge of the bed. She slewed around after him. He looked out of the window again.

'Oh, yes!' she said scornfully. 'I have had lots of boys, of course, and am quite familiar with what is known as the facts of life if that is what *you* mean. I know all about babies and what they call sleeping together. What I am interested in is if Catholics are all that strict what do they do when they fall in love?'

'They marry. Why are you asking me these questions?' He got up and went back to his chair. 'Sit on the bed, you'll get cold on that floor. What are you after?'

'It is Lorna Alleyn. She works at the bookstall. She is in love with a Catholic and she is not sure that he is not married. She does not know what to do about him. You would condemn her, wouldn't you, for going on with him?'

'I condemn nobody,' he said glumly. 'Everybody's case is different. We're all human.'

She sighed. They were silent for so long that she got up and said, 'I will put on that lovely *largo* again.'

It floated softly over them, part-dance, part-dream, part-dirge. She stood by the window looking up at the ashen and pink sky. Suddenly she found him by her side, his arm around her shoulder.

'Barbara! I want to be honest with you. I want you to know why I left the Gallery. I got mixed up with a loose woman. She used come after me at all sorts of times. She followed me into the Gallery. You know that fellow Rutchie in the Gallery? You must have seen him. He came over here during the war. He was down and out, like all those refugees. He got a job as a clerk in the railways, then he got a job as a clerk in the Gallery. He was over us warders. He caught her bothering me one day, and he threw her out. I had to leave. She follows me still. I'm terrified she'll find out I'm at Euston and come after me there. Every night going home I never dare get off the bus at my own door for fear she'd be waiting for me, wanting money.'

The pulse of the *largo* burst into the race of the *rondo*, into dancers, blue sea, blazing sun. They stood back from one another.

'Poor Tom! You never did have any luck with women, did you!'

'Not until I met you.'

'Oh, me? I'm only a girl. I'm only a kid. Why do you let yourself be persecuted like this, Tom? Why don't you clear out of London? Get a job somewhere else?'

He looked at her. He looked down into the street. He tapped the window with his forefinger. So sweet, so good, so innocent.

'So that is what you would advise. Is it?'

'You would be so much happier. It is better than staying here and being tormented.'

He looked at her. So cruel.

'You would advise that?'

'Yes, I would,' she said in a firm, practical tone. 'Have peace, Tom. Have peace.'

'In Birmingham? Liverpool?' He gave his sour, throaty chuckle. 'I'll think about it.'

'Poor Tom!'

'Don't give me pity!'

The music stopped. He grabbed his hat from the table and went out so fast that she could only wave to him over the banisters and, for fear of disturbing the house, whisper, 'Give me a ring, Tom, won't you, some time?'

She returned to her room and her window. Across the street the young man of last night was leaning on his elbows on the window-sill, smoking a big, crooked pipe, looking idly into the empty street, his shirt off – perhaps more.

She leaned her left temple against the window-pane and glared at the darkening sky over the chimney pots. If Rucellai were here now she would lever the truth out of him. But, first, she would praise him for not betraying Tom Dalton's secret to her. She would certainly ask him, please, really and truly, how old he was. But she could not mention Tom – he would never understand. He was sweet to give her the gramophone. She put on the *largo* again, first swathing the black box in her bath-towel so that the music could be barely heard in her room. She undressed, and lay down to sleep, letting the record play itself out. Was this the real Rucellai? Dreaming of Italy, and yellow MG's. He would never go back. He would never have a flat in Wigmore Street. And I am never going to ask him any questions, ever, about anything at all.

In October he gave her an engagement ring (telling her never to wear it at the Gallery: their secret for another while) and put her into a tiny top-storey flat in Wigmore Street: two tiny rooms, with a bed in one and a table and a chair in the other.

'It is all yours,' he said. 'I shall not intrude. Not very much.'

'Am I,' she thought as she looked about the almost bare room, 'a kept woman?'

'Now,' he said happily, 'you can tell Mamma.'

'But she will never allow it. I am only twenty!'

'You mean I am too old?' he asked angrily. 'Or is it too poor? I have always been poor. Because I fought for my country. Do you know that when the war ended I had to take a job as a clerk in the railways? Me! A Rucellai! Are you ashamed of me?'

'I will tell her at Christmas when I go home! Really and truly!'

Every week after that they went shopping for furniture; this week an armchair, next a rug, then a picture, then he could not resist a set of six Regency silver dessert-spoons, then he persuaded her that they would need this small silver salver 'for visiting-cards when our friends call on us.' She had to rebel to get a mirror. 'I am your mirror,' he throated like a wood pigeon. 'Besides we have so little money.' They met every evening, for dinner, or a film, or a concert, and afterwards there was a little Italian lesson, and a little Religion, and a little love, never going beyond, or stopping short of, a lowered strap and a kiss on the slope of her breast, usually followed by a roar from him like a lion from whom a joint of beef has been snatched, a rush and a banged door.

One night she moaned to him, 'But, Rucellai, why do you insist on tormenting yourself?'

'I am a man of deep feelings!'

'I have deep feelings, too!'

'Am I a brute?'

'I want to give you peace,' she whispered, sad for him. 'Besides you get me all upset! I don't know what you want from me!'

'Innocence,' he said, drawing himself upright, 'is a precious jewel. I never knew,' he groaned, just before he banged the door, 'how expensive it could be.'

He fled, and with a sigh she slowly unzipped her skirt and removed her blouse. The door crashed open and his eyeballs stared at her.

'I do not understand you,' she wailed.

His whole frame seemed to dissolve like a polar bear sitting down.

'I have sought you too long,' he said feebly, 'to lose you now,' and very slowly, and quietly, he closed the door, and flung it open again to growl, 'Lock it! Tight!'

She got a postcard from Tom Dalton, forwarded from Oakley Street. It was a coloured picture of Rossetti's *Annunciation* in the Tate Gallery. It was from Cardiff. 'I am among the dark Celts. I do this for you. One step nearer home? Tom.' She burned it. Then she got another, a postcard, in colour, of a railway engine. 'You do not reply. Where are you? I need you. Pray for me.' She burned this in the tiny grate, knelt and said an *Ave Maria* for him in Italian. That was November. The first week in December she got a telegram, at the gallery, from Naples. 'PLEASE MEET ME IN THE GREEN LION AT EUSTON TONIGHT AT EIGHT NEED YOU BADLY LOVE TOM.'

She had arranged to go with Rucellai to a concert that night, and went to his office to explain about Tom. She said, blushing to the roots of her hair, 'An old gentleman friend of Mamma's is suddenly come to town. I really must meet him tonight. Do you mind if I don't go to the concert?'

'Who is this man?' he asked irritably.

'A friend of Mamma. Old General Butterly.'

'Why didn't she write beforehand?'

'She thinks I have nothing to do at night, any night.'

'If you had told her about us months ago this deception need never have happened.'

'What deception? Whose deception?'

'Yours, ours, mine, to everybody, about everything, about me. How old is this man?'

'He is as old as a general.'

'I don't like old men taking you out. I know all about old men.'

'I'll be back after the concert. I'll be back by ten o'clock. I will tell Mamma at Christmas. Really and truly.'

'I wish we had got married last summer. You are too simple, too innocent. What are you going to talk to this general about?'

'I don't know, the war I suppose, he's always talking about the Dardanelles.'

'But that was the 1914 war! He must be ninety.'

'He's awfully old, very, very old, really and truly. He is much older than you.'

'I shall expect you,' he said severely, 'at ten-thirty. We have to do the Conjunctive Pronouns and the Tenth Commandment. You will then be ready to go for final instruction to my dear friend Father De La Poer at Farm Street. And not a minute too soon!'

He took up his pen. She almost said: 'Yes, Daddy.'

It was a dripping night. From beside the door of The Green Lion he saw her approach under the hazy light of a street lamp and knew her at once by the slim neck and the strong legs. She was wearing a tight-belted white raincoat and a little red beret on the back of her poll, her hands dug into the two big patch-pockets of her coat, her head bent against the rain. She knew him by the slouch of his back. He was wearing an old army raincape and a cap. When he took her two hands she saw that he was grey-faced, worn, tired and lined.

'The same old Barbara!' he said warmly.

'The same old Tom,' and she laughed to make it sound true.

'I've a surprise for you,' he said quickly, 'I'm just back from Naples. My wife . . .'

'Your wife?'

It came out in a rush:

'My wife was killed last week when a house collapsed in Naples. I'm not married any longer! I'm free! In the summer I'm going to bring back my little Gemma. She's about your age. You'd get on fine with her. I've got lots of plans. I have it all worked out in my head. You and everything.'

He led her into the pub; very different to The Cat and Cage – crowded, noisy, damp, smelly. No sooner had he set her on a bench by a plastic table than he jumped up and limped over to the counter for drinks. She got a disturbing feeling that he was glad to move away from her. She hoped he was not returning to live in London. As he moved back slowly, cap on poll, still in his waterproof cape, his head down, watching the glasses in his shaky hands, she saw that he was drinking whiskey and realized that he had been drinking before they met. When he sat down he clutched her hand. By the way his eyes kept sliding away from her as he talked she felt that he was afraid of something.

'It's this way, Barbara – I've been thinking about security. We all need security. I've thought it all out, all the way from Naples. I've never had a home. Gemma needs a home. I'm going over to Dublin tonight to look for a . . .'

He stopped dead and stared at her.

'You look terribly tired, Tom. Tell me everything.'

'I'm worn out. All this week in Naples – discussions. arguments, fighting day and night, the priest and the lawyer, her father and mother, brothers and sisters, grandmothers and grandfathers, uncles, cousins, aunts, all of them rubbing together in that coal-hole in a wall in a lane that they call a house, crushing around me like a lot of bloody damp dogs yapping at me. It was them, seeing them all together there, one family, all in a bunch, that made me see how much I need a home and a wife.'

She laughed. 'A wife? Good for you, Tom! Never say die!'

He waved her laughter away from him, roughly.

'I didn't know what they were saying, and all I could say – I was saying it all the time – was "I want a *mollyeh*", that's Italian for a wife, "I want a *casa*". Did you know the Italians have no word for a home? Only a *casa*. Like a bloody packing-case, and that's about all they have.

I can marry! I'm free! And I want that little girl of mine, to bring her up like you. That's where you're going to be so marvellous, Barbara. Look at you! Exactly the way I thought of you, the way I was dreaming of you there in the middle of them all, and all the way home in the train and the boat. Good, and lovely, and pure and innocent. No stinking Italian scent about *you*, no paint, no powder, no gewgaws. You will, won't you, Barbara? You'll be my little Barbara always? Say it, Barbara, say it!'

Inside in her she felt a big, choking breath that she could not breathe out. She heard her mamma saying it, and Donna and Lulu: 'My dear! How utterly squaliferous!' And, to her horror, she heard the words go ballooning out of her mouth, just the way Mamma would say it. 'I am afraid, Tom, we are a trifle intoxicated, aren't we? Don't you think it would be advisable for us to continue our chat on a more propitious occasion?'

'Stop that! Don't be snotty with me! I've had an awful time. All those bastards fighting me! But I'll get my rights. I'll get what I want, everything I've been dreaming of for months and months. I'll best them!'

'Sssh! Tom!'

His voice had risen. Two men at the near counter were looking over at them. He clutched her hand more tightly.

'Bloody Italians, they'd sell their souls to best you. But not me! Not me, thinking of you, Barbara! To Dublin, tonight! I have the "P" tickets. First-class. Once we get to Dublin and get a nice little house . . .'

She dragged her hand away, she half rose, he grabbed at her and knocked over his glass so that it spilled over the table, and his knees, and broke on the floor. She looked around for help. More people were looking at them now. A barman in a white apron was approaching.

'I must telephone,' she said.

She slipped into the booth and dialled the first letters of Rucellai's lodgings, and stopped. He wouldn't be in. And if she told him he would never trust her again. Through the misty glass she saw him feebly wiping the table, with his hands, and mopping his knees, and the barman upbraiding him. She dialled the complete number. A foreign woman's voice replied, 'No, Signor Rucellai is gone out.' She came back to the table and sat down helplessly.

'He isn't in.'

'Who?'

'I was trying to get Rucellai.'

He all but shouted the name: 'Rucellai?'

'I thought he might help.'

'Help who?'

'You, me, all of us.'

He was really shouting now. 'Why should you call that bloody skirt-chaser? What's he got to do with it? Is he butting in on me again? If that bastard butts in on me again . . .'

'Don't you dare talk about Rucellai like that.'

'Why the hell shouldn't I talk about him like that?'

'Rucellai is a gentleman.'

'Oh? So Mr Bloody Rucellai is a frigging gentleman? How long have you known Mr Bloody Gentleman Rucellai?'

'It's none of your damn business!'

(I'm arguing with a drunk. In a common pub.)

'It's very much my business. I found you first.' He sobbed it. He shouted again, 'If he's buttin' in again on me . . .' His grey face went white, completely white. 'What's between you and him?'

Like a woman putting down a trump card, she slapped her splayed fingers on the wet table, staring at him, waiting for him. He stared at her. Then slowly he lowered his eyes, and saw the ring. 'I'm marrying Rucellai.'

He looked up slowly and whispered it, evilly, 'You little bitch!'

'And you!' she cried, getting up, shaking all over. 'You dirty old ram!'

He scrambled up, his chair fell, this time her glass. The barman came back and grabbed his arm. 'Now then, out with you, both of you!' He struck at the barman. The whole pub was watching them, their glasses held immobile. The other barman rushed out and the two concentrated on hauling him, cursing at them, his heels dragging on the tiles, out through the cut-glass doors. One of them returned for his old suitcase and a brown-paper parcel and threw them out after him on the wet pavement.

With her palms to her cheeks she stood for a moment looking around at the indifferent crowd, and then she ran. She halted at the glass doors, looking between the two barmen at the street where, through the hazy rain, he staggered from one lamp-lit pool to the next, dragging his suitcase. One of the barmen glanced at her, and said coldly, 'Hop it!' She went out and stood with her back to the window of a closed shop and watched him move slowly towards the station. He would be all right in there. His old station. The friendly climate.

She followed him at a careful distance, hanging back under the porticos, now bustling with passengers. She watched him pass through the railings where an engine stood in a cloud of hissing steam, and pass out of sight behind it to the Irish Mail. She bought a platform ticket from the machine and went as far as the train's hither end, watching him move slowly along it, his cap falling, his paper parcel, and at last clamber into a carriage. She waited there for a long time, against the brick wall, out of the way of the travellers filing noisily into the train. She kept her eyes fixed on that one carriage until, at last, the porters slammed the last door, the guard lifted and waved his lamp, and all the lighted windows began to curve away, flickering like falling cards, out into the wet dark. Then her head sank, and she wept for him. She walked all the way down to the Strand and westward as far as Charing Cross. Her hair was a tangle, her shoes and stockings were sopping. She got a bus to Oxford Circus and walked home. When she got into the little flat she leaned her back against the door, and it seemed as if it was only then that she let out the pent-up breath of terror. She felt safe, cruel and bitchy, and filled with a deep longing for love.

She was still trembling as she lit the fire and drew a hot bath. She put her Secret of Venus in the bath. In her old blue dressing-gown, that she had had ever since she left Dublin, tied about her neck, she made coffee and sandwiches, and squatted with them before the fire. Full of guilt she heard her mamma's voice, 'London, my dear Babs, I warn you, is no place for little girls.' Resolutely she shook her head. 'I am not a little girl!' Feeling the warmth of the fire and the food steal over her she began to paint her toenails; made up her lips with a pale lipstick; tried on a pair of coral earrings that Rucellai had given her, turning her head now to the right, now to the left, straightening her Rossetti neck, holding back her Botticelli shoulders.

Maybe all he had meant was that she should cross with him to Dublin to ease the way for him? As he had done for her? But how long did he think . . . ? He must be crazy to think . . . The rain glistened in the street lights on the window. She looked at her watch where she had laid it on the mantelpiece. He would have a bad crossing. She put on the Cimarosa record and squatted again before the fire, and with the little gold scent-spray that Rucellai had given her she lightly dewed her hair, her shoulders and above her knees, which, Lorna Alleyn had said with an unlikeable covert smile, was the way you should do it. The wind sweeping down Wigmore Street rattled the windows. She saw the old *Hibernia*, all its lights ringed with mist, waiting at its moorings in Holyhead Harbour. She put on her Italian slippers and curled up in the armchair to do her fingernails. An hour later she was awakened by his insistent rapping on her door.

His black raincoat was shining, his black umbrella trickled, his black Homburg hat dripped on the mat. He looked big, grave , and – his pet-word whenever he felt melancholy – *tristuzzo*. She took his things and as she was stacking the umbrella upright in the kitchen sink, with his hat on top of it, she called out, 'Rucellai! I hope you aren't cross with me? I came back early specially for you.'

He was standing with one hand on the mantelpiece, one leg, held to the fire, already steaming, staring into the fire.

'Oh, my poor Rucellai! Your shoes are wet. Let me take them off. Sit down, darling.' As she untied them she said again. 'You're not cross with me? You don't think I am a naughty girl? Did you have a lovely night? You are sure you are not cross with me?'

'I did not think of you at all,' he said sombrely to the fire.

'Your socks are damp too! Let me take them off.'

She got a cushion and laid it near the fire, and laid a towel on it and tenderly laid each bare foot on the towel near the heat. She sat back on her hunkers and stroked his instep.

'I felt quite lonely,' she said to him as he looked down at her, looking up at him.

'I have never seen you look so beautiful, and so innocent.'

She laughed. 'You said that last night.'

'But you don't know how beautiful, and how good you are!'

'Let me make you some coffee.'

'Play me some music. It will calm my soul.'

She put on a Lully ballet suite that he often asked for and sat with her arm across his thigh looking at the fire.

'Nymphs and shepherdesses,' he murmured and stroked her hair. 'Enchantress. Wafted on a seashell as a gift from the Spring.'

'You said that last night, too.'

He clasped her to his side.

'Barbara! Promise me you will always be my little Barbara. Promise me you will never change. Say it!'

'I will always be me. And you, Rucellai? Promise you will never change.'

'I shall never change!'

She felt his fingers gently undo the silk knot of her dressing-gown for his usual ritual kiss. Drawing back her head to see better, she waited for the look in his eyes. The dressing-gown fell to her waist. She saw his eyes widen and then close with what, afterwards, she could only think of was despair. Three wild and rushing minutes later, during which he dragged on his socks and shoes, and ran for his coat, hat and umbrella, she found herself staring, defeated and ashamed, into the fire.

He was not at the Gallery the next day, nor the next after. On the third day she rang his lodgings and was told that he had left. On the fourth day she went to his office in the Gallery where she found a strange young man. 'I was looking for Mr Rucellai,' she said, wild-eyed.

'He has gone to Italy, I believe. Perhaps,' he said, smiling agreeably, 'I can be of service?' She said, 'Oh!' and, not taking in his question, she added, 'Thank you.' He said 'Not at all. Do come again.' She went away. Two days later she found a letter from him in her letterbox. The postmark said TORINO.

Dear beautiful, good Barbara,

I have fled from you because I am unworthy of you. I have betrayed you too often in the grossest ways. I am torn asunder by the hounds of Artemis for gazing at her beauty. My Hercules has been too strong for me. (Pollaiuolo. Formerly in the Uffizi Gallery, Florence.) Do not try to seek me out. I am a monster. The flat is all yours. The rent is paid to December 31st. I shall never live in Wigmore Street. I shall never have an MG. I shall never see your loveliness again.

Your despairing,

Rucellai

POSCRITTO. Corrupt as I may be your sweet innocence has corrupted me more than ever before. As the great Lord Acton said – All innocence corrupts, but absolute innocence corrupts absolutely.

Over and over she said aloud, 'It is extraordinary!' For days she kept saying it. Sometimes she said, 'It is really and truly extraordinary.'

Once she found herself saying it, standing in Trafalgar Square, and said to herself. 'I must stop it, I'm talking like old Aunt Edie!' An hour later she found herself holding a postcard out to a customer, her eyes on the window, thinking that it was really and truly the most extraordinary thing that had ever happened to her in her whole life. Only the customer saying with a smile, 'Please, may I have my card?' brought her back to where she was.

In the end she had to talk to somebody about it all, so she confided one day in Lorna Alleyn at the bookstall. She even showed her Rucellai's letter. Lorna, a dark, goat-toothed wench of whom it would be kind to say that she was largely endowed in every way, and frank to say that she was very fat, read the letter in wide-eyed glee. When she had read it she hooted with wicked laughter.

'Oh, gosh! "Dear, beautiful, good Barbara . . . " That's a tall order! To be beautiful is good, Babs. To be good is, I suppose, good too. But to be beautiful and good? Fatal! You will always attract the wrong kind of a man.' Then her black eyes narrowed and she said angrily, 'You kept all this to yourself very cleverly! You never uttered a word about Rucellai. You *are* a minx. And a silly, bloody little fool. I could have told you!'

'I did not want to hear!' she said proudly. 'In love the beloved has no faults.'

Lorna lifted dismayed paws.

'Beautiful. Good. Innocent. You poor kid!'

'But,' Barbara wailed, coming at last to the point, 'I am just like any other girl.'

'Of that, my dear, I have no least doubt, only you don't look it!'

'Then, what's wrong with me?'

Lorna went back to her postcards, banging and boxing them from Antonio da Messina to Zurbaran.

'Men!' she said furiously.

Appendix

These Tales
(Preface to *The Heat of the Sun*)

To these offerings I have given the subtitle *Stories and Tales* to point a distinction that has been in my mind when writing them, and which I think may be worth explaining.

As I see it a Short Story, if it is a good story, is like a child's kite, a small wonder, a brief, bright moment. It has its limitations; there are things it can do and cannot do but, if it is good, it moves in the same element as the largest work of art – up there, airborne. The main thing a writer of a short story wants to do is to get it off the ground as quickly as possible, hold it up there, taut and tense, playing it like a fish. The reader will never know how much time was spent on getting it airborne, how often it flopped, stumbled and dragged along the ground in all those first efforts, those discarded first drafts, those false beginnings, that were cut out once it was up – so much dismissed, forgotten but necessary labour. The limits of the Short Story are apparent. It may not wander far; it has to keep close to its base-point, within the bounds of place, time and character; it will only carry a few characters, three at least, at best not more than three; there is not time, or space, for elaborate characterization – we are flying a kite not a passenger-balloon or an aeroplane; and there is often no plot, nothing much more than a situation, and only just enough of that to release a moment or two of drama, enough to let the wilful kite swirl, change colour, catching the winds of mood. A short story is concentrated stuff. It is called a short story because it is short. An essentialist art. Maupassant and Chekhov invented it between them.

A Tale is quite different. Like a small plane it is much more free, carries a bit more cargo, roves farther, has time and space for more complex characterization, more changes of mood, more incidents and scenes, even more plot. Because it is more relaxed the reader may find the Tale easier reading, and he may even take more pleasure in it, but it is likely to give the writer-craftsman rather less pleasure, since what he always most enjoys is the fascination of what is most difficult. It has its own problems, however, for the writer, whose toughest task is to orchestrate his Tale into a single, satisfying shape of flight. For me, the greatest master of the Tale was Prosper Mérimée, even though he did not bother much about shape or form, not because he lacked the skill but because he nourished a certain, coy horror of seeming too much of an Artist. Hemingway was something of an American-style Mérimée, though never quite so tough, and no good with women. Compare any of his women with the Carmen of Mérimée.

The possibilities of both the Short Story and the Tale become evident when we compare them with that plane-carrier, the Novel, which can carry as heavy a load as the writer wishes, for as long and over as many seas. Yet the Novel, too, justifies itself only in the same moments of packed crisis as the Story and the Tale. These are the keychapters of its long voyage, when its planes go swoosh into the air. After they have returned to roost the slow, majestic pace begins again – until the next moment of dramatic crisis. It is such moments that the writer of the Short Story isolates.

I set out to write Tales in *A Sweet Colleen*, *£1000 for Rosebud* and *In the Bosom of the Country*. I was writing short stories when I wrote *The Heat of the Sun* and *Charlie's Greek*. Whichever is which, and the reader will easily distinguish, all I hope is that, now and again, the Story or the Tale 'levitates a little', like that endearing character The Flying Monk in Norman Douglas's *Old Calabria*. Any story, tale or novel that does not levitate a little is, as far as I am concerned, a grounded albatross. A prince of the air, all he can do on the earth is waddle a little because of his wings.

The Planets of the Years

I confess that I did not enjoy that winter of 1967 in Cambridge, Mass. My husband had too much to do and I had nothing to do: a common complaint, I have since gathered, with visiting professors' wives. Every morning while I faced an empty day he could go off happily to Widener Library researching for his biography of Henri Estienne, a character about whom I knew nothing except that he was a sixteenth-century French wit whose most famous *mot* is 'If youth but knew, if age but could.' I never got to like H.E., as we called him. His *mot* is out of date anyway, and his equally famous observation, that God tempers the wind to the shorn lamb, is complete baloney. I far prefer the man or woman (*Anon.*) who said that God never opens one door but he shuts another. And I like the other sad one, too, that says we are all as God made us, and some of us even worse.

When my happy man left me in the morning I rarely saw him again until dinnertime, and after dinner he so often buried himself in the study with H.E. that before the winter was out I took to calling him The Man Who Lives Upstairs. To be fair, he did, early on, introduce me to Boston, especially to its museums, and to two or three other disoccupied foreign wives. (American wives are never disoccupied.) But after that, apart from airily recommending me every morning to the delights of Boston, the only thing he did for me was to take me on Saturday nights to the Symphony, occasionally to a play, and, to my surprise – Are all newlywed wives constantly making these surprising discoveries about their husbands?— I found that not even H.E. could keep him away from a Western in Harvard Square or a Humphrey Bogart revival in Brattle Street. The only other way I could seduce him from H.E. was to make love with him – I will *not* tolerate the phrase make love 'to,' it is a ridiculous preposition – and as we were only four months married we made love a lot. It is my happiest memory of Cambridge, Mass. Still, no matter how much in love you are you cannot fill a whole winter's days that way. Certainly not in Widener Library. I was often lonely and mostly idle.

And then there was the house. It belonged to a friend of my husband, a professor in M.I.T., who in his turn was spending a sabbatical in Europe with, I am sure, his not at all disoccupied wife. I ought to have loved it, and in many ways I did. It was well furnished, well heated, well lit, contained lots of books, and it was delightfully roomy, far too big, really, for two people – it ought to have been full of noisy children. It was almost too quiet, tucked away on a side street flanked by a large if rather dank garden which I chiefly remember for the way its tall elms used to float up like seaweed every evening at twilight during those exquisite moments when the lights of the city are slowly turning the sky into a sullen, iridescent pink. I loved the house for its agreeably old-fashioned air of having been lived in for generations. I even liked the dust, the discarded matches, the lost coins, the bits of Christmas or Thanksgiving tinsel shining at the bottom of the hot-air registers in the floor. In fact, I liked everything about it except its situation – a long way up Massachusetts Avenue, bordering, across the railroad track, on the garish, noisy shopping centre of Porter Square, and the crumby neighbourhood behind it that looked anything but salubrious by day and, so my Cambridge friends warned me, was not particularly safe at night. Not being an American I suppose I dare mention the word Negroes. I do not mind mentioning Greeks, Italians and Syrians too. Like everybody in the world, I am nothing if not a racist – insofar as I accept every race but prefer my own. And I do not always trust the Irish either.

Now, I am not a nervous woman, but whenever The Man Who Lived Upstairs left Cambridge for a night to give a lecture elsewhere, and I lay in bed, reading myself to sleep, longing to have him by my side, hearing nothing but an occasional late car whistling along Mass Avenue, or the snow plopping softly from the roof, I could not help remembering that even back home in crimeless Ireland my parents' home had already been broken into three times in the previous three years. I could not also help thinking that the front door was partly glazed and that the downstairs windows were protected only by the weakest of hasps. Anybody who wanted to could, as the police say, have 'effected an entrance' without difficulty, and, the house being so tucked away, he could have done it unheard and unseen. Was that shuffling noise really the snow? On dusky afternoons I sometimes found myself rather shamefacedly putting the chain on the door.

Late one such snowy afternoon in November, I was alone in the house, writing home to my sister in Ireland. 'How I wish,' I had just written, 'we were together now, Nancy, gossiping over a drink or a pot of tea...' On the impulse, I had just risen to comfort myself with a solitary tea tray when, as I passed through the lighted hall towards the kitchen, I was startled to see two dark figures outside the glass door, outlined against the far street lights. I stood still and watched them. For quite a while they did not stir. Then the doorbell rang tentatively. I went forward, and saw through the muslin curtains what looked like two women. One was very small, the other was rather tall. I removed the chain and opened the door.

The small woman was ancient. Whenever I think back to her now I always see an old peasant woman wearing a black coif, bordered inside with a white goffered frill that enclosed a strong, apple-ruddy face netted by the finest wrinkles. I know this is quite irrational. She cannot have been dressed that way at all. I am probably remembering not her but my old grandmother Anna Long from the town of Rathkeale who came to live in our house in Limerick city when I was a child, and who was the first person I ever heard talking in Irish. The tall woman was middle-aged, and dressed conventionally. It was she who spoke first.

'I am sure,' she said diffidently, in unmistakable Boston-American, 'you will think this a very strange request that I am going to make to you. This is my aunt. She lives with me in Watertown. I brought her in to lunch in Cambridge for her eightieth birthday, and I promised her as a special treat that I would show her this house. You see, she got her first job here when she came over from Ireland sixty-three years ago...'

Here the old woman interrupted her niece. She spoke with a surprisingly rotund voice as if she were an oracle intoning from within the recesses of a cavern; but an oracle with an Irish brogue as thick as treacle and as rich as rum.

'We meant, ma'am,' she rumbled, 'only for to look at the outside of the house. But when I saw the lighted hall I made my niece ring the doorbell. For thirty-five years this was my door. It was a door-knocker we had. I'd love, ma'am, for to have wan tiny little peep into the inside of the house.'

I at once took her hand and drew her into the hall. At that moment nobody could have been more welcome.

'I was just putting down the kettle,' I said to them both. 'We'll have a nice cup of tea and be talking about home.'

When they had banged the snow from their boots I led them into the front drawing room. Tea, however, the old woman would not take, perhaps out of pure politeness, or from the delicate fear that I was only trying to compound her intrusion. She would not even sit on the chair I offered her. (I thought afterwards that in all her years as a servant she had never sat down in that house except in her kitchen or her bedroom.) Peering around her like a cat in a strange room, she started to talk about herself – again out of politeness? to cover her peering? – interrupting her flow only to say, every so often, like the warning croak of a bird, how much it had all changed:

''Tis changed entirely! We never had rugs on the floor like that. Carpets we always had, all over the house. Of course, when I landed in Boston it was the year nineteen-oh-four, and that is sixty-three years ago, and sure the whole world is changed since then! I was just turned seventeen. It was the month of January and I will never forget to my dying day the snow falling and falling. I never seen the like of it in all my life. From behind Slieve Callan I came, in the County Clare, and many's the time I seen Callan white with snow. Ye have the electric. Gas we had. But that Boston snow beat all I ever saw. It was like snow that started falling a long time ago and didn't know how to stop. Oh, dear! The blinds are changed too! It was my uncle Paudh met me off the boat, God rest his soul, and glad I was to get shut of it until I saw where he took me. To his home in South Boston. And a black, dark place South Boston was in them days. I was frightened out of my wits at all the rattle of the horsecars, and the trams, and the railway roaring like thunder and lightning all night long. I didn't sleep one wink with the fright and the strangeness of it all. Ma'am! Could I have a little peep at the back drawing room, if you please?'

We moved into it.

'Oh, no!' she said disapprovingly, peering down over the hummocked snow, indifferent to the beautiful sunset in the rusty sky, 'Look at the garden! Flowers we had, all the year round. We had a glasshouse. I can see no glasshouse! Have ye no glasshouse? The way I got the job was through my uncle Paudh's son, Patsy Coogan, my own first cousin. He was a coachman that time to a man named Newsom, a Quaker man, had a big country house out in Arlington. He had the job all lined up for me in this house with the three Misses Cushing. Are you sure there is no glasshouse? He came for me with the carriage the very next morning, and if I was frightened before, I was five and forty times more frightened the way we drove, and we drove and we drove. I that never saw any but the wan street of Miltownmalbay until I took the train straight down to the Queenstown docks ten days before. I was lost! There was no end to the streets. I was sure Patsy was lost too and was only taking me around in circles. I kept saying to him, "And where are we now, Patsy?" And Patsy kept saying, "In Boston! Where else?" I never in my life felt so cold as I did in that old horse carriage. It is very warm in here, God bless it! And no fires! It is the way ye have the central heating. The three Misses Cushing always insisted on a roaring log fire in every room. I was so cold I began to cry with the cold until Patsy said, "What the devil ails you and you going off to live in the finest house in Cambridge, Mass?" I said, "And where on earth is Cambridge Mass?" He got right cross with me. "Where is it?" he roars at me, "but in Boston! Where else?" Ma'am,' she pleaded, 'the one place I really wanted to see is my old kitchen.'

I led them into the kitchen.

'Oh, glory! Mind you, ma'am, I'm not faulting it. It is very nice. But somehow it is gone very small on me. God bless us, all the changes and innovations! I wouldn't know it at all, at all! Tiles on the floor we had. And where is my kitchen trough gone to? An electric stove! But where is my old kitchen range? Oh, the grand meals I cooked on that old range! For all the dinner parties! Yards long it was. And as bright as a battleship. Where can it be gone to? Am I in the right house at all?'

I showed her where I could only presume it must once have been, behind a walled-up part of the kitchen lined now with shelving.

'It was at that black divil of a range I learned how to cook. Oh, you have no idea of the kindness of the three Misses Cushing teaching me how to cook. The goodness of them! The patience of them! Though, mind you, many's the rap of the rolling pin I got on the knuckles from Miss Caroline when she'd be bad with the megrim. The best of good food they had! Would you believe it, this was the first house where I ever ate fresh meat. And is it how ye have the table and chairs for to eat in the kitchen?'

'Like we have ourselves,' the niece said crossly. 'At home in Watertown.'

'Three breakfast trays I took up every morning, winter and summer, to the three Misses Cushing. At half past six I would rise, and it was dark and cold them winter mornings, to light the range, and the divil of hell it was to light sometimes, and clear out the three fireplaces, and set and light the big log fires, and make the three breakfasts and, while the kettle was boiling, to steal up like a mouse so as not to waken my ladies, and put a match to the three fires in their bedrooms that I set the night before, and come down then and carry up the three trays at the tick of eight o'clock. Oh, the three loveliest, kindest ladies you ever met! Saints they were! I never in my life met such goodness. They thought nothing was too good for me. When I think of the darling little bedroom they gave me up under the roof, it was like a babby house, only for being like an icebox in the wintry nights.'

'You must have been very happy here,' I said comfortably, and realized at once that I had made a mistake by the way her head jerked like a bird cocking an ear to a worm underground. I had used a word she would never use. I was being sentimental about an experience that had been outside, and apart and beyond all sentiment. 'I mean,' I said hastily, 'you were contented here.'

'Ho!' she smiled. 'I was contented all day and every day as I never was before or since. I found my first and only home in this blessed house.'

'You have a nice home now,' her niece said. But once more the old lady paid no heed to her.

'Ma'am! There is one last thing I'd love to see. The stone trough in the basement.' (She pronounced it *throw*, as if she was still living in the wilds of County Clare, or in Anglo-Saxon Wessex.) 'Oho, then, the baskets and baskets of washing I did in that old black trough! And no hot water either only for what I'd drag down the stairs from the kitchen range.'

Was there a stone trough in the basement? I could not remember. Or had there ever been? But this time the younger woman rebelled, looked at her watch and looked out at a neighbouring house pouring two beams of light between the black trunks of the elms.

'It is too late, Auntie. The dark is falling. And there will be more snow. Don't encourage her,' she whispered to me. 'She could never make her way down those stairs.'

'Maybe I could help her?' I whispered.

The old lady was not listening. She had gone to the window, her mouth breathing moist patches on the cold pane.

'Marmee, her name was,' she whispered.

'Who?' I asked.

'The cat they gave me.'

It was only when she turned and began to sway, and we both ran to support her to a chair, that I realized the tiring day they must both have had.

'I won't let you go without the cup of tea!' I ordered, and put on the kettle, spread out the supermarket oilcloth, the rented china, the American biscuits and the Danish spoons, while her niece knelt beside her and looked worriedly at her pallid face and rubbed her knobbly hands. 'I only wish,' I laughed, 'that I had a nice hot slice of soda bread for you, cooked in the bastable, and tea smelling of the turfsmoke.'

They looked at me uncomprehendingly. Had they never seen a bastable pot or smelled turfsmoke? The old woman's eyes and mind had begun to stray away from me on the long journey homeward.

'Did you never go back to Ireland?' I asked. 'Didn't you ever go home?'

'Home?' she asked, and dropped her voice a pensive octave. 'Home?'

'I took her home,' the niece said curtly, 'in 1957. When my husband was killed working in the subway. It was my first visit to Ireland. And,' she said bitterly, 'my last.'

'Didn't you enjoy it?' I asked the old woman, and wet the tea, and sat beside her while she sipped it. I so wanted her to talk to me about Ireland!

'Slieve Callan,' she murmured, and I saw its whiteness rising like music under the low clouds moving imperceptibly from twenty miles away across the wrinkled Shannon. 'Letterkelly,' she whispered, and I saw a dozen roofs huddled under the white mountain. 'Miltownmalbay,' she said, and that would be her nearest market town, with every slate in its one street rattling under the wind across Spanish Point, where, I had so often been told, three ships of the Armada went down under tons of sea. 'County Clare,' she sighed, and I saw its grey lava, its tiny lochs, and its cowering white cottages with their pigs' eyes of windows glinting in the sun.

'No, girl,' she said, 'I did not enjoy it. It was not the way I remembered it to be. Whenever you go back to any place,' she said, and

I marvelled at the phrase, 'across the planets of the years, nothing is the way it was when you were young. Never go back, girl! I thought when I was going back that, maybe, I might stay there and end my days there. But it was not me they wanted. I took home all my savings. One thousand dollars I had. The savings of fifty years. They were dragging it out of me and dragging it out of me until it was all but gone. Ayeh! God help us! They were poor and they couldn't help it. When it was all gone I said to my niece here, "Now, we must go home."'

I looked at her niece, she looked sullenly at me, we both looked at the old woman.

'You are Irish,' the niece said after a while.

'Yes,' I said. 'I am Irish.'

She nodded, and the three of us looked out at the falling night and we understood everything.

We rose. The niece carefully muffled the old woman against the cold. As we went to the door they thanked me again and again for showing them the house. The farewells ended when I said, 'Goodbye, now, and come again any time ye like,' and closed the door, and replaced the chain.

I watched them through the muslin curtains cautiously descending the wooden steps to the brick pavement. They moved away carefully and slowly, arm in arm, towards the bright headlamps flying along Mass Avenue, and the bright windows of Sears, Roebuck across it, and the friendly telephone kiosk that I liked so much because it remained bright all through the night. At the end of the street they halted, turned for a moment and looked back. I saw with their eyes this lighted door behind which I stood unseen. The whole house behind me would be dark against the city's glow. I knew better than to fancy that the old woman would be rejoicing at her last backward look. She would be uttering her vatic croak, 'All changed!' Or the exhausted niece might even be saying crossly, 'Are you sure it was the right house at all? It didn't look so very grand to me!'

As they moved out of sight large flakes were sinking silently through the penumbra of a street lamp. I saw a black mountain mourning under a white veil. Somewhere there had been a lost childhood. Somewhere, at some time, in some house, there had been a vision of home. I returned to the letter I had been writing in the drawing room.

'How I wish we were together now, Nancy, gossiping over a drink or a pot of tea . . .' I wrote on quickly. 'I could be telling you my great news. I have suspected it for weeks but I only heard today from the doctor that it is true. Oh, Nancy, the spring will be here soon, and after that the months won't be long passing until it comes, and then the four of us will all be together, in Ireland . . .'

How gently the lighted snow kept touching that window-pane, melting and vanishing, and, like love, endlessly returning across the planets of the years.

A Dead Cert

Whenever Jenny Rosse came up to Dublin, for a shopping spree, or a couple of days with the Ward Union Hunt, or to go to the Opera, or to visit some of her widespread brood of relations in or around the city, or to do anything at all just to break the monotony of what she would then mockingly call 'my life in the provinces,' the one person she never failed to ring was Oweny Flynn; and no matter how busy Oweny was in the courts or in his law chambers he would drop everything to have a lunch or a dinner with her. They had been close friends ever since he and Billy Rosse – both of them then at the King's Inns – had met her together twelve or thirteen years ago after a yacht race at the Royal Saint George. Indeed, they used to be such a close trio that, before she finally married Billy and buried herself in Cork, their friends were always laying bets on which of the two she would choose, and the most popular version of what happened in the end was that she let them draw cards for her. 'The first man,' she had cried gaily, 'to draw the ace of hearts!' According to this account the last card in the pack was Billy's, and before he turned it she fainted. As she was far from being a fainter, this caused a great deal of wicked speculation about which man she had always realized she wanted. On the other hand, one of her rivals said that she had faked the whole thing to get him.

This Saturday afternoon in October she and Oweny had finished a long, gossipy lunch at the Shelbourne, where she always stayed whenever she came up to Dublin. ('I hate to be tied to my blooming relatives!') They were sipping their coffee and brandy in two deep saddleback armchairs, the old flowery chintzy kind that the Shelbourne always provides. The lounge was empty and, as always after wine, Oweny had begun to flirt mildly with her, going back over the old days, telling her, to her evident satisfaction, how lonely it is to be a bachelor of thirty-seven ('My life trickling away into the shadows of memory!'), and what a fool he had been to let such a marvellous lump of a girl slip through his fingers, when, all of a sudden, she leaned forward and tapped the back of his hand like a dog pawing for still more attention.

'Oweny!' she said. 'I sometimes wish my husband would die for a week.'

For a second he stared at her in astonishment. Then, in a brotherly kind of voice, he said, 'Jenny! I hope there's nothing wrong between you and Billy?'

She tossed her red head at the very idea.

'I'm as much in love with Billy as ever I was! Billy is the perfect husband. I wouldn't change him for worlds.'

'So I should have hoped,' Oweny said, dutifully, if a bit stuffily. 'I mean, of all the women in the world you must be one of the luckiest and happiest that ever lived. Married to a successful barrister. Two splendid children. How old is Peter now? Eight? And Anna must be ten. There's one girl who is going to be a breaker of men's hearts and an engine of delight. Like,' he added, remembering his role, 'her beautiful mother. And you have that lovely house at Silversprings. With that marvellous view down the Lee . . .'

'You can't live on scenery!' she interposed tartly. 'And there's a wind on that river that'd cool a tomcat!'

'A car of your own. A nanny for the kids. Holidays abroad every year. No troubles or trials that I ever heard of. And,' again remembering his duty, 'if I may say so, every time we meet, you look younger, and,' he plunged daringly, 'more desirable than ever. So, for God's sake, Jenny Rosse, what the hell on earth are you talking about?'

She turned her head to look out pensively at the yellowing sun glittering above the last, trembling, fretted leaves of the trees in the Green, while he gravely watched her, admiring the way its light brought out the copper-gold of her hair, licked the flat tip of her cocked nose and shone on her freckled redhead's cheek that had always reminded him of peaches and cream, and 'No,' he thought, 'not a pretty woman, not pretty-pretty, anyway I never did care for that kind of prettiness, she is too strong for that, too much vigour, I'm sure she has poor old Billy bossed out of his life!' And he remembered how she used to sail her water-wag closer to the wind than any fellow in the yacht club, and how she used to curse like a trooper if she slammed one into the net, always hating to lose a game, especially to any man, until it might have been only last night that he had felt that aching hole in his belly when he knew that he had lost her forever. She turned her head to him and smiled wickedly.

'Yes,' she half agreed. 'Everything you say is true but...'

'But what?' he asked curiously, and sank back into the trough of his armchair to receive her reply.

Her smile vanished.

'Oweny! You know exactly how old I am. I had my thirty-fourth birthday party last week. By the way, I was very cross with you that you didn't come down for it. It was a marvellous party. All Cork was at it. I felt like the Queen of Sheba. It went on until about three in the morning. I enjoyed every single minute of it. But the next day, I got the shock of my life! I was sitting at my dressing table brushing my hair.' She stopped dramatically, and pointed her finger tragically at him as if his face were her mirror. 'When I looked out the window at a big red grain boat steaming slowly down the river, out to sea, I stopped brushing, I looked at myself, and there and then I said, "Jenny Rosse! You are in your thirty-fifth year. And you've never had a lover!" And I realized that I never could have a lover, not without hurting Billy, unless he obliged me by dying for a week.'

For fully five seconds Oweny laughed and laughed.

'Wait,' he choked, 'until the lads at the Club hear this one!'

The next second he was sitting straight up in his armchair.

'Jenny,' he said stiffly, 'would you mind telling me why exactly you chose to tell this to *me*?'

'Aren't you interested?' she asked innocently.

'Isn't it just a tiny little bit unfair?'

'But Billy would never know he'd been dead for a week. At most he'd just think he'd lost his memory or something. Don't you suppose that's what Lazarus thought? Oh! I see what you mean. Well, I suppose yes, I'd have betrayed Billy. That's true enough, isn't it?'

'I am not thinking of your good husband. I am thinking of the other unfortunate fellow when his week would be out!'

'What other fellow? Are you trying to suggest that I've been up to something underhand?'

'I mean,' he pressed on, quite angry now, 'that I refuse to believe that you are mentally incapable of realizing that if you ever did let any other man fall in love with you for even five minutes, not to speak of a whole week, you would be sentencing him to utter misery for the rest of his life.'

'Oh, come off it!' she huffed. 'You always did take things in high C. Why are you so bloody romantic? It was just an idea. I expect lots of women have it, only they don't admit it. One little, measly wild oat? It's probably something I should have done before I got married, but,' she grinned happily, 'I was too busy then having a good time. "In the morning sow thy seed and in the evening withhold not thine hand." Ecclesiastes. I learned that at Alexandra College. Shows you how innocent I was – I never knew what it really meant until I got married. Of course, you men are different. You think of nothing else.'

He winced.

'If you mean me,' he said sourly, 'you know damned well that I never wanted any woman but you.'

When she laid her hand on his he understood why she had said that about Billy dying for a week. But when he snatched his hand away and she gathered up her gloves with all the airs of a woman at the end of her patience with a muff, got up, and strode ahead of him to the levelling sun outside the hotel, he began to wonder if he really had understood. He even began to wonder if it was merely that he had upset her with all that silly talk about old times. A side-glance caught a look in her eyes that was much more mocking than hurt and at once his anger returned. She had been doing much more than flirting. She had been provoking him. Or had she just wanted to challenge him? Whatever she was doing she had manoeuvred him into a ridiculous position. Then he thought, 'She will drive to Cork tonight and I will never be certain what she really meant.' While he boggled she started talking brightly about her holiday plans for the winter. A cover-up? She said she was going to Gstaad for the skiing next month with a couple of Cork friends.

'Billy doesn't ski, so he won't come. We need another man. Would you like to join us? They are nice people. Jim Chandler and his wife. About our age. You'd enjoy them.'

He said huffily that he was too damned busy. And she might not know it but some people in the world have to earn their living. Anyway, he was saving up for two weeks' sailing in the North Sea in June. At which he saw that he had now genuinely hurt her. ('Dammit, if we really were lovers this would be our first quarrel!') He forced a smile.

'Is this goodbye, Jenny? You did say at lunch that you were going to drive home this evening? Shan't I see you again?'

She looked calculatingly at the sun winking coldly behind the far leaves.

'I hate going home – I mean so soon. And I hate driving alone in the dark. I think I'll just go to bed after dinner and get up bright and early on Sunday morning before the traffic. I'll be back at Silversprings in time for lunch.'

'If you are doing nothing tonight why don't you let me take you to dinner at the Yacht Club?'

She hesitated. Cogitating the long road home? Or what?

'Jenny! They'd all love to see you. It will be like old times. You remember the Saturday night crowds?'

She spoke without enthusiasm.

'So be it. Let's do that.'

She presented her freckled cheek for his parting kiss. In frank admiration he watched her buttocks swaying provocatively around the corner of Kildare Street.

Several times during the afternoon, back in his office, he found himself straying from his work to her equivocal words. Could there, after all, be something wrong between herself and Billy? Could she be growing tired of him? It could happen, and easily. A decent chap, fair enough company, silent, a bit slow, not brilliant even at his own job, successful only because of his father's name and connections, never any good at all at sport – he could easily see her flying down the run from the Egli at half a mile a minute, the snow leaping from her skis whenever she did a quick turn. But not Billy. He would be down in the valley paddling around like a duck among the beginners behind the railway – and he remembered what a hopeless sheep he had always been with the girls, who nevertheless seemed to flock around him all the time, perhaps (it was the only explanation he ever found for it) because he was the fumbling sort of fellow that awakens the maternal instinct in girls. At which he saw her not as a girl in white shorts dashing to and fro on the tennis courts, but as the mature woman who had turned his face into her mirror by crying at him along her pointing finger, 'You are in your thirty-fifth year!' How agile, he wondered, would she now be on the courts or the ski runs? He rose and stood for a long time by his window, glaring down at the Saturday evening blankness of Nassau Street, and heard the shouting from the playing fields of Trinity College, and watched the small lights of the buses moving through the blueing dusk, until he shivered at the cold creeping through the pane. He felt the tilt of time and the falling years, and in excitement understood her sudden lust.

As always on Saturday nights, once the autumn comes and the sailing is finished and every boat on the hard for another winter, the lounge and the bar of the Club were a cascade of noise. If he had been alone he would have at once added his bubble of chatter to it. Instead he was content to stand beside the finest woman in the crowd, watching her smiling proudly around her, awaiting attention from her rout (What was that great line? *Diana's foresters, gentlemen of the shade, minions of the moon?*) until, suddenly, alerted and disturbed, he found her eyes turning from the inattentive mob to look out broodily through the tall windows. The lighthouse on the pier's end was writing slow circles on the dusty water of the harbour. He said, 'Jenny, you are not listening to me!' She whispered crossly, 'But I don't know a single one of these bloody people!' He pointed out the commodore. Surely she remembered Tom O'Leary? She peered and said, 'Not *that* old man?' He said, 'How could you have forgotten?'

Tom had not forgotten her, as he found when he went to the bar to refresh their drinks.

'Isn't that Jenny Rosse you have there?' he asked Oweny. 'She's putting on weight, bedad! Ah, she did well for herself.'

'How do you mean?' Oweny asked, a bit shortly.

'Come off it. Didn't she marry one of the finest practices in Cork! Handsome is as handsome does, my boy! She backed a dead cert.'

Jealous old bastard! As he handed her the glass he glanced covertly at her beam. Getting a bit broad, alright. She asked idly, 'Who is that slim girl in blue, she is as brown as if she has been sailing all summer?' He looked and shrugged.

'One of the young set? I think she's George Whitaker's daughter.'

'That nice-looking chap in the black tie looks lost. Just the way Billy used always to look. Who is he?'

'Saturday nights!' he said impatiently. 'You know the way they bring the whole family. It gives the wives a rest from the cooking.'

It was a relief to lead her into the dining room and find her mood change like the wind to complete gaiety.

'So this,' she laughed, 'is where it all began. And look! The same old paintings. They haven't changed a thing.'

The wine helped, and they were safely islanded in their corner, even with the families baying cheerfully at one another from table to table, even though she got on his nerves by dawdling so long over the coffee that the maids had cleared every table but theirs. Then she revealed another change of mood.

'Oweny! Please let's go somewhere else for our nightcap.'

'But where?' he said irritably. 'Not in some scruffy pub?'

'Your flat?' she suggested, and desire spread in him like a water lily. It shrivelled when she stepped out ahead of him into the cold night air, looked up at the three-quarter moon, then at the Town Hall clock.

'What a stunning night! Oweny, I've changed my mind! Just give me a good strong coffee and I'll drive home right away.'

'So!' he said miserably. 'We squabbled at lunch. And our dinner was a flop.'

She protested that it had been a marvellous dinner; and wasn't it grand the way nothing had been changed?

'They even still have that old picture of the Duke of Windsor when he was a boy in the navy.'

He gave up. He had lost the set. All the way into town they spoke only once.

'We had good times,' she said. 'I could do it all over again.'

'And change nothing?' he growled.

Her answer was pleasing, but inconclusive— 'Who knows?'

If only he could have her in the witness box, under oath, for fifteen minutes!

In his kitchenette, helping him to make the coffee, she changed gear again, so full of good spirits (because, he understood sourly, she was about to take off for home) that he thrust an arm about her waist, assaulted her cheek with a kiss as loud as a champagne cork, and said fervently (he had nothing to lose now), 'And I thinking how marvellous it would be if we could be in bed together all night!' She laughed mockingly, handed him the coffee pot – a woman long accustomed to the grappling hook – and led the way with the cups back into his living room. They sat on the small sofa before his coffee table.

'And I'll tell you another thing, Jenny!' he said. 'If I had this flat twelve years ago it might very easily have happened that you would have become my one true love! You would have changed my whole life!'

She let her head roll back on the carved moulding of the sofa, looking past him at the moon. Quickly he kissed her mouth. Unstirring she looked back into his eyes, whispered, 'I should not have let you do that,' returned her eyes to the moon, and whispered, 'Or should I?'

'Jenny!' he ordered. 'Close your eyes. Pretend you really are back twelve years ago.'

Her eyelids sank. He kissed her again, softly, wetly, felt her hand creep to his shoulder and impress his kiss, felt her lips open. Her hand fell weakly away. Desire climbed into his throat. And then he heard her moan the disenchanting name. He drew back, rose, and looked furiously down at her. She opened her eyes, stared uncomprehendingly around her, and looked up at him in startled recognition.

'So,' he said bitterly, 'he did not die even for one minute?'

She laughed wryly, lightly, stoically, a woman who would never take anything in a high key, except a five-barred gate or a double-ditch.

'I'm sorry, Oweny. It's always the same. Whenever I dream of having a lover I find myself at the last moment in my husband's arms.'

She jumped up, snatched her coat, and turned on him.

'Why the hell, Oweny, for God's sake, don't you go away and get married?'

'To have me dreaming about you, is that what you want?'

'I want to put us both out of pain!'

They glared hatefully at one another.

'Please drive me to the Shelbourne. If I don't get on the road right away, I'll go right out of the top of my head!'

They drove to the Green, she got out, slammed the car door behind her and without a word raced into the hotel. He whirled, drove hell for leather back to the Club, killed the end of the night with the last few gossipers, drank far too much and lay awake for hours staring sideways from his pillow over the grey, frosting roofs and countless yellow chimney pots of Dublin.

Past twelve. In her yellow sports Triumph she would tear across the Curragh at seventy-five and along the two straight stretches before and after Monasterevan. By now she has long since passed through Port Laoise and Abbeyleix where only a few lighted upper-story windows still resist night and sleep. From that on, for hour after hour, south and south, every village street and small town she passes will be fast asleep, every roadside cottage, every hedge, field and tree, and the whole widespread, moonblanched country pouring past her headlights until she herself gradually becomes hedge, tree, field, and fleeting moon.

Arched branches underlit, broken demesne walls, a closed garage, hedges flying, a grey church, a lifeless gate-lodge, until the black rock and ruin of Cashel comes slowly wheeling about the moon. A streetlamp falling on a blank window makes it still more blank. Cars parked beside a kerb huddle from the cold. In Cahir the boarded windows of the old granaries are blind with age. The dull square is empty. Her wheeling lights catch the vacant eyes of the hotel, leap the useless bridge, fleck the side of the Norman castle. She is doing eighty on the level uplands under the Galtee mountains, heedless of the sleep-wrapt plain falling for miles and miles away to her left.

Why is she stopping? To rest, to look, to light a cigarette, to listen? He can see nothing for her to see but a scatter of farmhouses on the plain; nothing to hear but one sleepless dog as far away as the moon it bays. He lights his bedside lamp. Turned half past two. He puts out his light and there are her kangaroo lights, leaping, climbing, dropping, winding, slowing now because of the twisting strain on her arms. She does not see the sleeping streets of Fermoy; only the white signpost marking the remaining miles to Cork. Her red taillights disappear and reappear before him every time she winds and unwinds down to the sleeping estuary of the Lee, even at low tide not so much a river as a lough – grey, turbulent and empty. He tears after her as she rolls smoothly westward beside its shining slobland. Before them the bruised clouds hang low over the city silently awaiting the morning.

She brakes to turn in between her white gates, her wheels spit back the gravel, she zooms upward to her house and halts under its staring windows. She switches off the engine, struggles out, stretches her arms high above her head with a long, shivering, happy, outpouring groan, and then, breathing back a long breath, she holds her breasts up to her windows. There is not a sound but the metal of her engine creaking as it cools, and the small wind whispering up from the river. She laughs to see their cat flow like black water around the corner of the house. She leans into the car, blows three long, triumphant horn blasts, and before two windows can light up over her head she has disappeared indoors as smoothly as her cat. And that, at last, it is the end of sleep, where, behind windows gone dark again, she spreads herself under her one true lover.

Neither of them hear the morning seagulls over the Liffey or the Lee. He wakes unrefreshed to the sounds of late church bells. She half opens her eyes to the flickering light of the river on her ceiling, rolls over on her belly, and stretching out her legs behind her like a satisfied cat, she dozes off again. He stares for a long time at his ceiling, hardly hearing the noise of the buses going by.

It is cold. His mind is clear and cold. I know now what she wants. But does she? Let her lie. She called me a romantic and she has her own fantasy. She has what she wanted, wants what she cannot have, is not satisfied with what she has got. I have known her for over twelve years and never known her at all. The most adorable woman I ever met. And a common slut! If she had married me I suppose she would be dreaming now of him? Who was it said faithful women are always regretting their own fidelity, never their husbands'? Die for a week? He chuckled at her joke. Joke? Or gamble? Or a dead cert? If I could make him die for a week it would be a hell of a long week for her. Will I write to her? I could telephone.

Hello, Jenny! It's me. I just wanted to be sure you got back safely the other night. Why wouldn't I worry? About anyone as dear and precious as you? Those frosty roads. Of course it was, darling, a lovely meeting. And we must do it again. No, nothing changes! That's a dead cert. Oh, and Jenny! I nearly forgot. About that skiing bit next month in Gstaad. Can I change my mind? I'd love to join you. May I? Splendid! Oh, no! Not for that long. Say . . . just for a week?

He could see her hanging up the receiver very slowly.

Hymeneal

1

Away back in 1929, a few months before they got married, Phil and
Abby Doyle had bought a red-and-yellow brick house, semi-detached,
with a small garden in front and a useful strip for vegetables at the rear,
on the North Circular Road. It stood about halfway between the Dublin
Cattle Market and the entrance to the Phoenix Park – to be precise a
bare 1300 feet, or 80 perches, from the Park Gate, as Phil had once
carefully established in his schoolmasterish way by means of a
pedometer attached to his left leg. All in all it was a pleasant quarter,
so convenient to the city that Abby could be down in O'Connell Street
by tram within ten minutes, and yet sufficiently remote for almost
unbroken quietness. On still summer nights she could sometimes hear
the morose growling of lions from the Zoological Gardens, the crazed
laughter of monkeys. Early in the morning, if the wind was from the
east, she might hear the mooing of cattle and the baaing of sheep from
the Market. Otherwise the only obtrusive noise was when an
occasional freight train from Kingsbridge came trundling along the
loop north of the city down to the quays and the cargo steamers for
England. But the greatest attraction of the North Circular for Abby was
that when her sister Molly married Failey Quigley in the following
year, they had bought an identical house next door. Abby, it soon
transpired, was to have no children, so that when Molly's family got
too long-tailed for their little terrace house, and Failey became a
Member of the Dail, and ultimately a Cabinet Minister, she was all the
more relieved that they moved only five minutes away, to a larger
house, at the corner of Infirmary Road.

There they all remained, then, close together for more than
thirty-five years, as much familiars of the North Circular as its
postmen, busdrivers, doctors, shopkeepers, milkmen, dustmen, priests,
beggarwomen, policemen and park-keepers; co-citizens of Oxman-

stown, veterans of the Arran Quay Ward, seasoned Dubliners. Abby could have walked blindfold between Doyle's Corner and the Park Gate. She knew every dog with its nose out through the bars of its garden gate, every crack in every pavement, every step up or down, as well as she knew every vagary of her house – the secondhand Frigidaire that grunted up to her so comfortingly during the night, her one-bar electric stove that warmed her toes in the morning (if she remembered to stick the scrubbing brush under its loose wall-plug), the four permanently stuffed jets of her gas stove, the electric bulb in the middle of the kitchen ceiling that she knew how to light and put out with a tap of her broom handle, or the plants in her tiny glasshouse outside the kitchen window, all stolen from the People's Gardens or the Botanics and dropped into the pouch of her umbrella with the quick sideways look of a born babysnatcher, every one of them to be palm-touched afterwards with maternal love in their tiny indoor garden. Outside and inside number 26 Saint Rita's Villas, she had put down her roots for life in the North Circular.

Unfortunately, when his retirement was about a year away, Phil had been forced to make some unsettling observations. Of these the most inexorable was that Abby was getting a bit beyond housekeeping; and on his modest pension he could never afford a full-time servant. On the other hand, as the cost of living went up and the value of his pension went down, the house had quintupled in value. Now, if ever, was the time to sell it and move out of Dublin to some place cheaper.

After much searching he found exactly what he wanted west of the Shannon in County Clare, about a mile from the tiny village of Corofin, some thirty-five miles from Limerick, and less than twenty from the Atlantic coast. It was a small old whitewashed cottage, standing on a quarter-acre of reedy ground, with a stout slate roof (only a few of its slates were missing), two and a half rooms, cement floors, and an open turf-shed leaning against the gable under a rusty corrugated iron roof. Without saying a word to Abby he bought it. He had the holes in the floor filled in, the broken glass in the windows restored, the walls whitewashed, the woodwork painted blue, a dry closet built at the end of a path to the rear, and a cold bath installed in the half-room. The fine new zinc cistern that he raised outside, level with the roof, would supply plenty of soft rainwater. For drinking water there was a well about a hundred yards away. For heat they had two fireplaces. In the nearby bogs turf abounded. For light they would use petrol lamps. Absolute perfection!

When it was all done he took some coloured photographs of it and for months he kept them in his wallet to peep at as secretively and happily as a youth might peep at a picture of his first girl. Then, at last, one night, like a conjurer, he whisked them out of the air and fanned them out on Abby's lap.

'Our new home!' he cried triumphantly, standing over her – six foot two and thin as a rake handle— 'Isn't it the perfect answer? Isn't it lovely? You will garden. I will fish, and shoot, and take long walks. Every night we will sit on each side of a blazing turf fire, you with a cat, me with a dog, as cosy as two kittens in a basket. You will be sewing or knitting. I will be writing my Autobiography. And when the night ends we'll fall asleep lulled by the lovely pattering of the rain on the tin roof of the turf-shed. Perfect peace. Philosophic calm. Fresh air. Lovely country. Content and serenity without end.'

Abby slowly put on her specs and looked carefully at the pictures, one after the other. Then she went through them again. When she had looked at them several times she held them between her palms without raising her head or saying a word. She was forcing herself to remember that whenever Phil got some lunatic idea into his head there had always been only one thing to do – let him alone and he might, he just might begin gradually to forget it. Cross him and it was stuck in his head forever.

'Well?' he cried at last. 'Isn't it wonderful? Isn't it what the doctor ordered?'

She slowly lifted her head and looked at him with eyes as moist and humble as a dog so old that even its whiskers have gone white.

'It looks very nice, Phil. Very nice. For the summer. But the rain, Phil? The rain battering on the tin shed?'

In a fury he snatched up the pictures.

'Chalk and cheese!' he roared, meaning that that was what they always were.

He roved up and down the room like a caged cheetah. He kicked the chair. He kicked the table. He took up a cushion from the sofa and hurled it to the end of the room. Then he stood in front of her with his ten fingers splayed flat against her.

'Say no more!' he said. 'I understand! You have made yourself perfectly clear! Don't say one other single word! But for God almighty's sake will you tell me what it is that you don't like about our cottage?'

'You haven't even told me, Phil,' she whispered meekly, 'where it is.'

''Tis in West Clare! And please don't try to tell me that you, who were once a National School teacher, don't know where West Clare is.'

Abby had been reared in Dublin. Anywhere beyond the Liffey, or west of the Phoenix Park or south of Bray was, to her, a wasteland.

'Oh, of course, Phil,' she wailed humbly, 'I often *heard* of West Clare! I even heard a song about it. *Are ye right there, Michael, are ye right? D'ye think that we'll get there before the night?* All about some queer railway they have that has to balance itself on one track like an acrobat. Phil! Will we have to travel to West Clare on that awful railway?'

He sank into his armchair and bowed his head in his hands. Bloodshot he looked up at her. He spoke to her gently.

'Abby! The railway that you are trying to describe was called the Artique railway. It was an engineering experiment made by a Frenchman in 1889 away down in the County Kerry. It was abolished twenty-five years ago.'

'But, Phil, in the song they have the railway in West Clare. I'm almost certain of that, Phil! I can sing it for you.'

Which, pipingly and inaccurately, she began to do while he contemplated her, undecided whether to admire the power of female stupidity or the profundity of female deceit. At the end her voice broke and she was singing croakingly through a veil of tears.

'*And as the train draws near Kilrush / The passengers get out and push . . . Are ye right there, Michael, are ye right / D'ye think we'll get there before the night? / Oh, it all depends on whether / The ould engine holds together . . . / But we might, then, Michael . . . So we . . .*'

He went and sat beside her and touched her wrinkled paw, remembering how sweetly she used to sing for him long ago.

'Abby,' he whispered, 'that old railway was broken up, donkeys' years ago, too. Listen to me, Abby! Let me tell you, calmly, simply and quietly, about West Clare. County Clare is one of the loveliest counties . . .'

She dried her eyes with one hand while he held the other and talked and talked about County Clare – to her as he thought, to himself as he was despairingly to discover, both that night and on every other night that he tried to interest her in Clare's fauna and flora, its archaeology, its geology, its ecology, its methods of husbandry, and all the wild sports of the West. Her trouble, he realized in the end, gazing at her opaque eyes, was not that she could not take in what he was telling her. It was simply that she thought that the less she knew about Clare the farther she kept it away from her. He might, he saw, as well be trying to sell her an unfurnished shack in the Great Mohave Desert.

2

For some twenty-five years before Phil had been due to retire from his post as Inspector of Schools he had planned his pensioned years around The Book as exultantly as an executioner sharpening his axe to wrap it around the neck of his favourite enemy.

'On the night,' he would say to Abby, 'of the day that I hand in my gun, to whatever half-witted idiot will at that time be Minister for Education, I am going to sit down on that chair, by that window, at that table, and I'm going to start writing The Book.'

Unmuzzled at long last, he was going to expose, in his Autobiography, all the miseries and humiliations, botcheries and bunglings, all the chicaneries, evasions and general lunacies that he had had to suffer in silence at the orders of one fool of a Minister after another through forty years of serfdom.

'Mind *you!*' he would roar at her. 'This book isn't going to be just any old book. There never was, there never will be a book like my Book. It's not going to be a Book at all! It's going to be a landmine. It's going to be an atom bomb. The day my Book comes out you will hear an explosion like the Trumpet of Judgment reverberating from one end of Ireland to the other, and the next thing you will see,' spreading his arms like wings and letting his voice fall to the gentlest whisper, 'will be the entire Department of so-called bloody Education floating over Dublin like black snow.'

It was all ready. It was all waiting, locked in his bookcase. Two hundred and fifty blank pages of it, bound in black cloth, with the words *Chapter One* written on the top of page one, and the title neatly typed and pasted across the black cover: *I Was Speechless for Forty Years*. On nights when he felt particularly hard pressed by some harder-to-bear-than-usual ministerial folly he would run his fingers lovingly down the spine of it, sigh expectantly and feel calm again.

Not that Abby ever heard him utter all these wild words of his in one breath. Normally Phil was a staid, disciplined and good-humoured man, who had made countless friends all over Ireland and enjoyed countless happy days with them. All the same, over the years, and over and over again, Abby had heard every one of those separate words, always in total and tactful silence; having learned by experience that if she uttered as much as one word in reply, even if she did no more than sigh a gentle 'Oh, Moses!' – her one and only expletive – he would at once start reciting what she called the Pome. And the Pome was even harder to bear than his wildest guff about the Book.

This poem was a set of satirical verses entitled *The Patriot* which she privately called 'That accursed ould rawmeysh of a thing by Frank O'Connor that started it all off.' These malevolent verses Phil – if crossed, or imagining he was crossed – would recite at her in a voice like a tuba at full blast, slowly goose-stepping up and down the worn carpet of their little sitting room in the North Circular.

> BEJASUS! (*forte*) Before ye inter me (*maestoso*)
> I'll show ye all up! (*fortissimo*)
> I've everything stored in me memory, (*con brio*)
> Facts, figures enough (*veloce*)
> Since I first swore an oath of allegiance (*spiritoso*)
> As a patriot boy (*diminuendo*)
> To avenge me maternal grandfather (*sforzando*)
> They hanged at Fermoy... (*vibrato*)

On down to the last sibilant bellow of,

> Ye think ye'll escape me? (*capriccioso*)
> Ha! 'Tis true that me sight's a bit shook, (*scherzo*)
> I was never no hand with a pen, (*allegro*)
> But I'll write One Terrible Book (*pianissimo*)
> Before, with gun-carriage and pipers – (*affettuoso*)
> Ye dastardly crew! – (*parlante*)
> Ye bring to his grave in Glasnevin (*legato*)
> The ONE man that was true! (*tremolo*)

The only time Abby had ever spoken out about the Pome was one night after she had complained to her sister Molly that he must have recited that accursed pome to her at least once a month for the last twelve years, which made some one hundred and forty-four times in all – enough, Molly commented, to make even a gravedigger get a bit fed up with *An Elegy Written in a Country Churchyard*.

'But it's your own fault!' Molly had flashed at her out of her black gypsy's eyes. 'You're too soft with him! I tell you, if my Failey did that to me I'd soon put a stop to his gallop. Why don't you just tell him to put a sock in it? The man must be mad. But, sure, those fellows in the Department of Education are all mad. 'Tis well known! 'Tis given up to them! Every one of them is half-crazy from having to deal with priests and bishops from morning to night. You can't tell me anything about those fellows. If I didn't put my foot down on Failey at least once a month he'd be making speeches at me every night of the week – speeches that he'd never dare to give out in public but that I have to listen to just to let him blow off steam. The next time Phil Doyle recites that old stuff to you just tell him to put it where the woman told the monkey to put the nuts.'

Three nights later, like the fool she was, Abby took Molly's advice. When Phil had completed the Pome she gazed up at him pensively, allowed him his marital due of one minute's silence, and then gave a babyish little titter.

'Phil! Do you know what I think whenever I hear that pome? I think that it's a very nice pome. But somehow it always reminds me of that other lovely pome, "*The curfew tolls the knell of parting day, the lowing herd...*"'

'That thing,' he roared at her, 'has no guts in it!'

'Maybe,' she persisted tremblingly. 'But 'tis apt, Phil! 'Tis very apt. I mean if you ever do get around to that book of yours, and I'm sure, Phil, it will be a very nice little book too, it will be our parting day with a lot of old friends. That is if, God help me, I ever live to see it.'

'See it?' He charged at her with his finger pointing at her like a bayonet. 'You wait! And you know, too, who's going to get the worst lash of my whip in it – your lovely brother-in-law. Our longest reigning so-called Minister for Education. Ireland's beardless Palmerston! The original inventor of Total Inaction and Absolute Non-intervention in Anything Whatsoever! The blind boshtoon! The total botch! The braying polthacawn! Oho! If I was never to write another word but that fellow's obituary I'll show him up for the eedjut he is, was and always will be. He's going to be the linch-pin of my Book. The core, and kernel, fulcrum and omphalos of it! You just wait and see!'

Shaking like a poplar leaf, she still dared to persist.

'Oh, Moses! Is it poor Failey? Who was always and always so fond of the pair of us!'

'Fond?' At that Phil laughed in three descending, mocking brays, like the devil in *Faust*. 'Ho, ho, ho! That's a new one. Fond? I don't want fondness! I want action. But will I get it from Failey? Any more than I ever got one spark of it from any single one of his rubber-stamp predecessors? Let me give you one simple example. Look at this frightful case that cropped up only last week in Mullaghabawn East over a teacher named Hooligan! A fellow that, as every living soul in Mullaghabawn East, and West, well knows, hasn't been sober since he switched from his mother's paps to his father's poteen. And his wife as bad as him. Fighting in the schoolroom, the pair of them. Before the children's eyes. Throwing mollyers of stones at one another in the schoolyard. Calling one another bitch and bastard at the tops of their voices! But do you think your fond, and fair and lovely Failey will take any action about that? And why not, pray? Answer me! Why not?'

Wishing to the Lord God she had never opened her mouth about either the Pome or the Book, or that she had Molly there to talk up to him, she moaned:

'Phil! What do I know about any Hooligan or Booligan? You're the one who knows everything about these things.'

'You know damn well why Failey won't take action.'

'I don't, Phil. I'm sure it's some awful reason. I suppose 'tis because her mother is his aunt, or his cousin is his nephew, or his sister is the Reverend Mother of Mullinavat, or her uncle is a titular bishop in Africa, or . . .'

'Failey will take no action because he hasn't the GUTS, that's why, and he never had, nor never will have, and that's why!'

At which point in their sad comedy – where any normally intelligent member of the audience would have begun to roll up his programme and fish for his coat, and the doorkeepers would be signalling out to the cloakroom girls – what must Abby do but produce her last little weapon, pull the trigger, and let her feeble fan of protest puff out of it:

'Failey,' she whispered, 'is *kind!* It's through his kindness,' she began to weep, 'that you weren't retired like everybody else at sixty. And that leaves the pair of us with our one last year of peace and comfort here in Dublin. *And leaves the world to darkness and to me.*'

Curtain! With Phil falling back into his armchair behind his shivering newspaper; gassed, silenced, chokingly whimpering to himself at the insoluble mystery of why in God's name he had ever married a woman who knew nothing whatsoever about Education; and, if *she* was like that, in spite of listening to him day in and day out, how could he ever hope to liberate anybody or anything at all in Ireland? It was not, however, the end of their row. It never was. That always came as a final apotheosis, showing Phil deep in hell, growling through Greek fire and blue smoke – that is to say, locked upstairs in the bathroom, obscening at her as he never in his life obscened at anybody in public, strangling her with his two fists, shoving her head down into the W.C. and pulling the chain on her for good and all. That done, he straightens his four-inch stiff collar, tidies his thin dust of hair, and emerges on the landing to call amiably down the stairs, 'Abby! What about a nice little cup of tea and a few of those old arrowroot biscuits of yours?'

'Well,' Molly duly asked her, 'did you shut him up about the Pome?'

'I did,' Abby lied. 'I said the reason Failey kept him on, and every lunatic like him in the Department, was out of sheer kindness and nothing else.'

'And what did his Royal Irish Lordship say to that?'

'He said, "He kept me on because he knows I'm the best Inspector of Schools in Ireland."'

The two of them smiled wisely at one another. They knew that Failey had kept Phil on only because he adored him. The best storyteller, the funniest yarner, the only decent bit of company in the whole Department, the one man who knew the country inside out and from edge to edge, every parish priest in it, every jarvey, every tinker, every taxi driver, every bush in every bog, every sparrow on every telegraph wire, a man always ready with a comical tale about every one of them, a man to be welcomed with open arms whenever he came into the office in Marlborough Street, shaken heartily by both hands, ordered to 'sit down there, my old pal from far-off days and tell us the latest lunacy from the hinterland,' and straightway given a generous jar from the bottle of Irish that Failey kept in his bottom drawer for the few, the very few visitors that he could more or less completely trust. The sisters knew furthermore, having told him of it themselves, that Failey knew about the Book and that he did not like the smell of it at all.

'Not,' he once privately confided to Abby, 'that I care a damn what he puts into it. Give and take, I'm used to hard knocks. But Phil isn't. And he'll get plenty of them if he ever writes that book!'

To the end Abby built high hopes on those words. Maybe, she innocently hoped, Failey might extend Phil's retiring age to seventy, and by then all this lunacy about leaving Dublin would have 'frizzled out.' She spent her last few months pleading with him not to take her away. He spent them reassuring her that it was best to go. Then, his time up, he led her westward across the Shannon.

3

It took them a whole day to get from Dublin to the cottage. They went by taxi, by train to Limerick, by bus to Ennis, by a second bus to the village of Córofin, and finally by a hired car from the village to the cottage, the month being March, the day misty and windy, the daylight barely holding its own against the shrouds of the sun. When she got out of the hired car and stood under her umbrella on the roadside, cold and stiff, she saw a white box in a field, oblong, one-storied, wet-slated with two blank eyes. It was backed by a low wall through whose lacy chinks she saw the sunset. She saw rocks, she saw a dark lough blown into froth by the wind. She could barely discern the limestone-grey uplands that she was to come to know as the elephant's hide of the Barony of Burren. That night, from their bed, she listened for hours to the rain pattering on the tin roof of the turf-shed.

A couple of days later, during a dry, windy hour, she ventured alone on her first walk. She saw a small village huddled below the corrugated uplands. She followed a slim road. On a low rise she came on a ruined castle with six motionless goats on the tiptop of it, their beards blown by the wind. In the far distance she saw a broom of rain gradually blot out a tiny belfry. She saw two cottages whose smoke streamed sideways like two small ships in a gale vanish under the broom. When she got back to the cottage she went into their bedroom to weep in secret. Nor was she converted in May when the entire expanse of lava became lit up by millions of tiny gentians that brought the blue sky down into every sheltering furrow. She was not even comforted by the one blessed hot spell the Burren enjoyed that August when she could watch scores of small black cows wandering slowly over it to lick the tender grass from its marrowbones. Cows to her had always meant only two white bottles tinkling on her front step in Saint Rita's Villas.

She had nobody to consult except Molly. She did not write to her until the grunting September wind under the door warned her that winter would soon be counting her bones. Even then she wrote only because of a fright she got one frosty night, hard with stars and silence, when she was sitting on one side of the fire gazing into it, and Phil was at his table on the other side bent over the terrible Book. Hearing that vast autumnal silence of the Burren, broken only by the faint hiss of their petrol lamp and an occasional purr from the great fire of burning peat, it suddenly came to her with a pang of regret, as if for one other precious thing she had left behind her in Dublin, that he had never recited the Pome to her since they came to Corofin. She turned to him to ask him to recite it to her, and was startled to find him staring blankly into the globe of the lamp. She stole another glance, and yet another glance. Each time she looked he was still staring fixedly at the white globe. At last, as if he felt her eyes on him, he turned his head towards her, threw down his pen, said, 'I think I'll go for a stroll, it's a fine frosty night for a ramble,' put on his long greatcoat, took his stick and went out.

She waited until his footsteps faded down the ringing road. Then, she dared to peep at the Book. In his minute but beautiful handwriting he had, so far, covered only four pages – all, she gathered, skimming quickly over them, about his youth in Dublin. She also found, pasted inside the front cover, a calendar of dates and events. These she read with as much fear as if she was reading an account of his death in a newspaper:

Philip Ignatius Doyle, MA, D.Litt. Born in Dublin, February the fourth, 1901. Educated at the Christian Brothers' school in Synge Street, 1914 to 1918. Studied at Saint Patrick's Training College for teachers, Drumcondra, from 1918 to 1921. I taught school in Drumcondra from 1921 to 1926. I met Failey Quigley there in my last year. He was then aged twenty. Already balding, ingratiating, devious, ambitious, convivial. I attended evening courses at University College, Dublin, for my BA and MA, 1922 to 1927. In my last year there I met Failey again, studying for his BL. I duly completed my doctoral thesis on 'The Folk High Schools of Denmark.' I became Inspector of Primary Schools in 1928.

She looked a long time at the next three entries:

Met Abby (Abigail) Goggin with Molly (Máire) Goggin at the Gaelic League in Parnell Square. Striking contrast. Molly dark. Abby blue-eyed, Danish hair, the colouring of a young seagull. She sang sweetly in Irish. A small but perfect voice. I married Abby in 1929. Failey married Molly in 1930.

In, she remembered, the University church on Saint Stephen's Green, with Phil as the best man. But that was in their good days when they were all still on warm terms with one another, before Failey went into politics.

She closed the book and returned, shaken, to the fire. He came back from his walk as silently as he left. On the three following nights exactly the same thing happened. She bore with it for a few more days and then she wrote to Molly. This place was getting them both down. The Book was a flop. He had not spoken to her for a week. What in God's name was she going to do?

4

Another week passed and then, to her delight, he told her, grumbling mightily about it, that he had to go to Dublin to clear up some damnfool remnant business in the Department. 'The change will do you good,' she said, but he only huffed and puffed at the very idea. On his return, three days later, she was hurt to notice how much good it had done him, how talkative he was again, full of gossip and guff, relaxed, looking ten years younger. Then the lone walks and the silent nights came back again, unless he had met somebody on his wanderings, even if it was only the breadman, or a tinker, or even a child herding cows – he, who had always been used to travel and company of every kind.

One bright Sunday evening, in the last week of October, he returned from one of those walks, full of excitement because he had come on a few late gentians among the rocks.

'Look!' he cried, holding out the pallid blue flowers. 'Autumn gentians! I never knew they even existed. I came on them by pure chance up there on the hill behind Kilnaboy. Shining in the full moon. Aren't they miraculous?'

She looked indifferently at the pale flowers, and for the first time since they came there she summed up her feelings about everything.

'They make me feel like one myself.'

Startled, he looked at her pallid eyes and at her white head, hearing far away a young girl with gentian eyes and fair hair, singing a fluting love song in Irish. Slowly he laid the few flowers down on the black cover of the Book. He said, 'I must go back to the village, I forgot my tobacco. I'm forgetting everything these days. I'll soon be forgetting my own head,' and went out again.

He did not rightly know where he was going, or what he was remembering, until the little road brought him to the side of a moonlit lough where he paused to rest. There, he remembered that one of the things he had been looking forward to doing in Clare was fishing, and that another was shooting. He had done neither. And yet, when he used to be telling his colleagues in the Department about all the things he would do when he retired he had always boasted that 'that wrist' could drop a dry fly lighter, longer and later than any fisherman he ever met on Corrib or on Mask; and what a marvellous place Clare was for wild duck, planing down on their orange legs to the lakes at evening. He looked about him. What exactly was he remembering? He slashed a ghostly head off a ragweed. What the hell exactly was he trying to write about in his book? Why wasn't it blazing? Why wasn't he getting on to Failey? And leaning his two hands on the stick, he recalled that absurd talk he had with him three weeks before, in Dublin, about those two teachers in Mullaghabawn East.

'Failey!' he had said. 'I can call you Failey now, not "Minister" as I used to have to. I don't quite know exactly why you asked me to come back up here to talk about these two people. Unless it's just that, as usual, you want to find some pleasant way out of a nasty problem! If that is what you want, there is no way out of it! Because what that report of mine is really about,' tapping the grey folder on the desk, 'is

Love. And as an old fellow in Kerry once said to me, all love is just
"shteam" condensed by the cold air of marriage.'

Failey had ruffled his grey poll and laughed delightedly.

'Phil! You haven't changed one iota since the first day we got to know
one another. Always the same old cynic!'

'I am not a cynic. I am a stoic. Look! All that is wrong with those
two stupid and thoroughly worthless people is that they got married
before they knew one another. They found out their mistake too late.
Live with me and know me, as the old Irish proverb says. This clod
Hooligan is forty-one. His fool of a wife is thirty-five. I knew that fellow
when he first came to that school at the age of twenty-three. A decent
poor hoor of a fellow with no other interest in life bar football and his
occasional pint. The first time I knew her she was a junior teacher in
Blackrock. She wasn't bad-looking. In fact she was quite good-looking.
And all she was interested in was golf. They were perfectly happy with
their football and their golf until they fell in love – whatever the hell
that means – and got married. Now look at them! He's drinking like a
fish. You could cut cheese with her nose. And they hate the living sight
of one another.'

Failey had scoffed.

'Come off it, Phil! Married people don't live like that. Squabble? Yes!
Have a row? Sure! We all have rows. But married people don't hate one
another to that extent, not anyway in Ireland! You know that!'

'I know it's the way with these two people. All marriage ever did for
the pair of them was to ruin their lives.'

'It gave them five sturdy children,' Failey pointed out sensibly, and
insensitively, to his childless friend.

'I wouldn't know anything about that side of it. How many have you,
Failey?'

'Eleven.'

Phil noted how proudly he threw out the figure. That for the Book.
'Our beardless Palmerston, active in only one Department!'

'Phil, what are we going to do with these two unfortunates?'

'It's in my report. Dismiss them. And at once!'

'My God, I can't sack a man of forty-one with five children?'

'It's up to you. It is a question of principle. Or are you more interested
in cohabitation than in co-education?'

(That for the Book, too – a darling phrase.)

Failey put a ministerial look on himself, calculating, would-be wise, his mind plainly as restless as his ten fingers. He got it out in bits:

'I was thinking. Principles are one thing, Phil. Human beings are another. What may be wrong. With those two unfortunate people. Is the place where they're living. Suppose now we could shift them? To some big town? Or even to some place like Galway city? You see, it must be very hard for any city girl, born and bred to the sights and sounds of the streets...'

And while he went on expatiating Phil had got so angry at the absurdity of the proposal that it never occurred to him what Failey was aiming at until now, by the glittering lake, savagely whipping the heads off stalk after stalk of ragweed. So mistress Abby had been conspiring against him with this unprincipled botch and boshtoon. And Molly, no doubt, with her!

He whirled for home, a thousand angry snakes writhing in his head, so possessing him with hatred of all three of them that he scarcely noticed the boy cycling away from his cottage gate. He strode down the moonlit path and with a bang flung the door open. Abby's face was twisted up with tears as she handed him the telegram.

'It's Failey,' she wept. 'Killed in a car crash!'

He snatched it from her and read it down to ' ... funeral eleven on Tuesday morning to Glasnevin Cemetery.' Glaring at his own dim face in the window, hearing Abby behind him, weepily talking and talking about the old days when they used to be so happy together in Dublin, all he wanted to say was, 'This is the ultimate interference. This is logical, a botch in life and a botch in death.' Quietly he said, 'Ah, well! Another poor devil whose dancing days are done. The Lord be kind to him. This means, I suppose, that we must put on our hats and coats tomorrow morning and go up to Dublin for another miserable jaunt to Glasnevin.' And to get away from her whining he went into the back room, took down his suit of clerical charcoal, removed the mothballs from its pockets, and started to brush the dust from his black homburg that he had worn for the interment of so many other public men whom he had neither liked nor admired.

5

The next morning ghost after ghost of mist went sheaving past their crucified window. At every pause on the journey it caressed their ankles, wrists and throats. They went by taxi (late and smelling of fish), by bus (late and damp), by another bus (so prompt that they barely managed to board it), by train (slow), finally by another taxi in Dublin shrouded by the same mist. They did not talk much on the way, yet, by the little that was spoken, each could guess at the unspoken thoughts of the other. Abby had talked again about their young days in Dublin. Once she was so frank as to say expectantly, 'I hope it won't look much changed.' He spoke twice about Failey's latter-day career, drily and ironically. Once he said outright, 'Everything can come out now! All will be revealed.' It was like him at his solitary worst and his sensitive best to insist that they must not stay with Molly. 'The house will be full of his country relatives.' She was disappointed at first, but she liked the small hotel he chose, on the Liffey, near the station and the old North Circular. After supper they called on Molly to pay their respects, and as he always did on such occasions he said all the proper, kindly things. He even said, 'Happy the corpse the rain falls on,' though he made up for it to his conscience the following morning by adding to Abby as the cortege moved slowly through the mist to Glasnevin, 'And miserable the mourners!'

The sky was low, wet and matted. It darkened every headstone, cobwebbed every yew and made the massed umbrellas about him look like barnacles. He had to stand at the graveside in line with Molly, and Abby, Failey's nearest relatives and his family of eleven, ranging from a middle-aged man of about thirty-five down to a young woman in her first twenties. With one glance from under his umbrella he ranked this as a Class B funeral. It was understandable that the President had not come; it was a bad day and he was an old man. But there were only three members of the Cabinet, including the Taoiseach. The leader of the Opposition had managed to rally only two members of his party. The Labour Party was not represented at all. He discounted the six priests, the three Franciscans and the two nuns. Relatives. The general public was small. The usual flock of civil servants, glad to take the day off. He frowned at the tricolour clinging wetly to the coffin. He lifted his eyebrows wearily when the surpliced priest, conducting the burial service from under an umbrella held by a mute, said the last few prayers in Irish – a language that, to his knowledge, Failey had never spoken in his life. He had to lower his umbrella to hide his amusement when he saw, among the wreaths that the gravediggers were now strewing on their wet hummock, a garland of bays. (What scoundrel, what embittered clerk, had the wit to think of that one?) He bowed his head in agony as the Taoiseach began the formal words of farewell.

' . . . a colleague who did Ireland and me the honour of accepting without demur the arduous duties of a post of the greatest import to our country's future. Yet when he did so, Phelim Patrick Quigley did no more than he had always done, in the same spirit of devotion that, from his earliest years, inspired him to serve and suffer for Ireland. A man who . . .'

Suffer? The reference, he presumed, could only be to the occasion when Failey, by the greatest stroke of political good luck, had been arrested on suspicion during the Civil War, at the age of twenty, and detained for three nights in the Bridewell. When the oration finished, he glared quickly around to see if there was going to be a firing squad or a bugler sounding the last post. Seeing that there was not, he relaxed; and then wished there had been – it would have made a lovely chapter ending for the Book, which he was at last free to write without quarter.

It was all over. The crowd began to dissolve with a seemly slowness that did not conceal from him their eagerness to regather in The Crossed Guns for the usual elegaic hot toddy. He was peeping at his watch, about to drag Abby away to the afternoon train for the west, when he felt her softly pulling his sleeve and whispering that Molly wanted them both to stay with her for a night or two. If she had not known him so well she might have mistaken his fright for anger.

'I will do nothing of the kind!' he was growling down at her. 'Stay alone in a house with two wailing women for two nights? I have no more to say, to Molly. Anyway it isn't me she wants, it is you. You can stay if you like, but I am going home.'

'She does want you. She's worried about the future. Failey had some investments. There's the insurance. And the will. The house will have to be sold. All sorts of money matters. And the relatives will be all gone, Phil. She will be left all alone. You must come.'

'She has lawyers. She has a son of thirty-five. Why pick on me? Am I never to be shut of that man?'

'She trusts you. And Failey was always kind to us. You can't refuse her.'

With a groan he surrendered.

'Alright. But I'll stay only one night. I want to get back to my Book.'

Abby recoiled.

'Oh, Phil! What a time to be thinking of that!'

After the funeral the feast. They found the house on the Infirmary Road crowded with half a hundred people enjoying, as the old sagas loved to say, 'the freshest of every food and the oldest of every drink'; secular priests, the three Franciscans, country relatives, greying politicians, lots of young people whom he took to be the Dublin friends of the family, and a gaggle of civil servants who welcomed him so eagerly that he forgot himself in their cascade of talk, argument, and gossip whispered behind palms with sidelong glances towards the politicians. It was four o'clock before the crowd began to thin out. By six all that remained were Molly, Abby, himself, two unmarried daughters and a young man who was obviously courting the older of them. When the young man took her away, the three women began to tidy up the house and prepare the usual Dublin supper of 'Tea and Something' – the Something tonight being the remains of the funeral feast. It was eight o'clock before the remaining daughter went out. To the chapel? Or to meet another young man? Molly and Abby sat reminiscing before the drawing room fire. By nine o'clock he was deep in gloom.

'Where are those papers, Molly?' he finally asked, glad of any excuse to get away by himself for the rest of the night.

'I'll show you,' she sighed. 'They're all in the engine room. It is what Failey always called his study. Where he did his homework at night. I have the fire lit for you and a bottle of Irish on the table.'

She led him upstairs. In the return room he saw an old rolltop desk, a green-shaded reading lamp on top of it. He saw shelves of books, a table, an old-fashioned mahogany wardrobe, a couch with a plaid rug on it and an armchair by the turf fire. As she closed the long rep curtains he saw raindrops gleaming on the windowpane. The wet wind was still blowing from the west, down the Liffey. Tonight the sea would be covered with white horses.

'Pay no heed to me,' he ordered her. 'You two can go off to bed when ye want to. I'll stay up until I finish this job.'

'Ayeh!' she sighed. 'As poor Failey often did until three in the morning. He was as strong as a bull. If it wasn't for that damned accident he'd have lived to be ninety.'

6

There was no doubt whose room he was in. The wall above the fireplace was covered with black-framed photographs of Failey, massed shoulder to shoulder and head to tail. Failey, with a face like a boy, dressed in cap and gown, holding a scroll. Failey wearing a barrister's wig. Failey in a cutaway coat, holding a grey topper in the crook of his left arm, standing beside Molly in a wedding dress whose train curved in a white stream about her feet. Failey as Parliamentary Secretary to the Minister for Roads and Railways opening a factory. Failey as Minister for R. and R. opening another factory. Failey as Minister for Education opening a new school. Failey grinning on the golf course. Failey addressing Rotary. Failey in a Franciscan robe with a white cincture roped around his belly recalled the press announcement of his death. 'Phelim Patrick Quigley, B.L., T.S.O.F.' Third Order of Saint Francis. To what other order, association or society had he belonged? The Knights of Columbanus? Probably. The Knights of Malta? But you'd have to be at least a doctor to get into them. There were at least a hundred of those black-edged pictures. Vanity? Or just a cool awareness of the value of publicity? The bookshelves were untidy, disorderly, and wholly predictable. Rows of the official records of parliamentary debates; books and pamphlets about railroads, canals, and aeronautics; paperback thrillers, *A Portrait of the Artist as a Young Man*, books on religion, the odd Yeats, a book entitled *How to Make a Million Dollars a Year*, a rhyming dictionary.

He rolled up the hood of the desk and found what he expected. Chaos. He filled himself a stout glass of malt, lit his pipe, seized a pad of writing paper and set to work. The first pile he made was of the unopened letters, most of them from constituents. He read them all conscientiously: begging letters, abusive letters, grateful letters. It took him an hour to sweep them one by one into the waste-paper basket. He wrote on his pad the word *Investments* and started to search for them. He found only five in all. He humphed as he noted that Failey had not invested a penny in Irish Government Stock or Irish Industrials. He had favoured English gilts and equities. Unaccustomed to such matters, it took him another hour to work out whether Molly should keep or sell them, poorly helped by a three-day-old *Irish Times* that he found on the floor beside the desk. If Molly kept them they would not bring her in £200 a year, though the real wonder was that the man had been able to invest anything with such a long-tailed family and the modest salary of a Minister.

He was just about to pass on from Investments to Insurance when he came on a wallet containing a broker's contract notes of sales and purchases. These showed that, at one time, Failey must have invested much more. Only two weeks before he had sold over £4000 worth of stock. He looked for and found the bank sheets, and there it was duly credited, and on the same day a corresponding debit of £4310. He tumbled everything about in his eager search for Failey's cheque book, found it, riffled the stubs, and there was what he was looking for. The sum had been made payable to a well-known Dublin firm of solicitors. But what on earth was it for? Debts? The sum was too large for debts. A property purchase?

Thoughtfully, he wrote down on his pad the word *Insurance* and started to look for the policies. There were two, each for £1000, each taken out many years ago. He added the sums to Molly's credit. He next wrote down on his pad the word *Property* and started to search for the indentures, if any. He found two. To his relief the first one was for the house. This, at least, would be something of real value for poor old Molly. What Failey had paid for it he had no idea, and he would have to wait until the morning to find out precisely, but he had guessed ever since last February, when he had sold his own house at 26 Saint Rita's Villas, that this place, standing in an acre of land, must be now worth at least £12,000. He wrote down the sum £12,000, followed by a cautious query mark, to Molly's credit, reached for his glass, and found it empty.

He rose, stretched himself, and looked at his watch. Past midnight. He refilled his glass, went to the curtains, and parted them. The windowpanes were still speckled with rain, the sky over the city a sodden pink sponge. He returned to the desk, picked up the second grey document, also headed in large decorative gothic letters with the word INDENTURE, relit his pipe and puffing easily began to read it. Abruptly he laid down his pipe and began to reread. There was no question about it. The document did witness that in consideration of the usual this, that and the other 'the Lessor doth hereby DEMISE unto the Lessee ALL THAT the plot of ground known as 26 Saint Rita's Villas, North Circular Road, in the City of Dublin . . .'

For a while he sat as rigid in his chair, staring as fixedly in front of him, as if he had suddenly died there. Galvanized he whirled to the last page to see the date. Two weeks ago. He grabbed the cheque book again and compared the stub. The dates agreed. Two weeks ago? Molly must have known of it. If Abby had not known of it before the funeral she did now. But why the secrecy?

He strode to the door, opened it, and listened. Not a sound from downstairs. The two of them must have gone to bed. He opened the door of the bedroom allotted to Abby and himself, and seeing it empty bethought himself. She would, naturally, be sleeping tonight in the same room as Molly. He moved down the corridor to its door and bent his head to listen. Through the door he could hear a soft whispering, lifted now and then to an audible feminine murmur. He was about to put his hand on the doorknob when he heard the sound of one or other of them crying. At the same moment he thought of the will. He hurried back to the desk to look for it. Two hours ago he would have blandly assumed that there would, characteristically, be no will. He now knew better. He went carefully through every pigeonhole and drawer again. It was not in any of them. Then he saw what had earlier seemed to him to be a long, slim horizontal panel, slightly protruding along the top of the pigeonholes, eased it forward, and there was the buff envelope, duly inscribed *My Will*. He drew out the document. In the usual benignant legal language of all wills everything had been left 'to my dear wife Molly for her own use absolutely.' He added everything up and found that if she sold the house well, she would enjoy an income of about two thousand pounds.

The pictures over the fireplace, the shelves of books, even the old-fashioned furniture suddenly possessed an ominous solidity. He had belittled Failey. This room, this home that he had created, the family he had reared were all about him. The man had been a rotten Minister, but he had been a good husband. To reassure himself he looked again at the massed photographs over the fireplace. He felt humiliated to notice that the wedding photograph hung in the middle of them.

When he came to himself he found that the hour was approaching two o'clock. To be certain that he had performed his task completely he returned to the desk, now tidily in order, and checked off each of its seven small drawers and eight pigeonholes, running his fingers back into their recesses to be sure he had missed nothing. He had missed nothing. The last central compartment had a small door like a tabernacle. It was empty, but as his fingers groped in the rear of it they entered a crevice, and at once a small upright panel to the side of it moved slowly forward a half-inch. He drew it towards him, one of those so-called secret receptacles that are sometimes to be found in old desks. He pulled it out and turned it upside down. It was empty. He did the same with the opposite crevice of the tabernacle, drew out its second panel, turned it upside down, and out of it fell a book. It was a small black book. Inside it was an envelope marked *Private*. On its black cover was pasted a white label bearing the written words:

THE DARK AND FAIR
1930–1935

A Sequence in Quatrains
by
PHELIM PATRICK QUIGLEY, BL

He found that it contained a gathering of verses, each one a numbered quatrain, each on a single page. Between embarrassment and pity he took it to the armchair by the sinking fire, threw on a few sods of turf from the turf-basket, relit his pipe and started to read the first verse.

> Think not, who reads these tortured lines, I pray,
>   Of Dark or Fair. To me they symbolize
> Lost dreams of love or none, night after day,
>   A dream I dreamed, a forfeit prize.

He turned the leaf indifferently. Unprepared, he felt the knife slip in:

> This fool once suffered eyes of midnight hue,
>   And gypsy-coloured ringlets to betray
> A heart that burned for eyes of gentian blue,
>   And virgin smiles, and primrose-coloured hair.

He tautened too late. He felt his skull crawling as he ran through the third, the fourth and the fifth quatrains to find out for certain who was who in this farrago.

> Until, with gypsy smiles and wiles, she wound
>   Her hair about my eyes and drew me deep
> Into her gypsy flesh where passion crowned
>   Desire, and Love cast out could only weep.

He was sweating when he came to the eighth quatrain. He read it several times, reliving every single one of those nights of his betrayal:

> Yet, every night as that last train drew out
>> For Bray, two girls backward waving, someday,
> I swore, I'd hold her in my arms, and mouth
>> To mouth on fire, my Fair would whisper, Stay!

Forty years ago. On the platform of Amiens Street Station smelling of midnight dust, fish, steam, petrol. The two of them joking upwards to the two girls in the lighted carriage, holding their hands until the very last moment when the engine shook itself and chugged slowly out. Then two white hands waving back through the steam until train and lights and hands vanished around the curve like falling cards. Out, then, mocking one another's ardour, into the empty streets for the slow walk back to their lodgings on the North Side, and the usual prolonged last talk or argument on the canal bridge, often not parting until two in the morning with cheery backward calls of farewell.

Did she? Ever? Let her hot mouth stay? He had to read on to the thirteenth quatrain before he knew.

> At last, the moonlight on the waves' soft sigh,
>> We kissed. Then bracken-deep in love we lay,
> Until 'Too late!' I heard her sobbing cry.
>> 'Last night, in bed, he said, "Our wedding day!"'

The one secret of his life! His one lovely, imperious, flaming passion shared with that lying clod!

'The poor bastard!' he said, and laid the book aside. 'What have his private sins to do with me?'

It was only when he found himself standing in the rain on the pavement outside 26 Saint Rita's Villas, peering at the TO LET sign pasted inside the lamplit window that he knew that he was out of control. He was carrying Abby's ridiculous blue umbrella. He was wearing no overcoat. He removed his hat, looked at it, and found that he had taken Failey's. He had no key to let him back into the house.

He began to return quickly, but after walking for half an hour stopped dead. He was lost in a suburban maze. Not a soul in sight, nor a sound to be heard except the rain spitting into him like arrows. Had he been making for Glasnevin? He listened. A sighing wind down the concrete avenue made him turn in fright. He halted and listened again, and again he heard that sifting sigh. He started to run, gripped himself, and hurried as quickly as he could walk, back on his tracks. He calmed only when he had found his way to the door, shocked to see that he had left it so wide open that the rain was blowing into the hall as if it were a deserted house.

He closed the door silently behind him, and crept carefully up to the engine room, halting at every creak of the old stairs. The fire had melted into grey ash. With the box of firelighters beside the turf-basket, a bundle of Failey's discarded papers and fresh turf he made a blazing fire, and stripped to his skin; he hung the shirt by its sleeves from the mantelpiece, outspread like a crucifix, and sat naked before the fire watching the steam begin to rise from the clothes that he had strewn to dry on the brass fender.

It was then that his uplifted eye saw, peeping down at him over the corner of the mantelpiece, the envelope that he had found in the black book. He snatched it down and ripped it open. It contained two letters. He had at one time smiled at her handwriting for being so simple and childlike. Later he had frowned at it for being quavering and old. But, for years now, everything she said and did had made him think of her as somebody who had never had any proper womanhood between her girlhood and her age. The first letter was dated December 20, 1934, five years after they had married. As he read it, in spite of the fire mottling his shinbones, his whole body began to exude cold sweat.

DEAR FAY,

How kind you were to write to me in my great unhappiness. I have read your letter so many times that I have it all off by heart. I will never forget one word of it as long as I live. I am sure you are right in everything you say about Phil, and there can be nobody living or dead who knows him better. You are right in another thing. He is not an unkind man by nature and he can be very warm, and giving, and loving. But there is something in him, or maybe in me, that brings out the worst in him and turns him into what you call an irate man full of cold principle. But it is all very well for you, Fay, to say that that is what makes him the most honest and reliable civil servant you ever met. You do not have to live with him night and day. God knows I don't ask much. If only he would not be so contemptuous of me. If only he'd make a few allowances for me. If only he would not turn all his anger on to me. The way he is I just can't go on with it. I feel I will have to leave him or have the life crushed out of me. I am terribly sorry Fay to have poured all this over you but I have nobody else to confide in. Molly is so strong and so dominating that whenever I have tried to hint any of this to her she just laughs and tells me to slap back at him. I can't write any more tonight, I am so miserable. God bless you for trying to understand. I pray that you and Molly and the children may have a happy, happy Christmas.

Ever,
ABBY

He tried to remember that Christmas, but it was too long ago. The second letter was dated New Year's Day, 1935.

DEAR FAY,
Thank you and bless you for all you said to me yesterday in Wynne's Hotel. I have thought it over and over and as always I see that you are dead right. I must stick it out. I will always remember specially two things you said. I hope it *is* true that he needs me, though I'll never know what he saw in me to want to marry me at all. The other thing you said was how wonderful he is with the schoolchildren and how tough he is with their teachers. I wish I could have given him children. It might have made him a bit more kind to me. As it is I must look on him now as my only child. I will not bother you any more, Fay. I promise. Not a word to Molly about any of this. And may you and yours all have a very, very happy New Year.

ABBY

The letter fell from his hand, he closed his eyes, crumpled into his armchair and swooned out of the memory of man.

He woke, shivering. It was six o'clock. With a groan he remembered, rose, stiff in all his bones, laid another couple of firelighters into the seed of the ashen fire, the two letters on top of them, then the book of verses, then a pyre of turf, and watched until the flames embraced them all. Then he opened the wardrobe door, found a worn woollen dressing gown, and an overcoat, and put them both on. He went to the window and drew the curtains apart. The rain had stopped. By the city's glow and the presence of a few stars he could see that the clouds were breaking up. Once, for a moment, between their torn edges, he saw the moon, a steaming rag hung there to dry. To the north east the sky was becoming paler. Inside an hour morning would be creeping in across the plain of Swords, over Drumcondra and Glasnevin. After that it would soon be touching the city's spires.

A mile away, up there, he was lying where they had left him, a man he had never known, a life he had failed to share. He did not feel guilty. He felt only the barrier. Of late years he had noticed that his old friends no longer died. He would ask casually after one of them and be told in some surprise, that it must be a year or so since the poor chap had disappeared around some corner. Looking out at the paling sky he felt the pain of loss, the brevity of life and its challenge that never stops. He turned to the couch, lay and wrapped the rug about him.

When he woke again it was ten o'clock, the room filled with blinding sunlight, nearby roofs exuding a faint steam more soft than pity. A Saint Martin's summer? He found the bathroom, gave himself a cold shower, shaved, put on his dried clothes and went slowly downstairs in search of the Dark and the Fair. He found them in the kitchen, two white-haired old ladies talking quietly over their late breakfast. Molly got up to greet him. She was hooped even when she stood.

'Come in, Phil,' she said warmly. 'I hope you got some kind of a sleep on that old couch. Sit down there by Abby and we'll all have a fresh pot of tea. And you are going to eat a good plate of bacon and eggs, Master Philip, and none of your old arguments about it, if you please!'

'I will eat them,' he said obediently and watched her gather the soiled china on a tray. 'Anyway, I deserve them. I've done a good night's work for you. And to be shut of it at once, you are going to be alright, Molly. That is if you can live on fifteen hundred a year, tax-paid. Failey looked after you well.'

'Thank you, Phil. It's a great relief to me.'

As she lifted the tray and turned to go out to the scullery he held her.

'There is one thing I must ask you, Molly. Did you know that Failey had bought our old house on the North Circular?'

She half-turned.

'Yes, of course. He bought it two weeks ago when he saw it was up for sale again. He was going to write to you about it. He told me I should rent it. But he did say that if you and Abby want it you should have first call on it. At,' she added briskly, 'a nominal rent of five pounds a week,' and went out.

Abby was staring at the milk jug. Her left hand was trembling. He laid his hand on it and spoke as slowly and softly as if he were talking to a child.

'Abby! Do you want very much to go back to that house?'

Still looking at the milk jug she whispered, 'Yes.'

'Very well. Let's do it.'

Her hand closed tightly on his. He could see her throat gulping, and then the tears were creeping down her face, and she was sobbing into her palms. She raised her wet face to say, 'Oh, Phil, how soon can we go back there?'

'Right away, I suppose. We should be well settled in by Christmas.'

Molly came bustling in with the teapot.

'You can start on that, the bacon is sizzling, how do you like your eggs, basted or turned?'

'He likes them basted,' Abby said comfortably. 'And he likes two. With a nice little slice of fried bread, and a touch of parsley on it.'

'Ha!' Molly said sourly, but with a grin to take the harm out of it. 'You've spoiled him,' and bustled off again.

When she came in and out again with the toast he felt it to be sure it was not too crisp. 'She makes good toast,' he said and buttered it and began to eat, vaguely aware that Abby was babbling on and on about the house.

'We'll be doing it up,' he heard her saying, 'between now and Christmas. I'll be sitting on one side of the fire making new curtains. And you will be sitting on the other side writing the Book.'

'The what?' he said, startled. 'Oh! That? Pour me out a cup of tea, will you? Milk first. You always forget it. I see she has lump sugar. Why don't we always have lump sugar?'

'You will, Phil,' she said as she poured, forgetting the milk again.

'You'll have the best of everything. And peace, Phil. And calm, Phil. And philosophical content, Phil. And serenity without end.'

He munched silently, looking at the sun in the back garden. Saint Martin? He sniffed at the absurd legend: a soldier-saint who saw from horseback two beggars shivering in the snow, took off his cloak, cut it in two, and gave half to one beggar; then looked at the other beggar, took what was left of his cloak, divided it with his sword and gave half to him – so that now all three of them were shivering, until God, in pity, sent back the summer. And people believe things like that can really happen! Staring out he did not hear one word of the childish prattle by his side. He sniffed again. He smelled the rashers frying.

The Talking Trees

There were four of them in the same class at the Red Abbey, all under fifteen. They met every night in Mrs Coffey's sweetshop at the top of Victoria Road to play the fruit machine, smoke fags and talk about girls. Not that they really talked about them – they just winked, leered, nudged one another, laughed, grunted and groaned about them, or said things like 'See her legs?' 'Yaroosh!' 'Wham!' 'Ouch!' 'Ooof!' or 'If only, if only!' But if anybody had said, 'Only what?' they would not have known precisely what. They knew nothing precisely about girls, they wanted to know everything precisely about girls, there was nobody to tell them all the things they wanted to know about girls and that they thought they wanted to do with them. Aching and wanting, not knowing, half guessing, they dreamed of clouds upon clouds of fat, pink, soft, ardent girls billowing towards them across the horizon of their future. They might just as well have been dreaming of pink porpoises moaning at their feet for love.

In the sweetshop the tall glass jars of coloured sweets shone in the bright lights. The one-armed fruit-machine went zing. Now and again girls from Saint Monica's came in to buy sweets, giggle roguishly and over-pointedly ignore them. Mrs Coffey was young, buxom, fairhaired, blue-eyed and very good-looking. They admired her so much that one night when Georgie Watchman whispered to them that she had fine bubs Dick Franks told him curtly not to be so coarse, and Jimmy Sullivan said in his most toploftical voice, 'Georgie Watchman, you should be jolly well ashamed of yourself, you are no gentleman,' and Tommy Gong Gong said nothing but nodded his head as insistently as a ventriloquist's dummy.

Tommy's real name was Tommy Flynn, but he was younger than any of them so that neither he nor they were ever quite sure that he ought to belong to the gang at all. To show it they called him all sorts of nicknames, like Inch because he was so small; Fatty because he was so puppy-fat; Pigeon because he had a chest like a woman; Gong Gong because after long bouts of silence he had a way of suddenly spraying them with wild bursts of talk like a fire alarm attached to a garden sprinkler.

That night all Georgie Watchman did was to make a rude blubberlip noise at Dick Franks. But he never again said anything about Mrs Coffey. They looked up to Dick. He was the oldest of them. He had long eyelashes like a girl, perfect manners, the sweetest smile and the softest voice. He had been to two English boarding schools, Ampleforth and Downside, and in Ireland to three, Clongowes, Castelknock and Rockwell, and had been expelled from all five of them. After that his mother had made his father retire from the Indian Civil, come back to the old family house in Cork and, as a last hope, send her darling Dicky to the Red Abbey day-school. He smoked a corncob pipe and dressed in droopy plus fours with chequered stockings and red flares, as if he was always just coming from or going to the golf course. He played cricket and tennis, games that no other boy at the Red Abbey could afford to play. They saw him as the typical school captain they read about in English boys' papers like *The Gem* and *The Magnet*, *The Boy's Own Paper*, *The Captain* and *Chums*, which was where they got all those swanky words like Wham, Ouch, Yaroosh, Ooof and Jolly Well. He was their Tom Brown, their Bob Cherry, their Tom Merry, those heroes who were always leading Greyfriars School or Blackfriars School to victory on the cricket field amid the cap-tossing huzzas of the juniors and the admiring smiles of visiting parents. It never occurred to them that *The Magnet* or *The Gem* would have seen all four of them as perfect models for some such story as *The Cads of Greyfriars*, or *The Bounders of Blackfriars*, low types given to secret smoking in the spinneys, drinking in the Dead Woman's Inn, or cheating at examinations, or, worst crime of all, betting on horses with redfaced bookies' touts down from London, while the rest of the school was practising at the nets – a quartet of rotters fated to be caned ceremoniously in the last chapter before the entire awe-struck school, and then whistled off at dead of night back to their heartbroken fathers and mothers.

It could not have occurred to them because these crimes did not exist at the Red Abbey. Smoking? At the Red Abbey any boy who wanted to was free to smoke himself into a galloping consumption so long as he did it off the premises, in the jakes or up the chimney. Betting? Brother Julius was always passing fellows sixpence or even a bob to put on an uncle's or a cousin's horse at Leopardstown or the Curragh. In the memory of man no boy had ever been caned ceremoniously for anything. Fellows were just leathered all day long for not doing their homework, or playing hooky from school, or giving lip, or fighting in class – and they were leathered hard. Two years ago Jimmy Sullivan had been given six swingers on each hand with the sharp edge of a metre-long ruler for pouring the contents of an inkwell over Georgie Watchman's head in the middle of a history lesson about the Trojan Wars, in spite of his wailing explanation that he had only done it because he thought Georgie Watchman was a scut and all Trojans were blacks. Drink? They did not drink only because they were too poor. While, as for what *The Magnet* and *The Gem* really meant by 'betting' – which, they dimly understood, was some sort of depravity that no decent English boy would like to see mentioned in print – hardly a week passed that some brother did not say that a hard problem in algebra, or a leaky pen, or a window that would not open or shut was 'a blooming bugger'.

There was the day when little Brother Angelo gathered half a dozen boys about him at playtime to help him with a crossword puzzle.

'Do any of ye,' he asked, 'know what Notorious Conduct could be in seven letters?'

'Buggery?' Georgie suggested mock-innocently.

'Please be serious!' Angelo said. 'This is about Conduct.'

When the solution turned out to be *Jezebel*, little Angelo threw up his hands, said it must be some queer kind of foreign woman and declared that the whole thing was a blooming bugger. Or there was that other day when old Brother Expeditus started to tell them about the strict lives and simple food of Dominican priests and Trappist monks. When Georgie said, 'No tarts, Brother?' Expeditus had laughed loud and long.

'No, Georgie!' he chuckled. 'No pastries of any kind.'

They might as well have been in school in Arcadia. And every other school about them seemed to be just as hopeless. In fact they might have gone on dreaming of pink porpoises for years if it was not for a small thing that Gong Gong told them one October night in the sweetshop. He sprayed them with the news that his sister Jenny had been thrown out of class that morning in Saint Monica's for turning up with a red ribbon in her hair, a mother-of-pearl brooch at her neck and smelling of scent.

'Ould Sister Eustasia,' he fizzled, 'made her go out in the yard and wash herself under the tap, she said they didn't want any girls in their school who had notions.'

The three gazed at one another, and began at once to discuss all the possible sexy meanings of notions. Georgie had a pocket dictionary. 'An ingenious contrivance'? 'An imperfect conception (*US*)'? 'Small wares'? It did not make sense. Finally they turned to Mrs Coffey. She laughed, nodded towards two giggling girls in the shop who were eating that gummy kind of block toffee that can gag you for half an hour, and said, 'Why don't you ask *them*?' Georgie approached them most politely.

'Pardon me, ladies, but do you by any chance happen to have notions?'

The two girls stared at one another with cow's eyes, blushed scarlet and fled from the shop shrieking with laughter. Clearly a notion was very sexy.

'Georgie!' Dick pleaded. 'You're the only one who knows anything. What in heaven's name is it?'

When Georgie had to confess himself stumped they knew at last that their situation was desperate. Up to now Georgie had always been able to produce some sort of answer, right or wrong, to all their questions. He was the one who, to their disgust, told them what he called conraception meant. He was the one who had explained to them that all babies are delivered from the navel of the mother. He was the one who had warned them that if a fellow kissed a bad woman he would get covered by leprosy from head to foot. The son of a Head Constable, living in the police barracks, he had collected his facts simply by listening as quietly as a mouse to the other four policemen lolling in the dayroom of the barracks with their collars open, reading the sporting pages of *The Freeman's Journal*, slowly creasing their polls and talking about colts, fillies, cows, calves, bulls and bullocks and 'the mysteerious nachure of all faymale wimmen'. He had also gathered a lot of useful stuff by dutiful attendance since the age of eleven at the meetings and marchings of the Protestant Boys' Brigade, and from a devoted study of the Bible. And here he was, stumped by a nun!

Dick lifted his beautiful eyelashes at the three of them, jerked his head and led them out on the pavement.

'I have a plan,' he said quietly. 'I've been thinking of it for some time. Chaps! Why don't we see everything with our own eyes?' And he threw them into excited discussion by mentioning a name. 'Daisy Bolster?'

Always near every school, there is a Daisy Boister – the fast girl whom everybody has heard about and nobody knows. They had all seen her at a distance. Tall, a bit skinny, long legs, dark eyes, lids heavy as the dimmers of a car lamp, prominent white teeth, and her lower lip always gleaming wet. She could be as old as seventeen. Maybe even eighteen. She wore her hair up. Dick told them that he had met her once at the tennis club with four or five other fellows around her and that she had laughed and winked very boldly all the time. Georgie said that he once heard a fellow in school say, 'She goes with boys.' Gong Gong bubbled that that was true because his sister Jenny told him that a girl named Daisy Bolster had been thrown out of school three years ago for talking to a boy outside the convent gate. At this Georgie flew into a terrible rage.

'You stupid slob!' he roared. 'Don't you know yet that when anybody says a boy and girl are talking to one another it means they're doing you-know-what?'

'I don't know you-know-what,' Gong Gong wailed. 'What what?'

'I heard a fellow say,' Jimmy Sullivan revealed solemnly, 'that she has no father and that her mother is no better than she should be.'

Dick said in approving tones that he had once met another fellow who had heard her telling some very daring stories.

'Do you think she would show us for a quid?'

Before they parted on the pavement that night they were talking not about a girl but about a fable. Once a girl like that gets her name up she always ends up as a myth, and for a generation afterwards, maybe more, it is the myth that persists. 'Do you remember,' some old chap will wheeze, 'that girl Daisy Bolster? She used to live up the Mardyke. We used to say she was fast,' The other old boy will nod knowingly, the two of them will look at one another inquisitively, neither will admit anything, remembering only the long, dark avenue, its dim gaslamps, the stars hooked in its trees.

Within a month Dick had fixed it. Their only trouble after that was to collect the money and to decide whether Gong Gong should be allowed to come with them.

Dick fixed that, too, at a final special meeting in the sweet-shop. Taking his pipe from between his lips, he looked speculatively at Gong Gong, who looked up at him with eyes big as plums, trembling between the terror of being told he could not come with them and the greater terror of being told that he could.

'Tell me, Gong Gong,' Dick said politely, 'what exactly does your father do?'

'He's a tailor,' Tommy said, blushing a bit at having to confess it, knowing that Jimmy's dad was a bank clerk, that Georgie's was a Head Constable, and that Dick's had been a Commissioner in the Punjab.

'Very fine profession,' Dick said kindly. 'Gentleman's Tailor and Outfitter. I see. Flynn and Company? Or is it Flynn and Sons? Have I seen his emporium?'

'Ah, no!' Tommy said, by now as red as a radish. 'He's not that sort of tailor at all, he doesn't build suits, ye know, that's a different trade altogether, he works with me mother at home in Tuckey Street, he tucks things in and he lets things out, he's what they call a mender and turner, me brother Turlough had this suit I have on me now before I got it, you can see he's very good at his job, he's a real dab...'

Dick let him run on, nodding sympathetically – meaning to convey to the others that they really could not expect a fellow to know much about girls if his father spent his life mending and turning old clothes in some side alley called Tuckey Street.

'Do you fully realize, Gong Gong, that we are proposing to behold the ultimate in female beauty?'

'You mean,' Gong Gong smiled fearfully, 'that she'll only be wearing her nightie?'

Georgie Watchman turned from him in disgust to the fruit-machine. Dick smiled on.

'The thought had not occurred to me,' he said. 'I wonder, Gong Gong, where do you get all those absolutely filthy ideas. If we subscribe seventeen and sixpence, do you think you can contribute half-a-crown?'

'I could feck it, I suppose.'

Dick raised his eyelashes.

'Feck?'

Gong Gong looked shamedly at the tiles.

'I mean steal,' he whispered.

'Don't they give you any pocket money?'

'They give me threepence a week.'

'Well, we have only a week to go. If you can, what was your word, feck half-a-crown, you may come.'

The night chosen was a Saturday – her mother always went to town on Saturdays; the time of meeting, five o'clock exactly; the place, the entrance to the Mardyke Walk.

On any other occasion it would have been a gloomy spot for a rendezvous. For adventure, perfect. A long tree-lined avenue, with, on one side, a few scattered houses and high enclosing walls; on the other side the small canal whose deep dyke had given it its name. Secluded, no traffic allowed inside the gates, complete silence. A place where men came every night to stand with their girls behind the elm trees kissing and whispering for hours. Dick and Georgie were there on the dot of five. Then Jimmy Sullivan came swiftly loping. From where they stood, under a tree just beyond the porter's lodge, trembling with anticipation, they could see clearly for only about a hundred yards up the long tunnel of elms lit by the first stars above the boughs, one tawny window streaming across a dank garden, and beyond that a feeble perspective of pendant lamps fading dimly away into the blue November dusk. Within another half-hour the avenue would be pitch black between those meagre pools of light.

Her instructions had been precise. In separate pairs, at exactly half past five, away up there beyond the last lamp, where they would be as invisible as cockroaches, they must gather outside her house.

'You won't be able even to see one another,' she had said gleefully to Dick, who had stared coldly at her, wondering how often she had stood behind a tree with some fellow who would not have been able even to see her face.

Every light in the house would be out except for the fanlight over the door.

'Ooo!' she had giggled. 'It will be terribly oohey. You won't hear a sound but the branches squeaking. You must come along to my door. You must leave the other fellows to watch from behind the trees. You must give two short rings. Once, twice. And then give a long ring, and wait.' She had started to whisper the rest, her hands by her sides clawing her dress in her excitement. 'The fanlight will go out if my mother isn't at home. The door will open slowly. You must step into the dark hall. A hand will take your hand. You won't know whose hand it is. It will be like something out of Sherlock Holmes. You will be simply terrified. You won't know what I'm wearing. For all you'll know I might be wearing nothing at all!'

He must leave the door ajar. The others must follow him one by one. After that . . .

It was eleven minutes past five and Gong Gong had not yet come. Already three women had passed up the Mardyke carrying parcels, hurrying home to their warm fires, forerunners of the home-for-tea crowd. When they had passed out of sight Georgie growled, 'When that slob comes I'm going to put my boot up his backside.' Dick, calmly puffing his corncob, gazing wearily up at the stars, laughed tolerantly and said, 'Now Georgie, don't be impatient. We shall see all! We shall at last know all!'

Georgie sighed and decided to be weary too.

'I hope,' he drawled, 'this poor frail isn't going to let us down!'

For three more minutes they waited in silence and then Jimmy Sullivan let out a cry of relief. There was the small figure hastening towards them along the Dyke Parade from one lamp-post to another.

'Puffing and panting as usual, I suppose,' Dick chuckled. 'And exactly fourteen minutes late.'

'I hope to God,' Jimmy said, 'he has our pound note. I don't know in hell why you made that slob our treasurer.'

'Because he is poor,' Dick said quietly. 'We would have spent it.'

He came panting up to them, planted a black violin case against the tree and began rummaging in his pockets for the money.

'I'm supposed to be at a music lesson, that's me alibi, me father always wanted to be a musician but he got married instead, he plays the cello, me brother Turlough plays the clarinet, me sister Jenny plays the viola, we have quartets, I sold a Haydn quartet for one and six, I had to borrow sixpence from Jenny, and I fecked the last sixpence from me mother's purse, that's what kept me so late . . .'

They were not listening, staring into the soiled and puckered handkerchief he was unravelling to point out one by one, a crumpled half-note, two half-crowns, two shillings and a sixpenny bit.

'That's all yeers, and here's mine. Six threepenny bits for the quartet. That's one and six. Here's Jenny's five pennies and two ha'pence. That makes two bob. And here's the tanner I just fecked from me mother's purse. That makes my two and sixpence.'

Eagerly he poured the mess into Dick's hands. At the sight of the jumble Dick roared at him.

'I told you, you bloody little fool, to bring a pound note!'

'You told me to bring a pound.'

'I said a pound note. I can't give this dog's breakfast to a girl like Daisy Bolster.'

'You said a pound.'

They all began to squabble. Jimmy Sullivan shoved Gong Gong. Georgie punched him. Dick shoved Georgie. Jimmy defended Georgie with 'We should never have let that slob come with us.' Gong Gong shouted, 'Who's a slob?' and swiped at him. Jimmy shoved him again so that he fell over his violin case, and a man passing home to his tea shouted at them, 'Stop beating that little boy at once!'

Tactfully they cowered. Dick helped Gong Gong to his feet. Georgie dusted him lovingly. Jimmy retrieved his cap, put it back crookedly on his head and patted him kindly. Dick explained in his best Ampleforth accent that they had merely been having 'a trifling discussion', and 'our young friend here tripped over his suitcase'. The man surveyed them dubiously, growled something and went on his way. When he was gone Georgie pulled out his pocketbook, handed a brand-new pound note to Dick, and grabbed the dirty jumble of cash. Dick at once said, 'Quick march! Two by two!' and strode off ahead of the others, side by side with Tommy in his crooked cap, lugging his dusty violin case, into the deepening dark.

They passed nobody. They heard nothing. They saw only the few lights in the sparse houses along the left of the Mardyke. On the other side was the silent, railed-in stream. When they came in silence to the wide expanse of the cricket field the sky dropped a blazing veil of stars behind the outfield nets. When they passed the gates of the railed-in public park, locked for the night, darkness returned between the walls to their left and the overgrown laurels glistening behind the tall railings on their right. Here Tommy stopped dead, hooped fearfully towards the laurels.

'What's up with you?' Dick snapped at him.

'I hear a noise, me father told me once how a man murdered a woman in there for her gold watch, he said men do terrible things like that because of bad women, he said that that man was hanged by the neck in Cork Jail, he said that was the last time the black flag flew on top of the jail. Dick! I don't want to go on!'

Dick peered at the phosphorescent dial of his watch, and strode ahead, staring at the next feeble lamp hanging crookedly from its black iron arch. Tommy had to trot to catch up with him.

'We know,' Dick said, 'that she has long legs. Her breasts will be white and small.'

'I won't look!' Tommy moaned.

'Then don't look!'

Panting, otherwise silently, they hurried past the old corrugated iron building that had once been a roller-skating rink and was now empty and abandoned. After the last lamp the night became impenetrable, then her house rose slowly to their left against the starlight. It was square, tall, solid, brick-fronted, three-storeyed, and jet-black against the stars except for its half-moon fanlight. They walked a few yards past it and halted, panting, behind a tree. The only sound was the squeaking of a branch over their heads. Looking backwards, they saw Georgie and Jimmy approaching under the last lamp. Looking forwards, they saw a brightly lit tram, on its way outward from the city, pass the far end of the tunnel, briefly light its maw and black it out again. Beyond that lay wide fields and the silent river. Dick said, 'Tell them to follow me if the fanlight goes out,' and disappeared.

Alone under the tree, backed still by the park, Tommy looked across to the far heights of Sunday's Well dotted with the lights of a thousand suburban houses. He clasped his fiddle case before him like a shield. He had to force himself not to run away towards where another bright tram would rattle him back to the city. Suddenly he saw the fanlight go out. Strings in the air throbbed and faded. Was somebody playing a cello? His father bowed over his cello, jacket off, shirt-sleeves rolled up, entered the Haydn; beside him Jenny waited, chin sidewards over the viola, bosom lifted, bow poised, the tendons of her frail wrist hollowed by the lamplight, Turlough facing them lipped a thinner reed. His mother sat shawled by the fire, tapping the beat with her toe. Georgie and Jimmy joined him.

'Where's Dick?' Georgie whispered urgently.

'Did I hear music?' he gasped.

Georgie vanished, and again the strings came and faded. Jimmy whispered, 'Has she a gramophone?' Then they could hear nothing but the faint rattle of the vanished tram. When Jimmy slid away from him, he raced madly up into the darkness, and then stopped dead halfway to the tunnel's end. He did not have the penny to pay for the tram. He turned and raced as madly back the way he had come, down past her house, down to where the gleam of the laurels hid the murdered woman, and stopped again. He heard a rustling noise. A rat? He looked back, thought of her long legs and her small white breasts, and found himself walking heavily back to her garden gate, his heart pounding. He entered the path, fumbled for the dark door, pressed against it, felt it slew open under his hand, stepped cautiously into the dark hallway, closed the door, saw nothing, heard nothing, stepped onward, and fell clattering on the tiles over his violin case.

A door opened. He saw firelight on shining shinbones and bare knees. Fearfully, his eyes moved upwards. She was wearing nothing but gym knickers. He saw two small birds, white, soft, rosy-tipped. Transfixed by joy he stared and stared at them. Her black hair hung over her narrow shoulders. She laughed down at him with white teeth and wordlessly gestured him to get up and come in. He faltered after her white back and stood inside the door. The only light was from the fire.

Nobody heeded him. Dick stood by the corner of the mantelpiece, one palm flat on it, his other hand holding his trembling corncob. He was peering coldly at her. His eyelashes almost met. Georgie lay sprawled in a chintzy armchair on the other side of the fire wearily flicking the ash from a black cigarette into the fender. Opposite him Jimmy Sullivan sat on the edge of a chair, his elbows on his knees, his eyeballs sticking out as if he just swallowed something hot, hard and raw. Nobody said a word.

She stood in the centre of the carpet, looking guardedly from one to the other of them out of her hooded eyes, her thumbs inside the elastic of her gym knickers. Slowly she began to press her knickers down over her hips. When Georgie suddenly whispered 'The Seventh veil!' he at once wanted to batter him over the head with his fiddle case, to shout at her to stop, to shout at them that they had seen everything, to shout that they must look no more. Instead, he lowered his head so that he saw nothing but her bare toes. Her last covering slid to the carpet. He heard three long gasps, became aware that Dick's pipe had fallen to the floor, that Georgie had started straight up, one fist lifted as if he was going to strike her, and that Jimmy had covered his face with his two hands.

A coal tinkled from the fire to the fender. With averted eyes he went to it, knelt before it, wet his fingers with his spittle as he had often seen his mother do, deftly laid the coal back on the fire and remained so for a moment watching it light up again. Then he sidled back to his violin case, walked out into the hall, flung open the door on the sky of stars, and straightway started to race the whole length of the Mardyke from pool to pool of light in three gasping spurts.

After the first spurt he stood gasping until his heart had stopped hammering. He heard a girl laughing softly behind a tree. Just before his second halt he saw ahead of him a man and a woman approaching him arm in arm, but when he came up to where they should have been they too had become invisible. Halted, breathing, listening, he heard their murmuring somewhere in the dark. At his third panting rest he heard an invisible girl say, 'Oh, no, oh no!' and a man's urgent voice say, 'But yes, but yes!' He felt that behind every tree there were kissing lovers, and without stopping he ran the gauntlet between them until he emerged from the Mardyke among the bright lights of the city. Then, at last, the sweat cooling on his forehead, he was standing outside the shuttered plumber's shop above which they lived. Slowly he climbed the bare stairs to their floor and their door. He paused for a moment to look up through the windows at the stars, opened the door and went in.

Four heads around the supper table turned to look up inquiringly at him. At one end of the table his mother sat wearing her blue apron. At the other end his father sat, in his rolled-up shirt-sleeves as if he had only just laid down the pressing iron. Turlough gulped his food. Jenny was smiling mockingly at him. She had the red ribbon in her hair and the mother-of-pearl brooch at her neck.

'You're bloody late,' his father said crossly. 'What the hell kept you? I hope you came straight home from your lesson. What way did you come? Did you meet anybody or talk to anybody? You know I don't want any loitering at night. I hope you weren't cadeying with any blackguards? Sit down, sir, and eat your supper. Or did your lordship expect us to wait for you? What did you play tonight? What did Professor Hartmann give you to practise for your next lesson?'

He sat in his place. His mother filled his plate and they all ate in silence.

Always the questions! Always talking at him! They never let him alone for a minute. His hands sank. She was so lovely. So white. So soft. So pink. His mother said gently, 'You're not eating, Tommy. Are you all right?'

He said, 'Yes, yes, I'm fine, Mother.'

Like birds. Like stars. Like music.

His mother said, 'You are very silent tonight, Tommy. You usually have a lot of talk after you've been to Professor Hartmann. What were you thinking of?'

'They were so beautiful!' he blurted.

'What was so bloody beautiful?' his father rasped. 'What are you blathering about?'

'The stars,' he said hastily.

Jenny laughed. His father frowned. Silence returned.

He knew that he would never again go back to the sweetshop. They would only want to talk and talk about her. They would want to bring everything out into the light, boasting and smirking about her, taunting him for having run away. He would be happy forever if only he could walk every night of his life up the dark Mardyke, hearing nothing but a girl's laugh from behind a tree, a branch squeaking, and the far-off rattle of a lost tram; walk on and on, deeper and deeper into the darkness until he could see nothing but one tall house whose fanlight she would never put out again. The doorbell might ring, but she would not hear it. The door might be answered, but not by her. She would be gone. He had known it ever since he heard her laughing softly by his side as they ran away together, for ever and ever, between those talking trees.

The Time of their Lives

Before Miss Gogan finished her fifth lunch in the Grand Hotel Villa Serbelloni she had made a dreadful scene in the dining room – and on a Sunday afternoon at that! It was not that there had been anything wrong with the lunch; not in a hotel honoured by the red print of the *Guide Michelin* for its exquisite situation, gardens, decor, food and unbroken silence. It was simply that as she was finishing her usual excellent *scaloppine*, at her usual table, in the corner of the dining room, with her volume of *The Forsyte Saga* open before her – her fork poised over Soames proposing marriage to the reluctant Irene – seven or eight boys and girls in coloured wraps and sandals came crowding in from the lake, sun-bronzed and wet-haired, to occupy a large table at her elbow, laughing and babbling as noisily as if they were still cavorting on the sunblanched beach.

More annoying still, her old waiter who had hitherto been so attentive to her began to neglect her and cosset them, jocosely called them 'my little daughters' and 'my little sons.' It took her fully ten minutes to persuade him to remove her plate. It took him another ten minutes to bring her the fruit dish. And when she had eaten her peach she found herself beckoning and calling to him in vain for her coffee until she became so cross with him that she could not remember the Italian for waiter and began calling him *garsone*, *waitore*, and *monsignore*. In the end she got into such a frenzy of irritation that she seized Aunt Rosa's thirty-year-old phrase book and her own new pocket dictionary, composed and rehearsed a speech of protest, got up, slapped her books closed, walked over to the old man, tapped him on the shoulder, and let him have it.

He whirled, wide-eyed, to find the fat little woman with the lovely blue eyes and black eyelashes, the one dressed in red like a robin redbreast, all bosom and bum, announcing (insofar as he could make out at all what she was trying to say) that she had come here from (was it Iceland or Holland?) to search with a skewer (*con fuscellino*) for the peace and the repose, but now, 'Thy fault, O hunter, I go forth alone *abbandonata* to search for a coffeepot in the piazzetta!' Which said, she threw a ferocious, blueblack glare at him – who raised his hands aloft as if to bless her departure – and strode out between the staring diners, most of whom, she observed with chagrin, seemed chiefly interested in her long red cotton dress (bought last week at a sale at Cannocks' in Limerick) that she could feel flapping about her calves at every step like a bloody flag.

The sun in the whirling glass doors blinded her. The heat smote her. Below her lay the piazzetta, shadowless, overexposed, empty. Taking courage from her anger, she decided that she really would have her coffee there and bravely descended to it. To her relief every one of the little round tables outside the cafe was unoccupied. The only person in sight was a beautiful boy in a white apron, shading his eyes to look at a white steamer slowly crossing from Cadenabbia. Looking at him, so young, so lightly poised on one leg, his hand lifted so gracefully to his brow, she felt Italy returning in all its former plenitude. When, with a start, he came hurrying towards her, she knew again that this must be the most simple, innocent, warm and welcoming country in the whole world.

'Signora?' He smiled eagerly.

The word, so clearly implying that she had long ceased to qualify for the younger title, had irked her a little in the mouths of the waiters and chambermaids of the hotel. Coming from this child it accentuated his youth rather than her age.

'Oh, very well!' she laughed. 'As the song says, "Call me Madam," I suppose, anyway, once you turn forty . . .'

'Signora?' he asked again, not understanding a word.

'*Un caffè, per favore.*'

While she waited she stared at the approaching steamer. Why on earth had she made that awful exhibition of herself? It could be nothing to do with the hotel. He was really a very nice poor old waiter. And it could, most certainly, be nothing to do with lovely Bellagio. She looked about her questioningly. Or could it? The quayside was as silent as it was blank. When she heard the hoot of the steamer, she thought for a moment of crossing back on it to pass an hour in Cadenabbia, but a second hollow hoot extended the same sense of blankness up and down the entire lake from north to south. It would be the same story over there. Every shutter closed. A dog stretched panting in the shade.

A boatman asleep beside his boat. She received her answer from a third hollow hoot. 'Pao-o-la,' it said, and she repeated it aloud.

'Who has not rung me since last Friday!'

Unnoticed, her beautiful boy laid her coffee on the table, offered her an unseen smile, retired with an unacknowledged bow. She had snatched up her letter to Aunt Rosa on which she had spent the entire morning, and was lost in the reading of it, very slowly and very carefully, watching now not for the meaning of the words but, as she knew Aunt Rosa would also do, for their tell-tale tone:

> *Bellagio*
> *Lago di Como*
> *Sunday, June 14th*

MY DEAREST AUNT ROSA,

I am sure you got my telegram saying I arrived safely. Now I must tell you all my news. But before I do, I must tell you how wildly grateful I am to you for arranging this wonderful trip for me to your dear, darling Italy. For years and years whenever you spoke of Italy I used to imagine, afterwards, what it must be really like. Now that I have, thanks to you, laid eyes on it I can assure you that it has surpassed my wildest dreams. How right you were! Lake Como is truly a vision of delight. Bellagio is, as you have always said, out of a child's picture book, winding back and up under the bluest sky to the loveliest country walks. Every moment I am enchanted by the magnificent views over the lake, with its dear little white steamers coming and going, offering to transport me to other delights, and its hundreds of darling pink villas dotted like flowers on every hillside. The hotel, the food, the service are beyond description. But I do not need to tell any of this to *you!* I cannot believe that a single thing has changed here since you and poor, dear Sir Julian, may God rest him, came to this very same hotel on your honeymoon thirty-odd years ago. But now I must at once explain to my dear benefactor how it has happened that I am spending the holiday here on Lake Como in this super hotel and not, as you so kindly planned, with Paola Buononcini in the villa at Forte dei Marmi. Well, this is the extraordinary thing that happened, and I can only hope and trust that in the circumstances I have acted just as you would have wished me to act. If I have not done so please write to me at once and I will obey you in every respect.

When I got off the plane at Milan on Tuesday afternoon, there indeed was Paola waiting for me, as you said she would be, as ravishingly elegant and lovely as when she stayed at the Castle last October, wearing pink raw-silk slacks, so tight that I could not imagine either how she got into them or out of them – zipped, do you suppose? – with openwork gold sandals, silver toenails, her fair hair down about her shoulders, looking about seventeen instead of, is it twenty-three? Before she said a word I knew there was something wrong. I could see it in her tragic eyes and the way she kissed me on both cheeks, which she never did in Limerick, and the way she at once began to gesticulate and talk like a machine gun. She told me, half in English, half in Italian, about the terrible *disgrazia* (this, I gather, is the Italians' curious word for an accident) that had happened to their villa in Forte dei Marmi only the night before.

It appears that their villa caught fire in the middle of the night and, though nobody was hurt, her mother had to be taken back at once to Milan suffering badly from shock. So, very apologetically, and sweetly, she really is the sweetest girl, she asked me would I mind if just we two spent the holiday together in this marvellous hotel on Lake Como, where she would be near her mamma in Milan, rather than in some seaside hotel in Forte dei Marmi where she would be very far away from her. Well, I said that I was terribly upset about the loss of the villa, and the shock to her mamma, but that I did not mind the change at all, though I was privately much more worried lest in saying so I might not be acting as you would have wished me to act. Still, looking back at it, I do not really see what else, at that moment, I could have said or done except to take the next plane home, an abrupt action that might well have seemed rather cavalier to the good Buononcinis. Nevertheless, I repeat, if you do not approve of my staying here, please do say so and I will follow your instructions in every particular.

Paola was accompanied by a very tall man, an old friend of the family, one Count Algradi, who had his car waiting outside the airport. In this great, long, white, shining vehicle, called I believe an Alfa-Romeo, like Romeo and Juliet, he at once whirled the pair of us off at a speed which frightened the very life out of me, in through the suburbs of Milan and out and on and up through the lakeside town of Como for my first view of the real Italy. On we drove, over the hills and far away, to this ritzy hotel on the edge of the lake, at the point of a peninsula, surrounded by flowers and gardens, tucked away from all traffic which, Paola told me, can be quite noisy on Sundays and holidays on these narrow roads.

Paola could not, unfortunately stay with me that night as she had to go back to reassure her mother in Milan. On Wednesday night she rang to say her mother was much better though still so shaken that she, Paola, would not be able to join me for another couple of days and would I be alright by myself until then? Of course, I said yes, and of course I am. I mean how could anybody be otherwise in this exquisite place of peace, joy and total relaxation? She could not, apparently, call me on Thursday but on Friday morning she did ring again to explain that her poor mamma was still feeling a little down, but she, Paola, would ring again on Saturday, and join me as soon as possible...'

Were those last four words a giveaway? More cold than whatever that Italian phrase was that Paola had used?

It is now Sunday morning and here I am happily sitting in the sun on the hotel terrace awaiting her call. It will, I am sure, come any minute now...

The steamer bumped against the pier. She sipped her coffee. It had gone cold. Two motorcars came lumbering on to the quay. A few pedestrians disappeared into the shadows of the village. She wondered again if she ought to cross back on the ferry to Cadenabbia. Those roads behind Bellagio were all the same. Besides, it was really the evenings that got her down. Reading Galsworthy in the hotel lounge, while that chinless, chain-smoking young man doodled at the piano. She glanced over the rest of her letter.

So very, very, very grateful... All my love to my dear cousins... I do hope the new paying guests are nice, I wish I were there to help... I wonder would somebody be so very, very, very kind as to water my white jasmine? Unless there has been more rain? My goodness, it was wet the morning I left... Endless love to you all.

Your devoted niece,
MARY ANNE

She folded it and put it into its envelope and looked at the address. *Lady Alleyn, Doon Castle, Castledoon, near Croom, Irlanda.* Limerick's long Sunday afternoons. The black eye of a raincloud glowering over the flat plain. So lush. So level. Damp potholes in the avenue. Tree trunks green on the windy side. Every single one of the battlements along the top of the house a bucket of rain. Water her white jasmine? Nobody's shoes would leave green marks on the grey dew of her lawn these mornings. Her twelve-year-old lawn behind the gate lodge. Where she had lived with old grandaunt Jenny until that Sunday afternoon last March when the poor, silly old soul sat down on a chair that was not there and broke her skull. She sighed, licked a mauve stamp and walloped it on to the envelope so passionately that she toppled her Galsworthy off the table. A cadaverous elderly man who, unobserved, had seated himself at the next table politely restored it, saying in perfect English, with a ghastly lower-lip smile, 'Your book, Miss Gogan.' She turned to stare at him.

'Good gracious!' she cried, enchanted to meet somebody she knew, and who could talk English. 'If it isn't Count Algradi!'

He was dressed in a metallic pink-grey suit, with big gold links in his long white cuffs. He rose above her, a pink flamingo, took her proffered hand by the fingertips and lowered his lips to the back of it. His splendid grey eyes stared frighteningly at her. He was the thinnest man she had ever seen.

'I am so pleased, Miss Gogan,' he said rapidly, precisely and sweetly, 'that you have not forgotten me.'

He resumed his seat, his panama perched on his pointed knee.

'Of course, I remember you,' she smiled, and involuntarily touched her letter to Aunt Rosa. 'But I do not remember your talking English to me at the airport?'

He smiled another lower-teeth smile.

'I did not talk to you at all, Miss Gogan. Paola Buononcini did all the talking. As she always does. Quite a chatterbox, isn't she? I think I should introduce myself again. My name is Federico Algardi. Not Algradi. But everybody calls me Freddy. My father had an enormous admiration for England. He sent me to an English school at Lausanne. They all called me Freddy there too. I went for two years to the University of Nottingham just before the war. Everyone there called me Freddy. Everybody in Milan knows me as Freddy Algardi. But I can talk Scots, too, ye know. I can recite your great poet Shelley in Scots. Shall

I do it for you? *Hael taw thee, bliuthe speerutt! Burrd thaw neverr wurt,
With thay baded bobbles winkin' at thay brrum, and thay purple-
stained mourth!* Quite good, don't you think? I learned my Scots from
the pastor at the Church of Saint James in Cadenabbia. I was there this
morning. He is the Reverend Jamie Macandrew, from Aberdeen, an
awfully nice fellow, though he does talk an awful lot of rot about
hellfire. I am afraid in Nottingham we would have called him a bally
ass. Mark you,' he said, and liked the phrase enough to repeat it, 'mark
you, he really does believe in hellfire. He almost makes me believe in
it.' He laughed another toothy laugh. '"To hell with the Pope!" They
taught me how to say that in Nottingham. When I came home and said
it to my mamma she was absolutely enchanted. Ye see, my mamma
believed strongly in hellfire and she loathed all the popes. They taught
me to say it because, like all the English, they think that all Italians
are Catholics. It's not true, ye know, I'm not a Catholic. I'm a kind of
Protestant. Actually I'm a Waldensian. Ye see, my mamma was not a
Milanese. She came from Torino, a great stronghold of the Walden-
sians. The Scots of Italy, a severe people. Born Manichaeans. The
persecuted devoted to persecution. My mamma was a tremendous
persecutor. She persecuted me for years and years. Oh, my dear Miss
Gogan, I cannot tell you how pleased I am to meet a lady from England.
I adore Englishwomen.'

'But, Count Algardi,' she demurred. 'I am Irish!'

His bony fingers flashed gold.

'Same thing! Scots, English, Welsh, Irish. All British.'

He was nut-brown from the sun and, on a second glance, not so
bad-looking. In fact, with those greying wings over his ears, he looked
quite distinguished, even if he was as thin as a pencil. Aunt Rosa had
warned her that all Italian counts are rakes. ('A lot of bad hats,' she
had said, remembering Italy under Mussolini. 'Watch out for them,
even if you are forty-one. All the more so because you look it.')

'Oh, dear!' he said, and put his bony hand to his mouth, remembering
his joke about the pope. 'If Irish, then Catholic? I've made an awful
bally bloomer, what, what?'

'Count Algardi,' she said primly, 'all the Irish are not British. And
like the Italians, not all the Irish are Catholics. I am a member of the
Church of Ireland.'

'Please explain to me Church of Ireland.'

She explained feebly. He waved his wrist again.

'You mean the Church of England in Ireland. I am so relieved. My father greatly admired the Church of England. So do I! In fact, when I was in Nottingham I thought of joining the Church of England, but my mamma put her foot down. She said it was too lax. I have always regretted that I obeyed her. But, I have spent my life regretting that I ever obeyed her in anything. She really *was* an old tyrant.'

He sighed, regretting, and she, feeling also at a loss, stared sidelong at him over imaginary spectacles. Bad counts she could understand. Were there also mad counts? He roused himself from his gloom.

'Mark you, I know a lot about Ireland. The Irish Sweepstakes. Your great patriot De Valera. Your great English writers, Giose, Occasi, Becchetta. How lovely that poem by your great poet Giatsa! *I will rise up and go now far away to Ginnitsfrié*. Miss Gogan, I adore Ireland! The land of ghosts and goblins, of castles and kilts, of murderous queens and murdered kings. Macbeth!'

Miss Gogan decided to take him in hand.

'Count Algardi,' she said. 'What is your news of Paola Buononcini?'

He shifted his chair closer to her table.

'Signorina Gogan, I want very much to talk to you about dear Paola. In fact I badly need your advice about dear Paola. In fact I would like to talk with you about many things. I have a suggestion to make to you. Would you honour me by joining me for dinner tonight? I could collect you at your hotel at six o'clock, we could cross over to Cadenabbia on the ferry, and I would drive you from there to dinner at the Villa d'Este. It is a hotel but it is not a hotel. It is a house that is not a house. It is the most delightful mansion in Europe south of the Alps. I promise to have you back in your hotel by ten o'clock sharp. Please, Miss Gogan, I do so need your help. And your advice. Please join me for dinner.'

She looked into his pleading grey eyes. She thought of those boring hill roads that she had walked and walked. She thought of those empty hours after dinner.

'Thank you, Count,' she said sedately. 'I should be most pleased to join you for dinner.'

'Splendid!' he cried joyfully. 'Until six, then. At your hotel' – and lifted her hand again by the fingertips, bowed over it, and, with long, swift heron steps stooped rapidly away, folded himself into his white car and whirled from the empty quay.

The lake was rippled like a fish by the prow of the steamer. The mountains wavered in the water. She had never met a real count before. Rapidly she changed that. She had never met any sort of count before. Nobody had ever kissed her hand before. Nobody had ever asked her advice about anything, except about such things as whether the paying guests could be fobbed off with ·liver and bacon. Bad counts? Aunt Rosa must have been joking. Anyway, Aunt Rosa did not have to know every damn thing. She became aware that her beautiful boy was hovering, a bottle in one hand, in the other a tiny glass.

'*Una Strega, signorina?*' (Signorina!) '*Complimenti del Padrone.*'

She glanced where he was glancing, behind him. The portly *padrone* was bowing to her from the door of his café. Bad or mad, the count apparently counted.

'*Grazie,*' she whispered, wondering as she watched him pour out the golden liquor what a Strega was, and was she doing something absolutely awful again? Guardedly she sipped the sweet liqueur. She stayed there quite a while gazing happily around her. Once she slipped her bookmarker under the flap of her letter to add a postcript, paused, and thought better of it. If Limerick only knew! She tossed back her liqueur, and tossed her head. To hell with them! Let them know! She rose, turned and bowed towards the watching *padrone* and the watching boy beside him, and walked back slowly to the Grand Hotel Villa Serbelloni. On the way she deftly consigned her conscience to the red letterbox fixed to the wall of the shuttered tobacconist. To her relief there was no telephone call from Paola.

He came on the first stroke of the angelus, looking, she thought, like a broken thermometer with his white hair, his black dinner jacket, white front, black tie, white socks. She, after two hours of trying on and casting off every rag she possessed, had settled for her shortest frock – black satin, with great, walloping hand-painted roses, a light shawl of pink wool, an evening bag in silvered calf, a trifle cracked, green evening shoes with red Spanish heels. He looked her over, said, 'You look marvellous! I adore English clothes,' and bowed her into his car. There, seated beside her, on the steamer, he at once began to gabble in his rapid way about the vanity of human wishes.

'Today,' he said, 'the air was so dry you could see a golf ball two hundred yards away. The Reverend Macandrew was very good about that this morning. He said, "Life is like a man's breath on a wintry day, appearrring and vonishing. It reminds him of his mortality. Listen," he said to us, "to what the summer says to us. Last week we had a showurr of rain. Now the earth is as dry as snuff. Our life is like the rrain that the earrth cannot hold. It vonishes into the sky. All things tend upwarrds. Here under the great sunlight of Italy we may dream of a life that will last for everrr, but the lakes are more wise. They dream of the sky."'

She agreed that it was a verra, verra beautiful thought. 'But a bit melancholy?' He startled her by saying that all life is melancholy, bumped off the ferry and began to drive so fast past countless other roaring cars, along a road suitable only for cows in single file, that all conversation was out of the question. He tore within inches of pink villa walls whose hanging bougainvillea swayed in their wind at their shoulders and whose plaster had been scored by the axles of generations of previous roaring drivers. She devoutly hoped that they had all long since evaporated into the sky. She looked sideways at him. He was beaming wildly ahead of him. There could be no doubt about it. The man was as mad as a brush. After that she did not dare open her eyes again until she felt the car slowing on the gravel of what she hoped was his Villa d'Este. When she glared at him she found him gazing at her in happy self-admiration and thought of the drive back, through the night, along those awful donkey-roads. The next moment she forgot everything. He had led her, tottering on her fears, through the foyer out to the terrace. Seeing her delight, he pressed her bare arm. This, also, nobody had ever done to her before. She liked it.

'But this,' she cried, 'knocks the Villa Serbelloni into a cocked hat. This must be the most beautiful place in the whole world. This must be Italy at its very, very, very . . .'

'At its verra, verra, verra?' he laughed, and in her relief she laughed back at him.

'At its verra, verra, verra best!'

It was an opinion she was to abandon heartlessly two days later in favour of a smelly hatbox of a place they discovered halfway to Lugano, a fisherman's trattoria where they ate the freshest of sprats and drank horripilous draughts of a nameless wine under an occluded sky whose low clouds sliced the tops of the mountains. A shutter kept banging in the wind. An invisible cat lapped the shore. At its edge there stood the most romantic figure she had ever seen, a young man in black knee gaiters, a black-brimmed hat and a black cloak. While they ate the young man stood there unstirring.

'Do you think he is a poet?' she asked.

He said that he might be a spy for the Swiss customs. It would not have surprised her if the spy had broken out into an aria from *Il Trovatore*.

He released her arm, to her regret. She touched it where he had held it.

'Now for an aperitif! While we watch the shadows creeping over the lake, and the lights coming up across there in Belvio, and the stars envying us from the mountains.'

By her second martini Miss Gogan felt so much at her ease in Zion that she dared to chide him for his driving.

'Count!' she begged. 'Would yeh tell me wan thing and tell me no more, do you always drive as fast as that? Some day you'll break your blooming neck, so ye will! I'm sure it's very bad for yer nerves.'

'*Noi altri Italiani*,' he said proudly, 'have no nerves. It is why we drive like angels, fight like devils, climb like goats, die like heroes and live without a thought for tomorrow. Besides,' he added casually, 'driving is my business. I sell racing cars.'

'Go along with you! Is that really true? A count? Selling motor cars?'

'My dear signorina, counts, as we would have said at Nottingham, are ten a penny these days. We all have to work,' and he nodded towards the affluent-looking gentlemen seated around them under the vines with their low-backed bulbous wives.

'They look very rich,' she said shyly. 'Look at the pearls. They must have paid hundreds of pounds for those evening dresses.'

'Don't let them impress you,' he laughed. 'That is why all these men have to work. And for those,' he added, nodding towards a frieze of golden youth in bottomy bikinis and coloured wraps strolling against the balustrade of the terrace into the hotel. 'But don't let us waste our time talking about these silly people. I want to talk about you. First of all please tell me your first name.'

'Mary Anne.'

'Marianna! How beautiful! The Madonna and Santa Anna all in one. I have a better idea still, let me talk to you about you. I will tell you all about yourself. You are Marianna Gogan. You live with your dear aunt, Lady Rose Alleyn, the widow of the late Sir George Alleyn, in an ancient castle called Doon Castle. Yes?'

She cocked a wary eye at him.

'You mean,' he laughed, 'who told me? Paola. While we were waiting for you at the airport on Tuesday.'

(How much else, she wondered, did that little monkey tell him?)

'But, you see, our dear Paola is such a dreadful liar I never know how much to believe from her. Let me go on. Your ancient castle stands behind high walls and iron gates in the middle of a great, green rolling plain . . .'

'Not so rolling!'

' . . . dark with woods that are full of foxes, stags, hares and boars specially preserved for the hunt. Yes?'

'Did Paola tell you all that too?'

'She did not enlarge, but I have second sight. Like my mother. But I am right about the woods? Yes?'

She saw the rusty gates that were never shut, the gapped walls that were never mended, the big house at the end of the avenue against the wet sunset, old dotty grandaunt Jenny clucking like a hen after her pet tortoise under the bushes, and, for no reason, she wondered who was now carrying the bathwater upstairs in the tall tin containers clad in red padded wickerwork to be poured by astonished American P.G.'s into brown sitbaths.

'Well,' she temporized, 'it is all certainly very green around Doon Castle.'

'You see!' he cried happily. 'I do have second sight! Now! Your castle. It is so very old that it is covered with ivy. It has turrets and battlements. From its highest turret a flag flies in the wind of every Saint George's Day. And it is lighted only by tiny gothic windows, yes?'

She wove her fingers. A flag, my bottom! And what the hell does he want turrets and battlements for? The next thing he will want is a belfry. He ought to go and live there like a bat. She emptied her glass, he clicked his fingers and one of the white-jacketed waiters immediately refilled it. Old? Doon Castle? *Doon* is the Irish for a fort, and wherever that old thing was it must be ancient.

'Doon Castle,' she smiled at him, 'is indubitably very ancient.'

He creaked back in his wickerwork armchair and gazed up at the vine trellis.

'There,' he intoned dreamily, 'I see young Marianna Gogan, in pig's tails, leaning out of a gothic window in the early morning, awakened by the horn of the huntsman. You are wearing a pink peignoir. You are looking out of your wide, blue eyes down at the line of huntsmen in red coats, the hounds baying before them, the red fox streaking ahead of them across the dewy fields. But then,' he raced on, his hand on hers to silence her, 'as you grow older I see you amongst the huntsmen, riding sidesaddle, in your long black skirt, wearing your tall black hat, and at one of the mighty jumps your hat flies off on its string and your black hair floats behind you like a thundercloud. Am I right? Yes?'

She gulped half her third martini. 'Christ!' she moaned to herself (long since infected by all the more colourful vices of Catholicism). 'If he only got one look at the East Limericks! The Master would have a red coat. And I know Corney Costigan the vet has one because he bought all Sir George's old castoffs ten years ago. And I did see Father Binchy one time in a black riding coat with a cravat. And some of the youngsters would have jodhpurs and hunting caps. But if he saw the farmers' sons! Leggings and berets, that's all they'd rise to. And as for the ragtag and bobtail...'

But he was galloping on and on again, breathless, to the kill, while she was seeing the old rooky-rawky house in Dublin where she might still be living if her mammy and pappy had not died, and if Sir Julian had not died, and if Aunt Rosa had not had to take in P.G.'s, and get somebody to look after grandaunt Jenny in the gate lodge.

'When I was in Nottingham,' he was sighing, and she was wishing to God he had never left it, 'I once drove over to Melton Mowbray with a fellow named Ranjit Singh to see the hunt. The car broke down. We never saw it. But I have seen it on television, and in the movies. Didn't you love *Tom Jones?*'

She threw back the second half of her martini.

'Count Algardi! *Please* talk to me about Paola Buononcini.'

'Later! At dinner. Let us have a sherry this time. I forgot that in England you always take sherry before dinner. *Xeres*, ye know, is the Italian for sherry, but nobody ever says it. Domenico! *Due* sherry. *Molto secco!* You remember your Homer?' he asked her. 'How Helen threw a drug into the wine and they forgot all their sorrows. As your great Shakespeare says, "Let our joy be unconfined."'

'Count Algardi,' she giggled. 'I think I'm a bit tiddly already. Look't! Leave us be talking about you thish time. Tell me every single bluddy thing about yourself!'

'Everything? I can tell you that in one sentence. I am a poor, half-crazy fellow who sells cars, dreams dreams, and wishes he had a glorious youth like you, and,' he added gloomily, 'remembers his own.'

But to remember is also to forget. Her memories of the rest of that night would be as gapped as her memories of the nights that followed it. She would never remember how she got to the dinner table. She would know only that she found herself under a red and white marquee, crowded with diners, surrounded by boxes of paw-pink begonias, scarlet zinnias, purple lobelias and white geraniums; under great billowing loops of nasturtiums. On every table a small pink lamp gleamed on the silver, the glass, the napery. The shadows had by then climbed to the far tip of Monte Beletto, twilight had become dusk, one vast star sat in a hollow between two peaks, and across the lake a steamer slowly carried past them a cargo of fairy lights and faint music. But she would remember that the ink-blue night and the skin-pale wine so fumed in her head that whenever a white-haired man in a black tie passed their table with a bare-backed lady and nodded and smiled at him she nodded and smiled back boozily at them, and that presently she was calling him Freddy, and he, with equal amiability, was calling her Marianna. Nothing else stayed with her except the moment when he uttered the name Paola. He did it just after he had risen from his chair – for nobody else had he done this – and bowed deeply to a powerfully built lady with blued hair, and to a gentleman of equal size with a tri-coloured button in the lapel of his dinner jacket.

'They,' he whispered to her over his glass of Soave, the lamplight below his nose hollowing his cheeks, 'are the father and mother of Paola Buononcini.'

Startled sober, she stared at him.

'But that is impossible! Her mother is ill in Milan. Freddy! Tell me at once. Where exactly is Paola?'

Feebly he raised his elbows and his eyebrows.

'In Forte dei Marmi.'

'You mean she has been lying to me?'

He laid his lean hand on her chubby hand.

'Marianna! You do not understand Paola. I have known her for years. I have been devoted to her since she was sixteen. And I am not sure that I even still understand her. You see, you British . . .' (She let it pass with an exasperated breath.) '. . . have all the honesty, truthfulness and straightness of your noble race. Your yes means yes, and your no means no. With *la bella* Paola yes means perhaps, and no means maybe.

Paola is young, wilful, selfish, greedy for life. She never decides what she wants until the last minute. At Linate airport, five minutes before your plane arrived, she suddenly left me, telephoned Bellagio, reserved a room for you, came back and told me that I must stay here and look after you for ten days.'

She could hardly speak for rage and shame.

'Are you telling me that the villa was never burned?'

He shook his head sadly.

'Oh! I know. She has always done it. She uses me. She uses everybody. You and I are in the same boat. She has ditched the pair of us. After all, I too was supposed to have gone to Forte dei Marmi. I was to have driven the three of us down there that Tuesday afternoon and stayed for a fortnight. My holidays.'

'I shall take the next plane home,' she said instantly.

His hand tightened on her hand.

'Marianna, please don't be angry with Paola.'

'Angry with her? I could kill the little bitch.'

'No, no! I have as much reason to be cross with her. But I am grateful to her. Because she made me meet you. Besides, she was right about Forte. What is Forte but miles upon miles of coloured *cabane* and umbrellas? Young people shouting, laughing, babbling and flirting all day long, sunbathing or sleeping half the day, dancing or playing canasta half the night. You would have felt out of everything. Paola would not have known what to do with you. Anyway, she probably has a young man there.'

'Then why did she invite me?'

At that he curled.

'Well . . . She didn't really, you know.'

'But Aunt Rosa told me . . .'

'If Paola was telling me the truth, she really invited your cousin, Geraldine. But your cousin could not come. Paola said something about a young American. So, Lady Alleyn suggested you.'

She covered her face in her hands, then slowly parted them and looked at him.

'I see,' she said quietly, 'I was second best – and not wanted. And Aunt Rosa fixed nothing for me. I shall take the plane home tomorrow.'

To her horror, he straightway began to sob like a child who has been struck. He clutched her hands.

'Marianna,' he wailed, while her eyes darted around to see how many people were noticing. 'Please, do not leave me. If you go away, what shall I do without you?'

'You mean I'm to be second best even for that bitch Paola?'

Why, in God's name, had she ever had anything to do with him? With any of them? Filthy Italians! All liars! The whole damned pack of them, all liars. Wops!

'If you go away I'll drink like a fish all day long. I'll do terrible things. I'll drown myself in the lake if you abandon me. I was so happy to meet you again. I came to Bellagio this afternoon solely to meet you. I was looking forward to being your guide, to showing you everything, little villages, little lakes, hidden corners that no foreigner ever sees. Everybody on the Lakes knows me. They are all my dear friends. I owe money to all of them. I owe thousands upon thousands of lire to the old pirate who runs the restaurant on the island of Comacino. We can lunch there every day. I owe millions to the casino at Campione. We will gamble there together and make pots of money. We will visit the Prince Borromeo on Isola Bella – my father was a great business friend of his. He often said it to me, 'I will never, simply *never* forget your father!' We will eat in little *trattorie* around the lakes where I owe nothing and they'll only be delighted to let me run up enormous bills. Marianna! Don't abandon me!'

Her rage sank to the bottom of a sea of pity.

'But if Aunt Rosa finds out that Paola never joined me, what will I do? I'd be disgraced in Limerick if they got one word of the wind of all this.'

'Seal your mouth like a fish. Don't tell anybody. If you knew the things I've done that I never told to anybody. Not even to my own mother.'

They argued and argued, though again about what she would never remember, except only that, there among the pink lights, the scurrying waiters, the elegant diners, the flowers, his eyes as melancholy and his face as long as a wet hake's, she found herself blurting out a terrible thing.

'Freddy! Why are you making yourself out to be a wicked man? Are you a bad man? Aunt Rosa says all Italian counts are bad men.'

He blenched. She curled. Then, for the first time since they had met, he threw himself back and laughed with his whole mouth, and in her relief at his relief she started to weep for the pair of them.

'Your Aunt Rosa!' he laughed, 'she must be just like all the other grownups I've ever known – my mother, my father, the Reverend Macandrew . . .'

'You mean,' she said, 'she is a bally ass? Oh, Freddy, you are a scream! I always thought that about Aunt Rosa but I never had the courage before to say it' – at which he knew that she would stay. He deftly halted the scurrying wine waiter.

'Sesto! Champagne! The Bollinger. Forty-seven.'

With a single flourishing gesture the young man blessed their happiness and saluted the champagne. 'The first champagne, signorina,' he whispered to her, for there was a table of Germans near them, 'that the Germans did not drink,' and hastened away to serve them.

'He likes us!' she cried.

'He likes you!'

'Me?' eyes wide, looking around her.

'And why not?' he asked haughtily.

'All these elegant women! And fat me!'

'Pfoo! Bought elegance. But you are genuine, you are true, you are the real thing,' and took both her hands. 'Oh! My dear, dear Marianna! We are going to have the time of our lives.'

They were the last to leave the marquee. Over their brandies he spoke with a sad dignity.

'You asked me, Marianna, if I am a bad man. I am.'

'I refuse to believe it,' she cried passionately. 'I think you're a grand fellow.'

'I am bad,' he insisted. 'And growing old in my badness! How old do you think I am?'

'I am thirty-five,' she said. 'If not more!'

'I am a hundred. I go back too far. I must tell you that my grandmamma was a Princess Levashov. One of those mad Russian revolutionaries who fled to Switzerland in the sixties and led such wild lives there that she ran away from them all to live in the Vaud and become a Waldensian. From one craziness to another. She had only one child. My mamma. In Torino my mamma met my papa. She, too, had only one child. I was not born until they had been married for six years, and I swear that she never once slept with my papa before that, and I swear that after I was born she never again let him make love to her. She was a monster! A woman who hated and despised everything to do with the body and with pleasure. Shall I tell you what she did to me when I was fifteen?'

Over the pink lamp he whispered it to her. By its underlight he looked like Mephistopheles.

'It was Easter. She found out through her spies that I was going out every night with the girl who sold cigarettes in the railway station in Milan. She went down into our garden and she cut two of her loveliest madonna lilies. She took her paint box and she daubed black paint all over one of the white chalices, and daubed a hideous red paint all over its golden pistil. She put the two flowers into a vase in my bedroom, and, pointing at them with her bony finger, she said, "That candid lily was you before you met that slut. This horrible thing is what you are now!" She left them in my bedroom for a month. I can still smell their stink.'

She took his hand in both her hands and her eyes filled with pity for him.

'Poor little boy! But, Freddy, you must have had lots of nice girls since then?'

'Only the kind I dare not talk about. Even while I longed only for girls who were pure, and sweet, and innocent and *oneste*. Seven years ago when I first met Paola she was sweet, pure and innocent. Or was she? How do I know? Now she is greedy, thinks only of herself, lies like a trooper and makes a fool of me all the time. Yet, I never once blamed her. I blamed only this corrupt south where we live. Until last Tuesday at the airport when I saw her deceiving you, a trusting, truthful, honourable, straightforward, candid, open woman from the honest north. The scales fell from my eyes. I realized then that all I long for comes only with the years.'

She did the only thing she could do. She closed her eyes and uttered a soft ancestral moan.

'Freddy!' she whispered. 'I'm dhronk! Take me home.'

She woke at ten o'clock to insistent tom-toms, in her head and from the telephone. It was Freddy. She confided about her head.

'I will attend to that. And I have fixed your appointment with Toni for half-past eleven.'

'With Toni? Who is Toni?'

'I told you about him last night. Have you forgotten? You asked me about a hairdresser. He is the best *parruchiere* on the Lakes. You will find him in Bellagio, near the church. He is my second cousin. And you asked me, too, about a boutique, though why I cannot imagine; you dress so beautifully. You will find one two doors away from Toni's, called La Fiorella. She is my uncle's sister. Goodbye, dear Marianna. I will call for you at half-past twelve.'

She fell on her pillow with a groan, dedicating her life to cold water, total abstinence and, even if he was an RC, Father Theobald Mathew, Ireland's apostle of temperance – as her papa used to do long ago in Dublin whenever he woke up after a bad skite. Five minutes later a young waiter knocked and entered. He bore on a silver tray a glass of brown liquid that looked like Mother Siegel's Syrup.

'Compliments of Count Algardi, signorina. Throw it back.'

She did so and he laughed amiably at her face of disgust, assured her with all the sympathy of one who had in his time also paid wages to Bacchus, that she would feel fine within three minutes, and retired with a nod of comradely approval. And, indeed, by the time she had risen, reeled around for a bit, vomited, bathed and vomited again, she did feel better; so much so that when she fared out into the sunshot village in search of his Toni and his Fiorella she was in a state of happy expectation. She saw, blazing in the window of the boutique, a frock so brilliant that it would have seduced a parakeet. Without hesitation she went in, spent half her pocket money on it, and emerged in it feeling half-naked, depraved, a fool, and utterly delighted. Two doors on there was Toni, ready and waiting for her, as hairy, tiny and garrulous as a Yorkshire terrier. He conducted her to a throne, swished pink curtains about her and began to walk around her as if she were a horse, prattling saucily to her about the superiority of all northern Italians to the rest of the entire world in matters of hairdressing and of love.

'We are as hotta as Siciliani. But more *intelligente*. I love plenty. I have five kids. Three masculine, two feminine. Siciliani not *intelligente*. Millions of kids!'

Whereupon he fell into a gloomy silence, clicked his fingers to summon two pink-robed handmaidens, pointed to her and spread his hands in despair. At once the three of them began to argue passionately about her face. As suddenly he switched off their torrent and began to snip and snap. One of the handmaidens stripped her of her stockings, and sat by her feet to manicure her toes and her fingers. The other came and went with trays of powders, creams and golden lipsticks which she matched and rematched to her skin, all the while (or so it sounded) cursing softly under her breath. The rising heat crept through the open door. Drowsing smells invaded her. Far away she heard the drone of a buzzbike. A distant steamer cock-crowed. Voices from the village carried on the thin air. 'Air,' she begged, 'can I have some air?' and they swished back the curtains and there was the wide, metallic light of Italy, powerful, penetrating, pitiless and inviting. Part of her said, 'What am I doing this for?' Part said, 'What can they do for me?' Part said, 'How much is this going to cost?' Part said, 'Are we both out of our minds?' Part said, 'What does he see in me?' Part said, 'Poor Freddy!' And part of her said, 'He may be mad, but I do like him.'

She blew bubbles into the washbasin. As she surfaced, a church bell rang away the half hour. Anaesthetized under the dryer, she was barely aware of fingers touching, drying, dabbing her, and those soft murmuring curses going on all the time. She felt the dryer being lifted and Toni behind her again. Then, just as the church bell was striking the angelus Toni was presenting her with a hand mirror and slowly twirling her throne so that she could see herself from every angle, the girls exclaiming at one another's art, and embracing one another in delight, while she thought, 'Sacred Heart of Jesus! I look like a whore!' She was coffee-brown. Her eyelids were as blue as the lake. Her hair was a blue-black helmet. She had eyelashes a yard long. Her mouth was as big as a letterbox. She beamed at them, clapped her paws, babbled thanks and began to rummage in her handbag, at which Toni gave her the Fascist salute with his right hand and machine-gunned her with a hundred no's.

'The friend of my best friend! *Impossibile*! In the winter I work in Milano. Freddy send me every woman he know.' (Oh, does he?) 'But,' waving his hand royally to the two girls, 'if you wish . . .'

Fishing for two modest notes she gave each girl a thousand lire. They almost palanquined her to the door. There, one of them suspended her stockings above a waste basket, mimicked 'Yes?' with her painted eyebrows, displayed her own pretty, coffee-dyed legs, and smilingly taking her answer for an 'Oh, yes!' discarded her best Cantreces. (Three and sixpence in Cannocks'! And brand new!) More showers of thanks, smiles, wavings, and farewells pursued her as she went scurrying back to her hotel, her handbag to her nose like a yashmak, her other hand feeling her bare thighs, hastening to rub all this stuff off before Freddy saw her. For, in the newfound wisdom of an admired woman, she knew that this could not possibly be what he wanted at all. Unless he really was a bad man? Before her mirror she ruffled her hair, wiped her mouth, and did what she could with the blue eyelids and the coffee face. She hesitated a long time over the beautiful eyelashes. She finally peeled them off, carefully trimmed them with her nail scissors, stuck them back again, and approved. To finish, she started to draw on a fresh pair of stockings and fell back in her chair red with shame. They had painted her *all* the way up. The telephone rang.

'Signorina Gogan? Count Algardi has arrived.'

With a groan she abandoned her stockings and her modesty, slipped on her shoes, covered her naked back with her auntie shawl and went forth to meet him, smilingly holding her hand straight out from her shoulder in the hope that when he bowed over it he would not see her legs. He gave her one quick all-over glance.

'Perfect! As Cicero says, when unadorned the most adorned. But, of course,' he added as he bestowed her into his car, 'it is one of the most extraordinary things about women – I once waited two hours outside a *parruchiere* for Paola and when she came out she was exactly the same as when she went in.'

'Perhaps,' she said tartly, 'you did not see her. You didn't notice my new frock,' she pouted, thinking with annoyance of all the money she had paid for it. 'Freddy, I don't think you see me at all! Or do you?'

'Your frock is wonderful,' he said, giving it a casual look as, with three fingers on the wheel, he halted within inches of the edge of the dock. 'As for seeing you? The Reverend Macandrew said a beautiful thing a few weeks ago. "Love, my dear bretherrn," he said to us, "is a secret that grows within the soul."'

She looked hopelessly over the lake. *More* guff? Her look changed to a quick apprehension as he went on.

'"But, dear bretherrrn, the body is love's open book." Now that we are friends, Marianna, we shall have no secrets from one another.'

From that moment on she never looked forward. A woman without a past can read only the present. A woman with no future must ignore it. Even the sun conspired against foresight. Its heat shrivelled the pages of her calendar. Like a moth under a glazed dome of breathless air, wine-fumy and sticky, she began to move slower and slower. Each morning she woke later, stretched out an arm reluctantly for the telephone, breakfasted in bed, bathed as languidly as an odalisque, had to struggle against the temptation to roll back into bed again. She spent hours over a face that, in Limerick, she would have washed in three minutes out of a basin of rainwater from the barrel outside her door. She never wore stockings again. She left her clothes strewn around the bedroom floor. She lost her *Forsyte Saga*. Only once did she manage to squeeze out five lines to Aunt Rosa (who never wrote) telling her about the sweetness and kindness of Paola Buononcini (who never rang), taking her everywhere, showing her everything.

Every noon she kept Freddy waiting when he called to whirl her off to a long, guffy lunch, after it whirling her back to the Grand Hotel Villa Serbelloni for her siesta, during which he, in his panama hat, would snore in a deckchair directly under her window. They drank afternoon tea on so many different terraces that their names became a jumble in her memory – Stresa, Cannobio, Lugano, Varese, Bellano... Having eaten, between them, as many pastries as six children of fourteen, he would drive on to some other terrace for their aperitif; and on to a third for dinner, which always finished so late – especially if there were dancing; he was like a stork waltzing with a robin – that she was never in bed until long after midnight.

Debauched by pity, corrupted by kindness, demoralized by all the deceits he forced on her, she had no desire but to please him, to be his friend, nurse, slave, handmaiden, ayah, confidante, governess, scheherazade, or – her own words, spoken silently one exasperated night through the wide-open windows of her bedroom to the gigantic stars – whatever in God's name it was that this poor, good, kind, dignified, dotty, deceived man wanted her to be or to do. For him she only wanted one thing: to fatten him – whence those piles of pastries that served only to fatten her. From him she wanted only one small thing: that he might kiss her just once before they parted forever.

As the days and the nights peeled away and she could not do the first and he apparently had no desire to do the second, she became so frustrated, nervous and bewildered – Could he be what they call impotent? – that she led him, one night after dinner, up into the dark gardens behind the Villa d'Este, hoping that the stars, the dark and the view might inspire him to do something else beside talk to her. Whereupon, as they sat on a stone bench among the plumes of the cypresses, under a statue that was more shade than stone, a fountain more whisper than water, the light across the lake quivering in the warm air like the fireflies at their feet, dance music thrumming far below them, she became terrified to recall how, in her teens, in their basement kitchen in Dublin, their old servant Molly Power had told her, screaming with laughter, about the night in her own teens when her fellow took her up into the dark of Killiney Hill, and made her lie among the furze and take off every stitch of her clothes so that he could have a good look at her. ('And the blooming furze sticking into me bottom like needles!') Heart pounding, she waited. At last he touched her hand.

'Look, Marianna, how the stars lie in the laps of the mountains like little babies! See how the night passes. So our life passes. As the Reverend Macandrew says, only truth, like love, lasts forever.'

Then he led her gently back, down to the lakeside, to sit and talk some more on the terrace, while she felt as wicked as if she had been trying to seduce a vicar and as exhausted as if she had succeeded.

So far as she could see he appeared to want nothing at all but to take her life in exchange for his. But what was his life? There were mornings when, breakfasting drowsily, she doubted everything about him. How did she know he was even a count? Paola could have lied about that. But unless everybody else, in the Villa d'Este, the Villa Serbelloni, on the Isola Comacina, in all the other grand places he took her to were also taking part in a conspiracy to deceive her ... Poor and odd he might be. He *was* Count Algardi. But all this talk about his miserable youth? If she even knew where he lived. If, instead of wandering with her around these lakes he was walking with her around Milan, showing her where he lived, and worked; the house where he grew up as a boy; where he went to school; the garden where his mamma cut the lilies.

She thought of writing to Paola Buononcini. 'Dear Paola, I know that this must sound a curious request that I am about to make to you. Yet, you are a woman of the world who knows the hearts of men, and you will, I am sure, sympathize with the strange predicament of an older woman who ...' Who what? 'Dear Paola, I feel myself impelled to thank you with all the sincerity of my heart for so generously sharing with me the friendship of your charming friend, Freddy Algardi, who ...' Who what? Who nothing! 'Yet, I must also confide to you that in my heart I find him ...' She could see Paola showing the letter around among her gang in Forte dei Marmi. They would crowd over her shoulder. They would roll on the sand laughing themselves sick over her. She thought of calling on Toni. But Toni was related to him, and indebted to him, and there, in terror, she suddenly felt the ultimate isolation of every traveller who, no matter how well he may speak a foreign tongue, can be defeated by the movement of a thumb.

She tried to probe and trap him.

'Freddy, have you written to Paola?'

'Why should I?'

'Have you rung her? Has she rung you?'

He smiled. A shoulder stirred. An eyelid moved.

'Why should she? She has fixed everything the way she wants it. Or so she thinks.'

'Did you always dance as well as this, Freddy?'

'My mamma disapproved of dancing. I had to take lessons secretly. Even when I was thirty I still had to steal out to dancehalls. I never dared go to invitation dances. Her spies would have told her at once.'

'Were they nice dancehalls?'

'Nice? They were rough, gay, noisy places. Nice?' A hand stirred. '*Popolare*. Away out beyond the cemeteries. I used to wear an old trenchcoat and a cap, and go there on the tramway, through the fog. She drove me to such places. It was her own fault. But you? Ah, you! You went to Hunt Balls! Yes?'

'Of course! Every year. Twice a year sometimes.'

'With pipers? And harpers? I can see the whirling kilts. The tartan shawls flying. And other dances? Tell me about them all!'

'You mean Harvest Home dances? And there were Birthday dances, too. And there were the Pony Club dances. And we always had Coming of Age dances, with all the tenantry lighting great bonfires down the avenue. Freddy! Are there brothels in Milan?'

'What a question!'

'But are there?'

'By the score! Or so I would guess.'

She was afraid to pursue the subject.

'Did you ever get drunk, Freddy?'

'That reminds me. What exactly does go into a stirrup cup?'

'Mulled wine. Freddy, you must have enjoyed something! The opera? Used you to take your girl friend to the opera?'

'A girl? To the opera? Alone? In Milan? My dear Marianna, nobody is ever alone in Milan! We went to the opera *en famille*, and only on opening nights, and only to certain operas of which my mamma approved. And while I was doing that, bored to death, think of what you were doing! Wandering with a lantern through your dark fields, spying on elves, goblins, ghosts and fairies. Oh, please tell me all about them, Marianna.'

'Well, it is more in the mornings, you know, that one sees the fairies. Ghosts only at night. Banshees at any time. Elves, very rarely.'

'Tell me!'

Indulgently, she led him by the hand on summer mornings, at sunrise, over the dew-grey grass to pick newborn mushrooms, and watch the leprechauns running away in all directions. She told him every fairy story she had ever read. He listened with her to the dogs at dawn, baying death-warnings, to ghostly whisperings winding down the chimneys on stormy nights. He straightway demanded brigands. She drew the line at that. Instead, she let him see the I.R.A. peeping from behind every tree. Weakly, since he insisted so strongly on it, she allowed them a dirk or two.

'Freddy, there is one thing I'd love to do with you – visit your mamma's grave in Milan.'

'My mamma is buried in Turin.'

'Your father's grave?'

'He was drowned while sailing off Genoa. The body was never recovered.'

She gave it up. She felt, if not happiest, most content, or at least most relieved, when they did not talk at all; seasoned comrades who only needed a glance or a smile to feel the pulse in one another's veins: as when they saw the crescent moon, whose fullness they knew they would not share, look tenderly at itself in the mirror of Orta; or when they stood hand in hand before an orange sun slowly drowning into the mist of Mergozzo; though she did mock him amiably for showing her such expansive lakes and, out of Italian vainglory, calling them small.

'You should see my little loch at Doon Castle! It is hardly big enough for the coots to swim about without bumping one another. I swim there in my pelt every morning.' Just for that, he roused her very early on the morning of their last day, drove her up into the Val Tellina and on and up to the Val del Bitto as far as the village of Gerola Alta. There he left the car and bullied her into panting and puffing, protesting every foot of the way, for another thousand feet to a dammed loch on the northern base of a mountain that he called the Three Men. As they lay there, beside one another, after eating the sandwiches and drinking the white wine that he had brought in an Alitalia carry-all, gazing either into one another's eyes or beyond one another's shoulder at the serrated snow-tipped Alps, her heart burned with happiness that he should have gone to so much trouble to share his lakes with her down even to this last, lost, tiny loch. She became even more happy and more fond of him when he boasted that there was not a pass in Lombardy that he had not climbed on foot when he had been young enough to do it – this at least the poor, unhappy boy had wrested from his miserable youth. They stood up, arms about waists, while he indicated, far and wide, some of the ways that he had gone. Just then a drone in the sky made her lift her swimming eyes to a plane that might be her plane tomorrow, which made him look down at her, say, 'Now your blue lakes tend upwarrrds,' and kissed her parted lips. At once her arms snapped tight about his neck, gripping him close until their mouths had to part for air. 'Again!' she implored, her hand pressing him by his poll into so wild and prolonged a kiss that he became lost to everything until she released him with a gasp. He then saw that she had shaken out her black hair and that her unzipped parakeet frock was shivering to the ground.

'Marianna! What on earth are you doing?'

'The heat! The sun! The wind!' and dragged his hands by the wrists about her bare waist. 'My darling, I want to take off everything for you!'

And even before he had disengaged himself she had unfastened her brassiere, dragged down one strap and exposed one bursting nippled breast.

'Marianna!' he cried, his joined palms jigging in imploration. 'Not now! Not yet! Not here! We must wait until we get Aunt Rosa's permission. When I come to Ireland next month!'

In the silence – even the high drone of the plane had faded – she felt a cold wisp of fog creeping about her thighs. She drew back from him, her arms across her bosom, her eyes staring up at him like a terrified Magdalen.

'What did you say?' she whispered. 'Until you come to *Ireland*? To ask Aunt Rosa *what*?'

Solicitously he knelt to draw up her fallen frock about her hips.

'Aunt Rosa is your guardian, Marianna. I must naturally ask her permission to marry you.'

'To . . . Did you say to marry me?'

'Dress, my darling, there's a sudden fog coming.' And when they both looked about them every hollow was a white lake and the whole plain back to Milan a grey sea. 'You must have known, Marianna! I have been thinking of nothing else since the first moment I saw you!'

'You must be out of your mind, Freddy, I could never marry you. It would be... It would be... It would be most unsuitable, it would be ridiculous, it would be impossible in every way. Me? You? Ireland? I am an old, middle-aged woman. O God, I didn't even tell you the truth about that. I'm forty-one, Freddy. And I have nothing.'

Embarrassed, horrified, ashamed, weeping, she began to dress, and tie up her hair into a knot because she had lost all her hairpins. He lifted his arms to the sky.

'And what have I? I live down there,' throwing one arm back across the plain, 'in three rooms with my mamma's old sister Tanta Giuletta. I am so poor I eat pasta twice a day. I wash my own shirts. I press my own trousers. I go shopping with a little basket. I say to the butcher, "Give me some cheap meat for my little dog", and he knows well that I have no little dog, but because he has known me for years he throws in a good piece of meat for myself and Tanta Giuletta. If you marry me you would live with us. And after all, old Tanta Giuletta can't live forever. I would be happy with you if we lived in a cave. We could make such a lovely world together. We would imagine our world so beautifully that everybody who knew us would think that any other sort of world is a lie.'

She turned her back on him. She looked at the Alps, cold, pure, lofty, remote. She spoke quietly to them.

'I told you lies. I don't live the way I told you I live. I made it all up. I deceived you in everything.'

Behind her back he spoke just as quietly.

'You deceived me in nothing. I know all about you. Paola told me. All mothers are spies. Her mother wrote to her about us. Paola is a bitch in the manger. Even when she doesn't want a thing or a person for herself she hates anybody else to have it. She wrote to me five days ago, a mean, bitchy, jealous letter. About Castle Doon, and the paying guests, and you living in the gate lodge.'

'A penniless retainer?'

'She did not use the word. She wrote in Italian. She said *una stipendiata.*'

She turned on him, blazing.

'Then why did you drag me down like that? Why did you go on making me tell you those stupid, stupid, stupid lies?'

His hands pleaded.

'They were not lies, Marianna. It was just a game we began to play that first night in the Villa d'Este. You were so shy, and so innocent, and so lovely – and all those puffed-up, snobby Milanese about us, bloody Fascisti the whole lot of them – I knew them, my father knew them – and you and I worth a thousand of them. It was my way of telling you what we both really are. Then I went on with it to make our holiday more fun.'

The veined nose, the baggy eyes, the hollow cheeks and stooped back of a defeated old man. His white hair blew across his forehead like dust. She touched his hanging hand. Hopelessly she shook her head.

'Let's go down, Freddy. I must pack. Thank you for everything. You gave me a lovely time. But you made one mistake. You gave me the last thing on earth that I want from anybody. You pitied me.'

And ran through the mist down the path to Gerola farther and farther from his wild, beseeching cries to come back to him, to wait for him, to come back to him, to come back. He must have stumbled as he leaped after her, for it was a long time before he appeared beside his white car, his beginning and his end. His trousers were torn, there was dried blood on his cheek, his right hand was wrapped in his silk handkerchief. In the silence of a fallen tower they drove back to the hotel, where, as he scrambled from the car, he called after her that he would come for her at eight o'clock.

'Our last dinner, Marianna!'

When he came he was handed a note from her saying that she was too upset to join him. All he could do was to leave a note for her saying that he would call for her at eleven in the morning to drive her to the airport. When he did come, the majordomo had to tell him, sympathetically, that she had taken the seven o'clock steamer for Cadenabbia; from there, one presumed, gone by bus to Milan. Freddy glanced at his lean wrist. He could still catch up with her. He descended to the *piazzetta* for a coffee. He had his pride.

For months she expected that he would write, was relieved when he did not, half-hoped for a Christmas card and was again glad that he sent none. She had almost succeeded in putting him out of her mind when, one May morning at the family breakfast table, she heard Aunt Rosa utter an exclamation of surprise and looked up to see her beaming over her half-moon glasses and holding up a big gilt-edged card for them all to see.

'A wedding! And guess who? Our little Paola Buononcini.' (Mary Anne felt her heart go burp.) '*To*,' Aunt Rosa read out, '*il conte Federico Amadeo Emmanuele Levashov-Algardi*.' She turned eagerly to her niece. 'Mary Anne, surely you wrote to me last June that when you met Paola she was with a Count Something-or-other. Could he be the same man? But you said he was an old man. Or did you? What was his name?'

'Count Federico Algardi. I said he was an old friend of the family.'

'What an extraordinary coincidence! Was he, in fact, old? What was he like? Tell us all about him. Is he very rich? If I know anything about Paola Buononcini he must be stinking rich. Or else his pedigree must go back to Romulus and Remus.'

'No, he is not old. Though he is not young, either. He is very handsome, and very dashing. He could be forty-five. I took it that he was very wealthy. He drove an immense white car. An Alfa-Romeo, I think it was. But he did not speak at all. It was at the airport and he just drove us to the Hotel Serbelloni. After that he vanished.'

'Mary Anne, how tiresome of you! You never do notice anybody.' She looked again at the card. 'Well, well, so our little Paola is about to become a countess.'

She glanced at Geraldine, sighed, spread her ringed fingers and, with a long accusatory look, passed the card to her. And this, Mary Anne thought, staring sidewards at his printed name, is the man who once dreamed of innocence, and purity, and honesty and true love. She cradled her teacup in her palms and looked across its rim at the snow-tipped Alps, the sun burning the valleys to dust, the blue lakes dreaming of the sky. He had whispered, 'Now your blue lakes tend upwarrrds,' and kissed her. She closed her eyes and smiled.

'I see,' Aunt Rosa said brightly to Geraldine, 'that she is going to be married next month.'

'Sweating,' Geraldine laughed coarsely, 'like a June bride.'

She opened her eyes wide. Another Paola? Jealous, greedy and envious, and in that second she understood it all. His kiss had been his one, last feeble cry for help. She hesitated. Then, imperceptibly, her head shook. It would not have been honest, and it would not have worked. But nothing he had ever done ever had worked. Nothing ever would work. However! He'd had something. They had both had something. Something precious, brief and almost true that, she felt proudly certain, neither of them would ever forget.

Feed My Lambs

It is about eleven o'clock of a sunny September morning in late September. The unfrequented road that crosses the level bogland from skyline to skyline passes on its way a few beech trees, a white cottage fronted by a small garden still bright with roses and snapdragons, a cobbled path and a small wooden gate bearing, in white celluloid letters, the name *Pic du Jer*. In the vast emptiness of the bog these unexpected and inexplicable beech trees, the pretty cottage, the tiny garden, the cobbled path suggest only a dream in the mind of somebody who, a long time back, thought better of it, or died, or gave up the struggle with the bog.

A young woman in an apron as blue as the sky is sweeping a few fallen beech leaves along the cobbles. She is bosomy, about thirty, with amber hair, and eyelids as big as the two half-domes of an eggshell. Looking idly towards the west she observes, far away, a flash of sunlight. She gives it one thoughtful glance and resumes her sweeping. Whoever the motorist is, he will come and go as slowly as a dot of light emerging from one mirror and as slowly dwindling into another. The bog is as immense as it is flat. It swallows everything.

Pic du Jer? A mountain peak? Asked why, Rita Lamb always says, in her usual saucy, self-mocking way, one quizzical eyebrow cocked: 'Yerrah, it's an old mountain near Lourdes. You go up to it in the funicular. It's where I climbed to the pic of my career. It's where I met Jer.' If she admitted that she really met Jer at the foot of the peak, in the waiting funicular, it would spoil the joke. It would be no joke at all if she said, 'It's where I met Father Tom.'

Under the final whisk of her broom the leaves rustle out through the garden gate. She looks again. The car is half a mile away. Her hands tighten on the broom handle. The cups of her eyelids soar, she runs indoors, tearing off her blue apron, looks at herself in the mirror, punches the cushions of her minute parlour, looks into the sideboard to be sure there is a bottle or two there, and out at the gate again just in time to greet Father Tom with a delighted grin. He has never failed her. He drops in at least three or four times a year, either on his way up to Dublin or on his way back to his parish on the far side of the Shannon. She takes his overcoat, indicates the settee, and begins to make his usual drink, Irish coffee.

'Now!' she says pertly as a parrot. 'What's y'r news? Tell me everything.'

'I'll tell you one thing, Rita,' he laughs. 'You haven't changed one iota since the first day I met you.'

That day, waiting for the funicular to start, the four of them had got talking at once: the two priests, herself and Jer. The older priest – rosy, bony and bald, easygoing and poorly dressed, his waistcoat flecked brown from his scented snuff – simply leaned across and took her paperback from her hand: Franz Werfel's *Song of Bernadette*.

'Not bad,' he conceded, 'For a modern novel. Tell me, my child, did you ever read a novel by Canon Sheehan called *My New Curate?*'

At this, the young priest had pulled down his elegant white cuffs, and all in one breath laughed, groaned, sighed and said, 'Here we go again. Poor old Tom Timlin off to the guillotine once more.'

'Indeed and I did read it,' Rita gushed. 'I think I've read every single thing Canon Sheehan wrote.'

Father Jordan patted her knee.

'Good girl! Most of ye read nothing nowadays but dirty books like the one his reverence here gave me the other day by some young trollop named . . . What was this her name is, Father Timlin?'

'Miss Edna O'Brien,' the young priest said, his natural courtesy qualified by an over-patient smile.

'A fine Irish name! It was the only decent thing about her rotten book. I nearly shoved it behind the fire it made me so mad! Upon my word, Father, I don't know for the life of me what you want to be reading books like that for.'

Father Tom folded the crease of his trousers over his knee and observed urbanely that it is one's duty to know what young people are thinking nowadays.

'After all, one belongs to one's contemporaries, Father Jordan, as Simone de Beauvoir puts it.'

'I read her, too!' Rita exclaimed, and blushed wildly, suddenly remembering the picture of a completely naked woman on the cover of her contraband copy of *The Second Sex*, and how its first chapter was all about the machinery of the inside of a woman and the outside of a man. 'I forget now what book by her it was that I read. I think it was a travel book about France.'

'You probably read *The Second Sex*,' Father Tom said dryly. 'Quite an interesting study. It's a pity she has no sense of humour. Sex can be funny, too.'

The old man threw him a cold look. 'In this excellent novel by the late Canon Sheehan,' he persisted, 'there is a poor old parish priest like myself who has the life plagued out of him by his new curate.'

'I remember the two of them well,' said Rita, patting his knee as approvingly as he had patted hers, 'and, do you know, I felt very sorry for the pair of them.'

'The part I love,' he said with relish, 'is where this poor old P.P. walks in one day into his curate's room and finds him if you please, playing the piano and singing some sloppy German love song about "Roselein, Roselein, Roselein buck – Roselein auf dem heiden"? Wasn't that how the song went, Father?'

Father Tom coughed and said that, yes, it was, indeed, something on those lines.

'Well! Father Timlin here is *my* new curate and he has me plagued out with Italian. Always playing Italian operas on the gramophone. In Italian if you please! Always throwing around words like *Giovannismo*, and *ecumenismo*, and *aggiornamento*, and what's that other word you have, Father, that sounds like an Italian racing car?'

'*La gioventù!*' Father Timlin cried eagerly, and threw his hands out to the two young people seated opposite them. 'And here we have them! Youth at the helm!'

The old priest winked at them.

'He is ancient, you see. He is twenty-six.'

'Ah!' Father Tom said enthusiastically. 'There's nothing like youth. Married or engaged?' he asked.

Rita and the young man beside her looked at one another. He observed that she had eyes as big as a cow, eyelids as sleepy as a cow, soft hair the colour of a Jersey cow, and that she was very well made around the brisket. She liked his grin, his white teeth and his warm voice as he answered. 'We are not even acquainted yet, Father. We just met this minute.'

Father Jordan roared with delight.

'There you are,' he nudged his curate. 'Crashing in as usual.'

'Only anticipating, maybe,' the young priest said, unabashed, and they all introduced themselves. Father Malachy Jordan, P.P., and Father Tom Timlin, C.C., from the parish of Annabwee in the County Galway; Jerry Lamb, farmer and butcher, from Barron in the County Kildare; and Rita Lyons, schoolmistress, from Doon in the County Westmeath; at which point the funicular gave a jolt and they started to climb.

'Talking of marriages,' said Father Tom, paying no attention at all to the descending landscape, 'I suppose ye know that Lourdes is a great place for matchmaking? The best Catholic families in France come here with their children. We have a count, and a prince, and their wives and children in our hotel. The idea is that the best young people in France meet, and if they like one another ... well, you never know your luck.'

Jerry Lamb chuckled.

'It would be one of the unrecorded miracles of Lourdes if I met a princess here and took a shine to her – and she to me!'

Father Tom waved his hand with a man-of-the-world air.

'It would be no miracle at all! We get all kinds in Lourdes. All sorts and sizes come here to see the pilgrimages, Buddhists, Jews, Muslims, Communists, atheists, everybody!'

Rita turned sideways to consider Mr Lamb.

'Wouldn't that be a good joke,' she said, 'if your Catholic princess met a Communist who was a roaring atheist and took a shine to him?'

The old priest's palms applauded silently, but the young priest was unquashable.

'It might be an excellent thing for them both. She might convert him and he might broaden her.'

'Ha!' said his PP sourly. 'She might! And so might a mouse! And supposing they did get married? A mixed marriage! And what about the children? If they had any children!'

Father Tom smiled benevolently.

'Ah, now, Father, you must admit that since the *Concilio* the attitude of the church to mixed marriages has greatly relaxed. And as for the question of having children, that will come too. Do you believe in large families, Mr Lamb?' he asked their butcher.

'I wouldn't be averse to two or three. Or at most four.'

'Two or three?' Father Jordan said sadly. 'I was the youngest of twelve. Brought up on a scrawny thirty-five-acre farm west of Ballinasloe. An acre to the cow, they say, and three acres to the child, we cut it fine.'

'I was the youngest of six myself,' from Father Tom.

'Ai, ai, ai! Father Jordan sighed. 'I suppose this is your *aggiornamento*.' He gazed into a distant valley. 'My mother was one of fifteen. Twelve of us. Six of you. Mr Lamb here would like three. And if you have three I suppose they will want one apiece. We progress!'

'What I'd like,' Rita said, looking pensively out over the distant Pyrenees, 'would be to have a boy and a girl.'

'Two?' Father Tom asked her amiably. 'Four?' he asked Jerry Lamb. 'Why don't ye split the difference and make it three?' – at which Father Jordan asked him if he was getting a percentage on this, and all four of them laughed, and the funicular stopped and all the passengers except Rita looked down.

'Maybe they want us to enjoy the view?' Jer suggested.

'My sister Joanie has seven children,' Rita said to the sky. 'She is married to a clerk. He gets eleven pounds a week. Seven children. And they are only married seven years.'

'Fine!' Father Jordan said to the valley. 'Splendid! A proud and happy mother!'

Rita's mouth tightened. Father Tom was watching her closely.

'Is she happy?' he asked, stressing quietly.

'Tell me, Father,' Rita said to him, 'what's all this about the Pill?'

'It is forbidden,' the old priest said shortly.

'Well, now,' the young priest temporized, 'it is certainly not authorized. But it is still under discussion. I hope,' he added, looking around at the crowded carriage, 'we're not stuck forever?'

'Are we stuck?' Father Jordan asked an old Frenchwoman across the aisle from him, and her husband turned back from where he was looking up the peak to say that the one coming down was stuck too. Jer and the old priest crossed over to look out. Father Tom was left with Rita. She was staring moodily at the sky. He leaned forward, elbows on thighs.

'You are very silent, Rita.'

She said nothing.

'What is on your mind?'

'Nothing.'

'There is something. What is it?

Struck by the kindness in his voice, she slewed her eyes towards him, and for the first time took stock of him. He had sandy hair; his eyelashes were golden fair; his eyes were as bright blue as a Siamese cat's; he reminded her of her brother who was a sailor. She hesitated. Then she spoke very softly: 'I was remembering why I came to Lourdes.'

'Why did you?'

'Everybody comes to Lourdes to pray for something. I prayed that my sister Joanie won't have any more children. And if I ever get married that I'll only have two.'

He looked at her mischievously. She was to become familiar with that mischievous, mocking way of his – his way of calming her, of calling her to use her commonsense.

'When I was young, Rita, I had a small sister who was mad about a sort of sweet called bull's-eyes. The nuns told her one day to pray to the Blessed Virgin to break her of the habit.'

'And did she?' Rita asked with interest.

'She got a terrible pain in her stomach one day and that cured her. Rita! Which are you? Dying to be married, or afraid to be married?'

'I don't want to have a child every year for the rest of my blooming life.'

He smiled at her. She looked away, annoyed.

'Father, you're like every priest. Ye know all about theology and ye know nothing about feelings. Would you like to have a child every year of your life?'

'Not unless I was a rabbit. Still, nathless, and howbeit, and quid pro quo, and all things being carefully considered, and so on, you would like to get married?'

'I'm human.'

'I should hope so, if that means that you are a normal woman with the normal longings and desires of a woman.'

She faced him crossly, at a disadvantage. If he had been a man she could tell him!

'How do I know what I am?'

'Everybody knows what he is. You've had boy friends, haven't you?'

'Yes.' Then she said coldly, 'Am I going to confession to you?'

'Oh, come off it, girl! This talk about confession that women go on with! Why wouldn't you have boy friends? Anyway, nobody confesses any more to a priest. The priest today is only a kind of spiritual telephone operator. To what part of the otherworld do you want a trunk call today, madam? For all faults, inquiries and difficulties kindly dial Tom Timlin, C.C.'

She laughed.

'But you listen in!' she pointed out.

'And interpret now and again. And add up the charges. Come now, Rita! Face up to yourself.' He chuckled at her. '*Vide, visse, amò*. She saw, she lived, she loved. You embraced. You kissed. And you hated it like poison!'

'I did not!' she said furiously. 'I liked it.'

'As *il buon Dio* intended you to. "So long as things are", Saint Augustine said, and he was a tough man, "they are good". Kissing is like Guinness, Rita. It's good for you. The *osculum...*'

'The what?'

'The kiss on the cheek.'

His eyes were mocking her again. She waved an airy hand.

'The *basium*. On the lips.'

Even more jauntily, she waved the other hand.

'The *suavium*?' and he shrugged.

She waved both her hands and was enraged with herself for blushing; and more enraged when he laughed delightedly.

Jer turned back to them and shouted, 'I think it is a life sentence!'

'Anyway,' she protested, 'that's all damn fine,' not quite knowing what was fine, 'but seven kids in seven years? Eight in eight? Nine in nine?'

He glanced across the carriage to where Father Jordan and Jerry Lamb were now trying out their French on the old French lady and her husband.

'You can only do your best, Rita,' he said gently. 'When any man or woman comes to me with your problem all I ever say is, "You can only do your best". If I was speaking as your spiritual telephone operator I'd always say, "He is saying, you can only do your best".'

She glared down at the huddled red roofs of Lourdes until he thought she was going to throw herself out. Then she breathed out a long sigh of exasperation.

'These last three days,' she said, 'I was so happy down there.'

He gave her a melancholy laugh. He looked down at the basketful of roofs.

'Ai! Ai! – as Father Jordan says. Such a mixture! The lovely and the tawdry, sincerity and sentimentality, lies and truth, God and Mammon. It would remind you of life! And here we are now like Mahomet's coffin slung halfway between . . . Where was it slung? I always imagine it was held up between walls of magnetic forces. Impossible?' He paused. 'You mustn't be afraid, Rita.' She kept staring sulkily down at the roofs. 'No woman can do more than her best.' This time he was silent a long while. 'I'd say that to you anytime, anywhere.'

He watched her. She got the point. She smiled at him:

'I have a car. Sometime I might pay you a visit.'

'Do!'

'But you will never know.'

'I will never know. All I will hear will be a voice. It will come and go. Like a bird singing in flight.'

The carriage jolted a little, started to move, and the whole carriage cheered and laughed. Father Jordan and Jer rejoined them.

'*E pur si muove!*' Father Tom cried. 'Galileo. The world does go around the sun. Though I'm not sure Father Jordan entirely believes it. George Bernard Shaw,' he went on, 'once said that in Ireland we still believe that the world, if not exactly flat, is only very slightly removed from the spherical.'

They all chuckled and began to discuss such important things as whether they could get a cool refreshing drink on top of the mountain.

From the peak they gazed far and wide about them, silenced by the gleaming wings of the Hautes Pyrénées, still snow-covered, and the eyes of the lakes in the far valleys, and Father Tom, who knew his Lourdes, pointed out famous peaks like the Pic du Midi de Bigorre that local mountaineers had mastered at the risk of their lives.

'Glory be to God,' said Father Jordan, 'but it's a hard country! Is it good for anything at all?'

'Sheep,' said Jer. 'And I bet you there's fine grazing up there for the cattle in the summertime.'

'I read in the paper this morning,' said Father Tom, 'that the shepherds are complaining that the wolves aren't being shot.'

'Feed my lambs,' said the old priest, and the two of them drifted around, and Rita and Jer went in search of a beer.

Sitting on a rough bench a little apart from the other tourists, she amused him by telling him what it is like to teach in a nun's school, and he entertained her by telling her what it is like to be a farmer-butcher in a small village in the middle of a bog as flat as a slate. When Father Tom and Father Jordan came by, the old man looked as if he were going to join them, but the curate took him firmly by the arm and pointed off into the distance and drew him away around the corner. Presently Mr Lamb was asking Miss Lyons if she had ever been to Biarritz and when she said no, Mr Lamb said he was going by bus the day after tomorrow, and Miss Lyons said she wondered if she ought not to visit it someday.

'Yerrah, why don't you? You earned it. If you like you could come with me. I'm all on my own.'

'But, Mr Lamb,' she said, floating her eggshell eyelids wide open, 'we are hardly acquainted!' – and when his laugh showed his splendid teeth she laughed too, and he went on laughing because she looked so happy, and had such big droopy eyelids and was well made around the brisket.

Father Tom advanced his empty glass of Irish coffee to Rita sideways along the settee, laughed and clinked it with hers.

'So there you have it! That's all my news. Nothing at all since July. I'm the same old three-and-fourpence I always was and always will be.'

She looked at him affectionately.

'We have no news either! Jer goes on with his butchering. I go on with my sweeping. If you are worth three-and fourpence, then between the three of us we're worth exactly ten bob.'

She took up the empty glasses, the bottle, the cream, and the percolator and started to tidy them on the small dining room table by the window. He looked appreciatively at her straight back and her trim legs.

'Rita!'

She turned, observed him and cocked an alert eye.

'You look as if you are about to give birth to a profound thought?'

'Divil a profound thought! It's just that ever since I came within sight of this little cottage of yours this morning I was thinking how you once said to me, five years ago, "I have a car". And you have never once paid me a visit?'

She came back and sat on the settee.

'You are a low scoundrel, Father Tom. You only thought of that just half an hour ago? And in all those five years you never once thought of it before? The truth isn't in you.'

'Well, I admit I did give it a passing thought now and again. I'm not probing, Rita!'

'You are. And I don't mind. Sure we're always probing one another. When we have no news it's all we ever do.'

'Why didn't you?'

'Do you really want to know? I'll tell you. But I think you will be sorry you asked me. One reason I didn't visit you was because I had no need to. I had nothing to tell you. Or to tell any other priest. Now you know!'

Her left hand lay supine on the settee near his. He laid his right hand on her palm. The palm slowly closed on his fingers.

'Poor Rita! I guessed it must be that way. I'm afraid your family hasn't had much luck with Our Lady?'

'Not with three more babies for my sister, and none for me.'

'And poor Jer, too!'

'Oh, he's accepted it now. At first, he minded an awful lot.'

'What was the other reason?'

She looked down at their two hands. She gave him a long silent look – so long that he peered questioningly at her. She leaned over a little and castled her right hand on his.

'Did it ever occur to you, Father,' she said, 'that from the first day we met you called me Rita? Because you're a priest and that made it all right – for you. But I have never once called you Tom. Because I'm a woman, and that mightn't be quite so safe – for me. I love it when you drop in here, Father, and pop off again after an hour or so. I love the chat. I love the way I can say anything I like to you. I love the way you say anything you like to me. I love all the things we argue about. I look forward to it for weeks. I think about it for weeks after you've gone. And that's not just because it's lonely out here on this empty old bog. Now and again friends of Jerry's drop in, and I like them to call too, but I never think of them when they're gone, and if they never came again I wouldn't miss them. I love you to come because you are you. Still, so far, I've always managed to remember that you are a priest and I am a married woman. The other reason I did not visit you is because if I started meeting you outside of here it would be very different. It would be admitting to myself that I am fond of you as a man.'

His golden eyelashes fell. She removed her hand. He laid his on his knee.

'Well?' she asked tartly. 'What's wrong with you? Am I to be the only one to tell the truth today? Or did none of this ever occur to you?'

'You are a wonderful woman, Rita! You are the most honest being I have ever met.'

'Is that all you can say to me?'

'It is all I dare say to you. What the hell is the good of anybody saying anything if he can do nothing about it? What would you want me to say? That I love you? When neither you nor I can ever prove it!'

She shook her amber head at him.

'Well, there's the cat out of the bag at last! Tom! You should never have been a priest. The first day I met you I knew it.'

'Why didn't you say so then?'

'Would it have made any difference?'

He jumped up, walked away from her, whirled and cried, 'I don't know! I was younger then!'

She rose and went over so close to him that he could hear her breathing.

'And now,' she taunted, 'you are a feeble old man?'

He flung his arms around her and kissed her on the mouth. She held his kiss. Then she drew away from him and laid her finger gently but imperatively on his mouth.

'The *basium?*' she mocked. 'You've come a long way in five years, Tom.'

'Do you realize you are the first girl I ever kissed!'

'I do. And I'm the last. You can never come here again.'

He walked away from her and looked angrily at her.

'Is that what you wanted, talking the way you did on that settee?'

'I merely answered your question. I warned you that you might be sorry. You asked for the truth. And you put an end to our story.'

'You didn't have to answer me!'

'I had to. Because immediately you asked me I knew what I'd never let myself know before. And I knew that we both knew it. And I knew something else too. That if it didn't end one day we would explode, and then we'd be torturing one another for the rest of our lives.'

He stared wildly around him.

'There is no sense nor meaning to this. It doesn't hang together. All I ever wanted was a bit of friendship. A bit of companionship. There's nobody else in the world I can talk to but you. That day I first met you I knew that here was somebody at last that I could talk to. Maybe that I could help. That I'd be a better priest if I could . . .'

'Tom! It's long ago that I told you that you knew all about theology and all that stuff, and nothing about feelings. Now you know better! This is what love is like.'

He glared at her in misery and longing. Then, suddenly, he calmed, and then as suddenly broke into a long peal of laughter, at himself, at both of them, at the whole of life.

'Honest to God, Rita! You're worth fifty priests. You're worth a thousand of us. And I that began it all by trying to educate the simple, ignorant schoolteacher! Well, I may have learned slow, but you learned damn fast. Where the hell, Rita, did you learn all you know?'

'Where every woman learns everything. In bed. Am I shocking you? Because if I am, then you really are getting very old.'

He considered her answer bitterly.

'The one classroom no priest ever visits. And I suppose the only one that ever tells anyone anything about the nature of love. So! That's it. I'm never to see you again?'

'Why not? I will go my way. You will go yours. If I live I will become an old woman. If you live you will become an old, old parish priest like poor old Father Malachy Jordan.'

'My God! If Father Jordan was alive today and knew about you and me he'd break his heart laughing at me for a botch of a priest and a fool of a man!'

She flashed out angrily at him. He had never seen her so angry.

'Stop that, Tom! Stop it at once! Never say that again! Never think it! I liked you that day in Lourdes because you were honest with me. I grew fond of you, I fell in love with you if you want the whole bloody truth, because you went on being honest with me. You will always be honest, and you will always be a better priest than old Jordan ever was because you will always remember that, if it was only for one minute of your life, you loved your woman and kissed her. When you run yourself down you are only cheapening yourself and cheapening me. I won't have that! I'm not sorry for anything we've done. I'm proud of it.'

Far away a bell gently, faintly tolled. She listened. 'There's the angelus bell in Barron.' Suddenly she became the bright, capable housewife. 'Jer will be back in an hour. Will you stay and have lunch with us, Tom?'

'No!' he said brusquely, and grabbed his overcoat and dived into it. 'But there's one thing I'll tell you, Rita!' He snatched up his hat and gloves. 'If I met you not five years ago but ten I'd have given up God Himself for you!'

He went out the door and down the cobbled path. She followed slowly after him. At the wicket-gate he paused and looked up and down the long, empty road.

'I'll never pass this road again.' He flipped his gloves against the white celluloid letters on the gate. 'Why did you call it Pic du Jer?'

He watched her great eyelids drooping. He watched the sinking of her amber head. She spoke as softly as if she were whispering to the three foreign words.

'To remind me of you.'

She did not raise her head again until his car started and his wheels spurned the gravel of the road. Then she walked out to the middle of the road to watch him dwindling away, from her into infinity, diminishing like a dot of light until he vanished out of sight.

She looked around the level bog. Miles away the blue smoke of a turfcutter's fire rose out of the flat emptiness straight up into the blue sky. She heard nothing. Then she heard a soft wind and raised her eyes to the blue above her. A host of swallows were flying south. She watched them until they, too, became lost to sight. Soon it would be winter. The rains and the fogs. She turned briskly indoors to prepare a meal for her man.

Only once did she pause in her task, the knife in one fist, the apple in the other, to look out of the window and murmur aloud to herself, 'I know what he'll do. It's what I'd do. Drive past me every time he goes to Dublin.' She added, 'Until it wears off,' and went on with her work.

Our Fearful Innocence

My name is Jerry Doyle. J. T. Doyle, B.E. I am the County Engineer for W——. I have made this town my home since I first came here as Assistant C.E. twenty-one years ago. I am a bachelor. Aged forty-six. I live in this half-comfortable converted flat on the first story of Jack Jennings's old wreck of a house on Martin's Quay. He lives above me. Our housekeeper lives above him, although she is beginning to say that the stairs get longer every year. Below me is Jack's shop. He is a ship chandler. Or was.

It is such a warm evening that I am sitting in my shirtsleeves by the open window, with my pipe, and a glass of whiskey in my fist – and this old red-covered notebook of Jill Jennings's on my lap. I have been playing golf all day, our own course, above the town, the bay and the sea, my lungs so full of fresh air that I feel too lazy to do anything but look out at the seagulls wheeling like ... well, as Jill once said, wheeling like seagulls. The smoke from Ed Slator's house half a mile away on Rock Point is as steady as if it was part of the chimney. Children playing below on the quay. The canon strolling back as usual to his presbytery, which means that in about fifteen minutes the bell of Saint Killian's will begin to ring for Benediction. Not that I shall attend. I do turn up to mass every Sunday, but purely *pro forma*. As the C.E. I have to keep up appearances. Since what happened to Jill I believe neither in God nor the Devil. And neither does Jack, whom I have just heard shuffling about upstairs. The poor old bastard ...

When I first met Jack Jennings he was about forty-two or forty-three; the grandson of the *Jennings and Son* spelled out in marbled chinaware lettering on the fascia board over his shop window. He never altered the form of name on the board. This was stupid of him, and typically insensitive, because he and Jill had no children. But it was just like him not to change it – an obstinate, cantankerous old cuss if there ever was one. After all, when he married Jill Slator he knew he was marrying into a dynasty famous for long-tailed families. Some of them must often have given that sign a glance that was as good as a process.

I liked Jack from the start, in spite of the seventeen years between us. While he was able to do it we played golf together every weekend. We were never really close to one another, although sometimes we exchanged confidences, mostly about what we chose to call our philosophies. My nickname for him was Zeno because I maintained that he was a born cynic. In revenge he called me Pangloss, the eternal optimist, who 'felt best after meals.' We got on, give and take, kidding, jabbing now and again, never really quarrelling. We got on – the way people always do in small towns. In a big city we might never have bothered about one another. We were an odd pair. We still are. I only gradually realized that Jill was the real bond between us. As she still is.

She was ten years younger than him when she married him. She was about thirty-two when I first met her, and in spite of the fact that she was much older than me I thought her the most attractive woman I had ever met. I must have said so once too often to my secretary May Hennessy because she infuriated me one day by snorting, 'Of course you're in love with Jill Jennings.' I was so mad with her that I nearly ate her. Then, realizing that nobody would ever call her attractive – the poor thing is no oil painting – I had to explain that all I meant was that what I found 'attractive' about Jill was her personality. At which May snorted again. She is a good secretary but she does speak her mind. Which I like now. In this shut-mouthed town everybody else goes around hinting at things they have not the guts to say straight out the way she does. I used to think that it might be because she travelled abroad every summer, and was always full of talk about France or Portugal or Italy and how free life is there compared to Ireland.

Actually, what first attracted me to Jill Jennings was the way she, too, used to burst out with whatever came into her head. She had wide-open eyes, earnest and challenging. Her profile went with that eagerness, face and figure advanced like a ship's figurehead by the slope of her neck, an effect accentuated by the way her beautifully curved upper lip protruded a shade over her lower lip. I loved the way she greeted me whenever we met in the street, the eyelids lifted delighted to see me but abusing the hell out of me for not visiting her more often.

At thirty-two she still had the face of a girl just let out of convent-school, looking everywhere for this wonderful thing called Life that she and her pals had been talking about, and whispering about, and making big eyes about ever since they realized that within a matter of months they would be – heaven help the poor kids – free. How enchanting young girls are at that age, before vanity: unaware of their own looks, their school berets flat as plates on their heads, their pigtails tied with venom, as uninterested in the crowds on the shore as the morning sea. Within a year it is all gone, they have become demons, vulgarians, simpering at every male across the mirrors of their compacts.

Jill never knew vanity. She had glossy hair, the finest and lightest, always untidy, loosely pinned at the nape of her neck in tiny, wandering downy curls that delighted and disturbed me. If she had any fault her skin was too white. On hot days when her arms and shoulders were exposed I used to feel excited to think that all her body was just as white. She dressed in soft, fluffy blouses, light as shadows, or smoke, billowing carelessly. Being so good-looking, she had no need to bother about dress. Her eyes were as grey-green as that sea out there. There was something of the mermaid about her, so free, so fresh, so restless, landlocked, always hearing sounds or voices beyond the town, outside the harbour, this shallow bay.

I loved this old fabric of a house where she and Jim lived. It is now as rundown as Jim's shop but it must have been a fine house and a good business a hundred years ago before the bay became silted up. Now only a couple of coal-tubs and small cargo vessels occasionally moor at the quays, and even they have to wait on the tide to come in. I see one waiting outside the harbour now. High tide will be around ten o'clock. Then it will have to wind carefully through the buoys marking the channels to the quayside.

I loved to visit them on nights when the east wind rattled their windows or blew white spindrift across the water, nights when the three of us would sit before the fire and drink a jorum, and have long wandering arguments about the craziest things, always started off by her. 'What is true happiness?' 'Free Will versus Determinism.' One night after she had been reading some advanced book about religion she suddenly asked, 'Should Faith be based on Life or should Life be based on Faith?' Another night she burst out with 'What is Reality, anyway?' We kept at that one until three o'clock in the morning. Last winter I took down one of her books, *Madame Bovary*, by Flaubert, and when

I came on Emma and her lover talking for hours about Great Art I thought to myself, 'That fellow had us cold!' There was no other house in town where I could have arguments like that. All they talk about is golf, and bridge, and business. But I liked best of all to visit her when she was alone. Otherwise, she tended to take possession of me, ignoring Jack – I do not believe he had read a dozen books in his whole life – lounging on the other side of the fire, puffing his pipe, staring glumly into the fire.

Like that wild March night, in my third year in W——. A force-ten gale howling outside, the rain turning to sleet that threatened any minute to become snow. Jill and I were gabbling away about a performance of *The Three Sisters* that I had driven her up to Dublin to see two months before. Jack, who had obstinately refused to come with us, was saying nothing. Just staring into the fire. From that she went on to talk about the Russian ballet – she had been reading Karsavina's memoirs and she had once been to see a ballet in London. I was not saying much. I was lying back in the old armchair before the fire, between the two of them, enjoying her chat, the fire roaring up the chimney at my feet, and the occasional spat of sleet against the windows, pleasantly aware that every street in the town was empty, when, all of a sudden, Jack jumps up, says, 'I think I'll drop down to the Club,' and walks out on us. We listened to him clumping down the stairs and the front door banging. Then I heard the old Jennings and Son signboard below the window twanging and banging like a drum and I realized that on a night like this there would not be a sinner in the Club – unless it was old Campbell the caretaker sitting by the fire gushing smoke every three minutes into the musty billiard room.

'I'm afraid we've been boring Jack,' I said.

For a few moments it was her turn to stare glumly into the fire. Then as if the wind had hit her into a shiver, she shook herself all over, looked wildly all around the room, and cried, 'Then why does he go on living here? This bloody place is choking the life out of the pair of us. It will choke me like a wood if I don't clear out of it. And clear out of it quick!'

'Aha!' I laughed. 'To Moscow? To Moscow?'

She glared, tossed her head, then leaned forward over the arm of my chair and gripped my hand.

'Did it ever cross your mind, Jerry, that if the three sisters in that play had gone to Moscow they might have been just as unhappy there?'

I barely stopped myself from saying that their brother was not all that unhappy – he at least had the comfort of his child. Instead I said hurriedly that, after all, Jim's business was rooted here, and she could not expect him at the drop of a hat to open up another chandler's store in some place where nobody knew him, and she had all her relations here, and after all, this was not such a bad town, it was lovely in the summer, with the bay, and the sea . . .

She threw away my hand and said crossly:

'Jerry! There is no such place as Moscow. If I went to Moscow I would hear nothing there but the same stupid, empty chitter-chatter that I hear day after day in this bloody town – and nothing at all going on inside me. That play about the three sisters is marvellous because it is all chatter outside, and all silence inside. The summer! Don't talk to me about the summer! On summer evenings I sit by that window for hour after hour looking at the seagulls wheeling like seagulls, or a yacht manoeuvring in or out, or some little cargo boat with Cardiff or Bristol painted on the stern coming alongside Harry Slator's coalyard, or edging out past the lighthouse, and I watch it until it rounds Rock Point past the chemical factory, out to sea. And what do I think of? Nothing! Unless it is about somebody like you whom I know and like. Like you, or May Hennessy who came here a couple of years before you. Another stranger. People who come and who go before this rotten town knocks the truth and the honesty and the guts out of them.'

'Well, it is a fact that May Hennessy is always coming and going. The most travelled woman in W——!'

She snorted at me.

'Is that all you know? May is a friend of mine. I know a lot about May. And May knows a lot about me. May Hennessy hasn't been out of this town for five years.'

'But she is always telling me about her travels! She knows the Continent like the palm of her hand.'

'All out of books. Five years ago May went to Brittany. I said, "Did you enjoy it?" She said, "All I used to do was to walk along the quay and look at the names at the backs of the ships, and think wouldn't it be nice to be going home." Home! All May Hennessy found in Brittany was this town.'

'Then why are you talking about leaving here? I hope you're not serious about that?'

'I am! I am going somewhere where there are no ships coming and no ships going, where there is nothing except me. No! Not even me! Someplace where I will be born all over again.'

I sat straight up.

'You don't mean by any chance that you are thinking of leaving Jack?'

She nodded, took my hand again and stroked it. Completely misunderstanding her, I felt as if the wind had burst roaring in through every window, door and cranny of the house and that it was sinking like a ship under us both.

'Jerry,' she said. 'You are an ambitious man. Aren't you? You want to be the County Engineer. Don't you? To be king of the castle? If you don't go away from here soon, and very soon, you will get exactly that – and this place will knock the truth and the honesty and the guts out of you too.'

On the instant I knew she was right. Because while one side of me was thinking what an honest, outspoken woman she was, the other part of me was thinking all the mean, petty things they would all be thinking, but not saying openly if she did leave Jack – the behind-the-hand whispering, the consternation of the Slators, and finally that total silence when the town would deliberately forget what it did not dare acknowledge.

She rose. I leaped up, and clipped her in my arms. The little curls on her neck seemed so tender and helpless that I wanted to bury my face in them. The smell of her skin overpowered me. I looked into her eyes and noticed what I had never seen before, the way hard, green little flecks pricked their softness. Before I could say what I wanted to say, her fingers stopped my mouth. Then she kissed me, chastely, not the way a woman kisses a man but the way a mother kisses her child. She held me away from her and shook her head.

'No, Jerry! Don't say it! You are not in love with me. You are only in love with an imaginary me. Somebody you've made up inside in your head. I saw it the first day we met.'

'But,' I cried, 'I have only just discovered the real you!'

'And before that? What real me were you in love with then? I am not real, Jerry. I have no world to be real in. Not yet! Now you had better go, before he comes back.'

I was in such a turmoil I could not have stayed near her. I ran out of the room. I felt that if I stayed there for another minute I would start tearing the blouse off her.

When the hall door banged behind me I could hear it echoing up through the hollow house with that muffled sound that always means snow. The quay was already white with it. The whole town was being smothered in it. It clung to the gaslamps. When I came to the door of the Club I could barely see the light through the snow on its fanlight. Just as I passed it I became aware of a stream of light behind me and, turning, I saw him come out and start to beat his way home, head bowed, the snow flecking his hat and his shoulders. He walked against the wind and snow with the gait of an old man. In a moment he vanished into the darkness, as silently as the snow.

Before April ended she had vanished. I did not need to ask anybody what the Slators thought. One day as I was passing Tom Slator's coalyard he hailed me cheerfully and delivered the agreed formula.

'Hello, Jerry! Did you hear the great news? Jill is after buying a country mansion in County B——.' His laughter pealed. Falsely. 'Ach, it's only an old lockhouse on the canal. A little hideaway for themselves. To get away from the roar and the rumble of W——! Hahaha! Of course between you and me I don't believe she'll ever persuade Jack to go down there. It's just another one of her artistic notions.'

It would work, and she would pay for it. To the 'men's club' side of the town she would henceforth be 'odd,' 'queer,' 'difficult,' 'hard to get on with.' The man who remained would always be defended. What a town!

I did not dare visit her until that July. It was not an easy place to find, a small two-story canal house, of no special distinction apart from its age, in a valley between pinewoods filled with shadows and sunbeams, silence and sloth. The noisy humming of flies or bees. A coot clucking. A heron flapping away. The only real sound was from the water gushing between the timbers of the lock gates. For a mile right and left of her cottage the sky dreaming in the smooth water of the canal. For the dozen or twenty days we get of hot summer it would be as lovely a retreat as it was on that warm day. But in the winter?

She was more beautiful than ever. I knew that she was thirty-five – a middle-aged woman – but she looked about twenty-five. She seemed what I can only call triumphantly lighthearted. Yet our talk was not the old, easy freewheeling talk of three months ago. I felt a distance of reserve in her. There were long silences when we walked, with her little Yorkshire terrier trotting before us along the towpath, or when

I was driving her to the nearest village to do some shopping, or when, once, a Guinness barge passed slowly through the lock and we watched the men lean against the gates to slew them slowly open, and then watched it go slowly dud-dudding away from us along the perspective of the canal until it looked no bigger in the distance than a toy boat. That was the only time I probed her.

'Are you never lonely here?' I asked her.

'Not at all!' she said, in astonishment. 'I have so much to do! Reading about the antiquities around here. I have an old bicycle to visit them. Studying the river flowers. Watching the birds. And it is extraordinary how much time I can spend on the house. It will take me years to get it the way I want it. Dreaming and thinking.'

The only word that held me was *thinking*. Thinking what?

As I was about to leave her she asked me if I would drive her as far as the next lock. (When I said she could drive with me to the end of the world, she laughed and said, 'That *is* the end of my world.') She wanted to buy freshly laid eggs from the wife of the lock-keeper with whom, now and again, if she wanted to hear a voice, she would pass the time of day and, perhaps, glance at the daily newspaper.

'Though it is always,' she smiled, 'yesterday's newspaper!'

This lockhouse was an exact replica of her own. Like the cells of certain monastic orders that are identical the world over, so I suppose is every lockhouse on these decaying canals that slowly creep across Ireland. We sat for a while in its poky kitchen chatting with the woman. Then she did something that I can never forget. She had brought a few sweets for the two small children there, and as she sat, the sweets in her lap, the two little girls standing on either side of her, she put an arm around each, saying, 'One for you' and 'Now one for you,' until the few sweets were evenly shared. The mother fondly watched the group. I went to the door to look out. I could not bear to watch it.

During the three years that she stayed there I never let two months pass without visiting her. I never again spoke to her of my feelings for her. There was no need to. We both knew. Nobody else from W—— visited her. Two or three times I told Jack I had 'dropped in' on her. Each time he asked if she was well – no more. She told me he had written once inviting her to return, and that she had several angry letters from her family telling her it was her duty to return. In the spring of her third year I thought she looked ill and said so to Jack. The next

I heard was from May Hennessy, who told me that she had suddenly been taken to the County Hospital of B——, in an advanced stage of leukaemia.

From that on the family became full of solicitude and pity for her, telling us all that the one wish she and Jack had was that she should leave the hospital and come home. I guessed that she would be too weak to resist them. And that, in fact, was how, in the end, everything was done, all the whispering ended, the scandal smothered and forgotten, if not forgiven.

The last time I saw her was on a June afternoon, just like this one, lying in this front room, her bed near the window so that she could look out over the bay. She was thin and pale, her eyes made wider and brighter by the smallness and pallor of her face. There were half a dozen Slators there, keeping up a cheerful chatter about her. She was not talking, but once she smiled joyfully at the lace curtains blowing in through the open window, and said to me, 'They are like a ballet.' At which I remembered that snowy night three years back when she and I had been talking about *The Three Sisters*, and Jack had suddenly gone off in a sulk to the Club, and she said she was going to go away and be born again, and I began to wonder if she saw all life in the forms or shapes of a ballet that you cannot explain or reason about, but that, somehow, in their own way, say, 'This is right, this is the way it all is really when it is right.' But even as she said it, my eye fell on the black, gold-edged missal by her bed and I wondered if she had, in her weakness, surrendered to all the habits and ways against which she had once decided to rebel. A moment later her face contorted and she said, 'I must ask you all to leave now. I must ask nurse to do something for me.' I never laid eyes on her again. Two mornings later May Hennessy told me she was gone.

It was the right word. Gone she has but I have never felt that she has died. I don't believe it still. All my memories of her are of a vital living woman. I have no other image of her. As I looked out of my office window that morning at the sea, I felt what I still feel – she has gone back into it.

For everybody in the town except Jack and me that was the end of her story. Her death broke him. I never met him that he did not start talking about how lovely and spirited a creature she was, a great-hearted woman. In my misery I began to haunt him, though I was never sure from one day to the next whether it was through friendship or hate. Still there must have been some compassion in it because when he said to me one day, 'Jerry, I can't go on living in that empty house,' I said, 'It's too big for you. Why don't you break it up into two flats and rent one to me? We'd be company for one another.' He jumped at it. He retired to live on the third floor, we put his old housekeeper up under the roof, and he rented me these rooms over the shop, furnished as they stood with all the bits and pieces of antiques she used to buy at auctions, and the shelves full of her books, even the ones she had taken with her to the lockhouse on the canal. He said he didn't want any of them near him. They only kept on reminding him of her.

That is fifteen years ago now, and I never stop thinking of her, coming back and back to all those questions that began to torment me from the morning she left us. Did she win? Or did she lose? What, in God's name, was she thinking during those three years of solitude when she was trying to be born again? What, in God's name, did she think could, should or would happen to her? Did, in fact, anything at all happen to her? Not, of course, that I think of her all day long. I haven't the time – the year after she died I became (as she prophesied) the County Engineer. I am overworked. There are more things I want to do for this town than would keep any man busy for twenty hours a day. And not even a man as madly in love with a woman as I was and as I still am with her can think for every moment of his beloved. But often, on evenings like this and at odd moments, at noon, or late at night, she ambushes me. I see her again gabbling in this room, or walking in that lost valley, under the rain or the sun, and I wonder again what went on inside her, or whether the leaves, or the clouds or the mist ever told her what she wanted to know.

I sometimes now believe they said nothing, because, one night, I found among her books this red-covered notebook – a handwritten journal that she kept during those three years. I stayed awake half the night reading it over and over again hoping to find the answers to whatever it was she wanted to know. Not a clue! She had divided each year into the four seasons, and in each section she had merely written such pointless, passing things as 'I saw a kingfisher today,' followed by the details of the place and the hour and the weather. Or she wrote, 'It is raining, the drops slide down my window, through it the trunks of the pine trees look wavy and puckered and corrugated. The water of the canal is pockmarked. The reeds are bowed down by the wind and rain.' Or she has scribbled down some quotations from whatever book she had been reading, like: '*A little kingdom I possess / Where thoughts and feelings dwell, / And very hard the task I find / Of governing it well.* By Louisa May Alcott, when aged 13.' Or this one: '*The longest journey / Is the journey inward.* By D. H.' whoever he is! Or there are small sums of housekeeping money added up. Or she wrote down some details about some old abbey she had visited on her bicycle. A schoolgirl could have written it all.

The next morning I brought the journal to my office and threw it on May Hennessy's desk.

'I found this last night among Jill Jennings's books. It's apparently her journal. She kept it when she was living by herself in Buna-hown.'

I watched her open it at random, reluctantly, almost with distaste. She read a bit. She turned over another thumbful of pages and read another bit.

'I thought,' I said, 'there might be something in it about what she used to be thinking. But there isn't!'

She looked up at me sullenly.

'What would you,' she asked, 'be thinking, if you were her?'

'I might be thinking of God, or Life, or "What is Reality?" or I might be thinking why I could not get on with *him*. Wouldn't you?'

She lowered her head, turned another clutch of pages, and spoke without raising her head.

'She had only one thing against Jack Jennings.'

'What?'

She slapped the book shut and handed it to me with 'This is all about birds.'

'What was the one thing she had against Jack?'

'He is impotent.'

I shouted it at her:

'You have absolutely no right to say a thing like that! It's not true!'

'It is true. I have every right. She told me.'

For a moment we glared at one another.

'But if that was so she could have had an annulment of the marriage in five minutes! Annulments are granted every week of the year for that!'

'And would you,' she said, with contempt, 'expect her to expose him before the whole town? To shame him for the rest of his life?'

I walked from her to the window and looked down into the busy square. How many of them knew?

'So,' she said quietly to my back, 'she went away. It's as simple as that.'

I heard her typewriter clacking away behind me. I snatched up the book and left her. I didn't do a stroke of work that day.

But it is not as simple as that! She never really did go away! She remained. He remained. Both of them remained. She still remains. You cannot just toss aside two lives with 'A man and a woman who married badly,' or 'If she lived anywhere else she could have divorced him and married again.' If! You can do anything, if... And if... And if... There is always that human and immortal If. God's curse on it! Am I one of those damfool Americans who think there is nothing on earth you cannot do? There are things nobody can do! The number of times I have wanted to do something as simple as widen a road, and knew I could only do it if I bulldozed some old woman's cottage that stood in the way, and that she would not give up, not if we gave her a new house a hundred times more comfortable. I once heard that in the middle of Chicago, where real estate is worth millions, there is an old fellow with a farm that he simply will not sell. How often have I wanted to dredge that bay out there, and I could do it in three months if the money was not wanted worse for something else. To build houses, to clear the slums. Why are there slums in America as bad as anything in Singapore? Why are there wars? How many men and women in the world wish to high heaven they had never married and yet they cannot leave one another because of their children, or their compassion, or pity, or their memories of their first happiness that is stronger than the cold years that, God knows why, froze their love to death.

Is that my answer? That she did not marry him for love. Only for pity. Did he tell her before they were married? But that is incredible. The poor bastard probably did not know until he married her. How long did it take her to understand? Years? Of bewilderment, then terror, then misery and pity for them both. But I still do not know what she meant by being born again.

'I bought four eggs today from Mrs Delacey at the lockhouse. Four lovely brown eggs with a feather clinging to one of them.' 'Poor Jerry visited me again today, I wonder what brings him so often.' She knew perfectly well what brought me. 'My wild cherry is a cloud of white blossoms.' What the hell have feathers and cherry blossoms to do with anything?

There's a plane passing over. To London? To Paris? To Rome? If anyone in it looked down at us what would he see? Nothing but an empty harbour, a huddle of roofs, a membrane of blue smoke. He would not see the Slators, or me, or Jack, or the tumbledown backyards, with their rusty sheds, and the valerian growing out of old walls, places I'm going to tear to bits some day if . . . If! And if!

That grey moon up there won't be bright for two more hours. Nor the lighthouse blink. Nor the tide in. The bay looks lovely when the tide is in. A skin of pure water. Moon-tracked. On a moony night like this, when the whole town is sound asleep, what would I not give to see her come floating in, look, and look, and wave one white arm to me before she turns for home again?

Brainsy

The night Tom Kennedy landed off the bus in the long street of Coonlahan to begin his career as a teacher in the Abbatian Brothers' College (popularly known as the A.B.C.) it was raining softly but implacably. He passed no remarks on the rain. He gave one look at Coonlahan and noted the hour: exactly seventy minutes before closing time. The next thing he did was to ask the driver if he could trouble him to show him where the hotel was. The driver laughed. No trouble at all. No hotel. But he might get some class of a room in that tall house down the street that old Mrs Gaston called a Guest House. 'Don't give her more than a quid. She never has any guests.' The old lady showed him by candlelight to a room high up under the roof, large, damp and cold as an aerial vault. That done, he went out at once, shot another despairing look around him and turned into the first pub he met to drown his shame. That telegram from the Brother Superior—'COME AT ONCE BEGIN DUTIES TOMORROW' – could mean only one of two things. Either somebody else had come before him, looked at Coonlahan, and spat on it; or nobody had wanted to come there at all. He drank steadily until the barman put out the oil lamps, clambered up to his room, emptied his pockets on the bed and counted his coins with a shaking finger to see if he had the price of his fare back to Dublin. He found that of the five pounds with which he had started from Dublin all he had left was eleven shillings and two pennies, and stared down through the mist around the street lamp opposite his window at his past and his future...

One look at him, a couple of questions, and any stranger would have had it all. He looked about forty-five (he was thirty-six); his hair was grey as a badger; his lower eyelids were as pink as a bloodhound's; his trousers gave him legs like an elephant; he walked like a seal; and he had been on the booze for some fifteen years. As for his qualifications to be a teacher of English: he had, some eight years before, managed to scrape up a B.A. (pass level), by attending night courses at

University College, Dublin, while concurrently (also previously and subsequently) failing at every odd job he had tried – clerk in a travel agency, copywriter for an advertising agency, door-to-door canvasser for the *British Encyclopaedia*, sub-editor for *The Irish Digest*, sub-sub-editor for a comic weekly called *Hullaballoo*, an auctioneer's clerk, a bookie's sidekick, and a collector for a pious organization advocating total abstinence from all spirituous liquors. Only three days ago he had been sacked from that job for arriving on the doorstep of the Parish Priest of Killiney at eleven o'clock at night, speechless and footless. It was then that he decided that there was only one thing left for him to do – take up teaching. Searching the next morning through the small ads in the educational column of *The Irish Independent* he had come on one for the post of English Teacher in the A.B.C. of Coonlahan, in County Kerry. He had written off at once to the Brother Superior saying that he held a first class honours B.A. and had had three years' experience in England, adding, truthfully, that twenty years ago in Cork he had himself been a pupil of the Abbatians. He sent off the letter and prayed that something else except teaching would turn up in the meantime. To his dismay all that turned up was the telegram.

When old Mrs Gaston woke him up in the morning, groaning at her long stairs, he found that although the village consisted of a single Main Street it was a fine, wide street of multi-coloured houses, and the sun shone so warmly on it that roofs exhaled a gentle steam. From his high window he saw a majestic range of mountains, a vast moorland broken here and there by tiny farms, and he could just see a gleaming spit of ocean away off to the west. Better still, when he found the school – grey, square, two-storied, cross-crowned – down a side road, beyond the church that concluded the street at that end, the Superior, one Brother Angelo Harty, turned out to be a kindly, hulking old man who welcomed him warmly, asked him no questions, and, before introducing him to his own pupils, courteously led him around the other seven classrooms to meet his future colleagues – six Abbatian brothers in the old blue-black soutanes with the bony collars, and one lay teacher, Dicky Talbot, a cheerful, skinny little man, wearing pince-nez glasses on a promising prawn-red nose. They all greeted him in the most friendly manner.

'And this,' said Angelo, as he threw open the seventh door, 'is Brother Regis. Our history teacher.'

Tom stared through the ageing mask before him and slowly held out his hand to his oldest schoolboy pal, Brainsy Carty. As slowly, Brother Regis did the same, and then it was a cheerful 'Hello, Tom!' and an astonished 'So it really is you?' and he was back in the Abbatian Brothers' College in Cork, aged thirteen.

For four years – the purest, sweetest, loveliest years of his life – he and Brainsy had sat side by side on the same bench, for every class, every day. They used to meet every afternoon after school. They spent every holiday together. Days of Damon and Pythias. Exchanges of soul years: their diaries, their dreams, their heroes, their poems. Brainsy's 'All hail to Napoleon, dreamer and doer of might,' for Tom's 'O sweetest Virgin, free me of my fetters, / Send my prayer upward to the sky, / That I may suffer among the lonely lepers, / As Father Damien did in far-off Molokai.' Years when Brainsy's ambition was to climb the mountains of India or explore 'the untracked Amazon'; when Tom, if he could not be another Father Damien, wanted to be a Trappist monk, pray all night, work all day, never speak, and dig a foot of his grave every week. Years when, because Tom had no father and Brainsy's mother was also dead, they agreed that it would be marvellous if Tom's mother married Brainsy's father and they would always live together like brothers. They had wept openly when at seventeen Brainsy's father sent him to Dublin to be trained as a teacher, and Tom's mother sent him off to a seminary in County Limerick to become a Capuchin priest. From that moment the pattern of their lives was set. Brainsy got what he wanted, a teacher's job in Dublin, and Tom was fired from the seminary, his Master of Novices dryly intimating to him that his mother (who had died, in the meantime) might have had a vocation for the priesthood, but he . . . Well, he was turned twenty-one now. He had better go up to Dublin and look for a job.

Dublin? Tom's first thought was of Brainsy.

They were soon sharing a small flat, going halves in everything, eating and drinking together, chasing girls together, loyally deceiving them for one another, agreeing that if either of them wanted to bring a girl to the flat the other would walk the streets until he saw the window blind up and an umbrella standing against the light to show that the storm was over; though, in practice, it was always Tom who walked the streets. He liked the company of girls but, as the saying goes, he never 'touched' them. As for their arguments – Brainsy being Brainsy – they were never in short order. For the time was now long gone since Brainsy's hero was Buonaparte at Lodi, or since he wanted to climb great mountains and explore great rivers. His obsessive interest now was in the marvels of modern science. His heroes were men like Bohr, Rutherford, Thomson, Einstein, Planck and Millikin. His villains were every priest, nun, monk, bishop and archbishop on up to the Vatican and the cardinals of the curia. It was a change that bewildered Tom until he remembered those odd questions at school that had won Brainsy his nickname. ('But, Brother, if it is a sin to kill, what about the glories of the religious wars?' Or 'But, Brother, if birds have wings why haven't we?' Or 'But, Brother, if we become dust when we die why can't Catholics be cremated?')

Their dissent only troubled Tom when their roles began to interchange, like a castling in chess; as when Brainsy might yield that if there ever was any truth in religion the last time it was seen was when it was hiding in the catacombs; and Tom would find himself conceding that, yes, it was there alright, but maybe it was really to be found only in our memories of a divine shadow passing along the shores of Galilee? Which would take them on to the analysis of the Gospels until, in agony, Tom began to find his shadow slowly turning to a wisp of smoke. One July night he came tramping home eagerly from his job to have it out, once and for all. He found a note on the table saying, 'Goodbye, we will meet in the great Hereafter.' Since then he had had neither sight nor sound of him until this minute.

Brainsy's smile went back into his mouth. His hair became grey, his back stooped. All that was left of his youth was the broken perpendicular furrow that used to come and go between his eyebrows like wind on water. It seemed now to be dug in there as permanently as the broken line of life in a man's palm. Or, Tom thought, as Angelo led him out of the classroom, like a sentence that starts one way and ends another– Was that an anacoluthon? – like, say, 'If I don't mend my boozy ways what, in God's name, is going to be the end of *me*?' Though, God knows, he thought, following Angelo's broad back down the corridor, anacoluthing like blazes as he went, the truth is isn't it an extraordinary fact, like Brainsy and me, why must everybody in Ireland live like an express train that starts off for heaven full of beautiful dreams, and marvellous ambitions and, halfway, bejasus, you switch off the bloody track down some sideline that brings you back to exactly where you began, with all your machinery falling out of you in bits, and every wagon branded 'What's-the-use-of-doing-any-thing-at-all?'

Angelo paused with his hand on the doorhandle of Tom's classroom. He turned to say curiously, 'So you know Brother Regis?' A soft babel went on inside. Tom said, cautiously, not knowing what Brainsy might have told him about his own past, that, yes, they had both been at school together in the A.B.C. in Cork.

'But, of course, that was years and years ago. He was a very clever boy at school. Oh, very talented! One of the stars of the A.B.C. And friends in Dublin tell me that he became a marvellous teacher.' He smiled ingratiatingly. 'At school the boys used to call him Brainsy. A nickname, like that, from boys, don't you think, Brother Angelo, is a great compliment?'

Looking steadily at his new teacher, the old man took out his snuffbox, opened it, dabbed in one fat thumb and slowly approached the nicotine to each hairy nostril. Still looking steadily at his man, he slowly replaced the box in his trousers pocket through a slit in his soutane.

'Brainsy? That's not bad, you know. It's extraordinary how penetrating boys can sometimes be. And how cruel!'

'He has been a monk now for how long?'

'Twelve years.'

'Always here?'

'He spent nine years in his old school in Cork.'

Nine years in a big city? And now shunted down to this back-of-beyond? Puzzled as well as worried, Tom ventured a probe.

'I never expected to find him down here.'

There was a sudden silence behind the classroom door. Had the boys heard them talking? In the silence, through the open window of the corridor, he heard the juniors downstairs repeating in unison the voice of a teacher guiding them through a reading lesson, first his deep voice, phrase by phrase, then their piping voices repeating the words after him:

'THE RHINE-O-SAYROS,' the deep voice boomed. 'The rhine-o-sayros,' the children piped. 'IS A WILD BASHTE.' 'Is a wild bashte.' 'HE WOULD ATE YOU.' 'He would ate you.' 'AND DESHTROY YOU.' 'And deshtroy you.'

When Angelo's answer came it was a shade too delicate.

'Well, you see, our Superior General thought he might find it a bit more easy away down here in the quiet of the country.'

It was the word *away* that gave him away. Whenever somebody has what we politely call a nervous breakdown we always say, 'He has been away.'

For several weeks all that Tom saw of his friend was when they passed one another in the corridor between classes, and without halting, Brainsy would lift a hand, smile faintly and say something like 'All going well, I hope?' or 'Bad weather, isn't it?' Tom, deeply hurt, decided finally that if this was the sort of relationship the fellow wanted now he could play that game too – 'Morning, Brother! Nice day, isn't it?' – until, bit by bit, he began to get a hint here and a hint there of the kind of tensions that tauten life in small communities like the A.B.C.

He got his first small shock the day he overheard two boys refer to Regis as Brainsy. It could only mean that Angelo had, unguardedly, mentioned the nickname to one of the brothers who had, at once and maliciously, passed the arrow on to his boys. For a boy to give a nickname like that to another boy was a chummy thing to do. To give it to a teacher was like sticking a firecracker into his tail. He got a more painful hint the day he was trying to persuade his class that when Oliver Goldsmith was writing *The Deserted Village* in his miserable London garret he was all the time sadly remembering the village where he was born, in Ireland.

'Take, for example, the lines...'

At once an ink-fingered hand shot up. It was Micky Brennan, the son of a local publican, a boy he had already come to recognize as one of the smartest boys in the class.

'I know the lines, sir,' Micky said eagerly, and started to quote them fluently and feelingly, from

> In all my wanderings round this world of care,
> In all my griefs – and God has given my share—
> I still had hopes my latest hours to crown,
> Amidst these humble bowers to lay me down...

on down to:

> And, as an hare whom hounds and horns pursue,
> Pants to the place from whence at first she flew,
> I still had hopes, my long vexations past,
> Here to return – and die at home at last.

Immediately Brennan had begun to recite the lines the whole class began to titter. (At what?)

'That's very good, Brennan. But how do you happen to know the lines so well?'

Another boy spoke up, a rough fellow named Harty, the duffer of the class and, Tom suspected, the bully of the school – he had already had to stop him, one day in the yard, from punching a boy half his size and weight.

'He knows them lines, sir,' Harty growled, with an envious look at Brennan, 'only because Brainsy . . .' There was a general titter at this slip of the tongue; if it was a slip. 'I mean Brother Regis, sir, is always quoting them to us at History. He says he's very fond of 'em.'

The whole class laughed openly; Tom understood; and in his fright passed quickly on to something else. If these giggling brats had been smart enough to read Brainsy for Goldsmith he had no need to persuade them to read Lissoy for Auburn. As he looked around at their innocent-wicked-probing eyes he knew that it would not be long before they saw through him too. What nickname had they, maybe already, given him? And did this sort of thing run through the whole school, through the monastery, all through Coonlahan?

Where he now lodged was with a young carpenter and his wife in a tiny pink house rising directly from the pavement that ended with the school and the monks' dwelling place. Beyond that the road became grass-edged and the countryside began; though within a month, merely by facing the window of the small front room of his lodgings as he ate his dinner – at half past three every afternoon – watching the rare cart or the rare pedestrian that passed slowly by, it came to him that Coonlahan was a place where the life of the country had neither beginning nor end. Like any one of the little whitewashed farmhouses on the level bogland that he could see through his window it was just another dot in space and time. That donkey cart trundling slowly by with its roped pyramid of turf to be sold from door to door brought the bogland into the Main Street. The pasturers plodded in every evening with a small herd of black cows, their udders dripping, eager to be milked in somebody's backyard. Coonlahan's one water pump stood on top of three rectangular steps at a fork in the road just beyond the school, its timber casing always wrapped in posters advertising hay or land for sale, so that he occasionally saw the waterman's two barrels, covered with wet sacking, pass his window to the lazy cry of

'Pennyabucketthewa-a-ather!' The carpenter's wife, like many other women in Coonlahan, kept chickens in her backyard – he once saw a hawk swoop down on the hen run to carry off a chicken between its claws; and one hard, wintry morning he found her in floods of tears – a fox had stolen in at night and killed them all. 'I'm beginning to think,' he said to her, 'that the whole village ought to be stockaded!' Yet, one lovely afternoon in the following April he was to see a host of swallows pour in at one end of the Main Street and out at the other as if there were no village there at all. No wonder that old bus driver had laughed at him the night he asked for 'the hotel'! In a place where there was no railway, no cinema, no library, no bookshop, no dancehall, nothing but a handful of shops and pubs? Where, all through the long autumn nights, he soon found that there was nothing whatever to do – after he had corrected his pupils' homework or prepared his own – but to read, or sit with the carpenter and his wife in the back kitchen playing cards, or listening to voices from Dublin fading and returning on the dying batteries of the radio.

At such dead hours he would occasionally wonder what Brainsy was doing at that moment down the road. What did they all do once school was over? One afternoon he had seen two of them playing handball against the gable of the school. Another day he had watched a few of them aimlessly pucking a hurling ball in an empty field, shouting like boys, their soutanes doffed, their bony collars scattered on the grass like crescent moons. On fine afternoons he regularly saw some of them passing his window in pairs to walk, as he sometimes did himself, out some country road until the sun set. Coming on Dicky Talbot one October night in Brennan's pub, he asked him, 'How do ye pass the winter nights here in Coonlahan?' Dicky, married, with eight kids, said he had never needed to consider the problem.

'I mean, the brothers,' Tom said testily. 'Do they play cards? Do they ever read? And if so what?'

'I suppose they read the newspaper. Though it must be a bit of rag by the time it has passed through all their hands? I imagine they read *Our Boys*, or look at the clerical weeklies. They have some sort of a ragtime library of their own but I have no idea what's in it. Textbooks? Lives of the saints? As you know, there's no library here. All the County Librarian can do is dump a couple of cases of books in the back porch of the chapel once a month. A couple of years back he offered them the run of everything he has in his H.Q. in Killarney, but only one of them ever availed of the offer.'

'I bet that was Regis!'

'The very man. But they soon put a stop to his gallop.' Dicky laughed at the happy memory. 'They caught him one night reading a book called *Is There an Afterlife?* by some Calvinist divine named Vaughan. They raised blue hell and bloody murder over it. They complained the poor old County Librarian to the Parish Priest and to the County Committee. A bright boyo, he said he thought the author was Cardinal Vaughan.'

'You're surely not suggesting that Regis was having religious doubts? I mean, did the book deny the existence of immortality?'

'Amn't I after telling you the book was by a Calvinist? And the world knows that no Calvinist could exist for one minute without heaven for himself and hellfire for everyone else. Doubts? Not at all. It was simply the question mark after the title. They weren't going to stand for that! Doubts? Regis have doubts? You obviously don't know our Regis. His trouble is that he's full to the butt of the lugs with certainties. He's the Savonarola of Coonlahan. He's the scourge of the monastery. He thinks they're all a soft, flabby, half-pagan lot, and he's always telling them so. You should hear him saying, "He that is neither hot nor cold I spe-e-ew him out of my mouth." Or you should have been here last year when he made them all agree to give up cigarettes for Lent, and then caught one of them sucking a butt in the jakes. He reported the poor bastard to the Superior, the P.P. and the Bishop. What do they do at night? Sit around and eat one another, I would imagine. Have another pint.'

Tom brooded over that conversation. 'Simply the question mark after the title . . .' That would be right up Brainsy's alley. He decided that he must have a talk with him alone.

It was a frosty afternoon in mid-November before he got his chance. He had finished his dinner and was reading the Dublin paper (it never came in before three o'clock) when his eye was lifted by the lone pencilled shadow of one of the brothers passing swiftly outside the lace curtains. He recognized Nessan, the man who taught the kids Irish, and was just deciding that he was hurrying on some errand down the street when he saw Brainsy slowly passing by, also alone. He seized his umbrella, hat and overcoat and hastened after him. Ahead of him he saw Nessan turning right for the open country, with Brainsy about a hundred yards behind him. He caught up with him.

'Hello, Regis.'

'Hello, Tom.'

'You seem to have lost your companion.'

'He's my non-companion,' Brainsy said gruffly. 'I prefer my own company.'

'Oh? Am I intruding on some great thoughts?'

Brainsy relaxed into a smile as frosty as the grey field beside the road.

'Divil a thought, great or small. Walk along with me and leave us be talking. All that fellow,' nodding his chin towards Nessan's back, 'ever talks about is crossword puzzles. "What is a four-legged domestic animal in three letters beginning with C?" If you say cat he says cow. If you say cow he says cat. Lovely afternoon, isn't it? How's everything with you? Getting along alright?'

Tom let him talk school talk for a bit. Then he drew closer.

'You know that boy Micky Brennan?'

Brainsy's smile became a trifle softer and sadder.

'A bright boy, an inquiring boy, he reminds me sometimes of myself when I was his age.'

'He stood up in class one day and recited a whole chunk of *The Deserted Village* for me. *In all my wanderings round this world of care . . .* You know the lines. He tells me you taught them to him. I never knew you were a Goldsmith fan.'

'As a matter of fact, I am very fond of that poem. Every historian ought to be. It touches on quite a number of modern problems. *Ill fares the land, to hastening ills a prey.* And so on. Poor Oliver knew it all. An exile himself.'

'Who always wanted to go home in the heel of his days? I often wondered whether he had a home to go to. As well I might. Since my mother died I have no home to go to. Is your dad still alive?'

Brainsy said, 'No,' and halted and looked off to where the far mountains rose clear and sharp against the frosty twilight.

'Home?' he said softly. 'The word has various meanings, of course. *Lead, kindly light . . . The night is dark and I am far from home.*'

'Newman. The lighthouse in the Strait of Bonifacio. A great stylist.'

'A great teacher. When I read him I feel the next world revolving about me.'

'But you believe in the next world.'

'Meaning?'

'Meaning that I gave up all that sort of thing years ago. Thanks to you, Brainsy.' Brainsy lifted shocked eyes to him. 'You haven't forgotten all our talks in Dublin? Day after day. Night after night. Year in and year out. After you left Dublin I stopped going to church, chapel or meeting. I hope you won't report that to your superior? I don't want to lose my job – just yet.'

They walked on in the frosty silence. After a bit Brainsy spoke.

'I accept no responsibility for your state of mind. You are a grown man. But if that is your state of mind what are you doing here?'

'It's a living.'

Their feet rang on the hard road.

'Well! You are a layman. So I suppose a living is a good enough reason for you to be here. I might do better to ask what am I doing here?' He pointed forward with his umbrella to his lone chaperon. 'Or what is that fellow doing here? Or what are they all doing here?'

'Teaching?'

Brainsy halted again. The line between his eyebrows went red as a scar. His voice became hoarse with fury.

'Teaching what? Isn't that the beginning and end of it? Isn't that what I'm always saying to these fellows? If every single thing we say and do and teach doesn't give the youngsters the feeling that this ball of the world is carrying us inch by inch towards another world where is the sense in any one of us giving up everything to become brothers? But do we do it? Angelo teaches them Latin. Perhaps you can tell me, because he can't, since when did Cicero or Ovid become pillars of Christianity? Oh, laugh away! That's what they do! That man there teaches the Irish language. He thinks he's doing great work for Ireland. He might just as well be teaching them pagan Greek. This year your lads will be reading *Macbeth* or *Julius Caesar*. What's so very Christian about either of them? It may all be a great joke to you. You've just said you have no beliefs. But I have my beliefs. And it's no laughing matter for me.'

He shivered and they resumed their walk.

'Tom! Do you know why I left you that time in Dublin? I'll tell you why. It's not nice. But I'll tell you. It was a Saturday. If you remember?

You were working that day, I wasn't. It was a lovely sunny day. I took a girl down to Brittas Bay. She was eighteen. A sweet, lovely, innocent girl. I sometimes still pray for her. It was a real Irish July day, little showers of rain, great steamy clouds rising up all around us, everything bruised black and blue, the hills, the white fields, the blue sky. We swam and we lay down on the cool sand. Not a soul along the beach for miles and miles. The usual opening gambit. Slipping the strap of her bathing dress off her shoulder. When I did it she looked up at me and I never saw such terror, such contempt, such disgust, such disappointment in any human being's eyes. She looked at me as if I was filth. I put back the strap and I said, "Forget it." I couldn't think what else to say or do. After a while she got up and said, "We'd better go home now, Jerry, you've spoiled everything." The whole way back to Dublin we didn't say one word. When she left me I went back to the flat and I looked at it. Everything ready. The half-bottle of whiskey. The two glasses. The couch in the corner. The sun pouring into the room. It looked exactly what it was. Sordid. That was my moment on the road to Damascus. It came to me like lightning that I was a bad influence on everybody, including you, Tom, and that if I didn't leave the world entirely I was done for. Inside a year I became an Abbatian brother.'

Ahead of them Nessan halted on the brow of a little hill looking at the sky. Hesperus. He could have been one of the Magi. They paused to let him walk on.

'And you have been happy ever since?'

'Within three years I realized that all I'd done was to jump out of the frying pan into the fire. I had thought I had a vocation . . .'

'Like me in the Capuchins!'

' . . . Instead, all I was doing, year after year, was shoving a few score of boys through some examination or other to get some lousy job. Would you give up the whole world just for that? After that it became more and more clear to me every year that if that was all my vocation was good for I was a fool, we were all a lot of fools, and the whole blooming thing was a cod.'

Whom hounds and horns pursue. Until the hare is torn to pieces. They thought he might find it more easy down here in the quiet of the country. Or was it because he was the kind of brainy teacher they couldn't afford, or the expensive makings of one? One small head that, as Goldsmith did not say about the village teacher, could never carry all he thought he knew?

That month ended it. A leak in the roof of the school made Tom's class uninhabitable, and for three weeks, while they were replacing the slates, he had to keep moving his class from room to room. For those three weeks he had a chance to watch them all teaching. None of them interested him except Brainsy, and he was a magician. With him the boys were not in a class at all; they were in a circus, on an ice-hockey rink. His trick, though it was his nature rather than a trick, was to keep them doubling after him all the time, never letting them rest for a minute. He was so good that Tom used to set his class to some written exercise so that he could pretend to be looking out the window while listening, entranced, to the chase going on at the other end of the room.

One such day he was standing like that, looking down into the kitchen-garden of the monastery, with Brainsy behind him luring them on to discuss the suppression of the monasteries. For forty minutes he started argument after argument. 'Sullivan, how would you like it if you saw your father's grazing land being taken away from him?' 'Yes, but supposing it didn't belong to him? Supposing that it originally belonged to the Church?' 'Brennan, what about all those executions of multitudes of poor people wandering all over the country, driven to terrible crimes by hunger? How far was it just, or unjust, to hang them?' Then, at a great leap, he was on to the humanity of John Howard and his plans for Prison Reform. 'Cassidy, what do you make of that idea?' 'Whelan, have you any idea where that humane spirit began in England?' 'Walsh, what about the Church, for example? Was it a humane idea when the Church began to teach that hell is not just fire eating the body but torment eating the soul?' 'Foley, what do you think? Was that a humane idea? Or was it even more inhumane?' 'What do you all think? Which was the more humane in that terrible century, the Pope or the King?' It was then that Tom heard the doorhandle click and, turning, saw old Angelo slide out as softly as he had, apparently, come in.

The very next day Angelo called Tom out of his class and informed him, in the corridor, that after the Christmas holidays he must, in addition to English, teach History.

'But,' Tom cried, 'I never studied History. And Brother Regis is a dab at History. He's marvellous at it. You heard him yourself.'

'I have heard him many times, Mr Kennedy.'

'Then you can see for yourself that I couldn't come within a thousand miles of the way he does it. Compared to him I'm a complete ignoramus! And the boys are mad about his ideas on History!'

Angelo let out an exasperated sigh. He took out his snuffbox, but he was too upset to use it.

'I am very sorry, Mr Kennedy, but you will just have to do what I say. All you need do is to read the set texts and keep a couple of pages ahead of the class. And,' suddenly and uncharacteristically getting excited, 'I want you to know that I don't care two pins whether the boys are interested in Brother Regis's ideas, or your ideas, or anybody else's ideas, or not. My position is quite simple. I want my boys to get through their examinations, and that is all I want. And the plain fact of the matter is that since Brother Regis came here three years ago we have had more failures in History than in any other subject on the entire curriculum. And I'm not one bit surprised. Unless you can explain to me what on earth History has to do with such matters as whether there is real fire in hell or not. Look!' He was trembling in every limb, and his round, soft face had become as purple as a swede turnip. 'This little community of ours was as cosy and happy a little community as you could find in the length and breadth of Ireland until Brother Regis was sent down here on top of us to enjoy the peace and quiet of the country. Peace and quiet? God help us! Since that man joined us there has been neither peace nor quiet in this place. Do you know that last night, in our quiet little library, he and Brother Nessan, two brothers in religion, literally, literally I say, came to blows – I never thought I'd live to see it – before all the brothers. And about what, Mr Kennedy? About the nature of hellfire!' He gripped his soutane across his chest as if he were getting a grip of himself. On the spot he became quiet. 'You will take History in the New Year. Have no fears – you can't be worse than your predecessor. And for the rest of the year I will raise your salary by twenty-five per cent.'

That night Tom decided, over his fourth pint of porter, that Angelo could sack him if he wanted to; but he could not and would not do this to his best friend. In the morning he found he had no option. An ambulance stood outside the monastery door. The sergeant of the Guards and a plainclothesman were talking with Angelo and Nessan inside the gate. Every window in the school was full of white faces. Dicky Talbot whispered to him that Regis had been missing since midnight and that the Guards and the brothers had been out searching for him with lamps until three hours ago, when he was found, unconscious, in a ditch beside the road, presumably knocked down by some yob in a passing motorcar. He was now lying in his bed in the monastery, still unconscious, about to be taken to the County Hospital in Tralee.

He was still unconscious when Tom went to Dublin that Christmas; he was unconscious on his return; he remained unconscious for, in all, sixty-six days. A month later he was discharged from hospital, as well as ever, meaning, as he himself said over a cup of tea in Tom's lodgings, 'Hale and hearty! Except for a bruised liver, a broken leg, two smashed fingers, three ribs that creak whenever I try to touch my toes, and a silver plate in my skull.'

'Well,' Tom joked, in the merry tone we all reserve for such doleful occasions, 'you gave us a nice fright! I expected to hear any day that you were dead.'

From his armchair Brainsy gave him a queer look.

'So I was,' he said quietly.

'Was what?'

'Dead.'

'You look very much alive now, anyway.' Tom laughed uncomfortably.

Brainsy's mouth went tight. The frown between his eyes caved in. This, apparently, was no laughing matter either.

'There is no least doubt about my death, Tom. I have had plenty of time since I came back from the grave to think the whole matter out completely. I have been asking myself a great many interesting questions. And I have arrived at a very simple conclusion. When I was knocked down that night on the highway I was given a blow on the head that plunged me into a state of total oblivion for sixty-six days. I lost all my faculties. I fail to see what more could have happened to me if my heart had stopped beating. I was, in a word, humanly speaking, dead.'

With anybody else Tom would have scoffed or made polite, meaningless noises. He opened his mouth to make one, leaned forward, leaned back; did the same again, did it a third time; and sank back into his armchair. He felt like a lunatic rowing an imaginary boat. You always had to come to the point with Brainsy.

'But your soul was alive!' he said at last.

Brainsy smiled and to enforce the smile adopted, at one and the same moment, a Kerry brogue and what used to be called an Oxford accent

– the common Irish way of being superior without seeming to be lofty.

'Oho! Aren't we a darlint boy! So, now, oo doo believe in the sowl, eh?'

'Well, no! Or, only as a metaphor. Such as, "Brevity is the soul of wit." Shakespeare. Or, "O God, if there is such a thing as a God, please save my soul, if I have such a thing as a soul." Renan. But, I don't believe in the soul in your sense of the word.'

Brainsy sighed.

'After my experience on the road to Tralee I don't believe in anything any longer. How could I? A material man, with no material faculties whatever, but endowed with a soul? That's not a man, that's a vegetable. Are we horseradishes or potatoes? Of course,' he mused, 'there were philosophers who believed, and some may even still believe, that vegetables and animals have souls.'

'God knows,' Tom conceded, 'there are times when I think the one half of me isn't much better than a potato.'

Brainsy waved a languid hand.

'Now you are postulating two souls. One rational, the other irrational. The heresy of Photius. Condemned by the Council of Constantinople in 869.'

'But, surely,' Tom pleaded, 'my soul isn't working all the time? I mean when a pint of porter is flowing down my gullet. Or when my eye looks at you now drinking that cup of tea . . .'

'You are now denying the principle of unity. Condemned by the Council of Vienne in the thirteenth century. Recondemned by Pius the Ninth in 1857. It is the whole man who sees and drinks, not your boozy, bloodshot eyes or your big thirsty mouth. Soul and body drink together. "I drink," said Aristotle, "therefore I am."'

Tom stared goiterously at his friend.

'Brainsy! I'm lost. Would you mind telling me what exactly we are talking about?'

'About a fantasy. Believed in by millions. Real to millions. I sometimes wonder,' he considered, pulling his left ear, 'whether the idea had any existence at all in Western Europe before Aristotle?'

Tom's voice rose to a squeak of desperation.

'Are you saying now that Aristotle invented my soul – if I have such a thing as a soul?'

'The origin of your soul? If you have a soul? That is very difficult.

Saint Augustine suggested that it may have come out of your father's cock. *Incorporeum semen* was his elegant phrase. That was called Generationism. Others thought that God creates the soul and pops it into the embryo in, I can't remember, was it the third or the fourth month? That is Creationism. But that raises an extremely awkward problem. It means that God would have had to stain it deliberately with Original Sin beforehand. No, Tom! It's all a lot of scholastic nonsense. Man was born with a brain. Without a brain he is a beast. Or he is dead as a man. When that fellow left me that night on the road I was no more than a rabbit that somebody took by the hind legs to bash its head against a rock. I died.'

'But your doctor,' Tom cried, 'will tell you that your organs remained alive, your heart, your guts, you were fed intravenously, you breathed, you aged, your tissues went on growing.'

'As your whiskers will keep on growing in the grave. As snakes galvanize after you cut them in two. What is it to be dead? Tom, if anybody knows I should know. I went into black darkness. And there was nothing there.'

The image of Brainsy lying in black nothingness flooded such horror into Tom that he leaped up and, as if he was at a retreat, or a mission, or a revival meeting, or listening to Billy Graham, he shouted out, 'I believe! I believe in the soul! I cannot believe in a man without one!' and he banged the polished round table that the carpenter had made for his wife, with its lace doily under a little silver vase bearing its one artificial rose.

'Anyway!' he cried triumphantly. 'The simple proof of the matter is that you are here now, alive and kicking. If you died, tell me who or what is this sitting there now in front of me talking all this balderdash?'

Brainsy rose on his walking stick and took his black hat.

'I do not know, Tom. I do not know who I am. Or where I came from. Or what I am. That is something I shall have to find out. I'd better go. Whatever I do and wherever I go I seem to have a bad influence on everybody, and upset everybody.'

'Everybody?' Tom asked fearfully, following him to the door. 'Have you been talking like this to anybody else?'

'Why not? I explained it all to Angelo. I explained it all to the Bishop. Oh, yes,' he beamed, seeing Tom's eyes widen, 'they brought the Bishop to me.'

'And what did his Lordship say to you?'

'What could he say? He just kept looking at me. He mentioned Lazarus. "But, my Lord," I said, "Lazarus was not dead. If he was dead when Christ came, you must believe that he was already judged by God and either resting in what your Lordship calls heaven, or suffering in hell. Or can your eternal God upset his own eternal judgments?" That floored him. He left me without another word and I have not seen or heard from him since. Oh, by the way, Tom, I'm forgetting my manners. I never thanked you for that nice cup of tea.'

It was this cheerful mention of the cup of tea that most frightened Tom. The man had no idea at all of what lay ahead of him.

'What are they going to do to you now?' he asked, at the front door.

'Angelo tells me I'm to teach Geography. A safe subject? "What are the chief rivers of France? What's the highest mountain in the world?" Or that's what he thinks. Geography has changed completely since his day. It is everything now – anthropology, sociology, the study of environments, economics, human values, history, religion, science. I'm going to have a lovely time with Geography.'

He waved a hand and limped away back to the monastery.

'I'll pray for you,' Tom called after him, and slowly closed the door.

He did not see him for three weeks. One reason was that since Lent began he had gone completely off the drink, but all this so upset him that every time he neared a pub in the Main Street he had to rush past it and start counting the days to Easter Sunday. The man *was* a bad influence! Nevertheless he could not help wondering how far the story had travelled. On the Sunday before Good Friday he met Dicky Talbot as he came out from mass, and asked him for news of Regis. Dicky stared at him, laughed long and loud, and then fell silent for a full half-minute, staring at him.

'You know,' he said at last, 'Coonlahan must be one of the most extraordinary little places in the whole world. It has one street, one large church, one small convent, one monastery of microscopic proportions, four pubs, it contains about fifteen hundred people, and I'm sure every person here thinks he knows everything about everybody. And he mostly does. But as for what goes on in the convent or the presbytery, or the A.B.C., the three of them might as well all be in Siberia. I swear that at this moment there could be three nuns nailed up by the ears to the back wall of the convent and nobody would know anything about them for six months. Look at you! You are teaching here, and you actually have to ask me where Regis is! For the last week he's been out in the kitchen-garden working as a lay brother.'

'You mean they wouldn't even let him teach Geography?'

'Angelo watched him doing it for a week and whipped him out of it like a shot to go downstairs teaching spelling to the kids. You know the way the kids chant their spelling after the teacher. "C.A.T. Cat. C.A.T. Cat. C.A.T. Cat." Sometimes it's about the only sound you'd hear from one end of Coonlahan to the other. Angelo went into Regis's spelling class one day and he nearly had a fit. Regis had them chanting, "D.O.G. God. D.O.G. God. D.O.G. God."'

Tom wiped his forehead. Dicky looked up and about the sky.

'Grand day, thank God!' he said. 'The first week of April. Nice time for planting spuds. If you go out into the walled garden any afternoon you'll probably find him hard at it.'

It took Tom until Thursday to overcome his dread of the encounter; then, miserably, when he knew the brothers would be out walking, he made his way to the kitchen-garden. It was a warm, sunny day. The remnant white plaster and exposed sandstone of the backs of the houses in the Main Street were islands of red sausage-meat in seas of snow. The gate twanged behind him. The lovely evocative smell of manure. The tops of the new potato ridges already beginning to whiten in the sun. In one corner an old, whitehaired brother digging stolidly. Brainsy sitting on an upturned bucket apparently lost in the passing clouds. His dusty soutane was rucked up by a cincture of twine, his sleeves and his trousers' ends were turned back, heavy boots on his stockingless feet. When he heard the gate he lowered his head to see who his visitor was, waved, got up with the help of his stick and, as graciously as if he were welcoming Tom into his drawing room, indicated a grassy patch where they could lie in the sun and out of the turn of the spring wind.

Tom looked at him apprehensively. He seemed entirely at his ease. Even the furrow between his eyebrows was pale and shallow. They laid down, facing one another, each on his elbow. Tom produced cigarettes, lit for them both, and it was all suddenly as cosy as if they were back in Dublin years ago, talking from bed to bed about the doings of the day, or about girls, or the gossip of the pubs, or the days when they were boys together in Cork.

'How's the old leg?' he asked.

'It works. It will never be up to much. I'll always have to use the stick.'

'And how's the old head?'

'Oh! That never stops. Around and around like a mill horse. Clop. Clop.'

'And how's all the old rest of you?'

'Fine! I get pains now and again. But when they're bad I take pills.'

'At this rate you can't be much use as a gardener, can you?'

'Paul,' nodding to the far corner, 'does all the hard work. I plant, or weed, or anything I can do on my knees. I've got very interested in cooking, too. They used to have a lay brother doing that – he was a ship's cook before he joined the Order – but they've promoted him to teaching the infants. Within a month or two I bet you they will all be eating better than they ever did in their lives. Oho! There's plenty of work in the old horse still.'

It seemed to Tom that he was being much too chipper about it all.

'And how are they treating you?'

'I rarely see them. Lay brothers can, if they want to, sit in the library, but in practice they rarely do. Paul and I live, eat and amuse ourselves in the kitchen. In there at night we are like an old farmer and his son. Reading, or listening to the radio, or playing draughts or chess – he's very good at them both. I read a lot. The County Librarian has promised to keep me well supplied in that quarter.'

'And they don't mind?'

'They don't mind anything I do any longer. I am a man who has lost his faculties. I am off my chump. They are alright. They're a dull bunch. But never forget it, Tom, there is such a thing as Christian charity. I have never in my life experienced such kindness as I have since they shunted me out here.'

Away in his corner Paul's spade rang on a stone. A swallow did a jet dive down and out of the garden. Brainsy was talking of how Paul and himself spent their day. Ten mouths for breakfast, washing up after it, making the beds, sweeping and dusting the whole place, and then off down the Main Street with two big woven shopping bags.

'We're not the most popular customers.' He grinned. 'Probably because they are afraid to cheat us.'

Their shopping done, they might leave the bags behind some counter and go out the road for a stroll, but not before Paul had satisfied his one secret vice.

'He loves his bottle of stout. So, in with us by the back door to Brennan's pub, upstairs to his parlour, and he has his little tipple there like a lord.'

'And you?'

'As you know, I never drink stout. And we can't afford anything else.'

'That's where the ferryboat left you, Brainsy! Guinness and godliness, it's a great combination. You can't whack it.'

'Meaning that you are back on the booze?'

'I wish I was. I'm dying for Easter Sunday to come. Four more days! My stomach thinks my throat is cut. It's very decent of them to give you money for the stout.'

'They give us no money. Poverty, Chastity and Obedience. That's the rule. But we cheat them a bit on the shopping.'

They gossiped about the town. Little gossip. About the tiniest things. Paul knew every hole and corner of the place, every man, woman and child in it. Towards the end Tom said, 'I hope you're not corrupting poor old Paul with all your wild talk. Aren't they afraid you might?'

'I can say anything I like to him. In fact, I say the most outrageous things to him. And they don't mind. He is stone deaf. He's far more likely to corrupt me. He cheats like the devil at chess. There last night when I was waiting for him to make his move I saw a mouse coming out of its hole along the floor under the wainscoting. It had an eye like a robin. I winked at it. It winked at me. I said *Ouutch*! The next thing there was old Paul saying, "Checkmate!" I swear to high heavens he pocketed a pawn while I wasn't looking. We fought all night over it.'

He laughed so heartily that Tom's heart sank. What a way to pass a life! There was a long silence between them. Another swallow swooped in and out of the garden.

'They're coming back,' Brainsy said and Tom, thinking he meant the brothers, got up to go. Brainsy showed him where they were having the peas, and the cauliflowers, and the scarlet runners. Tom looked at them and did not see any of them. When they came, at last, to the gate Brainsy held his hand in a long, hard grip and the furrow between his eyes became intense.

'Look, Brainsy!' Tom cried, holding the holding hand just as tightly. 'If you don't believe in any of this stuff why don't you for God's sake chuck it all up and clear out?'

'And where,' Brainsy asked sadly, 'would I go?'

'Come back with me to Dublin. I'll be quitting here in June. We'll start together all over again.'

'And what would I do? All I'm any good for is teaching. And they've taken that away from me. After all this hullabaloo you know well that I'd never get another job again.'

Their hands parted. He opened the rasping gate. Tom passed through it. They looked at one another through it.

'Don't worry about me, Tom. You know where I live. Come and see me anytime. I'll be alright. All I'll ever miss will be the old chat.'

He raised his hand as if in blessing, and went back to his garden. Tom watched him limping away, turned, went out to the road and shuffled down to the Main Street, where he saw a great host of swallows blowing in through one end of it and out through the other. He went into the first pub he met, and he drank there until he was drunk. It was a habit that would stick to him all his life, always sober as a judge through Lent, always as drunk as an owl on the eve of the Crucifixion. In the dark pool of his pint he saw what the swallows would see: the wide bogland, brown-yellowy, seaweedy green, and the small road driving through it, and the far mountains with their clouds, and a few clustered roofs far below with one or two specks of humans moving between them, and one upturned garden with thickly ivied walls, good for nesting, and a man lying there on his back gazing up at them.

But, O swallow, swallow, swallow! That is the only man I have ever loved. And he is dead.

Thieves

From the beginning it was Fanny Wrenne's idea. The whole gang must go up in a bunch to the cathedral for their Easter Communion. This time a real pilgrimage! It would be like walking to Jerusalem. What was more, they must go up there for first mass. Clamorously the gang danced around her.

'Six o'clock mass! We'll have to get up at four. It'll be pitch-dark. There won't be a soul abroad. We'll be all alone. We'll have all Cork to ourselves. Everybody but us snoring.' Fanny added her masterstroke. 'And after mass, do ye know what we'll do? Buy a bag of broken biscuits and be munching them all the way home.'

It was one stroke too many, as they found when they scattered, racing in all directions to beg pennies from their fathers and mothers, their uncles and their aunts, for the bag of broken biscuits.

Were they gone clean out of their little heads? Were they mad? Kids of nine and ten walking halfway across Cork in the dark of an April morning? To a cathedral that was miles away? Supposing it was raining! And what about if they lost their way? Whose idea was this anyway? Fanny Wrenne's. That kid was ever and always creating trouble.

In the end only two of them met at the bridge that morning. Fanny, because she always got her way, because her mother was dead, and her father away at sea, and she an only child, and her old Aunt Kate was a softie. And Dolly Myles, because her father neither knew nor cared what any one of his eleven children did, and because her mother knew that Fanny Wrenne could be relied on to look after anybody anywhere – a dark, sturdy, bosomy, bottomy boss of a robin who would spend her life bullying every other little bird in the garden away from the crumbs that God meant for all. As for poor Dolly, she was born to be bossed. Eyes as blue and as blank as a doll's, her hair as fair, her cheeks as pink, and her adenoidal lips hanging from her nose in such a sweet little triangle that old gentlemen were always stopping her in the street to pat her curly poll.

They approached one another across the bridge like two dwarf ghosts. Upriver all they could see was the bright window of the waterworks shining down on the smooth curve of its lasher. All they could hear was the faint hum of turbines, and even that came and went on the morning wind. Downriver they saw nothing at all but the daffodil of the first gaslamp, and, far away, one vast cloud reflecting the night glow of the city. Overhead the sky was as black and blue as a mackerel.

Fanny had brought her Aunt Kate's best umbrella. It was red, it bore a red tassel, its handle was a scarlet bird's beak with a glassy eye embedded on each side of its head. She brought it because Dolly had told her the night before that her mother had a good friend named Mrs Levey who lived near the cathedral in a place called Flatfoot Lane. Fanny immediately said they would call on Mrs Levey on the way to mass, and give her the umbrella as an Easter present. In return she would be certain to give them a penny each as an Easter present, and with the two pennies they would buy the broken biscuits on the way home.

The gaslamps were no better than candles. Between their wavering scraps of light they could not so much see the footpath as feel for it with their feet. They walked hand in hand. They did not speak at all. They met nobody. They heard nothing but their own footsteps. Every house was as dark as a prison wall. Then, suddenly in one house they saw a lighted upstairs window. It made them speak. Who could be awake at this hour? Somebody sick? Somebody dying? Staring up at it, Dolly put her arm around Fanny's waist and Fanny clutched the umbrella to her like a baby. Could it be a robber? They hurried on fearfully. Soon they began to dawdle. Once, they looked back towards the west and were glad to see a star floating behind a black cloud. Ahead of them the sky was paling and opening but there was no star to be seen there at all. They sat on a low wall to rest and began to argue about how many broken biscuits you could get for tuppence. They started off again, still arguing, took two wrong turnings, and were only halfway up the long sloping street to the cathedral when Shandon Tower exploded into the three-quarters chime so close to them that Dolly let out a squeak of fright. *Do, So. La. Re ... Re. La ...*

'It's alright,' Fanny soothed. 'We've lots of time. So long as you know where Ma Levey's house is. And,' threateningly, 'I hope to God you do!'

Dolly looked down a dark laneway to their right. 'I know it's up here somewhere.' She looked across the street at the maw of another alley. 'Or could it be that way?' Blankly she looked back down the hill. 'Or did we come too far?' With a wild rush of assurance she chose the first laneway, and in a second, they were swallowed into its black gullet, running around and around in a whale's belly, through dusky gullies and dark guts, thin defiles and narrow, whirling shafts, dead-end lanes and turn-back cross trenches, all nameless and all smelly, only to find themselves ejected exactly where they began just as a soft sprinkle of April rain began to fall. Seeing that Fanny was about to shout, Dolly got her shout in first. 'It must be the other way!' Again they were blown about like two bits of white paper through more revolving lanes, dykes, alleyways and passages, lined with more dwarfs' houses and white-washed cabins, some thatched, some slated, each with its holland blind drawn down tightly, all of them so close together that a woman could, without moving her body, have stretched her hand from her own door to her neighbour's for the loan of a sup of milk or to return yesterday's newspaper. In every one of those cobbled lanes there was a runnel, already trickling with rainwater. There was barely room for it between the lines of cabins. There was no room at all for a footpath. They circled and descended, climbed and came down again, twisted and turned until a vast giant suddenly soared up above them with a great black clock face that silently said five minutes to six. At the sight of Shandon Tower where she least expected to meet it, Dolly burst into tears and Fanny, in a rage, pointed the bayonet of her umbrella at her belly.

'The house!' she screamed. 'Or I'll spit you up against that wall.'

'But,' Dolly wailed, 'I was only up here once. And I was with me mudder. And it was two years ago. And I was only seven.'

'Find that house!'

'If we could only find Flatfoot Lane, I know I'd know the house.'

'How would you know it? This place is maggoty with houses.'

'It have a white card in the window with Mrs Levey's name on it.'

'March!'

Dolly snuffled and pleaded.

'Why can't we keep the umbrella. It's not your umbrella. You stole it. And if it goes on raining we'll be drowned.'

At this sign of grace the sky ceased to weep, but the devil smiled. By magic there appeared, just above their heads, a bright red board that said FLATFOOT LANE. Here there were real houses, small but two-storied, in red brick, with two windows above and one window and a door below. More cobbles, no pavement, another gurgling refuse-runnel, and at the end of it a blank wall. They raced up one side of it and down the other, and, at last, there, between looped lace curtains, was the white card. It said in black print MIRIAM LEVEY. Beneath the name it said LOANS. On its green door there was a brassy knocker shaped like an amputated hand. Fanny seized it, sent a rattle of gunfire echoing up and down the lane, and looked at the upstairs window expectantly. Nobody stirred. She looked across the lane and could just see the tiptop of the clock tower, a tiny green dome carrying a big golden salmon, its weathervane gleaming in the risen sun and stirring faintly in the morning wind. Still, no sound, not a breath, not a thing stirring except when a white cat flowed along the base of the enclosing wall and leaped over it like a wave.

'Maybe,' Dolly said hopefully, 'she's dead?'

Fanny sent another dozen rounds of riflefire up and down the lane. They heard the upper window squeak open, saw ten bony fingers slide over the windowsill and Mrs Levey's tiny witch's face, yawning up at the sky from underneath a cellophane bag full of white hair in blue curlers. She yawned for so long that they thought she would never close her gummy mouth again. When she had finished her yawning she peered sleepily around the lane, said, 'Pusspuss! Pusspuss!' and finally looked down at the two white children. Fanny cheerfully waved the red umbrella at her.

'Good morning, Mrs Levey. Me Aunt Kate sent us up to you with this gorgeous umbrella for a present for Easter.'

'Your Aunt who?' she asked, and the word 'who' turned into another prolonged yawn. She peered down at the pair of them, shook her head, said, 'I'm afraid, child, I don't know no aunts at all. But, anyway, whoever she is . . .' Another yawn. 'Or whatever it is, leave it there on the windowsill and I'll get it when I wake up,' and withdrew, and the window banged.

Fanny gazed reproachfully at Dolly, who, knowing what was coming, lifted her blonde eyebrows, put her hand on her hip, and, self-dissociatingly, began to examine the architecture of every house along the opposite side of the lane.

'So that,' Fanny said scornfully, 'is your ma's lovely friend?'

'That,' Dolly piped, without as much as a backward glance, 'is your aunt's lovely umbrella.'

'A mangy ould maggoty ould moneylender.'

'Our credit was always good,' Dolly said loftily.

Fanny looked imploringly at the sky. The great gong saved her, booming the full hour, and all over the valley lesser bells softly announcing the angelus.

'We'll be late,' she shouted, threw the scarlet object on the windowsill and they scurried off back to the open street of the hill.

In the valley spires and chimneys were not tipped by the sun. Between these hill-houses the only sign that the night was going was a man who raced before them, lamplighter by night, lampquencher in the morning, plucking the head off every daffodil as he ran.

They hastened into the cathedral, panting. It blazed with lights, candles and white chrysanthemums. Not more than a couple of dozen worshippers. The priest, robed in the violet of Lent, was standing with his back to the altar, reading from a book the gospel story of the woman caught in adultery. ('What does that mean?' Dolly whispered, and Fanny whispered, 'Watering the milk.') Afterwards, Dolly said the bit she liked was where Jesus said to her, 'Run along with you, now, but don't do that any more,' but Fanny said the bit she liked was where Jesus kept stooping to the ground, writing some strange words whose meaning, the priest said, nobody will understand to the end of time. After that the sermon began and it went on so long that their heads began to nod, and they had to nudge and kick at one another to wake up, then making shocked faces and giggling, or, for fun, pretending to yawn like Ma Levey in the window. At last the priest ended his sermon, throwing his white wings open to say, 'Three weeks after He forgave that unfortunate woman they murdered Him, calling Him a criminal, but three weeks from now He will rise again as, in a few minutes, He will appear amongst us in the shape of a white circle, shining and immortal. Leave ye all kneel down now and prepare to welcome Him as He descends from heaven.'

The time for communion came. Side by side, their hands joined like the angels in holy pictures, their eyes modestly cast down, they walked slowly to and from the altar rails, as Sister Angelina at school had taught them to do. Slowly, the mass ended. There were more public prayers after it, and then they were standing in the porch, the city below them, the morning about them, the gaslamps all quenched, the pavements dancing with rain. A postman's black cape shone. A milkman, hooped against the wind and the rain, raced from his cart to pour milk into a saucer-covered jug on a doorstep, leaped back into his chariot and drove off with his whip sailing behind him like a flag.

'What about the umbrella?' Dolly said accusingly, and, because of the rain, longingly.

'Why don't we take it back?' Fanny cried, and hand in hand they galloped down the hill and back into Flatfoot Lane. The trickle of rainwater still ran whispering down the central runnel. In an upstairs window an old man, slowly and dexterously shaving one side of his face before a small square mirror balanced on top of the window sash, suspended his razor to watch them gallop through the rain, halt before the white card, and stare at the empty windowsill. Fanny rattled the hand on the green door and peered upward, the rain pouring down her face. The upper window squeaked open and Mrs Levey looked down.

'Oh, Law!' she said mildly. 'Is it ye again?'

'We made an awful mistake, Mrs Levey, we brought you the wrong umbrella, would yeh ever throw it down to us and we'll bring yeh the right one tomorrow morning at exactly the same time.'

The old face withdrew. After a moment the red object came sailing out through the window over their heads, plonked on the wet cobbles, and the window banged shut.

The umbrella was as old as sin. It bulged like a carrot. It was tied by a bit of string. It had a black bamboo handle. The old man in the opposite window, one half of his face red, the other half white, hailed them.

'Use it, girls,' he shouted. 'That's rain! Oho!' he assured them, waving his frothy razor, 'I seen it all. Ye gave her yeer lovely new umbrella and she throws ye back her leavings. Just like her!' he roared at the top of his voice across the lane. 'The bloody ould Jew' and returned to his tender shaving.

Fanny picked up the carroty umbrella, untied the bit of string, shot the gamp open above her head, and from it there showered scores and scores of pieces of paper that the wind at once sent blowing wildly all over the cobbles. The old man, watching, let out a roar of delight that drowned the last strokes of the seventh hour. Others who must also have been watching from behind their curtains, slammed up their windows, leaned out, cheered and bawled and pointed joyfully to one another.

In astonishment the two children stared around them at what they had done. Up and down the lane, more and more doors opened and more people pointed, laughing and shouting in chorus, 'Levey the thievey, the dirty ould sheeny, rob ye and leave ye!' Overhead the old woman's window opened. She leaned out, screamed like a peacock, vanished, and the next minute shot past them, a man's overcoat over her head and her nightdress like a shawl, racing hither and thither barefooted over the wet cobbles after her dockets. As she raced and stooped and picked, the whole lane kept bawling their horrid chorus at her. Only once did she pause and that was to shake her skinny fist at them. Then, suddenly, there was total silence. She had collapsed on her hunkers in the middle of the lane, her withered arms raised to the pouring sky, her mouth wide open, pleading to it in some strange language. As suddenly she fell silent, her head and her hands sunk into her lap. Slowly, a handsome young man came forward in his bare feet to lift her. After him an old woman came, and then another, and another, began to pick up the bits of paper, until one by one all the watchers were silently gathering up her dockets and pressing them into her crumpled hands. The two children ran.

Not until they halted at the river did Fanny notice that the rotten scarlet thing had accompanied them. She threw it over the quay wall, where, by stretching up on their toes to look, they could see it floating slowly away on the outgoing tide.

'Down the river!' Fanny hooted.

'Under every bridge,' Dolly giggled.

'Out to sea!' Fanny shouted.

Laughing they turned for home, stamping into the puddles of the rain, screaming with delight as they kicked arcs of water at one another. They lifted their wide-open mouths to the trees along the Mall trying to catch the falling drops. When they came to the iron railings opposite their own parish church of Saint Vincent they swung on them like two white wheels to see the rain falling up, and the church spires pointing down, the whole world standing on its head. By the time they came to their own bridge the rain had petered out, the sky was white and blue, the river water was smooth, the fields beyond it were empty and wet.

'Anyway,' Fanny said, 'even if we got the pennies we couldn't have bought broken biscuits. Not a shop open.'

They saw a light in a cottage, and a light in a villa on the side of the hill, and one window in a house beside the river was reflected longingly in the pure water. Dolly cocked her head.

'Listen!' she said.

They listened. Far away, around the bend of the road, from maybe half a mile away they could barely hear it. It would be lighted, and empty. The first tram.

Of Sanctity and Whiskey

As Luke Regan drove down to Saint Killian's for the first sitting he kept shifting around the fading cards of his schoolboy's memories of the place and wishing the press had never got on to this thing. It was a pleasant idea, of course, and he could understand the columnists playing it up – but the stupid things they wrote about it! 'Former pupil returns to his old school to paint his old teacher... This portrait of a distinguished Headmaster by a distinguished Academician is certain to reflect two sensibilities in perfect rapport with one another... This new portrait by Mr Luke Regan, RHA, of Brother Hilary Harty, the retired Head of Saint Killian's College, should record not one journey but two journeys from youth to maturity...' He had already confided to his boozing friends that he found the whole bloody thing extremely embarrassing; not least because he could see that they thought he was just boasting about it. He had only been in that school for three years, between the ages of twelve and fifteen. It was forty years ago. He had not the slightest recollection of this Brother Hilary Harty, and he felt sure that old man could not possibly remember him.

Hilary Harty? He hoped he was not that old snob they used to call Dikey, a fellow with a face like a coffin and eyes like a dead hen. Could he be Flossy, who used to collect jokes in a notebook as fat as a Bible: head and a face like a turnip; purple, orange and green – that would be a nice palette to have to work with! Without affection he remembered Popeyes, always blinking at you like the flicker of a motorcar that the driver had forgotten to turn off. But his name was Hurley. Now, little Regis would be a marvellous subject – a pink-and-white angel face with a fierce furrow between the eyebrows. That would be a challenging puss – if your were lucky enough, and had time enough to get him talking about himself. But Hilary? The name rang no chime, sweet, cracked or otherwise. 'Two sensibilities in perfect rapport with one another...' Had none of these fellows ever been to school themselves? Didn't they know well that no boy ever knows anything human at all about his teachers? Men dressed in black soutanes and bony collars, with names like ships, or stars, or horses – Hyperion, Aquarius, Berengarius, Arkel – floating into your classroom every morning, saying, 'Irregular verbs today!' or 'Did we polish off Queen Anne yet?' and if you didn't know your stuff, giving you three on each hand with the leather strap stuck in their black belts like a policeman's truncheon. All any boy ever wants from any teacher is that he might give you a bit of a chance now and again; understand, or know, or guess that the real reason you did not know your history, or your maths, was not because you lost the book, or had a headache, or broke your pen but because you saw Molly Ryan yesterday with high leather boots halfway up her fat legs and you simply had to dodge out that night to be gassing with her under the gaslamp by the back gate, watching her swinging her pigtails and admiring her toes just to provoke you. Little Regis would have understood; he was the only one of them who understood anything. He would give you a good clout on the ear, look at you hard and say, 'I'll give you this one chance, Master Regan, but if you ever do it again I'll have the hide off you.' And you loved him for it. But the rest of them? Human? The shock he got the day he saw Popeyes laughing with a woman in the Main Street! (Jesus! I must have been a right little prig in those days!) Not to mention the evening he saw Monsieur Joffre, their French teacher, coming out of a pub wiping the froth off his Clemenceau moustache. And by the same token not a drop must pass his lips while he was doing this portrait. Not with two hundred quid from the Past Pupils' Union depending on it. Anyway, he had been off the booze for four months now. 'Drop it, Luke!' – his doctor's last words. 'Or it will drop you into a nice, deep, oblong hole up in Glasnevin. Ninety per cent of your bloodstream is pure alcohol, and you know where that finally lodges?' – and he had tapped his forehead. 'DT's. Epilepsy, Neuritis, Insanity, God knows what!' The memory of it frightened him so much that when he was passing through Kilcrea he halted for one last, one absolutely last quick one before he arrived. And, just for precaution's sake, he packed a bottle of Paddy Flaherty in his hold-all in case he got a cold, or needed a little nightcap to send him to sleep after a day's revving-up at the easel.

The only change he could see, guess, presume or infer in Coonlahan was the rows of cars parked on each side of the Main Street. Surely, in his time, there were only a few horse-drawn carts or donkey-butts?

Chromium everywhere now and neon strips. The street's surface, asphalted, recalled mud and cowdung on market days. With relief he saw a neat-looking hotel called The Shamrock, and booked himself in there.

'How long, Mr Regan?' the freshfaced young woman said with a welcoming smile.

'How did you know my name?'

'Ah, sure the whole town knows about the painting.'

He winced.

'Four nights, please.'

'Only four?'

He winced again. In the Academy his colleagues called him Luca Fa Presto, after a certain Neapolitan painter who could finish any picture in twenty-four hours.

'It's a small portrait. Head and shoulders.'

Did she think he was going to live in the monastery? All the same he felt a bit ashamed that he was not. There were painters who would have done it, toiling to reveal the habits of a lifetime in a face. Degas must have done it before he began his *Uncle and Niece*. Manet must have known every damned thing about those three people he imprisoned behind the green railing of *The Balcony*. Courbet had put a whole countryside into those three men in *Bonjour, Monsieur Courbet*. Still, when he had driven out of the town and come to the big iron gateway, with SAINT KILLIAN'S COLLEGE half-mooned across it in gilded lettering, and saw the half-mile of avenue leading straight as a ruler up to the barrack-bare front of the college, grim as a tombstone against the sinking sun, he wondered whether Degas, or Monet, or Courbet, or Rembrandt, or Holbein or any of them would have wanted to soak himself in so dreary a joint as this either in the name of literal truth or ideal beauty. Wishing that he had had another drink in The Shamrock before facing this Brother Hilary Harty, he rang the bell.

A cheerful little lay brother, spry and bright as a monkey, showed him into the front parlour where, with painful clarity, he remembered the evening his mother had handed him over there to a matron named Miss Wall and with a face like one. The literal truth of the room leaped to the eye: linoleum on the floor, horsehair chairs, a round table glistening with a mock walnut veneer, a gas-fire unlit. As for ideal beauty: pictures in monochrome, *The Agony in the Garden*, the ghostly face of Christ on the pious fraud called *The Veil of Veronica*, somebody's *Annunciation*, and was that Breughel's *Tower of Babel* lifting the clouds? The Past Pupils' Union was going to make him earn every penny of this two hundred quid. The door was hurled open, a powerful-bodied old brother strode in, jolly-faced and beaming, and on the spot the setting sun hit face and everything became joyous, and splendid and okay.

'Luke Regan!' he all but shouted. 'After all these years!'

And the two of them were laughing and shaking one another's hands as energetically and boisterously as only two men can do who do not know one another from Adam. But what a head! Ripe for marble! For marble and porphyry! Nose rubicund, eyes blue as gentians, and an astonishingly protruding lower lip, the sure sign of a born talker. Hair white, thin on top but curling like the last of the harpers around his neck. Manet be blowed! Poor old Rembrandt! It was going to be the portrait of his life. Green curtain behind, ochre streaks of sunlight, buckets of carmine, lumps of it laid on with bold hard brushstrokes – half-inch brushes at that. Energy, strength, tenderness, humour! No more of that blasted pink toothpaste enamel that he had been floating all over the gobs of endless company directors for the last ten years. Not, to be fair, to flatter them but to flatter their stupid wives. 'Oh, Mister Regan, I think Eddie is much younger than you are making him out to be!' Or 'D'ye think, Mister Regan, you could make the tie a bit smoother like? The way you have it makes him look old and careless like.' Meaning, 'My God, man, do you want people to think *I'm* that old?'

'Brother Hilary, when do you think we can begin?'

He was so excited that when he got back to The Shamrock he had to go into the bar for a large one to calm his nerves. In its gold pool he saw the title on the catalogue of the Academy, where the portrait would be shown publicly for the first time. *The Old Dominie*. By Luke Regan, RHA. Not for Sale. Or what about *The Good Shepherd*? Or maybe, *Ex Cathedra*. Or *Post Multos Annos*? With a neat gold tab at the bottom of the frame saying, *Gladly wolde he lerne and gladly teche*. Tactile values? His fingers involuntarily began to mould the face. The man sitting beside him said, 'Hello, Mister Regan.' He sighed and did not deny it.

'My name is Halligan, Harry Halligan. We all knew you were coming. All Ireland knows about the painting. You have a great character there in old Leatherlip.'

'Leatherlip?'

Far away a bell chimed harshly, curtains parted on a small red light at the end of a mile-long corridor.

'Don't you remember? Or didn't ye call him that in your day?'

'How extraordinary! We did call one fellow that. But surely, not *this* man?'

'*Tempus fugit.* It's twenty-five years since I was at Saint Killian's. He was slim then, bushy black hair, eyes like a razor blade. You knew him in his thirties. And you really can't remember him?'

'He will come back to me. I'll quarry him out. That's how a painter works, working in and in, burrowing, excavating. It's like archaeology, you don't know what you are looking for until you find it. Sooner or later the face speaks.'

Halligan half-turned to the woman on his left: a bosomy, high-coloured little blonde. Horsy type.

'Let me introduce you to my wife. Valerie, this is Luke Regan the famous painter.'

She gave a cool hand and a cooler 'Howdyedo?' in a loud Anglo-Irish voice. No smile. Regan could feel the antagonism in her, and wondered at it. They had two more quick ones together before Mrs Halligan abruptly hauled her husband off with her. Regan took a last one by himself for the road to sleep.

Because of the light he decided to use the front parlour for a studio. It had three tall windows facing north. He could come and go without bother. By two o'clock, when his man would be free and the light good for two hours or so, he had managed to get a throne fixed up, a green curtain hung for background, his easel and work table ready and the inflatable lay figure that he always travelled with (one of his neatest Fa Presto tricks) draped with a black soutane that he would be working on every morning.

'I can't believe, Brother Hilary,' he laughed, as his charcoal lightly and rapidly sketched in the outline, 'that you are really seventy-five. You look about fifty.'

He always talked while he worked to keep his subject from stiffening or sagging.

'Aha!' the old boy laughed triumphantly. 'Mixing with youth all my life, that's what does it. That,' finger magisterially aloft, 'and the regular life. A dull life I suppose, not like you, out in the world, travelling, meeting interesting people, doing interesting things. But I have had my compensations. No worries, no regrets, no tensions. The rut, Luke. The beaten path. The ascetic discipline. Simple food. Good country air. Constant exercise. No excesses of any kind. You wouldn't grow fat on my kind of life, my boy. But that's what turns every monk into a man.'

When he came to the mouth he stared long and hard at the protruding lower lip. Again that far-off bell. Leatherlip? The eyes were curiously small but they gave out sparks when he talked. He would have given anything for an early photograph of the softer eyes of the boy buried behind those sharp orbs. He saw that the nose was red because it was veined all over. If this were a company director he would have said at once, 'Chronic alcoholic.' He knew rosacea when he saw it. Chiefly in elderly women. The wages of virtue. Chronic tea-drinkers. Gastritis. Monastery food. Probably an ulcer. Teeth browning from age and pipe-smoking. There would be black centres on the tip of every one of them. He frowned again at the big lip. A hard mouth in a jolly face. Now, what in hell did that portend? Silence. A good subject – he held the pose patiently.

'The rut?' he murmured, looking up, looking down. 'The beaten path? "The path of the just is as the shining light that shineth more and more unto the perfect day."'

'I'm glad to see that you read your Bible, Luke.'

'Now and again, Brother. A little to the left, Brother. Thank you, Brother.'

The light on the lip threw an interesting shadow. The nose became gory.

'Ah, yes!' concentrating on the jutting lip. 'Now and again... "Return, return O Shulamite. Thy belly is like a heap of wheat set about with lilies... Thy neck is as a tower of ivory... Many waters cannot quench love, neither can the floods drown it."'

He glanced up. The eyes were blazing, the whole expression of the face had changed, the brows gathered down fiercely, the cheeks as scarlet as the nose. His charcoal flew, dragging down the eyebrows. That revealing wet light on the lip, thrust out a whole inch – that, above all, *that* he must keep.

'I think, Mister Regan, I think, Luke, it might have been better if you had concentrated on the New Testament.'

By a forty-year-old reflex he glanced at the black belt around the belly to see if he still carried the strap. No time for that now. Now? Memory was now!

'Now, Brother, I begin painting.'

As he mixed his colours he cooled, a sign that he was in tiptop form. He knew they called him Luca Fa Presto. Bloody fools! You boil at the inspiration. You go cold as ice in the execution.

'You're dead right, Brother,' he said soapily. 'The new Covenant. There is the true wisdom. I learned that here in Saint Killy's.' (Funny how the old slang name came back to him. It was all creeping back to him.) 'I often think, Brother, of those wonderful words of Saint Matthew. "Behold the birds of the air . . . They sow not, neither do they reap . . . Consider the lilies of the fields . . . Even Solomon in all his glory was not arrayed like one of these."'

To his relief the mollified voice quoted back to him.

'"Behold, a greater than Solomon is here."'

He looked up at the veined nose. The tuning fork for a study in *rouge et noir*. He touched the canvas with carmine.

'Oh, a beautiful saying, Brother! A darlint saying, Brother. And so wise, Brother. So very wise.'

Not too red now, for Christ's sake. No wife, but the Past Pupils' Union would have to be pleased. And, after all, two hundred johnny-o'goblins in this job! A long silence.

'And there's another fine phrase. Muscular Christianity. A Jew invented that. Disraeli. A great man in lots of ways.'

'A Jew?' said the voice coldly.

'By the way, Brother,' he said hurriedly. 'Talking of muscle. When I was here in twenty-six, Brother, the Gaelic Football team was going great guns. How is it doing these happy days?'

The old man beamed and told him. The rest of the sitting went as smooth as milk. The only other little lurch came when he looked out at the sky, threw down his brushes, and said that the light was going.

'Can I see what you have done so far, Luke?'

He handled it with expert joviality.

'We never do, Brother, not until we've polished off the victim.'

They parted in laughter and with warm handshakes. He took the key of the parlour with him; he would be working on the lay figure in the morning.

Halligan was waiting for him in the bar; alone this time. Seeing that his glass was at low tide, Regan invited him to freshen it up.

'I won't say no. How's the masterpiece doing?'

A stocky man. Heavy hands, but they could be a craftsman's. A fawn waistcoat with brass buttons. Ruddy cheeks. A gentleman farmer? A fisherman? Not a doctor – no doctor would dare drink at a public bar in a small town like this. The wife had had the smell of money.

'He's coming back to me slowly. Another sitting and I'll have him smoked out.'

'What,' eagerly, 'are you finding?'

Regan eye-cornered him. This fellow might be a member of the Past Pupil's Union.

'A splendid character. I was just wondering did he ever teach me history?'

'Were you a senior?'

'I was only what we used to call a gyb. A Good Young Boy. I came here when I was twelve. Straight from the nuns. Our Ladies of the Holy Bower. You wouldn't think it now to look at me, but I used to be their little angel. Curly hair. They used to make me sing solo at Benediction. In a lacy surplice, purple soutane, red tie. They spoiled me. It was only by the blessing of God I didn't turn into a queer. I may tell you the change from there to here was pretty tough. I only stayed three years.'

'No, you wouldn't have had him. And,' surveying him humorously, 'you may have been a little angel, Mister Regan, but you've put on a bit of weight since then. Thirteen and a half stone? He only taught the seniors, and after he became Headmaster he had no fixed classes at all. Anyway, his particular obsession was English Grammar. He was dotty about it. He was a bit of a megalomaniac, really. Couldn't give it up. Even after he became Head he used to rove around the school from class to class leathering it into us. Of course he's retired now, but I'm told he still does it. Did he never come into your classroom to wallop *I seen* out of you and *I saw* into you?'

Halligan laughed as if in happy memory of the walloping, and, on the spot, Regan had his man whole and entire. The terror of his very first day at Saint Killy's often repeated, seeing the lean black ghost come floating in. Like a starved wolf. One hand waving the leather strap behind his back like a black tail. The rasping voice. 'What is a relative clause? What is an adverbial clause? Decline the verb *see* in the past tense. No, it is not! Hold out your hand. Take that. And that. And that.' And, always, the one thing all boys loathe in teachers, as sarcastic as acid. Oh, a proper bastard!

'Do I take it, Mister Halligan, that you didn't particularly like it at Saint Killy's?'

'I got on there all right. I was good at games. And Leatherlip was mad on games. "The Irish," he was always telling us, "are famous all over the world as sportsmen. Strong men." It was he started boxing at Saint Killy's. He used to knock the hell out of me in the ring. I got so mad at him one day that I deliberately gave him one right under the belt. And I could hit hard that time. When he got his wind back he nearly murdered me. He was the only fly in the ointment.' He leaned over and whispered: 'I often thought afterwards that he was the only wasp in the ointment.' He glanced quickly around the bar and said in a loud voice, 'Mind you, Brother Hilary is a great organizer. He built up a great school here. We are all very proud of Saint Killian's in this town.'

('Fuck *you*!' Regan thought.)

'And most justifiably so, Mister Halligan. By the way, are you a member of the Past Pupils' Union?'

Halligan smiled crookedly. His voice fell.

'I didn't tell you I'm the local vet. I look after the Jersey herd up there.' He beckoned to the barmaid. 'The same again, Miss Noble.'

'Family?' Regan asked.

'Three boys.'

'They at school here?'

Halligan shuffled his glass a bit.

'Not exactly. You see . . . Well, the fact is Valerie is a Protestant. We met at the hunt. Actually, she's a niece of Lord Boyne's.' (A good connection for a vet, Regan thought.) 'Before I married her I knew I'd have to do something to smooth the way for her. For myself, of course, I didn't give a damn. To hell with them. But for poor little Valerie . . . You live up in Dublin, you can do what you like there, you don't understand what it's like in small places like this. But,' he winked, 'there's always ways and means. Two months before I got married, do you know what I did?' He nudged and again winked. 'I joined the local Knights of Columbanus. And, by God, it worked. Though I'll never forget the first time I went to the Club after the wedding. The Grand Knight got up and he says, "Since our last meeting I suppose you all know that one of our brothers got married." Christ Almighty, I thought, here it comes! He's going to give me hell for marrying a Protestant. I'm going to be ruined for life in this place. Far from it! He complimented me most warmly. I drove home that night singing like a bird. I knew I'd done one of the smartest things in my life. After a year I dropped them. But when it came to where we'd send the boys to school, Valerie and myself had one hell of a fight. I said we simply had to send them to Saint Killy's. We started with the oldest boy. The very first day he came home from school with his two hands red as pulp from Leatherlip's strap. After that Valerie put her foot down. We came to a sensible compromise. We sent them all to school in England. One of the finest Catholic schools in the world. Nobody could object to that.'

'Very shrewd. Very wise move. And after that, no opposition? Miss Noble, fill 'em up again.'

'Not half! The day I whipped Tommy out of school Leatherlip wrote me a stinker. He went all around town saying I was a snob, and a lah-di-dah, and an Anglicized Irishman, and a toady, and God knows what else. Just to show you – it wasn't until he retired that I got the job of looking after the college herd.'

Regan laughed.

'Elephants never forget.'

'It's no joke,' Halligan whispered solemnly. 'Don't delude yourself. That man never forgets anything. Or anybody.'

'I wonder,' Regan said uncomfortably.

Just then Valerie Halligan came in. He noted that after one quick one she hauled her husband away. From her manner it was plain that she did not approve of his latest drinking companion. This time Regan did not wonder why.

Not that he had ever been much leathered by anybody at Saint Killy's, and never once by Leatherlip. On the contrary, he had often wished he would leather him after the day he called him out of the class and sat him on his knee, and said to the rest of them after he had leathered them all, 'Look at this clever little boy. He knows what a dependent clause is. And he's only twelve, and straight from the nuns, as small and fresh and rosy as a cherry. Why don't you slobs know it as well as he does?' His nickname became Cherry. They called him Leatherlip's Lapdog or Leatherlip's Pet. They used to corner him and say things like, 'Cherry, if *he* comes in today for more frigging grammar your job is to suck up to him. Get him into a good humour or he'll leather us and we'll puck the hell outa you.' He used to try, but it was always the same, 'See this bright little boy!' And, after school, they would shove him, and taunt him and puck him. Once he deliberately tried to get leathered by failing to write out six sentences that night before on *shall* and *will*. The strap swished, the brows came down, a grey spittle appeared at each corner of the big lip. Terror shook his bones.

'"I *will* go there tomorrow." Is that correct?'

'No, Brother. Plain future statements in the first person must always have *shall*.'

'"We would not win a single match with a team like that." Is that correct?'

'No, Brother. Plain conditional statements in the first person must have *should*.'

'Come here to me, boy. Now, listen to that bright little boy, straight from the nuns...'

For three years he had suffered hell from the benign approbation of that accursed old fathead.

'Miss Noble, the same again. No, make it a double this time.'

He went to bed plastered.

'Well, Brother Hilary, I hear nothing all over the town but people singing your praises. You've made a great job of this college. The doyen of Saint Killian's.' The old monk beamed softly.

'Ah, well, Luke, I've done my humble best. But, mind you,' rather less softly. 'I had to fight all the way.' Far from softly: 'Opposition. I had to keep my hand on my dagger every moment of the day.'

'Aha, but you fought well, Brother. You fought the good fight, Brother. "To give and not to count the cost, to fight and not to heed the wounds."'

'Who said that?' – suspiciously.

The lip out again with the lovely wet light on it. Porcine. Sensual. Lickerish. Loose. Deboshed by pride and righteousness. Daringly he slapped on a fleck of viridian. And, by God, it was just right. He kept him waiting for the answer.

'Saint Ignatius Loyola said that. A great body of men, the Jesuits.'

The two eyes cold. Turquoise? No! Pine-needle blue? Hell's bells, snow and ice are the one thing no Irish painter can ever get right. Nor the British. Nor the Italians. You have to live with the stuff like the Dutch and the Scans. The gore of the cheeks would have to bring it out. Cherry? Damn you, I'll give you cherry. No ablation here. Warts and all. Maxillae of an anthropomorph. Ears of a bat. That time he had to sit on his lap in class! The hair stuck out of his ears.

'Have you ever had any Protestants in Saint Killy's, Brother?'

The little finger dug into a hairy ear and wagged there twenty times.

'I don't approve of mixed marriages and I don't approve of mixed schooling. Protestants haven't our morality, Luke. The morality of every Protestant I ever met was written into his cheque-book. They are completely devoid of our mystical sense of the otherworld. Not like you and me. I don't like Protestants. You mentioned some Jew yesterday. I'll be frank with you, Luke. I don't like Jews either.'

'Oh, you're on to something there, Brother. A cunning bloody race. Very able, though. I was talking about Disraeli.' He seized his palette knife for the coarse, oily skin of the cheeks. 'Do you remember what he said the time Dan O'Connell taunted him with being a Jew. "Yes, I *am* a Jew, and when ancestors of the right honourable gentleman were brutal savages in an unknown island, mine were priests in the temple of Solomon."'

The old warhorse out on grass. Teeth bared. Sepia? Burnt sienna?

'For Heaven's sake, Luke! I do wish you'd stop talking about Solomon!'

'All the same, Jesus was a Jew.'

'One of the mysteries of the world!'

'And he chose the Jews.' Laughing delightedly at the furious face on his canvas he quoted. '"How odd/That God/Should choose/ The Jews."'

In laughter the ritual answer pealed from the throne.

'"Oh no, not odd./They hoped to God/Some day/He'd pay."'

They both cackled.

'Ah, Brother, you understand it all!'

'We understand one another, Luke. Two comrades in Christ!'

He worked on. From the distant playing fields young voices cheered. A long silence. When he looked up he saw a profile. The old man was gazing at the moony face of Christ looming through the Veil of Veronica.

'Do you know Greek, Luke? A pity! There is a wonderful Greek word. *Archiropito*. It is the perfect word for that image of Christ. Painted by no human hand. Painted by the angels. The day I became Headmaster I bought three dozen copies of that angelic image. I put one in every classroom. I gave one to every brother to hang over his bed.'

He sighed. Regan looked at the fraud. Then he looked at his portrait.

Never had he felt such a sense of power, energy, truth to life. The light was fading. 'Tomorrow is Sunday. I might do a little work on the background. Then on Monday we'll have the last sitting.'

'And then,' as eagerly as a boy, 'I can see it?'

A laggard nod. As they parted the old man put his arm around his shoulder.

'My dear friend!' He sighed affectionately. 'Take care of yourself, Luke,' who gave one backward glance at his easel; the face was virtually finished, the body half finished, the soul naked. Areas of bare canvas at the edges surrounded it all like a ragged veil.

That evening the Halligans came together, had one quick one and left, promising to call on Sunday afternoon and go out to the college for a secret look at the unfinished masterpiece. He stayed on alone. The Saturday night crowd was dense. He felt he was drinking with half the town. He was the last to leave the bar, pushed out, blind drunk, by the barman and old Noble. He took a bottle of whiskey to bed with him. He woke late. The angelus was slowly tolling and under his window hollow feet were echoing along the pavement to last mass. He drank some more and slept some more. He was wakened by the maid knocking at his door to ask him did he want to eat something. He ordered her to bring him a bottle of whiskey. When she returned she stamped the bottle distastefully on his chest of drawers and banged the door after her. Halligan came up at four, refused to drink with him, said that Valerie was waiting outside in the station wagon, helped him to dress and all but carried him downstairs. He was tolerantly amused by his stumblings and fumblings as he tried to get into the car, but Mrs Halligan was not. 'Oh, for Christ's sake!' she growled at her husband. 'He needs to be pumped!'

When they had pushed open the hall door of the college and crept cautiously across the empty hall to the parlour, she had to take the key from his helpless hand to open the door. They entered twilight. Regan dragged back the window curtains, bade Halligan switch on the light, and with one forensic arm presented them to the easel. For one minute's silence he watched Halligan's mouth fall open and his eyelids soar. Her eyelashes peered.

'God almighty!' Halligan whispered. 'You have him to a T.'

'T for Truth,' he cried triumphantly.

Halligan turned to his wife.

'What d'ye think, Valerie?'

She looked at him, she looked at Regan, she looked at the portrait. Then she edged Halligan aside, stood before the portrait, and, one hand on her hip, extended her silence to two minutes.

'Isn't it stu – PEN – dous, Valerie?'

She walked away to the window, did a tiny drum roll with her nails on the glass, turned to them and spoke, quietly, coldly and brassily.

'Don't be a damn fool, Halligan. Mister Regan! I know nothing about painting, but I know one thing, for certain, about that painting. Nobody will buy it. Not here, anyway. Are you, Halligan, going to get up in the committee of the Past Pupils' Union and say that portrait is stupendous? Vote for it? Pay for it? And hang it? And where? There's only one place in this town where you could hang that picture – in the bar of the Shamrock Hotel, where everybody would laugh their heads off at it and then go out and say it is a public disgrace. And do you think even old Noble would dare hang it? You can vote for that picture, Halligan, over my dead body – we've had trouble enough in this town and I don't want any more of it. And I'll tell you one other little thing about that picture, Mister Regan. If you show it anywhere in this country you might just as well go out and hang yourself because it would be the last portrait you'd be asked to paint as long as you live.'

Regan laughed at her.

'To hell with their money. I'll show it at the Academy. I'll sell it there for twice the price. It'll be reproduced in every paper in Dublin! In every art magazine in the world!'

Halligan looked at him with funky eyes.

'Luke!' (And if Regan had been sober he would have known at once by that use of his first name how grave the issue was.) 'Valerie is right. Listen! Would you do one thing for me, and for yourself and for God's sake. There must be a second key to this room. Anyone might come in here at any moment.' He cocked a frightened ear. 'Any second that door might open. Would you take it back to the hotel for the night, and tomorrow morning look at it calmly and coldly and make up your own mind what you're going to do about it. You know,' he wheedled, 'they might even start pawing it!'

'Pawing? Wise man! Shrewd man! Monkey, monkey,' he approved. 'See all, hear all, say nothing. Let's get it out of here.'

They restored the twilight, the hallway was as empty as before; they drove fast, back to the empty, Sunday afternoon Main Street. Outside

The Shamrock she put her head out through the window of the wagon to say, 'I'll give you one minute, Halligan, no more.' They were lucky. They met nobody on the way to the bedroom. They stood the portrait on the mantelpiece. They sat side by side on the bed and looked at the scarlet, scowling, wet-lipped face of their old master staring down at them. Halligan accepted one slug from the neck of the bottle, slapped his companion on the back, and ran for it. Regan lay back on his pillow, emptying the bottle gulp for gulp, rejoicing strabismally at the face on the mantelpiece that, like a wavering fire, slowly faded into the veils of the gathering dusk.

'*Archiropito!*' he wheezed joyfully as he drained the bottle on its head, let it fall with a crash on the ground and sank into a stupor.

It was dark when he woke. He had no sense of time, of date, of day or night. He thought he heard noises downstairs. He groped for the bell, found it and kept pressing it until the door opened and, against the light, he saw the burly figure of old Noble.

'Mishter Noble, shend me up a bottle of whishkey if you please.'

Silence. Then:

'I will do no such thing, Mister Regan. If I was to do anything I'd send for a doctor. Sleep it off.'

The door closed and he was in darkness again.

'The bitch!' he growled, knowing that she had tipped off the old man. *Must* have a drink! If only . . . Suddenly he remembered. That bottle he had bought on the way down from Dublin. Had he drunk that too? He rolled out of bed, crawled on all fours to the light switch, at last found his hold-all, and there was his golden salvation. The colours of the little map of Ireland on the label swam – purple, and red, and yellow and green. With his teeth he tore off the thin metal covering on the neck, wrested out the cork, twisting its serrated edge, lifted the bottleneck to his mouth, engorged the sweet liquor as if it were water, and sank on the floor in a coma. The maid found him there in the morning, and ran from him down the stairs, screeching.

He recovered his senses only for the few minutes during which he was being put to bed in the monastery. Hilary had him brought there immediately he was informed of his sorry condition by old Noble, then by the community's doctor who had driven him at once to the college door, wrapped in blankets, still in a stupor, his breath coming in gasps, his forehead glistening with cold dots of sweat. It took three brothers to lift him from the car and carry him upstairs to Hilary's bedroom.

Harry Halligan and Valerie Halligan, also alerted by Noble, came after them, carrying his few belongings stuffed into his suitcase and his hold-all. As they packed them, her eye roving about the room saw the portrait on the mantelpiece.

'Halligan,' she ordered. 'Take that thing down and burn it.'

He looked at her, looked at the closed door, told her to lock it, took out his clasp knife and cut the canvas from its frame. But when he approached the empty grate his nerve failed him.

'I can't do it, Valerie. It's like murder.'

She snatched it from him, tore some paper linings from the chest of drawers, crumpled the canvas on top of them in the grate, put her cigarette lighter to the paper and they watched everything burn to ashes. They drove to the college, laid his two cases inside the door, and drove rapidly down the drive for home and a couple of stiff ones. In the middle of her drink, and her abuse of him, she looked at him and laughed, remembering from her schooldays.

'"To be thus is nothing, but to be safely thus,"' jumped up to ring old Noble and warn him never to mention their names to anybody in the college about this affair.

'Rely on me,' the old voice replied. 'We're all in it together,' from which she knew that he, too, had seen the portrait.

Hilary sat by his bed during his few, limp moments of consciousness.

'My poor Luke,' fondling his icy palm. 'What on earth happened to you at all, at all?'

'Brother,' he said faintly. 'Can I have one, last little drink?'

The old man shook his head, sadly but not negatively.

'Of course you can, Luke. I'll leave you a glass of the best here beside your bed for the night. Tomorrow we'll cut it down to half a glass. Then, bit by bit, between us, with God's help,' glancing up piously at the veiled face over the bed, 'we'll wean you back to your old self.'

In the morning a young lay brother stole into the room with a nice hot cup of tea for the patient. He found the glass dry and the body an empty cell. Touched, it was like stuffed leather.

The obituaries were invariably kind. They all stressed the burned portrait, the symbol of every artist's indefatigable pursuit of unattainable perfection. They slyly recalled his convivial nature, his great thirst for friendship, the speed with which he could limn a character in a few lines, the unfailing polish of his work. But as always, it was some wag in a pub who spoke his epitaph.

'Well, poor old Lukey Fa Presto is gone from us. He wasn't much of a painter. And he had no luck. But what a beautiful way to die! In the odour.' His glass raised. All their glasses lifted. 'Of sanctity and whiskey.'

With solemn smiles they drank.

The Kitchen

I was there again last night; not, I need hardly say, deliberately. If I had my own way I would never even think of that house or that city, let alone revisit them. It was the usual pattern. I was in Cork on some family business, and my business required that I should walk past the house and, as usual, although it was the deep middle of the night the kitchen window upstairs was dimly lit, as if by a lamp turned low, the way my mother used always fix it to welcome my father home from night duty. She usually left a covered saucepan of milk beside the lamp. He would put it on the stove to heat while he shook the rain from his cape on the red tiles of the kitchen, hung his uniform on the back of the door, and put on a pair of slippers. He welcomed the hot milk. It rains a lot in Cork and the night rain can be very cold. Then, as happens in dreams, where you can walk through walls like a pure spirit and time gets telescoped, it was suddenly broad daylight, I was standing in the empty kitchen, and that young man was once again saying to me with a kindly chuckle, 'So this is what all that was about?' It was five past three in the morning when I sat up and groped wildly for the bedside light to dispel the misery of those eight dismissive words that I am apparently never going to be allowed to forget, even in my sleep.

It is a graceless lump of a house, three stories high, rhomboidal, cement-faced, built at the meeting point of a quiet side street curving out of an open square and a narrow, noisy, muddy, sunless street leading to one of the busiest parts of the city. Every day for over twenty years I used to look down into this narrow street from the kitchen window – down because of the shop beneath us on the ground floor, occupied in my childhood by a firm of electrical contractors named Cyril and Eaton. Theirs was a quiet profession. Later on, when the shop was occupied by a bootmaker we could hear his machines slapping below us all day long.

My guess is that the house was built around 1870; anyway, it had the solid, ugly, utilitarian look of the period. Not that my father and mother ever thought it ugly. They would not have known what the word meant. To them, born peasants, straight from the fields, all the word 'beautiful' meant was useful or prolific; all 'ugly' meant was useless or barren – a field that grew bad crops, a roof that leaked, a cow that gave poor milk. So, when they told us children, as they often did, that we were now living in a beautiful house all they meant was that it suited our purposes perfectly. They may also have meant something else: because they had been told that the house had originally been put up by a builder for his own use they considered it prime property, as if they had come into possession of land owned by a gentleman farmer for generations. Few things are more dear to the heart of a peasant than a clean pedigree. It keeps history at bay. Not, of course, that they owned the house, although they sometimes talked dreamily about how they would buy it someday. What a dream! Landless people, in other words people of no substance, they had already gone to the limit of daring by renting it for twenty-six pounds a year, a respectable sum in those days for a man like my father – an ordinary policeman, rank of constable, earning about thirty bob a week.

Their purpose in renting so big a place was to eke out his modest income by taking in the steady succession of lodgers who were ultimately to fill the whole house with the sole exception of the red-tiled kitchen where the six of us lived, cooked, idled or worked. I do not count as rooms the warren of attics high up under the roof where we all, including the slavey (half a crown a week and her keep), slept with nothing between us and the moon but the bare slates. Still, we were not really poor. Knowing no better life, we were content with what we had.

During some forty years this was my parents' home; for even after my brothers and I grew up and scattered to the corners of the compass, and my mother grew too old to go on keeping lodgers, and my father retired, they still held on to it. So well they might! I was looking at my father's discharge papers this morning. I find that when he retired at the age of fifty his pension was £48. 10s. 8d. a year. Fortunately he did get a part-time job as caretaker of a garage at night which brought him in another £25. 5s. 5d. a year. Any roof at ten bob a week was nicely within his means. It must also have been a heartbreak to his landlord, who could not legally increase the rent.

One day, however, about a year before I left home – I was the last of us to go – my father got a letter which threatened to end this agreeable state of affairs. When he and my mother had painstakingly digested its legal formalities they found to their horror that the bootmaker downstairs had, as the saying goes, quietly bought the house 'over their heads,' and was therefore their new landlord. Now, forty-odd years in a city, even in so small a city as Cork, can go a long way towards turning a peasant into a citizen. My father, as a lifelong member of the Royal Irish Constabulary, then admiringly called the Force, had over the years imbibed from his training and from the example of his officers, who were mostly Protestants and Gentlemen, not only a strong sense of military, I might even say of imperial, discipline but a considerable degree of urban refinement. My mother had likewise learned her own proper kind of urban ways, house-pride, such skills as cooking and dressmaking, and a great liking for pretty clothes. At times she even affected a citified accent. When they read this letter and stared at one another in fright, all this finery fell from their backs as suddenly as Cinderella's at the stroke of midnight.

They might at that moment have been two peasants from Limerick or Kerry peering timidly through the rain from the door of a thatched hovel at a landlord, or his agent, or some villainous land-grabber driving up their brambled boreen to throw them out on the side of the road to die of cold and starvation. The kitchen suddenly became noisy with words, phrases and names that, I well knew, they could not have heard since their childhood – evictions, bum bailiffs, forcible entry, rights-of-way, actions for trespass, easements, appeals, breaches of covenant, the Land Leaguers, the Whiteboys, Parnell and Captain Boycott, as if the bootmaker downstairs slept with a shotgun by his bed every night and a brace of bloodhounds outside his shop door every day.

Nothing I said to comfort them could persuade them that their bootmaker could not possibly want to evict them; or that, far from being a land-grabber, or even a house-grabber, he was just an ordinary, normal, decent hardworking, citybred businessman, with a large family of his own toiling beside him at his machines, who, if he wanted anything at all, could not conceivably want more than, say, one extra room where he could put another sewing machine or store his leather. And, in fact, as he patiently explained to my father, that was all he did want; or perhaps a little more – two rooms, and access for his girls to our private W.C. on the turn of the stairs. He must have been much surprised to find himself thrown headlong into the heart of a raging rural land war.

I left home that year, so I cannot tell if there was or was not litigation at this first stage of the battle. All I knew for certain is that after about a year and a half of argufying, both parties settled for one room and access to the W.C. The rest I was to gather and surmise from their letters to me. These conveyed that some sort of growling peace descended on everybody for about three years, towards the end of which my father died, my mother became the sole occupant, and the bootmaker, seeing that he now had only one tenant over his head, and that with expanding business he was even more cramped for space than before, renewed his request for a second room.

At once, the war broke out again, intensified now by the fact that, as my mother saw it, a bloody villain of a land-grabber, and a black Protestant to boot, was trying to throw a lonely, helpless, ailing, defenceless, solitary poor widow woman out on the side of the road to die. The bootmaker nevertheless persisted. It took him about two more years of bitter struggle to get his second room. When he got it he was in possession of the whole of the second floor of his house with the exception of the red-tiled kitchen.

Peace returned, grumbling and growling. Patiently he let another year pass. Then, in the gentlest possible words, he begged that my mother might be so kind, and so understanding, as to allow one of his girls, and only one, to enter the kitchen once a day, and only once, for the sole purpose of filling a kettle of water from the tap of her kitchen sink. There was, to be sure, he agreed, another tap downstairs in his backyard – a dank five-foot-square patch of cement – but it stood outside the male workers' outdoor W.C., and she would not, he hoped and trusted, wish any girl to be going out there to get water for her poor little cup of tea? I am sure it was the thought of the girl's poor little cup of tea that softened my mother's heart. She royally granted the humane permission, and at once began to regret it.

She realized that she had given the black villain a toehold into her kitchen and foresaw that the next thing he would want would be to take it over completely. She was right. I can only infer that as the bootmaking business went on expanding, so did the bootmaker's sense of the value of time. At any rate he was soon pointing out to my mother that it was a dreadful expense to him, and a hardship to his staff, to have to close his shop for an hour and a half every day while his workers, including his family, trudged home, in all weathers, some of them quite a long distance, for their midday meal. If he had the kitchen they could eat their lunch, dryshod and in comfort, inside half an hour. He entered a formal request for the kitchen.

Looking back at it now, after the passage of well over a quarter of a century, I can see clearly enough that he thought he was making a wholly reasonable request. After all, in addition to her kitchen my mother still possessed the third floor of the house, containing three fine rooms and a spacious bathroom. One of those rooms could become her kitchen, another remain her bedroom, and the third and largest, which she never used, would make a splendid living room, overlooking the square's pleasant enclosure of grass and shrubs, and commanding an open view up to the main thoroughfare of the city – all in all as desirable an apartment, by any standards, as thousands of home-hungry Corkonians would have given their ears to possess.

Unfortunately, if I did decide to think his request reasonable, what I would have to forget, and what he completely failed to reckon with, was that there is not a peasant widow woman from the mountains of west Cork to the wilds of Calabria who does not feel her kitchen as the pulse and centre of her being as a wife and a mother. That red-tiled kitchen had been my mother's nest and nursery, her fireside where she prayed every morning, her chimney corner where she rested every night, the sanctum sanctorum of all her belongings, a place whose every stain and smell, spiderweb and mousehole, crooked nail and cracked cup made it the ark of the covenant that she had kept through forty years of sweat and struggle for her lost husband and her scattered children.

Besides, if she lost her kitchen what would she do when the Bottle Woman came, to buy empty bottles at a halfpenny apiece? This was where she always brought her to sit and share a pot of tea and argue over the bottles and talk about the secret doings of Cork. Where could she talk with the Dead Man, collecting her funeral insurance at sixpence a week, if she did not have her warm, red-eyed range where he could take off his damp boots and warm his feet in the oven while she picked him dry of all the gossip of the narrow street beneath her window? She had never in her life locked the front door downstairs except at night. Like the door of any country cottage it was always on the latch for any one of her three or four cronies to shove open and call out to her, 'Are ye there, can I come up?' – at which she would hear their footsteps banging on the brass edgings of the stairs while she hastily began to poke the fire in the range, and fill the kettle for the tea, or stir the pot of soup on the range in preparation for a cosy chat. All her life her neighbours had dropped like that into her kitchen. They would be insulted if she did not invite them into her kitchen. She would not have a crony in the world without her kitchen. Knowing nothing of all this, the bootmaker could argue himself hoarse with her, plead and wheedle with her to accept the shiniest, best-equipped, most modern American-style kitchenette, run by electricity, all white and gleaming chromium. Even if it was three stories up from the hall door it seemed to him a marvellous exchange for this battered old cave downstairs where she crouched over a range called the Prince Albert, where the tiles were becoming loose, where he could see nothing to look at but a chipped sink, one chair, a table, one cupboard, a couple of old wooden shelves, and a sofa with the horsehair coming out of it like a moustache. He might just as well have said to a queen, 'Give me your throne and I'll leave you the palace.' While as for proposing as an alternative that she could keep her old kip of a kitchen if she would only let him make a proper kitchen upstairs for himself, his family and his workers . . .

'Aha, nah!' she would cry at me whenever I visited her; and the older and angrier she became the more did her speech revert to the flat accent of her flat West Limerick, with is long vanishing versts of greasy limestone roads, its fields of rusty reeds, its wind-rattling alders, and its low rain clouds endlessly trailing their Atlantic hair across the sodden plain. 'Is it to take me in the rear he wants to now? To lock me up in the loft? To grind me like corn meal between the upstairs and the downstairs? A room? And then another room? And after that another? And then what? When he'd have me surrounded with noise, and shmoke, and shmells, and darkness and a tick-tack-turrorum all day long? Aha. My mother, and my grandmother before her didn't fight the landlords, and the agents, and the helmeted peelers with their grey guns and their black battering rams for me to pull down the flag now! It's a true word, God knows it, them Proteshtants wouldn't give you as much as a dry twig in a rotten wood to light your pipe with it. Well and well do I remember the time ould foxy-whiskers, Mister Woodley the parson, died of the grippe away back in Crawmore, and my uncle Phil stole out the night after his funeral to cut a log in his wood! While he was sawing it didn't the moon come out from behind a cloud, and who do you think was sitting on the end of the log looking at him out of his foxy eyes? Out of my kitchen I will not stir until ye carry me out on a board to lie in the clay beside my poor Dinny. And not one single minit before.'

Which was exactly what happened, six years later.

All in all, from start to finish, my mother's land war must have lasted nearly fourteen years. But what is fourteen years to an old woman whose line and stock clung by their fingernails to their last sour bits of earth for four centuries? I am quite sure the poor bootmaker never understood to the day of his death the nerve of time he had so unwittingly touched.

After the funeral it was my last task to empty the house, to shovel away – there is no other word for it – her life's last lares and penates to a junk dealer for thirty shillings. When it was all done I was standing alone in the empty kitchen, where I used to do my homework every evening as a boy, watching her cooking or baking, making or mending, or my father cobbling a pair of shoes for one of us, or sitting at his ease, smoking his pipe, in his favourite straw-bottomed chair, in his grey constabulary shirt, reading the racing news in the pink *Cork Evening Echo*.

As I stood there I suddenly became aware that a young man was standing in the doorway. He was the bootmaker's son. Oddly enough, I had never spoken to his father, although years ago I had seen him passing busily in and out of his shop, always looking worn and worried, but I had once met this son of his in the mountains of west Cork – fishing? shooting? – and I had found him a most friendly and attractive young fellow. He came forward now, shook hands with me in a warm, manly way and told me how sorry he was for me in my bereavement.

'Your mother was a grand old warrior,' he said, in genuine admiration. 'My father always had the greatest respect for her.'

We chatted about this and that for a while. Then, for a moment, we both fell silent while he looked curiously around the bare walls. He chuckled tolerantly, shook his head several times and said, 'So this is what all that was about?'

At those eight words, so kindly meant, so good-humoured, so tolerant, so uncomprehending, a shock of weakness flowed up through me like defeat until my head began to reel and my eyes were swimming.

It was quite true that there was nothing for either of us to see but a red-tiled floor, a smoke-browned ceiling and four tawny distempered walls bearing some brighter patches where a few pictures had hung and the cupboard and the sofa used to stand. The wall to our right had deposited at its base a scruff of distemper like dandruff. The wall to our left gaped at us with parched mouths. He smiled up at the flyspotted bulb in the ceiling. He touched a loose tile with his toe and sighed deeply. All that! About this? And yet, only a few hours before, when I had looked down at her for the last time, withdrawn like a snail into her shrivelled house, I had suddenly found myself straining, bending, listening as if, I afterwards thought, I had been staring into the perspective of a tunnel of time, much as I stared now at him, at one with him in his bewilderment.

I thought I had completely understood what it was all about that morning years ago when they read that letter and so pathetically, so embarrassingly, even so comically revealed their peasants' terror at the power of time. I had thought the old bootmaker's mistake had been his failure to understand the long fuse he had so unwittingly lighted. But now – staring at this good-humoured young man who, if I had said all this to him, would at once have understood and have at once retorted, 'But even so!' – I realized that they, and that, and this, and he and I were all caught in something beyond reason and time. In a daze I shook hands with him again, thanked him again for his sympathy, and handed him the keys of victory. I was still dazed as I sat in the afternoon train for Dublin, facing the mile-long tunnel that burrows underneath the city out to the light and air of the upper world. As it slowly began to slide into the tunnel I swore that I would never return.

Since then I must have gone back there forty times, sometimes kidnapped by her, sometimes by my father, sometimes by an anonymous rout of shadowy creatures out of a masked ball, and sometimes it is not at all the city I once knew but a fantastically beautiful place of great squares and pinnacled, porphyry buildings with snowy ships drawing up beside marble quays. But, always, whatever the order of my guides, captors or companions, I find myself at the end alone in a narrow street, dark except for its single window and then, suddenly, it is broad daylight and I am in our old kitchen hearing that young man say in his easy way, 'So this is what all that was about?' and I start awake in my own dark, babbling, clawing for the switch. As I sit up in bed I can never remember what it was that I had been babbling, but I do understand all over again what it was all about. It was all about the scratching mole. In her time, when she heard it she refused to listen, just as I do when, in my turn, I hear her velvet burrowing, softer than sand crumbling or snow tapping, and I know well whose whispering I had heard and what she had been saying to me.

She was a grand old warrior. She fought her fight to a finish. She was entirely right in everything she did. I am all for her. Still, when I switch on the bulb over my head I do it only to banish her, to evict her, to push her out of *my* kitchen, and I often lie back to sleep under its bright light lest I should again hear her whispering to me in the dark.

The Faithless Wife

He had now been stalking his beautiful Mlle Morphy, whose real name was Mrs Meehawl O'Sullivan, for some six weeks, and she had appeared to be so amused at every stage of the hunt, so responsive, *entrainante*, even *aguichante*, that he could already foresee the kill over the next horizon. At their first encounter, during the Saint Patrick's Day cocktail party at the Dutch embassy, accompanied by a husband who had not a word to throw to a cat about anything except the scissors and shears that he manufactured somewhere in the West of Ireland, and who was obviously quite ill at ease and drank too much Irish whiskey, what had attracted him to her was not only her splendid Boucher figure (whence his sudden nickname for her, La Morphée), or her copper-coloured hair, her lime-green Irish eyes and her seemingly poreless skin, but her calm, total and subdued elegance: the Balenciaga costume, the peacock-skin gloves, the gleaming crocodile handbag, a glimpse of tiny, lace-edged lawn handkerchief and her dry, delicate scent. He had a grateful eye and nose for such things. It was, after all, part of his job. Their second meeting, two weeks later, at his own embassy, had opened the doors. She came alone.

Now, at last, inside a week, perhaps less, there would be an end to all the probationary encounters that followed – mostly her inventions, at his persistent appeals – those wide-eyed fancy-meeting-you-heres at the zoo, at race-meetings, afternoon cinemas, in art galleries, at more diplomatic parties (once he had said gaily to her, 'The whole diplomacy of Europe seems to circle around our interest in one another'), those long drives over the Dublin mountains in his Renault coupé, those titillating rural lunches, nose to nose, toe to toe (rural because she quickly educated him to see Dublin as a stock exchange for gossip, a casino of scandal), an end, which was rather a pity, to those charming unforeseen-foreseen, that is to say proposed but in the end just snatched, afternoon *promenades champêtres* under the budding leaves and closing skies of the Phoenix Park, with the first lights of the city springing up below them to mark the end of another boring day for him in Ailesbury Road, Dublin's street of embassies, for her another possibly cosier but, he selfishly hoped, not much more exciting day in her swank boutique on Saint Stephen's Green. Little by little those intimate encounters, those murmured confessions had lifted acquaintance to friendship, to self-mocking smiles over some tiny incident during their last meeting, to eager anticipation of the next, an aimless tenderness twanging to appetite like an arrow. Or, at least, that was how he felt about it all. Any day now, even any hour, the slow countdown, slower than the slow movement of Mendelssohn's Concerto in E Minor, or the most swoony sequence from the Siegfried Idyll, or that floating spun-sugar balloon of Mahler's 'Song of the Earth,' to the music of which on his gramophone he would imagine her smiling sidelong at him as she softly disrobed, and his ingenious playing with her, his teasing and warming of her moment by moment for the roaring, blazing takeoff. To the moon!

Only one apprehension remained with him, not a real misgiving, something nearer to a recurring anxiety. It was that at the last moments when her mind and her body ought to take leave of one another she might take to her heels. It was a fear that flooded him whenever, with smiles too diffident to reassure him, she would once again mention that she was a Roman Catholic, or a Cat, a Papist or a Pape, a convent girl, and once she laughed that during her schooldays in the convent she had actually been made an *Enfant de Marie*. The words never ceased to startle him, dragging him back miserably to his first sexual frustration with his very pretty but unexpectedly proper cousin Berthe Ohnet during his lycée years in Nancy; a similar icy snub a few years later in Quebec; repeated still later by that smack on the face in Rio that almost became a public scandal; memories so painful that whenever an attractive woman nowadays mentioned religion, even in so simple a context as, 'Thank God I didn't buy that hat, or frock, or stock, or mare,' a red flag at once began to flutter in his belly.

Obsessed, every time she uttered one of those ominous words he rushed for the reassurance of what he called The Sherbet Test, which meant observing the effect on her of some tentatively sexy joke, like the remark of the young princess on tasting her first sherbet:— 'Oh, how absolutely delicious! But what a pity it isn't a sin!' To his relief she not only always laughed merrily at his stories but always capped them, indeed at times so startling him by her coarseness that it only occurred to him quite late in their day that this might be her way of showing her distaste for his diaphanous indelicacies. He had once or twice observed that priests, peasants and children will roar with laughter at some scavenger joke, and growl at even a veiled reference to a thigh. Was she a child of nature? Still, again and again back would come those disturbing words. He could have understood them from a prude, but what on earth did *she* mean by them? Were they so many herbs to season her desire with pleasure in her naughtiness? Flicks of nasty puritan sensuality to whip her body over some last ditch of indecision? It was only when the final crisis came that he wondered if this might not all along have been her way of warning him that she was neither a light nor a lecherous woman, neither a flirt nor a flibbertigibbet, that in matters of the heart she was *une femme très sérieuse*.

He might have guessed at something like it much earlier. He knew almost from the first day that she was *bien élevée*, her father a judge of the Supreme Court, her uncle a monsignor at the Vatican, a worldly, sport-loving, learned, contriving priest who had persuaded her papa to send her for a finishing year to Rome with the Sisters of the Sacred Heart at the top of the Spanish Steps; chiefly, it later transpired, because the convent was near the *centre hippique* in the Borghese Gardens and it was his right reverend's opinion that no Irish girl could possibly be said to have completed her education until she had learned enough about horses to ride to hounds. She had told him a lot, and most amusingly, about this uncle. She had duly returned from Rome to Dublin, and whenever he came over for the hunting, he always rode beside her. This attention had mightily flattered her until she discovered that she was being used as a cover for his uncontrollable passion for Lady Kinvara and Loughrea, then the master, some said the mistress, of the Clare-Galway hounds.

'How old were you then?' Ferdy asked, fascinated.

'I was at the university. Four blissful, idling years. But I got my degree. I was quick. And,' she smiled, 'good-looking. It helps, even with professors.'

'But riding to hounds as a student?'

'Why not? In Ireland everybody does. Children do. You could ride to hounds on a plough horse if you had nothing else. So long as you keep out of the way of real hunters. I only stopped after my marriage, when

I had a miscarriage. And I swear that was only because I was thrown.'

A monsignor who was sport-loving, worldly and contriving. He understood, and approved, and it explained many things about her.

The only other ways in which her dash, beauty and gaiety puzzled and beguiled him were trivial. Timid she was not, she was game for any risk. But the coolness of her weather eye often surprised him.

'The Leopardstown Races? Oh, what a good idea, Ferdy! Let's meet there... The Phoenix Park Races? No, not there. Too many doctors showing off their wives and their cars, trying to be noticed. And taking notice. Remember, a lot of my college friends married doctors... No, not *that* cinema. It has become vogueish... In fact, no cinema on the south side of the river. What we want is a good old fleabitten picture house on the north side where they show nothing but westerns and horrors, and where the kids get in on Saturday mornings for thruppence... Oh, and do please only ring the boutique in an emergency. Girls gossip.'

Could she be calculating? For a second of jealous heat he wondered if she could possibly have another lover. Cooling, he saw that if he had to keep a wary eye in his master's direction she had to think of her bourgeois clientele. Besides, he was a bachelor, and would remain one. She had to manage her inexpressibly dull, if highly successful old scissors and shears manufacturer, well past fifty and probably as suspicious as he was boring; so intensely, so exhaustingly boring that the only subject about which she could herself nearly become boring was in her frequent complaints about his boringness. Once she *was* frightening – when she spat out that she had hated her husband ever since the first night of their marriage when he brought her for their honeymoon – it was odd how long, and how intensely this memory had rankled – not, as he had promised, to Paris, but to his bloody scissors and shears factory in the wet wilds of northern Donegal. ('Just me dear, haha, to let 'em see, haha, t'other half of me scissors.')

Ferdy had of course never asked her why she had married such a cretin; not after sizing up her house, her furniture, her pictures, her clothes, her boutique. Anyway, only another cretin would discourage any pretty woman from grumbling about her husband: (a) because such grumblings give a man a chance to show what a deeply

sympathetic nature he has, and (b) because the information inciden-
tally supplied helps one to arrange one's assignations in places and at
times suitable to all concerned.

Adding it all up (he was a persistent adder-upper) only one problem
had so far defeated him: that he was a foreigner and did not know what
sort of women Irish women are. It was not as if he had not done his
systematic best to find out, beginning with a course of reading through
the novels of her country. A vain exercise. With the exception of the
Molly Bloom of James Joyce the Irish Novel had not only failed to
present him with any fascinating woman but it had presented him
with, in his sense of the word, no woman at all. Irish fiction was a lot
of nineteenth-century *connerie* about half-savage Brueghelesque
peasants, or urban *petits fonctionnaires* who invariably solved their
frustrations by getting drunk on religion, patriotism or undiluted
whiskey, or by taking flight to England. Pastoral melodrama. (Giono
at his worst.) Or pastoral humbuggery. (Bazin at his most sentimental.) Or, at its best, pastoral lyricism. (Daudet and rosewater.) As for
Molly Bloom! He enjoyed the smell of every kissable pore of her
voluptuous body without for one moment believing that she had ever
existed. James Joyce in drag.

'But,' he had finally implored his best friend in Ailesbury Road,
Hamid Bey, the third secretary of the Turkish embassy, whose amorous
secrets he willingly purchased with his own, 'if it is too much to expect
Ireland to produce a bevy of Manons, Mitsous, Gigis, Claudines,
Kareninas, Oteros, Leahs, San Severinas, what about those great-
thighed, vast-bottomed creatures dashing around the country on
horseback like Diana followed by all her minions? Are they not
interested in love? And if so why aren't there novels about them?'

His friend laughed as toughly as Turkish Delight and replied in
English in his laziest Noel Coward drawl, all the vowels frontal as if
he were talking through bubble gum, all his r's either left out where
they should be, as in *deah* or *cleah*, or inserted where they should not
be, as in *India-r* or *Iowa-r*.

'My deah Ferdy, did not your deah fatheh or your deah mamma-r
eveh tell you that all Irish hohsewomen are in love with their hohses?
And anyway it is well known that the favourite pin-up gihl of Ahland
is a gelding.'

'Naked?' Ferdinand asked coldly, and refused to believe him,
remembering that his beloved had been a hohsewoman, and satisfied

that he was not a gelding. Instead, he approached the Italian ambassador at a cocktail party given by the Indonesian embassy to whisper to him about *l'amore irlandese* in his best stage French, and stage French manner, eyebrows lifted above fluttering eyelids, voice as hoarse as, he guessed, His Excellency's mind would be on its creaking way back to memories of Gabin, Jouvet, Brasseur, Fernandel, Yves Montand. It proved to be another futile exercise. His Ex groaned as operatically as every Italian groans over such vital, and lethal, matters as the Mafia, food, taxation and women, threw up his hands, made a face like a more than usually desiccated De Sica and sighed, 'Les femmes d'Irlande? Mon pauvre gars! Elles sont d'une chasteté...' He paused and roared the adjective, '... FORMIDABLE!'

Ferdinand had heard this yarn about feminine chastity in other countries and (with those two or three exceptions already mentioned), found it true only until one had established the precise local variation of the meaning of 'chastity.' But how was he to discover the Irish variation? In the end it was Celia herself who, unwittingly, revealed it to him and in doing so dispelled his last doubts about her susceptibility, inflammability and volatility – despite the very proper Sisters of the Spanish Steps.

The revelation occurred one night in early May – her Meehawl being away in the West, presumably checking what she contemptuously called his Gaelic-squeaking scissors. Ferdy had driven her back to his flat for a nightcap after witnessing the prolonged death of Mimi in *La Bohème*. She happened to quote to him Oscar Wilde's remark about the death of Little Nell that only a man with a heart of stone could fail to laugh at it, and in this clever vein they had continued for a while over the rolling brandy, seated side by side on his settee, his hand on her bare shoulder leading him to hope more and more fondly that this might be his Horizon Night, until, suddenly, she asked him a coldly probing question.

'Ferdy! Tell me exactly why we did not believe in the reality of Mimi's death.'

His palm oscillated gently between her clavicle and her scapula.

'Because, my little cabbage, we were not expected to. Singing away like a lark? With her last breath? And no lungs? I am a Frenchman. I understand the nature of reality and can instruct you about it. Art, my dear Celia, is art because it is not reality. It does not copy or represent nature. It improves upon it. It embellishes it. This is the kernel of the classical French attitude to life. And,' he beamed at her, 'to love. We make of our wildest feelings of passion the gentle art of love.'

He suddenly stopped fondling her shoulder and surveyed her with feelings of chagrin and admiration. The sight of her belied his words. Apart from dressing with taste, and, he felt certain, undressing with even greater taste, she used no art at all. She was as innocent of makeup as a peasant girl of the Vosges. Had he completely misread her? Was she that miracle, a fully ripe peach brought into the centre of the city some twenty years ago from a walled garden in the heart of the country, still warm from the sun, still glowing, downy, pristine, innocent as the dew? He felt her juice dribbling down the corner of his mouth. Was this the missing piece of her jigsaw? An ensealed innocence? If so he had wasted six whole weeks. This siege could last six years.

'No, Ferdy!' she said crossly. 'You have it all wrong. I'm talking about life, not about art. The first and last thought of any real Italian girl on her deathbed would be to ask for a priest. She was facing her God.'

God at once pointed a finger at him through the chandelier, and within seconds they were discussing love among the English, Irish, French, Indians, Moslems, Italians, naturally the Papacy, Alexander the Sixth and incest, Savonarola and dirty pictures, Joan of Arc and martyrdom, death, sin, hellfire, Cesare Borgia who, she insisted, screamed for a priest to pray for him at the end.

'A lie,' he snarled, 'that some beastly priest told you in a sermon when you were a schoolgirl. Pray! I suppose,' he challenged furiously, 'you pray even against me.'

Abashed, she shook her autumn-brown head at him, threw a kipper-eyed glance up to the chandelier, gave him a ravishingly penitential smile, and sighed like an unmasked sinner.

'Ah, Ferdy! Ferdy! If you only knew the real truth about me! Me pray against you? I don't pray at all. You remember Mimi's song at the end of the first act? "I do not always go to Mass, but I pray quite a bit to the good Lord." Now, I hedge my bets in a very different way. I will not pray because I refuse to go on my knees to anybody. Yet, there I go meekly trotting off to Mass every Sunday and holy day. And why? Because I am afraid not to, because it would be a mortal sin not to.' She gripped his tensed hand, trilling her r's over the threshold of her lower lip and tenderly umlauting her vowels. Dürling. Cöward. Li-er. 'Amn't I the weak cöward, dürling? Amn't I the awful li-er? A crook entirrrely?'

Only a thin glint of streetlight peeping between his curtains witnessed the wild embrace of a man illuminated by an avowal so patently bogus as to be the transparent truth.

'You a liar?' he gasped, choking with laughter. 'You a shivering coward? A double-faced hedger of bets? A deceiving crook? A wicked sinner? For the last five minutes you have been every single one of them by pretending to be them. What you really are is a woman full of cool, hard-headed discretion, which you would like to sell to me as a charming weakness. Full of dreams that you would like to disguise as wicked lies. Of common sense that it suits you to pass off as crookedness. Of worldly wisdom still moist from your mother's nipple that, if you thought you would get away with the deception, you would stoop to call a sin. My dearest Celia, your yashmak reveals by pretending to conceal. Your trick is to be innocence masquerading as villainy. I think it is enchanting.'

For the first time he saw her in a rage.

'But it is *all* true. I *am* a liar. I *do* go to Mass every Sunday. I do *not* pray. I *am* afraid of damnation. I . . .'

He silenced her with three fingers laid momentarily on her lips.

'Of course you go to Mass every Sunday. My father, a master tailor of Nancy, used to go to Mass every Sunday not once but three times, and always as conspicuously as possible. Why? Because he was a tailor, just as you run a boutique. You don't pray? Sensible woman. Why should you bother your *bon Dieu*, if there is a *bon Dieu*, with your pretty prattle about things that He knew all about one billion years before you were a wink in your mother's eye? My dearest and perfect love, you have told me everything about Irishwomen that I need to know. None of you says what you think. Every one of you means what you don't say. None of you thinks about what she is going to do. But every one of you knows it to the last dot. You dream like opium eaters and your eyes are as calm as resting snow. You are all of you realists to your bare backsides. Yes, yes, yes, yes, yes, you will say this is true of all women, but it is not. It is not even true of Frenchwomen. They may be realists in lots of things. In love, they are just as stupid as all the rest of us. But not Irishwomen! Or not, I swear it, if they are all like you. I'll prove it to you with a single question. Would you, like Mimi, live for the sake of love in a Paris garret?'

She gravely considered a proposition that sounded delightfully like a proposal.

'How warm would the garret be? Would I have to die of tuberculosis? You remember how the poor Bohemian dramatist had to burn his play to keep them all from being famished with the cold.'

'Yes! Ferdy laughed. 'And as the fire died away he said, "I always knew that last act was too damned short." But you are dodging my question.'

'I suppose, dürling, any woman's answer to your question would depend on how much she was in love with whoever he was. Or wouldn't it?'

Between delight and fury he dragged her into his arms.

'You know perfectly well, you sweet slut, that what I am asking you is, "Do you love me a lot or a little? A garretful or a palaceful?" Which is it?'

Chuckling she slid down low in the settee and smiled up at him between sleepycat eyelashes.

'And you, Ferdy, must know perfectly well that it is pointless to ask any woman silly questions like that. If some man I loved very much were to ask me, "Do you love me, Celia?" I would naturally answer, "No!", in order to make him love me more. And if it was some man I did not like at all I would naturally say, "Yes, I love you so much I think we ought to get married," in order to cool him off. Which, Ferdy, do you want me to say to you?'

'Say,' he whispered adoringly, 'that you hate me beyond the tenth circle of Dante's hell.'

She made a grave face.

'I'm afraid, Ferdy, the fact is I don't like you at all. Not at all! Not one least little bit at all, at all.'

At which lying, laughing, enlacing and unlacing moment they kissed pneumatically and he knew that if all Irishwomen were Celias then the rest of mankind were mad ever to have admired women of any other race.

Their lovemaking was not as he had foredreamed it. She hurled her clothes to the four corners of the room, crying out, 'And about time too! Ferdy, what the hell have you been fooling around for during the last six weeks?' Within five minutes she smashed him into bits. In her passion she was more like a lion than a lioness. There was nothing about her either titillating or erotic, indolent or indulgent, as wild, as animal, as unrestrained, as simple as a forest fire. When, panting beside her, he recovered enough breath to speak he expressed his surprise that one so cool, so ladylike in public could be so different in private. She grunted peacefully and said in her muted brogue, 'Ah, shure, dürling, everything changes in the beddaroom.'

He woke at three twenty-five in the morning with that clear bang so familiar to everybody who drinks too much after the chimes of midnight, rose to drink a pint of cold water, lightly opened his curtains to survey the pre-dawn May sky and, turning towards the bed, saw the pallid streetlamp's light fall across her sleeping face, as calm, as soothed, as innocently sated as a baby filled with its mother's milk. He sat on the side of the bed looking down at her for a long time, overcome by the terrifying knowledge that, for the first time in his life, he had fallen in love.

The eastern clouds were growing as pink as petals while they drank the coffee he had quietly prepared. Over it he arranged in unnecessarily gasping whispers for their next meeting the following afternoon—'*This* afternoon!' he said joyously – at three twenty-five, henceforth his Mystic Hour for Love, but only on the strict proviso that he would not count on her unless she had set three red geraniums in a row on the windowsill of her boutique before three o'clock and that she, for her part, must divine a tragedy if the curtains of his flat were not looped high when she approached at three twenty o'clock. He could, she knew, have more easily checked with her by telephone, but also knowing how romantically, voluptuously, erotically minded he was she accepted with an indulgent amusement what he obviously considered ingenious devices for increasing the voltage of passion by the trappings of conspiracy. To herself she thought, 'Poor boy! He's been reading too many dirty books.'

Between two o'clock and three o'clock that afternoon she was entertained to see him pass her boutique three times in dark glasses. She cruelly made him pass a fourth time before, precisely at three o'clock, she gave him the pleasure of seeing two white hands with pink fingernails – not, wickedly, her own: her assistant's – emerge from under the net curtains of her window to arrange three small scarlet geraniums on the sill. He must have hastened perfervidly to the nearest florist to purchase the pink roses whose petals – when she rang his bell five cruel moments after his Mystic Hour – she found (to her tolerant amusement at his boyish folly) tessellating the silk sheets of his bed. His gramophone, muted by a bath towel, was murmuring Wagner. A joss stick in a brass bowl stank cloyingly. He had cast a pink silk headscarf over the bedside lamp. His dressingtable mirror had been tilted so that from where they lay they could see themselves. Within five minutes he neither saw, heard nor smelled anything, tumbling, falling, hurling headlong to consciousness of her mocking laughter at the image of her bottom mottled all over by his clinging rose petals. It cost him a brutal effort to laugh at himself.

All that afternoon he talked only of flight, divorce and remarriage. To cool him she encouraged him. He talked of it again and again every time they met. Loving him she humoured him. On the Wednesday of their third week as lovers they met briefly and chastely because her Meehawl was throwing a dinner at his house that evening for a few of his business colleagues previous to flying out to Manchester for a two-day convention of cutlers. Ferdy at once promised her to lay in a store of champagne, caviar, *pàté de foie* and brioches so that they need not stir from their bed for the whole of those two days.

'Not even once?' she asked coarsely, and he made a moue of disapproval.

'You do not need to be all that realistic, Celia!'

Already by three fifteen that Thursday afternoon he was shuffling nervously from window to window. By three twenty-five he was muttering, 'I hope she's not going to be late.' He kept feeling the champagne to be sure it was not getting too cold. At three thirty-five he moaned, 'She *is* late!' At three forty he cried out in a jealous fury, glaring up and down the street, 'The slut is betraying me!' At a quarter to four his bell rang, he leaped to the door. She faced him as coldly as a newly carved statue of Carrara marble. She repulsed his arms. She would not stir beyond his doormat. Her eyes were dilated by fear.

'It is Meehawl!' she whispered.

'He has found us out?'

'It's the judgment of God on us both!'

The word smacked his face.

'He is dead?' he cried hopefully, brushing aside fear and despair.

'A stroke.'

She made a violent, downward swish with the side of her open palm.

'*Une attaque? De paralysie?*'

'He called at the boutique on his way to the plane. He said goodbye to me. He walked out to the taxi. I went into my office to prepare my vanity case and do peepee before I met you. The taxi driver ran in shouting that he had fallen in a fit on the pavement. We drove him to 96. That's Saint Vincent's. The hospital near the corner of the Green. He is conscious. But he cannot speak. One side of him is paralysed. He may not live. He has had a massive coronary.'

She turned and went galloping down the stairs.

His immediate rebound was to roar curses on all the gods that never were. Why couldn't the old fool have his attack next week? His second thought was glorious. 'He will die, we will get married.' His third made him weep, 'Poor little cabbage!' His fourth thought was, 'The brioches I throw out, the rest into the fridge.' His fifth, sixth and seventh were three Scotches while he rationally considered all her possible reactions to the brush of the dark angel's wing. Only Time, he decided, would tell.

But when liars become the slaves of Time what can Time do but lie like them? A vat solid-looking enough for old wine, it leaks at every stave. A ship rigged for the wildest seas, it is rustbound to its bollards on the quay. She said firmly that nothing between them could change. He refuted her. Everything had changed, and for the better. He rejoiced when the doctors said their patient was doomed. After two more weeks she reported that the doctors were impressed by her husband's remarkable tenacity. He spoke of Flight. She now spoke of Time. One night as she lay hot in his arms in his bed he shouted triumphantly to the chandelier that when husbands are imprisoned lovers are free. She demurred. She could never spend a night with him in her own bed; not with a resident housekeeper upstairs. He tossed it aside. What matter where they slept! He would be happy sleeping with her in the Phoenix Park. She pointed out snappishly that it was raining. 'Am I a seal?' He proffered her champagne. She confessed the awful truth. This night was the last night they could be together anywhere.

'While he was dying, a few of his business pals used to call on him at the Nursing Home – the place all Dublin knows as 96. Now that the old devil is refusing to die they refuse to call on him anymore. I am his only faithful visitor. He so bores everybody. And with his paralysed mouth they don't know what the hell he is saying. Do you realize, Ferdy, what this means? He is riding me like a nightmare. Soaking me up like blotting paper. He rang me four times the day before yesterday at the boutique. He rang again while I was here with you having a drink. He said whenever I go out I must leave a number where he can call me. The night before last he rang me at three o'clock in the morning. Thank God I was back in my own bed and not here with you. He said he was lonely. Has terrible dreams. That the nights are long. That he is frightened. That if he gets another stroke he will die. Dürling! I can never spend a whole night with you again!'

Ferdy became Napoleon. He took command of the campaign. He accompanied her on her next visit to 96. This, he discovered, was a luxury (i.e., Victorian) nursing home in Lower Leeson Street, where cardinals died, coal fires were in order, and everybody was presented with a menu from which to choose his lunch and dinner. The carpets were an inch thick. The noisiest internal sound heard was the Mass bell tinkling along the corridors early every morning as the priest went from room to room with the Eucharist for the dying faithful. The Irish, he decided, know how to die. Knowing no better, he bore with him copies of *Le Canard Enchaîné*, *La Vie Parisienne*, and *Playboy*. Celia deftly impounded them. 'Do you want him to die of blood pressure? Do you want the nuns to think he's an Irish queer? A fellow who prefers women to drink?' Seated at one side of the bed, facing her seated at the other, he watched her, with her delicate lace-edged handkerchief (so disturbingly reminiscent of her lace-edged panties) wiping the unshaven chin of the dribbling half-idiot on the pillow. In an unconsumed rage he lifted his eyebrows into his hair, surveyed the moving mass of clouds above Georgian Dublin, smoothened his already blackboard-smooth hair, gently touched the white carnation in his lapel, forced himself to listen calmly to the all-but-unintelligible sounds creeping from the dribbling corner of the twisted mouth in the unshaven face of the revolting cretin on the pillow beneath his eyes, and agonizingly asked himself by what unimaginably devious machinery, and for what indivinable purpose the universe had been so arranged since the beginning of Time that this bronze-capped, pastel-eyed, rosy-breasted, round-buttocked, exquisite flower of paradise sitting opposite to him should, in the first place, have matched and mated with this slob between them, and then, or rather *and then*, or rather AND THEN make it so happen that he, Ferdinand Louis Jean-Honoré Clichy, of 9 *bis* rue des Dominicains, Nancy, in the Department of Moselle et Meurthe, population 133,532, altitude 212 metres, should happen to discover her in remote Dublin, and fall so utterly into her power that if he were required at that particular second to choose between becoming Ambassador to the Court of Saint James's for life and one night alone in bed with her he would have at once replied, 'Even for one hour!'

He gathered that the object on the pillow was addressing him.

'Oh, Mosheer! Thacks be to the ever cliving and cloving Gog I khav mosht devote clittle wife in all Khlistendom... I'd be chlost without her... Ah, Mosheer! If you ever dehide to marry, marry an Irikhwoman... Mosht fafeful cleatures in all exhishtench... Would any Frenchwoman attend shoopid ole man chlike me the way Chelia doesh?'

Ferdy closed his eyes. She was tenderly dabbing the spittled corners of the distorted mouth. What happened next was that a Sister took Celia out to the corridor for a few private words and that Ferdy at once leaned forward and whispered savagely to the apparently immortal O'Sullivan, 'Monsieur O'Sullivan, your wife does not look at all well. I fear she is wilting under the strain of your illness.'

'Chlstrain!' the idiot said in astonishment. 'What chlstrain? I khlsee no khlsignch of kkchlstrain!'

Ferdy whispered with fierceness that when one is gravely ill one may sometimes fail to observe the grave illness of others.

'We have to remember, Monsieur, that if your clittle wife were to collapse under the chlstr ... under the *strain* of your illness it would be very serious, for *you*!'

After that day the only reason he submitted to accompany his love on these painful and piteous visits to 96 was that they always ended with O'Sullivan begging him to take his poor clittle, loving clittle, devoted clittle pet of a wife to a movie for a relaxation and a rest, or for a drink in the Russell, or to the evening races in the park; whereupon they would both hasten, panting, to Ferdy's flat to make love swiftly, wildly and vindictively – swiftly because their time was limited, wildly because her Irish storms had by now become typhoons of rage, and he no longer needed rose petals, Wagner, Mendelssohn, dim lights or pink champagne, and vindictively to declare and to crush their humiliation at being slaves to that idiot a quarter of a mile away in another bed saying endless rosaries to the Virgin.

Inevitably the afternoon came – it was now July – when Ferdy's pride and nerves cracked. He decided that enough was enough. They must escape to freedom. At once.

'Celia! If we have to fly to the end of the world! It won't really ruin my career. My master is most sympathetic. In fact since I hinted to him that I am in love with a *belle mariée* he does nothing but complain about his wife to me. And he can't leave her, his career depends on her, she is the daughter of a Secretary of State for Foreign Affairs – and rich. He tells me that at worst I would be moved off to some place like Los Angeles or Reykjavik. Celia! My beloved flower! We could be as happy as two puppies in a basket in Iceland.'

She permitted a meed of Northern silence to create itself and then wondered reflectively if it is ever warm in Iceland, at which he pounced with a loud 'What do you mean? What are you actually asking? What is really in your mind?' She said, 'Nothing, dürling,' for how could she dare to say that whereas he could carry his silly job with him wherever he went she, to be with him, would have to give up her lovely old, friendly old boutique on the Green where her friends came to chat over morning coffee, where she met every rich tourist who visited Dublin, where she made nice money of her own, where she felt independent and free; just as she could never hope to make him understand why she simply could not just up and out and desert a dying husband.

'But there's nothing to hold you here. In his condition you'd be sure to get custody of the children. Apart from the holidays they could remain in school here the year round.'

So he had been thinking it all out. She stroked his hairy chest.

'I know.'

'The man, even at his best, you've acknowledged it yourself, over and over, is a fool. He is a moujik. He is a bore.'

'I know!' she groaned. 'Who should better know what a crasher he is? He is a child. He hasn't had a new idea in his head for thirty years. There have been times when I've hated the smell of him. He reminds me of an unemptied ashtray. Times when I've wished to God that a thief would break into the house some night and kill him. And,' at which point she began to weep on his tummy, 'I know now that there is only one thief who will come for him and he is so busy elsewhere that it will be years before he catches up with him. And then I think of the poor old bastard wetting his hospital bed, unable to stir, let alone talk, looking up at his ceiling, incontinent, with no scissors, no golf, no friends, no nothing, except me. How *can* I desert him?'

Ferdy clasped his hands behind his head, stared up at heaven's pure ceiling and heard her weeping like the summer rain licking his windowpane. He created a long Irish silence. He heard the city whispering. Far away. Farther away. And then not at all.

'And to think,' he said at last, 'that I once called you a realist!'

She considered this. She too no longer heard the muttering of the city's traffic.

'This is how the world is made,' she decided flatly.

'I presume,' he said briskly, 'that you do realize that all Dublin knows that you are meanwhile betraying your beloved Meehawl with me?'

'I know that there's not one of those bitches who wouldn't give her left breast to be where I am at this moment.'

They got out of bed and began to dress.

'And, also meanwhile, I presume you do *not* know that they have a snotty name for you?'

'What name?' – and she turned her bare back for the knife.

'They call you The Diplomatic Hack.'

For five minutes neither of them spoke.

While he was stuffing his shirt into his trousers and she, dressed fully except for her frock, was patting her penny-brown hair into place before his mirror he said to her, 'Furthermore I suppose you do realize that whether I like it or not I shall one day be shifted to some other city in some other country. What would you do then? For once, just for once in your life tell me the plain truth! Just to bring you to the crunch. What would you really do then?'

She turned, comb in hand, leaned her behind against his dressing table and looked him straight in the fly which he was still buttoning.

'Die,' she said flatly.

'That,' he said coldly, 'is a manner of speech. Even so, would you consider it an adequate conclusion to a love that we have so often said is forever?'

They were now side by side in the mirror, she tending her copper hair, he his black, like any long-married couple. She smiled a little sadly.

'Forever? Dürling, does love know that lovely word? You love me. I know it. I love you. You know it. We will always know it. People die but if you have ever loved them they are never gone. Apples fall from the tree but the tree never forgets its blossoms. Marriage is different. You remember the day he advised you that if you ever marry you should marry an Irishwoman. Don't, Ferdy! If you do she will stick to you forever. And you wouldn't really want that?' She lifted her frock from the back of a chair and stepped into it. 'Zip me up, dürling, will you? Even my awful husband. There must have been a time when I thought him attractive. We used to sail together. Play tennis together. He was very good at it. After all, I gave him two children. What's the date? They'll be home for the holidays soon. All I have left for him now is contempt and compassion. It is our bond.'

Bewildered he went to the window, buttoned his flowered waistcoat. He remembered from his café days as a student a ruffle of aphorisms about love and marriage. Marriage begins only when love ends. Love opens the door to Marriage and quietly steals away. *Il faut toujours s'appuyer sur les principes de l'amour – ils finissent par en céder.* What would she say to that? Lean heavily on the principles of love – they will always conveniently crumple in the end. Marriage bestows on Love the tenderness due to a parting guest. Every *affaire de coeur* ends as a *mariage de convenance.* He turned to her, arranging his jacket, looking for his keys and his hat. She was peeking into her handbag, checking her purse for her keys and her lace handkerchief, gathering her gloves, giving a last glance at her hat. One of the things he liked about her was that she always wore a hat.

'You are not telling me the truth, Celia,' he said, quietly. 'Oh, I don't mean about loving me. I have no doubt about you on that score. But when you persuade yourself that you can't leave him because you feel compassion for him that is just your self-excuse for continuing a marriage that has its evident advantages.'

She smiled lovingly at him.

'Will you ring me tomorrow, dürling?'

'Of course.'

'I love you very much, dürling.'

'And I love you too.'

'Until tomorrow then.'

'Until tomorrow, dürling.'

As usual he let her go first.

That afternoon was some two years ago. Nine months after it he was transferred to Brussels. As often as he could wangle special leave of absence, and she could get a relative to stay for a week with her bedridden husband, now back in his own house, they would fly to Paris or London to be together again. He would always ask solicitously after her husband's health, and she always sigh and say his doctors had assured her that 'he will live forever.' Once, in Paris, passing a church he, for some reason, asked her if she ever went nowadays to confession.

She waved the question away with a laugh, but later that afternoon he returned to it pertinaciously.

'Yes. Once a year.'

'Do you tell your priest about us?'

'I tell him that my husband is bedridden. That I am in love with another man. That we make love. And that I cannot give you up. As I can't, dürling.'

'And what does he say to that?'

'They all say the same. That it is an impasse. Only one dear old Jesuit gave me a grain of hope. He said that if I liked I could pray to God that my husband might die.'

'And have you so prayed?'

'Dürling, why should I?' she asked gaily, as she stroked the curly hair between his two pink buttons. 'As you once pointed out to me yourself all this was foreknown millions of years ago.'

He gazed at the ceiling. In her place, unbeliever though he was, he would, for love's sake, have prayed with passion. Not that she had said directly that she had not. Maybe she had? Two evasions in one sentence! It was all more than flesh and blood could bear. It was the Irish variation all over again: never let your left ass know what your right ass is doing. He decided to give her one more twirl. When she got home he wrote tenderly to her, 'You are the love of my life!' He could foresee her passionate avowal, 'And me too, dürling!' What she actually replied was, 'Don't I know it?' Six months later he had manoeuvred himself into the consular service and out of Europe to Los Angeles. He there consoled his broken heart with a handsome creature named Rosie O'Connor. Quizzed about his partiality for the Irish, he could only flap his hands and say, 'I don't know what they have got. They are awful liars. There isn't a grain of romance in them. And whether as wives or mistresses they are absolutely faithless!'

Something, Everything, Anything, Nothing

1

Somebody once said that a good prime minister is a man who knows something about everything and nothing about anything. I wince – an American foreign correspondent, stationed in Rome, covering Italy, Greece, Turkey, Corsica, Sardinia, Malta, Libya, Egypt and the entire Middle East.

Last year I was sent off to report on pollution around Capri, steel in Taranto, which (as journalists say) 'nestles' under the heel of the peninsula, the Italo-American project for uncovering the buried city of the Sybarites, which is halfway down the coast from Taranto, the political unrest then beginning to simmer in Reggio di Calabria, around the toe of the continent, and, of course, if something else should turn up – some 'extra dimension,' as my foreign editor in Chicago likes to call such unforeseens...

Summer was dying in Rome, noisily and malodorously. Down south, sun, silence and sea. It was such a welcome commission that it sounded like a pat on the head for past services. I was very pleased.

I polished off Capri in two hours and Taranto in three days – a well-documented subject. After lunching at Metaponto, now one of Taranto's more scruffy seaside resorts, I was salubriously driving along the highway beside the Ionian when, after about an hour, 'something else' did crop up. It happened in a place too minute to be called a village, or even a hamlet, an Italian would call it a *loguccio* (a rough little place), named Bussano. I doubt if many travellers, not natives of these parts of Calabria – barring Karl Baedeker some sixty years or so ago, or the modern Italian Touring Club guide, or a weary Arab peddler – had ever voluntarily halted in Bussano. The Touring Club guide is eloquent about it. He says, and it is all he says:—'At this point the road begins to traverse a series of monotonous sand dunes.' Any guide as reticent as that knows what he is not talking about.

Bussano consists of two lots of hovels facing one another across the highway, one backing on that wild stretch of the Calabrian Apennines called La Sila, the other on an always empty ocean; 'always' because there is no harbour south of Taranto for about a hundred and fifty miles, nothing but sand, reeds, a few rocks, the vast Ionian. I presume that during the winter months the Ionian Sea is often shaken by southwesterly gales. In the summer nothing happens behind those monotonous sand dunes except the wavelets moving a foot inward and a foot outward throughout the livelong day, so softly that you don't even hear their seesaw and you have to watch carefully to see their wet marks on sand so hot that it pales again as soon as it is touched. The *loguccio* looked empty.

The only reason I halted there was that I happened to notice among the few hovels on the sea side of the road one two-storied house with a line of brown and yellow sunflowers lining its faded grey-pink walls on which, high up, I could barely decipher the words *Albergo degli Sibariti*. The Sybarites' Hotel. It must have been built originally for travellers by stagecoach, first horse then motor, or by hired coach and horses, or by private carriage, or in later years by the little railroad along the coast that presently starts to worm its slow way up through those fierce mountains that climb seven thousand feet to the Serra Dolcedorme where, I have been told, snow may still be seen in May. It was the same friend who told me about a diminutive railroad in this deep south – could it be this one? – grandiosely calling itself *La Società Italiana per le Strade Ferrate del Mediterraneo-Roma*, five hundred miles from the smell of Rome and barred by the Apennines from the Mediterranean. The *Albergo degli Sibariti* would have flourished in the youth of Garibaldi.

I was about to move on when I glanced between the hotel and its nearest hovel at a segment of sea and horizon, teasingly evoking the wealth of centuries below that level line – Greece, Crete, Byzantium, Alexandria. Once again I was about to drive off, thinking how cruel and how clever of Mussolini, and also how economical, to have silenced his intellectual critics (men like, for instance, Carlo Levi) simply by exiling them to remote spots like this, when an odd-looking young man came through the wide passageway, halted and looked up and down the highway with the air of a man with nowhere to go and nothing to do.

He was dark, bearded and longhaired, handsome if you like mushy

Italian eyes, dark as prunes, eyelashes soft and long, cheeks tenderly browned, under his chin hung a great, scarlet blob of tie like a nineteenth-century Romantic poet, his shirt gleaming (washed and ironed by whom?), his shoes brilliantly polished (by whom?), pants knife-pressed (by whom?), on his head a cracked and tawny straw hat that just might have come many years ago from Panama, and he carried a smooth cane with a brass knob. His unshaven jaws were blackberry blue. His jacket was black velvet. His trousers were purple. All in all more than overdressed for a region where the men may or may not wear a cotton singlet, but a shirt never except on Sundays, apart from the doctor if there is one, or the teacher if there is one, or the local landowner, and there is always one of them.

What on earth could he be? Not a visitor, at this time of the year, and in this non-place. An adolescent poet? More likely an absconding bank clerk in disguise. (Joke. In empty places like this the sand-hoppers for fifty miles around are known by their first names.) The local screwball? I alighted. He saw me. We met in the middle of the road – the roads down here are wide and fine. I asked him if he might be so kind as to tell me where I might, if it were not too much to ask, find the lost city of the Sybarites. At once he straightened his sagging back, replied eagerly, rapidly and excitedly, 'Three kilometres ahead fork left after the gas station then first right along a dirt track can I have a cigarette where are you from may I show you my pictures?'

Well, I thought, this is odd, I am on Forty-second Street, Division, Pigalle, the Cascine, the Veneto, Soho, Pompeii, show me his dirty pictures, what next? His sister? A pretty boy? Cannabis? American cigarettes? I told him I was an insurance salesman from Chicago and bade him lead on. He led me rapidly through the passage to a wooden shack in the untidy yard behind the house, where, as he fumbled with the lock, he explained himself.

'I am a Roman I am a great painter I came down here two years ago to devote my life to my art I have been saving up for years for this a professor of fine arts from New York bought four of my paintings last week for fifty thousand lire apiece.'

I knew this last to be not so immediately he flung open the door on lines of paintings stacked around the earthen floor – there were three or four canvases but he had mostly used chipboard or plywood. His daubs all indicated the same subject, mustard yellow sunflowers against a blue sea, each of them a very long way after van Gogh, each the same greasy blob of brown and yellow, each executed (appropriate word!) in the same three primary colours straight from the tube, chrome yellow, burnt umber, cerulean blue, with, here and there as the fancy had taken him, a mix of the three in a hoarse green like a consumptive's spittle. They were the most supremely splendid, perfect, godawful examples of bad art I had ever seen. As I gazed at them in a Cortes silence I knew that I simply must possess one of them immediately.

Snobbery? A kinky metropolitan taste? I know the feeling too well not to know its source in compassion and terror. To me bad art is one of the most touching and frightening examples of self-delusion in the world. Bad actors, bad musicians, bad writers, bad painters, bad anything, and not just the inbetweeners or the borderliners but the total, desperate, irredeemable failures. Wherever I have come on an utterly bad picture I have wanted to run away from it or possess it as a work of horror. Those 'original' gilt-framed pictures in paper elbow guards displayed for sale in the foyers of big commercial hotels, or in big railroad terminals. A quarter of a mile of even worse 'originals' hanging from the railings of public parks in the summer. Those reproductions that form part of the regular stock of novelty stores that sell china cuckoo clocks, nutcrackers shaped like a woman's thighs, pepper pots shaped like ducks' bottoms. The poor, sad, pathetic little boy with the one, single, perfect teardrop glistening on his cheek. Six camels forever stalking across the desert into a red ink sunset. Three stretched-neck geese flying over a reedy lake into the dawn. That jolly medieval friar holding up his glass of supermarket port to an Elizabethan diamond-paned window as bright as a five-hundred-watt electric bulb.

We know the venal type who markets these *kitsch* objects and we know that they are bought by uneducated people of no taste. But if one accepts that these things are sometimes not utterly devoid of skill, and are on the edge of taste, who paints them? Looking into the earnest, globular eyes of this young man in Bussano (who insofar as he had no least skill and no least taste was the extreme example of the type) I felt once again the surge of compassion and of fear that is always the prelude to the only plausible answer I know: that he was yet another dreaming innocent who believed that he had heard the call to higher things. His type must be legion: young boys and girls who at some unlucky moment of their lives have heard, and alas have heeded that far-off whir of wings and that solitary midnight song once heard, so they have been told, in ancient days by emperor and clown, the same voice that flung magic casements open on the foam of perilous seas and faery lands forlorn. The frightening part of it is that there can be very few human beings who have not heard it in some form or another. If we are wise we either do nothing about it or do the least possible. We send a subscription, join something, vote, are modest.

As I offered him a cigarette I felt like the man in charge of a firing squad; not that I, or anybody else ever can kill such lethal innocence. As he virtually ate the cigarette I saw that his eye sockets were hollowed not by imagination but starvation. He was a living cartoon of the would-be artist as a young man who has begun to fear that he possibly may not be the one and will certainly never again be the other. To comfort him I irresponsibly said, 'You might one day become the van Gogh of Calabria,' to which he said quickly, 'I sell you any one you like cheap.' Should I have said they were all awful? I said I liked the one that, in characteristic burlesque of the real by the fake, he had labelled *Occhio d'oro, Mar' azzurro*. 'Golden Eye, Azure Sea.' Whereupon he said, 'Fifty dollars,' and I beat him down to two. As he pouched the two bills I asked him what he was proposing to do with all that lovely money. He laughed gaily – the Italian poor really are the most gutsy people in the world, as well as the most dream-deluded– 'Tonight I will bring my wife to the hotel for two brandies to celebrate my first sale in two years. It is an omen from heaven for our future.'

All this, and a wife too? I invited him into the hotel for a beer, served by a drowsy slut whom he had imperiously waked from her siesta. I asked him about his wife.

'Roman,' he said proudly. 'And *borghese*. Her father works in a bank. She believes absolutely in my future. When we married she said, "Sesto" – I was a sixth child, my name is Sesto Caro— "I will follow you to the end of the world."' He crossed two fingers. 'We are like that.' He crossed three. 'With our child, like that. The first, alas, was stillborn.'

(The harm innocence can do!)

He said that he, also, was a Roman. And he was! He knew the city as well as I do, and I have spent twenty years living there as a nosy reporter. I found him in every way, his self-delusion apart, an honest young man. He agreed that he had done all sorts of things. Run away from home at fourteen. Done a year in the galleys for stealing scrap.

Returned home, spent two years in a seminary trying to be a monk, a year and a half in a *trattoria* in the Borgo Pio. Was arrested again and held for two years without trial for allegedly selling cannabis. Released, he spent three years in Germany and Switzerland to make money for his present project. Returned home, was apprenticed as an electrician's assistant... He was now twenty-nine. She was now twenty-one. When she was turned off by her father they had come down here to beg the help of her godfather-uncle Emilio Ratti, an engineer living in what I heard him lightly call 'the Cosenza of Pliny and Varro.' I looked out and upward towards the Sila.

'Cosenza? A godfather so far from Rome?'

'He was exiled there by Mussolini and never went back.'

Unfortunately, or by the whim of the pagan gods of Calabria – he contemptuously called it *Il Far Ovest* – his wife, then nineteen, and big with child, got diarrhoea so badly in Naples ('Pollution around Capri?') that they finally tumbled off the train at a mountainy place called Cassano in the hope of quickly finding a doctor there; only to be told as the train pulled away into the twilit valleys that the station of Cassano was hours away from the village of Cassano, whereas their informant, a carter from Bussano, offered to drive them in one hour to his beautiful village by the sea near which (equally untrue) there was a very good doctor. So, with their parcels, their cardboard suitcases, their paper bundles and bulging pillowcases they had come to this *casale* and stayed. Uncle Emilio had visited them once. Still, like her father, he occasionally disbursed small sums of money on condition that they stayed where they were.

2

We shook hands cordially, I gathered my bad painting and drove off fast. I had walked into the middle of a frightening story and I had no idea what its end would be. Murder? Suicide? If I could wait for either that could be a good something else for Chicago. Not now. No lift. No human interest. I looked eagerly ahead of me along the straight highway to my meeting with the skilled Italo-American technicians and archaeologists at Sybaris. About this, at least, van Gogh was accurate. After exactly three kilometres I saw the yellow and black sign of a gas station, whose attendant directed me, without interest, towards a dirt track leading into a marshland of reeds and scrub.

As I bumped along this dusty track I could see no life whatever, nothing but widespread swamp, until I came around a bend in the track and saw ahead of me a solitary figure leaning against a jeep, arms folded, pipe-smoking, well built, idly watching me approach. High boots to his knees, riding breeches, open-necked khaki shirt, peaked cap, sunglasses, grizzled hair. In his sixties? I pulled up beside him, told him who and what I was and asked him where I could see the buried city of Sybaris. Immobile he listened to me, smiled tolerantly, or it might be boredly, then without speaking beckoned me with his pipe to follow his jeep. I did so until he halted near a large pool of clear water surrounded by reeds and mud. Some ten feet underwater I perceived a couple of broken pillars and a wide halfmoon of networked brick.

'Behold Sybaris,' he said and with amusement watched me stare at him, around the level swamp at the immensity of the all-seeing mountains and back to him again.

'You mean that's *all* there is to see of it?'

'All, since, if you believe the common legend, its enemies deflected its great river, the Crathis,' he in turn glanced westward and upward, 'to drown it under water as Pompeii was smothered in volcanic ash. Crathis is now brown with yellow mud. "Crathis the lovely stream that stains dark hair bright gold."'

He smiled apologetically at the quotation.

'But the archaeologists? I was hoping to find them all hard at work.'

He smiled unapologetically. He relit his pipe.

'Where is the hurry? Sybaris has been asleep a long time. They have finished for this year. They have had to work slowly. They have been experimenting with sonic soundings since 1964. They have had to map the entire extent of the city with their magnetometers. It was six miles in circumference. But I am only an engineer. Consultant engineer. Of Cosenza.'

I stared unhappily at the solitary eye of the once largest and most elegant city of the whole empire of Magna Graecia. I recalled and mentioned an odd detail that had stuck in my mind's tooth, out of, I think, Lenormant, supposedly typical of the luxury of the city in its heyday – its bylaw that forbade morning cocks to crow earlier than a stated number of hours after sunrise. He shrugged dubiously. I did know that it was Lenormant who a hundred years ago looked from the foothills of the Sila down at this plain and saw nothing but strayed bulls, long since gone wild, splashing whitely in its marshes. He said he had been much struck by this legendary picture.

'Legendary? You *are* a sceptical man.'

'In this country legend is always posturing as history. We are a wilderness of myths growing out of myths. Along the coast there, at Crotone, my wife, as a girl, walked to the temple of Juno, the Mother of the Gods, in a procession of barefooted girls singing hymns to Mary, the Mother of God. Here Venus can overnight become Saint Venus. *Santa Venera*. A hill once sacred to Cybele becomes sanctified all over again as Monte Vergine. I do not deride any of this. Some myths point to a truth. Some not. I cannot always distinguish. And I have lived in Calabria for thirty years.'

'Not a born Calabrese, then?'

'I am a Roman. I was exiled here by the Fascisti in 1939. Not in this spot! Back up there in a small village called San Giovanni in Fiore. A pretty name, situated beautifully, poor and filthy when you got there. The night they arrested me in Rome they allowed me five minutes and one suitcase. I grabbed the biggest book I could find. It was *Don Quixote*. That winter I reread it by daylight and by candlelight three times. I had nothing else to read, nobody to talk to, nothing to do. Every fine day I tramped over those mountains, sometimes twenty and more miles a day.' He laughed cheerfully. 'Wearing out the Fascist spies detailed to follow me. Today the same men, as old as I am now, joke with me over it. They were bastards every one of them. And would be again if it suited them. They say, "Ah, the good old days, Emilio! You were so good for our bellies. If only we could lead one another that dance all over again!" I came everywhere on old stories written on old stones – myths, charms, omens, hopes, ambitions. The cerecloths of Greece. The marks of Rome. Those bits in that pool are probably Roman. You can tell it by the *opus reticulatum* of the bricks. That was only uncovered in '32. They call this place the *Parco del Cavallo*. What horse? Whose horse? I came on remnants of Byzantium, the Goths, the Saracens, the Normans. Our past. When my spies saw what I was after they stopped following me – I had become a harmless fool – doors opened to me, a landowner's, then a doctor's, even a schoolmaster's, a learned priest's in Rossano. I met and fell in love with a doctor's daughter from Crotone. It was a charming little port in those days.

Good wine of Ciro. Good cigars. Very appealing. One day in September 1943 the British Fifth Army entered Crotone and we were married. Well before then,' he laughed, 'every Fascist of San Giovanni in Fiore had burned his black shirt and started shouting *Viva il Re*. The old woman with whom I had lodged sold me for ten thousand lire to the doctor, who sold me for twenty thousand to the police marshal, who sold me for fifty thousand to a landowner who drove me into Crotone to show the British commanding officer the victim of Fascism whom he had protected for the last four years. I did not give him away. I had fallen in love so much with Calabria that I even liked its ruffians. I settled in Cosenza.'

Why was he unburdening himself like this to a stranger? I said that in September 1943 I was with the American Eighth Army across those mountains.

'My God!' I wailed, throwing a bit of silver wrap from my chewing gum into the pool of the horse. 'Do you realize that all that is over a quarter of a century ago?'

He smiled his tender, stoic's smile.

'I realize it very well. My youngest son is a lieutenant in the Air Force. His brother is studying medicine in Palermo. My eldest child is due to have her first baby at any hour.'

'Why did you not return to Rome?'

He again glanced towards Cosenza. The sun, I observed, sinks early behind those Apennines. For no reason there flashed across my eyes the image of this plain covered by sheets of water made of melting snow.

'I have told you why I never went back to Rome. Because I had fallen in love with a woman and a place, with a woman who was a place. I saw my Claudia as a symbol of the ancientness, the ancestry, the dignity, the unforgettable beauty of Calabria, of its pedigree, its pride, its arrogance, its closeness to the beginning of the beginnings of man and the end of the ends of life. I believed then and believe still that outside Calabria it would be impossible to find such a woman as my Claudia.'

I did not suggest that fifty million Italians might not agree. If a young man in love, and an old man remembering his young love is not entitled to his dreams, who is? I merely suggested that there is also some 'ancientness' in Rome.

'In museums? In Rome the bridge is down. It has no living past. It is just as venal, vulgar, cowardly, cynical and commercial a city as any other in the world.' He jerked his body to a soldierly attention. 'I must get back to Cosenza. We have been warned by the doctor that the birth may be difficult. There may have to be a caesarian. My wife will be praying for an easy birth. When I get back she may have more news.'

No relatives? Ageing both. Alone. I did not say that my own daughter has married far away from me into another continent. All dreams have an ending somewhat different from their beginnings.

'Your daughter is in Cosenza?' I asked hopefully, but he waved his right hand towards the south.

'No. She married a splendid young man in Reggio, an *avvocato*. Bartolomeo Vivarini. It is not very far but it is far too far for my wife and me at a time like this.'

We shook hands warmly. We had in some way lit in those few minutes a small flame to friendship. He waved and went his way. I continued along the coast, deeper into his South, his beloved Past.

I slept in Crotone, badly, woke wondering if I had been as unwise about my food as one so easily can be anywhere south of Rome, or dreamed oppressively, or failed to do something along the road that I ought to have done. It was not until I had dived into the sparkles of the sea and been driving fast for a good hour that the reason for my dejection struck me. I had caught the *mal du pays*. Four days out of Rome and I was already homesick for it. And why not? I am not married to Old Calabria. I am a political animal, a man of reason, interested in the world as it really is. My job is to do with today, occasionally with tomorrow, never with yesterday. I had been seeing far too many memorials to that incorporeal, extramundane, immaterial, miasmic element that is food and drink to men like Emilio Ratti and that Carl Sandburg called a bucket of ashes.

One ancient temple had been exciting, like those fifteen Doric columns at Metaponto deep in weeds and wild flowers. The next, less than a mile away, had been too much. A cartload of stones. Decline, decay, even death is Beauty's due. Never defeat. This South is littered with decay and defeat. Farther on a bare few megaliths recorded another defeated city. A duck pond to call up great Sybaris! Not even a stone had marked another lost city. Juno's great church had been worn by time, weather and robbery to a naked column on the edge of a bleak moor and a bare cliff outside Crotone. All as empty now as the sea, except for ageing women remembering the garlanded girls who once walked there in a line singing hymns in May. At Locri I had paused for gas and found the local museum ill-kept and dusty. *Aranciata Pitagora*. One of Greece's greatest philosophers advertising orange juice over a wayside stall.

I covered my final forty miles in half an hour. I swept into a Reggio bristling with carabinieri, local police, armed troops, riot squad trucks crackling out constant radio reports. The hotel was like a Field H.Q. with pressmen and photographers, cinema crews and TV crews. All because it was widely and furiously feared that Rome intended to pass Reggio over in favour of either Cosenza or Catanzaro as the new provincial capital. Posters all over the walls announced that at four o'clock there would be a Monster Meeting in the Piazza del Popolo. This would leave me just enough time to interview the chief citizens of Reggio: mayor, archbishop, city councillors, parliamentary deputies, labour bosses, leading industrialists if any. For some five hours, lunchless, I patiently gathered from them thousands of flat-footed words, to which at the afternoon meeting a sequence of bellowing orators added their many more.

Weary, hungry and bored I remembered with a click of my fingers the name Vivarini.

3

Twenty minutes later, in a quarter of the city far removed from the noisy piazza, I was admitted by an elderly woman in black – wife? housekeeper? secretary? – to the presence of a very old man in a dusky room cluttered with antiquated furniture, bibelots, statuettes in marble, alabaster and bronze, old paintings, vases, boxes of papers, books, bowls, crystal paperweights, signed photographs in silver frames. It was the kind of room that made me wonder how he ever found anything he might require there. A Balzac would have been delighted to list all its telltale signs, markers or milestones of the fortunes of a business and a family, especially those signed photographs – King Vittorio Emmanuele III, Dr Axel Munthe, one Peter Rothschild, Prime Minister Giolitti (the one who held out against Mussolini until 1921), Facta (who fell to Fascism in 1922), Mussolini's son-in-law Galeazzo Ciano, Marshal Badoglio. As for me, one look and I knew what I was in for. And I was!

'Ah, *signore*, this was once a city of the rarest elegance. My son whom you must meet – he is at the hospital – does not realize this, he is too young. But I myself heard d'Annunzio say that our *lungomare* is one of the most gracious seaside promenades in Europe. What do you think of that?' (I refused to say that if the so-called Prince of Montevenoso ever said so he must have said it before 1908 when this city was flattened by its terrible earthquake, and at that date Signor Vivarini would have been a very small boy indeed.) 'But, now, alas, *signore*, we have been taken over by the vulgar herd, the *popolazzo*. Corruption. Vendettas. Squabbles for gain. Maladministration. And all because our natural leaders, our aristocracy, the landed gentry of Calabria, started to abandon Reggio immediately after the earthquake of 1908 . . .'

In the distance an irritable rattle of rifle fire. He did not seem to hear it. He went on and on. And I should be back there at the rioting.

'Nothing can save us now but a miracle . . . When I was a youth . . .'

I rose at the sound of a distant, dull explosion, ready to run from him without ceremony, when from the doorway I found myself transfixed by the stare of a man whom I took to be his son – a tall, thin, challenging, cadaverous man of about thirty-five, eyes Atlantic grey, peering through eyelashes that hid nothing of his patent awareness of his own merits, his inquisitorial mistrust, his cold arrogance of a pasha. I would have been utterly repelled by him if his clothes were not so much at odds with his manner. His lean body was gloved in a light, metallic, bluish material suggestive of shimmering night and stars, his skintight shirt was salmon pink, his lemon tie disappeared into the V of a flowered waistcoat, the silk handkerchief in his breast pocket lolled as softly as a kitten's tail, or as its eyes, his shoes were sea-suede, and his smoke of hair was blued like a woman's. After all those big mouths in the piazza he looked so promisingly ambiguous that I introduced myself at once, name, profession, nationality. In a courteous and attractively purring voice, and in the unmistakable English of Cambridge (Mass.), i.e., of Harvard, he replied that he had also spent some time in America. In return I told him that I had begun my career as a journalist on *The Crimson*. His laugh was loud, frank, open and delighted. We shook hands amiably. I was on the point of deciding that he was really a most engaging fellow when I recalled his first ice-cold air, his arrogance and his suspicion. I glanced at his clothes and I looked at his face, where now it was the mouth that impressed me: a blend of the soft, the mobile, the vulpine, the voracious, the smiling that made me suddenly think that the essence of his first effect on me had been the predatory and the self-protective nature of a born sensualist. Obviously a man capable of being very attractive to women, but also, I feared, capable in his egoism of being cruel.

'You enjoyed America,' I stated cheerfully.

For a second or two his peering mask returned and he smiled, not unhappily, yet not warmly either, the way I fancied an inquisitor might when watching a heretic slowly gyrating over the flames that would soon deliver his soul to paradise. He said that he had endured the arid rigidities of Harvard University for three years. He laughed gaily at another rattle of gunfire, saying, 'That nonsense will be over in an hour.' He did not so much invite me to dine with him, as insist that I should give him the pleasure.

'And the consolation. I am going through a difficult time.'

The next second he was blazing with fury at his father's tremulous question, 'How is Angelica?' This – I had observed in some embarrassment – had already been iterated four times.

'She has been in labour now for eight hours!' he ground out savagely. 'If she has not given birth within three more hours I insist upon a caesarian.' The old man waved protesting hands. 'My dear father!' he raged at him in a near whisper. 'I have told you twenty times that there is nothing scientifically wrong with a caesarian.'

He turned suavely to me. 'I do wish my dear father would realize that even after three caesarians my wife could still bear him a long line of grandchildren.' He laughed lightly. 'Of course there is no truth in the legend that Julius Caesar was so delivered. I will call for you at your hotel – The Excelsior I presume? – at half past seven. We will dine at the Conti. It is not very much but it is our best.'

I would have preferred to catch the plane for Rome. But I remembered, and shared, some of Emilio Ratti's quiet troublement over his daughter. My own daughter had not had an easy time with her first. There bounced off my mind the thought that a nameless young woman in Bussano had lost her first. Actually it was none of these things decided me but the sound of more shots. I ran from the pair of them.

The rioting was well worth it, water cannon, baton charges, rubber bullets, the lot, women howling Jesu Marias, hair streaming, children bawling, fat men behaving like heroes, the finest fullest crop of De Sica clichés, vintage 1950, and not a cat killed. And all for what? For, at least, more than Hecuba, if for less than Hector. For pride, honour, family, home, ancient tradition, *Rhegium antiquum* so often raped by Messinaians, Syracusans, Romans, Goths, Normans, Saracens, Pisans, Turks, Aragonese, Fascisti, Nazis, and the liberating armies of Great Britain and the USA. Also, no doubt, for something to do with real estate, tourism, air travel, emigration, IRI, Bernie Cornfield's *fonditalia*, Swiss hooks in Chiasso, the Mafia, the *Cassa per il Mezzogiorno*, the Demochristians' majority in parliament... But the journalist's classical symptom is cynicism, the boil of his inward frustration, the knowledge that he will never get at that total truth reserved for historians, novelists and poets who will reduce his tormented futilities to a few drops of wisdom.

By the time Vivarini called for me I was calmed, and if apart from Crotone's morning moonshine coffee still unfed, I was by now not unslaked, braced by two martinis which I insisted that he and I, at the bar, make four; as, in Conti's, he at once ordered not one but two litres of *vino di Ciro* – reminding me of that drunken night, it was in Peking (Oh! Jesus!) years and years ago, that I first became a father.

'No!' he groaned aloud to the totally empty restaurant. (Its usual clients afraid to emerge at night?) 'No baby yet!'

His father ('Don't touch the *scampi!* Even here we have possible pollution!') was a Polonius, a foolish, fond old man whom nobody would mistake for his better, three generations out of date. A sweet, kind man. With fine sensibilities. But, like all Italians, a besotted sentimentalist.

'By comparison I, Bartolomeo...'

'Hi, Bart! Call me Tom!'

'Hi, Tom ... am a cold Cartesian. My wife,' he informed me secretively, evidently making some point, 'is a mortal angel. I have selected her with the greatest care. For I have also had my sorrows. My betrayals. But she is an angel with a Gallic mind. She also loathes all this traditional nonsense of her father's and of my father, all this ridiculous adoration of the Past. Down with Tradition! All it is is confusion! Mythology! Obfuscation!' He hammered the table, a waiter came running and was dismissed. 'I insist on a caesarian! Those two old men with their folksy minds think it bad, wrong, a threat to the long line of children they dream of as their – *their!* – descendants. Excuse me,' he said quietly. 'May I telephone?'

He returned, swaying only a very little, shook his head, looked at his watch, while I thought of my engineer and his wife waiting by the telephone in Cosenza, and that agonized girl hauling on a towel tied to the end of a bedpost, and the old lawyer somewhere up the street moaning to himself among his portraits and his trophies of the dead and I said, 'Look't, for Chrissake, forget me! I know you want to be back in that hospital, or nursing home, or whatever it is. Do please go there!' – to which, intent on behaving as calmly as a Harvard man, that is to say as a Yank, that is to say as an English gentleman (period 1850) would have behaved, he replied that if his papa was irrational his father-in-law Emilio was far more so.

'I can guess how my father explained those riots to you. The decay of the aristocracy? All that shit? But did he once mention the Mafia? With whom, of course, he worked hand in glove all his life? Whereas, on the other hand, Emilio would know all about the Mafia, but he would also tell you that the rioting would have been far worse if it had not been for,' here one could almost hear his liver gurgling bile, 'the "wisely restraining hand of Mother Church." Two complementary types of total unreason.'

At this he bowed his face into his palms and moaned into them.

'If only my love and I could get out of this antiquated, priest-ridden, Mafia-ridden, time-ridden, phony, provincial hole!'

He quickly recovered control of himself sufficiently to beg me, concernedly, to give him the latest news from the States. I did so, keeping it up as long and lightly as I could since the narration seemed to soothe him. But it was only a seeming, because he suddenly cried out, having obviously not heeded one word I had been saying:—

'The Church here is, of course, a master plotter and conspirator. Have you seen their latest miracle?' – as if he were asking me whether I had seen the latest Stock Exchange reports. 'You must. It is a masterpiece. It is only five hundred metres away. A weeping Madonna. Weeping, of course, for Reggio. Like Niobe, from whom the idea most certainly derives. What a gullible people we are! Madonnas who weep, bleed, speak, go pale, blush, sway, for all I know dance. Did you know that before the war Naples possessed two bottles of milk supposed to have been drawn off the breasts of the Virgin which curdled twice a year? Excuse me. May I telephone?'

He disappeared. This made the restaurant twice as empty. The patron asked me solicitiously if all was well. Signor Vivarini seemed upset? I said his wife was expecting a baby.

'A baby!'

Within a minute the restaurant came alive. A fat female cook bustled from the kitchen. After her came a serving woman. The *padrone*'s wife appeared. Two small children peeped. An old man shuffled out in slippers. In a group they babbled about babies. It was nine o'clock. I had lost my plane. I had not yet written my report on Reggio. But he did not come back and he did not come back, and I was cross, bothered, bored and bewildered. The restaurant again emptied – the whole company of family and servitors had gone off in a gabble to regather outside the telephone booth. I had decided to pay the bill and leave when a mini-riot burst into the place, all of them returning, cheering and laughing, to me, as if I was the fertile father, and in their midst Bartolomeo Vivarini, swollen as the sun at noon, beaming, triumphant, bestowing benedictions all around, proclaiming victory as smugly as if he was the fertile mother.

'*Un miracolo gradito!*' he laughed and wept, 'a son! I am the father of a son! I have telephoned my father and my mother, my father-in-law and my mother-in-law. They are all such good people. Are they not?'

The company laughed, clapped, declared that it was indeed a miracle, a splendid miracle, a *miracolo gradito*.

'There will be more children!' the cook assured him.

'And more sons,' the *padrone*'s father assured him.

He sat, sobbed, hiccuped, called for champagne, but this I firmly forbade.

'You haven't yet seen your wife!' I pointed out. 'She must have suffered terrible pain,' at which his sobs spouted like champagne.

'I had forgotten all about her!' he wailed and punished his bony breast. 'I must light a candle for my wife to the Madonna. To the weeping Madonna! Let us go, my dear friend. To the Madonna! She, perhaps, may make them give me one peep at my son. You will drive me? I dare not! It is not far away.'

So, we left, led noisily by all to the door. And nobody asked us to pay the bill.

His car was a Lancia. I drove it furiously to somewhere up the hill, this way, that way, until, above the nightness and lightness of the city, of the straits, of all Calabria and all Sicily, we halted on the edge of a tiny *piazza* crowded with worshippers or sightseers, where there stood an altar, and on the altar a pink and blue commercial statue of the allegedly lachrymose Virgin Mary. A hundred breathless candles adored her, and four steady electric spotlights. Bartolomeo crushed me through the crowds to the altar, bought two candles, one for himself, one for me, refusing to take any change from his thousand-lire bill, lit his candle, fixed it in position and knelt on the bare ground to pray, his hands held wide in total wonder and belief.

As far as I was concerned the miracle was, of course, like every popular Italian miracle preposterous – a word, I had learned at high school, that means in Ciceronian Latin arse-to-front. The object was to me simply an object, bought from some statue vendor in Reggio, with, if even that ever happened, a drop or two of glycerine deposited on its painted cheek by some pious or impious hand. But why should anybody want a miracle so badly, and gradually, as I looked about me and felt the intensity of the human feeling circling the altar like a whirlpool of air, or bees in a swarm, or butterflies over a wave, or fallen leaves whispering in a dry wind, I began to feel awed and even a little frightened. As I moved through the murmuring or silent crowds, conscious of the eloquent adoration of the old, the unexpected fervour of the young, the sudden hysteria of a woman carried away screaming, the quiet insistent stare of two Franciscans fixed on the painted face, I became so affected that at one point I thought that I, too, could, might, perhaps – or did I? – see one single, perfect teardrop gleaming in the spotlights on the face of the mother of their God. I blinked. 'It' vanished.

But had it ever been there? Who had the proof that it had not been an illusion for us all? The night was inflammable, the country explosive, I had too much respect for my skin to ask why even one teardrop had not been looked at through a microscope capable of distinguishing between glycerine, that is to say $C_3H_5(OH)_3$, and the secretions of the lachrymal gland. I might as well have committed instant suicide as suggest that a similar test could be applied to the wine said to change during their Mass into the blood of their God. I found myself beside the two motionless friars. I cautiously asked one of them if he had seen, or knew anybody who had seen, a tear form in the Madonna's eye. He answered skilfully that this was not wholly relevant since if one saw the tear it was so, and if one did not see a tear it was not so, which, he took pleasure in explaining to me courteously, but at some length, marks the difference in Kantian philosophy between the *phenomenon* and the *noumenon*. My mind swam.

Bartolomeo had vanished. I stayed on in that haunted *piazzetta* until well after one in the morning. I collected some opinions, two asserted experiences, stories of miraculous cures. The crowds thinned, but at no time was the statue unattended by at least one worshipping believer. Only when a palsied dumb woman asked me the time by tapping my watch with her finger did I remember that by now the huntsmen might be asleep in Calabria but the foreign editors of America would be wide awake, for who could be drowsy at that hour whose first edition frees us all from everlasting sleep? A few steps away I found a lighted café whose owner must have nourished the same views as Sir Thomas Browne. There, over a couple of Stregas, I disposed in twenty minutes of Reggio's political troubles. Inside another half an hour I evoked the miracle of the Madonna in one of the most brilliant pieces I have written during my whole life. The best part of it was the coda, which I doubted I would ever send – they would only kill it at once. In it I asked Chicago, still daylit, still dining or well dined, rumbling like old thunder, smelling as rank as a blown-out candle, how it is that the Mediterranean never ceases to offer us new lamps for old. I opined that it is because it is in the nature of that restless Mediterranean mind to be divinely discontent with this jail of a world into which we are born. It is always trying to break out, to blow down the walls of its eyes, to extend time to eternity so as to see this world as nobody except the gods has ever seen it before.

No! Not for Chicago. Not that I cared. What is every journalist anyway but an artist *manqué* spancelled to another, who is tethered to a third, and a fourth and a fifth up to the fiftieth and final *manqué* at the top?

I passed slowly back through the little *piazza*. The candles were guttering, the spotlights still shone, it was empty except for one man kneeling in the centre of it before the sleepless statue. I bade her a silent farewell, Juno, Hera, Niobe, Venus, or the Virgin, and went on walking through the sleeping streets downhill to the shore. It was a still night. The sky gleamed with stars like Vivarini's blue coat. I thought of my dauber of Bussano, my van Gogh *manqué*, and I decided that the distinction between Emperor and Clown is irrelevant. Every virtue is woven into its opposite, failure built into ambition, despair into desire, cold reason into hot dreams, delusion into the imagination, death into life, and if a youth does not take the risks of every one of them he will not live long enough to deserve peace.

I paused. In the straits was that a purring motorboat? Not a sound.

Here, at about five twenty o'clock one equally silent morning sixty-one years ago – it was in fact December 28th – people like the father and mother of old Mr Vivarini the lawyer felt their houses sway and shiver for thirty-two seconds, and for twelve miles north and south every house swayed and shook in the same way for two months. At widening intervals the earthquake went on for a year and a half. The entire city vanished. Like Sybaris. Like Pompeii. I looked at my watch. In a few hours another green sheen would creep over the straits. Another pallid premorning lightsomeness would expand behind Aspromonte.

I walked on smiling at the fun the Vivarinis would have disputing over the name of their newborn child.

An Inside Outside Complex

So then, a dusky Sunday afternoon in Bray at a quarter to five o'clock, lighting up time at five fifteen, November 1st, All Souls' Eve, dedicated to the suffering souls in Purgatory, Bertie Bolger, bachelor, aged forty-one or so, tubby, ruddy, greying, well-known as a dealer in antiques, less well-known as a conflator thereof, walking briskly along the seafront, head up to the damp breezes, turns smartly into the lounge of the Imperial Hotel for a hot toddy, singing in a soldierly basso 'my breast expanding to the ball.'

The room, lofty, widespread, Victorian, gilded, over-furnished, as empty as the ocean, and not warm. The single fire is small and smouldering. Bertie presses the bell for service, divests himself of his bowler, his vicuna overcoat, his lengthy scarf striped in black, red, green and white, the colours of Trinity College, Dublin (which he has never attended), sits in a chintzy armchair before the fire, pokes it into a blaze, leans back, and is at once invaded by a clearcut knowledge of what month it is, and an uneasy feeling about its date. He might earlier have adverted to both if he had not, during his perambulation, been preoccupied with the problem of how to transform a twentieth-century Buhl cabinet, now in his possession, into an eighteenth-century ditto that might plausibly be attributed to the original M. Boulle. This preoccupation had permitted him to glance at, but not to observe, either the red gasometer by the harbour inflated to its winter zenith, or the haybarn beside the dairy beyond the gasometer packed with cubes of hay, or the fuel yard, facing the haybarn, beside the dairy beyond the gasometer, heavily stocked with mountainettes of coal, or the many vacancy signs in the lodging houses along the seafront, or the hoardings on the pagoda below the promenade where his mother, God rest her, had once told him he had been wheeled as a coiffed baby in a white pram to hear Mike Nono singing 'I do liuke to be besiude the seasiude, I do liuke to be besiude the sea,' or, most affectingly of all, if he had only heeded them, the exquisite, dying leaves of the hydrangeas in the public gardens, pale green, pale yellow, frost white, spiking the air above once purple petals that now clink greyly in the breeze like tiny seashells.

He suddenly jerks his head upright, sniffing desolation, looks slowly about the lounge, locates in a corner of it some hydrangeas left standing too long in a brass pot of unchanged water, catapults himself from the chair with a 'Jaysus! Five years to the bloody day!', dons his coat, his comforter and his bowler hat, and exits rapidly to make inland towards the R.C. church. For days after she died the house had retained that rank funereal smell. Tomorrow morning a Mass must be said for the repose of his mother's soul, still, maybe – Who knows? Only God knows! – suffering in the flames of Purgatory.

It is the perfect and pitiless testing date, day and hour for any seaside town in these northern islands. A week or two earlier and there might still have been a few lingering visitors, a ghost of summer's luke-warmth, a calmer sea, unheard waves, and, the hands of the Summer Time clocks not yet put backward, another hour of daylight. This expiring Sunday the light is dim, the silence heavy, the town turned in on itself. As he walks through the side avenues between the sea and the Main Street, past rows of squat bungalows, every garden drooping, past grenadiers of red brick, lace curtained, past ancient cement-faced cottages with sagging roofs, he is informed by every fanlight, oblong or halfmoon, blank as night or distantly lit from the recesses behind each front door, that there is some kind of life asleep or snoozing behind number 51, *Saint Anthony's*, *Liljoe's*, *Fatima*, 59 (odd numbers on this side), *The Billows*, *Swan Lake*, 67, *Slievemish*, *Sea View*, names in white paint, numbers in adhesive celluloid. Every one of them gives a chuck to the noose of loneliness about his neck. I live in Dublin. I am a guest in a guest house. I am Mister Bee. I lunch of weekdays at the United Services Club. I dine at the Yacht Club. Good for biz. Bad for Sundays, restaurants shut, homeless. Pray for the soul of Mrs Mary Bolger, of Tureenlahan, County Tipperary, departed this life five years ago. Into thy hands, O Lord.

On these side avenues only an odd front window is lit. Their lights flow searingly across little patches of grass called front gardens, privet-hedged, lonicera-hedged, mass-concrete hedged. Private. Keep Off.

As he passed one such light, in what a real estate agent would have called a picture window, he was so shaken by what he saw inside that after he had passed he halted, looked cautiously about him, turned and walked slowly back to peep in again. What had gripped his attention through the unsuspecting window had been a standing lamp in brass with a large pink shade, and beneath its red glow, seated in an armchair with her knees crossed, a bare-armed woman reading a folded magazine, one hand blindly lifting a teacup from a Moorish side table, holding the cup immobile while she concentrated on something that had detained her interest. By the time he had returned she was sipping from the cup. He watched her lay it down, throw the magazine aside and loop forward on two broad knees to poke the fire. Her arms looked strong. She was full-breasted. She had dark hair. In that instant B.B. became a *voyeur*.

The long avenue suddenly sprang its public lights. Startled he looked up and down the empty perspective. It was too cold for evening strollers. He was aware that he was trembling with fear. He did not know what else he was feeling except that there was nothing sexy to it. To calm himself he drew back behind the pillar of her garden gate whose name plate caught his eye. *Lorelei*. He again peeped around the side of the pillar. She was dusting her lap with her two palms. She was very dark, a western type, a Spanish-Galway type, a bit heavy. He could not discern the details of the room beyond the circle of light from the pink lamp, and he was glad of this: it made everything more mysterious, removed, suggestive, as if he was watching a scene on a stage. His loneliness left him, his desolation, his longing. He wanted only to be inside there, safe, secure, and satisfied.

'Ah, good evening, Bertie!' she cried to the handsome man who entered her room with the calm smile of complete sangfroid. 'I am so glad, Bertie, you dropped in on me. Do tell me your news, darling. How is the antique business? Come and warm your poor, dear hands. It is going to be a shivering night. Won't you take off your coat? Tea? No? What about a drink? I know exactly what you want, my pet. I will fix it for you. I have been waiting and waiting for you to come all the livelong day, melting with longing and love.'

As he gently closed the door of the cosy little room she proffered her hand in a queenly manner, whereupon our hero, as was fitting, leaned over it – because you never really do kiss a lady's hand, you merely breathe over it – and watched her eyes asking him to sit opposite her.

The woman rose, took her tea tray, and the room was suddenly empty. Her toe hooked the door all but a few inches short of shut. He was just as pleased whether she was in the room or out of it. All he wanted was to be inside her room. As he stared, her naked arm came slowly back into the room between the door and the jamb, groping for the light switch. A plain gold bangle hung from the wrist. The jamb dragged back the shoulder of her blouse so that he saw the dark hair of her armpit. The window went black.

He let out a long, whistling breath like a safety valve and resumed his long perambulation until he saw a similar light streaming from the window of an identical bungalow well ahead of him on the opposite side of the roadway. He padded rapidly towards it. As he reached its identical square cement gate-pillars he halted, looked backward and forward and then guardedly advanced a tortoise nose beyond the edge of the pillar to peep into the room. A pale, dawnlike radiance, softly tasselled, hinted at comfortable shapes, a sofa, small occasional chairs, a pouffe, a bookcase, heavy gleams of what could be silver, or could be just electroplated nickel. Here, too, a few tongues of fire. In the centre of the room a tall, thin, elderly man in a yellow cardigan, but not wearing a jacket or tie, stood so close beside a young girl with a blonde waterfall of hair as to form with her a single unanalysable shape. He seemed to be speaking. He stroked her smooth poll. They were like a still image out of a silent film. They were presumably doing something simple, natural and intimate. But what? They drew apart abruptly and the girl, while stooping to pick up some shining object from a low table, looked in the same movement straight out through the window. B.B. was so taken by surprise that he could not stir, even when she came close to the window, looked up at the sky, right and left, as if to see if it was raining, turned back, laughed inaudibly, waved the small silver scissors in her hand.

In that instant, at that gesture, some time after five fifteen on the afternoon of November 1st, the town darkening, the sky lowering, his life passing, a vast illumination broke like a sunrise upon his soul. At the shut-time of the year all small towns become smaller and smaller, dwindle from out-of-doors to in-of-doors; from long beaches, black roads, green fields, wide sun, to kitchens, living rooms, bedrooms, locked doors, drawn blinds, whispers, prayers, muffling blankets, nose-hollowed pillows; from making to mending; to littler and littler things, like this blonde Rapunzel with a scissors and a needle; all ending in daydreaming, and nightdreaming, and dreamless sleeping. How pleasant life could be in that declension to a white arm creeping between a door and a jamb, bare but for a circle of gold about a wrist and a worn wedding ring on one heavy finger. But I am outside. When the town is asleep in one another's arms I will sleep under the walls. No wife. No child. Mister Bee.

The headlamps of a motorcar sent him scurrying down an unlighted lane that may once have led to the mews of tall houses long since levelled to make room for these hundreds of little bungalows. In this abandoned lane the only window-light was one tiny, lofty aperture in the inverted V of a gable rising like a castle out of tall trees. Below it, at eye level the lane was becoming pitch dark. Above it, a sift of tattered light between mourning clouds. Hissing darkness. A sheaving wind. The elms were spiky as if the earth's hair was standing on end. He stiffened. A bird's croak? A sleepless nest? A far-off bark? He stared up at the tiny box of light whose inaccessibility was so much part of its incitement that when it went black like a fallen candle he uttered a 'Ha!' of delight. He would never know who had put a finger on the switch of that floating room. A maidservant about to emerge into the town? To go where? To meet whom? A boy's den? An old woman lumbering down the long stairs?

That Monday morning B.B. was laughing happily at himself. Bertie Bolger, the well-known dealer! The Peeping Tom from Tipperary! That was a queer bloody fit I took! And Jaysus, I forgot all about the mother again: well, she will have to wait until next year now though surely to God they'll let her out before then? Anyway, what harm did she ever do bar that snibby way she treated every girl I ever met; if it wasn't for her I might have been married twenty years ago to that Raven girl I met in 1950 in Arklow. And a hot piece she was, too . . . Mad for it!

The next Sunday evening he was padding softly around the back roads of Bray. He could not locate the old-man-blonde-girl bungalow. He winked up at the little cube of light. But *Lorelei* was dark. The next two Sundays were raining too heavily for prowling. On the fourth Sunday the window of *Lorelei* was brilliantly lighted, and there she was plying a large dressmaker's scissors on some coloured stuff laid across a gate-legged table under the bare electric bulb whose brightness diminished the ideality of the room, increased the attractions of the dressmaker. Broad cheekbones, like a Red Indian; raven hair; the jerky head of a blackbird alert at a drinking pool. He longed to touch one of those fingers, broad at the tip like a little spade. Twice the lights of an oncoming car made him walk swiftly away, bowler hat down on nose, collar up. A third time he fled from light pouring out of the door of the adjacent bungalow and a woman hurrying down its path with her overcoat over her head and shoulders. Loping away fast he turned in fright to the running feet behind him and saw her coat-ends vanish under the suddenly lighted door lamp of *Lorelei*. Damn! A visitor. Spoiling it all. Yet, he came back to his watching post, as mesmerized as a man in a vast portrait gallery who returns again and again to *Portrait of Unknown Woman*, unable to tell why this one unidentified face makes him so happy. The intruder, he found, made no difference to his pleasure.

'Jenny! Isn't that a ring at the door? Who the devil can that be?'

'I bet that will be Mrs Ennis from next door, she promised to give me a hand with these curtains, you don't mind, darling, do you?'

'Mind! I'm glad you have friends, Molly.'

'Hoho! I've lots of friends.'

'Boyfriends, Katey?'

'Go 'long with you, you ruffian, don't you ever think of anything but the one thing?'

'Can you blame me with a lovely creature like you, Peggy, to be there teasin' me all day long, don't stir, I'll let her in.'

In? To what? There might be a husband and a pack of kids, and at once he had to sell his *Portrait of Unknown Woman* for the known model, not being the sort of artist who sees a new face below his window, runs out, drags her in, and without as much as asking her name spends months searching for her inner reality on his canvas.

Every Sunday he kept coming back and back to that appealing, rose-pink window until one afternoon, when he saw her again at her tea, watched her for a while, and then boldly clanged her black gate wide open, boldly strode up her path, leaped up three steps to her door, rang her bell. A soft rain had begun to sink over the town. The day was gone. A far grumble of waves from the shingle. She opened the door. So close, so solid, so near, so real he could barely recognize her. His silence made her lift her head sideways in three slow, interrogatory jerks. She had a slight squint, which he would later consider one of her most enchanting accomplishments – she might have been looking at another man behind his shoulder. He felt the excitement of the hunter at her vulnerable nearness. He suddenly smelled her. Somebody had told him you can always tell a woman's age by her scent. *Chanel* – and Weil's *Antelope* – over sixty. *Tweed* – always a mature woman.

Madame Rochas – the forties. The thirties smell of after-shave lotions: *Eau Sauvage, Moustache.* Wisps of man scent. The twenties – nothing. She had a heavy smell. Tartly she demanded, 'Yes?' Unable to speak, he produced his business card, handed it to her spade fingers. *Herbert Bolger/ Antiques/ 2 Hume Street, Dublin.* She laughed at him.

'Mister Bolger, if you are trying to buy something from me I have nothing, if you are trying to sell me something I have even less.'

He was on home ground now, they all said that, he expected it, he relied on them to say it. His whole technique of buying depended on knowing that while it is true that the so-called Big Houses of Ireland have been gleaned by the antique dealers, a lot of Big House people have been reduced to small discouraged houses like this one, bringing with them, like wartime refugees, their few remaining heirlooms. Her accent, however, was not a Big House accent. It was the accent of a workaday countrywoman. She would have nothing to sell.

'Come now, Mrs Eh? Benson? Well, now, Mrs Benson, you say you have nothing to sell but in my experience a lot of people don't know what they have. Only last week I paid a lady thirty pounds for a silver Georgian saltcellar that she never knew she possessed. You might have much more than you realize.'

He must get her alone, inside. He had had no chance to see her figure. Her hair shone like jet beads. Her skin was not a flat white. It was a lovely, rich, ivory skin, as fine as lawn or silk. He felt the rain on the back of his neck and turned up his coat collar. He felt so keyed up by her that if she touched him his string would break. She possessed one thing that she did not know about. Herself.

'Well, it is true that my late husband used to attend auctions. But.'

'Mrs Benson, may I have just one quick glance at your living room?' She wavered. They always did. He smiled reassuringly. 'Just one quick glance. It will take me two minutes.'

She looked up at the rain sifting down about her door lamp.

'Well? Alright then . . . But you are wasting your time. I assure you! And I am very busy.'

Walking behind her in the narrow hallway, he took her in from calves to head. She was two women: heavy above, lighter below. He liked her long strong legs, the wide shoulders, the action of her lean haunches, and the way her head rose above her broad shoulders. Inside, the room was rain-dim, and hour-dim, until she switched on a central hundred-and-fifty-watt bulb that drowned the soft pink of the standing lamp, showed the furniture in all its nakedness, exposed all the random marks and signs of a room that had been long lived in.

At once he regretted that he had come. He walked to the window and looked out through its small bay up and down the avenue. How appealing it was out there! All those cosy little, dozing little, rosy little bungalows up and down the avenue, these dark trees comforting the gabled house with its one cube of light, and, her window being slightly raised above the avenue, he could see the scattered windows of other cosy little houses coming awake all over the town. An hour earlier he might have been able to see the bruise-blue line of the Irish Sea. *I could live in any one of those little houses out there,* and he turned to look at her uncertainly – like a painter turning from easel to model, from model to easel, wondering which was the concoction and which was the truth.

'Well?' she asked impatiently.

His eye helicoptered over her cheap furniture. Ten seconds sufficed. He looked at her coldly. *If he were outside there now on the pavement, looking in at her rosy lamp lighting . . .*

'There is,' she said defensively, 'a mirror.'

She opened the leaves of large folding doors in the rear wall, led him into the room beyond them, flooded it with light. An electric sewing machine, patterns askew on the wall, a long deal table strewn with scattered bits of material, a tailoress's wire dummy and, incongruously, over the empty fireplace, a lavish baroque mirror, deeply bevelled, sunk in a swarm of golden fruit and flowers, carved wood and moulded gesso. Spanish? Italian? It could be English. It might, rarest of all, be Irish. Not a year less than two hundred years old. He flung his arms up to it.

'And you said you had nothing! She's a beauty! I'd be delighted to buy this pretty bauble from you.'

She sighed at herself in her mirror.

'I did not say I have nothing, Mr Bolger. I said I have nothing for you. My mirror is not for sale. It was my husband's engagement present to me. He bought it at an auction in an old house in Wexford. It was the only object of any interest in the house, so there were no dealers present. He got it for five pounds.'

He darted to it through an envious groan. He talked at her through it.

'Structurally? Fine. A leaf missing here. A rose gone there. Some scoundrel has dotted it here and there with commercial gold paint. And somebody has done worse. Somebody's been cleaning it. Look here and here and here at the white gesso coming through the gold leaf. It could cost a hundred pounds of gold leaf to do it all over again. Have you,' he said sharply to her in the mirror, 'been cleaning it?'

'I confess I tried. But I stopped when I saw that chalky stuff coming through. I did, honestly.'

He considered her avidly in the frame. So appealing in her contrition, a fallen Eve. He turned to her behind him. How strongly built and bold she was! Bold as brass. Soft as silk. No question – *two* women!

'Mrs Benson, have you any idea what this mirror is worth?'

She hooted at him derisively.

'Three times what you would offer as a buyer, and three times that again for what you would ask as a seller.'

He concealed his delight in her toughness. He made a sad face. He sighed heavily.

'Lady! Nobody trusts poor old B.B. But you don't know how the game goes. I look at that mirror and I say to myself, "How long will I wait to get how much for it?" I say, "Price, one hundred pounds," and I sell it inside a month. I say, "Price, two hundred pounds," and I have to wait six months. Think of my overheads for six months! If I were living in London and I said, "Price, three hundred pounds," I'd sell it inside a week. If I lived in New York, I could say, "Price fifteen hundred dollars," and I'd sell it in a day. If I lived on a coral island it wouldn't be worth two coconuts. That mirror has no absolute value. To you it's priceless because it has memories. I respect you for that, Mrs Benson. What's life without memories? I'll give you ninety pounds for it.'

They were side by side, in her mirror, in her room, in her life. He could see her still smiling at him. Pretending she was sorry she had cleaned it! Putting it on! They do, yeh know, they do! And they change, oho, they change. Catch her being sorry for anything. Smiling now like a girl caught in fragrant delight. Listen to this:—

'It is not for sale, Mr Bolger. My memories are not on the market. That is not a mirror. It is a picture. The day my husband bought it we stood side by side and he said,' she laughed at him in the mirror, '"We're not a bad looking pair."'

He stepped sideward out of her memories, keeping her framed.

'I'll give you a hundred quid for it. I couldn't possibly sell it for more than a hundred and fifty pounds. There aren't that many people in

Dublin who know the value of a mirror like yours. The most I can make is twenty-five percent. You are a dressmaker. Don't you count on making twenty-five percent? Where are you from?' he asked, pointing eagerly.

'I'm a Ryan from Tipperary,' she laughed, taken by his eagerness, laughing the louder when he cried (untruthfully) that he was a Tipp man himself.

'Then you are no true Tipperary woman if you don't make fifty percent! What about it? Tipp to Tipp. A hundred guineas? A hundred and ten guineas? Going, going...?'

'It is not for sale,' she said with a clipped finality. 'It is my husband's mirror. It is our mirror. It will always be our mirror,' and he surrendered to the memory she was staring at.

As she closed the door on his departure there passed between them the smiles of equal strangers who, in other circumstances, might have been equal friends. He walked away, exhilarated, completely satisfied. He had got rid of his fancy. She had not come up to his dream. He was cured.

The next Sunday afternoon, bowler hat on nose, collar up, scarfed, standing askew behind her pillar, the red lamp glowing, will now always glow above the dark head of Mrs Benson, widow, hard-pressed dressmaker, born in Tipperary, sipping Indian tea, munching an English biscuit, reading a paperback, her civil respite from tedious labour. How appealing! She has beaten a cosy path of habit that he lusts to have, own, at least to share with her. 'I can make antiques but I can't make age, I could buy the most worn bloody old house in Ireland and I wouldn't own one minute of its walls, trees, stones, moss, slates, gravel, rust, lichen, ageing.' And he remembered the old lady in a stinking dry-rotted house in Westmeath, filled with eighteenth-century stuff honeycombed by wood-worm, who would not sell him as much as a snuffbox because, 'Mister Bulgey, there is not a pebble in my garden but has its story.'

Bray. For sale. Small modern bungalow. Fully furnished. View of sea. Complete with ample widow attached to the front doorknob. Fingerprints alive all over the house.

He pushed the gate open, smartly leaped her steps, rang.

A fleck of biscuit clung childishly to her lower lip. Her grey eye, delicately defective, floated beyond his face as disconcertingly as a thought across surprise.

'Not you again!' she laughed lavishly.

'Mrs Bee! I have a proposition.'

'Mister Bee! I do not intend to sell you my mirror. Ever!'

'Missus Bee! I do not want your mirror. What I have to propose will take exactly two tics. I swear it. And then I fly.'

She sighed, looked far, far away. Out over the night sea?

'For two minutes? Very well. But not *one* second more!'

She showed him into the living room and, weakening – in the name of hospitality? of Tipperary? of old country ways? – she goes into the recesses of her home for an extra cup. In sole possession of her interior he looks out under the vast umbrella of the dusk, out over the punctured encampment of roofs. Could I live here? Why does this bloody room never look the same inside and outside? Live *here*? Always? It would be remote. Morning train to Dublin. In the evenings, this, when I had tarted it up a bit, made it as cosy, lit inside, as it looks from the outside.

'My husband,' she said, pouring, 'always liked China tea. You don't mind?'

'I am very partial to it. It appeals to my aesthetic sense. Jasmine flowers. May I ask what your husband used to do?'

'Ken was an assessor for an English insurance company. He was English.'

He approved mightily, fingers widespread, chin enthusiastically nodding.

'A fine profession! A very fine profession!'

'So fine,' she said wryly, 'that he took out a policy on his own life for a bare one thousand pounds. And I am now a dressmaker.'

'Family?' he asked tenderly.

She smiled softly.

'My daughter, Leslie. She is at a boarding school. I am hoping to send her to the university. What is your proposition?'

Her profile, soft as a seaflower, changed to the obtuseness of a deathmask, until, frontally, its lower lip caught the light, the eyes became alert, the face hard with character.

'It is a simple little proposition. Your mirror, we agree, is a splendid object, but for your business quite unsuitable. Any woman looking into it can only half see herself. What you need is a great, wide, large, gilt-framed mirror, pinned flat against the wall, clear as crystal, a real professional job, where a lady can see herself from top to toe twirling and turning like a ballet dancer.' He smiled mockingly. 'Give your clients status.' He proceeded earnestly. 'Worth another two hundred pounds a year to you. You would be employing two assistants in no time. I happen to have a mirror just like that in my showrooms. I've had it for six years and nobody has wanted it.' He paused, smiling from jawbone to jawbone. 'I would like you to take it. As a gift.'

Shrewdly he watched her turning her teacup between her palms as if she were warming a brandy glass, while she observed him sideward just as shrewdly out of an eye as fully circled as a bird's. At last she smiled, laid down her cup, leaned back and said, 'Go on, Mr B.'

'How do you mean, "go on"?'

'You have only told me half your proposition. You want something in return?'

He laughed with his throat, teeth, tongue and gullet, enjoying her hugely.

'Not really!'

She laughed, enjoying him as hugely.

'Meaning?'

He rose, walked to the window, now one of those black mirrors that painters use to eliminate colour in order to reveal design. The night had blotted out everything except an impression of two or three pale hydrangea leaves wavering outside in the December wind and, inside, himself and a lampshade. He began to feel that he had already taken up residence here. He turned to the woman looking at him coldly under eyebrows as heavy as two dark moustaches and flew into a rage at her resistance.

'Dammit! Can't you give me credit for wanting to give you something for your own sake?' As quickly he calmed. The proud animal was staring timidly, humbly, contritely. Or was she having him on again? She could hide anything behind that lovely squint of hers. He demanded abruptly, 'Do you ever go into Dublin?'

She glanced at the doors of her workroom.

'I must go there tomorrow morning to buy some linings. Why?'

'Tomorrow I have to deliver a small Regency chest to a lady in Greystones. On my way back I could call for you here at ten o'clock, drive you into Dublin and show you that big mirror of mine, and you can take it or leave it, as you like.' He got up to go. 'Okay?'

She gave an unwilling assent but as she opened the front door to let him out added, 'Though I am not at all sure that I entirely understand you, Mister B.'

'Aren't you?' he asked with an impish animation.

'No, I am not!' she said crossly. 'Not at all sure.'

Halfway across her ten feet of garden he turned and laughed derisively, 'Have a look at the surface of your mirror,' and twanged out and was lost in a dusk of sea-fog.

She returned slowly to her workroom. She approached her mirror and peered over its surface. Flawless. Not a breath of dust. With one spittled finger she removed a flyspeck. What did the silly little man mean? Without being aware of what she was doing she looked at herself, patted her hair in place, smoothed her fringe, arranged the shoulder peaks of her blouse, then, her dark eyebrows floating, her bister eyelids sinking, her back straight, her bosom lifted, she drawled, 'I really am afraid, Mister B., that I still do *not* at all understand you,' and chuckled at the effect. Her jaw shot out, she glared furiously at her double, she silently mouthed the word, 'Fathead!' seized her scissors and returned energetically to work. She would fix him! Tomorrow morning she would let the ten o'clock train take her to Dublin.

He took her to Dublin, and to lunch, and to her amused satisfaction admitted that there was a second part to his proposition. He sometimes persuaded the owners of better class country hotels to allow him to leave one or two of his antiques, with his card attached, on view in their public rooms. It could be a Dutch landscape, or a tidy piece of Sheraton or Hepplewhite. Free advertisement for him, free decor for them. Would she like to cooperate? 'Where on earth,' some well-off client would say, 'did you get that lovely thing?' – and she would say, 'Bolger's Antiques.' She was so pleased to have foreseen that there would be some such *quid pro quo* that she swallowed the bait. So, the next Sunday, though he did not bring his big mirror, he brought a charming Boucher fire screen. The following Sunday his van was out of order, but he did bring a handsome pair of twisted Georgian candlesticks for her mantelpiece. Every Sunday, except during the Christmas holidays when he did not care to face her daughter, Leslie, he brought something: a carved, bronze chariot, Empire style, containing a clock, a neat Nelson sideboard, a copper warming pan, so that they always had something to discuss over their afternoon tea. It amused and pleased her until the day came when he produced a pair of (he swore) genuine Tudor curtains for her front window and she could no longer conceal from herself that she was being formally courted, and that her living room had meanwhile been transformed from what it had been four months ago.

The climax came at Easter when, for Leslie's sake, she weakly allowed him to present her with two plane tickets for a Paris holiday. In addition he promised to visit her bungalow every day and sleep there every night while she was away. On her return she found that he had left a comic 'Welcome Home' card on her hall table; that her living room was sweet with mimosa; that he had covered her old-fashioned wallpaper with (he explained) a hand-painted French paper in (she would observe) a pattern of Notre Dame, the Eiffel Tower, the Arc de Triomphe and the Opéra; replaced her old threadworn carpet – she and Ken had bought it nearly twenty years ago in Clery's in O'Connell Street – by (he alleged) a *quali* Persian carpet three hundred years old; and exchanged her central plastic electric shade for (he mentioned) a Waterford cluster. In fact he had got rid of every scrap of her life except her mirror, which now hung over her fireplace, her pink lamp and, she said it to herself, 'Me?'

The next Sunday she let him in, sat opposite him, and was just about to say her rehearsed bit of gallows humour— 'I am sorry to have to tell you, Bertie, that I don't particularly like your life, may I have mine back again please?' – when she saw him looking radiantly at her, realized that by accepting so many disguised gifts she had put herself in a false position, and burst into tears of shame and rage. Bertie, whose many years of servitude with his mother had made all female tears seem as ludicrous as a baby's squealing face, laughed boomingly at her, enchanted to see this powerful woman so completely in his power. The experience filled him with such joy that he sank on his knees beside her, flung his arms about her, and said, 'Maisie, will you marry me?' She drew back her fist, gave him such a clout on the jaw that he fell on his poll, shouted at him, 'Get up, you worm! And get out!'

With hauteur he went.

She held out against him for six months, though still permitting him to visit her every Sunday for afternoon tea and a chat. In November, without warning, her resistance gave out. Worn down by his persistence? Or her own calculations? By her ambitions for Leslie? Perhaps by weariness of the flesh at the prospect of a life of dressmaking? Certainly by none of the hopes, dreams, illusions, fears and needs that might have pressed other hardpressed women into holy wedlock; above all not by the desires of the flesh – these she had never felt for Bertie Bolger.

He made it a lavish wedding, which she did not dislike; he also made it showy, which she did not like; but she was soon to find that he did everything to excess, including eating, always defending himself by the plea that if a man or a woman is any good you cannot have too much of them; a principle that ought to have led him to marry the Fat Lady in the circus, or led her to marry Paddy O'Brien, the Irish giant, who was nine feet high and whose skeleton she had once seen preserved in the College of Surgeons. 'Is he all swank and bluff?' she wondered. Even on their honeymoon she discovered that after a day of boasting about his prowess compared with all his competitors, it was ten to one that he would either be crying on her shoulder long past midnight, or yelping like a puppy in one of his nightmares; both of which performances (her word) she bore with patience until the morning he dared to give her dogs' abuse for being the sole cause of all of them, whereat she ripped him with a kick like a cassowary. She read an article about exhibitionism. That was him! She read a thriller about a manic-depressive strangler, and peeping cautiously across the pillows, felt that she should never go to bed with him without a pair of antique duelling pistols under her side of the mattress.

Within six months they both knew that their error was so plenary, so total, so irreducible that it should have been beyond speech – as it was not. He said that he felt a prisoner in this bloody bungalow of hers. He said that whenever he stood inside her window (and his Tudor curtains) and looked out at those hundreds of lovely, loving, kindly, warm, glowing, little peaked bungalows outside there he knew that he had picked the only goddam one of the whole frigging lot that was totally uninhabitable. She said she had been as free as the wind until he took forcible possession of her property and filled it with his fake junk. He said she was a bully. She told him he was a bluffer. He said, 'I thought you had brains but I've eaten better.' She said, 'You're a dreamer!' He said, 'You're a dressmaker!' She said, 'You don't know from one minute to the next whether you want to be Jesus Christ or Napoleon.' He shouted, 'Outside the four walls of this bungalow you're an ignoramus, apart from what little I've been able to teach you.' She said, 'Outside your business, Bertie Bolger, and that doesn't bear close examination, if I gave you three minutes to tell me all *you* know, it would be six minutes too much.' All of it as meaningless and unjust as every marital quarrel since Adam and Eve began to bawl with one voice, 'But *you* said . . . ,' and 'I know what *I* said, but you said . . . ' 'Yes but then *you* said . . .'

His older, her more recent club acquaintances chewed a clearer cud. At the common table I once heard three or four of them mentioning him over lunch. They said next to nothing but their tone was enough. Another of those waxwork effigies that manage somehow or other to get past the little black ball into the most select clubs. Mimes, mimics, fair imitations, plausible impersonations of The Real Thing, a procession of puppets, a march of masks, a covey of cozens, a levee of liars: chaps for whom conversation means anecdotes, altruism alms, discipline suppression, justice calling in the police, pleasure puking in the washroom, pride swank, love lust, honesty guilt, religion fear, patriotism greed and success cash. But if you asked any of those old members to say any of this about Bertie? They would look you straight in the top button of your weskit and say, without humour, 'A white man.' And Maisie? 'A very nice little wife.'

Dear Jesus! Is life in all clubs reduced like this to white men and nice little wives? Sometimes to worse. As well as clubbites there are clubesses to whom the truth is told between the sheets and by whom enlarged, exaggerated, falsified, and spread wide. After all, the men had merely kicked the testicles of his reputation; the wives castrated him. They took Maisie's part. A fine, natural countrywoman, they said; honest as the daylight; warm as toast if you did not cross her, and then she could handle her tongue like the tail end of a whip; a woman who carried her liquor like a man; as agile at Contract as a trout; could have mothered ten and would never give one to Bertie, whom she had let marry her only because she saw he was the sort of weakling who always wants somebody to lean on, and did not find out until too late that he was miles away from what every woman really wants, which is somebody she can rely on. Their judgment made him seem much less than he was, her much more. The result of it was that he was soon feeling the cold wind of Dublin's whispering gallery on his neck and had to do something to assert himself unless he was to fall dead under the sting of its mockery.

Accordingly, one Sunday afternoon in November, a year after his marriage, he packed two suitcases, called a cab, and drove off down the lighted avenue to resume his not unimportant role in life as the Mister

Bee of some lonely guest house. It had not, at the end, been her wish. If she had not grown a little fond of him she had begun to feel a little sorry for him. Besides, next autumn Leslie would be down on her fingers and up on her toes at the starting line for the university, waiting eagerly for the revolver's flat 'Go!'

'This is silly, Bertie!' she had shrugged as they heard and saw the taxi pulling up outside their window. 'Husbands and wives always quarrel.' He picked up his two suitcases and looked around the room at his lost illusions, a Prospero leaving for the mainland. 'It's nothing unusual,' she had said, to comfort him. 'It happens in every house,' she had pleaded, 'but they carry on.'

'You bitch!' he had snarled, making for the door. 'You broke my heart. I thought you were perfect.'

She need not have winced, knowing well that they had both married for reasons the heart knows nothing of. Nevertheless she had gone gloomily into her dining room, which must again become her workroom. The sixty pounds that he had agreed to pay her henceforth every month, though much more than she had had before they met, would not support two people. Looking about it she noted, with annoyance, that she had never got that big mirror out of him.

So then, a dusky Sunday afternoon in Bray, at a quarter to five o'clock, lighting up time five fifteen, All Soul's Eve, dedicated to the souls of the dead suffering in the fires of Purgatory, Bertie Bolger, half Benedict half bachelor, aged forty-four, tubby, ruddy, greying, walking sedately along the seafront, sees ahead of him the Imperial Hotel and stops dead, remembering.

'I wonder!' he wonders, and leaning over the promenade's railings, sky-blue with orange knobs, rusting to death since the nineteenth century, looks down at the damp pebbles of the beach. 'How is she doing these days?' and turns smartly inland towards the town.

At this ambiguous hour few houses in Bray show lighted windows. The season is over, the Sunday silent, landladies once more reckoning their takings, snoozing, thinking of minute repairs, or praying, in *Liljoe's, Fatima, The Billows, Swan Lake, Sea View*. Peering ahead of him Mr B. sees, away down the avenue, a calm glow from a window and feels thereat the first, delicate, subcutaneous tingle that he has so often felt in the presence of some desirable object whose value the owner does not know. Nor does he know why those rare lighted windows are so troubling, suggestive, inviting, rejecting, familiar, foreign, like any childhood's nonesuch, griffin, mermaid, unicorn, hippogriff, dragon, centaur, crested castle in the mountains where there grows the golden rose of the world's end. Not knowing, he ignores that first far-off glow, turns from it as from a temptation to sin, turns right, turns left, walks faster and faster as from pursuing danger, until his head begins to swim and his heart to drumroll at the sight, along the perspective of another avenue, of a lighted roseate window that he knows he knows.

As he comes near to *Lorelei* he looks carefully around him to be sure that he is not observed by some filthy Paul Pry who might remember him from that year of his so-called marriage. He slows his pace. He slowly stalks the pillar of his wife's house. He peeps inside and straightway has to lean against the pillar to steady himself, feeling his old dream begin to swell and swell, his old disturbance mount, fear and joy invade his blood at the sight of her seated before the fire, placid, self-absorbed, her teacup in her hand, her eyes on her book, the pink glow on her threequarter face, more than ever appealing, inciting, sealed, bonded, unattainable.

I *have* neglected her. I owe her restitution. He enters the garden, twangs the gate, mounts the steps, rings the bell, turns to see the dark enfold the town. A scatter of lights. The breathing of the waves. The glow of a bus zooming up Kilruddery Hill a mile away, lighting the low clouds, bare trees, passing the Earl of Meath's broken walls, his gateway's squat Egyptian pillars bearing, in raised lettering, the outdated motto of his line, LABOR VITA MEA.

'Bertie!'

'Maisie!'

'I'm so glad you dropped in, Bertie. Come in. Take your coat off and draw up to the fire. It's going to be a shivering night. Let me fix you a drink. The usual, I suppose?' Her back to him: – 'As a matter of fact I've been expecting you every Sunday. I've been waiting and waiting for you.' She laughed. 'Or do you expect me to say I've been longing and longing for you since you abandoned me last November?'

He looks out, shading his eyes, sees the window opposite light up. They, too, have a pink lampshade.

'That,' he said, 'is the Naughtons' bungalow, isn't it? It looks very cosy. Very nice. I sometimes used to think I'd be happy living there, looking across at you.'

She glances at it, handing him the whiskey, sits facing him, pokes the fire ablaze.

'We're all alike, in our bungalows. Why did you come today, Bertie?'

'It's our marriage anniversary. I didn't know what gift to send you, so I thought I would just ask. Hello! Your mirror is gone!'

'I had to put it back in my workroom. If you want to give me a present give me your mirror.'

'Jesus, I never did give it to you, did I? Next Sunday, I swear! Cross my heart! I'll bring it out without fail. If the van is free.'

In this easy way they chatted of this and that, and he went on his way, and he came back the next Sunday, though not with his mirror, and he came every Sunday month after month for tea or a drink. On his fourth visit she produced, for his greater comfort, an old pair of felt slippers he had left behind him, and on the fifth Sunday a pipe of his that she had discovered at the bottom of a drawer. He did not come around Christmas, feeling that Leslie would prefer to be alone with her mother. Instead he spent it at the Imperial Hotel. In a blue paper hat? She refused to let him send them both to Paris for Easter but she did let him send Leslie. For her own Easter present she asked, 'Could I possibly have that mirror, Bertie?' – and he promised it, and did not keep his promise, saying that someday she would be sure to give up dressmaking and not need it, and anyway he was somehow getting attached to the old thing, it would leave a big pale blank on his wall if he gave it away, and after all she had a mirror of her own, but he promised, nevertheless, that he would sometime give it to her.

The music of the steam carousel played on the front, the town became gay, English tourists strolled up and down the lapis lazuli and orange promenade, voices carried, and now and again he went for a swim before calling on her, until imperceptibly it was autumn again, with the rainy light fading at half past four and her rosy window appealing to him to come inside, and in her mirror he would tidy his windblown hair and his tie, and look in puzzlement around the room, and speculatively back at her behind him pouring his drink, just as if he were her husband and this was really his home, so that it was a full year again, and November, and All Souls' Eve before she saw him drive up outside her gate, accompanied by his man Scofield, in his pale blue-and-pink van, marked along its side in Gothic silver lettering, BOLGER'S ANTIQUES, and, protruding from it his big mirror, wrapped in felt and burlap. She greeted it from her steps with a mock cheer that died when Scofield's eye flitted from the mirror to her door, and from door back to mirror, and Bertie's did the same, and hers did the same, and they all three knew at once that his mirror was too big for her. Still, they tried, until the three of them were standing in a row in her garden looking at themselves in it where it leaned against the tall privet hedge lining the avenue, a cold wind cooling the sweat on their foreheads.

'I suppose,' Bertie said, 'we could cut the bloody thing up! Or down!' – and remembering one of those many elegant, useless, disconnected things he had learned at school from the Benedictines, he quoted from the Psalms the words of Christ about the soldiers on Calvary dicing for his garments: – '*Diviserunt sibi vestimenta mea et super vestem meam miserunt sortem.*'

'Go on!' he interpreted. 'Cut me frigging shirt in bits and play cards for me jacket and me pants,' which was the sign for her to lead him gently indoors and make three boiling hot toddies for their shivering bones.

He was silent as he drank his first dram, and his second. After the third dram he said, okay, this was it, he would never come here again, moving with her and Scofield to the window to look at his bright defeat leaning against the rampant hedge of privet.

And, behold, it was glowing with the rosiness of the window and the three of them out there looking in at themselves from under the falling darkness and the wilderness of stars over town and sea, a vision so unlikely, disturbing, appealing, inviting, promising, demanding, enlisting that he swept her to him and held her so long, so close, so tight that the next he heard was the pink-and-blue van driving away down the avenue. He turned for reassurance to the gleaming testimony in the garden and cried, 'We'll leave it there always! It makes everything more real!' At which, as well she might, she burst into laughter at the sight of him staring out at himself staring in.

'You bloody loon!' she began, and stopped.

She had heard country tales about people who have seen on the still surface of a well, not their own hungry eyes but the staring eyes of love.

'If that *is* what you really want,' she said quietly, and kissed him, and looked out at them both looking in.

Murder at Cobbler's Hulk

It takes about an hour of driving southward out of Dublin to arrive at the small seaside village of Greystones. (For two months in the summer, it calls itself a resort.) Every day, four commuter trains from the city stop here and turn back, as if dismayed by the sight of the desolate beach of shingle that stretches beyond it for twelve unbroken miles. A single line, rarely used, continues the railway beside this beach, on and on, so close to the sea that in bad winters the waves pound in across the track, sometimes blocking it for days on end with heaps of gravel, uprooted sleepers, warped rails. When this happens, the repair gangs have a dreary time of it. No shelter from the wind and spray. Nothing to be seen inland but reedy fields, an occasional farmhouse or abandoned manor, a few leafless trees decaying in the arid soil or fallen sideways. And, always, endless fleets of clouds sailing away towards the zinc-blue horizon.

Once there were three more tiny railway stations along these twelve miles of beach, each approached by a long lane leading from the inland carriage road to the sea. The best preserved of what remains of them is called Cobbler's Hulk. From a distance, one might still mistake it for a real station. Close up, one finds only a boarded waiting room whose tin roof lifts and squeaks in the wind, a lofty signal cabin with every window broken and a still loftier telephone pole whose ten crossbars must once have carried at least twenty lines and now bear only one humming wire. There is a rotting, backless bench. You could scythe the grass on the platform. The liveliest thing here is an advertisement on enamelled sheet metal, high up on the brick wall of the signal cabin. It showed the single white word STEPHEN'S splashed across a crazy blob of black ink. Look where one will, there is not a farmhouse nor cottage within sight.

It was down here that I first met Mr Bodkin one Sunday afternoon last July. He was sitting straight up on the bench, bowler-hatted, clad, in spite of the warmth of the day, in a well-brushed blue chesterfield with concealed buttons and a neatly tailored velvet half collar that was the height of fashion in the Twenties. His grey spats were as tight as gloves across his insteps He was a smallish man. His stiff shirt collar was as high as the Duke of Wellington's, his bow tie was polka-dotted, his white moustaches were brushed up like a Junker's. He could have been seventy-three. His cheeks were as pink as a baby's bottom. His palms lay crossed on the handle of a rolled umbrella, he had a neatly folded newspaper under his arm, his patent-leather shoe tips gleamed like his pince-nez. Normally, I would have given him a polite 'Good day to you' and passed on, wondering. Coming on him suddenly around the corner of the waiting room, his head lowered towards his left shoulder as if he were listening for an approaching train, I was so taken by surprise that I said, 'Are you waiting for a train?'

'Good gracious!' he said, in equal surprise. 'A train has not stopped here since the Bronze Age. Didn't you know?'

I gazed at his shining toes, remembering that when I had halted my Morris Minor beside the level-crossing gates at the end of the lane, there had been no other car parked there. Had he walked here? That brambled lane was a mile long. He peeked at the billycan in my hand, guessed that I was proposing to brew myself a cup of tea after my solitary swim, chirruped in imitation of a parrot, 'Any water?' rose and, in the comic-basso voice of a weary museum guide, said, 'This way, please.' I let him lead me along the platform, past the old brass faucet that I had used on my few previous visits to Cobbler's Hulk, towards a black-tarred railway carriage hidden below the marshy side of the track. He pointed the ferrule of his umbrella.

'My chalet,' he said smugly. 'My *wagon-lit*.'

We descended from the platform by three wooden steps, rounded a microscopic gravel path, and he unlocked the door of his carriage. It was still faintly marked FIRST CLASS, but it also bore a crusted brass plate whose shining rilievo announced THE VILLA ROSE. He bowed me inward, invited me to take a pew (his word for an upholstered carriage seat), filled my billycan from a white enamelled bucket ('Pure spring water!') and, to expedite matters further, insisted on boiling it for me on his Primus stove. As we waited, he sat opposite me. We both looked out the window at the marshes. I heard a Guard's whistle and felt our carriage jolt away to nowhere. We introduced ourselves.

'I trust you find my beach a pleasant spot for a picnic?' he said, as if he owned the entire Irish Sea.

I told him that I had come here about six times over the past thirty years.

'I came here three years ago. When I retired.'

I asked about his three winters. His fingers dismissed them. 'Our glorious summers amply recompense.' At which exact moment I heard sea birds dancing on the roof and Mr Bodkin became distressed. His summer and his beach were misbehaving. He declared that the shower would soon pass. I must have my cup of afternoon tea with him, right there. 'In first-class comfort.' I demurred; he insisted. I protested gratefully; he persisted tetchily. I let him have his way, and that was how I formed Mr Bodkin's acquaintance.

It never became any more. I saw him only once again, for five minutes, six weeks later. But, helped by a hint or two from elsewhere – the man who kept the roadside shop at the end of the lane, a gossipy barmaid in the nearest hamlet – it was enough to let me infer, guess at, induce his life. Its fascination was that he had never had any. By comparison, his beach and its slight sand dunes beside the railway track were crowded with incident, as he presently demonstrated by producing the big album of pressed flowers that he had been collecting over the past three years. His little ear finger stirred them gently on their white pages: milfoil, yarrow, thrift, sea daisies, clover, shepherd's-needle, shepherd's-purse, yellow bedstraw, stone bedstraw, great bedstraw, Our-Lady's-bedstraw, minute sand roses, different types of lousewort. In the pauses between their naming, the leaves were turned as quietly as the wavelets on the beach.

One December day in 1912, when he was fifteen, Mr Bodkin told me, he had entered his lifelong profession by becoming the messenger boy in Tyrrell's Travel Agency, located at 15 Grafton Street, Dublin. He went into Dublin every morning on the Howth tram, halting it outside the small pink house called The Villa Rose, where he lived with his mother, his father, his two young sisters and his two aunts...

The Villa Rose! He made a deprecatory gesture – it had been his mother's idea. The plays and novels of Mr A. E. Mason were popular around 1910. He wrinkled his rosy nose. It was not even what you could call a real house. Just two fishermen's cottages joined front to back, with a dip, or valley, between their adjoining roofs. But what a situation! On fine days, he could see, across the high tide of the bay, gulls blowing about like paper, clouds reflected in the still water, an occasional funnel moving slowly in or out of the city behind the long line of the North Wall; and away beyond it, all the silent drums of the Wicklow Mountains. Except on damp days, of course. The windows of The Villa Rose were always sea-dimmed on damp days. His mother suffered from chronic arthritis. His father's chest was always wheezing. His sisters' noses were always running. His aunts spent half their days in bed.

'I have never in my life had a day's illness! Apart from chilblains. I expect to live to be ninety.'

The great thing, it appeared, about Tyrrell's Travel Agency was that you always knew where you were. The Tyrrell system was of the simplest: Everybody was addressed according to his rank. (Mr Bodkin did not seem to realize that this system was, in his boyhood as in mine, universal in every corner of the British Empire.) Whenever old Mr Bob wanted him, he shouted 'Tommy!' at the top of his voice. After shouting at him like that for about five years, Mr Bob suddenly put him behind the counter, addressed him politely as 'Bodkin' and shouted at him no longer. Five years passed and, again without any preliminaries, Mr Bob presented him with a desk of his own in a corner of the office and addressed him as 'Mr Bodkin.' At which everybody in the place smiled, nodded or winked his congratulations. He had arrived at the top of his genealogical tree. He might fall from it. He would never float beyond it. Very satisfactory. One has to have one's station in life. Yes?

The summer shower stopped, but not Mr Bodkin. (In the past three years, I wondered if he had had a single visitor to talk to.) There were, I must understand, certain seeming contradictions in the system. An eager ear and a bit of experience soon solved them all. For example, there was the case of old Clancy, the ex-Enniskillener Dragoon, who opened the office in the morning and polished the Egyptian floor tiles. Anybody who wanted him always shouted, 'Jimmy!' Clear as daylight. But whenever old Lady Kilfeather came sweeping into the agency from her grey Jaguar, ruffling scent, chiffon, feather boas and Protestant tracts, she clancied the whole bang lot of them.

'Morning, Tyrrell! Hello, Bodkin! I hope Murphy has that nice little jaunt to Cannes all sewn up for myself and Kilfeather? Clancy, kindly read this leaflet on Mariolatry and do, for heaven's sake, stop saying "Mother of God!" every time you see me!'

The aristocratic privilege. The stars to their stations; the planets in their stately cycles about the sun; until the lower orders bitch it all up.

Meaning old Mrs Clancy, swaying into the office like an inebriated camel, to beg a few bob from Clancy for what she genteelly called her shopping. Never once had that woman, as she might reasonably have done, asked for 'Jim.' Never for 'Mr Clancy.' Never even for 'my husband.' Always for 'Clancy.' Mr Bodkin confessed that he sometimes felt so infuriated with her that he would have to slip around the corner to the Three Feathers, to calm his gut with a Guinness and be reassured by the barman's 'The usual, Mr B.?' Not that he had ever been entirely happy about that same B. He always countered it with a stiff, 'Thank you, Mr Buckley.'

It was the only pub he ever visited. And never for more than one glass of plain. Occasionally, he used to go to the theatre. But only for Shakespeare. Or Gilbert and Sullivan. Only for the classics. Opera? Never! For a time, he had been amused by Shaw. But he soon discarded him as a typical Dublin jackeen mocking his betters. Every Sunday, he went to church to pray for the king. He was nineteen when the Rebellion broke out. He refused to believe in it. Or that the dreadful shootings and killings of the subsequent Troubles could possibly produce any change. And did they? Not a damned thing! Oh, some client might give his name in the so-called Irish language. Mr Bodkin simply wrote down, 'Mr Irish.' Queenstown became Cobh. What nonsense! Kingstown became Dun Laoghaire. Pfoo! Pillar boxes were painted green. The police were called Guards. The army's khaki was dyed green. All the whole damned thing boiled down to was that a bit of the House of Commons was moved from London to Dublin.

Until the Second World War broke out. Travel stopped dead. The young fellows in the office joined the army. He remembered how old Mr Bob – they ran the office between them – kept wondering for weeks how the Serbians would behave this time. And what on earth had happened to those gallant little Montenegrins? When the Germans invaded Russia, Mr Bob said that the czar would soon put a stop to that nonsense. Mind you, they had to keep on their toes after 1945. He would never forget the first time a client said he wanted to visit Yugoslavia. He took off his glasses, wiped them carefully, and produced a map. And, by heavens, there it was!

There had been other changes. His mother had died when he was forty-three. His two aunts went when he was in his fifties. To his astonishment, both his sisters married. His father was the last to go, at the age of eighty-one. He went on living, alone, in The Villa Rose, daily mistering thousands of eager travellers around Europe by luxury liners, crowded packet boats, Blue Trains, Orient Expresses, Settebellos, Rheingolds, alphabetical-mathematical planes. He had cars waiting for some, arranged hotels for others, confided to a chosen few the best places (according to 'my old friend Lady Kilfeather') to dine, drink and dance, and he never went anywhere himself.

'You mean you *never* wanted to travel?'

'At first, yes. When I could not afford it. Later, I was saving up for my retirement. Besides, in my last ten years there, the whole business began to bore me.'

He paused, frowned and corrected himself. It had not 'begun' to bore. His interest in it had died suddenly. It happened one morning when he was turning back into the office after conducting Lady Kilfeather out to her grey Jaguar. Observing him, young Mr James had beckoned him into his sanctum.

'A word in your ivory ear, Mr Bodkin? I notice that you have been bestowing quite an amount of attention on Lady Kilfeather.'

'Yes, indeed, Mr James! And I may say that she has just told me that she is most pleased with us.'

'As she might well be! Considering that it takes six letters and eight months to get a penny out of the old bitch. That woman, Mr Bodkin, is known all over Dublin as a first-class scrounger, time waster and bloodsucker. I would be obliged if you would in future bear in mind three rather harsh facts of life that my aged parent seems never to have explained to you. Time is money. Your time is my money. And no client's money is worth more to me than any other client's money. Take it to heart, Mr Bodkin. Thank you. That will be all for now.'

Mr Bodkin took it to heart so well that from that morning on, all those eager travellers came to mean no more to him than a trainload of tourists to a railway porter after he has banged the last door and turned away through the steam of the departing engine for a quick smoke before the next bunch arrived.

Still, duty was duty. And he had his plans. He hung on until he was sixty-five and then he resigned. Mr James, with, I could imagine, an immense sense of relief, handed him a bonus of fifty pounds – a quid for every year of his service, but no pension – shook his hand and told him to go off to Cannes and live there in sin for a week with a cabaret dancer. Mr Bodkin said that for years he had been dreaming of doing exactly that with Mrs Clancy, accepted the fifty quid, said a warm goodbye to everybody in the office, sold The Villa Rose and bought the tarred railway carriage at Cobbler's Hulk. He had had his eye on it for the past five years.

The night he arrived at Cobbler's Hulk, it was dry and cold. He was sweating from lugging two suitcases down the dark lane. The rest of his worldly belongings stood waiting for him in a packing case on the grass-grown platform. For an hour, he sat in his carriage by candlelight, in his blue chesterfield, supping blissfully on the wavelets scraping the shingle every twenty seconds and on certain mysterious noises from the wildlife on the marshes. A snipe? A grebe? A masked badger?

He rose at last, made himself another supper of fried salty bacon and two fried eggs, unwrapped his country bread and butter and boiled himself a brew of tea so strong that his spoon could almost have stood up in it. When he had washed his ware and made his bed, he went out on to his platform to find the sky riveted with stars. Far out to sea, the lights of a fishing smack. Beyond them, he thought he detected a faint blink. Not, surely, a lighthouse on the Welsh coast? Then, up the line, he heard the hum of the approaching train. Two such trains, he had foreknown, would roar past Cobbler's Hulk every twenty-four hours. Its headlamps grew larger and brighter and then, with a roar, its carriage windows went flickering past him. He could see only a half a dozen passengers in it. When it died away down the line, he addressed the stars.

'O Spirits, merciful and good! I know that our inheritance is held in store for us by Time. I know there is a sea of Time to rise one day, before which all who wrong us or oppress us will be swept away like leaves. I see it, on the flow! I know that we must trust and hope, and neither doubt ourselves nor doubt the good in one another... O Spirits, merciful and good, I am grateful!'

'That's rather fine. Where did you get that?'

'Dickens. *The Chimes.* I say that prayer every night after supper and a last stroll up the lane.'

'Say it for me again.'

As he repeated those splendid radical words, he looked about as wild as a grasshopper. 'Thinner than Tithonus before he faded into air.'

Had he really felt oppressed? Or wronged? Could it be that, during his three years of solitude, he had been thinking that this world would be a much nicer place if people did not go around shouting at one another or declaring to other people that time is money? Or wondering why

Mother should have had to suffer shame and pain for years, while dreadful old women like Kilfeather went on scrounging, wheedling, bloodsucking, eating and drinking their way around this travelled world of which all he had ever seen was that dubious wink across the night sea? He may have meant that in his youth, he had dreamed of marriage. He may have meant nothing at all.

He leaned forward.

'Are you sure you won't have another cup of tea? Now that I can have afternoon tea any day I like, I can make a ridiculous confession to you. For fifty years, I used to see Mr Bob or Mr James walk across Grafton Street every day at four-thirty precisely to have afternoon tea in Mitchell's Café. And I cannot tell you how bitterly I used to envy them. Wasn't that silly of me?'

'But, surely, one of the girls on the staff could have brewed you all a cup of tea in the office?'

He stared at me.

'But that's not the same thing as afternoon tea in Mitchell's! White tablecloths? Carpets? Silverware? Waitresses in blue and white?'

We looked at each other silently. I looked at my watch and said that I must get going.

He laughed happily.

'The day I came here, do you know what I did with *my* watch? I pawned it for the sum of two pounds. I have never retrieved it. And I never will. I live by the sun and stars.'

'You are never lonely?'

'I am used to living alone.'

'You sleep well?'

'Like a dog. And dream like one. Mostly of the old Villa Rose. And my poor, dear mamma. How could I be lonely? I have my beautiful memories, my happy dreams and my good friends.'

'I envy you profoundly,' I said.

On which pleasant lying coda we parted. For is it possible never to be lonely? Do beautiful memories encourage us to withdraw from the world? Not even youth can live on dreams.

He had, however, one friend.

One Saturday evening in September, on returning from the wayside shop on the carriage road, he was arrested by a freshly painted sign on a gate about two hundred yards from the railway track. It said FRESH

EGGS FOR SALE. He knew that there was not a house nor a human being in sight. Who on earth would want to walk a mile down this tunnelled lane to buy eggs? Behind the wooden gate, there was a grassy track, leading, he now presumed, to some distant cottage invisible from the lane. He entered the field and was surprised to see, behind the high hedge, an open shed sheltering a red van bearing, in large white letters:

FLANNERY'S

HEAVENLY BREAD

After a winding quarter of a mile, he came on a small, sunken freshly whitewashed cottage and knocked. The door was opened by a woman of about thirty-five or forty, midway between plain and good-looking, red-cheeked, buxom, blue-eyed, eagerly welcoming. She spoke with a slight English accent that at once reminded him of his mother's voice. Yes! She had lovely fresh eggs. How many did he want? A dozen? With pleasure! Behind her, a dark, heavily built man, of about the same age, rose from his chair beside the open turf fire of the kitchen and silently offered him a seat while 'Mary' was getting the eggs.

Mr Bodkin expected to stay three minutes. He stayed an hour. They were the Condors: Mary, her brother Colm – the dark, silent man – and their bedridden mother lying in the room off the kitchen, her door always open, so that she could not only converse through it but hear all the comforting little noises and movements of her familiar kitchen. Their father, a herdsman, had died three months before. Mary had come back from service in London to look after her mother, and poor Colm (her adjective) had come home with her to support them both. He had just got a job as a roundsman for a bakery in Wicklow, driving all day around the countryside in the red van.

Mr Bodkin felt so much at ease with Mary Condor that he was soon calling on her every evening after supper, to sit by the old woman's bed, to gossip or to read her the day's news from his *Irish Times* or to give her a quiet game of draughts. That Christmas Day, on Mary's insistence, he joined them for supper. He brought a box of chocolates for Mary and her mother, one hundred cigarettes for Colm and a bottle of grocer's sherry for them all. He recited one of his favourite party pieces from Dickens. Colm so far unbent as to tell him about the bitter

Christmas he had spent in Italy with the Eighth Army near a place called Castel di Sangro. Mary talked with big eyes of the awful traffic of London. The old woman, made tipsy by the sherry, shouted from her room about the wicked sea crossing her husband had made during 'the other war,' in December of 1915, with a herd of cattle for the port of Liverpool.

'All travelled people!' Mr Bodkin laughed, and was delighted when Mary said that, thanks be to God, their travelling days were done.

As he walked away from their farewells, the channel of light from their open door showed that the grass was laced with snow. It clung to the edges of his carriage windows as he lay in bed. It gagged the wavelets. He could imagine it falling and melting into the sea. As he clutched the blue hot water bottle that Mary had given him for a Christmas present, he realized that she was the only woman friend he had made in his whole life. He felt so choked with gratitude that he fell asleep without thanking his spirits, the merciful and the good, for their latest gift.

What follows is four fifths inference and one fifth imagination; both, as the event showed, essentially true.

On the Monday of the last week in July, on returning from the roadside shop with a net bag containing *The Irish Times*, tea, onions and a bar of yellow soap, Mr Bodkin was startled to see a white Jaguar parked beside the level crossing. It was what they would have called in the travel agency a posh car. It bore three plaques, a GB, a CD and a blue-and-white silver RAC. Great Britain. *Corps Diplomatique*. Royal Automobile Club. He walked on to his platform to scan the beach for its owner. He found her seated on his bench, in a miniskirt, knees crossed, wearing a loose suede jacket, smoking a cigarette from a long ivory holder, glaring at the grey sea, tiny, blonde (or was she bleached?), exquisitely made up, still handsome. Her tide on the turn. Say, fifty? He approached her as guardedly as if she were a rabbit. A woven gold bangle hung heavily from the corrugated white glove on her wrist. Or was it her bare wrist? Say, fifty-five? Her cigarette was scented.

'Fog coming up,' he murmured politely when he came abreast of her and gave her his little bobbing bow. 'I do hope you are not waiting for a train.'

She slowly raised her tinted eyelids.

'I was waiting for you, Mr Bodkin,' she smiled. (One of the sharp ones?)

Her teeth were the tiniest and whitest he had ever seen. She could have worn them around her neck. Last month, he saw a field mouse with teeth as tiny as hers, bared in death.

'Won't you sit down? I know all about you from Molly Condor.'

'What a splendid woman she is!' he said and warily sat beside her, placing his net bag on the bench beside her scarlet beach bag. He touched it. 'You have been swimming?'

'I swim,' she laughed, 'like a stone. While I waited for you, I was sun-bathing.' She smiled for him. 'In the nude.'

Hastily, he said, 'Your car is *corps diplomatique!*'

'It is my husband's car. Sir Hilary Dobson. I stole it!' She gurgled what ruder chaps in the agency used to call the Gorgon Gurgle. 'You mustn't take me seriously, Mr Bodkin. I'm Scottish. Hilary says I am fey. He is in the F. O. He's gone off on some hush-hush business to Athens for a fortnight, so I borrowed the Jag. Now, if it had been Turkey! But perhaps you don't like Turkey, either? Or do you? Athens is such a crumby dump, don't you agree?'

'I have never travelled, Lady Dobson.'

'But Molly says you once owned a travel agency!'

'She exaggerates my abilities. I was a humble clerk.'

'Eoh?' Her tone changed, her voice became brisk. 'Look, Bodkin, I wanted to ask you something very important. How well do you know Molly Condor?'

He increased his politeness.

'I have had the great pleasure of knowing Miss Mary Condor since last September.'

'I have known her since she was twenty-two. I trained her. She was in my service for twelve years. But I have never looked at Molly as just a lady's maid. Molly is my best friend in the whole world. She is a great loss to me. Of course, as we grow older, the fewer, and the more precious, our friends become.'

He considered the name, Molly. He felt it was patronizing. He had never lost a friend – never, before Mary, having had one to lose. He said as much.

'Too bad! Well! I want Molly to come back to us. My nerves have not been the same since she left.'

He looked silently out to sea. He was aware that she was slowly turning her head to look at him. Like a field mouse? He felt a creeping sensation of fear. Her nerves seemed all right to him. He watched her eject her cigarette, produce another from a silver case, insert it, light it smartly with a gold lighter and blow out a narrow jet of smoke.

'And then there is her brother. Condor was our chauffeur for five years. It would be simply wonderful if they both came back to us! I know poor old Hilary is as lost without his Condor as I am without my Molly. It would be a great act of kindness if you could say a word in our favour in that quarter. Hilary would appreciate it no end. Oh, I know, of course, about the mother. But that old girl can't need the two of them, can she? Besides, when I saw her this morning, I had the feeling she won't last long. Arthritis? *And* bronchitis? *And* this climate? I had an old aunt just like her in Bexhill-on-Sea. One day, she was in splendid health. The next day, her tubes were wheezing like bagpipes. For six months, I watched her, fading like a sunset. In the seventh month...'

As she wheedled on and on, her voice reminded him of a spoon inside a saucepan. He listened to her coldly, with his eyes, rather than his ears, as for so many years he used to listen to old ladies who did not know where exactly they wanted to go nor what they wanted to do, alert only to their shifting lids, their mousy fingers, their bewildered shoulders, their jerking lips. Crepe on her neck. French cigarettes. Sun-bathing nude. Bodkin. Condor. Molly. 'Poor old Hilary.' What did this old girl really want? Coming all this way for a lady's maid? My foot!

'And you know, Bodkin, Molly has a great regard for you. She thinks you are the most marvellous thing she ever met. I can see why.' She laid her hand on his sleeve. 'You have a kind heart. You will help me, if you can, won't you?' She jumped up. 'That is all I wanted to say. Now you must show me your wonderful *wagon-lit*. Molly says it is absolutely fab.'

'I shall be delighted, Lady Dobson,' he said and, unwillingly, led her to it.

When she saw the brass plate of THE VILLA ROSE she guffawed and hastened to admire everything else. Her eyes trotted all over his possessions like two hunting mice. She gushed over his 'clever little arrangements.' She lifted potlids, felt the springiness of the bed, penetrated to his water closet, which she flushed, greatly to his annoyance because he never used it except when the marshes were very wet or very cold, and then he had to refill the cistern with a bucket every time he flushed it.

'I find it all most amusing, Bodkin,' she assured him as she powdered her face before his shaving mirror. 'If you were a young man, it would make a wonderful weekend love nest, wouldn't it? I must fly. It's nearly lunchtime. And you want to make whatever it is you propose to make with your soap, tea and onions. Won't you see me to my car? And do say a word for me to Molly! If you ever want to find me, I'm staying in the little old hotel down the road. For a week.' She laughed naughtily. 'Laying siege! Do drop in there any afternoon at six o'clock for an aperitif,' and she showed half her white thigh as she looped into her car, started the engine, meshed the gears, beamed at him with all her teeth, cried, '*A bientôt*, Bodkin,' and shot recklessly up the lane, defoliating the hedges into a wake of leaves like a speedboat.

Watching her cloud of dust, he remembered something. A chap in the office showing him a postcard of *Mona Lisa*. 'Ever seen her before? Not half! And never one of them under fifty-five!' Indeed! *And* indeed! 'I am afraid, Lady Dobson, we must make up our minds. A cool fortnight in Brittany? Or five lovely hot days in Monte Carlo? Of course, you *might* win a pot of money in Monte Carlo . . .' How greedily their alligator eyelids used to blink at that one! He returned slowly to his *wagon-lit*, slammed down the windows to let out the smell of her cigarette, washed the dust of yellow powder from his washbasin, refilled his cistern and sat for an hour on the edge of his bed, pondering. By nightfall, he was so bewildered that he had to call on Mary.

She was alone. The old lady was asleep in her room. They sat on either side of the kitchen table, whispering about the hens, the up train that had been three minutes late, the down train last night that was right on the dot, the fog that morning, both of them at their usual friendly ease until he spoke about his visitor. When he finished, she glanced at the open door of the bedroom.

'I must say, she was always very generous to me. Sir Hilary was very kind. He went hard on me to stay. He said, "You are good for her." She had her moods and tenses. I felt awfully sorry for him. He spoiled her.'

'Well, of course, Mary, those titled people,' Mr Bodkin fished cunningly and was filled with admiration for her when she refused to bite.

All she said was, 'Sir Hilary was a real gentleman.'

'They are married a long time?'

'Fifteen years. She is his second wife. She nursed his first wife. But I *had* to come back, Mr Bodkin!'

'You did quite right. And your brother did the right thing, too. I mean, two women in a remote cottage. Your brother is never lonely?'

She covered her face with her hands and he knew that she was crying into them.

'He is dying of the lonesome.'

From the room, the old woman suddenly hammered the floor with her stick.

'Is he back?' she called out fretfully.

Mary went to the bedroom door and leaned against the jamb. It was like listening to a telephone call.

'It's Mr Bodkin . . . He went up to the shop for cigarettes . . . I suppose he forgot them . . . About an hour ago . . . He may be gone for a stroll. It's such a fine night . . . Och, he must be sick of that old van . . .' She turned her head. 'Was the van in the shed, Mr Bodkin?' He shook his head. 'He took the van . . . For God's sake, Mother, stop worrying and go to sleep. He maybe took the notion to drive over to Ashford for a drink and a chat. It's dull for him here . . . I'll give you a game of draughts.'

Mr Bodkin left her.

A nurse? It was dark in the lane, but above the tunnel of the hedges, there was still a flavour of salvaged daylight. He started to walk towards the road, hoping to meet Condor on his way back. The air was heavy with heliotrope and meadowsweet. A rustle in the ditch beside him. Far away, a horse whinnied. He must be turned forty by now. Behind him, Africa, Italy, London. Before him, nothing but the road and fields of his boyhood. Every night, that solitary cottage. The swell of the night express made him look back until its last lights had flickered past the end of the lane and its humming died down the line.

But I have lived. An old man, now, twice a child.

By the last of the afterlight above the trees of the carriage road, he saw the red nose of the van protruding from the halfmoon entrance to the abandoned manor house. He walked to it, peered into its empty cabin, heard a pigeon throating from a clump of trees behind the chained gates. He walked past it to the shop. It was closed and dark. He guessed at a lighted window at the rear of it, shining out over the stumps of decapitated cabbages. Condor was probably in there, gossiping. He was about to turn back when he saw about one hundred yards farther on, the red taillights of a parked car. Any other night, he might have given it no more than an incurious glance. The darkness, the silence, the turmoil of his thoughts finally drew him warily towards it along the grassy verge. Within fifteen yards of it, he recognized the white Jaguar, saw the rear door open, the inner light fall on the two figures clambering out of it. Standing on the road, they embraced in a seething kiss. When he released her, she got into the driver's seat, the two doors banged and everything was silent and dark again. She started her engine, floodlit the road and drove swiftly away around the curve. Crushed back into the hedge, he heard Condor's footsteps approach, pass and recede. In a few moments, the van's door banged tinnily, its headlamps flowered, whirled into the maw of the lane, waddled drunkenly behind the hedges, down towards the sea.

Before he fell asleep that night, Mr Bodkin heard a thousand wavelets scrape the shingles, as, during his long life, other countless waves had scraped elsewhere unheard – sounds, moments, places, people to whose lives he had never given a thought. *The Irish Times* rarely recorded such storms of passion and, when it did, they broke and died far away, like the fables that Shakespeare concocted for his entertainment in the theatre. But he knew the Condors. This adulterous woman could shatter their lives as surely as he knew, when he opened his eyes to the sea sun shimmering on his ceiling, she had already shattered his.

It was his custom, on such summer mornings, to rise, strip off his pyjamas, pull on a bathing slip and walk across the track in his slippers, his towel around his neck, down to the edge of the sea for what he called a dip: which meant that since he, too, swam like a stone, he would advance into the sea up to his knees, sprinkle his shoulders, and then, burring happily at the cold sting of it, race back to the prickly gravel to towel his shivering bones. He did it this morning with the eyes of a saint wakened from dreams of sin.

On Tuesday night, he snooped virtuously up the lane and along the carriage road. The red van was not in its shed. But neither was it on the road. Lascivious imaginings kept him awake for hours. He longed for the thunderbolt of God.

On Wednesday night, it was, at first, the same story; but on arriving back at the foot of the lane, there were the empty van and the empty Jaguar before him, flank to flank at the level crossing. He retired at once to his bench, peering up and down the beach, listening for the sound of their crunching feet, determined to wait for them all night, if necessary. Somewhere, that woman was lying locked in his arms. The bared thigh. The wrinkled arms. The crepey neck.

Daylight had waned around nine o'clock, but it was still bright enough for him to have seen shadows against the glister of the water, if there had been shadows to see. He saw nothing. He heard nothing but the waves. It must have been nearly two hours later when he heard their cars starting. By the time he had flitted down to the end of the platform, her lights were already rolling up the lane and his were turning in through his gateway. Mr Bodkin was at the gate barely in time to see his outline dark against the bars of the western sky. As he looked at the van, empty in its shed, it occurred to him that this was one way in which he could frighten him – a warning message left on the seat of the van. But it was also a way in which they could communicate with each other. Her message for him. His answer left early in the morning at her hotel.

On Thursday night, the van lay in its shed. But where was Condor? He walked up the grass track to the cottage and laid his ear to the door. He heard Mary's voice, his angry voice, the mother's shouting. He breathed happily and returned to his bed.

On Friday morning, the Jaguar stood outside Mary's wooden gate. Laying siege? That night, the scarlet van again lay idle in its pen. Wearied by so much walking and watching, he fell asleep over his supper. He was awakened around eleven o'clock by the sound of a car. Scrambling to his door, he was in time to see her wheeling lights hit the sky. He went up the lane to the van, looked around, heard nothing, shone his torch into the cabin and saw the blue envelope lying on the seat. He ripped it open and read it by torchlight. 'Oh, My Darling, for God's sake, where are you? Last night and tonight, I waited and waited. What has happened? You promised! I have only one more night. You are coming back with me, aren't you? If I do not see you tomorrow night, I will throw myself into the sea. I adore you. Connie.' Mr Bodkin took the letter down to the sea, tore it into tiny pieces and, with his arms wide, scattered them over the receding waves.

That Saturday afternoon, on returning from the shop with his weekend purchases in his net bag, there was the Jaguar beside the level crossing, mud-spattered and dusty, its white flanks scarred by the whipping brambles. Rounding the corner of the waiting room, he saw her on his bench, smoking, glaring at the sparkling sea. She barely lifted her eyes to him. She looked every year of sixty. He bowed and sat on the bench. She smelled of whiskey.

'What an exquisite afternoon we are having, Lady Dobson. May I rest my poor bones for a moment? That lane of mine gets longer and longer every day. Has everything been well with you?'

'Quite well, Bodkin, thank you.'

'And, if I may ask, I should be interested to know, you have, I trust, made some progress in your quest?'

'I could hardly expect to with that old woman around everybody's neck. I have laid the seeds of the idea. Molly now knows that she will always be welcome in my house.'

'Wait and see? My favourite motto. Never say die. Colours nailed to the mast. No surrender. It means, I hope, that you are not going to leave us soon.'

'I leave tonight.'

'I do hope the hotel has not been uncomfortable.'

'It is entirely comfortable. It is full of spinsters. They give me the creeps.'

He beamed at the sea and waited.

'Bodkin! There is one person I have not yet seen. For Hilary's sake, I ought to have a word with Condor. Have you seen him around?'

Her voice had begun to crumble. Eyes like grease under hot water. Cigarette trembling.

'Let me think,' he pondered. 'On Thursday? Yes. And again last night. We both played draughts with his mother. He seemed his usual cheerful self.'

She ejected her cigarette and ground it into the dust under her foot.

'Bodkin! Will you, for Christ's sake, tell me what do young people do with their lives in Godforsaken places like this? That lane must be pitch dark by four o'clock in the winter!'

He looked at his toes, drew his handkerchief from his breast pocket and flicked away their dust.

'I am afraid, Lady Dobson, I no longer meet any young people. And, after all, Condor is not a young man. I suppose you could call him a middle-aged man. Or would you?'

She hooted hoarsely.

'And what does that leave me? An old hag?'

'Or me? As the Good Book says, "The days of our years are threescore years and ten; and if by reason of strength they be fourscore years, yet is their strength labour and sorrow; for it is soon cut off, and we fly away."'

She spat it at him:

'You make me sick.'

From under her blue eyelids, she looked at the clouds crimped along the knife of the horizon. He remembered Mary's twisted face when she said, 'He is dying of the lonesome.' She turned and faced him. Harp strings under her chin. Hands mottled. The creature was as old as sin.

'Do you happen to know, Bodkin, if Condor has a girl in these parts? It concerns me, of course, only insofar as, if he has, I need not ask him to come back to us. Has he?'

Mr Bodkin searched the sea as if looking for a small boat in which to escape his conscience.

'I believe he has,' he said firmly.

'Believe? Do you know? Or do you not know?'

'I saw them twice in the lane. Kissing. I presume that means that they are in love.'

'Thank you, Bodkin,' she said brightly. 'In that case, Hilary must get another chauffeur and I must get another lady's maid.' She jumped up. He rose politely. 'I hope you all have a very pleasant winter.' She stared at him hatefully. 'In love! Have you ever in your life been in love? Do you know what it means to be in love?'

'Life has denied me many things, Lady Dobson.'

'Do you have such a thing as a drink in that black coffin of yours?'

'Alas! Only tea. I am a poor man, Lady Dobson. I read in the paper recently that whiskey is now as much as six shillings a glass.'

Her closed eyes riveted her to her age like a worn face on an old coin.

'No love. No drink. No friends. No wife. No children. Happy man! Nothing to betray you.'

She turned and left him.

The events of that Saturday night and Sunday morning became public property at the inquest.

Sergeant Delahunty gave formal evidence of the finding of the body on the rocks at Greystones. Guard Sinnott corroborated. Mr T. J. Bodkin was then called. He stated that he was a retired businessman residing in a chalet beside the disused station of Cobbler's Hulk. He deposed that, as usual, he went to bed on the night in question around ten o'clock and fell asleep. Being subject to arthritis, he slept badly. Around one o'clock, something woke him.

CORONER: What woke you? Did you hear a noise?

WITNESS: I am often awakened by arthritic pains in my legs.

CORONER: Are you quite sure it was not earlier than one o'clock? The reason I ask is because we know that the deceased's watch stopped at a quarter to twelve.

WITNESS: I looked at my watch. It was five minutes past one.

Continuing his evidence, the witness said that the night being warm and dry, he rose, put on his dressing gown and his slippers and walked up and down on the platform to ease his pains. From where he stood, he observed a white car parked in the lane. He went towards it. He recognized it as the property of Lady Constance Dobson, whom he had met earlier in the week. There was nobody in the car. Asked by a juror if he had seen the car earlier in the night, before he went to bed, the witness said that it was never his practice to emerge from his chalet after his supper. Asked by another juror if he was not surprised to find an empty car there at one o'clock at night, he said he was but thought that it might have run out of petrol and been abandoned by Lady Dobson until the morning. It did not arouse his curiosity. He was not a curious man by nature. The witness deposed that he then returned to his chalet and slept until six o'clock, when he rose, rather earlier than usual, and went for his usual morning swim. On the way to the beach, he again examined the car.

CORONER: It was daylight by then?

WITNESS: Yes, sir.

CORONER: Did you look inside the car?

WITNESS: Yes, sir. I discovered that the door was unlocked and I opened it. I saw a lady's handbag on the front seat and a leather suitcase on the rear seat. I saw that the ignition key was in position. I turned it, found the starter and the engine responded at once. At that stage, I became seriously worried.

CORONER: What did you do?

WITNESS: I went for my swim. It was too early to do anything else.

Mr Bodkin further stated that he then returned to his chalet, dressed, shaved, prepared his breakfast and ate it. At seven o'clock, he walked to the house of his nearest neighbours, the Condors, and aroused them. Mr Colm Condor at once accompanied him back to the car. They examined it and, on Mr Condor's suggestion, they both drove in Mr Condor's van to report the incident to the Guards at Ashford.

CORONER: We have had the Guards' evidence. And that is all you know about the matter?

WITNESS: Yes, sir.

CORONER: You mean, of course, until the body was found fully clothed, on the rocks at Greystones a week later; that is to say, yesterday morning, when, with Sir Hilary Dobson and Miss Mary Condor, you helped identify the remains?

WITNESS: Yes, sir.

CORONER: Did you have any difficulty in doing so?

WITNESS: I had some difficulty.

CORONER: But you were satisfied that it was the body of Lady Constance Dobson and no other.

WITNESS: I was satisfied. I also recognized the woven gold bangle she had worn the day I saw her. The teeth were unmistakable.

Dr Edward Halpin of the sanatorium at Newcastle having given his opinion that death was caused by asphyxiation through drowning, the jury, in accordance with the medical evidence, returned a verdict of suicide while of unsound mind. The coroner said it was a most distressing case, extended his sympathy to Sir Hilary Dobson and said no blame attached to anybody.

It was September before I again met Mr Bodkin. A day of infinite whiteness. The waves falling heavily. Chilly. It would probably be my last swim of the year. Seeing him on his bench – chesterfield, bowler hat, grey spats, rolled umbrella (he would need it from now on), his bulging net bag between his feet, his head bent to one side as if he were listening for a train – I again wondered at a couple of odd things he had said at the inquest; such as his reply to a juror that he never emerged from his railway carriage after supper; his answer to the coroner that he was often awakened at night by his arthritis ('I sleep like a dog,' he had told me. 'I have never in my life had a day's illness, apart from chilblains'); and he had observed by his watch that it was five past one in the morning ('I live by the sun and the stars'). Also, he had said that from the platform, he had noticed the white car parked at the end of the lane. I had parked my Morris a few moments before at the end of the lane and, as I looked back towards it now, it was masked by the signal box.

He did not invite me to sit down and I did not. We spoke of the sunless day. He smiled when I looked at the sky and said, 'Your watch is clouded over.' I sympathized with him over his recent painful experience.

'Ah, yes!' he agreed. 'It was most distressing. Even if she *was* a foolish poor soul. Flighty, too. Not quite out of the top drawer. That may have had something to do with it. A bit spoiled, I mean. The sort of woman, as my dear mother used to say, who would upset a barrack of soldiers.'

'Why on earth do you suppose she did it? But I shouldn't ask; I am sure you want to forget the whole thing.'

'It is all over now. The wheel turns. All things return to the sea. She was crossed in love.'

I stared at him.

'Some man in London?'

He hesitated, looked at me shiftily, slowly shook his head and turned his eyes along his shoulder towards the fields.

'But nothing was said about this at the inquest! Did other people know about it? Did the Condors know about it?'

His hands moved on his umbrella handle.

'In quiet places like this, they would notice a leaf falling. But where so little happens, every secret becomes a buried treasure that nobody mentions. Even though every daisy on the dunes knows all about it. This very morning, when I called on Mary Condor, a hen passed her door. She said, "That hen is laying out. Its feet are clean. It has been walking through grass." They know everything. I sometimes think,' he said peevishly, 'that they know what I ate for breakfast.'

(Was he becoming disillusioned about his quiet beach?)

'How did you know about it? Or are you just guessing?'

He frowned. He shuffled for the second time. His shoulders straightened. He almost preened himself.

'I have my own powers of observation! I can keep my eyes open, too, you know! Sometimes I see things nobody else sees. I can show you something nobody else has ever seen.'

Watching me watch him, he slowly drew out his pocketbook and let it fall open on a large visiting card. I stooped forward to read the name. LADY CONSTANCE DOBSON. His little finger turned it on to its back. There, scrawled apparently in red lipstick, was the word *Judas*. When I looked at him, he was smiling triumphantly.

'Where on earth did you find it?'

'That morning at six o'clock, it was daylight. I saw it stuck inside the wind-screen wipers' – he hesitated for the last time – 'of the Jaguar.'

My mind became as tumbled as a jigsaw. He was lying. How many other pieces of the jigsaw were missing? Who was it said the last missing bit of every jigsaw is God?

'You did not mention this at the inquest.'

'Should I have? The thought occurred to me. I decided that it would be more merciful not to. There were other people to think of. Sir Hilary, for one. And others.' He replaced his pocketbook and rose dismissively. 'I perceive that you are going for a swim. Be careful. There are currents. The beach shelves rapidly. Three yards out and the gravel slides from under your feet. And nobody to hear you if you shout for help. I had my usual little dip this morning. Such calm. Such utter silence. The water was very cold.'

He bobbed and walked away. I walked very slowly down to the edge of the beach. I tested the water with my hand. He was right. I looked around me. I might have been marooned on some Baltic reef hung between an infinity of clouds and a lustre of sea gleaming with their iceberg reflections. Not a fishing smack. Not even a cormorant. Not a soul for miles, north and south. Nobody along the railway track. Or was somebody, as he had suggested, always watching?

If he were concealing something, why had he admitted that he had come out from his railway carriage at all? Why did he choose to mention one o'clock in the morning? Did he know that she had died around midnight? Was he afraid that somebody besides himself might have seen her lights turn down the lane? A timid liar, offering a half-truth to conceal the whole truth?

Above the dunes, I could just see the black roof of his railway carriage. I measured the distance from where I stood and let out a loud 'Help!' For ten seconds, nothing happened. Then his small, dark figure rose furtively behind the dunes. When he saw me, he disappeared.

Foreign Affairs

1

Georgie Freddy Ernie Bertie Atkinson's mature speech style when holding forth at the bar of the Hibernian United Services Club went something like this – though he would doubtless dismiss it complacently as a vulgar parody of an inimitable original; a pastiche, or, if he were in his Italian vein *un pasticcio*, or in his French mood *un pastichage*, or in his Old French humour a *pasté* ('As the Old French used to say'), or if in a Latin frame of mind a *pasta* ('As Cicero might have said'), or if in his Greek role a παστή.

'Hear *my* case!' he might orotundate to the bar. 'When I, at the tender age of approximately twenty minutes and an unspecified number of seconds, at or around ten in the morning on November 11th, 1918, was tenderly deposited in my father's outstretched and trembling arms by the woman who had for so long borne me, none other, I am relieved to be able to say, than his dear wife Eliza, it is not surprising, in view of the day and the hour, forever after to be remembered as Armistice Day, that the bloody old fool should have instantaneously decided to christen me George Frederick Ernest Albert, to express his fervent gratitude, not to the Lord God, in which case he might prophetically have christened me Lord Atkinson, but to King George the Fifth, Reigning Majesty of the United Kingdom of Great Britain and Ireland, head of the once more triumphant Empire, as well as of a whole lot of other institutions ranging from titular admiral of the Royal Fleet to Colonel of the Canadian Mounties, titles and subtitles all, as anyone may absorb in a twenty-five minutes' perusal of any half-decent British almanack spelled with a K.

'Now, when I say that my dear fathead of a father decided thus to label me for life I do not wish to suggest that he calmly made up his mind to do so, and that having made it up he did so. In my experience my father was as nearly mindless as it is possible for any man to be while engaged in selling insurance policies with, it would appear, unusual success, to the normally improvident Irish. I merely wish to convey that he did what he did as absently as one winds one's watch at midnight after heaving one's beloved to the other side of the bed to unwind herself as best she can. Yet, I do assure you gentlemen that, even after I discovered to my cost what exactly he had done to me, I could not find it in my heart to blame him for his folly, nor – and here I do raise my index finger in solemn oath – can I fault him for it even now.

'After all, in that far-off Dublin of 1918 how much common sense could one reasonably expect from a man of his class, origins, upbringing and religious beliefs? Royalist to his rappers, bourgeois to his boots, primitive Methodist Connexion, spelled if you please with an X. Open-air revivalist meetings. Second cousins to the Salvation Army. Hymns in the street under black bowler hats. Belting the Bible like a drum. Come to Jesus! Total certainty of one's own salvation and an even more serene certainty of the damnation of everybody else. How could any such man have foreseen all the political upheavals that within two brief years would turn this British Isle of his fathers' adoption into a free, roaring Irish Republic? Nevertheless, though I forgive the old boy for not having been able to foresee all this political faldirara when he tied "Georgie Freddy Ernie Bertie" to my tail like a firecracker I do blame him, and most severely blame him for having been so unobservant of the meaning and trend of everything happening under his eyes in the years after as to have gone on bestowing on his next four unfortunate children, all distaff, the names of four further members of the English Royal Family. The result is that my eldest sister is now Alexandra Caroline Marie Charlotte Louise Julie. We used to call the second, in my boyhood, Amelia Adelaide and All That Stuff. The third we knew as C.A.I., meaning Caroline Amelia Inc. He christened his fourth and last after that unfortunate bitch Queen Marie Charlotte Sophia of Mecklenburg-Strelitz who was obliged to present her husband King George III with fifteen brats before, as we all know, his imperial Anglo-Teutonic Majesty went completely off his chump.

'I do not know what agonies my sisters may have had to endure at the hands, or tongues, of their school friends because of those outrageous prefixes. I vividly recall the taunting tones in which, even at school, my more nationalistic fellow Mountjoyians used to hail me as loudly as possible with a "Hello, Georgie Freddy Ernie Bertie," accompanied, when affected by the current xenophobia, by a blaze of homicidal scorn in their green Irish eyes or, if a little less categorically patriotic, the clearest flicker on their lips of what I can only describe as *l'équivoque sympathique . . .'*

A monologuist? That was his form, all right! So infectious that one wants to describe it as port winy, portentous, pompous, pomaded. Any other P's? Patchouli? Well, it is, he was, he *is* an Edwardian hangover. Nevertheless, give the man his due. If he had not had an unfortunate knack of delivering his monologues with such a hang-jawed pelican smile, an archness perilously close to the music hall leer, wink, nudge, lifted eyebrow, he might have ranked with the best of Dublin's legendary monologuists. He lacked their professional self-assurance. However carefully guffers like Wilde, Shaw, Stephens, Yeats or Gogarty prepared their *dits* they always threw them away, assured that there would be an infielder to catch them, an audience to applaud. With Georgie Freddy you were aware of a touch of insecure self-mockery, as if he were always trying to kick his own backside before somebody else did it for him.

'Basta!'

It was his common finale when he wished to indicate that he had made a good point with unusual felicity. Enough on this theme, anyway, to establish that his father was not only a fool but an insuppressible outsider, unusually lucky to have escaped a tarring and feathering, if not assassination, during the revolutionary troubles of the Twenties. And he went on inviting slaughter for years after by bragging every single working day of the year about Georgie Freddy to his eyes-up-to-the-ceiling colleagues during their regular lunch in the crowded basement of Bewley's Oriental Café in Grafton Street. The location is relevant: that it was a café, not a club or restaurant, gives the modest measure of the old chap's commercial standing. Still, though paternal boasting can be boring it can also be touching – one man's daydream is another man's despair. His bored colleagues, remembering their own sons, could sadly shrug. Unfortunately the most aggravating side of the old man's bragging was that Georgie Freddy's career really was outstandingly brilliant from the day he entered Trinity College, Dublin, as a poor sizar to the day he left it with a first class degree in classics, a gold medal in Greek, a sound command of modern Italian and French language and literature, and a good reading knowledge of German. Even more aggravatingly, his career went on being brilliant after he exchanged the university for the British Army in 1942, starting as a lieutenant, promoted to staff-captain in the desert, finally elevated to major in Italy.

With Italy old Bob Atkinson elevated himself to the rank of God the Father. He was now able, thanks to Georgie's dispatches, to gas the whole lunch table of insurance men with prolonged, detailed, hour by hour, beach by beach, blow by blow accounts of how Georgie landed in Sicily at the head of the Eighth Army, advanced to Catania and Messina and crossed between Scylla and Charybdis to the Italian mainland. There, surpassing all, an event occurred that sent the old man into a blazing, vertical takeoff from Bewley's perfumed basement up through every floor and out through the slates of the roof into Dublin's sea-gulled September air.

This event was Georgie's personal encounter with General Alexander, the commander of the Eighth Army, in a war-battered Calabrian hamlet called Galiana at one o'clock of a warm, sticky morning in September shortly after the capture of the city of Reggio di Calabria.

'Think of it, gentlemen!' the old buffer embraces the coffee table with a gleeful laugh. 'There is our brave bucko, Captain George Frederick Ernest Albert Atkinson, my son, my very own son, lying flat on his ass on the upstairs floor of a fleabitten hut in the volcanic mountains of Calabria, dead to God and the world, sound asleep, white as a statue from the dust, and the dirt and the brunt of the battle, shagged from fighting the Eyties the whole bloody sweating day, when he is suddenly shaken awake by one of his fellow officers and a blaze of light blinding his eyes through the windows. He thinks it's the rising sun. It is the headlamps of a military jeep.

'"What in the hell's blazes," says he, "is up now?"

'"Up," sez the officer. "Did you say *up?* You'll soon know what's up," sez he, "if you're not down in five seconds," sez he, "because it's the general that's up," sez he, "that is to say down them ladders thirsting for your blue Oirish blud."

'"What flaming general, for God's sake?" sez our young hero, still lost in the arms of Murphy.

'His comrade stands to attention and sings out the answer as if he was on a barrack square.

'"I refer to General Harold Rupert Leofric George Alexander Irish Guards Military Cross Companion of the Order of the Star of Indiar

ADC to His Majesty whom God preserve since 1936 born in Tyrone in good ould Oireland . . .'

'Well, I needn't tell ye, gentlemen, that at the mention of the general's name it didn't take Georgie boy a week of Sundays to get down that ladder, buttoning his uniform. He clatters into the kitchen, salutes to attention, wondering what in God's name Alexander can have let go wrong with the campaign while he was catching a wink of sleep, and gets the usual polite lift of the finger in return.

'"Captain Atkinson," says Alex very quietly, for he is on all occasions most polite and courteous, one of nature's gentlemen, one of the real old Irish stock. "I regret to have to tell you, Captain, that to my nostrils this village stinks. From the point of view of the health and morale of my troops, such dirt is not a good thing. Can you, as the officer in charge of the area, explain to me why it is so?"

'Gentlemen! Does Georgie tremble? Does Georgie blench? Is Georgie rattled? No, gentlemen. Georgie stares Alex straight in the eye, as cool as that cucumber sandwich there on me plate. "Dirty?" sez he, and now don't let us forget that Georgie was a gold medallist in Ancient Greek when he was at Trinity College, Dublin. "I entirely agree with you, sir. This village stinks to high heaven. It is an absolutely filthy hole. But, sir, if you would care to recall from your days at Eton your Herodotus, book three, chapter four, paragraph one, I think you will remember, sir, that this village has been dirty, evil-smelling and nauseating since the year 434 B.C." Well, gentlemen, do you know what Alex did, at three minutes past one o'clock in the morning in that battered ould canteen in Calabria? He laffed. And he laffed. And he laffed! "I perceive, Captain," he decides at last, "that you are a linguist and a scholar. What other languages do you command besides Greek?" Georgie replies that as well as being a gold medallist in Ancient Greek he speaks fluent Italian, fluent French and has a useful knowledge of German. The general raises the one finger. "The very man for me! Consider yourself promoted from this moment to the rank of major. Report to me at Field H.Q. this morning at seven, ready to assume the post of Military Commander of the City of Reggio di Calabria until further orders." And with that he turns on the leather heel of his brown, polished high boots, climbs into his jeep, leaving Major Atkinson stunned – stunned, gentlemen – as he watches its lights vanishing like a kangaroo into the blackness of the Eyetalian night. And that is how my boy became a major, in command of the first city in Italy taken by Allied troops. Is that, gentlemen, or is that not an astonishing ringside view of contemporary history?'

Undeniably! The coffee cups toast him. If true! The cups are sipped silently. But . . .

Now, we Irish, like certain other peoples honed hard by history – some of them our best friends – are a double helix of softness and hardness, of passion and calculation, which is why one of the men at that table, an envious, nosy, aquiline character named Cooney got so fed up to his zinc-filled molars (insurance salesmen cannot afford gold) with this oft-repeated yarn about Alex and Georgie that he snuck off to consult a professorial friend in the clerical College of Maynooth, who in turn snuck off to an Irish Catholic archaeologist friend in the Dublin Institute for Advanced Studies, about this Methodist yarn about a Calabrian village called Galiana said to have been unflatteringly mentioned by the great Herodotus in the fifth century B.C. After prolonged searching through the entire corpus of the historian's works none of the three of them could find any mention whatever of any such settlement in any known part of Magna Graecia.

Cooney – for even the most cooneyish Cooney in the world has a heart – was far too kind to mention this fact to old Bob Atkinson. Instead, he waited for four years, and for the appropriate jovial company, to tax the then retired major with his lie. The answer he got made him blush slowly from his neck to his chin, to his eyes, to the peak of the rampant cupola of his bald skull.

'There is, of course,' Georgie declaimed, *ore rotundo* as always, 'no mention of any such place in Herodotus. Indeed, only an illiterate would expect to find it there. I simply embellished a trivial but actual encounter to give a little harmless pleasure to an old man, who, by the way, if, sir, the matter is of any interest to you, we moved late last night into Sir Patrick Dun's Hospital, situated beside the canal once justifiably acclaimed as The Grand Canal. It now barely moves. Weedy. Muddy. Tin cans. Dead cats. He moves not at all. His doctor tells me he has not the strength left to die. He will probably float away, like Joyce's last Liffey leaf, to join his cold, old, dreary fathers tonight.'

'You told a lie,' Cooney insisted coldly.

'Mr Cooney, I did speak to General Alexander. I was promoted major. I was O.C. in Reggio di Calabria. And that is not a world away from the ruins of Thurii, on the Italian Ionian, which Herodotus helped to found, and from which, by then a great and famous city, as famous at least as Dublin, he is believed to have finally floated into his own history. May I, Mister Cooney, give my father your kind wishes, whether false or true, before he in his turn returns to his proper sea?'

'Having told one lie,' Cooney said, 'I am sure you can manage another.'

'I admit,' Georgie replied ever so gently, 'that I did allow my imagination a little latitude. It is a national failing. You, unfortunately, do not appear to suffer from it.'

2

Ex-major. Home to roost. Portly. Savile Row suit, blue and grey pinstripe, blue weskit, mother-of-pearl buttons, T.C.D. tie, rolled gamp, *Times*, of London not Dublin, flat folded under right oxter, pallid blue Peep O'Day handkerchief in breast pocket, Italian shoes. At thirty a man with a past, to be taken seriously, for the moment, another wandering fighter returned reluctantly to stay-at-home Dublin. War-scarred by a bullet that grazed his inside right thigh at Potenza. ('Another inch and I'd be a *castrato*.') Far travelled, through France as a beggarly student, through Greece as a frayed-at-the-cuffs classicist, sweating under North Africa's steely sun, Sicily baked him, Magna Graecia rained on him, England demobbed him, Ireland reopened her arms to him. Pensionless.

'My *epikedeion*,' he liked to sigh and to translate. 'My threnody. My graveside oration.'

He was already inventing his own legend to fortify himself, an alien in a city that had been his ever since he burst upon it on that historic morning thirty years ago via Saint Assam's Nursing Home off Hatch Row, in Ballsbridge.

The place is relevant: the prelude to his myth, his *domus omnium venerum*, to be flourished with bravura on all suitable occasions as Dublin's most famous house of pleasure, patronized by procreative jockeys, trainers, handicappers, bloodstock exporters, breeders (also of horses), dignitaries of the Turf Club, pouring in at all hours of the day and night to view the offspring of their loins, as laden with flowers as if Ireland were Hawaii; wine merchants' messenger boys constantly bearing cases of champagne in and out of the wrong bedrooms; lean, goitre-eyed greyhounds lolloping up and down deeply upholstered, much urinated on stairs; a home less given to displaying umbrellas in its hall stands than bridles, hunting crops, horse blinkers as rigid as leather bras. The city of his pimpled and impoverished schoolboy years under the switch of Parson Magee in Mountjoy Square. He recalls the ribald smiles of his bare-kneed fellows whenever they mentioned the double-meaning name of a square whose latter-day decline from Georgian *piazza* to Joyceian slum both betrayed and confirmed (pure and total legend this) his ruttish teens. His personal city, his *dolce domum* from the day it flowered superbly, generously, ubertosely (he invented the word) as a metropolis of the mind during his student days in its major university, founded by Elizabeth the First. The scene and source of his proudest achievements, his *alma noverca* whose knighting queen had transformed (first battering break) this poorborn Methody into newborn gentleman, man of the world, soldier of the Empire, inheritor of all the ages of the world . . .

'Behold me now!' he loved to groan. 'Back in Ithaca, fatherless, motherless, wifeless, loveless, homeless. Our old family home in Mount Pleasant Square sold! O God!' At this his voice would break. 'With the military barracks to the west of us, bugle-calling at dawn, and the monastery to our east, hymning hymns, and the road through Windy Arbour, Dundrum, Sandyford, Golden Ball, to the lovely, lonely moors beyond the Scalp; and the canal floating seaward silently past its Dickensian tenements on Charlemont Place, every bum painter's delight; and Harcourt Terrace around the corner, odorous of Saint John's Wood, frankincense, classic grace and decadent nineteenth-century vice!

'And now? Not a relative left. My four sad sisters scattered through the British Isles, nursing, typing, clerking, married or otherwise gone to the bitches. As witness my dearest, youngest sister Charlie, she homonymously of Mecklenburg-Strelitz, obliged to marry at seventeen, when apparently – the adverb sounds aerie but is accurate – pregnant by a hot theological student at Trinity. Thereafter obliged, like her famous eponym, to bear his reverence one infant per annum, a fair excome on a poor investment, exiled in a sea-sprayed parsonage on the coast of West Cork, facetiously called "a living," endlessly fertile because, again apparently, neither of them can think of anything better to do when the paraffin ebbs in the pink glass bowl of the lamp, and the hearth goes grey and the Atlantic waves claw at the naked shingles of the western world.'

Such groans were masochist – apart from that sincere reference to Mount Pleasant Square. Names like that fell on the ears of his generation like far-off music, the horns of elfland; especially so for every boy come up from the provinces to a Dublin that had been a promise and a legend. For these, now grown men, Dundrum, Windy Arbour, Sandyford, Golden Ball would always happily evoke days of idleness and pleasure in the mountains with their lost girls and their faded youth. They fell like a knell on the memory of the ex-major; he had been too poor, pressed, and pimply for girl-play. Those nostalgic place-names suggested to him the youth he had never had.

Nevertheless! No regrets! Chin up! He was a man! He had campaigned! He had travelled and proved himself! He dismissed his non-youth without an audible sigh, and smartly unpacked his *elegantissimi* bags, purchased in vanquished Rome, in the bedroom of a modest Leeson Street guest house, called *The Anchor*, directly opposite the nuns' hospital, and from this base began thoughtlessly, blissfully, improvidently to live the life of a clubman. The United Services, five minutes across the Green, ten if he dawdled to watch the geese, ducks, seagulls. Its paths were, in the summer, lined with deck chairs, female legs to glance at covertly, an extra paper to buy, a sixpence for the old woman with the flowers outside the Saint Stephen's Green Club who always flattered him with her, 'Ah! God be good to you, *Colonel!*'

At lunch, at the Round Table, there was always somebody to talk to. He could easily kill time after it in the reading room, if lucky in the billiard room, then over afternoon tea in town. He lived extravagantly – his well-earned due – even slipped in a couple of expensive visits to Paris and Cannes. Before the year was out he had the beginnings of a duck's belly. For ten months he flourished. Then, suddenly, always an ominous word, while still abed one damp March morning he found on his breakfast tray, beside his London *Times*, three envelopes that caused his pleasant life to stammer, hiccough, wobble, shake and halt like a car out of petrol. His monthly bank sheet drew his eye swiftly to a total in red.

'Aha!' he laughed. '*Enfin, je suis dans le rouge.*'

The secretary of his Club also politely requested £50 in renewal of his annual subscription, plus £75. 6. 10 for drink and food consumed on the premises during the previous quarter. ('And well worth it!') His London tailor's bill brought him to the ground.

He steadily perused his *Times*, lit a cigarette and gazed calculatingly across the street at the nuns' hospital. Long before he was halfway through his cigarette he agreed that he possessed only one solid asset. His scholarship was unsaleable. Nobody except headmasters of schools would want his gift of languages. Majors were as little in demand in the Dublin of 1949 as Jesuits in the Geneva of 1549. His one solid asset was Moll Wall. He sent her an invitation to dinner at his Club. She agreed happily. With her usual shrewdness she had been expecting it for months.

3

Moll Wall was an Irish-speaking, Dublin-born Jewess whose father was known all over the world to every serious collector of Irish glass and silver. He ran a small antique business on one of the Dublin quays, a widower, the doyen of his profession, respected as a man of knowledge and probity. Alas for his only child, he took so much delight in his craft that he never had time to make money out of it. Accordingly Moll had had to work her way into college by winning scholarships, and knew that when she finished she would always, like her father, be comparatively poor. She worked now in the Department of External Affairs.

At Trinity she had been Georgie Atkinson's only female friend. He had been happy to spend months of hours with her over morning coffees or cups of afternoon tea in cheap cafés – he could never afford to take her to lunch – exchanging carefully prepolished student repartees and epigrams, solemnly discussing politics and languages, especially ancient tongues. They used to talk most warmly about loyalties, which at that time chiefly meant family loyalties and college personalities; spreading out later to international personalities; which in turn gradually hardened into political principles. They talked of religion, especially of its history. Here she had the edge on him, a Jewish mind ranging aeons behind Christianity into the vast Asiatic desert between the world-mothering rivers, finding everything he associated with the nineteenth century already matured four thousand years before in the thoughts of Ur and Babylon. He never dared to discuss love with her—

How could he? He so poor, she so proper – though she did attract him: lean, hard, lank, black, bony, muscular – they first met at the Foils Club. She was his senior, due to leave college before him, stern of character, good humoured, but also unpredictably puritanical, a woman whose moral force he frankly feared, whose Jewish sense of what is righteous and just he burningly admired, whose chosen vocation he wished he had dared to imitate. But even at college he was already (that English Connexion) hearing not the far-off echoes of Babylon but the imminent bellowings of Hitler, reading Houston Stewart Chamberlain, wondering how 'his' Empire and 'her' race would fare in the years before them.

Her real name was not Moll. It was Miriam, but since in her excessive efforts to nationalize herself she always signed her name not only in Gaelic but in an outmoded script, Máire de ball, her fellow students called her Moira, or Maurya, or Maureen, until she ended up by being universally known as Moll Wall. Whenever she lapsed into one of her more solemn moods they called her The Wailing Wall. He always respectfully called her Miriam. She always kindly called him George.

As he watched her sip her abstemious aperitif ('A small dry sherry, please') he guessed at her age. Thirty-five? Halfway to three score and ten. Perhaps more? Why had she never married? Took love too solemnly? Warned chaps off? She had always warned him off. Or was it he who warned her off? No beauty, yet she did unarguably have her fine points, even if each of them suffered a 'but' from the poor company it kept. Her skin was delicate, but tinged like a quarter gypsy's; her black hair was rich, oily and luxuriant, but it hung straight as threads beside her fine eyes; which were as lightly blue as two morning glories but set in eyelids as misshapen as scalene triangles recumbent against the bridge of her Hebraic nose; her teeth were as healthy and white as the teeth of a hound, but the canines and incisors crossed voraciously; her lips, if set in a gentler face, might have been prettily described as bee-stung, but in her strong countenance their pouting suggested not an insatiable kisser but an insuppressible talker. He liked her best when she laughed with a zany triumph that lit up her whole being. He had seen it often behind the flashing foils. She was at her best there – breastless, black from masked face to hissing foot, strong-calved, aggressively competitive, swift as her mind that was as sharp as a pitiless diamond in the hand of a glasscutter. How often had he not seen her at a public debate in college slash through some speaker's clever sophistry with one clean, arrogant stroke and casually chuck his bits into the rubbish bin beside her. He feared her – she was female. She envied him – he was male.

'You look very well,' he quizzed, raising his glass to her. 'How is life in your wicked Quai d'Orsay?'

'In order,' she smiled.

'Meaning in your order. I do congratulate you, Miriam. You always have ordered your life. Unlike those of us who have lived not wisely but too well, you have lived most wisely if not too well.'

'Where did you steal that piece of wit?'

'Othello. But he said "loved." He, too, admired a dark skin.'

'He too?' She smiled crookedly – it was as far as he would ever go. Timid? Shy? Unsexy? Androgynous? Selfish, like all bachelors? Frightened of women, like all Irishmen. But with her racial humility, her Jewish submissiveness – a female Job, *I have said to the worm Thou art my mother and my sister* – she had long since accepted that for him a wife would always be a poor substitute for the cosy filial relationship that always seemed sufficient for so many Irish *goyim* and so many Jewish Jews. And what if I *have* ordered my life? Had I any alternative? And how well I did it! His useless Greek, my useful Semitic languages, Arabic, Hebrew, even that spot of Aramaic, and then modern Irish, and that second degree in political science.

She could read his mind as if she were sitting inside it.

'George! What is the English for *cul-de-sac*?'

'Blind alley?' he suggested.

Years before he went marching off down his blind alley to the sound of guns and drums, and drums and guns, in defence of an Empire that even one of his father's actuaries could have told him would be stone dead within ten years, I was within steps of the top in External Affairs. I'd be an ambassador now if I were a man. Some woman once said of penis-envy, 'Who wants the stupid thing anyway?' O God! It must be worth five thousand pounds a year at least. Certainly worth an ambassadorship.

As if he could read her thoughts he told her sympathetically that with her Talmudic mind, so regulative, so legalistic, she was far too honest for foreign service, and, of course, far too idealistic, too romantic, much too sentimental. She hooted with laughter, well used to male romantics boasting of their realism. Ireland is full of them. She calmly declared her role – the *Eminence rose* of Ireland, guiding it knowledgeably through all its conflicts with the wicked world; at which they laughed so merrily that they ended by casting flickering glances of mistrust at one another. It was how they always sparred, advancing, receding to and from some sort of understanding, affinity, or intimacy that seemed to be regarded as best left undefined. One of their comrades once summed it up with, 'They are completely different and they are two of a kind.' And had she not once told him, with the air of somebody passing on a clue in a game, the sad story of the Egyptologist who, on finding a tiny flower in a freshly opened tomb, scooped it out of the dusk, into the sun, where it straightway died.

'I see you have settled back into Dublin all right,' she stated so firmly that he frowned. Had the witch been bugging him for the last ten months?

'I am back,' he shivered at her, 'in the cold bosom of Mother Ireland. Surrogate paps.'

She raised an eyebrow, observed that he had been drinking a lot of wine. On top of three martinis. Lacking courage? To pop his question? Whose nature she foresaw from his joke, disconnected, about owing a debt to his tailor and to society. Through the smoke of his cigar, over his port, her brandy, he finally posed the problem with a blend of bluster and nonchalance, so transparent that her heart was touched. Poor kid! Up against it?

'Miriam, I've come to the end of this bloody city. If you were me what would you do to keep boredom profitably at bay?'

'Join the army.'

'They sacked me a year ago!'

'The Irish army.'

'My God!' he cried rudely. 'A joke army! They are about as martial as the Pope's Swiss Guards. They haven't fought since 1922.'

'Snob! And ignoramus! It is for its size as good an army as any in the world. It also happens that the Swiss Guards have in their time fought skilfully and died bravely. Anyway,' glancing at his midriff, 'most of your fighting was conducted in an office. I must fix you up with some fencing soon. Think about it, George. Good quarters, a good mess – those we have inherited from your British Army – good pay, no expenses, all your financial troubles solved. Okay?'

'Well,' he mumbled, abashed by her penetration, 'I know my merits. I am quite sure I could teach those chaps a thing or two. But what about my deplorable genealogy? Even my name marks me as what your race would call "a gentile."'

'If you have the luck to be even so much as considered by them at all it will be solely because of your deplorably Saxon background. Consider! Our army is aggressively patriotic, ninety-five percent Roman Catholic, one hundred percent proletarian. Can't you see the kick we would get out of introducing you with deadpan faces to some visiting foreign brass? "Our Captain Atkinson." The brass looks at you superciliously. You turn out to be a first class Greek scholar, from a sixteenth-century university, a practising Methodist, ex-British Army, widely travelled, an Oxford accent, commanding five languages. You would be our prize exhibit. Our Uncle Tom.'

His cheeks blazed. She raised two palms and pouted at him with her shoulders, chin, eyebrows, lower lip, even with that shrugging of the bottom known as the *cul de poule*.

'It's what I am, George. Their Auntie Tom. It does not prevent me from doing my job as well as anybody in the department, indeed a hell of a sight better.'

For a while he was too aghast to speak. Finally:—

'I am *not*,' he insisted, 'a practising Methodist. And I do *not* speak five languages. I speak only Greek, French, Italian and English.'

She laid her hand on his wrist. His throat gobbled. He looked in astonishment at her radiant eyes and triumphant mouth. She could be damned attractive sometimes.

'The fifth language is the quintessence of our plot. It will be our master stroke. You must also be able to talk Gaelic to visiting brass. In fact I wonder could we put you into kilts?'

'Me?' he railed in his most haughtily offensive tone – excusable, she felt, in a man whom she had been deliberately kicking in the balls. 'I don't know a word of your bloody lingo.'

'My lingo,' she yielded gently, 'is Hebrew. You are a good linguist, George. Almost as good as I am. In six weeks I can teach you enough Irish to get you through the interview. With the strings I can pull for you they will see that you are on a plate for them. After that, the more you behave like a bally ass the more they will love you. But I am afraid you simply must also be some sort of a Protestant because it so happens that by pure luck we just now badly need one to represent the President and the army on such sad occasions as the funerals of such alien sects as Jews, Methodists, Jehovah's Witnesses, Baptists, Orangemen, Free

Masons, Buddhists, members of the Church of Ireland and all that pagan lot.'

He gazed at her lean and yellow abstinence. Sardonic bitch! A victim of genes. Also sexual frustration. And a countervailing lust for power. He said grandly that he would 'look them over.' Her sable eyelids drooped. She did not say it but he heard it. 'Good doggy!' Was this the beginning of his servitude or his success?

4

Those army years proved to be the best years of his life. Financed, fed, clothed, housed, flattered, fathered and, he was right, he *could* teach them a thing or two. They asked his views about lots of things – about cigars, wines, cricket, social protocol, Methodism, French letters, the English public school system, cocktails, gloves, ties, polo, English whores, John Wesley, The Royal Family, London clubs. Splendid fellows. Most intelligent. Some of my best friends.

If only, he sighed sincerely to her – and she smoothly agreed – they had some cultural interests. To remedy this, being unmarried and with no more than a peripheral interest in Woman and none in Marriage he was able to afford a secret, tiny, pink-papered bedsitter in the city where he could store his L.P. records, his beloved Loeb Classics, his French novels, relax in his Hong Kong pyjamas, sip a *pastis*, or a *Punt e Mes*, or a *retsina*, or a *Chambéry vermouth*, or a *cassis vin blanc*, unfold his *Times*, smoke a ten-shilling cigar, even entertain a rare female acquaintance. Naturally he never told Moll about this hideaway. She would have closed her bistre eyelids and laughed with her blue serpentine tongue at his rosy refuge. She would have known at once that he would have lost more battles there with Dublin's virgins than would bankrupt the honour of an entire army in any other part of the globe except Uganda, Israel and Maoist China. She was pleased that he did, now and again, take her to dinner at his Club. There he always had the grace to thank her for what she had done for him. Secretly he wished she had less moral character and more immoral flesh.

Those lovely fat years ended the day he heard her, to his bewilderment, abruptly telling him on the telephone that he was wasting his talents in the army and that he must stop it at once. He invited her to dinner in the Club. There she repeated her extraordinary opinion. He bluntly told her to mind her own damned business, he was hunkydory where he was, he had every intention of going on being hunkydory, and thank her VERY much! He saw her lower lip curl. He saw her slanted canines. He also noted, with an ingenuous satisfaction, that she seemed to have no ready reply – she merely changed the subject. That, he decided, was the way to do it. Treat them rough. A month later he discovered from a chummy note slipped under his door that he was about to be transferred to a civilian post in the Department of Defence. He at once sent her a dispatch, by motor cyclist, marked *Supremely Urgent*, informing her that as soon as he had put his affairs in order he would resign. The final haughty sentence of this dispatch recalled Alfred de Musset. *On ne badine pas avec moi!* Unfortunately a month of frantic search showed him that Fate *could* trifle with him. She had rightly assumed penury, hoped for boredom, was satisfied that he would not succeed in locating any alternative income. She had experienced it all herself.

He suffered in the Department of Defence. Why had he ever been so foolish as to return home to this mist-shotten island? If only, he groaned, there were another war, another lovely, bloody, muddy, dusty, murderous war to free him from this womb! Nevertheless, as a man of courage, an Odysseus, he must suffer Ithaca! And Penelope! He gave up his London *Times*. He had to surrender his pink-papered hideaway, sell his Loebs, wear cotton pyjamas, even have his suits off the rack. But he clung, by God, he clung to his Club. *On ne badine pas*... It should be the motto of the arms of the Atkinsons. He endured his lot until, perceptibly, some secret powers realized his true worth. He gradually found himself being used as a liaison between External Affairs and Defence, involving certain (not always intelligible, but nonetheless always welcome) explorations of the continent of Europe, for four weeks at a time and not less than four times a year. Bit by bit his bitter blood became sweeter, until, on a day no different to any other, he decided now that he had taught the foolish woman a lesson – namely that his worth would always be appreciated by somebody – he could afford to be generous. He took her back into his favour. He invited her to dinner at his Club.

5

Before the night was out she realized sadly that the Civil Service had taught him only a little. She knew his age to the hour, as who did not, forty-two on November 11th. He was as portentous as if he were still twenty-seven, a trifle less supercilious, capable at last of an occasional two minutes' silence. He found her as alert as always, regrettably one of those women who bear the lineaments of unsatisfied desire, as garrulous as ever but, now that he had learned what a desk and a dictaphone can do to the human spirit, he had to admire the way she had preserved her identity over the years *senza rancor*. It was the foils, he presumed, that preserved her sanity. No swordsman can feel rancour against an opponent who slips a blade under his defence.

All in all it was a most pleasant evening. Warmed by the wine he was so daring as to say to her as they parted on the pavement outside her flat, 'As Mr Churchill once said to Mr Roosevelt, *Amantium irae amoris integratio est.*' He cautiously spoiled it by adding, 'The maxim is also found in Publilius Cyrus, Maxim twenty-five. Speaking also of the quarrels of lovers as a renewal of friendship's bond.' She was to recall the moment as a missed opportunity. If only she had said – even with so shy a man, so conditioned a Methody, so late in the game – 'Aren't you going to kiss me good night?' she might have saved him some shame and herself some misery. Her excuse could only have been that at that moment she was gazing past him at the lamps of the square like a painter before his landscape, a sculptor before his model, a writer before his theme, wondering what the hell to do next to, with or for so intractable a subject. She merely said, 'Thanks for a delightful dinner, George! Good night!'

Sin loomed. Pride, vainglory, hubris, even some of that very bumptiousness that she held against him. It was natural, to be sure, that she should want not only to have his apple on her tree but to pluck it, feel it in the palm of her hand, under her eye, shining on her own desk, in her own department – she managed it easily even though she was well aware that it is the one department whose men are supposed to be mobile, even nomadic. 'But not our George!' George was no pilot; he was ground staff, a born adjutant, no more. She was amusedly confident of it – until, against her vehement, fervent, pleading, even irascible advice her superiors insisted on posting him as Second Secretary to the Paris embassy. When, in a drawling voice, he told her that, after careful consideration, he had agreed to accept this minor post, she foresaw with satisfaction that within a month Paris would return him to her lap.

To her rage he succeeded brilliantly there. A year later the powers beyond her control (and understanding) decided to send the boy to Oslo. He succeeded there as impeccably. Two years later she shudderingly saw him depart as First Secretary in the embassy to the Quirinal. Within a month he was the toast of Rome's diplomatic corps. (*Questi Irlandesi! Argutissimi! Spiritosi! Un gros gaillard. Ces Irlandais! Jolly able chap, take him for an Englishman any day. Ein so witziger Kerl.*) She gave in. Anyway she knew that the whispering gallery of the department had long since marked him down as their *Eminence rose's* personal creation. She had no option left but to pilot him to greater and greater achievements. An embassy? But not too far away! Canberra was mentioned. She cursed the Corona Australis in Irish. Africa offered. She Hebrewed it into a fog. Canada produced an obscenity in Arabic. The hand of chance crept forward on two fingers towards the E.E.C. The United States of Europe? *Chef de cabinet* in the Commission for Culture and Civilization? That would be worthy of her. But there was one danger. The U.S.E. is supranational. Its officers serve Europe, not their own country. She could have him sent on a string – seconded. Even so, to recall him might not be easy. Threatened by Australia, Canada and Africa, she yielded.

Brussels. 1972. *And Belgium's capital had gathered then her beauty and her chivalry. A few miles north of Waterloo. To arms! And there was mounting in hot haste . . . Or whispering with white lips, 'The foe! They come! They come!'*

6

She came one sunny November morning. Her cold camera's eye smilingly interrupts and startingly arrests one of his slow and stately steps as, bearing his fawn gloves, rolled gamp, bowler hat, he strolls from and now proudly leads her back to his modest but elegant three-roomed apartment on the Avenue des Arts.

'I chose it myself as befitting my not inconsiderable rank in the bureaucratic hierarchy of the new supranational Europe.'

His housekeeper, a lean, dark, sallow Flamande of middle age, makes them some excellent fresh French coffee, and Moll settles back to consider her protégé.

To her knowledge, she informs him, he is now fifty-four.

'Matured and wise?' she hopes.

She is, he flatters her, by his reckoning fifty. 'Would I wish any contemporary older?'

His living room she finds most untidy: letters, newspapers, books, magazines, reports on this and that all strewn about.

'My fingers itch.'

He is, she mocks, bloated from vanity and luxury. She is, he quips, lean from unsatisfied desire. She retorts with the fat weed that roots itself in ease on Lethe's wharf. He pulls in his gut.

'An elegant suit, it flatters your figure, George.'

'A charming frock. Do I perceive one teeny grey hair? The vanity of that necklet must have set you back at least a hundred pounds.'

Husband and wife could not have sparred more equivocally, each with reason. He would have preferred an ambassadorship and is sure she has denied it to him. He is behaving arrogantly just to show that he has slipped out of my power. He owes her more than his pride approves. She could do so much, oh, so very much more for him if only he would be a tiny bit more accommodating. At which point they both suddenly experienced a painful revelation of shared loss. In small countries like the green island to which they both belonged – as in all small cities, towns, houses, offices, institutions, workshops throught-out the world – familiarity breeds envy, and that conspiracy, and that skulduggery – it is their greatest disadvantage. However, just because they are so close, so small, so familiar, so personal, so intimate, one understands their skulduggery – it is one of their greatest advantages. Here? One can never keep track of the conspiracies of impersonal, ever-shifting Babels like the League of Nations, The United Nations, The Council of Europe, the E.E.C. They both suddenly begin to talk about Dublin, its gossip, its personalities, its plotters and planners, its news, its . . . It was she who, in the end, had to rise, and sadly send him about his business. Still, as she went her way she was humming, *He might have been a Rooshian,/ A French or Turk or Prooshian/ Or perhaps Itali-AN,/ But in spite of all temptations/ To belong to other nations,/ He still remains an Irishman.*

In high good humour she fished among her own informants around the city – the U.S.E. had already brought some four hundred Irish to

Brussels – took stock, weighed up, relaxed, expanded and returned to Dublin satisfied at long last with her offspring, her everything, husband, uncle, aunt, father, mother, sister, brother, fat, folly, power, freedom, fame. She began to boast of My Man in Bruxelles. She paced the corridors of power, moved across the chessboard of mirrored Europe, equipped with almost a dozen western and eastern languages, dropping amiably into this office and that, thriving on all those old Dublin yarns, legends, memories, characters, another Irish wit. From that on she flowered in the sun of his delightfully regular, secret dispatches from the front, intimate vignettes, witty, salted by a touch of the malicious, the flirtatious, even the salacious. He revelled in hers, so full of naughty local gossip. For them both it was like being back in T.C.D. all over again, except that she began to dress more and more carefully, had her straight hair waved every week, favoured restaurants where the headwaiter called her Madame, flaunted costume jewellery, wore Chamade scent and, the department groaned, talked like a bloody minister. During the next nine months she visited him there four times and he returned four times to Dublin. It was his heyday, her green period, his mature style period, the time when from Dublin she possessed Europe. A year passed. Never the tiniest spray of yew.

It was around the second quarter of his second year that the dry palmetta leaves of gossip began to clack. Long accustomed to such mutterings she made nothing of them. A woman? She laughed sardonically. The palm leaves still rattled their loose skin in the wind. What woman? She laughed in hysterical relief. She had met the poor creature five times. His hard-working, middle-aged, plain, surly, dark, unprepossessing, skinny housekeeper! Her assurance persisted until the September afternoon when:

Dear Miriam,

I have last week been here for exactly a year and a half, and I can say in all modesty that we have left our mark on Europe. I have now decided to show the flag. Accordingly I have taken a roomy apartment at 132 *bis*, two blocks farther along the avenue where I can suitably house a visitor or entertain a colleague. There are three bedrooms, one for me, one for a guest, one for my housekeeper, Miss Virginie Nieders. You may remember Ginnie. Or did you ever notice her at all? She is a splendid cook and, as I have just discovered, a superb if expensive shirtmaker, a marvellous find. She is Flemish and in many ways a remarkable creature. Lean as a greyhound, blackhaired, sallow as tallow, a coiled spring of energy, eyes shadowed as if by a gauze of libidinous soot, filled with a proud, Aristophanic scorn of all mankind, most entertainingly outspoken about my international colleagues, and especially about their wives. Where *does* she collect all this scandal? Moody if reproved, even thunderous, but absolutely devoted to me. And what a vocabulary! You would enjoy it. Yesterday evening I said that it was a charming sunset. She cried, '*C'est transcendant.*' Last week when she was fitting one of her splendid shirts on me I mentioned to her that it was rather tight under the armpits. What did this child of nature reply? She cried out in agony, in Walloon – though she can speak French too – that her soul was lacerated. Can you imagine any woman of any other race relating souls and shirts? Except perhaps an Italian? '*Mi straccia l'animal!*' But these Flemish women can be highly tempestuous creatures. If I did not accept this as a fact of nature I do not think I could, or even should have put up with some of her more outspoken remarks about our visitors. Anyway, it is a charming apartment and the next time you come to Brussels you must bring a chaperon and stay with us.

Ever, G.

Another woman reading this letter might have merely raised a speculative eyebrow, wonderingly turned down the corners of the mouth. Moll, who knew her man to the backbone, not so much turned the pages as whirled them. At the imprecise word 'our' in 'our visitors' she stopped breathing. At the final sentence she became taut, at the final word 'us' her spring snapped. 'Our' visitors? Her finger accused him. Rage blinded her. The fool wondered where the woman got her amusing scandals? She saw one of those inevitable international *kaffeeklatschen* of valets, hall porters, cooks, maids, chauffeurs, housekeepers, remembered her first glance about his earlier apartment, the untidy desk, the letters and papers strewn about it, covered her face in fury at the thought of her letters to him being eagerly deciphered over so many full-breasted and elbowed kitchen tables. She pulled herself up, and back. The essential word was not 'our.' It was the final word 'us.' When he wrote that word he convicted himself.

She must make certain. But could anybody ever know for certain what exactly, if anything, had happened between these two idiots? Not even he, perhaps he least of all, for when men of his age compromise themselves they lose all touch with reality. Her brain went cold and her heart went hard for one concentrated hour by which time she had established five points.

1. Though nothing is impossible in this area, it was unlikely that he had slept with her.

2. Even if he had she was not affected by the slightest feeling of jealousy – on this she had to be clear, and was.

3. Something either had happened, was happening, or was about to happen, well-known to Brussels, as the gossip at home showed, implying enough laughter in the *coulisses*, the *couloirs*, the cafés to show her that he was letting down the side.

4. The crunchy bit. An international U.S.E. aide is beyond the direct control of his home country: unless, *a*., he has made such a fool of himself as to embarrass his resident Minister or, *b*., deeply offended his own resident racial community (in this case the proper, puritanical, R.C., inferiority-complexed and supersensitive Irish), or, best/worst of all, *c*., created gross scandal or ribald laughter at home.

5. There was one way in which he just might be persuaded to do Number 4, *c*.

She sat to her typewriter and wrote to him, in French, her thanks for his invitation, and of her joy and delight at all the dear letters he had been sending to her over the last year or so. She had at last broken their secret code, she had lifted the curtain of their timid and, for that very reason, all the more delightful intimations. She understood, at last, all that his dear, fond heart had so tremulously been trying to say. 'How blind I have been! How my heart burns to think of all the days and nights we shall have together!' She would be in his arms in Brussels by next Friday night, happy that they need no longer conceal their passion from the world. Of course, she would be charmed to stay with him, *sans* chaperon. In fact he must send that silly old housekeeper on a holiday for the weekend. *Je me prends a pleurer de joie. Je t'embrasse.* M.

It was Wednesday. She posted her letter, to his new flat, before noon. She left the flap open. He (they) should be reading it by Friday morning. She had left him no time to reply by letter. He would not risk telephoning. The answer must be a telegram, and everything would now depend on its tone. It would be a blisterer if he was completely innocent; a blusterer if he was half innocent; evasive if he were guiltily unsure about whatever the hell he had or had not been up to. If he was guilty he would rush across to Dublin at once to find out what precisely he had been guilty of in his sleep.

His telegram came on Friday afternoon. AM FLYING TO DUBLIN FRIDAY SOONEST WILL TELEPHONE FROM CLUB SATURDAY MORNING SOONEST. EVER, GEORGE.

She no sooner read it than she found herself unable to swallow. Could the idiot – she was prepared to swear in open court that the possibility had not occurred to her before – could he, whether innocent or guilty, have taken her declaration *au pied de la lettre?* She suffered a night of sleeplessness, nightmare and nervous indigestion while pondering on all the uncomfortable as well as on some of the pleasing if also tormenting implications of the idea. He did not telephone on Saturday morning. Instead, the hall porter at his Club did, to tell Miss Miriam Wall that The Major had arrived, after a bad crossing, had a cold and neuralgia, was confined to his room, but would ring her in the afternoon. An hour later a great heap of red roses arrived from the florist near the Club. She extra-mured them in her hall. What was this all about? Oozing courage? For what? Up to some trickery? She waited indoors all day. He did not telephone.

He had decided to let her wait, which is to say that – like his old father long ago who could never make up his mind about anything – he was cowering in his room, not with a bad cold and neuralgia but with a bad conscience and nerves. He had already had a scene with one woman in Brussels; he could not bring himself to face another scene in Dublin. Let her be the one to telephone! Dammit! Was he a man or a mouse? (His honest insides whispered, 'Mouse!') Around five o'clock, being just about to descend to the bar for a bracer, a knock at his door and the page boy outside informed him that a lady of the name of Wall was inquiring for him downstairs.

He had always said it! Treat them rough! He tremblingly brushed back the greying wings of his green fifties, checked the lie of his tie, plucked the dark red handkerchief in his breast pocket an inch higher and then with stately tread slowly descended the winding stairs to meet the wench. There below him, foreshortened in the middle of the tesselated hall, stood Virginia Nieders, black-clothed, blackhaired, her black spring wound tight, the aureoles about her eyes as brown as thunder. Cornered, even a mouse will bare its tiny teeth. Reverting instantly to type Major Atkinson strode past her to the porter's glass box, whipped out his wallet, slipped a fiver into the man's hand, said, 'Get rid of her at once,' emerged, howled at her in Walloon, French, Flemish, English and Italian, 'Go away!', while bounding in long leaps like an obese giraffe for the stairs. Behind him the porter's brass-buttoned tails did such an effective flying tackle about her whirling waist that two arriving diners, both rugby threequarters, cheered his grappling speed. A lifted telephone, a Guard opportunely passing, peacock screams in Walloon, French and Flemish diminuendoed into the street. Calm returned to the Hibernian United Services Club. The porter stood staring at her through the barred glass door. The Guard stood warily watching her from the balcony of the double steps. Georgie leaned from the tiptop bedroom of the club peering at her glistening poll until God sent the miracle of a cloudburst whose downpour washed her ark away.

The Major galloped downstairs, rang for a taxi, drove to his old Guest House on Leeson Street. They were delighted to see him. But there was no room in the inn. Oh! A foreign lady, they slyly said, had been asking after him only an hour ago. Phew! Being without his address book he drove on to External Affairs, on Saint Stephen's Green, to collect a few friendly telephone numbers from the usual solitary Casabianca holding the Saturday fort. He had barely time to shout 'Full speed ahead' to the cabby before she bounded like a dripping mermaid from the portico down to the pavement to shriek in Walloon after him. He remembered an old Irish army friend who had a base on Earlsfort Terrace, around the corner from the Green. Terror poured its adrenaline all over his kidneys at the sight of her black, spearlike figure under the spotlight of that portico too. 'Down the Hatch!' he roared, and with whistling tyres down the Hatch they went. Were there ten of her? He must think. He must have a drink. He must eat. Round the Green to the Unicorn. Or had he by chance spoken to her of that estimable restaurant as a haunt of his legendary student days? He evidently had. Peeping from his knees on the floor of the taxi, he saw her against the restaurant's lighted, curtained window. He surrendered. Back to the Club! There for the first time in his life he was relieved to find the bar empty. It took him half an hour and three brandies to clarify the situation.

What were the simple facts? He shook his head wildly. Damnation! What WERE the simple facts? He had been lonely. Right? She had been lonely. Right? What more natural than that he should want to comfort her, be kind to her? Right? And if he ever had gone beyond that whose business was it but his own? Anyway everybody knew that half the international population of Brussels was living in sin – except the cagy Irish. It would all have been hunkydory if the cow hadn't pulled the teat out of the baby's bottle. Chasing him over here in broad daylight! And God knows what she had been saying to whatever junior she had found across the Green in External Affairs! And, no doubt, she would be back there on Monday morning screaming fit for a French farce. Right? No! Yes!!!

He was a ruined man.

A third brandy was needed to give him the courage to ring for the firing squad.

'Miriam! It is me. I'm simply dying to see you.'

'George!'

She sounded sad. Could she be shy? How dicey was this going to be? He tried to make his own voice sound neither soft nor hard. It came out as hoarse as an old hinge.

'I needn't tell you, Miriam, that I'd have rung you at once if it hadn't been for this wretched cold.'

'Your poor cold! Caught, I presume, racing around Dublin from that woman.'

His stomach fell a foot.

'How soon can I see you, Miriam?'

'I am afraid not tonight, George. Nor tomorrow. Ever since your housekeeper arrived in Dublin she has been telephoning me every half hour. You must have confided greatly in her, she is so accurately informed about this city. Have you been telling her all about your golden youth? Also you left your address book behind you. For all I know she may have rung the Secretary. Even the Minister. Perhaps the entire Cabinet? Some little while ago she took up her position on the pavement opposite my flat, parading up and down under the rain between two lampposts like an unemployed whore. After watching her through my curtains for half an hour I brought her in. Soaked to the skin, poor slut! I gave her a stiff drink, let her pour some of her European despair over me, gave her some dry clothes and sent her to soak in a hot bath where she is wallowing at this moment. When she emerges I suppose I shall have to listen to a few more lurid revelations about our man in Bruxelles before I park her in some modest guest house where she can prepare herself for her interview with the Secretary on Monday morning.'

'But the woman is daft, Miriam! You can't, nobody can believe a word she says!'

'It is not only what she says, it is what she sees. She says you have a mole in the small of your back. Have you, George?'

'She makes shirts for me!'

'How intimate! And that you have a scar on the inside of your right thigh.'

'I must have mentioned it to her.'

'She has a letter you wrote to her from Paris two months ago. It almost made me blush.' Her voice became soft and sad again. 'I am sorry, George. You ought to have stayed in Trinity and become a tutor in Ancient Greek. I realize now that what you are is a man so afraid of the lonely, little Irish boy in you that you have grown fold after fold of foreign fat to keep him in. Just as this poor woman may well have had an exuberant Peter Paul Rubens goddess bursting to get out of her skinny body ever since the day she was born. O dear! I sometimes wonder how many Ariels were imprisoned in Caliban. And how many Calibans were imprisoned in Ariel? It is a thought that makes one feel sorry for the whole human race.'

'Well!' he blustered, 'since you are so damned sorry for the whole human race would you kindly tell me what I had best do now?'

'That is quite simple. You have only two alternatives. The first is to resign and return. You would have to accept a spot of demotion. But, never fear, we will find a cosy berth for you somewhere. A consulate in South America? In Africa? Say in Uganda? We won't let you starve. The other possibility you must surely have gathered from my letter. If you should still wish me to announce that we have been privately engaged for the past six months you can blow the whole business out like a candle. But you must decide at once so that I may ring up the Secretary, or the Minister, and a gossipy friend or two, and have it published in Monday's *Irish Times*, and break it gently to the poor slut upstairs, and drive her to the airport tomorrow. You could then break off our engagement at your convenience. Only, in that case, George, please do, I beg you, return my letter. It puts me so completely in your power as a woman.'

She knew that the flattery of that last bit would be irresistible.

'You mean ... I mean ... You mean you meant all that in your letter?'

'George! Do you not realize how attractive you are to women?'

He answered her without hesitation in the voice of a small boy saying, 'Mummy! May I go to the pictures?':—

'Miriam! Let us be married at once.'

'I hear her bath water running out. At once cannot be too soon, George. I must hurry. Get on a plane for Brussels *il più presto*. If you don't she will strip our flat naked and then set fire to it. Goodnight, darling. Ring me from Brussels.'

For a long time he looked with a dazed smile into the mouth of the receiver. He carried the same smile to his mirror. Attractive to women? Well! He brushed his greying wings, chucked his lapels, arranged his lolling peony handkerchief, smilingly went downstairs to dinner. What a woman! Such tact, ability, foresight! He would have ample time for dinner before catching the last plane for London. His concierge in Brussels would do the rest. Touching his empty *boutonnière* at the turn of the stairs his descent was halted by a memory: her story of the rash Egyptologist whose frail flower wilted at the sight of day.

She, hit at that precise moment by a memory of a different sort, hastily concluded a swift goodnight to her most gossipy gossip –

'Happy? I remember what happened to poor Pygmalion. He worked for years on a statue of the perfect woman and found himself left with a chatterbox of a wife. I think of all the years I have devoted to my chatterbox.' She laughed philosophically. 'Never mind. I am really very fond of poor old George. I always have been. And he needs me. I must fly. Tell the world!'

As she replaced the receiver she turned in her chair to watch the china handle of the door slowly turning. When it was thrown wide open her eyes stared at her dark visitor staring at her, wearing the long, soft, white, woollen shawl, interwoven with gold thread, always kept in tissue in her tallboy, the gold torque that had so diverted George, three bracelets from her dressing table on each scraggy arm, and a red rose in the black mat of her hair. For one statuesque second the door became a bevelled mirror asking, 'And who is who, now?' Then, resolutely conquering her weakness, she rose and advanced with her arms wide open.

'Virginia!'

They sat side by side on the cosy sofa beside the fire. There, speaking ever so gently, but firmly, she tenderly, gradually, almost absentmindedly, woman to woman, stripped her guest of her dreams and her plumes. From both a few tears, a shrug, a hug and, in three or four languages, 'Men!'

Falling Rocks, Narrowing Road, Cul-de-Sac, Stop

The day Morgan Myles arrived in L—— as the new county librarian he got a painful boil under his tongue. All that week he was too busy settling into his new quarters to do anything about it beyond dribbling over his mother's hand mirror into a mouth as pink and black as a hotel bathroom. Otherwise he kept working off the pain and discomfort of it in outbursts of temper with his assistant, Marianne Simcox, a frail, long-legged, neurotically efficient, gushingly idealistic, ladylike (that is to say, Protestant) young woman whom he hated and bullied from the first moment he met her. This, however, could have been because of his cautious fear of her virginal attractiveness.

On his fourth day in the job he was so rude to her that she turned on him, called him a Catholic cad, and fled sobbing behind the stacks. For fifteen minutes he went about his work humming with satisfaction at having broken her ladylike ways; but when she failed to come trotting to his next roar of command, he went tearing around the stacks in a fury looking for her. He was horrified to find her sitting on the floor of the Arts Section still crying into her mouse-sized handkerchief. With a groan of self-disgust he sat on the floor beside her, put his arm around her shoulder, rocked her as gently as if she was a kid of twelve, told her he was a bastard out of hell, that she was the most efficient assistant he had ever had in his life and that from this time on they would be doing marvellous things together with 'our library.' When she had calmed, she apologized for being so rude, and thanked him so formally, and so courteously, and in such a ladylike accent that he decided that she was a born bitch and went off home in a towering temper to his mother who, seeing the state her dear boy was in, said, 'Wisha, Morgan love, why don't you take that gumboil of yours to a doctor and show it to him. You're not your natural nice self at all. You're as cranky as a bag of cats with it.'

At the word 'doctor' Morgan went pale with fear, bared his teeth like a five-barred gate and snarled that he had no intention of going next nor nigh any doctor in this one-horse town. 'Anyway,' he roared, 'I hate all doctors. Without exception of age or sex. Cods and bluffers they are, the whole lot of them. And you know well that all any doctor ever wants to do with any patient is to take X-rays of his insides, order him into hospital, take the clothes down off of him, stick a syringe into his backside and before the poor fathead knows where he is there'll be half a dozen fellows in white nightshirts sawing away at him like a dead pig. It's just a gumboil. It doesn't bother me one bit. I've had dozens of them in my time. It's merely an Act of God. Like an earthquake, or a crick in the neck. It will pass.'

But it did not pass. It went on burning and smarting until one windy sunstruck afternoon in his second week when he was streeling miserably along the Dublin Road, about a mile beyond the town's last untidy lot, beside its last unfinished suburban terrace. About every ten minutes or so, the clouds opened and the sun flicked and vanished. He held the collar of his baggy, tweed overcoat humped about his neck. His tongue was trying to double back acrobatically to his uvula. Feeling as lost and forlorn as the grey heron he saw across the road standing by the edge of a wrinkled loch, he halted to compose. '*O long-legged bird by your ruffled lake/ Alone as I, as bleak of eye, opaque . . .*' As what? He unguardedly rubbed his under-tongue on a sharp tooth, cursed, the sun winked, and he was confronted by one of destiny's infinite options. It was his moment of strength, of romance, of glamour, of youth, of sunshine on a strange shore. A blink of sunlight fell on a brass plate fastened to the red-brick gate pillar beside him, DR FRANCIS BREEN.

The gate was lined with sheet metal. Right and left of it there was a high cutstone wall backing on a coppice of rain-black macrocarpa that extended over the grassgrown border of the road. The house was not visible. He squeaked the gate open, peered timidly up a short curved avenue at it, all in red brick, tall, turreted and baywindowed. An empty-looking conservatory hooped against one side of it (intended, presumably, for the cultivation of rare orchids). Along the other side, a long veranda (intended, doubtless, to shelter Doctor Francis Breen from Ireland's burning tropical sun). He opened his mouth wide as he gazed, probed with his finger for the sore spot, and found it.

It did not look like a house where anybody would start cutting anybody up. It did not look like a doctor's house at all. It looked more like a gentleman's residence. Although he did remember the American visitor to Dublin who said to him that every Irish surgery looked as if it had been furnished by Dr Watson for Sherlock Holmes. As he cautiously entered the avenue he observed that the gate bore a perpendicular column of five warning signs in blue lettering on white enamel. NO DOGS. NO CANVASSERS. NO HAWKERS. NO CIRCULARS. SHUT THE GATE. He advanced on the house, his fists clenched inside his overcoat pockets, his eyebrows lifted to indicate his contempt for all doctors. Twice on the way to the front door he paused, as if to admire the grounds, really to assure himself that no dog had failed to read the NO DOGS sign: a born cityman, he feared all living animals. He was very fond of them in poetry. He took the final step upward to the stained glass door, stretched out his index finger, to tip, to tempt, to test, to press the brass bellknob. (An enamel sign beneath it said, TRADESMEN TO THE REAR.) His mother had spoken of a deficiency. She had also mentioned pills. He would ask this sawbones for a pill, or for a soothing bottle. He would not remove his shirt for him. And he would positively refuse to let down his pants. 'Where,' he foresaw himself roaring, 'do you think I have this boil?'

A shadow appeared behind the door. He looked speculatively over his glasses at the servant who partly opened it. She was grey and settled, but not old, dressed in black bombazine, wearing a white starched apron with shoulder frills. When he asked for the doctor she immediately flung the door wide open as if she had been eagerly expecting him for years and years; then, limping eagerly ahead of him, dot and carry one down a softly upholstered corridor, she showed him into what she called 'the dachtar's sargery,' quacking all about 'what an ahful co-eld dayeh it iss Gad bliss itt' in what he had already scornfully come to recognize as the ducks' dialect of this sodden, mist-shotten dung-heap of the Shannon's delta.

Left to himself he had time only to be disturbed by the sight of one, two, three barometers side by side on the wall, and one, two, three, four clocks side by side on the mantelpiece; relieved by an opposite wall lined with books; and enchanted by a dozen daintily tinted lithographs of flying moths and half a dozen hanging glass cases displaying wide-winged butterflies pinned against blue skies, when the door was slammed open by a tall, straight, white-haired, handsome, military-looking man, his temper at boiling point, his voice of the barrack-square, the knuckles of his fist white on the doorknob as if he were as eager to throw out his visitor as his Bombazine had been to welcome him in. Morgan noted that his eyes were quiet as a novice of nuns, and that his words were as polite, and remembered hearing somewhere that when the Duke of Wellington gave his order for the final charge at Waterloo his words to his equerry had been, 'The Duke of Wellington presents his compliments to Field Marshal von Blücher and begs him to be so kind as to charge like blazes.'

'Well, sir?' the doctor was saying. 'Would you be so kind as to tell me what you mean by entering my house in this cavalier fashion? Are you an insurance salesman? Are you distributing circulars? Are you promoting the Encyclopaedia Britannica? Are you a hawker? A huckster? A Jehovah's Witness?'

At these words Morgan's eyes spread to the rims of his lake-size glasses. He felt a heavenly sunlight flooding the entire room. He raised two palms of exultant joy. More than any other gift of life, more than drink, food, girls, books, nicotine, coffee, music, more even than poetry and his old mother (whom he thought of, and saw through, as if she were a stained glass image of the Mother of God), he adored all cranks, fanatics, eccentrics and near-lunatics, always provided that they did not impinge on his personal comfort, in which case he would draw a line across them as fast as a butcher cuts off a chicken's head. More than any other human type he despised all men of good character, all solid citizens, all well-behaved social men, all mixers, joiners, hearty fellows and jolly good chaps, always provided that he did not require their assistance in his profession as librarian, in which case he would cajole them and lard them and lick them like a pander, while utterly despising himself, and his job, for having to tolerate such bores for one moment. But, here, before his eyes was a figure of purest gold. If there were any other such splendid crackpots in L—— then this was heaven, nor was he ever to be out of it.

'But,' he protested gaily, 'you are a doctor! I have a gumboil! We are the perfect match.'

The old man moaned as if he had been shot through by an arrow of pain.

'It is true that I am, by letters patent, a man licensed to practise the crude invention called medicine. But I have never practised, I have never desired to practise and I never do intend to practise medicine. I know very well, sir, what you want me to do. You want me to look down your throat with an electric torch and make some such solemn, stupid and meaningless remark as "You have a streptococcal infection." Well,' he protested, 'I will do nothing of the kind for you. Why should I? It might be only a symptom. Next week you might turn up with rheumatic heart disease, or a latent kidney disease, as people with strep throats have been known to do. You talk airily of a gumboil. You may well be living in a fool's paradise, sir. Even supposing I were to swab strep out of your throat and grow it on a culture medium, what would that tell me about the terrible, manifold, creeping, subtle, lethal disease-processes that may be going on at this moment in the recesses of your body as part of that strep infection, or set off by it? The only thing I, or any other doctor – bluffers and liars that we all are – could honestly say to you would be the usual evasion. "Gargle with this bottle three times a day and come back in a week." By which time Nature or God would have in any case cured you without our alleged assistance. I know the whole bag of tricks from the Hippocratic collection, the treatises of Galen and the Canon of Avicenna down. I suppose you imagine that I spent all my years in Dublin and Vienna studying medicine. I spent them studying medicos. I am a neurologist. Or I was a neurologist until I found that what true medicine means is true magic. Do you know how to remove a wart? You must wait on the roadway to the cemetery until a funeral passes, and say, "Corpse, corpse, take away my wart." And your wart will go, sir! That is true medicine. I believe in miracles because I have seen them happen. I believe in God, prayer, the imagination, the destiny of the Irish, our bottomless racial memory – and in nothing else.'

Morgan's left hand was circling his belly in search of manifold, creeping, secret diseases.

'But, surely to God, doctor,' he whined, 'medical science can do *something* for a gumboil?'

'Aha! I know what you're up to now. X-rays! That's the mumbo-jumbo every patient wants. And neither will I suggest, as you would probably like me to suggest, that you should go to hospital. All you would do there would be either to pass your infection to some other patient or pick up his infection from him. I will have nothing to do with you, sir. And please keep your distance. I don't want your beastly infection. If you want to mess about with your gumboil you will have to go to a doctor. If you wish me to pray for your gumboil I will pray for it. But I refuse to let you or anybody else turn me into the sort of mountebank who pretends he can cure any tradesman's sore toe or any clerk's carbuncle in one second with a stroke of his pen and a nostrum from the chemist's shop. Good afternoon to you, sir. You are now in the hands of God!'

Morgan, stung by arrogance and enraged by fear, roared back a line fit for his memoirs.

'And good afternoon to you, sir! From one who is neither clerk nor tradesman, higgler nor hawker, huckster nor hounddog but, by God's grace, a poet whose poems will live long after,' hand waving, 'your butterflies have been devoured by the jaws of your moths.'

The old man's rage vanished like a ghost at cockcrow. He closed the door gently behind him.

'A poet?' he asked quietly. 'Now, this is most interesting.' Courteously he indicated a chair. 'Won't you sit down? Your name is?'

'Morgan Myles,' Morgan Myles boomed as if he were a majordomo announcing Lord Byron.

'Mine is Francis Breen. Yours is more euphonious. I can see it already on your first book of verses. But a poet should have three names. Like American politicians. Percy Bysshe Shelley. George Gordon Byron. Thomas Stearns Eliot. William Butler Yeats. Ella Wheeler Wilcox. Richard Milhous Nixon. You have a second name? Taken at your Confirmation? Arthur? There we have it! *First Poems.* By Morgan Arthur Myles!'

Morgan, like most men who are adept at flattering others, could never resist flattery himself. He waggled his bottom like a dog. His grin was coy but cocksure. Three minutes later the doctor was tenderly parting his lips and illuminating the inside of his mouth. He extinguished the torch. He lifted his eyes and smiled into Morgan's.

'Well, Doc?' Morgan asked fearfully. 'What did you see there?'

'You are not even,' his new-found friend smiled, 'about to give birth to a couplet. Just a blister.' He sat to his desk. 'I will give you a prescription for a gargle. Rinse your mouth with this three times a day. And come back to me in a week. But if you wish to get better sooner come sooner, any evening for a drink and a chat. I have no friends in L——.'

'Nor have I!'

Within a week they were bosom cronies.

From start to finish it was a ridiculous friendship. Indeed, from that day onward, to the many of us who saw them every day after lunch walking along O'Connell Street arm in arm like father and son, or nose to nose like an ageing ward boss with a young disciple, it seemed an unnatural business. Can the east wind, we asked one another in wonder, lie down with the west wind? A cormorant mate with a herring? A heron with a hare? An end with a beginning? We gave their beautiful friendship three months. As a matter of fact we were only two years and eleven months out.

Even to look at they were a mismatch: the doctor straight and spare as a spear, radiating propriety from every spiky bone of his body, as short of step as a woman, and as carefully dressed from his wide-brimmed bowler hat to the rubber tip of his mottled, gold-headed malacca cane; the poet striding beside him, halting only to swirl his flabby tweeds; his splendid hydrocephalic head stretched behind his neck like a balloon; his myopic eyes glaring at the clouds over the roofs through the thick lenses of his glasses; a waterfall of black hair permanently frozen over his left eye; his big teeth laughing, his big voice booming, he looked for all the world like a peasant Yeats in a poor state of health. The only one of us who managed to produce any sort of explanation was our amateur psychiatrist, Father Tim Buckley, and we never took him seriously anyway. He said, with an episcopal *sprinkle me O Lord with hyssop* wave of his hand, 'They have invented one another.'

Now, we knew from experience that there was only one way to handle Tim Buckley. If he said some fellow was a homosexual because he had fallen in love with his hobbyhorse when he was five you had to say at once, 'But, Tim, why did he fall in love with his hobbyhorse when he was five?' If he said that it was because the poor chap hated his mother and loved his father you had to say, at once, 'But, Tim, why did he hate his ma and love his da?' If he then said that it was natural for every child to prefer one parent to another, you had to say at once, 'But, Tim, why . . .' And so on until he lost his temper and shut up. This time, however, he was ready for our counterattack.

'They have invented one another,' he said, 'for mutual support because they are both silently screaming for freedom. Now what is the form of slavery from which all human beings most want to be free?'

'Sex,' we conceded, to save time, knowing our man.

'Passion!' he amended. 'For this agony there are only three solutions. The first is sin, which,' he grinned, 'I am informed on the best authority is highly agreeable but involves an awful waste of time. I mean if you could hang a girl up in the closet every time you were finished with her that would be very convenient, but. Then there is marriage, which as

Shaw said is the perfect combination of maximum temptation and maximum opportunity. And there is celibacy of which, I can say with authority, as the only member of the present company who knows anything at all about it, that it bestows on man the qualified freedom of a besieged city where one sometimes has to eat rats. Of our two friendly friends the older man needs approval for his lifelong celibacy. The younger man needs encouragement to sustain his own. Or so they have chosen to imagine. In fact neither of them really believes in celibacy at all. Each has not only invented the other. He has invented himself.'

Our silence was prolonged.

'Very well,' he surrendered. 'In that case thicken your own plot!'

Of course, we who had known Frank Breen closely ever since we were kids together in L——, knew that there was nothing mysterious about him: he had simply always been a bit balmy, even as a four-eyed kid. When his parents sent him to school in England we saw much less of him; still less when he went to Dublin for his MB, and from there on to Austria for his MD. After he came back to L—— to settle down for life in the old Breen house on the Dublin Road on the death of his father, old Doctor Frank, and of his mother, we hardly saw him at all. We knew about him only by hearsay, chiefly through the gossip of his housekeeper, Dolly Lynch, passed on to Claire Coogan, Father Tim Buckley's housekeeper, and gleefully passed on by him to the whole town.

That was how the town first heard that the brass plate on his gate pillar – his father's, well polished by chamois and dulled by weather – would never again mean that there was a doctor behind it; about his four clocks and his three barometers; about his collection of moths and butterflies; about the rope ladder he had coiled in a red metal box under every bedroom window; about his bed always set two feet from the wall lest a bit of cornice should fall on his head during the night; about the way he looked under the stairs for hidden thieves every night before going to bed; that his gold-knobbed malacca cane contained a sword; that he never arrived at the railway station less than half an hour before his train left; that he hung his pyjamas on a clothes hanger; had handmade wooden trees for every pair of his handmade boots; that he liked to have his bootlaces washed and ironed; that his vest-pocket watch told the time, the date, the day, the year, the points of the compass, and contained an alarm buzzer that he was always setting to remind him of something important he wanted to do later on, but whose nature he could never remember when the buzzer hummed over his left gut – very much the way a wife will leave her wedding ring at night on her dressing table to remind her in the morning of something that by then she has incontinently forgotten.

So! A bit odd. Every club in the world must have elderly members like him – intelligent and successful men of whose oddities the secretary will know one, the headwaiter another, the bartender a third, their fellow members smile at a fourth. It is only their families, or if they live for a long time in a small town their townsfolk who will, between them, know the lot. Frank Breen might have gone on in his harmless, bumbling way to the end of his life if that brass plate of his had not winked at Morgan Myles, and if Father Tim Buckley – was he jealous? – had not decided to play God.

Not that we ever called him 'Father Tim Buckley.' He was too close to us, too like one of ourselves for that. We called him Tim Buckley, or Tim, or even if the whiskey was fluming, Bucky. He was not at all like the usual Irish priest who is as warm as toast and as friendly and understanding as a brother until you come to the sixth commandment, and there is an end to him. Tim was like a man who had dropped off an international plane at Shannon; not a Spencer Tracy priest from downtown Manhattan, all cigar and white cuffs, parish computer and portable typewriter, fists and feet, and there is the end to him; perhaps more like an unfrocked priest from Bolivia or Brazil, so ungentlemanly in his manners as to have given acute pain to an Evelyn Waugh and so cheerful in spite of his scars as to have shocked a Graham Greene; or still more like, among all other alternatives, a French workers' priest from Liège; or in other words, as far as we were concerned, the right man in the right place and as far as the bishop was concerned, a total disaster. He was handsome, ruddy and full-blooded in a sensual way, already so heavy in his middle thirties that he had the belly, the chins and (when he lost his temper) something of the voracity of Rodin's ferocious statue of Balzac in his dressing gown; but he was most himself when his leaden-lidded eyes glistened with laughter, and his tiny mouth, crushed between the peonies of his cheeks, reminded you of a small boy whistling after his dog, or of some young fellow saucily making a kiss-mouth across the street to his girl. His hobby was psychoanalysis.

His analysis of the doctor was characteristic. He first pointed out to us, over a glass of malt, the sexual significance of pocket watches, so often fondled and rubbed between the fingers. He merely shrugged at the idea of ladders unfolding from red containers, and said that swords being in sword sticks needed no comment. Clocks and barometers were merely extensions of pocket watches. (The wristwatch, he assured us, was one of the great sexual revolutions of our age – it brought everything out in the open.) But, above all, he begged us to give due attention to Frank Breen's mother complex – evident in his love of seclusion behind womblike walls, dark trees, a masked gate; and any man must have a terrible hate for his father who mockingly leaves his father's brass plate on a pillar outside his home while publicly refusing to follow his father's profession inside it. ('By the way, can we ignore that NO DOGS sign?') The looking for thieves under the stairs at night, he confessed, puzzled him for the moment. Early arrival for trains was an obvious sign of mental insecurity. 'Though, God knows,' laughing in his fat, 'any man who doesn't feel mentally insecure in the modern world must be out of his mind.' As for this beautiful friendship, that was a classical case of Narcissism: the older man in love with an image of his own lost and lonely youth.

'Any questions?'

No wonder he was the favourite confessor of all the nubile girls in town, not (or not only) because they thought him handsome but because he was always happy to give them the most disturbing explanations for their simplest misdemeanours. 'I kissed a boy at a dance, Father,' they would say to some other priest and, as he boredly bade them say three Hail Marys for their penance, they would hear the dark slide of the confessional move dismissively across their faces. Not so with Father Tim! He would lean his cheek against the grille and whisper, 'Now, my dear child, in itself a kiss is an innocent and beautiful act. Therefore the only reason prompting you to confess it as a sin must refer to the manner in which the kiss was given and the spirit in which it was received, and in this you may be very wise. Because, of course, when we say *kiss*, or *lips*, we may – one never knows for certain – be thinking of something quite different...' His penitents would leave his box with their faces glowing, and their eyes dazed. One said that he made her feel like a Magdalen with long floating hair.

Another said he made her want to go round L—— wearing a dark veil. A third (who was certain to come to a bad end) said he had revealed to her the *splendeurs et misères de l'amour*. And a fourth, clasping her palms with delight, giggled that he was her Saint Rasputin.

We who met him in our homes, with a glass in his fist and his Roman collar thrown aside, did not worry about what he told our daughters. We had long since accepted him as an honest, innocent, unworldly man who seemed to know a lot about sex-in-the-head – and was always very entertaining about it – but who knew sweet damn all about love-in-the-bed, not to mention love at about eleven o'clock at night when your five kids are asleep and the two of you are so edgy from adding up the household accounts that by the time you have decided once again that the case is hopeless all 'to go to bed' means is to go sound asleep. But we did worry about him. He was so outspoken, so trustful of every stranger, had as little guard over his tongue as a sailor ashore, that we could foresee the day when his bishop would become so sick of getting anonymous letters about him that he would shanghai him to some remote punishment-curacy on the backside of Slievena-muck.

We would try to frighten him into caution by telling him that he would end up there, exiled to some spot so insignificant that it would not be marked even on one of those nostalgic one-inch-to-the-mile British Ordnance maps of 1899 that still – indifferent to the effects of time and history, of gunshot and revolution – record every burned out constabulary barracks, destroyed mansion, abandoned branch-rail-way, eighteenth century 'inn,' disused blacksmith's hovel, silenced windmill, rook-echoing granary or 'R.C. Chapel,' where, we would tell him, is where our brave Bucky would then be, in a baldface presbytery, altitude 1750 feet, serving a cement-faced chapel, beside an anonymous crossroads, without a tree in sight for ten miles, stuck for life as curator, nurse and slave of some senile parish priest. He would just raise his voice to spit scorn at us; like the night he gobbled us up in a rage:—

'And,' he roared, 'if I can't say what I think how the hell am I going to live? Am I free or am I not free? Am I to lie down in the dust and be gagged and handcuffed like a slave? Do ye want me to spend my whole life watching out for traffic signs? Falling rocks! Narrowing Road! Cul-de-sac! Stop! My God, are ye men or are ye mice?'

'Mice!' we roared back with one jovial voice and dispelled the tension in laughter so loud that my wife looked up in fright at the ceiling and said, 'Sssh! Ye bastards! If ye wake the kids I'll make every one of ye walk the floor with them in yeer arms till three in the morning. Or do ye think ye're starting another revolution in yeer old age?'

'We could do worse,' Tim smiled into his double chin.

Whenever he smiled like that you could see the traffic signs lying right and left of him like idols overthrown.

It was a Sunday afternoon in May. The little island was deserted. He was lying on the sunwarmed grass between the other two, all three on their backs, in a row, their hats on their faces. They were neither asleep nor awake. They were breathing as softly as the lake at their feet. They had driven at their ease that morning to the east side of the lake past the small village of Mountshannon, now looking even smaller across the level water, rowed to the island (Tim Buckley at the oars), delighted to find every hillocky green horizon slowly bubbling with cumulus clouds. They had inspected the island's three ruined churches, knee-deep in nettles and fern, and its tenth-century Round Tower that had stood against the morning sun as dark as a factory chimney. They had photographed the ruins, and one another, and then sat near the lake and the boat to discuss the excellent lunch that Dolly Lynch always prepared for 'the young maaaster' on these Sunday outings: her cold chicken and salad, her handmade mayonnaise, her own brown bread and butter, the bottle of Liebfraumilch that Frank had hung by a string in the lake to cool while they explored the island, her double roasted French coffee, flavoured, the way the maaaster always liked it, with chicory and a suspicion of cognac. It was half an hour since they had lain back to sleep. So far everything about the outing had been perfect. No wonder Morgan had jackknifed out of bed that morning at eight o'clock, and Frank Breen wakened with a smile of special satisfaction.

Before Morgan came, exactly two years and eleven months ago, it had been the doctor's custom, at the first call of the cuckoo, to take off now and again (though never too often to establish a precedent), on especially fine Sundays like this, with Father Timothy Buckley in Father Timothy's roomy secondhand Peugeot – Frank did not drive – in search of moths and butterflies, or to inspect the last four walls, perhaps the last three walls, of some eighth-century Hiberno-Romanesque churchlet, or the rotting molar of some Norman castle smelling of cow dung, purple mallow, meadowsweet and the woodsmoke of the last tinkers who had camped there. After Morgan came he had begun to drive off every fine Sunday with Morgan in Morgan's little Ford Prefect. Still, *noblesse oblige*, and also if the journey promised to be a rather long one, he had about twice a year suggested to Morgan that they might invite Father Timothy to join them; and Tim had always come, observing with amusement that they indulgently allowed him to bring his own car, and that they would, after loud protestations, allow him to do all the driving, and that he also had to persuade them forcibly to allow him to pack the luggage on the seat beside him, so as to leave plenty of room – at this point they would all three laugh with the frankest irony – for their lordships' bottoms in the soft and roomy rear of the Peugeot. This luggage consisted of Frank's two butterfly nets, in case one broke, three binoculars and three cameras, one for each, two umbrellas for himself and Morgan, the bulging lunch basket for them all, two foam-rubber cushions, one for his poor old back, one for Morgan's poor young back, and a leather-backed carriage rug so that the dear boy should not feel the cold of the grass going up through him while he was eating his lunch and enjoying – as he was now enjoying – his afternoon siesta.

Retired, each one, into his own secret shell of sleep, they all three looked as dead as they would look in fifteen years' time in one of the photographs they had just taken of themselves. The day had stopped. The film of the climbing towers of clouds had stopped. The lake was silent. The few birds and the three cows they had seen on the island were dozing. Thinking had stopped. Their three egos had stopped. Folk tales say that when a man is asleep on the grass like that, a tiny lizard may creep into his mouth, devour his tongue and usurp its power. After about an hour of silence and dozing some such lizard spoke from the priest's mouth. Afterwards he said that he had been dreaming of the island's hermits, and of what he called the shortitude and latitude of life, and of how soon it stops, and that those two selfish bastards beside him were egotistical sinners, too concerned with their comfort as adolescents to assert their dignity as men. 'And I?' he thought with a start, and woke.

'In Dublin last month,' his lizard said hollowly into his hat, 'I saw a girl on a horse on a concrete street.'

'What?' Morgan asked drowsily, without stirring.

'A girl on a horse,' Tim said, removing his hat, and beholding the glorious blue sky. 'It was the most pathetic sight I ever saw.'

'Why pathetic?' Morgan asked, removing his hat and seeing the blue Pacific sweep into his ken.

'She was riding on a concrete street, dressed as if she was riding to hounds. The fantasy of it was pathetic. Miles away from green fields. But all the girls are gone mad on horses nowadays. I wish somebody would tell them that all they're doing is giving the world a beautiful example of sexual transference. They have simply transferred their natural desire for a man to a four-legged brute.'

'Balderdash,' said Morgan, and put back his hat as Frank patiently lifted his to ask the blueness what all the poor girls who haven't got horses do to inform the public of their adolescent desires.

'They have cars,' Tim said, and sat up slowly, the better to do battle. Morgan sat up abruptly.

'So,' he demanded, 'every time I drive a car I become a homosexual?'

Tim considered the matter judicially.

'Possibly,' he agreed. 'But not necessarily. There are male cars for women, and female cars for men. For women? Clubman, Escort, Rover, Consort, Jaguar, Triumph. Fill 'em up and drive them at seventy miles an hour! What fun! For men? Giulietta. Whose Romeo? Morris Minor. The word means moor – symbolical desire for a small negress. Mercedes? Actually that is Mrs Benz's name. Also means Our Lady of Mercy. Symbolical desire for a large virgin. Ford Consul? Consuela, Our Lady of Consolations. Volvo? Vulva. Volkswagen. Double V. Symbolical...'

'Well of all the filthy minds!' Morgan roared.

The doctor sat up with a sigh. His siesta was ruined. His anger was hot upon his humour and his honour.

'I do think, Father Timothy, that you, as a priest of God...'

Tim scrambled to his feet, high above him, black as a winetun against the pale sheen of the lake.

'A priest, a presbyter, an elder, a sheikh, an old man, a minister, a pastor of sheep? What does that mean? Something superior, elegant, stainless and remote from life like yourself and Master Poet here? An angel, a seraph, a saint, a mystic, a eunuch, a cherubim, a morning star? Do I look like it? Or like a man fat from eating too much, wheezy from smoking too much, sick and tired from trying to do the job he was called on to do? A priest of God is a man with a bum and a belly, and everything that hangs out of a belly or cleaves it, with the same appetites and desires, thirsts and hungers as the men and women, the boys and the girls he lives and works with. It may be very nice for you to look at us before the altar in Saint Jude's all dressed up in our golden robes, swinging a censer, and to think, "There is heavenly power, there is magic." But I have no power. I'm nothing alone. I merely pretend to a power that is an eternity beyond me. When I was in Rome, as a student, a priest in Southern Italy went mad, ran down to the bakery to turn the whole night's baking into the body of God, and from there to the wine factory to turn every flask and vat of flowing wine into the blood of the Lord. But did he? Of course not. Alone he hadn't the power to make a leaf of basil grow. But I will pretend to any boy or girl who is troubled or in misery that I have all the power in heaven to cure them, do mumbo-jumbo, wave hands, say hocus pocus, anything if it will only give them peace. And if that doesn't work I tell them the truth.'

'You are shouting, Father,' Doctor Frank said coldly.

Tim controlled himself. He sat down again. He laughed.

'Ye don't want to hear the truth. Too busy romanticizing, repressing, rationalizing, running away, when everybody knows the pair of ye think of nothing but women from morning to night! Your moths, Frank, that come out in the twilight, your easy girls, your lights o' love, fluttering against your windowpanes? Do you want me to believe that you never wish you could open the window to let one in? I saw you, Morgan, the other day in the library fawning over that unfortunate virgin Simcox, and a child could see what was in the minds of the pair of ye. And what do you think she thinks she's doing every time she goes out to the yard to wash the backside of your car with suds and water? Why don't you be a man, Morgan, and face up to it – one day you'll have to be spliced. It's the common fate of all mankind.'

'It hasn't been yours, Father,' Frank snapped.

'Because I took a vow and kept to it, logically.'

'Pfoo!' Morgan snarled at him. 'You know damned well that logic has as much to do with marriage as it has with music.'

Tim looked at him with the air of a small boy who is thinking what fun it would be to shove his Auntie Kitty down the farmyard well.

'You know,' he said slyly, 'you should ask Fräulein Keel about that the next time she is playing the Appassionata for you,' and was delighted to observe the slow blush that climbed up Morgan's face and the black frown that drew down the doctor's eyebrows. The silence of his companions hummed. He leaned back.

It was about two months ago since Frau Keel had come to L—— with her daughter Imogen and her husband Georg, an electrical engineer in charge of a new German factory at the Shannon Free Airport complex. He was about fifty and a Roman Catholic, which was presumably why he had been chosen for this Irish job. His wife was much younger; blonde, handsome, curlyheaded, well-corseted, with long-lashed eyes like a cow. Hera-eyed, Morgan said; dopey, Frank said; false lashes, Tim Buckley said. She was broad of bosom and bottom, strong-legged as a peasant and as heavy-shouldered, one of those abundant, self-indulgent, flesh-folding bodies that Rubens so loved to paint in their pink skin. Imogen was quite different; small, black-avised, black-haired, her skin like a bit of burned cork. She was a *belle laide* of such intensity, so packed and powerful with femininity that you felt that if you were to touch her with one finger she would hoop her back and spring her arms around you like a trap. Morgan had met her in the library, let her talk about music, found himself invited by her mother to hear her play, and unwisely boasted about it to Tim Buckley.

In the sullen silence he heard the lake sucking the stones of the beach. The clouds were less bright. The doctor said primly that he wanted to try his hand with his butterfly net. Morgan said gruffly that he wanted to take some more pictures before the sun went down. Together they walked away across the island. Tim reached for his breviary and began to read the office of the day. 'Let us then be like newborn children hungry for the fresh milk . . .'

The delicate India paper of his breviary whispered each time he turned a page. Presently a drop of rain splashed on his knuckles. He looked about him. The sun still touched the island but nowhere else. The lake hissed at the shore. He stood on a rock but could see no sign of his companions. Were they colloguing with the seventh century? He packed the lunch basket, rolled up the rugs, loaded the cargo, sat in the stern of the boat, opened an umbrella, lit his pipe and waited. He was sick of them. No doubt when slaves fall in love they feel more free . . .

They returned slowly and silently. Little was said as he rowed them to the mainland, and less on the way back to L—— because the rain became a cloudburst, and he was alone peering into it. On previous excursions he had always been invited to dine with them. He knew he would not be this evening: a snub that Morgan aggravated by assuring

him that they must all meet soon again 'on a more propitious occasion.'
He gave them a cheerful goodbye and drove off along the rain-dancing
asphalt. To the devil with their four-course dinner. His freedom was
more important to him. Anyway there were a dozen houses in town
where the wife would be delighted to give him a plate of bacon and
eggs.

Frank said nothing until he had poured their usual aperitif – a stout
dollop of malt.

'That,' he said as he handed the glass of whiskey to Morgan deep in
the best armchair on the side of the turf fire, 'is probably the last time
we shall meet his reverence socially.'

Morgan looked portentously over his glasses at the fire.

'A terrible feeling sometimes assails me,' he said, smacking each
sibilant, 'that Timothy John Buckley has a coarse streak in him.'

Frank took the opposite armchair.

'I would call it a grave lack of tact. Even presuming that La Keel has
not already told him that she is a patient of mine.'

'Imogen?' said Morgan, sitting straight up. 'Good God! Is there
something wrong with her?'

'Imogen? Oh, you mean the child? I was referring to the mother.'

Morgan sat back.

'Oh, and what's wrong with that old battle-axe? Are you beginning
to take patients?'

Frank frowned.

'I have done my best to avoid it. The lady, and her husband, ever
since they heard that I studied neurology in Vienna, have been very
persistent. As for what is wrong, I should not, ethically speaking as a
doctor, discuss the affairs of any patient but, in this case, I think I may
safely speak to you about the matter. Aye. Because I can trust you. And
Bee. Because there is nothing whatsoever wrong with the lady.'

'Then why did she come to consult you?'

Frank answered this one even more stiffly.

'She speaks of her cycles.'

Morgan, like an old lady crossing a muddy road, ventured between
the pools of his inborn prudishness, his poetic fastidiousness and his
natural curiosity:—

'Do you by any chance mean she has some sort of what they call
woman trouble?'

'If you mean the menopause, Madame Keel is much too young for that. She means emotional cycles. Elation-depression. Vitality-debility. Exultation-despair. The usual manic-depressive syndrome. She says that ever since she came to Ireland she has been melancholy.'

'Jaysus! Sure, aren't we all melancholy in Ireland? What I'd say that one needs is a few good balls of malt every day or a dose or two of cod liver oil. If I were you, Frank, I'd pack her off about her business.'

The doctor's body stirred restively.

'I have made several efforts to detach myself. She insists that I give her comfort.'

Morgan looked over his glasses at his friend.

'And what kind of comfort would that be?' he asked cautiously.

'That,' his friend said, a trifle smugly, 'is scarcely for me to say.'

Morgan glared into his glass. For a moment he wished Bucky was there to crash through the ROAD NARROWS sign, the CUL-DE-SAC, the FALLING ROCKS.

'It is a compliment to you,' he said soapily.

'I take small pride in it, Morgan. Especially since she tells me that she also gets great comfort from her pastor.'

Morgan rose to his feet, dark as a thundercloud, or as a Jove who had not shaved for a week.

'What pastor?' he demanded in his deepest basso.

'You have guessed it. Our companion of today. The Reverend Timothy Buckley. He also gives great comfort to Herr Keel. And to the girl. He holds sessions.'

Jehovah's thunder-rumble rolled.

'Sessions?'

'It is apparently the latest American-Dutch ecumenical idea. Group confessions.'

'The man,' Morgan boomed, 'must be mad! He is worse than mad. Who was it called him Rasputin? He was born to be hanged! Or shot! Or poisoned! That man is e-e-e-evil. Frank! You must stop this monstrous folly at once. Think of the effect on that innocent poor child.'

'I have no intention whatsoever of interfering,' Frank fluttered. 'It's a family affair. I have no least right to interfere. And I suspect she is not in the least innocent. And she is not a child. She is eighteen.'

'Frank!' Morgan roared. 'Have you NO principles?'

A mistake. It is not a nice question to be asked by anybody. Suppose

Morgan had been asked by somebody if he had any principles himself! How does any of us know what his principles are? Nobody wants to have to start outlining his principles at a word of command.

'I begin to fear,' Frank said huffily, 'that in all this you are not thinking of me, nor of Frau Keel, nor of Herr Keel, nor of my principles, nor of any principles whatever but solely of the sexual attractions of Fräulein Keel. She has hairy legs. A well-known sign of potency.'

At which moment of dead silence Dolly Lynch opened the door, put in her flushed face and in her slow, flat, obsequious Shannon voice, said, 'Dinner is i-now-eh sarvedeh, Dachtar.' Her employer glared at her. Why was she looking so flushed? The foul creature had probably been outside the door for the last three minutes listening to the rising voices. By tomorrow the thing would be all over the town.

They entered the dining room in silence. She served them in silence. When she went out they maintained silence, or said small polite things like, 'This spring lamb is very tender,' or 'Forced rhubarb?' The silences were so heavy that Morgan felt obliged to retail the entire life of Monteverdi. Immediately after the coffee, in the drawing room, he said he had better go home to his mother, and, with fulsome thanks for a splendid lunch and a marvellous dinner, he left his friend to his pipe and, if he had any, his principles.

Morgan did not drive directly to his cottage on the Ennis Road. He drove to the library, extracted from the music section a biography of Monteverdi and drove to the Keels' flat in O'Connell Square. It was Frau Keel, majestic as Brünnhilde, who opened the door, received the book as if it were a ticket of admission and invited him to come in. To his annoyance he found Buckley half-filling a settee, winking cheerfully at him, smoking a cigar, a coffee in his paw, a large brandy on a small table beside him. Herr Keel sat beside him, enjoying the same pleasures. Through the dining room door he caught a glimpse of Imogen with her back to him, clearing the dinner table, her oily black hair coiled as usual on either side of her cheeks. As she leaned over the table he saw the dimpled backs of her knees. She was not wearing stockings. The dark down on her legs suggested the untamed forests of the north.

'Aha!' Herr Keel cried, in (for so ponderous a man) his always surprising countertenor. 'It is Mister Myles. You are most welcome.

May I offer you a coffee and a good German cigar? We had just begun a most interesting session.'

Morgan beamed and bowed ingratiatingly. He almost clicked his heels in his desire to show his pleasure and to conceal the frightening thought: – 'Is this one of Bucky's sessions?' He beamed as he received the cigar and a brandy from Herr Keel, who bowed in return. He bowed as he accepted a coffee from Frau Keel who beamed in return before she went back to her own place on a small sofa of the sort that the French – so he found out next day from a History of Furniture – call a *canapé*, where she was presently joined by Imogen. Thereafter he found that whenever he glanced (shyly) at Frau Keel she was staring anxiously and intently at Buckley, and whenever he glanced (shyly) at Imogen she was looking at himself with a tiny smile of what, crestfallen, he took to be amusement until she raised her hairy eyebrows and slowly shook her midnight head, and he heard a beautiful noise like a bomb exploding inside his chest at the thought that this black sprite was either giving him sympathy or asking sympathy from him. Either would be delightful. But, then, her eyebrows suddenly plunged, she shook her head threateningly, her smile curled, anger and disapproval sullied her already dark eyes.

'As I was saying,' Father Tim was saying, magisterially waving his cigar, 'if adultery is both a positive fact and a relative term, so is marriage. After all, marriage is much more than what The Master of the Sentences called a *conjunctio viri et mulieris*. It is also a union of sympathy and interest, heart and soul. Without these marriage becomes licensed adultery.'

'I agree,' Frau Keel sighed. 'But no woman ever got a divorce for that reason.'

Buckley pursed his little mouth into a provocative smile. 'In fact people do divorce for that very reason. Only they call it mental cruelty.'

'Alas,' said Brünnhilde, 'according to our church, there is no such sin as mental cruelty and therefore there is no divorce.'

'There are papal annulments,' Herr Keel said to her coldly, 'if you are interested in such things.'

'I am very interested,' she said to him as frigidly, which was not the kind of warm domestic conversation that Morgan had read about in books.

'You were about to tell us, Father Tim,' Imogen said, 'what you consider unarguable grounds for the annulment of a marriage.'

Sickeningly Buckley beamed at the girl; fawningly she beamed back. *She!* The Hyrcanian tigress! Had this obese sensualist mesmerized the whole lot of them? But he could not, as Buckley calmly began to enumerate the impediments to true wedlock, centre his mind on what was being said, so dumbfounded was he to find that nobody but himself seemed to be forming images of the hideous realities of what he now heard. All he could do was to gulp his brandy, as any man of the world might in such circumstances, and struggle to keep his eyes from Imogen's hirsute legs. (Where had he read that Charles XII had a woman in his army whose beard was two feet long?)

'It is not,' Buckley said, 'a true marriage if it has been preceded by rape. It is not a true marriage if either or both parties are certifiable lunatics. It is not,' here he glanced at Keel, 'a genuine marriage if the father marries the daughter,' smiling at Imogen, 'or if the sister marries the brother. It is not marriage if by error either party marries the wrong person, which can happen when a number of people are being married simultaneously. If either party has previously murdered the wife or husband of the other party it is not really a very good marriage. Nor if either party persuades the other party into adultery beforehand by a promise of marriage afterwards. It is not marriage if the male party is impotent both antecedently and perpetually. Nor if a Christian marries a Jew or other heathen...'

At which point they all started talking together, Imogen declaring passionately, 'I would marry a Jew if I damn well wanted to,' and Georg Keel demanding, 'How can you prove impotency?', and Frau Keel protesting with ringed fingers, 'Kein Juden! Kein Juden!', Buckley laughingly crying out, 'I agree, I agree,' and Morgan wailing that it was all bureaucratic balderdash, all quashed suddenly into silence by the prolonged ringing of the doorbell. Keel glanced at his watch and said testily, 'Who on earth...?' Imogen, unwilling to lose a fraction of the fight, rushed to the door and led in the latecomer. It was the doctor.

Morgan had to admire his comportment. Though he must have been much taken aback to see all his problems personified before him, the old boy did not falter for a moment in his poise and manners. He formally apologized for his late call to Frau Keel, who revealed her delight in his visit by swiftly patting her hair as she passed a mirror, making him sit beside her, fluttering to Imogen to sit beside Morgan, and yielding him a brandy glass between her palms as if it were a chalice. He accepted it graciously, he did not allow it to pass over him, he bowed like a cardinal, he relaxed into the company, legs crossed, as easily as if he were the host and they his guests. Morgan observed that the cuffs of his trousers were wet. He had walked here in the rain. He must be feeling greatly upset.

'Are you a friend of this dirty old doctor?' Imogen whispered rapidly to Morgan.

'I know him slightly. I like you very much, Imogen.'

'He is a vurm!' she whispered balefully. 'You are another vurm. You both turned Father Tim from the door without a meal.'

'Neither,' said Tim, resuming control, 'is it a marriage if it is clandestine, that is, performed secretly.'

'I would marry in secret if I wanted to,' like a shot from Imogen.

'It wasn't my house,' Morgan whispered. 'I wanted him to stay.'

'What does "secret" mean?' Keel asked petulantly.

'I know you lie,' she whispered.

'It means failing to inform your parish priest.'

'That's more bureaucratic fiddlesticks!' Morgan said, and an electric shock ran up his thigh when Imogen patted it approvingly.

'So,' Tim said dryly to him, 'the Empress Josephine thought, but her failure to obey the regulation meant that the Pope was able to allow the Emperor to eject her from his bed and marry again.'

'Then,' Keel agreed, 'it is a wise precaution.'

'It's bosh!' Morgan declared. 'And cruel bosh.'

'Good man!' said Imogen, and gave him another shock, while Frau Keel turned inquiringly to her pastor who said that the rule might be useful to prevent bigamy but was really no reason for dissolving a marriage, whereat she said, 'Then it is bosh!' and her husband, outraged, proclaimed, 'In my house I will allow nobody to say I am defending bosh!'

She waved him aside, clasped her paws, beamed at Father Timothy and cried, 'And now, for adultery!'

'Alas, Madame, adultery by either party is not sufficient cause to annul a marriage.'

'So we women are trapped!'

'While you men,' charged Imogen, glaring around her, 'can freely go your adulterous ways.'

The doctor intervened mildly.

'Happily none of this concerns anybody in this room.'

'How do you know what concerns me?' she challenged, jumping to her feet, her gripped fists by her lean flanks, her prowlike nose pointing about her like a setter. 'I, Imogen Keel, now, at this moment, vant to commit adultery with somebody in this room.'

Morgan covered his face in his hands. O God! The confessions! She means me. What shall I say? That I want to kiss her knees?

'Imogen!' Keel blazed at her. 'I will not permit this. In delicacy! Not to say, in politeness!'

'Please, Georg!' his wife screamed. 'Not again!' She turned to the company. 'Always I hear this appeal to politeness and delicacy. It is an excuse. It is an evasion. It is an alibi.'

'Aha!' Imogen proclaimed, one hand throwing towards her father's throat an imaginary flag or dagger. 'But he has always been excellent at alibis.'

Keel slammed his empty brandy glass on the coffee table so hard that its stem snapped. 'How fiery she is!' Morgan thought. What a heroic way she has of rearing her head back to the left and lifting her opposite eyebrow to the right. A girl like that would fight for her man to her death – or, if he betrayed her, to his. Has she, he wondered, hair on her back? Father Tim, amused by the whole scene, was saying tactfully but teasingly, 'Imogen, there is one other injustice to women that you must hear about. It is that you will in most countries not be permitted to marry, no matter how much you protest, until you have arrived at the age of twelve and your beloved at the age of fourteen.'

She burst into laughter. They all laughed with relief.

'Finally,' he said tristfully, 'priests may not marry at all.'

'They are nevertheless doing so,' the girl commented pertly.

He looked at her, seemed to consider saying something, drank the last drop of his coffee, and did not say it. Frau Keel said it for him, compassionately.

'Only by giving up their priesthood.'

'Or more,' he agreed in a subdued voice.

'The whole caboodle,' Imogen mocked.

They talked a little about current examples of priests who had given up everything. The subject trailed away. Keel looked at the window. 'Rain,' he sighed, in so weary a voice that the doctor at once rose, and all the others with him. As the group dissolved towards the entrance hall of the apartment Morgan found himself trailing behind with Imogen.

'What have you against the doctor?' he asked her.

'He is just like my father. And I hate my father. The only good thing I say about your doctor is that he helps my mother to put up with my father.'

He must drive old Frank home – he must go on helping Frau Keel; they must talk about the best way to handle Buckley in future; they must have Georg Keel on one of their excursions; if the girl was lonely perhaps Keel would like to bring her with them. She was a superb, a wonderful, a marvellous girl, so heroic, so wild, so passionate. The very first thing they must do was to have Buckley to dinner, and maybe Buckley would bring the girl with him . . . Just then he heard Frank ask Keel if it was too late for them to have a brief word together before he left. If this meant the old fool was falling back on some ridiculous, bloody point of principle about treating Frau Keel . . . As he was making his way towards his friend to offer him a lift home Frau Keel absently shook his hand, handed him his hat, opened the door, bade him good night and the door closed on her voice suggesting to Imogen to drive the good Father to his presbytery in her little car. A minute later he was in the street cursing.

There was not a soul in sight. The rain hung like vests around the lamplights of O'Connell Street. When his car refused to start his rage boiled against that stupid cow Marianne Simcox who must have let water (or something) get into the petrol. After many fruitless zizzings from the starter he saw Imogen's little blue car with the priest aboard shoot past in a wake of spray. More zizzings, more pulling at the choke, a long rest to deflood the carburettor and the engine roared into life, just as Keel's Mercedes, with the doc aboard, vanished through the rain towards the bridge and the Dublin road. He circled wildly, followed their taillights, halted twenty yards behind them outside Frank's house, dowsed his lights, saw him get out and Keel drive away. He ran forward to where Frank was unlocking his iron gate, and clutched his arm beseechingly.

'Frank! I simply must talk to you about Buckley. What is he doing to all those people? What is he doing to that Imogen girl? For God's sake what's going on in that Keel family? I won't sleep a wink unless you tell me all you know about them.'

The doctor marvelled at him for a moment and then returned to his unlocking.

'I do not feel disposed,' he said in his haughtiest voice, holding the gate six inches ajar for the length of his reply, 'to discuss such matters at twelve o'clock at night, on an open road, under a downpour of rain, and all the less so since, so far as I can see, nothing is, as you so peculiarly put it, "going on" that is of any interest to me. Everything seems perfectly normal and in order in the Keel family, except that Herr Keel is a total idiot who seems unable to control his wife, that she seems to me to have developed a most unseemly sexual interest in Father Timothy Buckley, that she is intent on divorcing her husband, that their daughter, who is both impertinent and feckless, is a nymphomaniac, who has quite obviously decided to seduce you, and that I am very glad to say that I need never again lay eyes on them for the rest of my natural life. And, now, sir, goodnight to you.'

With which he entered his drive, banged the metalled gate behind him, and his wet footsteps died into a voice from his front door wailing, 'Oh, dachtar, dachtar! Wait for me! I have the umberella here for you. You'll be dhrowneded all together with that aaahful rain...'

Morgan spat on the gate, turned and raced for his car, which resolutely refused to start. He implored it until its exhausted starter died into the silence of a final click. He got out, kicked its door soundly, and then overwhelmed by all the revelations he had just heard, especially the one about Imogen and himself, he walked home through the empty streets of L——, singing love songs from the *Barber* and *Don Giovanni* at the top of his voice to the summer rain.

One of the more pleasantly disconcerting things about wilful man is that his most table-thumping decisions rarely conclude the matter in hand. There is always time for a further option. Every score is no better than half-time. *Viz:*—

1. That July our poor, dear friend Tim Buckley left us for a chin-pimple of a village called Four Noughts (the vulgarization of a Gaelic word meaning Stark Naked) on the backside of Slievenamuck. We loyally cursed His Lordship the bishop, while feeling that he had had no option. For weeks the dogs in the streets had been barking, 'Im-o-gen Keel.' At the farewell party Tim assured us that the bish had neither hand, act nor part in it. He had himself asked His Lordship for a transfer. He asked us to pray for him. He said sadly that he believed

he was gone beyond it. The die was cast, the Rubicon crossed, it was the Ides of March, and so forth and so on.

One effect of this event (Dolly Lynch reporting, after her usual survey of her master's wastepaper basket) was that Mister Myles had been invited to dinner with the dachtar at his earliest convenience.

2. That August we heard that Frau Keel was claiming a separation from her husband *a mensa et a thoro;* that she was also applying for a papal annulment of her marriage on the ground of his impotence, which meant that she was ready to swear that Imogen was not his child. Herr Keel, we gathered, had knocked her down, broken one of her ribs with a kick and left for Stuttgart swearing that he would foil her if it cost him his last deutschmark.

Mister Myles was by now dining every week with the doctor, who was also (Dolly Lynch's knuckle suspended outside the dining room door) seeing Frau Keel regularly, who (Dolly Lynch's hand on the doorknob) was also in constant consultation, through Imogen, with Father Tim Buckley in his exile on Slievenamuck.

3. That September Tim Buckley disappeared from Four Noughts, Imogen Keel disappeared from the Keel flat, and both were reported to have been seen at Shannon Airport boarding a plane for Stockholm. This blow brought us down. Tim's way of living life had been to tell us how to live it. Now that he was starting to live it himself he was no better than any of us. He was the only one of us who had both faced and been free of the world of men, of women, of children, of the flesh. Now we knew that it cannot be done. You must not put your toe into the sea if you do not want to swim in it.

Myles was by now dining with Frank Breen three times a week, friendship glued by gossip.

4. October. Dreadful news from Stuttgart. Herr Keel had accidentally killed himself while cleaning a shotgun. When the news came Morgan was having tea with Frau Keel. She collapsed, calling for the doctor. Morgan drove at once to Frank's house and brought him back to her. For the rest of that month Myles was dining every night with the doctor.

5. By November Dolly Lynch reported that Mister Myles had stopped dining with the doctor, but Mrs Keel, she spat, was coming as often as 'tree taimes every bluddy wee-uk.' When we heard this we looked at one another. Our eyes said, 'Could it be possible?' We asked Morgan. He was in no doubt about it.

'Buckley was right!' he stormed. 'The man is a sexual maniac! A libertine! A corrupter of women! A traitor and a liar. As that foolish woman will discover before the year is out.'

It was a spring wedding, and the reception was one of the gayest, most crowded, most lavish the town had ever seen. The metal sheeting was gone from the gate, the cypresses cut down, the warning signs inside the gate removed, the brass plate removed, the conservatory packed with flowers, the only drink served was champagne. The doctor became Frank to every Tom and Harry. For the first time we found out that his wife's name was Victorine. With his hair tinted he looked ten years younger. Long before the reception ended he was going around whispering to everybody, as a dead secret, that Victorine was expecting.

6. Morgan, naturally, did not attend the wedding. He took off for the day with Marianne Simcox, and they have since been taking off every fine Sunday in her red Mustang, together with Morgan's mother, in search of faceless churchlets in fallow fields where the only sound is the munching of cattle. His mother prepares the lunch. Marianne reads out his own poems to him. They both feed him like a child with titbits from their fingers. But who knows the outcome of any mortal thing? Buckley – there is no denying it – had a point when he insisted that man's most ingenious invention is man, that to create others we must first imagine ourselves, and that to keep us from wandering, or wondering, in some other direction where a greater truth may lie, we set up all sorts of roadblocks and traffic signals. Morgan has told his Marianne that he has always admired the virginal type. It is enough to put any girl off her stroke. A wink of a brass plate in a country road set him off on one tack. A wink from her might set him off on another. What should she do? Obey his traffic signs, or acknowledge the truth – that he is a born liar – and start showing him a glimpse of thigh?

Heaven help the women of the world, always wondering what the blazes their men's next graven image will be.

How to Write a Short Story

One wet January night, some six months after they had met, young Morgan Myles, our country librarian, was seated in the doctor's pet armchair, on one side of the doctor's fire, digesting the pleasant memory of a lavish dinner, while leafing the pages of a heavy photographic album and savouring a warm brandy. From across the hearth the doctor was looking admiringly at his long, ballooning Gaelic head when, suddenly, Morgan let out a cry of delight.

'Good Lord, Frank! There's a beautiful boy! One of Raphael's little angels.' He held up the open book for Frank to see. 'Who was he?'

The doctor looked across at it and smiled.

'Me. Aged twelve. At school in Mount Saint Bernard.'

'That's in England. I didn't know you went to school in England.'

'Alas!'

Morgan glanced down at twelve, and up at sixty.

'It's not possible, Frank!'

The doctor raised one palm six inches from the arm of his chair and let it fall again.

'It so happened that I was a ridiculously beautiful child.'

'Your mother must have been gone about you. And,' with a smile, 'the girls too.'

'I had no interest in girls. Nor in boys either, though by your smile you seem to say so. But there was one boy who took a considerable interest in me.'

Morgan at once lifted his nose like a pointer. At this period of his life he had rested from writing poetry and was trying to write short stories. For weeks he had read nothing but Maupassant. He was going to out-Maupassant Maupassant. He was going to write stories that would make poor old Maupassant turn as green as the grass on his grave.

'Tell me about it,' he ordered. 'Tell me every single detail.'

'There is nothing to it. Or at any rate, as I now know, nothing abnormal. But, at that age!' – pointing with his pipestem. 'I was as innocent as . . . Well, as innocent as a child of twelve! Funny that you should say that about Raphael's angels. At my preparatory school here – it was a French order – Sister Angélique used to call me her *petit ange*, because, she said, I had *"une tête d'ange et une voix d'ange."* She used to make me sing solo for them at Benediction, dressed in a red soutane, a white lacy surplice and a purple bow tie.

'After that heavenly place Mount Saint Bernard was ghastly. Mobs of howling boys. Having to play games; rain, hail or snow. I was a funk at games. When I'd see a fellow charging me at rugger I'd at once pass the ball or kick for touch. I remember the coach cursing me. "Breen, you're a bloody little coward, there are boys half your weight on this field who wouldn't do a thing like that." And the constant discipline. The constant priestly distrust. Watching us like jail warders.'

'Can you give me an example of that?' Morgan begged. 'Mind you, you could have had that, too, in Ireland. Think of Clongowes. It turns up in Joyce. And he admired the Jesuits!'

'Yes, I can give you an example. It will show you how innocent I was. A month after I entered Mount Saint Bernard I was so miserable that I decided to write to my mother to take me away. I knew that every letter had to pass under the eyes of the Prefect of Discipline, so I wrote instead to Sister Angélique asking her to pass on the word to my mother. The next day old Father George Lee – he's long since dead – summoned me to his study. "Breen!" he said darkly, holding up my unfortunate letter, "you have tried to do a very underhand thing, something for which I could punish you severely. Why did you write this letter *in French?*"' The doctor sighed. 'I was a very truthful little boy. My mother had brought me up to be truthful simply by never punishing me for anything I honestly owned up to. I said, "I wrote it in French, sir, because I hoped you wouldn't be able to understand it." He turned his face away from me but I could tell from his shoulders that he was laughing. He did not cane me, he just tore up the letter, told me never to try to deceive him again, and sent me packing with my tail between my legs.'

'The old bastard!' Morgan said sympathetically, thinking of the lonely little boy.

'No, no! He was a nice old man. And a good classical scholar, I later discovered. But that day as I walked down the long corridor, with all its photographs of old boys who had made good, I felt the chill of the prison walls!'

'But this other boy?' Morgan insinuated. 'Didn't his friendship help at all?'

The doctor rose and stood with his back to the fire staring fixedly in front of him.

(He rises, Morgan thought, his noble eyes shadowed. No! God damn it, no! Not noble. Shadowed? Literary word. Pensive? Blast it, that's worse. "Pensive eve!" Romantic fudge. His eyes are dark as a rabbit's droppings. That's got it! In his soul . . . Oh, Jase!)

'Since I was so lonely I suppose he *must* have helped. But he was away beyond me. Miles above me. He was a senior. He was the captain of the school.'

'His name,' Morgan suggested, 'was, perhaps, Cyril?'

'We called him Bruiser. I would rather not tell you his real name.'

'Because he is still alive,' Morgan explained, 'and remembers you vividly to this day.'

'He was killed at the age of twenty.'

'In the war! In the heat of battle.'

'By a truck in Oxford. Two years after he went up there from Mount Saint Bernard. I wish I knew what happened to him in those two years. I can only hope that before he died he found a girl.'

'A girl? I don't follow. Oh yes! Of course, yes, I take your point.'

(He remembers with tenderness? No. With loving kindness! No! With benevolence? Dammit, no! With his wonted chivalry to women? But he remembered irritably that the old man sitting opposite to him was a bachelor. And a virgin?)

'What happened between the pair of ye? "Brothers and companions in tribulation on the isle that is called Patmos"?'

The doctor snorted.

'Brothers? I have told you I was twelve. Bruiser was eighteen. The captain of the school. Captain of the rugby team. Captain of the tennis team. First in every exam. Tops. Almost a man. I looked up to him as a shining hero. I never understood what he saw in me. I have often thought since that he may have been amused by my innocence. Like the day he said to me, "I suppose, Rosy," that was my nickname, I had such rosy cheeks, "suppose you think you are the best-looking fellow in the school?" I said, "No, I don't, Bruiser. I think there's one fellow better-looking than me, Jimmy Simcox."'

'Which he, of course, loyally refused to believe!'

The old doctor laughed heartily.

'He laughed heartily.'

'A queer sense of humour!'

'I must confess I did not at the time see the joke. Another day he said, "Would you like, Rosy, to sleep with me?"'

Morgan's eyes opened wide. Now they were getting down to it.

'I said, "Oh, Bruiser, I don't think you would like that at all. I'm an awful chatterbox in bed. Whenever I sleep with my Uncle Tom he's always saying to me, 'Will you for God's sake, stop your bloody gabble and let me sleep.'" He laughed for five minutes at that.'

'I don't see much to laugh at. He should have sighed. I will make him sigh. Your way makes him sound a queer hawk. And nothing else happened between ye but this sort of innocent gabble? Or are you keeping something back? Hang it, Frank, there's no story at all in this!'

'Oh, he used sometimes to take me on his lap. Stroke my bare knee. Ruffle my hair. Kiss me.'

'How did you like that?'

'I made nothing of it. I was used to being kissed by my elders – my mother, my bachelor uncles, Sister Angélique, heaps of people.' The doctor laughed. 'I laugh at it now. But his first kiss! A few days before, a fellow named Calvert said to me, "Hello, pretty boy, would you give me a smuck?" I didn't know what a smuck was. I said, "I'm sorry, Calvert, but I haven't got one." The story must have gone around the whole school. The next time I was alone with Bruiser he taunted me. I can hear his angry, toploftical English voice. "You are an innocent mug, Rosy! A smuck is a kiss. Would you let *me* kiss you?" I said, "Why not?" He put his arm around my neck in a vice and squashed his mouth to my mouth, hard, sticky. I thought I'd choke. "O Lord," I thought, "this is what he gets from playing rugger. This is a rugger kiss." And, I was thinking, "His poor mother! Having to put up with this from him every morning and every night." When he let me go, he said, "Did you like that?" Not wanting to hurt his feelings I said, imitating his English voice, "It was all right, Bruiser! A bit like ruggah, isn't it?" He laughed again and said, "All right? Well, never mind. I shan't rush you."'

Morgan waved impatiently.

'Look here, Frank! I want to get the background to all this. The telling detail, you know. "The little actual facts" as Stendhal called them. You said the priests watched you all like hawks. The constant discipline, you said. The constant priestly distrust. How did ye ever manage to meet alone?'

'It was very simple. He was the captain of the school. The apple of their eye. He could fool them. He knew the ropes. After all, he had been there for five years. I remember old Father Lee saying to me once, "You are a very lucky boy, Breen, it's not every junior that the captain of the school would take an interest in. You ought to feel very proud of his friendship." We used to have a secret sign about our meetings. Every Wednesday morning when he would be walking out of chapel, leading the procession, if that day was all right for us he used to put his right hand in his pocket. If for any reason it was not all right he would put his left hand in his pocket. I was always on the aisle of the very last row. Less than the dust. Watching for the sign like a hawk. We had a double check. I'd then find a note in my overcoat in the cloakroom. All it ever said was, "The same place." He was very careful. He only took calculated risks. If he had lived he would have made a marvellous politician, soldier or diplomat.'

'And where would ye meet? I know! By the river. Or in the woods? "Enter these enchanted woods ye who dare!"'

'No river. No woods. There was a sort of dirty old trunk room upstairs, under the roof, never used. A rather dark place with only one dormer window. It had double doors. He used to lock the outside one. There was a big cupboard there – for cricket bats or something. "If anyone comes," he told me, "you will have time to pop in there." He had it all worked out. Cautious man! I had to be even more cautious, stealing up there alone. One thing that made it easier for us was that I was so much of a junior and he was so very much of a senior, because, you see, those innocent guardians of ours had the idea that the real danger lay between the seniors and the middles, or the middles and the juniors, but never between the seniors and the juniors. They kept the seniors and the middles separated by iron bars and stone walls. Any doctor could have told them that in cold climates like ours the really dangerous years are not from fifteen up but from eighteen to anything, up or down. It simply never occurred to them that any senior could possibly be interested in any way in a junior. I, of course, had no idea of what he was up to. I had not even reached the age of puberty. In fact I honestly don't believe he quite knew himself what he was up to.'

'But, dammit, you must have had some idea! The secrecy, the kissing, alone, up there in that dim, dusty box room, not a sound but the wind in the slates.'

'Straight from the nuns? *Un petit ange?* I thought it was all just pally fun.'

Morgan clapped his hands.

'I've got it! An idyll! Looking out dreamily over the fields from that dusty dormer window? That's it, that's the ticket. Did you ever read that wonderful story by Maupassant – it's called *An Idyll* – about two young peasants meeting in a train, a poor, hungry young fellow who has just left home, and a girl with her first baby. He looked so famished that she took pity on him like a mother, opened her blouse and gave him her breast. When he finished he said, "That was my first meal in three days." Frank! You are telling me the most beautiful story I ever heard in my whole life.'

'You think so?' the doctor said morosely. 'I think he was going through hell all that year. At eighteen? On the threshold of manhood? In love with a child of twelve? That is, if you will allow that a youth of eighteen may suffer as much from love as a man twenty years older. To me the astonishing thing is that he did so well all that year at his studies and at sports. Killing the pain of it, I suppose? Or trying to? But the in between? What went on in the poor devil in between?'

Morgan sank back dejectedly.

'I'm afraid this view of the course doesn't appeal to me at all. All I can see is the idyll idea. After all, I mean, nothing happened!'

Chafing, he watched his friend return to his armchair, take another pipe from the rack, fill it slowly and ceremoniously from a black tobacco jar and light it with care. Peering through the nascent smoke, Morgan leaned slowly forward.

'Or did something happen?'

'Yes,' the doctor resumed quietly. 'Every year, at the end of the last term, the departing captain was given a farewell dinner. I felt sad that morning because we had not met for a whole week. And now, in a couple of days we would be scattered and I would never see him again.'

'Ha, ha! You see, you too were in love!'

'Of course I was, I was hooked,' the doctor said with more than a flicker of impatience. 'However... That Wednesday as he passed me in the chapel aisle he put his right hand in his pocket. I belted off at once to my coat hanging in the cloakroom and found his note. It said,

"At five behind the senior tennis court." I used always chew up his *billet doux* immediately I read it. He had ordered me to. When I read this one my mouth went so dry with fear that I could hardly swallow it. He had put me in an awful fix. To meet alone in the box room was risky enough, but for anybody to climb over the wall into the seniors' grounds was unheard of. If I was caught I would certainly be flogged. I might very well be expelled. And what would my mother and father think of me then? On top of all I was in duty bound to be with all the other juniors at prep at five o'clock, and to be absent from studies without permission was another crime of the first order. After lunch I went to the Prefect of Studies and asked him to excuse me from prep because I had an awful headache. He wasn't taken in one bit. He just ordered me to be at my place in prep as usual. The law! Orders! Tyranny! There was only one thing for it, to dodge prep, knowing well that whatever else happened later I would pay dearly for it.'

'And what about him? He knew all this. And he knew that if *he* was caught they couldn't do anything to him. The captain of the school? Leaving in a few days? It was very unmanly of him to put you to such a risk. His character begins to emerge, and not very pleasantly. Go on!'

The doctor did not need the encouragement. He looked like a small boy sucking a man's pipe.

'I waited until the whole school was at study and then I crept out into the empty grounds. At that hour the school, the grounds, everywhere, was as silent as the grave. Games over. The priests at their afternoon tea. Their charges safely under control. I don't know how I managed to get over that high wall, but when I fell scrambling down on the other side, there he was. "You're bloody late," he said crossly. "How did you get out of prep? What excuse did you give?" When I told him he flew into a rage. "You little fool!" he growled. "You've balloxed it all up. They'll know you dodged. They'll give you at least ten on the backside for this." He was carrying a cane. Seniors at Saint Bernard's did carry walking sticks. I'd risked so much for him, and now he was so angry with me that I burst into tears. He put his arms around me – I thought, to comfort me – but after that all I remember from that side of the wall was him pulling down my short pants, holding me tight, I felt something hard, like his cane, and the next thing I knew I was wet. I thought I was bleeding. I thought he was gone mad. When I smelled whiskey I thought, "He is trying to kill me." "Now run," he ordered me, "and get back to prep as fast as you can."'

Morgan covered his eyes with his hand.

'He shoved me up to the top of the wall. As I peered around I heard his footsteps running away. I fell down into the shrubs on the other side and I immediately began to vomit and vomit. There was a path beside the shrubs. As I lay there puking I saw a black-soutaned priest approaching slowly along the path. He was an old, old priest named Constable. I did not stir. Now, I felt, I'm for it. This is the end. I am certain he saw me but he passed by as if he had not seen me. I got back to the study hall, walked up to the Prefect's desk and told him I was late because I had been sick. I must have looked it because he at once sent me to the matron in the infirmary. She took my temperature and put me to bed. It was summer. I was the only inmate of the ward. One of those evenings of prolonged daylight.'

'You poor little bugger!' Morgan groaned in sympathy.

'A detail comes back to me. It was the privilege of seniors attending the captain's dinner to send down gifts to the juniors' table – sweets, fruit, a cake, for a younger brother or some special protégé. Bruiser ordered a whole white blancmange with a rosy cherry on top of it to be sent to me. He did not know I was not in the dining hall so the blacmange was brought up to me in the infirmary. I vomited again when I saw it. The matron, with my more than ready permission, took some of it for herself and sent the rest back to the juniors' table, "with Master Breen's compliments." I am sure it was gobbled greedily. In the morning the doctor saw me and had me sent home to Ireland immediately.'

'Passing the buck,' said Morgan sourly, and they both looked at a coal that tinkled from the fire into the fender.

The doctor peered quizzically at the hissing coal.

'Well?' he slurred around his pipestem. 'There is your lovely idyll.'

Morgan did not lift his eyes from the fire. Under a downdraft from the chimney a few specks of grey ashes moved clockwise on the worn hearth. He heard a car hissing past the house on the wet macadam. His eyebrows had gone up over his spectacles in two Gothic arches.

'I am afraid,' he said at last, 'it is no go. Not even a Maupassant could have made a story out of it. And Chekhov wouldn't have wanted to try. Unless the two boys lived on, and on, and met years afterwards in Moscow or Yalta or somewhere, each with a wife and a squad of kids, and talked of everything except their schooldays. You are sure you never did hear of him, or from him, again?'

'Never! Apart from the letter he sent with the blancmange and the cherry.'

Morgan at once leaped alive.

'A letter? Now we are on to something! What did he say to you in it? Recite every word of it to me! Every syllable. I'm sure you have not forgotten one word of it. No!' he cried excitedly. 'You have kept it. Hidden away somewhere all these years. Friendship surviving everything. Fond memories of...'

The doctor sniffed.

'I tore it into bits unread and flushed it down the W.C.'

'Oh, God blast you, Frank!' Morgan roared. 'That was the climax of the whole thing. The last testament. The final revelation. The summing up. The *document humain*. And you "just tore it up!" Let's reconstruct it. "Dearest Rosy, As long as I live I will never forget your innocence, your sweetness, your..."'

'My dear boy!' the doctor protested mildly. 'I am sure he wrote nothing of the sort. He was much too cautious, and even the captain was not immune from censorship. Besides, sitting in public glory at the head of the table? It was probably a place-card with something on the lines of, "All my sympathy, sorry, better luck next term." A few words, discreet, that I could translate any way I liked.'

Morgan raised two despairing arms.

'If that was all the damned fellow could say to you after that appalling experience, he was a character of no human significance whatever, a shallow creature, a mere agent, a catalyst, a cad. The story becomes your story.'

'I must admit I have always looked on it in that way. After all it did happen to me... Especially in view of the sequel.'

'Sequel? What sequel? I can't have sequels. In a story you always have to observe unity of time, place and action. Everything happening at the one time, in the same place, between the same people. *The Necklace. Boule de Suif. The Maison Tellier.* The examples are endless. What was this bloody sequel?'

The doctor puffed thoughtfully.

'In fact there were two sequels. Even three sequels. And all of them equally important.'

'In what way were they important?'

'It was rather important to me that after I was sent home I was in the hospital for four months. I could not sleep. I had constant nightmares, always the same one – me running through a wood and him running after me with his cane. I could not keep down my food. Sweating hot. Shivering cold. The vomiting was recurrent. I lost weight. My mother was beside herself with worry. She brought doctor after doctor to me, and only one of them spotted it, an old, blind man from Dublin named Whiteside. He said, "That boy has had some kind of shock," and in private he asked me if some boy, or man, had interfered with me. Of course, I denied it hotly.'

'I wish I was a doctor,' Morgan grumbled. 'So many writers were doctors. Chekhov. William Carlos Williams. Somerset Maugham. A. J. Cronin.'

The doctor ignored the interruption.

'The second sequel was that when I at last went back to Mount Saint Bernard my whole nature changed. Before that I had been dreamy and idle. During my last four years at school I became their top student. I suppose psychologists would say nowadays that I compensated by becoming extroverted. I became a crack cricket player. In my final year I was the college champion at billiards. I never became much good at rugger but I no longer minded playing it and I wasn't all that bad. If I'd been really tops at it, or at boxing, or swimming I might very well have ended up as captain of the school. Like him.'

He paused for so long that Morgan became alerted again.

'And the third sequel?' he prompted.

'I really don't know why I am telling you all this. I have never told a soul about it before. Even still I find it embarrassing to think about, let alone to talk about. When I left Mount Saint Bernard and had taken my final at the College of Surgeons I went on to Austria to continue my medical studies. In Vienna I fell in with a young woman. The typical blonde fräulein, handsome, full of life, outgoing, wonderful physique, what you might call an outdoor girl, free as the wind, frank as the daylight. She taught me skiing. We used to go mountain climbing together. I don't believe she knew the meaning of the word fear. She was great fun and the best of company. Her name was Brigitte. At twenty-six she was already a woman of the world. I was twenty-four, and as innocent of women as . . . as . . .'

To put him at his ease Morgan conceded his own embarrassing confession.

'As I am, at twenty-four.'

'You might think that what I am going to mention could not happen to a doctor, however young, but on our first night in bed, immediately she touched my body I vomited. I pretended to her that I had eaten something that upset me. You can imagine how nervous I felt all through the next day wondering what was going to happen that night. Exactly the same thing happened that night. I was left with no option. I told her the whole miserable story of myself and Bruiser twelve years before. As I started to tell her I had no idea how she was going to take it. Would she leave me in disgust? Be coldly sympathetic? Make a mock of me? Instead, she became wild with what I can only call gleeful curiosity. "Tell me more, *mein Schätzerl*,' she begged. "Tell me everything! What exactly did he do to you? I want to know it all. This is *wunderbar*. Tell me! Oh do tell me!' I did tell her, and on the spot everything became perfect between us. We made love like Trojans. That girl saved my sanity.'

In a silence Morgan gazed at him. Then coldly:—

'Well, of course, this is another story altogether. I mean I don't see how I can possibly blend these two themes together. I mean no writer worth his salt can say things like, "Twelve long years passed over his head. Now read on." I'd have to leave her out of it. She is obviously irrelevant to the main theme. Whatever the hell the main theme is.' Checked by an ironical glance he poured the balm. 'Poor Frank! I foresee it all. You adored her. You wanted madly to marry her. Her parents objected. You were star-crossed lovers. You had to part.'

'I never thought of marrying the bitch. She had the devil's temper. We had terrible rows. Once we threw plates at one another. We would have parted anyway. She was a lovely girl but quite impossible. Anyway, towards the end of that year my father fell seriously ill. Then my mother fell ill. Chamberlain was in Munich that year. Everybody knew the war was coming. I came back to Ireland that autumn. For keeps.

'But you tried again and again to find out what happened to her. And failed. She was swallowed up in the fire and smoke of war. I don't care what you say, Frank, you *must* have been heartbroken.'

The doctor lifted a disinterested shoulder.

'A student's love affair? Of thirty and more years ago?'

No! He had never enquired. Anyway if she was alive now what would she be but a fat, blowsy old baggage of sixty-three? Morgan, though shocked, guffawed dutifully. There was the real Maupassant touch. In his next story a touch like that! The clock on the mantelpiece whirred and began to tinkle the hour. Morgan opened the album for a last look at the beautiful child. Dejectedly he slammed it shut, and rose.

'There is too much in it,' he declared. 'Too many strands. Your innocence. His ignorance. Her worldliness. Your forgetting her. Remembering him. Confusion and bewilderment. The ache of loss? Loss? *Lost Innocence?* Would that be a theme? But nothing rounds itself off. You are absolutely certain you never heard of him again after that day behind the tennis courts?'

They were both standing now. The rain brightly spotted the midnight window.

'In my first year in Surgeons, about three years after Bruiser was killed, I lunched one day with his mother and my mother at the Shelbourne Hotel in Dublin. By chance they had been educated at the same convent in England. They talked about him. My mother said, "Frank here knew him in Mount Saint Bernard." His mother smiled condescendingly at me. "No, Frank. You were too young to have met him." "Well," I said, "I did actually speak to him a couple of times, and he was always very kind to me." She said sadly, "He was kind to everybody. Even to perfect strangers."'

Morgan thrust out an arm and a wildly wagging finger.

'Now, *there* is a possible shape! Strangers to begin. Strangers to end! What a title! *Perfect Strangers.*' He blew out a long, impatient breath and shook his head. 'But that is a fourth sequel! I'll think about it,' as if he were bestowing a great favour. 'But it isn't a story as it stands. I would have to fake it up a lot. Leave out things. Simplify. Mind you, I could still see it as an idyll. Or I could if only you hadn't torn up his last, farewell letter, which I still don't believe at all said what you said it said. If only we had that letter I bet you any money we could haul in the line and land our fish.'

The doctor knocked out the dottle of his pipe against the fireguard, and throating a yawn looked at the fading fire.

'I am afraid I have been boring you with my reminiscences.'

'Not at all, Frank! By no means! I was most interested in your story. And I do honestly mean what I said. I really will think about it. I promise. Who was it,' he asked in the hall as he shuffled into his overcoat and his muffler and moved out to the wet porch, the tail of his raincoat rattling in the wind, 'said that the two barbs of childhood are its innocence and its ignorance?' He failed to remember. He threw up his hand. 'Ach, to hell with it for a story! It's all too bloody convoluted for me. And to hell with Maupassant, too! That vulgarian oversimplified everything. And he's full of melodrama. A besotted Romantic at heart! Like all the bloody French.'

The doctor peeped out at him through three inches of door. Morgan, standing with his back to the arrowy night, suddenly lit up as if a spotlight had shone on his face.

'I know what I'll do with it!' he cried. 'I'll turn it into a poem about a seashell!'

'About a seashell!'

'Don't you remember?' In his splendid voice Morgan chanted above the rain and wind: – "*A curious child holding to his ear/ The convolutions of a smoothlipped seashell/ To which, in silence hushed . . .*" How the hell does it go? " *. . . his very soul listened to the murmurings of his native sea.*" It's as clear as daylight, man! You! Me! Everyone! Always wanting to launch a boat in search of some far-off golden sands. And something or somebody always holding us back. "The Curious Child". *There's* a title!'

'Ah, well!' the doctor said, peering at him blankly. 'There it is! As your friend Maupassant might have said, "*C'est la vie!*"'

'*La vie!*' Morgan roared, now on the gravel beyond the porch, indifferent to the rain pelting on his bare head. 'That trollop? She's the one who always bitches up everything. No, Frank! For me there is only one fountain of truth, one beauty, one perfection. Art, Frank! Art! and bugger *la vie!*'

At the untimely verb the doctor's drooping eyelids shot wide open.

'It is a view,' he said courteously and let his hand be shaken fervently a dozen times.

'I can never repay you, Frank. A splendid dinner. A wonderful story. Marvellous inspiration. I must fly. I'll be writing it all night!' – and vanished head down through the lamplit rain, one arm uplifted triumphantly behind him.

The doctor slowly closed his door, carefully locked it, bolted it, tested it, and prudently put its chain in place. He returned to his sitting room, picked up the cinder that had fallen into the hearth and tossed it back into the remains of his fire, then stood, hand on mantelpiece, looking down at it. What a marvellous young fellow! He would be tumbling and tossing all night over that story. Then he would be around in the morning apologizing, and sympathizing, saying, 'Of course, Frank, I do realize that it was a terribly sad experience for both of you.'

Gazing at the ashes his whole being filled with memory after memory like that empty vase in his garden being slowly filled by drops of rain.

Liberty

Three men are seated on a low grassy wall opposite the high, white, wide, double, wooden, open gates and porter's lodge of a mental institution a mile from the modest town of B—— in the province of D——. Once it was frankly called The Madhouse, later more delicately The Asylum, still later, more accurately, The Mental Hospital, finally, less candidly, Saint Senan's Home. Two of the three men are fat and wear peaked-cap uniforms. The third, thin and tall, wears another kind of uniform, the usual, grey, hirsute, tweed suit, hairy grey cap, woollen shirt and the boots without laces worn by all housebound patients. A few, so-called 'good' patients, who are encouraged to walk freely about the neighbouring town and countryside, dress like you and me. This man is privileged to sit just outside the gates of the Home.

The three men are looking at the ground under their feet, considering whether, without spoiling this favoured spot, it would be feasible to have some gravel spread there as an insurance against the fog, damps and miasmas rising under their boots when the ground tends to become soft and muddy. The patient, answering to the name Mister Cornfield, has just suggested that the low wall would be a more comfortable seat if paved with flagstones. This suggestion meets with a majority disapproval.

'Cold flags,' says the fatter of the attendants, slowly and paternally circling his belly with his open palm, 'could give you piles.'

Mr Cornfield argues quietly that damp grass and damp earth are 'just as conducive to haemorrhoids.'

At this the two attendants begin to discuss the meaning of the words *piles* and *haemorrhoids*. Mr Cornfield, for whose knowledgeability and cleverality they entertain a very proper respect (he was once a journalist) informs them that the word *piles* comes from Old English and etymologizes from the same source as the word *pellets*, or as the Spanish form of tennis known as pelota. 'By God!' says the fatter attendant whose paw is still comfortably navigating his belly. 'You could get tennis balls from piles all right!' Soon after this an obese woman from the lodge inside the gates appears on her doorstep with her right index finger placed horizontally on her left index finger to symbolize Tea. The attendants at once abandon their patient who hangs his hands, clasped, between his thighs and contemplates the earth they have been discussing until a refined Saxon female voice says, 'Good awfternoon, Mister Cornfield.'

He rises and bows.

'Good afternoon, Miss Huggard.'

The lady and the lunatic sit side by side. Some three miles farther on, she teaches in a tiny rural Protestant school a few remnant children of the Reformation. He sees her almost every day, in fine weather, at this hour, appearing underneath the tunnel of trees that mark the penultimate stage of her daily three-mile trudge out to the school and back to the old family home of the Huggards, a tall weather-slated house that has stood in its own grounds outside the town for four generations, and of which she is now the only occupant. She stretches out her feet and surveys her brogues. He knows what she is about to say: she says it every time.

'Those skates won't lawst me another month. Every yeah I weah out three paihs of boots going east and west. So you are back?' she adds in astonishment and admiration. 'I missed you, you know. Back from London!' she annotates, as if he were Marco Polo. 'It was naughty of you, I gathah, to have run away?'

'The caged bird always flies away,' he laughs.

'And how is good old London?' she asks as breezily as a games mistress – if games mistresses ever reach fifty.

'Not much different really since I saw it last. Which was eleven years ago. Too many people. More coloureds. Noisier. When did you see London last, Miss Huggard?'

'I was there only once, Mister Cornfield. When I was fifteen. Just before the war. Daddy met me at Victoria Station, and took me by Underground down to the docks. The next place I set foot on was the Barbados. As a rule, women, it appears, are not very popular aboard ships, but I had great fun. But of course I was not a woman. I was just Captain Huggard's little girl.'

The word 'Barbados' had visibly excited him.

'Are they wonderful, the Barbados?'

'Rather Britishish. Of course in a long, long ago way. A bit ungainly. I suppose they are all changed now.'

She grimaced and spread her hands in a long, long ago way. Rather ungainly, with her sand-grey hair, her humble spinster's eyes, her stooped back. He wished she did not have to feel that the one adventurous image of her life had altered.

'My father was drowned in 1943. I had just got my teacher's diploma. It was very fortunate. I was free to look after Mummy.'

The walls had closed early on her. She smiled, looked towards the distant outline of her home.

'There was a First World War song called "The Last Long Mile." I've got to face it. Tell me! Does your recent escapade mean that now that you have shown that you can travel you may at last be allowed to visit the town? Walk the roads? You might even visit my school? Wouldn't that be jolly!'

'It may work the other way around. They may now feel confirmed in their notion that I am irresponsible.'

'Oh, dear! I do hope not, Mr Cornfield.'

She rose. He rose.

'I have stolen some begonia bulbs for you,' he said in a naughty-boy voice. 'If you come up to the corner by the land steward's house this evening before the supper bell I'll have them for you.'

'I will come. I do hope you may continue to help the gardener, Mr Cornfield. Your trouble is you do not occupy your mind enough. Work is good for the soul. It is always pleasant talking with you, Mr Cornfield.'

She smiled again, he lifted his cap as she walked away from him. How Protestant!

His two caretakers presently returned and sat on either side of him. Over their tea they had decided that flags underneath their bottoms and flags underneath their feet would be best of all, about which they became so excited that they had barely time to salute Doctor Reynolds in her scarlet sports Triumph, her black curls leaping in the wind as she whirled through the gateway so sharply that her front fender barely missed its left pillar.

Her eyebrows soared with pleasure. He was back! She had a snapshot of him in her side mirror rising to bow after her the way he always used to do. As she sped up the avenue she was still chuckling at his cap lifting sedately from his head inclining baronially, as if he owned the whole blooming madhouse. Odd how that those old-fashioned ways of his got on the nerves of every doctor in the place except herself. 'Cornfield's *folie de grandeur!*' – until she gave them their answer one night at dinner.

'So far as I can see the only unusual thing about his manners is that they are so good: the one man in the place who knows how to treat a lady properly.'

They had guffawed of course, but she knew she had drawn a spot of blood: also from herself, who had taken a whole year to pick him out from among the hopeless herds brought in here from the moors, the mountains and the dying islands, mooing as softly and ceaselessly as a village pound. Yet all he had done that morning four years ago had been to waist-bow to a nurse who had responded with a wink and provocative cock of the ankle. A nurse had known how to handle him. She had never known whether to treat him as a patient or as a man.

She braked in the doctors' parking space at the top of the avenue, got out, banged the door and stood glaring across the river valley ridges of Magharamore. She conjured up from behind it the narrow glen of the Owenaheensha. She had fished both rivers many times but there was really no good fishing that way until you came to the lakes at Laoura. She slewed her head eastward to a round hill, ten miles away, horned like Moses by two beams of upthrown sun. Every horizon shouldered white clouds that shouldered more white clouds, that shouldered still more clouds up and up into the deepening blue. Below her the daffodils scattered about the grounds did not sway. The air smelled freshly of the Easter rains. In exasperation she ruffled her poll. She would give it to him straight this time.

'Jack, you damned fool! You've balloxed it for keeps. For years you've been telling us that all you want is to be allowed to stroll around the roads and into the town for an hour a day. Solid John C. Reliable John C. To prove it he runs away from us to London. And then, after six months of AWOL here he comes crawling back like the Prodigal Son.' She knew that what she would actually say would be, 'Welcome home, Mister Cornfield. I trust you know that you were mad to have left this madhouse. In your five years among us nothing became you less than your leaving us, and nothing more than your return to the village pound.' He would laugh politely. He always saw through her defensive jokes. The one thing she would not dare to say would be, 'I missed you.'

She started to empty her car, furiously throwing the stuff on the cement – rod, waders, basket, suitcase. She became aware of a familiar smell. That would be Mac, pipe smoking, delivered through the revolving glass doors, his lean cheeks insucked, his heavy eyelids lowering at her legs. He would not speak until she deigned to turn. She finally did. He lifted his pipe silently. She noted that he was not coming forward to help her with her gear. If she had been a pretty nurse...

'Nice holiday, Doctor Reynolds?' he asked circumspectly.

'Yes, if you don't mind lashing rain, and a force ten gale. If I'd been a flying fish I might have caught a flying fisherman. I played poker, drank Irish, chain smoked and read six whodunits.'

'And won every game hand down I bet? And drank them all under the table? And had the villain spotted by page fifteen?'

'One has to shine at something.'

'You shine! Your boyfriend is back.'

She stared him down.

'So London didn't work?'

'We warned them, didn't we? Six months to the day. I'd have given him six weeks. He stayed with his daughter, that fat, rich American Jewess who kidnapped him from us in October. Four days ago he bombed her. Two black eyes, a crushed rib and a broken septum.'

'Good for him! She is a right bitch.'

'On that, doctor, if on little else we are of one mind. There were occasions when even I felt my toe itching. However, you and I, not being mental patients – so far – can afford to dream violently. With him, an itch today, a black eye tomorrow, a knife the day after.'

She faced him full and crossly, her yellow sou'wester in one fist, her gaff in another.

'I have repeatedly pointed out to you, Doctor MacGowan, that Cornfield is as sane as I am. Even if you think that's not saying very much.'

Furiously she turned her back on him, threw down gaff and sou'wester, rummaged for her bookbag. He would be looking at her bottom now. He spoke pleadingly.

'Judy!'

She turned.

'I missed you.'

'Lookit, Mac. Are you by chance jealous of Cornfield?' He scoffed defensively. 'Then why can't you lay off me? The place is full of passionate nurses mad for it.' She switched herself off. 'How did he get back?'

'His American son-in-law threw him on a plane at London airport last Sunday morning. With a fiver stuffed into his vest pocket. At a quarter to one this Tuesday morning I was awakened by somebody at my doorbell. An old hand, he knows all the ways in. I hauled up the window. There was your ladyship's lordship below on my doorstep shouting against the wind and rain for God's sake to let him in. He was like a water rat with his big, effluent knob of a nose. We had quite an interesting chat, roaring up and down to one another at the tops of our voices. I've never seen such a night. I wouldn't have left a milk bottle out on such a night. No hat. No overcoat. He'd eaten nothing since he left the plane. Hiked the whole way. He was carrying a cardboard suitcase containing dirty linen, a large photograph of his daughter and two small pictures of her that he had been painting. I let him in, poked up the fire, gave him a hot toddy and watched him steam larger than life. That man has a superb constitution. You saw him just now, fresh as a daisy after being storm-battered for nearly forty hours.' One side of his knife-edged mouth smiled. 'While I am deciding what to do with him next I have sent him up to Ward Three.'

Her voice soared.

'Now why the hell should I have the silly bugger under my care?'

He looked paternally at her over his glasses.

'We all have our special babies, Judy. Admit you are pleased to have him back.'

'Not particularly,' she said, sulkily lowering her owl-lidded eyes. 'I have lost interest in his case. He is simply a sound, healthy, ordinary, bad-tempered man whom we have ruined by domesticating, national-izing, habituating, acclimatizing or, in the neologistic gobbledygook of our bombastic profession, institutionalizing so thoroughly that he is now afraid to live a normal life. We have turned him into that well-established male Irish type, the baa-ram bleating for his mummy's teats. Which we provide. Self-absorbed? Self-pitying? Egocentric? Chip on the shoulder? Truculent? Timid? Incurably self-referential? All that, but even if he really did give his blond cow of a daughter a couple of shiners does that make him insane? Any more than it would if you were to marry me as you say you would like to, but would not, and gave me two pandas when you discovered the sort of bitch you would sooner or later decide I am? That would not be you walloping me. It would be your dear little ego revenging itself on the whole monstrous regiment of women from Old Mother Hubbard, and Old Mother Goose, and Holy Mum the Church, down to Mother Ireland and your own dear departed and long-suffering Mother Machree. Doctor MacGowan!' She said it sweetly and gently. 'Why have I to explain these elementary things to you so often? Did you never, when younger perhaps, think of taking up plumbing, or dentistry, or some other study a bit more obvious than psychiatry?'

'Some day, Judy,' he said quietly, 'I will black your fucking eye without the blessing of either Father Freud or Mother Church and it might do you a power of good. Meanwhile...'

She barely felt the trap snap on her neck.

'... I have been rereading your dossier on Cornfield. This afternoon, in fact. You stress that he should be allowed a limited freedom. I think you are on the right track. If this man can travel once to London why should he not travel twice? Turn the matter over again in your mind, Doctor Reynolds. If we are in accord I propose to tell Mrs Reuther that she must henceforth accept full custody and responsibility for her father. In London. Or in New York. Or wherever else she damned well likes.'

He turned to go. The shrillness of her voice halted and turned him.

'Mac! You can't do this! You can't encourage this poor devil to get attached to us -- and then boot him out into the streets of London.'

'Isn't it what you have always been asking for on his behalf? Freedom of the city?'

'Not of London! What is he going to do in the purlieus of Sloane Square, Lowndes Street, Kinnerton Street, Eaton Square, Belgravia? A man who has been accustomed for five years to sitting on the side of a country road watching that evening sun go down, chatting with passers-by, looking at a spider in the grass, the drops of dew hung out to dry on a cobweb, able to sit in the gate-lodge by the fireside in the winter with Patrice's fat wife, poke the coals, lift the curtains, look at the flooded river, look...'

With a sob, incoherently, she waved around to the grey-stemmed daffodils and the climbing clouds.

His voice became precise and hateful.

'This may be pointed out to his daughter. We have done our bit. See you at dinner,' and the glass valves of the door whirled the blues and whites of the sky behind his back.

'Damn you!' she said bitterly at the slowing doors. Then, luggage-laden, she bumped up the stairs to her rooms.

At the window she took up her old bird-watching binoculars. He was there still, a blurred figure sitting on the low wall, alone. She focused him to sharpness. His back to the fields, his hands hanging between his knees, he was looking at the earth. Suddenly he rose, straightened, braced his aching back, lifted his Atlas arms to grasp the sky. A fine figure of a man, six foot one, red nose like a sailor, brisk black hair. Aged fifty? Not much in his head. Soft-cored. Too gentle. A bit of a coward? She hungered to eat him. She had never seen him stripped but Mac, who had checked his condition several times, reported that he had the physique of a man of thirty. My soul thirsts for him in this wet and rainy land where there is no sun. I want him where every woman longs for the leap of a child. What do I see in him? Myself.

She laid down her field glasses, drew a hot bath, stripped, and filled herself a glass of Irish. She glanced at her mirrored face, her bulldog nostrils, pocked skin, big mouth, prognathous jaw, laid herself in her hot bath and slowly sipped her liquor. She glanced along her full fish-length in the bath, calmly aware that the gods had never created a more preeminently beautiful body, as far as the neck. She cheerfully informed her wriggling toes, 'If I had been dug up in marble two hundred years ago as a headless Venus I'd be in the Louvre now under spotlights.'

Her eyes wandered out of her bathroom to her bookbag squatting like a black cat in the middle of the carpet of her living room. *Jessica's Daughter.* According to his publisher, 'John Cornfield's magnificent 100,000 words cry for Freedom.' He should have been dug up as a brainless gladiator. Four months it had taken her to wheedle it out of his besotted daughter, and then only under a solemn promise that nobody else, not even he, must know that a copy of the novel still existed.

Now, it may be agreed that every visible and celestial achievement is, in the nature of nature, flawed. That thing was an embarrassment. Autobiographical as she had expected, which was why she wanted it; and almost straight autobiography at that, which was why it was a failure. When she was a student at Westminster Hospital she had had a lover who was a real writer who had made her see that the truth is always much too complicated to be told straight out. Here everything was as implacably grim as grime. The hero, like the author, a lone child. Named Shawn. Scene, a grey English mining town. Father and mother Irish-born, Roman Cats, elementary school teachers. At twenty Shawn flies from insensitive and brutal England to warmhearted, kindly Ireland. She snorted. What John-Shawn had fled from was the War, the blackout, roving searchlights, ack-ack, austerity. End of Book One. Dublin. Our hero is found working in Dublin. On an R.C. magazine. That word had always amused her: a storehouse for explosives, the part of a rifle where you put bullets, French for a shop. This shop provokes his last wild cry for freedom when he meets a Jewish girl, named Jessica, visiting Ireland from New York, loses his virginity to her, marries her, gets booted out by his warm-hearted and kindly employers, disowned by his father and mother and angrily returns to cruel, cloddish England. End of Book Two. Fleet Street. Updating obituaries and checking sports results. Lives in a flat in a semi-detached in Crouch End. Constant quarrels with wife. Conscience in flitthers. Drinks. A chaste and tender friendship with an Irish prostitute whose conscience is also in flitthers. And then, casually, simultaneously and without warning he fathers a beautiful daughter and a highly successful novel. Peace? Achievement? Freedom?

In real life *Jessica's Daughter* had been a flop.

To his credit, by the time she was compiling his original dossier, he was able to refer to this fiasco with a bitter humour. But he could not remember even the titles of his four subsequent, unpublished novels.

'Four? What persistence, Mr Cornfield! Still, I hope you enjoyed writing them?'

'I hated every moment of them. Every one of those bloody things,' his cassette recorded, 'was written under the whip of the most characteristically bossy conceited insensitive ambitious misanthropic egomaniacal woman who ever issued out of the loins of Abraham.'

A pity he did not wait another few years before writing these failures. He would have had at least a splendid ending for one of them.

The cassette again:

'We came back to Ireland on holidays eleven years ago she started nagging at me to write a sixth novel one morning I saw red for ten seconds I've often timed it I went for her with a loose brick we had to keep the door of the kitchen open a cottage we hired a small pink Georgian brick six inches by three it didn't do her any harm only for all that blood streaming down her face and she running around in a circle like a dog with the distemper and poor little Beryl staring.'

His wife was probably right to commit him to a private clinic and go back to New York with the kid. Five years later she died, the cash stopped, they had to take him in.

She sucked down the last drops of her whiskey, deposited the glass on the bath mat, sat up and slowly and softly began to soap her armpits and her lavish breasts. Eleven years behind walls and, in her view, only one symptom of abnormality: the pathetic smallness of his protest against his life of a castaway – his plea to be granted sixty minutes a day alone. Crusoe would probably have got that way in the end, with no more than an occasional dreamy wish to walk on Tower Hill or Cheapside. Still, Crusoe had coped, made a new world. There was nothing wrong with Jack Cornfield except that at some time his wish to cope had got a knockout blow. In what part of him, why, where, nobody would ever know, unless some psychiatrist had him every week for five years, breaking him down and down until he was a little naked man at the bottom of a deep, dark cone begging for the last cruel drop of truth to be squeezed from him – the price of his release to the upper air.

Am I his female Orpheus?

She clambered out of her bath, grumbling 'Cure thyself,' towelled herself with energy, began to dress. She leaned to her mirror to test her upper lip. 'The passing shadow on her upper lip . . . Blown hair about her mouth . . . Thy shadow, Cynara . . . Swan's neck and dark abundant hair . . .' She stiffened. Her watch said six thirty. She rang the head nurse of Ward Three. If it was convenient could Mr Cornfield be sent to her surgery at eight o'clock for ten minutes. No, nothing special.

'But we may have to have a conference about him tomorrow morning.'

He was waiting in her office. She lifted down the overcoat hanging on the back of the door.

'I think, Mr Cornfield, we might stroll. It is still bright. I shan't keep you ten minutes.'

They strolled to the highest and quietest corner of the grounds, just below the farm and the land steward, Billy Victory's, house. He recognized the clatter from the kitchens after the usual tasteless meal. If he could only have a glass of beer sometimes with his supper. The country slowly expanded. Soon it would be veiled. She talked about her fishing. He asked if it was very far away and she waved towards the horizon. He asked in which direction, and when she pointed he paused and stared. She waited and watched.

They came to the white seat, cast iron, where he had sat an hour ago with Elsie Huggard, giving her six corms of gladioli in a cardboard box marked *Saint Senan's Confectionery*. The name was a common eponym in the town – Saint Senan's Maternity Home, School, Church, Bridge, Furnishing, Insurance, Credit Union, Hospital, Cemetery. The old Huggard home had the Saint's name carved on the pillars of its entrance gate.

'I'm glad to see you back, Mr Cornfield. I hope you realize how mad you were to have left this madhouse.' (Like her to call it that. Honest. No palaver.) 'In all your years nothing became you less than your leaving us and nothing more than your return to the fold.' He laughed obligingly. Who did she think she was fooling? 'Why did you let Mrs Reuther kidnap you away from us?'

He smiled his crooked smile, replied circumspectly:—

'Beryl is half-Irish, half-American. And a hundred per cent Jewish. Married to a Jew. Eat your spinach. Drink your chicken soup. One obeys.'

A plane hummed over. Its wingtips blinked. Escaping to London, New York, Amsterdam, or Paris, Brussels?

'I missed you,' she said to the grass.

'I thought of you many times,' he said to the sky, and accepted one of her cigarettes. Her lighter ran a line down the shinbones of her legs. It incised the aquiline face of a revolutionary sucked dry by years of jail. At the sense of so much helplessness in so strong a body a surge of power hit her like a contraction of the womb, a four-beat stoppage of the heart. Her cigarette flew in an arc of anger against the deepening sky. She spoke out of the corner of her mouth like a gangster's moll.

'What are you going to do, Mr Cornfield, when we send you back to your daughter in London?'

'Could you?' he demanded so fiercely that she slewed her head a full hundred and eighty degrees the better to relish his smell of fear, sweat, tobacco.

'If you can travel once you can travel again.' She sweetened her voice. 'You have a very pretty daughter. A lovely girl.'

'Isn't she though?' Eagerly.

'You must be very proud of her.'

'She's all I have in the world.'

'Then why did you go for her, break her nose, crack her ribs, black her pretty eyes?'

He patted her knee. She dribbled for him.

'Me go for Beryl? I just said I did that in order to get back to my featherbed.'

'In that case you should not be here. Perhaps you never even attacked your wife?'

'Now her I did do! With a hammer.'

'You said with a brick, six by three, pink, Georgian.'

'I can't remember. Do you think I'm lying?'

'If you can't remember it's probably true.'

'But little Beryl! For God's sake, not Beryl! It wasn't she pushed me out of that flat in Sloane Square, it was her husband, not that I blame him, he got me four jobs, I couldn't keep any of them, he was quite nice about it, really. One day he even called me "chum." He has his own life to lead, and Beryl is expecting. He had a drink with me at the airport, he stuffed two fivers into my pocket, I drank them in Dublin. I tell you this because you are the only person I can trust in this bin. Will I be chucked out?'

She looked around her. All she could see clearly was a row of lighted windows.

'Mr Cornfield, you did attack your wife with intent to kill. Please let us be clear about that, and no nonsense. You did attack your daughter. And let us have no shilly-shallying about that either. You put them both in mortal danger. You gave your Beryl two shiners, broke her septum, cracked two of her ribs, in a word went off your chump again. Do you understand?'

'I am not,' he said furiously, 'I repeat *not*, off my chump.'

She lifted her eyes imploringly to the one great planet in the sky.

'In that case you wish me to report that you are as gentle as a mouse? That you never really went berserk? That you never will, that you are fit to pack your bag, leave this featherbed and earn your living out there in that dark, wide, windy world? Do you understand all that, you great, big stupid slob?'

He became as gentle as a mouse.

'I am not insane and I will never say otherwise. It simply happens that I do not like this horrible world. And that is your own word. Or, you said it, quoting Bertrand Russell, "This world," you said he said, "is horrible! Horrible! Horrible! Once we admit that we can enjoy the beauty of it."'

'I ought not to have repeated the witticism to somebody only too eager to take my every lightest word seriously. After all, His Lordship might just as well have said, "This world is lovely! Lovely! Lovely! Once we admit that we are ready to suffer the horrors of it." I find plenty of pleasant things sandwiched between the horrors of life. Good fishing. Good drink. Good friends.'

'I do not fish. I do not drink. I have no friends.'

She considered the bizarre angle of his hairy cap against the stars. She wished only that she could strip him, scrub him in a hot, hot bath, and dress him like a free man.

'So be it, Mr Cornfield. You must make your own miserable decisions. And if you still do not like this horrible ship we are sailing in there is a very simple way to solve your tiny problem.'

She drew her index finger across his bristly throat, shivered at the nutmeg-grater feel of it, jumped up and abruptly walked away. 'Damn you!' he shouted after her and sulkily watched her stately figure sink from sight down the hill.

She felt her pulse banging in her right ear. Her calves were groggy. Mac's black house rose against the ash of the Easter moon. Their passionate widower. Twice married. Father of seven. If I became his third they certainly would not become fourteen. She halted to reconnoitre. Doctors were entitled to receive friends in their rooms provided they were not patients or nurses, whether M or F, but in this fortified village everybody saw, suspected, invented, scoffed, hinted. Even as she looked around she saw a white edge of skirt, a shoe, a stocking, a black cloak slide through young Carty's door. In such matters Mac was neither a Puritan nor a Paul Pry, but if he suspected her of trying to saddle him with Cornfield he would not give her a grass blade of leeway.

There was no corner inside these walls where they could meet after dark. No corner where some eye, some fly, some spy would not sooner or later surprise them. But would either of us dare to? Can a bird fly with a broken wing? A man who had not had a woman for eleven years? That story he told about himself when he was a kid and the fledgling jackdaw that their yard-cat in Stockport struck down with a crooked claw. How he capped it under a cardboard box, and then put this box into a larger box, and then covered that larger box with wire netting, and found a worm for the bird, and gave it a saucer of water, hoping it would recover from the shock, and its wing would mend and it would be able to fly away again.

'But in the morning it was on its side, its eyes glazed, half-closed, its claws and feet extended. Even my worm was dead. The nights in the North can be bitter.'

Well, Judy? And how is our precious cornfed baby? You have become a cat who walks by night. You never drop in for a drink with me these nights. If I may make so bold, Dr Reynolds, am I wrong in imagining that you have, so to speak, been avoiding me lately? Damn you, Jack Cornfield, you know the form just as well as I do. No, Mac! For the hundredth time. No! And if I did let you that night after Easter it was not, I assure you, because I was madly in love with you but simply that I felt randy as hell and sorry for all poor, bloody mankind. Oh, yes indeed, Dr MacGowan, I cannot tell you how happy I am here, safe from all temptations and troubles, all of us together in this cosy little world of our own. Oh, you just reminded me, Mr Cornfield, I have a book about the South Pacific that you might like to collect from my office this evening . . .

A week later she applied for a post in Dublin. On the night she told him so eleven years of celibacy fell from his back. Hand in hand, like children, they ran for their lives. Three weeks later they were married. To establish his pride his Beryl settled a generous income on him. Elsie Huggard said to him, 'While you are looking for a house why don't you rent my ground floor? "Saint Senan's" is big enough the Lord knows, built to house ten children at least. I shan't butt in on you.' He accepted without even examining the house, but when the two of them first entered it he was as boastful and triumphant as if he had inspected it as carefully as a real estate broker.

'I couldn't have chosen better. See! A ship's bell, with the name engraved on it. PYLADES. A Turkish hookah. A sailing ship inside a Barbados rum bottle. An Indian coffee table, brass inlaid. A Moroccan tapestry. Junk from all over the globe. I bet you we'll come on a fifty-year-old album of photographs. The place smells of the seven seas.'

She laughed at his zany laughter, told him he was like a lark in the air, whereupon, without embarrassment, he recited, and at the end slid into song: – '*Dear thoughts are in my mind/ And my soul soars enchanted/ When I hear the dear lark sing/ In the clear air of the day./*

For a tender, beaming smile/ To my hopes has been granted/ And I know my love tonight will come/ And will not say me nay.'

'You entertain strong feelings, Mr Cornfield.'

'And what other feelings would you expect your husband to entertain for his wife, Dr Reynolds?'

Every day he wandered the streets of the town, or along the tunnelled, bud-bright roads of Spring. Every evening, over dinner, her first question was always, 'What sage did you meet today? What wisdom did you collect?' and he would empty a pocketful into her lap, a word, a leaf, a stone, a broken eggshell, a sound, a chestnut, a colour, an acorn, a feather. For a long time she puzzled over the inordinate amount of satisfaction he could get out of the slightest bit of chat on a road, in a field, a side street. She decided in the end that he was extending, expanding, marrying everybody and everything, giving birth by communion with other selves. For eleven years he had been imprisoned on a barren island. At last, she smiled proudly, her odd man was out, coupling like an unspancelled goat.

She watched him intently. She knew her man better than he her. She observed that his strolls changed from walks to expeditions, extending farther and farther. He bought a bicycle to go farther still. She noted that he would not come salmon fishing with her, hating, so he said, that prolonged playing of the hooked fish in from the wide ocean; but she noticed that when she took down her trout rod he came, she teased, illogically, although he insisted that he came then only because he liked the long drive across the parallel ridges of Magharamore, and the Owenaheensha on to Lough Laoura. She noted further that on their return he would always ask her to pull up on some ridge where he would alight and look back.

One day he asked the question outright. 'What's out there behind those Laoura mountains?' and was patently astonished when she just said, 'Another county. No fishing. Shallow streams.'

The testing time came with the winter, cold, wet and seemingly endless. Work and fishing sufficed to distract her. He felt bottled up. The town offered few distractions. She suggested a trip to London but the look he gave her silenced her. The wintry roads discouraged him although he was abashed every morning to see Elsie Huggard start off on her three-mile trudge, head bowed into the weather, cowled under a shining black mackintosh down to her ankles. He watched television all day, or sat reading by the fire, mostly historical biographies, histories of exploration, travel books. He developed a taste for astronomy, had a brief craze for books on mountaineering. She hated to think of him sitting there in silence, his book sinking to his lap, his eyes facing an unseen fire, and for the first time a truth about him that she had always known in an abstract way became visually real – he had been beaten into subjectivity by years of loneliness. They had not killed his spirit, but he would always be at risk.

Driving home one dank, dusky, February afternoon, the hood of her red Triumph closed tight, she was startled to see him standing beside the gate-lodge greeting her with his old polite bow and raised hat. He sat in beside her; for one second, perhaps for as long as two, he smiled at her dilated eyes and then burst into a laugh.

'It's all right, darling. I am not suffering what is known as a regression to a chronologically earlier pattern of feeling. I just came up to have a chat with old Dawson the cook.'

'About what?' Suspiciously.

'He used to be a ship's cook. He sailed the seven seas in his heyday. I've been reading a book about Gauguin in Tahiti. Are you going fishing this weekend?'

'Come?'

'Yes. I could leave you at the lake and drive on. I want to see what's beyond those Laoura hills.'

'But you don't drive!'

'I've been taking lessons secretly,' he said with his naughty-boy grin. 'I got my licence yesterday.'

She said nothing for a long minute. Then she said that that was a fine idea. All the same he really might have mentioned it to her? He asked her if she would not, in that case, have wanted to teach him herself; at which she admitted that it is apparently, all too easy for a wife to begin behaving like a wife.

He duly drove her to her chosen corner of the lake, promised to meet her in the afternoon at the local pub, drove away. Twilight came. He did not. She had a drink while waiting. He did not come. She had another drink. She kept glancing at her watch. Her hands were tight. He came. When he did not say he was sorry for being late she found it hard not to behave like a wife; wondered was he finding it hard to behave like a husband. He asked her easily as they drove away how she had fared.

'Nothing worth talking about. A couple of brown trout. Under a pound each. You?'

'In the distance between two clefts of hills like breasts I saw a V of sea.'

'That,' she said sourly, 'means you were only ten thousand miles away from Tahiti.'

He comforted her knee.

'When Gauguin was a child he went to Peru, came home, sailed with the merchant marine and the French navy, chucked it, got a job, married, chucked it when he was thirty-six, tried Brittany, sailed for Martinique, chucked it, tried Paris again, chucked it, tried Brittany again, sailed to Tahiti, lived and painted there, chucked it, sailed for the Marquesas, and died. Let's fry our brown trout.'

For some fifteen miles the windscreen wipers hissed. Then the mist stopped, the sky cleared, and for the rest of the drive they were aware of a vast tumescence of moon in command of all wintry life. Immediately they got into their dusty old living room in 'Saint Senan's' he lit the laid fire. When it was blazing they sat before it with two whiskeys, exchanging trifles about their day. Presently he got up and went into the kitchen – old, flagged, vast, that nobody had refurbished for forty years. He came back wearing her butcher's blue-and-white apron, and went to her fishing basket for the two fish. She got up to help, but he waved her back commandingly.

'You stay there. I'm going to gut'em and cook'em. *Meunière?* Fresh butter just turning brown. A touch of lemon? A spot of parsley? Plates straight from oven to table.' He winked at her over his disappearing shoulder. 'This I *can* do.'

'But I'd like to help!'

'I need no help,' he said arrogantly and left her.

She sank back into her armchair and, without relish, finished her drink. Presently she heard him humming over his chopping block. To command her feelings she inhaled slowly and slowly exhaled, aware that something far less than a chorus ending from Euripides or a sunset touch would be more than enough to make her burst into tears at her Grand Perhaps singing over her two fish. Suddenly he reappeared in the door of the kitchen with a look of farcical helplessness, advanced, turned his shoulders to her and asked her to tighten those damned strings, so she knotted the cords more tightly and with an approving pat on the bottom sent him on his way.

When he was gone she covered her face with her palms and began blowing into them like waves dying in caves. This was, no doubt, since it had so happened, and, after all, Saint Augustine once said that whatever is is right, exactly what was to be expected, but it was not at all what she had wanted. She blew one last mighty wave of discontent into her hands, rose and listened to him tra-la-la-laing merrily through the Blue Danube waltz. Then, with a philosophic smile she dutifully began to lay the table. For what, as Aeschylus says, can be more pleasing than the ties of host and guest? To drown his tra-la-la-laing she murmured to herself certain famous lines by another prisoner that had always entertained her:—

> If I have freedom in my love,
>   And in my soul am free,
> Angels alone that soar above
>   Enjoy such libertee.

Marmalade

When Ellie slammed the front door he slowed his cup's approach to the coffee table to glance across his shoulder at the clock on the mantelpiece. Six forty-five? Of course. Monday. Her night for bridge, his for the art class. His coffee made a smooth landing. He sank into his armchair, carefully unfolded his evening paper, looked blindly at its headlines for a while, let it sink into his lap. If only! If only! If only they had had a child! All day she had not spoken one word to him since she said at breakfast, 'May I have some marmalade, please?' And now she was gone for the night.

Which of them first mooted this crazy idea of one night a week apart? She had been sarcastic about it. 'Divorced weekly? A comedy in 52 acts.' He had been sour. 'The road back to celibacy? Act Five.' Probably neither of us began it. Just another Knight's move, another oblique assertion of another imaginary speck of precious bloody personality threatened by some other imaginary attack by one on t'other. *Quid pro quo.* My turn now. Tit for that. Even Stephen. Omens common to every failing marriage? Like her insistence on rising early every Sunday morning for first Mass and his on staying in bed late. His demanding roast leg of lamb on Fridays against her preference for black sole – not that he did not always let her have her way – he liked black sole; or her wanting flowers before her Madonna's statue all through May. It was not the flowers he minded; it was the silent betrayal of her man who had given up 'all that' for... For what? At which, as if an earth tremor made the ornaments on the mantelpiece tremble, he heard all around him for miles and miles the tide of Dublin's suburban silence. Out there how many mugs like himself were enjoying the priceless company of their own personalities? He flung the newspaper on the carpet, tore off his grey tie and pink shirt, went into his bedroom, dragged on his old black roll-neck Pringle pullover, groped for his old black Homburg hat and began to brush it briskly. As good today as the day I bought it in Morgan's in Westmoreland Street for the mother's funeral. He curled a black scarf around his neck, felt for his car keys, switched off the Flo-Glo fire and the electric candles on the walls, checked the bathroom taps and the taps of the electric cooker, put out the hall light and slowly drew the front door behind him until he heard the lock's final click. Fog. A drear-nighted February. Every road lamp on the estate had its own halo. He drove with care. Bungalow, bungalow, bungalow. Some lighted, most caverns of television flicker. Exactly the kind of night he had first persuaded Father Billy Casey to doff their Roman collars, black jackets, black overcoats, black hats, put on sports jackets, chequered caps, jazzy ties and set off for some, any lounge bar in the city, in search, Father Billy had said, rocking with amusement, of what laymen call Life.

He was able to accelerate a bit on the yellow-lighted bus route. After fifteen minutes or so he felt space and damp on his right. The sea. The new hospital. Lights in a church for Benediction. Inner suburbia's exclusive gateways. The US embassy. He crossed the canal. The city's moat.

'Whither tonight?' Casey had always said at this point, rubbing his palms. Anywhere west of O'Connell Bridge used to be safe from episcopal spies; the east was less safe, too many people coming and going between the big cinemas, the bars of hotels, the Abbey Theatre, the Peacock, the Bus Arus theatre. There was the same contrast on the other side of the bridge between Dublin's only pricy hub, the cube of Grafton Street, Nassau, Dawson and Saint Stephen's Green on to the east, and the old folksy Liberty's off to the West. Once you got that bit of geography clear in your head you knew the only danger left was the moment of exit from the presbytery and your return to it. Holy Smoke! Supposing the Parish Priest caught you dressed in civvies! As Father Billy once put it a priest in a check cap is as inconceivable as a pope in the bowler hat or, suddenly remembering some scrap of his seminarian's philosophy, if not inconceivable at least unimaginable. He had enjoyed and hated these small risks so much so that he could still groan and laugh at the thought of their hairbreadth escape the night they were nearly spotted by the P.P.'s housekeeper coming home late from what she always spoke of as her Fwhishte Diriuve. That was the night Father Billy had in his Edenish innocence all unknowingly pushed him out of the Church.

'Here's to us!' Billy had cheered from where he lay strewn like a podgy Pompeian on the triclinium of his secondhand sofa, his nightcap of malt aloft. 'To us! Who have at this triumphant moment once more unarguably demonstrated the undeniable truth that privacy is the last and loveliest of all class luxuries. Look at us! Boozing to our hearts' content in peace and privacy and nobody one penny the wiser, whereas all that the most overpaid, socialist, lefty poor working man can do when he is thrown out of his pub at closing time is to take home half a dozen bottles of beer in a pack. In a pub, Foley! That's the key word. In a pub! A public house. Subject to public inspection, permission to drink only in public, get drunk in public, puke in public, under the public eye, to public knowledge. But you and I, Foley, privileged nobs by virtue of our exclusive, élitist rank as officers of the Pope's *Grande Armée* can sit here at our ease, luxuriating in the lordly privacy of Father William Casey's personal sitting-room in Saint Conleth's Roman presbytery and not another soul one penny the wiser.'

He had replied coldly:

'You've got it all wrong, Father Billy. We do not drink in lordly privacy. We drink in abject secrecy.'

One word and he became aware of the duplicity of all institutions, the Law, the Army, Medicine, the Universities, Parliament, the Press, the Church dominated by the one iron rule, *Never let down the side*. There was only one kind of people from whom you might get a bit of the truth, not because they are more moral but because they have no side to let down. Outlaws. Join any organization and Truth at once takes second place. They went on arguing it down to the bottom of the half-bottle of Irish. 'Sleep on it, Billy,' he had said. 'In whishkey weritas.'

The kindled traffic light halted him as he approached O'Connell Bridge. He peered up at the Ballast Office clock, 7.32, and remembered the night – *The* Night – when he had answered Father Billy's ritual 'Whither tonight?' with the dare-devil cry of 'Why don't we try the Long Bar in the basement of the old Met.?' which – bang in the middle of O'Connell Street – spelled maximum danger. He was still chuckling at Casey's reply when the green let him through: 'The Long Bar? The short life! Onward to booze, death and glory.' Poor Billy! Poor in every sense. All a 'booze' meant to him was a large whiskey, or two glasses of ale. He remembered how the two of them had cheered like kids that night when they found a parking spot directly opposite the Long Bar of the Met. And, behold! Here it was waiting for him again. He slid smoothly into its arms, sighing 'This is what I should be doing every night instead of staring into bloody TV or an electric fire!'

He halted at the foot of the stairs, pushed open the glass door, three semi-circular steps above the floor of the saloon, and surveyed the babble. He saw one vacant table and his mistake. A mob of youngsters. Mere boys and girls. Pint drinkers. Years of tobacco smoke. Life? Gaiety? Unconventional? Bohemian? It was just any ordinary bar. Or had it changed? Or had he? Or was it she who had transformed it that night? He edged down to the vacant table and gave his order to the bar curate. After two slow dry martinis he surrendered. He took up his homburg – no other man or woman in the rooms wore a hat – felt for his car key, foresaw fog, the drive, the empty bungalow. How Father Billy had stared around that night at all the pairs and quartettes!

'Well, here it is, Foley! Life! And I can't tell you how glad I am to see it because only last night I found myself going through the dictionary to find out what the devil the word means. I was as nearly off my rocker as that! I can now reveal to you Father Foley that Life is, quote, unquote, that condition which distinguishes animals and plants from inorganic objects and dead organisms by growth through AH metabolism, BEE adaptability and CEE reproduction. Look around you. Look at us. They are growing up. I put on seven pounds since Easter. Look at their fancy dress. Look at our fancy caps and jackets. We all adapt. Reproduction? Look at 'em, every single one of 'em with a one way first class ticket for the double bed. All booked!'

'Not all! Or don't I see over there in the corner two unaccompanied young women. The dark one isn't at all bad looking. Four people spoiling two tables who could be improving one? Maybe those two young ladies are in search of Life? Come on, Billy Casey! Let's ask them over for a drink.'

He had not meant one word of it. What they had already done on half a dozen nights was, every time, an act of the gravest indiscipline. Two soldiers of a victorious Empire frolicking in taverns with conquered barbarians? At the sight of Casey's terrified eyes he had leaned back and laughed so heartily that the dark young woman had looked across and smiled indulgently at their happiness. One second's thought and he would have merely smiled back and resumed his chatter with Casey. He spontaneously lifted his glass to her. Her smile widened whitely. His questioning eyebrows rose, his eye and thumb indicated his table invitingly, hers did the same to hers, he said 'Come on Billy, in for a

penny in for a pound!' and the unimaginable of five minutes before
became reality.

'Ellie,' her companion apologized admiringly for her friend, 'is very
saucy'. She was herself a striking redhead, but he thought the dark one
much more handsome and she had by her laugh and gesture across the
bar suggested a touch of dash and character. As for her looks she had
only one slight flaw; her mouth was by the faintest touch awry, and
even this was in itself an attraction, that delicate, that charming fleck
of imperfection that never fails to impress a woman's looks unforget-
tably. Her black hair, divided down the centre of her skull, was drawn
back boldly like two curtains. Her eyes were as clear as her clarid
speech. Their large brown irises, shining like burred chestnuts,
harmonized with her willow coloured skin. She was dressed entirely in
black apart from the little white ruff on her high neck that somehow
made her look like a nun. He confided to himself the next day that her
smiles came and went like the sly sunshine of April. He introduced
himself as Frederick Cecil Swinburne and his companion, to Casey's
grinning delight, as Arthur Gordon Woodruffe, both of them final
medicals at Trinity College. She said, 'I am Ellie Wheeler Wilcox, and
my friend is Molly Malone'; both of them private secretaries to directors
of The Irish Sweep. They passed what any casual observer would have
seen as a merry hour, as light, bright and gay as a joking and laughing
scene in an operetta. On parting they all four said they might meet
again the next Monday night. He said a couple of hours later in Father
Billy's rooms in the presbytery that the only thing missing was that
those two young women should have been nuns in disguise and they
should all have burst out into an Offenbach quartette. Casey's solemn
reply had infuriated him:

'I am afraid, Father Foley, we went a bit too far tonight. We deceived
those two young ladies. We pretended. We were guilty of bad faith.'

He responded in exasperation with a whisper of 'Well, I'll be
damned!'

This restored Father Billy's sense of humour far enough to let him
disagree about the damnation bit though, possibly, there might be an
extra couple of thousand years of Purgatory in store for them both. All
the same he kept coughing dramatically the following Monday
morning to indicate the onset of a bad cold.

The corner table was empty. No Miss Wilcox. No Miss Malone. He
sat at the table that he had shared the week before with Father Casey

prolonging three tasteless Martinis for an hour. Thereupon, cursing his silliness he had clapped on his homburg and risen to his feet and there she was on the platform of the last three semicircular steps of the entrance door, tall and slim, dressed in black, her eyelashes overflowing her cheeks, her hair as closefitting as a cap, her high neck extended to assist her searching gaze. He flung up his hand. Smiling back at him she slowly edged her way between the tables. She sat opposite him though still looking about her, explaining that she had expected to meet her friend Molly Malone, although Molly did mention something today about feeling a cold coming on, but he felt so happy in her presence that he heeded little she said until he got her to talking about herself, her girlhood in the country, in County Offaly, where her father was a National Teacher, her two younger sisters, her brother Fonsy, short for Alphonsus, who had emigrated to England and was now married in Birmingham; not that he attended to her chat half so much as he did to the fleeting mobility of her features, her contralto laughter, her vivacious gestures, though he did heed her carefully when she described her Auntie Nan with whom she was lodging in a little house in Ranelagh, and her friends, working mostly in the Irish Sweep, which led her in turn to ask him about what it is like to be a final medical in Trinity College and about his plans when he became a doctor, a question that instantaneously reminded him of Father Billy's words about bad faith. She listened to his lies with such a transparent expression of belief that he felt thrown down beneath her feet by a whirlwind of shame that kept gnawing at him for the rest of the night, until the moment came when he had halted outside her aunt's little red brick home in that terraced *cul de sac* at Ranelagh. There, drawn up beside the kerb, he gripped her hand not, as she obviously thought and by her warm smile showed, to say a grateful goodnight but to plead for her trust. He must confess the truth about himself.

'Miss Wilcox, I have been deceiving you.'

'The truth? Deceiving me?'

Staring, frightened by his intensity and tone.

'I am not a medical student. I made all that up.'

If only he could have stopped there. Neither, she could laugh, was she Ella Wheeler Wilcox. He had to tell her the essence of him. He kept pressing her hand tighter and tighter.

'I am a clerical student. Trying to become a priest. You have been a revelation from heaven to me. I can't go on with it. I no longer want to be a priest.'

Her eyelids shot open at that last word. While he went on to half explain they opened wider and wider as if she were opening the doors of her soul to him. In the silence that followed she kept staring at him and he at her. In his celibate ignorance he was feeling for the first time the full blast of power that Woman when reduced to one special woman possesses by the mere fact of being female. She in her virginal ignorance was transfixed by the power that Man in the person of this one man held over her by the mere fact of being male. Each was at that moment so evenly conqueror and conquered that if the essential god of all lovers had in that blind alley breathed over them even so delicately as would not have shaken the filaments of a dandelion in full cloud of seed they would have sunk into one another's arms. That they did not, he often thought later, was due less to the gods than to her aunt, or to whatever other hand suddenly lit the fanlight. What she may have said before she jumped from the car and ran up the brief concrete path to the door beneath the light he was never after to remember verbatim except for the petals of her voice declaring with unarguable clarity that they must never meet again, and her 'Very well!' to his wild pleading that they must meet just once more so that neither of them should remember the other ungratefully. So, they did meet just once again, and went on meeting just once again for the whole of the next year, propelled as gently and as irresistibly as a yacht before a summer breeze by sympathy, chivalry and self-immolation until to his astonishment, one gentle May evening in the stodgy bedroom of her Auntie Nan's dim house in Ranelagh, while the old lady was away on holidays in County Cork, a typhoon of passion swallowed them both. After another year, marked by more agonizing and less passion, he extricated himself from his priestly vows. They married.

All that was five years ago and he had long since accepted that he was never to understand what estranged them, he who had so often in his presbytery given counsel and comfort to young marrieds lost in the same fogged wood. All he knew for certain was that that anticipatory year of waiting, of tenderly comforting one another, of trying to decide what he should do had been the happiest year of his life, conjoined by the misery of separation, divided now by the disaster of domesticity.

They had never really quarrelled, never violently confronted one another, though of course they now and again 'had words', the worst being the night he had evaded her clamant desire on the eve of Good Friday, the anniversary of the execution of a great man in whose alleged godliness he no longer believed, and she had spat at him, 'Your very skin is dyed black! You will never wash yourself of your precious stigmata!' to which he had retorted, 'You? You of all people dare say that to a man who has cast off every last trace of what you call black? You with your getting up at dawn, your statues and your flowers and your evening benedictions and all the rest of your pietistic falderals and fandangos, you say that to me?'; all of which she dismissed haughtily with the passionate observation that God's world is one – joy and pain, crocuses and the crucifixion, love and lust, desire and denial, human passion and prayer.

'Dare you deny it?'

Weaponless he did not.

The only clear hint he ever got anywhere about how marriages break had been vouchsafed to him one morning a bare month ago in the little shop of convenience near their bungalow, managed by an ageing man and wife. He had always found each of them normally friendly and loquacious. This day the two were in the shop together. The old man, before attending to him, quietly asked his wife some trivial question concerning their stock, was it about firelighters or washing soda? She answered him in the voice of *ancien régime* courtesy, in the softest voice, with all the formality of a duchess from the good old days before the Revolution. She said between politeness and hauteur, 'I beg your pawrdon?' He had fled from the shop, horrified by the revelation that this old pair were living out their last days in a state of savage war. Passion ends in politeness. After that he added to his 'If only we could have had a child' the wish that they could have one blazing, battering, bloody row.

He jingled his car keys, rose to face the fog, the bungalow, the evening paper already out of date, clapped on his homburg, and saw a vision. His wife was standing on the platform at the end of the stairs, dressed in black, her hair as black as thunder, her midnight lashes enlarging her eyes that roved the rooms in search of... In search of whom? He flung up the arm of a drowning man. For a moment she looked across the rooms at him, then her eyelids sank, her eyebrows shot upwards, she looked at him again, she decided, smiled her small crooked smile at him and edged forward between the tables. She held out her hand, with, 'Well, after all these years if it isn't Mr Swinburne! And what have you been doing with yourself all this time? Medicine?'

'Miss Wilcox!' he said and shook her hand. 'You will join me in a drink?' She gave him her sly smile, took the proffered chair and let silence fall between them as she slowly removed her gloves finger-tip by finger-tip. He as slowly extracted a cigarette and lit it. At their first far-off meeting when he had taken her to be an ingenuous miss of about twenty he had been struck by this same air of complete assurance. They both asked simultaneously, 'Do you often come here?' and chuckled into a fresh silence which she quickly took hold of with, 'I have been told that some gentlemen have their pet pubs. Is this one of yours, Mr Swinburne?'

Two seconds' silence during which he wondered if it was one of hers.

'I have no pet pub. I used to come here years ago to meet a girl I used to know.'

'What happened to her?'

'She just disappeared.' The bar curate stood silently beside them. 'Your usual, Miss Wilcox? A Dry Martini? – Make it two. On the rocks.'

'Nice of you to remember my favourite drink, Mr Swinburne.'

'I have a good memory. When you stood in that doorway just now you reminded me very much of my friend. Oddly enough she also liked a Dry Martini. Like you she was tall, dark and queenly.'

She lowered her head sideways to deprecate the compliment, smiled to accept it.

'This is odd. When I saw you just now you reminded me of a man I first met in this bar several years ago. I have not seen him for a long time either. He, as you say, disappeared.'

'What happened to him?'

Three seconds pause.

'I have wondered. My friends and I have never been able to agree about what happens to make these people disappear.'

'Your friends?'

Four seconds' pause during which she slowly turned her head to look towards a large round table, in an alcove which he had not previously noted, occupied by five or six women of varying ages. They were all looking her way. Her left wrist lifted her palm an inch to greet them. Her chin nodded an unspoken agreement. She turned back to him.

'My friends.'

'Your bridge club?'

Five seconds' pause.

'I never play bridge. But we are a club. All married, all botched, all of us working now in The Irish Sweep. We came together by chance. Last summer I got chatting with Mrs Aitch, that is the jolly fat woman in the orange head scarf with her back to us. Angela Hanafey. She is about 46. Her husband was, is, always will be an AA case. She has four sons all but one grown up. She just happened to be walking beside me one evening when we were pouring in our hundreds out of the Sweepstake offices at five o'clock. We had never laid eyes on one another before. "God!" she said to me. "I'm starved for a drink. Come and have a quick one on me at the Horseshoe." We met Mrs King there. She's the slim, handsome blonde, don't let her see you looking. She is still bitter of her ex. He left her holding three children and slid off to get lost somewhere in England with a slut of seventeen. It was she brought along Kit Ferriter, the baby of the bunch, six months married and glad to be living alone again in her virginal bedsit. Kit studied sociology for three years at Trinity. She says she learned far more about it in six months of marriage. Three or four others drop in and out. All sorts. One is married to an army captain who batters her. Another to a briefless barrister. Mrs Aitch calls us the Missusmatched. Monday is club night. No other rules. No premises.'

'And you talk about men and sex and marriage.'

'Sex? Never. Men? No. Marriage? Occasionally. Not as an important subject. We mostly talk about woman things. Food, cooking, dress, make-up, kids, the cost of living, our jobs, nothing in particular.'

'And in your club's view why do those marrieds have this odd way of disappearing?'

'Why?'

Her eyebrows threw a shrug over her left shoulder. Her eyelids lowered a curtain on the shrug. The corners of her mouth buttoned it down. She leaned back to consider either the question or him. When she tinkled the ice in her glass it sounded like his idea of Swiss cowbells in far-off valleys. When she laughed her contralto laugh it hurt him that he had not heard it for a long long time.

'Yes, why?'

'Why? We solved that months ago when we invented The Seven C's. Every marriage, we decided, sinks or swims on any three of,' right finger, left thumb checked them off, 'Concupiscence, Comradeship, Contact, Kids, Cash, high or low Cunning, and not to give a tinker's Curse about everything in general and anything in particular.'

'Ye have left out Love!'

'Mrs Aitch, our mother hen, dealt ably with that. "I made a fatal mistake" says she, "with my fellow. I led him to think I was the reincarnation of the Blessed Virgin. On our honeymoon I got a sudden, terrible thirst for tangerines. Afterwards we both found out, too late, that pregnant women get these odd hungers. He would have done anything for me, of course, on our honeymoon. He went to a power of trouble to get me the tangerines but get them he did! When we were back home I got a sudden wish for apricots. He rumbled and bumbled about it but still and all the poor devil did get me the apricots. A month later I got an unquenchable longing for nothing less than wild strawberries. Well, by that time I had a belly on me like a major. He told me to go to hell and find out for myself where anyone could find wild strawberries in the month of November and I knew at once that my dear love had vanished from the earth as if the fairies had got him." Kay Ferriter, our expert on sociology, told her she was lucky that he didn't batter the other fellow's baby out of her. The dear child insists that Love, which you say we have omitted from our Seven C's, is a mass-invented delusion with a life-expectation of three weeks.'

She rose, holding out her hand. 'Nice meeting you again, Mr Swinburne. It was very pleasant. Now I must join my friends.' He held her hand pleadingly. 'Can't we meet again? Say next Monday night. Just for a quick drink?' She looked around the rooms, said, indifferently, 'Alright,' and joined her welcoming group. As he walked out he heard behind him again her miraculously joyous laughter.

Back home he kicked aside the evening paper, switched on his fire, sank into his armchair and fell into a stunned sleep. In the morning the only time either of them spoke over their breakfastette in their kitchenette across their hinged tablette was when she said, 'May I have some marmalade please? ... Thank you.' On their way into town to work, he as always driving, he did say that next Monday night he would be as usual at his art class and she with an air of slight surprise replied that she would of course as usual be playing bridge with her friends.

Accordingly, on the following Monday night she again left home before him to walk to the bus, and he, after taut calculations followed

her in time to be in the Long Bar before her arrival, seated facing the
glass doors. Now and again he glanced furtively towards the women's
table in the alcove to his far left. His jury? His judges? His amused
witnesses? Again, after two slowly sipped drinks, he jumped to his feet
between rage and regret just as she appeared in the doorway. For a
moment she stood there motionless, then slowly descended to the level
of the bar, edging between the tables towards him with, 'So we meet
again, Mr Swinburne,' sat, began calmly to deglove. Of the precious ten
minutes she allowed him that night he could afterwards recall clearly
only one sequence, which he initiated:

'Did they ask if we were related?'

'No. And I did not vouchsafe. You could be only one of two
things.'

He worked it out.

'Or I could be a new friend?'

'Here? So briefly?'

'Did they say nothing at all about me?'

'Mrs King said, "He looks like a priest, all in black, even to the hat."
I said that the first time I met you seven years ago, here, you were
dressed in the colours of the rainbow. I left them guessing. I said,
"Maybe he has become a priest since then."'

Ten seconds' silence, looking at one another. She swallowed her last
piece of ice, put down her glass smartly, picked up her gloves and
handbag, rose, said, 'Have you?' and turned to go. He winced but held
her hand to beg for next Monday. He pleaded for it. They had talked
so very little. 'And I have nowhere else to go.'

'Except', she said sympathetically, 'back? Alright. Then they *will*
know!', and left him for her beaming friends.

In this fashion he had continued to meet her every week into the first
green promises of spring until by early May these extemporaneous
meetings took on the character of regular assignations and, since they
were never mentioned at home, the clandestine air of a double life. He
looked forward to these encounters more and more eagerly; as we say
he lived for them, suspected that she enjoyed them equally; he noted
with excitement that they extended themselves on occasion to fifteen
minutes, even to nearly twenty minutes and on one memorable night
to fully twenty-five minutes – this being the night when he asked for
her opinion as to which of her club's Seven C's of marriage was the most
important of all. She answered promptly.

'The first three of course. Concupiscence, Camaraderie, and Contact. Some people think Camaraderie comes first, but that is just Con disguising itself as Cam. Kids inevitably follow. Then Cash edges forward. Then more and more need arises for High Cunning. But on all occasions thereafter there is the need for not caring a damn, for the indifference of a divorce court judge.'

Naturally they started to argue, and they might have gone on arguing if she had not suddenly become aware of radiations of impatience from across the room. The next morning she said, 'May I have the marmalade please? Thank you.' But then, as lightly as she pasted the preserve on her toast she added, 'By the way I understood you to say some time ago that your art class meets twice a week. My bridge club is proposing to meet on Mondays and Fridays.' He at once decided that their relations had completely changed and on that following Friday the women's alcove contained only two elderly men drinking stout. His chest swelled with triumph. She arrived on time. Unasked he clicked his fingers for the bar attendant and ordered their drinks. Presently he observed with a tolerant amusement at the transparency of the feminine mind that the conversation had returned to last Monday's question about the primacy in marriage of feelings of fellowship or of desire, to which she referred as 'passion' and rather brazenly (he thought) as 'lust'. In the course of their conversation she said:

'Of course in all this one should first agree about the general principle of the thing. I mean is it not all largely a question of what in life does one most believe in, in Poetry or in Prose? I happen to see the world as a complex of things beyond all understanding, far too bewildering to be confined or defined by human laws or rules, shalls and shalt nots. I look at it all as a miracle and a mystery, a place of beauty and horror, a spring flower, a tree in bud, a dead child, a husband dying of cancer— Mrs Aitch's boozy husband is dying that way and she has fallen in love with him again – a lottery like the Irish Sweep, chance, fate, the gods, God, the Madonna, love, lust, passion, a baby at the breast. Everything is one thing. That is why I love to have flowers for the Madonna who had a baby, miraculously according to you, not that it matters how she had it, why I rise in the morning for the first dark mass where they celebrate again the execution of a god, or of God, not that that matters either, why I like to come in the evening for the last benediction before the dark night, why I used to let that friend of mine whom I loved years ago go to bed with me because I thought he saw life the way I do as a poem that anybody can read and that nobody can understand.'

Staring at her, taken again by her passion, yes, he could remember those wild talks during that year of blissful agony before . . .

'Alas!' she smiled her hurt smile. 'When we got married he changed. Looking at him then I was often reminded of the marvellous thing Keats once said about the greatest quality any human being can possess – the power to live in wonder and uncertainty, and mystery and doubt without ever reaching out after fact and reason. My friend turned out to be a man always looking for fact and reason, a law maker, a law giver, a law explainer, a policeman, a judge, a proseman, a prosy priest longing for his pulpit.'

The bar's chatter, rumble, clinking, talk, laughing stopped dead. Silence isolated them. Then:

'Did you never consider, Miss Wilcox, that this friend of yours may nevertheless have once dearly loved you?'

She pounced.

'Once? Yes. Once! One night in my aunt's house in Ranelagh while she was on holidays in County Cork with her sister. For a whole year after that night my wild lover wandered around and around in his head in search of fact and reason. I,' she smiled crookedly, 'was left waiting for the poetry of love.'

Unguardedly he laid a hand on her hand, said 'Ellie!' saw that he had blundered, withdrew. There was a staring silence. Then she looked at the ceiling as if she were listening to a plane passing over Dublin, looked at him once again, drew back her cuff from her wristlet watch with her index finger, seized her bag and rose.

'You have reminded me, Mr Swinburne, I promised my Auntie Nan to keep an eye on her little house in Ranelagh while she is gone to Derbyshire to stay with a niece. Would you mind leaving me there on your way home?'

He threw up his palms. Outside it was raining. They did not speak in their car. She became proprietress of his homburg hat, nursing it on her lap. When they arrived outside the tiny red-brick house he offered Miss Wilcox to wait and drive her to wherever she lived, it was no night for bussing, she had no hope of getting a taxi. She said that that would be most kind of him, 'But do come in! This is real rain,' and clapped his black hat comically on her head and ran through the rain beside the new mown patch of grass. He was relieved to see her laughing gaily at him as he also ran, hatless and stooped, through the rain. She left him in the parlour while she went off to do her checking room by room. He could recognise only two items in the parlour: the aquatint of Christ with the Samaritan woman at the well, its frame painted in ugly commercial gilt (his mind clicked, *They shall not thirst any more*), and the corded old sofa where he had put his arms around her for the first time. He heard her steps on the linoleum overhead. The photograph of a bearded man on the mantelpiece. What relative? He went into the kitchen. Her aunt's kingdom. An antique iron range. A stoneware sink. A crucifix. Tidy. Cold. He wandered to the stairs. On its side walls lithographs of castles. He identified Ross Castle in Killarney. Then Blarney Castle in Cork. He paused longest at Reginald's Tower in Waterford still seeing that corded sofa in the parlour. It had been raining that night too. That, too, had been May. Through a little shower they had raced for the door.

From the front bedroom she called him. 'Mister Ess?' When he reached the half open door he saw through the vertical aperture between the panelled door and its jamb an object that he recalled clearly, and with emotion, a tall mirror so mounted on its mahogany frame as to be able to tilt forward or backward. In this cheval mirror he had, that first night, seen her completely undressed. Now, modestly undressed, in black bikini and black brassiere, she was smiling into the mirror in the direction of the slowly opening door. He entered, became aware that she was deliberately modelling female allurement, his hat tilted on her head, one wrist back-twisted on her left hip, right knee forward, the other hand airily held aloft.

'Well?' she invited him in the mirror with her minx's smile. 'Do you really still love me?'

Between incomprehension and revelation, desire and revulsion, passion and despair he gestured wildly around the room. Over the bedhead Pope Pius X in black and white stared like an intolerant boy from under black eyebrows. His mind clicked: Giuseppe Sarto, that bitter anti-modernist. By the bed on the wall a Holy Water font. Last thing before sleep. His mind clicked: daring seminarian joke – *Here I lay me down to sleep, upon my little bed, but if I die before I wake how will I know that I am dead*? On the dressing-table a tiny Infant of Prague, gaudy, pyramidical, pagan.

'Yes!' he said defiantly. 'I do still love you. But not this way! Not here! Where everything smells of spinster and sanctity!'

She turned to him. She handed him back his black hat. He was prepared for her to spit that there is no other way; or that 'This room was once heaven to you.' If she had said that he would have said, 'Yes! But then I was defying it, now I would be accepting it.' Or she might in memory of lost hope say nothing. She said nothing. She looked from his eyes to his feet, and from his feet up to his eyes, and with one fast swing of her fist she crashed him across the face. Her engagement ring drew a red line in blood across his jaw. He returned the blow, they grappled, swaying and stumbling, screaming bitch and bastard, fell across the bed where her nails tore at his face until he found himself mastering her on her back and suddenly she was kissing his slavering mouth and groaning over and over, 'Give it to me.'

Whether it was the morning sun milliarding through the window into his face or the boom of a plane just taken off from Dublin, or the sound of a neighbouring churchbell that woke him he found himself sitting up in bed bewildered until he was informed by a hand stroking his bare back and her voice soothing him with 'It is alright, Swinny! This is Saturday. Neither of us has to work.' He sank back on the pillow, closed his eyes, remembered, turned his head towards her face on her palm on her pillow watching him quizzically. Beyond her on the floor he saw his homburg hat battered flat.

'I'm starving,' he announced querulously.

'Love always does that.'

Always?

'Can we have breakfast?'

'Here? There's nothing in this house. No bread, milk, butter. Nothing. Water and power turned off. No shave, no shower. Where do you live, Swinny? Let's have brekker in your place.'

At this inane question his eyes widened. His lips tightened. He could say, 'What the hell is this game you are playing?', or, 'I am sick and tired of this falal,' or, 'How long more are we going to act the parts of cat and mouse?' He said sourly, 'I live near Ballybrack. Half an hour away.' While they were hurrying into their clothes she toed his black hat with, 'You might as well throw that out.' He lifted it, dusted it affectionately, punched it, said, 'One never knows' and put it on. 'Hadn't we better make the bed?' he asked in his disciplined way. She waved a paw. 'She won't be back for a week, I'll drop in some day.' He held her wrist when she was unlocking the street door. 'The neighbours?' She ushered him out. 'You are the gas man come to measure the meter.'

He took the six-lane Bray Road. She murmured, 'I am still sleepy,' and leaned back her head and closed her eyes. The morning traffic was floating inward on his right. His outward lane was empty. He would be home in twenty minutes. He pondered on the coming confrontation. Home, she silently prepared breakfast. While he showered and shaved he was phrasing his ultimatum. His cheek needed a slim strip of plaster. Back in the kitchen he found a changeling who spoke silently, as all long-marrieds can, ignoring words, hearing thoughts, interpreting silence, speaking runes. He sat to table and waited for it. Her open palm politely indicated his dish of marmalade. His belly went red with rage. He accepted the challenge. He withheld his marmalade. She looked at him mildly. He yielded the dish and waited. Slowly she stroked his marmalade to and fro. Do come a little early. Before the others. My aunt will not be home until Saturday. He was almost certain that the extreme corner of her upper lip stirred. A speck of marmalade clung to her cheek. It made her look agreeably silly. He rubbed brisk palms, grabbed three slices of toast, surveyed his favourite dish of bacon and tomatoes, poured himself coffee, faced a hearty breakfast. But wait! Hold it! Half a sec.! This woman? His fists closed like castles on either side of his breakfast. Who is she? My wife? Somebody else's? Nobody's? Is she a bit crazy? Does she mean all this? His memory clicked. Who said *Love is a mood to a man, to a woman life or death?* It was Ella Wheeler Wilcox! Without raising her eyes or ceasing to munch her toast she slowly pushed the marmalade back to him. He considered the move, and her. The snippet of marmalade kept seductively moving up and down. He remembered his old Parish Priest saying to him as they parted, 'Once a celibate . . .' Pensively he plastered his toast. Impassively she watched him.

From Huesca with Love and Kisses

A handsome young woman of about thirty, her black hair straight and shining as if it had just been pomaded, her eyes as brown as polished mahogany, her complexion of the warmest, her figure dangerously near to portly, is lying on a deck-chair in the gardens of a small but well thought of Irish rural hotel called, after the nearby village, Carrigduv House. Before her there stretches one of the vast bays, really an inland sea, that the Atlantic has clawed out from between the mountains of this westerly end of Europe. She does not see the bay. Her eyelids are closed tight. When she clinches them more tightly a tear oozes. Her name is Ruth Goodman. She is Jewish. She is in despair.

Ruth had known that the instant she opened her mouth in Carrigduv everybody would think that she was English, which was only half-true; just as they would think when they saw her painting before her easel on one of their blank beaches, or in one of their ragged fields, that she was a painter; and if they had questioned her directly about those things she would not in politeness have denied either, least of all the second, despite her reservations and doubts. Otherwise she had so far truthfully answered every conjecture advanced towards her in the circumlocutory, devious way that an Irish acquaintance had amiably warned her to expect: the jokes about her name, Goodman, Good-woman, Goodgirl, Goodwife, as a delicate way of finding out if she were married; where and for how long had she lived in London, curious about the source of her sallow complexion; would she call painting real work, meaning had she another job; and did she not think that if one can afford it, is it not much easier nowadays to fly to Cork than have to come by train and boat, a way of probing her income. The technique amused her. She was familiar with it from her travels in various remote parts of Europe from her native Spain to inland Greece. In fact she would have liked many more such questions, interchanges (from which she always got as much as she gave), being convinced that nobody can paint anything anywhere, a pig in a sty, a cart in a stable, a lamp in a lane, a tree in a field, a busted zinc bucket being rolled by the wind in a backyard, without first merging oneself intimately into the rustic local life where the humblest household object gradually becomes so familiar as to be no longer seen.

Her obsessive exemplar of this credo was the seventeenth-century Dutch painter Paul Potter whose painting of four bulls had overwhelmed her five years before when she happened to notice it amid a lot of junk displayed in the Flemish-Dutch room of the Galleria Sabaudia in Turin. During the hour or so that she had spent wandering through this old building she found herself coming back again and again to that room trying to make out what it was that had so deeply impressed her about those four bulls, two of them wholly white, one black-rumped and the fourth a Holstein mapped in black and white. Three were standing, one lying motionless, beside an almost defoliated willow in the forefront of thousands of acres of flat land obviously reclaimed from the sea. Otherwise clouds filled nine-tenths of the canvas; that is if the word 'filled' could possibly have any meaning in face of that infinity of light sifted through clouds as chequered as those four tiny bulls down below on their vast pinch of salvaged land.

She had been the last visitor to leave the gallery. That afternoon as she wandered through its once-royal city (modern travellers find it more famous now for motor cars than for kings) she saw only the bulls and the clouds. They followed her even when she extinguished the light in her bedroom. They were her first thought the next morning, so teasingly that although it had been her plan to take the earliest train to Genoa she suddenly changed her mind in order to have one more look at a canvas that implacably challenged her to decide what set it so magically above the hundreds of other pieces of Dutch naturalism that she had admired soberly and tranquilly ever since she had decided in her teens that the one thing she wanted to do with her life was to be a painter. She barely caught her second choice of train, feeling by now thrown quite off her course by those damned bulls.

As she glared out of her carriage window, she pondered on what, she feared, might become an obsession if she did not get some sort of reasonable answer to her question. She was still glaring as the train crept through the Monferrato down to the wide Alessandrian plain manufactured, like the whole series of plains between Turin and the Adriatic, by aeons of river-borne Alpine dust which first became mud and ultimately Venice. Rice country? Cow country? Transformed marshland? Had Time something to say to her problem? If Venice could be based on mud, if beauty could be born of dust... At which an informing rocket exploded in her dark. She had espied far away across the sunburned plain, hazy under the heat – soporific, shadowless, brutal – a tiny pink campanile right in the middle of the limitless globe of blue sky surrounding it on all sides. Seeing it, defining it, she at first angrily sniffed 'How picturesque!' in much the same scornful voice as she would have dismissed anybody's 'picturesque' explanation of any other equally obvious fact of life, and was the second after suddenly back in London fifteen years ago, a girl of 17, applying for entry to the Slade, listening – she was later assured that it had been a great privilege – to a well known or at least a well established painter chatting to one of the assessors about her 'Examples of Recent Work' as if (she thought furiously) she were stone deaf.

'Oh, not again!' the old painter had sniffed as another of the water colours she had done on the Italian Lakes that summer was placed on the easel. 'You know, Kenworthy, I can never so much as think of those bloody Lakes without feeling that I am back again at a Parochial Sale of Work trying to raise funds for the dry rot in the crypt or wood-worm in the chantry. When I was a youngster you could never go to one of those eleemosynary affairs without seeing at least one water colour of the Lakes on sale. Glass dusty. Frame cracked. Colours faded. Perpetrated by the late wife of the late vicar on their late honeymoon on Lake Como...'

The assessor yielded him a polite smile; lifted to her apologetic eyebrows! Afterwards he assured her that the old boy always treated new students this way, and a day later could be as kind to them as if they were stray kittens.

'Always the same. See! Here we have it again, sixty years after I was in short pants. The quaint boat moored beside the quaint steps. The quaint garden gate under its quaint arch. The veils of purple bougainvillaea ordered by the yard from Harrods. The good old pretty old pots of geraniums lining the old path from the old boat to the old gate. And of course the inevitable picturesque Swiss mountains as a backdrop to it all. Oh! Well! Never mind! The brush work is vigorous. The drawing is accurate. Time and the Slade will knock the nonsense out of him, or her. Make 'em realize that the picturesque boat was also useful to fish from. That one can get pickled capers from nasturtiums to flavour the perch. That those pretty mountains can send some pretty snow storms all over the lakes when the tourists have all gone home. Why the devil is it that no young person ever realizes that in any part of the world what is picturesque to visitors is a mere fact of life to the natives? Something so familiar that they never see it, not even when they use it. Oh, of course they can feel a presence! Or an absence? A boat, a goat, a dog, a cat, a son, a daughter. If one of these chaps lost his wife he would see with a heart-breaking clarity a face he might not have noticed for forty years. I suppose nothing but experience makes a student realize that nobody can paint anything until he feels it rather than sees it, better still not until he remembers it long after he buried the mere image of it in his memory. He will pass by some place, some corner, some house, some face a thousand times after he first saw it and not notice it in the way a painter notices things until, only God knows why, years and years after he looks at it and at once wants to shove it into a picture. The past is always a bit of the present. After all isn't that the kind of stuff every artist deals in? Scraps found at the bottom of a boot-box, stuck in a book like a marker, or where a fellow I used to know used always keep his cheese, rolled up in a sock in the hot press. I'm sure that is where the Mona Lisa came from. Every Madonna worth a damn. The half forgotten. I must leave you. I have to drop in at the nursing home.'

The old boy's voice trailed away gently, just as he not so much walked away as shuffled to the door while Ruth blushing to her guts with vexation, stood glaring at her shameful water colour, barely hearing the exchange at the door: the younger man asking how was 'she' today and the old man replying, 'Not well. Not at all well', in a bewildered tone as if he were trying to remember some face to which he had not given a thought these forty years.

It was this moment at the Slade that she recalled as the little pink campanile began to move in a slow half-circle to the north. Never looked at by the people living around it? Invisible even to the few who regularly prayed in it? Some presence, some familiar, some memory that if one of those locals were to emigrate to Manhattan or Boston might bring tears; like its one electric light bracket, its one village tree, its old busted zinc bucket they used to be so accustomed to hear rolling in the pastor's backyard of windy nights that they no longer heeded it. Like one of their goats, dogs, cats. Like Paul Potter's four bulls that he had resurrected from his memories not of bulls but of beer houses, of days and nights with the herring fleet, of those boring years when his country seemed to be always at war with Spain, of fat serving girls in fat feather beds, of mornings after when the bells tolling down from the Zuydertorn hammered his sore head. Potter had seen bulls galore but never exactly just like these. And anyway how the blazes could any painter have persuaded four bulls to hold the pose for all the hours during which he recorded them? The man had recreated a thousand moments of his life in a candle-lit attic packed with hastening clouds and infinite space and wandering herds and northern light and called his life-story 'Four Bulls'.

The campanile had floated out of sight, already a nest of memory, and she was open to agree that it is perhaps in that broody nest that all art wherever engendered breaks its shell, opens its yellow maw to be fed by its begetter, and expertly spreads its furry wings for its first flight, already alert, thanks to some ancestral memory, for the magpie and the neighbour's cat.

Ever since that conjunction of a grumpy old painter in the Slade, and Paul Potter's bulls, and a tiny pink campanile seen from a stuffy carriage creeping across a Piedmontese plain, the idea that familiar experiences are the easiest to forget and the most fruitful to recall had nestled in her phylactery. Presently she added to the importance of the familiar a phrase she came on in a poem by Yeats praising 'heart-revealing intimacy'. The words now stayed in her phylactery as things, as ideas never to be exposed, as she had found out when she first tried to talk about her credo in a pub to four other would-be painters. One of them, a woman devoted to abstract art, pretended to assume that by words like 'familiar' and 'intimacy' she meant illicit sexual relations, and two of the other three mercilessly followed her lead. After that she kept her mouth shut about forgotten memories, intimacy and the familiar, excepting only for one of the three others, an Irishman, who seemed to sympathize with her; and after all they were both descendants of lost tribes, conquered peoples ground into the dust, wanderers aware that it takes centuries of forgotten memories to turn a new local habitation into an old home. In all she met him again in their alien metropolis only three times. She heard then that he had weakly surrendered, become first a commercial artist, then moved to Manchester, finally emigrated to Western Australia, married and settled in Perth. She, fortunate to have got a job in one of the well-known, small London galleries, stubbornly held on, now not so much a Sunday painter as a secret painter, as coy about her passion as if art were a glorious young god desirable beyond the reach of all but the barely perceptible few.

Now and again she would get an amiably satirical card from her confidant in Perth (W.A.) signed Liam, she had forgotten his patronymic and he never gave an address nor said anything more intelligible than 'How is your HRI doing?', meaning her Heart Revealing Intimacy. These cards were all aimed to arrive on such self-mocking occasions as Mothers' Day, or April Fools' Day. Once on Saint Valentine's Day he became loquacious enough to claim that the remains of this wandering saintly *Irishman*, that word underlined, are NOT, that word underlined three times, to be found in Rome but under the high altar of the Carmelite Church in Aungier Street in Dublin. She was relieved that he never expected an answer. Her HRI was not doing well, neither in nor out of London. She could paint, yes. So can thousands upon thousands. She could execute a happy design, yes. But the ultimate break through custom and convention to what she still called intimacy (and maybe that sour woman in that pub was right about intimacy being a sexual power) she had never achieved, no matter where or how she sought it. Italy mocked her. To her horror she found that Holland also was picturesque. She did once hear a whisper in Spain. Then last March, she got from Perth a postcard commemorating the common birthday of Saint Patrick and one Bobby Jones. It bore a sketch of an Irishman in kneebreeches, tails, a comic hat with a vast shamrock stuck in it, leading a small pig and waving a shillelagh, saying 'For God's sake send me a sketch of some corner of ould Oireland'. This time it did carry an address, and the full signature, Liam Clancy. It also showed a stain with an arrow pointing to it, saying 'Teardrop?'

So three months later here she is, lying in a deck-chair outside a hotel called Carrigduv House in South-West Cork hiding behind her eyelids. She has been here ten days, is due to return to London inside four more, and every canvas she attempted each day was daubed over every morning after, once spiked again and again in a fury by her Spanish heels. She is not weeping because her holiday has been a failure: she is in a state of terror, because she at last feels certain that she is.

For her first few days in Carrigduv she had overflowed with happiness. 'This', she felt, 'is exactly what I have always been looking for': immediate cognition, doors thrown wide open on Liberty Hall, a fortress of coequality in friendship, tolerance, understanding, warm compassion, a Land of Cockaigne indifferent to, unaware of the venal world beyond the surrounding mountains. After four days her painting informed her that if all this were truly so it did not show in her work. Alerted she began to feel uneasy. She became suspicious. Each new expert, heartless painting, dismissed, denied, destroyed, put her on guard. She presently became inescapably aware of one of those all-too-recognizable flavours that might fling open the eyes of any guest anywhere at the end of an otherwise flawless banquet. Was it instant coffee? Japanese Cognac? Staffordshire port? The peculiar aroma of Scottish cigars? 'All-too-recognizable' because she was by now far from unfamiliar with this experience of betrayal, estrangement, alienation. Had it always been her error to have asked too much? Even though all she had ever wanted was a little of the smell and touch of that familiar experience that so many people call Home? And yet she had to admit that Ireland had some virtues. A certain coequality of feeling between her fellow-residents in Carrigduv House did operate perfectly, even though she had also finally become aware that it worked only after the manner of continental guidebooks that graduate the virtues of hotels by means of crossed forks: five forks for Traditional and Luxurious coequality; four forks for Top Class equality; three for Very Comfortable, two for Comfortable, one for Plain but Adequate, and none at all for places where, like Mimi in *La Bohème*, the visitors did not attend the egalitarian mass even if they did pray a lot to the good Lord.

True, she had had to concede, in her rational Jewish way, that she had noted on her very first night that a priest (a monsignor she presumed from the triangle of purple between his chin and his vest) sat at the head of the long table while she had been seated at the end. However, not being a contentious woman, she attributed this to what she tolerantly called their religion. She had been rather more disturbed by frequent long-distance telephone calls broadcast all over the house by the roaring maids who mediated them. 'Who's that calling? Speak up! Dublin? Louder! Who do you want and what d'yeh want him for? Jamesy, there's somebody here wants the doctor. I'm asking you where the divil the doctor is. Out fishing? Oh, Jasus! Are ye there Dublin? The doctor is gone to Cork on a life and death job. Do that! I'll tell him you'll call again after six o'clock.' Or:— 'Who's calling? London? Who do you want and what d'yeh want him for? He's out. What name did you say? Fiddle and Rich? Riddle and Fitch? Speak up please. Brokers? What message? Cold? Old? Gold? It's what? Roaring? Soaring? I'll tell him. And good luck to you, too.' Whereupon the world would disappear again for a while.

In the end it was the silences that broke the spell. There was nothing, she found, about which she could not talk freely with anybody so long as the two of them were alone and that she or the other were quick to add, at an appropriate moment, a dollop of oily jocosity to soften the salad-dressing of their conversation. If a third joined them the conversation became more guarded. In a foursome, unless the subject mentioned were the weather, sport, fish, drink or politics the talk in hollow murmurs died away. At first she genially thought, 'Oh, well! If they want to live insulated from whatever it is they want to be insulated from why should they not?' But today, so close as she was to total despair, she rebelled. These Irish bastards were just like every other set of bastards whose job was to sell illusions: the Spanish Tourist Board, the Italian Tourist Board, the stolid Dutch, the solid Swiss, the jolly Germans, the fervent Indians, the honest English. These Irish were of all the worst insofar as they believed their own illusions, and at that moment here down the finely-wooded avenue to the hotel there most aptly and appropriately came a new bit of their make-believe – a horse-drawn caravan, painted in the gaudiest, jokeyest, gypsyiest, shamrock-green colours trundling between sentries of trees elegantly planted generations ago by some now forgotten English-into-quarter-Irish-into-halfIrish-into-threequartersIrish-into AngloIrish who had in the beginning come here to grab, to settle, to build, to boss, to farm, to nurture, to plant, to live for ever and ever, until their very last generation saw that what had been for three centuries a homestead had become a mere Departure Lounge and took off for the England they must for centuries have considered their more real home.

As the caravan drew to a halt before the hotel joyous screams from the kitchen preceded the billowing outrush of two white aprons. One apron ballooned to the van. The other, seeing their English guest lying on the deck chair, deflected excitedly towards her. 'Miss Goodman, it is Mister Caraway! All Ireland is out looking for him!' and ran to join her companion who, clutching the gaudy vehicle, was meantime screaming to its driver, 'Mister Caraway, the Guards are out looking for ye!' The daughter-of-the-house came forward to explain sedately:

'It was a police message, Miss Goodman, on the Radio this morning. "Would Mr Roger Caraway of Bristol believed to be touring in the southwest of Ireland in a horse-drawn caravan immediately contact his home in Bristol where Mrs Caraway lies seriously ill, or contact any Garda station." Actually we were expecting him, he telephoned last night asking for a double room and by sheer luck we had had a drop-out, but I doubt if after all this hullabaloo he will occupy it tonight.'

The man who leaped from the caravan was about forty or fifty, smiling widely, sure of his welcome, eyes quizzical, face lean, very much what used to be known as a man's man, the sort who might once have been a boxer, or a reliable hand on the rudder of a yacht, extrovert, born for action in the open air. After him clambered a younger woman, dark haired, shapely enough to wear jeans seductively, her features pleasant but undistinguished. Only a partial friend would call her handsome and only a confirmed enemy plain. Ruth admired the agility with which the manageress defused the embarrassing police message while transferring it to its addressee:

' ... "contact your home in Bristol where your mother Mrs Caraway lies seriously ill ...'''

The Englishman looked his dismay at his dismayed companion. She, palms up, indicated that he had no option. He glared back at the gypsy caravan.

'Cork is the nearest airport. Hire a car? Taxi? Bus? With this contraption it would take me four days to get back to Cork. What on earth can I do with the blessed thing?'

From a deck-chair on the lawn a black-haired, brown-eyed, sallow-faced young woman told him.

'You could have it collected. Cost you a lot! Or, if it is any help to you I could take it over from you. I was in any case proposing to return to Cork in three days' time.'

'I would be most grateful. But can you manage a horse?'

'If that were a racehorse I could ride it in the Grand National. My people bred fighting horses, and fighting bulls, for generations in Spain.'

Within hours she had entered into a conspiracy of scandalous laughter with the entire parish. The situation suited them down to the ground. It was a perfect image of their concept of life – a web of illusion and disaster, farce and factuality. Even the monsignor enjoyed their sidelong jokes about adultery. She became singled out by her conspicuous absences from the hotel and her observable presences in the wicked caravan now moored beside the wall of their venerable graveyard; warmly welcomed to the hotel for meals and drinks; identifiable by every local; courteously escorted at night across two dewy fields by never less than two residents of the hotel. It did not accordingly surprise her on her third and last afternoon in the caravan, seated on its steps writing to her friend in Australia to confess her own failure as a painter, that two men should appear behind the portion of the low graveyard wall she overlooked, begin forthwith to dig and, on observing her, wave amiably. In their urban clothes, they looked incongruous among the ancient yews and mossy headstones. Presently two more men arrived with shovels to help with the digging of the grave. They also wore citified suits and pointed shoes. Had they come from England for the funeral? They too gave her such a cheerful salute, which she as cheerfully returned though she also felt so sensitive about her nearness, immediately across the wall, to so gravely intimate a ceremony that she retired to her tiny table by her tiny window to complete her letter. Then, still observing them cheerfully at work and observing that she was so observed, she emerged when the grave was some four feet deep to ask whom were they burying. One of the four, a brawny, blue-eyed, white-toothed giant, handsome in a bullish peasant way, nodded cheerfully towards one of the other three.

'Mick's father-in-law.' His eyes danced mischievously over his companions, and in a tone that revealed that they had been discussing her he went on. 'Jo Canty his name was. Oho! Jo was a wild one in his day, so he was! We were just saying that you'll have good company every night from this on.' Being four feet down his appreciative eyes were level with her legs. 'Jo was a rover in his day. You'd do well to lock your door tight once the dark falls.'

Relaxed, laughing, she sat on her caravan's steps and watched and heard them gasp occasional jokes about the late Jo, smack shovels on clay and stone, sink slowly to their bent backs. At last the grave was dug. It had been hard work, the day hot, they paused, a bottle was produced with a yarn or two about the dead Rover's thirst. The giant fellow held up the bottle and invited her to join them. She agreed eagerly, proffered glasses and the bucket of well-water beside her, cool still under its moist napkin. At once the giant and a fair fellow who was as tall but not so broad, vaulted the wall to help her over. There were no introductions. She just stood glass in hand among the four wiping their foreheads, dusting their Sunday clothes, flecking their

English-looking shoes, exchanging more scabrous memories of the Rover's life. By her feet she noted two big-eyed skulls of older relatives of the deceased culled from the dirt so as not to startle the women of the family the next day when Jo's coffin would be lowered and covered. Presently the giant clambered down into the grave to try it for length. Lying face up to her he asked her, 'Were you ever in a grave?' She laughed, 'Not yet!' He asked her would she like to see how it feels. She said she would, whereupon, helped by the others, he clambered up and she was slowly lowered to lay herself full length on the dry earth, looking up past their four faces at the racing clouds. She had never felt the sky so strongly, nor its dark and white herds passing so swiftly away. No more words were spoken. A hush came over them all as if death had suddenly become real or some tabu broken. She realized this when she heard one of them say earnestly to the others, 'Don't any of ye, for God's sake, let Janie hear one word about this!' She stood, held her hands up, was lifted out. The four gathered their forks and shovels, helped the stranger back over her wall. Then all separated with silent waves.

She at once set up her easel and canvas and began to paint with concentration. She painted first an oblong frame of Vandyke brown to represent the band of crumbling earth that had enclosed the perspective she had seen upward from her grave. She painted at the centre of each side of this oblong a head laughing down at her. She then concentrated on the centre of the canvas, covering it vigorously but accurately with white and dark clouds moving swiftly westward across the sky. By the time she had finished she was hours late for dinner at Carrigduv House, had not eaten all day, was unaware of hunger, kept raising and lowering her eyes between the twilit clouds and her twilit picture like a woman in prayer. She was aware that something had happened inside her that never had happened before. She looked dazedly around her. It would soon be dusk. Her grey horse head-bowed stood as motionless in the middle of the field as if it had been let out to grass a hundred years ago. The dusk was as silent as that grave behind. She went into her van, found the remains of a packet of biscuits, ate them, drank a glass of water, lay on the bed and became unconscious.

She woke at six to full sunlight. It was time for her to depart. She delayed. She set up her easel to sketch a quick reminder of her clouds, vertically this time, above a foreground of beach slit by a fish-shaped pool placidly reflecting the floaters above it. This one would be a beauty. A copy of it would be the envy of Australia. She was presently startled by the funeral bell from the village church but insisted on one last record: a cumulo-nimbus of whiteness erupting tower upon tower from the volcano-peak of a mountain the colour of a bruise.

A basso roll of thunder made her turn her head to the east. The sky had darkened. Rain was coming. She barely had time to tackle her horse and start on the road for Cork before the cloud burst. It battered her roof like hailstones. She could see little between her horse's ears but the fog of rain dancing madly on the tarmac, and she saw this only by constantly wiping her eyes, but not this time to efface tears: she was laughing joyfully at the memory of how her father back in Spain used to laugh whenever he remembered his father's laughter at the memory of the way her great-grandfather used simultaneously pray and curse whenever a thunderstorm came rolling down the Pyrenees over his woods and crops, shaking his clasped hands to plead with God in the bewildered words of Job: 'Who can master the clouds in wisdom? Who can stay the battles of heaven? Who maketh the clouds his chariot?'

From this on she would watch them from her high Hampstead windows sailing in over London before the south-easters, slanting misty rain on the city's million roofs and parks, or unloading downpours as straight as stair-rods, or blowing white and sun-polished out past Land's End to the Atlantic, there at the last drawing their light shadows over that grave where she had been ravished by Huesca.

The Wings of the Dove

A Modern Sequel

(To rewrite a great novel as a short story can only be regarded either as an impertinence or an experiment. I have made the experiment with The Wings of the Dove to find out what is gained or lost by writing fiction briefly or at length. I have made no great discoveries, and it is more than possible that my reader will have made them all long ago without going to any bother at all. They are: that the writer of a short story does not travel – he is content, like an astronaut, or somebody on a package tour, to be shot to his destination; that he then, unlike the gregarious novelist, can proceed to operate quite successfully with as few as two or three characters; and that the novelist, again like the astronaut or the package tourer, does not always arrive at journey's end. Stendhal's Charterhouse is a famous example of a delightful journey some of whose travellers are to this day floating loosely in the air. It seemed to me that The Wings of the Dove cries out for a sequel telling us what happened in the end to its two lovers Kate Croy and Morton Densher, whom James ruthlessly abandoned to the elements when he considered that he had squeezed them dry.

To bring the characters closer to our cameras I have dated my sequel in or around 1970 and everybody in the novel may be taken as rejuvenated accordingly. When the sequel opens Densher is seated beside his wife dining in the old Café Royal – which has also been rejuvenated accordingly.)

'Well? What pretty girl are you staring at now?' Densher's wife asked him with a frown half way between amusement and suspicion.

No man a hero to his wife, nor even, the sudden memory warned him, to his mistress. His eyebrows directed her attention across the restaurant to an elderly couple of about his own age squabbling with the head waiter over their bill. Kate Croy, forty years after he first laid eyes on her in this same restaurant! It was her throat that had alerted him. 'Thy swan's neck and dark abundant hair.' Tower of ivory. Or it used to be a tower of ivory, as smooth as her roll of black hair falling over her white shoulders.

'You who know everybody who are they?'

'Read Morton Densher the best-informed social columnist in London. The Man who Knows Everybody. They are Lord and Lady Macbane. She was once a much photographed beauty. Clever too. Marked out for success, which, as you see, she achieved.'

'She has also achieved a stoop. Who was she?'

'That is a rather more delicate question. She was what people used to call A Nobody in the good old days before the '39 – '45. Bonny Prince Churchill and all that. When every man and woman knew his/her station in life. Those happy years before the Revolution. Sic., as we say in the trade. A *sic.* joke. She was not only A Nobody but a penniless Nobody. Name? It escapes me. Crew? Craw? Croy! That's it. Katherine Croy. Irish originally, I believe, her father had been a quartermaster-sergeant or something. In charge of military stores. Got into trouble, fired, cashiered. Some dark shadow. In fact I may have been the first man to talent-spot her when she cannot have been more than nineteen, one wet day during the war, here in this Café Royal, taking in umbrellas, mackintoshes, gas masks, handing out numbered tabs. That evening I gave her a couple of lines of accolade in my column. 'They Also Serve.' Even then she was ravishing.'

From the Latin *rapere*: rapture; also rape. The film whistled backwards until its tail flipped off the white screen. Seeing her home to grubby Chirk Street. Meetings in pubs. Discreet approaches in parks. That garret he got her in Paddington. His bachelor flat on the King's Road. Jesus!

'From taking in parcels to taking in peers? She must have learned fast.'

'An Irish gift? Or just the usual colonial gift? Indians do it. Blacks do it. Australians do it. Jews do it. Let's fall in love. I swear Becky Sharp was some little copy-cat adventuress Thackeray met in Dublin or Glasgow or Aberystwyth, which is the only word I know that has eight consonants in a row. The only other time I saw the future Lady Macbeth – I beg her pardon, Lady Macbane – was two or three months later, in a B.B.C. canteen dishing out cups of wartime tea made of sawdust. She was doing it as loftily as a lady to the manor born. Feeding starving refugees. Practising?'

He should know who had by then already started to lead her through the golden mirrors of this old Café, or of what was left of its original old Anglo-French rococo pillars, painted ceilings, velvet benches, marble tables, emanations now of a century of painters, writers, scribblers, composers, few of them more than names to him in his twenties, meaningless to Chirk Street. Max, Wilde, A.R. Orage, Koteliansky, Middleton Murry, C. Carswell, K. Mansfield, Augustus John, Acton, Connolly, on down through Roy Campbell, Dylan Thomas, Louis MacNeice to what V. Woolf bitchily called 'the literary underworld'. The lower Brewer Street end was more staid (one of her picked-up words) than the marble-topped tables up front. Back there a sanctity of white linen for diners and lunchers. Learned fast? It took her only one visit to decide that she preferred the quarters aft. 'More solid' had been her decisive phrase. 'More pricey' had been his practical thought. When he said so she pretended she had meant 'more cosy'. And after all there were those masked streets outside, darkness probed by hooded hand-torches, padding feet, perhaps a rare taxi, distant bumps of anti-aircraft fire down river. With a paternal amusement, as time went on, he came to interpret her secret-if-real reason for by-passing the front deck: he loved the catlike way she used to snuggle down among what she once called 'important people', as if all those diners about her had only just emerged for the first time that day from secret underground bunkers humming day and night to conquer the brute conditions of life overhead. Analogues of her own battle in her lofty Paddington garret? He would glance around him with the cynical smile appropriate to his profession and note how lecherously all those spivs, flashers, profiteers, general hangers-on of the actual London under-world kept on savouring her beauty. But would anybody ever be able to resist those wonder-enlarged brown eyes, that midnight cloud, her blend of the artless child and the womanly appraiser, as when her two big eyes would peer at him excitedly when he waved aside such wartime lures as 'Fillet of hake, sir? Very nice, very fresh'; or 'Sirloin of beef, sir?', or 'Jugged hare, sir?', with such sidelong sniffs to her as 'Whale meat, my dear', or 'Horse for certain!', or 'Common rabbit, my darling!', in favour of seagulls' eggs and their moderately decent Australian Moselle. It was this guttersnipe innocence that had first evoked his protective affection. Gradually compassion, then passion, finally admiration for her sheer guts reduced him to complete subjection as he became aware of the dear girl's determination to be free forever of beastly Chirk Street. Inevitably, after a bad bomber's night-raid, a bloody thing that went on for hours, squads and squads of them, he chose to discover in her an ascetic heroine, self-disciplined, will-powered, when she casually mentioned the following morning that she had spent most of the night looking through her garret window at the searchlights sweeping beautifully through the stars in search of the Gerries. 'Well?' she had protested when he protested. 'What else was I to do? Crawl downstairs to that cheery, dreary, beery crowd of men, women, kids, babies singing in a stinking basement?'

Learned fast? Within six months of their becoming lovers she had come to know herself so to a nicety that everyone he casually introduced her to, would sooner or later assure him that she was regularly clever, a lady, as one shrewd woman put it, who would never judge herself cheap. For his part he was delighted to watch her develop, though it would probably have taken one of her own countrywomen to appreciate fully the skill of yet 'another wild wan' smoothly changing gear to match the speed of the emotional traffic around her. How long, by contrast, it had taken him to notice her speedometer! Colleen to climber, dreamer to darer, temptress to huntress, gambler to *grande dame*, artless Kate, admirable Kate, an ambitious, acquisitive, predatory – My God! he had been blind! – adventuress.

'What on earth did he see in her?' his wife asked staring across the white tables. 'Or was she all that pretty then? How could he possibly have thought that she would suit him?'

But, to be sure, if one had understood those changing times properly at the time, had taken their measure coldly, it would not have seemed such a great jump for either of them to ride beside the other. Is there all that difference between gamblers? He did have his ancestral home somewhere in the highlands, and a couple of thousand acres that probably did feed a snipe or two. He was handsome. A gallant soldier. Decorated twice. A member of White's, or the Carlton, or the Burlingham. Holding a seat on the board of a company or two. A man with a fine past, a hopeful future, and no cash.

'What did he see in her? Well, her considerable looks. And it would have helped that by then she had become a model.'

'A model? Only a model?'

His own stupidity to have put it into her head, far-seeing for her, not for himself. Still, the times again! Those extraordinary years after the war ended when life in London became a mixture of austerity and life hunger such as had not been known since the Gay Nineties. In those hungry 'forties and 'fifties a man was not permitted by law to have pockets in his jackets (to save material); everybody virtually ate by meal-ticket; women who for years had been tying kitchen dusters under their chins for scarves, mending torn panties over and over, ferreting for silk stockings on the Black Market, wearing Blitz grey day after day until they could at last at least look at pictures of frills, furbelows, great silly hats, flounced frocks divinely, wastefully, unpatriotically designed by chaps who only a couple of years ago had been shock commandos and kamikaze pilots. 'Only a model?' Only a perambulating sunflower? A fair comparison. Time was when to be a model you could be as fat as a Rubens so long as you wore no clothes. Now a model meant an exquisitely emaciated Botticelli loaded with clothes. Does some post-Churchill Socialist grumble, 'Only a lord?' True; but a lord transformed suddenly into vintage 1880 when both his worse and better off ancestors hung around stage doors hoping to carry off an actress or a dancer, as it were on horseback, to some lost keep in Cumberland, or the Cambrian hills or Connemara. Now squabbling over a bill.

With an inner shrug he told himself that the whole story should be dropped at once; but the barber of Midas had to tell about his master's asses' ears to somebody even if it were only to a hole in the ground; meaning, how the hell could anybody possibly have foreseen that his love's widowed, bloody old Aunt Maud Lowder would, on hearing of her impoverished sister's death, at once have ordered her chauffeur to drive her across the Park to miserable Chirk Street out of her tall, rich, heavy, lonely, empty house at Lancaster Gate – she certainly had never judged herself cheap – taken one astounded look at her exquisite young niece and carried her back forthwith, to live with her in luxury and loneliness. Still, it was a good investment all round: a bounteous new interest for herself, fresh opportunities for Miss Croy, a novelty for her guests, who included Lord Macbane, in short for everybody except this who-ever-he-was Mister Morton Densher, some Fleet Street scribbler by whom the girl, with as little regard for her future as her fool of a mother had ever shown for herself, had apparently (What was the vulgar modern phrase?) allowed herself to be 'picked up'. Mr Densher was nevertheless permitted, very rarely, to make formal calls, either for watchful inspection, or as a demonstration of Aunt Maud's consanguineous tolerance of these extraordinary topsy-turvy post-war years, or perhaps because she was operating some impenetrable sisterly strategy on behalf of her niece. The lovers were otherwise reduced to discreet strolls in the Park, stealthy *billets doux*, exasperatingly brief assignations in his flat. After all he could not in decency expect Kate to push her luck too far, nor did she encourage him to do so.

'That, Merty,' said his wifely hole-in-the-ground, 'was an excellent Fleuris. The old Café Royal never lets you down, does it?'

He raised a finger to the wine waiter for the red, and looked across at Lady Macbane.

'So! A beautiful and ambitious girl, a worldly aunt, a door regularly opened to important people such as Macbane, or interesting chance visitors, like that wealthy young woman from Boston. What was her name? Theale, Millicent Theale. Who took such an enormous shine to our Miss Croy that they became heart-friends, became you might almost say mirror models. In fact that was where our Miss Croy's public career began.' He nodded across the restaurant. 'And there you have the end of it.'

'Have I? You said "wealthy". Was she also pretty?'

'The Theale girl? Oh, quite reasonably good-looking.'

'A helpful aunt? A handsome heiress? A poor but very pretty young woman from Chirk Street? And the noble lord chose the beggarmaid. Well, *good* for him!'

'I'm only guessing you realize? For all I know it may have been as Wellington said of Waterloo a damned close thing.'

'Tell me more about *la belle Americaine*. Did you ever meet her?'

'Once. At some big formal gathering for ... for what I can't now remember. I also heard about her later on from acquaintances of associates of friends who moved in Mrs Lowder's set. Their impression of her one way and another was that she was just a sweet, shining little New England dove with jewelled wings, filled with what somebody described as an embarrassing determination to see everything, meet everybody, do everything, go everywhere, to gleam, to glow, to live. You see, the real object of her visit to London was to consult a famous specialist in Portland Place. In the event her trajectory was of the briefest.'

'That,' his wife remarked with a shrewdness that startled him, 'may have been why our Cinderella over there took such a shine to her. Both dying to live. Life has its meanings.'

The wine waiter had broached the red wine, poured a taste,

proffered, observed. In admiration he raised his glass to his wife, nodded absently to the waiter. Milly Theale.

'True! One of them poor in cash the other in health? Rival backgrounds. The prosperity of Louisburg Square, Aunt Maud Lowder's upholstered house in Lancaster Place.'

La Croy was repairing her make-up in her hand mirror; her rolling eyes were still chestnut brown, her rolling lips were gone thin. Give her her due, it was inevitable that she should have outdone everybody in her attachment to Milly, not only in envy of her new American friend's prodigious position in the world but in admiration and pity of her courage in the face of the oncoming night. Envy. Pity. Admiration. People have done terrible things out of sheer envy. Pity has known its own violence. Admiration can inspire. Like a ghost Lady Macbane had vanished. Kate Croy was gathering up her purple gloves and a couple of elegantly bound packages preparatory to rising.

It stabbed his pride yet once again that for all his efforts over the years he had never been able to say exactly 'That was the moment' when she had floated the seed of her terrible plan into his mind so softly that he became only half aware of its poison three months after it had begun to discolour his blood stream. Even then all he had been driven to say, during one of their assignations in his minute flat on the King's Road, lying on his back, hands clasped behind his head, all passion spent, was 'Have I noticed, Kate, or do I imagine it, that you have begun to be rather cryptic with me these last few weeks? Do tell me why are we two, acknowledged lovers, at least so acknowledged by ourselves,' glancing at their clothes laid across his two chairs, 'temporising about finally declaring our love to the world?' That was all he had said but he was so troubled by the half-memory of a whisper, or a frown, or a suggestive earlier smile about pretty Milly the Millyonaire, and by his agreeing that it must indeed be galling for anybody to be the mere companion of a rich old lady, and his saying 'We were so happy when you were all on your own in that garret in Paddington', that he added firmly, 'We have simply got to make a move!' at which she flung the sheet aside, cried 'We?', rose and dressed. They parted in virtual silence.

It was not until the following day that he weighed between two steps that last word of hers, failing even then to observe that by his use of a mere pronoun he had accepted some involvement, however involuntary, in whatever she was being cryptic about. That he was entangled in some sort of strategy did not truly occur to him until a couple of weeks later, one windy afternoon in the Park, when, under a browning beech, he spoke sympathetically of Milly's falling leaves and Kitty said tempestuously, 'Oh please do *please* let our poor darling have her little adventure,' to which he of course warmly agreed, saying 'She really is prodigious in her determination to live.' They had walked on in silence for a while. Then, tardily he said that he did not see how he particularly could help, or indeed why he should be put forward in her fight for life. They walked on again, Kate now kicking the leaves before her, until at a passionate groan beside him, he clasped his beloved's hand in admiration of her feelings of pity for their poor friend. Kate threw away his hand, halted, faced around, cried that all she was doing was trying to break him into what, in Milly's heartbreaking circumstances, everybody around him must clearly expect of him. He had stared at her in bewilderment laced for the first time by a fleck of fear. 'Expect? Everybody?' He had looked vacantly around the Park. After all Kate had assured him, and on his rare, formally permitted calls to Lancaster Gate he had observed for himself, that Milly was always modestly, shyly undemanding, almost retiring, grateful for any attention, however ferociously she might secretly be importuning the gods for yet another and another sip of the wine of life. Anyway what special relief could he, Merton Densher, a mere journalist, bring to this doomed citadel? That autumn afternoon in the Park Kate had not pursued his portentous question; but within a week the sybil herself answered it in a manner dramatic enough to redouble his mounting fears. Quite simply, casually, gaily in fact, as if it were just one more of her childish 'adventures' she had it conveyed to him, that she had taken over a Venetian palace on the Grand Canal, the Palazzo Leporelli, and was inviting everybody, 'including you, of course,' Kate transmitted unmistakably, to tread its stage.

Coming up as it were out of the *caves* beneath the Café Royal – although he had long since learned that wives also can be sibylline – his echo at his side was saying, 'Darling, why are you so dead set against celebrating our silver anniversary in Venice? You say you are bored with Paris. I am fed up with Florence. Rome is as raucous as a fun fair. The Riviera is a mob. It is odd really that we have never tried Venice!'

'All Venice is good for is a Thomas Mann film about dying!'

But she went on rattling about 'all those exciting plans to keep Venice alive and floating, plans that everybody is always...'

In fact everybody loaned a hand to float Milly's Venetian plan: visitors homeward bound for Boston and New York, Aunt Maud's regulars from London, desultory ambassadors from the Home Counties or farther, Kate and Macbane of course, and how could anybody for whatever different reason refuse Milly's invitations? He, however, quite differently to any of all these preferred not to stay at the *palazzo* but in modest lodgings up-canal from the Rialto for the sake ostensibly of memories from his student days, privately to be alone occasionally with his Kitty, most of all in order to be at once sufficiently close to Milly for kindness and good manners yet not so close as to overheat those alleged expectations of him that Kitty continued to press upon him just so near to once too often that he found himself driven brutally to press her to come out into the open once and for all from beyond her vague swayings, suggestions, implyings, encouragements, to speak out, to define exactly what were her hopes for her ailing dove. He gripped her wrists. Her stare forbade him. He stared her down.

'Merty, you must surely see it by now?'

'Is it this then? That you have bit by bit so arranged the condition of things, that she has confided in you that she has come to like me?'

'You cannot be so blind as not to see that she likes you very much. And more. And you know that she is doomed.'

He released her. Quietly, fatefully, fearfully:

'I begin to see. Since she is to die soon you mean that I should show love for her betimes?'

'I have begged you to let her have her little adventure.'

'You? My only love! Say this?'

She slowly lowered her chin but her eyes still fixed his from beneath her brows. He at last unravelled her terrible code, at last spoke it.

'I am to join then in her very last adventure? I am to love her even into marriage? So that when death has taken place you and I shall have her money?'

It struck him as fine in her that even in that moment she had not flinched or minced.

'I mean so that in the natural course of things you and I shall at last be free.'

What did not occur to him until too late was that because he did not then and there turn and leave her he tolerated that word 'free'. He had walked with her in silence back to the precincts of the Palazzo Leporelli. On his way to his lodgings he thought, at every glance that he gave to a passing face, 'Free? Who is free?' Not Kitty certainly, bound by ropes of passion to him, and by her equal passion for the freedom that he had called money; just as he was bound both by his passion for her and his compassion for a dying girl who even as she slowly folded her wings still implored life to yield her the experience of one selfless love.

He stayed on in Venice, loyal to whom or what he would never understand. He tried it, his own phrase, for six weeks, badgered by his London editor, daily counting his pennies, stayed long after both Aunt Maud and Kitty tactfully left this autumnal city of virtually empty hotels where only a few stubborn tourists lingered in hope of one last · hour of romance until all their dreams of a Saint Martin's summer collapsed under downpours that leaped back a foot high over the fogged expanses of the lagoons and winds from the Adriatic that rocked the most sheltered *sandalo* in the most greasy gully of this streetless city. He had nothing to do but wander collar up, opened umbrella at the lance, between museum, *caffè* and church, miserably aware that she did not care a jot about this beastly weather so long as she had her dear Merton's afternoon visits to the *palazzo* and his nightly presence alone with her at and after dinner to keep at bay far worse demons than these winds and rains besieging every window in the streaming city outside. His sense of shame and weakness, his futile two-faced pity for a young woman whose beauty gleamed through the frail eggshell of her body not now like a springtime sunrise but like a winter sunset, became final despair, utter defeat on one unusually inclement afternoon as he sought shelter from a cloudburst under the wet, crowded, shuffling arcade of the great Piazza. There he was halted by a familiar face espied through the window of Florian's restaurant. It was Lord Macbane seated by a small table before a neglected glass, not reading the copy of the *Figaro* on his knee, glaring in front of him at the rococo wall.

One glance in through that misty window and he identified a spy. Macbane's astonishing presence was clearly a sequel to some equally fruitless earlier approach in London to the little heiress. He passed on his way through the crowds wandering blindly for two hours before he dared to face the Palazzo Leporelli. Yet, hopeless though he was against the horror that he knew was awaiting him there, he was still, up to the last second after he pulled the chain of the old inward-echoing bell, prepared to enter as usual without being announced. He knew that the game was up when the great door squeaked open just a few inches and he was quite held-off by her x-ray-eyed *major duomo*, her 'great' Eugenio, the personification of Venice's heavy-lidded concept of life as one long clandestine, venal intrigue, informing him through the chained crack politely, which is to say insinuatingly, mockingly, that *la signora padrona* was not receiving today, and slowly closed the door on one who up to a few hours ago had been of all callers the prince.

Standing on the palace steps by the flopping canal he surrendered to the fact. Macbane, unable to tolerate that anybody should win what he had lost had told her, no doubt in the most gentlemanly manner, about her charming Merton's manifest relations with her dear Kate. Milly, upstanding American freewoman, would have gratefully thanked him, graciously got rid of him, then alone with the winds, and the rain, and the waters turned her face to the wall. She was up there now, facing it.

'So?' Kate had greeted him, poised as always and smiling, three weeks before Christmas. 'You have been in London rather a while before calling on me.'

He stood close to her before the warming fire, looking intensely into those lovely brown eyes that looked neutrally into his. He drew from his pocket a long, pale-blue envelope, unopened, franked in Venice, and not ceasing to look into her eyes held up the envelope before them. Almost invisibly lowering her lids she intimated to him that she recognized the hand and foresaw what its frail fingers had written. That there should be no doubt about the matter this time he said it.

'In her prodigious generosity she would have us rich enough to be free to marry.'

Still poised, she stared at him. He crumpled the blue letter and tossed it into the yellow and red fire and said strongly:

'Mind you, Kate, I'd still marry you inside an hour.'

'As we were?'

'As we were!' he answered firmly.

Their silence was not too painfully long. She glanced at the door, went towards it and, with one hand on the knob, said quietly:

'We shall never again be as we were.'

Kitty was leaving the restaurant. Not Kitty! Kitty's back had always been as straight as an undrawn bow. Macbane was bald. As his eyes followed them out he felt a hand, as cool as if it had come out of the night air, softly stroke his. How much had he revealed? How much had she inferred between the white wine and the red?

'Darling!' she murmured. 'I don't really mind if we do not go to Venice. And, after all, she was a long time before me. If life always has its meanings, it also has its pasts.'

'She? Who?' He protested large-eyed. 'I don't follow you.'

She stroked even more delicately.

'But you really were just a teeny bit in love with her weren't you? Any man as kind as I know you are might well be. Alone. Dying in a rainy city.'

He slowly turned the stem of his empty glass.

An Unlit Lamp

When it became known that a woman from Dublin named Goggin was about to open a private nursing home in Ballybun, in that old Georgian house on De Valera Square that had been empty for years, it is doubtful if many of the locals were greatly interested, excepting to be sure our hard core of addicted gossips who are always inquisitive about everything. The sergeant of the Guards may have as a matter of routine made a genial enquiry. One of our seventeen publicans drawing a careful pint may have said to his customer, his eye fixed on the slowly rising froth, 'I hear we are getting a Private Nursing Home now, if you please,' meaning by this last piece of Socratic irony that Ballybun is rising in the world. Or the owner of the Imperial Hotel, a building wizened by the Atlantic mist ever since such hotel names as Imperial, Royal, Continental, Ambassador and the like used to evoke images of luxury rather than, as they do now, of tractors, gas cookers, brassières, motor cars or lavatory bowls, may have said as he looked out at two cows ambling down the Main Street, 'Well, I hope the poor woman will get enough business to fill *her* beds!': a fair remark since Ballybun, according to the official census, contains only 3,426 residents, and lies on the direct road to nowhere, south, north or east and as a local wag has sourly said there is nothing much west of it except the United States of America and more rain.

In this indifferent mood Ballybun's 3,427th resident became generally accepted on her arrival as Nurse Goggin or Miss Goggin. Gradually, that is to say within a year, she became known to some as Judith Goggin, a sure sign of her provisional acceptance as a citizen. After about two years she became known to her very few close acquaintances as Judy Goggin. To the town's gossips, however, she was disparagingly known, almost from the start as Gog, to express their annoyance with her for never coming to the town's café, called *Le Bon Bouche*, never playing bridge, or taking part in the town's monthly Whist Drive, or in any of the many doings of the Ballybun branch of the Irish Countrywomen's Association. Who was she anyway to be so stuck up? Out of what sky did she parachute into Ballybun? Who were her backers in this Nursing Home? Where did she get the cash for all its new shiny medical equipment? They were nettled, felt put down, challenged, and of course in the end they caught their mouse, and caught her in such a neat way that their pleasure in their corporate skill dissipated their annoyance with her as a snobby outsider. Their sense of grievance was also modified by compassion.

What happened was that one of them reported one morning at the round table of the tea shop that a patient in Saint Dympna's Home had mentioned to her that whenever Gog was asked any slightly difficult question she would look up at the ceiling as if seeking advice from another planet, and start to caress the bare first joint of the third finger of her left hand with the thumb and fingers of her right hand. Experimentally the Bong Butchers around the table began to perform the same gesture and at once they pounced. Why had they not guessed it before? But married into which dynasty of Goggins? They knew Goggin families scattered up to Galway, down to Limerick, over into Tipperary. They settled for the Limerick branch: two doctors, one in Galway, one in Gort, an influential Reverend Mother in Kilkee, a chemist's shop in Nenagh, a home-farm near Patrickswell, and had not a Goggin doctor from Athlone been killed in a car crash on the day of his wedding to a Dublin *nurse*? At that everything fell into place: Gog's reticence, retirement, her exile, aloofness, her intense – they did not say, though it was what they meant – 'compensatory' concentration on making a success of Saint Dympna's which, four years after she opened it, was already being recommended by every doctor within fifty miles of Ballybun. Thereafter the gossips lost interest in their Gog, much as a sated cat does with a dead mouse after panting for weeks to lay it low.

Or they did until one day this last winter when, with a lack of discretion quite out of character, Judy casually threw out to somebody, who repeated it to somebody else, who etc.: 'You know! There are times when I really don't know what I am. A spinster, a widow, a married woman or an old maid?' On the spot the Butchers again became, as one of them had the wit to say, agog. They knew her now for a widow, and no spinster, but she had become both so narrowly that they could see how easily she could convey the impression that she was neither absolutely. Was she under that same impression herself? What, otherwise, was this bit about *not* being an 'old maid'? Just exactly how old was milady? They answered it on their finger tips. Say around 40? Whereupon like mice their eyes stole about the table. Around 40. But how round is around? And when does around 40 start being around 50? When does 50...? They sipped their instant coffee and sucked their low-tar cigarettes, unwontedly silenced by a question so fascinating that it would be a crime to dispose of it by answering it: namely, when ought the most reasonably presentable widow or spinster admit that the party is over? It would be fun to let Gog herself answer that question, fun to watch for the slightest sign of friendship, not to mention intimacy, between her and the least likely bachelor in sight. What they did not realize was that the last person to bear witness to what is going on in a battle is somebody lost in the thick of it. If they had read *War and Peace*... Or recalled from *The Charterhouse* that plaintive cry of Fabrizio del Dongo after he nearly lost his life on the plain of Waterloo: 'Was that really a battle? And did I take part in it?' But if gossips were to read such truthful fictions where would they get the time to make up their own? She had, they knew, already found one male friend. But he...

The first time Judy Goggin laid eyes on the Reverend Thomas Tully, C.C., without the slightest personal interest, was on a savagely cold December morning last year when she found him in her best bed, with a temperature of 101°, three cracked ribs, a twisted shoulder and a black eye. This quadruple achievement, Mrs O'Dea her fat old night nurse dryly informed her, was the result of his reverence's unskilful effort to skate down the town's frozen Main Street between midnight and one o'clock in the morning. Dr Cantwell, the clergy's regular doctor, had set the shoulder and plastered up his chest. It had been such a straight-forward job that they had not disturbed her. The patient had had a good night. He had eaten a hearty breakfast. All of which may have been why the somewhat weary night nurse ended her report by whispering as she left the room that Father Tully had been transferred to Ballybun only a few hours before his accident 'Probably for some similar misdemeanour in some other part of the parish.'

Judy, left alone with the patient, observed with professional disapproval that the curve of the bedclothes over his belly implied very little figure skating, or any other exercise, and at least two inches of yellow fat, and she shared every surgeon's distaste for fat. If she had been a surgeon she too would have taken pleasure in cutting through clean muscle. She looked at the card hanging at the end of his bed. Her own age, 39. At her third glance she met two small, blue, piggy eyes glittering up at her like a small boy contemplating mischief, noted his tiny mouth pursed forward like those fat-cheeked cherubs on old maps that are for ever blowing winds of laughter from the four corners of the compass. On the instant she diagnosed him exactly, inspired by his naughty smile, his puppy fat, his gleaming eyes, his puss-mouth and his age: another of those clerical Peter Pans who are a scourge of God to every bishop, vicar general and parish priest, to every layman a bloody good scout, to women a surrogate son to be admired, advised, indulged, protected and sometimes – if (on a fourth glance) he is as handsome as this Father Thomas Tully, in spite of his yellow fat – to be virginally loved by early widows and foiled spinsters.

His first words confirmed her guess. He asked her if she was aware that her Saint Dympna was the patron saint of lunatics. At this she burst out laughing, as he did too with a spasm of pain, confessed that she did not even know that a Saint Dympna existed, and that the only reason she had given this name to her Nursing Home was in the hope that it would 'impress our humbler goodies and intrigue our richer baddies'.

'And are there,' he asked hopefully, also diagnosing a kin soul, 'rich baddies in this bog town?'

It may be a measure of her calm confidence in her knowledge of human nature that she thereupon sat unprofessionally on the edge of his bed and opened up an indiscreet chat the like of which she had not enjoyed during her four years in Ballybun. That frank half-hour chat made bits of the professional barriers between nurse and patient, the proprietress of a Home and a priest without a home. It started a friendship. When he was off the sick list he visited her patients so conscientiously that before July they had become not only trusting friends but . . . Well, what else in the circumstances could they become? Soul friends? Affinities? Conspirators contra Ballybun? Yes! That certainly. Every time he left Saint Dympna's after a sherry in her sitting-room on the top floor she would draw the net curtain an inch aside in the embrasure of her window, look after him as he crossed the square and think, 'What a waste!'

Nevertheless the nearest she ever came to chaffing him in an even slightly intimate way was the July of the following year. After all, business is business, meaning that discretion is also business. He had gone on what she now knew was his annual summer holiday to Italy (he had been Rome-educated) and out of that blue width, heat, noise and wonder of Rome he had sent her a paperback selection of the previous year's Nobel winner, Eugenio Montale. He did it, she knew, because he knew that she had begun trying to learn some tourist Italian on her own in the hope of some day also escaping to 'his' Rome. She smiled patiently when she saw the book. To have sent her this Montale was just the kind of silly, impractical, dreamy, juvenile thing he could always be expected to do. She could not get to the end of even the first poem in the anthology. For a beginner the going was much too tough. To her pleasure, however, she noted (because it made him a bit less silly) that the book had been published in Manchester, edited by a Belfast professor, had notes and a vocabulary in English. With these aids she did, for his sake, partially decode in the first poem, *In Limine*, two lines that hit her across the face like a smack from a wet fish. The two lines said, 'Search always for the weak thread in the nets that so tightly bind us...' [Nets of what? Chance? Fate? Memories?] ... 'And jump! Fly! Escape! Be free! For this, for you, I pray to God.' *Cerca una maglia rotta nelle rete che ci stringe, tu balza fuori, fuggi...* She thought for a moment of tearing out the page, underlining the two lines in red ink, and sending the wet fish back to him, but at once thought, 'No! For God's sake! Montale could say that sort of thing to one of his journalist chums in Milan, Florence, Genoa, to himself, to his life, to his mistress if he had one but not, NOT to some poor bastard of a fly caught in the cobweb of an Italian Ballybun.' Nevertheless on his return from Rome to his cloister she did, in all innocence, say something to him along the lines of those words of Montale that made him behave like Vesuvius in a temper.

She had watched him alight from the 5 p.m. Dublin bus and come directly across the Square to Saint Dympna's. She was touched, although she could have wished him a little more prudent, but she excused him knowing that he knew that she was going off for her own modest holidays to Dublin on the same bus in half an hour's time. He brought with him an Italian tan, a dozen tiny papal yellow and white flags to distribute among the boys in his church choir, and a small bottle of the most vulgar scent. She thought his Roman bronze becoming; it went splendidly with the first few grey hairs brushed back from his temples. His holiday had taken years off him, so many that she suddenly wondered if he had not badly needed it. Had he since they first met, or perhaps long before they met, been under strains unknown to her? Every priest must at some time in his life find it tough to be cut off from the warmth of common life, as isolated as a desert monk inside his mud-hut in the vasty desert. After all, when a young man becomes a priest he flings all his dearest friendships at the feet of Christ like the bundle of clothes a swimmer lays on a beach before diving into a lonely lake to swim to some calm solitude, only to meet on the nearest island a smiling figure warmly welcoming him, a familiar friendly figure – his own boring self. She was happy that he had his brief escape from this Rome in that Rome, sad only because she would have so dearly enjoyed being shown over his Rome by him; but as she deftly poured him out a welcoming glass she surrendered to her commonsense. Snatched moments like this one were the most they would ever share; at which as if to measure its fragility he happened to mention the name of an Italian colleague whom he had known in his Roman days but whom he had in vain hoped to re-meet for a chat about old times. 'Ah, well!' he laughed. 'That's Rome. The Paradise, the Grave, the City and the Wilderness as who-was-it, Shelley-was-it, said. Seclusion and Faith.'

She misunderstood that last word, her eye on the clock, and chaffed him: 'You and your nonsense about fate. Fate is just Chance.'

She had never seen him angry before, wondered a lot afterwards at this sudden eruption.

'My faith,' his teeth clenched, 'is my own free choice! I chose to be a priest with my eyes and my mind as clear as the sky. Proud to belong to a Church that is wide, spacious and open. Room for all sorts in it. Rome and room enough for all of us. When I stood again last Sunday in Saint Peter's and looked away up, and up, around and about it, it came to me that the very size and width and height of it was a symbol of the liberty, the space, the . . .'

The compensatory images whirled, transparently. She read them easily. She clutched her fist behind her back until it shook.

'Ho! Ho!' she jeered. 'Have a bit of commonsense, Tom! After one week back here you will be singing another tune. Railing at the gossips. Cursing the prudes. Belabouring the pietists. Growling about the P.P. I have heard you at it. You see-saw! You great big bundle of contradictions!'

'Hoho, yourself!' he laughed at her. 'And I suppose you never tilt your nurse's bonnet this way that way a dozen times between morning and midnight, and your nightcap after that? Praying to your Saint Dympna to save you from going balony in this madhouse?'

And, to her relief, there he was once again happily wobbling in his fat and she like a kite swaying to the wind on the string of his caprice, delighted to see her smart nurse's cap through his piggy blue eyes lidded with fat, or fate, or faith – she did not give a damn which; although this was the worst of the many exasperating things she had observed about every priestly innocent – that in the pulpit any one of them will appear as steady as an oak tree and be as fickle as an aspen leaf out of it, an overgrown boy all over again, a shrugging fathead, a feeble fool, a child elated by the smallest blessing, hurt by the lightest blow, intemperate as a gypsy, no resting place, up-down down-up, the typical Irish manic depressive, constant in only one thing, his endless power to evoke protection from others. 'Holy God!' she groaned to herself, gathering up her handbag, gloves, small parcels from around and under the feet of and beside her elated traveller back from the blazing sun of Rome, her cheek to the window watching for the bus that would take her for ten days to white-skied Dublin: 'How unjust! Any other priest doing his job as obediently as a circus seal could at the very most count on my sympathy. I would mount the barricades to fight for this fat-bottomed fat-head, waving his sherry glass all over my carpet! Booming away to me about the power and the grandeur of 'my' Rome!' He looked as if he might even lay a condescending hand on her knee, or did she detect a certain (Roman?) look in his eye? If he dared to as much as touch her she would slap his face, and then, God help her, maybe sob on his shoulder?

'All right!' she granted him sourly. 'Room for the whole of Ballybun in heaven! You can stuff them all inside that famous high-walled city in Paradise where Saint Patrick stuffs the Irish so that they can go on thinking they are the only ones who reached heaven. I wish you joy of your fond parishioners. They are still growling at the sermon you gave them last month about their Miraculous Medal being no more miraculous than the pennies people throw into that old fountain in Rome for good luck. And I especially wish you joy of their latest campaign – against the naked Madonna. Good-bye!'

He followed her to the door, touched her arm, said gently:

'What Madonna did you say?'

'Don't you remember? The statue the goodies have been wanting for 20 years to run up on some rock in Galway Bay? That national competition they had to decide on the sculptor? While you were away Foxer O'Flaherty, Ballybun's one, only and therefore greatest-in-the-world sculptor won it. He is using a nude model. I expect he is over there this minute with her,' nodding through her window towards the stables of the Imperial Hotel. 'Working on his masterpiece.'

His eyes became as wide as plates at the idea of a female model in Ballybun.

'A nude model? Of the Madonna? Foxer O'Flaherty? In this town?'

His laughter howled. She did hers remembering by sympathy the sort of sculpture Foxer loved to produce; what she called Giacometti spaghetti, lean, skeletous symbols of starvation. She looked at the frail model of one such on her mantelpiece, bought out of sheer comparison for poor Foxer. Sculptors don't become rich in Ireland. If they choose to live in its wild west they invite Famine. Her hand on the door-knob, she explained rapidly:

'He says he always starts with the undraped figure and moulds the drapery about it. He says sculptors have always done this. He says "I make the flesh vanish into the clay. I finish only when I have produced the shadow of an angel, a female drawn up to heaven like a whistle of air."'

He followed her downstairs. This cultivated Roman did not, she observed, offer to carry her suitcase.

'But where,' he implored her, 'did he get a nude model within two hundred square miles of Ballybun?'

'He got her simply by advertising in that paper in your fist.' He looked unbelievingly at his *Clare Champion*. 'He had them queueing up for the job! And why not? Five pound for doing nothing but stand in your pelt on a box. Times have changed, Tom Tully, since you were a clerical student. Even in this wilderness they see English TV. They read the English Sunday papers. The old prudishness is gone. What's more, he told me he got exactly the sort of woman he wanted, big shoulders, maternal bosom, thighs like an elephant, hips like a mare, muscular arms. Don't ask me why he likes them so fat when they always end up as skin and bones. But I can tell you this, the town doesn't approve of it one little bit. There's my bus hooting!'

She raced for it.

Two weeks later, at five in the evening, she alighted from the same bus, pleased to find him sitting, waiting for her in her office, smoking her cigarettes.

'You've a lovely tan,' he approved. She gave him marks for saying so and took them back on noting that he did not stand up when she came in. Celibacy!

'Marvellously we had sun. I did nothing but sunbathe. That's the advantage of having relatives scattered around Dublin Bay. You still have your Roman bronze. And you have been slimming.' She just stopped herself from saying, 'I missed you'.

He had lost all his tan. He had also lost pounds of fat. His skin looked dry as well as pale. She produced the old bottle of gold and two glasses. She wondered what he had been like as a boy. A rascal? A scamp? A wilder? A little devil? Up to every mischief? His mother's despair? Or pale, slim, young, blushing Tommy Tully? Mother's darling. The morning shadow of a priest? A thin flame drawn up to heaven like a whistle? She banished the happy image with a mock-cheery:

'And how has life been in the wild west since I have been away?'

'I can tell you in five famous words. Out of *Paradise Lost*. Did you know that it was John Milton who first said them? "All hell has broken loose." That is what life has been here since you left. This nude model of Foxer O'Flaherty's has the town in bits. The Parish Priest has thrown it all over to me. "You're young. You can cope. You are the new generation."

'Judy! I need moral rearmament. I need help. Every morning the letter-box in the presbytery stuffed with anonymous letters. A woman without a stitch on her in the Imperial Hotel? Children trying to peep in at the Mother of God naked? Threats to picket the hotel. Two windows of Foxer's cottage smashed one night. Another day he couldn't get out, they had jammed the door. Graffiti on his walls. This morning was the last straw; he called on me in the presbytery with a face like a sheet. He couldn't talk. He just handed me this box.'

He handed her a matchbox. On a piece of paper pasted on one flat side of it was Foxer's name and address, typewritten. The other side bore a tenpenny stamp commemorating some famous Irish nun. She pushed open the little drawer of the matchbox. A revolver cartridge. Brass case. Grey bullet. He annotated:

'It fits a forty-five revolver. You could kill a bull with it. Of course whoever sent it is out of his mind. He would never use it. But still!'

'What did you say to Foxer?' she asked fearfully.

'I said I would protect them both. Him and her. I said, leave this matter entirely to me.'

He spoke like a Napoleon. He collapsed when he glanced across the Square at the hotel archway that led into the cobbled yards to the disused stables that Foxer had rented as his studio.

'There is Biddy Cash now,' he said. 'The madonna.'

She was emerging from the archway, fastening a green kerchief around her head. Young. Say eighteen. No beauty; a splendid image of female strength; a bosom a man could sit on, brawny arms, peasant legs, haunches fit to breed heroes. As she strode she was confronted by the woman who owned *Le Bon Bouche*, given to elegant tropes like 'Ooh, lala!' and 'Commong sa va?' She halted the great creature frontally and said something to her. Biddy Cash at once thrust her fat red tongue between lips that make the contemptuous sound known as a raspberry, and walked on. Judy laughed. 'Well, Father Tom? We don't seem to have much control over our congregation, do we?'

Tully threw back his drink and leaped to his feet.

'I have made up my mind! I will show these bigots that times *have* changed. The Church will show up these prudes for the ignorant slobs they are. Dammit, half the angels in the city of Rome have hardly a rag on them. Baby *putti* flying around every altar in their skins! Countless madonnas all over Italy painted with their breasts bare to the world! Christ crucified like every common malefactor not only naked but stark naked! What's wrong with the body that these... I am going to visit that studio publicly tomorrow morning. I am going to show the flag. Will you join me?'

'Flag? What flag?'

'Any flag; the papal flag. The green, white and gold, the red, white and blue, the green, white and red, the fifty stars.'

Three minutes too late, Judy knew that she should have immediately replied: 'Look't, Tom! I run a private Nursing Home for the public. I cannot have a private life in public any more than you can. Do you want to make a public scandal out of the pair of us?' Instead, without her volition, obscene words began to pour from her mouth: words like Worldly Wisdom, Tact, Expediency, Diplomacy, Politic, Bread and Butter, Temporize, until she suddenly heard herself saying 'Tricks of the Trade' and in horror she clapped her hand to her mouth.

'Did I say that? I'm possessed. Tom. Exorcise me.'

He said he would call for her tomorrow morning at ten-thirty exactly, and left her to stay awake long after midnight going through what in her childhood, submissive, Catholic, conformist, filled to the gullet with guilt, she used to call An Examination of Conscience. She was now aged 39. A lie! She was 40. A lie! She was into her forties. He was the same. She had a job, a career, a role in life, but she was not tied to one place: if she threw her nurse's bonnet over the windmill here she could start again elsewhere tomorrow. But could he? One o'clock struck from the Town Hall. He had his attractions. Two o'clock struck from the Town Hall. She wasn't all that bad looking herself. Did he ever look at any woman as a woman? Three struck from the Town Hall. She got up, looked across at the hotel, went back to bed, took a Mogadon tablet whose effect was to open her hazeing mind to the beautiful clarity of the unarguably reasonable decision that if a widow married a priest they would accumulate such world-wide publicity that they could run any Horseing Nome at a great Prophet and no schloss, whereupon the Mogadon kindly hit her with its padded mallet.

At twenty-five minutes after ten he was waiting for her at her front door. She knew that he was a priest of Heaven but he looked like Hell. In his white-knuckled fist he held a white and yellow paper papal flag, three inches square, about the size of a packet of twenty cigarettes. He saluted her with it, glared at her, surveyed the empty square as if at one wave of his paper flag his troops would at once pour out from every side-lane and side-street.

The only visible sign of life was the broad backside of a woman on all fours outside the entrance to the hotel scrubbing its steps. Shoulder beside her shoulder, he marched and Judy undulated across the vacant square to the arch and across the cobbled stable yards that were all that remained of the glorious coaching days of the Imperial Hotel. There was nobody in its yard. He led the way across its cobbles, rapped firmly on the door of the particular stable, mews, barn or coachman's house that had temporarily become Foxer O'Flaherty's studio. Presently Foxer unbolted the door, slowly drawing behind him on its curved rail a heavy curtain made, it seemed, of potato sacks stitched together, once dyed red, now approaching the tint of pink potatoes gone dusty with dried clay. His hands were orange with a rather more creative clay, his eyes, enlarged like a man awakened from a visionary dream, looked blankly from one to the other. Somewhere in the town a cock crowed plaintively. Judy felt Tom's elbow jab her ribs.

'Good morning, Foxer,' she said amiably.

'Good morning, Nurse Goggin,' Foxer said, returning crossly to earth.

Her comrade nudged her again.

'Gorgeous weather we're having,' she smiled to Foxer.

'It's all that,' said Foxer, looking towards the archway. Half looking back she saw a small boy of about four looking in. His presence did not suggest any danger of immediate violence. In the silence the distant cock doodledooed again. She got another jab in the ribs from her comrade.

'They'll be cutting the hay soon,' she informed Foxer pleasantly.

At this the Church thrust forward, flung aside the faded curtain and marched through the outstretched arms of the now loudly protesting Foxer. Judy cursing herself, limping after them, beheld with a shock of delight the naked, white buttocked, young Biddy Cash, standing on a low platform, about five foot eleven on her bare feet, angled slightly away from them, maternal, uberous, noble. Tom was still insisting something about 'friends'. Foxer was shouting something like 'God save us from our friends'. The girl's pose was a bit like that of Michelangelo's David: her left thigh splayed to the left, her right hand hanging loose. Her left hand did not however, as in the David, hold a sling-strap over her shoulder. It was a sign of Foxer's genius that he had made her left palm support the back of her head just above the neck thus both indenting a curve in the long black hair that hung down her back, and forcing her to look slightly upward – a gesture that gave to her whole person the moon-staring stance that he considered right for a girl who knows that she is about to become a mother while still a virgin.

Looking at her beauty nobody spoke any further, but the great girl, hearing and sensing their alien presence, slowly lowered her hand from the back of her head and slowly turned to look, saw the rotund black-clothed figure and with the scream of 'A priest!' leaped as lithely as a wild animal for the ladder leading to the loft overhead, her buttocks right-lefting out of sight. Tully roared to Judy. Foxer shouted after Biddy. Judy, vanished after her, knelt by her side where she had thrust herself back into the loose hay, arms hiding breasts, knees updrawn, moaning in horror again and again, 'A priest? A priest?'

'But what about it, Biddy! He's only just a man! Like Foxer!'

In denial the young woman shook her great head of black hair.

'A priest that never seen a woman?'

Judy, silenced, remembered suddenly her own man's astonishment and delight when on their marriage night they stood facing one another naked for the first and last time. She rose, blindly dusted hay from her skirt and arms. Shaking all over she climbed back down the ladder.

They had waited for that night: for eight years, two months and one week. He had been the youngest of his family, the four others had married and had left to him the care of a virtually bedridden father, and a mother soon to become crippled with rheumatoid arthritis, both begging him not to put them into a Home. He had been a second year medico when they met, he twenty, she twenty-two. They did not become engaged until he was still two years short of his medical degree. They waited also for that. They waited again, the old people still on his hands, for two more years while he got his M.D. His father died two years later. Even so Judy could not bear to ask him to put his mother into a Home and anyway few Homes would want to receive her at her age in a now quite crippled condition. The old lady, for her part, used to beg him to send her away, but when she said it there was a look in her eyes that begged him please *not to*. They buried her two years later.

That night in their hotel, at the very moment when they were on the brink of total love there had come a wild hammering on their door and the voice of the proprietress calling for help. A man had come cycling from a cottage a mile away, his wife far gone in labour, a breech birth, a hopeless midwife, for God's sake come. One of the two village doctors was attending a call five miles away. The other was on holidays. He had stared at Judy. She had said, 'You must go'. Years after she came on a line of poetry by Robert Browning that, she felt, condemned them both: the line imputed to every frustrate ghost the sin of 'the unlit lamp and the ungirt loin'. He dressed fast. He drove away fast. She did not see him alive again. When racing his car back to her at speed an hour later, he had run full tilt around a bend into a halted truck.

At the bottom of the ladder she found that Father Tom was gone. The sculptor lifted the curtain for her to follow him. She beheld Tully standing under the arch of the hotel yard, profiled against the morning sun, his head lowered as if in converse with his toes. She watched him raise his head and look northwards towards the open countryside; then look east across the square at her Nursing Home; then southwards towards – she translated with mocking indifference to grammar – Ballybun's *campanili, palazzi, torri, ponti, fontani*. He finally walked their way. As she went out under the arch she saw on the ground at her feet his little papal flag with the crossed keys and triple crown.

In her sitting-room in Saint Dympna's she went directly to her heavy red album of photographs and sat beside her window slowly turning its stiff pages until she came to the wedding group. For a long while she studied his face, felt an impulse to press the page to her lips, resisted, shut the book and shoved it back on its shelf. It was with profound relief that she heard her house telephone's tinkle and Nurse Clane begging her to come quickly to have a look at old Mrs Cronin in Number Six. From that on – it became a ragged day – she was saved from thinking of anything but the job until well after supper.

It was still daylight when she sat before her desk in her bay-window sipping a coffee and smoking her first cigarette of the day. She glanced across at the spire of the church rising above the slates and chimneys about it. It would be a couple of weeks before she got any more signals of distress from that quarter! And would he by then be as full as ever of his jellybelly jokes about Ballybun? And if he were how on earth could she stand him? The night nurse, old Mrs O'Dea, knocked and came in to report her arrival and ask her usual 'All well?' Judy was always glad to see Ma O'Dea, a fat, bosomy mother of seven, with a gusty laugh and full of good cheer. She poured her out a cup of coffee and proffered a cigarette. They chatted a nice little while. Or it was nice except for one remark Ma dropped about meeting Father Tully a couple of hours back in the Main Street. 'A lovely man. Everybody in the town likes him. A funny thing though, I'd swear I nearly thought did I maybe get a smell of you know what?': she raised an imaginary glass to her lips, and winked and nodded solemnly. But, perceiving that this bit of local news was unwelcome she washed the slate clean with a shower of exculpations, and cheerily took herself off to her quarters for the night.

Was the blue of the sky beginning to darken? The evening star above the spire of the church was as clear as a dot over an i. Looking at it she leaned back in her desk-chair, drew on her cigarette deep and slow, and as slowly outbreathed pensive smoke. Venus? Sweet beyond all imagining as friendship and love. Of all mortal promises and pleasures the most fickle. Faithless as a friend, faithful as an enemy. Bitter beyond bearing when it dies. Offering us as Lucifer a brightness that it steals from us before the night. A far from ally, trusting friend,

comrade, pal ... She picked up her telephone and dialled the presbytery, frightened to hear the empty buzz-buzz, buzz-buzz.

'Hello!' his voice said harshly, impersonally and, old Ma O'Dea was
right, thickly. 'Father Tully speaking.'

'Hello, Tom. This is me. I'm just ringing to say why don't you drop
in here tomorrow evening, say about this time, to visit some of my
ailing patients? We might have a drink and a chat afterwards. Right?
Good. See you. Good night, Tom.'

She replaced the receiver gently. The dusk was gathering. The star
was much brighter. She heard the voices of children playing below her
in the square.

After all! Two of a kind?

One Fair Daughter and No More

For well over a quarter of a century Lizzy Langford, wife of Dr Richard Langford, a – or the – long-established and well-known Belfast physician must (I have calculated in my pedantic Insurance Inspector's way) have struck between 25,000 and 35,000 of her husband's patients as the ideal wife for any doctor. She has always been decorous, sedate, soothing, interested delicately but never inquisitively in every body (not, my joke, everybody) needing Dick's professional attentions. She is not too pretty, meaning that she is not likely to arouse any patient's envy; indeed she is a good deal less than pretty, which could console a female client not feeling up to the mark herself; and lastly she is always dressed so simply, though also so elegantly that even I, a bachelor of many summers, can tell that every frock she wears must have cost at least four virus pneumonias. She may perhaps have one weakness: to be so very correct in every way that it is common Belfast knowledge that some other doctors' wives privately refer to her as Milady Longford.

Last August, therefore, we, the inner circle of the aforesaid 25,000 to 35,000 people who know the Langfords intimately were bewildered to hear that she had begun to berate *in public* none other than her husband Dick's oldest professional colleague and friend, Mr Carl Carson. Mister, not Doctor, he being a surgeon. In fact she had most uncharacteristically begun to behave like a scold, a word which, I gather, means a notoriously abusive woman, saying without regard to the company listening to her such monstrous things, according to the general gossip, as:

'I shall never understand how that nice woman Norma Carson married that ugly man. He must be the ugliest man in all Belfast – hobby-horse nostrils, horse's teeth, piggy eyes, donkey's ears. Oh, he may be a very good eye surgeon, and he has a good physique, we've seen him on the beaches, and there are even people who in their kindness pretend that he has quite a way with him, although I have never seen it, but even if all that were true can you imagine having to face that ugly mug every morning across the breakfast table? Not to say imagine every night having to... And the funny side of it is that when he spotted Norma – she was then just a simple nurse, and it *was* rather a number of years ago – she had just won a beauty competition as the prettiest nurse in Northern Ireland. How *could* she? That ugly, ugly...'

Naturally the first question that occurred to every one of us was what had happened; what bomb through Lizzy's front window had knocked her elegant manners to bits? Jealousy? Not surely of Norma Carson's frail, pink, girly-sweet, long since faded prettiness? Some social grudge? It is true that we were told that she had called Carl Carson 'common in looks and common in origin.' But Carl never made any bones about being a prole, and a Belfast prole at that. He used to make jokes about it. 'My dad used to say when he'd be cleaning out the Sandy Row sewers...' Was she harking back again to her own aristocratic pedigree? 'My grandfather, the Lord Mayor of Belfast... My dear father, the rural dean... All my people were settled in Ulster since King Billy took possession of this place three and a half centuries ago...' On down to her one chick Anita, studying Baroque architecture in Rome after coming down from Oxford 'with a First'. So? Not jealousy, scorn, envy, certainly not religion, and least of all rivalry; because there is only one single thing in which those two families are not absolutely on a par: the Carsons have six children, the Langfords have only Anita, whom they adopted from her cradle. I did, being unable to think of any other sort of 'difference' between the two couples that I liked best in all Belfast, once let the thought flit past me, like a whiff of smoke from some remote autumn garden, that some childless couples do, sometimes, intimate, half conceal and thereby half reveal... But not those two, surely, after so many years? One cannot, simply, imagine any of those four decent people concocting comparisons. It is true that Carl's skill as an ophthalmic surgeon is so constricted by its very concentration on the tiniest of worlds that no doctor, such as Dick Langford, could rival the wonder of his work; but, then, think of the greater variety of challenges that Dick has to cope with every day. Carl may beat off an immediate dark, but only that. Dick staves off the black-out of life. And Carl has other limitations: he dares have only one hobby, that of playing the violin, which I happen to be able to say authoritatively he does with a sensitivity remarkable in an amateur.

Dick has a tin ear, but, then, Dick golfs, fishes, plays a ferocious game of tennis and he has sailed his *Norma I* to Iceland, rounded the Faroes, nosed into half the fjords of Norway and, I am told, is pretty certain any year now to become commodore of the Royal Ulster Yacht Club. No wonder I crumpled the whole silly gossip into a ball and threw it into the waste-paper basket of memory until the next time I went to Belfast and could smell out the truth for myself. Insurance Inspectors have sharp noses.

I did not get my chance until rather late that October simply because although my visits to Belfast as Claims Inspector have become much more frequent since that unhappy city became a centre of violence of every kind those visits have latterly become much more bustling. So, when I at last drove myself to ring the Langfords it was only to give Dick and Lizzy my apologies, my greetings, and an 'Hello both of you, see you soon – I *hope*!' I was distressed by the pitch and the strain of Dick's voice. I could see him gripping the receiver, leaning across his desk in his surgery, staring fiercely at nothing, begging me to come across and see the pair of them if it were only for ten minutes, they were in big trouble. Please, please... I replied that it could only be for five minutes; I had three more clients to see that day and I wanted to be out of his beastly, bombers' city before night. I was unlucky; held up twice by patrols searching cars, so that I would have arrived in Malone Road in a very bad temper indeed if I had not suddenly recalled on the way that gossip about Lizzy's feud with Carl Carson. Had that blown up again? Dick Langford's strained voice made me think even of libel actions between them. Was Lizzy having a nervous breakdown?

As I stood on the Langfords' sill, being inspected first through the eyehole in the door, and then through the three perpendicular inches permitted by the restrictive door-chain, finally opened by their sixty-year-old housemaid Lena, dressed in the usual Langford canonicals of starched apron, shoulder-frilled, full-busted, cap with tails, I heard what, if I had only understood it at the time, could have given me the key to the whole business. I heard a gramophone upstairs playing some puzzlingly familiar Italian music which I should have been able to identify – I am among my many other accomplishments a bit of a musician. Flutes and harpsichord? Boccherini? Scarlatti? Cimarosa? I kept worrying over it as Lena led me, not as I had expected, into Dick's surgery for our five minutes' talk, but to my dismay upstairs to their drawing-room, which meant Lizzy, explaining to me as she led the way that the Doctor (which, being one of the old, rural Catholic minority, she naturally mispronounced 'Duckthur') had been called out suddenly to attend a girl badly burned by an incendiary bomb. However, she explained further, the Duchesse Oriane de Guermantes was expecting me in her drawing-room whose white door she now opened wide without knocking (well trained) announcing me by my full name as if I were a complete stranger: a little formality at which the two of us exchanged a tiny collusive smile. Nevertheless I could not help admiring Lizzy's insistence, bombs or no bombs, on preserving every possible little punctilio of earlier times in her besieged bit of Belfast's suburban Saint Germain des Près. The music stopped abruptly when my name was announced.

Once inside her white door I turned left, familiar with the geography of the house, leaving to my right the extension known as The Garden Room which could be as it now was secluded by folding doors. It was, I guessed, in this garden-fronting room that the Italian music had been choked into silence on the announcement of my name, meaning, I further guessed, that their daughter Anita was returned from her university studies in Rome and, this being latish in October, returned for good. I also remembered in a flash that I had not seen the girl since the June of the previous year. No! I had not actually seen her even then, I had heard her; or, rather, I had heard that very same slow movement from a *concerto* by – I suddenly identified it – Boccherini, floating through the open window of the Garden Room down to Liz, Dick, Carl, Norma and myself drinking iced champagne on the lawn of the garden below. It had already become an eyebrow-quivering family joke that Anita played this same nostalgic *Andante* three times a day before meals every time she returned on holiday from Italy. Small wonder that the hair on the back of my neck stiffened like a pointer's tail at the smell of game when I observed now that Liz, while glancing over her half-glasses (at me) in poorly-simulated surprise and rising from her escritoire, threw a crumpled ball of paper into her leather wastepaper drum, precisely as I had metaphorically done three months before when I despaired of my guessings about her row with Carl Carson. Shaking her hand I apologized, rather gracefully if I say so myself, for 'interrupting both musical and literary pursuits'. She sat on her chintz-covered sofa and waved her queenly, wrinkling fore-arm towards the opening doors of the Garden Room, snuffling 'You, of course, remember our Anita' with what she obviously thought was a gracious smile, nobody since her schooldays having told her that whenever she smiles she wrinkles her snout in so odd a way that one can never be sure whether she is expressing delight in your presence or disgust at finding you still alive. I turned to greet Anita.

Now I do not think I flatter myself when I say that I am a matured celibate who can appreciate a beautiful female, whether fully dressed in real life or disrobed in art, as a purely aesthetic object. In fact I had already taken notice of the girl in her late schooldays, and more than a couple of times during her college years, always in judicial approval of her good looks and shapely figure. Lately however she had just become a family statistic with its hair up. In astonishment I now saw before me a grown young woman, erect as a statue, breastful if I may invent an apt word, tall, long necked, with two blue-blue eyes so skilfully recessed by Mother Nature as to make them seem at one moment spring blue, at another a rich moonlit midnight. I have never seen blue eyes change colour like that before or since. The effect was hypnotic. Her skin was like warmed marble, such as one only sees and feels in southern latitudes. Her hair was likewise an Italianate black, and so cleverly upcoiled that just one tress sank restfully to her shoulder. My first idea? Naturally: who had her parents been? What genes had given Italy to Ireland? As I reached out my hand to take hers I half-looked back at her mother to compliment her, though instantaneously embarrassed by the awareness that so beautiful a creature could never have come from that progenitor. Before I could fully complete my half-circle from her back to Anita with a cheery 'So we have polished off Rome?' I knew that already, unseen by me, her blue eyes had flashed from light to dark to light again. Implying?

Now, I know I am an odd cuss: a fisherman, a music lover, an Insurance Inspector, a bit of a naturalist, a bit of a traveller with a keen interest in history and especially antiquity, really a bit of everything like a lot of lone bachelors who pass their lives in amassing incomplete collections of information about various segments of life; so much so that I do sometimes astonish my friends with *trouvailles* from my store of universal if, I humbly admit it, incomplete information. My point is that I suddenly realized where elsewhere I had seen that sudden darkening and lightening and at once I had the secret of her beauty in my hand; she was unarguably pretty, but pretty young women are a thousand a penny – she had an extra thing that made her beauty special: she had force, thrust, vibrancy, eagerness, livingness, I suppose what that famous French philosopher whose name I forget, no, I have it, Bergson called *élan vital*. She had in her a powerful will to live. It was this quality in her that reminded me of where I had seen that sudden darkening and lightening of her eyes before. Early of May mornings in the middle of lakes in the west of Ireland, as still and large as mirrors of infinity I had seen away out on the surface of the water a tiny ripple, so tiny that only very keen eyes like mine can spot it, or the eyes of practised fishermen. That ripple reveals what one can only call a shadow of those ephemeridae called may-flies. Some people speak of this shadow as a cloud, but it is by comparison invisible. The ripple is made by a lethal trout. The fisherman aims to simulate the shadow to catch the trout. I had been too slow in turning back to her from her mother to catch her ripple but, by God, I knew that the shadow of a challenge from life and her instinctive leap in response had flitted across her face when I said, 'So we have polished off Rome?' And I saw the proof it in that residual thunder in her eyes. The rest was easy. Any man of my age and experience would have to be a dullard not to understand her response. Two years in Rome. Doing nothing else every day but listen to lectures? Going in and out of Rome's packed wealth of baroque palaces and churches? Really? Every day? Ask any Roman, any Italian, any man at all who has had daughters, especially one so appealing as Anita, and watch his heavy-lidded eyes smile sardonically. I tried hastily to retrieve my mistake.

'But, of course,' I cried heartily, 'there is no real end to Rome, is there?'

'Never!' with a tiny jerk of the head that darkened her lakes again.

Her mother crossed and recrossed her feet and said, 'Don't you think, Anita, you should offer our guest a sherry?' which I cut down at once with my (by now) six people whom I had to see before leaving for Dublin. It was enough. Our lovely smiled at me and the white door clicked to behind her. I said I must go. I said I regretted not meeting Dick. I said she had a pretty daughter. I said she must be proud of her. I said again I must go. I was not heeded. Liz was glaring at the telephone beside her. An extension? Did she want to listen in? She asked me absently where I had spent my summer holidays. I told her I had flown direct to Palermo from Dublin, hired a car there and 'done' the Greek temples around the southern shores of Sicily and the footsole of the peninsula. When she heard the word Sicily she echoed it in such a hiss of disgust that I was hard put to keep from assuring her that all-in-all

Sicily was a safer place to live in than Belfast. Instead I did worse, I asked her, while casually fingering one of her Chinese figurines, where she and Dick had spent their holiday, or were to go for the coming spring. She stared, was lost, gasped, made a contorted face, moaned, 'Us? On holiday?', clasped her hands to her eyes as if to avoid a bomb exploding, sank back into the corner hollow of the sofa and began to wail like a beaten child. In a fright, I slid in beside her, wondering what had I said now, put an arm about her shoulder to soothe her, called out for Anita, begged her again and again to tell me what was wrong, what had I said, for God's sake speak out. She turned, lowered her ringed hands from her tomato-coloured sponge of face, opened her mouth and Milady vanished.

'It's that bastard! That bloody quack, Carson! He did it all, my poor poor Nita, my poor, foolish little girl!'

She should talk about Sicily? Her wails would have done credit to the back lanes of Santa Lucia. What stopped her from wailing merely changed her into shouting – my silence of incomprehension.

'You are a bachelor. You could never understand. You have no idea what she, what all of us have been going through since last June!'

I cannot say that she calmed. She merely shut up; strode to the right hand door of her desk, pulled out from the back of one of its shelves a foolscap wallet marked ANITA, containing presumably every letter she had written since she left for Rome, and dragged out from it helter-skelter to show me from among the general mess of envelopes, picture postcards, letters, tourist folders, telegrams, what I still think of as the remnant papyri of her first and probably unmatchable love affair, or is it another instance of my celibate's ignorance that I hold that the wonder of a first love affair can never repeat itself? Once I was in that kind of love, or I thought I was; I regret to say it came to nothing and that the illusion never repeated itself. For the moment, however, hungrily scanning the papers Liz was passing under my eyes, trying with my fingers to slow their passage, I was far too inquisitive to consider feelings of sympathy or regret for anyone, following a word here or catching a sentence there from three telegrams from Rome, two letters in Italian, a crumpled letter in red ink on pale blue paper partly in English partly in Italian, getting a flash now of a gaudy picture postcard, now of the flying telegram in Italian that repeated its cry of agony so loudly that I still recall its, *Cinque giorni senza notizie devo darmi alla disperazione Giovanni.* 'Five whole days without a word of news must I despair? Giovanni.'

I asked Liz where she got those tell-tale leaves.

'Anywhere, everywhere, they don't care where, forgotten in books, stuffed into shoes, at that stage of madness they despise secrecy, they want to tell the world, scatter their joys and miseries in the streets, write beauty recipes on the backs of them for their friends, add up their debts on them, they are in whatever the hell the bloody goddam words mean IN LOVE!'

The only one of all those pages that I can now record fully is a crumpled one in red ink that she never finished. I have it here on my desk. It obviously got mixed up on that chintz sofa with papers that slipped from my portfolio in the haste of my departure. It is addressed from that house in Belfast and dated a week before. Apart from its *Caro Giovanni* it begins in English, describing the place where she is writing it. She is in the University library. It is a damp, autumnal, northern afternoon. She has come there to get away from 'them', to read something by some 'European'. She had first tried for Giraudoux. Lo and behold! Not one single thing in the catalogue under his name! *Perchè no?* Provincialism? Insularity? He, as a Sicilian, another islander, a sea between him also and the Continent, should know what it means to be cut off from Europe. She searches the catalogue for anything that will carry her mind out of her dreary prison, something by say Gide, something passionate, intimate, say *Et Nunc Manet in Te*, about his awful non-marriage, but of course Gide will not be here either. Lo and behold! They have every single word Gide ever wrote! Here she breaks into Italian which, like any old Susannah-watcher, I translate as best I can with dictionary and the help of my own not half-bad Italian:

'*Clearly this magnificent city of Sodomites ... I look around me. Green-shaded reading lamps. Pale Irish green faces. Bony Belfast masks. Each in an individual lake of lights. Each an island in an island in an island. Silence. Broken occasionally by small noises, a page turning, somebody blowing his nose. Yesterday when out riding I bit my tongue so I cannot now either eat or speak – the result of which is that I find myself in a state of gentle lethargy. I do not even want to write you a fulminating letter to match your verbal silence. All the same I have it in for you my beloved. You are neglecting me. Are you beginning to forget our love? Or has the Roman post office gone*

haywire again? Dear, dear Giovanni, remember our pact to say so at once if either of us ceased to feel in love with the other. Would you have the courage to say it? Yes! I am uneasy. I am afraid. My dear one, tell me immediately if it is so. I would prefer a million times to know the truth. Am I boring you? I do know for sure that I love you dearly but'
      End of letter.

      The lines of street lamps along the Malone Road lit up. Liz was going on and on and on.

      'If you had seen her in June! She had left Rome finally. Sulking and skulking around the house. Playing that stupid Italian record all day long. Hating Belfast, hating us. By July she was unbearable.' Liz shook her jangling wrist over the telephone. 'For long distance calls alone last quarter our bill ran into three figures. In August she was insisting that come what may she was going back to Rome. We said we would not give her the money. She said she would borrow it from her college friends, as she could and would, blackmail us in this small city with the scandal of it. One day Dick was so miserable about her that he confided our trouble to of all people Carl Carson who at once offered to talk sense to the girl. It shows you how desperate we were that we let him try. He drove her out into the country in his car and, we thought it very generous indeed of him, talked to her there for two precious hours. He reported back to us that the only thing to do with her was to let her fly back to Rome just for two days to straighten things out with her *inamorato* but not, *not*, NOT he insisted to let her go alone, have Dick go with her, that as far as violence and terror was concerned Belfast was in the kindergarten stage compared to Rome – the Red Brigade, the Mafia, the *Primo Linea*, Neo-Nazis, and God knows what this boy-friend was. The smarty ass! As if we had not already made contact through the British Embassy to the Quirinal. They comforted us immensely, oh enormously, put us quite at our ease by telling us that this young man in whom our daughter is so interested is on the Italian police lists as a suspected Sicilian left-wing activist. Well, we tried our dear, sweet, good, generous, kind Carl's advice. We told her we would let her go to Rome for two days provided we went with her. If I may make a bright little joke of it her answer was a flat 'No go!' Dick offered to go alone with her, that he would stay at a separate hotel, just be there at hand as a friend that she could contact if she got into trouble. Another 'No go!' The scenes! The arguments! At that point Mister Carson told us that he was due to attend an international congress of ophthalmologists in Zürich the first week in September, and that it had occurred to him that the Dublin-Zürich plane goes on to Rome. If she was agreeable he was willing to go on with her to Rome for just forty-eight hours, keep out of her way, stay strictly in the background, not see her or interfere with her in the least bit, just be there if she wanted help of any kind, and then at the end of the forty-eight hours back with the two of them, he to Zürich, she home to Dublin.'

It was a very old woman who looked at me, and nodded wearily when I asked, 'She went?', and when I said, 'And?':

'And she came home after the two days, beaming, glowing, triumphant. So happy that she revealed to me that on the day Carson drove her into the country to advise her on our behalf – on *OUR* behalf! – he told her he was all on her side, to stick to her guns, that every girl should follow her own star, that he himself was wildly in love with a German-Swiss woman, an eye specialist like himself, living in Zürich.' Liz again put her hands to her face and moaned into their smother, 'I felt like a fly caught in a spider's web of filthy concupiscence.'

Which said, she took a sudden hold of her dignity. Milady rose, wrinkled her tomato nose above her usual ambivalent smile and held out her hand at such a height that it was hard to decide whether she wished it to be shaken or breathed upon. Then, as she started to scoop up her documents from her chintz sofa, I helping, I was taken by surprise to notice the date and location of the post-office stamp on the gaudy postcard. It was *Ottobre X*, and the place of origin was not Rome but Caltanissetta, a name I had noticed last summer bang in the middle of my touring map of Sicily. As I slowly pushed the card Liz-wise I read its message. Four words without a signature. *La mia propria patria.* 'My fatherland.' What had that conveyed to her? It could have been friendly, ironical or dismissive. Was his signature withheld from conspiratorial caution or from coldness? For a moment I dearly wished I had visited this particular *patria* of her lover, remote though it was from my templed coastline, though I would not have needed to go there, I had passed through too many Caltanissettas already not to know what to expect in yet another. Two hotels less remarkable for their comfort than for their declamatory names, a *Zeus*, a *Minerva*, a *Paradiso* or some barbaric oriental name with an X in it or a Z, or a final accented ò or ù; one *trattoria*; a *giardino pubblico*, dusty, parched, flowerless commanding in Baedeker's blurb language 'striking views of the surrounding mountains and valleys'. There might be a decent

Norman church, or a sulphur mine or a salt mine, for there always had to be some explanation for places otherwise distinguished only by some sidelong reference to some quondam Demeter myth or to some Punic War still recorded in the local Museum, meaning a couple of rooms in some public building with shelves of cracked vases, bits of statuettes and other such antiquities displayed in an ambience of dust, graffiti, entwined hearts, cheers for a local football team. Whenever I had paused at such Sicilian townlets I had always assumed that the natives live there in a state of discouraged content, but I had also always remembered that novel of E.M. Forster's about the English woman whose imagination of Italy caused her to marry the local dentist. A wren that ventured where an eagle might fear to tread.

'But do tell me how you find her now?' I pressed Liz, eager to extract the last drop out of my little discovery that at the moment when the daughter was dying of thirst for 'his' sweet Rome, her beloved had already preferred violence in his Caltanissetta.

Before Liz could answer me I saw over her shoulder her drawing room door opening and there was Anita leading in her father and Carl Carson. Liz, to follow my stare, rotated her damp tomato face. When none of the four of us stirred the young woman took command. Young? Certainly by contrast with us her greying elders. For herself in full leaf and flower, though not yet enough so to dethrone her mamma, as she gaily tried to do with, 'Well, well, no introductions necessary here! Right? Elizabeth, a sherry for you I think.' (Did she always first-name her parents like this, or was this a sudden mutiny, a final declaration of independence?) 'Dick? A dry Martini. Right? Carl, something stronger for you, a double Bushmills. Right? And for our Southern Irishman here a double Irish. Right?' Even as a parody of her mother's style it was too much of a bad thing to serve. Liz would have known better than to overdo it. Only hams over-act. She put her daughter down simply by ignoring her.

'Is it a very bad case?' she asked Dick in a voice of such solicitude that she almost sounded sincere. His back-of-the-hand gesture intimated what Carl worded:

'Too soon to say how bad. My interest of course is to protect the girl's sight, if she has any left. The eyes themselves seem okay. She apparently clapped her hands to them at the moment of explosion. Interesting. It is always people's first instinct in the face of violence. The doctors are now spraying what is left of skin and flesh on the rest of her face. Which is not much. Nose gone. Ears gone. Hair of course all gone. The worst of all is the mouth. A few years of grafting and surgery will give her back some kind of nose and ears, but those lips can never really be restored. Thanks, Anita, for your offer of a drink but I am on the job, and I happen to know her father, he lives not far from here, I promised Matron to soften the bad news that they have already 'phoned to him and his wife. That is if I can get a lift.'

'His car,' Dick sighed. 'Rushing into the hospital he forgot to lock it, and you know what "they" are, always on the look-out for cars, especially Cortinas. The spare parts they need. He will never see that Cortina again.'

Liz turned to me.

'Unfortunately Dick ought to be in his surgery by now. Can you possibly give Carl a lift? It won't take you long.'

The four of us started for downstairs. Last out of the drawing-room Dick hastily drew me back to whisper his worry about Anita and also about his wife's unfortunate feud with 'our mutual friend'. I could hear Liz having words with him as they descended to the hall although I was relieved to get the impression that her tone did not suggest a totally broken friendship. When all four of us were together in the hall, amid much searching for hats, scarves, overcoats, medical bags and my own errant portfolio Carl and I kept reassuring the other two about Anita until I realized that I had left my portfolio on the couch upstairs and ran back to get it.

I was halted outside the drawing-room door by that lovely Boccherini. Guardedly I opened the door, so gently that I was not observed by Anita standing before the window of the Garden Room gazing out at a tranquil twilight descending over the lights of Belfast, her palms held out in the posture of a priestess either accepting something with a sigh or invoking it with a tremble; or, I had an old man's fancy to think, like a young goddess balancing two emblems of Time, the human and the immortal; the baroque melody, so elaborate, so civil, so consciously contrived, so adorned, one could even say so full of artifice, and out there the vanishing northern daylight that for a moment seemed, however deceitfully, both pastoral and simple. I was held rigid by the manner in which they enhanced one another and the listening girl. On tiptoe I retrieved the object I wanted and unseen withdrew. Still I paused, on the landing, my fist withholding the door's bevelled click until I might hear the start of that lovely movement which she had earlier choked on hearing old Lena announce me at the door. It came. Again she guillotined it. Why? Unbearable? She wanted the southern sun? Life, not music?

Carl impatiently ran upstairs to call me down. From the pavement we waved and received goodbyes. The door closed. Its chain rattled into place. As I switched on the lights, fastened seat belts, pushed starter, let out the brakes and went into gear I said, 'They can think what they like but if that unfortunate girl does not clear out of that house and this city before Christmas she will go off her head.' Clear out? But to where? To the Leonardo da Vinci airport? Nobody there. Bus into Rome. Ring from the terminal. Nobody she knew answering. Ring another number. Nobody. Ring another number. Nobody. Ring. '*Pronto. Chi parla?* ANITA! *Chi? Ma e andato via.* Gone home. *Sicilia.* Oho, no! He is not coming back *here*! Didn't you know? *E scappato.*' A red light halted us. I looked sidewards at Carl's knotted face. He did not say anything. Then he said: 'She will go. And she will never know how lucky she will have been to get away. Anyhow. Any way. Any where.' He flicked me forwards. The lights had changed. 'Third turn on your left. Number 34.'

It was a quiet *cul de sac* between two level rows of small redbrick houses, each with its tiny garden in front, its brief concrete drive and its garage, each with its own colour of railing. We drew up outside a house whose lighted fanlight bore the white celluloid figure 34. Carl told me not to wait. 'They will want . . .' He banged my door, stepped to the garden gate. As I turned my car to drive away my whirling headlights flooded Carl's back and the faces of a man and woman who had already thrown open their door and were rushing down the drive to meet him with outstretched hands and staring eyes. He was holding out his hands like a priest to comfort them.

A Present from Clonmacnois

It is noon in late May. The only bit of the monastery of Clonmacnois left intact after countless Viking raiders, local Irish robbers, English reformers and over a thousand Irish winters is its tall round tower, bare as a factory chimney. Its other remaining bits and pieces are now in the safe keeping of the Public Works Commissioners under the rubric 'A National Monument'. At this hour the gnomon of the tower casts no shadow. The only sound comes from a lawn-mower man from the Board of Works who is trimming the grass near the river. These last few months have been abnormally rainy, the grass is unusually succulent and thick, the Shannon is unusually high among the reeds along its banks, the surrounding fenlands are sure to be flooded again this coming winter. He halts his engine, takes off his hat, measures the hour by the sun, says the Angelus, wipes his poll whose central bald patch might remind one of a monk's tonsure, and peers up the slopes to where a young man and an old man are picnicking on a flat tombstone. They are the sole visitors so far today. He may advert to his own flask of hot tea and his sandwiches locked in the brown Board of Works van at the entrance to the site, or he may animadvert sourly on the toughness of this accursed grass, or he may be thinking of his wife who prepared his lunch, or of his five children, or of anything at all except the past of Clonmacnois. About this the most learned know no more than a barber does about the past in some grey poll under his scissors.

The younger of the two picnickers glances without interest at him down the slopes as between two large bites of his ham sandwich he mouths passionately, even high-handedly to his elderly companion:

'Owen! I don't know what you see in this bloody place. You have been boosting it to me all the winter and now that I am here it says nothing at all to me. It has no echoes. Its bridge is down. For Ever! That river there has become an ocean. This place is a far away Then. You and I belong to Now. And you know it, Owen! The primitive Church that created this sort of place has lost all meaning for the modern world.

To any rational man all this,' waving his tooth-gapped sandwich, 'is just so much antiquarian nonsense.'

The older man replies placidly.

'This spot has echoes for me. In its hey-day it was a midwife to the Irish imagination. It is one of the sacred places of Ireland. You speak like a young man who might have fallen in love with a girl of an unusual beauty if he had studied her more closely. You have not studied Clonmacnois.'

'My dear Owen, beware! Beware of enthusiasm, above all of patriotic enthusiasm. It could be the ruination of even our finest Celtic scholar!

Our finest Celtic scholar looks admiringly at his companion's head, sculpted by the gods for a prophet or a poet, relishes again the young man's splendid voice that tolls like a basso bell. He pours some more cool Liebfraumilch from his thermos flask into his neophyte's plastic cup. He strokes his greying beard outwards from his chin, looks over the ruins. He replies courteously.

'My dear Donal, beware! Beware of scepticism, above all of patriotic scepticism. It could be the ruination of even our finest Irish poet.'

The young man, obviously flattered by those last three words gulps down his wine, scatters its last drops in an arc over the grass ('A libation?' smiles the scholar) and proceeds with immense enthusiasm:

'I'll tell you, Owen, what we must do. We must exchange roles. You shall henceforth play the part of the sceptic and I the part of the believer. "My true love hath my heart and I have his," as Sir Philip Sidney put it, "by just exchange one for the other given". But that alchemy can't possibly take place in a wilderness like this. My God, even that poor devil from the Board of Works clacking away down there like a corncrake can hardly cut the grass of the place it is gone so wild and thick. Does the air in this place ever dry? A river like the Mississippi! Sodden boglands all around it! I swear half the monks here died of TB.'

'Saints died here. The grass is well manured. The air is numenous.'

'Well, whatever happened here it happened too long ago to break the time barrier. I'm telling you the bridge is down. Only last night I scribbled the rough draft of a poem about that barrier and that bridge. I call it "Rags to Riches". Shall I recite it for you? Mind you it is only a draft. It will take polishing.' And without formal leave he began to bell out his poem:

> Time was, Dark Head, we wore you like a flower,
> Prayed God and Mary nightly to fulfill
> Your longing to be our queen once more.
> For this, for you, for years we died pell-mell
> Until the night we overheard you groan
> 'How many generations more to spell
> My dowry as a queen?' Plainly the dower
> That gave your breath that night a rich-bitch smell
> Of envy was the wealth that taunted you before
> We burned down that town to an empty shell,
> Castles, churches, towers, morgues of power.
> Small wonder that your Wild Geese chose to sell
> Their swords abroad for honour sake, leaving us poor
> To claw barehanded at the citadel
> And free our queen. Ten centuries and more
> Have passed. A happy boy leads to a hill
> An old white-haired woman. Look where she will,
> Only ruins. A roofless church, a quondam tower,
> Tombstones leaning, a fallen bridge long reft and still.
> Laughing joyously he waves. 'All ours!'

The poet ended blushing with chagrin. More bloody rhetorical verse? The old man opened his tobacco pouch and pinch by pinch refilled his pipe, tamping each pinch with his fourth finger. He lit carefully. Then, between tiny puffs, he quoted:

'"Perhaps in this neglected spot is laid/Hearts once pregnant with celestial fire..." Did you know that one of the finest scholars of the eighth century came to this spot with gifts from the court of Charlemagne? The poet Alcuin. And he was not the sort of man who would have travelled far without good reason.'

'Did he write anything that was any damn good?'

'He wrote, my dear boy, what you normally write. Charming lyric poetry. In Latin of course. He wrote about his lost nightingale. About Spring's harbinger, the cuckoo. About his lonely monastic cell.'

'Can you,' his friend asked, a trifle more cautiously, 'quote me any of his verses? Owen, why did we come to this place? The cold of this gravestone is going up through my backside.'

'There is somebody beneath it who is colder. Alcuin's verse? You flatter my old man's memory. Moreover I am a Celtic not a classical scholar. But that splendid North of Ireland woman Helen Waddell, whom I once knew so well, and who translated so many medieval Latin lyrics, did render Alcuin's verse about the cuckoo something like this... I agree that such verses were possibly a common classical convention. "Green branches begin to give their shade to tired men, the goats come to their milking with full udders." It comes back to me. *Tu iam dulcis amor, cunctis gratissimus hospes, omnia te expectant.* "Come, O cuckoo, come! Thou art love himself, the guest on whom all things wait, the sea, the earth, the sky."'

'And man?' annotated the poet, glancing stealthily at his tutor, thinking that he must later enquire elsewhere about this splendid North of Ireland woman whom the old man had evidently once admired.

'Alcuin,' the other went on, 'wrote more than once about the cuckoo. *Carmina deducunt forte.* "Song brings the cuckoo home." *Sis memor et nostri.* "Sometimes remember us. Love, fare you well."'

The old scholar fell silent. The mower stopped. Far away a cuckoo imitated itself.

'Mind you,' the scholar went on, 'Helen inserted that word *love*. All the Latin says is *Semper ubique vale*. She did something similar to Alcuin's lament for his strayed nightingale. "So dim and brown thy little body was./ But none could scorn thy singing./ What a depth of harmony in such a tiny throat!"' He paused, puffed his pipe, looked in a troubled way across the monastery's rotted teeth at a remnant building grandiosely known as the Cathedral. The word implied a bishop's throne. Was there ever a bishop here? 'There is no word *little* in the Latin. Nor is there the word *tiny*. "Tiny throat." *Angusta*, yes. Narrow throat. Helen seemed to like the image of smallness, as if she were writing about a baby. "To thee, O small and happy, such a grace was given." The nightingale is not such a small bird. It measures about seventeen centimetres. Not that she would have known this. The nightingale is not heard west of the Severn.'

His pipe had gone out. He sighed.

'Yes, I suppose it *was* a long time ago!'

The mower stopped again. Silence. 'Cucu!' This time farther away. The poet shifted restlessly.

'Your Alcuin,' he snorted, 'was an Englishman, writing in Latin. Do we know whether even one poem in Irish came out of this place?'

'We cannot know but it is more than likely.'

'How likely?'

'You have, of course, heard of Priscian?'

'By name.'

'A man of no importance, really. A grammarian. A contemporary of that Roman citizen Cassiodorus who became a chief consul in Rome under the Goths. The Marshal Pétain of his day? Well, centuries afterwards some learned Irishman came on one of Priscian's grammarian's texts and started to copy it in an Irish-Swiss monastery near Lake Constance. He got so bored by the grammarian that to relieve the boredom he wrote on the margin of his vellum a little poem that goes like this... "A hedge of trees surrounds me..."'

The young man became excited.

'I know that poem. I have translated it myself. It goes like this in my version. "Birds chatter above my dull pages,/Trees surround me like a green wall./Over and over the cuckoo counts my wages,/Just now I hear a blackbird call."'

From behind the pair of them a loud burst of laughter. It was the man from the Board of Works.

'By Jiminy!' he swore. 'I must have heard translations of that poem a dozen times. Whenever a bunch of tourists come here there is always somebody who recites it. But the shape you have put on it, young sur, is the besht I ever heard. "Over and over the cuckoo counts my wages." Shtop!' he commanded, finger aloft, ear cocked.

Was it near? Or was it far? That fluting call.

The young 'sur' had become flamelike from pride: a troubadour bonding centuries. His laughter and the rustic's drowned the trailing monastic voice of the scholar:

'We cannot tell how far that Priscian manuscript wandered. Did it come from here? All we can say for certain is that at one stage in its life a wandering Irish scholar wrote a verse on its margin.'

He drained his thermos on the grass. He began to pack their lunch basket.

It was some months before those two amiable inapposites met again, though in the meantime they had communicated through some gay verses from the one and a suspiciously scholarly-looking volume from the other. The young man's first glance judged this volume to be nothing more than an early Calendar of Irish Saints prefaced by about a hundred quatrains in Old Irish which were, he decided after reading six or seven pages of them, the kind of pietistic doggerel to be expected from any unlettered coenobite in any desert in the world under the influence of prolonged mental starvation. Between aversion and puzzlement he fluttered the pages muttering to himself, 'Why the hell did Owen send me this heap of rubbish?' He re-examined the volume. Its Gaelic title was *Félire Oengusso Céli Dé*, translated as 'The Martyrology of Oengus the Culdee'. He noted that the Old Irish text had been 'critically edited from 10 manuscripts, with a preface, translation, notes and indices by Whitley Stokes.' He was aware that Stokes had been a scholar of repute, saw that the work had been published in London in 1905 by a Society with which he was not familiar, The Henry Bradshaw Society, and that it was numbered XXIX of a series.

Culdee? His encyclopedia refreshed his memory. In Irish *Ceile De*. A companion, mate, servant or spouse of God. In modern Irish *Dia. Dieu. Deus.* Zeus. The Shining One? A spouse of Zeus? A bit thick. More likely servant, menial, lay brother, cleaner-up, cook. At best somebody to do with the intoning or droning of hymns in some ruined monastery like Clonmacnois.

He became so bored with his encyclopedia that he returned to his monastery bore, the culdee called Oengus, and was once again on the point of becoming bored by his pietistic verses when, suddenly, as if he had been transformed into a pile of autumn leaves dosed with petrol into which Owen had thrown a lighted match he burst into a flame of enthusiasm at the quatrain following line 209. To anybody else the quatrain might not have seemed of any interest. All that the four lines said, in Mr Whitley Stokes's careful translation, was: '*The cells* (old monastic cells) *that have been taken by pairs and by trios, they are Romes with multitudes, with hundreds, with thousands.*' With a gulping throat he evoked from these four lines a dear image of his childhood in Cork: a tiny, impoverished cottage in a long, narrow city lane that went winding as a goat or a cow wanders, surrounded by multitudes, by hundreds, by thousands of similar cells, and himself and his mother kneeling at night beside the dying fire of her small kitchen, saying the Rosary. As he read again the tears trickled down his face. Poverty. Power. Rome. Empire. War. His pen had of its own will already written:

> Little places taken
> First by twos and threes
> Are like Rome reborn
> Peopled sanctuaries.

He hurled back the pages to see at what unperceived point this dreary doggerel had magically turned into poetry and at once found the answer. Two rivals had been at work on this job: a pietistic old (he insisted on the 'old') fool of a pedant, and a superb young artist. His guess was confirmed when Mr Whitley Stokes in his quiet Anglican way blew ashes into flame:

'Heathendom has been destroyed, though it once was widespread, the kingdom of God the Father has filled heaven and earth and air.'

Kings *had* been destroyed! Saints *had* been crowned! Fiercely the artist lashed his racer. Quietly Mr Stokes tapped out the hoof beats of the old tongue. *Múchta.* (Stifled.) *Plághta.* (Plagued.) *Rígtha.* (Kinged.) *Mártha.* (Glorified.) Which, in his Dublin bed-sitter, the poet, bursting with excitement, his voice tolling louder than the buses and the cars outside, transmogrified for the glory of Faith and Fatherland into:

> Sing the kings defeated!
> Sing the Domhnalls down!
> Clonmacnois triumphant,
> Cronan with the crown.
>
> All the hills of evil
> Level now they lie;
> All the quiet valleys
> Tossed up to the sky.

That was his winning post, even though the monkish poetaster behind him went on wheezing around the course again and again for 25 rounds more. Not that a great deal of work did not yet remain to be done before he finally winnowed this thousand-year-old celebration of a triumph to which his calmer hours would have given no more than the most transitory belief. Nor would he have been disconcerted if at any moment during those ardent weeks somebody had upbraided him for his inconsistency. 'And how many,' he would have boomed, 'of those exquisite Madonnas of the Renaissance do you suppose were just street girls of Florence or Rome? Think of the most profoundly religious painter of his age, Pietro Perugino, a man,' here he would have pounded his modest breast, 'who was well known to his contemporaries as a villain, an atheist and a genius!'

It was almost September before he was prepared to show his translation and return its source to its owner, his inspiration. To his disappointment he had to leave both with a wizened housekeeper who proudly explained that the 'professor' had gone off to 'speechify' at Clonmacnois. 'About what? About what but the pattern! Doesn't the world know it? Won't the world be there? The feast day of the Saint!'

Still, he thought as he disconsolately turned away from the suburban door, remembered by multitudes, by hundreds, by thousands coming from all over the suckling, Shannon shore in their Cortinas, Ford Eights, second hand Mercedes, to honour the *genius loci*.

But what a letter of praise he got three days later! 'The most superb poem ever composed on the deaths of Wotan and Thunder, of Goll and Manannaan, of all the pagan gods, Celtic and Germanic alike. For this is your very own poem, not to be treated as a mere translation – leave all that to pedants like Stokes and myself – so splendid a re-creation as not to be a translation at all.' The letter went on: 'Alas! My dear friend! How I envy you your faith! So much so that I forgive you for having by one word at our last meeting, beside the Shannon, shaken mine. We spoke then of the poet and scholar Alcuin. He whose great patron was Charlemagne, King of the Franks, Emperor of the West, who came with costly gifts to Clonmacnois, and of whom you said scornfully that he was *an Englishman*. That fatal word stuck...'

'O God!' the poet groaned. 'His patriotism has broken out again.'

'I have not been able to forget it, and I am thereby in your debt for forcing me to consider whether all those costly gifts that Charlemagne scattered among the monasteries of Ireland and Britain may demonstrate not his warm generosity but his cold eagerness to dominate this island and its neighbour. Was Alcuin just another tool in this imperialistic design? Was he first and last an English spy? What *am* I to believe? Whom trust? Could there have been some Irish accomplice in Clonmacnois who...'

At this the young man roared with laughter, threw his tutor's crazy letter into the air, following its floating leaves with uplifted hands that slowly sank back on his thighs. Belief? Could it be true that if any man wants badly enough to believe in anything he will believe for the pure relief of belief itself.

'Take that poem of Oengus the Culdee. I translated it. Owen says I did not. That it is my very own. I believe there were two poets at work on it. He makes me a third. Then who did write it?'

At which all his pride in his poem evaporated into the thought that everything created is recreated, that it takes many generations to write a poem, many lives, many grass-grown ruins. All humanity has but one song to sing and that written in many forms by life itself. Was that what Paul Valéry meant by his *La mer, la mer, toujours recommencée?* Life renews itself endlessly. The artist is a mere tiller of ancient soil.